THE MARK TWAIN PAPERS

AUTOBIOGRAPHY OF MARK TWAIN
VOLUME 3

The Mark Twain Project is an editorial and
publishing program of The Bancroft Library,
working since 1967 to create a comprehensive
critical edition of everything Mark Twain wrote.

This volume is the third one in that edition to
be published simultaneously in print and as an
electronic text at http://www.marktwainproject.org.
The textual commentaries for all Mark Twain
texts in this volume are published *only* there.

AUTOBIOGRAPHY OF MARK TWAIN

VOLUME 3

BENJAMIN GRIFFIN AND
HARRIET ELINOR SMITH, EDITORS

Associate Editors
Victor Fischer
Michael B. Frank
Amanda Gagel
Sharon K. Goetz
Leslie Diane Myrick
Christopher M. Ohge

*A publication of the Mark Twain Project
of The Bancroft Library*

UNIVERSITY OF CALIFORNIA PRESS

Frontispiece: Clemens departing for England on the SS *Minneapolis,* 8 June 1907. Photograph by Albert Bigelow Paine in the Mark Twain Papers.

University of California Press, one of the most distinguished university presses in the United States, enriches lives around the world by advancing scholarship in the humanities, social sciences, and natural sciences. Its activities are supported by the UC Press Foundation and by philanthropic contributions from individuals and institutions. For more information, visit http://www.ucpress.edu.

University of California Press
Oakland, California

University of California Press, Ltd.
London, England

Library of Congress Cataloging-in-Publication Data

Twain, Mark, 1835–1910.
  [Autobiography]
  Autobiography of Mark Twain, Volume 3 / editors: Benjamin Griffin , Harriet Elinor Smith ;
associate editors: Victor Fischer, Michael B. Frank, Amanda Gagel, Sharon K. Goetz, Leslie Diane Myrick, Christopher
M. Ohge
      p. cm. — (The Mark Twain Papers)
  "A publication of the Mark Twain Project of The Bancroft Library."
  Includes bibliographical references and index.
  ISBN 978-0-520-27994-0 (cloth : alk. paper)
    1. Twain, Mark, 1835–1910.   2. Authors, American—19th century—Biography.   I. Griffin, Benjamin, 1968–
II. Smith, Harriet Elinor.   III. Fischer, Victor, 1942–   IV. Frank, Michael B.   V. Gagel, Amanda.   VI. Goetz,
Sharon K.   VII. Myrick, Leslie Diane.   VIII. Ohge, Christopher M.   IX. Bancroft Library.   X. Title.
  PS1331.A2   2010
  818'.4'0924dc22   2009047700

Manufactured in the United States of America
23 22 21 20 19 18 17 16 15
10 9 8 7 6 5 4 3 2 1

The paper used in this publication meets the minimum requirements of ANSI/NISO z39.48–1992 (R 2002) (*Permanence of Paper*).

Editorial work for this volume has been supported by a
generous gift to the Mark Twain Project of The Bancroft
Library from the

KORET FOUNDATION

and by matching and outright grants from the

NATIONAL ENDOWMENT
FOR THE HUMANITIES,
an independent federal agency.

Without that support, this volume could not
have been produced.

The Mark Twain Project of The Bancroft Library at the University of California, Berkeley, gratefully acknowledges generous support for editorial work on all volumes of the *Autobiography of Mark Twain,* and for the addition of important new documents to the Mark Twain Papers, from the following:

The University of California, Berkeley, Class of 1958
Members of the Mark Twain Luncheon Club
The Barkley Fund
Phyllis R. Bogue
The Mark Twain Foundation
Robert and Beverly Middlekauff
Peter K. Oppenheim

The Beatrice Fox Auerbach Foundation Fund at the
    Hartford Foundation for Public Giving
The House of Bernstein, Inc.
Helen Kennedy Cahill
Kimo Campbell
Lawrence E. Crooks
Mrs. Henry Daggett
Les and Mary De Wall
Mr. and Mrs. Morley S. Farquar
The Renee B. Fisher Foundation
Ann and David Flinn
Peter B. and Robin Frazier
Virginia Robinson Furth
Edward and Andrea Hager
Stephen B. Herrick
The Hofmann Foundation

Don and Bitsy Kosovac
Watson M. and Sita Laetsch
Edward H. Peterson
Roger and Jeane Samuelsen
The Benjamin and Susan Shapell Foundation
Leslie E. Simmonds
Janet and Alan Stanford
Montague M. Upshaw
Jeanne and Leonard Ware
Sheila M. Wishek
Patricia Wright, in memory of Timothy J. Fitzgerald
Peter and Midge Zischke

and

The thousands of individual donors over the past fifty years
who have helped sustain the ongoing work
of the Mark Twain Project.

The publication of this volume has been made
possible by a gift to the University of California
Press Foundation by

WILSON GARDNER COMBS

FRANK MARION GIFFORD COMBS

in honor of

WILSON GIFFORD COMBS
BA 1935, MA 1950, University of California, Berkeley

MARYANNA GARDNER COMBS
MSW 1951, University of California, Berkeley

The University of California Press
gratefully acknowledges the support of

The Mark Twain Foundation

The Sydney Stern Memorial Trust

John G. Davies

and the Humanities Endowment Fund
of the UC Press Foundation

CONTENTS

LIST OF DICTATIONS

ACKNOWLEDGMENTS

As we complete work on the third and final volume of the *Autobiography of Mark Twain,* we are deeply mindful of the extraordinary support this work has received for more than a decade. After an initial five years of intensive labor, Volume 1 was published in 2010 (the centennial of Mark Twain's death), Volume 2 in 2013, and now the present volume just two years later. The indispensable core of support for this edition has come from the National Endowment for the Humanities, an independent federal agency, and through it, from the American people who have contributed their tax dollars. We renew our thanks to both, especially for the Endowment's two most recent grants of outright and matching funds, as well as its longstanding support of the edition, which reaches back as far as 1967. With equal warmth we renew our thanks to the Koret Foundation for its generous grant in 2008, all of which has gone to matching the Endowment's grants. That combination of federal and private-sector funding has made this edition possible.

The individuals and institutions acknowledged above (pages ix–x) have supported the Mark Twain Project for many years, sometimes for decades. So many people have lent their support, financial and otherwise, that we are obliged to thank them collectively. More than half of the Endowment's support has been in the form of dollar-for-dollar matching grants, which could not have been accepted or used without the generous gifts of thousands of individuals and foundations. Without all our loyal supporters, the Project would long ago have ceased to exist, and we would certainly not now be completing the *Autobiography*. Special thanks are in order for an ambitious undertaking by the members of the University of California, Berkeley, Class of 1958, who in 2008 gave the University a fiftieth-reunion gift of $1 million to support the Mark Twain Project. Led by Roger and Jeane Samuelsen, Edward H. Peterson, and Don and Bitsy Kosovac, this extraordinary class has helped to make completion of the Project's work a distinct possibility. We renew our thanks to each and every member of the Class of 1958 for their generosity. The future of the Mark Twain Project is likewise ensured by the estate of Phyllis R. Bogue and the estate of Peter K. Oppenheim, who have created similar endowments.

Central to our recent fundraising efforts has been the Mark Twain Luncheon Club, organized fourteen years ago by Watson M. (Mac) Laetsch, Robert Middlekauff, and the late Ira Michael Heyman. We thank them, and we thank the nearly one hundred members of the Club for their tireless financial and moral support; likewise the dozens of distinguished speakers who have addressed the Club on the subject of our mutual interest, Mark Twain. Our gratitude goes also to David Duer, the director of development in the Berkeley University Library, for his always wise and judicious counsel, and for his heroic efforts to raise funds for and awareness of the Project. Our home institution has provided us a place to work, and all essential equipment and services. We are grateful for these and other forms of support from the staff of the University Library and The Bancroft Library. In particular we thank Dan Johnston, head of the Library Digital Imaging Lab, for providing high-quality images for reproduction in the book. We especially want to acknowledge Thomas C. Leonard, University Librarian; Elaine Tennant, the James D. Hart Director of The Bancroft Library; and Peter E. Hanff, its Deputy Director, all of whom serve on the Board of Directors of the Mark Twain Project. To them and to the other members of the Board—Frederick Crews, Mary C. Francis, Michael Millgate, Alison Mudditt, George A. Starr, G. Thomas Tanselle—we are indebted for every kind of moral and intellectual support.

Scholars and archivists at other institutions have also been vital to the work on this volume. We wish to acknowledge the contributions of the following scholars to our understanding of Mark Twain and his *Autobiography*: Richard Bucci, Dianne McCutcheon, Takuya Kubo, and Bernard Baycroft. Barbara Schmidt, an independent scholar, maintains an invaluable website devoted to Mark Twain research (www.twainquotes.com), which has become an important source of information for our explanatory notes. Kevin Mac Donnell, an expert dealer and collector of Mark Twain documents, has given much-appreciated support and is always generous with information. We would also like to thank the following scholars, librarians, and archivists who assisted us with research, documents, and permissions: Christine Colburn, University of Chicago Library; Eva Tucholka and Harriet Culver, Culver Pictures; Halli Yundt Silver, Hannibal Free Public Library; John Walker, City University, London; Jonathan Eaker, Library of Congress; Lyndsi Barnes, Berg Collection of the New York Public Library; Mark Woodhouse and Barbara Snedecor, Elmira College; Melissa Barton and George Miles, Beinecke Library, Yale University; Patti Philippon and Steve Courtney, Mark Twain House and Museum, Hartford; Danielle M. Rougeau, Middlebury College, Middlebury, Vermont.

The enthusiasm of our sponsoring editor at UC Press, Mary C. Francis, has been an inspiration to us; our new sponsoring editor, Kim Robinson, has assumed her role with equal enthusiasm. We are grateful for the assistance of Kathleen MacDougall, our highly skilled copy editor and project manager, whose zeal has improved the accuracy of the editorial matter. Her expertise has helped us deal with the typographical challenges presented by the use of "plain text" to transcribe "The Ashcroft-Lyon Manuscript," and she has guided us at every stage of the production process. Lia Tjandra at UC Press has ensured photographic reproductions of the highest possible quality.

The Mark Twain Project's editions are created through a process of complex and sustained collaboration. Associate editors Victor Fischer and Michael B. Frank have contributed to every aspect of the editing process. The newest members of our editorial team, Amanda Gagel and Christopher Ohge, joined us while the texts and notes were in preparation, and have assisted with the work with great diligence and skill. Sharon

K. Goetz and Leslie Diane Myrick are essential to the creation of the digital edition (at www.marktwainproject.org), and provide the editors with technical support in pursuit of previously unimagined kinds of archival and bibliographical research.

Finally, we wish to acknowledge our administrative assistant of fourteen years, Neda Salem, who has moved on to another position with the university. During her tenure, she organized the daily operations of our office, and served as the gateway to Mark Twain information for scholars and fans alike.

B. G.   H. E. S.

AUTOBIOGRAPHY OF MARK TWAIN

Dictated March 1, 1907

Reminiscences of the Beecher family—Miss Clara Clemens singing in North Attleboro, Massachusetts, a place noted for manufacture of cheap jewelry—Anecdote of the feather-duster man, told to Mr. Clemens by Professor Sloane.

Isabella Beecher Hooker is dead. I first made her acquaintance about forty years ago; she and her sister, Harriet Beecher Stowe, were near neighbors of ours in Hartford during eighteen years. I knew all the Beecher brotherhood and sisterhood, I believe. The men were all preachers, and all more or less celebrated in their day. I knew Reverend Henry Ward, Reverend Thomas K., Reverend Charles, and Reverend James, very well; they all rank as conspicuously able men, but of course none of them was as able, or as internationally famous, as Henry Ward, that first of American pulpit orators. They are all dead. There was not an ungifted Beecher among all those brothers and sisters, and not one that did not make a considerable name.

But the Beecher talent is all gone now; the last concentration of it went out of the world with Isabella Beecher Hooker. I knew Reverend Thomas K. Beecher intimately for a good many years. He came from Connecticut to Elmira in his early manhood, when he was a theological fledgling, to take charge of a Congregational church there whose chief financial support was Jervis Langdon, my to-be father-in-law, and he continued in that charge until he died, a few years ago, aged seventy-four. He was deeply versed in the sciences, and his pulpit eloquence fell but little short of that of his great brother, Henry Ward. His was a keen intellect, and he was brilliant in conversation, and always interesting—except when his topic was theology. He had no theology of his own, any more than has any other person; he had an abundance of it, but he got it all at second-hand. He would have been afraid to examine his subject with his own fine mind lest doubts should result, and unsettle him. He was a very frank, straightforward man, and he told me once, in the plainest terms, that when he came on from Connecticut to assume the pastorship of that Elmira church he was a strenuous and decided unbeliever. It astonished me. But he followed it with a statement which astonished me more; he said that with his bringing up he was aware that he could never be happy, or at peace, and free from terrors, until he should become a believer, and that he had accepted that pastorate without any pangs of conscience for the reason that he had made up his mind to compel himself to become a believer, let the cost be what it might. It seemed a strange thing to say, but he said it. He also said that within a twelvemonth or two he perfectly succeeded in his extraordinary enterprise, and that thenceforth he was as complete and as thorough a believer as any Christian that had ever lived. He was one of the best men I have ever known; also he was one of the best citizens I have ever known. To the end of his days he was looked up to in that town, by both sinner and saint, as a man whose judgment in matters concerning the welfare of the town was better and sounder than any one else's, and whose purity and integrity were unassailable. He was beloved and revered by all the citizenship.

Isabella Beecher Hooker threw herself into the woman's rights movement among the earliest, some sixty years ago, and she labored with all her splendid energies in that great cause all the rest of her life; as an able and efficient worker she ranks immediately after those great chiefs, Susan B. Anthony, Elizabeth Cady Stanton, and Mrs. Livermore. When these powerful sisters entered the field in 1848 woman was what she had always been in all countries and under all religions, all savageries, all civilizations—a slave, and under contempt. The laws affecting women were a disgrace to our statute book. Those brave women besieged the legislatures of the land, year after year, suffering and endur- ing all manner of reproach, rebuke, scorn and obloquy, yet never surrendering, never sounding a retreat; their wonderful campaign lasted a great many years, and is the most wonderful in history, for it achieved a revolution—the only one achieved in human history for the emancipation of half a nation that cost not a drop of blood. They broke the chains of their sex and set it free.

Clara is singing in New England. I have a letter from the stage management in North Attleboro, Massachusetts, asking me in a matter-of-course way—not to say in a com- manding way—to come up there and introduce her to her audience, gratis, of course. I think that that must be their idea, because they did not ask me for my terms; still that may be only an oversight, so I have sent the terms—five thousand dollars—but I don't hear from those people, although they have had a good three days in which to jump at my offer. Maybe they don't want me after all; but I don't care; I don't want to go, anyway. However, the North Attleboro letter has brought that town back to my mind after an interval of twenty or twenty-five years, during which spacious spread of time its name has never happened to drift across the field of my memory, so far as I recollect.

Away back there at the further verge of that vast interval, I had a talk about North Attleboro one day with Professor William M. Sloane, then of Princeton, now of Columbia University. He told me that North Attleboro was a place apart: that it was the centre of a unique industry—an industry not to be found elsewhere in the United States; an industry whose office was to furnish cheap gimcrack jewelry to our nation—jewelry of a flashy and attractive aspect, jewelry built out of fictitious gold and real glass; and sold honestly *as* imitationry. He said that the jewelry factories were many and large, and employed hundreds and hundreds of girls and boys and men—in fact the bulk of the community; he said that in the city of New York there was a vast warehouse stocked from roof to cellar with that jewelry, and that from that building this product was forwarded to every State in the Union, and in truly surprising quantity. Then he told me this curious tale.

One day he was passing by that New York building and he entered it, out of curiosity, to see what he might see. He found much jewelry on exhibition in show-cases; on the out- side of each parcel there was a sample of the parcel's contents, and also the parcel's price in figures. It was a villainous March day—muddy, slushy, damp, misty, drippy; and cold and raw. Presently, meek and drooping, entered a sad-faced man of about forty, who seemed to be a tramp. His shoes were broken, and down at the heel, and soaked with slush; his hat was a battered and shapeless slouch; the rest of his clothing was poor and threadbare and patched; altogether he was a pathetic spectacle. Under his left arm he carried four feather-dusters of the commonest and cheapest pattern. He came timidly forward to a show-case near which Sloane was standing, and pointed to a parcel marked $7.00—but only pointed, he didn't say anything. The clerk got it out and handed it to him without saying anything; the tramp put it in his pocket and handed out seven dollars, still without saying anything; then he moved, meek and drooping, to the door and disappeared. It was a great surprise to Sloane to see such a looking creature as that transact business; and not only transact it but concrete the transaction with cash; and not only cash, but an entire seven dollars' worth of it. Sloane was interested, and he said to the clerk,

"You don't seem surprised. Do you know that tramp? Have you ever seen him before?"

"Oh yes," said the clerk, "we know him; he is called the Feather-Duster Man; he is a regular customer of ours."

"Tell me about him, won't you?"

But the clerk couldn't. He said it would be a breach of confidence; that the feather-duster man did not wish to be known.

I cannot now remember by what arts Sloane got hold of the man, a little later, and won his confidence and got his story out of him, but I can well remember the story, as the man told it to Sloane. It was about like this:

The Man's Story.

I am not a tramp, but I dress the part for business purposes. I earn a good and sure living in my occupation; I own property, and I have a good balance always in the bank. My business is not followed in exactly my way by any other person in the land; I planned it out myself; I practised it upon the people; I revised it, corrected it, improved it, and finally perfected it; and now I never change it, for it needs no change. I sell pinchbeck jewelry, and pinchbeck jewelry alone; I peddle it on foot far and wide, sometimes as far west as Ohio and as far south as the Gulf; at first I used to go out with a good many kinds of jewelry, so as to meet the requirements of all tastes, but gradually I discarded one kind and then another, as experience suggested, until at last my plan was perfect and unimprovable, and my stock was weeded down to just two articles—two, and no more; and since then I have never peddled any but just those two—engagement rings and wedding rings. That market never slacks; people never stop getting engaged, and they never stop getting married. It's a trade that's like undertaking—sure and steady, no fluctuations in good times or bad, the demand always the same.

Sloane interrupted to say,

"But aren't you forgetting about the feather-dusters?"

No, the man said, that is only a blind. I always carry them with me; I always offer them for sale, but never urgently, for I don't want anybody to buy; now and then I can't help it; somebody buys a duster and I have to stand it, but it's an inconvenience, because

I've got to send and get another one to put in its place. The duster is a good protection. A tramp, pure and simple, is an offence, and he drives his trade in a thick atmosphere of prejudice and aversion all the time, whereas everybody is favorably inclined toward a ragged and hungry poor fellow who has something to sell, and who is apparently doing the best he can to earn an honest living. These feather-dusters are an invaluable protection to me; they keep off prejudice the same as an umbrella keeps off rain; nobody ever receives me ungently.

The feather-duster man's story continued. He tells how he engraves skewered hearts and initials on wedding rings.

I've got a trade—engraving on silversmiths' work—but it furnished me only a poor living and I gave it up, ten years ago, in order to try commerce, for I felt that I had a talent for commerce. From that day to this I have walked the earth distributing North Attleboro jewelry to the farmers and villagers of our country. You saw me buy twelve dozen very good-looking wedding rings for seven dollars—say about five cents apiece; they have good weight, they have dignity, they are handsome, and they have a convincing 24-carat aspect; if they were gold, they would be worth ten dollars apiece, retail. To begin with, I take them home and engrave two sets of initials on the inside of them, with two hearts on a skewer between. Those hearts are very fetching. I have tried other devices, but for business, out in the country, where sentiment reigns and has its home, they are worth all the rest of a person's viscera put together, lungs and all; skewered with an arrow, you know; you would think hearts skewered on a fork would be exactly the same thing, but it's not; the trade would go to hell in a minute. It shows the power of sentiment; it shows what human beings are, out in the country—and I know all about them by this time; I don't make any mistakes with my customers.

I always engrave the skewered hearts in the wedding rings, and I always put initials on each side of them; any initials will answer; I could use the same ones all the time if I wanted to; you will presently see that it wouldn't hurt the business any. I do use variety in the matter of initials, but it's only to rest myself; it isn't necessary. You notice I bought only twelve dozen this time; it's because I shan't go any distance from New York for a couple of weeks till I'm ready to start South when April comes and the sunshine; I'll lay in a big stock then, and be gone two months. You didn't see me buy any engagement rings. It is because I've got a bucketful or two at home. When you buy several thousand at a time you get them at a large discount, and it's worth while. Each engagement ring has a small glass diamond in it, and is a very pretty thing, and captivating to the eye of young persons who are dangling on the brink of matrimony. If the ring was genuine, it would be worth seventy-five dollars; what I can get for it over fifteen cents is profit, and I always suit the price to the emotions of the customer; sometimes his emotions reach fifteen dollars, but if I land him for seven, or eight, or nine, I am satisfied, for where a young person's heart is engaged I couldn't be any way but tender if I tried; it's the way I am made. I myself have loved, and I know how it feels.

⁕

You might think the engagement ring was the daisy in this trade, but you would be mistaken; it's a close second, but the wedding ring stands first, for business, and I will tell you why: you may run a geodetic survey of farm-houses for a week on a stretch and not strike more than two or three engagements, or such a matter, but it's a most unusual circumstance when you strike a farm-house where there's no trade for a wedding ring. Then take a village, for instance: an ordinary village won't fetch more than three or four engagements, and maybe not be worth more than forty dollars to me; you can hunt them out and supply them in a day, as a rule—unless it's down South amongst the niggers; then the village trade is better; it's because in the North a man won't buy an engagement ring until he's engaged, but a nigger will take one anyway, so as to be prepared for the worst. Yes, you can work off all the engagement trade of a village in a day, but sometimes I've had to put in a whole week to supply just one village with wedding rings. I remember one village out in Indiana that had only eight hundred and forty grown-up people in it, but amongst them they took two hundred and sixty-four wedding rings.

Sloane broke in with,

"Do you mean to say that there were two hundred and sixty-four married women in so small a community as that that had never been provided with the certification and protection of a wedding ring?"

I never said that, did I? The statistics look strange to you at present, but they won't look strange after I have got done explaining.

The feather-duster man's story concluded.

You see, the procedure is this: for instance, I am languoring along a village street looking tired, and maybe discouraged; if it's a little muddy and drizzly and dismal, all the better, for then you are most likely to catch the womenkind at home—at home, and maybe one or another of them sitting by the window sewing. If there's a woman sitting by the window sewing, it means that in this modest cottage they are able to keep a hired girl; but they'll not interrupt her work to tend door. Understand, a hired girl at the door is well enough if you can't do any better, but you can't depend on her being worth more than about 25 per cent of what the average woman of the household would be. Of course you don't throw a hired girl over your shoulder, which would be flying in the face of Providence, and could bring bad luck; no, you accept what is sent, and be thankful, and don't grumble; you learn this kind of philosophy in the course of time. Very well, while you're moping along apparently absorbed in your cares, you've got a furtive eye out for business, and you see the woman at the window before she sees you; she's there to see what she can, and she doesn't get much to look at. There's a little yard in front of the cottage, and a paling fence, and a gate, and a walk that goes straight through to the front door, about five steps. Just as you are passing the gate, and looking your saddest, your face suddenly lights up, and you stoop down and apparently snake something eagerly out of the mud. The woman sees that episode—you needn't glance at her to make sure, you know by experience that she's always taking care of her end of the dramatics.

You examine that thing you've found, on the sly, she watching you all the time and you apparently not aware of it; then you slip it into your vest pocket and start briskly along; but when you've gone only two or three steps you stop and begin to reflect—you begin to look doubtful; you do a kind of struggle with your conscience, showing that you have been brought up in a godly family and are wavering between the right and the wrong at this moral crisis of your life—understand, the woman has her eye on you, and she is interpreting it all—then you kind of straighten up and heave a return-to-virtue expression into your style, and turn and go reluctantly back. Along at first, you can't do a really good sample of reluctance, but after a little practice you can do it so well, you can give it such a genuine aspect, that sometimes you deceive yourself; sometimes you really think for a moment that you are reluctant. Now when you strike that gait you know that your education is complete, and that you are all right for the future. As I was saying, you go back reluctantly and fumble the gate a little, in an undecided way; finally you enter and approach the door; you knock; if it was another person he would have to wait till that woman puts her sewing in the basket and sets it aside before she comes to the door, but in your case it is different; she is there already, and the minute you knock she opens, and her face is full of interest, and expectancy too. But you mustn't see that; no, you are intent upon another matter, and you don't observe it; you are going to disappoint her—that's the game. You begin to tell her, meekly and humbly, how long you have been without anything to eat, and haven't been able to find any opening for a feather-duster, and how many children you've got depending on you—arranging the number, of course, to suit the circumstances and the weather—and whether your wife is sick or not, and what is the matter with her, and what the chances are—and all that kind of thing—which doesn't interest the woman because her mind is on your vest pocket; and meantime you're taking each feather-duster in its turn and giving it a shake before her face and explaining how much better it is than any other feather-dusters that are on the market now, and how cheap these feather-dusters are, and so on, and so on. At last, when you a give her a chance to get in a word edgeways, she says just what you were expecting her to say, and just what you wanted her to say, to wit: that she doesn't need a feather-duster; she's sorry; she wishes she did need one, for she would like to help any honest poor person who is in trouble; and she follows that right up by offering to give you a feed. This is your chance. You turn sadly away, thanking her deeply, fervently, with considerable emotion in it, but saying it would not be right for you to eat bread which you had not earned; that you may have to come to it, but you feel it would not be honorable in you to succumb while you have yet strength to go on and seek further for a customer. This is very fetching, and it works that woman hard, but you don't let on to see it; you turn sorrowfully away and proceed toward the gate, feeling the gaze of her pitying eye beating upon your back, and—well, you mustn't carry it too far; half way to the gate is far enough; she is trying to pull her resolution together and shut the door and try to forget you and your sick children, and your other sorrows, and if you go one step too far she'll manage it; no, just at the right time, as determined for you by experience, you turn and go back and begin to fumble in your vest pocket as you go, which makes you welcome. You say,

"Madam, I am under sore temptation, but have been mercifully granted strength to resist. I have found a heavy gold wedding ring just outside your gate; I cannot keep it, it is the property of another. You have been kind to me; your sympathy has done me good; it's probably yours; if so I know you will grant a poor fellow some little reward for returning it. I was once a goldsmith's journeyman, in my better days, and I am aware that the ring must have cost ten or twelve dollars."

Meantime, I have been torturing that woman by dilatorily polishing the mud off the ring while she is itching to get her hands on it. I pass it to her now, and she turns it over and over with delight and desire. Presently she finds the initials and the skewered hearts, and then one of two things happens, according to the character, training, and social environment of the woman: she either pretends to recognize the ring as her own, by the testimony of the initials, or she frankly says it isn't her own—or rather her aunt's; it is most customary for the woman to leave herself out, in these conditions, and make use of an aunt; but it's all one to me; I'm not particular as to whose ring it's going to turn out to be. It's rather unusual for the woman to recognize the ring—with absolute certainty; in rare instances she does, and says it belongs to her aunt, who must have lost it off her finger this morning; but in all the other instances she recognizes it as the property of a friend from the other side of the village, who has been visiting her and has just gone. You mustn't let that incautious remark go by unobstructed, for you can suffer a damage by it. You must ask her to please give you the address, so that you can go and return the ring and hope to get four or five dollars' reward for it. You do this because you know that the thought has already entered her mind to propose to keep the ring and restore it to its imaginary owner herself, a thing which she can do by giving you a pretty economical reward; but you have made trouble when you ask for the address, because, in the first place, there isn't any address, and, in the second place, you may slip through her fingers if she doesn't raise the stake. You don't need to propose to go and hunt up that woman yourself, for she is not going to permit that; she is going to hold on to the ring and satisfy your requirement in the matter of a reward if she can.

There now, don't you see what a good trade it is, and how certain it is? It doesn't make any difference to you whether the woman is representing herself, or an aunt, or whether she is representing a friend on the other side of the town; she's going to keep the ring and arrange the terms with you at the best figure she can. I am never hard with those people. I generally know by the look of the woman, and her clothes, and the house, and all that, about how much of an outlay she can stand, and so I trade on that basis. She is good for two dollars, always, for that five-cent ring, and a meal into the bargain if I want it—which I don't. According to her style and make, she is good for two dollars, three dollars, four dollars; and it's not so infrequent as you might suppose, for me to find women that will add one, two, and even three dollars to those figures. Taking a season straight through, my accounts show that my average is three dollars and thirty-five cents for a wedding ring. Sometimes it takes me forty minutes to negotiate one; sometimes it takes fifteen minutes. Every now and then I pull off a trade in five minutes; but take the day through, the average is twenty-two minutes—call it four rings per hour. In the long summer days I can put in twelve or fourteen hours quite comfortably, and clear forty dollars or more on wedding rings; and in the meantime I am pretty sure to cash in ten or twenty or thirty dollars on engagement rings, according to the state of the market. You probably understand, now, how it is that in a population of eight or nine hundred grown-ups I have been able to find two hundred and sixty-four married women that were willing to strike up a trade with me for a wedding ring. Such is my history, sir, and I believe I have nothing to add to it.

Wednesday, March 6, 1907

The Frenchman's scheme for working off pewter watches on pawnbrokers, thereby making a large profit; his clever plan for reimbursing the pawnbrokers; who is the thief in the several transactions involved?

That cunning rascal's curious history brings back to me, out of the mouldy past of twenty-five years ago, a matter which is in some degree akin to it. It was a story which was discussed a good deal at the time, because there was what seemed to be a pretty difficult moral question involved in it. A young Parisian gentleman fell heir to a fortune and ran swiftly through it, by help of the customary aids furnished by fast living. When he realized that all his fortune was gone except his watch, he promptly made up his mind to pawn the watch, spend the resulting proceeds upon a single orgy, and then commit suicide. He was in London at the time. The watch was a Jürgensen, and worth six or eight hundred dollars. He took it to a pawnbroker; the pawnbroker examined it carefully outside, then opened it and as carefully examined the works; finally he dipped a camel's-hair brush into a liquid, touched the ball of the stemwinder with it, paused a moment for the effect—then he indicated by his manner that he was satisfied. He granted the young fellow a loan, at three months, of a hundred and fifty or two hundred dollars, and kept the watch.

The Frenchman dropped into a brown study on his way out of the shop, and before he had gone far he had made a radical change in his plans, and was resolved to postpone the orgy and try an experiment, and see what would come of it. The touching of the gold ball of the stemwinder with the camel's-hair brush had caught his attention; without doubt the liquid upon the brush was an acid, and perhaps that slight application of it was a pawnbroker's common and only test of the genuineness of the gold of a heavy hunting-case watch. At any rate, one could find out whether this was the custom or not, and it might be profitable to examine into the matter in a practical way. That was the young man's thought.

He was soon on his way to Switzerland. There he bought two or three sets of watch-works of unimpeachable excellence, and carried them to a competent and obscure constructor of watches and got them enclosed in heavy cases of fine gold—apparently;

but in fact the cases were of base metal, gold-washed; still there was one detail which was of good gold, real gold, gold able to stand the test of an application of acid and come out of it with credit; that detail was the knob of the stemwinder. He carried the watches back to London and distributed them among the pawnbrokers, and had no trouble; they touched the gold knobs with acid and handed him his money and his pawn tickets. He perceived that he had invented a way whereby he could make a reasonably good living, since he could calculate upon a clear profit of about eighty dollars on each watch. He sent to Switzerland for some more watches and unloaded them upon the pawnbrokers. He husbanded his profits carefully, and was presently able to order watches by the dozen. Naturally, he never went back to a pawnbroker to reclaim a watch. Pewter watches could not excite his passions.

Even in London there is a limit to pawnbrokers—they are not inexhaustible as to numbers. In the course of time they would all be supplied—then what should he do? Would it be safe to try to furnish them a second supply? Or must he go elsewhere and seek fresh markets in the other European capitals? He thought he would prefer to remain in London, if he could think of a safe way to manage it. He contrived one. It was very simple. He tried the experiment and it succeeded. He hired a cheap assistant to pawn the watches to pawnbrokers who had previously been supplied, and fetch home the money and the pawn tickets.

Now then, we arrive at the most curious and interesting part of this whole business— and that is this: at bottom that young Frenchman was very sensitive in the matter of morals; he could not bear the thought of cheating those pawnbrokers out of their money; they had done him no harm; they had offended him in no way, and he could not, and must not, have them on his conscience. He was deeply troubled; along at first he could not sleep. Every day he added two or three hundred dollars to his accumulation of cash, and so the distress at his heart grew daily heavier and heavier.

At last a saving thought occurred to him, and his troubles vanished away. He went out at mid-afternoon with a hatful of pawn tickets in his pocket and started down Regent street. He drifted through the moving crowd of men and women, watching for the right face—the face which should indicate the presence of a treacherous and dishonest heart in its owner's bosom, the face of a person who would rob his fellow man if he could, therefore the face of a person who ought to be made to suffer, and whom nothing but sorrow and loss could reform. Every time the Frenchman, eager to lift up his fallen fellow man and make him better and purer, saw that kind of a face, he dropped a pawn ticket on the pavement—apparently accidentally. There was always one unvarying result: that dishonest man glanced sharply around to see if the Frenchman had noticed his loss, but always saw—or thought he saw—that the Frenchman was not aware of the disaster that had happened to him; always, also, the dishonest man instead of flying to the Frenchman and restoring to him his lost property, as a clean and righteous person would have done, eagerly hid the ticket in his pocket and got away with all dispatch. In the course of time, the Frenchman dropped some thousands of pawn tickets in front of that class of persons, and as not one person of them all ever tried to restore a ticket to him he knew quite well that all of those shabby people had gone, each in his turn, and passed in his ill-gotten ticket and taken out a pewter watch and paid about two hundred dollars for it—but without doubt had been in a considerable measure purified and reformed by that bitter experience.

You will easily perceive that there is a defect of morals here somewhere, because somebody cheated somebody, and somebody got robbed; but who was it that did the cheating? And who was it that got robbed? The Frenchman never claimed that he was pawning a gold watch; he could never have brought himself to make such a statement; he merely offered the watch without saying anything about its character, and asked for a loan. The pawnbroker estimated the watch's value for himself and limited the loan to that valuation, therefore the Frenchman did not cheat the pawnbroker. Very well, did anybody cheat him? No. He got all his loan back with interest, from the dishonest finder of the pawn ticket, therefore he suffered in no way. The pawnbroker did not cheat the dishonest finder of the ticket, for the pawnbroker did not know it was a pewter watch. The fact remains, first and last and all the time, that there was a thief present in this transaction somewhere, and it now seems perfectly plain that the dishonest finder of the ticket was the only improper person connected with the transaction anywhere. He saw the ticket dropped, he could have restored it to the dropper, but he preferred to keep it; therefore he stole it. In paying to the pawnbroker a hundred and fifty or two hundred dollars for what he knew to be another man's watch, he perpetrated a glaring swindle, and since he was himself the person swindled there is no occasion for regrets, because he was also reformed and made clean, at the same time, and this was worth a hundred pewter watches to him. However, I will not try to go on any further with this. There are so many different kinds of morality mixed up in it that I find myself getting confused, I not being familiar with any but one kind.

Tuesday, March 26, 1907

Mr. Clemens has been taking another vacation, and a flying trip to Bermuda—His experiences with his eighty thousand dollars in 10 per cent stock—Miss Clemens's singing on the concert stage a success; she has learned how to please her audiences—Thomas Bailey Aldrich dead; none of the gay company of old left but Mr. Howells and Mr. Clemens—Mr. Clemens has completed the work which remained for him to do—his Autobiography—or enough of it to accomplish his object in writing it: to distribute it through his books and thus secure a new copyright life for them.

I have been taking another vacation—a vacation for which there was no excuse that I can think of except that I wanted to get away from work for a while to appease a restlessness which invades my system, now and then, and is perhaps induced by the fact that for thirty-five years I have spent all my winters in idleness, and have not learned to feel natural and at home in winter-work. I seem to have been silent about a month. Many things have happened in the meantime, and as I recall them I perceive that each incident was important in its hour, and alive with interest; then quickly lost color and life, and is now of no consequence. And this is what our life consists of—a procession of episodes and experiences which seem large when they happen, but which diminish to trivialities as soon as we get a perspective upon them. Upon these terms a diary ought to be a curious record, for in it all the events ought to be large, and all of the same size—with the result that by and by the recorded events should still be nearly all of one size, and that size lamentably shrunken in bulk.

This is a sordid and commercialized age, and few can live in such an atmosphere and remain unaffected by it; but I find that even the stock market is like the other interests—it cannot hold my attention long at a time. I have eighty thousand dollars in a 10 per cent stock, and I was not thinking of selling it, although I bought it to sell. While I was not noticing, it crept up, point by point, each point representing a profit of fifteen hundred dollars, and in the course of two or three weeks it climbed twenty-six points, each point, as I have said, standing for a profit of fifteen hundred dollars. If I had been awake I would have sold out and captured that thirty-nine thousand dollars to build the house with—for John Howells has been architecting a house for us, to be built upon the farm near Redding, Connecticut, which we bought a year and a half ago—but I was asleep, and did not wake up again until yesterday: meantime that stock had been sliding down, and in its descent it had sponged out the entire twenty-six points by yesterday afternoon. Then I bought some more of it, and made an order for a further purchase this morning if it should fall two or three points lower. I was hoping it would, but it didn't. It has started up again and I have recorded one more mistake. I hoped it would go 'way down, but since it has concluded to go up, I will try to get a sort of satisfaction out of watching its flight. Each ascending point now represents a profit of seventeen hundred and fifty dollars and it has accomplished two points since yesterday afternoon.

The next incident of importance was another trip to Bermuda a week or two ago. We went and came in the same ship, as before. The passages to and fro, and the twenty-four hours' sojourn in those delightful islands, were matters of high importance and enchanting interest for the time being, but already they have shriveled to nothing, and taken their place among the rest of the trivialities of life.

Clara has been barnstorming on the concert stage in New England the past few weeks, and at last she has learned her trade and is qualified to succeed, and will succeed—a great event for her, and a great event for me. By learning her trade, I mean that by normal processes her theories, which naturally seemed made of boiler-iron or some other indestructible substance, have been blown to the four winds by experience, that best of all teachers. According to her theories, her first duty was to be faithful to the highest requirements of her art and not move upon any plane but the highest; this meant classical music for all audiences, whether they were qualified to appreciate it and enjoy it or not. Experience has taught her that she and her audiences are in a tacit co-partnership, and that she must consider their share of the business and not arrange her performances to please herself alone. She has found, indeed, that her first duty is really to forget herself and give all her attention to pleasing her house. She has found that in striving to please the house she has accomplished several important things: her heart goes out to the house; by natural law the hearts of the house meet it half way; all hands are pleased; all dread and all anxiety have disappeared from her spirit, and life upon the platform has become to her a delight, and as pretty as a fairy-tale. She takes an undaughterful pleasure in noting that now the newspapers are beginning to concede with heartiness that she does not need the help of my name, but can make her way quite satisfactorily upon her own merits. This is insubordination, and must be crushed.

Thomas Bailey Aldrich has passed from this life, seventy years old. I was not back from Bermuda in time to attend the funeral, and the physicians would not allow Howells to go, he being but lately recovered from a wasting attack of the grippe. He was here yesterday, and naturally we called the roll. So many are gone! Of the gay company of us that used to foregather in Boston, thirty-five years ago and more, not one is left but himself and me; and of the New York contingent of that day we could call to mind no conspicuous member still in the flesh except Stedman. We had a right to complain of the order of the procession—disorder is its right name—for almost every one of those old-time friends got his release before he was fairly entitled to it. Howells and I have been postponed, and postponed, and postponed, until the injustice of it is becoming offensive. It is true that Aldrich was entitled to go before Howells, because he achieved his threescore and ten last November, whereas Howells only attained to that age on the 1st of the present month; but I am seventy-one and four months over—thus I ranked Aldrich by sixteen months—and was entitled to the precedence in the great procession. I do not need to stay here any longer, for I have completed the only work that was remaining for me to do in this life and that I could not possibly afford to leave uncompleted—my Autobiography. Although that is not finished, and will not be finished until I die, the object which I had in view in compiling it is accomplished: that object was to distribute it through my existing books and give each of them a new copyright life of twenty-eight years, and thus defeat the copyright statute's cold intention to rob and starve my daughters. I have dictated four or five hundred thousand words of autobiography already, and if I should die to-morrow this mass of literature would be quite sufficient for the object which I had in view in manufacturing it.

That very remarkable woman and exceedingly valuable citizen, Mrs. Kinnicutt, dined with us two or three nights ago, and that other very remarkable woman, Mrs. Draper, would have come also but an engagement prevented it. Mrs. Kinnicutt said—but I will refer to this later.

Wednesday, March 27, 1907

Mr. Clemens's experience with his copper stock as advised by
Mr. Rogers; his determination to exploit his stocks and bonds
according to his own intuitions—Pecuniarily the last twelvemonth
would have been more profitable than 1902 if he had acted on
his own inspirations—Mr. Clemens buys a hundred shares of
wireless telephone stock.

I wish to go on for a while cataloguing the things which have happened to me recently, for I find it very interesting to note how important each of them was in its turn, and how quickly it dropped to the rear and became of no consequence. I note one circumstance with high gratification, and that is this: that whereas Mr. Rogers's fiscal knowledge is better than mine, my fiscal ignorance is better than his fiscal knowledge, every now and then, and that whereas his caution is better than mine, my destitution of it is worth six of it. For instance: a year and a half ago, when he told me to buy that copper stock which I have been talking about, and said that the price would be certain to advance, I wanted to take two thousand shares, which would cost eighty-six thousand dollars, and would come near to exhausting my bank-balance. He said no, take the half of it. To my mind this was not good reasoning. If the price was sure to advance, why shouldn't one buy all of that stock that he could pay for? However, I respected his judgment, and I took a thousand shares instead of two thousand. I took it at 43; 50 was par. It was a 6 per cent stock and would soon pay 8. Copper was more precious than gold, and not all the mines in the world could supply the demand. I kept the thousand shares nine months; I collected one 8 per cent dividend and one 10 per cent dividend; then the market price had climbed to 79. I thought I would sell out. Thirty-two thousand dollars' profit on an investment of forty-three thousand, all in nine months, with four or five thousand in dividends added, seemed to me good enough for so humble a financier as I; but no, Mr. Rogers said, "Sell half; you couldn't possibly have anything better than that stock. Sell half, keep the rest." I obeyed. By luck, I had bought at the lowest figure; by luck again I sold at the highest figure—79¾. As soon as I withdrew my support from that excellent stock it began to drop along down, a point at a time, until two or three months ago, when it seemed to have reached the low water mark at 58. I consulted Mr. Rogers, and he said yes, buy. I thought of taking the whole mine, but again he was conservative; again he was cautious. He said, "take what you can pay for and no more, and leave as much money in the bank as you take out of it." So I took a thousand shares at 58. I still had five hundred at 43, and so the average cost of the whole was 53. I made up my mind to sell those fifteen hundred shares sure if the price ever reached 79 again. It did reach that figure, but, as I have already explained in an earlier chapter, I was asleep at the time and failed to secure the forty thousand dollars due me on my judgment. As I have said, the stock began to soar along down until it struck bottom day before yesterday, when I bought two hundred and fifty shares at 53, and of course by this maneuver I sent it up. It went up because I wanted to buy another two hundred and fifty, but I was proposing to pay less for it. Yesterday afternoon it had gone up five points and a half. I seem to be one of the most formidable persons in the financiering business, for I can't sell without sending the stock down, and I can't buy without sending it up. By my count, my pocket is much damaged through Mr. Rogers's expert judgment. I estimate that if I had bought and sold every time that I proposed to buy and sell, I should now have a profit of ninety thousand dollars in the bank, whereas, my intentions being defeated by Mr. Rogers's superior judgment, that money failed to arrive at the bank—and yet I do not see but that I get as much satisfaction out of it as anybody could get out of ninety thousand dollars that he didn't own, for I have already in fancy spent it several times, and have gotten very real pleasure out of spending it; also I allow myself luxuries which I could not afford at all if I didn't have that imaginary ninety thousand to draw upon. I am so pleased with my financial superiorities over Mr. Rogers's that I am resolved to exploit them now and see what will come of it. Within a week this temporary panic will be over, and the sound and safe dividend-paying stocks will be up again; then I shall sell my hoard, both stocks and bonds, that I have been holding these six or seven years; and I mean to put the money in the bank and leave it there at 3 per cent until the next flurry comes, even if it be six months that I must wait. Many a time, in these six or seven years, each stock that I own has gone up ten or twenty points above what I paid for it, and later each of them has gone ten points or more below what I paid for it. Hereafter I mean to sell them out at normal rates, then buy them back and sell them again, and keep this game going. I cannot hurt myself, because if they get left on my hands some time or other, no harm will be done, because their dividends will continue, and not fail. Pecuniarily, this last twelvemonth would have been more profitable to me than was the year 1902, if I had acted upon my fine inspirations and let Mr. Rogers's educated judgment alone, for the royalties on my old books have paid me forty thousand dollars, which is about eight thousand more than they have been in the annual habit of paying; also the *North American Review* is paying me thirty thousand for a hundred thousand words of my Autobiography; indeed I should have beaten 1902 considerably but for the miscarriage of that ninety thousand dollars.

There is a new invention. Apparently it is a wireless telephone. Everybody can have the machine in his house, and it has one or two advantages over the telephone that uses a wire. For instance: it records the messages which it receives, and it is able to do this when no one is present; therefore you can call up a friend, deliver your message into his house with none to receive it but the machine; when he returns home he can reverse the spool and listen to the message; also it keeps its secrets; they do not pass through a central station to be listened to by the telephone girl and distributed abroad. Some of the Company's circulars and other advertisements reached me yesterday by mail. I found that I could get a hundred shares of the stock at ten dollars a share, if I wanted it, but that I was not privileged to take any more than that. That has a suspicious look; it looks like fishing for widows and orphans, and the clergy. You can float any speculation that is inventable if you offer its stock at ten dollars a share, with a prediction that it will later sell for a million; then you get all the widows and orphans and clergymen that are floating around. They will pledge their very children and their Bibles to raise money enough to buy. However, I am no better, myself, than a widow, or an orphan, or a clergyman, when it comes to a chance for a clear, straight, unmitigated and inexcusable gamble; I always want to take a hand in that. Instantly I wanted a hundred of those shares; then I thought, no, I should have to conceal the matter from Mr. Rogers; then, later, I could not keep my secret; I should be sure to reveal it to him, and then there would be sarcasms. However, at this point in my reflections I picked up one of the advertisements which had thitherto escaped me. It was a facsimiled letter from a man of high fame in science, and of acknowledged and unassailable probity. In this letter he asked for a hundred shares, and said that he wanted to use them in rectification of a mistake which he made twenty-eight years ago when twenty-five hundred shares of Bell Telephone stock were offered to him for five hundred dollars and he didn't take them. Dear me, I knew how that poor wise ass was feeling! His wail brought back to me my own experience of twenty-nine years ago with Bell Telephone stock—an experience which I have already recorded, with many pangs, in one of the early chapters of this Autobiography. He remarked in his letter that if he had taken the twenty-five hundred shares it would have paid him twenty million dollars before this. It hurt me to the marrow to hear this man go into these quite unnecessary particulars, for it called back to my memory, out of that distant past, how in 1877 or '78 I had twenty-three thousand dollars in my pocket which I had no particular use for, and the Bell Telephone people tried to trade me a couple of tons of stock for it. I was fully as wise as this other smarty, and they did not succeed; but if they had succeeded I would pay off our national debt now, and let the country take a fresh start.

Upon reflection, I sent a thousand dollars this morning and captured a hundred shares of this gamble. I was not going to be caught out again. I shall not live to pay the national debt, but in my dying moments I shall instruct Clara and Jean to attend to it.

Thursday, March 28, 1907

The Russian Count's luncheon at the St. Regis and his political speech in response to Mr. Clemens's speech in behalf of the ladies present.

It was my intention to continue and complete the list of important-unimportant happenings which have fallen to my share lately, and no longer ago than yesterday afternoon there was a basketful of them in my head, but to my astonishment they are all gone this morning, and the basket is empty. I am sorry, for as far as I had proceeded in recording them they were a revelation to me of what a diary is, and of necessity must be: fine and precious gold to-day, ashes, and valueless, to-morrow. Never mind—let it go.

Yesterday I went to the plutocratic St. Regis Hotel to lunch with the Russian Count who dined with us a week ago. There were about thirty ladies and gentlemen present, all prominent people and all useful people; people not only distinguished for high place in society, but also for achievement—the women as well as the men. I knew nearly all of them, and the time passed very pleasantly. Toward the end of the function the Count did a rather startling thing; he sent a member of the Russian Embassy to me to ask me to get up and make a speech. It was a startling proposition only because it came from the giver of the feast. Properly there could be but one text for a speech on such an occasion, and that text would be the host himself, and the speech an irruption of compliments to that person. By the custom of our country, some conspicuous guest does always use that text, and produce that kind of a speech, but he either does this of his own motion or at the suggestion of another guest; the suggestion never comes from the host.

Some occult instinct seemed to inform me that I was in an embarrassing position, and so I thought it best to secure a moment or two in which to collect my judgment and determine what to do. Then the saving idea came to the rescue, and I went to the Count and said I was gratified by the honor which he had done me, but that it would not be quite properly deferential in me to take precedence of Mr. John Bigelow in so important a matter, I never having served a public office of any kind in my life, whereas Mr. Bigelow had represented the United States in ambassadorial capacities at foreign courts with high and memorable distinction; and I also observed that his age gave him another right of precedence over me, he being past ninety, and I only seventy-one—and so, for these various reasons, I ought to follow Mr. Bigelow, not precede him. I offered to go and say these things to Mr. Bigelow, and invite him, in the Count's name, to speak. The Count thanked me, and I went to Mr. Bigelow with my mission. I can't help admiring my smartness. It makes me proud every time I think of it—not because I was any smarter than usual, for I wasn't; I am always smart. Let other people think as they may, I privately know that I am always smart, and as a rule considerably smarter than anybody else—but with this defect: that my smartness heretofore has always arrived a matter of twenty-four hours too late, when it couldn't do any good, nor attract any attention, nor furnish me any self-admiration; but this time I was smart right on the spot, and I couldn't have been smarter if I had had a week to arrange the smartness in. I delivered the message to Mr. Bigelow, and his reply almost snuffed out my admiration of my own smartness, because of the suddenness of his responding smartness and the deep and wise and superior character of it. His training as a diplomat showed out very conspicuously. Through my inexperience I had been caught unprepared, and had been stunned, and had been obliged to procrastinate and gain time in which to find out what I would better do; but his trained and educated sagacity had qualified him to be ready on the moment to meet any exigency, and he was ready this time. He reminded me that this Russian Count and Major General must naturally be on the imperial side in Russia's present great quarrel with the people of Russia; that I was publicly known to be on the side of the revolutionists, where all right feeling Americans ought to be; that the imperialists and the revolutionists were laboring hard, both for the same object—to win the sympathies of the American people. He said,

"It is possible that if you and I should speak the Count would use the opportunity to introduce Russian politics into his reply; then if his speech should get into print, it could make you and me seem to be in sympathy with the Czar's side of the question, and certainly neither of us would enjoy that. I am not saying that the Count *would* do this; I am only saying it is a possibility; but no matter, a possibility is enough; the barest possibility is argument enough and reason enough for you and me to keep silent—but particularly me. I have no text; I cannot speak without one. It is different with you; you are at your best when you haven't a text and when you don't know anything about the subject you are instructing your audience upon. I give you leave to speak, but you mustn't by any accident make an opening for any political remarks in return. You may praise the Count himself, if you want to, but you are not to say anything about the Czar or the revolution—not even a word."

I went back to my place and reported results to the ladies in my neighborhood. They said it was quite too bad to leave the matter so; somebody ought to get up and say a pleasant thing about this sumptuous luncheon and pay the Count a handsome compliment or two, and that I ought to do it, and must do it. I said I had no text; that I could not do this complimenting on my own motion; it would be as difficult as it would be for me to get up and compliment myself—in fact more difficult, twice as difficult. They said, "But couldn't you make the speech and the compliment in our behalf—in behalf of the ladies?" I said, "Certainly, I can do that; that will be simple and easy, and I can do it with very real pleasure."

So I got up and made the speech. Of course it hadn't a reference in it to the Czar, or to Russia, or to the Duma, or to the revolution, or to the daily slaughter of the helpless Jews that that infamous Government has been carrying on daily for two years. It confined itself strictly to the ladies, and their thanks.

Then straightway the wisdom of that old diplomat was confirmed: the Count got up and made a political speech! It was ludicrously out of harmony with the light stuff which I had been delivering there. It was odd enough to hear a man respond to a batch of gilded and lightsome personal compliments with a flowing stream of memorized adulations of the Russian Emperor, and his great and good and divine nature and noble and beneficent intentions. Certainly a memorized speech can be a grotesque thing when you can't know what sort of a speech it is destined to respond to. A practised talker like Choate would make a memorized speech look convincingly as if every word of it had been suggested by some remark in the speech which preceded it. Choate would have found a word somewhere in my speech—even if he had to invent that word himself and insert it—that would have made the Count's speech look quite satisfactorily impromptu, but the Count lacked that art. Without a single preliminary word, and without a single reference to what I had been saying, he jumped right into his memorized adulations, and I think it was the funniest incident of the kind I have ever seen in an after-dinner experience of forty years.

**Mr. Clemens walks home from the St. Regis luncheon; on the
way he thinks about the *Christian Union* article and wishes
he had a copy of it; at 42d street a stranger puts the clippings
concerning that article into his hand, saying he was just going
to mail them to him.**

Some months ago I commented upon a chapter of Susy's Biography wherein she very
elaborately discussed an article about the training and disciplining of children, which I
had published in the *Christian Union,* (this was twenty-one years ago), an article which
was full of worshipful praises of Mrs. Clemens as a mother, and which little Clara, and
Susy, and I had been hiding from this lovely and admirable mother because we knew
she would disapprove of public and printed praises of herself. At the time that I was
dictating those comments, several months ago, I was trying to call back to my memory
some of the details of that article, but I was not able to do it, and I wished I had a copy
of the article so that I could see what there was about it which gave it such large interest
for Susy.

Yesterday afternoon I elected to walk home from the luncheon at the St. Regis, which
is in 55th street and Fifth Avenue, for it was a fine spring day and I hadn't had a walk for a
year or two, and felt the need of exercise. As I walked along down Fifth Avenue the desire
to see that *Christian Union* article came into my head again. I had just reached the corner
of 42d street then, and there was the usual jam of wagons, carriages, and automobiles
there. I stopped to let it thin out before trying to cross the street, but a stranger, who
didn't require as much room as I do, came racing by and darted into a crack among the
vehicles and made the crossing. But on his way past me he thrust a couple of ancient
newspaper clippings into my hand, and said,

"There, you don't know me, but I have saved them in my scrap-book for twenty years,
and it occurred to me this morning that perhaps you would like to see them, so I was
carrying them down town to mail them, I not expecting to run across you in this accidental way, of course; but I will give them into your own hands now. Good-bye"—and
he disappeared among the wagons.

Those scraps which he had put into my hand were ancient newspaper copies of that
Christian Union article! It is a handsome instance of mental telegraphy—or if it isn't
that, it is a handsome case of coincidence.

Monday, April 8, 1907

**The battles of Navarino and Lepanto and the princes of
Montenegro: all an annoyance to Mr. Clemens—Mr. William
T. Stead appoints Mr. Clemens a member of the International
Peace Convention; he and Mr. Stead discuss the appointment—
President Roosevelt the most popular human being that ever**

sojourned in America—Copy of letter in form of essay bearing on subjects recently discussed by Mr. Clemens.

I note with satisfaction that the last survivor of the battle of Navarino is dead. Perhaps we shall now have a rest from that battle. I seem to be including everybody, but it is merely a manner of speech; I am meaning only myself. The battle of Navarino has been an annoyance to me all my life. I cannot remember back to the time when the mention of that battle did not irritate me. It is not that I had any grudge against the battle itself; it is only that I never could separate it from the battle of Lepanto. I know of nothing that is more troublesome than a confusion of that kind; we all have them; no one is free from them; they embitter life and make existence a weariness. I have always known that it was in one of these battles that Cervantes was wounded, but I never could tell which battle it was without consulting the Cyclopedia again. I have worn out many and many a Cyclopedia in settling which battle it was, but I never could make the information stay after I had acquired it. I have consulted the Cyclopedia again, and this time I find, as usual, that it was in the Lepanto fight that Cervantes was wounded. It is the hundred and fiftieth time that I have found that out, and it is about the hundredth time that I have wished he had been wounded in both those battles; then I could keep his record clear and my own mind at rest. The fact that one of the battles was older than the other by about three centuries is of no help to me; in my muddled head they stick together, and I cannot separate them. But the thing that interests me is the curious fact that I should get a personal satisfaction out of the death of the last survivor of Navarino, for I had nothing against him; I was only tired of his battle. Now then—but never mind, let it go; it is not worth while to try to analyze my feeling; I should never be able to do it; it is like the feeling which I have harbored against the princes of Montenegro for forty years. That name always irritates me; still there is something like a definite reason for it—a trivial one, and yet, in effect, a reason. Forty years ago, when a party of us representing the *Quaker City* Excursion were examining the sights of Paris and arrived at the tomb of Napoleon, we were halted outside and informed that the Prince of Montenegro was visiting the tomb and we must wait until he was done with it. We were kept outside half an hour, and time was very precious to us cheap pilgrims. I had never heard of him before, but I inquired and found that he owned a farm in the neighborhood of Turkey somewhere, and raised rocks on it—not an important farm, but since it was a principality it made the Prince of Montenegro a person of consequence and set him up among the royalties. Years afterward, when I had acquired a family and we were traveling about Europe, I engaged rooms by telegraph in a hotel in Venice and when we arrived there, tired and worn, we found our quarters occupied. The landlord explained that he had been obliged to give them to the Prince of Montenegro, who had arrived unexpectedly. These were the beginnings of a procession of interruptions of my comfort and repose, by the princes of Montenegro, which has extended down to the present time. I do not go to Europe any more, on account of the princes of Montenegro. They have stepped into my way as many as a dozen times; they have been one of the chief annoyances of my life;

their name is a perennial disturbance to me whenever and wherever I see it. Lepanto, Navarino, Montenegro: these have permanently embittered me against all names that end with *o*. It seems a trivial thing that I should be affected by such small matters as these, and yet it is only natural, since all human concerns are trivial, and these are as large as any of them.

And this reminds me that I came across William T. Stead yesterday. He is over here to take part in an International Peace Convention which is to assemble a week or ten days from now. His project is to select one or two widely known men in each country and band them together in a commission, which shall visit all the presidents and crowned heads and persuade them to endorse and support a proposition to be laid before this year's Hague Tribunal. The idea is to have that Tribunal pass an international law requiring quarreling States about to go to war to postpone overt action until thirty days after they shall have made up their minds to draw the sword. This is to give time for the other States of Christendom to try to pacify the belligerents and compromise the quarrel, and prevent the war. As one of the members of the American contingent of this roving commission, Mr. Stead had nominated me, but I told him I could not serve; that my active days were over, and that even short journeys were a distress to me, and I could not think of venturing a long one. He said it was hardly my privilege to decline this great service; that it was my duty to do everything that in me lay to advance the human race, as long as the breath should remain in my body. But I said it was not worth while, for the reason that you can't advance the human race and make it stay advanced; that every time you propped up its wobbling form on one side it toppled over on the other; that all its affairs are transitory and unstable, and none of them important, for that reason; that all ameliorations of the condition of the human race are impermanent; as soon as you reform them in one particular the race breaks out, in another place, worse than ever; that it is a weary and unprofitable enterprise to keep on calking a rickety old ship that springs a new leak every time you calk an old one—and so on, and so on, a long chapter of discussion between us without a result, he holding that the affairs of the human race are important, worth our best efforts for their improvement and our loyal belief in the proposition that the improvement can be made permanent, and I denying these things in detail and in mass. Stead has a large reverence for the human race and a strong belief in its far-reaching intelligence and wisdom; I don't know where he got it, but that is his affair, not mine. Stead is a strong man and a good man, and I think he is almost always in the right. Stead is not popular in England, where he belongs. This is sufficiently good evidence that both his head and his heart are right—at least I look at it in that way. President Roosevelt is to-day, by very long odds—overwhelming odds—the most popular being, human or divine, visible or invisible, that has ever sojourned in America. I think it is a very damaging fact, and ought to make the President distinctly uncomfortable.

In view of the things which I have just been saying, the following letter has an odd interest for me. It arrived this morning from Canada, and was written three days ago.

I will leave out the introductory remarks and present the meat of the letter, which is in the form of an essay.

The Broader View.

Calm, fearless, imperturbable, the observer of world history should stand amid the travail of events.

Knowing that all forms however dear and all ideas however cherished must change, he should behold their mutations without emotion.

Things were real to Alexander. He had his social and political ideas and his gods.

He undoubtedly looked upon them as important enough to be permanent. To us these things are little more than names.

Caesar, we are taught, was a great military genius. He conquered a world. His time also possessed gods and social and political systems.

His gods we call mythological, his social arrangements we could not abide for he dressed and fed and otherwise lived like a barbarian. His language we call dead. We do not even know it's accent. Things were very real to Caesar.

Napoleon, perhaps the greatest reservoir of human energy that ever existed, was here and is gone.

Although so recent, historians already differ materially regarding many of the events of his career.

History itself begins but a few thousand years back and in that time has shown kaliedescopic changes in every department of human affairs.

It has been stated by Mark Twain, the deepest philosopher America has produced, that "The altar-cloth of one age becomes the door-mat of the next."

We, that have no scarcity of door-mats yet cling trustingly to our altar-cloths.

We hope against all experience that our's shall be the ones to cohere.

Does any really acute thinker believe that they shall? In it's self-consciousness the present may be personified as a stupendous egotist as blind as big.

It is as though at each second the clock ticked out "I am THE second, I am eternity."

The seconds grow into minutes, the minutes into hours, the hours into days, the days into years, the years into eons, the end is not yet.

Down the long procession, reaching into the dim mists beyond the beginning of history, march multitudes of errors of belief and practice. Those errors were solemn facts in their respective days.

Jah, Baal, Ra, Jove, Thor were names by which was called that infinite abstraction, God, source, power and director of the universe.

When the conceptions of today have taken their places in the march of centuries, shall they too be considered as in the dark catalog of errors?

With our lesson can we be so egotistic, so foolish, so ignorant as to believe otherwise?

From the crude stone phallus and the gilded sun, through every anthromorphic modification down to the intangible abstraction of the most diaphanous deist, there has not yet been discovered one iota of knowledge, one definite idea, however minute, or one useful relation between existence and that for which man has so diligently and so blindly searched.

Teachers of the people today, with an assurance that is astounding, pronounce upon the great problems of existence forgetting that almost with the last echo of their voices, they are the uncatalogued clods of a forgotten race.

Ages ago men pronounced as positively what we now regard as arrant nonsense.

Augurs were employed to watch the flight of birds before the departure of an army of conquest. Omens were to them realities.

Later Cromwell began his battles with prayer. In our day, Chinese Gordon was deeply imbued with the idea of the personal management of the universe by a God.

Was any one more absurd than the others? All of our inventions, our arts and our sciences seem powerless to teach to the multitude the evanescence of any point in history.

All they have succeeded in doing has been to change the names of the fetishes as they carry them down the highway of time.

Mark G. McElhinney

Dictated April 9, 1907

The "Wapping Alice" story.

At the banquet in honor of Ambassador Tower, last night, I encountered a guest, who greeted me with a formula which I hear pretty often, particularly from elderly people—

"You don't remember me?"

I confessed. Then he told me his name. The name did not help me, I still did not remember him. He said he would give me a pointer: which he did with a remark in which he lightly dropped a name—"Wapping Alice." Full lightly he dropped it, yes, but in my private breast it made a bang like a bombshell! I remembered him then; he was a minor character in a very dramatic episode which enacted itself in our house many many years ago—twenty-seven, to be precise. It came back to me with a sharp and sudden vividness, and I saw the whole thing again, just as it had happened so long ago; it flashed upon me bright and intense, like a midnight landscape revealed by a flood of lightning. I saw all the actors in the event, too, even to the clothes they wore, though they are all dead these many years, except this banquet-guest and me—yes, and one other.

I do not remember the real name of the Swede who figures in the drama, I only remember the fantastic name our servants furnished him with, but it will answer, for it is a plenty good enough name, for him or for anybody else. The time was 1880.

It was on the 2d of January of that year that we added Wapping Alice to our household staff. According to her story she was born and reared in that part of London which is called Wapping, and the other servants soon got to calling her Wapping Alice to distin-
1880   guish her from our other Alice, the colored cook. She came to us fresh from England; she brought no recommendations, but we took her on her face. She soon made her way. She was good-hearted and willing, she fitted neatly into her place, the children grew fond of her, everybody on the place had a good word for her, and we were glad of the luck that threw her in our way. She was a little frisky with her *h*'s, but that was nothing.

Some of the ridiculous features of the incident which I am going to speak of presently will be better understood if I expose Wapping Alice's secret here and now, in the beginning—for she had a secret. It was this: she was not a woman at all, but a *man*.

It is very creditable to his ingenuity that he was able to masquerade as a girl seven months and a half under all our eyes and never awake in us doubt or suspicion. It must not be charged that a part of the credit is due to our dulness; for no one can say that our friends and neighbors were dull people, and they were deceived as completely as we were. They knew Alice almost as well as we knew him, yet no suspicion of the fraud he was playing ever crossed their minds. He must have had years of apprenticeship in his part, or he could not have been so competent in it. Why he unsexed himself was his own affair. In the excitement of the grand climax in August the matter was overlooked and he was not questioned about it.

For convenience, now, I will stop calling him "he." Indeed, with that fair and modest and comely young creature framed before me now in the mirror of my memory, it is awkward and unhandy to call it anything but "she."

Wapping Alice took up her abode with us on the 2d of January. The kitchen was an independent annex, built against the north side of the house; the house-entrance to it was from the dining room. It consisted of two stories and a cellar; this latter was a laundry, and communicated with the house-cellar. It also had a door which opened upon the steep hillside, above the brook. All about our house was open ground; so it stood by itself. When it was locked up for the night, communication with the kitchen-annex was shut off, and the annex became in effect an independent establishment. After that, if the occupants of it wished to indulge in privacies of their own they had their opportunity: we should know nothing about it.

Wapping Alice and the cook had adjoining bedrooms on the second floor of the annex, over the kitchen. At five in the morning, February 2d, the burglar alarm let go with an urgent clatter, and I was out on the floor before I was awake. Before I was fairly into the bath-room the clatter stopped. I turned up the gas and looked at the annunciator. One of the metal tabs was down, and was still wagging with excitement. The number exposed by it indicated the laundry door which opened upon the hillside. That was a curious thing. What was there in the annex that a burglar might want? And why should he want it so early in the morning? And the weather so bitter cold, too. Ought I to go all the way down there and inquire? My curiosity was strong, but not strong enough for that. I went back to bed, and reported progress. I said there was no present danger. We could wait, and listen for the alarm again. In case it should indicate that the burglar was breaking into the dining room, we could collect the children and climb out of the front window. Then we went to sleep.

At five the next morning the alarm rang again. I went in the bath-room and looked, and it was the laundry door once more. At breakfast I told George about it. He could not account for it, but thought maybe Patrick had taken a notion to come at that strange hour and fertilize the furnace because of the exceeding sharpness of the weather. It turned out that Patrick had better sense. All the same the laundry rang us up at five on the succeeding morning. The mystery was not wasted on the family; it made plenty of good talk for us at breakfast. And for George, too, of course; for whatever interested the rest of the family interested him, for that is the way with the colored servant when he is built in the right and usual way. Let me explain George—with just a word or two; otherwise you may presently think that my ways with him and his ways with me were not ceremonious enough, not distant enough. Put that all out of your mind, in justice to us both. Each of us knew his place, quite well, and was in no danger of forgetting it. Let me throw some light—then you will understand: he was an institution—he was a *part* of us, not an excrescence—we had a great affection for him, and he for us; when he said to people "my family" are well, or "my family" are away, now, and so on, he meant *my* family, not his. But to go back to the breakfast-table discussion of that burglar alarm matter. Wapping Alice was in the room during this discussion. After breakfast she asked George what a burglar alarm might be. George explained it to her, and showed her how the opening of a door or a window would set it off. Well, the laundry door troubled us no more. For a while we wondered at that; then the matter dropped out of our minds. The 9th of June we went away for the summer. Something more than two months afterward I happened to be within a hundred miles of home, and I thought I would run up and see how things were getting along there. I arrived in the gloaming and walked out from the station. On the way, a horse-car came loafing by, and a friend hailed me from its rear platform—

"I thought that would fetch you! How much did they get?"

"What do you mean?"

"Don't you know your house has been burglarized?"

"No."

"George wanted it kept out of the papers—so it didn't get in; but I supposed he telegraphed you."

"No, I haven't heard of it."

The house and the grounds had a lonesome and forsaken look. I rang, and got no answer. I walked all about the place, but found no one. The horses were in the stable, but Patrick and his family were gone. I went back and was going to open the front door with a latch-key, but concluded to try the knob first. The door swung open! It seemed an odd state of things for a house that had so lately had experience of burglars. I went all over the house and the annex. Everything was in good order, but there were no human beings anywhere. So I lit up, in the library, and sat down to read and smoke, and wait.

I waited until ten at night, then George arrived. When he opened the door and saw me and the other lights, he was astonished.

"Why, when did you come, sir!"

I answered with austerity—meaning to impress him—

"More than three hours ago—and found the house absolutely unprotected. The whole tribe away; no one left to take care of the place. What do you think of that kind of conduct? A burglar could have emptied the house, unmolested."

George was not impressed. He laughed a comfortable, care-free laugh, and said—

"This house ain't in no danger, Mr. Clemens, don't you worry. There ain't a burglar that don't know there's a burglar alarm in this house. It's business for them to know where there's alarms, and they know it, you can 'pend upon that. No, sir, they don't tetch no house that's got a—"

"Do you mean to say that you keep the alarm *on,* day and night both?"

"No, sir, don't keep it on at all, generally. Just the *fact* is a plenty. They ain't going to meddle here."

"You think so, do you? Where have you all been?"

"Been down the river on the excursion boat."

"All of you?"

"Yes, sir, the whole bilin'."

"I think it's scandalous. Even if there *is* a burglar alarm, I think you might at least lock the front door when you desert the house."

George smiled a placid smile, and said, almost languidly—

"Well, now, we ain't quite so far gone as all that, Mr. Clemens. Whenever we go we always lock the front door, and—"

"George, I came in without a latch-key."

George caught his breath with a gasp, and reeled in his tracks. The next moment he was flying up stairs like a rocket. I was almost as much startled as he was. He was gone five minutes, then he came drooping into the room, limp and weak, and swabbing his face, which had paled to the hue of old amber. He came and leaned against the book-shelves near me, and waited a little to get his breath, his breast rising and falling with his pantings. Then he gave his face a final wipe, and said—

"My souls, Mr. Clemens, what a turn you did gimme! The front door not even on the latch, and fifteen hundred dollars hard-earned money up there betwixt my mattresses!"

"Oh," I said, "I see! To leave *my* things unprotected is a small matter; but when it imperils yours it's quite another matter. I'm ashamed of you, George."

"Well, now I come to look at it, I dunno but I feel mostly the same way."

"How did you come to have all that money in the house?—you that let on to be so careful about always banking the results of your pious robberies. Have you been betting on the revival-catch again? Is there another religious epidemic in your African church?"

I could see that that wounded him—poor old George. I knew it would, for it was probably true. It had been charged against him by the brother whom he supplanted as deacon of the church, and it was a sore spot with George, who always said it was a slander; but as he never went quite far enough to say it was a lie, and as he was something of a purist in language, this subtle discrimination was noticed by the family, to his damage. Out of love, they did not twit him with it; but out of love, I did—and rubbed it in, sometimes.

"Mr. Clemens, you oughtn't to talk so—because I never done it. I do bet on horse-races, and elections, and sprints, and base ball, and foot-ball, and everything that ain't sinful and got money in it, but I never done that."

"You didn't, didn't you? Well, let it go, for this time—though I suppose you did. Where did you get this fifteen hundred?"

"At the Rochester races, day before yistiddy."

"George! do you mean to say that you have been five hundred miles from home and left nobody but women in the house all that time?"

But George was not much troubled. He said—

"I only went for three or four days, and it ain't likely that anybody would break into the house in that little time. Especially where there's an alarm. And Patrick was right there in his house, anyway, and nothing to do but ring him up."

I had now artfully worked George up to the right place to spring my surprise upon him, and I touched it off:

"George, you haven't telegraphed anything to me lately; through your happy relations with the press, the papers have been muzzled. And so you think you have managed to hide something away which you didn't want me to find out. But your hand was not well played. George, I know everything. This house has been burglarized! And on top of this, you all go off larking and leave it to be burglarized again. *Now* what do you think of yourself!"

It didn't phaze him. It didn't start a hair. It left him as serene as a summer morning. He was the most provoking creature about making a person's calculations all go for nothing. A pleasant smile allowed a wink of his white teeth to show for a moment, and he said, comfortably—

"There hain't been no burglars here, Mr. Clemens. Nary a burglar."

"Now you know better. Mr. C— told me, as I came up from the station."

"Yes, sir. Well, he done right. *I* put that up on him. I done it for a purpose."

"You did, did you? Well, what was your purpose?"

"I'm going to tell you all about it, Mr. Clemens. You see, there was something happened here in the house, and it was a mystery. Yes, sir, that is what it was; it was a mystery. I reckoned it would get out, and get in the papers, and then the family would be worried, and you would come flying here, four hundred miles, and no use in it. Fact is, I knowed the other servants couldn't keep it, and I knowed they would ruther have something big to tell than something little, so I come flat out and told them to say it was a burglar. That pleased them, of course, and they done it. Then the rest of it was easy for me. I went down to the papers and told them a noble good lie—because that ain't no sin when you are trying to do good by it—and asked them to keep still and not scare the burglars out of town, for I was right on their track; and so they done it. Now then, the thing that *did* happen was like this. Last Sunday we all went up to Northampton on a little excursion—"

"Well, by gracious! The whole tribe, of course."

"No, sir, not all, that time. Three or four of Patrick's children warn't very well, but most of the others went, and Bridget and Patrick. And the rest of us went, except Wapping Alice. She allowed she'd stay at home and take care of the house, and she done it."

"She shall have a monument."

"Yes, sir. Well, we missed the connection at Springfield, so we come back home. We got here about three in the afternoon, and there warn't nobody in sight anywhere in these regions—just the way it always is out here Sunday afternoons in the summertime—lonesome; perfectly gashly. It was awful hot. So we come in by the ground-floor bedroom window, because it was handier than the annex, and come in here where it was cool. We set down here and begun to chat along. Now I had put the front door on the alarm that morning, and didn't say anything about it. I most always done so when we went on excursions—sometimes, anyway, if I thought of it. So we was setting here chatting, and the doors into the dining room was spread apart a piece—about a foot. I was setting just where you are now, and could see through that crack. All of a sudden I see a man go past it! It give me such a start I couldn't get my breath for as much as ten seconds; then I sung out 'By jimminy, there's a man!' and we jumped for the hall door. Just then, *zzzzzip!* went the alarm, then the front door banged to, and it stopped. I was there in a second, and out; and see a young man sailing over the sward like a deer. Now whatever went with him I couldn't make out; but when I got to the upper gate he warn't anywhere in sight.

"So then we come back, and looked the house over, and nothing was gone. That is, I told them to search the house and I would search the annex. We set here and talked it over, and over, and over, and *over*. Couldn't seem to get enough of it. I told them everything was all right, in the annex, and Wapping Alice sleeping like a graveyard; nothing hadn't disturbed *her*. So then we agreed on burglary, and they said they would go out and take a walk. I *judged* they would. And I judged it would be a long one, if they met up with a good many friends that was interested in burglaries.

"I had a chance to set down and think, now. I turned this and that and t'other thing over in my head for about an hour, and pieced them together, and when I was done I had made up my mind. What do you reckon it was, Mr. Clemens?"

"I don't know. What was it, George?"

"Well, sir, this was it. I says to myself, I don't want to wrong nobody, and anybody that knows me knows it ain't my disposition; but it's my opinion that Wapping Alice ain't what she ought to be."

"Oh, nonsense!"

"I hope it is, Mr. Clemens; there wouldn't be anybody gladder than me; for I am like the rest—I like Wapping Alice, and wouldn't hurt a hair of her head for the world. And she's far from her home and her people, too, poor thing, and I ain't no dog, and can feel for that."

"What things did you piece together, George, to build up that wild idea?"

"Well, sir, it's curious. The first thing that come into my head didn't seem to have any business there, and took me by surprise. Do you remember, sir, the time the alarm went off three mornings last February, long before daylight? That was it. You know it warn't ever accounted for."

"I know, but how does that connect itself with this remote matter?"

"Well, the third morning, Wapping Alice was in the breakfast room when we was all talking about it; and she asked me what a burglar alarm was, and I told her. Now, Mr. Clemens, the landry didn't wake you up any more after that."

"Come, that was well thought out. Go on."

"The next thing that come into my head was this. Last January the plumbers ripped out some wood-work to get at a leaky pipe, and a young carpenter was here a couple of days putting it back. A young Swede he was, by the name of Bjurnsen Bjuggersen Bjorgensen. Turrible name, and oversized him considerable, so it seemed to me, but that was it—or in that neighborhood. He set around in the kitchen a good deal, chatting, because he was working by the day and that always makes a person tireder than the other kind, and so we all got to know him pretty well, and liked him. About the 1st June I went into Wapping Alice's room one morning, and there was a suit of men's clothes laying there, and she was half-soling the seat of the pants. I asked her about it and she said she was mending them up for the young carpenter—he asked her to do it. So that come into my head, now, I didn't know why.

"Thinking it over, I remembered another thing. When I was telling her about the burglar alarm that morning, I smelt her breath, and there was liquor on it. That was curious, because there ain't any but locked-up liquor in this house, and I keep the key. She got that liquor outside. I never thought any more about it then; but this time when it come up in my mind, I reckoned maybe she turned out at five in the morning, being dry, which is natural to the English, and tramped down to the Union and moistened up. Well, it would have made a fine stir if she had done it in women's clothes. So I judged maybe she disguised herself as a man and done it. How does that seem to strike you?"

"Pretty thin, George. Still, it will do for a link if you can't find anything better."

"But I reckon I can. I told the girls I found Wapping Alice sleeping like a graveyard. It warn't strictly true, Mr. Clemens. She warn't in her room; she warn't in the house at all."

"Is that so?"

"She warn't in the house at all. Now, then, when I had thought out my think, I says to myself, it stands like this: Wapping Alice knowed we was to be off on the excursion two days—"

"Two days! Well, I'll be—"

"Mr. Clemens, you oughtn't to swear."

"I *didn't* swear, and I wasn't even thinking of it. But a person could be forgiven for it if he did, considering the way things go on in this house the minute we turn our backs. Go on!"

"Well, as I was saying, sir, I says to myself it stands like this: Wapping Alice couldn't know we were back and down there chatting in the library, and so, being dry, she reckoned she was perfectly safe to slip on her breeches and things and go out and oil up. If it *was* her, she heard me shout, and knowed she was out of luck this time. And if it was her, she would know we wouldn't be in the house long, but would go out excursioning around somewhere and passing the time, then she could slide back and get into her own clothes again. So I just set still and waited. Well, sir, sure enough, just as it was getting most dark, here she comes stretching and yawning into the library in her own clothes, and let on to be astonished to see me back from Northampton, and said she had most slept her head off, and I said, pretty sharp, 'Blame your cats you ought to slept it *clear* off; it ain't any good to you in a time of trouble; there's been a man in the house, and if we had all been as sleepy-headed as you he would have got away with the whole place.' She pretended to be ever so sorry she was asleep, but I reckoned she got considerable comfort out of the notion that she hadn't been found out. Now, then, Mr. Clemens, that is the case the way it stands. You see, yourself, that it warn't of any importance, and not worth disturbing the family about. And so I put it up on the papers for a burglary, and got them to keep still and give it a chance to blow off and pass away. I warn't thinking about myself, I done it for the family's sake, to save them from worry. Wasn't I right?"

"George, you are *always* right. Half the time I don't believe it, but to keep peace in the family it is safest to let on to. It's an idiotic family, and thinks you know more than the dictionary. You have figured this matter out pretty well, for an unprofessional, but it is pretty hard on Wapping Alice, George. To sum up, what do you think of her now?"

"Well, Mr. Clemens, I still think what I said before: she ain't what she ought to be."

"You don't think there is anything really bad about her, do you?"

"Yes, sir, I do. I think she drinks."

"Is *that* all?"

George was speechless for a moment, then he said, with deep solemnity—

"*All?* Mr. Clemens, ain't that enough?"

I had a reason for asking the next question.

"George, are you sure—I mean are you perfectly sure—that you aren't a little prejudiced against Alice?"

It made George uncomfortable. I was expecting it would. He coughed an embarrassed cough or two, loosened his collar with his fingers, and presently found speech.

"You mean the joke she played on me, Mr. Clemens?"

"Yes."

"Well, sir, I give you my word I done quit worrying 'bout it. It was scanlous—it was just scanlous—but she didn't mean no harm. There ain't no malice in her. She's the best-hearted girl there is; and if a person is pore or in trouble there ain't nothing she won't do for them. They can have everything she's got; and everything anybody else has got, too, if she can get aholt of it. *But*—when it comes to joking—oh, my land! Mr. Clemens, she can't help it; it's born in her. She ain't got no resisting power. If she see a chance to play a joke and couldn't play it, I believe it would kill her. She keeps the kitchen in a sweat; we don't ever know what's acoming next. Now then—"

"George, you are wandering from the subject. You always do, when I bring up that joke. I never can manage to pump your version of it out of you. You always go palavering off on side issues. Why is that?"

"Now Mr. Clemens, I don't like to talk about that joke. It was just scanlous. Why, it went all over this county; yes, sir, and clean out to Gilroy. Everybody knows me in this town, little and big; and I hardly das't to show up anywheres for four weeks, they kept at me so. Now Major Kinney, and Mr. Bunce, and Mr. Robinson, and Mr. Hubbard, and Gen'l—"

"Well, never mind, George, let it go. I see I am never going to bring you to book. I think you would dodge around that joke a year and never step over the outside edge of it. Tell me—have you ever examined that laundry door?"

George cheered up and looked relieved.

"No, sir, not as I remember. What would I do it for?"

"Well, your tale makes me think it will bear it. I wonder at you, George. Such a good detective and not think of that."

We went down and examined; and sure enough the ends of the metal pegs which made the electric connection had been filed off till they no longer touched the plate when the door was swung open.

"George, you explained the function of these pegs to Wapping Alice?"

"Yes, sir; and of course she went and filed them off, and that door hain't been on the alarm since the first week of last February. I ain't got no more to say; I'm just a fool."

"No, you mustn't say that, because it includes me, and isn't respectful. I ought to have examined the door last February."

II

Up to this time this whole matter had seemed trifling to me, but it suddenly began to look cloudy, now. The laundry door had been tampered with for a purpose. George said—

"Yes sir; and it was done so as Wapping Alice could put on men's clothes and slide out whenever she wanted to, and liquor up. I am more set, now, than ever, that that girl ain't what she ought to be. Mr. Clemens, if I had *my* way, I'd make her take the pledge before she's a day older; I'd do it as shore as I'm a standing here."

Privately, I went further than that. I believed that Alice was harboring sneak-thieves. I felt sure that an exhaustive search of the house would show that a thousand little things had been carried off.

I resolved to hold a court in the morning, and fan out the evidence and get at the bottom facts of this dark episode. I woke refreshed, and ready for business. Eager to begin, too; all alive with the novelty and interest and mystery of the situation, and sure I could manage it in as imposing style as any detective in the land, except George. When George brought up my breakfast we discussed and matured the plans; then he went down and sent up the witnesses, one at a time, and I questioned them separately. Last of all came Wapping Alice. She had on a white summer gown, with a pink ribbon at the throat, and looked very neat and comely and attractive and modest; also troubled and downcast. I questioned her gently, on this, that and the other point, and found her cautious, evasive and reluctant. She kept slipping through my fingers all the time; I never could quite catch her, anywhere. I was forced to admire her penetration and her ingenuity. I was not able to arrange any trap which she would walk into. Still I was making progress, and she could see it. She did not know what the previous witnesses had said, and this was a hindrance to her. Every now and then, consequently, I was able to drop a surprise on her which disordered her story and made difficulties for her. She was determined she wouldn't know that there had been a man in the house. No, it could be that there had been a man, and of course there *had* been, since the others said so, but she had no personal knowledge of it.

However, I gradually drove her into a corner; and at last when I thought the right time had come, I sprung my final surprise and showed all my cards. I wove the stories of the servants into a clear and compact narrative, and reeled it off like a person who had been behind the door and seen it all. The astonishment that rose in her face, and grew, and grew, as I went along—ah, well, it was an inspiration to me! It was as if I was plucking the secretest privacies out of her heart, one by one, and displaying them before her amazed eyes. When I had finished she seemed dazed, and said humbly—

"I see it is no use, sir; you know all. I am a poor friendless girl. I do not know what to do," and she stood there pitifully twining and untwining her fingers and gazing down at the carpet. And to tell the truth, it brought the moisture to my eyes.

"Make a clean breast, Alice; it is the only wise and honest thing to do."

After a struggle she said she would do it, and she began. This is the substance of her story.

That young Swede, Bjurnsen Bjuggersen Bjorgensen, did some joiner-work in the house in January, and when it was finished he was out of work and remained so. In the kitchen they all liked him and were sorry for him. Presently he had nowhere to sleep and nothing to eat. She took pity on him and secretly allowed him to sleep in our main cellar—in a part of it which had been walled off for a bowling alley and afterwards neglected and never used, and never visited. She made a pallet for him there. Also she carried food there for him. She warned him to enter, nights, before Patrick went his final rounds—ten o'clock—and get out before he came in the morning to replenish the furnace. There was a lock on the laundry door, but it was never used; the burglar alarm was protection enough. She knew the lock was not used, but she knew nothing about the burglar alarm. She learned about it the third time that it raised me out of bed. George explained the thing to her; then Bjurnsen Bjorgensen filed off the ends of the metal pegs, and after that he came and went at any hour he pleased.

"Ever since?"

"Yes sir; he has slept in the cellar all these months. When there was excursions he would come daytimes. He was free of the whole house, then. But he never took anything, sir. He was perfectly honest. I mended his clothes for him, I made that pallet for him, I fed him all these months. I hope you will forgive me, sir; I'm but a poor girl and I never meant any harm."

"Forgive you? Why, hang it, you poor good-hearted thing, you haven't done anything to forgive. I was afraid he was a thief, that's all. And so there's been all this pow-wow about just nothing. I thought there was going to be something dramatic, something theatrical, and now it's all spoilt; it's enough to make a man swear. You ought to be taken out and drowned for it. But never mind, let it go; there's nothing but disappointments in this world, anyhow. Go along about your work, and leave me to my sorrows.

But there's one thing—that young fellow ought to be very grateful to you; you've been a good friend to him, Alice."

She suddenly broke down and burst out sobbing as if her heart would break.

"Grateful? *Him?* Oh, sir, he—he—" Through the breaks in her sobs words escaped which conveyed a paralysing revelation.

"What!"

"Oh, dear-dear, it is too true, sir—and now he won't marry me! And I a poor friendless girl in a strange land."

"Won't marry you! Oh, he won't, won't he? We'll see about that!"

The rage I was in—well, a rage like that exhausts a person more in half an hour than a forty-mile walk. I sent the girl away and got back to bed. I told her to keep her secret to herself and tell George I wanted to see him. When he came I spread the ghastly facts before him, and they nearly straightened his wool with horror and indignation. And he was astonished and grieved at young Bjorgensen's conduct. He said he was as nice and good-hearted and manly a young fellow as he ever saw, and he couldn't ever have dreamed such things of him.

First, we telephoned for Reverend Thomas X.; next, we laid plans for the marriage of that couple. I said I would teach that scamp a lesson that he wouldn't forget till he was a widower. By the time the plans were completed, Mr. X. was with us. The Reverend Joe Twichell was off on his vacation, and Tom was supplying his pulpit. Next to Joe, he was the choicest man in the world for this kind of a circus. He was lovely, all through, like Joe, and he had Joe's luxuriant passion for adventure and doing good. He was fatter than Joe; a good deal fatter, and the hot weather made a kind of perennial water-works of him; but no matter, his good heart was touched by the tale we told him, and he was ready to shed his last drop of perspiration in the cause, for he knew our Alice well, and liked her, and was outraged by her pitiful fate. He took the names and ages of the couple, and went off down to the town clerk's to get the license. He was to arrive at our house at seven sharp, in the evening, and shut himself up in the bath-room attached to what we called the schoolroom, and sweat there till he was wanted; it was on the second floor, over the library.

Wapping Alice was to send a note by hand to her unintentional intended, and invite him to come out at eight o'clock sharp, and spend the evening.

George was to telephone the chief of police and ask him to furnish me an officer in plain clothes, and have him at the house at sharp seven thirty, where George would be on the lookout for him and shut him up in the library. He was to stay there until I should ring a bell—one stroke.

I was to be alone in the schoolroom at eight; Wapping Alice was to receive Bjuggersen Bjorgensen at the front door, betray him into the schoolroom, where I was, and then glide into the nursery, adjoining, and leave him to me.

At six in the evening the servants were to be let into the secret. They were then to dress in gala; then shut themselves up in the kitchen and stay there until I rang three bells—the signal that the wedding was ready to begin, and witnesses wanted.

On the dining room table there was to be moisture for the crowd, to finish up the wedding with, and no charge for corkage.

My native appetite for doing things in a theatrical way feasted itself with a relish on this spectacular program. George admired the arrangement, too, and was proud of his share in contriving it. He said it was one of the showiest things he had ever helped to put together. Then we fidgeted around and waited. It was a feverish long afternoon for us, but it dragged itself through, and the twilight began to gather and deepen at last.

No hitch occurred anywhere. Each actor was in his place at his appointed time. At seven the Reverend Tom arrived, and was shown up stairs and shut into the bath-room; at seven thirty the policeman arrived and was shut up in the library; at seven forty-five I was in the schoolroom; at eight the bridegroom was with me, and the bride had taken post in the nursery. The curtain was up, the performance ready to begin.

Bjorgensen was startled when he saw me, and began to apologize, supposing there had been a mistake; but I said it was all right, I was expecting him. He did not want to sit down, and said he should feel more comfortable standing; but I insisted persuasively, and presently he yielded and took a chair—the edge of it. He seemed a good deal perplexed, and a trifle uneasy.

He was a handsome young fellow, with a good face and a clear eye, and I noticed with some concern that he was able to throw me out of the window in case he should want to. His Alice had fed him well. I opened up the conversation with ordinary topics, for it was my purpose to thaw him out and get him into a comfortable and persuadable frame of mind before I should enter upon the main business. I meant to keep at him until I made him laugh, if it took all night. It was hard work, and long; but it won. At the end of half an hour he let go a hearty and unconstrained laugh, and I recognized that things were in shape now to call game.

So then I drifted along gradually into a revealment of the fact that I knew he had been sleeping in our cellar for months; that he had been seen to pass through the house; and that he had destroyed the electric connection which guarded the laundry and indeed the whole establishment. I told the story sorrowfully, and in a reproachful voice, and the cheerfulness gradually faded out of his face, and his head drooped in shame.

There was a painful silence now, for some moments, for I paused to let the effects work up; then I said—

"Alice was your benefactor—your *benefactor,* do you understand? She saved you, she nourished you, she protected you when you were friendless. And for reward—you take away her purity!"

He jumped as if he had been shot, and his face was transfigured with fury.

"I? Who says I did!"

"She says so."

"She lies! To the bottom of her soul she lies!"

Confound him, he almost convinced me. He went raging up and down the room, denying, protesting, almost crying; and really it was pitiful to see. But I had my duty to perform for that poor girl, and I hardened my heart and held to my purpose. Now and then I said a soothing word, and urged him to tranquillize himself and sit down and let us have a quiet, reasonable talk over the matter and see if we could not arrive at an adjustment that would be fair and satisfactory to both parties. And I said—

"You see, there is really only one right and honorable thing for you to do—only one—you must marry her."

It warmed his fury up to boiling-point again.

"Marry her! I'd see her hanged a hundred times, first, and *then* I wouldn't. Marry her! Why in the nation should I marry her?"

"Why, what objection have you?"

"Objection! Oh, great guns! Why *I* don't care anything for her beyond warm friendship—there's no love. Why in the world should I marry her?—*I* don't want a wife."

I said, coaxingly—

"Ah, but consider the hard circumstances. Here she is, a poor girl far from home, and her good name gone; surely you will have pity on her. Think—to you is granted a gracious and noble privilege: you can make an honest woman of her."

"But I don't *want* the privilege; and I won't *have* it! If her character needs coopering up, *I* can't help that. It isn't any affair of mine. Why am *I* selected out for the job. *Privilege,* you call it! It just makes me want to rip and curse—that's what it does."

I soothed him further. At least I meant it for that.

"Mind, Bjorgensen, I am not blaming you for denying it—far from it. Anybody would—first off; I would myself. For when we are excited we say things which we are not really responsible for. I am not blaming you. You are excited, now; but when you get cool, and are your own honest, honorable self again—"

He threw up his hands in a sort of agony of despair, and said—

"Ah, how did I ever get into this awful mess! Mr. Clemens, *don't* you believe me?— *can't* you believe me?"

Hang it, I was touched; but I had a duty to perform, and I put my weakness aside and kept my grip. By gentle persuasions I at last got the young fellow to come and sit down again; and with a proper delicacy I turned my head away, for the tears were running down his face. I said—

"Well, you know, Bjorgensen, that I haven't merely Alice's testimony. It is formidably backed up—*more* than that—convincingly backed up—made unshakable—"

"How?"

"By circumstantial evidence. You spent a hundred and fifty nights in our cellar; your presence was known to only one person; that person secretly fed and bedded you there; that person was a simple, confiding, unprotected girl. Answer me, now, out of your own common sense: with these facts back of Alice's testimony, what would a jury say?"

It wrung a groan from him.

"Lord help me!" he said. "I never thought of that; never thought how it would look." He sat silent a while—hunting for a straw to catch at. Then he said, in an aggressive tone,

"But it wouldn't be *proof*, say what you may; a court would have to admit that I could have been there for—for—"

"Burglary, for instance?"

It made him jump.

"Mr. Clemens, I make solemn oath that I never took even so much as a straw; I swear that I—"

"Yes—but that is not to the purpose. And it is not important. Quite aside from that, you were guilty,—by your own admission five minutes ago—of a crime which can send you to State prison for ten years."

"Who? I?"

"You."

"What was it?"

"House-breaking. You entered by unlawful means. You destroyed the safeguard of the laundry door."

He was quaking all over, now, and his breath was coming and going in gasps.

"Mr. Clemens, is that a penitentiary offence? Oh, take it back, take it back! *Don't* say it!"

"But I must. It is only the truth."

He dropped his elbows on the table, and his head in his hands, and moaned and grieved. Presently, all of a sudden he looked up and set his eyes on mine with such a fierce light in them that it gave me a start.

"This is a game!" he shouted, and brought his fist down on the table with a crash. "It's a game that you've put up on me; that's what it is—a game to force me to marry that lying baggage. I see it all. Now deny it if you can!"

"I am not denying it. It *is* a game; and I am playing this end of it."

"You mean you *have* played it. And you've lost, too. I'll *never* marry that girl—no, not if I live a thousand years! *Now,* then, what are you going to do about it!"

"You will be a married man inside of an hour. Or—"

"Or *what?*" he scoffed.

"Go to jail. Take your choice."

That warmed up his scorn. He rose, took his hat, and made a fine and rather elaborate bow, and said—

"I wish you a very good evening, sir. When you start out another time to play a game, you want to look at your cards, first, and see how much they are worth. And next time you start in to scare a man, you want to select better. Pleasant evening, to you, dear sir. Good-bye."

"Good-bye. Pleasant evening. Allow me—I will touch the bell. You will find a policeman down stairs who will help you out."

I put my finger on the button, and waited. The color went out of the young fellow's face, and he said, with a rather dubious attempt at bluster—

"*That* don't scare, either."

"All right. Shall I ring?"

He hesitated, then his confidence forsook him, and he said—

"No. Wait." He came and sat down. He mused a moment or two, then said, "Mr. Clemens, I put it to you on your honor: *is* there an officer down there?"

"There is. Your time is short. Look at the clock. It is five minutes to ten. You may have the lacking five to make up your mind in. At ten you marry, or go to jail."

It was time to walk the floor again. Any person in his circumstances would know that. He got up and did it. Sometimes moaning, sometimes swearing; always trying to find some way out of his bitter toils, and not succeeding. At last I put my finger on the button, and began to count, solemnly—

"One—two—three—"

"Damn her eyes, I'll marry her! Oh, it's awful—awful. But I've got to do it, and I will. I'll marry her next winter, I give you my word."

"Why not now?"

"*Now?* I reckon you are forgetting one or two details?"

"Which ones?"

"License—preacher—witnesses—and so on."

"Oh, you think so! Tom! Alice!" They entered. I touched the bell—three times, then once—to fetch the others. The whole gang burst in on the instant, policeman and all; they had been listening at the keyhole.

Alice was dressed to kill; so were her mates. The Reverend Tom was melted away to half his size, and had hardly strength enough to get about. It must have been a frightful two hours in that little blistering bath-room for a fat man like that. In my time I have seen millions of astonished carpenters, but not all of them put together were as astonished as our bridegroom. It knocked him groggy; and he was a married man before he knew what he was about. At the preacher's suggestion he kissed the bride—it didn't seem to taste over-good to him—and said to me, with a sigh—

"It's your game, sir. What a hand you held!"

Then they all cleared for the dining room below and the refreshments, and Tom and I sat down, I to smoke and he to fan; and we talked the whole grand thing over, and were very, very happy and content. And he put his hand in blessing on my head, and said, with tears in his voice—

"Mark, dear boy, you will be forgiven many a sin for the noble deed you have done this night."

I was touched, myself.

Just then George staggered in, looking stunned and weak, and said—

"That Wapping Alice—blame her skin, she's a *man!*"

And so it turned out. She explained that it had never occurred to her to make that dire charge against poor Bjorgensen till I complained that the outcome of the original episode wasn't theatrical enough. She thought she could mend that defect. Well, her effort wasn't bad—you see it, yourself. I keep calling her *she*—I can't help it; I mean *he.*

The couple never lived together, nor had any family.

Wednesday, April 10, 1907

Mr. Clemens removes the fictions from the "Wapping Alice" tale and tells the facts; also recalls his meeting with Alice and the Swede three years afterwards. The Thaw trial drawing to a close; part of Mr. Delmas's speech in summing up the case for the defence.

I am aware that yesterday's dictation reads like a farcical fairy-tale and looks like an invention; but never mind how it reads or how it looks, it is neither a fairy-tale nor an invention. There is not an essential detail in it that is fictitious. There is one considerable detail which is fictitious, but it is a nonessential. In that instance I diverged from fact to fiction merely because I wanted to publish the thing in a magazine presently, and for delicacy's sake I was obliged to make the change. But this Autobiography of mine can stand plainnesses of statement which might make a magazine shiver; it has stood a good many already, and will have to stand a good many more before I get through. For my own pleasure, I wish to remove that fictive detail now, and replace it with the fact. This considerable but not essential fact was this, to wit: Wapping Alice was a *woman*, not a man. This truth does not relieve or modify by even a shade the splendid ridiculousness of the situation, but the temporary transformation of Alice into a man does soften the little drama sufficiently to enable me to exploit it in a magazine without risk of overshocking the magazine's readers.

What actually occurred was, that when Alice stood before me sobbing, and emptied herself of her embarrassing evidence, she told me that by persuasion of the Swede's damnable fascinations she had "fallen;" that her time was approaching, and that she should presently become a mother. She said she had implored the young Swede to marry her and save her from disgrace, but that he had refused. It never occurred to me to doubt her story; nothing occurred to me but to fire up and boil with indignation, which I did. She played her part well; in fact she played it to perfection. I was not only immeasurably angry, but was saturated with evil joy, for I knew that I held all the cards and could make a most satisfactorily miserable man out of that Swede. So I told Alice to get ready for the wedding. Then I dismissed her and called George, and we laid the plans, detail by detail, as already described. In the evening, when I had the poor Swede in my trap, and he was raging up and down the room and trying to imagine some way to get out of those dreadful toils, I tried to interest him in that impending child. I made a moving appeal to his parental instincts and to his duty toward that blameless little creature, but it only raised his fury a couple of thousand degrees higher than it was before. He said he would allow no man's bastards to be foisted upon him, and said that if I were in his place I could see how cruel it was to insist upon such an outrage.

The marriage came off, with all its theatrical accompaniments, precisely as already described, and the couple, and the servants, and the policeman, retired to the dining room below to feast and rejoice; then the clergyman put his hand on my head and in a voice quivering with emotion, and with happy tears in his eyes, beatified me with the moving and noble blessing which I have already quoted. But this clergyman was not "Tom." Tom is a fiction. The real clergyman was Reverend Joseph H. Twichell, who still lives—and may he long continue with us! I have used the fiction "Tom" for magazine purposes. By and by, when Joe was ready to go home we went down to the dining room to say good night to the victims of our stern ideas of justice and morality, and I told them they need not indulge in any more clandestine conduct in the house, but that they could make themselves free, and at home, and temporarily occupy any room on the premises except my own.

The family did not return to Hartford that summer, nor the next, nor the next. I suppose we were in Europe, but I do not remember. However, in the third of these summers we were again in Elmira, New York, and I went to Hartford on a flying trip to see how George and the other servants were getting along. I remained several days. On a bright Sunday afternoon I was walking leisurely down the flagged walk toward the upper gate, when I saw a carriage stop in the street; next I noticed that there was a lady and a gentleman in it, and that they were looking intently and apparently expectantly toward me. The carriage was an open one—a fine new Brewster; the horses were coal black and shiny and proud; the occupants of the carriage were finely and fashionably dressed and gloved, and the gentleman had on his head a silk hat which was as shiny as the coats of the horses. I quickened my pace, and when I got to the carriage the gentleman lifted his hat, the lady bowed and smiled; then, after a moment, recognition burst upon me—these splendid birds were Alice and the Swede! The Swede's face broke into smiles of a glad and happy sort, and he said—

"Mr. Clemens, when you made me marry Alice that time three years ago I could have killed you, but I want to thank you now! it was the greatest favor anybody ever did me. I hadn't a cent; I hadn't any work; I hadn't a friend, and I couldn't see anything in front of me but the poor house. Well, Alice is the girl that has changed all that; she saved me, and I thank you again. She got work for me, all I could do, from Garvie and Hills, the contractors who built your house; she started a little restaurant down in Main street, and got Mr. Bunce and Mr. Robinson and General Hawley and Mr. George Warner, and all your other influential friends who had known her in your house, to come and try her bill of fare. They liked it, and brought everybody else, and pretty soon she had all the custom she could attend to, and was making money like a mint, and it's still going on yet. She took me out of wage-work and made a contractor and builder out of me, and that is what I am now, and prospering. This is our turnout; these are our clothes, and they are paid for. We owe it all to you, Mr. Clemens, and your arbitrary and mistaken notions of justice, for if you hadn't forced me to marry Alice or pack up and go to the penitentiary it never would have happened." He paused; then he added, without any bitterness in his tone, "But as to that child, it hasn't ever arrived, and there wasn't the damnedest least prospect of it the time that she told you that fairy-tale—and never *had* been!"

Then he laughed, and Alice laughed, and, naturally, I did the same. Then we parted.

I have now told all the facts and removed all the fictions, and to my mind the facts make a plenty good enough tale without any help from fiction.

The tremendous Thaw trial is approaching its end. Mr. Delmas delivered a part of his argument for the defence yesterday. I append an extract from it.

He began with the birth of Evelyn Nesbit, passing over her infant years, strangely enough, with only a word or two. He said:

> When she was 10 years of age the family began to feel the pinch of want, the sufferings of poverty and the gnawing of hunger. At 12 she became the family drudge, assisting her mother in such household duties as a brave, courageous child of her age could perform. In this condition the family continued, moving from place to place, with no fixed habitation, wandering like Arabs upon the face of the earth.
>
> But this did not continue forever. Nature had endowed the child with the fatal gift of beauty, in which her mother saw the means of supporting the family. And so at the age of 14 years in Philadelphia she embarked her daughter upon the perilous career of an artist's model. Soon afterward to New York the family came, and by procurement of her mother the employment which Evelyn had in Philadelphia was resumed here, and the beautiful child wended her way through the city streets from morn till eve, day after day, going from one studio to another and from artist to artist, and at the end of the week turning over to her mother the scanty dollars which she had earned and which went to support the family consisting of herself, her brother and her mother.

Appearance of the Tempter.

Mr. Delmas then traced the young girl's drifting progress from the studios of artists to the stage, following the lines marked out by her own testimony on the witness stand. About this time, he remarked, the tempter arrived. He went on:

> He saw, he desired and with the consummate skill of a man whose hair had grown almost gray, though he had a family in which his excellent wife and his gifted son sat by his side about the hearth, he determined to make her his.

Mr. Delmas went on to tell how, as Evelyn had testified, Stanford White ingratiated himself with her mother and induced her to go to Pittsburg, leaving her daughter in the care of the architect. After expressing a wish that he could pass over the night of Evelyn Nesbit's ravishment without any reference, he continued:

> Into one of those dens fitted with all the taste and splendor and dazzling beauty with which this man of genius could endow his surroundings this child was one night lured, under the pretence that others were to be there. When she arrived she found herself alone with this man, who was old enough to be her father and who had pledged himself to protect her during her mother's absence.

Need I recall to your memories how the child was led from one step to another until overcome, plied with wine and drugs, she became unconscious and the victim of the man who had lured her there to her undoing?

Need I recall to you the terrible scene you heard torn from the lips of the unfortunate victim. O, better for Stanford White if he had never been born, rather than that he should have seen that day! Better that his ears had never opened than that they should have heard the shriek of horror and anguish of the victim that lay mangled and devoured before him! For what had he done? He had perpetrated the foulest, the most cowardly, the most dishonorable of the sins and crimes that can stain or deface the image of God. He, the strong, the powerful, had lured a poor, little child to her undoing and to gratify a moment of passion and lust had crushed the poor little flower that was struggling toward the light and toward Heaven.

He had committed a crime that the law declares a felony and which in the old Anglo-Saxon language is labelled by the ugly name of rape. It is that cowardly crime which the Chief Magistrate of this nation recently said in a message to Congress was a crime which everywhere should be punished by death. He who had erected churches and sanctuaries crowned by the symbol of redemption had forgotten the word of the Redeemer when he called a little child and sat him in the midst of them and said: "Whoso receiveth such a little child in my name receiveth Me, but whoso shall offend one of these little ones, it were better for him that a millstone were hanged about his neck and that he were cast into the sea."

Oh, Stanford White, did you in the impiety of your hard heart imagine that the cry of this fatherless child heard that night in the silence of this great city—the cry of a child deserted by her mother, left alone in this city of millions—did you imagine that God would not hear that cry or believe that retribution would not come? Far better were it for Stanford White had he died before that day. For then he might have died at the meridian of his splendor, then public mourning might have attended his obsequies, then he might have died before his name became a byword and his memory would not have survived only to be execrated.

Debauched Her Mind, Too.

Mr. Delmas made a considerable pause here, as the vigor with which he pronounced this excoriation seemed to take a good deal of his strength. When he had recovered he went on to tell how Stanford White, having outraged Evelyn Nesbit's body, proceeded to do what he could to debauch her mind. He said:

He went to her and knelt on the floor at her side and kissed the hem of her dress and told her to dry her tears, that what she had done all women did and that the only sin was to get found out. He told her that if she could only keep the thing locked in her breast all would be well—that all women were wicked, only some succeeded in concealing their vices and others were found out. And so he lured her again and again to the same den or to others that he had and thus induced her to continue those unholy relations for a period of a couple of months.

Thursday, April 11, 1907

Items from the Children's Record: Susy's quaint sayings; Clara's innumerable damp-nurses, and description of Maria McManus, one of these nurses.

Many months ago I extracted a chapter from the old manuscript-book which we call the Children's Record—a book in which Mrs. Clemens and I rather desultorily set down remarks made by the children when they were little. We were accustomed to make the entries in the book while the sayings were fresh, wherefore the Record reads like a diary, and not like bygone history. When I extracted that chapter I observed that the Record has now attained to a value which we had not foreseen in those early days—not a value to persons outside the family, perhaps, but a value to me, because the thoughtless remarks of those innocent babblers, in which their tempers and characters were revealed, turned out to be such an accurate forecast of what their characters were to be when they should be grown-ups. I wish to quote from the Record again. When Susy was something over three years old, her religious activities began to develop rapidly. Many of her remarks took color from this interest. Instances:

> She was found in the act of getting out her water-colors, one Sunday, to make vari-colored splotches and splashes on paper—which she considered "pictures." Her mother said—
> "Susy, you forget it is Sunday."
> "But, mamma, I was only going to paint a few pictures for Jesus, to take up with me when I go."

It was reverently said, though it does not sound so at this distant day.

> Her Aunt Sue used to sing a hymn for her which ended:
> "I love Jesus because He first loved me."
> Susy's mother sang it for her some months afterward, ending it as above, of course. But Susy, the just, the conscientious, corrected her, and said—
> "No, that is not right, mamma—it is because he first loved Aunt Sue."
> The word "me" rather confused her.

> One day, on the ombra, she burst into song, as follows:
> "Oh Jesus are You dead,
> So You cannot dance and sing?"
> The air was exceedingly gay—rather pretty, too, and was accompanied by a manner and gestures that were equally gay and chipper. Her mother was astonished and distressed. She said—
> "Why Susy, did Maria teach you that dreadful song?"
> "No mamma, I made it myself, all out of my own head—nobody helped me."
> She was plainly proud of it, and was going to repeat it, but refrained, by request.

This reference to Maria brings that remarkable woman vividly before me, after all these slow-drifting years. The Record says:

Maria McManus was one of Clara Clemens's innumerable damp-nurses—a profane devil, and given to whisky, tobacco, and also to some other vices. From Clara's first birthday till some months had passed, her chances were uncertain. She could live on nothing but breast milk, and her mother could not furnish it. First we got Mary Lewis, the colored wife of John T. Lewis, (the colored lessee of Quarry Farm,) to supply it a couple of weeks; but the moment we tried to put her on prepared food she turned blue around the mouth and began to gasp. We thought she would not live fifteen minutes. When Mary Lewis's tank was exhausted, we next got Maggie O'Day from Elmira, who brought her child with her and divided up her rations—not enough for the two; so we tried to eke out Clara's share with prepared food, and failed—she turned blue again and came near perishing.

We never tried prepared food any more. Next we got Lizzie Botheker. When she went dry, we got Patrick's wife, Mary McAleer, to furnish the required milk. In turn, she went bankrupt. Then we got Maria—Maria McManus—and she stayed a year, until Clara was weaned. To me, but not to Mrs. Clemens, Maria was a delight, a darling, a never failing interest. She smoked all over the house; in the kitchen she swore, and used obscene language; she stole the beer from the cellar and got drunk on it and on stronger liquors, every now and then, and was a hard lot in every possible way—but Clara throve on her vices right along. In the shortest month in the year she drank two hundred and fifty-eight pints of my beer, without invitation, leaving only forty-two for me. I think it was the dryest month I ever spent since I first became a theoretical teetotaler.

By certain arts and persuasions I enabled Clara to believe that every time she acquired a damp-nurse she also acquired the nurse's name, and added it to her own. I taught her to rattle off the list glibly, and as she was not able to pronounce any of the names correctly, but butchered them all, I got great satisfaction out of hearing her do her little stunt. She did it gravely, and with innocent confidence that it was all right, and just so; and so whenever a stranger asked what her name was, she turned the whole battery loose on him, to wit: Clara Langdon Lewis O'Day Botheker McAleer McManus Clemens, and was not aware that she was playing any deception upon that stranger.

Maria was proprietor of a baby, which was boarded at a house on the Gillette place and by and by died. Mrs. Clemens gave her twenty dollars, out of sympathy and to enable her to make a worthy and satisfactory funeral. It had that effect. Maria arrived home about eleven o'clock that night, as full as an egg and as unsteady on end; but Clara was as empty as she was full, so after a steady pull of twenty minutes her person was full to the ears of milk-punch constructed of lager-beer, cheap whisky, rum, and wretched brandy, flavored with chewing-tobacco, cigar-smoke, and profanity; and the pair were regally "sprung" and serenely happy. Clara never throve so robustly on any nurse's milk as she did on Maria's, for no other milk had so much substance to it. It always had lemon-pie and green apples in it, and such other prohibited things as were believed by doctors to be fatal to children when administered to them through the breast of a nurse, but Clara always liked those things and prospered upon them.

Maria was one of the most superb creatures to look at I have ever seen. She was six feet high, and perfectly proportioned; she was erect, straight; she had the soldierly stride and bearing of a grenadier, and she was as finely brave as any grenadier that ever walked. She had a prodigal abundance of black hair; she was of a swarthy complexion, Egyptian in its tone; her features were nobly and impressively Egyptian; there was an Oriental dash about her costume and its colors, and when she moved across a room with her stately stride she was royal to look at—it was as if Cleopatra had come again.

Out of idle curiosity, I once made a search of her room to see if there was anything interesting in it. Between her mattresses I found apples, pears, oranges—and the other fruit of the season—and enough of my cigars, smoking-tobacco, and beer, to start a shop with. Another would have reproached her, but I didn't; I only admired her provident care of herself; I believed I would be just as thoughtful if I were a wet-nurse myself. A couple of years after Clara was done with her, in Hartford, she applied for a place as wet-nurse in an Institution in New York, and gave me as a reference. The President wrote and asked me if this was correct. I said it was, and gave her reference enough to elect the eleven thousand Virgins of Cologne, if they had been in Maria's line of business. I said, give her all the beer and whisky and brandy and tobacco and green fruit and lemon-pie she might want, and turn her loose on the nursery, and have no solicitude about the results.

More items from the Record: Susy and Mr. Millet—Mr. Clemens speaks of Millet: his beautiful character, his service as war correspondent, his marriage, his painting the first oil portrait of Mr. Clemens, etc.—Items from the Record, ending with Susy's letter to Mr. Millet.

Susy four and a half years old.
    Frank D. Millet, the young artist, came here some time ago, to paint my portrait, and remained with us a fortnight. A day after his arrival Susy asked her mother to read to her. Mr. Millet said:
    "I'll read to you, Susy."
    Susy said, with a grave, sweet grace, and great dignity—
    "I thank you, Mr. Millet, but I am a little more acquainted with mamma, and so I would rather she would do it."

Millet's hair was black then; it isn't now. My head was brown then; it is white now. Millet was unknown then; he is widely known now. Neither of us was acquainted with trouble then; we are familiar with it now. We were so young then! we are so old now. Millet was the dearest and most lovable human being of his sex anywhere to be found in that old day. He holds that beautiful supremacy yet, and can maintain it against all comers; age has not soured him; the sweetness that was born in him was born to stay. He has always had troops of affectionate friends; he still has troops of them, and not in America alone, but in England and in France. I don't suppose he knows what an enemy is; I cannot conceive of his knowing how to acquire an enemy.

Am I describing a male Miss Nancy? No, he was never that. Being an artist, and a good artist, he necessarily has a deal of poetry and sentiment in him, and they find expression upon his canvases; but he is also wise and practical, and also most masculinely brave. A year and a half after he painted my portrait, in Hartford, I encountered him rushing down the Boulevard des Italiens, in Paris, and asked him what was his hurry. He had in that hour been appointed war correspondent by the London *Daily News,* and was getting ready to start for the seat of war. A couple of hours later he had made all his arrangements, and was on the way. He was all through the war, and his closest and most admiring comrades were MacGahan and Archibald Forbes, those daring knights of the pen. He was in the centre of the hottest fire at Plevna, all day long; he was in the rest of the fights; he was a valued comrade of the grand dukes and generals; the Emperor was his friend, and decorated him on the field, for valor. Deadly peril seemed to have a charm for him, and for MacGahan and Forbes, and they had many a thrilling success in hunting it up and enjoying it; wherever news was to be had they proceeded to that place, let the distance and the dangers be what they might. Millet had a dozen subordinates under him, and twenty-three horses, and he developed great executive ability in handling these resources.

When the war was over he returned to Paris, resumed his painting, and got married. We were at the wedding and added our share to the display of wedding presents. I contributed a stick of fire-wood decorated with pretty ribbons, and of course it ranked as jewelry, as any one will know who had to pay for wood fires in the French capital in those days.

Millet's business ability exploited itself again at the World's Exposition in Chicago in honor of Christopher Columbus, in 1893. The decorating of the White City was placed in his hands; he had a great company of artists of repute under him; he ordered everything, superintended everything, finished his great work on time, did it thoroughly well, and kept peace in his art-family all the way through. The executive capacity which he displayed brought him an abundance of compliments; among others, he was offered, at a great salary, the chief managership of the largest and wealthiest coal business in Chicago; but he preferred his art to riches, and declined that and other fine offers of the kind.

When Millet came to Hartford to paint the first oil portrait that was ever made of me, he gave me a small picture—a Dutch interior, which was his earliest effort in oils, and I have it yet. At our first sitting he dashed off a charcoal outline of me on his canvas which was so good and strong and lifelike that Mrs. Clemens wouldn't allow him to add any paint, lest he damage it. She bought it. He had brought but the one canvas from Boston, so he had to go down town and get another. I remained outside on the sidewalk while he went into the art shop to stretch the canvas on the frame. It was dull out there, and I tried to think of some way to put in the time usefully. I was successful. There was a barber shop near-by, and I went in there to get the ends of my hair clipped off; I fell into a reverie, and when I woke up there was a bushel of brown hair on the floor and none on my head. When I joined Millet he took one glance, realized the disaster that had befallen, and said he wanted to go to some private place and cry. He devoted a couple of diligent weeks to the portrait and made a good one, if you don't count the hair; but as there was no hair, he had to manufacture it, and his effort was a failure. I have the portrait yet, but the hair it wears is not hair at all; it is tarred oakum, and doesn't harmonize with the rest of the structure.

One day at dinner Millet told a charming little story. On a bleak and sleety day two men were drifting here and there over an old and neglected cemetery, and evidently seeking something. Sometimes they were wide apart, sometimes they crossed each other's path, and at last they spoke. One said:

"You do not seem to succeed."

"No."

"Neither do I."

"Whom do you seek?"

"The dearest soul, the sweetest nature, the lovingest friend and the faithfulest, a man ever had. And you?"

"I am seeking the hatefulest scoundrel the human race has ever produced; I want to curse his ashes."

They separated, and searched again far and wide; at last they came together, and together they scraped the moss from a gravestone and revealed the inscription: both had been seeking the same man!

Of course the moral of the story is that there is a good side and a bad side to most people, and in accordance with your own character and disposition you will bring out one of them and the other will remain a sealed book to you. Millet had painted himself without knowing it. He is not capable of bringing out the bad side of anybody. He would bring out the good and lovable side every time, and never find out that there was any other.

> *January, 1877.*
> The other evening after the children's prayers, Mrs. Clemens told Susy she must often think of Jesus, and ask him to help her to overcome bad impulses. Susy said:
> "I do think of him, mamma. Every day I see His cross on my Bible and I think of Him then—the cross they crucified Him on. *It was too bad—I was quite sorry.*"
>
> *May 4.*
> When Miss Hesse ceased from her office of private secretary and took final leave of us to-day, Susy said gravely—
> "I am losing all my friends."
> This is rather precocious flattery.

As little as Susy was, she was a diligent reader, and in at least one particular she was like the rest of the human race, grown-ups and all; that is to say, she was likely to take the color of the latest book she had read and whose style she had admired. As a result of this she sometimes delivered herself of impressive formalities of speech which sounded quaintly enough coming from such a small person. I quote:

May 4.
Yesterday Susy had a present of a new parasol, and hit Clara a whack with it—to see if it was substantial, perhaps. Rosa, the nurse, took it away from her and put it in the blue-room. Susy was vastly frightened, and begged Rosa not to tell on her, but her pleadings failed. In the evening Susy said, with earnestness—

"Mamma, I begged, and begged, and *begged,* Rosa not to tell you—*but all in vain.*"

A month or more ago, Clara was naughty in the nursery and did not finish her dinner. In the evening she was hungry, and her mamma gave her a cracker. I quote now from a letter written to me by her mother when I was in Baltimore two or three days ago.

"Last night after George had wiped off Clara's sticky fingers in the china closet she came out, with her little sad, downcast look, and said, 'I been litte naughty up 'tairs, can I have a cracker?' I found that the naughtiness had been invented for the occasion."

The next paragraph in the Record is of date—

July 4, at the Farm.
There would be a grand display of fireworks down in Elmira, and the adult members of the farm tribe would sit in the grass on the hilltop and look out over the valley and enjoy the show:
Susy being ordered to bed, said thoughtfully—
"I wish I could sit up all night, as God does."

Letter to Millet, from Susy, March 1877:

"Dear Mr. Millet
Clara and I has both got valentines, I have a new fan and a German book and Clara's got a new carrage— Papa teached me that tick, tick—my Grandfather's clock was too large for the shelf so it stood 90 years on the floor. Mr. Millet is that the same clock that is in your picture— Dear Mr. Millet I give you my love, I put it on my heart to get the love out."

She refers to the little picture already mentioned, which was Millet's first effort with the brush, and contains an old-fashioned stand-up-in-the-corner clock.

Dictated April 20, 1907

In the morning paper I have once more come across that phrase which—considering its awful meaning—I think is the blackest one that exists in any language. It always unseats my self-possession. I wish to utter my feeling about it, and my contempt for the law-makers that invented it, and for the law it stands for. I will imagine a dialogue—a conversation between the President of the United States and an Ignorant Citizen who is seeking light:

President of the United States. You have desired to consult me upon a matter which you conceive to be of national importance. Be seated. Proceed.

Ignorant Citizen. It is indeed a matter which deeply concerns the nation, your Excellency, and this emboldens me to lay it before the head of the people, the source of justice and power, the protector of the weak. I am ignorant, I find myself perplexed, I stand in need of guidance. In this, my situation and the nation's is the same. I will state my case. In the family of a neighbor of mine there is a lad of sixteen for whom I have a warm affection, and he has the like feeling for me. I have long desired to kill him, and—

Pr. What!

I.C. I have long desired to kill him, but—

Pr. Man, you are not in your right mind!

I.C. Bear with me, your Excellency; hear me patiently, and you will presently cease to doubt my sanity. I can convince you of this without difficulty, sir, if you will but listen to what I have to tell, and give it a kindly and unprejudiced hearing.

Pr. It is so strange, so amazing, that—very well, go on, it promises to be interesting, at any rate.

I.C. Thank you sir. Like some other men, I am so constituted, by nature, that the desire to do murder is in certain circumstances a passion with me, and is not resistible when I can do it with safety to myself. As I have already said, sir, I have long desired to kill this boy. For many months he was unwilling. And so—

Pr. Unwilling? Do you mean to say that you *asked* him to let you take his life?

I.C. I used importunities and persuasions to that end, and bought things for him such as boys like, and took him to shows and picnics and such things, but often when he might have consented, his mother's tears and agonies and supplications turned the scale in her favor and he refused. She is a widow, and he is her only child, and she has often begged me on her knees to be merciful and spare him, and not break her heart. It is the way with mothers, it is natural, and I do not find fault, but they make it difficult. However, sir, to be brief, I at last got his consent, and all was well, and I was happy: I only needed to wait a little while, until he should be sixteen.

Pr. It is a noble forbearance, indeed! Why should you wait?

I.C. Ah, your Excellency is aware that if I should kill him before he reached the age of consent it would put me in danger, for the law could punish me for it, since his consent to be murdered, if granted before the age of sixteen would not be valid and therefore would not sufficiently protect me. But I am in great trouble, great perplexity; for now that he is sixteen and willing, I am told by a lawyer that there is no such thing as an "age of consent" where murder is concerned. Surely he must be in error, your Excellency, it cannot be that he is right, it is incredible, it is impossible. You must know, better than he, you are the embodiment of the nation's law and the nation's justice, and I beg you to clear away the doubt and tell me he is in the wrong.

Pr. This is an amazing business! It is inconceivable that a sane person can calmly entertain so atrocious an idea as that in a Christian land, a civilized land, an enlightened land, a citizen could give away his life to a murderer at *any* age between cradle and grave and the murderer go unhanged because of that consent! An "age of consent" for murder? Cannot you see that the idea is preposterous? You were going to convince me that you are in your right mind; you have convinced me that you are insane.

I.C. But I have not finished, your Excellency. What I have been telling you is fancy, imagination, fable; I will now tell you a thing which is true. Suppose I should kill, after calculated deliberation, a lad of seventeen, either with his consent or without it—what would happen? I should be hanged for it, and all would say I got my just deserts. The lad's family would be steeped in grief—but only in grief—there would be no disgrace. Time would heal their sorrow. But put the lad out of your mind, sir, and take the case of a girl—an innocent and trusting child of sixteen, the joy of her family and their idol. Beguiled by the devilish arts of a coward and a villain she consents and is seduced. She is deserted, she is disgraced, she is forsaken by her friends, she is pointed at, scorned, despised, gossiped about, her life is ruined, and this ruin falls also upon her unoffending family; they are disgraced, and the disgrace is permanent; their hearts are broken, existence is a misery and will so continue through all the heavy years until the refuge of the grave is reached. That poor girl has been murdered! Murdered—*once?* She has been murdered a million times! And her mother, her father, her brothers and sisters—they also have suffered a thousand deaths. And because that ignorant child of sixteen *consented* to these innumerable murders—including the destruction of unoffending people over whose lives she could have no sort of authority—that master-idiot *the law,* holds the assassin guiltless and sets him free! Indeed it is not I that am insane, your Excellency, it is the legislature; it is the law-makers who visit with death the light offence of a sole murder, and infamously place the fate of an inexperienced girl and of her family in her irresponsible hands to do as she pleases with; to turn that fate into a very hell, if she shall so choose, while the real criminal, a bowelless scoundrel, is turned loose unpunished to carry desolation and living death to other hearthstones. It is my hope sir, that the ass who invented the "age of consent"—*any* age of consent between cradle and grave—is with his progenitors in hell, and that the legislatures that are keeping the resulting law in force will follow him soon. Women are denied the suffrage, your Excellency. If they had it, how long do you think this most infamous of all laws would continue to defile the statute books?

Tuxedo, May 18, 1907

**Taking up the thread of dictation again after a silence of a month
or more—Four hundred thousand words of Autobiography
already dictated—The opening of the Actors' Fund Fair—The trip
to the Jamestown Exposition in Mr. Rogers's yacht—The proposed
trip to England on June 8th to receive honorary degree from
Oxford University—Copy of poem "To Mark Twain."**

It seems a long time since I have done any dictating; and it really is a long time, though not so long as it seems, perhaps. In March, after a second trip to Bermuda, I made a pretense of working, but it probably amounted to nothing more than a pretense, substantially. But I am not grieving about it; I am not reproaching myself. If I could have gotten more pleasure, more comfort, more satisfaction, out of dictating autobiography than I could get out of other forms of play, I should have gone on dictating, instead of seeking other forms of amusement. During a stretch of thirty-five years I exercised my pen, in my trade of authorship, in the summertime and in the summertime only. I worked three months in the year and amused myself in other ways during the other nine. My average literary output for the thirty-five years was short of seventy thousand words a year; but since I began to dictate, on the 9th of January 1906, I have not limited myself to the summer vacation as a working time but have spread my labors over all the months. Last March, when I went to Bermuda the second time, I estimated that I had dictated four hundred thousand words in the previous thirteen or fourteen months; I recognized that I had put together enough Autobiography, if spread through my existing books, to secure for those books a twenty-eight years' renewal of copyright life, and as that renewal, in the interest of the bread and butter of my daughters, had been the Autobiography's main object, I did not care whether I added anything to that Autobiography or not; indeed I rather formally retired from all human industries and set apart the remaining weeks or years of my life to be observed and enjoyed by me as a holiday—the first very real one in a lifetime of seventy years and upwards. This has a nonsensical sound, for I am not able to disguise from myself the fact that my life for the past thirty-five years and more has really been nothing more nor less than one long holiday, with three months' scribbling in each year which other people dignified with the great name of "work," but which to me was not work at all, but only play, delicious play, and was never a result of compulsion or of the prodding of conscience, but only of a strong desire to entertain myself.

Many things which I have wanted to talk about have happened in the past month or two, but they are ancient history now—let them go. I helped to open the Actors' Fund Fair on the 6th of this present month. We raised seventy-five thousand dollars for the Fund. I went down to Jamestown in Mr. Rogers's yacht, the *Kanawha,* and saw the opening of the World's Fair there. Two or three days of fog followed, and Mr. Rogers and all the guests except Mr. Broughton and I got tired and went back home by rail, but we waited a couple of days; then the fog lifted in the night for a moment and we got to sea and came through to New York without any trouble, although the newspapers said the vessel had gone to the bottom and carried us along with it.

Meantime, I have been invited by Oxford University to receive an honorary degree on the 26th of June, and shall sail on that quest on the 8th. I have made no effort to conceal the fact that I am vain of this distinction. Sometimes they catch an illustrious American who has wandered to the English shores on his own affairs, and Oxford transfigures him with a degree, but I am one of the very few that have been sent for from over the ocean.

I like compliments, praises, flatteries; I cordially enjoy all such things, and am grieved and disappointed when what I call a "barren mail" arrives—a mail that hasn't any compliments in it. I am always trying to find plausible excuses for copying these tributes into this Autobiography, but at cost of a good deal of pain I refrain from doing it. However, I mean to break the rule, to-day, for yesterday's mail brought me from Texas a complimentary poem which is so fine and so sincere—and I hope I may say affectionate—that I want it to live, and am not willing to suppress it. It is by a judge on the bench.

To Mark Twain.
We crave as guerdon of our unsought birth,
    Some height to scale, some glory to attain;
And in our march we fill the wayward earth
    With monuments portraying joy or pain,
Or the cold factors of some loss or gain,
    As Selfishness or Love our being sways.
How few are they who reach that higher plane
    Of Life's broad triumph, where its quiet days
Shine with more light and hope, and far serener rays.

But thou hast gained an eminence thine own,
    Beyond the reach of envy or of blame;
And of all human passions, love alone
    Will cherish and perpetuate thy name,
With other mortals of immortal fame,
    As bearer of the tidings that on earth
Our hopes, our dreads, our sorrows are the same;
    And he the only gainer from his birth
Who mingles with his toil God's boon of joy and mirth.

The sunny humour of thy useful life
    Hath filled with gladness many a cheerless mind,
Equipped it for a nobler, better strife,
    Against the faults and follies of mankind.
Philosopher and humourist combined!
    To whom at last a Voice shall cry "well done."
By thee e'en wretchedness shall solace find,
    For thou hast brought—and thereby glory won—
Good will to all thy kind, and malice unto none.

The world is happier in that thou wert born:
　　Thy gift to man is never draped in woe,
But diamonded in laughter, as the morn
　　With dew drops greets the Day-King's early glow;
And we would have thee, while in life, to know
　　How strong from every warm and buoyant breast
Love and love's attributes around thee grow.
　　If these beget a blessing—thou art blessed,
As in our hearts thou liv'st an ever welcome guest.

　　　　　　　　　　　　　John A. Kirlicks.

Dictated Thursday, May 23, 1907

The Oxford degree of Doctor of Letters to be conferred upon Mr. Clemens on June 26th, and some of the other degrees which he has received.

A cablegram arrived from England three weeks ago inviting me to come to Oxford and receive an honorary degree on the 26th of next month. Of course I accepted, and without any waste of time. During the past two years I have been saying with great decision that my traveling days were permanently over, and that nothing would ever induce me to cross the ocean again, yet I was not surprised at the alacrity with which I put that resolution behind me when this flattering invitation came. I could have declined an invitation to come over and accept of a London town lot, and I could have done it without any difficulty, but a university degree is a quite different matter; that is a prize which I would go far to get at any time. I take the same childlike delight in a new degree that an Indian takes in a fresh scalp, and I take no more pains to conceal my joy than the Indian does. I remember the time that I found a battered old-time picayune in the road, when I was a boy, and realized that its value was vastly enhanced to me because I had not earned it. I remember the time, ten years later, in Keokuk, that I found a fifty-dollar bill in the street, and that the value of that bill also was vastly enhanced to me by the reflection that I had not earned it. I remember the time in San Francisco, after a further interval of eight years, when I had been out of work and out of money for three months, that I found a ten-cent piece in the crossing at the junction of Commercial and Montgomery streets, and realized that that dime gave me more joy, because unearned, than a hundred earned dimes could have given me. In my time I have acquired several hundred thousand dollars, but inasmuch as I earned them they have possessed nothing more than their face value to me, and so the details and dates of their capture are dim in my memory, and in many cases have passed from my memory altogether. On the contrary, how eternally and blazingly vivid in my recollection are those three unearned finds which I have mentioned! Now then, to me university degrees are unearned finds, and they bring the joy that belongs with property acquired in that way; and the money-finds and the degree-finds are just the same in number up to date—three: two from Yale and one from Missouri University. It pleased me beyond measure when Yale made me a Master of Arts, because I didn't know anything about art; I had another convulsion of pleasure when Yale made me a Doctor of Literature, because I was not competent to doctor anybody's literature but my own, and couldn't even keep my own in a healthy condition without my wife's help. I rejoiced again when Missouri University made me a Doctor of Laws, because it was all clear profit, I not knowing anything about laws except how to evade them and not get caught. And now at Oxford I am to be made a Doctor of Letters—all clear profit, because what I don't know about letters would make me a multimillionaire if I could turn it into cash.

Oxford is healing a secret old sore of mine which has been causing me sharp anguish once a year for many, many years. Privately I am quite well aware that for a generation I have been as widely celebrated a literary person as America has ever produced, and I am also privately aware that in my own peculiar line I have stood at the head of my guild during all that time, with none to dispute the place with me; and so it has been an annual pain to me to see our universities confer an aggregate of two hundred and fifty honorary degrees upon persons of small and temporary consequence—persons of local and evanescent notoriety, persons who drift into obscurity and are forgotten inside of ten years—and never a degree offered to me! In these past thirty-five or forty years I have seen our universities distribute nine or ten thousand honorary degrees and overlook me every time. Of all those thousands, not fifty were known outside of America, and not a hundred are still famous in it. This neglect would have killed a less robust person than I am, but it has not killed me; it has only shortened my life and weakened my constitution; but I shall get my strength back now. Out of those decorated and forgotten thousands not more than ten have been decorated by Oxford, and I am quite well aware—and so is America, and so is the rest of Christendom—that an Oxford decoration is a loftier distinction than is conferrable by any other university on either side of the ocean, and is worth twenty-five of any other, whether foreign or domestic.

Now then, having purged myself of this thirty-five years' accumulation of bile and injured pride, I will drop the matter and smooth my feathers down, and talk about something else.

Friday, May 24, 1907

A description of Tuxedo Park; also of the invasion of Mr. Clemens's house by the first burglar known to the Park.

Tuxedo Park is unique—in America. It is what may be called the American San Marino. Like San Marino, it is set apart in a holy seclusion far from the madding crowd; also like San Marino it is a wee little miniature republic, with an excellent system of government of its own devising. I think that in territory it is about the twin of San Marino.

If I remember rightly, San Marino's territorial spread covers thirty-six square miles of the planet, and I believe the Tuxedo Park State covers just about the same amount of soil. By these statistics the reader will perceive that San Marino is no longer the smallest independent State in the world, but only one of the smallest.

There is a village of Tuxedo, and it is not new, but Tuxedo Park is not more than a quarter of a century old, and has no connection with the village. Tuxedo Park is ideally situated. It is only an hour from New York City by rail. Coming from New York the train flies through a level of flats and marshes for thirty or forty minutes, then comes suddenly upon a barrier of high and rocky and forest-clad hills, and plunges into the heart of this barrier; it climbs up through a beautiful gorge—the whole of which gorge is a part of the sovereignty of Tuxedo Park—and arrives at Tuxedo village station; thence you drive through a massive and towered granite gateway and enter the sacred ground—that is if the uniformed guards on sentry duty at the gateway are satisfied with your credentials, and are convinced that you are honest, and are on an honest errand; otherwise you will not get in. You ascend gradually, by winding and perfect roads, past fine and widely separated villas and private gardens, and the further you climb the more beautiful are the views that enchant your eyes; you look down upon a pair of lakes framed in the embrace of the lovely hills, upon whose surfaces the clouds and the forests and the scattered villas paint pictures of themselves in the softest and tenderest colors.

The whole population of the State is concentrated upon the hillsides around and about these lakes, and between the first villa of the processional series and the furthest one the distance is not more than three miles. The surrounding territory was bought by the corporation, not for use but merely to keep undesirable people out. The whole population of the miniature republic probably does not exceed fifty families, with an average of four members and five servants to the family. If you live in Tuxedo Park America takes it for granted that you are rich, it not being regarded as possible for a moderate income to survive there.

It is a pleasant place to live in; substantially the population is a club; it has a large and well conducted club house, and all the families are entitled to its privileges by right of residence. However, this right has a limit, in the case of a newcomer; if he rents, or buys, or builds, a house, he is a member of the club during that year without an election; but the community will take a vote upon him when the year is out, and if he has proven unsatisfactory they blackball him and close the club against him; he finds himself isolated and uncomfortable, and presently removes to some other place. In the course of the years eighteen newcomers have been blackballed, and have retired from the Park.

The Park's neatly uniformed policemen are on duty along the Park roads night and day, but as it is claimed that no tramp or burglar, or peddler, or beggar, or gambler, or improper lady, or any other undesirable person, can get by the guards at the granite gateway, the police have nothing to do but walk around and keep awake. It is held that locks and bolts and window-catches are not needed in the Park, and that you need not be afraid to let your doors and windows stand open night and day. If noises disturb you you telephone Captain Bush, and he squelches them. No noise has interrupted the dead stillness of my nights except in one instance: on the other side of the lake there was a remote dog with a deep voice, who complained all night long about something or other, and out of compassion for his troubles I lay awake and sympathized with him; but when I found that there was one concentration of power and authority who could comfort him and quiet him with a word, and that that concentration was Captain Bush, we applied to him by telephone and he conferred a sudden dumbness upon that dog which has lasted until now.

Apparently this is my season for high distinctions: Oxford the other day, and now a burglar—the first burglar that has ever been heard of in Tuxedo Park since the beginning of its existence. He entered the house at one o'clock this morning, and went all over it at his leisure, examining every room in it, at his leisure, by the light of a candle, and marking his route everywhere with candle drippings. He was in every room but mine; my bath-room door was wide open, and he stood in it and dripped candle-grease, but he came no further, or if he did, he dripped no grease; there were bank-bills on my night table, and a handful of silver; he did not touch them. At half past one he entered the cook's room, and she rose up and asked him what he wanted; he did not answer, but fled. I could have told her you can't get information out of a burglar by asking for it. I have had experience of burglars, and know all about them, but the cook is young and inexperienced; she called to Nellie, one of the maids, and that fetched both maids; they heard the burglar running, and heard him leave the house by the front door; three hours and a half later they got up in a body and examined the house all over, finding candle drippings everywhere, but not an asset missing—not a thing missing except three rolls which were to have been my breakfast, and whose loss reduced me to corn bread for that meal. At five o'clock I got up to fill a pipe, and I saw a policeman passing by my part of the house. The front door was standing wide open, but he probably attached no significance to that, as it is religion and tradition, here, that there are no burglars, and that a door is doing just as well when it is open as when it is closed. He gave the open door no attention, but passed by, like the Gentile, on the other side—if it was the Gentile; I think it was the Gentile; anyway I know it was either the Gentile or the Shunammite, or the good Samaritan; I am rusty in these things, but it is no matter; he passed by not on the other side, but on our side. It was a few minutes afterward that the servants examined the house. They found an extinguished candle on the floor close to the threshold of the open door; they found my overcoat-closet standing open and candle drippings on its floor, but no overcoats gone; they found the row of pictures on the staircase wall twisted askew—suggesting that the burglar was drunk, because a sober man would find plenty of room without crowding the pictures—and they found nothing missing except those three rolls. Now then, I come to something which hurts my feelings. On the table in the front hall were two boxes of my cigars—cost four cents apiece; one of them stood open, and six cigars of the top row were gone. When the three girls invaded my room at a quarter to six, with their great news of the burglary, and assured me that not a single asset was gone except the three rolls and six cigars, I felt a mingled thrill of gratitude and pride, for at last I seemed to have found somebody magnanimous enough to be willing to risk my kind of smokes; but the thrill did not last, it wavered off into doubt and then disappeared in a pang of disappointment and humiliation, for I remembered that it was I that had removed those six cigars.

We telephoned for Captain Bush, and he came and made a thorough examination; then reported to me. He said that that burglar was evidently an amateur, not a professional; also, it was his belief that this visitor was not a burglar at all, and had never intended to steal anything, but was some one who had a grudge against the owner of this house and made his visit merely out of revenge. Captain Bush had an idea that this amateur was most probably some former manservant who had been discharged by the owner of this house. I didn't say anything, but I had a quite different idea about the matter, and I have it yet. I think that my visitor was some young society gentleman; that his elaborate visitation was a joke, and that his purpose was to put a sarcasm upon the police and the community, a satire upon the Park's vaunted immunity from the visits of tramps and burglars. I think he will consider that his joke was successful beyond his utmost hopes, when he learns that the guardian of the night went by the wide open door at five in the morning and did not see it. Privately, I expect to get those missing rolls back, with a courteous letter of explanation.

Dictated May 26, 1907

Jim Gillis's death—Mr. Clemens pictures him as he knew him years ago in Jackass Gulch—The episodes of the boiling and tasting of the wild fruit, and the challenging of the impertinent stranger to fight a duel for having criticised Jim Gillis's clothing.

Through Mr. Paine I learn that Jim Gillis is dead. He died aged seventy-seven, in California, about two weeks ago, after a long illness. Mr. Paine went with Mr. Goodman to see him, but Jim was too ill to see any one. Steve Gillis's end is also near at hand, and he lies cheerfully and tranquilly waiting. He is up in the sylvan Jackass Gulch country, among the other Gillises whom I knew so well something more than forty years ago— George and Billy, brothers of Steve and Jim. Steve and George and Billy have large crops of grandchildren, but Jim remained a bachelor to the end.

I think Jim Gillis was a much more remarkable person than his family and his intimates ever suspected. He had a bright and smart imagination, and it was of the kind that turns out impromptu work and does it well; does it with easy facility, and without previous preparation; just builds a story as it goes along, careless of whither it is proceeding, enjoying each fresh fancy as it flashes from the brain and caring not at all whether the story shall ever end brilliantly and satisfactorily or shan't end at all. Jim was born a humorist, and a very competent one. When I remember how felicitous were his untrained efforts, I feel a conviction that he would have been a star performer if he had been discovered, and had been subjected to a few years of training with a pen. A genius is not very likely to ever discover himself; neither is he very likely to be discovered by his intimates; in fact I think I may put it in stronger words and say it is impossible that a genius—at least a literary genius—can ever be discovered by his intimates; they are so close to him that he is out of focus to them and they can't get at his proportions; they cannot perceive that there is any considerable difference between his bulk and their own. They can't get a perspective on him, and it is only by a perspective that the difference between him and the rest of their limited circle can be perceived. St. Peter's cannot be impressive for size to a person who has always seen it close at hand and has never been outside of Rome; it is only the stranger, approaching from far away in the Campania, who sees Rome as an indistinct and characterless blur, with the mighty cathedral standing up out of it all lonely and unfellowed in its majesty. Thousands of geniuses live and die undiscovered—either by themselves or by others. But for the Civil War, Lincoln and Grant and Sherman and Sheridan would not have been discovered, nor have risen into notice. I have touched upon this matter in a small book which I wrote a generation ago, and which I have not published as yet—"Captain Stormfield's Visit to Heaven." When Stormfield arrived in heaven he was eager to get a sight of those unrivaled and incomparable military geniuses, Caesar, Alexander and Napoleon, but was told by an old resident of heaven that they didn't amount to much there as military geniuses; that they ranked as obscure corporals only, by comparison with a certain colossal military genius, a shoemaker by trade, who had lived and died unknown in a New England village, and had never seen a battle in all his earthly life. He had not been discovered while he was in the earth, but Heaven knew him as soon as he arrived there, and lavished upon him the honors which he would have received in the earth if the earth had known that he was the most prodigious military genius the planet had ever produced.

I spent three months in the log cabin home of Jim Gillis and his "pard," Dick Stoker, in Jackass Gulch, that serene and reposeful and dreamy and delicious sylvan paradise of which I have already spoken. Every now and then Jim would have an inspiration, and he would stand up before the great log fire, with his back to it and his hands crossed behind him, and deliver himself of an elaborate impromptu lie—a fairy-tale, an extravagant romance—with Dick Stoker as the hero of it, as a general thing. Jim always soberly pretended that what he was relating was strictly history—veracious history, not romance. Dick Stoker, gray-headed and good-natured, would sit smoking his pipe and listen with a gentle serenity to these monstrous fabrications and never utter a protest. In one of my books—"Huckleberry Finn," I think—I have used one of Jim's impromptu tales, which he called "The Tragedy of the Burning Shame." I had to modify it considerably to make it proper for print, and this was a great damage. As Jim told it—inventing it as he went along—I think it was one of the most outrageously funny things I have ever listened to. How mild it is in the book, and how pale; how extravagant and how gorgeous in its unprintable form! I used another of Jim's impromptus in a book of mine called "The Tramp Abroad," a tale of how the poor innocent and ignorant woodpeckers tried to fill up a house with acorns. It is a charming story, a delightful story, and full of happy fancies. Jim stood before the fire and reeled it off with the easiest facility, inventing its details as he went along, and claiming, as usual, that it was all straight fact, unassailable fact, history pure and undefiled. I used another of Jim's inventions in one of my books—the story of Jim Baker's cat, the remarkable Tom Quartz. Jim Baker was Dick Stoker, of course; Tom Quartz had never existed; there was no such cat—at least outside of Jim Gillis's imagination.

Once or twice Jim's energetic imagination got him into trouble. A squaw came along one day and tried to sell us some wild fruit that looked like large green gages. Dick Stoker had lived in that cabin eighteen years, and knew that that product was worthless and inedible; but heedlessly, and without purpose, he remarked that he had never heard of it before. That was enough for Jim. He launched out with fervent praises of that devilish fruit, and the more he talked about it the warmer and stronger his admiration of it grew. He said that he had eaten it a thousand times; that all one needed to do was to boil it with a little sugar and there was nothing on the American continent that could compare with it for deliciousness. He was only talking to hear himself talk; and so he was brought up standing, and for just one moment, or maybe two moments, smitten dumb, when Dick interrupted him with the remark that if the fruit was so delicious why didn't he invest in it on the spot? Jim was caught, but he wouldn't let on; he had gotten himself into a scrape, but he was not the man to back down or confess; he pretended that he was only too happy to have this chance to enjoy once more this precious gift of God. Oh, he was a loyal man to his statements! I think he would have eaten that fruit if he had known it would kill him. He bought the lot, and said airily and complacently that he was glad enough to have that benefaction, and that if Dick and I didn't want to enjoy it with him we could let it alone—he didn't care.

Then there followed a couple of the most delightful hours I have ever spent. Jim took an empty kerosene can of about a three-gallon capacity and put it on the fire and filled it half full of water, and dumped into it a dozen of those devilish fruits, and as soon as the water came to a good boil he added a handful of brown sugar; as the boiling went on he tested the odious mess from time to time; the unholy vegetables grew softer and softer, pulpier and pulpier, and now he began to make tests with a tablespoon. He would dip out a spoonful and taste it, smack his lips with fictitious satisfaction, remark that perhaps it needed a little more sugar—so he would dump in a handful and let the boiling go on a while longer; handful after handful of sugar went in, and still the tasting went on for two hours, Stoker and I laughing at him, ridiculing him, deriding him, blackguarding him all the while, and he retaining his serenity unruffled. At last he said the manufacture had reached the right stage, the stage of perfection. He dipped his spoon, tasted, smacked his lips, and broke into enthusiasms of grateful joy; then he gave us a taste apiece. From all that we could discover, those tons of sugar had not affected that fruit's malignant sharpness in the least degree. Acid? It was all acid, vindictive acid, uncompromising acid, with not a trace of the modifying sweetness which the sugar ought to have communicated to it and would have communicated to it if that fruit had been invented anywhere outside of perdition. We stopped with that one taste, but that great-hearted Jim, that dauntless martyr, went on sipping and sipping, and sipping, and praising and praising, and praising, and praising, until his teeth and tongue were raw, and Stoker and I nearly dead with gratitude and delight. During the next two days neither food nor drink passed Jim's teeth; so sore were they that they could not endure the touch of anything; even his breath passing over them made him wince; nevertheless he went steadily on voicing his adulations of that brutal mess and praising God. It was an astonishing exhibition of grit, but Jim was like all the other Gillises, he was made of grit.

About once a year he would come down to San Francisco, discard his rough mining costume, buy a fifteen-dollar suit of ready-made slops, and stride up and down Montgomery street with his hat tipped over one ear and looking as satisfied as a king. The sarcastic stares which the drifting stream of elegant fashion cast upon him did not trouble him; he seemed quite unaware. On one of these occasions Joe Goodman and I and one or two other intimates took Jim up into the Bank Exchange billiard room. It was the resort of the rich and fashionable young swells of San Francisco. The time was ten at night, and the twenty tables were all in service, all occupied. We strolled up and down the place to let Jim have a full opportunity to contemplate and enjoy this notable feature of the city. Every now and then a fashionable young buck dropped a sarcastic remark about Jim and his clothes. We heard these remarks, but hoped that Jim's large satisfaction with himself would prevent his discovering that he was the object of them; but that hope failed; Jim presently began to take notice; then he began to try to catch one of these men in the act of making his remark. He presently succeeded. A large and handsomely dressed young gentleman was the utterer. Jim stepped toward him and came to a standstill, with his chin lifted and his haughty pride exhibiting itself in his attitude and bearing, and said, impressively—

"That was for me. You must apologize, or fight."

Half a dozen of the neighboring players heard him say it, and they faced about and rested the butts of their cues on the floor and waited with amused interest for results. Jim's victim laughed ironically, and said—

"Oh, is that so? What would happen if I declined?"

"You will get a flogging that will mend your manners."

"Oh indeed! I wonder if that's so."

Jim's manner remained grave and unruffled. He said—

"I challenge you. You must fight me."

"Oh really! Will you be so good as to name the time?"

"*Now.*"

"How prompt we are! Place?"

"*Here.*"

"This is charming! Weapons?"

"Double-barreled shotguns loaded with slugs; distance, thirty feet."

It was high time to interfere. Goodman took the young fool aside and said—

"You don't know your man, and you are doing a most dangerous thing. You seem to think he is joking, but he is not joking, he is not that kind; he's in earnest; if you decline the duel he will kill you where you stand; you must accept his terms, and you must do it right away, for you have no time to waste; take the duel or apologize. You will apologize of course, for two reasons: you insulted him when he was not offending you; that is one reason, the other is that you naturally neither want to kill an unoffending man nor be killed yourself. You will apologize, and you will have to let him word the apology; it will be more strong and more uncompromising than any apology that you, even with the most liberal intentions, would be likely to frame."

The man apologized, repeating the words as they fell from Jim's lips—the crowd massed around the pair and listening—and the character of the apology was in strict accordance with Goodman's prediction concerning it.

I mourn for Jim. He was a good and steadfast friend, a manly one, a generous one; an honest and honorable man and endowed with a lovable nature. He instituted no quarrels himself, but whenever a quarrel was put upon him he was on deck and ready.

Dictated Wednesday, May 29, 1907

Copy of letter from California lawyer regarding Jim Gillis— Roosevelt's attack upon Dr. Long, the naturalist, and newspaper clippings regarding it.

A letter has arrived from a lawyer resident in Sonora, California, which gratifies me because it speaks well of Jim Gillis, and because it proves to me that Jim remained, to the end, the same Jim whom I last looked upon thirty-nine years ago. I will insert it here.

> Dear Sir:—
> Your acquaintance with me is about the same as mine with the President, I know him but he does not know me that I know of, or at least the chances are about 1 in 80,000,000 that he would not remember me, having never met me personally.
> However, I am a native of Tuolumne County, for 45 years, at least that is what I am told, for the first few years of my stay here were a little hazy. Perhaps it was owing to the fact that I was under the care of a nurse and allowed a milk diet.
> Now laying alleged jokes aside, I simply want to tell you in an old-fashioned way that Jim Gillis, of Jackass Hill, passed over the Great Divide.
> If "Jim" wasn't a mighty good man, I would not take the pains to let you know this. He has enjoyed the peculiar habit of being strictly honest. Told truths about himself and his friends, when perhaps a lie would have been better appreciated. On all occasions looked Dame Nature square in the face. But he is gone, and I know that you will be sorry to hear it.
> He had a letter from you once, and it was the prize of his heart. He did not wear it out, as might an ordinary autograph fiend have done, but it was exhibited only to rare old cronies. About the greatest compliment he could offer, was to show one that letter of Mark Twain's.
> Now, I send this in good faith, without any design to creep into your acquaintance by the back door. But in honor to "Jim."
>
> Very kindly,
> Crittenden Hampton.

President Roosevelt has been having a scrap with the Rev. Dr. Long, who is a natural-ist equipped with a pleasant and entertaining pen. Mr. Long is not a heavy-weight like John Burroughs, and has never intimated, as John has seemed to intimate, that he knows more about an animal than the animal knows about itself. Mr. Long's books are very popular, particularly among the young people. He tells many amusing and interesting things about the wild creatures of the forest, and he does not speak from hearsay, but from observation. He tells what *he* has seen the animal do, not what it is reported to have done. If he misinterprets the actions of the animals and infers from them intellectual qualities of a higher order than they perhaps possess, is that a crime? I think not—although the President of the United States thinks it is. I think it is far from being a crime. Ninety-six per cent of our newspapers, and 98 per cent of our eighty million citizens, believe that the President is possessed of high intellectual qualities. Is that a crime? I do not think so. I think it is merely stupidity, and stupidity is not a crime. The other day the President allowed the affairs of the universe to stand unmolested during thirty minutes, while he got himself interviewed for the *Outlook,* and launched a devastating assault upon poor obscure little Mr. Long, and made a noise over him the like of which has not been heard on the planet since the hostile fleets opened upon each other with two thousand shells a minute, in the Japan Sea. What had Mr. Long been doing? He had merely been telling how he had found a deer whose breast had just been fatally torn by a wolf; and how he had also seen a wild bird mend its broken leg by smart devices invented by itself and successfully consummated without anybody else's help. No doubt these were extraordinary incidents, but what of that? Does their unusualness make them incredible? Indeed it does not. Wild creatures often do extraordinary things. Look at Mr. Roosevelt's own performances. Did he not fling the faithful Bowen out of office, and whitewash and deodorize the mephitic Loomis? Didn't he promulgate the illegal Order 78? Hasn't he tunneled so many subways under the Constitution that the transportation-facilities through that document are only rivaled, not surpassed, by those now enjoyed by the City of New York? Didn't he send a bouquet and a broken heart to lay upon the corpse of Mr. Quay? Hasn't he tacitly claimed, some dozens of times, that he is the only person in America who knows how to speak the truth—quite ignoring me, and other professionals? Hasn't he kept up such a continual thundering from our Olympus about foot-ball and base ball, and molly-coddles, and all sorts of little nursery matters, that we have come to stand in fear that the first time an exigency of real importance shall arise, our thunders will not be able to attract the world's notice or exert any valuable influence upon ourselves? And so on, and so on—the list of unpresidential things, things hitherto deemed impossible, wholly impossible, measure-lessly impossible for a president of the United States to do—is much too long for invoicing here. When a president can do these extraordinary things, why can't he allow a poor little unoffending bird to work a marvelous surgical operation without finding fault with it? That surgical operation is impossible, at first glance, but it is not any more impossible than is Order 78. It is not easy to believe that either of them happened; but we all know that Order 78 happened, therefore we are justified in believing in the bird's surgery. Order 78 should make it easy for us to believe in anything that can be charged against a bird. I should think that if a person were offered his choice as between risking his character upon the bird-story or upon the authorship of Order 78, he ought not to have any difficulty about which of the two to choose. I should think that a judicious person would rather father all the lies that have ever been told about the animal world than have it found out that he invented Order 78. Perhaps it is a marvelous thing for a bird to mend its broken leg; but is it half as marvelous, as extraordinary, as incredible, as that the autocrat over a nation of eighty millions should come down from his summit in the clouds to destroy a wee little naturalist who was engaged in the harmless business of amusing a nursery? Is it as extraordinary as the spectacle of a president of the United States attacking a private citizen without offering anything describable as evidence that he is qualified for the office of critic—and then refusing to listen to the man's defence, and following this uncourteous attack by backing out of the dispute upon the plea that it would not be consonant with the dignity of his great office to further notice such a person?

The President is badly worsted in the scrap, and I think he is wise in backing out of it. There was no respectable way out, and I think it was plainly best for him to accept and confess defeat, in silence. And he would be safe in any course he might pursue, whatever that course might be, for the newspapers would praise it, and admire it, and the nation would applaud. It is long since the head of any nation has been so blindly and unreasoningly worshiped as is President Roosevelt by this nation to-day. If he should die now, he would be mourned as no ruler has been mourned save Nero.

I wish to copy here a part of this pitiable fight, of the dates May 22 and May 28, and I wish I could be here fifty years hence and listen while some sane person should read these notes, and get him to tell me how they impress him. I feel quite sure that in that day the mention of Theodore's name will excite laughter—laughter at the eighty millions as well as at himself.

ROOSEVELT ONLY A GAMEKILLER—LONG

Stamford Naturalist Strikes Back at Criticism of His Nature Books.

ASSERTS IT WAS ANIMUS

Dogmatic Utterances Without a Shred of Positive Evidence— Attacks the President's Own Writings.

Special to The New York Times.

STAMFORD, Conn., May 22.—The Rev. Dr. William J. Long to-day gave out an interview in reply to President Roosevelt's criticism of his nature books. He intimates that the President is angry because he dared to criticise his method of slaughtering game promiscuously. He also says the President is taking up cudgels in behalf of John Burroughs, the naturalist, with whom Dr. Long carried on a bitter controversy in magazines and newspapers a few years ago. Burroughs and President Roosevelt are close friends.

"A Man Named Roosevelt."

"I have no desire for a controversy with the President of the United States," said Dr. Long. "I have a profound respect for that office, which is not modified or changed in the least by any man occupying the office. The point is that a man named Roosevelt has gone out of his way to make a violent attack upon me and my books. Ordinarily, I would ignore such an attack. If you read the article, even carelessly, you will see it is personal and venomous in spirit, while its literary style makes it fit for the waste basket.

"The title of this article is 'Roosevelt on the Nature Fakirs.' The first thing I notice about the article is that it is itself a fake. Mr. Roosevelt has frequently declared, in the midst of his endless personal squabbles, that the President must not enter into a personal controversy. In the present case, this alleged interview is one of the transparent modesties behind which he conceals his colossal vanity.

"Mr. Roosevelt arranged this interview, and, as I am informed by the magazine, revised the proofs, from the gross personal flattery at the beginning to the unfounded charge at the end. In concealing himself behind an alleged interview, and using his position to attack a man of whose spirit he knows nothing, his article seems to me not only venomous but a little cowardly—just as when he hides behind a tree and kills three bull elks in succession, leaving their carcasses to rot in the woods. That in itself is incomprehensible to sportsmen. But what jars you altogether is the preaching which follows on the heroism and high moral qualities developed by hunting.

"The next thing manifest in the article, even to the most casual reader, is the personal animosity. He devotes three-quarters of his attack to me, and, as I am the only one whose books are used in the public schools—which, by the way, he considers an outrage—the whole weight of his attack falls upon one man.

The Motive Behind It.

"Now, the reasons for this are perfectly plain. Some years ago a violent attack was made upon me and my books by one of Mr. Roosevelt's friends. That attack was met, and every honest argument it contained was frankly answered. But that was not enough. Mr. Roosevelt, with that love of peace which characterizes him, immediately jumped into the conflict, and in the preface to his last book he goes far out of his way for the sake of repeating his friend's attack.

"Then, again, a short time ago I wrote a series of articles which attempted to look at human life from the animal's standpoint, and in one of these I considered the subject of hunting. In this article it seemed to a simple mind, without prejudice, as if the promiscuous slaughter of game which, as Roosevelt claimed, develops heroism and manly virtue, was in reality a sort of brutal thoughtlessness.

"Mr. Roosevelt has never forgiven the poor animal who dared to criticise his hunting, and twice to my knowledge has declared to his associates that he would 'get even' and would even 'do me up.'

"The magazine article is the fulfillment of his declaration. Hence we can understand its spirit perfectly. As for the argument of the article, it is precisely like its predecessors—a series of dogmatic utterances and denials, without a shred of positive evidence to support them. He calls for evidence, but forgets the fact that his predecessors, in their attacks, did the same thing, and that the evidence was instantly produced. They took the most improbable thing I ever wrote—a story of a woodcock setting its own broken leg in a clay cast—and called this a gross deception, verging on lunacy, and demanded that I produce evidence or witnesses. I at once published a record of five cases, with the sworn testimony of eight witnesses.

Lynx and White Wolf.

"Mr. Roosevelt, in the same spirit, makes attacks upon certain statements concerning the Canada lynx and the great white wolf of the north, declaring positively that certain things recorded of them never happened."

Dr. Long, opening one of Mr. Roosevelt's books, continued:

"Now see what Mr. Roosevelt himself says: 'Wolves show an infinite variety in spite and temper.' Again: 'The differences between related animals are literally inexplicable.' It seems almost unkind to point out that Mr. Roosevelt never saw either the Canada lynx or the white wolf in their own woods. What he knows about lynxes and wolves he has learned in chasing different animals in different parts of the country, with a pack of savage dogs to help him understand their individual peculiarities.

"The one thing he declares to be a mathematical impossibility is that a huge wolf should kill a small deer by biting into the deer's chest. Now, those who have ever dressed a deer have noticed that the lower part of the chest narrows to a wedge shape, and when the shoulder-blades slide forward or back—as they do easily, the blades not being attached to the skeleton—it leaves a narrow part of the chest exposed, and it would be the simplest thing in the world for any large animal to get in a deadly bite."

Dr. Long then takes up the assertion of the President that a wolf could not kill a deer by biting into the deer's chest, and explains how the shifting shoulder blades allow a soft cartilage to be unprotected. He says he has seen deer which have been killed this way, and Indian guides have confirmed this.

"So much for the mathematical possibility. Now for facts. I once came upon a small deer lying in the snow, still living, but bleeding from tooth wounds in the under side of its chest. From the deer the tracks of a large wolf led off into the woods. It had probably heard or smelled me, and had slunk away within a few moments of the time I found its victim. More than this, the Indian with whom I explored the interior of Newfoundland tells me he has twice seen a huge white wolf kill caribou fawns this way. That this is an unusual method of killing goes without saying, but that it is both possible and probable remains a fact, despite Mr. Roosevelt's denial. It is a pity that animals and men do not conform their habits to the President's dictates, but the fact is they don't.

"There are several other points in the article worthy of attention, and in two or three of them Mr. Roosevelt lays himself open to attack by the utter absurdity of his dogmatic assertions. I shall answer these fully in a special article on the subject."

Quotes His Records.

Dr. Long opened in succession two of Mr. Roosevelt's books, and quoted a dozen records from Mr. Roosevelt's own "nature books."

"It seems," continued Dr. Long, "almost impossible that such a variety of atrocious records could be found by scores in these books, but such is the fact. I suggest that one who would understand Mr. Roosevelt's attack read Roosevelt's 'Wilderness Hunter,' and then read 'Wild Ways,' which he condemns. Mr. Roosevelt will then understand perfectly why he has no sympathy with any brand of nature study except his own.

"In a word, Mr. Roosevelt is not a naturalist, but a gamekiller. Of the real spirit of animal life, of their habits as discovered by quiet watching with no desire to kill, he knows nothing, and never will learn until he goes into the woods, leaving his pack of dogs, his rifle, his prejudice, and his present disposition behind him."

LONG ASKS APOLOGY FROM THE PRESIDENT.

——

Demands That He Retract "Fakir" Statements or Prove Them.

——

Stamford, Conn., May 28.—Dr. William J. Long to-day made public an open letter he has written President Roosevelt, which adds an interesting chapter to their "nature fakir" controversy. In part it is as follows:

"Stamford, Conn, May 28, 1907.

His Excellency, Theodore Roosevelt, President of the United States:

Dear Sir: The issue between you and me is no longer one of animals, but of men; it is not chiefly a matter of natural history, but of truth and personal honor. As President of the United States you have gone out of your way publicly to injure a private citizen who was attending strictly to his own business. As a man you have accused of falsehood another man whose ideas of truth and honor are quite as high as your own.

If I have spoken falsely, if in any book or word of mine I have intentionally deceived any child or man regarding animal life, I promise publicly to retract every such word and never to write another animal book. On the other hand, if I show to any disinterested person that you have accused me falsely you must publicly withdraw your accusation and apologize. As a man and as President no other honorable course is open to you."

Dr. Long submits an affidavit to sustain the truth of the story President Roosevelt calls a mathematical impossibility, and then he continues:

"You cannot at this stage, Mr. Roosevelt, take refuge behind the Presidential office and be silent. You have forfeited your right to that silence by breaking it, by coming out in public to attack a private citizen. If your talk of a square deal is not all a sham, if your frequent moral preaching is not all hypocrisy, I call upon you as President and as a man to come out and admit the error and injustice of your charge in the same open and public way in which you made it. Very sincerely yours,

W. J. Long."

SECY. LOEB CALLS IT A "DRAW."

——

The President Will Not Reply to the Rev. Dr. Long's Retort.

(Special to The World.)

WASHINGTON, May 28.—Private Secretary Loeb is willing to call the match a draw, it seems.

The Rev. Dr. Long's retort on the President was shown to Mr. Loeb to-night by a representative of The World, who asked him to show it to Mr. Roosevelt. Mr. Loeb declined to do so, saying:

"The President will pay no further attention to Dr. Long."

Nor will the President appoint anyone to investigate the truthfulness of S. J. (Sporting Judge) Hepidan, the educated Sioux Indian, who is Dr. Long's second and who swears he saw a horse a wolf had killed by tearing its breast to the heart.

Dictated Thursday, May 30, 1907

More about the Roosevelt-Long natural-history controversy; and Mr. Clemens's story of the turkey-gobbler that hatched out a doll's tea-set from a porcelain egg—The curious incident which happened to Mr. and Mrs. Clemens in Vienna, when they were detained in the Countess's house by the porter.

I think it is not wise for an emperor, or a king, or a president, to come down into the boxing-ring, so to speak, and lower the dignity of his office by meddling in the small affairs of private citizens. I think it is not even discreet in a private citizen to come out in public and make a large noise, and by criticism and fault-finding try to cough down and injure another citizen whose trade he knows nothing valuable about. It seems to me that natural history is a pretty poor thing to squabble about anyway, because it is not an exact science. What we know about it is built out of the careful or careless observations of students of animal nature, and no man can be accurate enough in his observations to safely pose as the last and unassailable authority in the matter—not even Aristotle, not even Pliny, not even Sir John Mandeville, not even Jonah, not even Theodore Roosevelt. All these professionals ought to stand ready to accept each other's facts, closing one eye furtively now and then, perhaps, but keeping strictly quiet and saying nothing. The professional who disputes another professional's facts damages the business and imperils his own statistics, there being no statistics connected with the business that are absolute and unassailable. The only wise and safe course is for all the naturalists to stand by each other and accept and endorse every discovery, or seeming discovery, that any one of them makes. Mr. Roosevelt is immeasurably indiscreet. He accepts as an established fact that the ravens fed Elijah; it is then bad policy in him to question the surgical ability of Mr. Long's bird. I accept the raven's work, and admire it. I know the raven; I know him well; I know he has no disposition to share his food, inferior and overdue as it is, with prophets or presidents, or any one else—yet I feel that it would not be right nor judicious in me to question the validity of the hospitalities of those ravens while trying to market natural-history marvels of my own which are of a similar magnitude. I know of a turkey-hen that tried during several weeks to hatch out a porcelain egg, then the gobbler took the job and sat on that egg two entire summers and at last hatched it. He hatched out of it a doll's tea-set of fourteen pieces, and all perfect, except that the tea-pot had no spout, on account of the material running out. I know this to be true, of my own personal knowledge, and I do as Mr. Roosevelt and Mr. Burroughs and Jonah and Aristotle, and all the other naturalists do—that is to say, I merely make assertions and back them up with just my say-so, offering no other evidence of any kind. I personally know that that unusual thing happened; I knew the turkey; I furnished the egg, and I have got the crockery. It establishes, once and for all, the validity of Mr. Long's statement about his bird—because it is twice as remarkable as that bird's performance and yet it happened. If I must speak plainly, I think it is rank folly for the President, or John Burroughs, or any other professional, to try to bear any other naturalist's stock in the public market. It is all watered—I even regard some of my own discoveries in that light—and so it is but common prudence for those of us who got in on the ground floor to refrain from boring holes in it.

Something has brought to my mind a curious incident of our sojourn in Vienna, nine years ago. I lectured for one of the great charities one afternoon. At the front, in the seats of honor, sat several young members of the imperial family, and with them a grand duchess whose married title was the Countess di Bardi. When I had finished my instructions Mrs. Clemens and I were introduced to this lady by a valued friend of ours whom I have already mentioned once or twice in this Autobiography, Madame Laszowska, wife of a lieutenant general. A pleasant conversation in English followed, lasting perhaps a quarter of an hour, then we parted. We met the Lieutenant Generalin again that evening and asked her if we were under any responsibilities and obligations imposed by court etiquette. She said, yes, but that they were quite simple and unburdensome: we must call about noon next day, write our names in the Countess's visiting-book, which we would find in a small office on the ground floor—that was all; then we could go peaceably about our business.

The Countess was sojourning at the time in the palace of another grand duchess of the imperial family. At noon next day we drove thither in a cab. We did not drive in, but stopped at the sidewalk abreast of the lofty arched doorway, and got out. A couple of soldiers with their muskets stood rigid and erect guarding that imposing entrance, with their backs against the masonry; also there was another guardian—the usual huge porter who in Vienna serves princes and such, and who is clothed from chapeau to heel in military splendors and bears a tall staff of office like that one which the drum-major of a regiment carries in front of the band. He approached us, bowing in the courtliest way, and conducted us through the great doorway, and was going to march us still further, but Mrs. Clemens was alarmed, and spoke to him. We had gone by the little office where our errand lay, and she explained, and said we merely wanted to write our names in the visitor's book; but the porter most politely informed her that we were expected up stairs, and he tried to march us forward again. But Mrs. Clemens assured him that that could not be so, and almost begged him to let us do our modest errand and go away. But he insisted that we were expected; adding that he had his orders, that it was his duty to produce us up stairs, and that he must do it. Mrs. Clemens was getting badly worried, and she assured him again that there was a mistake, and that it could not be possible that we were expected. He said—

"But madam, you are Americans?"

"Yes," my wife replied.

"Then there is no mistake, madam. The Countess expects you. She commanded me to deliver you up stairs, and beg you to wait for her, saying she was obliged to go out but would be back very soon."

Mrs. Clemens pleaded again, and said there was unquestionably a mistake, and added—

"It is not us, it is some other Americans."

But the vast creature was immovable; he had had his orders; it was his business to produce two Americans; he had got them, and evidently he was not going to trade Americans in the hand for Americans in the bush, and risk getting into trouble by it; all he needed was Americans; he had them, and evidently he was not going to take any chances. He moved forward, blazing the way with polite bows, and we followed, of course, realizing that his bulk and his two soldiers were arguments which had to be respected. At the foot of a grand staircase he delivered us into the custody of some powdered and silk-and-satin and yellow-velveted footmen who were distributed along up and down the stairs, then made his bow and went back to his post to see if he could catch some more unprotected stragglers.

Do you know that expression, "what larks!" It describes what I was feeling as we climbed the stairs. No fine and high and noble act that I could have done could have given me so much pleasure, so much joy, so much frivolous delight, as I was getting out of this accidental and unstudied circumventing of those other Americans, who had done me no harm and had not earned the frosty reception they would get from the big porter when they should presently arrive. I imagined that spectacle and enlarged it, and inflated it, and put into it every detail that could make it charming and spectacular, even to getting them shot by the sentries. I wished I could have a sight of it, but of course I couldn't. Mrs. Clemens's state of mind was very different from mine; she was distressed and ashamed, and profoundly unhappy. By nature she was refined, and gentle, and kindly, and she could find no pleasure in the thought of the humiliation of those other Americans; moreover, she was distressed on her own account, and on mine, for she was aware that our situation was not a desirable one, and could presently furnish us considerable discomfort.

We were conducted through two or three great salons on the first floor (or what an American would call the second floor); in the second—or the third, whichever it was—the lackey begged us to be seated, and bowed himself out. Mrs. Clemens sat down and mourned; but the curious adventure had so charged me with happiness that I could not sit—I had to keep moving. The place was a treasure-house of rare and beautiful things, and I sauntered around exclaiming over them and saying, time and again—

"Look at this, Livy," and "look at that, Livy," and "come and see this, Livy, you'll never find its like again."

But she wouldn't. She could not enjoy beautiful things when she was distressed. She said—

"How can you be so flippant when we are in such a serious situation? We can't get out—you know that; we have to stay, there is no help for it; they can come home at any moment and find us here—then what can we say?"

"Why Livy, we don't have to say anything; it is those other Americans that are in trouble; we are not out of luck; this is the delightfulest thing that could ever happen; it is just like a play; it couldn't be arranged better on the stage. You ought to be grateful; this couldn't happen to you twice in a century; you ought to make the most you can of it now that Providence has thrown it in our way. Livy, I wouldn't have missed this romantic adventure for anything; think how unusual it is—how rare, how extraordinary, and how fortunate and charming is our end of it. You ought to mourn for those other Americans; they are the ones that are in hard luck. They will try to get by the big porter; he will head them off; they will plead and beg and rage and storm, and try to flank him, and they can't succeed, of course; they can't dodge around a continent like that—it isn't such an easy matter. He will call the soldiers and they will charge bayonets on those Americans, and right at that crucial moment the grand duchesses will arrive, and at their order the soldiers and the porters will seize those Americans and throw them over their cab into the street. I would give a thousand dollars to see it, if I had it."

But she said sorrowfully—

"Don't talk so. It isn't a trifling matter; it is a serious one, and most distressful. You tell me to think of those other Americans. I do think of them; I can't help thinking of them. We are putting shame upon them, a humiliation which they will remember all their lives, and they have not done us any harm, nor meditated any."

I said—"Oh don't be troubled, Livy, it is going to come out some way or other—I don't know just how—but it is going to come out—don't you fret. This is better than any play on any stage, because it was unpremeditated; it was not invented; it has happened its own self without anybody's help, and there isn't a dramatist alive that could improve on it. Try to enjoy it; it was not sent for our sorrow, but for our entertainment, and we ought in gratitude to get the most out of it that we can. If you will stand at that window I'll stand at this one, and when they throw those Americans out——"

Just then the grand duchesses appeared at the head of the stairs, in the distance, and took up their line of march toward us. We stood up, respectful in attitude, and waited. As soon as they had arrived within good speaking distance the Countess di Bardi exclaimed in English—

"Oh I am so sorry we had to keep you waiting, Mrs. Clemens;" and the other duchess said the equivalent of it in German.

It seemed too good to be true, and Mrs. Clemens had to reassure herself with the question—

"Was your Highness expecting us?"

"Why yes, we sent a note to your hotel inviting you. Didn't you get it?"

The explanation was easy—to wit: we had missed the messenger, therefore we had not come to pay a visit, but only to write our names in the visitor's book according to the instructions of Madame Laszowska—and so when we arrived and found that we were rather evidently being mistaken for a couple of Americans who *had* had the honor of an invitation I was glad that we had gotten in ahead of those others and defeated them, but that Mrs. Clemens was sorry for them, I didn't know why.

We remained half an hour and had a quite lively time; in fact one might properly describe it as even a jolly time. When we finally proposed to go we were asked to wait a little and see the children, because the children wanted to see us. They presently came, and they proved to be very entertaining and interesting little talkers. The eldest was a little lady of fourteen; the youngest was a handsome little lad of seven years. I felt a mighty respect for that little duke, for he was the son of that widely and justly honored and revered grand duke of the imperial house who had given his life to the study of diseases of the eye, and whose office doors were always open to the poor whose eyes needed his healing services. He charged nothing, yet his rewards were rich, for they were paid in gratitude.

By all rules we ought to have retired from the presence backward, but the grand duchesses were as kindly and as thoughtful in this matter as the Emperor was to me on a later occasion: they went all the way to the head of the stairs with us, and thus spared us the necessity of attempting a mode of progress which we could not have essayed successfully and to our satisfaction, for lack of practice. After the good-byes one of the grand duchesses said—

"Mr. Clemens, you will have to wait a moment. This boy has been devouring you with his eyes all the time, and I can see that he has been wanting to ask you a question, out of the deeps of his heart, and has been afraid to utter it. He has whispered it to me, and I have encouraged him to speak it out and not be afraid."

And so, being thus encouraged, the little duke did speak it out, and eagerly, and with his heart in it. He said—

"Mr. Clemens, did you ever see a real red Indian?"

I answered, with a justifiable feeling of pride and self-admiration, that I had seen that kind of an Indian; and as we passed from the presence I saw by the light in that little duke's eyes that in one person's regard, at least, I was a hero for once in my life.

Dictated July 24, 1907

**Dictated after an interval of six weeks—The journey to England on
the *Minneapolis;* events that transpired on board, and the English
welcome by the stevedores.**

There has been an interval of six weeks. Originally I had intended to stay in England only ten or twelve days, but circumstances compelled me to add a fortnight to that. I sailed for London in the *Minneapolis* on the 8th of June, and took with me as temporary secretary and professional nurse Mr. Ashcroft—Ashcroft the Indelible. That name has grown out of an accident of speech. Ashcroft is a young business man and knows how to do everything that I am incapable of doing, and whatever he undertakes to do he does promptly and in the best and most effective way; hence he never fails, and cannot fail. I have long thought of him privately in my mind as Ashcroft the Infallible, but the first time that I tried to utter that phrase I made a mistake in the word and told Miss Lyon to call up Ashcroft the Indelible. That is, call him up on the telephone and place the pending impossibility in his hands and leave the result to him. Ashcroft has remained Ashcroft the Indelible ever since.

We had a lazy, comfortable, homelike, nine-day passage, over smooth seas, with not enough motion in a thousand miles to make a baby sick. The ships of that line are very large and very steady, and most satisfactorily slow and deliberate. They have spacious decks, and every passenger has a deal more room than he needs; they are freight ships, and have accommodation for only a handful of passengers. This one was full, with only a hundred and fifty-four. Fifty-one of them were college girls, with their protectors, going out on vacation to study Europe. This was pleasant to me, who am rather abnormally partial to young girls. I took care of the most of these, and did it very well, as everybody conceded. The pick of the flock was a very pretty and very sweet child of seventeen who looked only fourteen, and who seemed only fourteen, and remained only fourteen to me to the end of the voyage. I selected her before we were out of sight of land, and borrowed her from her three elderly aunts and placed her at my side at the captain's table, and from that time until the end of the voyage she had no occasion to miss her mother—if I do say it myself that shouldn't. Her name was Carlotta, but I changed it to Charley, which seemed to me to improve it. She was a gifted and cultivated little creature. On the last night out there was the usual concert in the dining room, for the benefit of the Seamen's Hospital. Charley played a violin solo to admiration, and astonished everybody. She wasn't much bigger than her fiddle, but she made it talk a moving and majestic language. I made a speech; other excellent people sang songs, and punished the piano. Rev. Dr. Patton, that verbal and intellectual wonder, twenty-five years President of Princeton University, conducted the concert, then finished his services with a brilliant exhibition of what a university president can do when he turns himself into an auctioneer. There was a jack-legged draughtsman on board who made some unimaginably poor caricatures of me on six post-cards; I autographed them, and Rev. Dr. Patton set himself the task of auctioneering off the six for eighty dollars. It furnished him a stubborn job, but he is not of the easily discouraged kind and he stayed faithfully by his enterprise until he accomplished it. In my talk I departed from the humorous for a while, and was greatly gratified with the result. I was expecting those people to cry, and they did. Afterward a deputation of ladies visited me on deck, and the spokeswoman said—

"We admired you before, but we love you now."

I did not suspect that a note was struck then whose gracious music was to continue to fall upon my grateful ears day and night, unceasingly, through all my stay in England. It made that journey of mine rich beyond expression in words. I am old, but I would repeat the journey not merely once, but ten times, for the like compensation.

At the end of nine days we reached the dock at Tilbury, and the hearty and happy and memorable English welcome began. Who began it? The very people of all people in the world whom I would have chosen: a hundred men of my own class—grimy sons of labor, the real builders of empires and civilizations, the stevedores! They stood in a body on the dock and charged their masculine lungs, and gave me a welcome which went to the marrow of me.

Dictated Thursday, July 25, 1907

A few words about Brown's Hotel, where Mr. Clemens stopped—
His active life in England compared with his former lazy one at
home—The many letters, telegrams, etc., to be answered—The
numerous calls to be returned—The dinner at Dorchester House,
and some of the guests who were present—The Pilgrims' luncheon,
and copy of the London *Telegraph* account of it.

At the railway station in London we had a moment's glimpse and a word or two of talk with that brilliant Irishman, Bernard Shaw, who was waiting there to receive his biographer, our fellow voyager, Mr. Henderson. I lunched at Mr. Shaw's house a week or two afterward, and expanded the acquaintanceship. I will speak of that entertaining episode further along. Charley's parents were waiting at the station for their charming little rascal, and into their hands the aunts and I delivered her.

By letter and cable, before leaving America, we had secured a parlor and two bedrooms in Brown's Hotel, Dover street, a placid, drowsy, subdued, homelike, old-fashioned English inn well known to me years ago, a blessed retreat of a sort now rare in England and becoming rarer every year. The tourist seeks the Hotel Cecil, the Savoy, and the other vast modern hotels now, and infests them multitudinously.

We found a great many letters and telegrams awaiting us, and Ashcroft engaged an assistant, and the two began the work of answering them. During the first week they worked from nine in the morning until midnight, but after that they did not have to do very much night work. The messages were from both sexes and of all ages, and there was hardly one whose prevailing note was not affection. One could not read those simple, unstudied, and hearty outpourings and not be moved. I may say with truth that I lived many happy lifetimes in a single week, in those days. Surely such weeks as those must be very rare in this world; I had seen nothing like them before; I shall see nothing approaching them again. I will leave room in this place for a sample or two of those letters and poems, and will decide later whether to insert them or not.

My habits underwent a sudden and lively change. At home they had been of a lazy sort, for a year or two—to wit: breakfast in bed at eight o'clock, newspapers and the pipe until about eleven, still in bed; then dictation for an hour or two with my clothes on; then down stairs to drink a glass of milk while the rest of the family ate their luncheon; back to bed at three in the afternoon to read and smoke and sleep; dinner down stairs at seven-thirty; billiards until midnight, if Mr. Paine was on the premises—otherwise back to bed at half past eight, not to sleep, but to read and smoke until one o'clock and then sleep if convenient. In London it was different. I breakfasted in bed, then got up and breakfasted with somebody else somewhere else; then took luncheon at somebody's house, and tea and dinner at other people's houses, and was usually home again, and asleep, by half past ten or eleven. It was a strenuous life, but it hardly ever furnished me any fatigue. The teas were accidental, and not by invitation. From four o'clock until six, every day, I returned calls. In all previous years the women of the family had attended to this duty, and I had been spared it, and was grateful; but I was alone now and had to carry out this formidable duty myself. The thought of it was irksome and distasteful, and for three days I made excuses to myself and shirked it. I should probably have gone on shirking it but for a happy accident. In the hotel I stumbled upon one of those college girls; I had not known before that she was in the house. She was a lovely creature of sixteen, and I borrowed her of her mother at once. After that I paid calls every day, and she went with me. She saw the inside of many beautiful English homes and got a world of petting homage, which pleased me as much as it pleased her. The next time I have a wilderness of calls to make it will have no distresses for me, for I will borrow another sweet Francesca.

As regards public functions, I had accepted two by cable before leaving America, and had declined the others; later the list was augmented by four, but by that time I was fairly broken in and did not mind it. The first of the functions was a dinner at Dorchester House on the 21st of June, the palace inhabited by our Ambassador, Whitelaw Reid, and was altogether delightful. There were twenty-five or thirty guests, all men of distinction in literature, art, science, and scholarship, and there were no speeches. We chatted until toward midnight, and even then were reluctant to break up and go home. I knew all of the guests by reputation, and I had known Abbey, the artist, and Sir Norman Lockyer, the astronomer, and several others, long and intimately. Among the guests were these: Lord Tennyson, President of the Royal Literary Fund; Sir E. Poynter, President of the Royal Academy; Sir E. Waterlow, President of the Royal Society of Painters in Water-Colors; Sir G. T. Goldie, President of the Royal Geographical Society; Lord Glenesk, President of the Newspaper Press Fund; Mr. R. N. Crane, acting chairman of the American Society in London; Sir G. Reid, ex-President of the Royal Scottish Academy; Professor Herkomer, R.A.; the Poet Laureate; Lord Macnaghten, treasurer of Lincoln's Inn; Mr. C. Willis, K.C., treasurer of the Inner Temple; Sir Arthur Conan Doyle, Mr. Anthony Hope Hawkins, Sir Lawrence Alma-Tadema, R.A., Mr. Sidney Lee, and Mr. H. W. Lucy, of *Punch*.

The next function was set for the 25th. It was a luncheon tendered by the London Society of the Pilgrims, and was to have place at the Savoy Hotel and be followed by the conferring of the degrees at Oxford, next day.

I will insert here the London *Telegraph*'s report of the Pilgrim affair:

There are two bands of Pilgrims. One foregathers in New York, the other in London. Both have learned the art of entertaining right well. So soon as a distinguished American sets his foot on these shores he finds a messenger awaiting him with a card of invitation for a feast, whereat he may learn in his mother tongue all that the Old Country may say in favour of him. It is a pleasant custom and one calculated to improve the common understanding of peoples whose ideals are the same. Mark Twain could not escape the Pilgrims if he would, and probably the honour of being the guest of so interesting a body afforded as much pleasure to him as his charmingly humorous speech was welcomed by his entertainers. The luncheon was served in the Savoy Hotel. The Right Hon. Augustine Birrell, Chief Secretary for Ireland, presided over a company of over two hundred gentlemen. The menu contained an excellent representation of the features of the guest, and facing the list of those for whom seats were reserved were the lines, the authorship of which could be recognised by all from the letters "O.S.":

> Pilot of many Pilgrims since the shout
> *"Mark Twain!"*—that serves you for a deathless sign—
> On Mississippi's waterway rang out
> Over the plummet's line—
>
> Still where the countless ripples laugh above
> The blue of halcyon seas long may you keep
> Your course unbroken, buoyed upon a love
> Ten thousand fathoms deep!

The company included:
Lord Glenesk, the Earl of Granard, Viscount Morpeth, M.P., the Hon. Harry Lawson, Archdeacon Sinclair, Mr. Owen Seaman, Sir Alfred Arnold, Mr. Butler Aspinall, K.C., Sir William Bell, LL.D., Mr. A. Shirley Benn, Mr. T. H. D. Berridge, M.P., Major H. P. Blencowe, the Right Hon. Sir Rowland Blennerhassett, K.C.M.G., Commodore F. G. Bourne, Mr. Harry E. Brittain, Major W. Broadfoot, R.E., Sir Thomas Brooke-Hitching, Sir Ernest Cable, Sir Vincent Caillard, the Hon. Colin H. Campbell, K.C., Mr. J. W. Comyns Carr, Mr. H. R. Chamberlain, General H. C. Cook, U.S.A., Captain Percy Creed, Mr. Thomas W. Cridler, Mr. A. S. Crockett, the Hon. Chauncey M. Depew, Lieut.-General C. W. Douglas, C.B., Mr. H. J. Duveen, Mr. Joseph Duveen, Mr. Louis Duveen, The Master of Elibank, M.P., Sir David Evans, Mr. George Faber, M.P., Surg.-General Sir Benjamin Franklin, K.C.I.E., Sir Frederick Fryer, K.C.S.I., Mr. John Fuller, M.P., Mr. J. L. Garvin, Colonel P. B. Giles, the Right Hon. Sir George Taubman Goldie, K.C.M.G., Mr. Hamar Greenwood, M.P., Mr. Francis O. Grenfell, Mr. R. N. Grenfell, Mr. H. A. Gwynne, Mr. H. Rider Haggard, Mr. Donald C. Haldeman, Mr. Charles A. Hanson, Sir Robert Harvey, the Hon. Claude Hay, M.P., Mr. Anthony Hope Hawkins, Sir Francis Hopwood, K.C.B., Colonel Millard Hunsiker, Major-General H. D. Hutchinson, C.S.I., Mr. E. B. Iwan-Muller, Rev. J. R. James, Mr. Charles Jacoby, Sir Alfred Jones, Mr. John Lane, the Hon. Charles Lawrence, Sir Joseph Lawrence, Sir Thomas Lipton, Bart., Mr. W. J. Locke, Canon Joseph McCormick, D.D., Major-General MacKinnon,

Mr. Donald Macmaster, K.C., Captain A. H. Marindin, Dr. Mayo-Collier, the Hon. Charles Murray, Sir George Newnes, Lieut.-Colonel N. Newnham-Davis, Lieut.-General Sir W. G. Nicholson, Sir Harry North, Mr. T. P. O'Connor, M.P., Lieut.-Colonel G. S. Ommanney, Sir John Ottley, K.C.I.E., Sir Gilbert Parker, M.P., Mr. Louis N. Parker, Colonel C. Parsons, Mr. C. Arthur Pearson, Mr. J. A. Pease, M.P., Sir Frederick Pollock, the Hon. Robert P. Porter, Mr. Arthur Priestley, M.P., Sir John Puleston, Mr. Henry Phipps, Sir Boverton Redwood, Sir Alfred Reynolds, Mr. John Morgan Richards, Mr. James W. Ritchie, Sir William Robson, K.C., M.P., Mr. H. H. Rogers, Sir Albert K. Rollit, Sir Percy Sanderson, Captain E. M. Sawtelle, Sir Bruce Seton, Mr. Charles D. Seligman, Captain Leveson E. Scarth, Canon H. Gibson Smith, Sir Edgar Speyer, Bart., Sir Douglas Straight, Mr. Alfred Sutro, Colonel the Hon. Milo Talbot, R.E., Mr. Charles Temperley, Mr. H. Beerbohm Tree, Mr. T. Fisher Unwin, Colonel Sir Howard Vincent, M.P., Professor Charles Waldstein, Sir Charles Walpole, Sir James Walker, Count Ward, Dr. Sylvester Willard, Mr. J. Leigh Wood, Mr. W. Basil Worsfold, and the Hon. Robert J. Wynne.

Mr. Harry Brittain, the secretary, read the following telegrams:

To Mark Twain greeting.—Even if the weather is inclement, our welcome will be warm. Best of luck now and always.—Undergraduates of Oxford.

All together, now, for three ripping, joyous hurrahs to your merry guest and the rest of you. American Pilgrims join in tribute to that champion dispenser of sunshine and good cheer, known to the gods and mortals as Mark Twain.—George Wilson, Pilgrims, New York.

Mr. Birrell, after proposing "The King and the President of the United States," said: I now have to give you the toast of our guest—Mr. Clemens, known to all good men and women in both hemispheres and to all boys and girls who are good for anything anywhere as Mark Twain. (Cheers.) Although, being as I am, still bound by the conditions of time and space, which I confess are beginning to get a little on my nerves—(laughter)—I am always at any given moment of time bound to be somewhere, I feel greatly surprised and deeply honoured at finding myself here. How I came here I will not ask. In the hurry and scurry of life I have long ceased to put to myself those momentous questions, "Why and wherefore?" and, indeed, I think the austerest moralist will admit that the man who is for the moment the Irish Chief Secretary is free from any obligation to ask himself any questions. (Loud laughter.) We are here this afternoon to do honour to a great and remarkable author, who writes in a language which is both his and my mother tongue. We have in our friend a remarkably fine specimen—I think the finest specimen extant—of a living author. (Cheers.) Authors may be divided roughly— very roughly—they are accustomed to rough treatment—into two classes—the living and the dead. (Laughter.) Gentlemen, you have already misunderstood me; I speak according to the flesh. If there be any dull author here, I beg to assure him that he need not be affronted, for I include him for this purpose, and this purpose only, in the ranks of the living. (Laughter.) Dead authors are indeed a mighty army. In the British Museum, in the Vatican library, in the Bodleian, nay, even on the humble shelves of an impoverished but persistent book-buyer like myself, they have a tendency to crowd us out. I know it has been said of them that they rule us from their urns, but I will have you bear in mind the fact that that observation was made by a nobleman who was himself an author. (Laughter.) This is how the grand tradition of literature is preserved from one generation to another. With regard to our distinguished friend, what is it necessary for any of us to say of him? As I was remarking, he is a living author; dead authors are bound on our shelves. I myself as a boy was a great reader. Chilly silence! (Loud laughter.) But don't judge me too harshly. I was from my cradle shortsighted. The preferably glorious career of Huckleberry Finn was from the beginning closed against me. I had no choice but to read, and my favourite reading was the lives of authors—dead authors—for in those days you had to be dead before your biography was written, even in one volume. (Laughter.) I therefore had no choice but to read the lives of dead authors, and my favourite day-dream—many happy hours have I spent in it—was to fancy myself, whilst reading the life of any particular dead author, his most contemporary admirer, the ministering angel who rushed to his assistance, and who was ever ready to supply his very numerous wants. Ah! gentlemen, those were happy days. It would surprise you the marvellous things that I was able to do in the imagination. I thrust a quartern loaf within reach of poor Otway, who, you will remember, died of starvation—probably that is all you do remember of him. (Laughter.) Had I had my way, Otway would not have died of starvation, and you would never have heard of him at all. (Laughter.) I delighted to picture myself acting the part of a judicious, friendly, tactful, and experienced Maecenas to poor Chatterton, that "marvellous boy who perished in his prime." Had I had my way, he would not have perished in prime, but would have lived to become the ablest and most critical editor we have ever had of Early English poetry. I was able also by a few strokes of the pen to liquidate the whole of the great burden of debt which played so tragic a part in the life of the man who was perhaps of all English authors the best—I mean the great and good Sir Walter Scott. (Cheers.) Nobly have I discharged my debt to the dead; but what about the living author, what have we, any of us, ever done for him? (A Pilgrim: "Bought his books.") Someone suggests we have bought his books. I am glad to meet that rare person. (Laughter.) I wonder by what art or subterfuge he obtained entrance into this literary circle. (Laughter.) It is much easier in imagination to be kind to the dead author than it is to endure the living one. (Laughter.) It is no easy matter, that; it is quite a different kettle of fish. The odds are that, albeit he be your friend, you cannot for the life of you read his books. There are hosts of living authors whose names I do not propose to mention—(laughter)—whose books I cannot read. Yet it may be that they have their necessities, and it cannot be denied that there have been Otways and Chattertons in our own day, men of genius but not of good fortune, who have need of all the assistance any kindly nature can render to them. But it is far more difficult to be good to the living author than it is to patronise the dead. Therefore, these are melancholy reflections. That is why we are all so rejoiced to be here to-day to do honour to a great and a living author—(cheers)—who we all unaffectedly love and admire. I know no wiser maxim of behaviour than this "love me, and tell me so." Did we only observe it more in all our relations of life I believe the misery of mankind would be partially mitigated. We all love Mark Twain, and we are here to tell him so. There is one more point. All the world knows it, and that is why it is dangerous to omit it. Our guest is a distinguished citizen of the great Republic beyond the seas. (Cheers.) In America his "Huckleberry Finn" and his "Tom Sawyer" are what "Robinson Crusoe" and "Tom Brown's Schooldays" have been to us. (Cheers.) They are racy of the soil. They are books of which it is impossible to place any period of termination. I will not speak of the classics—reminiscences of much evil in our early days. We do not meet here to-day without appreciations and depreciations of our "tupenny" little prefaces or our forewords. I am not going to say what the world a thousand years hence will think of Mark Twain. Posterity will take care of itself, will read what it wants to read, will forget what it chooses to forget, and will pay no attention whatsoever to our critical mumblings and jumblings. Let us, therefore, be content to say to our friend and guest that we are here speaking for ourselves and for our children to say what he has been to us. (Cheers.) I remember in Liverpool in 1867 first buying the copy, which I still preserve, of the celebrated "Jumping Frog." It has a few words of preface which reminded me that our guest in those days was called "the wild humorist of the Pacific Slope," and a few lines later down "the moralist of the Main." That was some forty years ago. Here he is, still the humorist, still the moralist. His humour enlivens and enlightens his morality, and his morality is all the better for his humour. That is one of the reasons why we love him. I am not here to mention any book of his; that is a subject of dispute in my family circle—which is the best and which is the next best. But I must put in a word lest I should not be true to myself—a terrible thing—for his "Joan of Arc"— (cheers)—a book of chivalry, of nobility, and of manly sincerity, for which I take this opportunity of thanking him. (Cheers.) But you can all drink this toast, each one of you with his own intention. You can get into it what meaning you like. Mark Twain is a man whom English and Americans do well to honour. He is the true consolidator of nations. His delightful humour is of the kind which dissipates and destroys national prejudices. (Cheers.) His truth and his honour, his love of truth and his love of honour overflow all boundaries. He has made the world better by his presence. We rejoice to see him here. Long may he live to reap the plentiful harvest of hearty, honest, human affection. (Loud cheers.)

The toast having been pledged in truly British fashion,

MARK TWAIN replied as follows: Pilgrims, I desire first to thank those undergraduates of Oxford. When a man has grown so old as I am, when he has reached the verge of seventy-two years, there is nothing that carries him back to the dreamland of his life, to his boyhood, like recognition of those young hearts up yonder. (Cheers.) And so I thank them out of my heart. (Cheers.) I desire to thank the Pilgrims of New York also for their kind notice and message which they have cabled over here. (Cheers.) Mr. Birrell says he does not know how he got here. But he will be able to get away all right—he has not drunk anything since he came here. (Laughter.) I am glad to know about those friends of his—Otway and Chatterton— fresh, new names to me. (Laughter.) I am glad of the disposition he has shown to rescue them from the evils of poverty, and if they are still in London I hope to have a talk with them. (Laughter.) For awhile I thought he was going to tell us the effect which my books had upon his growing manhood. (Laughter.) I thought he was going to tell us how much the effect amounted to, and whether it really made him what he now is—(laughter)—but with the discretion born of Parliamentary experience he dodged that, and we do not know now whether he read the books or not. He did that very neatly. I could not do it any better myself. My books have had effect, and very good ones, too, here and there—and some others not so good. There is no doubt about that. But I remember one monumental instance of it years and years ago. Professor Norton, of Harvard, was over here, and when he came back to Boston I went out with Mr. Howells to call on him. Norton was allied in some way by marriage with Darwin. Mr. Norton, who was very gentle in what he had to say, and almost delicate, said, "Mr. Clemens, I have been spending some time with Mr. Darwin in England, and I should like to tell you something connected with that visit. You were the object of it, and I myself would have been very proud of it, but you may not be proud of it. At any rate, I am going to tell you what it was, and to leave to you to regard it as you please. Mr. Darwin took me up to his bedroom and pointed out certain things there—pitcher plants and so on, that he was measuring and watching from day to day, and he said, 'The chambermaid is permitted to do what she pleases in this room, but she must never touch those plants and never touch those books on the table by the candle. With those books I read myself to sleep every night.' Those were your own books." (Laughter.) I said, "There is no question to my mind as to whether I should regard that as a compliment or not. I do regard it as a very great compliment, and a very high honour, that that great mind labouring for the whole human race should rest itself on my books. I am proud that he should read himself to sleep with them." I could not keep that to myself—I was so proud of it. As soon as I got home to Hartford I called up my oldest friend, and dearest enemy on occasion, the Rev. Joseph Twichell, my pastor, and I told him about that, and of course he was full of interest and venom. (Laughter.) Those people who never get any compliment like that feel like that. (Laughter.) He went off, he did not issue any applause of any kind, and I did not hear of that subject for some time. But when Mr. Darwin passed away from this life and some time after "Darwin's Life and Letters" came out, the Rev. Mr. Twichell procured an early copy of the work and found something in it which he considered applied to me. He came over to my house—it was snowing, raining, sleeting, but that did not make any difference to Twichell. He produced a book, turned over and over until he came to a place where he said, "Here, look at this letter from Mr. Darwin to Sir Joseph Hooker." What Mr. Darwin said, I give you the idea, was this: "I do not know whether I ought to have devoted my whole life to these drudgeries in natural history and the other sciences or not, for while I may have gained in some way I have lost in another. Once I had a fine perception and appreciation of high literature, but in me that quality is atrophied." "That," said Mr. Twichell, "was reading your books." Mr. Birrell has touched lightly—very lightly, but in not an uncomplimentary way, on my position in this world as a moralist. (Laughter.) I am glad to have that recognition, too, because I have suffered since I have been in this town. (Laughter.) In the first place, right away, when I came here a newsman was going around with a great red, highly-displayed placard in the place of an apron. He was selling newspapers, and there were two sentences on the placard which would have been all right if they had been punctuated; but they ran those two sentences together without a comma or anything, and that would naturally create a wrong impression, because it said, "Mark Twain Arrives Ascot Cup Stolen." (Laughter.) No doubt many a person was misled by those sentences joined together in that unkind way. (Laughter.) I have no doubt my character has suffered from it. I suppose I ought to defend my character, but how can I defend it? I can say here and now, and anybody can see by my face that I am sincere—(laughter)—that I speak the truth. I have never seen that cup. I have not got the cup—I did not have a chance to get it. (Laughter.) I have always had a good character in that way. I have hardly ever stolen anything, and if I did steal anything

I had discretion enough to know about the value of it first. I do not steal things that are likely to get myself into trouble. I do not think any of us do that. I know we all take things—that is to be expected; but, really, I have never taken anything, certainly in England, that amounts to any great thing. I do confess that when I was here seven years ago I stole a hat, but it didn't amount to anything. (Laughter.) It was not a good hat, and was only a clergyman's hat anyway. (Loud laughter.) I was at a luncheon party, and Archdeacon Wilberforce was there also. I daresay he is archdeacon now—he was a canon then—and he was serving in the Westminster Battery, if that is the proper term. (Laughter.) I do not know, as you mix military and ecclesiastical things together so much. He left the luncheon table before I did. He began this thing. I did steal his hat, but he began by taking mine. I make that concession because I would not accuse Archdeacon Wilberforce of stealing my hat—I should not think of it. (Laughter.) I confine that phrase to myself. He merely took my hat. (Laughter.) And with good judgment, too; it was a better hat than his. (Laughter.) He came out before the luncheon was over and sorted the hats in the hall, and selected one which suited. It happened to be mine. He went off with it. When I came out by-and-bye there was no hat there which would go on my head except his, which was left behind. My head was not the customary size just at that time. (Laughter.) I had been receiving a good many very nice and complimentary attentions, and my head was a couple of sizes larger than usual, and his hat just suited me. The bumps and corners were all right intellectually. (Laughter.) There were results pleasing to me, possibly so to him. He found out whose hat it was, and wrote saying it was pleasant that all the way home, whenever he met anybody, his gravities, his solemnities, deep thoughts, his eloquent remarks were all snatched up by the people he met, and mistaken for brilliant humourisms. (Laughter.) I had another experience. It was not unpleasing. I was received with a deference, which was entirely foreign to my experience, by everybody whom I met—(laughter)—so that before I got home I had a much higher opinion of myself than I have ever had before or since. And there is in that very connection an incident which I remember at that old date which is rather melancholy to me, because it shows how a person can deteriorate in a mere seven years. It is seven years ago. I have not that hat now. I was going down Pall Mall, or some other of your big streets, and I recognised that that hat needed ironing. I went into a big shop and passed on my hat, and asked that it might be ironed. They were courteous, very courteous—even courtly. (Laughter.) They brought that hat back to me very sleek and nice, and I asked how much there was to pay. They replied that they did not charge the clergy anything. (Laughter.) I have cherished the delight of that moment from that day to this. The first thing I did the other day was to go and hunt up that shop and hand in my hat to have it ironed. I said, "How much?" when it came back. They said "ninepence." (Laughter.) In seven years I have acquired all that worldliness, and I am sorry to be back where I was seven years ago. (Laughter.) But now I am chaffing and chaffing and chaffing here, and I hope you will forgive me for that; but when a man stands on the verge of seventy-two you know perfectly well that he never reached that place without knowing what this life is—a heart-breaking bereavement. And so our reverence is for our dead. We do not forget them, but our duty is towards the living, and if we can be cheerful, cheerful in spirit, cheerful in speech, and in hope that is benefit to those who are around us. (Cheers.) My history includes an incident which will always connect me with England in a pathetic way, for when I arrived here seven years ago with my wife and daughter we had gone around the globe lecturing to raise money to clear off a debt. My wife and one of my daughters started across the oceans to bring to England our eldest daughter. She was twenty-four years of age, and in the bloom of womanhood, and we were unsuspecting, when a cablegram—one of those heart-breaking cablegrams which we all in our days have to experience—was put into my hand. It stated that my daughter had gone to her long sleep. And so, as I say, I cannot always be cheerful, and I cannot always be chaffing; I must sometimes lay the cap and bells aside, and recognise that I am of the human race. I have my cares and griefs, and I therefore am very glad to have Mr. Birrell say something that was in the nature of those verses here, at the top of this programme:

> "He lit our life with shafts of sun,
> And vanquished pain.
> Thus two great nations stand as one
> In honouring Twain."

I am very glad to have those verses. I am very glad and very grateful for what Mr. Birrell said in that connection. I have received since I have been here, in this one week, hundreds of letters from all conditions of people in England—men, women, and children—and there is compliment, praise, and, above all, and better than all, there is in them a note of affection. (Cheers.) Praise is well, compliment is well, but affection—that is the last and final and most precious reward that any man can win, whether by character or achievement, and I am very grateful to have that reward. All these letters make me feel that here in England, as in America, when I stand under the English flag, I am not a stranger, I am not an alien, but at home. (Loud cheers.)

Dictated Friday, July 26, 1907

Paragraph copied from "England's Ovation to Mark Twain" by Sydney Brooks, in regard to Mr. Clemens's speech at the Pilgrims' dinner—Speeches can be conveyed in print, but talks cannot—The ceremony of conferring the degree of D. Litt., and copy of Sydney Brooks's account of it.

The fine verses quoted in that account are from the hand of Owen Seaman, of the *Punch* editorial staff. It sounds that same deep note of affection, which I so prize.

In an article entitled "England's Ovation to Mark Twain" Sydney Brooks has a paragraph which calls to mind a chapter of this Autobiography which I dictated a couple of years ago when Clara made her début on the concert stage at Norfolk, Connecticut, and I made a talk—not a speech. This is the quotation:

It would have done you good to hear the storm of cheers that greeted Mark Twain when he rose to respond. His first words had reference to two telegrams of greeting, one from the undergraduates of Oxford, the other from the New York Pilgrims. I was never more conscious of the difference between the spoken and the written word than in reading over in print the speech which I heard Mark Twain deliver. You get indeed the words, but the atmosphere of the occasion that made each point so inevitably appropriate and telling, the presence and gestures of the veteran speaker, his incomparably effective and dramatic drawl—all this you miss.

It is as I have said in the autobiographical chapter just referred to: *speeches* can be conveyed in print, but not *talks*. Speeches consist of literarily phrased and completed sentences, and they read smoothly and intelligibly, but this is not the case with talks. The soul of a talk consists of action, not words; action, gesture, inflection—the unvoiced expression of the thought. These felicities escape the stenographer; they are an aroma; he cannot concrete them into words; the words are not there; none but the inconsequential sentences are completed; the happy ones break off in the middle because the audience has got the point, it is not necessary to finish the sentence, and the house would not hear the finish anyhow. But the stenographer cannot leave the sentences in that broken condition, for the result would be ragged, incoherent and incomprehensible; therefore he finishes the broken sentences with words of his own, and the result is stupendously unhappy. A talk cannot be conveyed in print successfully; there is no way to do it, and the attempt should never be made. Oh look at that Pilgrim talk of mine! It was an exceedingly good talk when it was uttered, but how flat it is in print!

I was in Oxford by seven o'clock that evening (June 25, 1907), and trying on the scarlet gown which the tailor had been constructing, and found it right—right and surpassingly becoming. At half past ten the next morning we assembled at All Souls College and marched thence, gowned, mortar-boarded, and in double file, down a long street to the Sheldonian Theatre, between solid walls of the populace, very much hurrah'd and limitlessly kodacked. We made a procession of considerable length and distinction and picturesqueness, with the Chancellor, Lord Curzon, late Viceroy of India, in his rich robe of black and gold, in the lead, followed by a pair of trim little-boy train-bearers, and the train-bearers followed by the young Prince Arthur of Connaught, who was to be made a D.C.L. The detachment of D.C.L.'s were followed by the Doctors of Science, and these by the Doctors of Literature, and these in turn by the Doctors of Music. Sidney Colvin marched in front of me; I was coupled with Sidney Lee, and Kipling followed us; General Booth, of the Salvation Army, was in the squadron of D.C.L.'s.

Our journey ended, we were halted in a fine old hall whence we could see, through a corridor of some length, the massed audience in the theatre. Here for a little time we moved about and chatted and made acquaintanceships; then the D.C.L.'s were summoned, and they marched through that corridor and the shouting began in the theatre. It would be some time before the Doctors of Literature and of Science would be called for, because each of those D.C.L.'s had to have a couple of Latin speeches made over him before his promotion would be complete—one by the Regius Professor of Civil Law, the other by the Chancellor. After a while I asked Sir William Ramsay if a person might smoke here and not get shot. He said "Yes," but that whoever did it and got caught would be fined a guinea, and perhaps hanged later. He said he knew of a place where we could accomplish at least as much as half of a smoke before any informers would be likely to chance upon us, and he was ready to show the way to any who might be willing to risk the guinea and the hanging. By request he led the way, and Kipling, Sir Norman Lockyer and I followed. We crossed an unpopulated quadrangle and stood under one of its exits—an archway of massive masonry—and there we lit up and began to take comfort. The photographers soon arrived, but they were courteous and friendly and gave us no trouble, and we gave them none. They grouped us in all sorts of ways and photographed us at their diligent leisure, while we smoked and talked. We were there more than an hour; then we returned to headquarters, happy, content, and greatly refreshed. Presently we filed into the theatre, under a very satisfactory hurrah, and waited in a crimson column, dividing the crowded pit through the middle, until each of us in his turn should be called to stand before the Chancellor and hear our merits set forth in sonorous Latin. Meantime, Kipling and I wrote autographs until some good kind soul interfered in our behalf and procured for us a rest.

I will now save what is left of my modesty by quoting again from Sydney Brooks's "Ovation."

> On Wednesday, June 26, he received his degree of D. Litt. He was not the only American so honored. Mr. Whitelaw Reid was also present, the degree awarded him being the D.C.L.; and it is pleasant to be able to record that his reception was one of unforced heartiness and cordiality. The Oxford degrees are conferred in the Sheldonian Theatre, a circular building, built by Sir Christopher Wren after a Roman model, and though apparently small, capable of holding nearly four thousand people. On Wednesday all the tiers and galleries were filled to the uttermost, the lower ones by ladies and dons, the topmost ones by undergraduates, while on the floor stood the graduates and strangers, clustering round a passageway through which the procession was to pass. Shortly after eleven o'clock the Chancellor, Lord Curzon, in his black and gold state robes, attended by two pages, and followed by the heads of the colleges in their scarlet gowns, entered the theatre and passed up to the platform. The list of proposed degrees was at once read out by the Chancellor and the pleasure of the house asked in the time-honored Latin form. The mightiest bursts of applause were for the Prime Minister, the American ambassador, "General" Booth, Sir Evelyn Wood, Mark Twain, and Mr. Rudyard Kipling. Those on whom the degree of Doctor of Civil Law was to be conferred were then summoned into the theatre and took their seats in the reserved passageway. One by one they were presented to the Chancellor by the Regius Professor of Civil Law in a series of Latin speeches describing their achievements. The Chancellor replied in a few complimentary words that often concealed a shrewd pleasantry and formally admitted each nominee to the degree. The person so honored then mounted the platform, shook hands with the Chancellor, and took his appointed seat to the

right or left. When Mr. Whitelaw Reid's turn came round the Regius Professor of Civil Law hailed him as the distinguished son of a kindred race, famous for his eloquence and a marked journalist, whose worth and repute among his own countrymen were attested by their choice of him to represent them as Ambassador to Great Britain. But it was not only as a kinsman and an Ambassador that they greeted him, but as a man of learning and proficiency in all the arts. While this greeting was being declaimed in sonorous Latin an undergraduate voice from the gallery, affecting what passes in England for an American accent of the worst buzz-saw character, shouted out, to the huge merriment of all present, "I guess that's about right, pardner." Mr. Reid was most warmly cheered as the Chancellor, after addressing him as *vir honorate, magni populi legate, litteras diurnas magno labore multos annos molite, ingens inter consanguineas gentes amicitiae aut simultatis momentum,* pronounced the words admitting him to the degree of civil law and shook him cordially by the hand.

But unquestionably it was Mark Twain who of all the recipients of degrees roused the greatest enthusiasm. The whole building broke into a roar of applause when he stood up to be presented to the Chancellor. "What have you done with the Ascot Cup, Mark?" asked a voice from the gallery, and the assembly shook with laughter. "Have you got that jumping frog with you, Mark?" asked another voice, and peal upon peal of cheers rang out. The speech in which Mark Twain was presented was perfectly inaudible, but the professor who delivered it, being some-what bald, and standing within a foot or two of Mark Twain's magnificent mane, gave point to the coaxing query that floated down from the galleries, "Couldn't you spare him some of your hair, Mark?" I doubt whether Mark Twain has ever been more severely tried than as he stood there, condemned by all the proprieties to silence and a more or less passive demeanor, while the jests flew fast and all the spectators shook with laughter and applause. A tremendous and most moving ovation punctuated the Chancellor's address. *Vir jucundissime* [loud cheers], *lepidissime* [louder cheers], *facetissime* [frantic cheers], *qui totius orbis terrarum latera nativa tua hilaritate concutis* [prolonged cheers], during which Mark Twain advances to the Chancellor's rostrum, shakes hands, and passes to a seat on the left, smiling and gratified except for the thought of all the good things he might have said in reply. And it was the same wherever he went in Oxford. When the presentations were over and the newly made Doctors filed out of the theatre and went to lunch at All Souls College, the people in the streets singled out Mark Twain, formed a vast and cheering body-guard around him and escorted him to the college gates. But before and after the lunch it was Mark Twain again, whom everybody seemed most of all to want to meet. The Maharajah of Bikanir, for instance, finding himself seated at lunch next to Mrs. Riggs (Kate Douglas Wiggin) and hearing that she knew Mark Twain, asked her to present him—a ceremony duly performed later on in the quadrangle. At the garden party given the same afternoon in the beautiful grounds of St. John's, where the indefatigable Mark put in an appearance, it was just the same—every one pressed forward for an exchange of greetings and a hand-shake. On the following day, when the Oxford Pageant took place, it was even more so. "Mark Twain's Pageant" it was called by one of the papers. Wherever he went he received from the people of Oxford the warm affectionate welcome that greeted him in London, and that will continue to greet him in every town he visits in these islands.

Dictated July 30, 1907

**A dinner at one of the colleges, at which Mr. Clemens
was to respond to a toast. He wears evening dress when
he should have worn his scarlet robe—His opinion of dinners
and speech-making in general.**

There was to be a dinner of high dignity that night at one of the colleges. I was to occupy a place at the high table with the Chancellor, the heads of colleges, Ambassador Reid, and some other distinguished personages, and respond to a toast. I had asked and received permission to stay at home until the banquet should be over and speech-making time at hand. I had been asking and acquiring this privilege in America for six years, and valued it beyond price. A banquet is probably the most fatiguing thing in the world except ditch-digging. It is the insanest of all recreations. The inventor of it overlooked no detail that could furnish weariness, distress, harassment, and acute and long-sustained misery of mind and body. These sorrows begin with the assembling of the clans half an hour before the dinner. During all that half hour one must stand on his feet with the crowd, amid a persecuting din of conversation, and must shake hands and exchange banalities and "I am so glad to see you sirs" with apparently seven millions of fellow sufferers. Then the banquet begins, and there is an hour and a half of that. It is an hour and a half of nerve-wrecking clamor; of intolerable clattering and clashing of knives and forks and plates; of shrieking and shouting commonplaces at one's elbow-mates, and of listening to the like shriekings and shoutings from them in return; and when there is a band—and there usually is—the pandemonium is complete, and there is nothing to approach it but hell on a Sunday night. During that awful hour and a half the faces of certain of the men are a study, and are pathetically interesting. These are the men who have been damned—that is to say, they are under sentence to make speeches. The faces of these are drawn and troubled, and exhibit a distressed preoccupation. Such of the damned as have come with memorized speeches are trying to say them over privately and talk to their neighbors at the same time, and also at the same time try to look interested in what the neighbors are saying. The result is a curious and piteous jumble of expressions and vacancies in the faces, an exhibition which compels the deep and sincere compassion of any beholder who has been of the damned himself and knows what it is like. The other men under sentence are the men who have not been appointed to speak, but who know they are likely to be called upon, and who are now trying their best to think up something to say; if they are not succeeding they are no better off than those others, as far as comfort goes. It is unquestionably best to stay away from the banquet until the feeding and the racket are over and the time arrived for the speaking to begin; and so, as I have said, I had long ago adopted the policy of staying away until the banquet should be over and the speech-making ready to begin. This judicious policy has saved my life, I suppose.

That banquet at the College was to begin at seven o'clock. At eight nobody was able to tell me what kind of clothes I ought to wear; some said evening dress, others said the scarlet gown. We sent a messenger to the College to inquire, and he came back and said evening dress. It was an error. I was fairly within the place before I noticed that it was just one wide and flaming conflagration of crimson gowns—a kind of human prairie on fire. I had to pass through the centre of it in my black clothes, and I had never in my life felt so painfully and offensively and humiliatingly conspicuous before; and then I had to stand at the high table and look out over that fire and try to keep my mind on my business and make a speech. I could not have been in the least degree more uncomfortable if I had been stark naked. I called to mind a phrase which I had used ten years before when describing a great court function in the imperial palace at Vienna, a scene of dazzling color and splendor and gorgeousness, through the midst of which the American minister, in black evening dress, plowed his way, far and away the most conspicuous figure in that sea of flashing glories. I said he looked as out of place as a Presbyterian in hell. I was looking the same way now, and I knew how odiously showy and uncomfortable he must have felt.

Was it my conspicuousness that distressed me? Not at all. It was merely that I was not beautifully conspicuous, but uglily conspicuous—it makes all the difference in the world. If I had been clothed from helmet to spurs in plate armor of virgin gold and shining like the sun, I should have been entirely at ease, utterly happy, perfectly satisfied with myself; to be so thunderingly conspicuous, but at the same time so beautifully conspicuous, would have caused me not a pang—on the contrary it would have filled me with joy, pride, vanity, exaltation. When I appear clothed in white, a startling accent in the midst of a sombre multitude in mid-winter, the most conspicuous object there, I am not ashamed, not ill at ease, but serene and content, because my conspicuousness is not of an offensive sort; it is not an insult, and cannot affront any eye, nor affront anybody's sense of propriety. My red gown was brought to me just as I was leaving the place—oh infamously too late!

At three the next afternoon we headed for the Pageant, beyond the walls of Oxford, and at once encountered signs of what was coming.

The Oxford Pageant.

Most Americans have been to Oxford and will remember what a dream of the Middle Ages it is, with its crooked lanes, its gray and stately piles of ancient architecture and its meditation-breeding air of repose and dignity and unkinship with the noise and fret and hurry and bustle of these modern days. As a dream of the Middle Ages Oxford was not perfect until Pageant day arrived and furnished certain details which had been for generations lacking. These details began to appear at mid-afternoon on the 27th. At that time singles, couples, groups and squadrons of the three thousand five hundred costumed characters who were to take part in the Pageant began to ooze and drip and stream through house doors, all over the old town, and wend toward the meadows outside the walls. Soon the lanes were thronged with costumes which Oxford had from time to time seen and been familiar with in bygone centuries—fashions of dress which marked off centuries as by dates, and milestoned them back, and back, and back, until history faded into legend and tradition, when Arthur was a fact and the Round Table a reality. In this rich commingling of quaint and strange and brilliantly colored fashions in dress the dress-changes of Oxford for twelve centuries stood vivid and realized to the eye; Oxford as a dream of the Middle Ages was complete now as it had never in our day been complete; at last there was no discord; the mouldering old buildings, and the picturesque throngs drifting past them, were in harmony; soon—astonishingly soon!—the only persons that seemed out of place, and grotesquely and offensively and criminally out of place, were such persons as came intruding along clothed in the ugly and odious fashions of the twentieth century; they were a bitterness to the feelings, an insult to the eye.

The make-ups of illustrious historic personages seemed perfect, both as to portraiture and costume; one had no trouble in recognizing them. Also, I was apparently quite easily recognizable myself. The first corner I turned brought me suddenly face to face with Henry VIII, a person whom I had been implacably disliking for sixty years; but when he put out his hand with royal courtliness and grace and said, "Welcome, well-beloved stranger, to my century and to the hospitalities of my realm," my old prejudices vanished away and I forgave him. I think now that Henry VIII has been over-abused, and that most of us, if we had been situated as he was, domestically, would not have been able to get along with as limited a graveyard as he forced himself to put up with. I feel now that he was one of the nicest men in history. Personal contact with a king is more effective in removing baleful prejudices than is any amount of argument drawn from tales and histories. If I had a child I would name it Henry VIII, regardless of sex.

Do you remember Charles I?—and his broad slouch with the plume in it? and his slender, tall figure? and his body clothed in velvet doublet with lace sleeves, and his legs in leather, with long rapier at his side and his spurs on his heels? I encountered him at the next corner, and knew him in a moment—knew him as perfectly and as vividly as I should know the Grand Chain in the Mississippi if I should see it from the pilot-house after all these years. He bent his body and gave his hat a sweep that fetched its plume within an inch of the ground, and gave me a welcome that went to my heart. This king has been much maligned; I shall understand him better hereafter, and shall regret him more than I have been in the habit of doing these fifty or sixty years. He did some things, in his time, which might better have been left undone, and which cast a shadow upon his name—we all know that, we all concede it—but our error has been in regarding them as crimes and in calling them by that name, whereas I perceive now that they were only indiscretions. At every few steps I met persons of deathless name whom I had never encountered before outside of pictures and statuary and history, and these were most thrilling and charming encounters. I had hand-shakes with Henry II, who had not been seen in the Oxford streets for nearly eight hundred years; and with the Fair Rosamond, whom I now believe to have been chaste and blameless, although I had thought differently about it before; and with Shakspeare, one of the pleasantest foreigners I have ever gotten acquainted with; and with Roger Bacon; and with Queen Elizabeth, who talked five minutes and never swore once—a fact which gave me a new and good opinion of her and moved me to forgive her for beheading the Scottish Mary, if she really did it, which I now doubt; and with the quaintly and anciently clad young King Harold Harefoot of near nine hundred years ago, who came flying by on a bicycle and smoking a pipe, but at once checked up and got off to shake with me; and also I met a bishop who had lost his way because this was the first time he had been inside the walls of Oxford for as much as twelve hundred years or thereabouts. By this time I had grown so used to the obliterated ages and their best known people that if I had met Adam I should not have been either surprised or embarrassed; and if he had come in a racing automobile and a cloud of dust, with nothing on but his fig-leaf, it would have seemed to me all right and harmonious.

The Oxford Pageant continued.

The living pictures were to begin to appear toward four o'clock. Facing and commanding a wide prospect of meadow and winding river and scattered groups of venerable trees, with glimpses of dreamy blue distances between them, was the grand stand, and under its sheltering roof were banked like a slanting garden of flowers several thousand summer-clothed ladies and gentlemen. In the centre of the stand, down at the front, was a low-railed box with a sofa and chairs, capable of accommodating loosely and comfortably, twenty persons, perhaps. This choice place was for Royalty, but Royalty was detained, and did not come. Rudyard Kipling and his wife, and I, with two or three others, were substituted by the management, and we represented Royalty as well as we could in a sudden and unprepared way without opportunity for practice. Lord Curzon was presently added; then we did better; for he had been a king, (Viceroy of India), and a very great and competent one.

The situation, and the outlook, seemed vaguely familiar, for we seemed to be gazing into the swarded and wooded deeps and distances of the operatic stage; but that was as far as the seeming went: we realized, with a stirring and uplifting feeling, that these lovelinesses were not a painted fiction, but were real, splendidly real, and more noble and gracious and satisfying than any fiction could be; we realized that the little river winding here and there and yonder in the middle-ground, in the shadow of the June-clad old trees, was real water, fresh and sweet, and to our sense the very same water that had been gliding and glinting and whispering along between those banks in shadow and sunflash for unnumbered centuries and looking as it looked now—a winsome and worshipful allegory of eternal youth; the snowy swans that were diligently and contentedly breasting its surface, in the way of recreation or business, were real swans, not fictions worked with a string by a "supe" hidden behind a pasteboard tree; the country birds that were flitting and singing unafraid all about this bewitching sylvan theatre were real birds, not make-believes; and what a delightful feature they were, with their fearless intrusions, their impudent indifference to the swarming human life there present, and to the pomps and tragedies of Old English history which were soon being displayed under them! And why shouldn't they feel at home, and indifferent? They were full of inherited sentiment; their ancestors of the bygone centuries had actually seen the pomps and tragedies which were here reproduced as a dream and a memory, and no doubt these birds carried the recollection of those long-vanished scenes in their blood.

Here is the first scene; it dates back nearly twelve hundred years:

THE LEGEND OF ST. FRIDESWIDE.

Circa A.D. 727.

A flock of sheep are being driven by, when one of the Shepherds makes his way to a wattled hut by the river side, where fishermen are talking and jesting over their work as they draw their nets to the bank. One of the group catches sight of a boat in the distance, and calls the attention of his comrades to the strange vessel, which is being rowed towards them so swiftly as to suggest the fear of pursuit. It is Frideswide with her maidens, and the fishermen, realising her need for succour, offer their ready help in drawing her boat to shore. Then Frideswide, fainting with fatigue, is borne into the hut, but no sooner has she gained its shelter than two galleys heave in sight, manned with warriors, the thanes and chosen house-carles of Algar, Earl of Leicester. They put to land, and despite the protestations of the fishermen, Algar forces his way into the hut and attempts to carry off the maiden. But Frideswide, despairing of mortal help, sinks to her knees and implores a less uncertain aid; and not in vain, for the audacious noble is stricken with a sudden blindness from heaven. Terrified and repentant, he prevails upon her to plead for his sight to be restored; and laying his crown and arms on a shield, he makes a solemn vow to build upon that spot a convent for the maiden whose destruction he had planned. The scene closes with the departure of Frideswide, who is borne off on her return to Oxford in a waggon drawn by a team of oxen. Her bones still rest in the Cathedral built where the Convent stood, and round which the City of Oxford grew up.

Those were real sheep; they emerged from a forest some distance away on our left, beyond the river and the bridge, and a shepherd clad in skins drove them lazily across a meadow, the sheep taking their time and munching grass in a most real and natural way, and not ostentatiously and fictitiously and criminally and mechanically, as they would have done if they had been on the opera stage under salary. The swarm of skin-clad fishermen fussing at their nets had a genuine look also; and so had the commotions, likewise, which broke out when the beautiful and high-born young saint and her maidens arrived in a barge and scrambled up the shore in fright, closely followed by that savage earl and his savage men, who also scrambled ashore from their boat and started a furious fight and overcame the fishermen and captured the ladies. Everything was so well done that one was continually being thrilled and stirred as the events unfolded themselves and followed briskly one upon another.

In time the actors in this scene went drifting away across the meadows and among the trees to the right, and as they were disappearing in the distance cheering is heard far to the left, mingled with a singing of anthems, and the year 1036 has arrived; a swarming crowd of primitively armed cavalry and foot-soldiers and priests and civilian men and women and boys and girls of that ancient day comes marching by, and the coronation of Harold Harefoot takes place with bountiful pomp and ceremony.

Between the scenes there are no stage-waits; always while one multitude is marching away to the right and vacating the field, a fresh multitude is coming into view away to the left, a new date is arriving, and the picture presents new and fascinating splendors of costume and color. A multitude comes clothed in the fashions of 1110, and pictures the beginnings and institution of the University of Oxford; while these people are fading out of sight Henry II comes strolling along with the Fair Rosamond. Presently the gorgeous court comes flowing past, and in its midst one catches, with a distinct and lively thrill, a glimpse of a sweet and dainty little child, and recognizes and welcomes in that charming little figure a personage whom he has familiarly known all his life but had never once thought of him in that small and gentle and innocent form—for this is the formidable Richard of the Lion Heart, of deathless story!

Next comes Friar Bacon, (1270) illustrious and shining scientist in a dark time when scientists were few and far between; and he exhibits his legendary Brazen Head and makes it talk.

He and his crowd pass and disappear, and are followed by a riotous multitude, (1354) and a historic riot between town and gown takes place. I think I never saw a better riot on any stage. One of the marvels of these pageants was the easy and natural and competent and thoroughly satisfactory acting of these unprofessional multitudes of men and women and children—ordinary citizens of the little town of Oxford, every one of them—people who had never acted in their lives until they entered upon drill for these performances a year ago. There was never a hitch, never a stage-wait, never an awkwardness of any kind; the scenes had not the look of stage plays; they seemed distinctly real, and as if they were simply *happening*—happening by impulse, not studied invention.

Next scene—the Masque of the Mediaeval Curriculum, a fine allegorical piece, the creation of a young American.

Next, Wolsey receives Henry VIII at Oxford. (1518.) It was a brilliant and richly upholstered and multitudinous double procession marching from two different points and melting together at the centre of the stage. It was a sumptuous spectacle, a marvel of variety in costume, an undulating sea of flashing and flushing colors; when the head of the King's cavalcade came in sight it was so far away that it looked like a flower-bed gliding along the ground from among the distant trees; this was *real* perspective, real distance, and it made the mimic distances of the operatic stage seem very poor by comparison. I had never seen anything so fine and so remote and so moving as this before, and I shall not see its like again; but it has permanently spoiled the opera-perspectives for me.

The Oxford Pageant concluded.

The coming, and passing, and disappearing of dazzling pageants continued during the next two hours, without interruption. These great scenes are summarized as follows, in the Book of the Pageant:

THE FUNERAL OF AMY ROBSART.

A.D. 1560.

A mournful procession winds its way along the old Oxford Streets; the body of Amy Robsart, wife of Robert, Lord Dudley, is on its way to be interred with the most elaborate heraldic ceremony in St. Mary's Church. She has been found dead at the foot of a stone staircase in Cumnor Place, three miles from Oxford, on the very day when all the servants of the house had been granted special permission to visit Abingdon Fair. Her husband was in attendance at the Court of Queen Elizabeth at Windsor, and rumour said that he had connived at her death, and aspired to the hand of the Queen, whose principal favourite he had lately become. His wife had spent her life for the most part in country retirement, and was unaccustomed to join those courtly circles in which he was always found. He has caused her funeral to be conducted with great pomp and solemnity, but as the long procession, to the chanting of the choir, winds slowly past, there are not a few among the crowd who shake their heads and whisper to one another the dark tales of jealousy and murder which were current on every hand.

THE STATE PROGRESS OF QUEEN ELIZABETH.

A.D. 1566.

Heralded by trumpeters whose fanfare is heard before she comes in sight, the Queen makes her state entry into Oxford, and is met and welcomed by Robert Dudley, Earl of Leicester, and Chancellor of the University. He is preceded by the 'Esquires Bedell' with staves of office, and with him walk the Doctors of the University in their scarlet robes. The Queen advances, carried shoulder high by six of the gentlemen on a litter covered with a cloth of gold; and a gay crowd of brilliant courtiers throngs round their royal mistress. The Chancellor kisses the royal hand, and a speech of welcome is read in Latin by the University Orator. The civic authorities deliver up the city mace, and present the Queen with a rich silver cup, double gilt, and filled with old gold; and as the procession passes on through rows of kneeling scholars, Elizabeth smilingly replies 'Gratias ago!' to the loud 'Vivat Regina!' shouted by the crowd.

VISIT OF JAMES I.

A.D. 1605.

The expected visit of the first Stuart and his Queen has filled the city with excitement, and in St. Giles', just outside St. John's College, active preparations are afoot for the performance of the Three Witches of Macbeth. The stage management is in the hands of one Master William Shakespeare, who has been summoned from London for the special purpose of superintending a play which the next year is to see produced in the capital. Loudly acclaimed by the assembled citizens, the royal party makes its entry on horseback, guarded by a detachment of cavalry, and accompanied by a large and brilliant court. At the King's elbow is Francis Bacon, Lord Verulam, who has ridden over with him from Woodstock with the King; and on their way into the city they halt for a few minutes to watch the progress of the play.

CHARLES I. AT OXFORD.

The Happy Days. (A.D. 1636).

To the strains of musicians and minstrels on deck, a state barge is rowed slowly up the river, bearing the King and Queen Henrietta Maria, with the Princes Charles and James. Putting to shore, the Royal Party is received by Archbishop Laud and the Heads of Houses and Officials of the University, who have assembled at the riverside to give them welcome. A halt is made while a pavane is danced upon the bank, to the music of a band of players ensconced under the shadow of the trees; and after the measure is finished the barge moves slowly up the river with its royal burden.

The Early Days of the Civil War. (A.D. 1643).

The City by this time is the residence of the Court. With a bodyguard of troopers, Charles rides out of Oxford to meet his Queen, who arrives from the North in a coach of state. At the moment of their meeting news is brought of the Royalist victory at Roundway Down. The King dismounts, and enters the coach; the escorts join forces, and the two cavalcades return to the city in a triumphal progress with flags flying and drums beating. The gay dresses of the heralds and trumpeters of the various regiments make a brave show in the procession, and the pikemen and musketeers bring up the rear.

The Surrender of Oxford. (A.D. 1646).

Armed and in good order, with colours displayed, matches burning, and rattle of drums, the royal troops under Sir Thomas Glemham depart from Oxford between companies of Parliamentarian soldiers, who chant a puritan psalm and line their path on either side. They go out with all the honours of war, amid the scarcely concealed sorrow of the loyal academicians, who ever hated the Roundheads and gave all their sympathies to the Cavalier party.

THE EXPULSION OF THE FELLOWS OF MAGDALEN
BY KING JAMES II.

(A.D. 1687).

The King arrives with a small cavalry escort, and is received with honours by the City and University. Maidens clad in white strew flowers before him and his retinue, and on his way he is entertained with music, and the Waits of the City play before him. The Constables of the various parishes advance with their staves of office, followed by the guilds of the Glovers, Cordwainers, Tailors, and Mercers, on foot and on horseback, with the ensigns which bear the arms of their Company. A picturesque ceremony is seen when the monarch on his progress touches for the King's Evil poor folk who are brought to his presence. The Fellows of Magdalen are summoned before him, and are bidden to rescind their election of the Protestant, Dr. Hough, in favour of Mr. Farmer, the candidate favoured by James; and when they refuse to obey this unconstitutional demand, the King takes the law into his own hands and orders their immediate expulsion.

SCENE IN THE EIGHTEENTH CENTURY.

Circa A.D. 1785.

The last Scene gives a glimpse of Saint Giles' Fair in the Eighteenth Century. In the midst of a joyous scene of revelry the Royal Barge of George III. comes up the river; the King himself is on board, paying a brief visit to the city, and the strains of Handel's Water Music are heard as the barge advances. The King's arrival is greeted with great popular enthusiasm. The coaches of the country gentry and the sedan chairs of the townsfolk make a brave show among the crowd, and those gallants and belles who come out afoot to see the entry are conspicuous in the quaint dress of the period—the men bewigged and buckled, the ladies in towering head-dresses, and both in powder and in patches.

No one to whom was granted the privilege of seeing these great pictures can ever forget them; it was the Arabian Nights come again. The interest was so deep and intense and moving that the flight of time was not noticeable. There was seldom a time, during the four hours, when I had the feeling—a feeling seldom absent at the opera—that this was only a show, not reality; we seemed to be seeing the facts of history, not a mimicry of them. There was one little incident which proved to me that my sense of the reality, the flesh and blood concreteness of these passing shows, was shared by the whole multitude in the grand stand: when Royalty surrendered and the victorious Puritan troops came marching solemnly by, this multitude hissed them!

In a curving sweep of distant meadows beyond the curtaining trees that bordered the river, there were always glimpses of life and movement and color: there were knights in armor prancing along; there were bodies of brown-clad monks and white-clad nuns following on foot; there were crowds of peasants out of all the centuries drifting hither and thither; there were squadrons of infantry plodding along; there were regiments of cavalry flitting past them on the gallop. Always we were having these tinted and sparkling glimpses through the crevices and windows in the foliage, and always the movement was toward the left; always it was the marshaling of the clans to a point in the grove far up on our left, whence they would come streaming, at exactly the appointed moment, down upon our plain. One might well inquire how these movements could be so exactly timed, and kept in such perfect order, over distances so great. Kipling was moved to go out and inquire into this. When he came back he brought the solution of the mystery; he had been on the roof of the grand stand; from there the master of the show was dictating, by telephone, every slightest movement of his thousands, over a stretch of two miles. From his place up there he was conducting every motion, every movement of his host, with the order and system and precision of a general superintending and conducting a battle from a commanding point on the verge of the field. There was also a prompter up there. In front of us the crowds of actors were always uttering cries and delivering speeches appertaining to their parts, and it was matter of surprise that they never hesitated for a word, although there was no prompter out there to help them. It was a happy idea to put him on the roof. He used a megaphone there and easily made himself heard all about the field in front of us, yet no one in the grand stand could hear him.

I shall not try to describe the wonderful picture at the close, when the whole strength of the histrionic troop came streaming, with banners and music, from three different points of the compass, and fused themselves together, three thousand five hundred strong, in one splendid mass of motion and color. All that saw it can remember it, and vividly, but none that saw it can put that fine picture on paper.

Two incidents of the 28th of June: the visit to the University Press and the luncheon with Robert Porter and family, and interview with the butler who offered his services in order to have speech with Mr. Clemens.

The next day, (28th June) was a busy one. However that is a term which softly and moderately describes every one of the twenty-seven days which I spent in England. I was most pleasantly and satisfactorily and violently busy straight through each day, from breakfast until whisky punch; whisky punch occurs at 11 p.m., after I have been reading and smoking an hour in bed and am ready for sleep. One of the incidents of the 28th was a visit to the ancient, the vast, the illustrious University Press. Under the guidance of its superintendent, Dr. Hart, I went all over it. For seven years I had been feeling unkindly toward it, but when I found that it was flying the American flag from its staff, in compliment to me, my vanity was touched, and the same result followed that had followed my meeting with Henry VIII—a good deal of my prejudice was sponged out.

The buildings are very old, and they enclose a feature which is not possessed by any other printing-office on the planet, I suppose; and a darling feature it is—a roomy great court carpeted with the greenest grass, upon which falls the flooding sunshine, broken by the black shadows of venerable trees. From all the four sides, scores of windows look out upon this beautiful imprisoned patch of sylvan England, and through them pour the whir and clash of up-to-date steam presses. It was a curious conjunction, but it had its charm.

The University Press is not a thing of yesterday, it is an antiquity; it dates back to a time when there wasn't any such thing as a printing-press as yet. In the long ago, learned monks made books there—made them on vellum with the pen and illuminated them with the brush. At every case in the long composing-rooms stood a young compositor who was an erudite scholar; these young men were setting type in all the impossible languages known to erudition; they were setting up Egyptian hieroglyphics, (known by sight to you and me,) and other hieroglyphics which I had not seen before. With the deepest interest I examined many galleys of matter, but found none that I could read. There is an abundance of presses, and they are turning out hundreds of books, but they were all in tongues unintelligible to me. Apparently the bulk of these books were Bibles—Bibles in all sorts of languages, including the modern ones. Necessarily the expenses of such an establishment are prodigious, but when Dr. Hart casually observed that all these expenses were paid out of the profits on the Bibles, my prejudice experienced a sudden and acrid resurrection for a moment, for I knew, through Mr. John Murray, what not many people are aware of—to wit: that whereas the stingy and dishonest copyright laws of America and England steal the native author's book in its forty-second year, and make the publisher a present of it, a pious English Parliament has granted *perpetual* copyright to the Bible. Certainly this is one of the meanest discriminations that can be found in the statutes of any country, prodigally defiled as all statute books are with legalized crimes against the human race.

One of the other incidents of the 28th gave me peculiar pleasure, and reminded me of the prized welcome extended to me by the stevedores at Tilbury. In Oxford I was the guest of Robert Porter and his family; he had a luncheon party that day, and the butler of an Oxford don volunteered his services and superintended the function in order that he might have speech of me. After the guests had retired to the drawing-room I returned and talked with him and found, to my large contentment, that he knew ten or fifteen times as much about my books as I knew about them myself. He was an evidence that to me has been granted that rare and precious prize which Louis Stevenson and I dubbed the Suppressed Fame; and so I highly valued his frank and earnest homage. He did not spoil his compliments by adding what other and less gracious people are always adding—"But you are always hearing these things and are tired of them." It may be that there are persons in the world who get tired of compliments—a thing which I doubt—but I am not one of them; if I should run out of all other nourishment I believe I could live on compliments.

The Rhodes Scholars' Club, and similar benefactions.

There was still another incident of the 28th of which I wish to make a note: in the evening, after dinner, I went down by invitation to talk to the Rhodes scholars at their club—the American Rhodes scholars, I mean. As I understand it, the American Club is made up of American students, and not exclusively of Rhodes American students. There are about ninety American Rhodes scholars on the foundation all the time, for each of our States is privileged to send two.

Rhodes students come from many countries to enrich their minds and broaden and elevate and compact their characters by help of the mighty hand of that dead man, and this will go on, and on, and on, century after century, until this brisk and alert day of ours shall have drifted back, and back, and back, and melted into the times called ancient; and through all that stretch of time that dead hand will never have been idle, and never other than most nobly and beneficently active; it will have scattered, every year, those precious seeds out of which grow moral and intellectual depth and breadth of character; and year after year and century after century the world will have gathered and wholesomely nourished itself with the resulting harvests. It is a vast work, and a sublime work, that that dead hand is directing from the grave.

From the earliest days—from away back to the Crusades, with their generous hospitals for the diseased and helpless poor—the purse of the rich private citizen has wrought deeds of high and lasting benevolence for mankind—benevolences which have earned the title "great," and have deserved it—but perhaps it is only in our day, and within the past twenty-five years, that the benefactions of the private purse have been of a character to make the word "great" insufficient and supplant it with the more majestic and yet accurately descriptive word, "colossal." Our generation is indeed the generation of colossal private benefactions, and I am persuaded to believe it is the only one in history that is entitled to label itself with that great name. In our time Mr. Carnegie, Mr. Rockefeller, and a dozen other Americans, have given away millions upon millions of dollars for the uplifting of the less fortunate among the people; Mr. Carnegie's contributions in this interest have exceeded a hundred millions; Mr. Rockefeller's sixty millions; Mr. Stanford's twenty or thirty millions; Mr. Pierpont Morgan's many and many millions—how many I do not know; and the contributions of others, toward colleges and hospitals, have amounted to piles and pyramids of millions; but I believe that none of this money has been more wisely spent than the money which is being devoted to the Rhodes Scholarships. The Rhodes money promises to gather from the ends of the earth the brightest and best of the young intellect and character of every nation, and train it, educate it, elevate it, and send it back to diffuse itself like a stimulating and health-giving atmosphere all over the globe. There is indeed something sublime about it. Perhaps of all the millions contributed by Mr. Rockefeller and Mr. Carnegie, the ten millions with which Mr. Rockefeller has endowed that Institution in New York, and the one endowed with ten millions by Mr. Carnegie in Washington—both of these being devoted to medical research— promise the best and most beneficent results, on our side of the water, for the world. Within the past two or three months Mr. Rockefeller's Institution has removed one incurable malady from the list of the world's incurable diseases—cerebro-spinal meningitis—and thus at a single stroke has earned its costly endowment ten times over; for centuries to come it will go on in its gracious work of ameliorating the bitter conditions of the human race. Mr. Carnegie has contributed free public libraries, all over the globe, at cost of a hundred millions of dollars, and——but I will not go into that at present; I am getting too far away from the American Club of Oxford and the American Rhodes scholars.

I have uttered nothing but praises in speaking of the Rhodes benefaction, but they have been wrung from me; they have not come easily and fluently, for I always detested Mr. Rhodes; I never saw him, either in South Africa or in London; I avoided his vicinity; I never met him, and never wanted to meet him; my praises of what he has done must at least be granted the merit of sincerity. In several ways he was a very great sinner, but I think there is not a saint in the endless Roman calendar whom he could afford to trade halos with.

The conditions under which the benefits of the Rhodes endowment were to be extended to the Rhodes scholars were drafted by Mr. Rhodes himself; and while I was in Oxford a thing happened which showed what a wise and far-seeing document it was.

[*five pages (about 1100 words) missing*]

Dictated August 10, 1907

I take this paragraph from an editorial in this morning's *World:*

THE MORALS OF BOY READERS.

"Being a Boy" has its disadvantages in Worcester, Mass., where the directors of the Public Library have barred the books of Horatio Alger, jr., from their shelves as "untruthful" and "too sensational" for young readers. No more shall the Ragged Dicks and Tattered Toms be permitted to contaminate the innocence of budding minds. Why indeed should boys seek the companionship of those "undesirables," along with that of the Tom Sawyers and Huck Finns, the Gavroches and other gamins of juvenile fiction, when they may associate with Little Lord Fauntleroy and Rollo?

About once every year some pious public library banishes Huck Finn from its children's department, and on the same plea always—that Huck, the neglected and untaught son of a town drunkard, is given to lying, when in difficulty and hard pressed, and is therefore a bad example for young people, and a damager of their morals.

Two or three years ago I was near-by when one of these banishments was decreed and advertised, and I went over and asked the librarian about it, and he said yes, Huck was banished for lying. I asked,

"Is there nothing else against him?"

"No, I think not."

"Do you banish all books that are likely to defile young morals, or do you stop with Huck?"

"We do not discriminate; we banish all that are hurtful to young morals."

I picked up a book, and said—

"I see several copies of this book lying around. Are the young forbidden to read it?"

"The Bible? Of course not."

"Why not?"

"That is a strange question to ask."

"Very well, then I withdraw it. Are you acquainted with the passages in Huck which are held to be objectionable?"

He said he was; and at my request he took pen and paper and proceeded to write them down for me. Meantime I stepped to a desk and wrote down some extracts from the Bible. I showed them to him and said I would take it as a favor if he would attach his extracts to mine and post them on the wall, so that the people could examine them and see which of the two sets they would prefer to have their young boys and girls read.

He replied coldly that he was willing to post the extracts which he had made, but not those which I had made.

"Why?"

He replied—still coldly—that he did not wish to discuss the matter. I asked if he had some boys and girls in his family, and he said he had. I asked—

"Do you ever read to them these extracts which I have made?"

"Of course not!"

"You don't need to. They read them to themselves, clandestinely. All Protestant children of both sexes do it, and have been doing it for several centuries. You did it yourself when you were a boy. Isn't it so?"

He hesitated, then said no. I said—

"You have lied, and you know it. I think you have been reading Huck Finn yourself, and damaging your morals."

Once I was a hero. I can never forget it. It was forty years ago, when I was a bashful young bachelor of thirty-two. I lectured in the village of Hudson, New York, and was the guest of the village parson, there being no hotel in the place. In the morning I was summoned to the parlor for family worship. It began with a chapter from the Old Testament. Seated elbow to elbow around the walls were the aged clergyman's family of young folks, along with twenty-one maidens and youths from neighboring homes. I was pleasantly wedged between two young girls—sweet and modest and diffident lassies. The preacher read the first verse; a youth at his left read the second; a girl at the youth's left read the third—and so on down, toward me. I ran my finger down to my verse, purposing to familiarize myself with it, so that I could read it acceptably when my turn should come. I got a shock! It was one of those verses which would make a graven image blush. I did not believe I could read it aloud in such a company, and I resolved that I would not try. Then I noticed that the poor girl at my left had put her finger on that same verse and was showing signs of distress. Was it her verse? Had I miscounted? I counted again, and found it really was her verse, and not mine. By this time my turn was come. I saw my chance to be a hero, and I rose to the occasion: I braced up and read my verse and hers too! I was proud of myself, for it was as fine and grand as saving her from drowning.

Dictated August 16, 1907

The luncheon with Marie Corelli.

I met Marie Corelli at a small dinner party in Germany fifteen years ago, and took a dislike to her at once—a dislike which expanded and hardened with each successive dinner-course until, when we parted at last, the original mere dislike had grown into a very strong aversion. When I arrived in England, two months ago, I found a letter from her awaiting me at Brown's Hotel. It was warm, affectionate, eloquent, persuasive; under its charm the aversion of fifteen years melted away and disappeared. It seemed to me that that aversion must have been falsely based; I thought I must certainly have been mistaken in the woman, and I felt a pang or two of remorse. I answered her letter at once—her love-letter I may say; answered it with a love-letter. Her home is in Shakspeare's Stratford. She at once wrote again, urging me in the most beguiling language to stop there and lunch with her when I should be on my way to London, on the 29th. It looked like an easy matter; the travel connected with it could not amount to much, I supposed, therefore I accepted by return mail. I had now—not for the first time, nor the thousandth—trampled upon an old and wise and stern maxim of mine, to wit: "Supposing is good, but finding out is better." The supposing was finished, the letter was gone; it was now time to find out. Ashcroft examined the timetables and found that I would leave Oxford at eleven o'clock the 29th, leave Stratford at mid-afternoon, and not reach London until about half past six. That is to say, I would be seven hours and a half in the air, so to speak, with no rest for the sole of my foot, and a speech at the Lord Mayor's to follow! Necessarily I was aghast; I should probably arrive at the Lord Mayor's banquet in a hearse. Ashcroft and I then began upon a hopeless task—to persuade a conscienceless fool to mercifully retire from a self-advertising scheme which was dear to her heart. She held her grip; any one who knew her could have told us she would. She came to Oxford on the 28th to make sure of her prey. I begged her to let me off, I implored, I supplicated; I pleaded my white head and my seventy-two years, and the likelihood that the long day in trains that would stop every three hundred yards and rest ten minutes would break me down and send me to the hospital. It had no effect. By God I might as well have pleaded with Shylock himself! She said she could not release me from my engagement; it would be quite impossible; and added—

"Consider my side of the matter a little. I have invited Lady Lucy and two other ladies, and three gentlemen; to cancel the luncheon now would inflict upon them the greatest inconvenience; without doubt they have declined other invitations to accept this one; in my own case I have canceled three social engagements on account of this matter."

I said—

"Which is the superior disaster: that your half-dozen guests be inconvenienced, or the Lord Mayor's three hundred? And if you have already canceled three engagements, and thereby inconvenienced three sets of guests, canceling seems to come easy to you, and it looks as if you might add just one more to the list, in mercy to a suffering friend."

It hadn't the slightest effect; she was as hard as nails. I think there is no criminal in any jail with a heart so unmalleable, so unmeltable, so unphazeable, so flinty, so uncompromisingly hard as Marie Corelli's. I think one could hit it with a steel and draw a spark from it.

She is about fifty years old, but has no gray hairs; she is fat and shapeless; she has a gross animal face; she dresses for sixteen, and awkwardly and unsuccessfully and pathetically imitates the innocent graces and witcheries of that dearest and sweetest of all ages; and so her exterior matches her interior and harmonizes with it, with the result—as I think—that she is the most offensive sham, inside and out, that misrepresents and satirizes the human race to-day. I would willingly say more about her, but it would be futile to try; all the adjectives seem so poor, and feeble, and flabby, this morning.

So we went to Stratford by rail, with a car-change or two, we not knowing that one could save time and fatigue by walking. She received us at Stratford station with her carriage, and was going to drive us to Shakspeare's church, but I canceled that; she insisted, but I said that the day's program was already generous enough in fatigues without adding another. She said there would be a crowd at the church to welcome me, and they would be greatly disappointed, but I was loaded to the chin with animosity, and childishly eager to be as unpleasant as possible, so I held my ground, particularly as I was well acquainted with Marie by this time and foresaw that if I went to the church I should find a trap arranged for a speech; my teeth were already loose from incessant speaking, and the very thought of adding a jabber at this time was a pain to me; besides, Marie, who never wastes an opportunity to advertise herself, would work the incident into the newspapers, and I who could not waste any possible opportunity of disobliging her, naturally made the best of this one.

She said she had been purchasing the house which the founder of Harvard College had once lived in, and was going to present it to America—another advertisement. She wanted to stop at that dwelling and show me over it, and she said there would be a crowd there. I said I didn't want to see the damned house. I didn't say it in those words, but in that vicious spirit, and she understood; even her horses understood, and were shocked, for I saw them shudder. She pleaded, and said we need not stop for more than a moment, but I knew the size of Marie's moments, by now, when there was an advertisement to be had, and I declined. As we drove by I saw that the house and the sidewalk were full of people—which meant that Marie had arranged for another speech. However, we went by, bowing in response to the cheers, and presently reached Marie's house, a very attractive and commodious English home. I said I was exceedingly tired, and would like to go immediately to a bed-chamber and stretch out and get some rest, if only for fifteen minutes. She was voluble with tender sympathy, and said I should have my desire at once; but deftly steered me into the drawing-room and introduced me to her company. That being over, I begged leave to retire, but she wanted me to see her garden, and said it would take only a moment. We examined her garden, I praising it and damning it in the one breath—praising with the mouth and damning with the heart. Then she said there was another garden, and dragged me along to look at it. I was ready to drop with fatigue, but I praised and damned as before, and hoped I was through now and might be suffered to die in peace; but she beguiled me to a grilled iron gate and pulled me through it into a stretch of waste ground where stood fifty pupils of a military school, with their master at their head—arrangement for another advertisement. She asked me to make a little speech, and said the boys were expecting it. I complied briefly, shook hands with the master and talked with him a moment, then—well then we got back to the house. I got a quarter of an hour's rest, then came down to the luncheon. Toward the end of it that implacable woman rose in her place, with a glass of champagne in her hand, and made a speech! With me for a text, of course. Another advertisement, you see—to be worked into the newspapers. When she had finished I said—

"I thank you very much"—

and sat still. This conduct of mine was compulsory, therefore not avoidable; if I had made a speech, courtesy and custom would have required me to construct it out of thanks and compliments, and there was not a rag of that kind of material lurking anywhere in my system.

We reached London at half past six in the evening in a pouring rain, and half an hour later I was in bed—in bed and tired to the very marrow; but the day was at an end, at any rate, and that was a comfort. This was the most hateful day my seventy-two years have ever known.

I have now exposed myself as being a person capable of entertaining and exhibiting a degraded and brutally ugly spirit, upon occasion, and in making this exposure I have done my duty by myself and by my reader—notwithstanding which I claim and maintain that in any other society than Marie Corelli's my spirit is the sweetest that has ever yet descended upon this planet from my ancestors, the angels.

I spoke at the Lord Mayor's banquet that night, and it was a botch.

Dictated August 17, 1907

Mr. Clemens dines with Sir Gilbert and Lady Parker.

Ashcroft's next note says: "*Sunday, June 30th.* Dined with Sir Gilbert and Lady Parker."

It was a large company, with a sprinkling of titles, and also with a sprinkling of men and women distinguished for achievement; but the whole scene is abolished from my memory by one wonderful face, just as the stars sparkling upon the horizon are swallowed up in the glory of the rising sun and extinguished. I am referring in this prodigious way to the face of a young woman. By the figure which I have used I have intended to indicate that this young creature's beauty was of the sort which is called dazzling; it is the right word; that face dazzled all the other faces to extinction, and just blazed and blazed in a splendid solitude; and in that solitude it still goes on blazing in my memory to this day. Lady—Lady something—but the name has gone from me; names and faces will not stay with me; that name has departed, but I should know the face again anywhere. The style was English, the features were English, the complexion was English, the set of the head was English, the poise was English, the character was English, the dignity was English—all high-born English; but over it all, and pervading it and suffusing it with that subtle something which we call charm, was a friendly and outreaching good-fellowship and an easy and natural and unstudied grace of manner and carriage which was American—rare everywhere, and infrequent, but most frequent among our people, I think. I explained to her what I thought of her, and said England ought to be proud of such a product; but she smiled like a complimented angel, and rippled out a musical little laugh, and said she was an American product and destitute of English blood.

It was a very pleasant surprise. Later, at another dinner party, this pleasant surprise was repeated, where I mistook a couple of titled American ladies for English women; they were women whose looks, whose ways, and the set and style of whose upholstery was distinctly English. Those two ladies were grieved and disappointed; for they had hoped and believed that they had kept their beloved nationality unmodified and unalloyed by time and changed relations, and that it was visible on their outsides. These ladies had been living in England five years, and one cannot remain so long in an unaccustomed atmosphere without taking color from it.

There was talk of that soaring and brilliant young statesman, Winston Churchill, son of Lord Randolph Churchill and nephew of a duke. I had met him at Sir Gilbert Parker's seven years before, when he was twenty-three years old, and had met him and introduced him to his lecture audience, a year later, in New York, when he had come over to tell of the lively experiences he had had as a war correspondent in the South African war, and in one or two wars on the Himalayan frontier of India. Sir Gilbert Parker said—

"Do you remember the dinner here seven years ago?"

"Yes," I said, "I remember it."

"Do you remember what Sir William Vernon Harcourt said about you?"

"No."

"Well, you didn't hear it. You and Churchill went up to the top floor to have a smoke and a talk, and Harcourt wondered what the result would be. He said that whichever of you got the floor first would keep it to the end, without a break; he believed that you, being old and experienced, would get it, and that Churchill's lungs would have a half hour's rest for the first time in five years. When you two came down, by and by, Sir William asked Churchill if he had had a good time, and he answered eagerly, 'Yes.' Then he asked you if you had had a good time. You hesitated, then said without eagerness, 'I have had a smoke.'"

Dictated August 19, 1907

Dinner with Sidney Lee, and call afterwards at Mrs. Macmillan's to see Lord and Lady Jersey.

Well, to resume from Ashcroft's notes:

"*Monday, July 1.* Dined with Sidney Lee at the Garrick Club, and called at Mrs. Macmillan's, to see Lady Jersey, on the way home."

It was a distinguished company at the dinner, and once more I encountered J. M. Barrie; also once more he sat on the other side of the table and out of conversing distance. The same thing happened in London twice, seven years ago, and once in New York since then. I have never had five minutes' talk with him that wasn't broken off by an interruption; after the interruption he always dissolves mysteriously and disappears. I should like to have one good unbroken talk with that gifted Scot some day before I die.

The Garrick was familiar to me; I had often fed there in bygone years as guest of Henry Irving, Toole, and other actors—all dead now. It could have been there, but I think it was at Bateman's, thirty-five years ago, that I told Irving and Wills, the playwright, about the whitewashing of the fence by Tom Sawyer, and thereby captured a chapter on cheap terms; for I wrote it out when I got back to the hotel while it was fresh in my mind.

Sidney Lee's dinner was in a room which I was sure I had not seen for thirty-five years, yet I recognized it, and could dreamily see about me the forms and faces of the small company of that long-forgotten occasion. Anthony Trollope was the host, and the dinner was in honor of Joaquin Miller, who was on the top wave of his English notoriety at that time. There were three other guests; one is obliterated, but I remember two of them—Tom Hughes and Leveson-Gower. No trace of that obliterated guest remains with me—I mean the *other* obliterated guest, for I was an obliterated guest also. I don't remember that anybody ever addressed a remark to either of us; no, that is a mistake—Tom Hughes addressed remarks to us occasionally; it was not in his nature to forget or neglect any stranger. Trollope was voluble and animated, and was but vaguely aware that any other person was present excepting him of the noble blood, Leveson-Gower. Trollope and Hughes addressed their talk almost altogether to Leveson-Gower, and there was a deferential something about it that almost made me feel that I was at a religious service; that Leveson-Gower was the acting deity, and that the illusion would be perfect if somebody would do a hymn or pass the contribution-box. All this was most curious and unfamiliar and interesting. Joaquin Miller did his full share of the talking, but he was a discordant note, a disturber and degrader of the solemnities. He was affecting the picturesque and untamed costume of the wild Sierras at the time, to the charmed astonishment of conventional London, and was helping out the effects with the breezy and independent and aggressive manners of that far away and romantic region. He and Trollope talked all the time, and both at the same time, Trollope pouring forth a smooth and limpid and sparkling stream of faultless English, and Joaquin discharging into it his muddy and tumultuous mountain torrent, and— Well, there was never anything just like it except the Whirlpool Rapids under Niagara Falls.

It was long ago, long ago! and not even an echo of that turbulence was left in this room where it had once made so much noise and display. Trollope is dead; Hughes is dead; Leveson-Gower is dead; doubtless the obliterated guest is dead; Joaquin Miller is white-headed, and mute and quiet in his dear mountains.

I arrived at Mr. Macmillan's a little after ten o'clock, and found there a number of old friends besides Lord and Lady Jersey, and several strangers; one of whom had a special interest for me because he was of the blood of that fine creature and prized friend of forty years ago, "Charley," tenth Lord Fairfax, citizen of Maryland by birth and rearing, citizen of Nevada and San Francisco by adoption, a man whom I have said many praiseful and admiring things about in an earlier chapter of this Biography. This handsome young gentleman at the Macmillans' was either English or had been away from America long enough to acquire the English stamp.

I think that the successor of "Charley" of San Francisco was the last American lord, and was followed by a successor who moved to England and remained, thus leaving the great republic without a single hereditary lord, and extinguishing a distinction which the country had enjoyed for several generations. This present young bearer of the title was the successor of "Charley's" successor.

The dinner to Sidney Lee given by Andrew Carnegie
in New York, in 1902.

I had not seen Sidney Lee since 1902, when he made a flying visit to our side of the ocean and was banqueted by Andrew Carnegie, one night, in his new palace at 92d street and Fifth Avenue. He is not now a bashful man, but is as much at his ease in company as is anybody, whereas when he came to America that time there was only one other man on our soil who could successfully compete with him in bashfulness, and that was Joel Uncle Remus Harris. Sidney Lee's bashfulness spread out and covered the whole Northern half of the United States, and Harris's crowded the Southern half; there was no room in the republic for another man of this pattern. There were twenty men at Carnegie's; in the drawing-room, before dinner, they were introduced to Mr. Lee, one by one, and they were all struck by his extreme bashfulness. They were strangely bashful themselves at the dinner, yet there was no man present who had not been a long time before the public and accustomed to foregathering with all sorts of people under all sorts of conditions. That dinner afforded the strangest and most unaccountable exhibitions of timidity I have ever witnessed; I have never seen anything like it among grown-up men, either before or since then, in my long pilgrimage. Was Mr. Lee the cause of it? Or was it Mrs. Carnegie? I have asked myself that conundrum many a time, but have never yet been able to answer it to my satisfaction. Mrs. Carnegie was the only lady present. I took her out, and sat at her right, at the centre of the table; opposite me, across the table, sat Mr. Carnegie with Mr. Lee at his right; next to Lee sat John Burroughs, the naturalist; next to Burroughs sat Carl Schurz, great soldier and statesman; next to Schurz sat Melville Stone, head of the Associated Press of the planet; next to Stone sat Horace White, old and famous and able journalist. At Carnegie's left sat Mr. Howells; at Mr. Howells's left sat Gilder, of the *Century;* and so on—I will not try to name the rest of the assemblage. When the feast was finished and the black coffee and cigars installed, Mr. Carnegie—smiley and complacent little man!—rose in his place to speak. His smiliness, his complacency, his ease, his confidence—supports which had never failed him in his life, before, upon such an occasion—withered quickly away and vanished before he had uttered a word; it was a new and surprising and most interesting thing to see. Carnegie was in a bad stage-fright; everybody saw it, yet nobody was entirely able to believe it, I suppose. When he began to speak, the words came hesitatingly—gaspingly, one may fairly say—and with disastrous spaces between; he at once began to advertise his fright and his nervousness by that couple of age-worn indications which the distressed novice has unconsciously resorted to at banquets since the beginning of time: first he took up his wine-glasses one at a time, as a player takes up chessmen, and made a new arrange-ment of them on the cloth; then he took them up again, one at a time, and grouped them in a new way; again he took them up, and again changed the grouping—all this with a painful attention to detail that was most uncomfortable to witness, so charged was it with doubt and miserable anxiety; next he resorted to that other ancient sign, the fussing with his napkin. He folded it, kneaded it with his knuckles; he turned it around this way, then that way, then the other way, always kneading it and always stammering incoherently along. There was but four feet of table-cloth between him and me, yet his voice was so weak and his syllables so mumbled, so slurred, and so vacantly delivered, that I did not catch any more than half the words of any sentence; and when he sat down I was wholly ignorant of the matter of his speech, and even of the purpose of it. I knew he was introducing Mr. Lee, because I knew his speech could have no object other than that, but I got not a thing out of his remarks that I could not have gotten out of them if he had delivered them with the sign language of the deaf and dumb—a language with which I have no acquaintance. I noticed another thing: his hand quaked and quivered all the time that he was fumbling with his glasses and his napkin.

Sidney Lee got up and shivered—stood shivering the most of a minute, but not all of it—uttered three or four quite inaudible sentences, and sat down still alive but not noticeably so.

Mr. Carnegie got up and performed again with napkin and glasses, and with palsied lips and extinguished voice, and resumed his seat. I had not caught a word that I could understand. Apparently he had been introducing John Burroughs, for Burroughs got up and began to rock on his base, and quiver, and swallow the dry swallow which indicates distress and which compels the compassion of all witnesses. What he said was confused and disjointed, and marred with hesitations and repetitions, but one could at least hear it. He wandered hopelessly and helplessly for a minute or two, hunting for a text, skirmishing for an idea; then I spoke across and came to his rescue with the suggestion that he discard the conventions and step boldly out upon familiar ground and talk shop. I said that in a time gone by he had published an article in which he had offered the theory, with reservations, that the reason an oak forest always grew up in the place previously occupied by a pine forest when the pine forest had been removed, was because the squirrels had used the carpet of pine-needles as a hiding-place for acorns, and had forgotten them and left them there, with the result that when the pines were removed the sun had a chance to warm the acorns and make them sprout—and asked him to say whether he had since established the correctness of his theory. This text turned his language loose and he had no further trouble with his speech.

Carl Schurz, that marvelously ready and fluent and felicitous handler of our great English tongue on its highest planes, followed Burroughs and furnished us another surprise. He had never been frightened before, in all the history of his long and illustrious public career, but he was frightened now; all his noble and charming and exquisite phrasing was gone, and he stumbled pathetically along over a bumping corduroy road of disjointed commonplaces and poverties of expression, and soon reached the edge of his difficult world and fell over it and subsided, a defeated man.

Melville Stone rose, stammered, wandered, straggled, got lost, and was quickly vanquished and added to the muster-roll of the failures.

The very same fate befell Horace White.

Then Howells got up and bent over the table with his left hand supporting his curve, while he arranged and re-arranged his wine-glasses with his right, and gasped and stuttered and dripped disconnected and puerile words all around; next he turned to his napkin for help and heavily bore down upon it and pitilessly rolled it, unrolled it, and rolled it again, and presently cut an uncompleted sentence in two with something like a despairing gasp, and wilted into his seat, a target for everybody's heartfelt compassion.

Gilder followed, and failed; when he got through, any stranger could have told by the look of his napkin that it had been helping a scared man make a speech.

Mr. Hornblower, a celebrated advocate, followed Gilder. He tried to talk—indeed he made what could be justly called a heroic effort to do it—but he soon gave it up. He said he would frankly confess that his trouble was that he was frightened; that he was frightened to speechlessness; that he could not divine why, and was wholly unable to account for his curious and novel condition, but that the fact remained as stated: he was frightened, and couldn't go on. He said he could not remember ever having had a like experience since he had made his success at the bar. Then he sat down looking thankful that his ordeal was over.

I forgot to say that I followed Sidney Lee—but the omission is of no consequence; I was in the conflict before that deadly and mysterious contagion of fright had got well started, and so I escaped infection.

Dictated August 22, 1907

Luncheon with Henniker Heaton and discussion of cheap ocean postage—Mr. Clemens's postal check scheme.

Ashcroft's note:

"Lunched with Henniker Heaton, M.P., at the House of Commons; dined with Mr. and Mrs. Harry Brittain at the Savoy."

The luncheon had a purpose, and lasted two hours, but it didn't last long enough to get down to the purpose. The twelve or fifteen men present had been chosen with an eye to that purpose, which was political and commercial, and of international importance. Mr. Sydney Buxton, the Postmaster General, was present, also T. P. O'Connor, M.P., also the Earl of Crawford and Balcarres. I think all the rest were M.P.'s. I understood that all present favored the scheme—or rather the two schemes, for there were two; I had a scheme and Henniker Heaton had a scheme, and our idea was to join our strength and work for both schemes; both were to be freely discussed at the luncheon, and I was to have a private heart to heart talk with the Postmaster General afterwards. Henniker Heaton has for years been the diligent, acute, and tireless apostle of cheap ocean postage, and in spite of all kinds of official and parliamentary opposition—except the intelligent kind—he has carried the bulk of his dream to a successful conclusion. He had a hard time proving to doubting Parliaments and postmasters general that if postage to the British colonies and to far-off India should be reduced from five cents to two, the resulting tremendous addition to business and social correspondence would keep the revenue up to the high-water mark and secure the Government from loss, but by pluck and perseverance he succeeded. To-day you can send a letter to any British postoffice anywhere on the surface of the globe for two cents; no harm has happened to the revenue, the cheapened postage has formidably augmented export business, and the whole nation has profited thereby. Henniker Heaton is now laboring to establish a two-cent rate with all foreign countries, including the United States. Present conditions exhibit curious anomalies. For instance: the postage on a letter mailed direct from England to New York City is five cents; but if you send it to New York *by way of Canada,* the expense is only two cents, although the distance is greater. You can send merchandise in a liner from London to New York at ten dollars per ton, but the same ship charges ten times as much per ton for mail matter, while the expense involved in caretaking and transportation is no greater in the one case than in the other. Henniker Heaton is finding it as difficult to enlighten and convert our Congresses as if they were just British Parliaments, and no whit saner.

My project was a postal check—a notion which I conceived and elaborated in Vienna about the end of 1897, and further elaborated and ultimately completed in the summer and fall of 1898. Our minister at the Court of Vienna at the time was Charlemagne Tower, our present Ambassador to the Court of Berlin. He examined it carefully, in detail, and decided that it was good and workable, and that it would abolish our clumsy and stupid postal order system, and would also put a stop to the vast and growing and risky business of sending postage-stamps through the mail in payment for small purchases. A few days afterward I read my elaborated scheme to two other men—one of them an old friend in the insurance business, the other a new acquaintance. This document was intended for publication as a magazine article, and I have it yet, much scored by emendations, much damaged by handling, but still intact and legible. In London a year later, ('99, if my memory is sound), I came across a *Harper's Weekly* with a paragraph in it which interested me. It named a member of Congress, and said he was about to bring forward a bill for a postal check, and then went on and described my check with nice exactness. I judged that that young acquaintance of mine in Vienna had admired my scheme enough to talk about it, and that its details had finally wandered to America and fallen under the attention of that Congressman. My name was not mentioned, but the omission was of no consequence to me; I hoped the man would push the project in Congress and make a success of it. I thought I might be able to help him, so I sent a copy of my article to McClure for publication in his magazine; I also pinned to it the clipping from *Harper's Weekly.* I thought it likely that he might question the value of the article now that the clipping revealed the fact that what I was saying was lacking in freshness, and my conjecture was right; McClure did not publish it.

I never heard of that Congressman or his postal check afterward. I think he was a Tennesseean, but am not sure. A year or a year and a half ago, I read in the *American Review of Reviews* a description of a project by a Northern Congressman whereby the transmission of money by mail was to be much simplified, and at the same time rendered convenient and safe. It did not seem to me that this invention, as described and explained, was much of an improvement upon existing conditions, still it was a step in the right direction, and I was gratified. At my request, Dr. Shaw, editor of the *Review of Reviews,* called at my house and I gave him my battered article, explained it to him, and suggested that he send it to his friend, that Congressman, to the end that he might make use of it in case he should see his way to it.

I heard no more of the matter until four or five days ago; then a parcel reached me from the *Review of Reviews* containing my ancient article and some other documents concerning the matter of postal checks. Also, a fresh copy of my article with "emendations;" also an invitation to aid the good cause.

I find the documents interesting. One of them is House Bill 7053, entitled "A Bill to Prevent Robbing the Mail, to Provide a Safer and Easier Method of Sending Money by Mail, and to Increase the Postal Revenue. Introduced December 13, 1905, by Mr. Gardner of Michigan; referred to the Committee on the Post-Office and Post-Roads, and ordered to be printed." I like the bill very much. In all its essentials it is my scheme as mapped out in my article written in Vienna in '98 and '99.

There are some printed slips in which the various merits of a postal check are ably and urgently argued; they are the same ones used by me in my article; I do not perceive that one has been omitted. The earliest date mentioned is 1902—two or three years after my scheme leaked into print as per the paragraph published in *Harper's Weekly,* as heretofore mentioned.

In these documents the scheme is called the "invention" of a Mr. W. C. Post. It is stated, with a trace of conscious magnanimity, that he stands ready to confer it upon the Government as a free gift; he wants no money. Why, even that idea is not original. In '98 I wrote John Hay, from Vienna, and said I had invented a postal check scheme, and asked him to talk to the Postmaster General about it. I remarked that the Government would not be likely to be willing to buy it of me, because upon examination the War Department would perceive that you couldn't kill Christians with it, and therefore the Government would naturally take but a slight interest in it. Mr. Post heard about that, probably, from John Hay, or others in Washington, and it has admonished him to be magnanimous.

However, I am wandering far afield. I will inter that old postal-check article of mine in an Appendix, where the curious may find it if they want it—and now let us get back to London.

Dictated August 23, 1907

Henniker Heaton luncheon continued—Luncheon with George Bernard Shaw.

It was lively and interesting, was Mr. Henniker Heaton's luncheon—I mean the talk was—but we forgot all about the formidable world-questions which we were assembled there to settle, and when we broke up and scattered homeward they had not been mentioned.

Ashcroft's note:

"*Wednesday, July 3.* Luncheon with George Bernard Shaw; dined with Moberly Bell."

Bernard Shaw has not completed his fifty-second year yet, and therefore is merely a lad. The vague and far-off rumble which he began to make five or six years ago is near-by now, and is recognizable as thunder. The editorial world lightly laughed at him during four or five of those years, but it takes him seriously now; he has become a force, and it is conceded that he must be reckoned with. Shaw is a pleasant man; simple, direct, sincere, animated; but self-possessed, sane, and evenly poised, acute, engaging, companionable, and quite destitute of affectations. I liked him. He showed no disposition to talk about himself or his work, or his high and growing prosperities in reputation and the materialities; but mainly—and affectionately and admiringly—devoted his talk to William Morris, whose close friend he had been, and whose memory he deeply reveres. He again regretted that I had not known Morris, and again quoted Morris's colossal encomium upon "Huck Finn"—things which Mr. Shaw had already said to me in a letter. The luncheon was in his own apartment, overlooking the Thames, and there were only three guests. Some of the talking was done by the three, for form's sake, but we put the most of it upon Shaw, by preference, and to our own profit. One of the guests told me afterward that Shaw had had a troubled and discouraging and difficult time of it in acquiring a market for his literature in the beginning; that in the first nine years he earned only six pounds—five for an ingeniously worded patent medicine advertisement, fifteen shillings for an article in an obscure journal, and five for a verse which he contributed to a child's picture-book. He had been heard to say that he wrote the verse as a burlesque, and it was accepted seriously; adding "as many later writings of mine written seriously have been accepted as burlesques."

There was a choice company at Moberly Bell's, and by consequence it was a delightful evening. Mr. Bell is manager of the London *Times,* and therefore is in a sense deputy king of England. He has held this powerful office many years. Mrs. Clemens and I dined at his house many times when we were sojourning in London seven years ago. Those dinners were on a large scale; the guests numbered as many as forty; they were drawn from all ranks and were of all kinds and qualities, except the commonplace. At one of those gatherings there was a theatrical little episode: at Mr. Bell's right sat a handsome and stately and richly dressed lady, a Continental princess* of proud and ancient lineage—a person of special interest, at the time, for the reason that she had lately been making Cecil Rhodes's life uncomfortable for him in South Africa, she declaring with energy and passion that he had proposed to her and been accepted, and had then retired from the engagement without pretext or excuse. Rhodes called these statements nonsense, and denounced them, both publicly and privately, as fabrications. The noise that ensued was great, and it traveled far; because of this, the Princess was the centre of interest at Mr.

* Radziwill.

Bell's dinner that night. Among her ornaments was a long rope of very large and very fine pearls—the largest and finest and costliest to be found in England at the time, it was said. All the ladies present discussed them admiringly, and gazed upon them with fascinated eyes; by and by the string broke, and the great pearls gushed away in a brilliant freshet and went rolling and scattering everywhere. A dozen of the guests at that end of the table, together with the servants, hastened to seek and secure the gems and restore them to the Princess. She sat still and was not disturbed; as she received them she counted them, and finally pronounced the tale complete. Four hundred thousand dollars' worth, and none missing! I heard one lady speak across the table to another and say,

"How could she be so cool and so calm? She was perfectly indifferent."

The other answered, in a modified and confidential voice,

"She always breaks that string, and makes that display, when she has a good house—and besides, the real ones are in the bank; these are paste."

Dictated August 26, 1907

Luncheon at Sir James Knowles's.

Ashcroft's note:

"July 4. Lunched at Sir James Knowles's; attended the banquet in celebration of Independence Day, at the Hotel Cecil."

I perceived that at Sir James's I was upon familiar ground, for his house was situated just within the spacious court of the monster human hive called the Queen Anne Mansions, a caravansary which I and my family had helped to support and render prosperous during a fortnight or so, seven or eight years ago. Damn the place, I remember it well! In that court you stand as in a well whose dull-brown walls stretch away skyward, and so multitudinously perforated with windows is each wall that it looks like a colander. It was an easy mountain to get lost in, and I had that experience many times. There were guide-boards, but that was not sufficient; there ought to have been guides. It was said that in the course of time many persons had got lost in that place and were never found again, and this was true; for I often met their remains hunting around for their apartments and moaning. There were many dining rooms in that place and the food was good, and well served; one could not find fault with the service in bedrooms and private parlors, because there wasn't any; substantially speaking it did not exist. I acquired a prejudice against the place on the first day. Mrs. Clemens needed to go out and buy some necessary things, and she had not much time to spare. I sent down a circular check to the office to be cashed—a check good for its face in any part of the world, as any ordinary ass would know—but the ass who was assifying for the Queen Anne Mansions on salary didn't know it; indeed I think that his assitude transcended any assfulness I have ever met in this world or elsewhere. We waited, anxiously and impatiently, half an hour, then sent down to know what the trouble was. The answer returned was that the office had sent the check, by a boy, on foot, to a bank up town to find out whether it was good or not. I never said a word, but took other measures; I mean I never said a word that was proper—but just took other measures. I sent down a fresh, new, crisp fifty-pound Bank of England note and asked the office to retain it and send me some money on it—quick! There was also other security—twelve trunks and a sick child, which was Clara; at least I said she was sick, in order to inspire confidence in the office that we couldn't get away unobserved. They sent back the note and asked me to endorse it. Which I did, though it seemed to me that it was not any better or stronger then than it was before, when it had only the Bank of England back of it. I found afterward that it was a common thing, in Great Britain, to decline to take a Bank of England note from a stranger, unendorsed by him, but this was my first experience of the custom, and I thought it was meant as an affront. It was strange—it has always seemed strange, to me—that I did not burn the Queen Anne Mansions. As I stood now, at this distant day, gazing up the walls of that well, I found that the lapse of time had modified my bitterness, and that I was glad I had not burned it—not very glad, but glad, just glad.

As I stood there with my mind wandering back over the past I called to mind a very interesting conversation which I had had on the first night of our stay in that house—a conversation with an English gentleman who had sent in his card after dinner, then followed it in person by my request. It was the last day of September. Relations between England and the Transvaal were in a very strained condition, but that was all: that that little handful of Boers down there would actually stand out until war should become a necessity, was unthinkable; their high attitude must surely be only a "bluff." This gentleman surprised me by saying it was not a bluff, and that there would certainly be a war; I think he even said he knew it, but I am not quite sure as to that. He was a colonel in the British army and had seen long service in India, in the artillery. He uttered two predictions, and framed them in quite positive language: to wit, that the war would break out in eleven days, and that it would be an artillery war. It was uncommonly good prophesying, as the event showed: the war was proclaimed on the 11th of October, and it was an artillery war.

The luncheon at Sir James Knowles's was in honor of a Prussian princess of the blood. She was young and handsome and queenly, and was quite unroyally gifted intellectually; she seemed to know a good deal about everything, and to know it well; well enough to talk about it ably and entertainingly. She was an expert with the brush, and in music, and in designing and embroidery, and in several other fine arts; in fact in the matter of accomplishments she was a wonder, considering her place in the social world. London is certainly a wealthy place in distinguished human beings; no other city approaches it in this respect; she can furnish samples to several scores of dinners and luncheons at one time, and have more left.

Dictated August 27, 1907

Whitelaw Reid's reception, which Mr. Clemens was unable to attend—Remarks about Whitelaw Reid's career.

I was not able to go to Whitelaw Reid's afternoon reception of the American contingent, and so my ticket, (No. 2384), remained unused. The tickets suggest that the national function was conducted on a new plan. It was. It had not been the custom, before, to admit by ticket; any American could come that wanted to, and sometimes five hundred came, sometimes a thousand. In the present case, as usual, there was no restriction; any American could come who applied for a ticket; four thousand applied, and they were all there. It must have been that our Ambassador was proposing to provide refreshments, and needed to know what quantity would be required. Reid occupies the most palatial private residence in London, and a crush could be expected, for all the Americans would be eager to see it. It was indeed a crush, and half as many people were in it as were present at the King's great garden party at Windsor, which was attended by a multitude somewhat exceeding eight thousand; still the big house was equal to the emergency.

Reid's salary is $17,500, and it pays the hire of all his domestic servants except that of his cooks; I am speaking of the service in his town house—he has another great palace in the country. His town house rent is a hundred thousand dollars a year, and he has other expenses, but they are not a burden to him. He and his predecessor, John Hay, were salaried members of the New York *Tribune* staff when I first knew them; both married unnumbered millions of dollars. Hay was a man of great and varied talents and accomplishments, and was conspicuously well equipped for the several great national and international posts which he had filled in his brilliant career; and he climbed to several of them without the help of wealth, and would doubtless have climbed the rest of the way without that help, and all the public would have approved, and would also have affectionately applauded and rejoiced. But the like is not the case with Reid. He is educated but not accomplished; his talents are few and not distinguished; he is not actually and precisely commonplace, but comes dangerously near to being that; he can write out a good enough speech, and can deliver it well enough, and with dignity, but he cannot stir a house with it—it gives off no real fire, for there is no real fire in him, and his imitations of it are not effective; they are artificial, and they ring hollow. He is narrow, and hard, cold, calculating, unaffectionate, except toward his family and a very small circle of especial friends; his dislikes are strong and steady and lasting, and he is unforgiving. He was born with a good commercial head, and has improved it by experience, but he has no other talent that perceptibly rises toward distinction. It has served him well. By grace of it he moved up, step by step, from war correspondent to a staff position on the *Tribune* under Greeley; to managing editor; to part proprietor; to proprietor-in-chief; to political importance, by right of this powerful position; to minister to France and candidate for Vice President, partly by the same right but mainly by authority of the millions which he had meantime married; to special envoy to Queen Victoria's Jubilee, by right of these combined forces; and finally to his present post, the highest in the diplomatic service—again by authority of those forces. He was not shiningly equipped for any of the conspicuous positions which he has occupied; he has not made a shining record in any of them, but he has made a creditable record in all of them. He is disliked by many, liked by few, envied by a multitude, and admired by nobody. He is a typical American product—a product hardly producible elsewhere, but easily producible among us. He is a good sample of what money, push, steady-going energy, pertinacity, and a reasonably good business talent—unsubject to damaging excitements and gushing enthusiasms—can do for a man in our republic, where high ideals are not a requisite, nor indeed a help, but distinctly a hindrance. Probably it is only with us that a Whitelaw Reid can climb to the loftiest ambassadorship in the country's gift, a Leonard Wood to the highest position in the army, and a Theodore Roosevelt be implored by the whole nation to accept a third term and do his singular insanities all over again.

Dictated August 28, 1907

More remarks about Whitelaw Reid, and about Edward House: his bringing the injunction against the "Prince and Pauper" play, etc.

As a pendant to my closing remark of yesterday I wish to insert here, from this morning's paper, the following striking and photographically exact portrait of the President:

MR. ROOSEVELT'S EXACT PORTRAIT.

(Samuel W. McCall, Republican Congressman from Massachusetts.)
You are liable some day to have a President supremely lacking in the qualities of a statesman, and one who is egotistic, impulsive, of immature judgment, a mere glutton of the limelight, ready to barter away prosperity and even his country's freedom for momentary popular applause.
If he is an autocrat, such as he, for the time, will your country be. Instead of a mighty nation, great in her physical strength and greater in her moral qualities, you may have a strutting, confiscating, shrieking, meddling America.

In the early days Whitelaw Reid and I were friends, but in 1872 a coldness occurred. Reid and Edward H. House had a falling out. House told me his side of the matter, and at second-hand I got Reid's side of it—which was simply that he considered House a "blatherskite," and wouldn't have anything to do with him. I ranged myself on House's side, and relations between Reid and me ceased; they were not resumed for twenty-two years; and then not cordially, but merely diplomatically, so to speak; we have met at people's tables, and smiled and passed the time of day, but neither of us has much enjoyed even those slight love passages. I have never invited him, and he has never invited me, until he gave me that dinner at Dorchester House the other day. He did it because he couldn't help it, and he knew I accepted it because I couldn't help it. I was visiting England in the character of an unofficial ambassador, to receive and acknowledge an honor ostensibly conferred upon me, but really—at least mainly—upon the United States, and he, as the official representative of the nation, was obliged to take public notice of me. He wouldn't have invited *me,* but he *had* to invite the United States. I left a card on Lord Curzon as soon as I reached London, and went straight from there, in due and righteous accordance with ambassadorial etiquette and usage, to Dorchester House. Reid was diplomatically pleasant and friendly; I also was diplomatically pleasant and friendly, and it is quite likely that we shall remain in that condition until Satan wants one of us and the New Jerusalem the other; the final result is not in our hands, but each of us thinks he knows how it will be.

In justice to Reid I confess that many and many a year ago I found out that he was right concerning Edward H. House. Reid had labeled him correctly; he was a blather-skite. He was a tall and handsome creature, something over thirty years of age, and had a mobile, animated, and brightly intellectual face, and most charming and engaging manners. He went out to Japan in 1873, (his second trip thither, I think,) and he called upon me in London on his way. I had been helping the London newspaper men fetch the Shah of Persia over from Ostend, I being for forty-eight hours in the service of Dr. Hosmer, London representative of the New York *Herald.* I had dictated an account of the excursion covering two or three columns of the *Herald,* and had charged and received three hundred dollars and expenses for it—a narrative which seemed to the *Herald* to lack humor, a defect which the New York office supplied from its own resources, which were poor and coarse and silly beyond imagination. House was present when Hosmer came to me with the money, and he lightly borrowed it of me and changed the subject. A year or two afterward he wrote me from Japan that his New York banker had failed, at cost to him of twenty-five thousand dollars, all the money he had in the world, and he hoped I had been wise enough to cash the draft for three hundred dollars previously sent to me by him, while it still possessed value. This was the first time I had heard of the draft, and with this mention of it the incident closed.

But not the intimacy. I did not doubt that House had sent the draft, and that with my customary carelessness I had mislaid it and forgotten all about it. About 1882, or along there somewhere, House came back from Japan desperately knotted up and disabled by rheumatism. He brought with him a bright and good-natured and wonder-fully muscular Japanese lad who wheeled him about in a Bath chair, and who carried him in his arms from bed to chair and from chair to bed, weighty as he was, and did it with unfailing patience and serenity, although House gave him a vigorous cursing every time he got a jolt that gave him pain. I visited him in New York. I knew—at least by *his* testimony—that his alleged twenty-five thousand dollars had come from dramatic assistance rendered by him to Dion Boucicault. He said that he had done more than half of the literary work on "Arrah-na-Pogue," and that he had received the twenty-five thousand dollars as his share of the royalties. I believed the statement, and even went on believing it when a year later Boucicault laughed at it and said it was a straight lie, with not a vestige of truth in it.

However, when I visited House in New York I was looking for a dramatist for "The Prince and the Pauper," and this principal author of Boucicault's great play seemed to me to be the very man I wanted; so I proposed that House dramatize the book. He was indifferent, and declined. I hunted up another dramatist—Mrs. Abby Sage Richardson—and gave her the contract on a royalty. She hadn't ever dramatized anything, but knew she could; therefore she was satisfactory to me. She made a dramatization, and a marvel it was. She was sober enough, but her play was drunk—quite the drunkest play of the century, and quite the most impossible of representation, outside the madhouse, but Daniel Frohman's stage-manager took it in hand and reformed it, and little Elsie Leslie played it to the public satisfaction. Meantime, House had come to Hartford, bringing his Bath chair, his muscular little slave, and a young Japanese girl, Koto, whom he called his adopted daughter. I had invited them, and they were our guests during two or three months; then they returned to New York. After the play was put on the boards, House notified me, through his lawyer, Robert G. Ingersoll, to take it off or he would bring an injunction suit. He claimed that although there were no writings supporting the claim, I had asked him to dramatize the book and he had agreed to do it, and had now begun his task. He soon quarreled with Ingersoll, discharged him, and hired Howe and Hummel in his place. Birds of a feather, etc.; Hummel is in the penitentiary, now. Hummel renewed the notice to me; I declined to consider it; then he brought the suit. The case came before Judge Daly in chambers. I testified by deposition; so did House and Koto. House and Koto swore that when I talked with House in New York about the play, House had eagerly accepted my proposition; that a detailed contract was arranged, and that its terms were so definite and so perfectly understood by both parties that we agreed that to reduce it to writing was quite unnecessary. House and Koto also swore that House and I frequently took counsel together concerning the play while they were my guests in Hartford. To be brief, and also exact, the pair swore to not a thing that was not a lie. Judge Daly's decision went against me, upon one ground and upon one ground only—to wit, that the testimony upon the two sides utterly disagreeing, the veracity of a sick man, confined to his chamber, was more to be depended upon than the oath of a man who was well, and at large. It sounds odd, but I have truly stated Judge Daly's reason for deciding the case in House's favor.

A temporary injunction was put upon the box-office, and the play permitted to go on with its successful career, the royalties to be paid into the court and remain there, undisturbed, until House's suit for a permanent injunction should be decided one way or the other. Then House and his little family removed to Hartford and established themselves in the Isabella Beecher Hooker cottage in our neighborhood. House thought he would like to have two "Prince and Pauper" plays going, so he wrote one and put it in the hands of the parents of little Tommy Russell, a juvenile actor of good and growing reputation, House making himself responsible for the expense of staging it. It was to open in Brooklyn, and the date was advertised. On that day George Warner, brother of Charles D., came to our house with news: he had heard Charles Gross, lawyer, say that he had extradition papers and was going to descend upon House and ship him to France to answer a charge of swindling the Crédit Lyonnais out of a considerable sum by false pretenses. That night House and his tribe glided out of Hartford at a late hour, and when next they were heard of they were in Japan.

The new play opened in Brooklyn, and was a complete and perfect and irremediable failure; there was no second night; notice was sent to Hartford, with the request that House come forward and pay the bills, which were formidable—but he had already skipped, and was safe.

The temporary injunction on Mrs. Richardson's play was at once removed, and I was told that she went promptly forward and got her royalties out of the court's hands. I instructed Mr. Bainbridge Colby to go and get my share. At the end of two years I asked him about it and found that he had forgotten to attend to it. I then placed the matter in the hands of Whitford, that incomparable ass, and when I asked him about it, two or three years afterward, I found that he also had forgotten it; time went on, and I presently forgot all about it myself; I have never collected those royalties, and I do not now know what became of them.

I was wrong; Whitelaw Reid was right; House was a blatherskite.

Dictated August 29, 1907

The Fourth of July Banquet at the Hotel Cecil, and copy of the official report of Mr. Clemens's speech; also paragraph from President Murray Butler's speech.

The Fourth of July dinner that night was devoured in the great banqueting hall of the Hotel Cecil. Every chair on the floor was occupied by men, and all the seats in the gallery by ladies. It was a fine spectacle.

Banqueteering is becoming more and more endurable as the years go by, both in England and America, for the reason that not so many speeches are permitted now as was formerly the case. If the feeding-task could now be cut down two-thirds, reducing the usual menu from fourteen courses to three and a half or four, men would no longer be justified in ranking the fear of death and the fear of the banquet together. My first experience of a banquet in a foreign country was in England, thirty-four years ago. It was in the Guildhall, and it was said that there were nine hundred banqueteers present. I think it was the truth, for the din and crash and clash of a roaring and thundering and piercing confusion of sounds proceeding from an all-pervading storm of high-voiced conversation, and from the ceaseless collision of multitudinous knives and forks and plates, remains in my ears unto this day—dulled to a vague rumble and gnashing by lapse of time, but not wholly abolished, and never to be wholly abolished until I die.

I was there by appointment, to respond to a regular toast, of which there were nine!

Nine to be responded to, and mine in the place of honor—the last! It was a large distinction to confer upon a stranger, and I was properly proud of it; sorry for it too, for it broke my heart to wait so long; if I had had a hatful of hearts it would have broken them all. When at last the long, long, exhausting wait was ended, and my turn was come, and my gratitude rising up and pervading and supporting my whole system, a disaster befell: Sir John Bennett rose, uninvited, and began to speak. The indignation of the weary house burst out with the crash of an avalanche—a crash made up of shouts of protest and disapproval, powerfully aided and reinforced by deafening pounding of the tables with empty champagne bottles. But no matter—the gallant Sir John stood serene on the distant edge of the smoke and storm of battle and visibly worked his jaws and his arms, undismayed—and in silence, of course, for neither he nor any other man could hear a word that he was saying. He was one of the two outgoing sheriffs, and it was said that he always made speeches at the great banquets; that he was never invited to make them; that no one had ever been able to find out whether they were good or bad, or neither, because nobody had ever heard one of them, since the tempest of resentment always broke out with his rising and never ceased until he finished his pantomime and sat down again. It was the most picturesque thing I have ever seen at a banquet except one, and I have the impression that I witnessed that one at the same dinner—to wit, as a doxology and good-night, that multitude of guests got up in a body, with one impulse, and stood in their chairs, with hands joined and one foot on the table, and sang "Auld Lang Syne;" then each man reached for a glass of champagne, held it on high for a moment, then drank it down—all in unison; then in unison they smashed the glasses upon the table—a fine and spirit-stirring effect.

At the greatest of all American banquets—the banquet to General Grant, in Chicago in 1879 when he returned from around the world—there were actually *sixteen* regular toasts, and sixteen carefully prepared responses to them; again I had that high privilege, the place of honor—I was No. 16! If I remember rightly, that Guildhall banquet and the Grant banquet lasted from half past seven in the evening until after two in the morning; nobody died, but of course there were some close calls.

At this recent Fourth of July banquet that I have been talking about, there were but four regular toasts and four speeches in response to them, and the function was over by about eleven o'clock. First the King's health was drunk, standing, and in silence, in accordance with ancient and invariable custom; next the health of the President of the United States was drunk. Sir Mortimer Durand, late Ambassador to the United States, responded to it in a happy speech of considerable length; next, in a good and elaborate speech, Whitelaw Reid proposed "The Day We Celebrate." By appointment, I responded. I will here copy the official report of that effort, after striking out the bracketed "laughters" and "renewed laughters," and so on:

> Mr. Chairman, my Lords and Gentlemen,—Once more it happens, as it has happened so often since I arrived in England a week or two ago, that instead of celebrating the Fourth of July properly as has been indicated, I have to first take care

of my personal character. Sir Mortimer Durand still remains unconvinced. Well, I tried to convince these people from the beginning that I did not take the Ascot Cup, and as I have failed to persuade anybody that I did not take it, I might as well confess that I did take it, and be done with it. I don't see why this uncharitable feeling should follow me everywhere, and why I should have that crime thrown up to me on all occasions. The tears that I have wept over it ought to have created a different feeling than this—and besides, I don't think it is very right or fair that, considering England has been trying to take a Cup of ours for forty years, they should make so much trouble when I try to go into the business myself. Sir Mortimer Durand, too, has had trouble from going to a dinner here, and he has told you what he suffered in consequence. But what did he suffer? He only missed his train and had to sit all night in his regimentals—I don't know what they were. Why, that caused him only one night of discomfort, and he remembers it to this day. Oh, if you could only think what I have suffered from a similar circumstance! Two or three years ago in New York, with that society there which is made up of people from all British Colonies, and from Great Britain generally, who were educated in British colleges and British schools, I was there to respond to a toast of some kind or other, and I did then what I have been in the habit of doing from a selfish motive for a long time, and that is, I got myself placed No. 3 in the list of speakers—then you get home early. I had to go five miles up river and had to catch a particular train, or not get there. But see the magnanimity which is born in me, and which I have cultivated all my life. A very famous and very great British clergyman came to me presently, and said, "I am away down in the list, I have got to catch a certain train this Saturday night, if I don't catch that train I shall be carried beyond midnight, and break the Sabbath. Won't you change places with me?" I said, "Certainly I will." I did it at once. Now see what happened. Talk about Sir Mortimer Durand's sufferings for a single night—I have suffered ever since, because I saved that gentleman from breaking the Sabbath—saved him. I took his place, but I lost my train, and it was I who broke the Sabbath. Up to that time I never had broken the Sabbath in my life, and from that day to this I never have kept it.

Our Ambassador has spoken of our Fourth of July and the noise it makes. We have a double Fourth of July, a daylight Fourth and a midnight Fourth. During the day in America, as our Ambassador has indicated, we keep the Fourth of July properly in a reverent spirit. We devote it to teaching our children patriotic things, and reverence for the Declaration of Independence. We honour the day all through the daylight hours, and when night comes we dishonor it. Two hours from now, on the Atlantic coast when night shuts down, that pandemonium will begin and there will be noise, and noise, and noise, all night long, and there will be more than noise—there will be people crippled, there will be people killed, there will be people who will lose their eyes, and all through that permission which we give to irresponsible boys to play with firearms and firecrackers and all sorts of dangerous things. We turn that Fourth of July alas! over to rowdies to drink and get drunk and make the night hideous, and we cripple and kill more people than you would imagine. We probably began to celebrate our Fourth of July night in that way a hundred and twenty-five years ago, and on every Fourth of July night since, these horrors have grown and grown until now, in the most of our five thousand towns of America, somebody gets killed or crippled on every Fourth of July night, besides those cases of sick persons whom we never hear of, who die afterward as the result of the noise or the shock. They cripple and kill more people on the Fourth of July, in America, than they kill and cripple in our American wars nowadays, and there are no pensions for these folk. And, too, we burn houses. We destroy more property on every Fourth of July night than the whole of the United States was worth a hundred and twenty-five years ago. Really, our Fourth of July is our Day of Mourning, our Day of Sorrow. Fifty thousand people who have lost friends, or who have had friends crippled, receive that Fourth of July, when it comes, as a day of mourning for the losses they have long ago sustained in their families.

I have suffered in that way myself. I have had relatives killed in that way. One was in Chicago years ago—an uncle of mine, just as good an uncle as I have ever had, and I have had lots of them—yes, uncles to burn, uncles to spare. This poor uncle, full of patriotism, opened his mouth to hurrah, and a rocket went down his throat. Before that man could ask for a drink of water to quench that thing it blew up and scattered him all over the forty-five States, and—now, this is true, I know about it myself—twenty-four hours after that it was raining buttons, recognisable as his, the whole length of the Atlantic seaboard. A person cannot have a disaster like that and be entirely cheerful the rest of his life. I had another uncle on an entirely different Fourth of July who was blown up that way, and really it trimmed him as it would a tree. He had hardly a limb left on him anywhere. All we have left now is an expurgated edition of him. But never mind about these things, they are merely passing matters. Don't let me make you sad.

Sir Mortimer Durand said that you, the English people, gave up your Colonies over there—got tired of them—and did it with some reluctance. Now I wish you just to consider that he was right about that, and that he had his reasons for saying that England did not look upon our Revolution as a foreign war, but as a civil war fought by Englishmen. Our Fourth of July which we honour so much, and which we love so much, and which we take so much pride in, is an English institution, not an American one, and it comes of a great ancestry. The first Fourth of July in that noble genealogy dates back seven centuries lacking eight years. That is the day of the Great Charter—the Magna Charta—which was born at Runnymede in the next to the last year of King John, and portions of the liberties forced thus by those hardy Barons from that reluctant King are a part of our Declaration of Independence, of our Fourth of July, of our American liberties. And the second of those Fourths of July—also English—was not born until four centuries later, in Charles I's time, in the Bill of Rights, and that is ours by inheritance, it is part of our liberties. The next one was still English, conceived and secured by Englishmen in New England, where they established that principle which remains with us to this day, and will continue to remain with us—no taxation without representation. That Fourth is always going to stand, and that Fourth the English Colonists in New England gave us. The fourth Fourth of July, the one which you are celebrating now, born in Philadelphia on the Fourth of July, 1776, *is English, too*. It is not American. Those were English colonists, subjects of King George III, Englishmen at heart, who protested against the oppressions of the Home Government. Though they proposed to cure those oppressions and remove them, still remaining under the Crown, they were not intending a revolution. The revolution was brought about by circumstances which they could not control. The Declaration of Independence was written by a British subject, every name signed to it was the name of a British subject, there was not the name of a single American attached to it—in fact, there was not an American in the country in that day except the Indians out in the forests. They were Englishmen, all Englishmen—Americans did not begin to exist until seven years later, when that Fourth of July was seven years old and the American Republic established. Since *then* there have been Americans. So you see what we owe to England in the matter of Liberties.

We have, however, one Fourth of July which is absolutely our own, and that is that memorable proclamation issued forty years ago by that great American to whom Sir Mortimer Durand paid that just and beautiful tribute—Abraham Lincoln: a proclamation which not only set the black slave free, but set his white owner free also. The owner was set free from that burden and offence, that sad condition of things where he was in so many instances a master and owner of slaves when he did not want to be. That proclamation set them all free. But even in this matter England led the way, for she had set her slaves free thirty years before, and we but followed her example. We always follow her example, whether it is good or bad. And it was an English judge, a century ago, that issued that other great proclamation, and established that great principle, that, when a slave—let him belong to whom he may, and let him come whence he may—sets his foot upon English soil, his fetters by that act fall away and he is a free man before the world!

It is true, then, that all our Fourths of July, and we have five of them, England gave to us, except that one that I have mentioned—the Emancipation Proclamation; and let us not forget that we owe this debt to her. Let us be able to say to Old England, this great-hearted old mother of the race, You gave us our Fourths of July that we love and honour and revere, you gave us the Declaration of Independence, which is the Charter of our rights, you, the venerable Mother of Liberties, the Champion and Protector of Anglo-Saxon Freedom—you gave us these things, and we do most honestly thank you for them!

The next and last speech was made by President Murray Butler, of Columbia University, in response to the toast to "Our Guests." I will select, and insert here, a remark from his speech, because it pays me a compliment. The reason I do not put in the rest of his speech is because it dealt with other matters. Speeches which do not deal with me I regard as irrelevancies.

To my mind the most significant fact about this celebration of the Fourth of July is that the celebration is held with the greatest of cordiality and goodwill, and with the favouring and gracious presence of the leaders of British thought and action, in the capital of the British Empire itself. Is it possible for any one of us to think that such a gathering could take place anywhere else in the world as between a mother-land and a nation, once colonial, now independent? It is unthinkable, because the reasons which make possible this celebration in the British capital apply to Great Britain and America alone. Some of these reasons have been touched upon by Dr. Clemens in the very beautiful and eloquent passage at the close of his speech. He has pointed out with absolute fidelity to historical fact that we are celebrating, not something which Englishmen do not want and do not believe in, but something which England throughout its history has fought for and stood for. (Applause.)

Dictated August 30, 1907

Luncheon with Sir Norman Lockyer—Luncheon with the Plasmon directors—Paying calls with little Francesca—The *Punch* dinner.

Ashcroft's notes:

> *Friday, July 5*. Dined with the Earl and Countess of Portsmouth. Forty or fifty guests; two or three hundred came in afterward.
>
> *Saturday, July 6*. Breakfasted at Lord Avebury's. Among those present were Lord Kelvin, Sir Charles Lyell, and Sir Archibald Geikie.
> Quarters at the hotel occupied by invasion of photographers and portrait-sketchers during more than two hours; sat 22 times for photographs and 4 times for crayons; too exhausting, will sit no more.
> Savage Club dinner in the evening; white suit; "fake" Ascot Cup presented; Brennan mono-rail car exhibited in action.
>
> *Sunday, July 7*. Lunched with the astronomer, Sir Norman Lockyer.
> Except Linley Sambourne, the veteran *Punch* cartoonist, and Admiral Sir Cyprian Bridge, whom I had known in Australia in '95, all present were scientists.
> Drove two hours and a half returning calls, with little Francesca for company and support.
>
> *Monday, July 8*. Lunched with Plasmon Directors at Bath Club.
> Dined privately at Moberly Bell's.
>
> *Tuesday, July 9*. Lunched at the House of Commons with Sir Benjamin Stone. Many guests, chief among them Mr. Balfour, and Komura, the Japanese ambassador.
> *Punch* dinner in the evening.

No white-headed antiquity of my sex whose years exceed seventy, likes to pay social calls; he dreads to see the calling hour come round, he rejoices when the task is over for the day; he is often sensible of a guilty gladness when he finds the people "out." But I know a secret now that will make call-paying a delight to me hereafter. When I had been in England just a fortnight I had been constantly seeking and finding excuses for postponing return-visits, with the result that the accumulation of debts of this kind was so large that it had become a heavy and depressing burden upon my conscience; then I chanced to come across, in the hotel drawing-room, a sweet and pretty and charming little maid of sixteen whom I had known in the ship, and my depressing burden became at once a prized treasure, for I borrowed this child of her mother, and at four o'clock every day thereafter we drove about London during two hours paying calls. Never was a task so light. We presently got the best of the list, and after that we cleared the record every day, and kept it squared to date. That simple and honest and charming child made her way everywhere; she entered English homes of all ranks; she was petted by English people of all ages and all social degrees; she saw English home life in all its phases, from the humblest all the way up, and by grace of her winning ways and her sweet modesty she left friends behind her, and only friends, wherever she went. I was proud of my sample of the American country-bred girl, and perhaps did not take much pains to conceal it. She will enter Bryn Mawr presently, already possessed of one chapter of valuable knowledge which not many American country lassies have acquired at her age. We paid calls together every day for a fortnight, and when I sailed for home my score was clear.

The luncheon with the Plasmon directors was a business matter, and of a mutually congratulatory sort. Seven years ago I assisted in founding the Plasmon Company; I took five thousand pounds of its stock and paid par for it; it is worth eighty thousand dollars now, and will soon be worth more. Several years ago an American Plasmon Company was started, and in a little while was robbed, skinned, and reduced to bankruptcy by its own Board of Directors, one of whom—Henry A. Butters, a sharper hailing from Long Valley, California—swindled me out of my investment in it, amounting to thirty-two thousand dollars.

The *Punch* dinner will remain one of my pleasantest memories of my four weeks' sojourn in England. That dinner was a unique distinction—it has not had its fellow. For fifty years the *Punch* staff has assembled once a week in *Punch*'s own quarters, in *Punch*'s own private dining room, to dine, and, meantime, to consider and discuss and plan and arrange the literature and art for the next week's issue. *Punch* has always been hospitable to visiting foreigners of repute in the various walks of Literature and Art, and has dined and wined them; but never until now, on his own premises; never until now, in his own private dining room. In fifty years I am the only stranger unto whom has been extended the privilege of crossing that sacred threshold and sitting at that sacred board. I mean to remember this.

MARK TWAIN LEAVES ENGLAND FOR HOME

No Foreigner Ever Received So Warm a Welcome There.

CHEERED BY THE STEVEDORES WHEN HE LANDED, AND LATER HONORED BY ROYALTY.

Social Attitude of American Diplomats Attracts Attention Abroad—More Men of Brains and Fewer Rich Men in the Service Would Be Desirable—American-Japanese Situation Regarded Seriously in Most of the European Capitals.

N.Y. Sun-Syracuse Herald—Cablegram

LONDON, July 13.—Mark Twain sailed to-day, and it is fitting that a serious word should be said about his extraordinary month's visit to England. No foreigner has ever been treated as he has been treated by the English people. His welcome began as he walked down the gangplank when the stevedores on the dock broke into cheers. The highest and the greatest in the land had joined eagerly in all forms of tribute to this untitled friend of all mankind. He says himself that the universal welcome by the masses at every opportunity has pleased him most. The wonder is that a man of 72 or any age should go through the enormous programme of the past four weeks and live to tell the tale. Mr. Clemens not only lived but thrived upon it, and he goes home to write such a chapter of his autobiography as no other American was ever able to record.

If the truth must be told, Twain's popularity in England is of a warmer and more personal nature than even in his own country. He has won the hearts of Englishmen as no living writer has done, and they love to do him honor. The cheers at his departure to-day were of a different note from those on his arrival, and for once his emotion silenced him as he waved good bye.

Punch's Tribute to Mark Twain

Mr. Punch does himself the honor to drink your health, sir.

Dictated August 31, 1907

The *Punch* dinner continued—Little Joy Agnew presents Mr. Clemens with original of *Punch* cartoon—Copy of a letter from Joy Agnew to Mr. Clemens; also copy of his reply to it.

A few days earlier *Punch* had contained a cartoon in which that illustrious old gentleman was represented as "doing himself the honor" to drink my health.

The full strength of the *Punch* staff sat at the dinner, with Mr. Agnew, the editor-in-chief, at the head of the table. Nearly all the men were young, and new to me—in fact all except three: Linley Sambourne, Sir Francis Burnand, and Mr. Lucy. I had known Mr. Lucy a number of years, and Sambourne and Burnand a full generation. In these chairs had sat, fifty years ago, Leech, Tenniel, Douglas Jerrold, and others of the great departed, and I had a sort of sense that their viewless ghosts were present and approving. When all were seated and the napkins about to be lifted, I was warned in a low voice that a solemnity was about to take place. An impressive stillness and silence followed, which lasted as much as a minute, perhaps; then a closet door sprang open and out of it flitted a little fairy decked out in pink, like a rose, and came tripping toward me, her face all alive with smiles and excitement; and she bore in her hands the framed original of the *Punch* cartoon—a picture half as big as herself. She stopped near me, dropped a courtesy, and delivered, with charming grace and animation and well-taught expression, a touching and beautiful little speech in my honor. I took the picture from her hands, but before I could control my voice enough to even murmur a "Thank you" she had dropped another courtesy and flown to the refuge of her closet.

This is the prettiest incident of my long life, I think, and I cannot think of it yet without a thrill at my heart and quickened pulse-beat. The little sprite was Joy Agnew, eight years of age, daughter of the editor-in-chief. Naturally she got a unanimous recall, and so she came lightly tripping back and climbed up into her father's lap and sat there, rosy and sweet, and altogether adorable, and lit up the whole place with her fresh young loveliness and sanctified it with her innocence. She remained half an hour; then, under parental compulsion, she said her good-bye and was escorted away by a servant. She went reluctantly, and said she had never been allowed in that place before, and thought she wouldn't be allowed to come again. She was the feature of that banquet, the ever-memorable feature of it, the feature without rival or competitor—I confess it without jealousy. It took a while to get over the dazzle and exaltation of that bright vision; then we pulled ourselves together and had a lively time, with speeches and other hilarities.

I think Miss Joy asked me for an autographed portrait; at any rate I sent her one, and in return she wrote me a letter worth a hundred of it; I received it a few days after I reached home, in America. As a child's letter, I think it is perfect; perfect in its frankness, its simplicity, and in its unquestioning and well placed confidence that I would be interested in the deep concerns of the little writer's life. I will copy her letter here. In closing it she says "I hope you will remember me for I am yours ~~respec~~ affectionately Joy Agnew." She saw that that word was too distant, too cold, too formal, for the relations existing between her and me, so she stopped it in the middle and drove a single pen-stroke through it, which did not at all disguise it. An older and more artful person would have obliterated it, and pretended that he had had no such thought in his mind, but the child was open and honest, and in her heart there was no place for subterfuges.

15th of July 1907.
Monday

LITTLECOURT,
FARTHINGSTONE,
WEEDON.

My dear Mr. Mark Twain,
Thank you so much for the beautiful picture you sent me. It was very kind of you to think of me. We have a lovely garden, full of a lot of flowers We have also a good lot of pets too. I will tell you what they are. Mine are; three bantams, three goldfish, three doves, six canarys, two dogs and one cat My brother Ewan who is at Eton now has; nine goldfish, one cat, one dog, and a pony. My Daddy has one dog. Mummy has a lot of hens and some bees. We have a little garden of our own and Daddy is going to make us a see-saw. Ofcourse this is all in the country. I am going to a wedding on Thursday. I hope you will remember me for I am yours ~~respec~~ affectionately
Joy Agnew.

REPLY.

Tuxedo Park
New York.
1907

Unto you greeting and salutation and worship, you dear sweet little rightly-named Joy! I can see you now almost as vividly as I saw you that night when you sat flashing and beaming upon those sombre swallow-tails

"Fair as a star when only one
Is shining in the sky."

Oh, you were indeed the only one—there wasn't even the remotest chance of competition with *you,* dear! Ah, you *are* a decoration, you little witch!

The idea of your house going to the wanton expense of a flower garden!—aren't *you* enough? And what do you want to go and discourage the other flowers for? Is that the right spirit? is it considerate? is it kind? How do you suppose they feel when you come around—looking the way *you* look? And you so pink and sweet and dainty and lovely and supernatural? Why, it makes them feel embarrassed and artificial, of course; and in my opinion it is just as pathetic as it can be. Now then, you want to reform, dear, and do right.

Well certainly you are well off, Joy:
3 bantams;
3 goldfish;

3 doves;
6 canarys;
2 dogs;
1 cat.

All you need, now, to be permanently beyond the reach of want, is one more dog—just one more good, gentle, high-principled, affectionate, loyal dog who wouldn't want any nobler service than the golden privilege of lying at your door, nights, and biting everything that came along—and I am that very one, and ready to come at the dropping of a hat.

Do you think you could convey my love and thanks to your "daddy" and Owen Seaman, and Partridge, and those other oppressed and down-trodden subjects of yours, you darling small tyrant?

On my knees! These—with the kiss of fealty from your other subject—

Mark Twain.

Dictated September 4, 1907

Copy of letter from Professor Henderson in regard to Mr. Clemens's book, "What is Man?" Mr. Clemens tells of the writing of this book, the laying of one chapter of it before the Monday Evening Club, and the final publication of two hundred and fifty copies by Doubleday.

I shall continue the narrative of my adventures in England pretty soon, but my interest in that matter is for the moment pushed aside by a letter which has arrived this morning from Professor Henderson. Henderson was a fellow-passenger of mine when I sailed for England in June, and after I had come to know him, and like him, and trust him, I privately and confidentially gave him a copy of "What is Man?"

Many a time in the past eight or nine years I have been strongly moved to publish that little book, but the doubtfulness of the wisdom of doing it has always been a little stronger than the desire to do it, consequently the venture has not been made; necessarily it has not been made, for, according to my own gospel, as set forth in that small book, where there are two desires in a man's heart he has no choice between the two, but must obey the strongest, there being no such thing as free will in the composition of any human being that ever lived.

I have talked my gospel rather freely in conversation for twenty-five or thirty years, and have never much minded whether my listeners liked it or not, but I couldn't get beyond that—the idea of actually publishing always brought me a shudder; by anticipation I couldn't bear the reproaches which would assail me from a public which had been trained from the cradle along opposite lines of thought, and for that reason—which is a quite sufficient reason—would not be able to understand me. I had early proved all this, for I laid one chapter of my gospel before the Monday Evening Club in Hartford, a quarter of a century ago, and there was not a man there who didn't scoff at it, jeer at it, revile at it, and call it a lie—a thousand times a lie! That was the chapter denying that there is any such thing as personal merit; maintaining that a man is merely a machine automatically functioned without any of his help, or any occasion or necessity for his help, and that no machine is entitled to praise for any of its acts of a virtuous sort, nor blamable for any of its acts of the opposite sort. Incidentally, I observed that the human machine gets all its inspirations from the outside, and is not capable of originating an idea of any kind in its own head; and I further remarked, incidentally, that no man ever does a duty for duty's sake but only for the sake of the satisfaction he personally gets out of doing the duty, or for the sake of avoiding the personal discomfort he would have to endure if he shirked that duty; also I indicated that there is no such thing as free will, and no such thing as self-sacrifice.

The Club handled me without gloves. They said I was trying to strip man of his dignity, and I said I shouldn't succeed, for it would not be possible to strip him of a quality which he did not possess. They said that if this insane doctrine of mine were accepted by the world life would no longer be worth living; but I said that that would merely leave life in the condition it was before.

Those were the brightest minds in Hartford—and indeed they were very superior minds—but my little batch of quite simple and unassailable truths could get no entrance into them, because the entrances were all stopped up with stupid misteachings handed down by stupid ancestors, and docilely accepted without examination, whereas until those minds should be unstopped they would not be competent to intelligently examine my gospel and intelligently pass upon it. No mind, howsoever brilliant, is in a condition to examine a proposition which is opposed to its teachings and its heredities until, as pointed out by Lord Bacon some centuries ago, those prejudices, predilections, and inheritances shall have been swept away. I realized that night that since those able men were such children, such incompetents, in the presence of an unfamiliar doctrine, there could be but one result if my gospel should be placed before the general public: it would make not a single convert, and I should be looked upon as a lunatic, besides; therefore I put aside the idea of elaborating my notions and spreading them abroad in a book.

The sorrowful effort of that night consisted partly of a skeleton sketch, but mainly of talk. Years went by, and at last, in Vienna in 1898, I wrote out and completed one chapter, using the dialogue form in place of the essay form. I read it to Frank N. Doubleday, who was passing through Vienna, and he wanted to take it and publish it, but I was not minded to submit it to print and criticism. I added a paragraph or a chapter now and then, as time went by, and at last in 1902 I finished it; and I further finished it, in 1904, by destroying the concluding chapter, whose subject was "The Moral Sense." The fact is, I couldn't even stand that chapter myself; all the other chapters were sweet and gentle, but that one was disrespectful—in fact riotous.

Again Doubleday wanted to publish, but I remembered Hartford, and said no. He proposed a submerged and private circulation of the little torpedo, and I acceded to that. He got two hundred and fifty copies printed for me at the De Vinne Press, and J. W. Boswell, chief of one of De Vinne's departments, took out a copyright in his own name, by request, and doesn't yet know who wrote the book. Doubleday has sent ten or twelve copies to men here, and in England, through Mr. Boswell, (the authorship concealed, of course,) and I myself have given away four copies to discreet persons. The following is the Preface to "What is Man?"

> FEBRUARY, 1905. The studies for these papers were begun twenty-five or twenty-seven years ago. The papers were written seven years ago. I have examined them once or twice per year since and found them satisfactory. I have just examined them again, and am still satisfied that they speak the truth.
>
> Every thought in them has been thought (and accepted as unassailable truth) by millions upon millions of men—and concealed, kept private. Why did they not speak out? Because they dreaded (*and could not bear*) the disapproval of the people around them. Why have not I published? The same reason has restrained me, I think. I can find no other.

The italicized phrase is from the book, where it is maintained that men often do perilous things which they don't want to do, but are so constituted by nature that they can't bear to leave them undone, whereas a man differently constituted could leave them undone without any discomfort to himself. In this place I will insert Professor Henderson's letter:

> Salisbury, N.C.
> Aug. 26, 1907.
>
> My dear Mr. Clemens:
> I hope that by this time you have recovered from the effects of the magnificent ovation that was given you in England. Is it not Goethe who says that when a man becomes truly great, the world does everything it can to prevent him from doing other great things—with its receptions, dinners, and diversions of a thousand different kinds?
> I wish very much that it had been possible for me to run out to see you when I was in New York the other day; but, unfortunately, I was compelled to come straight home. Since I have been here, I have read the book—*What Is Man?*—which you most kindly sent me in London, and am startled to discover that your observations made from a close and direct study of man *au naturel,* so to speak, coincide at most points with the views of the greatest modern thinkers, who style themselves philosophers and who never write anything without conscious philosophic intention.
> I find that not only does Mr. Shaw agree with you in your general thesis: that from his cradle to his grave a man never does a single thing which has any *first and foremost* object but one—to secure peace of mind, spiritual comfort, for *himself;* he has actually written a play to epitomize this thesis. And the very point of departure of that play was the atmospheric enunciation of your doctrine that none but gods have ever had a thought which did not come from the outside. Dick Dudgeon, in *The Devil's Disciple,* becomes a devil's advocate because he has been driven to it by the excessive, outrageous puritanism of his family, and the soul-destroying religious narrowness of his environment. He deliberately goes to the scaffold to save the life of a man, a minister, for whom he has neither affection, devotion, loyalty, nor indeed

ties of any sort whatsoever. When the minister's wife, sentimentally fancying that Dick has made the sacrifice for her sake, goes to the prison and offers him her love, he staggers her by scorning her proffered love with more than Puritan asceticism. He has done it, i.e. saved the minister, not for her, not for any alien, but for himself. It was the law of his own nature that he obeyed. He had to satisfy that inner demand for spiritual contentment. With Dick, as with Martin Luther, the *mot d'ordre* was: *Ich kann nicht anders.* As Mr. Shaw once explained, Dick could no more refuse the imperious command of his own nature than a fireman could refuse to rescue a child from a burning building. And in the same play, the minister undergoes a like transformation—equally miraculous in the eyes of the world, but perfectly natural to himself, since it consisted in the discovery of the real Will which animated him.

Friedrich Nietzsche, Henrick Ibsen, and Bernard Shaw all insist, more or less explicitly, upon repudiation of duty. Nietzsche is intent upon doing away with the ordinary concepts of Good and Evil, and of entering upon a new dispensation of supermorality where abstract standards of right and wrong shall be replaced by relative standards, where conscience, so called, shall be superseded by an increased sense of personal responsibility. Throughout his entire work, Ibsen plainly insists that conformity to conventional notions of duty is just as likely to lead to evil as to good results, and that failure to fulfil the individual will is nothing short of a crime against oneself. The frequently employed Ibsenic phrase "to live one's own life" means this, if it means anything. He is the great Protestant, demanding everywhere private right of judgment in matters of conduct. Satisfaction of one's inner nature, not conformity to conventional standards of duty, is Ibsen's supreme test of conduct.

It is a fundamental theory of Mr. Shaw's that people never do anything for duty's sake only, or even primarily. Like Nietzsche, he believes that convictions are prisons, and that rationalism is bankrupt because sufficient reasons can always be found for the justification of any particular line of conduct. People do things, not at all because they ought to, but because they want to; and then they seek *ex post facto* excuses for their actions. But he is no mad advocate for the Rabelaisian motto, *Fais ce que tu veux,* for the man in the street. Institutions having fixed standards of duty must continue for a long time to come in order to do the thinking for the vast mass of people who will not think for themselves—to aid the individual to identify the individual will with the world-will. And I feel sure that his theory of Free Will is identical with your own.

It has been a great privilege to read your book, and to find that you have given explicit expression to the most fecund philosophic conceptions of this age. You have made perfectly concrete many notions which are only implicit in certain great works of modern art. And your *Admonition* is beyond praise: "Diligently train your ideals upward and still upward toward a summit where you will find your chiefest pleasure in conduct which, while contenting you, will be sure to confer benefits upon your neighbor and the community."

I enclose a copy of one of the three or four interviews with me in the New York papers of about a week ago.

Give my kindest regards to Mr. Ashcroft, and accept my sincerest good wishes for your health and happiness.

Faithfully,
Archibald Henderson.

Blythewood.

I have not read Nietzsche or Ibsen, nor any other philosopher, and have not needed to do it, and have not desired to do it; I have gone to the fountain-head for information— that is to say, to the human race. Every man is in his own person the whole human race, with not a detail lacking. I am the whole human race without a detail lacking; I have studied the human race with diligence and strong interest all these years in my own person; in myself I find in big or little proportion every quality and every defect that is findable in the mass of the race. I knew I should not find in any philosophy a single thought which had not passed through my own head, nor a single thought which had not passed through the heads of millions and millions of men before I was born; I knew I should not find a single original thought in any philosophy, and I knew I could not furnish one to the world myself, if I had five centuries to invent it in. Nietzsche published his book, and was at once pronounced crazy by the world—by a world which included tens of thousands of bright, sane men who believed exactly as Nietzsche believed, but concealed the fact, and scoffed at Nietzsche. What a coward every man is! and how surely he will find it out if he will just let other people alone and sit down and examine himself. The human race is a race of cowards; and I am not only marching in that procession but carrying a banner.

Dictated September 6, 1907

Call upon Lady Stanley; and upon Archdeacon Wilberforce, where Holy Grail is exhibited and story of its discovery related to Mr. Clemens by the Archdeacon.

Ashcroft's note———:

Mr. Clemens called on Lady Stanley, widow of the explorer, in the afternoon.

In fact, that was one of my earliest calls. Lady Stanley was as eager and impulsive as ever, and as free from any concealment of her feelings as she was when I first knew her, a proud and happy young bride, so many years ago. Stanley has been dead three years and a half, but I think all her days and nights are spent in worship of him, and I believe he is almost as present to her as he was in life. She is an intense spiritualist, and has long lived in the atmosphere of that cult. Mrs. Myers, her widowed sister, was the wife of the late president of the British Psychical Society, who was a chief among spiritualists. To me, who take no interest in other-worldly things, and am convinced that we know nothing whatever about them, and have been wrongly and uncourteously and contemptuously left in total ignorance of them, it is a pleasure and a refreshment to have converse with a person like Lady Stanley, who uncompromisingly believes in them; and not only believes in them but considers them important. She was as exactly and as comprehensively happy and content in her beliefs as I am in my destitution of them, and I perceived that we could exchange places and both of us be precisely as well off as we were before; for when all is said and done, the one sole condition that makes spiritual happiness, and preserves it, is the absence of doubt. Lady Stanley and I, and the black savage who worships a tar baby in the African jungle and is troubled by no religious doubts or misgivings, are just equals, and equally fortunately situated; either of us could change places with either of the others and be fully as well off as before; the trade would cost neither party the value of a farthing. Lady Stanley wanted to convert me to her beliefs and her faith; and there has been a time when I would have been eager to convert her to my position, but that time has gone by; I would not now try to unsettle any person's religious faith, where it was untroubled by doubt—not even the savage African's. I have found it pretty hard to give up missionarying—that least excusable of all human trades—but I was obliged to do it, because I could not continue to exercise it without private shame while publicly and privately deriding and blaspheming the other missionaries.

I found that Stanley had left behind him an uncompleted autobiography. It sets forth freely and frankly the details of his childhood and youth and early manhood, and stops with his adventures in our Civil War, if I remember rightly. Lady Stanley is preparing it for publication, and I was surprised, and also greatly gratified, to find that she was not purposing to suppress certain facts that used to sift around in whispers in Stanley's lifetime—to wit, that he was of humble origin and was born in a workhouse. No doubt there was a time when she would have been glad to see these things suppressed and forgotten, but she has risen above that; she lives upon a higher and worthier plane now; she perhaps realizes that those humble beginnings are matter for pride now, when one remembers how high the peerless explorer climbed in spite of them.

I will mix my dates again—this in order to bring into immediate juxtaposition a couple of curiosities in the way of human intellectual gymnastics. Lady Stanley believes that Stanley's spirit is with her all the time and talks with her about her ordinary daily concerns—a thing which is to me unthinkable. I wonder if it would be unthinkable to Archdeacon Wilberforce, also? I do not know, but I imagine that that would be the case. I imagine that the Immaculate Conception, and the rest of the impossibilities recorded in the Bible, would have no difficulties for him, because in those cases he has been trained from the cradle to believe the unbelievable, and is so used to it that it comes natural and handy to him—but that kind of teaching is no preparation for acceptance of other unbelievable things, to whose examination one comes with an untwisted and unprejudiced mind. Wilberforce is educated, cultured, and has a fine and acute mind, and he comes of an ancestry similarly equipped; therefore he is competent to examine new marvels with an open mind, and I think the chances are that he rejects the claims of spiritualism with fully as much confidence as he accepts Immaculate Conception. Is it possible that Mr. Wilberforce has been trained from the cradle up to believe in the Holy Grail? It does not seem likely; yet he does believe in it, and not only believes in it but believes he has it in his possession.

If I had had this astonishing fact at second-hand I could not have believed it, and would not have believed it, even if I had gotten it from the twelve apostles in writing, with every signature vouched for by a notary public. I should have said that to an educated, cultured, highly intellectual man who believes he has held the Holy Grail in his hand, complete and unquestioning belief in Münchausen's, and in all other conceivable extravagances, must come easy.

The text for what I am talking about now I find in this note of Ashcroft's:

> *Sunday, June 23.* In the afternoon Mr. Clemens visited Archdeacon Wilberforce, 20 Dean's Yard, Westminster. Sir William Crookes, Sir James Knowles, Mrs. Myers (widow of author of "Human Personality and its Survival of Bodily Death") and perhaps seventy-five or a hundred others were there.

As soon as I entered I was told by the Archdeacon that a most remarkable event had occurred—that the long lost Holy Grail had at last been found, and that there could be no mistake whatever about its identity! I could not have been more startled if a gun had gone off at my ear. For a moment, or at least half a moment, I supposed that he was not in earnest; then that supposition vanished; manifestly he was in earnest—indeed he was eagerly and excitedly in earnest. He leading, we plowed through the crowd to the centre of the drawing-room, where Sir William Crookes, the renowned scientist, was standing. Sir William is a spiritualist. We closed in upon Sir William, Mrs. Myers accosting me and joining us. Mr. Wilberforce then told me the rest of the story of the Holy Grail, and it was apparent that Sir William already knew all about it and was, moreover, a believer in the marvel. In brief, the story was that a young grain merchant, a Mr. Pole, had recently been visited in a vision by an angel who commanded him to go to a certain place outside the ancient Glastonbury Abbey, and said that upon digging in that place he would find the Holy Grail. Mr. Pole obeyed. He sought out the indicated spot and dug there, and under four feet of packed and solid earth he found the relic. All this had happened a week or ten days before this present conversation of June 23d.

Dictated September 12, 1907

The Holy Grail continued.

The Holy Grail was in the house. A proper spirit of reverence forbade its exhibition to a crowd, but Mr. Wilberforce offered to grant me a private view of it, therefore I followed him and Sir William; Mrs. Myers joined us. When we arrived at the room where the relic was, we found there the finder of it and one other man—a guardian of the place, this latter seemed to be. Mr. Pole brought a wooden box of a quite humble and ordinary sort, and took from it a loose bundle of white linen cloth, handling it carefully, and gave it into Mr. Wilberforce's hands, who proceeded to unwind its envelope—not hastily, but with cautious pains, and impressively; the pervading silence was itself impressive, and I was affected by it. Stillness and solemnity have a subduing power of their own, let the occasion be what it may. This power had time and opportunity to deepen and gather force, degree by degree, for the linen bandage was of considerable length. At last the sacred vessel which tradition asserts received the precious blood of the crucified Christ, lay exposed to view. In the belief of two persons present, this was the very vessel which was brought by night and secretly delivered to Nicodemus, nearly nineteen centuries ago, after the Creator of the universe had delivered up His life on the cross for the redemption of the human race; the very cup which the stainless Sir Galahad had sought with knightly devotion in far fields of peril and adventure, in Arthur's time, fourteen hundred years ago; the same cup which princely knights of other bygone ages had laid down their lives in long and patient efforts to find, and had passed from life disappointed—and here it was at last, dug up by a Liverpool grain-broker at no cost of blood or travel, and apparently no purity required of him above the average purity of the twentieth-century dealer in cereal futures; not even a stately name required—no Sir Galahad, no Sir Bors de Ganis, no Sir Launcelot of the Lake—nothing but a mere Mr. Pole; given name not known, probably Peterson. No armor of shining steel required; no plumed helmet, no emblazoned shield, no death-dealing spear, no formidable sword endowed with fabulous powers: in fact no armor at all, and no weapons but just a plebeian pick and shovel. Here, right under our very eyes, was the Holy Grail, renowned for nineteen hundred years—the longed-for, the prayed-for, the sought-for, the most illustrious relic the world has ever known; and there, within touch of our hand, stood its rescuer, Peterson Pole, whom God preserve! It was an impressive moment.

To be exact, it was not a cup at all; it was not a vase; it was not a goblet. It was merely a saucer—a saucer of green glass enclosing a saucer of white silver. Both surfaces of the saucer were adorned with small flower figures in soft colors pierced with open-work, and through these piercings the imprisoned silver saucer could be seen. In size and shape and shallowness, this saucer was like any other saucer. It may have been a cup, or a beaker, or a grail, once, but if so time has shriveled it.

Mr. Wilberforce said that it was the true Holy Grail; that there was no room for the slightest doubt about it; that no vessel like it was now in existence anywhere; that its age could not be short of four thousand years; that its place of concealment, under four feet of solid earth, was another indication of its antiquity, since it takes many centuries to form four feet of solid earth. It was evident that Sir William Crookes, who as a scientist will accept no alleged revelation of science until it has been submitted to the most exacting and remorseless tests—and has stood the tests and stands absolutely proven—was quite satisfied with these juvenile guessings and empty reasonings, and fully believed in the genuineness of this Holy Grail, and did not even doubt the authenticity of that angel of indigestion that brought the news to the grain-broker.

I am glad I have lived to see that half hour—that astonishing half hour. In its particular line it stands alone in my life's experiences; having no fellow, and nothing, indeed, that even remotely resembles it. I have long suspected that Man's claim to be The Reasoning Animal was a doubtful one, but this episode has swept that doubtfulness away; I am quite sure now that often, very often, in matters concerning religion and politics a man's reasoning powers are not above the monkey's. Mrs. Myers has lived in an atmosphere of spiritualism for many years, and subscribes to that cult's claims, still the Holy Grail was too large a mouthful for her; she indicated this in a private remark to me.

If this had been an American episode, the newspapers would have rung with laughter from one end of the country to the other, whether the sponsor of the Grail was at the bottom of the Church or at its summit—but Mr. Wilberforce is a great *English* Church dignitary, the episode is English also, and that makes all the difference. We followed custom, and kept still. So did the English press. Two or three weeks after the 23d a brief account of the finding of the Holy Grail was published in a London paper, along with the names involved, and this account was cabled over and published in the American papers; there the matter dropped, without comment on either side of the ocean; I have not seen nor heard of a single reference to it from that day to this.

Dictated September 13, 1907

World's recent exposure of fact that Roosevelt bought his election—Remarks about Roosevelt—His proposed trip down the Mississippi—Mr. Clemens declines to join the excursion and pilot President's boat—Copy of poem relating to this incident.

The King's garden party at Windsor——

But never mind about that now; I will take it up when to-day's latest and freshest and newest interest in President Roosevelt and his antics shall have had a chance to quiet down—in case he should give it one, which is not likely. Three days ago the *World* newspaper convicted him, beyond redemption, of having bought his election to the Presidency with money. That he committed this stupendous crime has long been suspected—ever since election day, in fact—but the proofs have never been furnished until now. Judge Parker, the opposition candidate, made the charge at the time, in courteous parliamentary terms, but Mr. Roosevelt fiercely denied it—thus adding falsehood to his burden of misconduct. However, that was not much of an addition—for him; he is accustomed to it, and has a talent for it, although he detests false speaking in other people, and cannot abide it. At one time and another, during the past three years, he has frankly charged a dozen of the cleanest men in the country with being unveracious, and in every instance has seemed almost really and sincerely shocked at it. Mr. Roosevelt is easily the most astonishing event in American history—if we except the discovery of the country by Columbus. The details of Mr. Roosevelt's purchase of the Presidency by bribery of voters are all exposed now, even to the names of the men who furnished the money, and the amounts which each contributed. The men are great corporation chiefs, and three of them are Standard Oil monopolists. It is now known that when the canvass was over, a week before election day, and all legitimate uses for election-money at an end, Mr. Roosevelt got frightened and sent for Mr. Harriman to come to Washington and arrange measures to save the State of New York for the Republican party. The meeting took place, and Harriman was urged to raise two hundred thousand dollars for the cause. He raised two hundred and sixty thousand, and it was spent upon the election in the last week of the campaign—necessarily for the purchase of votes, since the time had gone by for using money in any other way. In a printed statement, Judge Parker now says:

> Obviously in the closing hours of the campaign but one practical use could be made of it, and that was to swell the fund already accumulated to secure beyond peradventure the large floating vote, builded up by years of effort to corrupt the electorate by means of moneys contributed by those who were willing to buy favors from those willing to sell them.

Of the money subscribed, two hundred thousand dollars were spent in the City of New York, and Mr. Harriman claims that it changed the votes of fifty thousand floaters, thereby making a change in Mr. Roosevelt's favor of a hundred thousand votes.

For years the rich corporations have furnished vast sums of money to keep the Republican party in power, and have done this upon the understanding that their monopolies were to be shielded and protected in return. During all these years this protection has been faithfully furnished, in accordance with the agreement, but this time treachery intervened. Mr. Roosevelt saw that it would be popular to attack the great corporations, and he did not hesitate to retire from his contract and do it. Mr. Harriman and those others had bought him and paid for him, but that was nothing to a man who stands always ready to sell his honor for such a price as he can get for it in the market—for even a large advertisement, for that matter.

Mr. Roosevelt is now rejoicing in the possession of a federal judge, of Chicago, who is a man after his own heart. This judge has fined the Standard Oil Company twenty-nine million two hundred and forty thousand dollars, upon a quibble, and the President is delighted, for it is a large and showy advertisement. It is quite unlikely that a higher court will affirm the decision, on appeal, but the President will care little for that; he has had his advertisement.

He has sent Secretary Taft around the world on an electioneering trip—another advertisement.

He is sending the United States navy to San Francisco by way of the Strait of Magellan—all for show, all for advertisement—although he is aware that if it gets disabled on its adventurous trip it cannot be repaired in the Pacific, for lack of docks; but the excursion will make a great noise, and this will satisfy Mr. Roosevelt.

Mr. Roosevelt has done what he could to destroy the industries of the country, and they all stand now in a half-wrecked condition and waiting in an ague to see what he will do next. One more shake-up and they will go, perhaps. He will certainly provide that shake-up, if he can get a sufficient advertisement out of it. That San Francisco earthquake which shook the city down, and made such a noise in the world, was but a poor thing, and local; it confined itself to a narrow strip of the Pacific strand, and was a poor little back-settlement thing compared with Mr. Roosevelt; he is the real earthquake, and the most colossal one in history; when he quakes he convulses the entire land, from the Atlantic to the Pacific, and from Canada to the Gulf; not even a village escapes. In six months he has reduced the value of every species of property in the United States—in some cases 10 per cent, in others 20 per cent, in still others 50 per cent. Six months ago the country was worth a hundred and fourteen billions; it is not worth more than ninety billions now. The public confidence is gone; it is possible that the public credit may follow. Mr. Roosevelt is the most formidable disaster that has befallen the country since the Civil War—but the vast mass of the nation loves him, is frantically fond of him, even idolizes him. This is the simple truth. It sounds like a libel upon the intelligence of the human race, but it isn't; there isn't any way to libel the intelligence of the human race.

To descend to small matters: the President is about to start out on another advertising tour; two or three weeks hence he is going to review the Mississippi River—that poor old abandoned waterway which was my field of usefulness when I was a pilot in the days of its high prosperity, nearly fifty years ago. He will start at Cairo and go down the river on a steamboat, and make a noise all the way. He is ready to lend himself to any wildcat scheme that any one can invent for the bilking of the Treasury, provided he can get an advertisement out of it. This time he goes as cat's paw for that ancient and insatiable gang, the Mississippi Improvement conspirators, who for thirty years have been annually sucking the blood of the Treasury and spending it in fantastic attempts to ameliorate the condition of that useless river—apparently that, really to feed the Republican vote out there. These efforts have never improved the river, for the reason that no effort of man can do that. The Mississippi will always have its own way; no engineering skill can persuade it to do otherwise; it has always torn down the petty basket-work of the engineers and poured its giant floods whithersoever it chose, and it will continue to do this. The President's trip is in the interest of another wasted appropriation, and the project will succeed—succeed and furnish an advertisement.

Three or four weeks ago the Mayor of Cairo invited me to come out and join the conspiracy and be a guest, but I said I couldn't make so long a land journey at my time of life, I not being well able to endure such a strain upon my strength, and would therefore excuse myself. Memphis invited me also, and I excused myself upon the same plea. The next I heard was that I had accepted, and was going to steer the President's boat, with my venerable boss, Bixby, standing guard over me in the pilot-house to see that I didn't butt the boat's brains out and leave the country "shy" of a President, as the slang phrase has it. Next appeared a wandering telegram which said I had "declined" to pilot the President's boat. It was a gratuitous slur; I had made no remark which could be construed into a discourtesy to the Chief Magistrate; for the sake of my own self-respect I would not do that. However, some poetry has resulted—therefore I have my compensation. I love poetry—at least I love it when it advertises me.

MARK TWAIN TO THE PRESIDENT.
Note.—Mark Twain declines to pilot the steamboat which will take
President Roosevelt down the Mississippi.

I'm asked to steer that boat of yours,
Theodore! O Theodore!

Between the Mississippi shores,
    Theodore! O Theodore!
But hear me now before you go:
I shall not do it if I know
Myself, because I'll have no show,
    Theodore! O Theodore!

When at the wheel to steer I stand,
    Theodore! O Theodore!
You'll butt in there to take a hand,
    Theodore! O Theodore!
You'll bang that wheel around like—well,
You'll bang it as I cannot tell,
And I can only stand and yell:
    Theodore! O Theodore!

If I should say to you, "Get out,
    Theodore! O Theodore!
You do not know what you're about,"
    Theodore! O Theodore!
You'd gaze upon me fierce and glum;
You'd think that I was going some,
And say I was a liar, by gum,
    Theodore! O Theodore!

Nay, nay! no piloting for me,
    Theodore! O Theodore!
On board of any craft with thee,
    Theodore! O Theodore!
I'm rather old and on the shelf;
I do not care for fame and pelf—
Say, steer the darned old boat yourself,
    Theodore! O Theodore!
               W. J. Lampton.

Dictated September 26, 1907

The trip to Jamestown Fair in Mr. Rogers's yacht to celebrate Robert Fulton Day—Some of the details of what the program was to be, as originally planned.

I will resume the English excursion presently, but not yet, because I wish to talk now about an absurd matter which is of immediate and lively interest to me. As a sort of starting-point I will insert the following newspaper-account of a meeting which took place in New York yesterday evening, the 25th.

At a meeting of the New York Yacht Club last night, presided over by Commodore Cornelius Vanderbilt, the challenge of Sir Thomas Lipton to race a fourth time for the America's Cup was rejected.

This is the first time in the history of the club that a bona fide challenge to race for the historic cup has been declined. The motion to reject the offer of the Irish baronet who has three times so valiantly struggled to "lift the cup," was made by Lewis Cass Ledyard and seconded by J. Pierpont Morgan, both ex-commodores of the New York Yacht Club.

The rejection of the challenge is the result of a struggle that has been going on in the New York Yacht Club for the last five years. J. Pierpont Morgan, Mr. Ledyard, and other prominent men who have controlled its affairs for the last twenty years, have been leading this fight. They represented the owners of the steam yacht contingent in the club. Opposed to them were the owners of sailing yachts.

To Mr. Morgan, Mr. Ledyard and their friends, the *Columbia,* the *Reliance* and all other boats which have defended the cup in recent years have been "freak" yachts.

They believed that the construction of this design of boats did not contribute to the advancement of the science of navigation, and rather retarded it. The owners of sailing yachts have steadfastly upheld the building of racing machines and up to last night's meeting had successfully fought the others.

I have been having an experience which reminds me of a collapsed balloon. I once saw that kind of a balloon. It soared showily skyward, out of a sea of admiring upturned faces, and its aspect was quite sublime; its distended bulk was very impressive; then it exploded, and when it reached the ground it lay there a mere wrinkled and crinkled rag, with none so poor to do it honor.

Since early last May a World's Fair has been struggling along at Jamestown, Virginia, in commemoration of the settling of that village three hundred years ago by Englishmen—the first effort of white people to establish a colony in America. The village itself has disappeared, but the event remains, and still occupies a paragraph in the histories. I went down with Mr. H. H. Rogers, in his yacht, the *Kanawha,* in May, and witnessed the opening of the Fair. That was the President's Day, so called, and he was there and made one of his ten thousand speeches. Since then there has been an Army Day; also a Naval Day; also a Virginia Day; also a Georgia Day, and divers other Days—the usual plan for drawing crowds to World's Fairs in the hope of saving them from bankruptcy. Cornelius Vanderbilt is President of the Robert Fulton Monument Fund Association, and I am Vice President. I became Vice President a year or two ago upon the solicitation of Major General Fred Grant, the son of his father—a high and sufficient distinction; he has no other, but is a good man and a good citizen—virtues which not even his enemies, if he has any, will deny him. He did not earn his major-generalship, but neither did the horse-doctor, Leonard Wood, earn his; and neither did the dishonorable Funston earn his soiled brigadiership. However, those remarks in passing——they are not important. I stipulated that I should be merely a figurehead Vice President, with no duties to perform and nothing to do but pose; still the thing happened that has always happened in these cases—every now and then the Association has put a burden upon me, and I have wept and mourned, but have ended by carrying it.

In the grand stand at Jamestown, last May, Mr. Dearborn, second Vice President of the Association and its one active and energetic member and promoter, said that there was to be a Robert Fulton Day the 23d of the coming September, and that ex-President Grover Cleveland, whom I regard as the greatest and purest American citizen, and only American statesman now living, was to be the orator of the occasion, and I was asked if I would come to Jamestown on that occasion and introduce him to the multitude in the Auditorium. Mr. Rogers spoke up and said that if I would do it he would place the *Kanawha* at my disposal, and I could bring down Mr. Cleveland and his suite in proper state. I said I should be glad to invite Mr. Cleveland to be my guest in the yacht if Harry Rogers, junior, would accompany me as executive officer and relieve me of all responsibility as regarded the ship. Harry accepted, and the matter was settled there and then. I am fond of pomp and fuss and display, and when Mr. Dearborn went on to tell me the program for Robert Fulton Day I was intoxicated with it. Here are some of the details: there would be a squadron of seventeen yachts of the New York Yacht Club beside Commodore Cornelius Vanderbilt's *North Star* and our *Kanawha;* the squadron would sail from New York at two in the afternoon of the 22d of September, the *North Star* in the lead, the *Kanawha* second, and the others following after—a handsome, imposing, and snow-white spectacle. At eight the next morning the squadron would halt and form in the Bay off Old Point Comfort; Commodore Vanderbilt with his suite would pay a formal visit to Mr. Cleveland, on board the *Kanawha,* and be piped over the side like an admiral; he would return to the *North Star,* signal the advance and get under weigh, with his tail of eighteen yachts following in his wake, two hundred yards apart; at a considerable distance up the Bay we should see a double column of foreign and American battleships lying at anchor, with a space of four hundred yards between each two, and up the lane between these majestic creatures we should sail, all our yachts dressed in a fluttering wilderness of gay flags; at the moment that the *Kanawha* should find herself between the first two battleships those two would break out in flags from stem to stern, their invisible multitude of white-clad sailors would instantly appear, linked together, hand in hand, along the yards, and also at that moment those two battleships would thunder forth an ex-president's salute of seven guns. All this would be repeated, ship by ship, as we plowed our way up the mile-long lane; and then if one looked back he would see a striking picture, if it was a calm day, for on the water would lie two towering mile-long mountain-ranges of white smoke densely enveloping the battleships, and not one of them visible through it.

This stately ceremony accomplished, the yachts would come to anchor in a group off the Exposition pier, a mile from shore, and absorb breakfast; at ten o'clock I should convey my guest, and his suite, to the pier in the launch, Commodore Vanderbilt and suite following; on the pier we should be received in style by the minor officials of the Robert Fulton Association, with a military band to help; I should deliver my guest to these officials, and they in turn would deliver him to the President and chief officials of the Jamestown Fair; then all would proceed in carriages to the Auditorium and mount the platform; after music by the great organ I would introduce the ex-President, and he would deliver his oration; at twelve o'clock there would be a grand military review of infantry, cavalry, and artillery before the guest of honor, Major General Grant commanding in person; at one o'clock there would be a state luncheon, with the governors of sixteen States, with their suites, in uniform, present, along with the uniformed chief officials of the military contingent and those of the battleships; at three o'clock there would be a public reception in the Auditorium, by Mr. Cleveland, assisted by the grand-children and great-grandchildren of Robert Fulton, and by Commodore Vanderbilt and me; at seven-thirty in the evening Major General Grant would give a grand banquet to Mr. Cleveland and the others, at which there would be speeches—this in the big Hotel Chamberlin at Old Point Comfort; at half past ten, in the great ball-room of the same hotel, the President and other officials of the Jamestown Fair would give a grand ball in honor of Mr. Cleveland; also there was to be a race for the King of England's Cup; also fireworks; also races by the crews of the battleships—but I do not remember when these gayeties were to have place. However, it was to be a day or two of wonders and excitements and exalting and gratifying display, and I was glad that I was going to be in it.

But hang it, it was all a dream! The entire program was built, from the ground up, out of suppositions. But I didn't know that; I supposed that these handsome arrangements had all been actually made, not merely dreamed. As soon as I got back to Tuxedo I sent my invitation to Mr. Cleveland, at Princeton, and presently I sailed for England on my Oxford errand, and was gone until the 23d of July. Meantime I had learned by newspaper cablegrams, in London, that Mr. Cleveland had been stricken down with an alarming illness. Mrs. Cleveland wrote me that it would now be too great a risk for Mr. Cleveland to accept; that it would probably be long before he was fully recovered from his illness.

I then discovered an astonishing thing, to wit—that Mr. Vanderbilt had gone to Europe without sending the invitation to Mr. Cleveland, therefore I had offered transportation to him when he had not been invited to go and couldn't know whether he was going to need any transportation or not. It also transpired, presently, that when the invitation did go to Mr. Cleveland it went by mail, under a two-cent stamp, instead of being carried to him by an officer of the Association, or by some other properly qualified envoy. To treat an ex-president of the United States in this way was not merely shabby, it was indecent.

Very well, our orator had failed, the breaking down and disintegrating of our grandeurs had begun—begun never to stop. As the 22d of September drew fatefully near, and nearer, and still nearer, detail after detail of our great program crumbled away; toward the last Mr. Dearborn said it seemed impossible to secure an orator, and therefore it would now become a Mark Twain Day in spite of anything that could be done to prevent it—therefore I might as well take upon myself the oratorship; in fact I *must* do it. But I said "No." I said if they could get an orator I wouldn't give him transportation, but I would go down in the yacht and introduce him. An orator was finally secured, and he was a good one, too, and competent—although he was pretty nearly an unknown man.

Robert Fulton Day concluded.

It was Mr. Littleton, of New York. I feel sure he will not remain unknown; I shall watch his career with interest. He is young, but he will get over that; it is a point in his favor.

On the 21st we heard a rumor that the seventeen yachts were not going. It turned out later that this was true; true also that President Vanderbilt, of the Fulton Association, had forgotten to invite them. It was also said that he could have had twenty for the asking. At noon on the 22d Harry and his wife and I were on board and ready. We did not ask for orders, that being Mr. Vanderbilt's affair, not ours. Mr. Dearborn's secretary presently sent us word that the *North Star* would sail at two o'clock, but that Commodore Vanderbilt would not be able to go in her; that I was now *ad interim* President of the Fund Association and would have to act in Mr. Vanderbilt's place, and be chairman at the functions in Jamestown and introduce the speakers at the Auditorium in the daytime, and at the banquet at night. To this was added the information that this course had been determined at a meeting of the Fund officials by unanimous vote. This did not disturb me, for I would not have to act as chairman unless I wished to do it—and of course I should not wish to do it, and would therefore appoint another official to occupy that place.

The humors of the situation were growing: the fleet had shrunk from nineteen sail to two; its Commodore had taken to the woods, and it had no head; the much advertised gay festival had turned into a funeral, and the Commodore was sending his yacht to it as kings send an empty carriage to represent them at the obsequies of a distinguished servant.

The *North Star* sailed at two in the afternoon, and we followed at half past six. The *North Star* was slow, and it was our purpose to overtake her in the neighborhood of Old Point Comfort; but her slowness was beyond computation by our arithmetic, wherefore we passed her at two in the morning. We arrived off the Fair, and cast anchor at 10.25 in the forenoon, and the *North Star* arrived a couple of hours later. She had had no instructions and didn't know where to anchor, so she took up a position at such a distance that she hardly seemed to be a part of the marine display—by this large phrase I mean the display afforded by two war-ships, a pair of little black cheese-box models of Ericsson's *Monitor,* and the *Kanawha.* That part of the original program which was to afford us the spectacle of a double line of majestic battleships stretching toward the horizon and fading into spectral forms in the distance, had shrunk to this wee little handful of floaters. The question was, should the *Kanawha* form up in line of battle now and sail in state, and clothed in flags, up the lane formed by the pair of white war-ships, or would that performance detract from the due solemnity of the occasion and look like a sarcasm? Harry concluded to lie still and wait. Presently Admiral Harrington boarded us, and was soon followed by Captain Collins of the *Brooklyn*.

Properly it was a sad occasion, but there was no sadness in the air; properly Robert Fulton's Festival had turned itself into a funeral, and there ought to have been some tears, but none were shed. The most moving thing, the most uplifting thing, the most eloquent thing in the world, is *perfection*. We are always moved by the perfect thing, let it be what it may. Perfect beauty moves us; perfect ugliness moves us just as surely; perfect music satisfies us; perfect discord delights us; perfect grandeur, perfect majesty, perfect sublimity, always thrill and exalt and content us—and when you suddenly turn these three into an utterly and grotesquely perfect satire upon them, our happy souls are steeped in a drunken delight. After all the noise, all the advertising, all the gorgeous promises and anticipations, the great Robert Fulton Day had withered to this—a collapsed balloon, a prone and wrinkled rag. When I had grasped the whole matchless perfection of the failure, I was glad to be there, and would not have been elsewhere for anything.

In order that nothing might be lacking that could contribute to the splendor of the fiasco, the central day for the annual equinoctial tempest had been selected for Fulton Day. Black clouds came flocking in from the ocean and swept in ragged squadrons across the sky, heralded and accompanied by fierce lightnings and crashing thunders and deluges of rain. There was to have been a return visit to the *Brooklyn;* it had to be given up. There was to have been a luncheon at one o'clock on shore; it had to be given up. The oratory at the Auditorium was postponed until three o'clock, in the hope that the heavy seas might moderate sufficiently, by that time, to let us go ashore; it was not to be. At three, the seas were still so high that we could not be ferried ashore in an ordinary yachting launch and escape a thorough drenching; but at half past three a large government launch came for us and we managed to board it without breaking our necks. When we reached the Auditorium, at four, the audience had been waiting an hour and a half. I introduced Admiral Harrington; Robert Fulton Cutting consented to introduce the others, and in due course the function was over. Harry and my adoptive niece, his wife, went back to the yacht and I supposed they would consult their comfort and stay there, but they didn't; they came to the banquet at eight in the evening. If Mr. Vanderbilt had had some of their spirit—however, he hadn't.

The perfections continued. Fulton's boat, the *Clermont,* was to have been reproduced in fireworks—one of the grand spectacles of the occasion; it didn't happen. The banquet was to have been in the great banqueting hall of the Chamberlin, at Old Point Comfort; it didn't happen. It happened in the New York Building, on the Fair grounds, in a room which was full when two hundred guests sat down. There was a brilliant speech by Mrs. McLean, President General of the Daughters of the Revolution, and I replied to it. Other speeches followed; there was a deal of hearty jollity, and everybody had a good time. That function over, Robert Fulton Day was ended—the most extraordinary day of its kind I have seen in seventy-two years, and one of the most grotesque, and charming, and satisfactory.

The military review had been removed from the program days and days before—a happy inspiration, for if the soldiers had attempted one they would have been drowned. Major General Fred Grant telegraphed from New York that he was sick and couldn't come; Commodore Vanderbilt sent word that he was obliged to remain in New York on a matter of business of international importance.

Now look at that shrinkage! Six months before, we had set out with a prospective ex-President of the United States, a Major General in command of the Atlantic Department, a marine great gun in the person of the Commodore of the New York yacht fleet, a passage in state between a mile of foreign and domestic battleships clothed in bunting and vomiting fire and smoke and thunder; also we were to have a military review and fireworks, and a grand banquet, and as grand a ball—and behold, here was the result! Fulton Day was over and we hadn't had a damned thing!

Mr. Vanderbilt, that weak sister, had backed out because he was afraid to face those audiences and introduce the speakers, he being inexperienced and timid in such situations. Partly that—but mainly because he was afraid to face a fiasco. When he said he must be in New York on the 23d in the interest of a matter of international importance, he knew it wasn't so. The matter of international importance was a meeting of the New York Yacht Club to discuss Sir Thomas Lipton's challenge. In the first place, it was not at all a matter of international importance, and, in the second place, he knew that the meeting was not to take place until the 25th. The race for the America's Cup is in some small sense an international matter, but in an exceedingly small sense. It interests the one-hundredth fraction of 1 per cent of the population of England and America—these being rich sporting men—and stops there; it inflammatorily interests nobody else, and is of not the least value in any substantial way to our nation. As will be seen by reference to the newspaper clipping at the head of this chapter, it is nothing but a "freak" race, and a quite trifling matter. On the other hand, the Robert Fulton Centennial *was* a matter of international importance; and it was far more than that—it was a matter of planetary importance. That Centennial commemorates much the largest event in American history; the results proceeding from it have been more far-reaching, and will be more lasting, than those proceeding from any other event in our history. Our next greatest day is Independence Day, but Independence Day is temporary, whereas Robert Fulton Day is permanent. We are drifting steadily toward monarchy; we have been drifting slowly toward it for thirty years, and now, by help of Mr. Roosevelt, we may be said to be flying toward it; he has hastened the day; it will come—and when it comes, Independence Day will be removed from the national calendar—but Robert Fulton Day will remain, and not only upon our calendar, but upon the calendar of the world, and there it will abide for ages. Mr. Vanderbilt regards a "freak" race as a matter of international importance, and as of more importance than Robert Fulton Day. The innocent man has furnished us his own measure.

Dictated October 1, 1907

The King's garden party at Windsor.

Let us get back to England.

Mr. Ashcroft's note:

> *Saturday, June 22.* Mr. Clemens left at 2:45, with Mr. and Mrs. Henniker Heaton, for the King's garden party at Windsor; returned with the Heatons and Sir Thomas Lipton, and was motored from Paddington to the hotel by Sir Thomas.

The garden party at Windsor was a striking spectacle, and I was sharply reminded of it when I witnessed that memorable show, the Oxford Pageant, four days later—for the garden party itself was like a histrionic scene acted in the open air. When they repeat the Oxford Pageant, a thousand years from now, this garden party can be added to it with advantage—particularly if this part of the pageant shall be transferred to Windsor and exhibited upon that more spacious stage, for nine thousand finely dressed men and women must take part in it, and room will be needed. There will be plenty of it; there would be abundance of room for a hundred thousand, in those far-spreading lawns; also towering out of the lawns like a Gibraltar will be the vast bulk of the Castle, the most imposing and majestic pile of picturesque old architecture in Great Britain—an effect not to be lightly regarded. If it should chance to be mainly a ruin, in that distant day, the effect will rather gain than lose by that circumstance; already it is populous with the ghosts of seven centuries of English monarchs, and one cannot look at it without drifting into dreams of the bygone ages and in fancy seeing the robed and sceptred spectres flit dimly by the windows—and here, present in the flesh, was Edward VII, the latest of the line and the completion of the dreams to date, a fact which powerfully reinforced the impressiveness of the vision by concreting it into a reality, to a certain degree.

The multitude floated hither and thither over the sward, in groups and squadrons, making a gay and ever-changing color-scheme very beautiful to look upon. The first friend I chanced upon was the premier of England, Sir Henry Campbell-Bannerman, and in his company I wandered through the crowds for an hour, shaking hands right and left with strangers, and with an astonishing number of men and women whom I had known in earlier years—some as long ago as thirty-five. I had not supposed I knew so many. Among the oldest of these friends was Ellen Terry. She is fifty-nine, and with her was her new husband, aged thirty-four. She came charging down upon me with both hands extended, and looking as young as her husband, and twice as vivacious. I had known her thirty-five years; the first meeting was at a large dinner party at Mr. Bateman's house—the father of the "Bateman Children." I used to see that pair of pretty little girls frequently in St. Louis, in 1858, when their precocious acting was crowding the theatre nightly with charmed and worshiping admirers. At that time one of them was eleven years old, the other thirteen; they were beautiful little creatures, and a delight to look upon in that ancient day, forty-nine years ago; they are venerable old ladies now, with the snows of many winters upon their heads.

Henry Irving was present at that dinner party at Mr. Bateman's house. He had recently been promoted from comedy to tragedy. The promotion came about in a curious way, if the legend of the day was correct: Irving was a very popular comedian, and had never aspired to tragedy; he was a member of Bateman's company; for a good many years it had been the dream of Bateman's life to appear on the stage in high tragedy, but his managers would never allow him to do it; but he was his own manager now, and proprietor of a theatre, and he made up his mind to make the attempt. He chose as his venture either "The Bells" or "The Lyons Mail"—"The Bells," I think. He studied the part, advertised it widely—then, almost at the last moment, his courage vanished, and he gave up the project. He astonished Irving by asking him to take his place. Irving reluctantly consented, mastered the part in the brief time at his disposal, achieved a triumph, and never played anything but tragedy afterward, at least as a steady diet.

At the garden party, when the time came for presentations, the King and Queen stood in the shelter of a gay pavilion, and back of them were grouped His Royal Highness the Duke of Connaught and his heir; the King of Siam and his heir; and some other great personages and ladies of the court. The public were solidly massed in a semicircle in front of the pavilion, with a grassy space, ten yards wide, between them and it. Ambassador Reid presented me to the King, who shook hands with me cordially—"courteously," the newspapers said, a word not well chosen, for the King is a man who would not know how to be otherwise than courteous to anybody, therefore the word was quite unliterarily superfluous. One newspaper said I patted his Majesty on the shoulder—an impertinence of which I was not guilty; I was reared in the most exclusive circles of Missouri, and I know how to behave. The King rested his hand upon my arm a moment or two, while we were chatting, but he did it of his own accord. A newspaper said I recounted a funny incident of sixteen years before, when I met the King—then Prince of Wales—several times at Homburg. That was incorrect; it was the King that mentioned the funny incident, not I; and I didn't recount it; it was not necessary to recount it, for he evidently remembered it well enough, and I didn't need to refresh my memory about it. I dictated it more than a year ago, and it will be found, some day, in its place in this Autobiography.

When I turned to speak with the Queen I had my hat in my hand, of course—I would not accost any lady with my hat on; such conduct is not permitted in America, and I had my American manners with me. The newspaper which said I talked with her Majesty with my hat on, spoke the truth, but my reasons for doing it were good and sufficient—in fact unassailable. Rain was threatening, the temperature had cooled, and the Queen said, "Pray put your hat on, Mr. Clemens." I begged her pardon, and excused myself from doing it. After a moment or two she said, "Mr. Clemens, put your hat on"—with a slight emphasis on the word "on"—"I can't allow you to catch cold here." When a beautiful queen commands, it is a pleasure to obey, and this time I obeyed—but I had already disobeyed once, which is more than a British subject would have felt justified in doing;

and so it is true, as charged; I did talk with the Queen of England with my hat on, but it wasn't fair in the newspaper man to charge it upon me as an impoliteness, since there were reasons for it which he could not know of.

H.R.H. the Duke of Connaught introduced himself to me, then introduced the Prince his son, and afterward the King of Siam and his heir.

Dictated October 2, 1907

The journey to Liverpool with Tay Pay, and the Lord Mayor's banquet in the evening—Copy of the speech by Tay Pay, and extract from Mr. Clemens's reply to it.

My industries in England began at Tilbury, with the reporters at eight in the morning on the 18th of June, and continued without a break until midnight, the 10th of July. Ashcroft's note:

> To Liverpool with Tay Pay. Banquet in the Town Hall in the evening.

Tay Pay is Irish for T. P., and is a pet name familiar to the British nation; it is short for T. P. O'Connor, M.P. He is a gifted and charming Irishman, and has for many years represented Liverpool in the House of Commons, and is likely to continue to represent it while he lives. He had been invited by the Lord Mayor to introduce me, and we made the trip together—in quite unusual comfort, too, for his lordship had secured from the railway company for my use in going and returning the special car which it has provided for the Prince of Wales. I had not seen so satisfactory a car before, and am not likely to see its like again. It had one sumptuous bed-chamber, and another bed-chamber less sumptuous—the latter for servants, and beyond it a place for baggage; it also had a parlor and a dining room. We reached Liverpool a little after four in the afternoon, and I rested in bed until it was time to go to the banquet. The Lord Mayor was admirably hospitable; he sent his state carriage for me, with a most gorgeously clad captain and crew, consisting of coachman and footmen; and he received me at the municipal palace in his state costume, with his sword at his side and his cocked hat in his hand. I like these large attentions. The banquet was just over when he conducted me into the banqueting hall, so the speech-making began at once. After the usual toasts to the King and the President, and the reading of the usual letters and telegrams, the rest of the business of the evening was proceeded with. I copy from the newspaper:

> The Lord Mayor said that before calling on Mr. T. P. O'Connor to propose the toast of "Our Guest" he would like, on their own behalf and on behalf of all citizens of Liverpool, to offer a most hearty welcome to Dr. Clemens, the guest of the evening. Liverpool highly appreciated the honour which Dr. Clemens had done it in accepting his (the Lord Mayor's) invitation to meet such a body of Liverpool citi-

zens as he had the pleasure of seeing around him that evening. There was no man in the world to-day speaking the English tongue who had brought so much mirth and happiness to the citizens of this Empire and of the United States. That would be a red letter day in the annals of Liverpool. Mark Twain had, he thought, made his year of office to some extent famous, and he hoped that he might be remembered as being the Lord Mayor of Liverpool in Mark Twain's year.

The popular Tay Pay was received with enthusiasm when he rose. I will copy his speech here, because it is full of compliments for me and I shall want to read it over now and then. He said:

> Our friend has a name, our pet name, our family name for him. I will speak of him as Mark Twain. This is the manner in which we address him in our thoughts and private words. I feel it is a great honour to have to propose, in one of England's greatest cities, the toast of the most honoured and respected guest that England has had for many a year. Our guest of this evening has received a welcome of which an Emperor might be proud, and which I do not think any Emperor we know will be likely to receive. We honour him in the first place as a great man of letters. As a humourist he was known to the world many a day ago. His humour, when it first burst upon the horizon of literature, occasioned in this country, above all, the feeling that there was something new and original, and for a long time most people in this country would have thought of Mark Twain simply as a writer of our language who told the stories which gave everybody hours of happiness and mirth. But, as I ventured to say when writing about him some time ago, Mark Twain has come to his own, and people have recognised that what first appeared to be merely the exuberant humour of a great new country, and, to a certain extent, of a new literature, was destined to become one of the classics of the great English language, which is the heritage alike of America and England. It was, perhaps, a surprise to some, as time went on, to find that underneath the wild and exuberant gaiety of his early works our friend Mark Twain had always a serious and earnest purpose. Sometimes in the midst of what appeared to be the very recklessness of his fun you come across in his books some passage of serious purpose and sometimes of tragic earnestness. We know that one of the reasons why he holds so high a place in our esteem and affection is that he is a man who has always fought for the right and always hated the wrong. Within the last two or three years he has dealt stern and sturdy blows at the sordid superstition of Christian Science, and at the gross cruelty of a man who does not deserve the name of King.* In a speech which I heard him make at a banquet in London he uttered something approaching to an apology for the humour of his works. I will not say he deemed it necessary to explain—because no explanation was necessary—that a man may have a serious purpose and yet speak the language of laughter and cheerfulness. I don't know whether I will be right in laying it down as a theory of literature that while the authors of tragedies and melodramas are respected by mankind, it is the great humorist that is really loved by mankind. It is not because laughter is such a relief to a great deal of the necessary sombreness of life that the humorist is so loved, but it is because the man with the gift of humour has always the great gift of a sane and healthy point of view of

---

* Leopold of Belgium.

human life. I have no patience with those decadents who see nothing in life but its squalid side, its impure side, and its ignoble side. Men of that kind may be described as the Jack-the-Rippers of literature. Their influence was demoralising and bad, not teaching men the great lesson that the improvement of man's estate is illimitable, and that in any case it is our duty to live our lives in the best way we can, and to help future generations to higher and better things. I don't know of any writer who has preached the gospel of true, sincere, and genuine optimism better than our guest of this evening. If you were to ask me what has struck me as the most striking quality of Dr. Clemens as a man of letters, I would say it was his originality. There never was a Mark Twain before him, and there never will be again. He stands unique in the absolute originality of his genius and writings. The second quality which is eminently his is his Americanism. I have read a good deal about one of the greatest of Americans—Abraham Lincoln—and the eulogy that was the highest, and best, and shortest is contained in the poem of James Russell Lowell in which he speaks of Abraham Lincoln as the first American in the fullest sense of the word that had occupied the chair of President. As Lincoln came fresh and, as it were, bleeding from the soil, so Dr. Clemens came from the very roots of American life and experience. Beginning in the home of a lawyer, with a brother a journalist, he started in the State of California when that was in its teething stage. He has been a lecturer, traveller, publisher, inventor, and he has even been a financier. Cardinal Richelieu would not have been flattered if he had been told that he was one of the greatest statesmen of the world, but to insert in an obscure poet's corner one of his extremely bad poems he would have regarded as recognising his true genius. In the same way, if I could state that Mark Twain is as big a financier as his friend Mr. Rogers, of the Standard Oil, he would regard it as a compliment. However, I am not in a position to do that, nor, I believe, is Mr. Clemens himself. There was in his career an episode which has especially appealed to us, and was in some respects like an episode in the life of one of the heroes and martyrs of our literary history—I mean Sir Walter Scott. Sir Walter Scott became a member of a great publishing firm. So did Dr. Clemens some years ago, when he was making a large income in what I may be excused in calling one of the finest of human pursuits—that of a journalist. At an early age he started as a compositor, and in his teens he was an acting editor, and I believe there was a large accession of libel suits during that period. From that he went to the broad Mississippi, that great inland sea, and learned the work of pilot. Then he went to the West and became a mining prospector and pioneer. Walter Scott thought with Richelieu and Mark Twain that his true mission was publishing. Face to face with the dark spectre of ruin, he set to work and managed to rescue some of his fortune, but he died in his work. Our friend Dr. Clemens has had a similar experience, but with the tough and unconquerable energy of his race he successfully faced the situation. He travelled all over the world. Thousands of people were only too glad to help him, but he relied only on his own energy, his own unimpeachable integrity of purpose, and at the end of three years of hard drudgery, lecturing in all parts of the world, he was able to say that he was a free man, owing not a penny, and to give an example of a man of courage and energy and honesty in the face of calamity. But, gentlemen, when he travelled down the Mississippi, when he went from one town to another all through America, from office to office; when he saw the mines in Nevada and California, he was going through that great university of life which has made him the great man of letters he is to-day. And when he went down to Oxford I think there was a great meet-ing—I think I may say a great reconciliation—between two things which are apparently opposite. We all know and love Oxford, the greatest sanctuary and treasure-house of tradition and classical learning of many epochs in British his-tory—the representative and symbol of all that is old-world in tradition and his-tory. And when that old-world University held out its hand and gave its highest honour to this man representing a new land, modern traditions, an entirely unique genius untrammelled by the traditions of the old, I say that was a great reconcilia-tion which marked not only an epoch in the life of Dr. Clemens, but of Oxford itself. Finally, we welcome him as an American who has tried many trades. But there is one he has avoided—I don't know why he avoided it, or whether I ought to congratulate or condole with him—he has never been a politician. And why has he never been a politician? Because he occupies the higher and greater position of ambassador—an ambassador plenipotentiary in his omnipotence over our hearts and minds. A diplomatist cannot enter into the passing ferocities of party warfare. He represents something higher and better than one party in one State. He repre-sents all that seeks for the peace and goodwill among all parties in all States. And to-night we welcome him as a great American working for this goodwill between his own race and the races of all mankind. Therefore, I ask you to charge your glasses and wish many years of life to our friend—the glory of his own country and the delight of every other country.

In reply, I did what I seldom do—made a long speech. I did not mean to do it, but was incautious and heedless, and the time slipped by without my noticing it. I will copy only the close of it:

I don't think I will say anything about the relations of amity existing between our two countries. It is not necessary, it seems to me. The ties between the two nations are so strong that I do not think we need trouble ourselves about their being broken. Anyhow, I am quite sure that in my time, and in yours, my Lord Mayor, those ties will hold good, and, please God, they always will. English blood is in our veins, we have a common language, a common religion, a common system of morals, and great commercial interests to hold us together. Home is dear to us all, and now I am departing to my own home beyond the ocean. Oxford has conferred upon me the loftiest honour that has ever fallen to my share of this world's good things. It is the very one I would have chosen as outranking any and all others, the one more precious to me than any and all others within the gift of man or State. During my four weeks sojourn here I have had another lofty honour, a continuous honour, an honour which has flowed serenely along, without obstruction, through all these twenty-six days, a most moving and pulse-stirring honour—the heartfelt grip of the hand, and the welcome that does not descend from the pale grey matter of the brain, but rushes up with the red blood from the heart! It makes me proud and it makes me humble, too. Many and many a year ago I read an anecdote in Dana's "Two Years Before the Mast." It was like this. There was a presumptuous little self-important man in a coasting sloop engaged in the dried apple and kitchen furniture trade, and he was always hailing every ship that came in sight. He did it just to hear himself talk and to air his small grandeur. One day a majestic Indiaman came ploughing by with course on course of canvas towering into the sky, her decks and yards swarming with sailors, bearing a rich freight of precious spices, lading the breezes with gracious and mysterious odours of the Orient. It was a noble spectacle, and, of course, the little skipper popped into the shrouds and squeaked out a hail—"Ship ahoy! What ship is that? And whence and whither?" In a deep and thunderous bass the answer came through the speaking trumpet—"The Begum of Bengal—123 days out from Canton—homeward bound! What ship is that?" Well, it just crushed that poor little creature's vanity, and he squeaked back most humbly "Only the Mary Ann, fourteen hours out from Boston—with nothing to speak of." Oh, what an eloquent word that "only" to express the depth of his humbleness! That is just my case. Just one hour, perhaps, in the twenty-four— not more—I pause and reflect, and then I am humble. Then I am properly meek, and for a little while I am only the Mary Ann, fourteen hours out, cargoed with vegetables and tinware; but during all the other twenty-three hours my vain self-complacency rides high, and then I am a stately Indiaman, ploughing the great seas under a cloud of canvas and laden with the kindest words that have ever been spoken to any wandering alien in this world, and then my twenty-six happy days seem to be multiplied by five, and I am the Begum of Bengal, 123 days out—and (a sigh) homeward bound!

After the banquet there was a reception in one of the great salons, and there I talked with several hundred ladies and gentlemen, as many as twenty-five of whom I had seen in Liverpool before, without suspecting it—thirty-five years before. It was when I had once lectured there. Several of the twenty-five were able to quote remarks from that lecture—a very good feat of memory.

I returned to London on the 11th, and after some final dissipations on the 12th sailed from Tilbury on the morning of the 13th—homeward bound.

I believe that those four weeks in England were the delightfulest of my life.

Dictated October 3, 1907

The story of Mr. Clemens selling a dog to Lieutenant General Nelson A. Miles for three dollars, in Washington in 1867.

In some ways, I was always honest; even from my earliest years I could never bring myself to use money which I had acquired in questionable ways; many a time I tried, but principle was always stronger than desire. Six or eight months ago, Lieutenant General Nelson A. Miles was given a great dinner party in New York, and when he and I were chatting together in the drawing-room before going out to dinner he said,

"I've known you as much as thirty years, isn't it?"

I said,

"Yes, that's about it, I think."

He mused a moment or two and then said,

"I wonder we didn't meet in Washington in 1867; you were there at that time, weren't you?"

I said,

"Yes, but there was a difference; I was not known then; I had not begun to bud—I was an obscurity; but you had been adding to your fine Civil War record; you had just come back from your brilliant Indian campaign in the Far West, and had been rewarded with a brigadier-generalship in the regular army, and everybody was talking about you and praising you. If you had met me, you wouldn't be able to remember it now—unless some unusual circumstance of the meeting had burnt it into your memory. It is forty years ago, and people don't remember nobodies over a stretch of time like that."

I didn't wish to continue the conversation along that line, so I changed the subject. I could have proven to him, without any trouble, that we did meet in Washington in 1867, but I thought it might embarrass one or the other of us, so I didn't do it. I remember the incident very well. This was the way of it:

I had just come back from the *Quaker City* Excursion, and had made a contract with Bliss of Hartford to write "The Innocents Abroad." I was out of money, and I went down to Washington to see if I could earn enough there to keep me in bread and butter while I should write the book. I came across William Swinton, brother of the historian, and together we invented a scheme for our mutual sustenance; we became the fathers and originators of what is a common feature in the newspaper world now—the syndicate. We became the old original first Newspaper Syndicate on the planet; it was on a small scale, but that is usual with untried new enterprises. We had twelve journals on our list; they were all weeklies, all obscure and poor, and all scattered far away among the back settlements. It was a proud thing for those little newspapers to have a Washington correspondence, and a fortunate thing for us that they felt in that way about it. Each of the twelve took two letters a week from us, at a dollar per letter; each of us wrote one letter per week and sent off six duplicates of it to these benefactors, thus acquiring twenty-four dollars a week to live on—which was all we needed, in our cheap and humble quarters.

Swinton was one of the dearest and loveliest human beings I have ever known, and we led a charmed existence together, in a contentment which knew no bounds. Swinton was refined by nature and breeding; he was a gentleman by nature and breeding; he was highly educated; he was of a beautiful spirit; he was pure in heart and speech. He was a Scotchman, and a Presbyterian; a Presbyterian of the old and genuine school, being honest and sincere in his religion, and loving it, and finding serenity and peace in it. He hadn't a vice—unless a large and grateful sympathy with Scotch whisky may be called by that name. I didn't regard it as a vice, because he was a Scotchman, and Scotch whisky to a Scotchman is as innocent as milk is to the rest of the human race. In Swinton's case it was a virtue, and not an economical one. Twenty-four dollars a week would really have been riches to us if we hadn't had to support that jug; because of the jug we were always sailing pretty close to the wind, and any tardiness in the arrival of any part of our income was sure to cause us some inconvenience.

I remember a time when a shortage occurred; we had to have three dollars, and we had to have it before the close of the day. I don't know now how we happened to want all that money at one time; I only know we had to have it. Swinton told me to go out and find it—and he said he would also go out and see what he could do. He didn't seem to have any doubt that we would succeed, but I knew that that was his religion working in him; I hadn't the same confidence; I hadn't any idea where to turn to raise all that bullion, and I said so. I think he was ashamed of me, privately, because of my weak faith. He told me to give myself no uneasiness, no concern; and said in a simple, confident, and unquestioning way, "the Lord will provide." I saw that he fully believed the Lord would provide, but it seemed to me that if he had had my experience—

But never mind that; before he was done with me his strong faith had had its influence, and I went forth from the place almost convinced that the Lord really would provide.

I wandered around the streets for an hour, trying to think up some way to get that money, but nothing suggested itself. At last I lounged into the big lobby of the Ebbitt House, which was then a new hotel, and sat down. Presently a dog came loafing along. He paused, glanced up at me and said, with his eyes, "Are you friendly?" I answered, with my eyes, that I was. He gave his tail a grateful little wag and came forward and rested his jaw on my knee and lifted his brown eyes to my face in a winningly affectionate way. He was a lovely creature—as beautiful as a girl, and he was made all of silk and velvet. I stroked his smooth brown head and fondled his drooping ears, and we were a pair of lovers right away. Pretty soon Brigadier General Miles, the hero of the land, came strolling by in his blue and gold splendors, with everybody's admiring gaze upon him. He saw the dog and stopped, and there was a light in his eye which showed that he had a warm place in his heart for dogs like this gracious creature; then he came forward and patted the dog and said,

"He is very fine—he is a wonder; would you sell him?"

I was greatly moved; it seemed a marvelous thing to me, the way Swinton's prediction had come true. I said,

"Yes."

The General said,

"What do you ask for him?"

"Three dollars."

The General was manifestly surprised. He said,

"Three dollars? Only three dollars? Why that dog is a most uncommon dog; he can't possibly be worth less than fifty. If he were mine, I wouldn't take a hundred for him. I'm afraid you are not aware of his value. Reconsider your price if you like, I don't wish to wrong you."

But if he had known me he would have known that I was no more capable of wronging him than he was of wronging me. I responded with the same quiet decision as before,

"No—three dollars. That is his price."

"Very well, since you insist upon it," said the General, and he gave me three dollars and led the dog away, and disappeared up stairs.

In about ten minutes a gentle-faced middle-aged gentleman came along, and began to look around here and there and under tables and everywhere, and I said to him,

"Is it a dog you are looking for?"

His face was sad, before, and troubled; but it lit up gladly now, and he answered,

"Yes—have you seen him?"

"Yes," I said, "he was here a minute ago, and I saw him follow a gentleman away. I think I could find him for you if you would like me to try."

I have seldom seen a person look so grateful—and there was gratitude in his voice, too, when he conceded that he would like me to try. I said I would do it with great pleasure, but that as it might take a little time I hoped he would not mind paying me something for my trouble. He said he would do it most gladly—repeating that phrase "most gladly,"—and asked me how much. I said—

"Three dollars."

He looked surprised, and said,

"Dear me it is nothing! I will pay you ten, quite willingly."

But I said,

"No, three is the price"—and I started for the stairs without waiting for any further argument, for Swinton had said that that was the amount that the Lord would provide, and it seemed to me that it would be sacrilegious to take a penny more than was promised.

I got the number of the General's room from the office clerk, as I passed by his wicket, and when I reached the room I found the General there caressing his dog, and quite happy. I said,

"I am sorry, but I have to take the dog again."

He seemed very much surprised, and said,

"Take him again? Why, he is my dog; you sold him to me, and at your own price."

"Yes," I said, "it is true—but I have to have him, because the man wants him again."

"What man?"

"The man that owns him; he wasn't my dog."

The General looked even more surprised than before, and for a moment he couldn't seem to find his voice; then he said,

"Do you mean to tell me that you were selling another man's dog—and knew it?"

"Yes, I knew it wasn't my dog."

"Then why did you sell him?"

I said,

"Well that is a curious question to ask. I sold him because you wanted him. You offered to buy the dog; you can't deny that. I was not anxious to sell him—I had not even thought of selling him, but it seemed to me that if it could be any accommodation to you—"

He broke me off in the middle, and said,

"*Accommodation* to me? It is the most extraordinary spirit of accommodation I have ever heard of—the idea of your selling a dog that didn't belong to you—"

I broke him off there, and said,

"There is no relevancy about this kind of argument; you said yourself that the dog was probably worth a hundred dollars, I only asked you three; was there anything unfair about that? You offered to pay more, you know you did. I only asked you three; you can't deny it."

"Oh what in the world has that to do with it! The crux of the matter is that you didn't own the dog—can't you see that? You seem to think that there is no impropriety in selling property that isn't yours provided you sell it cheap. Now then—"

I said,

"Please don't argue about it any more. You can't get around the fact that the price was perfectly fair, perfectly reasonable—considering that I didn't own the dog—and so arguing about it is only a waste of words. I have to have him back again because the man wants him; don't you see that I haven't any choice in the matter? Put yourself in my place. Suppose you had sold a dog that didn't belong to you; suppose you—"

"Oh," he said, "don't muddle my brains any more with your idiotic reasonings! Take him along, and give me a rest."

So I paid back the three dollars and led the dog down stairs and passed him over to his owner, and collected three for my trouble.

I went away then with a good conscience, because I had acted honorably; I never could have used the three that I sold the dog for, because it was not rightly my own, but the three I got for restoring him to his rightful owner was righteously and properly mine, because I had earned it. That man might never have gotten that dog back at all, if it hadn't been for me. My principles have remained to this day what they were then. I was always honest; I know I can never be otherwise. It is as I said in the beginning—I was never able to persuade myself to use money which I had acquired in questionable ways.

Now then, that is the tale. Some of it is true.

Dictated October 5, 1907

Mr. Robert Porter's visit to Mr. Clemens, in Tuxedo; also Francesca's and Dorothy's—Copy of one of Dorothy's stories— an Indian tale.

Robert Porter arrived from England and Oxford a week or ten days ago, in the first trip of that wonderful ship which all the nations and all the newspapers have been admiring and talking about ever since—the *Lusitania*. Mr. Porter was my host during those days that I spent in Oxford. He is of the staff of the London *Times,* and has come over here on a special mission for that paper. He came out to Tuxedo for a day or two, and among other matters of interest he told us of his ingenious invention whereby he communicates with his family daily, by cable, without expense: whenever his wife and daughter take up the *Times* at breakfast, in Oxford, they eagerly seek the American cables and run their eyes down the column, paying no attention to any of its contents except the scattered names of our public men. The moment they light upon one of those names their interest is intensely concentrated there, and upon the word which precedes the name and the word which follows it; these two are always adjectives, and hidden in their insides is Porter's private and confidential message to the wife and daughter. Necessarily, the name which Mr. Porter has occasion to use oftenest is the President's; that name's attendant adjectives convey messages of affection, condition of health, and various other matters of a family nature—consequently the President's name appears in the cables with a good deal of frequency. The adjectives that precede and follow the names of our other public men convey information of other sorts to the Oxford household. Just as Mr. Porter was leaving Oxford a near neighbor, who is a friend of his family and is also an acquaintance of mine, ran over and gave him an errand to do for her in New York. She dearly hoped he could accomplish it for her, but she had her doubts. In any case, she wanted to be relieved of the misery of suspense as soon as possible, so she begged him to write her the result with all possible dispatch. Mr. Porter said,

"I'll cable it."

"Oh by no means," exclaimed the lady, in whose mind cabling is associated with ruinous expense, and so she was aghast at the idea, no matter whom the cost might fall upon.

"Yes," said Porter, "I'll cable it. You must not be kept waiting. It is too important for that; I will cable it at the expense of the *Times*."

The lady was distressed at such an idea, and also surprised. She said gravely,

"But will that be honest?"

"Oh no," said Porter, "but that is no matter. The *Times* will never find it out."

When Mr. Porter arrived in New York he carried the lady's affair through successfully, the first day. He wanted to send the good news at once, but in order to do it he was obliged to have the use of Mr. Bryan's name, and he couldn't get it, for the reason that the unexpected and the almost impossible happened: Bryan was quiet during two whole days, consequently there was no way to utilize him in a cablegram; but on the third day the permanent candidate for the Presidency did something, or said something, and at breakfast the next morning his name appeared in a cablegram in the *Times* in a sentence beginning "The irrepressible Bryan." That was the desired adjective, and Mrs. Porter at once telephoned that waiting lady, saying "The cablegram has come, and everything is as you wanted it."

When the *Lusitania* was half way across the Atlantic, Mr. Porter, assisted by the ship's engineers, made some nice and carefully worked-out calculations; then based some predictions upon the calculations and sent the predictions by wireless to the London *Times* and the New York *World*—to wit, that the new ship's average speed on the voyage would be twenty-three knots and two-tenths per hour, and that she would make the run to New York in so many days and so many hours—I have forgotten the precise details. The prediction as to knots was only *a tenth of a knot out of the way,* if my memory is right, and the prediction as to the length of the voyage missed the precisely correct figure by only *six minutes!* Prophecy has not arrived at this exactness before, I judge, either in ancient times or modern.

Francesca and her mother arrived from England ten days ago, and spent a couple of days with us. Ten days earlier Dorothy, my latest little shipmate, arrived here and we had her delightful society during seven days and nights. She is just eleven years old, and seems to be made of watch-springs and happiness. The child was never still a moment, when she wasn't asleep, and she lit up this place like the sun. It was a tremendous week, and an uninterruptedly joyful one for us all. After she was gone, and silence and solitude had resumed their sway, we felt as if we had been through a storm in heaven.

Dorothy is possessed with the idea of becoming a writer of literature, and particularly of romance, and it was a precious privilege to me to egg her on, and beguile her into working her imagination. She was intensely in earnest. I was her amanuensis; she did the dictating. I never betrayed myself with a laugh, but the strain which I had to put upon every muscle and nerve and tendon in me, to keep from breaking out, almost made a physical wreck of me sometimes. She is swift with the pen, she is hampered by no hesitations when she is dictating, and she is even a more desperate speller than ever Susy was. We began our mornings early—as early as half past eight—and from that time until nine in the evening there were no breaks in our industries. I say *our* industries because I always assisted her in them until I broke down at noon; then Miss Lyon stood a watch till about three; then I resumed my watch. In order to save myself from perishing, I usually persuaded Dorothy to devote this half-afternoon watch to literature. By grace of this subterfuge, I was enabled to lie down and perform; I lay on one lounge on the back porch and she on another one at my side; then she dictated her stories glibly, and I set them down. When a story was finished I dictated it back to her from my manuscript, and she wrote it down. I got around telling her why I observed this practice; I didn't want her to know my reason, which was that I wanted the tale in her own brisk and tumultuous handwriting, adorned with her own punctuation—I mean the absence of it—and steeped in the charm of her incomparable spelling. Her tales were of a highly romantic order, and she chose highly romantic scenes and episodes for them; but at that point romance usually took a rest; it didn't extend itself to the names of her characters; *any* sort of name would answer for her heroes—and five times in six they bore names of so plebeian and flat and pulpy a sort as to almost disqualify those persons from doing heroic things. But to me those forlorn names were golden, and I wouldn't have traded them for the most high-sounding ones in the world's romantic literature. One day she dictated an Indian romance, and I set it down. The little rascal was all innocence and candor, and was seldom suspicious, but it cost me many lies to keep her so, because every now and then as the sentences fell felicitously from her lips they hit me hard, and my suppressed laughter made my body shake; and when she detected that, I could notice a vague suspicion in her voice when she would ask what was the matter with me. The answer which came nearest to satisfying her was that I was feeling a little chilly; but that had also another effect, which was not a happy one for me, for it aroused her affectionate solicitude and she would not rest until I had taken some whisky to keep me from catching cold. Before we got through with the brief Indian tale—which I am going to insert here just as she wrote it, just as she spelled it, just as she punctuated it—the loving little creature had inflicted so many whiskies on me that my efficiency as an amanuensis was a little damaged and rickety; and if the tale had gone on a little longer I should have been incapable.

> in the very Depts of the forest the day was a sultry day and Henry Potter was tiered of hunting when suddenly a wild war hoop sounded very near him great heavens it's the Idains what can I do the hoop was comming nearer and nearer I must run for my life now he thought but then yes I must oh what can I do— the hoop was almost upon him now and from the other direction was comming another hoop good heavens it must be a band there is no chance I must hide in that hollow tree the indains by this time were there they at once began to camp then one of the Idains said we must have some wood for our fire there is a good tree there he pointed to the one where Henry was Hiding the men of the tribe began to approch the tree with tomahaks one of the Idains saw the hollow in the tree and said oh there must be an annimal in that tree I will get that for my supper Henry was thinking a nice supper you'll have out of me and even in all the danger that was around him he could not help smailing the Idains split the hole in the tree wider and when Henry saw his eye he knew no more———————————
> ————————————————————————————
> when he awoke he was in a large tent the tent of the chife who was glaring down upon him I wish I could make you see that tent with all the grim old warriors in thier coustans* ranged about thier chief eager to see what was to be done with this new captive—he will be burned cried some others he will be stoned with a lot of other opinons—at last the chief said put him under gaurd for tonight tomorrow we will decide what to do with him. Henry saw an indain girl in the ranks of women start and look toward him—then he was led away it was about 11 oclock that night when a gentle footstep came lightly into the tent then said a voice he thought he knew come with me at once who are you asked Henry I am Margearet oh Margearet cried Henry Margearet was a girl who had disseepered from the selte-met 2 years ago she was dressed as an Indain girl and was taned† she and Henry loved each other and were to be married she said we have no time for talking now come Henry followed her and she led him safely to the edge of the forest where they lived happily ever afterwards.

Dorothy reeled off this masterful tale just as she has punctuated it—without a pause anywhere, and just as if Henry's adventures were passing before her eyes at the moment and she was simply setting them down according to the facts. I was glad when "Margearet" got her young man safely out to the edge of the forest where they lived happily ever afterwards—without the formality of a marriage—for I thought for a moment that she was going to furnish the pair a family without any superfluous preliminaries and I would get another whisky-drench by consequence.

* Costumes.
† Tanned.

Dictated October 7, 1907

The manner in which Mr. Clemens is reported in Tuxedo to have declined and accepted a dinner invitation—Copy of postal from Sioux Falls relating little girl's remarks about Mr. Clemens's picture—Copy of postal from Mr. Twichell in regard to poem by Omar Khayyam.

It often pains me to note how this world is given to slander: that beautiful Mrs. M. was here yesterday afternoon, and she told a story which she said was on its rounds in Tuxedo Park; according to this story, I was called up on the telephone, a couple of weeks ago, by a lady for whom I have a strong but concealed aversion, who said,

"Mr. Clemens, can you come and dine with us to-night?"

"Oh I am unspeakably sorry, but I have an engagement which is imperative."

"Make it to-morrow night, then."

"It's too bad, and I am ever so sorry, but I have to be in New York to-morrow night."

"Well then what's the matter with Thursday?"

After a thoughtful pause—

"Oh hell, I'll come to-night!"

This whole legend is a lie on its face, by verdict of circumstantial evidence, which is the best of all testimony. Miss Lyon noticed a couple of discrepancies and pointed them out: she said,

"Mr. Clemens never goes to the telephone at all, and he never uses profane language in the presence of ladies whom he does not like."

That purified my reputation, as far as Mrs. M. is concerned, but of course it remains a wreck as far as regards the rest of the community. However, I must take the bitter along with the sweet, like the rest of our race. The bitter comes oftenest, perhaps, but when the sweet comes, in its turn, it heals our wounds and satisfies us with ourselves again. I was still suffering from that anecdote this morning, but the mail has brought me a healer, and once more I am glad to be alive. It comes from a very far country:

> Sioux Falls, S.D.
> Sept. 25.
>
> Dear Sir:
>
> The following true incident occurred in Sioux Falls: a little four-year-old girl who was one day visiting at the house of a friend, sat for a long time thoughtfully gazing at a picture of Mark Twain which stood on the mantel-shelf; at length, folding her hands and raising her eyes reverently, she said, "We have got a picture of Jesus like that, too, only ours has more trimmings on it."

Here is another post-card. This one is out of the long ago, and shows age in all its aspects. How strange it seems that there was once a time when I had never heard of Omar

Khayyam! The postmark is Hartford, and the card is from Reverend J. H. Twichell, and is addressed "Mark Twain. City."

> Wed. morning.
> Read (if you haven't) the extracts from Omar Khayyam on the first page of this morning's Courant. I think we'll have to get the book. I never yet came across anything that uttered certain thoughts of mine so adequately. And it's only a translation. Read it, and we'll talk it over. There is something in it very like the passage of Emerson you read me last night, in fact identical with it in thought.
> Surely this Omar was a great poet. Anyhow he has given me an immense revelation this morning.
> Hoping that you are better,
>
> J. H. T.

Our Post-Office Department is still something of a lame duck, in our day, as it was then. The postmark on this card gives the date December 22, and stops there, neglecting to furnish the year. The year must have been 1879, I think—indeed I feel almost sure of it, by persuasion of several circumstances of that time which remain in my memory.

When the card arrived, I had already read the dozen quatrains in the morning paper, and was still steeped in the ecstasy of delight which they had occasioned; no poem had ever given me so much pleasure before, and none has given me so much pleasure since; it is the only poem I have ever carried about with me; it has not been from under my hand for twenty-eight years.

Dictated October 10, 1907

The horizon likened to the Deity's mouth, laughing at the human race—Series of newspaper headlines showing what He may be laughing at—Mr. Clemens comments upon No. 10, and No. 11— The President's hunting of tame bears.

I must get that stupendous fancy out of my head. At first it was vague, dim, sardonic, wonderful; but night after night, of late, it is growing too definite—quite too clear and definite, and haunting, and persistent. It is the Deity's mouth—His open mouth— laughing at the human race! The horizon is the lower lip; the cavernous vast arch of the sky is the open mouth and throat; the soaring bend of the Milky Way constitutes the upper teeth. It is a mighty laugh, and deeply impressive—even when it is silent; I can endure it then, but when it bursts out in crashing thunders of delight, and the breath gushes forth in a glare of white lightnings, it makes me shudder.

Every night He laughs, and every morning I eagerly search the paper to see what it is He has been laughing at. It is always recorded there in the big headlines; often one doesn't have to read what follows the headlines, the headlines themselves tell the story sufficiently; as a rule, I am not able to see what there is to laugh at; very frequently the occurrences seem to merely undignify the human race and make its acts pitiful and pathetic, rather than matter for ridicule. This morning's paper contains the following instances:

No. 1.

SPECIAL TRAIN TO SAVE HER DOG'S LIFE.

———

Rich, Childless Woman Spent Thousands in Vain Efforts for Her Pet.

It is matter for pity, not mirth. No matter what the source of a sorrow may be, the sorrow itself is respectworthy.

No. 2.

MOTHER AND CHILD FOUND STARVING.

———

Mrs. Engel Subsisted on Dry Crusts that Her Daughter, Aged Three, Might Live.

No. 3.

CHRISTIAN SCIENCE ON TRIAL AGAIN.

———

Watsons Charged with Letting Son Die— Defense: "We Firmly Believed We Were Right."

No. 4.

MASKED MAN BOUND GIRL.

———

Left Her Gagged and Nearly Unconscious While Robbing House.

No. 5.

STRANGLED BOY WITH SHOESTRING.

———

Child's Body, with Arms Bound, Found in a Lonely Spot Near Bridgeport.

No. 6.

KNOCKED PREACHER DOWN AFTER FUNERAL SERVICE.

———

Husband Was Angry Because Clergyman Failed to Mention His Name.

No. 7.

Children See Mother Murdered.

COLUMBUS, O., Oct. 9.—Fred Butt, a hard drinker, who had beaten his wife till she separated from him and applied for a divorce, broke into her room to-day.

"Won't you let me live with you any more?" he asked.

"No," she replied.

Butt then shot her to death, shot himself slightly and drank acid while their two children screamed in terror. The husband will die.

No. 8.

BIG GANG ROBBING EUROPE'S CHURCHES.

American Collectors Get Spoils, an Antiquary Says, Paying Very High Prices.

No. 9.

JUMPS FROM HOME TO HOLY JUMPERS.

Miss Cole, Crossed in Love, Joins Strange Sect, but Father Finds Her.

Miss Arabella Mae Cole, a pretty girl of seventeen, was found by her father at Zarepath, the headquarters of the Pentacostal Union Church, near Bound Brook, N. J., yesterday. Miss Arabella Mae, rather sentimental and romantic, jumped her fine home in Philadelphia three weeks ago and joined the sect whose members the worldly and wicked call "The Holy Jumpers," because they dance during their supplications, even as did the original David. Miss Arabella Mae's father, a retired merchant, took her all unwilling to Philadelphia.

No. 10.

Humanity to Deer Promoted by Hunting Them with Hounds.

PLATTSBURG, N. Y., Oct. 9.—A resolution favoring the passage of a law providing for a period when deer may be hunted with hounds was unanimously adopted by the Essex County Republican Convention to-day. The resolution declares it to be the "sense of the Republican party that safety to man, humanity to deer and sport for hunters would be all furthered by two weeks' hounding of deer."

No. 11.

GOOD BEAR WEATHER FOR THE PRESIDENT.

He Ought to Have Captured One Bruin Yesterday if Ever, the Natives Say.

O'HARA'S SWITCH, near Stamboul, La., Oct. 9.—Not since early morning have any tidings been received from the President's hunting camp, and then they were confined to a mere statement that preparations had been made for a busy day.

The best local judges of the conditions are of the opinion that the day must have been one of activity if not of results. The rain has left a faultless sky and the temperature is all that could be desired. These circumstances, taken with the softened condition of the ground, the residents say, should make it possible for a party who go well equipped to get a bear if there is one in the Bayou Tensas.

I have to grant that Nos. 10 and 11 are properly matters for laughter, they being distinctly and charmingly ridiculous. There is something fresh and touching about that Republican Convention's idea of humanity. When we read of red Indians chasing a helpless white girl who is fleeing for her life, with bullets and arrows whizzing around her, the Indians' humanity is not apparent to us; the Indians seem to us only cruel and brutal, and all our sympathies are with the frightened girl. The fleeing deer is just as frightened, just as timid, just as void of offence; the deer's sharp agony and the girl's is the same, and it would seem to be logical that if the Republican hunter's performance is sport, and legitimate, the Indian's performance must be also regarded as sport, and legitimate.

If the bears were not in danger, instance No. 11 would be humorous; as it is, however, only the President's side of it is funny. Those are tame bears down there—at least they are quite without courage—and no considerable amount of glory can be gotten out of murdering them. When they see a man they turn and flee. Bears are the bogy of children—and even the children are not afraid of those poor canebrake bears down there; they are as helpless and as harmless as the flying girl and the fleeing deer; but bear hunting has a large and heroic sound to a President who was manifestly brought up on dime-novels, and he greatly enjoys having the eyes of two continents fixed upon him while he valiantly marches against a tame bear with a cloud of dogs and a cloud of armed body-guards and fellow sports and sutlers and secretaries, and finds his bear and murders him at long distance, giving him no chance to fight for his life even if he should have the disposition to do it. The President is taking too much trouble; he could get the same sport, and the same large advertisement, and the same immunity from personal danger, by slaughtering helpless bears in a menagerie—and the travel and fatigue would be less. Those bears are doing no harm; they are not wrecking a nation's prosperities to buy the votes of the ignorant, the envious, and the malicious; their lives are precious to them; no good is done to any one by taking them away. There is other game to be had where the taking of life can be justified, on the ground that the animals are hurtful, where the pursuit of them is not less dignified than is the pursuit of tame bears, and where the sport to be had is really exciting and exhilarating. The President of the United States ought to hire a squaw and a comb and get at it.

Dictated October 11, 1907

The impending marriage of Gladys Vanderbilt to Count Széchényi—The danger to American girls in marrying titled

Latterly, the newspapers are full of the impending marriage of Gladys, sister of
Commodore Cornelius Vanderbilt, with Count Széchényi. It is a love match—of this
there is no doubt. Two years ago the bride accomplished her twenty-first year and came
into her fortune of twelve million five hundred thousand dollars—but the groom is
very rich, and could have supported her without that. His is a great and old house.
I knew the head of it in Vienna nine or ten years ago, a charming man, and of high
character. He told me how to pronounce his name. He said that in my long residence
in the Territory of Nevada I must have become acquainted with the one wild bird in
America which prefers sand and sage-brush to a Christian life, and therefore inhabits
Nevada instead of stepping over into California, which it could do at no cost of time
or trouble. He was referring to the sage-hen. He said that if you pronounce sage-hen
swiftly, and add about half a syllable onto the end of it, the result would be a close
resemblance to his name.

It is well enough for American girls to marry Englishmen, Scotchmen or Irishmen,
but they ought to draw the line there, as regards foreigners. When they marry a foreigner of any other nationality the chances are nine to one that they will regret it—if
the foreigner be a Frenchman, an Italian, a German, a Russian or a Turk; and when he
is an Austrian, a Hungarian, or a Bohemian, of noble degree, the chances are ninety-
nine to one that in time the girl will wish she hadn't made the venture. In other foreign
countries she takes her husband's rank; in the last three mentioned she has no rank at
all, and is a nobody. Her husband is in society, but she isn't. He attends court functions,
the ambassadorial functions, and the dinners, luncheons, and teas, of the nobility, while
she abides lonely and homesick in her palace and rocks the baby. She could have social
relations with the merchant class, but she mustn't; it would be out of character, out of
taste, and the nobility would frown upon it. John Hay told me these things many years
ago, after he had served a term at the Austrian court as our chargé d'affaires, and they
were repeated to me in Vienna by persons qualified to testify.

In Vienna Mrs. Clemens and I visited with some frequency the American wife of an
Austrian nobleman, a lady whom I had known when she was a young girl. Her husband
went everywhere, she went nowhere; she was marooned in her home, and her only society,
her only companionship in her solitude, was her little boy aged seven. Her husband was
poor when she married him; she enriched him with a great fortune. She loved him, and
he loved her dearly, and would gladly have taken her into society if he could have done
it, but it was out of his power.

I was told of a case which strikingly exhibits the boiler-iron rigidity of the rule: in
the Revolution of 1848 a young Scotch officer in the imperial guard saved the young
Emperor's life at desperate risk to his own; he was rewarded with promotion after promotion; he was retained near the monarch's person; he was *Hof-fähig*, and was thus entitled
to the privileges enjoyed by the nobility. He was courted, he was envied, he was exceed-

ingly popular, and was regarded as the most fortunate man of his time. He had been poor, but he was able to marry now. His untitled Scotch sweetheart had been faithfully waiting for him; he went home and married her and brought her to Vienna, and laid all his honors at her feet. They had to stay where he laid them, for it was not her privilege to pick up any one of them and wear it. The society in which he moved was barred against her. She had been a plebeian, she was still a plebeian, yet the custom which forbade her to associate with the aristocracy also forbade her to associate with plebeians; she was as hopelessly marooned as was ever a castaway on a desert island in the ocean; neither the Emperor's gratitude nor the nation's could ameliorate her desolate estate. But—behold, and give praise! Glory and high fortune had not deteriorated her gallant Scot; he was gallant still: he flung his honors, his dignities, his offices and his emoluments out of the window, so to speak, and shook the dust of Austria off his feet and departed with his bride to begin life again and make a home elsewhere. If he had been an Austrian, instead of a foreigner, his case would have been different, and pleasanter. All that his wife needed would have been to become *Hof-fähig,* and this could have been promptly and easily managed by conferring hereditary nobility upon her great-grandfather in his grave, a procedure which had been in use in China ages before Austria adopted it. But this poor Scotch girl's great-grandfather was a foreigner, and not eligible.

Speaking of Vienna reminds me that I am invited to give a public reading, next week, in the village of Tuxedo, which is clustered around the little railway station just outside the Park. Reading on the platform is an art by itself, and I learned it all of a sudden in Vienna—and purely by accident—after having practised it in a lame and incompetent way for several years all over America and all round the globe. This education came late, for when I had made my good-night bow to an audience in a South African town two years before, I took my farewell of the platform for good and all. I reserved the privilege of reading and talking gratis, for charities, when I should wish to do it, but I was resolved never to talk for pay again. I have read and talked many times since, in these eleven years, but never for pay. It is a delight to read and talk when one is not charging anything for it, for that condition sets you free from all sense of responsibility, and you are quite sure to have a good time.

When I read for a charity the first time, in Vienna, I was still ignorant; it was when I read there the second time that I learned the art. No, I am making a mistake. I had long known the art of reading when one knows his chapters by heart and has in the course of many repetitions of them thoroughly weeded them, revised them, perfected them, and learned exactly the right way to deliver them; his art is perfect then, and cannot be improved. But it was another form that I learned in Vienna. It was there that I learned to read effectively without knowing my lesson. This art is just as good as the other one, just as telling, just as satisfactory, just as sure and just as triumphant, and has one great merit—to wit, that it requires little or no preparation, and possesses also another great merit, which is this: since you are acquainted with nothing but the outline of your piece and must invent the phrasing on the spot, this fresh and unstudied phrasing is pretty frequently happy—not to go further and say sparkling.

Platform "readings" continued—a Dickens reading as seen by Mr. Clemens.

What is called a "reading," as a public platform entertainment, was first essayed by Charles Dickens, I think. He brought the idea with him from England in 1867. He had made it very popular at home, and he made it so acceptable and so popular in America that his houses were crowded everywhere, and in a single season he earned two hundred thousand dollars. I heard him once during that season; it was in Steinway Hall, in December, and it made the fortune of my life—not in dollars, I am not thinking of dollars; it made the real fortune of my life in that it made the happiness of my life; on that day I called at the St. Nicholas Hotel to see my *Quaker City* Excursion shipmate, Charley Langdon, and was introduced to a sweet and timid and lovely young girl, his sister. The family went to the Dickens reading, and I accompanied them. It was forty years ago; from that day to this the sister has never been out of my mind nor heart.

Mr. Dickens read scenes from his printed books. From my distance, he was a small and slender figure, rather fancifully dressed, and striking and picturesque in appearance. He wore a black velvet coat with a large and glaring red flower in the buttonhole. He stood under a red-upholstered shed behind whose slant was a row of strong lights—just such an arrangement as artists use to concentrate a strong light upon a great picture. Dickens's audience sat in a pleasant twilight, while he performed in the powerful light cast upon him from the concealed lamps. He read with great force and animation, in the lively passages, and with stirring effect. It will be understood that he did not merely read, but also acted. His reading of the storm scene in which Steerforth lost his life, was so vivid, and so full of energetic action, that his house was carried off its feet, so to speak.

Dickens had set a fashion which others tried to follow, but I do not remember that any one was any more than temporarily successful in it. The public reading was discarded after a time, and was not resumed until something more than twenty years after Dickens had introduced it; then it rose and struggled along for a while in that curious and artless industry called Authors' Readings. When Providence had had enough of that kind of crime the Authors' Readings ceased from troubling and left the world at peace.

Lecturing and reading were quite different things; the lecturer didn't use notes, or manuscript, or book, but got his lecture by heart, and delivered it night after night in the same words during the whole lecture season of four winter months. The lecture field had been a popular one all over the country for many years when I entered it in 1868; it was then at the top of its popularity; in every town there was an organization of citizens who occupied themselves in the off season, every year, in arranging for a course of lectures for the coming winter; they chose their platform people from the Boston Lecture Agency list, and they chose according to the town's size and ability to pay the prices. The course usually consisted of eight or ten lectures. All that was wanted was that it should pay expenses; that it should come out with a money balance at the end of the season was not required. Very small towns had to put up with fifty-dollar men and women, with one or two second-class stars at a hundred dollars each as an attraction; big towns employed hundred-dollar men and women altogether, and added John B. Gough, or Henry Ward Beecher, or Anna Dickinson, or Wendell Phillips, as a compelling attraction; large cities employed this whole battery of stars. Anna Dickinson's price was four hundred dollars a night; so was Henry Ward Beecher's; so was Gough's—when he didn't charge five or six hundred. I don't remember Wendell Phillips's price, but it was high.

I remained in the lecture field three seasons—long enough to learn the trade; then domesticated myself, in my new married estate, after a weary life of wandering, and remained under shelter at home for fourteen or fifteen years. Meantime, speculators and money-makers had taken up the business of hiring lecturers, with the idea of getting rich at it. In about five years they killed that industry dead, and when I returned to the platform for a season, in 1884, there had been a happy and holy silence for ten years, and a generation had come to the front who knew nothing about lectures and readings and didn't know how to take them nor what to make of them. They were difficult audiences, those untrained squads, and Cable and I had a hard time with them sometimes.

Cable had been scouting the country alone for three years with readings from his novels, and he had been a good reader in the beginning, for he had been born with a natural talent for it; but unhappily he prepared himself for his public work by taking lessons from a teacher of elocution, and so by the time he was ready to begin his platform work he was so well and thoroughly educated that he was merely theatrical and artificial, and not half as pleasing and entertaining to a house as he had been in the splendid days of his ignorance. I had never tried reading as a trade, and I wanted to try it. I hired Major Pond, on a percentage, to conduct me over the country, and I hired Cable as a helper, at six hundred dollars a week and expenses, and we started out on our venture. It was ghastly! At least in the beginning. I had selected my readings well enough, but had not studied them. I supposed it would only be necessary to do like Dickens—get out on the platform and read from the book. I did that, and made a botch of it. Written things are not for speech; their form is literary; they are stiff, inflexible, and will not lend themselves to happy and effective delivery with the tongue—where their purpose is to merely entertain, not instruct; they have to be limbered up, broken up, colloquialized, and turned into the common forms of unpremeditated talk—otherwise they will bore the house, not entertain it. After a week's experience with the book I laid it aside and never carried it to the platform again; but meantime I had memorized those pieces, and in delivering them from the platform they soon transformed themselves into flexible talk, with all their obstructing precisenesses and formalities gone out of them for good.

One of the readings which I used was a part of an extravagant chapter, in dialect, from "Roughing It" which I entitled "His Grandfather's Old Ram." After I had memorized it it began to undergo changes on the platform, and it continued to edit and revise itself, night after night, until, by and by, from dreading to begin on it before an audience I came to like it and enjoy it. I never knew how considerable the changes had been when I finished the season's work; I never knew until ten or eleven years later, when I took up that book in a parlor in New York one night to read that chapter to a dozen friends of the two sexes who had asked for it. *It wouldn't read*—that is, it wouldn't read aloud.

I struggled along with it for five minutes, and then gave it up and said I should have to tell the tale as best I might from memory. It turned out that my memory was equal to the emergency; it reproduced the platform form of the story pretty faithfully, after that interval of years. I still remember that form of it, I think, and I wish to recite it here, so that the reader may compare it with the story as told in "Roughing It," if he pleases, and note how different the spoken version is from the written and printed version.

The story of "His Grandfather's Old Ram" as recited by Mr. Clemens.

The idea of the tale is to exhibit certain bad effects of a good memory; the sort of memory which is too good; which remembers everything and forgets nothing; which has no sense of proportion, and can't tell an important event from an unimportant one, but preserves them all, states them all, and thus retards the progress of a narrative, at the same time making a tangled, inextricable confusion of it and intolerably wearisome to the listener. The historian of "His Grandfather's Old Ram" had that kind of a memory. He often tried to communicate that history to his comrades, the other surface miners, but he could never complete it, because his memory defeated his every attempt to march a straight course; it persistently threw remembered details in his way that had nothing to do with the tale; these unrelated details would interest him and sidetrack him; if he came across a name, or a family, or any other thing that had nothing to do with his tale, he would diverge from his course to tell about the person who owned that name, or explain all about that family—with the result that as he plodded on he always got further and further from his grandfather's memorable adventure with the ram; and finally went to sleep before he got to the end of the story, and so did his comrades. Once he did manage to approach so nearly to the end, apparently, that the boys were filled with an eager hope; they believed that at last they were going to find out all about the grandfather's adventure and what it was that had happened. After the usual preliminaries, the historian said:

"Well, as I was a-sayin', he bought that old ram from a feller up in Siskiyou County and fetched him home and turned him loose in the medder, and next morning he went down to have a look at him, and accident'ly dropped a ten-cent piece in the grass and stooped down—so—and was a-fumblin' around in the grass to git it, and the ram he was a-standin' up the slope taking notice; but my grandfather wasn't taking notice, because he had his back to the ram and was int'rested about the dime. Well, there he was, as I was a-sayin', down at the foot of the slope a-bendin' a-way over—so—fumblin' in the grass, and the ram he was up there at the top of the slope, and Smith—Smith was a-standin' there—no, not jest there, a little further away—fifteen foot perhaps—well, my grandfather was a-stoopin' 'way down—so—and the ram was up there observing, you know, and Smith he . . . . (musing) . . . . . the ram he bent his head down, so . . . . Smith of Calaveras . . . . . no, no it couldn't ben Smith of Calaveras—I remember now that he—b' George it was Smith of Tulare County—course it was, I remember it now perfectly plain. Well, Smith he stood just there, and my grandfather he stood just here, you know, and he was a-bendin' down just so, fumblin' in the grass, and when the old ram see him in that attitude he took it fur an invitation—and here he come! down the slope thirty mile an hour and his eye full of business. You see my grandfather's back being to him, and him stooping down like that, of course he—why sho! it *warn't* Smith of Tulare at all, it was Smith of Sacramento—my goodness, how did I ever come to get them Smiths mixed like that—why, Smith of Tulare was jest a nobody, but Smith of Sacramento—why the Smiths of Sacramento come of the best Southern blood in the United States; there warn't ever any better blood south of the line than the Sacramento Smiths. Why look here, one of them married a Whitaker! I reckon that gives you an idea of the kind of society the Sacramento Smiths could 'sociate around in; there ain't no better blood than that Whitaker blood; I reckon anybody'll tell you that. Look at Mariar Whitaker—there was a girl for you! Little? Why yes, she was little, but what of that? Look at the heart of her—had a heart like a bullock—just as good and sweet and lovely and generous as the day is long; if she had a thing and you wanted it, you could have it—have it and welcome; why Mariar Whitaker couldn't have a thing and another person need it and not get it—get it and welcome. She had a glass eye, and she used to lend it to Flora Ann Baxter that hadn't any, to receive company with; well, she was pretty large, and it didn't fit; it was a No. 7, and she was excavated for a 14, and so that eye wouldn't lay still; every time she winked it would turn over. It was a beautiful eye and set her off admirable, because it was a lovely pale blue on the front side—the side you look out of—and it was gilded on the back side; didn't match the other eye, which was one of them browny-yellery eyes and tranquil and quiet, you know, the way that kind of eyes are; but that warn't any matter—they worked together all right and plenty picturesque. When Flora Ann winked, that blue and gilt eye would whirl over, and the other one stand still, and as soon as she begun to get excited that hand-made eye would give a whirl and then go on a-whirlin' and a-whirlin' faster and faster, and a-flashing first blue and then yaller and then blue and then yaller, and when it got to whizzing and flashing like that, the oldest man in the world couldn't keep up with the expression on that side of her face. Flora Ann Baxter married a Hogadorn. I reckon that lets you understand what kind of blood she was—old Maryland Eastern Shore blood; not a better family in the United States than the Hogadorns. Sally—that's Sally Hogadorn—Sally married a missionary, and they went off carrying the good news to the cannibals out in one of them way-off islands round the world in the middle of the ocean somers, and they et her; et him too, which was irregular; it warn't the custom to eat the missionary, but only the family, and when they see what they had done they was dreadful sorry about it, and when the relations sent down there to fetch away the things they said so—said so right out—said they was sorry, and 'pologized, and said it shouldn't happen again; said 'twas an accident. Accident! now that's foolishness; there ain't no such thing as an accident; there ain't nothing happens in the world but what's ordered just so by a wiser Power than us, and it's always fur a good purpose; we don't know what the good purpose was, some-times—and it was the same with the families that was short a missionary and his wife. But that ain't no matter, and it ain't any of our business; all that concerns us is that it was a special providence and it had a good intention. No sir, there ain't no such thing as an accident. Whenever a thing happens that you think is an accident you make up your mind it ain't no accident at all—it's a special providence. You look at my Uncle Lem— what do you say to that? That's all I ask you—you just look at my Uncle Lem and talk to me about accidents! It was like this: one day my Uncle Lem and his dog was down town, and he was a-leanin' up against a scaffolding—sick, or drunk, or somethin'—and there was an Irishman with a hod of bricks up the ladder along about the third story, and his foot slipped and down he come, bricks and all, and hit a stranger fair and square and knocked the everlasting aspirations out of him; he was ready for the coroner in two minutes. Now then people said it was an accident. Accident! there warn't no accident about it; 'twas a special providence, and had a mysterious, noble intention back of it. The idea was to save that Irishman. If the stranger hadn't been there that Irishman would have been killed. The people said 'special providence—sho! the dog was there—why didn't the Irishman fall on the dog? Why warn't the dog app'inted?' Fer a mighty good reason—the dog would 'a' seen him a-coming; you can't depend on no dog to carry out a special providence. You couldn't hit a dog with an Irishman because—lemme see, what was that dog's name . . . . . (musing) . . . . oh yes, Jasper—and a mighty good dog too; he wa'n't no common dog, he wa'n't no mongrel; he was a composite. A composite dog is a dog that's made up of all the valuable qualities that's in the dog breed—kind of a syndicate; and a mongrel is made up of the riffraff that's left over. That Jasper was one of the most wonderful dogs you ever see. Uncle Lem got him of the Wheelers. I reckon you've heard of the Wheelers; ain't no better blood south of the line than the Wheelers. Well, one day Wheeler was a-meditating and dreaming around in the carpet factory and the machinery made a snatch at him and first you know he was a-meandering all over that factory, from the garret to the cellar, and everywhere, at such another gait as—why, you couldn't even see him; you could only hear him whiz when he went by. Well you know a person can't go through an experience like that and arrive back home the way he was when he went. No, Wheeler got wove up into thirty-nine yards of best three-ply carpeting. The widder was sorry, she was uncommon sorry, and loved him and done the best she could fur him in the circumstances, which was unusual. She took the whole piece—thirty-nine yards, and she wanted to give him proper and honorable burial, but she couldn't bear to roll him up; she took and spread him out full length, and said she wouldn't have it any other way. She wanted to buy a tunnel for him but there wasn't any tunnel for sale, so she boxed him in a beautiful box and stood it on the hill on a pedestal twenty-one foot high, and so it was monument and grave together, and economical— sixty foot high—you could see it from everywhere—and she painted on it 'To the loving memory of thirty-nine yards best three-ply carpeting containing the mortal remainders of Millington G. Wheeler go thou and do likewise.'"

At this point the historian's voice began to wobble and his eyelids to droop with weariness, and he fell asleep; and so from that day to this we are still in ignorance; we don't know whether the old grandfather ever got the ten-cent piece out of the grass; we haven't any idea what it was that happened, or whether anything happened at all.

The difference between reading and reciting, continued.

Upon comparing the above with the original in "Roughing It," I find myself unable to clearly and definitely explain why the one can be effectively *recited* before an audience and the other can't; there is a reason, but it is too subtle for adequate conveyance by the lumbering vehicle of words; I sense it, but cannot express it; it is as elusive as an odor—pungent, pervasive, but defying analysis. I give it up. I merely know that the one version will recite, and the other won't.

By reciting I mean, of course, delivery from memory; neither version can be read effectively from the book. There are plenty of good reasons why this should be so, but there is one reason which is sufficient by itself, perhaps: in reading from the book you are telling another person's tale at second-hand; you are a mimic, and not the person involved; you are an artificiality, not a reality—whereas in telling the tale without the book you absorb the character and presently become the man himself, just as is the case with the actor. The greatest actor would not be able to carry his audience by storm with a book in his hand; reading from the book renders the nicest shadings of delivery impossible—I mean those studied fictions which seem to be the impulse of the moment, and which are so effective: such as, for instance, fictitious hesitancies for the right word; fictitious unconscious pauses; fictitious unconscious side remarks; fictitious unconscious embarrassments; fictitious unconscious emphases placed upon the wrong word, with a deep intention back of it—these, and all the other artful fictive shades which give to a recited tale the captivating naturalness of an impromptu narration, can be attempted by a book reader, and are attempted, but they are easily detectable as artifice, and although the audience may admire their cleverness and their ingenuity as artifice, they only get at the intellect of the house, they don't get at its heart; and so the reader's success lacks a good deal of being complete.

When a man is reading from a book, on the platform, he soon realizes that there is one powerful gun in his battery of artifice that he can't work with an effect proportionate to its calibre: that is the *pause*—that impressive silence, that eloquent silence, that geometrically progressive silence which often achieves a desired effect where no combination of words howsoever felicitous could accomplish it. The pause is not of much use to the man who is reading from a book, because he cannot know what the exact length of it ought to be; he is not the one to determine the measurement—the audience must do that for him; he must perceive by their faces when the pause has reached the proper length, but his eyes are not on the faces, they are on the book; therefore he must determine the proper length of the pause by guess; he cannot guess with exactness, and nothing but exactness, absolute exactness, will answer. The man who recites without the book has all the advantage; when he comes to an old familiar remark in his tale which he has uttered nightly for a hundred nights—a remark preceded or followed by a pause—the faces of the audience tell him when to end the pause. For one audience, the pause will be short; for another a little longer; for another a shade longer still; the performer must vary the length of the pause to suit the shades of difference between audiences. These variations of measurement are so slight, so delicate, that they may almost be compared with the shadings achieved by Pratt and Whitney's ingenious machine which measures the five-millionth part of an inch. An audience is that machine's twin; it can measure a pause down to that vanishing fraction.

I used to play with the pause as other children play with a toy. In my recitals, when I went reading around the world for the benefit of Mr. Webster's creditors, I had three or four pieces in which the pauses performed an important part, and I used to lengthen them or shorten them according to the requirements of the case, and I got much pleasure out of the pause when it was accurately measured, and a certain discomfort when it wasn't. In the negro ghost story of "The Golden Arm" one of these pauses occurs just in front of the closing remark. Whenever I got the pause the right length, the remark that followed it was sure of a satisfactorily startling effect, but if the length of the pause was wrong by the five-millionth of an inch, the audience had had time in that infinitesimal fraction of a moment to wake up from its deep concentration in the grisly tale and foresee the climax, and be prepared for it before it burst upon them—and so it fell flat. In Susy's little Biography of me she tells about my proceeding to tell this ghost tale to the multitude of young lady students at Vassar College—a tale which poor Susy always dreaded—and she tells how this time she gathered her fortitude together and was resolved that she wouldn't be startled; and how all her preparations were of no avail; and how, when the climax fell, that multitude of girls "jumped as one man"—which is an indication that I had the pause rightly measured that time.

In the "Grandfather's Old Ram" a pause has place; it follows a certain remark, and Mrs. Clemens and Clara, when we were on our way around the world, would afflict themselves with my whole performance every night, when there was no sort of necessity for it, in order that they might watch the house when that pause came; they believed that by the effect they could accurately measure the high or low intelligence of the audience. I knew better, but it was not in my interest to say so. When the pause was right, the effect was sure; when the pause was wrong in length, by the five-millionth of an inch, the laughter was only mild, never a crash. That passage occurs in "His Grandfather's Old Ram" where the question under discussion is whether the falling of the Irishman on the stranger was an accident, or was a special providence. If it was a special providence, and if the sole purpose of it was to save the Irishman, why was it necessary to sacrifice the stranger? "The dog was there. Why didn't he fall on the dog? Why wa'n't the dog app'inted? Becuz *the dog would 'a' seen him a-comin'.*" That last remark was the one the family waited for. A pause *after* the remark was absolutely necessary with any and all audiences, because no man, howsoever intelligent he may be, can instantly adjust his mind to a new and unfamiliar, and yet for a moment or two apparently plausible, logic which recognizes in a dog an instrument too indifferent to pious restraints and too alert in looking out for his own personal interest to be safely depended upon in an emergency requiring self-sacrifice for the benefit of another, even when the command comes from on high. The absurdity of the situation always worked its way into the audience's mind, but it had to have time.

Dictated October 18, 1907

First Marconigrams sent across the Atlantic yesterday—President comes within three miles of flushing a bear—Mr. Clemens mentions the great comet of 1858, the year in which the first cablegram was sent.

I believe I have now arrived at that occasion in Vienna already spoken of when, by accident, I learned how to read on the platform without previous preparation—a most valuable discovery! As I recall it now—never mind it, let it go for the present; this morning's news possesses a larger and more immediate interest:

First Marconigrams Sent Across Atlantic to The World.

London (via Marconi wireless via Glace Bay, N. S.), Oct. 17, 1907.
To the New York World:
Greetings to the Americans through the New York World in the words of Burns:

> Man to man the world o'er
> > Shall brithers be for a' that.

(Lord) LOREBURN, Lord High Chancellor of England.

London (via Marconi wireless via Glace Bay, N. S.), Oct. 17, 1907.
To the New York World:
Greater miracles than those of old bewilder us to-day.

(Andrew) CARNEGIE.

London (via Marconi wireless via Glace Bay, N. S.), Oct. 17, 1907.
To the New York World:
I earnestly trust that this marvellous discovery may tend to enrich the mutual affection and confidence between the two great branches of the English-speaking race.

(Ven. William Macdonald) SINCLAIR,
Archdeacon of London and Chairman of the Pilgrims' Committee.

Two colossal historical incidents had place yesterday; incidents which must go echoing down the corridors of time for ages; incidents which can never be forgotten while histories shall continue to be written. Yesterday, for the first time, business was opened to commerce by the Marconi Company, and wireless messages sent entirely across the Atlantic, straight from shore to shore; and on that same day the President of the United States for the fourteenth time came within three miles of flushing a bear. As usual, he was far away, nobody knew where, when the bear burst upon the multitude of dogs and hunters, and equerries, and chamberlains in waiting, and sutlers, and cooks, and scullions, and Rough Riders, and infantry and artillery, and had his customary swim to the other side of a pond and disappeared in the woods. While half the multitude watched the place where he vanished, the other half galloped off, with horns blowing, to scour the State of Louisiana in search of the great hunter. Why don't they stop hunting the bear altogether, and hunt the President? He is the only one of the pair that can't be found when he is wanted.

By and by the President was found and laid upon the track, and he and the dogs followed it several miles through the woods, then gave it up, because Rev. Dr. Long, the "nature fakir," came along and explained that it was a cow track. This is a sorrowful ending to a mighty enterprise. His Excellency leaves for Washington to-day, to interest himself further in his scheme of provoking a war with Japan with his battleships. Many wise people contend that his idea, on the contrary, is to compel peace with Japan, but I think he wants a war. He was in a skirmish once at San Juan Hill, and he got so much moonshine glory out of it that he has never been able to stop talking about it since. I remember that at a small luncheon party of men at Brander Matthews's house, once, he dragged San Juan Hill in three or four times, in spite of all attempts of the judicious to abolish the subject and introduce an interesting one in its place. I think the President is clearly insane in several ways, and insanest upon war and its supreme glories. I think he longs for a big war wherein he can spectacularly perform as chief general and chief admiral, and go down to history as the only monarch of modern times that has served both offices at the same time.

Yesterday Marconi's stations on the two sides of the Atlantic exchanged messages aggregating five thousand words, at the rate of forty or fifty words per minute. It is a world event. I met Mr. Marconi in London seven years ago, in company with Sir Hiram Maxim; he was confident, at that time, that he would some day be able to send wireless telegrams across the ocean, without relays, but not many other persons shared this confidence with him. I am glad to have seen him and talked with him, and glad that I have seen and talked with Professor Morse, and Graham Bell, and Edison, and others among the men who have added the top story to the majestic edifice of the world's modern material civilization. No fuss was made over the great event of yesterday, either in England or America; the time for that will come later, as was the case with Morse's telegraph.

I remember the wave of jubilation and astonishment that swept the planet in the summer of 1858 when the first electric message was sent across the Atlantic under the sea, by cable. It did not seem believable; it seemed altogether unbelievable, yet we had to believe it and go through the several stages of getting reconciled to it and adjusted to it; then, as usual in these vast matters, it presently became a commonplace. That was the year of the great comet—the most illustrious wanderer of the skies that has ever appeared in the heavens within the memory of men now living. It was a wonderful spray of white light, a light so powerful that I think it was able to cast shadows—however, necessarily it *could*, there is no occasion to seek for evidence of that; there is sufficient evidence of it in the fact that one could read a newspaper by that light at any time in the night. I know this because I did it myself. I was a cub pilot in those days, and had the glory and the splendor of that great companionship for my solace and delight on my lonely watch in the pilot-house during many and many a night. More than once I read a newspaper by the light that streamed from that stupendous explorer of the glittering archipelagoes of space.

By and by Marconi, like Morse, will have his triumph. It was not my fortune to be present when Morse had his, but I remember the stir it made. Morse, clothed in stars and ribbons and crosses contributed in his honor by the chief scientific societies and sceptred rulers of the world, sat, old and bowed with age, upon the stage of the Academy of Music, in presence of several thousand persons, and worked the key himself and exchanged messages over land and under sea with monarchs and municipalities scattered far and wide around the rotundity of the globe. I missed that colossal event, but I hope to be present when it is repeated, with Marconi at the key.

Dictated October 21, 1907

Roosevelt kills his bear at last—or was it a cow?

Alas, the President has got that cow after all! If it was a cow. Some say it was a bear—a real bear. These were eye-witnesses, but they were all White House domestics; they are all under wages to the great hunter, and when a witness is in that condition it makes his testimony doubtful. The fact that the President himself thinks it was a bear does not diminish the doubt, but enlarges it. He was once a reasonably modest man, but his judgment has been out of focus so long now that he imagines that everything he does, little or big, is colossal. I am sure he honestly thinks it was a bear, but the circumstantial evidence that it was a cow is overwhelming. It acted just as a cow would act; in every detail, from the beginning to the end, it acted precisely as a cow would act when in trouble; it even left a cow track behind, which is what a cow would do when in distress, or, indeed, at any other time if it knew a President of the United States was after it—hoping to move his pity, you see; thinking, maybe he would spare her life on account of her sex, her helpless situation, and her notorious harmlessness. In her flight she acted just as a cow would have done when in a frenzy of fright, with a President of the United States and a squadron of bellowing dogs chasing after her; when her strength was exhausted, and she could drag herself no further, she did as any other despairing cow would have done—she stopped in an open spot, fifty feet wide, and humbly faced the President of the United States, with the tears running down her cheeks, and said to him with the mute eloquence of surrender: "Have pity, sir, and spare me. I am alone, you are many; I have no weapon but my helplessness, you are a walking arsenal; I am in awful peril, you are as safe as you would be in a Sunday-school; have pity, sir—there is no heroism in killing an exhausted cow."

Here are the scare-heads that introduce the wonderful dime-novel performance:

ROOSEVELT TELLS OF HUNTING TRIP

Ate All the Game, Except a Wildcat, and That Had a Narrow Escape.

Charged Into the Canebrake After Bear and Hugged the Guides After the Kill.

There it is—he hugged the guides after the kill. It is the President all over; he is still only fourteen years old, after living half a century; he takes a boy's delight in showing off; he is always hugging something or somebody—when there is a crowd around to see the hugging and envy the hugged. A grown person would have milked the cow and let her go; but no, nothing would do this lad but he must kill her and be a hero. The account says:

> The bear slain by the President was killed Thursday, and the killing was witnessed by one of the McKenzies and by Alex Ennolds.

These names will go down in history forever, in the company of an exploit which will take a good deal of the shine out of the twelve labors of Hercules. Testimony of the witnesses:

> They say that the President's bearing was extremely sportsmanlike.

Very likely. Everybody knows what mere sportsmanlike bearing is, unqualified by an adjective, but none of us knows quite what it is when it is extremely sportsmanlike, because we have never encountered that inflamed form of the thing before. The probabilities are that the sportsmanlike bearing was not any more extremely sportsmanlike than was that of Hercules; it is quite likely that the adjective is merely emotional, and has the hope of a raise of wages back of it. The chase of the frightened creature lasted three hours, and reads like a hectic chapter in a dime-novel—and this time it is a chapter of pathetically humble heroics. In the outcome the credit is all with the cow, none of it is with the President. When the poor hunted thing could go no further it turned, in fine and picturesque defiance, and gallantly faced its enemies and its assassin. From a safe distance Hercules sent a bullet to the sources of its life; then, dying, it made fight—so there *was* a hero present after all. Another bullet closed the tragedy, and Hercules was so carried away with admiration of himself that he hugged his domestics and bought a compliment from one of them for twenty dollars. But this résumé of mine is pale; let us send it down to history with the colors all in it:

> The bear slain by the President was killed Thursday, and the killing was witnessed by one of the McKenzies and by Alex Ennolds. They say that the President's bearing was extremely sportsmanlike. The animal had been chased by the dogs for three hours, the President following all the time. When at last they came within

hearing distance the President dismounted, threw off his coat and dashed into the canebrake, going to within twenty paces of the beast. The dogs were coming up rapidly, with the President's favorite, Rowdy, in the lead.

The bear had stopped to bid defiance to the canines when the President sent a fatal bullet from his rifle through the animal's vitals. With the little life left in it the bear turned on the dogs. The President then lodged a second bullet between the bear's shoulders, breaking the creature's neck. Other members of the party soon came up, and the President was so rejoiced over his success that he embraced each of his companions. Ennolds said: "Mr. President, you are no tenderfoot."

Mr. Roosevelt responded by giving Ennolds a $20 note.

There was little hunting yesterday, because the dogs encountered a drove of wild hogs, more ferocious than bears. One of the best dogs was killed by a boar.

There were daily swims in the lake by members of the party, including the President.

"The water was fine," he said, "and I did not have the fear of alligators that some seem to have."

Whatever Hercules does is to him remarkable; when other people are neglectful, and fail to notice a detail, here and there, proper for admiration and comment, he supplies the omission himself. Mr. Ennolds lost a chance; if he had been judiciously on watch he could have done the alligator compliment himself, and got another twenty for it.

The paragraph about the wild hogs naïvely furnishes a measure of the President's valor: he isn't afraid of a cow, he isn't afraid of an alligator, but—

Dictated New York, October 25, 1907

Mr. O. called, and left the regards of Baron Tauchnitz. Mr. O. is here to arrange terms with several authors and the heirs of authors. Terms for living copyrights, also terms for expired copyrights. So the honest son is following in the footsteps of the honest father. This father and this son have one prodigious distinction which I believe no other publishers have ever enjoyed—to wit, that they were never thieves. I have known a great many publishers, and have cordially liked them and have not been above associating with them, but with the exception of these two, I have never known one who was not a thief.

I will explain. The Moral Law is above the Constitution of the United States, and says "thou shalt not steal." That is final. From that verdict there is no appeal. The Constitution—which is a thief and the pal of thieves—forbids perpetual copyright. Under protection of this power, and by warrant of it, the United States Government becomes a thief in its turn, and steals an author's book in the 42d year of its age and gives it to the publishing trade. The publisher, in his turn, publishes the stolen book and steals the author's share of the profit along with his own. And thus he becomes a plain, straightforward, unmitigated thief, and no cunning casuistries, no ingenuities of argument can cleanse him from that stain. In spite of constitutions and statutes the book remains the author's perpetual property, and who so trespasses upon it without his consent belongs in jail.

Dictated November 1, 1907

Clipping from morning paper criticising President Roosevelt's connection with the recent panic—Mr. Clemens discusses the panic—Copy of letter which Mr. Clemens wrote to the Knickerbocker Trust Company—Incident which occurred in the home of Mr. L. (Mr. Clemens's lawyer) in the Knobs of East Tennessee, showing how primitive the natives are to this day.

It is like a breath of fresh air in the Black Hole of Calcutta to at last come across a sane remark about our insane President. I find it in the morning papers:

NEW HAVEN, Conn., Oct. 31.—President Roosevelt was in one breath pilloried and the next defended before the Economic Club of this city to-night. John W. Alling, a Connecticut lawyer, accused him of causing the panic last week, and F. R. Agar of this city also scored him.

Henry Clews, the New York banker, took up the cudgels in his defense, and asserted that unless America ceased to be controlled by the money power the country would go the way of the Cities of Sodom and Gomorrah and of the Roman Empire.

Mr. Alling said:

"Roosevelt is immensely popular with the masses. Mr. Roosevelt is essentially like the old Crusade leaders, powerful, arrogant, conceited, with a halo of heavenly inspiration, a born leader, bound by no party ties, himself the 'whole thing,' in search of valiant deeds, claiming a supernatural power to detect and uncover and punish 'the wealthy malefactor.'

"Followed, as he thinks, by the whole people, he is the most dangerous foe to constitutional liberty that has ever existed in this country. The financial panic calls for an opinion as to how far 'my policies' are responsible for it. He has been conscious that he was making a prodigious stir, and warned that it would bring on a panic. He has noticed how general market values, the true index of credit, would rise in the hope that he would listen to the suggestions made to him and would slump on hearing the same old warlike trumpet blasts.

"President Roosevelt is alone responsible for raising this railroad rate question. It was not a plank in the Republican platform. In the Senate it did not command a majority of the Republicans. In the Senate Committee a *minority of the Republicans* and the Democrats combined and this Rooseveltian measure was intrusted to the Democrat Senator Tillman.

"The overwhelming popularity of President Roosevelt jammed it through. Now what has been the result? It was patent to everybody from the instant it appeared likely that the power to fix rates was to be taken from the railroads and put into the hands of Commissioners in the interest of the shippers, Commissioners, every one of whom could be removed at once by Mr. Roosevelt for what he might deem inefficiency or neglect.

"The value of railroad properties began to decline and their credit to disappear. In the meantime, the business of the country enormously increasing, and just at the time when the railroads needed capital by the hundreds of millions to equip themselves for the work to be done, their power to raise the necessary capital vanished."

This has been a strange panic. It has not strongly resembled any other panic in the history of the country. The panic to which we have long been accustomed, is a tempest, a cyclone, a hurricane, which sweeps away values and lays industries waste much as the cyclone fells forests and leaves towns a tumultuous confusion of wreckage; but this new panic is of a new sort; it is a still panic, a noiseless panic, a smothered panic; it makes no noise, there are no hysterics, no frenzies; it is not like a storm; it is like a blight, a paralysis; it is as if the business activities of our eighty millions of people had suddenly come to a standstill, leaving everybody idle, frightened, wondering. The conditions make one think of a mighty machine which has slipped its belt and is still running by previous and perishing impulse, but accomplishing nothing. There has not been a single important failure in the financial world. There are no crashes, no thunder-bursts, no earthquakes; there is nothing but a creepy and awful stillness, and an atmosphere charged with apprehension.

The phrase "laying off" has become common, almost wearisomely so. We hear of this and that and the other vast concern laying off a thousand men, two thousand men, three thousand men—and this makes us familiar with the conditions obtaining among the multitude of millionaire industries of the country; but there is a far wider and more disastrous laying off that does not find its way into the newspapers; this is the laying off that is going on under the surface, all over the land—the discharging of one employee out of every three in all the humble little shops and industries from one end of America to the other—a laying off which is not to be counted by thousands, as in the case of the giant industries, but by hundreds of thousands, with an aggregate reaching into millions, and making the laying off by the great companies a trifle, and insignificant by comparison. The four-servant families are getting along with three now; the three-servant families are getting along with two; the two-servant families are getting along with one; the one-servant families are getting along without any. The day governess with six pupils has lost three of them; the day governess with three pupils has lost all of them; counter-clerks, male and female, have been discharged in shoals; there is not a single trade in the country that has not reduced its force and imperiled the bread and butter of one family or a thousand. A blight has fallen everywhere, and Mr. Roosevelt is the author of it.

Last week a prodigious and universal crash was impending, and but for one thing would have happened: the millionaire "bandits" whom the President is so fond of abusing in order to get the applause of the gallery, stepped in and stayed the desolation. Mr. Roosevelt promptly claimed the credit of it, and there is much evidence that this inebriated nation thinks he is entitled to it. The great financiers saved every important bank and trust company in New York but one—the Knickerbocker Trust Company. That one had no friends, and was obliged to suspend, with obligations amounting to forty-two millions—mainly deposits. No one will lose by the temporary suspension, but twenty-two thousand depositors are more or less inconvenienced by it. Its Board of Blunderers have been shilly-shallying for a week, and trying to invent ways to save its stockholders from an assessment. Of course I had to be a depositor in the only concern that got into trouble—it was just my luck. I had fifty-one thousand dollars there. I feel hurt, I feel abused; I feel a deep sympathy for that man who— I think I have spoken of that Young Christian long ago, in an earlier chapter of this Autobiography—I don't remember; however, this was the incident: I was to talk to a lot of Young Men's Christian Associations in the Majestic Theatre on a Sunday afternoon. Miss Lyon and I entered the place by the stage door and sat down in a box and looked out over a desert expanse of empty benches—wondering. Miss Lyon presently went to the main entrance in the other street, to see what the matter was; just as she started the Young Christians came pouring in like a tidal wave; she plowed through the wave, and by the time she reached the main door the place was full and the police, mounted and on foot, were struggling with a multitude of remaining Young Christians and keeping them back. The doors were being closed against the people. There was one last man, of course—there always is. He almost got his body into the closing door, but was pushed back by a big officer. He realized that his chance was gone. He was mute for a moment, while his feelings were rising in him, then he said: "I have been a member of the Young Men's Christian Association in good standing for seven years and never got any reward for it, and here it is again—just my God damned luck!" I do not feel as profane as that—still I sense the situation, and I sympathize with that man.

The directors of the Lincoln Trust Company were hard pressed by their depositors, but they promptly put their

[one page and all but two lines of the following page (about 420 words) are missing]

Mr. L. was here last night. He is a well-known young New York lawyer, and is prosperous, and rising rapidly to distinction. He told me about his early life, and I found it peculiarly interesting because he was born in the Knobs of East Tennessee, that remote and primitive region where my father and mother lived eighty years ago, along with Colonel Mulberry Sellers, and whose life and surroundings I have described in the first chapter of the book called "The Gilded Age." I perceived by Mr. L.'s account of his own young life there that the conditions have not changed in a single detail from what they were eighty years ago. The people are shrewd and smart, but untaught, unlettered, and ignorant almost beyond imagination. They know nothing about the outside world; they are not interested in it, they are entirely indifferent regarding its concerns; they have no books and they cannot read; they are religious, but after their own fashion; they have no churches; they have no denominations. Mr. L.'s father is eighty years old and can neither read nor write; his first wife could neither read nor write; his second wife was an educated woman, a school-teacher, and came there from afar; but after twenty years' association with the people around her her grammar was as atrocious as theirs, and her phrasing and her pronunciation as barbarous. In the family there were fifteen boys and four girls. The father wanted his boys to remain on the farm, according to custom—a custom which had hardly known a break in a century previously—but they disappointed him; all his boys went away to seek their fortune elsewhere, as fast as they reached young-manhood. Mr. L., who is now about thirty-five years old, went to Texas when he was twenty. He earned a dollar or two a week there in humble capacities for a while, and meantime educated himself; then he came to New York City and hung out his shingle as a lawyer, and very soon dropped into a remunerative practice. When he was presently satisfactorily established in New York he paid his boyhood home a visit. This was about seven years ago. He had just met and had had long conversations with one of the victorious Boer generals, and as his father had been a Confederate captain in our Civil War, he counted upon thrilling him with the Boer general's stirring adventures in the South African war. Now then, I arrive at a curious illustration of the profound interest which those primitives down there take in their local affairs, and the pallid interest which they take in anybody else's. Mr. L., with the family grouped about him, began his tale, and as he dashed off picture after picture of battle and retreat, of narrow escape, of blood and carnage in the South African veldt—he grew excited, and poured out his great story with a fire and eloquence which compelled his own admiration and which he supposed was compelling the admiration of everybody present; but just in the midst of one of his stirring and spectacular pictures his old Uncle William reached out and gave his aged father's leg a vigorous pinch and said, in a tone of strong excitement and gratification,

"Jimmy, Nip's come back! He come over the mountains all by hisself yiste'day and Jake's got him again!"

The amazement, the astonishment, the delight that flashed over the faces of the family was like a sunburst. Mr. L. was smitten dumb with humiliation to see his great war tale snubbed, extinguished, abolished, in this heartless way. He saw one of his brothers clap his hands to his chest as if to restrain a spasm of some kind, and then rise and retreat from the place. Mr. L. followed him, and found him outside, supporting himself against a woodpile and laughing the soul out of his body and the teeth out of his head. Mr. L. said,

"What is it? What is there to laugh about? I think it's shameful! What is Nip? Who is Nip? and why has the return of this prodigal thrown the whole family into such indecent hysterics of joy and gratitude?"

The brother said,

"I had to laugh—I've got to laugh. The change from the tribe's mild interest in your war to the dynamite explosion of interest in a local matter of *real* interest, of unfeigned interest, of sublime and colossal interest—that's what I'm laughing about. Nip is a frowzy old no-account gray horse, fifteen years old, that belongs to Jake Utterback. Two years ago he wandered off and was never seen again, nor heard of, until yesterday evening, when he came loafing back over the mountains. Uncle William was dying to be the first to tell the family the great news, and he was afraid all the time that somebody would come in with it and get ahead of him. He waited as long as he could for you to get through with your war, and he couldn't have waited another minute or he would have died in his tracks. The news about Nip is flying all over this region for miles, and there isn't a man or a woman that hears it that doesn't put down work and play, and duty and pleasure, and everything else, and rush off to try to be the first to tell it to somebody else."

No, the Knobs have not changed.

Dictated December 2, 1907

Mr. Clemens calls upon Mr. Carnegie, who has just been celebrating his seventieth birthday—Some characteristics of Mr. Carnegie; his desire to talk about himself, and the attentions shown him.

Yesterday I had a message for Andrew Carnegie, who has just been celebrating his seventieth birthday with the help of friends, and I went up town to deliver it, first notifying him by telephone that I should arrive at mid-afternoon, or thereabouts. I arrived at his palace a little after three o'clock and delivered my message; then we adjourned to a room which he called his "cosy corner" to have a general chat while I should wait for Mr. Bryce, the British Ambassador, who had gone to fill an appointment, but had left word that I must wait, as he would soon return. I was glad to comply, for I have known Mr. Bryce a good many years, mainly at his own hospitable table in London, and have always not only respected and esteemed him, but have also revered him. I waited an hour, and then had to give it up; but the hour was not ill spent, for Andrew Carnegie, long as I have known him, has never yet been an uninteresting study, and he was up to standard yesterday.

If I were going to describe him in a phrase I think I should call him the Human Being Unconcealed. He is just like the rest of the human race, but with this difference, that the rest of the race try to conceal what they are, and succeed, whereas Andrew tries to conceal what he is, but doesn't succeed. Yesterday he was at his best; he went on exposing himself all the time, yet he seemed to be unaware of it. I cannot go so far as to say he *was* unaware of it—seemed is the safer word to use, perhaps. He never has any but one theme—himself. Not that he deals in autobiography; not that he tells you about his brave struggles for a livelihood as a friendless poor boy in a strange land; not that he tells you how he advanced his fortunes steadily and successfully against obstructions that would have defeated almost any other human being similarly placed; not that he tells you how he finally reached the summit of his ambition and became lord over twenty-two thousand men and possessor of one of the three giant fortunes of his day; no, as regards these achievements he is as modest a man as you could meet anywhere, and seldom makes even a fleeting reference to them; yet it is as I say, he is himself his one darling subject, the only subject he for the moment—the social moment—seems stupendously interested in. I think he would surely talk himself to death upon it if you would stay and listen.

Then in what way does he make himself his subject? In this way. He talks forever and ever and ever and untiringly, of the **attentions** which have been shown him. Sometimes they have been large attentions, most frequently they are very small ones; but no matter, no attention comes amiss to him, and he likes to revel in them. His friends are coming to observe, with consternation, that while he adds new attentions to his list every now and then, he never drops an old and shop-worn one out of the catalogue to make room for one of these fresh ones. He keeps the whole list; keeps it complete, and you must take it all, along with the new additions, if there is time, and you survive. It is the deadliest affliction I know of. He is the Ancient Mariner over again; it is not possible to divert him from his subject; in your weariness and despair you try to do it whenever you think you see a chance, but it always fails; he will use your remark for his occasion and make of it a pretext to get straight back upon his subject again.

A year or two ago Gilder, of *The Century,* and I called at Mr. Carnegie's upon some matter connected with General Carl Schurz, who was very ill at the time. We arranged for a visit to the Schurz family with Mr. Carnegie, who was Schurz's nearest neighbor; then our business was over, and we wanted to get away, but we couldn't manage it. In the study Mr. Carnegie flew from photograph to photograph, from autograph to autograph, from presentation book to presentation book, and so on, buzzing over each like a happy humming-bird, for each represented a compliment to Mr. Carnegie. Some of these compliments were worth having and worth remembering, but some of them were not; some of them were tokens of honest admiration of the man for the liberal way in which he had devoted millions of dollars to "Carnegie libraries," while others were merely sorrowfully transparent tokens of reverence for his money-bags; but they were all a delight to him, and he loved to talk about them and explain them and enlarge upon them. One was a poem written by a working-man in Scotland. It was a good piece of literary work, and sang Andrew's glories quite musically. It was in the Scotch dialect, and Andrew read it to us, and read it well—so well that no one born out of Scotland could understand it. Then he told us about King Edward's visit to him at Skibo Castle in Scotland. We had heard him read the poem before and tell about the King's visit; we were doomed to hear him read that poem many times and also tell about that visit many times, afterward. When his study seemed to be exhausted we were hoping to get away, but it was not to be. He headed us off at this and that and the other room, and made us enter each and every room under the pretext that there was something important in there for us to consider—but it was always the same old thing: a gold box containing the freedom of the city of London, or Edinburgh, or Jerusalem, or Jericho; or a great photograph with the pictures of all the iron masters whom he had reared and trained and made millionaires of—a picture which they had presented him, along with a banquet; or it was shelves which we must inspect loaded to the guards with applications from everywhere in the world for a Carnegie library; or it was this or that or the other God-knows-what, in the form of some damned attention that had been conferred upon him; and one exasperating feature of it was that it never seemed to occur to him for a moment that these attentions were mainly tributes to his money, and not to himself.

Andrew Carnegie—his characteristics, etc. continued.

Am I dwelling too long on Carnegie? I think not. He has bought fame and paid cash for it; he has deliberately projected and planned out this fame for himself; he has arranged that his name shall be famous in the mouths of men for centuries to come. He has planned shrewdly, safely, securely, and will have his desire. Any town, or village, or hamlet on the globe can have a public library upon these following unvarying terms: when the applicant shall have raised one-half of the necessary money, Carnegie will furnish the other half, and the library building must permanently bear his name. During the past six or eight years he has been spending six or seven million dollars a year on this scheme. He is still continuing it; there is already a multitude of Carnegie libraries scattered abroad over the planet, and he is always making additions to the list. When he dies, I think it will be found that he has set apart a gigantic fund whose annual interest is to be devoted forever to the begetting of Carnegie libraries. I think that three or four centuries from now, Carnegie libraries will be considerably thicker in the world than churches. It is a long-headed idea, and will deceive many people into thinking Carnegie a long-headed man in other and larger ways. I am sure he is a long-headed man in many and many a wise small way—the way of the trimmer, the way of the smart calculator, the way that enables a man to correctly calculate the tides and come in with the flow and go out with the ebb, keeping a permanent place on the top of the wave of advantage while other men as intelligent as he, but more addicted to principle and less to policy, get stranded on the reefs and bars.

It is possible, but not likely, that Carnegie thinks the world regards his library scheme as a large and unselfish benevolence; whereas the world thinks nothing of the kind. The world thanks Mr. Carnegie for his libraries, and is glad to see him spend his millions in that useful way, but it is not deceived as to the motive. It isn't because the world is intelligent, for the world isn't; it is only the world's prejudice against Mr. Carnegie that protects it from being deceived as to the Carnegie motive. The world was deceived as to President Roosevelt's motive when he issued that lawless Order 78, but that was because the world was saturated with adoration of our small idol. Even half-intelligent persons, outside of the holy Republican communion, knew that Order 78 was merely a vote-bribing raid on the Treasury. It would be by no means fair to say that Mr. Carnegie never gives away money with any other object in view than the purchase of fame. He does not give money to any large extent with a non-advertising purpose in view, still there are instances on record—instances where the notice acquired is but momentary, and quickly forgetable and forgotten.

To return to the visit of yesterday to Mr. Carnegie in his palace. One of his first remarks was characteristic—characteristic in this way: that it brought forward a new attention which he had been receiving; characteristic, also, in this way: that he dragged it in by the ears, without beating around the bush for a pretext to introduce it. He said,

"I have been down to Washington to see the President."

Then he added, with that sort of studied and practised casualness which some people assume when they are proposing to state a fact which they are proud of but do not wish to seem proud of,

"He sent for me."

I knew he was going to say that. If you let Carnegie tell it, he never seeks the great—the great always seek him. He went on, and told me about the interview. The President had desired his advice regarding the calamitous conditions existing to-day, commercially, in America, and Mr. Carnegie furnished that advice. It was characteristic of Mr. Carnegie that he did not enter into the details of the advice which he furnished, and didn't try to glorify himself as an adviser. It is curious. He knew, and I knew, and he knew that I knew, that he was thoroughly competent to advise the President, and that the advice furnished would be of the highest value and importance; yet he had no glorifications to waste upon that; he has never a word of brag about his real achievements, his great achievements; they do not seem to interest him in the least degree; he is only interested—and intensely interested—in the flatteries lavished upon him in the disguise of compliments, and in other little vanities which other men would value, but conceal. I must repeat he is an astonishing man in his genuine modesty as regards the large things he has done, and in his juvenile delight in trivialities that feed his vanity.

Mr. Carnegie is not any better acquainted with himself than if he had met himself for the first time day before yesterday. He thinks he is a rude, bluff, independent spirit, who writes his mind and thinks his mind with an almost extravagant Fourth of July independence; whereas he is really the counterpart of the rest of the human race in that he does not boldly speak his mind except when there isn't any danger in it. He thinks he is a scorner of kings and emperors and dukes, whereas he is like the rest of the human race: a slight attention from one of these can make him drunk for a week, and keep his happy tongue wagging for seven years.

I was there an hour or thereabouts, and was about to go, when Mr. Carnegie just happened to remember by pure accident—apparently—something which had escaped his mind—this something which had escaped his mind being, in fact, a something which had not been out of his mind for a moment in the hour, and which he was perishing to tell me about. He jumped up and said,

"Oh, wait a moment. I knew there was something I wanted to say. I want to tell you about my meeting with the Emperor."

The German Kaiser, he meant. His remark brought a picture to my mind at once—a picture of Carnegie and the Kaiser; a picture of a battleship and a Brooklyn ferry-boat, so to speak; a picture of a stately big man and a wee little forkèd child of God that Goliath's wife would have pinned a shirt-waist onto a clothes-line with—could have done it if she wanted to, anyway. I could see the Kaiser's frank big face, bold big face, independent big face, as I remember it, and I could see that other face turned up toward it—that foxy, white-whiskered, cunning little face, happy, blessed, lit up with a sacred fire, and squeaking, without words: "Am I in heaven, or is it only a dream?"

I must dwell for a moment upon Carnegie's stature—if one may call it by that large name—for the sake of the future centuries. The future centuries will be glad to hear about this feature from one who has actually looked upon it, for the matter of stature will always be a matter of interest to the future ages when they are reading about Caesar and Alexander and Napoleon and Carnegie. In truth Mr. Carnegie is no smaller than was Napoleon; he is no smaller than were several other men supremely renowned in history, but for some reason or other he looks smaller than he really is. He looks incredibly small—almost unthinkably small. I do not know how to account for this; I do not know what the reason of it is, and so I have to leave it unexplained; but always when I see Carnegie I am reminded of a Hartford incident of the long, long ago—a thing which had occurred in a law court about a dozen years before I went there, in 1871, to take up my residence. There was a little wee bit of a lawyer there, by the name of Clarke, who was famous for two things: his diminutiveness and his persecuting sharpness in cross-questioning witnesses. It was said that always when he got through with a witness there was nothing left of that witness—nothing but a limp and defeated and withered rag. Except once. Just that one time the witness did not wither. The witness was a vast Irishwoman, and she was testifying in her own case. The charge was rape. She said she awoke in the morning and found the accused lying beside her, and she discovered that she had been outraged. The lawyer said, after elaborately measuring her great figure impressively with his eye,

"Now Madam what an impossible miracle you are hoping to persuade this jury to believe! If one may take so preposterous a thing as that seriously, you might even charge it upon me. Come now, suppose you should wake up and find me lying beside you? What would you think?"

She measured him critically and at her leisure, with a calm judicious eye, and said,

"I'd think I'd had a miscarriage!"

Andrew Carnegie, continued.

As I was saying, Carnegie jumped up and said he wanted to tell me about his meeting with the Emperor; then he went on, something like this:

"We went aboard the *Hohenzollern*, Tower and I, in a perfectly informal way, as far as I was concerned, for emperors and commoners are all one to me, and so I didn't care to have any announcement made that I was coming. Well, there on the deck stood the Emperor, talking, with the usual imperial crowd of gilded and resplendent naval and civil dignitaries standing a little apart and reverently listening. I stood to one side quietly observing, and thinking my own thoughts, the Emperor not conscious that I was there. Presently the Ambassador said,

"'There is an American here, your Majesty, whom you have more than once expressed a desire to see.'

"'Who is that, your Excellency?'

"'Andrew Carnegie.'

"With a start which might be translated into a 'God bless my soul,' the Emperor said,

"'Ha! a man I have so wanted to see. Bring him to me. Bring him to me,' and he advanced half way himself and shook me cordially by the hand and said, laughing, 'Ah, Mr. Carnegie, I know you for a confirmed and incurable independent, who thinks no more of kings and emperors than of other people, but I like it in you; I like a man that does his own thinking and speaks out what he thinks, whether the world approve or not; it's the right spirit, the brave spirit, and there's little enough of it on this planet.'

"I said,

"'I am glad your Majesty is willing to take me for what I am. It would not become me to disclaim or disown, or even modify, what your Majesty has said of me, since it is only the truth. I could not be otherwise than independent if I wanted to, for the spirit of independence is a part of my nature, and a person's nature is born, not made. But I have reverences, your Majesty, just the same. What I revere, respect, esteem, and do homage to is a *man!*—a man, a whole man, a fearless man, a manly and masculine and right-feeling and right-acting man; let him be born in garret or palace, it is the same to me—if he is a man he has my homage; your Majesty is a man, a whole man, a manly man, and it is for this that I revere you, *not* for your mighty place in the world.'"

And so on, and so on. It was a battle of compliments, appreciations, and almost indecently enthusiastic delight on both sides. One or two of the speeches which Mr. Carnegie made to the Emperor were of the soaring, high-voiced, ornate, and thunderously oratorical sort, and in re-delivering them now he acted them out with fire, energy, and effective gesticulation. It was a fine and stirring thing to see.

Andrew Carnegie continued—Some of the advice which he gives to Roosevelt when he visits him—by request—in Washington.

We are all alike—on the inside. Also we are exteriorly all alike, if you leave out Carnegie. Scoffing democrats as we are, we do dearly love to be noticed by a duke, and when we are noticed by a monarch we have softening of the brain for the rest of our lives. We try our best to keep from referring to these precious collisions, and in time some of us succeed in keeping our dukes and monarchs to ourselves; it costs us something to do this, but in time we accomplish it. In my own case, I have so carefully and persistently trained myself in this kind of self-denial that to-day I can look on calm and unmoved when a returned American is casually and gratefully playing the earls he has met; I can look on, silent and unexcited, and never offer to call his hand, although I have three kings and a pair of emperors up my sleeve. It takes a long time to reach this summit of self-sacrifice, and Carnegie has not reached it and never will. He loves to talk about his encounters with sovereigns and aristocracies; loves to talk of these splendid artificialities in a lightly scoffing and compassionate vein and try not to let on that those encounters are the most precious bric-à-brac in the treasury of his memory; but he is just a human being, and he can't even wholly deceive himself, let alone the housecat. With all his gentle scoffings, Carnegie's delight in his contacts with the great amounts to a mania; it must be as much as four years since King Edward visited him at Skibo Castle, yet it is an even bet that not a day has passed since then that he has not told somebody all about it, and enlarged with pride upon the fact that the visit was so small a matter to him that he was able to forget that it was impending, and so the King had to wait a moment until Mr. Carnegie was sent for. Mr. Carnegie cannot leave the King's visit alone; he has told me about it at least four times, in detail. When he applied that torture the second, third, and fourth times, he certainly knew that it was the second, third, and fourth time, for he has an excellent memory. I am not able to believe that he ever allows an opportunity to tell it to go by without getting out of that opportunity all it is worth. He has likable qualities and I like him, but I don't believe I can stand the King Edward visit again.

In his talk about his recent visit—by request—to the President, Mr. Carnegie very, very gently criticised a couple of Mr. Roosevelt's latest insanities: one of these is his departure from his last year's requirement of a new battleship per year and his substituted policy of last week, requiring four new battleships right away, at a cost of sixty-nine million dollars. Carnegie suggested to him, in a guarded and diplomatic way, that this amazing warlike outburst was not altogether in harmony with Mr. Roosevelt's laboriously acquired position in the world as the Dove of Peace, and as the recipient of the Nobel Prize of forty thousand dollars as the chiefest Dove of Peace on the planet. Mr. Carnegie also suggested, in cautious, diplomatic language, that the war-ships be postponed, and the sixty-nine millions be employed in improving the waterways of the country.

I said that the suggestion to drop the battleships was good advice, but that the President would not be influenced by it, because dropping the battleships would interfere with his policy—policy, not policies, since the President has only one policy, and that is to do insanely spectacular things and get himself talked about.

Mr. Carnegie toyed cautiously with that suggestion of insanity; he did not commit himself, and I didn't expect him to do it. He had no call to trade dangerous political confessions with me—and besides, he didn't need to tell me what I already knew; to wit, that there isn't an intelligent human being in America that doesn't privately believe that the President is substantially and to all effects and purposes insane, and ought to be in an asylum. I added, without fishing for a response, and not expecting one,

"Mr. Roosevelt is the Tom Sawyer of the political world of the twentieth century; always showing off; always hunting for a chance to show off; in his frenzied imagination the Great Republic is a vast Barnum circus with him for a clown and the whole world for audience; he would go to Halifax for half a chance to show off, and he would go to hell for a whole one."

Mr. Carnegie chuckled half approvingly, but didn't say anything, and I wasn't expecting him to say anything.

As I have said, Mr. Carnegie mentioned two incidents of his Washington visit: one of them was the one I have been talking about—the four battleships; the other was the "In God We Trust." Away back yonder in the days of the Civil War, a strong effort was made to introduce the name of God into the Constitution; it failed, but a compromise was arrived at which partially satisfied the friends of the Deity. God was left out of the Constitution, but was furnished a front seat on the coins of the country. After that, on one side of the coin we had an Injun, or a Goddess of Liberty, or something of that kind, and on the other side we engraved the legend, "In God We Trust." Now then, after that legend had remained there forty years or so, unchallenged and doing no harm to anybody, the President suddenly "threw a fit" the other day, as the popular expression goes, and ordered that remark to be removed from our coinage. Mr. Carnegie granted that the matter was not of consequence; that a coin had just exactly the same value without the legend as with it, and he said he had no fault to find with Mr. Roosevelt's action, but only with his expressed reasons for the act. The President had ordered the suppression of that motto because a coin carried the name of God into improper places, and that this was a profanation of the Holy Name. Carnegie said the name of God is used to being carried into improper places everywhere and all the time, and that he thought the President's reasoning rather weak and poor.

I thought the same, and said,

"But that is just like the President. If you will notice, he is very much in the habit of furnishing a poor reason for his acts while there is an excellent reason staring him in the face, which he overlooks. There was a good reason for removing that motto; there was, indeed, an unassailably good reason—in the fact that the motto stated a lie. If this nation has ever trusted in God, that time has gone by; for nearly half a century almost its entire trust has been in the Republican party and the dollar—mainly the dollar. I recognize that I am only making an assertion, and furnishing no proof; I am sorry, but this is a habit of mine; sorry also that I am not alone in it; everybody seems to have this disease. Take an instance: the removal of the motto fetched out a clamor from the pulpit; little groups and small conventions of clergymen gathered themselves together all over the country, and one of these little groups, consisting of twenty-two ministers, put up a prodigious assertion unbacked by any quoted statistics, and passed it unanimously in the form of a resolution: the assertion, to wit, that this is a Christian country. Why, Carnegie, so is hell. Those clergymen know that inasmuch as 'Strait is the way and narrow is the gate, and few—*few*—are they that enter in thereat' has had the natural effect of making hell the only really prominent Christian community in any of the worlds; but we don't brag of this, and certainly it is not proper to brag and boast that America is a Christian country when we all know that certainly five-sixths of our population could not enter in at the narrow gate."

Mr. Carnegie did not argue the point, and I did not expect him to do it, for he couldn't know what use I might make of unwise disclosures in case he should indulge himself in that kind of revelations.

Dictated December 10, 1907

Dinner to Mr. Carnegie given by the Associated Societies of Engineers—The speeches, and Mr. Clemens's remarks about Carnegie's Simplified Spelling.

I have been leading a quiet and wholesome life now during two entire banqueteering, speech-making seasons. These seasons begin in September and last until the end of April; it is half a year. Banquets run late, and by the end of the season the habitual banqueteer is haggard and worn, facially, and drowsy in his mind and weak on his legs. Three seasons ago I was still keeping up the banqueteering habit—a habit which had its beginning in 1869 or '70 and had been continued season by season, thereafter, over that long stretch of thirty-five or thirty-six years. I renounced that habit on the 29th of April, three seasons ago. I had been banqueteering and making speeches two or three times in every week for six months; I had tried to get out of this soul-wearing slavery every year for a long time, but had failed of my desire through the adoption of a mistaken system—the system of tapering off, used by hard drinkers. I said I would limit myself to three banquets in the season. This was naturally a mistake, for when a weak person has said yes once he hasn't grit enough to say no the rest of the time—but I adopted a better policy on that 29th of April just referred to; I took what may be called the teetotaler's pledge, and said I would not attend speech-making banquets any more. That pledge has saved me, and has given me a quiet and peaceful life; I think I have not broken it more than three times since I made it.

I broke it last night, and am not at all likely to break it again for a twelvemonth. I had good reasons for breaking it last night—I wanted to see some more of Andrew Carnegie, who is always a subject of intense interest for me. I like him; I am ashamed of him; and it is a delight to me to be where he is if he has new material on which to work his vanities where they will show him off as with a lime-light. The banquet last night was given him by the Associated Societies of Engineers, a wonderful organization with a membership of fifteen thousand engineers of all sorts and kinds, an organization whose industries cover every department of that extraordinary trade; that trade which by help of the inventor, has created the marvel of the ages—this modern material civilization of ours. Two hundred and fifty members were present, and not an unintellectual face visible anywhere—a most remarkable body of men to look at. The oldest member present, Mr. Fritz, aged eighty-six, hale and hearty, was the revolutionizer of the steel industries of the United States—a small affair when he took hold of it with Mr. Holley, but now vast almost beyond the power of figures to compute. Edison was there, looking young and plump; and there were others of high distinction present. The dinner was in honor of Mr. Carnegie, who had given to the Associated Societies their great building and the land it stands upon in 39th street, a present which cost his pocket-book twelve hundred thousand dollars.

I wonder what the banquet will be a century from now. If it has not greatly improved by that time it ought to be abolished. It is a dreadful ordeal, and in my long experience it has shown not a shade of improvement; I believe it is even worse now than it was a generation ago. The guests gather at half past seven in the evening, and stand and chat half an hour and weary themselves with the standing and the chatting; then they march out in procession, in double file, with the chairman and the chief guest in the lead, and the crashing and deafening clamor of the music breaks out; the guests seat themselves and begin to talk to each other softly, sanely, then a little louder, and a little louder, and still a little louder, each group trying to make itself heard above the general din, and before long everybody is shrieking and shouting; knives and forks and plates are clattering, and a man might as well be in pandemonium as far as personal comfort is concerned. This used to continue an hour and a half; then at half past nine the speaking began, and continued for an hour; then the insurrection ceased and the survivors went home. Years ago, in order to save my life, I adopted the system of feeding at home, then starting to the banquet in time to reach it when the banquet was over and the speaking ready to begin—say at half past nine; then leaving the place, upon one pretext or another, as soon as I had emptied my speech upon the assembled sufferers. But nowadays the menu is so intolerably long that the speaking is not likely to begin until fully ten o'clock, so I asked them not to come for me before ten and to allow me as early a place as they could in the list of speakers, so that I could get back home at a reasonable hour. But they came for me at nine, which cheered me and charmed me, because I supposed it meant that the banquet was about over. It was a mistake. I arrived at a quarter past nine, and the feeding was not over until a quarter to eleven. Then the intellectual labors of the evening began; the speeches of the chairman and Mr. Carnegie and Mr. Fritz occupied, altogether, thirty-five minutes; then I spoke ten minutes, and got away at half past eleven, leaving behind me half a dozen speakers still to be heard from. It is likely that the last one did not finish before one o'clock.

I hope I shall not see another banquet in this life until Mr. Carnegie is chief guest again. He made a good speech—sound, sensible, to the point, not a minute too long; and it had humor in it, and also quite distinct traces of modesty—but that was because it was a prepared speech and memorized; he had the typewritten manuscript on the table before him, but I did not see him refer to it; he trusted to his memory, and it was not strictly faithful to him; it failed him a couple of times when he tried to quote poetical passages from Kipling; they were forceful, and would have been very effective if he had reeled them off easily and comfortably, but as he was obliged to stop in the middle of them and stand and wait, and think, their effectiveness oozed out and was lost—but there was no other defect in his speech, and it was received with high and vociferous approval. When he sat down, Mr. Fritz was called up and read a quiet speech of considerable length, from manuscript, and sat down. Apparently it was my turn now, but there was an interruption—a framed certificate of honorary membership was brought forward to be presented to Mr. Carnegie by Mr. Fritz. The chairman held the big frame up where all the house could see it, and explained what it was, and everybody cheered;

then Mr. Carnegie rose and from his low altitude beamed up at the tall and stately Fritz, and reached up and took him by the hand and said,

"I will not call him Mister, it is too distant; he is not Mister to us, he is Uncle John," whereat everybody shouted approval, and one man shouted "Unser Fritz," and the house took that up and re-shouted it—Mr. Fritz has German blood in his veins—and altogether the incident was very pleasing and stirring. The little episode was highly dramatic, and if Mr. Carnegie had sat down then he would have scored the triumph of the evening; but no, he was Carnegie, and that could not happen. He was Carnegie, and being Carnegie of course he was bursting to tell about his recent contact with the Emperor of Germany. He played the same casualness that he had played upon me in his palace the other day, and in just about the same words—certainly in the same spirit. He pretended that he had been on the point of sitting down, but had suddenly remembered something—which was an acted lie; without any doubt he had come there intending to tell about himself and the Emperor, and he hadn't forgotten about it at all; it was fresh and boiling and steaming in his mind all the time; he was only waiting for a chance. He said, ever so casually—

"Oh I forgot to tell you about my recent reception by the Emperor of Germany."

I don't see how a man of such principled and practised veracity as Carnegie can lie in that easy and comfortable way and look just as if it came natural to him to do it. He went on at great length and told about the meeting with the Emperor in almost exactly the same words in which he had detailed it to me in his palace. I know that one sentence, at least, was in precisely the same words which I had heard him utter on that occasion; to wit,

"His Majesty said, 'Ah well, Mr. Carnegie, I know you. I have read all your books, and I know you hate kings.' I said, 'Ah yes, your Majesty, I am certainly a democrat of the democrats. I do hate kings; but, your Majesty, I admire and revere the man behind the king, when he is a man, and that is what your Majesty is.'"

I could see that Mr. Carnegie was tired and worn with the daily and hourly repetition of his encounter with the Emperor, and that his stupendous pride and joy in that imperial attention was shortening his life with pure ecstasy—but dear me, how full of it he was! How delighted he was to expose himself to those people while imagining that he was deceiving them all the time! He filled his talk with his brave scorn of royalties, and those people cheered those handsome and intrepid remarks to the echo, and in their kindness of heart they never once betrayed their perception of the fact that his only reason for remembering to tell them about that contact was that he might brag about it and intoxicate himself with it, and send them home filled with the immortal glory of having seen with their own eyes a man who had talked face to face with an emperor.

He was interrupted by the heartiest applause all the way through, and by and by he made a hit that almost fetched the house to its feet—and perhaps a hundred did rise and wave their napkins at him, while every man present made all the noise he could. Carnegie ought to have sat down then, but it wouldn't have been Carnegie if he had done that;

when he is happy he can't stop, he has to go on and wind up with an anti-climax—and that is what he did.

Well then we had some music, and at last the chairman called me up.

I said I had been chief guest myself, several times, and knew by experience what this one was suffering. He had said himself that he was embarrassed by the chairman's splendid compliments. I said that that was always what happened to the chief guest, and that it was a pity that he should be so treated; there ought always to be some friend present humane enough to act as devil's advocate in the preliminaries of a beatification and do the guest the kindness of calling some little attention to the uncomplimentable side of his career and character, since no man, not even Mr. Carnegie, has led a life that is wholly free from crime. I said,

"Look at him where he sits, his face softly, sweetly, benignantly scintillating with the signs and symbols of a fictitious innocence. Is he free from crime? Look at his pestiferous Simplified Spelling! It has disordered the minds of this whole nation and brought upon this people sorrow and disaster in a hundred forms; it has broken up families; it has ruined households; it produced the San Francisco earthquake; it has brought the vast industries of this country to a standstill and spread a blight of commercial stagnation and undeserved poverty, hunger, nakedness and suffering from Florida to Alaska and from the Great Lakes to the Gulf—and not even the solar system has escaped; the sun is blanketed as never before with sun-spots—sun-spots which will bring upon us cyclones, hurricanes, electrical storms of all descriptions throughout the coming year; and the astronomers lay all this to Mr. Carnegie's pernicious Simplified Spelling. He has attacked orthography at the wrong end; he has attacked the symptoms, not the disease itself. The real disease is in the alphabet: there is not a vowel in it that has a definite and permanent and inalterable value, and sometimes a consonant is placed where it has no value at all. The h in honor, honesty, gherkin, and in a multitude of other words, has no value, and it ought to be flung out; in wheat and which and what, and so on, it is misplaced: it should be the first letter of the word, not the second, for the sound of the h precedes the sound of the w; we don't say w-heat, we say h-weat; it isn't w-hich, it is h-wich—and so on. The consonants that begin mnemonics and pneumonia, and three of the consonants in phthisis, are wasted—and so on. Adequate reform would give each consonant a sole and definite office to perform, and restrict it to that. Adequate reform would give each vowel and its modifications a sole and definite office to perform, and restrict it to that. Then you wouldn't have to be taught spelling, you would only need to be taught the alphabet—then every word that fell upon your ear would instantly and automatically spell itself. After three hours' labor in mastering that reformed alphabet you could promptly and correctly spell every word in the Unabridged Dictionary with your eyes shut; whereas by reason of the immeasurable silliness of our present alphabet there isn't a man in this house that doesn't have to leave fifteen hundred words out of his correspondence every day because he doesn't know how to spell them—yet he spent many weary weeks, and many, many dreary months of his life trying to learn how to spell; it's as idiotic as trying to do a St. Vitus dance with wooden legs. Is there anybody here that knows how to spell pterodactyl? No, not one. Except perhaps the prisoner at the bar. God only knows how he would simplify it. When he got done with it you wouldn't know whether it was a bird or a reptile, and the chances are that he would give it tusks and a trunk and make it lay eggs.

"A system of accents assigning to each vowel its special and sole and definite shade of sound would enable us to spell rationally and with precision all kinds of words, let them come from what language they might; and that would be *real* simplifying, thorough simplifying, competent simplifying—*not* inadequate and half way simplifying by removing the hair, cauterizing the warts, lancing the tumors, medicating the cancers—leaving the old thing substantially what it was before, only bald-headed and unsightly. If I ask you what b-o-w spells you can't answer till you know which bow I am referring to; the same with r-o-w; the same with sore, and bore, and tear, and lead, and read—and all the rest of that asinine family of bastard words born out of wedlock and don't know their own origin and nobody else does; and if I ask you to pronounce s-o-w, instead of promptly telling me, as you would if we had a sane and healthy and competent alphabet instead of a hospital of compound comminuted cripples and eunuchs in the place of it, you have to waste time asking me which sow I mean, the one that is poetic, and recalls to you the furrowed field and the farmer scattering seed, or the one that recalls the lady hog and the future ham. It's a rotten alphabet! O Carnegie, O prisoner at the bar, reform, reform! There's never been a noble, upright, right-feeling prophet in this world, from David and Goliath down to Sodom and Gomorrah who wouldn't censure you for what you've done! And yet you have meant well; you have not been purposely criminal, and your Simplified Spelling is not destitute of virtue and value. It has a certain degree of merit—but I must be just, I must be sternly just, and I say to you this: your Simplified Spelling is well enough, but like chastity—*(artful pause of a moment or two, here, to let the word sink in and give the audience a chance to guess out where the resemblance lies)*—it can be carried too far!"

Dictated December 12, 1907

Carnegie continued—He gives two additional millions to Carnegie Institute—Everybody likes attentions—Prince of Wales once showed Mr. Clemens a match-box and told him it was presented to him by King of Spain.

The Carnegie Institute will be Carnegie's best monument. While he was performing at the engineers' banquet on the 9th, he was once more his very self as heretofore described by me—his very self in that he was eagerly and delightedly advertising an inconsequential attention which had been paid him, and at the same time overlooking, forgetting, holding of small consequence and leaving unmentioned, a very handsome and public-spirited act of his which almost any other man, in his place, would have found some means to bring to the notice of those banqueteers. But Andrew was Andrew—to give away millions upon millions to splendid causes cannot excite him, cannot accelerate the pulse of his vanity by so much as three beats per minute; his great achievements are nothing to him, the only events in his career that are really important in his eyes, and memorable and caressable, are the attentions shown him by his fellowmen. I clip the following telegram from the newspaper:

WASHINGTON, Dec. 10.—Andrew Carnegie has added $2,000,000 to the $10,000,000 endowment fund of the Carnegie Institute. The announcement was made at a dinner given to-night by the Board of Trustees at the New Willard.

Mr. Carnegie was unable to attend, and sent this letter from his home in New York to President R. S. Woodward:

"Dear Sir—I have watched the progress of the institution under your charge, and am delighted to tell you that it has been such as to lead me to add two millions of dollars more to its endowment. It has borne good fruit, and the trustees are to be highly congratulated. In their hands and yours I am perfectly satisfied it is going to realize not only our expectations but our fondest hopes, and I take this opportunity to thank one and all who have so zealously labored from its inception."

The dinner followed a business meeting of the trustees. For scientific research next year, $529,940 was allotted. The trustees decided to erect an administration building at Sixteenth and P streets, Northwest, to take the place of the present rented quarters.

We all like attentions. Mr. Carnegie is not any fonder of them than are the rest of us; he differs from the rest of us only in this: that while we try to advertise our accumulation of attentions while not seeming to be advertising them, he spreads his attentions on a thirty-foot hoarding with a long-handled brush, so to speak. No, I am all wrong; that is not the difference. The real difference is that Andrew's art in advertising his attentions while pretending that he is mentioning them for quite other reasons, is less delicate than ours, less subtly surreptitious. Even the purple is human—even the purple is pleased with small attentions under certain conditions. For instance, seventeen years ago, in Germany, I was one of the guests at a small dinner party of six men and two women, and I sat at the left of that excellent and very human man who was then Prince of Wales and is now King and Emperor. He had a small silver match-box, and he kept picking it up and handling it in a preoccupied way and then laying it down again. Gradually the impression was built up in my mind that he wanted to say something about that box and didn't know how to get at it. The impression was correct. Eventually he passed the box to me to look at, and mentioned with the artful casualness which we are all so well acquainted with in our own persons, that it was given to him by the King of Spain. It was a startling and light-throwing incident. It seemed almost unthinkable that the heir to the colossal British Empire could prize an attention from any human being in this earth, but it was so; that seventh-rate King was still a King and ranked the Prince; therefore the Prince prized an attention from that source.

I have several times said that I could live upon compliments alone, if I could get no other sustenance, and I think that in this I do not differ from the rest of the race, even the members of it that wear the purple.

Dictated January 13, 1908

Madame Elinor Glyn calls upon Mr. Clemens, and they discuss her book, "Three Weeks."

Two or three weeks ago Elinor Glyn called on me, one afternoon, and we had a long talk, of a distinctly unusual character, in the library. It may be that by the time this chapter reaches print she may be less well known to the world than she is now, therefore I will insert here a word or two of information about her. She is English. She is an author. The newspapers say she is visiting America with the idea of finding just the right kind of a hero for the principal character in a romance which she is purposing to write. She has come to us upon the storm-wind of a vast and sudden notoriety. The source of this notoriety is a novel of hers called "Three Weeks." In this novel the hero is a fine and gifted and cultivated young English gentleman of good family, who imagines he has fallen in love with the ungifted, uninspired, commonplace daughter of the rector. He goes to the Continent on an outing, and there he happens upon a brilliant and beautiful young lady of exceedingly foreign extraction, with a deep mystery hanging over her. It transpires, later, that she is the childless wife of a king, or kinglet—a coarse and unsympathetic animal whom she does not love. She and the young Englishman fall in love with each other at sight. The hero's feeling for the rector's daughter was pale, not to say colorless, and it is promptly consumed and extinguished in the furnace-fires of his passion for the mysterious stranger—passion is the right word; passion is what the pair of strangers feel for each other, and which they recognize as real love—the only real love, the only love worthy to be called by that great name—whereas the feeling which the young man had for the rector's daughter is perceived to have been only a passing partiality. The queenlet and the Englishman flit away privately to the mountains and take up sumptuous quarters in a remote and lonely house there—and then business begins. They recognize that they were highly and holily created for each other, and that their passion is a sacred thing; that it is their master by divine right, and that its commands must be obeyed. They get to obeying them at once, and they keep on obeying them, and obeying them, to the reader's intense delight and disapproval; and the process of obeying them is described, several times, almost exhaustively, but not quite—some little rag of it being left to the reader's imagination, just at the end of each infraction, the place where his imagination is to take up and do the finish being indicated by stars.

The unstated argument of the book is that the laws of Nature are paramount, and properly take precedence of the interfering and impertinent restrictive statutes obtruded upon man's life by man's statutes.

Madame Glyn called, as I have said, and she was a picture! Slender, young, faultlessly formed and incontestably beautiful—a blonde, with blue eyes, the incomparable English complexion, and crowned with a glory of red hair of a very peculiar, most rare, and quite ravishing tint. She was clad in the choicest stuffs and in the most perfect taste. There she is—just a beautiful girl; yet she has a daughter fourteen years old. She isn't winning; she has no charm but the charm of beauty, and youth, and grace, and intelligence and vivacity; she *acts* charm, and does it well; exceedingly well, in fact, but it does not convince; it doesn't stir the pulse, it doesn't go to the heart; it leaves the heart serene and unemotional. Her English hero would have prodigiously admired her; he would have loved to sit and look at her and hear her talk, but he would have been able to get away from that lonely house with his purity in good repair, if he had wanted to.

I talked with her with daring frankness, frequently calling a spade a spade instead of coldly symbolizing it as a snow-shovel; and on her side she was equally frank. It was one of the damnedest conversations I have ever had with a beautiful stranger of her sex, if I do say it myself that shouldn't. She wanted my opinion of her book, and I furnished it. I said its literary workmanship was excellent, and that I quite agreed with her view that in the matter of the sexual relation man's statutory regulations of it were a distinct interference with a higher law—the law of Nature. I went further, and said I couldn't call to mind a written law of any kind that had been promulgated in any age of the world in any statute book or any Bible for the regulation of man's conduct in *any* particular, from assassination all the way up to Sabbath-breaking, that wasn't a violation of the law of Nature—which I regarded as the highest of laws, the most peremptory and absolute of all laws—Nature's laws being in my belief plainly and simply the laws of God, since He instituted them—He and no other—and the said laws, by authority of this divine origin taking precedence of all the statutes of man. I said that her pair of indelicate lovers were obeying the law of their make and disposition; that therefore they were obeying the clearly enunciated law of God, and in His eyes must manifestly be blameless.

Of course what she wanted of me was support and defence—I knew that, but I said I couldn't furnish it. I said we were the servants of convention; that we could not subsist, either in a savage or a civilized state, without conventions; that we must accept them and stand by them, even when we disapproved of them; that while the laws of Nature—that is to say the laws of God—plainly made every human being a law unto himself, we must steadfastly refuse to obey those laws, and we must as steadfastly stand by the conventions which ignore them, since the statutes furnish us peace, fairly good government, and stability, and therefore are better for us than the laws of God, which would soon plunge us into confusion and disorder and anarchy, if we should adopt them. I said her book was an assault upon certain old and well established and wise conventions, and that it would not find many friends, and, indeed, would not deserve many.

She said I was very brave—the bravest person she had ever met; (gross flattery which could have beguiled me when I was very very young), and she implored me to publish these views of mine—but I said "No, such a thing is unthinkable." I said that if I, or any other wise, intelligent, and experienced person, should suddenly throw down the walls that protect and conceal his *real* opinions on almost any subject under the sun, it would at once be perceived that he had lost his intelligence and his wisdom and ought to be sent to the asylum. I said I had been revealing to her my private sentiments, *not* my public ones; that I, like all the other human beings, expose to the world only my trimmed and perfumed and carefully barbered public opinions and conceal carefully, cautiously, wisely, my private ones. I explained that what I meant by that phrase "public opinions" was *published* opinions—opinions spread broadcast in print. I said I was in the common habit, in private conversation with friends, of revealing every private opinion I possessed relating to religion, politics, and men but that I should never dream of *printing* one of them, because they are individually and collectively at war with almost everybody's public opinion, while at the same time they are in happy agreement with almost everybody's private opinion. As an instance, I asked her if she had ever encountered an intelligent person who privately believed in the Immaculate Conception—which of course she hadn't; and I also asked her if she had ever seen an intelligent person who was daring enough to publicly deny his belief in that fable and print the denial. Of course she hadn't encountered any such person. I said I had a large cargo of most interesting and important private opinions about every great matter under the sun, but that they were not for print. I reminded her that we all break over the rule two or three times in our lives and fire a disagreeable and unpopular private opinion of ours into print, but we never do it when we can help it; we never do it except when the desire to do it is too strong for us and overrides and conquers our cold, calm, wise judgment. She mentioned several instances in which I had come out publicly in defence of unpopular causes, and she intimated that what I had been saying about myself was not perhaps in strict accordance with the facts; but I said they were merely illustrations of what I had just been saying—that when I publicly attacked the American missionaries in China, and some other iniquitous persons and causes, I did not do it for any reason but just the one: that the inclination to do it was stronger than my diplomatic instincts, and I had to obey and take the consequences. But I said I was not moved to defend her book in public; that it was not a case where inclination was overpowering and unconquerable, and that therefore I could keep diplomatically still, and should do it.

The lady was young enough, and inexperienced enough, to imagine that whenever a person has an unpleasant opinion in stock which could be of educational benefit to Tom, Dick, and Harry, it is his *duty* to come out in print with it and become its champion. I was not able to get that juvenile idea out of her head. I was not able to convince her that we never do *any* duty for the duty's sake but only for the mere personal satisfaction we get out of doing that duty. The fact is, she was brought up just like the rest of the world, with the ingrained and stupid superstition that there is such a thing as *duty for duty's sake,* and so I was obliged to let her abide in her darkness. She believed that when a man held a private unpleasant opinion of an educational sort, which would get him hanged if he published it, he ought to publish it anyway, and was a coward if he didn't. Take it all around, it was a very pleasant conversation, and glaringly unprintable—particularly those considerable parts of it which I haven't had the courage to more than vaguely hint at in this account of our talk.

Some days afterward I met her again, for a moment, and she gave me the startling information that she had written down every word I had said, just as I had said it, without any softening and purifying modifications, and that it was "just splendid, just wonderful." She said she had sent it to her husband, in England. Privately I didn't think that that was a very good idea, and yet I believed it would interest him. She begged me to let her publish it, and said it would do infinite good in the world; but I said it would damn me before my time, and I didn't wish to be useful to the world on such expensive conditions.

She wanted to show me her report of our talk so that I could admire the accuracy of it. I said it wouldn't interest me, still she could fetch it some time or other, if she liked.

A friend of Mrs. Glyn brings to Mr. Clemens a report of Mr. Clemens's conversation with Mrs. Glyn, and urges him to allow it to be published.

Sure enough, her report came! It came several days ago, not by her hand but by the hand of another—by the hand of an American lady who is Mrs. Glyn's closest friend and most ardent admirer, a lady whom I know and like. She is young; she is beautiful; she has faultless taste in dress, and I know she would be charming if she hadn't a hobby; but often a hobby so possesses its rider that it sucks all the juices out of the rider's personality and leaves it dry and feverish and hot-eyed and unwholesome, unspiritual, unwinning, unpersuasive, and I may even say repellent. As a rule, a person under the dominion of a hobby cannot be satisfactorily dealt with. It is the hobby-rider's conviction that his own reasonings upon his subject are the only sane ones; it is his conviction that your counter-reasonings are either insane or insincere; they make not the least impression upon him, if he even hears them, which he generally doesn't, for while you are talking his mind is commonly busy with what it is going to say in reply to these reasonings which it has not been listening to—busy with what it is going to say when you make a temporary halt for breath and give it a chance to break in.

The lady had not been sent by Mrs. Glyn; she had come of her own accord, and without Mrs. Glyn's knowledge. She had studied Mrs. Glyn's report of our conversation, with Mrs. Glyn's permission, with the result that she felt it to be her duty to come and urge me to let it be published. The sense that it was her duty to do this was so commanding, so overpowering, that she was not able to resist it, but was obliged to surrender to its mastery and obey. She added that she was thoroughly convinced that it was my duty—a duty which I could not honorably avoid—to allow this conversation to be published, because of the influence it would have upon the public for good.

I said I was sorry to be obliged to take a different view of my duty, but that such was the case. I said I was so habituated to shirking my duty that I was able now to shirk it fifty times a day without a pang; that is, that I could shirk fifty duties a day without a pang if the opportunity to do it were furnished me; that I did not get fifty opportunities a day, but that I got an average of about that many a week, and that I had noticed a peculiarity, a quite interesting peculiarity, of these opportunities—to wit, that the opportunity to do a duty was always furnished me by an outsider, it seldom originated with me; it was always furnished by some person who knew more about my duties toward the public than I did. I said I believed that if I should become the champion of every cause that was brought to my attention and shown by argument that it was my duty to take hold of it and champion it, I shouldn't ever have any time left to punch up the China missionaries or revel in any of the other duties that were of my own invention and that were occupying all the spare room in my heart. "And yet," I said, "if you leave out the China missionaries, and King Leopold of Belgium, and the Children's Theatre, I am not working many duties of my own invention, but am mainly laboring at duties put upon me by other people." I said,

"I am really quite active in fussing at other people's good causes—by request. Let me show you—let me give you a list. At present my duty-mill is pretty persistently grinding in the interest of these several matters—to wit:

"The Fulton Memorial Fund, which has imposed upon me two voyages to Jamestown, several appeal-letters for publication, half a dozen speeches, and one lecture;

"The movement propagated by Miss Holt for raising a large fund to be devoted to the amelioration of the condition of this State's helpless and unsupported adult blind persons;

"The American movement in the interest of those Russian revolutionists whose hope is to modify the Czar and his blood-kin menagerie, and make life in Russia endurable for the common people.

"However, the full list would take up too much room. Let the rest go. It is only noon now, yet between yesterday noon and the present noon I have had more opportunities offered me in the way of assisting good causes than I could utilize, even if I should do my very best. For instance:

"Speech at the impending banquet in the interest of that great society which is endeavoring to promote more intimate relations between America and France than now exist. I had to decline it;

"Invitation to take a prominent part in another impending function in that same interest. I had to decline it;

"Invitation to take a prominent part in still another impending function in that same interest. I had to decline it;

"Invitation to attend a public meeting whose object is to obstruct the progress of Christian Science in the land. I had to decline it;

"Invitation to make a speech at a public meeting whose object is to raise funds in aid of another polar expedition. I had to decline it;

"That isn't the whole list—but never mind the rest. It is a sufficient indication that you have arrived late with your opportunity for me to do my duty toward the public in this matter of yours, and it will suggest to you that when a person gets so many chances, every twenty-four hours, to do good, he is bound to become callous eventually, and feel not a single responsive throb in his heart when a new chance, or a hundred of them, are offered him. You are very strongly interested in the matter which has brought you to me aren't you?"

"Yes, my heart is in it."

"Your whole heart?"

"Yes, my whole heart."

"It is the same with Mrs. Glyn, isn't it?"

"Yes, just the same."

"Both of you have been approached by people whose whole hearts were in other large causes and who wished to secure your sympathy and help in those causes—isn't it so?"

"Yes, that is true—there have been many instances."

"I don't need to ask you if you declined. I already know you did. It isn't human nature to feel a working sympathy in every good cause that is brought to one's attention, and without that warm sympathy in a person's heart he is not going to take hold of such things merely because somebody whose whole heart is in them wants him to do it. Now no part of my heart is in this matter of yours and Mrs. Glyn's, and I long ago stopped engaging my mouth in either good or bad causes where my heart was indifferent. You and Mrs. Glyn think it strange that since I have an opinion about this matter of yours I yet refuse to make that opinion public; you do think it strange, don't you?"

"Yes, we do."

"You think that if you were in my place you would consider a private opinion a public one as well, and that it was your duty to publish it, and that you could not refuse to publish it without being guilty of moral cowardice—isn't it so?"

"You have stated it in perhaps harsher terms than necessary, but substantially it is what we think."

"Don't you believe that there are often cases where you would do things in private which were without offence and yet which you would not be quite willing to do in public? For instance: you are the mother of three children."

"Yes."

Dictated February 12, 1908

Sample of foreign English discovered in New York—Mr. Clemens makes his fifth trip to Bermuda—His fad is collecting young girls.

Apparently we do not need to go abroad to find quaint and delightful samples of foreign English. I doubt if the English of Continental hotel-advertisements or Continental English local guide-books, or even the showy and wonderful English of the college-bred Babu of Calcutta, can surpass in charm and naïveté and felicity the following effort of a Hebrew tailor of our own city of New York. Mr. Paine came across it by accident, and gathered it in. It is a cheap and humble and rudely printed little circular:

I have been to Bermuda again; this is the fifth time; it was on account of bronchitis, my annual visitor for these seventeen or eighteen years. I have not come out of any previous attack so quickly or so pleasantly; the attack has always kept me in bed five weeks, sometimes six, and once eight. This time I got out of bed at the end of the first week, two days after a ten-inch snow-storm, and took the chances and went to sea in bitter winter weather. We made the passage in forty-five hours and landed in lovely summer weather. The passage itself came near to curing me, for a radical change is a good doctor. A single day of constant and delightful exposure to the Bermudian sun completed the cure; then I stayed eight days longer to enjoy the spiritual serenities and the bodily rejuvenations furnished by that happy little paradise. It grieves me, and I feel reproached, that I allowed the physicians to send Mrs. Clemens on a horrible ten-day sea journey to Italy when Bermuda was right here at hand and worth a hundred Italies, for her needs. They said she must have a warm and soft and gentle climate, and that nothing else could help her. The winter climate of Florence distinctly failed to meet the requirements; we had eight months of uncomfortable weather, with much chilliness, two months of rain, and very infrequent splashes of sunshine. She was not able to outlive these disasters, and she was never able to flee from them, for lack of strength. It astonishes me and grieves me to remember that when Italy was proposed Bermuda never once occurred to me; yet I knew Florence well, and I knew Bermuda well, and was aware that for climate Florence was a sarcasm as compared with Bermuda.

I suppose we are all collectors, and I suppose each of us thinks that his fad is a more rational one than any of the others. Pierpont Morgan collects rare and precious works of art and pays millions per year for them; an old friend of mine, a Roman prince, collects and stores up in his palace in Rome every kind of strange and odd thing he can find in the several continents and archipelagoes, and as a side issue—a pastime, and unimportant— has collected four hundred thousand dollars' worth of postage-stamps. Other collectors collect rare books, at war prices, which they don't read, and which they wouldn't value if a page were lacking. Still other collectors collect menus; still others collect playbills; still others collect ancient andirons. As for me, I collect pets: young girls—girls from ten to sixteen years old; girls who are pretty and sweet and naïve and innocent—dear young creatures to whom life is a perfect joy and to whom it has brought no wounds, no bitterness, and few tears. My collection consists of gems of the first water.

Dictated February 13, 1908

Bermuda, Margaret, Maude, Reginald, and the pedestrian excursions.

My first day in Bermuda paid a dividend—in fact a double dividend: it broke the back of my cold and it added a jewel to my collection. As I entered the breakfast room the first object I saw in that spacious and far-reaching place was a little girl seated solitary at a table for two. I bent down over her and patted her cheek and said, affectionately and with compassion,

"Why you dear little rascal—do you have to eat your breakfast all by yourself in this desolate way?"

She turned up her face with a sweet friendliness in it and said, not in a tone of censure, but of approval,

"Mamma *is* a little slow, but she came down here to get rested."

"She has found the right place, dear. I don't seem to remember your name; what is it?"

By the sparkle in her brown eyes, it amused her. She said,

"Why you've never known it, Mr. Clemens, because you've never seen me before."

"Why that is true, now that I come to think; it certainly is true, and it must be one of the reasons why I have forgotten your name. But I remember it now perfectly—it's Mary."

She was amused again; amused beyond smiling; amused to a chuckle, a musical gurgle, and she said,

"Oh no it isn't, it's Margaret."

I feigned to be ashamed of my mistake, and said,

"Ah well, I couldn't have made that mistake a few years ago, but I am old now, and one of age's earliest infirmities is a damaged memory; but I am clearer now—clearer-headed—it all comes back to me; I remember your whole name now, just as if it were yesterday. It's Margaret Holcomb."

She was surprised into a laugh this time; the rippling laugh that a happy brook makes when it breaks out of the shade into the sunshine, and she said,

"Oh you are wrong again; you don't get anything right. It isn't Holcomb, it's Blackmer."

I was ashamed again, and confessed it; then—

"How old are you, dear?"

"Twelve, New Year's. Twelve and a month."

"Ah, you've got it down fine, honey; it belongs to your blessed time of life; when we get to be seventy-two we don't reckon by months any more."

She said, with a fine complimentary surprise in her innocent eyes,

"Why you don't look old, Mr. Clemens."

I said I wasn't, except by the almanac—otherwise I was only fourteen. I patted her dainty brown hand and added,

"Good-bye dear, I am going to my table now; but after breakfast— Where are you going to wait for me?"

"In the big general room."

"I'll be there."

We were close comrades—inseparables in fact—for eight days. Every day we made pedestrian excursions—called them that anyway, and honestly they were intended for that, and that is what they would have been but for the persistent intrusion of a gray and grave and rough-coated little donkey by the name of Maude. Maude was four feet long; she was mounted on four slender little stilts, and had ears that doubled her altitude when she stood them up straight. Which she seldom did. Her ears were a most interesting study. She was always expressing her private thoughts and opinions with them, and doing it with such nice shadings, and so intelligibly, that she had no need of speech whereby to reveal her mind. This was all new to me. The donkey had always been a sealed book to me before, but now I saw that I could read this one as easily as I could read coarse print. Sometimes she would throw those ears straight forward, like the prongs of a fork; under the impulse of a fresh emotion she would lower the starboard one to a level; next she would stretch it backward till it pointed nor'-nor'east; next she would retire it to due east, and presently clear down to southeast-by-south—all these changes revealing her thoughts to me without her suspecting it. She always worked the port ear for a quite different set of emotions, and sometimes she would fetch both ears rearward till they were level and became a fork, the one prong pointing southeast the other southwest. She was a most interesting little creature, and always self-possessed, always dignified, always resisting authority; never in agreement with anybody, and if she ever smiled once during the eight days I did not catch her at it. Her tender was a little bit of a cart with seat room for two in it, and you could fall out of it without knowing it, it was so close to the ground. This battery was in command of a nice grave, dignified, gentle-faced little black boy whose age was about twelve, and whose name, for some reason or other, was Reginald. Reginald and Maude—I shall not easily forget those gorgeous names, nor the combination they stood for. Once I reproached Reginald. I said,

"Reginald, what kind of morals do you sport? You contracted to be here with the battery yesterday afternoon—on the Sabbath Day, mind you—at two o'clock, to assist in the usual pedestrian excursion to Spanish Point and Paradise Vale, and you violated that contract. What is the explanation of this conduct—this conduct which in my opinion is criminal?"

He was not flurried, not affected in any way; not humiliated, not disturbed in his mind. He didn't turn a feather, but justified his course as calmly and as comprehensively with his tranquil voice as Maude could have done it with her ears:

"Why, I had to go to Sunday-school."

I said with severity,

"So it is Bermudian morals, is it, to break contracts in order to keep the Sabbath? What do you think of yourself, Reginald?"

The rebuke was lost; it didn't hit him anywhere. He said, easily and softly and contentedly,

"Why I couldn't keep 'em both; I had to break one of 'em."

I dropped the matter there. There's no use in arguing against a settled conviction.

The excursioning party always consisted of the same persons: Miss W.,* Mr. Ashcroft, Margaret, Reginald, Maude and me. The trip, out and return, was five or six miles, and it generally took us three hours to make it. This was because Maude set the pace. Sometimes she kept up with her own shadow, but mostly she didn't. She had the finest eye in the company for an ascending grade; she could detect an ascending grade where neither water nor a spirit-level could do it, and whenever she detected an ascending grade she respected it; she stopped and said with her ears,

"This is getting unsatisfactory. We will camp here."

Then all the vassals would get behind the cart and shove it up the ascending grade, and shove Maude along with it. The whole idea of these excursions was that Margaret and I should employ them for the gathering of strength, by walking—yet we were oftener in the cart than out of it. She drove and I superintended. In the course of the first excursion I found a beautiful little shell on the beach at Spanish Point; its hinge was old and dry, and the two halves came apart in my hand. I gave one of them to Margaret and said,

"Now dear, some time or other in the future I shall run across you somewhere, and it may turn out that it is not you at all, but some girl that only resembles you. I shall be saying to myself 'I know that this is a Margaret, by the look of her, but I don't know for sure whether it is my Margaret or somebody else's;' but no matter, I can soon find out, for I shall take my half-shell out of my pocket and say 'I think you are my Margaret,

* A bright and charming lady with a touch of gray in her hair, head of a college in the University of Chicago, Margaret's most devoted friend, if I except myself.

but I am not certain; if you are my Margaret you will be able to produce the other half of this shell.'"

Next morning when I entered the breakfast room and saw the child sitting solitary at her two-seated breakfast table I approached and scanned her searchingly all over, then said sadly,

"No, I am mistaken; she looks like my Margaret, but she isn't, and I am so sorry. I will go away and cry, now."

Her eyes danced triumphantly, and she cried out,

"No, you don't have to. There!" and she fetched out the identifying shell.

I was beside myself with gratitude and joyful surprise, and revealed it from every pore. The child could not have enjoyed this thrilling little drama more if we had been playing it on the stage. Many times afterward she played the chief part herself, pretending to be in doubt as to my identity and challenging me to produce my half of the shell. She was always hoping to catch me without it, but I always defeated that game—wherefore she came at last to recognize that I was not only old, but very smart.

Dictated February 14, 1908

The many wonderful inventions that have had their birth since Mr. Clemens was born; the newest the autochrome—Mr. Clemens's picture is taken in Bermuda, with Margaret, by the Lumière process.

One's first contact with a fresh, new, thrilling novelty is for him a memorable event. I still remember quite clearly the wonder and delight that swept through me the first time I ever saw a daguerreotype; and along with it was the sense that there wasn't any reality about this miracle; that it was a dream, a product of enchantment—beautiful, astonishing, but impermanent. I still remember my first contact with the electric telegraph, and with the phonograph, and with the wireless, and with the telephone, and with the Hoe press—which with my own eyes I saw print twenty thousand newspapers on one side in an hour, and couldn't quite believe it although I was actually seeing it. Oh, compare that wee marvel with to-day's press! In Bermuda an addition was made to the list of these great first contacts, these splendid impossibles: it was the autochrome. I had never seen a sample of that lovely miracle before. A gentleman amateur there had half a dozen pictures, made by himself by the Lumière process, of Bermudian scenery, and a picture of his little girl reposing in the midst of tapestries and vases and rugs, and flowers, and other things distinguished for variety and beauty of coloring, and I was carried away with them. I was glad to have lived to see at last that old, old dream of the photographer come true—the colored photograph painted by the master, the sun.

How many wonderful inventions have had their birth since I was born! Broadly speaking, it is an interminable list. I was born in the same year that the lucifer match was born, and the latest link in this great chain is the dainty and bewitching Lumière.

The amateur whom I have spoken of was preparing an article about the Lumière process for one of the great magazines, and he wanted a picture of me for use as one of the illustrations. I was quite willing to sit, but said Margaret must be put into the picture with me. The picture was notably successful. I was in white, and so was Margaret. Her frock was a very white white, and her white jacket had broad lapels of an intense red; also she wore a red leather belt. My white clothes were of three slightly differing shades of white, and in the picture those shades were exactly reproduced—the coat one shade of white, the shirt-front a slightly whiter white, the necktie a slightly whiter white than the shirt-front. The Lumière had a sharper eye than myself; I had not detected those differences until it revealed them to me. . . . .

One day Miss W. betrayed to me one of Margaret's sweet little confidences. Margaret said to her,

"Is Mr. Clemens married?"

"No."

Margaret, after a little pause, said, with a dear and darling earnestness, and much as if she were soliloquizing aloud,

"If I were his wife I would never leave his side for a moment; I would stay by him and watch him, and take care of him all the time."

It was the mother instinct speaking from the child of twelve; it took no note of the disparity of age; it took no note of my seventy-two years; it noticed only that I was careless, and it was affectionately prepared to protect me from my defect.

I have already spoken at some length of a couple of other gems of my collection: Francesca and Dorothy—my New Jersey Dorothy, Dorothy Quick. I have two other Dorothies besides—an American one and an English one.

The collection of gems continued—Dorothy Quick—Her April Fools' Day anecdote, and Colonel Harvey's story of Naughty Mabel at the races—Dorothy's methods of playing games.

Dorothy Quick is eleven and a half years old now, and as tirelessly active, vivacious, energetic, bright, interesting, good, obedient, and sweet and companionable and charming as ever. When we were shipmates last summer, coming home from England, I discovered her the second day out, and took possession, leaving her mother, her grandfather and her grandmother to get along the best they could without her during the most of each day, for we were nearly inseparable. When the time for that ancient function, the "concert," approached—a paid show in aid of the sailor hospitals of England and America—the elected manager came to me and asked if I would take part in the performance and make a speech. I said, with asperity,

"It is strange that you should come to *me* with such an errand. I am a slave; I have no authority in the matter. Go to the source of power—go to the master. I will perform if the master permits."

"If I may ask, who is the master?"

"Dorothy."

The manager hunted Dorothy up and gravely laid the proposition before her, and was as gravely answered. The result appeared in the printed program, an hour later—thus:

"Mark Twain, speech. (By permission of Dorothy Quick)"

One day last September when Dorothy spent a week with us in Tuxedo, she sat at luncheon looking radiantly sweet and lovely in her bright summer costume, and I said,

"Dorothy, I am holding in—I am holding in all I can—but I don't think I can hold in much longer—I want to eat you!"

She responded promptly,

"Don't do it, Mr. Clemens, I should miss you so."

We fell to telling anecdotes, and Dorothy furnished one or two. One of hers was to this effect:

It was April Fools' Day, and little Johnny burst into the parlor, where a dozen ladies were taking a cup of five o'clock tea, and exclaimed excitedly,

"Mamma, there's a stranger up stairs kissing the governess!"

Mamma started indignantly toward the stairs, with battle in her eye, then Johnny cried out in triumphant delight,

"April fool! It ain't a stranger at all—it's only papa!"

Next day Colonel Harvey came down to spend the day. That charming man, that gifted man, has a certain peculiarity: sometimes a humorous thing carries him off his feet; at another time the same thing would merely set him to thinking, and there would be no indication that he had even heard it. We were used to this peculiarity, but it was new to Dorothy. The Colonel was in a happy mood, and he told several anecdotes. One of them was to this effect, an incident which had fallen under his personal observation:

Scene, the grand stand; occasion, a great horse-race; present, in their rich attire, ladies of high society; a little apart, a pretty creature, unattended, overdressed; under-bred, also, by the look of her. She was painstakingly looking the lady of culture and high degree, and she quite successfully kept up the calm dignity proper to the part until the flying horses began to draw near; then she forgot herself and began to get excited. Her excitement grew, and she further forgot herself and stood up—which made those other ladies transfer their attention from the race to her, though she was unaware of it. She craned her neck; her eager eyes began to flame with excitement; next she began, unconsciously, to soliloquize aloud. She uttered her thought in gasps:

"I'm going to win!——I'm going to win sure!......Go on—whip up—whip up!....... he's half a nose ahead!........ he's three-quarters of a nose ahead!.......... Oh he's dropping back! back, and back, and back!........ Damn his soul he's lost the race!"

Then she turned on a Vesuvian irruption of profanities and indelicacies that turned the air blue, and made those staring ladies gasp! There was a pause, then the soliloquizer

came to herself, took one pathetic glance—one self-reproachful glance—at those hor-
rified people, and ejaculated,

"Naughty Mabel!"

We thought it was about time to show off our Dorothy, so I asked her to tell us the
April Fool story. She told it in her dearest and sweetest and most winningly simple and
matter-of-fact fashion—and there was no result; that is, from the Colonel. His reflecting-
mill was at work; he probably had not heard Dorothy's effort. The child looked mortified,
but didn't say anything. The cut was deep—as appeared after a long, long interval; an
interval of twenty-four whole hours, during which Dorothy had not mentioned the
episode—but that it had been rankling all that time was evidenced in the fact that now
at last when she came to comment upon it there was no subject at all before the house,
yet she dropped her comment right into the midst of that vacancy without any word of
introduction, and didn't even couple the Colonel's name with it, but said "he"—

"He laughs at his own jokes, but he doesn't care for other people's."

Dorothy came last Saturday and stayed over Sunday, and she was her same old dear
self all the time. We occupied the billiard room all day; again Dorothy read Shakspeare
aloud, always selecting from each play her favorite passages and skipping the rest of
it—which is her fashion. Now and then, between billiard games, she browsed among
the books, making selection after selection, and always good selections; she would read
aloud about twenty minutes, then require me to read aloud for about twenty; then she
would inaugurate a game of "500" and discard it in twenty minutes; next she would
play euchre twenty minutes; next it would be a game of verbarium, and so on all the
day long—twenty minutes to each fleeting interest, with twenty minutes of billiards
sandwiched between every two of them. And all the day long, from nine in the morning
till her bedtime—nine at night—she was an immeasurable delight.

If you don't know what verbarium is I will explain. You write a great long word at the
top of a sheet of paper; then you begin with the first letter of that word and build words
out of the letters of the long word with that letter as a beginner; and the contestant who
builds the most words in a given length of time is the winner. Then you take the second
letter, and continue the process. Dorothy would laboriously harvest six or seven words;
then she would discover that the text-word needed another vowel or another consonant
to make it really effective, and she would suggest that we add the letter which she
needed. I never objected; I always said it would be a fortunate addition—and as I never
smiled, I never fell under suspicion. But there was opportunity to smile, for usually by
the time Dorothy was tired of the game the text-word which originally contained only
seventeen letters, had, in the course of the game, accumulated the rest of the alphabet.
She's a darling little billiard player; and when she plays the game you can recognize that
it is Dorothy, and not another, because under her sway all rules fail and new ones are
introduced—on her sole and sufficient authority and without any vote—which improve
that game beyond imagination. When the balls do not lie favorably she makes no remark,

but groups them in a better position and goes on with her performance without any comments.

Dorothy Quick, continued—copy of letter recently received from her.

A letter has come from Dorothy, and I will insert it here to show how much she hasn't improved in punctuation and in slowing her swift pen down, and in curbing and taming her dear headlong eagerness.

> My Dear Mr Clemens
> Thank you so much for your lovely valentine I had thirty-one when yours came so now I have thirty-two and they were all lovely every one has admired my belt that you brought me from Bermuda very much it is really beautiful I read in the paper all about Miss Clara's musical it must have been lovely I love Miss Clara she is so beautiful Will you write me soon I always rush for the mails they are delivered here three times a day always hoping I will get a letter from you but I know you are busy and cant write so often I suppose you went out for a walk today it was so lovely out here today I went to a party yesterday had a lovely played lots of silly games but it was great fun I didn't get one prize what do you think of that lots and lots of love and kisses
>
> your loving
Dorothy
>
> P.S. Please give my love to Miss Lyon

Her letter exposes another small defect or two, but they are like all her defects—for they go to make up Dorothy, and anything that goes to the making up of Dorothy is precious, and cannot be discarded without loss. What would a letter from Dorothy be if its express-train pace were obstructed and retarded at every milestone by commas, and semicolons, and periods; and if it didn't revel in tautologies; and if the rushing floods from the child's golden heart were tamed by cold literary calculation and made to flow in an orderly stream between the banks and never overflow them? I couldn't have it, it wouldn't be Dorothy. Dorothy is perfect, just as she is; Dorothy the child cannot be improved; let Dorothy the woman wait till the proper time comes.

Last summer I thoughtlessly gave Dorothy an instructive hint, and afterwards mourned about it; but the mourning was premature—the hint went wide of the mark and produced no result, achieved no damage. That hint was to this effect: I told her there was a wide difference between repetition and tautology; that she must never be afraid to repeat a word where the repetition could help to uncloud her meaning and make it clear, bright, distinct, and unmistakable, but that she must be cautious about repeating a word when it would not have that effect, for then the repetition would be tautological, and, by consequence, commonplace and slovenly in the result. This letter is evidence to me, with its prodigal repetitions of "love" and "lovely," that even to this happy day the difference between helpful repetition and tautology has no existence for Dorothy.

Dictated February 19, 1908

Mr. Clemens sails again for Bermuda three days hence—Copy of Mr. Clemens's letter to Miss Jean about Miss Clemens's musicale— The party at Sherry's, the interesting people there, and the many dissipations which precede the second trip to Bermuda.

I sail for Bermuda three days hence, but not for my health. Last Thursday I had an energetic day, followed by an equally energetic and stirring night. I wrote Jean about these wholesome dissipations next morning:

> Dearest Jean, I must snatch a moment to tell you about Clara's musicale of last night. It was very rainy, but no matter about 140 of the 160 guests invited came to the show—and very choice people they were, too, bright, and cultivated. Clara was beautiful to look at, and her voice was in great form. She was a picture of grace, and ease, and conscious mastery of the situation. Sometimes she was playful and cunning; sometimes she was sweetly and eloquently moving and pathetic, sometimes she was a storm, sometimes she was a majestic tragedy queen; and in all her moods she was an expert in expression, and carried the house! It was a splendid triumph. Everybody praised her singing, praised it with enthusiasm, and praised her acting in the same measure. They couldn't talk about anything else. Melville Stone, head of the Associated Press, was present, and he told Miss Lyon to furnish him any chance that might occur for him to be of service to Clara, and he would spread her merit from one end of the country to the other.
>
> Miss Nichols played divinely, and she and Clara did a duet that so delighted the house that they had to do it all over again. And there were other encores. It was a great night.
>
> At midnight I went to a big supper and ball at Sherry's, and enjoyed it thoroughly till 4.05 a.m., when I came away with the last of the rioters.
>
> I have been dictating, this morning, and am going to play billiards all the afternoon.
>
> I hope you are well and happy. With ever so much love, dear Jean—
>
> Father.

The party at Sherry's was continuously interesting, from the beginning to the end. It was given by Robert Collier. He, and that sweet and beautiful girl, his wife, were at Clara's musicale, and we departed for Sherry's in their automobile at midnight. It was a large company, and was made up of well-known names. Among them was John Hay's poet-daughter, Mrs. Payne Whitney. I had not seen her since she was a little child. Neither her mother's nor her husband's limitless millions have smothered her literary gift or beguiled her into neglecting it. Among them, also, was her sister-in-law, Mrs. Harry Payne Whitney, who is likewise staggering under weighty millions, but slaves daily and enthusiastically and faithfully at her statuary work, like the loftiest minded poor devotee of the great arts in the land. Twice, under the concealment of fictitious names, she has carried off the first prize in important public competitions. Prince Troubetskoi was there, a fine man and diligent and successful artist. I have known him some time. His wife is Amélie Rives, the poet. The lovely Ethel Barrymore, actress, was there. She is the sole support of her widowed mother's family, and has been working hard and making and saving a deal of money these many months, and now misfortune has befallen her. A few nights ago, when she was absent at the theatre, a burglar entered her apartment and carried off every valuable thing she had in the world, including her accumulated money, which she kept at home because in these disastrous and panicky days she was afraid to trust it in a bank. Nazimova, the illustrious Russian actress, was there, a most interesting character; I had not seen her before, either on the stage or elsewhere. She talks in easy and flowing and correct English, and she was playing in it acceptably two and a half months after her tongue's first contact with it. She said she was born and reared in Switzerland, and at eleven didn't know a Russian word; then she took lessons and acquired her native tongue by the same laborious processes required in mastering a foreign one.

I was at home by half past four in the morning, in bed at five, asleep at six, and ready for breakfast at eight—refreshed and ready for more activities. They were liberally furnished, and have been industriously carried on ever since. Yesterday I spent two pleasant and exciting hours witnessing a Ben Jonson masque performed at the Plaza Hotel by about twenty young and attractive creatures of the two sexes, and it was wonderful for rich and beautiful costumes, for excellent singing, and for acting which I had not seen approached before by amateurs. I dined out in the evening at the Doubledays', and went from there to the Guinnesses', in Washington Square. By eleven a great throng had gathered. There was fine instrumental music and fine singing. The illustrious Caruso was present. I had not seen him before, off the operatic stage. It was a highly fashionable company, but I went in white clothes, because that is my custom, and because everybody approves it. That bright and engaging and untamed young Virginian, a distant cousin of mine, Mrs. William Waldorf Astor, who is over from England on a visit to her people, was there, and at midnight she dragged me into the middle of the room and commanded the music to strike up and then she required me to dance with her. I was willing; I had never danced, but I always knew I could do it if I wanted to. Our performance brought down the house, as the phrase goes, and I privately thought it was rather unusually good myself—and I knew there was a sufficiency of life and activity in it, for one thing. We got an immense encore and responded to it, adding several fresh and hitherto unattempted and finely artistic variations. I promised to visit her in England next summer, and spend a few weeks at Cliveden. I probably can't go, but I would greatly like to see that wonderful place. Shortly after midnight I came away with Prince Troubetskoi and Peter Dunne ("Mr. Dooley"); many were departing, but many were arriving to take their places.

It is as I said, I am not leaving for Bermuda to build up my health, for there is nothing the matter with it; I am going because a change of scene and climate is absolutely necessary for H. H. Rogers, and he won't go unless I go too. I have divested myself of engagements until the 16th of April.

Return from Bermuda—Mr. Clemens's mistake in not recognizing the Chief Justice—Some characteristics of Earl Grey.

Miss Lyon and the Rogerses and I arrived back from Bermuda three days ago, after a delightful and health-restoring absence of seven weeks.

I talked twice in that fairyland—once for the benefit of the Hospital and once for the benefit of the Aquarium. Upon the latter occasion I came near to making a regrettable blunder. The Opera House has no stage door, therefore I was brought down the central aisle and temporarily located in a chair in the front row, whence I was to mount to the stage by a short step-ladder when my time should come. I knew that my performance was to be preceded by a speech by the Chief Justice in the nature of a report of the condition and prospects of the Aquarium; I also knew that he would do his speaking not from the stage but from the floor of the house, bracing his back against the stage and facing the audience. At my right was an empty chair; at my left were four others; these four were swathed in British flags and were the places of honor; they were to be occupied by their Excellencies Governor Wodehouse and wife and by their visiting Excellencies, Countess Grey and Earl Grey, Governor-General of Canada. From old experience in lecturing around the world in British colonies I knew that the official group would not arrive until after the rest of the house had assembled. After I had been seated a while the Chief Justice came in and sat down at my right. I had known him a year ago, but did not remember him. He was cordial, and I pretended to know him. I supposed that he was Jones, or Smith, or Brown, and that I was trespassing upon a seat which belonged by rights to his wife, or some other friend, so I hastened to assure him that I was going to occupy the seat only temporarily. I was meaning that for an apology, and I fully expected him to assure me that it was all right, and that his friend could wait, but he embarrassed me by not saying anything at all; necessarily my fraudulent cordiality had made him suppose that I knew him, and knew what he was there for, and so he naturally couldn't think of anything to say in answer to a remark which hadn't any sense in it. I was uncomfortable, and tried to think of something to talk about that could modify the awkwardness of the situation, but nothing occurred to me. I waited and waited, and fished around in my mind for something happy to say, but I didn't catch anything. At last the house was crammed; then after a brief pause and a waiting silence the orchestra struck up "God Save the King," and the house rose. I knew by this sign that the dignitaries had entered the place. They came down to the front and shook hands and took their seats, and I turned to my unknown and apparently new acquaintance at my right and started to say heartily, "Now if the damned Chief Justice would arrive and do his stunt the show could proceed," but Providence interfered and saved me—the first favor I have received from that source this year—for just as I had got out the first word of the remark his Excellency the Governor, with a bow and a smile and a wave of the hand toward my new friend, said:

"Mr. Chief Justice, please take the floor."

I was paralysed for a moment; then, as I came to, I felt as I had not felt before for sixty-five years—the time that the slave woman plucked me out of Bear Creek by the hair of my head when I was going down for the third time.

Earl Grey is a winning and lovable man and a fine and sterling character. He made the voyage back with us. He has lived a great deal upon the frontiers of the world and has been familiar with its rough life and its half-wild cowboys, gold-miners and ranchmen, and is unreservedly fond of those rude and manly men. He has no airs, and was ready to talk with anybody that came along; without effort he puts anybody and everybody at ease in a few moments—even young girls. One of my angel-fishes was along—a diffident Boston schoolgirl of sixteen years—and for five minutes after he joined us where we sat on the after-deck, in the sunshine, she was timid, and couldn't find her vocabulary; but after a little while she was at home, her self-consciousness disappeared, and she was eagerly and interestedly telling him a story which she had read, and requiring him to admire its several ingenuities in turn as she came to them—which he cordially did.

He travels the Dominion in plain clothes and with no attendants except an aide-de-camp and a couple of uniformed mounted police; his friendly face wins his way for him everywhere. His aide-de-camp furnished me several instances of this; one of them was to this effect: one day the little party rode up to a humble dwelling in the remotenesses of Canada, and a gray-headed Scotch-Presbyterian mother in Israel came out with a greeting for the horsemen and laid her hand upon the Earl's knee and looked sweetly up at his face and said:

"I see by the soldiers that you are the Governor-General, yet I seem to be no more afraid to talk to you than I would to talk to Christ."

Dictated April 17, 1908

Mr. Clemens's Club of ten angel-fishes—Headquarters to be in billiard room of new home in Redding—Letter to Mr. Twichell regarding the New Movement originating in Boston.

One day at Riverdale-on-the-Hudson Mrs. Clemens and I were mourning for our lost little ones. Not that they were dead, but lost to us all the same. Gone out of our lives forever—*as little children.* They were still with us, but they were become women, and they walked with us upon our own level. There was a wide gulf, a gulf as wide as the horizons, between *these* children and *those.* We were always having vague dream-glimpses of them as they had used to be in the long-vanished years—glimpses of them playing and romping, with short frocks on, and spindle legs, and hair-tails down their backs—and always they were far and dim, and we could not hear their shouts and their laughter. How we longed to gather them to our arms! but they were only dainty and darling spectres, and they faded away and vanished, and left us desolate.

That day I put into verse, as well as I could, the feeling that was haunting us. The verses were not for publication, and were never published, but I will insert them here as being qualified to throw light upon my worship of schoolgirls—if worship be the right name, and I know it is.

"In Dim and Fitful Visions They Flit Across the Distances."

―――

In Memory of

Olivia Susan Clemens

―――

Departed this life August 18, 1896.

―――

"I am old, poor lady.
If sympathy of one whose years—"

"*Experience* is age; not years!
Your face is ignorantly smooth, and ignorantly pink;
You have lived long, and nothing suffered.
You try to pity me, I see the good intent, I know it is your best;
But how shall you pay out in coin
What yet lies bedded in your ores?
The fires of grief—*they* lap the heart in flame,
They smelt the red gold free! It is the bleeding heart
That pays the due of woe in metal fire-assayed,—
Not kindly-meaning paper
Drawn upon an unexploited mine
Which one *may* find some day in case by malice of the fates
Misfortune shall so order it."

She dreamed a moment in her past,
With absent look, and mumbled, in her pain,
"Oh, I am old in grief—so old!" And presently began
The story of her wounds, as one who muses to himself,
Scarce knowing that he speaks:
"My curly-headed fay!
My baby girl—how long ago that was!—
'Tis five and twenty years—an age!
"There sat I, thinking of my happiness,
The riches garnered in my heart, my hopes
Fulfilled beyond my dreams, and wondering
If any in the world knew such content as I:
"And now, from out my veiling lids
I caught a flash of sun-lit golden hair,
But kept the secret to myself. I knew the game:
A bear was lurking there, I knew it well,
And knew its ways. All stealthily it crept
In shadow and concealment of the wood—
(Which others thought a sofa of the horse-hair type)—
Until it gained the nearest coign of vantage:

Then—out it burst upon me with a roar, and I
Collapsed in fright!—which was my part to play.
    "O, I can see my darling yet: the little form
In slip of flimsy stuff all creamy white,
Pink-belted waist with ample bows,
Blue shoes scarce bigger than the housecat's ears—
Capering in delight and choked with glee
To see me so becrazed with fright.
    "Then suddenly the laughter ceased—
Drowned, dear heart, in penitential tears—
She flew to me and hugged me close,
And kissed my eyes and face and mouth,
And soothed away my fears with anxious words,
'Look up, mamma, don't cry; it's not a *real* bear, it's only me.'

    "Ah me, ah me, how could I know
That I should look upon her face no more!"

      "Poor soul! She died? That very day?"

    "No. Lost, I think—or stolen away;
We never knew."
    It smote me cold; it smote me dumb;
There were no words to say. She noted not
Or if I spoke or no, but drifted on
Along her tale of griefs—that weary road
The wretched travel day and night,
From eve to dawn and dawn to eve again,
Whilst happier mortals toil or sleep:

    "No, I have not been spared.
So long ago it seems an age, misfortune came again.
'Tis sixteen years. Could I forget the count? Ah, no, ah, no.
The dearest little maid—scarce ten years old—
How strange it was—how strange—how strange!
    "It was a summer afternoon; the hill
Rose green above me and about, and in the vale below
The distant village slept, and all the world
Was steeped in dreams. Upon me lay this peace,
And I forgot my sorrow in its spell. And now
My little maid passed by, and she
Was deep in thought upon a solemn thing:
A disobedience, and my reproof. Upon my face
She 'must not look until the day was done;'
For she was doing penance. . . . *She?*
O, it was *I!* What mother knows not that?
And so she passed, I worshiping and longing. . . .
It was not wrong? You do not think me wrong?
I did it for the best. Indeed I meant it so.
And it was done in love—not passion; no,

But only love. You do not think me wrong?
'Twould comfort me to think I was not wrong. . . .
If I had spoken! If I had known—if I had only known!

    "As then she was, I see her still;
And ever as I look, awake or in my dreams,
She passes by. Unheeding me, she passes by!
    "By duty urged, I checked the hail all charged with love
That burned upon my tongue, and let her pass unwelcomed—
Sat worshiping, and let her pass unwelcomed. . . .
Ah, how was I to know that doom was in the air!

    "She flits before me now:
The peach-bloom gown of gauzy crêpe,
The plaited tails of hair,
The ribbons floating from the summer hat,
The grieving face, droop'd head absorbed with care.
O, dainty little form!—
I see it move, receding slow along the path,
By hovering butterflies besieged; I see it reach
The breezy top and show clear-cut against the sky. . . .
Then pass beyond and sink from sight—forever!"

        "To death?"

    "God knows. But lost to me;
To come no more, to bless my eyes no more in life.
Where now she wanders—if she wander still and live—
That shall I never know. . . . And there is yet
Another."

        "Gone?"
    "Taken while I stood and gazed!"
            "O, pitiful!"

    "In presence of a hundred friends
She vanished from my eyes! In my own house
It was. Within, was light and cheer; without,
A blustering winter's night. There was a play;
It was her own; for she had wrought it out,
Unhelped, from her own head—and she
But turned sixteen! A pretty play,
All graced with cunning fantasies,
And happy songs, and peopled all with fays,
And silvan gods and goddesses,
And shepherds, too, that piped and danced,
And wore the guileless hours away
In care-free romps and games.
    "Her girlhood mates played in the piece,
And she as well: a goddess, she,—
And looked it, as it seemed to me.

"'Twas fairyland restored—so beautiful it was
And innocent. It made us cry, we elder ones,
To live our lost youth o'er again
With these its happy heirs.
        "Slowly, at last, the curtain fell.
Before us, there, she stood, all wreathed and draped
In roses pearled with dew—so sweet, so glad,
So radiant!—and flung us kisses through the storm
Of praise that crowned her triumph. . . . O,
Across the mists of time I see her yet,
My Goddess of the Flowers!

        . . . . "The curtain hid her. . . .
Do you comprehend? Till time shall end!
Out of my life she vanished while I looked!

        . . . . "Ten years are flown.
O, I have watched so long,
So long. But she will come no more. . . .
No more. No, she will come no more."

    She sobbed, and dumbly moaned, a little time,
I silent, wanting words to comfort griefs like these;
Then, sighing, took she up her tale again:

        "Yet even this I over-lived
And in my heart of hearts gave thanks
That of my jewels one was left,
That of my jewels still the richest one
Was spared me to delight my eye
And light the darkness of my days.
        "My idol, she!
I hugged her to my dreading soul—my precious one!—
And daily died with fear. For now,
To me all things were terrors, that before
Were innocent of harm: the rain, the snow, the sun—
I blenched if they but touched her.
        "O, tall and fair and beautiful she was!
And all the world to me, and I to her. In her I lived,
And she in me. We were not two, but one.
And it was little like the common tie that binds
The mother and the child, but liker that
Which binds two lovers:
The hours were blank when we were separate;
The time was heavy and the sun was cold,
Life lost its worth. And when the blank was past,
And we drank life again from out each other's eyes
And lips and speech—oh, heaven itself could nothing add
To that contenting joy! . . .
        "I would you could have seen her.

If you, a stranger . . . But you will never see her now;
Nor I—oh, never more!
　. . . . "How beautiful she was!
Not outwardly alone,—within, as well. Her spirit
Answered to her face, her mind ennobled both. . . .
And now. . . .
O, now to know that in that wonder-working intellect
The light is quenched, the cunning wheels are still,
The eyes that spoke, the voice that charmed,
Have ceased from their enchantments!

　. . . . "How dear she was! how full of life!
A creature made of joyous fire and flame and impulse—
A living ecstasy! Ah who could dream
That she could die? . . . Two years—two little years ago. . . .
　"It seems so strange. . . . so strange . . .
Struck down unwarned!
In the unbought grace of youth laid low—
In the glory of her fresh young bloom laid low—
In the morning of her life cut down!
　"And I not by! Not by
When the shadows fell, the night of death closed down,
The sun that lit my life went out. Not by to answer
When the latest whisper passed the lips
That were so dear to me—my name!
Far from my post! the world's whole breadth away.
O, sinking in the waves of death she cried to me
For mother-help, and got for answer—
Silence!"
　"O, you wring my heart!
God pity you, poor lady! God pity you, and grant
That this hard stroke shall be the last
That in His providence—"
　I stopped—rebuked by something in her face.
She drifted into dreams—she did not hear;
Her thoughts were far away,
Wandering among the ruins of her life.
Then presently she muttered to herself,
　　"All gone.
All; and she, the last, my joy, my pride, my solace—
Dead. Dead, in the perfected flower of her youth."

　She rose, and went her way.
I questioned one who seemed to know her, and he said,
　"Poor lady, she is mad.
She is bereft of four, she thinks. There was but one."

　　Ah, God!
And yet, poor broken heart, she said the truth!
We that are old—we comprehend; even we

That are not mad: whose grown-up scions still abide,
Their tale complete:
Their earlier selves we glimpse at intervals
Far in the dimming past;
We see the little forms as once they were,
And whilst we ache to take them to our hearts,
The vision fades. We know them lost to us—
Forever lost; we cannot have them back;
We miss them as we miss the dead,
We mourn them as we mourn the dead.

                                                    S. L. C.
York Harbor, August 18, 1902.

After my wife's death, June 5, 1904, I experienced a long period of unrest and loneliness. Clara and Jean were busy with their studies and their labors, and I was washing about on a forlorn sea of banquets and speech-making in high and holy causes—industries which furnished me intellectual cheer and entertainment, but got at my heart for an evening only, then left it dry and dusty. I had reached the grandpapa stage of life; and what I lacked and what I needed, was grandchildren, but I didn't know it. By and by this knowledge came by accident, on a fortunate day, a golden day, and my heart has never been empty of grandchildren since. No, it is a treasure-palace of little people whom I worship, and whose degraded and willing slave I am. In grandchildren I am the richest man that lives to-day: for I *select* my grandchildren, whereas all other grandfathers have to take them as they come, good, bad and indifferent.

The accident I refer to, was the advent of Dorothy Butes, fourteen years old, who wanted to come and look at me. Her mother brought her. There was never a lovelier child. English, with the English complexion; and simple, sincere, frank and straightforward, as became her time of life. This was more than two years ago. She came to see me every few weeks, until she returned to England eight months ago. Since then, we correspond.

My next prize was Frances Nunnally, schoolgirl, of Atlanta, Georgia, whom I call Francesca for short. I have already told what pleasant times we had together every day in London, last summer, returning calls. She was sixteen then, a dear sweet grave little body, and very welcome in those English homes. She will pay me a visit six weeks hence, when she comes North with her parents Europe-bound. She is a faithful correspondent.

My third prize was Dorothy Quick—ten years and ten-twelfths of a year old when I captured her at sea last summer on the return-voyage from England. What a Dorothy it is! How many chapters have I already talked about her, and about her bright and booming and electrical ways, and her punctuationless literature and her adorably lawless spelling? Have I exhausted her as a text for talk? No. Nobody could do it. At least nobody who worships her as I worship her. She is eleven years and nearly eight-twelfths of a year old, now, and just a dear! She was to come to me as soon as I should get back from Bermuda, but she has an earlier grandpa, and he is leaving for Europe next Monday morning, and naturally he had to have the last of her before sailing. Is she still her old self, and is her pen characteristically brisk and her spelling and punctuation undamaged by time and still my pride and delight? Yes:

> Dear Mr Clemens
> I am very glad you are home and I am so glad I am to see you on Monday I will not be able to come Monday Morning but will come on the one-nine train I will be so glad to see you I am sorry not being able to be with you on Saturday but I really want to be with grandpa and now I must close.
> with love to you and miss Lyon
>
> Your loving
Dorothy
>
> P.S. Grandpa is going away that is why I must be with him on sunday
>
> Dorothy

Next is Margaret—Margaret Blackmer, New York, twelve years old last New Year's. She of the identification-shell. (See a previous chapter.) Those shells were so frail and delicate that they could not endure exposure on a watch-chain, therefore we have put them safely and sacredly away and hung gold shells enameled with iridescent shell-colors on our watch-chains to represent them and do the identifying with. Margaret's father will bring her down from her school at Briarcliff on the Hudson six days hence to visit me—as I learn per her letter of five days ago—and then she will go with me to a play at the Children's Theatre, where, as Honorary President of that admirable institution, I am to say a few words.

Next is Irene—Irene Gerken, of 75th street, New York, that beautiful and graceful and altogether wonderful child—I mean fairy—of twelve summers. To-morrow she will go to a matinée with me, and we are to play billiards the rest of the day. In Bermuda, last January, we played much billiards together, and a certain position of the balls is still known by her name there. When her ball backed itself against the cushion and became thereby nearly unusable, she was never embarrassed by that defect but always knew how to remedy it: she just moved it out to a handier place, without remark or apology and blandly fired away! Down there, now, when a ball lies glued to a cushion, gentlemen who have never seen that child lament and say, "O, hang it, here's another Irene!"

Next is Hellen Martin, of Montreal, Canada, a slim and bright and sweet little creature aged ten and a half years.

Next is Jean Spurr, aged thirteen the 14th of last March, and of such is the kingdom of Heaven.

Next is Loraine Allen, nine and a half years old, with the voice of a flute and a face as like a flower as can be, and as graciously and enchantingly beautiful as ever any flower was.

Next is Helen Allen, aged thirteen, native of Bermuda, perfect in character, lovely in disposition, and a captivator at sight!

Next—and last, to date—is Dorothy Sturgis, aged sixteen, of Boston. This is the charming child mentioned in yesterday's chapter when I was talking about Lord Grey.

On the voyage we were together at the stern watching the huge waves lift the ship skyward then drop her, most thrillingly H—alifaxward, when one of them of vast bulk leaped over the taffrail and knocked us down and buried us under several tons of salt water. The papers, from one end of America to the other, made a perilous and thunder-some event of it, but it wasn't that kind of a thing at all. Dorothy was not discomposed, nobody was hurt, we changed our clothes from the skin outward, and were on deck again in half an hour. In talking of Dorothy yesterday I referred to her as one of my "angel-fishes."

All the ten schoolgirls in the above list are my angel-fishes, and constitute my Club, whose name is "The Aquarium," and contains no creature but these angel-fishes and one slave. I am the slave. The Bermudian angel-fish, with its splendid blue decorations, is easily the most beautiful fish that swims, I think. So I thought I would call my ten pets angel-fishes, and their Club the Aquarium.

The Club's badge is the angel-fish's splendors reproduced in enamels and mounted for service as a lapel-pin—at least that is where the girls wear it. I get these little pins in Bermuda; they are made in Norway.

A year or two ago I bought a lovely piece of landscape of 210 acres in the country near Redding, Connecticut, and John Howells, the son of his father, is building a villa there for me. We'll spend the coming summer in it.

The billiard room will have the legend "The Aquarium" over its door, for it is to be the Club's official headquarters. There is an angel-fish bedroom—double-bedded—and I expect to have a fish and her mother in it as often as Providence will permit.

There's a letter from the little Montreal Hellen. I will begin an answer now, and finish it later:

> I miss you, dear Hellen. I miss Bermuda too, but not so much as I miss you; for you were rare, and occasional, and select, and Ltd., whereas Bermuda's charms and graciousnesses were free and common and unrestricted,—like the rain, you know, which falls upon the just and the unjust alike; a thing which would not happen if I were superintending the rain's affairs. No, I would rain softly and sweetly upon the just, but whenever I caught a sample of the unjust outdoors I would drown him.

Reverend Twichell is coming down from Hartford, and I will send him a word of welcome right now:

> I am glad, Joe—uncommonly glad—for you will tell me about the "new move-ment" up your way which your clergy have been importing from Boston. Something of it has reached me, and has filled me to the eyelids with irreverent laughter. You will tell me if my understanding of the New Movement is correct: to wit, that it is just Christian Science, with some of the ear-marks painted over and the others removed, after the fashion of the unanointed cattle-thieves of the wild, wild West. My word, how ecclesiastical history do repeat herself! The Jews steal a God and a Creation and a Flood and a Moral Code from Babylon; Egypt steals the like from a forgotten Antiquity; Greece steals the swag from Egypt; Rome steals it from

Greece; Christianity comes belated along and steals morals and miracles and one thing and another from Budh and Confucius; Christian Science arrives and steals the Christian outfit and gives it a new name; and now at last comes the Boston puritan—hater of Christian Science—and steals the plunder anew, and re-baptizes it, and shouts tearful and grateful glory to God for winking at the mulct and not letting on—according to His shady custom these thirty million years.

Oh yes, I am aware that the Science was emptying New England's churches, and that the wise recognized that something had got to be done or the Church must go out of business and put up its pulpits at auction; I am aware that the peril was forestalled, and *how;* I am aware that Christian Science, disguised and new-named, has arrived in Hartford and is being preached and thankfully welcomed—where? In the most fitting of all places: the Theological Factory, which was largely built out of stolen money. Money stolen from me by that precious Christian, Newton Case, and his pals of the American Publishing Company.

Oh, dear Joe, why doesn't somebody write a tract on "How to Be a Christian and yet keep your Hands off of Other People's Things."

Dictated April 27, 1908

Extract from District-Attorney Jerome's recent speech in which he declares that a democratic government won't work as long as we have government by the newspapers—Mr. Clemens comments upon this speech and upon the evil influence of the daily papers.

District-Attorney Jerome has been telling some straight truths at a banquet the other night. The newspaper report says:

Mr. Jerome was cheered when he arose and began by praising the British Ambassador, Mr. Bryce. He then said that Americans expected that their humor would tide them over the rough places.

"Nothing can be done," said Mr. Jerome, "if you men will not take more interest in public life. You take this great State of New York and turn it over to Pat. McCarren, Charley Murphy, Fingy Conners and Packy McCabe and then you sit down. I say God bless the Irish and I am glad you haven't conquered them. Still I don't want to see the State run by those four Irishmen."

The District Attorney then took another tack.

"I tell you," declared Mr. Jerome, "a democratic government won't work as long as you have government by the newspapers. No other form of government devised by the mind of man requires so much care from its citizens (meaning democratic government). You cannot make things right by statutes, you can only make them work by men. Men may say they don't care for approbation, but the man who tells you that is a fool and a liar.

"He tells you that he doesn't care for approbation and he lies and he is a fool if he thinks you will believe it. A democratic form of government should be based on universal suffrage, but it is now based on public opinion. What makes it so is that you men of education have not done your duty. You read the headlines in the newspapers and it makes no impression upon you. You read them again—the same headlines—for a few weeks and then you have a decided opinion without a single fact to substantiate it. I tell you a democratic government won't work as long as we have government by the newspapers.

"Here, only recently, the head of a great financial institution killed himself. He made what atonement he could, and then a great journal spread before the public his private life. He had two lovely daughters growing up. Did it concern the public in any way to read the story of his personal wrongdoing that was blazoned before the world? Did it make it more possible for us to work out our own institutions?

"It was done for what? It was for cash. And yet we read it and take in every detail that was spread before us. A large advertiser in Philadelphia guilty of a crime committed suicide here. Not a paper in Philadelphia chronicled it. A great and enterprising newspaper of New York owned by a great and enterprising citizen sent a special edition to Philadelphia with the fearful story blazing forth to wreck that home.

"Another instance—a prominent man in this city was shot dead in a department store. Not a paper in the city said where it was done. If I want a paper controlled where do I go?"

Mr. Jerome here mentioned the names of a number of large department stores of the city.

"The leading publications of this city are dictated to by the counting-rooms," continued the District-Attorney. "One of our great papers investigated ice. One of its men went up to Maine and looked around, and then he returned and went to the President of the company and said to him: 'I have got an option on a little ice; don't you want to buy it.' That was in 1906, when ice was scarce, and they might have been glad to get it.

"At any rate they put a price on that ice that netted the young man $5,000. These papers lead us by the glamor of their headlines and they trail into the dust the good name of a public officer trying to do his sworn duty—and they do it for personal reasons.

"I recently sat next to a great critic at a musical performance. I am not much of a musician, but I can sing. This great critic told me that his criticisms were blue pencilled in the office because of the advertising end of the paper.

"What do the libel laws of to-day amount to? I was called a thief, in so many words. For two years I have been trying to get that up in a suit. When the Public Service bill was up in Albany I found that hardly a man had given any consideration to that bill. They said they voted as they did for fear of the newspapers. The same was true of the Eighty Cent Gas bill—they were afraid of the papers. This passing of legislation under the whip is wrong. Maybe the judgment of a newspaper man is better than anybody else's, and if that is true the remedy is to send the editor to the Legislature."

What we call our civilization is steadily deteriorating, I think. We were a pretty clean people before the war; we seem to be rotten at the heart now. The newspapers are mainly responsible for this. They publish every loathsome thing they can get hold of, and if the simple facts are not odious enough they exaggerate them. There are twenty-five hundred daily newspapers in the country, and I know of only six whose conduct is not in accordance with what Jerome has said about them and with what I have just said concerning them. Jay Gould made commercial dishonesty a fashion, and respectable; all the attempts made to check the spread of the decay which he started have failed.

Our newspaper is a singular product. Its editorial page is morally clean; its ideals are high and fine, and its advocacy of them is able, eloquent, and convincing; then along with it, every day, we have seven pages of poisonous dirt in the form of news. Our newspaper is a kind of temple, with one angel in it and seven devils. The nation has become fond of the seven devils, and is feverishly interested, hungrily interested, in all they may have to say; but it is only the select few that listen to the angel. The seven devils wield a prodigious influence; they wield seven-eighths of the influence exercised by the nation's newspapers, and it is a damaging influence. The good accomplished by the other eighth certainly has a value, but it is the value of one to seven.

We are hearing from the Gould family again. Their doings constitute our court-circular. I take the following synopsis from a newspaper of last week:

SORROWS OF CUPID IN GOULD FAMILY.

Howard Gould.

Married Katherine Clemmons, an actress, in October, 1898.

Sued by her for a separation in May, 1907, and alimony based on an income of $1,000,000 a year, alleging cruelty and inhuman treatment.

His answer a charge that she was too friendly with "Buffalo Bill" and later with Dustin Farnum.

Awaiting further disclosures and trial.

Anna Gould.

Married Count Boni de Castellane in March, 1895.

He squandered a large part of her fortune and after a few years there were reports of trouble between them.

She sued him for an absolute divorce, naming many correspondents, and was freed from one Count only to wed another, if Count Helie de Sagan's prediction and hopes are fulfilled.

Frank Gould.

Married Helen Margaret Kelly, daughter of the late Edward Kelly, in December, 1901.

A love match which was soon broken by quarrels and finally culminated in a suit for a limited divorce and the angry separation of the couple.

Anna Gould remains in Europe. Yesterday's court-circular announces that she is in Naples, with that fragrant prince, and is going to marry him. She says she prefers Europe as a residence because it is only in Europe that Americans of the best class can find those refinements which make existence tolerable to that kind of Americans. That we should live to hear a Gould talk refinement and admire it!

Dictated April 28, 1908

"Lord Dundreary" as played by the elder Sothern and by his son.

Lord Dundreary has been revived, after an age-long silence, and is being played by Sothern's son. When my lord came on the stage the sight of him almost gave me a grave-yard shiver; for the reproduction in face, form, manner and costume, of the Dundreary of a quarter of a century ago was nearly perfect in every detail, and it seemed to me for a moment that this was the long-ago dead man up and around again. I can distinctly remember the last time that I saw the elder Sothern play Dundreary. It must be all of twenty-five years ago, I should say. It was in Hartford. The reason I remember it so well is, that I couldn't keep my laughter within reasonable bounds, and was presently pretty nearly, and very uncomfortably, dividing the house's attention with the actor—and so for decency's sake I got up and went out in the midst of the performance.

In those days it was the funniest thing I had ever seen on the stage, and I find that it is just as funny now as it was then. I saw it yesterday. I am old and intelligent now, and by earnest and watchful effort was able to keep from going into hysterics over it, but there were others present who had not my luck. A girl in the next box to me was a positive calamity to the actors. She kept up a continual shriek of laughter that made it difficult for them to look unconscious of her and keep their attention upon their work.

A generation ago, Dundreary made in London the first long-run record of modern times. Sothern played it there every night for a couple of years, at a time when a hundred nights was a long run, and two hundred an extraordinary one. It was said that Sothern's people became practically idiotic from saying and doing the same things every night for months and months on a stretch, and had to be laid off periodically to save their rotting mentality.

Daniel Frohman and his wife have been dining with us, and Frohman said that when Laura Keene accepted the play and staged it here in New York, she cast Sothern for Dundreary's part and he refused to play it. He was a stock actor on a moderate salary, but Dundreary was altogether too minor a part for even him. There were only seventeen lines of it, and nothing in the seventeen lines worth saying; besides they furnished no occasion for acting, and Sothern said that as between playing Dundreary and a deaf and dumb Roman soldier, he would prefer the gentleman in the tin armor. Frohman said that in this emergency Laura Keene did what no manager ought ever to do—she gave up her mastership and told Sothern that if he would play the part he might do whatever he pleased with it. Sothern accepted the terms and took such liberal advantage of them that before long he was become the chief figure on the stage, and presently almost the only figure, and was talking fifteen words to anybody else's one. The piece's name, "The American Cousin," sank out of sight and remained out of sight and hearing permanently. The piece came to be called "Lord Dundreary;" it is called so yet, and there is almost nothing left of the play; it isn't a play any longer, it is only a monologue, and nobody cares for anything in it but the idiotic and fascinating nobleman.

Dictated April 29, 1908

Mr. Clemens meets Dr. Van Dyke near Cathedral and talks with him concerning the human race—Copy of extract from one of Dr. Van Dyke's articles on fishing.

Last night I read in the *Atlantic* a passage from one of Rev. Dr. Van Dyke's books, and I cut it out, with a vaguely defined notion that I might need it some time or other, by and by. I like Van Dyke, and I greatly admire his literary style—this notwithstanding the drawback that a good deal of his literary product is of a religious sort. He is about thirty-five years old, he is a Presbyterian, he is a clergyman, he is a member of the faculty of Princeton University. Still, I like him and admire him, notwithstanding.

This forenoon I was lounging along Fifth Avenue, and I stopped opposite the Roman Catholic cathedral to contemplate the crowd massed in front of the edifice. It is a grand Catholic day—a grand Catholic week, in fact. There's a cardinal here with a message from the Pope, there are sixty bishops on hand, and there is to be great doings. A hand touched my shoulder—it was Van Dyke's! We hadn't met for a year. He nodded toward the multitude, and said:

"What do you think of it? Doesn't it warm your heart? They are ignorant and poor, but they have faith, they have belief, and it uplifts them, it makes them free. They have feelings, they have views, convictions, and they live under a flag where they have no master, and where they have the right and the privilege of doing their own thinking, and of acting according to their preference, unmolested. What do you think of it?"

"I think you have misinterpreted some of the details. You think that these people think. You know better. They don't think; they get all their ostensible thinkings at second hand; they get their feelings at second hand; they get their faith, their beliefs, their convictions at second hand. They are in no sense free. They are like you and me and like all the rest of the human race—slaves. Slaves of custom, slaves of circumstance, environment, association. This crowd is the human race in little. It is no trouble to love the human race, and we do love it, for it is a child, and one can't help loving a child; but the minute we set out to *admire* the race we do as you have done—select and admire qualities which it doesn't possess."

And so on and so on; we argued and argued, and arrived where we began: he clung to his reverence for the race as the grandest of the Creator's inventions, and I clung to my conviction that it was not an invention to be really proud of. We had settled nothing. We were quiet for a while, and loafed peaceably along down the street. Then he took up the matter again. He reminded me that there were certain undeniably fine and beautiful qualities in our human nature. To wit, that we are brave, and hate cowardly acts; that we are loyal and true, and hate treachery and deceit; that we are just and fair and honorable, and hate injustice and unfairness; that we pity the weak, and protect them from wrong and harm; that we magnanimously stand between the oppressor and the oppressed, and between the man of cruel disposition and his friendless victim.

I asked him if he was acquainted with this person.

He said he was—hundreds of him; that, broadly speaking, he had been describing a Christian; that a Christian, at his best, was just such a person as he had been portraying. I said—

"I know a very good Christian who cannot fill this bill—nor any detail of it, in fact."

"I must take that as a jest," he said, lightly.

"No, not a jest."

"Then as at least an extravagance, an exaggeration?"

"No, as fact, simple fact. And I am not speaking of a commonplace Christian, but of a high-class one; one whose Christian record is without spot; one who can take rank, unchallenged, with the very best. I have not known a better; and I love him and admire him."

"Come—you love and admire him, and yet he cannot fill any single detail of that beautiful character which I have portrayed?"

"Not a single one. Let me describe one of his performances. He conceived the idea of getting some pleasure out of deceiving, beguiling, swindling, pursuing, frightening, capturing, torturing, mutilating and murdering a child—"

"Im-possible!"

"A child that had never done him any harm; a child that was gratefully enjoying its innocent life and liberty, and not suspecting that any one would want to take them away from it—for any reason, least of all for the mere pleasure of it. And so—"

"You are describing a Christian? There is no such Christian. You are describing a madman."

"No, a Christian—as good a one as lives. He sought out the child where it was playing, and offered it some dainties—offered them cunningly, persuasively, treacherously, cowardly, and the child, mistaking him for one who meant it a kindness, thankfully swallowed the dainties—then fled away in pain and terror, for the gift was poisoned. The man was full of joy at the success of his ingenious fraud, and chased the frightened child from one refuge to another for an hour, in a delirium of delight, and finally caught it and killed it; and by his eloquent enthusiasms one could see that he was as proud of his exploit as ever brave knight was, of deceiving, beguiling, betraying and destroying a cruel and wicked and pestilent giant thirty feet high. There—do you see? Is there any resemblance between this Christian and yours? This one was not brave, but the reverse of it; he was not fair and honorable, he was a deceiver, a beguiler, a swindler, he took advantage of ignorant trustfulness and betrayed it; he had no pity for distress and fright and pain, but took a frenzied delight in causing them, and watching the effects. He was no protector of threatened liberty and menaced life, but took them both. And did it for fun. Merely for fun. But you seem to doubt me. Here is his own account of it; read it yourself; I clipped it out of the *Atlantic* last night. For 'fish' in the text, read 'child.' There is no other difference. It is a Christian in both cases, and in both cases the human race is exposed for what it is—a self-admiring humbug."

As a point of departure, listen to a quotation from Dr. Henry van Dyke:—

"Chrr! sings the reel. The line tightens. The little rod firmly gripped in my hands bends into a bow of beauty, and a hundred feet behind us a splendid silver salmon leaps into the air. 'What is it?' cries the gypsy, 'a fish?' It is a fish, indeed, a noble ouananiche, and well hooked. Now if the gulls were here who grab little fish suddenly and never give them a chance; and if the mealy-mouthed sentimentalists were here, who like their fish slowly strangled to death in nets, they should see a fairer method of angling.

"The weight of the fish is twenty times that of the rod against which he matches himself. The tiny hook is caught painlessly in the gristle of his jaws. The line is long and light. He has the whole lake to play in, and he uses almost all of it, running, leaping, sounding the deep water, turning suddenly to get a slack line. The gypsy, tremendously excited, manages the boat with perfect skill, rowing this way and that way, advancing or backing water to meet the tactics of the fish, and doing the most important part of the work.

"After half an hour the ouananiche begins to grow tired and can be reeled in near to the boat. We can see him distinctly as he gleams in the dark water. It is time to think of landing him. Then we remember with a flash of despair that we have no landing-net! To lift him from the water by this line would break it in an instant. There is not a foot of the rocky shore smooth enough to beach him on. Our caps are far too small to use as a net for such a fish. What to do? We must row around with him gently and quietly for another ten minutes, until he is quite weary and tame. Now let me draw him softly toward the boat, slip my fingers under his gills to give a firm hold, and lift him quickly over the gunwale before he can gasp or kick. A tap on the head with the empty rod-case,—there he is,—the prettiest land-locked salmon that I ever saw, plump, round, perfectly shaped and colored, and just six and a half pounds in weight, the record fish of Jordan Pond."

We had a very good time together for an hour. And didn't agree about anything. But it was for this reason that we had a good time, disagreement being the salt of a talk. Van Dyke is a good instance of a certain fact: that outside of a man's own specialty, his thinkings are poor and slipshod, and his conclusions not valuable. Van Dyke's specialty is English Literature; he has studied it with deep and eager interest, and with an alert and splendid intelligence. With the result that the soundness of his judgments upon it is not to be lightly challenged by anybody. But he doesn't know any more about the human being than the President does, or the Pope, or the philosophers, or the cat. I wanted to give him a copy of my privately printed, unsigned, unacknowledged and unpublished gospel, "What is Man?" for his enlightenment, but thought better of it. He wouldn't understand it.

Dictated May 21, 1908

**A son of "Buck" Brown writes requesting an interview—"Buck"
Brown attended Dawson's school—The magazine publishers'**

luncheon at the Aldine Club—Although probably every one of these publishers had said harsh things about the Standard Oil chiefs they gave them a hearty welcome at the luncheon, Mr. Doubleday and Mr. Clemens having effected the presence there of the two Rockefellers and Henry Rogers.

Yesterday morning brought a note from a son of a former schoolmate of mine requesting an interview. That schoolmate was W. B. Brown—"Buck" Brown, as we called him in that ancient time; ancient is the right word, for the school was Dawson's school, and the time could not have been later than 1846, when I was eleven years old, for my father died in the spring of 1847, and I was never in a school after that event. I remember "Buck" Brown very well, after all these sixty-two years. The school numbered twenty-five boys and girls; some of them were little children; others were older and larger, and "Buck" Brown was the oldest and largest of all; his age was twenty-five, and to the most of us he seemed not of our world, but a patriarch stricken with age, a relic of a hoary antiquity. He was very studious, very grave, even solemn; he had a kindly smile and a disposition in harmony with it; and he had a tongue, but he seldom used it. I shall be glad to talk with the son, and yet the talk, as I foresee, will only be about the tenants of the grave. He mentions the names of many of his father's schoolmates and mine, but they are all dead, most of them many years ago. With each name, as it came under my eye, there flashed before me, often with a sharp vividness, a fresh young face that had been familiar to me two generations ago; and in each case it was a face that is dust and ashes now, and from whose happy young eyes the light was quenched years and years ago.

"Buck" Brown was a most patient creature. At the noon recess he always remained at the schoolhouse to study his lessons while he ate his dinner, and Will Bowen and John Briggs and I always remained also, and sacrificed our dinner for the higher profit of pestering him and playing pranks upon him, but he never lost his temper. In fact I never knew him to lose his sweet serenity except once: there was an idiot slave girl in the town who could not go anywhere without being followed and jeered at, and mocked, and made fun of by the young boys of the place. It was a custom of the time to treat friendless lunatics and idiots in this way, and it attracted no attention; but one day a grown man joined the young ruffians in their persecutions. "Buck" Brown was passing by at the time. Suddenly he was transformed. All his serenities vanished in a moment, and he burst into a fury of passion that was amazing for its fierce intensity. He beat and banged the man until there was little left of him but pulp.

Yesterday the magazine publishers met together at a luncheon at the Aldine Club. They have been meeting there once a month for the last two or three years, with a very wise end in view—this end being to get acquainted with each other, become friendly, and work together for their mutual advantage, instead of each fighting for his own hand as in the days gone by. About forty of these men were present. These are the men who are responsible for the policy of their publications. Their editors are merely salaried servants, and have no authority, and in fact but little influence, perhaps, in the matter of policy. For years now, it has been policy for the magazines to make war, along with the newspapers, against the great corporations and monopolies, and this war has been carried on as such wars are always likely to be conducted where the persons assailed have to take what they get and can't talk back. It has been a cheap and easy matter to be bold and daringly ferocious in attacking the corporations, for the reason that they had no friends—at least no friends that were brave enough to face the general storm in their defence. It was always possible, of course, that the corporations had a defence worth examination and consideration if they could only get a hearing, but for several years such a hearing has been quite impossible. The hostility to the corporations was brought to its height by President Roosevelt's attitude toward them. The corporations were the creation of the atrocious tariffs imposed upon everything by the Republican party, and Mr. Roosevelt and his party have known all the time that all the burdensome monopolies could be squelched by the simple process of reducing the robber tariffs to a figure which would allow the rest of the nation to prosper, instead of conferring the bulk of the prosperity upon a few dozen multimillionaire producers—but neither the President nor the party has ever confessed that this was the case; they have persisted in attacking the symptoms and in letting the disease carefully alone. They have had their reasons for it: the vast election contributions of the money of stockholders have kept that party in power, and the President's ferocious attacks upon them of the last two or three years have been merely a sham and a pretense. He has inspired no real move against them in the courts, he has merely indulged in wordy bluster about what he was going to do.

Among mighty corporations the chief sinner selected for attack was the Standard Oil Company. For some years now, that Company has been freely and volubly charged with every crime and every villainy known to commercial oppression and misconduct, and anybody who could think of any vindictive thing to say about that corporation could promptly get a hearing in the newspapers and the magazines; and so the American world was brought to believe that the Standard Oil people were conscienceless criminals, one and all. The Standard Oil employs sixty-five thousand persons. The Company has been in existence about forty-five years, yet in all that time it has never had a strike. For years now, strikes have been persistently frequent in all the other industries of the country; the newspapers are always full of them; rioting and bloodshed are common because of the strikes. The fact that the Standard Oil Company has never had a strike might suggest to a sane person, here and there, that the Standard Oil chiefs cannot be altogether bad, or they would oppress their sixty-five thousand employees from habit and instinct, if they are so constituted that it is instinctive with them to oppress everybody else. But neither their good standing with their wage-earners nor any other testimony that exists in their favor, can get even a passing hearing in any newspaper or magazine in the United States.

Of the forty-five magazine publishers that were present at that luncheon yesterday, there was probably not one whose magazine had not had the habit, for the past few years, of abusing the Rockefellers, Henry Rogers, and the other chiefs of the Standard Oil, and without doubt those publishers had acquired the habit of heartily hating the said chiefs and of experiencing emotions of horror at the mere mention of their names—and so they must have had some curious sensations when John D. Rockefeller, senior, John D., junior, and Henry Rogers walked in in single file, yesterday, and sat down at the head of the table, elbow to elbow with the President of their Association. To me it was an interesting spectacle, and dramatic. Three-fourths of those magazine publishers had never seen those three persons in their lives before, except in a couple of million photographs and caricatures.

How did these notorious criminals come to venture their persons in this den of their deadly enemies? It happened in this way: Doubleday came here a few days ago and said he had been thinking it was time for somebody connected with the public prints to go and look at a Standard Oil magnate and see what kind of a devil he might seem to be, from an outside inspection; and time, also, for the said publisher to come into actual contact with the fiend and talk with him and try to get on the inside of him and see what he might look like in there. He had been moved to this strange and unchristian project by something he found in the Annual Report of Mr. Rockefeller's Institute for Medical Research—a Report which showed that the ten million dollars which Mr. Rockefeller had put into that Institute was bearing good fruit, such good fruit, in fact, that it would not be popular for the newspaper or magazine press to say much about it, and not good policy to notice it otherwise than in a three-line remark followed by a judicious permanent silence; a Report no paragraph of which could find its way into a newspaper where room was needed for an account of the latest rape. One of the facts in that Report was this: one of the results of the Institute's patient, continuous, and unflagging research into that awful malady, meningitis, was the reduction of its death-rate from 75 per cent of the persons attacked to 25, with the hopeful prospect that that death-rate would presently be still further reduced. There were other great things in that Report, and Doubleday told me about them, but I will not set them down at this time. Doubleday had been vaguely aware that Mr. Rockefeller had been known to make large contributions to charities and to good causes of one sort or another, privately, in addition to the one hundred and thirty-eight million dollars he has publicly contributed to such things. He hunted out some of these cases and found that the facts were in accordance with the rumors, therefore it seemed to Doubleday that perhaps Mr. Rockefeller was not giving away his tens of millions at a time wholly to buy public charity for his Standard Oil offences. Finally he concluded to go and get acquainted with Mr. Rockefeller and see how much of him was Standard Oil fiend and how much of him was average human being. He went to Rockefeller, got acquainted with him, down in the country, played golf with him every day, talked with him hour by hour, got acquainted with his sister-in-law and talked with her about Rockefeller, and it ended in his conceiving a great respect and liking for the man, and also in his conceiving a considerable degree of shame for disrespecting the man this long time upon evidence which presented only one side of his case.

Now then, the idea of Doubleday's visit to me was this: he wanted to bring Rockefeller face to face with all the magazine publishers—and did I think it would be wise for him to do this? He wanted to do Rockefeller a good turn, but possibly it might be a bad turn. The men who had lent their magazines to harsh criticisms of him might resent his appearance among them as an impertinence. He had asked Mr. Rockefeller if he would be willing to meet those men and Rockefeller said,

"Certainly. Why not? I am willing to meet and talk with any body of men, friends or enemies."

Doubleday asked me what I thought of the project—ought he to go on with it? I said I thought it was a very good idea; that I knew Mr. Rockefeller fairly well and was sure he would favorably impress those hostiles. Doubleday said he would go on with the project, but he wanted all the strength he could get; he would like to have Mr. Rogers there. What would I think of that? I said Mr. Rogers's face would destroy any harsh evidence that had ever been brought against him, he wouldn't need to say a word; those men would look at him and would recognize and realize that if he was a villain there wasn't anybody left in the country that wasn't.

Well, then, would I come to the luncheon? And would I get Mr. Rogers to come?

I said I didn't think he would decline; indeed I was quite sure he would accept, and that Doubleday could tell Mr. Rogers I would go if he would come and fetch me.

Mr. Rogers arrived at our house on time yesterday, and drove me to the Aldine Club, and that pleasant little dramatic surprise occurred which I have already mentioned: Rockefeller, his son John, Mr. Rogers and I, filed in and sat with the chairman on the firing line. After a speech from the chairman and a speech from an officer of the organization, explaining the nature of the organization and its purpose, I followed with a speech. Then Mr. Rockefeller was asked by the chairman to make a few remarks. Mr. Rockefeller got up and talked sweetly, sanely, simply, humanly, and with astonishing effectiveness, being interrupted by bursts of applause at the end of almost every sentence; and when he sat down all those men were his friends, and he had achieved one of the completest victories I have ever had any knowledge of. Then the meeting broke up, and by a common impulse the crowd moved forward and each individual of it gave the victor a hearty hand-shake, and along with it some hearty compliments upon his performance as an orator.

But I have forgotten one rather striking incident. This was the reading of a letter in which a physician described an impressively interesting surgical operation which was performed on a child last March. It was a physician's child; it was four months old; it had been stricken by a fearful malady which sometimes attacks grown persons and attacks children with some little frequency; it is an internal hemorrhage, whose details I am not able to describe, and is in almost all cases fatal. The attack was making rapid progress; the physicians in attendance knew of nothing that could be done; the child was evidently dying; the hour was midnight. Some one suggested that one of Mr. Rockefeller's Institute researchers had been making experiments upon kittens which promised a hope—at least a slight hope—for this child.* One of the doctors drove to the house of that physician, reached there at one o'clock, routed him out of his bed, and they drove to the Institute and gathered a few instruments but could not get all that were needed, because the others

* By blood-transfusion, the father to furnish the blood. To mingle old blood and infant blood had never been ventured before, nor considered worth the trial.

were locked up and the holder of the key was not there; but that Institute physician had with him, fortunately, one instrument which was absolutely essential; it was a needle so fine and delicate as to be next to invisible, and its thread was wholly invisible except when held against a black background. They proceeded to the house of the patient. The child was too young for the use of anesthetics, and none were given. The thing necessary to be done, if I remember the details rightly, was to sever a vein of the child and an artery of its father, sew the ends of these tubes together in an absolutely perfect way, making no mistakes in the joining of them, and renew the child's famished blood with the fresh blood of the strong and healthy father. The child was wasted and white and flabby, and it was so small a creature that it possessed no vein large enough for the operation except one hidden deep in the calf of its leg. When they were ready for the operation they could not tell, and had no way of finding out, with absolute certainty, whether the child was still alive or not, but it seemed to be dead. But they proceeded with the operation. The new blood was flushed into the child, and everybody stood by watching to see if there would be any effect. For a time no effect was apparent; then a faint rosy tinge appeared on the tops of the child's ears; after a little this rosy tinge appeared upon the ends of the child's fingers. After a little while the same tinge began to rise in the death-white cheeks; then presently that rosy tinge burst out in a sudden flash all over the little creature, and it threw up its hands and broke into a cry—with its grateful mother there to hear that music! This was nearly three months ago. The child is well and flourishing now. It owes its life to the ten million dollars which Mr. Rockefeller put into that Institute.

The reading of the letter was listened to in a deep and impressive silence, and the interest and emotion which it excited were visible in the faces of every person present, and there were times when those men seemed hardly to breathe. When the end came there was a pause and a deep breath, and then followed a burst of grateful and uplifting applause which was another triumph for the criminal at the bar.

Dictated May 22, 1908

The Harpers Mr. Clemens's publishers for four years—Sales of his books, amount of royalties during these four years, etc.—Copy of letter from young journalist telling of skipper who wrecks three ships while reading Mark Twain's books—Incident recalled by this letter, of Jack Van Nostrand finding only two books while he traveled in the West—a Bible and "The Innocents Abroad."

The Harpers have now been my publishers four years and a half, and I have been examining the details of their last Annual Statement which was furnished to me last December, at the end of the fourth year. They have done exceedingly well with all the books, although almost all of them are old, not young—many of them being books that range from fifteen to twenty-seven years old, and the oldest reaching back to thirty-five and forty.

Old as the books are, the sales have increased each year instead of diminishing, as is the custom. The aggregate of volumes sold in the first year by the Harpers was 90,328; in the second year 104,851; in the third year 133,975; in the fourth year—which was last year—the sale was 160,000 volumes. The aggregate for the four years is 500,000 volumes lacking 11,000.

Of the oldest book, "The Innocents Abroad"—now forty years old—the sales aggregated 46,000 copies in the four years; of "Roughing It"—now thirty-eight years old, I think—40,334 were sold; of "Tom Sawyer," 41,000. And so on.

There is one detail that is especially gratifying to me: the book called "The Personal Recollections of Joan of Arc" has also steadily increased its sales instead of diminishing. The gratification lies in the fact that it is a serious book, and therefore was quite unlikely to meet with favor, since it has always been the way of the world to resent gravity in a humorist. It is a little strange that this should be so, for an absolutely essential part of any real humorist's native equipment is a deep seriousness and a rather unusually profound sympathy with the sorrows and sufferings of mankind. In one sense that book is a novel; in another and graver sense it is history, and a conscientiously accurate one. This accuracy has been conceded by Andrew Lang, and one may fairly say that from his verdict there is no appeal. During twelve years I devoted much study to the Maid's career, and steeped myself in her words, her acts, and her personality. In the book I made one or two characters of my own invention do things that never happened, but I never attributed an act to the Maid herself that was not strictly historical, and I never put a sentence in her mouth which she had not uttered. I wrote the book for love, not money, and at first, when it appeared serially in *Harper's Monthly,* I concealed the authorship, because my name would have deceived the public into thinking it was a humorous work, and I did not wish to trade upon misplaced confidence. But the imaginary characters which I had introduced into it betrayed me; their acts and sayings were frequently of a humorous sort, and of a sort that too distinctly marked them as my children. When the serial had been running three months in the magazine, letters began to flow in charging me with the authorship, and it was soon evident that further concealment would not be worth while. As I have already said, I wrote the book for love, and was not expecting that it would sell; but to my great gratification my forecast was an error. The book is now fifteen years old, yet it not only sells quite well, considering that it is a serious book from the pen of a humorist, but the sales are steadily increasing. In 1904 it sold 1,726 copies; in 1905, 2,445; in 1906, 5,381; and last year—1907—the sale was 6,574 copies. Yet it is the highest priced book in the collection.

The royalties paid me by the Harpers in the four years were as follows: in 1904, $24,939; in 1905, $29,311.92; in 1906, $39,284.33; in 1907, $48,225.98. Aggregate for the four years, $141,761.23.

A letter has arrived this morning which brings to my mind an incident of forty years ago. The book called "The Innocents Abroad" is a history of the *Quaker City* Excursion of that long past time. Jack Van Nostrand was among the excursionists. He was a charming, good-natured, long-legged New York lad of seventeen, and belonged to our small clique on board the ship—a clique consisting of Dan Slote, now dead; Moulton, now dead; Davis, now dead; Church, now dead; young Jack, long ago dead; and myself, at the present day still alive. Two years after the completion of the excursion poor Jack was smitten with consumption, and his parents sent him to Colorado in the hope that a life in the open air there might save him—a hope which was disappointed. Meantime "The Innocents Abroad" had been published and distributed about the country. Jack rode two or three hundred miles, horseback, through the cattle ranches of Colorado all alone, and at the end of his trip he wrote back to Dan Slote and said substantially this:

"Tell Clemens I saw no human beings on that long trip but cattle ranchmen, and I fed and slept nowhere but in their mud cabins. Tell him that from the beginning to the end I saw only two books: one was a Bible, the other was 'The Innocents Abroad.' The Bible was in good condition."

The letter referred to as having arrived this morning quite naturally brought that ancient incident to my mind. It is to my secretary, and comes from a young journalist who visited us a year ago on his way from his home in Australia on a zigzag journey to the uttermost parts of the earth. He says, dating from Glasgow:

> I have a grudge against 21 Fifth Avenue and I want to make it known. In just completing a voyage on the tramp steamer "Charing Cross" from Seville to Glasgow, I have had to endure with a skipper whose library (a life collection) consists of one Bible in Welsh and three of Mark Twain's books in American. As I am the only shipmate this old Welsh skipper has had who has seen Mark Twain, I suppose my burden was really heavier than those who have gone before. At no time, waking or sleeping, fair weather or foul, was I safe from quotations, which after the second day out became repetitions. Meals I dreaded as an Inquisition. Coffee was never handed except with the remark "Can you see two fathoms in that?" (Pun: two-fathoms, mark twain.)
>
> In curiosity I investigated the career of this David Davies, master of the good ship "Charing Cross" out of London, and was not surprised to find that he has wrecked three ships in his day. At each time, when the "accident" happened, he was in his berth studying the humorous shelf of his library. Now I am to take one of two courses and I would be glad of your assistance in deciding. Either, as a preservation measure, in the interest of British shipping, must I commence an agitation for the enactment of a law prohibiting the sale of Mark Twain's books to master mariners, and compelling the circulating libraries at British seaports to remove his volumes from their shelves, or take this alternative—more profitable but hardly as decent as the one stated already. Why not? Secure an option on the remaining years of this David Davies, Master Mariner, and having secured this option, present him with three or four other volumes by Mark Twain—then find and interview the owners of such ships where the profits are light and the insurance heavy, and, for a consideration, make them acquainted with this David Davies, Master Mariner. Then finally study Loyd's shipping reports and collect dividends. The only running expenses of the Syndicate (I am assuming that you will take shares) would be the cost of three Mark Twain books for each steamer, say approximately 18 volumes a year. There's money in it.

Dictated June 3, 1908

Copy of Mr. Clemens's speech at booksellers' banquet in regard to sales of his books during last four years—Statement as to amount of royalties in last four years.

I clip the following from the newspapers:

In a speech delivered at the eighth annual banquet of the American Booksellers' Association Mark Twain quoted some remarkable statistics that show the popularity of his writings. Included in the association are practically all the booksellers of America. The banquet was held at the rooms of the Aldine Association, No. 111 Fifth Avenue, Wednesday evening, May 20. Among other things Mark Twain said:

"This annual gathering of booksellers from all over America comes together ostensibly to eat and drink, but really to discuss business; therefore I am required to talk shop. I am required to furnish a statement of the indebtedness under which I lie to you gentlemen for your help in enabling me to earn my living. For something over forty years I have acquired my bread by print, beginning with *Innocents Abroad*, followed at intervals of a year or so by *Roughing It, Tom Sawyer, Gilded Age,* and so on. For thirty-six years my books were sold by subscription. You are not interested in those years, but only in the four which have since followed. The books passed into the hands of my present publishers at the beginning of 1904, and you then became the providers of my diet. I think I may say, without flattering you, that you have done exceedingly well by me. Exceedingly well is not too strong a phrase, since the official statistics show that in four years you have sold twice as many volumes of my venerable books as my contract with my publishers bound you and them to sell in five years. To your sorrow you are aware that frequently, much too frequently, when a book gets to be five or ten years old its annual sale shrinks to two or three hundred copies, and after an added ten or twenty years ceases to sell. But you sell thousands of my moss-backed old books every year—the youngest of them being books that range from fifteen to twenty-seven years old, and the oldest reaching back to thirty-five and forty.

By the terms of my contract my publishers had to account to me for 50,000 volumes per year for five years, and pay me for them whether they sold them or not. It is at this point that you gentlemen come in, for it was your business to unload the 250,000 volumes upon the public in five years if you possibly could. Have you succeeded? Yes, you have—and more. For in four years, with a year still to spare, you have sold the 250,000 volumes, and 240,000 besides.

Your sales have increased each year. In the first year you sold 90,328; in the second year, 104,851; in the third, 133,975; in the fourth year—which was last year—you sold 160,000. The aggregate for the four years is 500,000 volumes, lacking 11,000.

Of the oldest book, the *Innocents Abroad*—now forty years old—you sold upwards of 46,000 copies in the four years; of *Roughing It*—now thirty-eight years old, I think—you sold 40,334; of *Tom Sawyer,* 41,000. And so on.

And there is one thing that is peculiarly gratifying to me: the *Personal Recollections of Joan of Arc* is a serious book; I wrote it for love, and never expected it to sell, but you have pleasantly disappointed me in that matter. In your hands its sale has increased each year. In 1904 you sold 1726 copies; in 1905, 2445; in 1906, 5381; and last year, 6574."

There were three hundred and fifty booksellers present, and they came from all parts of the United States. They wanted statistics, and I furnished them from Harper and Brothers' official statements. It was not necessary to tell how much my book-royalties had paid me in the four years and I did not do it; but I may say here that my income from the books was almost twice as much in the fourth year as it was in the first. The first year it was twenty-five thousand dollars, and last year it was some trifle over forty-eight thousand.

Dictated at Innocence at Home, June 26, 1908

Copies of two clippings from papers with Mr. Clemens's comments—Mr. Clemens speaks of Grover Cleveland's death.

We entered into occupation of this new house eight days ago.

In an earlier chapter I have told how Clara and I kept distressing things from Mrs. Clemens's knowledge by a kindly and justifiable system of lying. In that chapter I also introduced a sketch entitled "Was It Heaven or Hell?" in which a similar system of lying was used by a dying mother and a dying daughter and their attendants to keep the condition of each from becoming known to the other. I published that true story in a magazine, and approved the deceptions practised. As a consequence, I received letters from many offensively pious persons severely disapproving of me and my morals. But my reform was not achieved, and to me, therefore, the following incident is deeply pathetic, and will be so to the reader of this page fifty years from now, if I know human nature:

DOUBLE BLOW FOR FATHER.

——

Child Killed, He Hides Death from His Sick Wife to Prevent Her Death, Too.

Patrick McDermott hurried home to his apartment at 2,487 Second Avenue from his work last evening a little earlier than usual, for his wife was sick and he knew that he must help his fifteen-year-old daughter Anna prepare the supper. He turned into 126th Street, walking rapidly, but stopped when he saw an ambulance drawn up to the curb outside of the tenement at 206 East 126th Street.

A sudden fright seized the father and he pushed his way through the throng of children, and through the long hallway saw the white-coated ambulance surgeon in the back yard. McDermott ran through the hall and looked at the limp figure over which the surgeon was kneeling.

It was his daughter Anna, who had fallen from the fire escape of Mrs. Edley Craig's flat on the fifth floor, where the little girl had been visiting Mrs. Craig's children. The sight of his dead daughter crazed the father and two policemen had all they could do to hold him. Dr. Bennett of Harlem Hospital administered to the father, who was suffering from the effects of heat as well as grief. It was some time before the man became calm enough to talk intelligently. Then he told the physician of the sick wife at home, and declared that to break to her the news of Anna's death would kill her. Dr. Bennett said he would take the child's body to the police station instead of taking it home, and he did so.

McDermott, trying to conceal all signs of his grief, went home to tell his wife that Anna had gone to spend the night with friends. He declared piteously last night that he did not know what he could tell his wife this morning when the child failed to appear.

Here is another item which will still be of interest fifty years from now, and still be as competent then to exasperate the reader as it is to-day:

ARRESTS IN BALLOON CASE.

Two Vermonters Accused of Shooting at Mr. Glidden's Big Craft.

BRATTLEBORO, Vt., June 25.—Charged with assaulting Charles J. Glidden of Boston while Glidden was traveling over Brattleboro in a balloon with Leo Stevens of New York last Friday, William Murphy, aged 30, and Charles Rigaman, aged 33 years, of this city, were placed under arrest to-night by Deputy Sheriff Myron P. Davis. The complaint is made by Attorney General Clark C. Fitts, who gave his attention to the matter.

The balloon Boston was hit by a bullet on Friday. According to Mr. Glidden two bullets were fired, apparently from a white barn. The time of the shots and the exact location of the balloon were noted by the aeronauts. One bullet grazed the balloon, leaving a scar. The second passed completely through it, and the balloonists had to descend.

It is my belief that no crime, however cowardly and however shameless and cruel, can be imagined which there isn't somebody in Christendom willing to commit. It seems to me that an attempt to murder an aeronaut, with the risk of horribly mutilating him first, is as mean and vile and cruel a crime as can be imagined. I am opposed to harsh punishments, yet I think that if it can be proven that these two would-be assassins are really the ones who made the attempt, they ought to be dismembered while still alive and then boiled in oil.

A great man is lost to the country; a great man and great citizen, the greatest citizen we had and the only statesman left to us, after the death of Senator Hoar of Massachusetts. I speak of Grover Cleveland, twice President of the United States, who died yesterday. He was a very great President, a man who not only properly appreciated the dignity of his high office but added to its dignity. The contrast between President Cleveland and the present occupant of the White House is extraordinary; it is the contrast between an archangel and the Missing Link. Mr. Cleveland was all that a president ought to be; Mr. Roosevelt is all that a president ought not to be—he covers the entire ground.

It is said that Mr. Cleveland has left but little for his family to live on. His widow ought to have a life pension of twenty-five thousand dollars, but she will not get it. If she were the bastard of a bounty-jumper and had a vote to sell, Roosevelt and Congress would tumble and scramble over each other in their eagerness to confer the pension and buy that vote.

Dictated at Innocence at Home, July 3, 1908

What Mr. Clemens would name the Fourth of July—He speaks of the new home, the mantelpieces, rugs, etc.—The Aldrich Memorial, and some of Mrs. Aldrich's characteristics.

To-morrow is Hell-fire Day, that English holiday which we have celebrated, every Fourth of July, for a century and a quarter in fire, blood, tears, mutilation and death, repeating and repeating and forever repeating these absurdities because neither our historians nor our politicians nor our schoolmasters have wit enough to remind the public that the Fourth of July is not an American holiday. However, I doubt if there is a historian, a politician, or a schoolmaster in the country that has ever stopped to consider what the nationality of that day really is. I detest that English holiday with all my heart; not because it is English, and not because it is not American, but merely because this nation goes insane on that day, and by the help of noise and fire turns it into an odious pandemonium. The nation calls it by all sorts of affectionate pet names, but if I had the naming of it I would throw poetry aside and call it Hell's Delight.

But fortunately for us, we are far from that pandemonium, and shall neither see nor hear anything of it. For a couple of weeks now we have been occupying the pleasant and comely and roomy Italian villa which John Howells has built for me on lofty ground surrounded by wooded hills and valleys, and secluded by generous distances from the other members of the human race. I call the house "Innocence at Home," and I mean to provide the innocence myself, so that it shall be of an unchallengeable quality. Thirty-five years ago, in Edinburgh, Mrs. Clemens and I came across an old carved oak mantelpiece in a kind of general junk-shop and hospital for disabled furniture, and Mrs. Clemens was greatly taken with it and wanted to own it and put it into the house which we were then building in Hartford, Connecticut. It was fourteen feet high and finely and symmetrically proportioned, and beautifully carved. The lower half of it was a hundred and fifty years old and the other half something more than a hundred; it had been in a Scotch country mansion all that time and had now been on sale in that junk-shop a couple of years. The man said he had never had an offer for it; he had never come across anybody that wanted it, and he would now like to get it off his hands, for it was taking up a good deal of room to no purpose. He said he would take twenty pounds for it. We bought it and shipped it to America at once. When we sold the Hartford house, several years ago, Mrs. Clemens preserved the mantelpiece and stored it away for future use. It is in this house now; it handsomely ornaments the living-room, which is forty-one feet long by thirty-one wide—and I think that that room is just the right place for it. The lower half of it encloses the fireplace, and we have mortised the other half of it to the wall at the end of the room, where it fills the reserved space exactly; it looks as if it might have been originally designed for that place. In these thirty-five years that twenty-pound investment has done very well indeed commercially. If we should get this mantelpiece duplicated to-day by the best carver in New York he would charge eight thousand dollars for his labor, and then his product would cover only half the value of this one, because it would lack the rich coloring which this old mantelpiece has acquired by a century or so of exposure to the light and to wood-smoke and tobacco smoke, and other ennobling influences.

Also, thirty-five years ago, in Paris, Mrs. Clemens bought a number of old Oriental rugs; rugs which seemed to me a shabby and unpleasant property. Nobody was buying such things at that time, and nobody cared for them, but Mrs. Clemens's instinct was right, and her taste not to be challenged by anybody, for nobody was competent to challenge it. Every now and then, as the years went by, she bought other old Oriental rugs, until long ago we were sufficiently equipped and needed no more. By that time other people were buying them all around and about Christendom, and the prices were advancing of course; they have continued to advance ever since. Those old rugs have turned out to be a good investment commercially. I remember the cost of the most of them and I think that the whole of them together cost about eight thousand dollars. Several experts, native and foreign, examined them in New York last year and pronounced their present value to be forty thousand dollars. That is just the value of the new house itself, as per the builder's bills. An early chapter of this Autobiography exposes the fact that every time I have invested money I have lost it; I ought to have reserved my commercial talent and employed Mrs. Clemens's.

This house is now finished with the exception of one minor detail: some months ago citizens of the Sandwich Islands wrote me and said they would like to contribute a mantelpiece to this dwelling—a mantelpiece to be made of samples of the beautiful woods that are native to the Islands. The architect sent the measurements and the fireplace is waiting for that ornament.

Last Monday Albert Bigelow Paine personally conducted me to Boston, and next day to Portsmouth, New Hampshire, to assist at the dedication of the Thomas Bailey Aldrich Memorial Museum. – – – – – – – At this point I desire to give notice to my literary heirs, assigns, and executors, that they are to suppress, for seventy-five years, what I am now about to say about that curious function. It is not that I am expecting to say anything that shall really need suppressing, but that I want to talk without embarrassment and speak with freedom—freedom, comfort, appetite, relish.

As text and basis I will here introduce a few simple statistics: the late Thomas Bailey Aldrich was born in his grandfather's house in the little town of Portsmouth, New Hampshire, seventy-two or seventy-three years ago. His widow has lately bought that house and stocked it with odds and ends that once belonged to the child Tom Aldrich, and to the schoolboy Tom Aldrich, and to the old poet Tom Aldrich, and turned the place into a memorial museum in honor of Aldrich and for the preservation of his fame. She has instituted an Aldrich Museum Memorial Corporation under the laws of the State of New Hampshire, and has turned the museum over to this corporation which is acting for the City of Portsmouth, the ultimate heir of the benefaction, and she has injected the mayor of Portsmouth and other important people into that corporation to act as advertisement and directors. A strange and vanity-devoured, detestable woman! I do not believe I could ever learn to like her except on a raft at sea with no other provisions in sight.

The justification for an Aldrich Memorial Museum for pilgrims to visit and hallow with their homage may exist, but to me it seems doubtful. Aldrich was never widely known; his books never attained to a wide circulation; his prose was diffuse, self-conscious, and barren of distinction in the matter of style; his fame as a writer of prose is not considerable; his fame as a writer of verse is also very limited, but such as it is it is a matter to be proud of. It is based not upon his output of poetry as a whole but upon half a dozen small poems which are not surpassed in our language for exquisite grace and beauty and finish. These gems are known and admired and loved by the one person in ten thousand who is capable of appreciating them at their just value. It is this sprinkling of people who would reverently visit the memorial museum if it were situated in a handy place. They would amount to one visitor per month, no doubt, if the museum were in Boston or New York, but it isn't in those places—it is in Portsmouth, New Hampshire, an hour and three-quarters from Boston by the Boston and Maine Railway, which still uses the cars it employed in its early business fifty years ago; still passes drinking water around per tea-pot and tin cup, and still uses soft coal and vomits the gritty product of it into those venerable cars at every window and crack and joint. A memorial museum of George Washington relics could not excite any considerable interest if it were located in that decayed town and the devotee had to get to it over the Boston and Maine.

When it came to making fun of a folly, a silliness, a windy pretense, a wild absurdity, Aldrich the brilliant, Aldrich the sarcastic, Aldrich the ironical, Aldrich the merciless, was a master. It was the greatest pity in the world that he could not be at that memorial function in the Opera House at Portsmouth to make fun of it. Nobody could lash it and blight it and blister it and scarify it as he could do it. However, I am overlooking one important detail: he could do all this, and would do it with enthusiasm, if it were somebody else's foolish memorial, but it would not occur to him to make fun of it if the function was in his own honor, for he had very nearly as extensive an appreciation of himself and his gifts as had the late Edmund Clarence Stedman, who believed that the sun merely rose to admire his poetry and was so reluctant to set, at the end of the day, and lose sight of it, that it lingered and lingered and lost many minutes diurnally, and was never able to keep correct time during his stay in the earth. Stedman was a good fellow; Aldrich was a good fellow; but vain?—bunched together they were as vain as I am myself, which is saying all that can be said under that head without being extravagant.

For the protection of the reader I must confess that I am perhaps prejudiced. It is possible that I would never be able to see anything creditable in anything Mrs. Aldrich might do. I conceived an aversion for her the first time I ever saw her, which was thirty-nine years ago, and that aversion has remained with me ever since. She is one of those people who is profusely affectionate, and whose demonstrations disorder your stomach. You never believe in them; you always regard them as fictions, artificialities, with a selfish motive back of them. Aldrich was delightful company, but we never saw a great deal of him because we couldn't have him by himself. If anything was ever at any time needed to increase and crystallize and petrify and otherwise perpetuate my aversion to that lady, that lack was made up three years ago, at a time when I was to spend six days in Boston and could invent no plausible excuse for declining to visit the Aldriches at "Ponkapog," a few miles out, a house and estate wheedled out of poor old Mr. Pierce years ago by that artful lady, a number of years before the old gentleman died. By the time he was ready to die, eleven years ago, she had very comfortably feathered the Aldrich nest in his will. He had already given them a great dwelling-house at 59 Mount Vernon street, Boston, and had built for them a small cottage at the seaside; also he had already fed Mrs. Aldrich's appetite for jimcrack bric-à-brac, at considerable expense to his purse; also he had long ago grown accustomed to having her buy pretty much anything she thought she wanted and instruct the tradesmen to send the bill to him; also he had long ago grown accustomed to feeding the Aldrich appetite for travel, and had sent them in costly and sumptuous fashion all about the habitable globe at his expense. Once, in Europe, when I was a bankrupt and was finding it difficult to make both ends meet, Mrs. Aldrich entertained Mrs. Clemens and me by exploiting in a large way various vanities of hers, in the presence of Aldrich and of poor old Mr. Pierce—they apparently approving. She had projected a trip to Japan for Mr. Pierce, Mr. Aldrich and herself, and had been obliged to postpone it for a while because she was not able to secure anything better than the ordinary first-class accommodations in the steamer. She was full of a fine scorn for that kind of accommodation, and told how she made those steamer people to understand that they must do better than that if they wanted her further custom. She waited until they were able to sell her one of the two seven-hundred-and-fifty-dollar suites on the promenade deck—a suite with beds for only two in it, but she didn't explain what she did with Mr. Pierce. Shipped him in the steerage, I reckon. Then she got out half a dozen gorgeous gowns, worth several hundred dollars each, and told how she gave Worth, the celebrated Parisian ladies' tailor, a piece of her mind regarding those gowns. She showed him that he was taking up too much of her time in fitting them and fussing at them, and she added that she had never asked him the price of a gown, she didn't care what he charged, but she would not have her time wasted by his dalliances with the fitting of the things, and she told him quite plainly that her patience was exhausted and that he would never have any of her custom again.

Think of it!! Why damnation! she had been a pauper all her life, and here she was strutting around on these lofty stilts.

Dictated at Innocence at Home, July 6, 1908

Joel Chandler Harris's death—The incident which enlarged Mr. Clemens's prejudice against Mrs. Aldrich.

Joel Chandler Harris is dead; Uncle Remus, joy of the child and the adult alike, will speak to us no more. It is a heavy loss.

I must try to get back to the incident which enlarged and rounded out and perfected my prejudice against Mrs. Aldrich—a little thing which occurred three years ago at "Ponkapog," and to which I have already made vague reference. I had gone to Boston to spend a week with a friend. I did not want to go to "Ponkapog," but I could think of no good excuse, either truthful or otherwise, so I accepted an urgent invitation and went. I knew what would happen: the talk would be merely about "society,"—that is, wealthy society—just as in England when one is with titled people the conversation is nearly exclusively about people with titles, and what they were doing when the talkers met them last or heard of them last; I knew there would be a showy and exultant display of precious vanities acquired through the late Mr. Pierce's benevolence; I knew there would be occasional happy glimpses of the charming and lovable Tom Aldrich of early times, and that the Madam would be both occasionally and always her old time and ever-and-ever self-centred, self-seeking, self-satisfied, honey-worded, interesting and exasperating sham self. I knew all this would happen, and of course it turned out just so. They had an automobile; an automobile was a new and awesome thing then, and nobody could have it except people who could afford it and people who couldn't. This was a cheap 'mobile, but it was showy and had a high complexion; they had a steam yacht, but couldn't show it to me, which was a matter of no consequence because they had already shown it to me at Bar Harbor in July; it was a cheap little thing with accommodations for three passengers, but it looked as important as it could for the money, and it expressed pretense as with a voice that spoke; of course they would have a yacht, it is the sign and advertisement of financial distinction; the son was a polo player, in an indigent way, and I was taken out to the fields to see him and half a dozen other men play at that aristocratic game; the "Ponkapog" house would necessarily have to indulge in polo, because it is another symbol and advertisement of financial obesity; the men were up-to-date as regards polo costumery, but as they had only two ponies apiece of course the game was brief—brief and delightfully immature and incompetent; incompetent and dangerous, to everybody but the ball; nobody could hit it, and poor Aldrich was full of distressed explanations in amelioration of the pathetic miscarriages which constituted the exhibition. I have not yet reached the incident which I have been so long trying to overtake, but I think I have arrived at it now. I was shown all over the old farm-house, and I paid my way the best I could with shamelessly insincere compliments, when pumped. However there were two details which compelled sincere compliments, and I easily furnished them without any pumping. One of these details was the living-room, which was satisfyingly cosy and pretty, and tasteful in its colors and appointments, and was in all ways inviting and comfortable; the other detail was the sole and solitary guest room, which was spacious and judiciously furnished and upholstered and had a noble big bed in it. I was given that room, and was properly thankful, and said so; but a girl of twenty arrived unexpectedly in mid-afternoon and I was moved out of it and she into it; I was transferred to a remote room which was so narrow and short and comprehensively small that one could hardly turn around in it; it had in it a table, a chair, a small kerosene lamp, a wash-bowl and pitcher, a cylindrical sheet-iron stove, and no other furniture. It was the meanest cell, and the narrowest, and the smallest, and the shabbiest, I had ever been in since I got out of jail. The month was October, the nights were very cool; the little stove's food was white pine fragments fed to it a handful at a time; it would seize upon these with a fierce roar, turn red hot from base to summit in three minutes and be empty and hungry and cold again in ten; under the fury of its three-minute passion it would make the cell so hot that a person could hardly stay in it, and within half an hour the freeze would come on again. The little kerosene lamp filled the cell with a vague and gentle light while it was going, and with a cordial and energetic stench when it wasn't.

The reason I was transferred to that unwholesome and unsavory closet was soon apparent. Young Aldrich was a bachelor of thirty-seven; that young girl was daughter to an ex-governor of the State and was high up in "society." The match-making Madam was setting traps for her and working all the ingenuities of her plotting and planning and scheming machinery to catch her for her son. She was quite frank about the matter, and was feeling tranquilly sure she was going to succeed in her designs. But she didn't; the girl escaped.

I have at last disgorged that rankling incident. It makes me angry every time I think of it. That that woman should jump at me and kiss me on both cheeks, unsolicited, when I arrived, and then throw me down cellar, seventy years old as I was, to make sumptuous room for a mere governor's daughter, seemed to me to be carrying insult to the limit.

As to the memorial function, let us take that up again.

Dictated at Innocence at Home, July 7, 1908

**Murat Halstead's death—His life contrasted with that of
Mr. Clemens—The incident of Murat Halstead getting left on
steamer and going to Germany with Mr. Clemens and his family
and Bayard Taylor—The coincidence of Halstead and Taylor
thinking they had heart disease and the way in which they were
cured of that belief.**

But not now—after a few minutes.

Murat Halstead is dead. He was a most likable man. He lived to be not far short of eighty, and he devoted about sixty years to diligent, hard slaving at editorial work. His life and mine make a curious contrast. From the time that my father died, March 24,

1847, when I was past eleven years old, until the end of 1856, or the first days of 1857, I worked—not diligently, not willingly, but fretfully, lazily, repiningly, complainingly, disgustedly, and always shirking the work when I was not watched. The statistics show that I was a worker during about ten years. I am approaching seventy-three, and I believe I have never done any work since—unless I may call two or three years of lazy effort as a reporter on the Pacific coast by that large and honorable name—and so I think I am substantially right in saying that when I escaped from the printing-office fifty or fifty-one years ago I ceased to be a worker, and ceased permanently. Piloting on the Mississippi River was not work to me; it was play—delightful play, vigorous play, adventurous play—and I loved it; silver mining in the Humboldt Mountains was play, only play, because I did not do any of the work; my pleasant comrades did it and I sat by and admired; my silver mining in Esmeralda was not work, for Higbie and Robert Howland did it, and again I sat by and admired. I accepted a job of shoveling tailings in a quartz mill there, and that was really work, and I had to do it myself, but I retired from that industry at the end of two weeks, and not only with my own approval but with the approval of the people who paid the wages. These mining experiences occupied ten months, and came to an end toward the close of September 1862. I then became a reporter, in Virginia City, Nevada, and later in San Francisco, and after something more than two years of this salaried indolence I retired from my position on the *Morning Call,* by solicitation. Solicitation of the proprietor. Then I acted as San Franciscan correspondent of the Virginia City *Enterprise* for two or three months; next I spent three months in pocket-mining at Jackass Gulch with the Gillis boys; then I went to the Sandwich Islands and corresponded thence for the Sacramento *Union* five or six months; in October 1866 I broke out as a lecturer, and from that day to this I have always been able to gain my living without doing any work; for the writing of books and magazine matter was always play, not work. I enjoyed it; it was merely billiards to me.

I wonder why Murat Halstead was condemned to sixty years of editorial slavery and I let off with a lifetime of delightful idleness. There seems to be something most unfair about this—something not justifiable. But it seems to be a law of the human constitution that those that deserve shall not have, and those that do not deserve shall get everything that is worth having. It is a sufficiently crazy arrangement, it seems to me.

On the 10th of April, a little more than thirty years ago, I sailed for Germany in the steamer *Holsatia* with my little family—at least we got ready to sail, but at the last moment concluded to remain at our anchorage in the Bay to see what the weather was going to be. A great many people came down in a tug to say good-bye to the passengers, and at dark, when we had concluded to go sea, they left us. When the tug was gone it was found that Murat Halstead was still with us; he had come to say good-bye to his wife and daughter; he had to remain with us, there was no alternative. We presently went to sea. Halstead had no clothing with him except what he had on, and there was a fourteen-day voyage in front of him. By happy fortune there was one man on board who was as big as Halstead, and only that one man; he could get into that man's clothes but not into any other man's in that company. That lucky accident was Bayard Taylor; he was an unusually large man and just the size of Halstead, and he had an abundance of clothes and was glad to share them with Halstead, who was a close friend of his of long standing. Toward midnight I was in the smoking-cabin with them and then a curious fact came out: they had not met for ten years, and each was surprised to see the other looking so bulky and hearty and so rich in health; each had for years been expecting to hear of the other's death; for when they had last parted both had received death sentence at the hands of the physician. Heart disease in both cases, with death certain within two years. Both were required to lead a quiet life, walk and not run, climb no stairs when not obliged to do it, and above all things avoid surprises and sudden excitements, if possible. They understood that a single sudden and violent excitement would be quite sufficient for their needs and would promptly end their days, and so for ten years these men had been creeping and never trotting nor running; they had climbed stairs at gravel-train speed only, and they had avoided excitements diligently and constantly—and all that time they were as hearty as a pair of elephants and could not understand why they continued to live. Then something happened. And it happened to both at about the same time. The thing that happened was a sudden and violent surprise followed immediately by another surprise—surprise that they didn't fall dead in their tracks. These surprises happened about a week before the *Holsatia* sailed. Halstead was editor and proprietor of the Cincinnati *Enquirer,* and was sitting at his editorial desk at midnight, high up in the building, when a mighty explosion occurred, close by, which rocked the building to its foundations and shivered all its glass, and before Halstead had time to reflect and not let the explosion excite him, he had sailed down six flights of stairs in thirty-five seconds and was standing panting in the street trying to say "Thy will be done," and deadly afraid that that was what was going to happen. But nothing happened, and from that time forth he had been an emancipated man, and now for a whole week had been making up for ten years' lost time, hunting for excitements and devouring them like a famished person.

Bayard Taylor's experience had been of the like character. He turned a corner in the country and crossed a railway track just in time for an express train to nip a corner off the seat of his breeches and blow him into the next county by compulsion of the hurricane produced by the onrush of the train. He mourned and lamented, thinking that the fatal surprise had come at last; then he put his hand on his heart and got another surprise, for he found that it was still beating. He rose up and dusted himself off and became jubilant, and gave praise, and went off like Halstead to hunt up some more excitements and make up for ten years' lost time.

Bayard Taylor was on his way to Berlin as our new Minister to Germany; he was a genial, lovable, simple-hearted soul, and as happy in his new dignity as ever a new plenipotentiary was since the world began. He was a poet, and had written voluminously in verse, and had also made the best of all English translations of Goethe's "Faust." But all his poetry is forgotten now except two very fine songs, one about the Scotch soldiers singing "Annie Laurie" in the trenches before Sebastopol, and the other the tremendously inspiriting love song of an Arab lover to his sweetheart. No one has gathered together his odds and ends and started a memorial museum with them, and if he is still able to think and reflect he is glad of it.

He had a prodigious memory, and one night while we were walking the deck he undertook to call up out of the deeps of his mind a yard-long list of queer and quaint and unrelated words which he had learned, as a boy, by reading the list twice over, for a prize, and had easily won it for the reason that the other competitors after studying the list an hour were not able to recite it without making mistakes. Taylor said he had not thought of that list since that time, but was sure he could reproduce it after half an hour's digging in his mind. We walked the deck in silence during the half hour, then he began with the first word and sailed glibly through without a halt, and also without a mistake, he said.

He had a negro manservant with him who came on board dressed up in the latest agony of the fashion and looking as fine as a rainbow; then he disappeared and we never saw him again for ten or twelve days; then he came on deck drooping and meek, subdued, subjugated, the most completely wilted and disreputable-looking flower that was ever seen outside of a conservatory or inside of it either. The mystery was soon explained. The sea had gotten his works out of order the first day on board, and he went to the ship's doctor to acquire a purge. The doctor gave him fourteen large pills and told him, in German, to take one every three hours till he found relief; but he didn't understand German, so he took the whole fourteen at one dose, with the result above recorded.

Dictated at Innocence at Home, July 8, 1908

The Aldrich Memorial affair continued.

To resume about the Aldrich Memorial affair: I had not inquired into the amount of travel which would be required. It came near being great, for I had supposed we must go to New York and reship thence to Boston, which would have made a hard day of it, considering the character of the weather. And a long day—a very long day—twelve hours between getting out of bed at home and stepping into the hotel in Boston. But by accident we found out that we could change cars at South Norwalk and save four hours, so we reached Boston at two in the afternoon, after a dusty and blistering and rather fatiguing journey. We were to go to Portsmouth next day, June 30th. Printed cards had been distributed by mail to the invited guests containing transportation-information. Whereby it appeared that the nine o'clock express for Portsmouth would have a couple of special cars sacred to the guests. To anybody but me, to any reasonable person, to any unprejudiced person, the providing of special cars by the surviving rich Aldriches would have seemed so natural a thing, so properly courteous a thing—in fact so necessary and unavoidable a politeness—that the information would have excited no comment, but would have been unemotionally received as being a wholly matter-of-course thing; but where prejudice exists it always discolors our thoughts and feelings and opinions. I was full of prejudice, and so I resented this special train. I said to myself that it was out of character; that it was for other people, ordinary people, the general run of the human race, to provide the simple courtesy of a special train on an occasion like this and pay the cost of it, but it was not for Mrs. Aldrich to do such a thing; it was not for Mrs. Aldrich to squander money on politeness to guests, eleemosinarily rich as she is. It irritated me, disappointed me, affronted me, to see her rising above herself under the elevating influence of a high family occasion; in my malice I wanted to find some way to account for it that would take the credit out of it, and so I said to myself that she, the great advertiser, the persistent advertiser, the pushing and scrabbling and tireless advertiser, was doing this gaudy thing for the sake of spreading it around in the newspapers and getting her compensation out of it as an advertisement. That seemed a sort of plausible way of accounting for it, but I was so deeply prejudiced that it did not pacify me; I could not reconcile myself to seeing her depart from herself and from her traditions and be hospitable at her own expense—still, she was defeating me, and I had to confess it and take the medicine. However, in my animosity I said to myself that I would not allow her to collect glory from me, at an expense to her of two dollars and forty cents, so I made Paine buy tickets to Portsmouth and return. That idea pleased me; indeed there is more real pleasure to be gotten out of a malicious act, where your heart is in it, than out of thirty acts of a nobler sort.

But Paine and I went into one of the two special cars in order to chat with their occupants, who would be male and female authors—friends, some of them, the rest acquaintances. It was lucky that we went in there, the result was joyous. I was sitting where I could carry on a conversational yell with all the males and females at the northern end of the car, when the conductor came along, austere and dignified, as is the way of his breed of animals, and began to collect tickets! Several of the guests in my neighborhood I knew to be poor, and I saw—not with any real pleasure—a gasp of surprise catch in their throats and a pathetic look of distress exhibit itself in their faces. They pulled out of their pockets and their reticules the handsomely engraved card of invitation, along with the card specifying the special train, and offered those credentials to the unsympathetic conductor and explained that they were *invited* to the mortuary festival and did not have to pay. The smileless conductor-devil said with his cold and hollow Boston and Maine Railway bark, that he hadn't any orders to pass anybody, and he would trouble them for transportation-cash.

The incident restored my Mrs. Aldrich to me undamaged and just the same old thing she had always been, undeodorized and not a whiff of her missing. Here she was, rich by an old gull's alms, getting all the glory inseparable from the act of indulging in the imposing grandeur of a special train, and in the valuable advertising for herself incident to it, and then stepping aside and leaving her sixty hard-worked breadwinners to pay the bill for her. I realized that I had gotten back my lost treasure, the real Mrs. Aldrich, and that she was "all there," as the slang-mongers phrase it. There was another detail of this sorrowful incident that was undeniably pitiful: persons unused to the luxurious Pullman car and accustomed to travel in the plebeian common car, have the fashion of sticking their fare tickets in the back of the seat in front of them, where the conductor can see them as he goes along; on a New England railway the conductor goes along every few minutes, glances at the exposed tickets, punches some holes in them, and keeps that up all day, until the ticket has at last ceased to be a ticket and consists only of holes; but in the meantime the owner of the ticket has been at peace, he has been saved the trouble of pulling a ticket out of his vest pocket every two or three minutes. Now then, these special-train guests, naturally thinking that their engraved invitation-card was intended to serve as a pay-ticket, had stuck it in the back of the seats in front of them so that the conductor could turn it into a colander with his punch and leave the owner unmolested; and now, when they pointed out these cards to him with a confident and self-complacent and slightly rebukative air, and he responded, by his countenance, with a pointedly irreverent though silent scoff, those people were visibly so ashamed, so humiliated, that I think Mrs. Aldrich herself would have been almost sorry for them. I was noble enough to be sorry for them—so sorry that I almost wished I hadn't seen it. There were sixty guests, ten or fifteen of them from New York, the rest from Boston and thereabouts, and the entire transportation bill could have been covered by a hundred and fifty dollars, yet that opulent and stingy woman was graceless enough to let that much-sacrificing company of unwealthy literary people pay the bill out of their own pockets. When I used to see her hanging around poor happy old Mr. Pierce's neck and caressing and fondling him and kissing him on both cheeks, and calling him "dearie"— But let that go. I am often subject to seasickness on land, and nearly any little thing can give me the heaves.

At a way station the governor of Massachusetts came on board with his staff—these in modest uniform, with two exceptions; these exceptions were veritable birds of paradise for splendor. One of them was young Aldrich, the remaining child and heir. He is a nice and modest and engaging lad of thirty-eight, but his modesty goes for nothing; he is his mother's property, as his father was before him, and will have to be a staff officer, or any other kind of wax figure she may prefer, if so be there is an advertisement in it.

Every now and then in the special train some lamb, undergoing the slaughter, would inquire of some other lamb who this train was in charge of; there was never a lamb that could answer that question; manifestly the special train was not in charge of anybody; there was nobody at the Boston Station to tell any guest where to go or which were the special cars; there was nobody on board the train to see that the tin-pot boy came around, now and then, in the awful swelter of that scorching day; at Portsmouth there was nobody to take charge of any guests save the governor's party and about a dozen others. The Madam's motor car, which is now a real one, and a sumptuous and costly one, was there to fetch the governor—free of charge, I heard.

At the Opera House about three-fourths of the special-train guests were sent to seats among the general audience, while the governor and staff and several more or less notorious authors were marshaled into the greenroom to wait until the house should be full and everything ready for the solemnities to begin. The mayor of Portsmouth was there too, a big, hearty, muscular animal, just the ideal municipal mayor of this present squalid century. Presently we marched in onto the stage, receiving the noisy welcome which was our due. Howells and I followed the mayor and the governor and his staff, and the rest of the literary rabble followed us. We sat down in a row stretching across the stage, Howells sitting with me near the centre in a short willow sofa. He glanced down the line and murmured,

"What an old-time, pleasant look it has about it! if we were blacked and had sharp-pointed long collars that projected slanting upward past our eyebrows like railway bars, it would be complete; and if Aldrich were here he would want to break out in the old introductory formula of happy memory and say breezily, 'How is you to-night Brer Bones? How is you feelin', Brer Tambourine? How's yo' symptoms seem to segashuate dis ebenin'?' "

After a time the mayor stepped to the front and thundered forth a vigorous and confident speech in which he said many fine and deservedly complimentary things about Aldrich, and described the gentle and dreamy and remote Portsmouth of Aldrich's boy-hood of sixty years ago and compared it with the booming Portsmouth of to-day. He didn't use that word; it would have been injudicious; he only implied it. The Portsmouth of to-day doesn't boom; it is calm, quite calm, and asleep. Also he told about the gather-ing together of the Aldrich mementoes and the stocking of Aldrich's boyhood home with part of them, and the stocking of a fireproof building in the yard with the rest of them, and the placing of the whole generous deposit in the hands of an Aldrich Museum Corporation, with the privilege of saving it for posterity at the expense of the city.

Then Governor Guild——but let that go, until to-morrow.

Dictated at Innocence at Home, July 9, 1908

Aldrich Memorial affair concluded.

Governor Guild, talking at ease, made a graceful and animated speech, a speech well suited to the occasion, it having been faultlessly memorized. The delivery was free from halts and stumbles and hesitations. A person who is to make a speech at any time or anywhere, upon any topic whatever, owes it to himself and to his audience to write the speech out and memorize it, if he can find the time for it. In the days when I was still able to memorize a speech I was always faithful to that duty—for my own sake, not the hearers'. A speech that is well memorized can, by trick and art, be made to deceive the hearer completely, and make him reverently marvel at the talent that can enable a man to stand up unprepared and pour out perfectly phrased felicities as easily and as comfortably and as confidently as less gifted people talk lusterless commonplaces. I am not talking morals now, I am merely talking sense. It was a good beginning—those well memorized speeches, the mayor's and the governor's; they were happy, interesting, animated, effective.

Then the funeral began. Mourner after mourner crept to the front and meekly and weakly and sneakingly read the poem which he had written for the occasion; and read it confidentially, as a rule, for the voice of the true poet, even the voice of the third-rate poet, is seldom able to carry to the middle benches. Pretty soon I was glad I had come in black clothes; at home they had fitted me out in that way, warning me that the occasion was not of a festive character, but mortuary, and I must dress for sorrow, not for the weather. They were odiously hot and close and suffocating and steamy and sweaty, those black clothes there on that sad platform, but they fitted the poetry to a dot; they fitted the wailing deliveries to a dot; they fitted the weary, hot faces of the audience to another dot, and I was glad my outfit was in harmony with the general suffering. Poet after poet got up and crawled to the desk and pulled out his manuscript and lamented; and this went on, and on, and on, till the very solemnness of the thing began to become ludicrous. In my lifetime I have not listened to so much manuscript-reading before upon any occasion. I will not deny that it was good manuscript, and I will concede that none of it was bad; but no poet who isn't of the first class knows how to read, and so he is an affliction to everybody but himself when he tries it. Even Colonel Higginson, inconceivably old as he is, and inured to platform-performances for generations and generations, stood up there, bent by age to the curve of a parenthesis, and piped out his speech from manuscript, doing it with the ghostly and creaky remnant of a voice that long ago had rung like a tocsin when he charged with his regiment and led it to bloody victories. Howells's speech was brief, and naturally, and necessarily felicitously, worded, for fine thought and perfect wording are a natural gift with Howells, and he had it by heart and delivered it well; but he read his poem from manuscript. He did it gracefully and well, then added it to the pile and came back to his seat by my side, glad it was over and looking like a pardoned convict. Then I abolished my prepared and vaguely and ineffectually memorized solemnities and finished the day's performance with twelve minutes of lawless and unconfined and desecrating nonsense.

The memorial function was over. It was dreary; it was devilish; it was hard to endure; there were two sweltering hours of it, but I would not have missed it for twice the heat and exhaustion and Boston and Maine travel it cost, and the cinders I swallowed.

Dictated at Innocence at Home, July 10, 1908

Mr. Clemens writes letter to John Howells praising his work as architect of this house—Extracts from W. D. Howells's letter to Mr. Clemens—Mr. Clemens's theory as to reason for his own well preserved hair, and some remarks about the inconsistencies of the human race in regard to care of hair, diet, etc.

A few days ago I wrote John Howells some strong and spontaneous praises of his work as architect of this house. I remember John as a little child, and it seems strange and uncanny, and impossible, that I have lived, and lived, and lived, and gone on continuously and persistently and perpetually living, until at last that child, chasing along in my wake, has built a house for me and put a roof over my head. I can't realize that this is that child. I knew the child well; and I also know that child as it looked at the advanced age of seven, when it and its father came down to Hartford once to stay a day or two with us, it must have been thirty years ago. It was in the earliest years of our lost and lamented friend, the colored butler, George. Howells and John were put into the chamber on the ground floor that was called the mahogany-room. John was up early and searching the place over, tiptoeing softly and eagerly around on excursions of discovery. He was unfamiliar with the colored race, but, being seven years old, he was of course acquainted with the "Arabian Nights." At a turn in his voyage he presently caught a glimpse of the dining room; then he fled to his father, woke him up and said in awed half-gasps,

"Get up, papa, the slave is setting the table."

I meant to say my say to the architect in good and strong words and well put together, for in a letter received yesterday evening his father says:

> That was beautiful of you to write John of your pleasure in the house. I believe I would rather have such a letter than the most perfect villa.

I wish to quote still another paragraph from Howells's letter:

> I have been thinking how Aldrich would have enjoyed that thing the other day, and what fun he would have got out of us poor old dodderers. How old is Col. Higginson any way? He made you look young, and me feel so.

Speaking of youth, I am reminded that with some frequency people say to me, "You wouldn't look so young if you had the bald head proper to your time of life; how do you preserve that mop? How do you keep it from falling out?" I have to answer with a theory, for lack of adequately established knowledge. I tell them I think my hair remains with me because I keep it clean; keep it clean by thoroughly scouring it with soap and water every morning, then rinsing it well; then lathering it heavily, and rubbing off the lather with a coarse towel, a process which leaves a slight coating of oil upon each hair—oil derived from the soap. The cleansing and the oiling combined leave the hair soft and pliant and silky, and very pleasantly and comfortably wearable the whole day through; for although the hair becomes dirty again within ten hours, either in country or city, because there is so much microscopic dust floating in the air, it does not become dirty enough to be really raspy to the touch and delicately uncomfortable under twenty-four hours; yet it does become dirty enough in twenty-four hours to make the water cloudy when I wash it. Now then we arrive at a curious thing; the answer to my explanation always brings forth the same old unvarying and foolish remark, to wit—"Water ruins the hair because it rots the root of it." The remark is not made in a doubtful tone but in a decided one—a tone which indicates that the speaker has examined the matter and knows all about it. Then I say, "How do you know this?"—and the confident speaker stands exposed; he doesn't quite know what to say. If I ask him if he has ruined his own hair by wetting it it turns out that he doesn't wet it often lest he rot the roots of it, therefore he is not talking from his own experience; if I ask if he has personal knowledge of cases where the roots were rotted by wetting, it turns out that he hasn't a single case of the kind to offer; when I hunt him remorselessly home he has to confess at last that "everybody says" water rots the roots of the hair. Strange—it is just like religion and politics! In religion and politics people's beliefs and convictions are in almost every case gotten at second-hand, and without examination, from authorities who have not themselves examined the questions at issue but have taken them at second-hand from other non-examiners, whose opinions about them were not worth a brass farthing.

It is an odd and curious and interesting ass, the human race. It is constantly washing its face, its eyes, its ears, its nose, its teeth, its mouth, its hands, its body, its feet, its hind legs, and it is thoroughly convinced that cleanliness is next to godliness, and that water is the noblest and surest of all preservers of health, and wholly undangerous, except in just one case—you mustn't apply it to the hair! You must diligently protect the hair from cleanliness; you must carefully keep it filthy or you will lose it; everybody believes this, yet you can never find any human being who has tried it; you can never find a human being who knows it by personal experience, personal test, personal proof; you can never find a Christian who has acquired this valuable knowledge, this saving knowledge, by any process but the everlasting and all-sufficient "people say." In all my seventy-two years and a half I have never come across such another ass as this human race is.

The more one examines this matter the more curious it becomes. Every man wets and soaps and scours his hands before he goes to dinner; he washes them before supper; he washes them before breakfast; he washes them before luncheon, and he knows, not by guesswork but by old experience, that in all these cases his hands are dirty and need the washing when he applies it. Does he suppose that his bared and unprotected hair, exposed exactly as his hands are exposed, is not gathering dirt all the time? Does he suppose it is remaining clean while his hands are getting constantly dirty? I am considered eccentric because I wear white clothes both winter and summer. I am eccentric, then, because I prefer to be clean in the matter of raiment—clean in a dirty world; absolutely the only cleanly-clothed human being in all Christendom north of the Tropics. And that is what I am. All clothing gets dirty in a single day—as dirty as one's hands would get in that length of time if one washed them only once; a neglect which any lady or gentleman would scorn to be guilty of. All the Christian world wears dark colored clothes; after the first day's wear they are dirty, and they continue to get dirtier and dirtier, day after day, and week after week, to the end of their service. Men look fine in their black dress-clothes at a banquet, but often those dress-suits are rather real estate than personal property; they carry so much soil that you could plant seeds in them and raise a crop.

However, when the human race has once acquired a superstition nothing short of death is ever likely to remove it. Annually, during many years, Mrs. Clemens was promptly cured of desperate attacks of that deadly disease, dysentery, by the pleasant method of substituting a slice of ripe, fresh watermelon for the powerful and poisonous drugs used—frequently ineffectually—by the physician. In no instance, in the long list, did the eating of a slice of watermelon ever fail, in Mrs. Clemens's case, to promptly cure the dysentery and make her immune from it for another year; yet I have never been able to get a physician, or anybody else, to try it. During the Civil War any one caught bringing a watermelon into a military camp down South, where the soldiers were dying in squads from dysentery, was sharply punished. Necessarily the prejudice against the watermelon was founded upon theory, not experience, and it will probably take the medical fraternity several centuries to find out that the theory is theory only, and has no basis of experience to stand upon.

Dictated at Innocence at Home, July 14, 1908

Mr. Clemens comments upon Norman Hapgood's eulogy of President Roosevelt in *Collier's Weekly* for July 11th.

The principal editorial comment in *Collier's Weekly* for July 11th contains seven or eight sentences—short ones, therefore it is a brief paragraph. It is a wonderful accumulation of rubbish to be packed into so small a space. It is a burst of servile and insane admiration and adulation of President Roosevelt. It purports to be a reflection of the sentiment of the nation; that is to say, the Republican bulk of the nation. It ought to grieve me to concede that it does reflect the sentiment of the Republican bulk of the nation, but it doesn't. To my mind, the bulk of any nation's opinion about its president, or its king, or its emperor, or its politics, or its religion, is without value, and not worth weighing or considering or examining. There is nothing mental in it; it is all feeling, and procured at second-hand without any assistance from the proprietor's reasoning powers. On the other hand, it would grieve me deeply to be obliged to believe that any very large number of sane and thinking and intelligent Republicans privately admire Mr. Roosevelt, and do not despise him. Publicly, all sane and intelligent Republicans worship Mr. Roosevelt, and would not dare to do otherwise where any considerable company of listeners was present; and this is quite natural, since sane and intelligent human beings are like all other human beings, and carefully and cautiously and diligently conceal their private real opinions from the world and give out fictitious ones in their stead, for general consumption. Norman Hapgood wrote that paragraph. He is an able young man; well read, well educated, and as honest and honorable as any man whom I am as intimately acquainted with as I am with him. But do I believe that this diseased paragraph came out of his private heart, and reflects his real feeling toward this disgraced outgoing President? No, I am not able to believe that. If I had him here in private a while I should expect him to find it very difficult to put his finger on half a dozen considerable benefits conferred upon this country since he ceased to be President, four years ago, and became Czar. Hapgood's paragraph begins thus:

> MR. ROOSEVELT WILL LEAVE OFFICE secure in the hearts of his countrymen. The dexterity and sincerity with which he avoided a renomination for himself, and secured it for a believer in his policies, have solidified the affection and the confidence of mankind.

That sentence is itself about as dexterous as was the Presidential dexterity which it admired. The sentence mixes together a possibly creditable act and a distinctly discreditable one, and the mixing is so cleverly done as to divert attention from the discreditable one and make one or two important words seem to apply to it as well as to the other member of the sentence, when, in fact, no such application of those words is justifiable. That wily sentence should be bitten in two and each half of it chewed by itself: "The dexterity and sincerity with which he avoided a renomination for himself—"

That half of the sentence is true. No, that is putting it too strong; it isn't quite true. If we leave the "dexterity" out and put in "reluctance," then it is true. Mr. Roosevelt did avoid a renomination of himself, after trying for two years to find some decent way to get out of his bombastic pledges and renunciations of the great office for all future time. The public press kept after him like a swarm of bees, and they pestered and pestered him for two years before they were able to sting a definite and final renunciation out of him. And so we will leave the "dexterity" out of that half of the sentence and put "reluctance" in its place, as being some four hundred thousand miles nearer the truth—but "dexterity" comes good, and exceedingly good, in the last half of that sentence: "The dexterity with which he secured the nomination for a believer in his policies—"

Yes, he dexterously secured Mr. Taft's nomination. But dexterity doesn't cover the whole ground; it needs the help of some more words, in order that the whole truth may be arrived at. The dexterity itself needs these qualifying words; mere dexterity carries with it a suggestion of compliment, but no compliment is due in this case. The President's dexterity in the matter of Mr. Taft's nomination was a dishonest and dishonorable dexterity—the same kind used by him when he jumped that horse-doctor, Leonard Wood, over the heads of fifty regular army brigadiers, real soldiers, and made that Rooseveltian flunky a Major General by help of the famous "interval," a trick which was merely and simply a lie and a swindle; and also—so to speak—a criminal assault upon the Senate. The President's act was not superior in respectability to the raping of a blind idiot—a blind and very reluctant idiot, a pleading idiot, a beseeching idiot; in fact that was just about what the Senate was—a blind and rapable idiot, and upon her the President accomplished his hellish purpose, as the Western papers used to say, fifty years ago, in these cases.

Criticism of Norman Hapgood's eulogy of President Roosevelt, continued.

Examined by the facts of Mr. Roosevelt's Presidential career, the rest of Mr. Hapgood's paragraph becomes matter for laughter:

> Turned aside by none of the flattering and plausible arguments which were daily showered upon him, he gave up power, kept his word, and set a high example. Scarcely was Mr. TAFT nominated when the President gave another example of his quality by springing enthusiastically to the aid of HENEY, SPRECKELS, and their friends in San Francisco, at a time when the current had set strongly in the opposite

direction. A few days more, and, in his praise of CLEVELAND, Mr. ROOSEVELT once again struck with hearty truthfulness those notes which celebrate earnestness and the truth. He has been a good Police Commissioner, a good Governor, a good President, and a good man. Twenty years of active life may still be his. Meanwhile he has already done splendid service for a thankful nation.

In what way has Mr. Roosevelt given up power? He hasn't given it up; he has merely gone through the form of transferring it to his serf, Mr. Taft, who runs to him daily with the docility of a spaniel to get his permission to do things. Taft even carries his speech of acceptance to his master to be edited and made the utterance of the master, not the voice of the serf. In what way has the President set a high example? Is it a high example for a president of the United States to keep his word? Is keeping one's word such a very extraordinary thing, when the person achieving the feat is the first citizen of a civilized nation? It could be a compliment to say of a burglar that he has kept his word and has thereby set a high example for the other burglars, but it is probably the poorest compliment that has ever been fired at a president of the United States up to this time. And yet there is some little reason why Hapgood should consider it a compliment, and praiseworthy, in this President's case, for this President has never been servilely addicted to keeping his word. A man's acts are also his word. Look at Mr. Roosevelt. He is always vaporing about purity, and righteousness, and fairness, and justice, just the same as if he really respected those things and regarded himself as their pet champion, whereas there is little or nothing in his history to show that he even knows the meaning of those words. Mr. Roosevelt's character and conduct have undergone many changes since he rose upon the political horizon and became notorious, but the changes are not to his credit, since they have been persistently not for the better but for the worse. Years ago he was the champion and vigorous fighter for civil service reform, and in this character he won the strong and outspoken praises of a public sick unto death of the spoils system. This was before he was President. The other day this stately foe of the blending of public office with politics, sent three hundred federal office-holders to represent his interests at the Republican Convention in Chicago and help nominate his shadow. Mr. Roosevelt is always talking about his policies, but he is discreetly silent about his principles. If he has any principles they look so like policies that they cannot be told from that commodity, and they have that commodity's chiefest earmark—the quality of impermanency, a disposition to fade out and disappear at convenience. In the matter of justice and fairness, he evidently has no fixed idea; he talks fairness and justice noisily, but he is quite ready to sacrifice these things to expediency at any time, and apparently without a pang. He admires the dime-novel hero, and has always made him his model, but he has always failed to "make good," as the slang phrase has it; he has always been ready to do the fine and spectacular hero-act, and he has always been equally ready to wish he had let it alone when he found that it pleased only half of the people and not the other half. Six or seven years ago he had a chance to do some dime-novel heroics and he eagerly accepted the opportunity to make a big sensation and set the whole American world applauding—applauding his nerve, his courage, his daring. He invited a negro to lunch with him at the White House, and the negro did it. That was Booker T. Washington, a man worth a hundred Roosevelts, a man whose shoe-latchets Mr. Roosevelt is not worthy to untie. A negro feeding at the White House table! The storm that burst on us from one end of the country to the other must have enthused the circus soul of the little imitation cowboy to the utmost limit, for a few hours, for the whole eighty millions were helping to make that noise, but when the inspirer of it found that it wasn't all praise, but that the Southern half of it was furious censure, it was not in his nature to remain happy.

I am speaking as if I knew. I think I do know; I think I know he was an unhappy man over that incident. For this reason: there was a freshet of honorary degrees at Yale, and the President was there to get part of the ducking, and I was there on the same errand, and there were sixty more, gowned and hooded for baptism. The President asked me if I thought he was right in inviting Booker Washington to lunch at the White House. I judged by his tone that he was worried and troubled and sorry about that showy adventure, and wanted a little word of comfort and approval. I said it was a private citizen's privilege to invite whom he pleased to his table, but that perhaps a president's liberties were more limited; that if a president's duty required him, there was no alternative, but that in a case where it was not required by duty, it might be best to let it alone, since the act would give offence to so many people when no profit to the country was to be gained by offending them.

I didn't tell him all I thought about it—we never do that; we keep half of what we think hidden away on our inside and only deliver ourselves of that remnant of it which is proper for general consumption. Privately, I thought it a president's duty to refrain from offending the nation merely to advertise himself and make a noise, but I didn't say that. But I believed that he would not leave that mistake of his alone; I believed he would watch for a chance to rectify it and get himself back into Southern favor. His opportunity came, by and by, and he seized it with avidity, and instantly made himself as splendidly popular in the South as Alexander VI is in hell. It was the Brownsville incident that gave him his chance. Some unimaginable ass in the War Department—surely not Taft—and it couldn't be Taft anyway, because Taft was always away from home around the globe somewhere electioneering for Roosevelt at the nation's expense—ordered the 25th Colored Infantry to take post at Brownsville, on the Mexican border. The Brownsville people heard of this proposition, and they implored the War Department to not fling this firebrand into their midst; that the sight of a nigger soldier could not be endured by Texans and disaster must certainly follow if the colored soldiers came there. Whoever was doing the particular assing in the War Office at that time paid no attention to these appeals. The negro soldiers went into barracks there, and by and by the prophesied hatred and bad blood manifested itself between the two colors, and presently there was some shooting done at midnight, manifestly with government arms and by negro soldiers. To please the Brownsville folk, the Government did several strange and shabby things: it sent a commission of officers of the regular army down there to take testimony and they took it; took such of it as would go toward convicting some of the negro soldiers and stopped there—they were not interested in any testimony that could go to the favor of those men. By the testimony of Captain McDonald, Texan Ranger, a man whose character for veracity is well established, the Government and its agents acted in a shabby and dishonest and dishonorable way from the beginning to the end. Mr. Roosevelt was anxious to convict some of those soldiers and thus get back into Southern favor, but as he was not able to do it he did the next best thing; he convicted the entire command himself, without evidence and without excuse, and dismissed them from the army, adding those malignant and cowardly words, "without honor."

How long would it take me to set down a list of the acts and utterances of the President which are at variance with Norman Hapgood's estimate of Mr. Roosevelt as crystallized in his closing sentence? It would take me a good while; too long for this day and this weather, and so I will leave that interminable list unregistered until another time.

But meantime, I find this editorial in an old newspaper—a New York *Herald* of something more than a month ago. The writer of it seems to me to know Mr. Roosevelt pretty well:

PRESIDENT TAFT—Roosevelt's Reign of Terror Over.

William H. Taft is the next President of the United States—provided the Democratic National Convention nominates William J. Bryan.

It is an office for which Mr. Taft has conspicuous qualifications. But best of all, his nomination means the end of Roosevelt and Rooseveltism. It means the end of personal government, of autocratic régime, of militarism, of jingoism, of rough-riderism, of administration by shouting and clamor, tumult and denunciation. It means the end of the Roosevelt reign of terror and the restoration of the Presidency to its historical dignity under the Constitution.

Even Andrew Johnson, in his periods of sobriety, had more innate respect for the office itself, for its traditions and for appearances than Mr. Roosevelt has shown. Never before was there such a lawless President. Never before was the Presidency so deliberately lowered to gratify a love for studied and sensational theatricalism.

Mr. Taft's nomination means the end of the most shocking extravagance known in the history of the country; the most extraordinary contempt for economy and retrenchment that any Executive ever displayed; the most irresponsible clamor for bigger navies by absurd appeals to the war spirit and absurd threats of foreign enemies; the most reckless disregard of constitutional limitations and constitutional checks and balances. Every serious, thoughtful citizen can now breathe more freely, and feel that the Republic is safer, having withstood another searching test of its right to endure.

Dictated July 16 and September 12, 1908

Dictated July 16, 1908. Thirty-five years ago in a letter to my wife ostensibly, but really to Mr. Howells, I amused myself—and endeavored to amuse him—with forecasting the

Monarchy and imagining what the country would be like when the Monarchy should replace the Republic. That letter interests me now. Not because of anything *it* says—for there are no serious sentences in it—but because it refreshes my memory and enables me to recall the substance of a letter which preceded it and which treated the coming Monarchy seriously.

I was not expecting the Monarchy to come in my own time, nor in my children's time, nor at any period which one might forecast with anything approaching definiteness. It might come soon, it might come late; it might come in a century, it might be delayed two centuries, even three. But it would come.

Because of a special and particular reason? Yes. Two special reasons and one condition.

1. It is the nature of man to want a definite something to love, honor, reverently look up to, and obey: God and King, for example.

2. Little Republics have lasted long, protected by their poverty and insignificance, but great ones have not.

3. The Condition: vast power and wealth, which breed commercial and political corruption, and incite public favorites to dangerous ambitions.

The idea was, Republics are impermanent; in time they perish, and in most cases stay under the sod, but the overthrown Monarchy gets back in the saddle again by and by. The idea was—in other and familiar words,—history repeats itself: whatever has been the rule in history may be depended upon to remain the rule. Not because, in the case under present consideration, men would deliberately *desire* the destruction of their Republic and plan it out, but because *circumstances* which they create without suspecting what they are doing will by and by *compel* that destruction—to their grief and dismay. My notion was, that in some near or some distant day, circumstances would so shape themselves, unnoticed by the people, as to make it possible for some ambitious idol of the nation to upset the Republic and build his throne out of its ruins; and that then history would stand ready to back him.

But all this was thirty-five years ago. It seems curious, now, that I should have been dreaming dreams about a *Future* Monarchy, and never suspecting that the Monarchy was already present and the Republic a thing of the past. Yet that was the case. The Republic in name remained, but the Republic in fact was gone.

For fifty years our country has been a constitutional monarchy, with the Republican party sitting on the throne. Mr. Cleveland's couple of brief interruptions do not count; they were accidents, and temporary, they made no permanent inroad upon Republican supremacy. Ours is not only a monarchy, but a hereditary monarchy—in the one political family. It passes from heir to heir as regularly and as surely and as unpreventably as does any throne in Europe. Our Monarch is more powerful, more arbitrary, more autocratic than any in Europe, its White House commands are not under restraint of law or custom or the Constitution, it can ride down the Congress as the Czar cannot ride down the Duma. It can concentrate and augment power at the Capital by despoiling the States of their reserved rights, and by the voice of a Secretary of State it has indicated its purpose to do this. It can pack the Supreme Court with judges friendly to its ambitions, and it has threatened—by the voice of a Secretary of State—to do this. In many and admirably conceived ways it has so formidably intrenched itself and so tightened its grip upon the throne that I think it is there for good. By a system of extraordinary tariffs it has created a number of giant corporations, in the interest of a few rich men, and by most ingenious and persuasive reasoning has convinced the multitudinous and grateful unrich that the tariffs were instituted in *their* interest! Next, the Monarchy proclaims itself the enemy of its child the monopoly, and lets on that it wants to destroy that child. But it is wary and judicious, and never says anything about attacking the monopolies at their life-source—the tariffs. It thoughtfully puts off that assault till "after election." A thousand years after, is quite plainly what it means, but the people do not know that. Our Monarchy takes no backward step; it moves always forward, always toward its ultimate and now assured goal, the *real* thing.

I was not expecting to live to see it reach it, but a recent step—the newest advance-step and the startlingest—has encouraged me. It is this: formerly our Monarchy went through the form of electing its Shadow by the voice of the people; but now the Shadow has gone and *appointed* the succession-Shadow!

I judge that that strips off about the last rag that was left upon our dissolving wax-figure Republic. It was the last one in the case of the Roman Republic.

Dictated September 12. I shall vote for the continuance of the Monarchy. That is to say, I shall vote for Mr. Taft. If the Monarchy could be permanently abolished and the Republic restored to us by electing Mr. Bryan, I would vote the Democratic ticket; but it could not happen. The Monarchy is here to stay. Nothing can ever unseat it. From now on, the new policy will be continued and perpetuated: the outgoing President will appoint his successor, and the Party will go through the form of ratifying the appointment. Things will go on well enough under this arrangement, so long as a Titus succeeds a Vespasian, and we shall best not trouble about a Domitian until we get him. All in good time he will arrive. The Lord will provide—as heretofore. My humble vote is for Titus Taft, inherited insane Policies and all, and may it elect him! I do not believe he will appoint a Domitian to succeed him; I only know that if he shall disappoint us and appoint Domitian, Domitian will be elected. But I am not personally concerned in the matter; I shall not be here to grieve about it.

Evidently the spirit of prophecy is upon me again. It was upon me when, thirty-five years ago, I wrote the letter to Mr. Howells, while ostensibly writing it to my wife. Its date—1935—projects me into a still distant day, and makes some of the persons mentioned in it pretty old: for instance, the Earl of Hartford (myself,) 100; his grace the Duke of Cambridge, (Howells), 98; the Lord Archbishop of Dublin (Reverend Joseph H. Twichell) 96; John Howells (the Lord High Admiral) 65; Lady Hartford, (Mrs. Clemens—on whom be peace!) 90; and the Rt. Hon. the Marquis of Ponkapog (Thomas Bailey Aldrich—on whom be peace!) 98.

Here followeth the said letter:

Dear Livy:

You observe I still call this beloved old place by the name it had when I was young. *Limerick!* It is enough to make a body sick.

The gentlemen-in-waiting stare to see me sit here *telegraphing* this letter to you, and no doubt they are smiling in their sleeves. But *let* them! The slow old fashions are good enough for me, thank God, and I will none other. When I see one of these modern fools sit absorbed, holding the end of a telegraph wire in his hand, and reflect that a thousand miles away there is another fool hitched to the other end of it, it makes me frantic with rage; and then am I more implacably fixed and resolved than ever, to continue taking twenty minutes to telegraph you what I might communicate in ten seconds by the new way if I would so debase myself. And when I see a whole silent, solemn drawing-room full of idiots sitting with their hands on each other's foreheads "communing," I tug the white hairs from my head and curse till my asthma brings me the blessed relief of suffocation. In our old day such a gathering talked pure drivel and "rot," mostly, but better that, a thousand times, than these dreary conversational funerals that oppress our spirits in this mad generation.

It is sixty years since I was here before. I walked hither, then, with my precious old friend. It seems incredible, now, that we did it in two days, but such is my recollection. I no longer mention that we walked back in a single day, it makes me so furious to see doubt in the face of the hearer. Men were *men* in those old times. Think of one of the puerile organisms in this effeminate age attempting such a feat.

My air-ship was delayed by a collision with a fellow from China loaded with the usual cargo of jabbering, copper-colored missionaries, and so I was nearly an hour on my journey. But by the goodness of God thirteen of the missionaries were crippled and several killed, so I was content to lose the time. I love to lose time, anyway, because it brings soothing reminiscences of the creeping railroad days of old, now lost to us forever.

Our game was neatly played, and successfully. None expected us, of course. You should have seen the guards at the ducal palace stare when I said, "Announce his grace the Archbishop of Dublin and the Rt. Hon. the Earl of Hartford." Arrived within, we were all eyes to see the Duke of Cambridge and his Duchess, wondering if we might remember their faces, and they ours. In a moment, they came tottering in; he, bent and withered and bald; she blooming with wholesome old age. He peered through his glasses a moment, then screeched in a reedy voice: "Come to my arms! Away with titles—I'll know ye by no names but Twain and Twichell!" Then fell he on our necks and jammed his trumpet in his ear, the which we filled with shoutings to this effect: "God bless you, old Howells, what is left of you!"

We *talked* late that night—none of your silent idiot "communings" for us of the olden time. We rolled a stream of ancient anecdotes over our tongues and drank till the Lord Archbishop grew so mellow in the mellow past that Dublin ceased to be Dublin to him and resumed its sweeter forgotten name of New York. In truth he almost got back into his ancient religion, too, good Jesuit as he has always been since O'Mulligan the First established that faith in the Empire.

And we canvassed everybody. Bailey Aldrich, Marquis of Ponkapog, came in, got nobly mellow, and told us all about how poor Osgood lost his earldom and was hanged for conspiring against the Second Emperor—but he didn't mention how near he himself came to being hanged, too, for engaging in the same enterprise. He was as chaffy as he was sixty years ago, too, and swore the Archbishop and I never walked to Boston—but there was never a day that Ponkapog wouldn't lie, so he does it whenever by the grace of God he gets the opportunity.

The Lord High Admiral came in, a hale gentleman close upon seventy and bronzed by the suns and storms of many climes and scarred with the wounds got in many battles, and I told him how I had seen him sit in a high chair and eat fruit and cakes and answer to the name of Johnny. His granddaughter (the eldest) is but lately married to the youngest of the Grand Dukes, and so who knows but a day may come when the blood of the Howellses may reign in the land? I must not forget to say, while I think of it, that your new false teeth are done, my dear, and your wig. Keep your head well bundled with a shawl till the latter comes, and so cheat your persecuting neuralgias and rheumatisms. Would you believe it?—the Duchess of Cambridge is deafer than you—deafer than her husband. They call her to breakfast with a park of artillery; and usually when it thunders she looks up expectantly and says "Come in." But she has become subdued and gentle with age and never destroys the furniture, now, except when uncommonly vexed. God knows, my dear, it would a happy thing if you and old Lady Harmony would imitate this spirit. But indeed the older you grow the less secure becomes the furniture. When *I* throw chairs through the window I have a sufficient reason to back it. But you—you are but a creature of passion.

The monument to the author of "Gloverson and His Silent Partners" is finished. It is the stateliest and the costliest ever erected to the memory of any man. This noble classic has now been translated into all the languages of the earth and is adored by all nations and known to all creatures. Yet I have conversed as familiarly with the author of it as I do with my own great-grandchildren.

I wish you could see old Cambridge and Ponkapog. I love them as dearly as ever, but privately, my dear, they are not much improvement on idiots. It is melancholy to hear them jabber over the same pointless anecdotes three and four times of an evening, forgetting that they had jabbered them over three or four times the evening before. Ponkapog still writes poetry, but the old-time fire has mostly gone out of it. Perhaps his best effort of late years is this:

> "O soul, soul, soul of mine!
> Soul, soul, soul of thine!
> Thy soul, my soul, two souls entwine,
> And sing thy lauds in crystal wine!"

This he goes about repeating to everybody, daily and nightly, insomuch that he is become a sore affliction to all that know him.

But I must desist. There are drafts here, everywhere and my gout is something fright-ful. My left foot hath resemblance to a snuff-bladder. God be with you.

HARTFORD.

These to Lady Hartford, in the city and earldom of Hartford, in the upper portion of the city of Dublin.

1. That first paragraph is bad prophecy—very bad, indeed. But it is full of interest, for it calls sharp attention to an astonishing political change—astonishing when we reflect that it has taken only the brief space of thirty-five years to bring it about. Thirty-five or forty years ago the Irishman had been with us only about thirty years, yet had already become a formidable power, and was increasing his power by such leaps and bounds that a person prophetically inclined might with some sort of show of reason predict political supremacy for him after a further interval of a couple of generations, allowing him to remove the Papacy to New York and distribute Irish names about the country—Dublin, Limerick, etc.

It has not happened. No, the probabilities of thirty-five years ago have failed—and signally. In that day the Irishman was at the top of our foreign element, and the German came next. The other foreigners were few and unimportant. There were lots and lots of Americans in the city of New York, then—a thing unthinkable to-day! To-day we have to go around with an interpreter. To-day 85 per cent of Greater New York's four-and-odd millions are foreign, half-foreign, and foreign by one remove. The citizen with American great-grandparents—when found—is stuffed and put in the great museum in the park, along with the Brontosaur and the other impressive fossils. The Irishman still rules the city—like hell, so to speak!—but it is by grace of native genius, not by authority of numbers.

2. My second paragraph foresees a day when the telegraph is to be too slow, and we shall correspond by thought-transference—straight from brain to brain. That forecast has still twenty-seven years in which to make good. I repeat that forecast, and stand by it. Before 1935 it will cease to be a dream and become a fact. Wireless telegraphy has arrived; from sending thought on the wings of the air out of a battery made of metal to sending it out of a battery made of brain-cells is but a trifling step, and the Marconi is already born who will show us how to do it. The temper exhibited in paragraph No. 2 is another bad prophecy. I shall let fly no such outbursts when I am a hundred years old. I shall be a very quiet prophet then, and an example to the whole cemetery.

3. Paragraph No. 3 is good enough prophecy. If I live to be a hundred I know very well I shall verify it; for by that time I shall be sure to think I *did* walk from Hartford to Boston with Twichell, and that we *did* walk back in a single day—a hundred miles and more! Even now, when I tell about that walk I find it difficult to keep its marvels within bounds. That was a memorable excursion. It was a wretched idea. Twichell proposed it, and I thoughtlessly said yes to it, which shows that there was more than one ass in Hartford in those days. We walked twenty miles the first day, and I went to bed that night a physical wreck, though Twichell was as fresh as a new-blown flower, for he had been chaplain of

a marching regiment all through the war and by practice had acquired the endurance of a steel machine. The next morning we resumed the pedestrian exploit—on the train, not on foot. The Associated Press had informed the country about our start. Aldrich and Howells and Osgood and the others were full of enthusiastic interest in the matter and were on the lookout. When next day's telegrams informed the world that we should reach Boston by nightfall, those boys were proud of us and astonished, for they had not supposed we could walk the whole distance in two days, but would require three. So they got up a banquet for us at Young's Hotel, and when we entered the place on foot (from the station) they were insane with admiration of us and pride in us. I suppose we would have told them about the train if we had thought of it.

4. Paragraph No. 4 is good prophecy. Day before yesterday the air-ship of the brothers Wright broke the world's record. It did another thing, too: it demonstrated—for the first time in history—that a competent air-ship *can* be devised. For several years, now, the newspapers of the whole civilized world have daily been filled with the encouraging doings of the air-ship inventors, and now at last we perceive that the long-hoped-for day has come, and that we shall presently be flying about the skies with ease and confidence and comfort. No. 4 has another prophecy: that by 1935 we shall have Chinamen coming to us as missionaries. But I think that that was not really intended as a prediction, I think it merely embodied a *hope;* a hope that some day those excellent people would come here and teach us how to be at peace and bloodless for thousands of years without the brutal help of armies and navies. But that gentle dream is dead: we have taught them to adopt our sham civilization and add armies and navies to such other rotten assets as they may possess.

Paragraph No. 8 refers to poor Ralph Keeler—on whom be peace! He was a dear good young fellow, and we all loved him. He sailed for Cuba as correspondent for the New York *Tribune,* and never reached there. There was some evidence that he talked too freely in the hearing of some royalist Spaniards and was assassinated and his body flung into the sea. His novel, "Gloverson and His Silent Partners," is probably long ago forgotten, for Keeler's removal left only one person to remember it. I judge so, for he told me himself that only one copy was sold.

August 16, 1908

Samuel Erasmus Moffett

August 16. Early in the evening of the first day of this month the telephone brought us a paralysing shock: my nephew, Samuel E. Moffett, was drowned. It was while sea-bathing. The seas were running high, and he was urged to not venture out, but he was a strong swimmer and not afraid. He made the plunge with confidence, his frightened little son looking on. Instantly he was helpless. The great waves tossed him about, they flung him hither and thither, they buried him, they struck the life out of him. In a minute it was all over.

He was forty-eight years old, he was at his best, physically and mentally, and was well on his way toward earned distinction. He was large-minded and large-hearted, there was no blot nor fleck upon his character, his ideals were high and clean, and by native impulse and without effort he lived up to them.

He had been a working journalist, an editorial writer, for nearly thirty years, and yet in that exposed position had preserved his independence in full strength and his principles undecayed. Several years ago he accepted a high place on the staff of *Collier's Weekly* and was occupying it when he died.

In an early chapter of this Autobiography, written three years ago, I have told how he wrote from San Francisco when he was a stripling and asked me to help him get a berth on a daily paper there; and how he submitted to the severe conditions I imposed, and got the berth and kept it sixteen years.

As child and lad his health was delicate, capricious, insecure, and his eyesight affected by a malady which debarred him from book-study and from reading. This was a bitter hardship for him, for he had a wonderful memory and a sharp hunger for knowledge. School was not for him, yet while still a little boy he acquired an education, and a good one. He managed it after a method of his own devising: he got permission to listen while the classes of the normal school recited their abstruse lessons and blackboarded their mathematics. By questioning the little chap it was found that he was keeping up with the star scholars of the school.

In those days he paid us a visit in Buffalo. It was in the first year of our marriage, (1870) and he was ten years old. I was laboriously constructing an ancient-history game at the time, to be played by my wife and myself, and I was digging the dates and facts for it out of cyclopedias, a dreary and troublesome business. I had sweated blood over that work and was pardonably proud of the result, as far as I had gone. I showed the child my mass of notes, and he was at once as excited as I should have been over a Sunday-school picnic at his age. He wanted to help, he was eager to help, and I was as willing to let him as I should have been to give away an interest in a surgical operation that I was getting tired of. I made him free of the cyclopedias, but he never consulted them—he had their contents in his head. All alone he built and completed the game rapidly and without effort.

Away back in '80 or '81 when the grand irruption of Krakatoa in the Straits of Sunda occurred, the news reached San Francisco late in the night—too late for editors to hunt for information about that unknown volcano in cyclopedias and write it exhaustively and learnedly up in time for the first edition. The managing editor said, "Send to Moffett's home—rout him out and fetch him—he will know all about it, he won't need the Cyclopedia." Which was true. He came to the office and swiftly wrote it all up without having to refer to books.

I will take a few paragraphs from the article about him in *Collier's Weekly:*

If you wanted to know any fact about any subject it was quicker to go to him than to books of reference. His good-nature made him the martyr of interruptions. In the middle of a sentence, in a hurry hour, he would look up happily, and, whether the thing you wanted was railroad statistics or international law, he would bring it out of one of the pigeonholes in his brain. A born dispenser of the light, he made the giving of information a privilege and a pleasure on all occasions.

This cyclopedic faculty was marvelous because it was only a small part of his equipment which became invaluable in association with other gifts. A student and a humanist, he delighted equally in books and in watching all the workings of a political convention.

For any one of the learned professions he had conspicuous ability. He chose that which, in the cloister of the editorial rooms, makes fame for others. Any judge or cabinet minister of our time may well be proud of a career of such usefulness as his. Men with such a quality of mind as Moffett's are rare.

* * * * * * * * * * * *

Any one who discussed with him the things he advocated stood a little awed to discover that here was a man who had carefully thought out what would be best for all the people in the world two or three generations hence, and guided his work according to that standard. This was the one broad subject that covered all his interests; in detail they included the movement for universal peace, about which he wrote repeatedly; so small a thing as a plan to place flowers on the windowsills and fire-escapes of New York tenement-houses enlisted not only the advocacy of his pen, but his direct personal presence and cooperation; again and again, in his department in this paper, he gave indorsement and aid to similar movements, whether broad or narrow in their scope—the saving of the American forests, fighting tuberculosis, providing free meals for poor school-children in New York, old-age pensions, safety appliances for protecting factory employees, the beautifying of American cities, the creation of inland waterways, industrial peace.

He leaves behind him wife, daughter and son,—inconsolable mourners. The son is thirteen, a beautiful human creature, with the broad and square face of his father and his grandfather, a face in which one reads high character and intelligence. This boy will be distinguished, by and by, I think.

In closing this slight sketch of Samuel E. Moffett I wish to dwell with lingering and especial emphasis upon the dignity of his character and ideals. In an age when we would rather have money than health, and would rather have another man's money than our own, he lived and died unsordid; in a day when the surest road to national greatness and admiration is by showy and rotten demagoguery in politics and by giant crimes in finance, he lived and died a gentleman.

Mark Twain

Dictated at Stormfield, October 6, 1908

I called this house Innocence at Home but my daughter Clara has abolished that name and replaced it with Stormfield. This is well, and is satisfactory to me; for the whole strain of furnishing innocence enough to justify the other name was falling upon me, and was already beginning to tax me beyond my strength. The house stands high and lonely and exposed to all the winds that blow; consequently Stormfield is a rational name for it; besides, the loggia and the apartment over it, which is Clara's, was not to have been built until next year or the year after, for economic reasons; but when we found we could add it at once without expense, we added it. It cost us nothing because I got all of the necessary money for it out of a small manuscript which had lain in my pigeon-holes forty-one years, and which I sold to *Harper's Magazine*. The article was entitled "Captain Stormfield's Visit to Heaven." So I think that on the whole Stormfield is a more logical and more justifiable name than the other one.

Lately Stormfield has distinguished itself by getting broken into by burglars. It seems strange to me that a New York architect should have overlooked so glaring a necessity as a burglar alarm for so isolated a house as this is, when I reflect that New York is only an hour and a half away; that it contains four millions of people, and that the most of them are burglars. It would not have occurred to me to employ a dog, because a dog barks; he barks at anything and everything that comes along, and therefore is a nuisance; of course he would bark at a burglar, and I would rather have the burglar.

The house was entered at half past twelve, midnight, eighteen days ago. There were two burglars and they entered by the cellar door and came up to the dining room on the ground floor. Nobody sleeps on that floor, all the household sleep on the second floor. The burglars made a good deal of noise, but disturbed the sleep of no one but Miss Lyon my secretary. She went down stairs and discovered the burglars and shouted for the butler; the burglars disappeared at once through the dining room door, which they had opened for their convenience. They had already carried away some silver to the entrance gate, and had come back for the rest.

Here we have the whole reason for a burglar alarm: the whole function of a burglar alarm is to alarm burglars. It does it. The moment the burglar hears it begin to buzz he drops everything and flies. There was never yet a burglar who would remain after the alarm began its office, and there was never a burglar who would enter a house which he knew possessed an alarm. We are having an alarm put in now. A little late, but worth while.

Miss Lyon telephoned Mr. Lounsbury, our nearest neighbor; he telephoned Deputy-Sheriff Banks, who lives six miles away, and by a trifle after one o'clock both were here and ready for business. They set out upon the trail of the burglars, accompanied by Mr. Wark and the butler—a trail easy to follow by help of a lantern, because the dust was deep in the road and the burglars kept to the road instead of breaking for the woods. Following a trail by lantern light is slow work; it led the searchers a plodding and weary six miles, to a railway station. Presently a train came along and the searchers and the burglars boarded it simultaneously, the burglars from the one side, the searchers from the other. It was an accommodation train that carries almost exclusively people with whose faces the conductor is familiar. The Sheriff asked the conductor if he had any strangers aboard. He said he had only two, and pointed them out. The pair sat together, with a small hand-bag between them—a hand-bag with our silver in it, as it happened. When a highwayman accosts you in the way of business he says, "hold up your hands!" but when Sheriff Banks accosted this couple he changed that, and said "hold up your feet!" for he wanted to see if their unimmortal soles corresponded to the footprints he had been following. His remark was quite enough for the burglars, and they made a spring for freedom. A scuffle followed, in which one burglar fought his way to the rear of the car and jumped from the moving train unhurt by the pistol-shots which Mr. Wark sent after him; meantime the Sheriff had the other burglar down on the floor, and he secured him at cost of getting a bullet in his thigh and another one in the rest of his leg. An hour later the escaped burglar was captured. Both are in jail now, awaiting trial.

All the silver they had taken was in that hand-bag, and therefore we got it back. They had taken double as much plated ware; but they were old and experienced New York cracksmen, and as soon as dawn enabled them to examine it they recognized its character and hid it in the grass by the roadside, where it was found ten days later. I suppose one ought to feel sorry for these men, for they must spend about fifteen years in a penitentiary for their adventure yet they got nothing at all for the trouble they took.

But I will reserve my compassion, because certain aspects of this case have changed my mind about burglary, and have brought me to consider it a very high crime, even when the burglar inflicts bodily harm upon no one when committing it. In the course of thirty-five years of experience as a householder I have been visited in the night several times by burglars. They took whatever was handy and went away without disturbing us, and we were unaware that anything had happened—in all but one instance—until the next morning; and so the impression left behind them was not discomforting. No one in the house was in the least degree disturbed by the incident. I think, now, the saving thing was that they made no alarming noise. The present case was different. The heedless creatures woke up Miss Lyon, and she woke up the whole household except me. That was eighteen days ago, and I am the only member of the household that has had any valuable sleep since. Clara fled to New York, finding she could get no sleep here; Miss Lyon's nights are mainly sleepless; four days ago the butler gave up trying to sleep, and took his departure; the cook and the maids handed in their resignations the next day; yesterday one of the maids who has been with us four years, and was expecting to remain with us forty, resigned her position and told me that since the burglary she never gets more than three hours of sleep at one stretch, and whether the stretch be short or long she wakes out of it with a shriek and sits up in bed delivering cold perspiration from every pore—and always because of one and the same dream, repeated and repeated over and over again night after night, in which dream the burglars are always shooting her to death and she feels the bullets go through her. Since the burglary I have conversed with many persons who have had personal experience of burglaries, and I find that when the burglar makes a noise and frightens the women-folk of the household it takes those women years to get over the effects of it. For many months their sleep, when they get any, is filled with horrors, and their lives are made miserable. As I have already said, this new light makes burglary, to me, a particularly high crime—a much higher crime than it would be if the burglar had killed the sufferer; for death is much better than a life filled with terror.

And so, if I were privileged to alter the law, I would make the penalty light for noiseless burglary, and remorselessly hang the burglar who disturbed the peace of the family.

A couple of days after the burglary I put a notice on the front door. By the letters which are arriving now, I find that it has traveled through the European newspapers, and as it had already traveled through the American ones I think that most of the burglars of this world have read it and will see the wisdom of allowing themselves to be guided by it.

NOTICE.

To the next Burglar.

———

There is nothing but plated ware in this house, now and henceforth. You will find it in that brass thing in the dining room over in the corner by the basket of kittens. If you want the basket, put the kittens in the brass thing. Do not make a noise—it disturbs the family. You will find rubbers in the front hall, by that thing which has the umbrellas in it, chiffonier, I think they call it, or pergola, or something like that.

Please close the door when you go away.

Very truly yours,
S. L. Clemens.

Dictated October 31, 1908

Paragraph clipped from the news columns a day or two ago:

Widow Provided For, Butters Fortune Goes to Student Son.

(Special to The World.)
SAN FRANCISCO, Oct. 29.—Having been handsomely provided for by Henry Butters, the Oakland capitalist, before his death last Monday, the widow and her two daughters by a former marriage will not sue to break the will which leaves practically everything to Henry Butters jr, son, now a student at Phillips-Exeter Academy in New Hampshire. Butters's fortune is thought to be close to a million dollars. It was made in a South African tramway line.

So Butters has escaped. I seem to have no luck, lately. My case is like William C. Prime's. Prime was a gushing pietist; religion was his daily tipple; he was always under the influence. Seldom actually and solidly drunk with holiness, but always on the verge of it, always dizzy, boozy, twaddlesome. But there was another and a pleasanter side to him: when he wasn't praying, when he wasn't praising God intemperately, he was damning to the nethermost hell three or four men whom he hated with his whole heart, and imploring the Throne of Grace to keep them alive so that he could go on hating and damning them and be happy. Chiefest of these was Mr. Lincoln's great Secretary of War, Edmund M. Stanton.

When Stanton died, in 1869, Prime was doing the Nile with his brother-in-law, the distinguished philologist of Hartford, Hammond Trumbull. One day, when the dahabieh was tied up to the bank near Luxor, Prime was ashore lounging up and down in the rich gloaming and pouring out ecstasies of pious gratitude to the Creator for permitting His worm to see this sumptuous loveliness while yet in the flesh. An ascending dahabieh handed Trumbull the sad news of our nation's bereavement. He stepped ashore to break it to Prime. Then he stopped and respectfully waited, for Prime was doing an attitude—doing it in his best theatrical style, with one eye furtively cocked toward Heaven to see if it was being noticed up there. And he was working off his panegyric, and stacking up his grateful adorations mountains high. He finished with an eloquent burst and a self-satisfied nod of the head, as who should say, "There—put that in your archives." Then Trumbull told him.

There was a sudden change. Prime shook his fist at the sky and shouted venomously:

"You've taken him—taken my all and left me a pauper! Humbly and faithfully have I served You from the cradle up, and *this* is what I get for it!"

Butters has escaped, and now I am likewise poor indeed. He has been my pet aversion, my heart's detested darling, for nearly seven years; and now, for no sufficient reason, no even plausible excuse, he is taken from me. I would rather have lost thirty uncles. Butters was easily the meanest white man, and the most degraded in spirit and contemptible in character I have ever known; and next to him ranks his lawyer, William W. Baldwin, whom God preserve! He still lives. Still lives to compete with the polecat and outsmell him. He is my only comfort now.

Butters the millionaire came to me recommended by his devoted friend, an honorable and high-minded man, John Hays Hammond; and he at once set his traps and played a "confidence game" upon me. To what end? Merely to swindle me out of an infinitely trivial sum of money—twelve thousand dollars. He succeeded. The lies and the treacheries it cost him to achieve this small thing—why, an ordinary scoundrel would not have taken that amount of trouble for less than a million.

He escaped to California, and there he had to remain. He dearly wanted to live in New York, but he had to forego that delight, and has chafed and lamented in exile for six years. He knew he would retire to the penitentiary if he ventured into this State, and so he stayed out of it.

Three years ago, in a short story entitled "A Horse's Tale" I made one of the horses describe Butters by name and character; and for this bit of pleasantry Butters commissioned his legal serf in New York to bring against me a libel suit—and he placed the damages at fifty thousand dollars! Damage to his reputation, you understand. Whereas it couldn't be damaged, by any process known to science; there wasn't a place on it the size of a hydrogen molecule that wasn't already rotten. And now he is dead, and alas the suit is taken away from me; I am robbed of even that chance to be gleeful. It is an odious world. That suit, tried in open court, with the latitude which such suits permit, would have been the comedy of the century!

A Brooklyn evening paper of yesterday has a telegram from California which contains further tidings of the bereavement which has befallen me. To this effect: Butters, in his will, has cut off his wife (his second, who lately opened divorce proceedings against him) with nothing; has cut her daughters off with five dollars apiece, and has left the remainder of his swag to his son. Has left him his name, too—Butters—and so he is the worst off of the family after all, for the daughters are married and the widow can change her name, for she is young and handsome and good.

Dictated November 2, 1908

Several times in this Autobiography I have spoken of an unpublished philosophy of mine entitled "What is Man?" About three years ago I copyrighted the book in Mr. Bosworth's name and got a few copies printed and bound—four hundred. F. N. Doubleday attended to it for me. Bosworth is superintendent of a great printing-house in New York. He transferred the copyright to Doubleday, and Doubleday transferred it to me. In this way the authorship has been kept secret. I have disclosed the authorship to half a dozen special friends, safe people and trustworthy. Doubleday has possessed my secret ten or eleven years; I read a part of the manuscript to him in Vienna in '97 or '98. My idea in privately printing the four hundred copies was, to distribute them among thinking men, concealing the authorship, and in this way to get at their opinion of the book unmodified by prejudice. I felt entirely sure that no highly sane and intelligent person could read it understandingly and not accept its positions. But it turned out that I had a couple of serious difficulties to contend with. They were these: a sane man of high intelligence is sure to be a busy man, and is about equally sure to waste-basket a philosophy which comes to him untagged with a name commanding attention; the other was, that no man, howsoever sane and intelligent can read a new philosophy understandingly. His vision will be blurred by age-long preconceptions due to training and environment, and until somebody shall brush these away he will misinterpret the book, and misunderstand it. Doubleday sent a copy to Kipling's father, a very intelligent man, and his verdict was very amusing; also quite necessarily and quite naturally grotesque. For the book had not been explained to him; wherefore he saw it through spectacles falsely focussed by ancient and foolish preconceptions and superstitions. With Andrew Carnegie the result was the same. The same with Bernard Shaw's biographer, who wildly imagined a lot of resemblances between Shaw's philosophy and mine. It eventually became plain to me that to get intelligent verdicts from sane and intelligent men who had not been taught how to read the book, was an impossibility and I gave it up. But I found that whenever I read the small book myself to a person of good intelligence, of whatsoever age or sex, I always captured a disciple. Generally against the disciple's will, still the disciple was made, and remained my possession. Remained my possession, and presently became reconciled; later, had the wit to realize that I had set him free, and was properly glad and grateful for this service I had rendered him.

Ashcroft is a disciple. Some time ago he converted a Canadian friend of his, and that friend has been privately passing the book from hand to hand, and teaching people how to read it, with the result that he has added several converts to the list. He knows the authorship himself but conceals it from his clients.

Mr. Norris is on the right track. By his missionary methods he has accomplished in a few months about as much in the matter of acquiring disciples as I have accomplished in ten years. My gospel will get a good start yet. That is all it needs, then it will thrive and spread. I shall not live to see it, but that is no matter.

The following letters reached me this morning from Mr. Norris.

Toronto
October, 30th, 1908.

Dear Mr. Clemens:—

I enclose herewith carbon copy of letter today to David Grayson, which explains itself. You may know him as the author of the delightful articles appearing from time to time in "The American" Magazine, for 1907–8, under heading of "Adventures in Contentment" and "The Open Road," which indicate him a man of rare insight.

I have had made four typewritten copies of "What is Man" and expect to keep these and the original constantly in circulation. They are all out now.

It occurs to me you might have a copy available that you would want to loan Mr. Grayson. If so Mr. Ashcroft could mail it to him as indicated, care of The American Magazine. In one way I would like him to read my copy, because of my great regard for the spirit he expresses, but am more interested in obtaining results with the book, than in a matter of sentiment. I could then request him to return the book to Mr. Ashcroft. If, however, it coincides with your wishes better, not to do this, my copy cannot be doing better service.

Elbert Hubbard also writes me that he wants to see this book; that he will be in Toronto early in December, when I will hand it to him. I did not mention the title of the book in writing, yet I note a title of one of Hubbard's lectures, curiously, is "What is Man." Frankly, Mr. Hubbard's personality in some ways is not very pleasing to me. He seems too pronounced an egotist; but I cannot help admiring his candid plea of guilty; and no one can gainsay his independence and power.

I have also written, among others, Edward Carpenter, the English philosopher, whom you may know as the author of "Towards Democracy" (paterned after "Leaves of Grass,") and other books, and Count Leo Tolstoy. I thought perhaps you might wish to reveal yourself to Tolstoy before he reads the book. I have hardly had time to hear from these two as yet.

I believe it will not be necessary to explain that, in all this, my principle desire is service, and that every thing else with me must be subservient to one thing; and that is, to "content my spirit."*

Yours sincerely,
C. G. Norris

Toronto
October, 30th, 1908.

Dear David Grayson:—

Your short note of the 26th, reached me yesterday. The book, which is entitled "What is Man," had been mailed to Dr. Isaac K. Funk of New York City, who has also expressed a desire to see it, a few hours before. You probably know him as the author of that, to me, remarkable little spiritual-philosophical book "The Next Step in Evolution" and as managing editor of the "Standard Dictionary." Will request him to forward it to your publishers as soon as finished unless a New York friend of mine can spare his copy immediately.

Presenting the naked truth as the author has done, unadorned, not even with the garments of religion, how can the reader with any degree of spiritual intelligence fail to see the point?

I realize there is but one Spirit, one Power, one Life. I know it is not I that doeth anything, but this Spirit, this Master mentioned in the book, that worketh in me, whether I will or no. I know that, while my consciousness may choose or decide which is best (expressing free-choice as the author indicates), something in me, that is not I, doeth as It wills, not as I will. I believe the time is rapidly approaching when the will of this Master will be mine, if it is not so already.

Nothing, I find, contents my spirit—really satisfies me—except to do This Will. Moreover, I know that even then there is and could be only one motive for anything I do—to please myself.

If convenient, shall be glad if you can get at the book immediately as I may have another request for it and shall wish to respond as soon as you have examined it to your satisfaction. Needless to say I shall receive your verdict with very great interest; and, if favorable, I shall want permission to forward it to the author.

Sincerely yours,
C. G. Norris

Dictated November 5, 1908

Meantime a letter has arrived which continues this subject. It is to Ashcroft, and is from an accomplished lady who is a professor in one of the great female colleges. That odious form is common, and I submit and use it, though it offends me as much as it would to say female brickbat or female snow-storm or female geography. I will take a paragraph or two from that part of the letter which treats of "What is Man?" As follows:

---

* The primary law of human action, as proclaimed by the book.   S.L.C.

"I know I ought to return that wonderful book of his to you, but I simply cannot, yet; I want to read it again and digest it better. It is so new to me, that philosophy of his, that I rebelled at every page, and really fought my way through it all, but it was so damnably convincing that, by the time the end was reached, I sat dazed, but completely reconciled to his way of thinking, and can only say as your friend did that it is a shame the world does not know what great man wrote that great book. I truly will send it soon and I am mighty grateful to you for lending it to me."

(Ten days later.)

"I am returning by mail the best book I ever hope to read. I know it now almost by heart, and am mighty grateful to you for putting it into my life, for it has completely won me over. There's only one point I'd like to talk out with you—take, for example, that thief Mr. Clemens had before him in court not long ago, what right had he or the judge to sentence him when he was simply acting 'according to his make' and the outside influences of his life-long training which compelled him; yet what would become of law and government, if we did not hold him responsible? Tell me that."

Reply, dictated by Mr. Clemens; November 4th.

The question deals with *speculation,* thus it moves over the frontier-line, and enters a foreign land, a land with which the book does not concern itself. What might happen if this gospel were adopted by the world *is* certainly interesting matter for forecasting and speculation, but nothing definite or valuable ever results from guessings and prophecies; the results never in any case come out in accordance with the forecast. We cannot form the slightest idea of what would happen if this gospel were adopted. We only know, by the light of history, that the thing that would happen would be precisely the thing which we had imagined would *not* happen.

The book answers the question, but that is merely as it happens: the book's function is to state facts, caring nothing for anything but just that——the truth. Civilization has always claimed that what it wants, and all it wants, and all it values is the truth, and let the results take care of themselves. As usual, civilization is lying; its dearest care from the beginning has been to avoid the truth when it can, and fight it and destroy it when it can't. And yet the truth is valuable and proves itself so whenever it gets a chance. It is quite natural to wish to speculate on what would happen if a new gospel be accepted and adopted. The Terra del Fuegans can count only up to 10; when they attempt multiplying, the results of their cipherings are something extraordinary. Now suppose we imagine a Terra del Fuegan multiplication table wherein 4 times 1 are 14, 3 times 7 are 96, 9 times 5 are 150, and an educated white man goes there, and by intelligence, industry and persistence succeeds in proving to those people that their multiplication table is all wrong, and is a confusion and a falsity; then by further industry and persistence succeeds in showing them that our multiplication is accurate in all its details, and that it is in verity a fact and a *truth.* At this point, those savages would unquestionably exhibit apprehension and say:

"All our commerce, all our trade, all our business, have always been and are to-day still based upon the proposition that 4 times 1 are 14, etc.; will not this new multiplication table upset everything and throw our commerce into disorder?"

What would that intelligent white man answer? He would be obliged to say:

"God only knows; there is no way to find out but to wait and see what the result will be. I am here merely to bring you the truth, not to tell you what will happen if you accept it. My mission is plenty great enough and high enough without adding any extraneous and unrelated matter to it."

Put it in another form: a man is afflicted with delusions. A physician proves to him that they are delusions, and proposes to remove them, brush them away and leave him a healthy mind. But the dismayed patient says:

"But they have always been mine, I have believed in them, I have lived by them, what is to become of me if you brush them away?"

The physician would reply:

"I don't know; you will have to take the chances, then you will find out; I am merely here to give you a healthy mind, not to forecast what you will do with it when you get it."

The lady's compliments are strong but not too strong for my appetite. For several days I have been trembling for Prince von Bulow, for two days I have been trembling for Mr. Taft. Perhaps it is time for me to begin to tremble for myself now. Ten or eleven years ago, when I knew Prince von Bulow in Vienna—Graf, not yet Prince—he had already risen very high in the political world, and was still rising. He went on climbing and became Prime Minister and Prince. During some years now, the two hemispheres have been full of his great name, full of his praises, and of course he has been envied as being a most happy and fortunate man. And now, at last, he has committed a blunder—merely a blunder not a crime—and instantly he has gone tumbling and rumbling and fumbling and crashing down his mountain to the valley below with a noise that has reached to the uttermost parts of the earth. Another instance of a fact found out ages and ages ago that no man's glory is safe until he is dead. There is always a chance that some little ghastly accident will happen, unforeseen, unexpected, unpreventable, and turn it to a shame. Three months ago Senator Foraker of Ohio was a great man; a great man, and a useful man; very few of his colleagues in the Senate could show so fine and brave and independent and creditable a record as he; he seemed booked for the Presidency and likely to arrive at that position in due time. Very well, the other day that paragon of virtue and cleanliness, Mr. Hearst, bought some stolen private letters—bought them because he hadn't a chance to steal them himself—and he published them. Among them were a couple which seemed to show that Senator Foraker had had compromising relations with the Standard Oil Company a few years ago. That was enough, and more than enough. The nation didn't stop to find out whether Foraker was really guilty or not, it rose against him and he is a crushed man to-day, and will never rise again. Three months ago not a man in America doubted that at the election for Senator in the Ohio legislature, an election to be held in this present month, Foraker would succeed himself without opposition. Alas he could not be elected constable of a precinct now. The day before yesterday Mr. Taft was elected President of the United States, to-day both continents are shouting his praises and pelting him with congratulations by mail, telegraph, telephone, wireless and all the other ways, and his happy soul is swimming in painted sunsets. Very well I am trembling for him, and when I read and re-read and read again those delightful things in that lady professor's letter, by George I tremble for myself.

Dictated November 12, 1908

The following telegram appeared in the newspapers yesterday morning:

TWAIN'S BURGLARS ON TRIAL.

———

Author on Witness Stand Identifies Silverware They Stole from Him.

DANBURY, Conn., Nov. 10.—Charles Hoffman and Henry Williams were put on trial here to-day on the charge of robbing the home of Samuel L. Clemens (Mark Twain) in Redding several weeks ago. Against Williams, who resisted arrest and shot at the officer attempting to arrest him, the additional charge of assault, with intent to kill, was placed. The prisoners were guarded by three Deputy Sheriffs while they were in court, as they are believed to be desperate men.

Mr. Clemens came down from his place, Innocents at Home, in an automobile, accompanied by his secretary, Miss Lyon, and several neighbors. He was bundled up in furs, but in a room on the first floor he left his outer garments, and appeared in the courtroom attired in a light gray suit.

When called to the witness stand he was addressed as Dr. Clemens by Prosecuting Attorney Stiles Judson throughout his examination. Mr. Clemens identified a large part of the silverware which was recovered at the time the burglars were arrested on a train.

I have seldom been in a court room therefore my interest in the forms and aspects and impressivenesses which prevail in courts of justice has not been staled by use. There was a fine dignity and order about the proceedings of this Danbury court. They were formal, precise and venerable with age, for they have come down to us with our blood out of English ancient days. The lawyers did not make speeches, they merely talked and in low and respectful voices. The judge never raised his voice but said what he had to say quietly, calmly, judicially. In the beginning there was an incident: when the jury had been polled, and were ready for business, a bushy-headed, truculent-looking animal from the criminal haunts of New York rose and bowed to the judge: I knew by the look of him that he was there to defend the burglars, and I thought I knew by the look of him that he had been a burglar himself in happier days. He addressed the court most respectfully, and called attention to the fact that the two accused men were under guard of three deputy sheriffs and he suggested that this great show of force could give the jury the impression that his clients were desperate men and in that way could prejudice the jury against them; he closed by requesting that the force of deputy sheriffs be reduced.

Of course the jury had been sent out of the room while this appeal was being made. In response to the appeal, an appeal which was of the cheap East Side clap-trap order, and was intended to impress the burglars, not the court, the judge said reposefully,

"It is presumable that the sheriff knows his business and if he thinks a strong force necessary that is his affair. Call the jury back."

It made the house smile to see that missing link snuffed out, quiet and effective fashion, but it took the precaution to smile behind its hand and as privately as it could.

Before our case was called an incident occurred which carried me back thirty-five years and brought vividly before me, out of some long-forgotten corner in my memory, a scene in an English court. The thing that stirred this old memory to life was this; a trial was being concluded, and the prisoner was about to be sentenced, a humbly clad young woman twenty-five or thirty years old. Apparently she had no friends with her, she sat in the prisoner's box forlorn and melancholy. She had been convicted of a small theft, and was to go to prison for it. When she stood up with the tears running down her face to receive sentence, I perceived with a sort of shock that I had seen the essentials of this sorrowful picture before, and at once my memory transported me to Warwick in England, across an ocean and thirty-five years of time all in a moment. It was a court of assize. The court room was much like this Danbury one, the officials had fine intelligent faces like these Danbury officials, the English judge like the Danbury judge was a man with humanity and intellectuality writ large in his face. But the English court had one advantage over this American court, in that its formalities got an added emphasis and impressiveness from the judge's scarlet robe, the official costumes of the sheriff and his subordinates, from the rods of the ushers—things which appeal powerfully to the human race, compel its respect, and are of as high value in a democracy as they are in the monarchies. In the English court there was plenty of color, in the American court there was none, all was monotonous gray there. In the English court the prisoner at the bar was a meek and melancholy and humbly dressed young woman of thirty-five or perhaps forty, with a face and bearing which indicated that hers had been a hard and unhappy life. She never raised her face nor looked about her, but sat with her head bowed and her thoughts busy, perhaps, with her troubles and her shame. In sentencing her the judge spoke so pityingly and so gently and so kindly that all the house was moved. In closing his preliminary remarks he said in substance this:

"Yours is a distressing case and calls rather for compassion than for censure. You have uttered counterfeit coin, and this is a high crime under the law, but you did not do it of your own volition, you were forced to it by a brutal husband and his criminal comradeship. Morally it may be claimed for you that you are innocent; but technically you are guilty and the law cannot discriminate. The court has dealt by you with such generosity as was at its command; it has carefully concealed from the jury the fact that you have suffered before for the kind of offence of which you have just been adjudged guilty so that your past history might not imbue the minds of the jury with a prejudice against you. Once before in the same cruel circumstances that compelled you to commit the present crime you committed its like and suffered for it a long imprisonment. It is my duty now, and a most painful one it is, to sentence you to fourteen years' imprisonment at hard labor."

The woman broke into sobs and lamentations and moanings and beseechings and still crying and still lamenting was led from the place leaving behind her no heart that was untouched and no face that did not exhibit strong emotion, the judge's most of all.

Yesterday the trial of the burglars was concluded. I was not present and had no desire to be there, for according to my gospel the burglars were not guilty. They obeyed the law of their temperament, and the compulsions of their birth, their training, their associations and their circumstances. They had nothing to do with their birth, they did not create their temperaments, they had nothing at all to do with arranging their circumstances, their environment, their associations, these being all compulsory and not avoidable. For its protection society must restrain burglars, thieves, maniacs and natural murderers. This cannot be avoided, the men themselves are guilty of nothing, it is temperament, environment, association and circumstances that commit the crime but as these are things which cannot be called into court and tried and punished, society is obliged to try and punish the unfortunates whose ill luck has given them the ill luck of standing for these elusive and ungraspable criminals and of doing penance for them by proxy.

The burglars pleaded guilty and one of them was condemned to four years in the penitentiary on the single count of burglary, the other was condemned on two counts, burglary and shooting with intent to kill, and he goes to prison for nine years.

Dictated at Stormfield, November 24, 1908

Lord Northcliffe came up with Colonel Harvey to talk over my new copyright scheme, and spent the night. Considering his years, which are but forty-three, he is easily the most remarkable man of the day, I think. He has a smooth young face and frank and strong youthful enthusiasms, enthusiasms veiled under his native English reserve, but quite perceptible, nevertheless. When I first met him, eight or nine years ago, he was as fresh-faced as a boy, and indeed looked like a boy; yet he had already achieved his fortune, made his mark, and was a recognized power in the English world.

He began life under unpromising circumstances. He came up to London from the country, unacquainted with the world, destitute of friends competent to help him, a stranger, a waif, and without money. He presently got a humble place in a publication office, and as soon as his wage was increased to twenty dollars a month, he got married. He was about twenty-one or twenty-two years old then. Twelve years later, when I first knew him, he was proprietor of ten or twenty prosperous periodicals and daily news-papers, was burdened with more money than he knew how to spend, and had acquired a title—Sir Alfred Harmsworth. To-day, aged forty-three, he is Lord Northcliffe, is chief proprietor of that journal which for a hundred years has ranked with the sceptred sovereigns of the world as a political power, and he owns and conducts fifty-two other journals and magazines besides the one just mentioned, the London *Times*. He lives in various palaces which he owns, he is steeped in luxury and magnificence, he has money without limit, yet he is in no way spoiled but is simple and modest in his ways, and quite as unassuming as he was when he married the moneyless girl of his choice on an income of twenty dollars a month.

He liked my new copyright scheme, of course. I know it to be the only one not idiotic that has ever been devised. He said that if I would go to England with it he would work for it with zeal in Parliament and would support it with equal zeal with his entire battery of fifty-two guns including the London *Times*. I am aware that to pass a measure in Parliament would be the same as passing it in Congress, because Congress always imitates Parliament in matters of copyright and never ventures to initiate anything in that line itself, but I do not want to go to England with this enterprise yet for I believe I can work it through Congress this winter, and so at the judicious time I shall go to Washington and make the attempt. If I fail I shall go to England early next summer, or next spring, and take up the matter there with Northcliffe.

The following contains an embodiment of my scheme.

Copyright.

A Memorial respectfully tendered to the Members of the Senate and the House of Representatives.

Nineteen or twenty years ago, James Russell Lowell, George Haven Putnam, and the undersigned, appeared before the Senate Commitee on Patents in the interest of Copyright. Up to that time, as explained by Senator Platt of Connecticut, the policy of Congress had been to limit the life of a copyright by a term of years, with one definite end in view, and only one—to wit, that after an author had been permitted to enjoy, for a reasonable length of time, the income from literary property created by his hand and brain, the property should then be transferred "to the *public*" as a free gift. That is still the policy of Congress to-day.

The policy of Congress.

The purpose in view was clear: to so reduce the price of the book as to bring it within the reach of all purses, and spread it among the millions who had not been able to buy it while it was still under protection of copyright.

The purpose in view.

This purpose has always been defeated. That is to say, that while the death of a copyright has sometimes reduced the price of a book by a half, for a while, and in some cases by even more, it has never reduced it *vastly,* nor accomplished *any* reduction that was *permanent and secure.*

The purpose defeated.

The reason is simple: Congress has never made a reduction *compulsory.* Congress was convinced that the removal of the author's royalty and the book's consequent (or at least probable) dispersal among several competing publishers would make the book cheap by force of the competition. It was an error. It has not turned out so. The reason is, a publisher cannot find profit in an *exceedingly* cheap edition if he must divide the market with competitors.

The reason.

The natural remedy would seem to be, an amended law *requiring* the issue of cheap
editions.

I think the remedy could be accomplished in the following way, without injury to
author or publisher, and with *extreme advantage to the public:* by an amendment to the
existing law providing as follows—to wit: that at any time between the beginning of
a book's forty-first year and the ending of its forty-second the owner of the copyright
may extend its life thirty years by issuing and placing on sale an edition of the book at
one-tenth the price of the cheapest edition, thitherto issued at any time during the ten
immediately preceding years; this extension to lapse and become null and void if at any
time during the thirty years he shall fail during the space of three consecutive months to
furnish the 10 per cent book upon demand of any person or persons desiring to buy it.

The result would be, that no American classic enjoying the thirty-year extension
would ever be out of the reach of any American purse, let its *uncompulsory* price be what
it might. He would get a two-dollar book for twenty cents, and he could get *none but
copyright-expired classics* at any such rate.

At the end of the thirty-year extension the copyright would again die, and the price
would again *advance.* This by a natural law, the excessively cheap edition no longer carrying with it an advantage to any publisher.

*A clause of the suggested amendment could read about as follows, and would obviate the
necessity of taking the present law to pieces and building it over again:*

All books, and all articles other than books, enjoying forty-two years' copyright-life
under the present law shall be admitted to the privilege of the thirty-year extension upon
complying with the condition requiring the producing and placing upon permanent sale
of one grade or form of said book or article at a price 90 per cent below the cheapest rate
at which said book or article had been placed upon the market at any time during the
immediately preceding ten years.

Remarks.

If the suggested amendment shall meet with the favor of the present Congress and
become law—and I hope it will—I shall have personal experience of its effects very
soon. Next year, in fact: in the person of my first book, "The Innocents Abroad." For its
forty-two-year copyright-life will then cease and its thirty-year extension begin—and
with the latter the permanent low-rate edition. At present the highest price of the book
is eight dollars, and its lowest price three dollars per copy. Thus the permanent low-rate
price will be *thirty cents* per copy. A sweeping reduction like this is what Congress, from
the beginning, has desired to achieve, but has not been able to accomplish because no
inducement was offered to publishers to run the risk.

Respectfully submitted.

S. L. Clemens

Dictated at Stormfield, December 8, 1908

Speaking of burglars, here is a curious coincidence. I will lead up to it by inserting here a letter which I received about a week ago from the Connecticut Penitentiary. It is from the worst and toughest of our two burglars—Williams—who has just begun a nine-year term there for his midnight adventures in my house and with the sheriff on the train.

CONNECTICUT STATE PRISON.

WETHERSFIELD, CONN. Sunday Nov. 29. 1908
NAME, Henry Williams,
REGISTER NO., 2176 GRADE, 2d.

To MR. Dr. S. L. Clemens, L.L.D.
NO.   ,   STREET.
TOWN, Redding Conn.
Fairfield COUNTY.   STATE,   (Personal Matter)

WRITE ONLY ON RULED LINES.
THE PRISONER MUST CONFINE HIMSELF TO FAMILY OR BUSINESS MATTERS OF HIS OWN. NO NEWS OF OTHER PRISONERS OR REFERENCE TO CRIMINAL MATTERS MUST BE MADE, AND NO ALLUSIONS TO PRISON MATTERS OR PRISON OFFICIALS WILL BE MAILED OR RECEIVED.
NO LETTERS MAILED TO GENERAL DELIVERY IN LARGE CITIES.

TO THE PERSON RECEIVING THIS LETTER:—DO NOT VISIT FRIENDS ON SUNDAY, FOURTH OF JULY, FAST DAY, THANKSGIVING DAY OR CHRISTMAS. PRISONERS IN THE FIRST GRADE MAY RECEIVE ONE VISIT EVERY TWO WEEKS: IN THE SECOND GRADE, ONCE A MONTH. NO VISITS PERMITTED TO PRISONERS WHILE IN THE THIRD GRADE OR WHEN TICKETS HAVE BEEN TAKEN. FRIENDS MAY SEND PRISONERS, BY MAIL, SUSPENDERS, HANDKERCHIEFS, COMB, HAIR BRUSH, TOOTH BRUSH, SLIPPERS—BUT NOTHING ELSE. FRIENDS MAY BRING A SMALL QUANTITY OF FRUIT WHEN VISITING A PRISONER. FIRST GRADE PRISONERS MAY WRITE ONCE A WEEK. SECOND GRADE PRISONERS MAY WRITE ONCE A MONTH; THIRD GRADE PRISONERS CANNOT WRITE AT ALL. CERTAIN WEEKLY NEWSPAPERS AND MAGAZINES WILL BE ADMITTED, BUT NO DAILIES. ALL MAIL INSPECTED. ADDRESS PRISONER'S MAIL WITH FULL NAME AND REGISTERED NUMBER. FRIENDS MAY VISIT PRISONERS ON FRIDAY, AS ABOVE NOTED. NO EXPRESS PACKAGES RECEIVED.
ALL LETTERS TO AND FROM UNITED STATES
MUST BE WRITTEN IN ENGLISH

Most Honorable Sir:

In order to have a clear conscience and peaceful mind, which is so essential to human life, and as I firmly believe in your "genuine gentleness, honest symphaty, brave humanity and sweet kindliness" I take the boldness and ask of you the following respectful and humble request.

Since you know the weakness and frailty, the many struggles and temptations, and miseries of human life, better than most men, I humbly come to you and beg that you will forgive me and trust, that you will not be harsh with a repentant and regretful sinner and bear no malice or ill-will towards me. We are all human and therefore apt to make mistakes and fall into temptations and times come into our lives "when necessity knows no law" (to borrow one of your own expressions) and we perceive, when it is too late, what a terrible mistake we have made. But it is only:

"Old age and experience hand in hand, lead us to death and make us understand;
That after a search so painful and so long, our whole life had been in the wrong."

Since all is over, I cannot help to make mention of "a certain class of people" who did all in their power to prejudice and bias me against the long-eared, thoughtless and slow-minded public at large, and put me down as a low, hard-hearted, vicious and dangerous evil-doer, in order to gain notoriety and satisfy their pityful political ambition.— But, "Father forgive them, they know not what they did."— Being my first offence against the law, I have asked for a fair and square trial; but it was denied. I have pleated for mercy and clemency but received none. "Oh what a fatal time when society casts off and consummates the irreparable abandonment of a thinking being!" It is not for myself and my hard estate, that I am pleading; but for those I love and left behind and who are dear and true to me and whom I have so shamefully disgraced. Perhaps like me they struggle with, each feeling of regret; but it is my place to repent and ask you to forgive. It is in your power, most venerable sir, to relieve the painful and oppressed heart of a repentent sinner and have compassion with him. For: "I say unto you, that likewise joy shall be in heaven over one sinner that repenteth, more than over ninety nine just persons, that need no repentance." (Luke. 15–7.) My sole consolation lies in the verb "forgive."—

Your "Tramp Abroad" gives me much pleasure and—pain, for it recalls many scenes of my boyhood and one who saw "Alt Heidelberg" knows "warum ich traure in des Lebens Blüthezeit."

In the hope, that my appeal will not be rejected, not for my sake but for those I love, I once more implore your compassion an clemency and with a thankful and regretful heart I conclude these few and simple lines, giving you the repeated assurance of my gratitude and sincerety. I remain, most venerable sir, very respectfully yours,

Henry Williams.

When I began to read this letter, I also began to be touched. I could feel my heart softening. But the process was suddenly interrupted. There was something about the tone of the letter that seemed vaguely, dimly, remotely familiar: it was as if I had read such a letter ages ago, or had dreamed it; also I had the feeling that there was something unpleasant about that ancient experience. Without definitely knowing why, I began to chill towards the writer of this present letter.

Presently the feeling dawned upon me that I had come in contact with this kind of a letter before, at some time or other in the past. My mental machinery went on automatically digging deeper and deeper into my memory, and at last it uncovered the source of my present fancies and imaginings. I now remembered that I had once read such a letter; I also remembered that I had written about it in some book of mine. I did not know which book it was, but I could recall the very look of the room in which I wrote the book. Not the whole book, but the last two chapters of it, one of which chapters contained that reminiscence. I occupied that room only a fortnight but I remembered that it was during that fortnight that I wrote the chapter which contained that matter. That gave me the date—1882. This enabled me to identify the book—"Life on the Mississippi"—since I was busy with no other book during that year. I took down the volume and instituted a search; in chapter 52 I found what I was after. In that chapter there is a letter from an ostensible criminal who has acquired religion, to a brother rascal who is serving a term in a penitentiary for burglary. The letter is the work of apparently a phenomenally ignorant person, also an elaborately sweet and simple-hearted and permanently and perfectly converted person. The Reverend Joseph H. Twichell brought that letter to me in that old day and tried to read it to me, but its moving pathos broke him down and he could not finish it. I tried to read it and it broke me down. Copies of it were distributed around among the clergy, and they read it to their congregations, sobbing, and the congregations wept all through the ordeal.

By and by it was discovered that the letter was a humbug; it was written by the jailed convict himself, to himself; and that its ostentatious illiteracy was a pretense, for the rascal was an educated rascal. With this light upon the matter I read the letter again, this time without breaking down, and was amazed that so glaring a fraud, so transparent a fraud could ever have deceived anybody possessed of any vestige of insight or intelligence. I have re-read that old letter once more, ten minutes ago; and again I have marveled that it deceived Twichell and those other clergymen and me. Its bad spelling is preposterously, extravagantly, impossibly bad; bad but not ingeniously bad; sillily, stupidly, inartistically bad; as a piece of sham manufacture it is grotesquely poor and lubberly; even the housecat ought to have perceived at once that it was the product of a humbug.

The coincidence referred to above is this: the name used by the writer of that ancient letter was Williams. The name used by the writer of the letter to me from the penitentiary a week ago is Williams; the ancient Williams was a burglar, this present Williams is a burglar; the ancient Williams was sent up for nine years and the same thing happened to this present Williams two or three weeks ago: the tone of sweet repentance and pious sentimentality observable in the ancient letter pervades this present one. I wonder if penitentiary people always get to feeling like that. Two years ago Robert Fulton Cutting told me that there are men who make their living writing pathetic letters for prisoned convicts and that sometimes these writers do not find it necessary to write fresh letters for new clients but are content to use a really good and moving letter over and over again merely changing names and places to fit new circumstances and new clients. It may be that one of these experts helped to write the letter quoted above—I feel reasonably sure that he furnished the pathos, the sentimentality, the repentance, the piety, the humility and the Biblical and other quotations, for I cannot conceive of our Williams having any of this kind of merchandise in stock. He is a low and coarse and hard-hearted creature in all his fibres and sentiment and piety and repentance and humility are distinctly out of his line. The last thing he said upon leaving in charge of the officers for the penitentiary was, that when he got out of prison he would hunt down his fellow convict and kill him.

Dictated at Stormfield, December 10, 1908

It always distresses me when I do something sly and furtive which seems to me to be particularly and admirably smart to find that it has missed fire so to speak. These smartnesses of mine fail so often that I have finally been forced to the conclusion that the smartness is all on my side, and fails of recognition because smartness, and smartness alone, is able to perceive smartness. Sometimes when depressed by these failures, I have even wished that I was not so smart then I would not suffer so much and so often.

A short time ago, when I was trying to think up some way to save our little community of farmers the expense of building a house for our little library by putting that expense upon distant strangers in no way interested in that library, I hit upon a plan which I thought was very smart and would accomplish the end in view. On its face this plan was quite conspicuously innocent; it revealed no conspiracy against the distant stranger at all but seemed to interest itself in only the casual visitor to my house. Upon him it levied a tax of one dollar, to be applied to the building fund. It did not seem to interest itself in the distant stranger at all, yet the distant stranger was just the person it was after; for the reason that the distant stranger is very numerous, and his dollar equally numerous, whereas the visitor under my roof is necessarily not numerous and his dollar not swiftly cumulative. My guests average about twenty a month, and as half of these are women and I was proposing to tax only the men, it would take a painfully long time to gather together money enough by the tax to build even the most inexpensive library house.

In pursuance of my deep plan, I wrote out the communication for delivery to my guests explaining the purpose of the tax and justifying it; I had this communication nicely printed upon vellum paper and placed carelessly and casually so conspicuously in each room that no guest could overlook it—then I waited for results. The results were satisfactory as far as the guests were concerned; they promptly paid the tax and sometimes paid it twenty and thirty-fold, but there my scheme halted, there it failed, there it disappointed me. I was after the distant stranger, and I couldn't seem to get hold of him. The kernel of my deep scheme was shut up in a single sentence, but apparently I had shut it up so securely that nobody was ever going to discover it. That sentence, upon which I set such great store, and from whose ministrations I expected such wide pecuniary results was this:

"I desire that the money be paid to me personally."

Do you see? To pay the money to me personally would make an autographed receipt from me necessary. Now right there lies the admirable smartness of the whole great scheme. I had hoped and believed and expected that the distant stranger would hear of these autographed receipts and would be smitten with what would seem to him to be a bright and cunning and novel idea: the happy idea of sending a dollar and calling for an autographed receipt, without adding the formality of traveling to Stormfield to pay a personal visit. Here is a copy of that communication which I exposed in the guest-rooms.

To My Guests

Greeting and Salutation and Prosperity!
And Therewith, Length of Days. Listen:

MY fellow farmers of this vicinity have gathered together some hundreds of books and instituted a public library and given it my name. Large contributions of books have been sent to it by Robert Collier, of Collier's Weekly, by Colonel Harvey, of Harper & Brothers, and by Doubleday, Page & Company—all these without coercion; indeed upon the merest hint. The other great publishers will do the like as soon as they hear about this enterprise. The Harper Periodicals, Collier's Weekly, World's Work, Country Life in America, and other magazines are sent gratis to the library—this also without coercion, merely upon hint. The hint will in due time be extended to the other magazines. And so, we have a library. Also, my fellow farmers have arranged for the librarian's salary and the other running expenses, and will furnish the necessary money themselves. There is yet one detail lacking: a building for the library. Mr. Theodore Adams gives the ground for it. Mr. Sunderland furnishes, gratis, the plans and specifications, and will let the contracts and superintend the erection of the house. The library building will cost about two thousand dollars. Everybody will have a chance to contribute to this fund. Everybody, including my guests—I mean guests from a distance. It seems best to use coercion in this case. Therefore I have levied a tax—a GUESTS' MARK TWAIN LIBRARY BUILDING TAX, of one dollar, not upon the valuable sex, but only upon the other one. Guests of the valuable sex are tax-free, and shall so remain; but guests of the other sex must pay, whether they are willing or not. I desire that the money be paid to me, personally: this is the safest way. If it were paid to my secretary a record would have to be made of it, and the record could get lost.

The peace of the house be upon thee and abide with thee!

"STORMFIELD," REDDING, CONN., October 7, 1908.

Every day or two a guest paid his fine and carried away his autographed receipt. By now, about fifty of these receipts have gone out, I expecting all the time that the distant stranger would come across one of these baits and bite, but I was disappointed; it never happened until this morning. This morning I have a bite from Canada and a dollar along with it and my spirit is relieved and at peace at last; the scheme is going to win; it was deep, it was smart, it is going to succeed; we have captured the first stranger, we will get the others, it is as I foresaw when the spirit of prophecy was upon me: the distant stranger is going to build our library house for us. Here follows the letter from Canada which has brought me all this peace.

Toronto, December 7, 1908

Mr. Samuel M. Clemens,
"Stormfield,"
Redding, Conn.

Dear Sir:—

The last time I had the pleasure of hearing you was at the Princess Hotel, in Hamilton, Bermuda, last March, when you were speaking in aid of the Sailors' Hospital.

In the Toronto Saturday Night of December 5th I again find you assisting to build a library, and I herewith enclose cheque for $1.15, the 15¢ is for exchange, the dollar for the library building, but I must confess that I am sending you the cheque with the hope that when it comes back, it may have your valued autograph on the back. Do not stab my hopes by using a rubber stamp or letting somebody else sign it with a power of attorney, but let me have your real, genuine signature.

Hoping this letter may find you in a good humor, though I suppose I should "say you are always in a good humor," but I have read your autobiography and know that this would be base flattery.

Yours faithfully,

There are many interesting letters in this morning's mail. Among others there is one from a German schoolboy which I wish to copy here because of the engaging quaintness of its English. There is an elusive and darling and delightful something about a foreigner's use of a book-acquired language which is nearly always pleasant and fragrant and felicitous. This German boy's letter is certainly English, and as certainly not English, but its quaint handling of our language has a pungent charm, a charm that is all its own.

I am engaged with my school-fellows in reading your "A Tramp abroad" in my English lessons. I am very satisfied with it and have had till now much pleasure with all my fellow-pupils and our teacher, Mr. Yemusens. We have sometimes very much laughed at the humour, which is contained it. In our last lesson we have found a passage, which is not quite clear to us, which we are not quite understanding. In chapter III. near the middle of "Baker's blue-jay yarn" you make say the blue-jay at its examination of the hole on the log-house's roof: I wish I may land in a museum with a belly full of sawdust in two minutes. I beg to ask of you what you mean by these lines. Will you therefore kindly inform me, what you will express by this passage? Moreover your blue-jay has queer thoughts just so Jim Baker himself, whose style I find sometimes very comical.

I hope, you will spend a post-card for answer, for, of course, I cannot compensate you the postage by German post-stamps. Should you have pains to understand these lines, I beg to excuse me, as I am engaged in the English language only for two years and a half.

I have the honour to remain, Sir,

Your truly obliged,
Kurt Mönch
Realschüler

To Mr. Clemens.

Auerbach i. Vgtld., unterer Bahnhof
(Germany)

I have explained to him that when I was a boy in the wilds of Missouri, we supposed that the birds in museums were stuffed with sawdust; if any other material was used by the taxidermist, we were not aware of it.

Dictated at Stormfield, December 16, 1908

I passed my seventy-third birthday a couple of weeks ago and the usual annual congratulations and condolences have followed by mail and telegraph. This time the unusual has happened; a letter has come to me from a once intimate friend whom I have not seen for forty-five or fifty years,—Howard P. Taylor.

My Dear Sam:

I read in a 'Frisco paper yesterday that you had just celebrated your 73d birthday. Let your old friend of nearly 50 years ago throw a few congratulations over your old pompadour, with the fervent hope you may live to celebrate many more annuals, and continue to entertain the world with your pleasantries. I am but three years your junior, but feel fourteen years your senior, owing to a bunch of ingrowing rheumatism that has claimed most of my system since my advent among the "glorious fogs of California" shortly after the earthquake, and left me physically and financially "pinched" on a bargain-day mattress in Oakland, with a second-hand typewriter for company. I have read, too, of your frequent illnesses, and can only wonder at your extraordinary vitality, for when we were doing time on the old Enterprise in Virginia, you didn't seem "bigger than a paragraph," nor stalwart enough to pry up a carpet tack. I don't know your attitude on religion, or whether you ever had any (few of us had in the old days), but doubtless you are thankful to the Great Unseen for the blessed energies He has given you, for prolonging your days, and for making you the creature of cheerful usefulness to the world. It saddens "we old 'uns," though, to know that so few of our comrades of the past remain. A new, and still newer, generation has sprung up, and only a bent form and wrinkled face from among our youthful friends is occasionally seen wandering listlessly along the streets of San Francisco and Oakland. It makes one feel like the proverbial cat in the strange garret.

Nearly all the old newspaper editors, reporters and compositors that we knew have passed to the beyond, except Joe Goodman, whom I have been unable to locate, but hear he is somewhere in Southern California. Jim Townsend, I am told, died a year or two ago at Lodi, Cal., and Jim Gillis passed out last year—Dan de

Quille some time ago, as you know. Denis and Jack McCarthy, Pit Taylor, Jack McGinn, Mike McCarthy, George Thurston, and other of the old office boys, have all been gathered in, leaving but few of the old Comstockers to face the inevitable. My brother Billy, whom I believe you knew, is still on earth, here with me, but a paralytic. He is 76 years old. All very saddening; yet the retrospect is not so unpleasant, as I ponder over it, and doubtless the sanctities are still slumbering within both of us that make this life worth the living.

I am more than rejoiced to know that you are still on fair terms with your health. We are both left for a purpose, doubtless—yet yours has been at least partially accomplished in the pleasureable food you have furnished the world—while mine is still a speck on the disk of uncertainty, the difference being that you understood yourself—I didn't.

Let me again congratulate you.

The letter makes me seem older than I am accustomed to feel because of the list of names it has dug up out of so remote a past. We were all young fellows then and there were twenty-six of us in the Virginia *Enterprise* office, a most gay and cheerful and noisy lot. The paper went to press at two in the morning, then all the staff and all the compositors gathered themselves together in the composing-room, and drank beer and sang the popular war songs of the day until dawn. When I look back now, they do seem preposterously young, those boys; and now when I read what Taylor has said about the remnant of them in his letter they seem as preposterously and impossibly old. No doubt the great majority of them are in the cemetery long ago, and I suppose the rest of us will join them before long. Speaking for myself I am willing; in fact I believe I have been willing ever since I was eighteen years old; not urgent, but willing, merely willing.

Howard Taylor was a Southerner, with the pleasant South-twang in his speech; he was a handsome young fellow and graceful and full of life and jollity and good-nature and I think he had the blackest hair I have ever seen on the head of a person not an Indian. It is probably white enough now. He was foreman of the composing-room, and I suppose he was the inventor of a word which I have often used in my books when I was talking about poor literary stuff that had a good opinion of itself—when I was talking about it disparagingly and wanted to compress my disparagement into a single word. I was city editor and my duties kept me scribbling after the rest of the staff had finished theirs. Taylor used to come in and sit down near me and remark that the public were standing in ranks reaching from our front door to China and the rest of the corners of the earth waiting for my stuff, in fact crying for it and not willing to go to their beds until they got it. Presently he would take up a sheet of my manuscript, run his eye along down it, and then languidly ask:

"Aren't you nearly done? Don't you think this is enough hog-wash for to-day?"

A very good word. He never had any other name for my literature. Ten years ago, in London, Poultney A. Bigelow came to our house and said that an old, old and very affectionate friend of mine was living in handsome quarters at the West End and wanted me to come and dine with him and swap ancient reminiscences—name of the friend

Howard P. Taylor. I was electrified with joy. When Poultney and I arrived at the place, we entered an English lift of that day and generation—a lift which held the two of us and the lift boy by squeezing, and moved with impressive deliberation and solemnity— and when we stepped out on the fourth floor there stood Taylor eagerly waiting with his eyes sparkling and both hands out tended. We shook and shook and shook—most vigorously at first, less vigorously presently and with a quite pallid and failing energy at the last. I mean that this was my case; it wasn't Taylor's; Taylor shook vigorously all the way through. We sat down at his sumptuous table, and I began to talk pretty gay old reminiscences of the early days in Virginia City, and he began to respond with equally gay reminiscences of old times in Keokuk, Iowa. Mine didn't seem to hit him anywhere, and certainly his didn't ever hit me. Neither of us wanted to spoil this happy renewal of a fond old friendship; and so I never came out brutally and said I had never seen him in Keokuk and did not know before that he had ever been there; also I didn't say his reminiscences had never happened in my neighborhood. I pretended in a lame and poorly acted way to sort of dimly remember those things without being quite able to call back the particulars—"it was so long ago you know." At the same time he was doing the same charitable thing by my Virginia City reminiscences; he only just vaguely remembered them and could not call to mind any distinct particular except that he had never been in Virginia City. When this condition of things became at last unbearable I broke out and said:

"Oh come now call a halt. Let us throw off this humbuggery and come to an under-standing. Who are you anyway? Have we ever met before or is this all a blunder? I have been in Keokuk, I know what year it was when I left there. I have noticed that your reminiscences of those joyous Keokuk days all begin with the summer of 1857, whereas I have not seen Keokuk since the January of that year. Who are you? Who am I? Are you you, am I I? It looks to me as if it is neither of us."

An explanation promptly cleared the atmosphere and made everything pleas-ant and agreeable for the rest of the evening. He had known my brother Orion in Keokuk and probably hadn't known him well enough to notice so little a thing as the difference between his name and mine. When I had first begun to shake hands with him I was cordial and unsuspecting; unsuspecting and undoubting; but before the hand-shaking had been completed I was saying to myself dubiously "But can this be Howard Taylor?"

The first reminiscence I dealt him from my hand fell so flat that I could hear it slap the floor. It was this. I said:

"How would you like to have some hog-wash now?"

I have never seen a person look blanker than he did. He didn't look the kind of blankness that would indicate that he had forgotten about hog-wash, it was the kind of uncompromising blankness which indicated that he had never heard of hog-wash before in his life.

Now that three years have gone by and I am acclimated to old age and can look back upon its birth without any sentimental pangs, I think I will insert here (if I have not inserted it in some earlier chapter of this autobiography) the grand account of the banquet which Colonel Harvey gave in celebration of my seventieth birthday, and which appeared in *Harper's Weekly* a week later.

Dictated December 22, 1908

The mails bring me many interesting letters, and now and then a remarkable one. I save the remarkable ones, and shall by and by distribute them through my Autobiography, in order that my far-off future readers may have a chance to enjoy them as much as I have enjoyed them myself. I have now received a remarkable one from Holland which I want to share with the public at once; I cannot bring myself to inter it for years in the cold-storage vault with those others. In the storage vault are a number of letters from foreigners—letters remarkable only or mainly for their quaint and comic and startling English; but while the present one blazes with those merits it possesses others besides, as the reader will presently admit. It is from a born humorist, and his humor is so natural to him that not even the stubborn plate-mail of his book-acquired English is able to keep it in; it breaks its way out, and flashes through the chinks. He is so hampered by his imperfect speech-vehicle that he seldom succeeds in saying exactly what he is trying to say, but no matter, he always says his say felicitously, always quaintly and deliciously, and often brilliantly; and to be brilliant in a tongue not one's own is a rare feat indeed. We hear of it sometimes, but we don't personally encounter it. I think his English is perfectly charming, and I perceive that the personality back of it is charming, too.

It appears that his "bundle" (his book of humorous matter) fails of a market in Holland. Let him turn it into English—doing the translating with his own hand and allowing no one to mar it with corrections—and give it a trial and chance the result. I mean a free, unlabored, offhand translation, with no scrapings and filings and polishings, and other strivings after perfection. I think humor-lovers would enjoy the book and like the author.

Observe what Irwin has done, with his delightful Japanese schoolboy. That schoolboy's English is manufactured, yet how forceful it is, how hard it hits, how straight to its mark it goes. And all so innocently unconscious—apparently—of the havoc it is distributing, under the gentle protection of the broken speech. Mr. Bausch's broken speech could be effective, too, I think. Here is his letter:

> Most honoured and venerated Sir.
> It will probably wunder you very much to receive from a Netherlander a letter that is written in so bad English as this and only the circumstance that I am in reality not a true Netherlander, but that the blood of about the half of the European nations streams pure through my veins, may be able to explain somewhat this in each other case completely incomprehensible, few recommandable and totally unnational absence of knowledge of languages.
> Nevertheless I have done all that is possible to make this letter as good as I

might. When* I had been a true, pure Netherlander, then should I have succeeded without daught in so brilliant manner, that after years this letter should be considered by the linguists of your country as the most trusted source for the knowledge of your language, like she was in this time, but yet, now it is I, who has reached with my lessons in languages only this result that I am able to make myself ridiculous in three different languages for three different strangers—what a true Netherlander never can happen of course!—who has written the letter, I fear that the result will be somewhat less favourable.

I hope however that it will be you possible to conceive something about it and I do an appeal on your kindness and concurrence in this regard. But might it happen, in spite of all this consecration as well from your as from my side, that my presentiment appeared to be juste, and that you meand after conscientious study, that this letter looks more a composition in a by me for this occasion with purpose discovered dead language, or in a hitherto unknown dialect of the Esperanto or Volapück, so hope I nevertheless that you will not deprive me from the glory which me belongs therefore and that, when you dispatches this letter to the conductor of the rubric "Informations about the present abode of dead languages," or to them of the rubric "Observation of the natural growing crooked of artificial languages" of one of your local newspapers, my name will remain married with this work, so that I acquire always something with this letter.

And now the proper reason for this letter.

I ought to say that this is in reality a somewhat difficult question. I avow openhearted that I would have preferred to avoid this point, safe then in a note, placed at the underend of this letter, which should then have treated about all sorts of interesting questions, which had nothing to do with the affair self, but the fear that perhaps you will read only the half of this letter brought me back of this purpose and does me give the explaining of the question. You will also, even when you throw away this letter on the half, have read and have consented or refused the half of that what I have to write and to ask to you. In both cases is the half of that what I wish to beg you me also allowed at least not refused; I hasard also nothing, gain always somewhat and beg you also frankly: will you be so kind to write a preface for my first bundle of sketches?

That is a very strange demand indeed!, will you probably remark. For how can I write a preface for a book that I not have read and for a man that I never have seen?

I approve that this ask, when you put it indeed, would have some good reason under some circumstances, but yet, now the affair for what I ask you a recommandation is only a book and not a new mark of sausages, safety matches, an automatic self-slaughter-machine or something of this art, has this ask this reason not at all.

Why should it be necessary to know and to answer for the contents of a book, before one could recommend it? Have you then ever caused yourself an inflammation of your entrails by the reading of a book, like that can happen you with sausages? Did you then seen your children descends in the grave, the one after the other, like the guaranteed safety matches had caused without doubt, because you had given them a book? From such things has nobody even heard, is not it?

And then besides: since what time makes one name as author, artist or actor by his works? That happens certainly never, is not it! That is certainly contrary to the usance and good manners, is not it! That would certainly be a divergence of the

* German for *if.*—M. T.

good, old customs that never would be approved by the public and with which one who tried to introduce it would provoke the people and excite his hate and rage!

And how good has the existing customs not worked till to day! How many statesmen, who had else been delivered to the oblivion, do not thank their glory and their statue to the circumstance, that their wife could not endure their company and trickled away? How many singers, actors etc. are not very known, even famous, and have yet done in the service of their art nothing more than to wrench themselves the ancle, to lose their diamonds or to be arrested, all this with more sensibility then they ever had reached in their art! I myself know somebody, from a kind that you surely know also, who is praised by everybody and who are attributed all the virtues and endowments which are imaginable, only on account of the good case he has known to acquire a little belly* (Bauchchen) like we call that.

"From him have I the best hopes," says one in society's, when the happy owner of this belly goes away. "That is a worthy man! One who has endowments! One who will bring it far!"

And all they who speaks with so much appraising about this man, look with admiration to this remarkable, prosperitous belly, when they speak also, come under the influence of this strong argument for his good qualities and speaking from the man, they attribute him unconscious all that what they admire with so much enthusiasm in his belly. And is this not an irreproachable, beautiful manner to acquire the esteem and admiration of his countrymen?

No, most honoured Sir, I have the unshaken conviction that you will not maintain this argument of ignorance with my work, but that on the contrary it will be you a pleasure, to acquire the admiration and the agreement of the whole civilized world by the writing of a beautiful, thorough preface, which has nothing to do with my book.

And what a beautiful task is such a preface as for the rest! What a large field for all sorts of interesting contemplations offers she you! It has striked me, that since the author of this bundle conceived the project for it, the statistics indicate a notable diminution of crimes against the laws on the shoe of the beasts for draught can you say per exempel, criticising the affair of a large, economic point of view. Farther, returning to subjects of more local nature, you can remark that since the publishing of this work was resolved, the paving-stones of your domiciliary town are used less more on the outside and much more on the foot which is resting on the earth, so that the publishing of a work like this signifies for penurious communities a notable sparing in the expenses for the pavement and all such things more which you can say much more nice, juste and with more penetration then they here are written, of course.

But why does that man not ask such a preface to a well known humorist of his own country? Is that not somewhat suspected?, will you possibly remark to yourself.

Most honoured and venerated Sir, I avow openhearted that I annulate the whole admiration which I ever have showed for your logical power, your sagacity, your spirited look on all problems which are possible and that I retract all the declarations which I ever have done about this, when you put this ask indeed.

For what should I beginn with such a preface, that better could be calculated a funeral sermon?

* German pun on his own name.

Supposed that Netherland possesed a humorist, supposed even a well known humorist, stronger: supposed that you yourself were a Netherlandth humorist, do you mean that I should venture to appear with a preface of you? I should not dare it when my life were me precious! I should admirate you in this case as much as I do it now, yes, perhaps still more! For I should think: such a bad fate has the poor man not deserved! And I should regret at most that your were not born under more gracefull circumstances: that you were not a native of Greenland, not a citizen of the Nord Pole, not a man of Mars (the planet), but above all: that you were not an American.

And this cannot wunder you indeed! For it is you known of course, how much admiration my countrymen cherish for all the races, nations and peoples which I have enumerated and above all: how much admiration they cherisch for your countrymen.

Coming from your independent America, where narrow-mindednesses like these are unknown of course, you must have been striked double so strong on your travels through our country—you rambles it at all sides and know all his corners is not it? An American who does not run through our country is not a true American, as we learn on the school!—by the great predilection for all that is from you and your countrymen you saw here.

Or do not you know more with what a surprise each Netherlander used to listen, when you, speaking about the beautiful things that you had seen on your travels, told him somewhat from the curiosities of his own country, from which he never had heard till this day. In your own country is that quite otherwise of course. Your countrymen travel in the foreign only then, when they know their own country as good as their own house, but here is this just the contrary and does not exist anybody who knows exactly what there is to be seen in his native country. And stronger and stronger: when one says that it has indeed somewhat that is remarkable, they do not believe it at once, safe when it is an American who says that, for in this case is it the truth, of course!

And do you mean that I should dare to appear with a preface of a countryman under such circumstances? Sir, I do not think about it! Even when [if] I could obtain for my bundle a preface from the most orthodox and old fashioned clergyman which Netherland possesses then should I not yet think about it, though this is the best recommandation for all kinds of things that can be haved by us!

No most honoured Sir, only with a preface of you I can reach my aim. A recommandation of you, a humorist, the most famous humorist of your country, the most famous humorist of America and my success is certain! When I can show to an editor this, then undoubted is my bundle printed. Without my sketches, that is possible. But may hap are these then printed on the coverside (Umschlag), when no advertisements are received and when the editor is a generous man. Or possibly does he place them on loose papers between the pages of your preface, in variation with the announcements and with the intention to make the reading of these a few less monotonous. But in each case is the aim reached.

And should you refuse to grant your support therefore? Most honoured Sir, I cannot believe that. I do an appeal on your kindness! Your dollarkings sustain our painters for buying their pictures, from which they else never were delivered and even in a much greater quantity then ever has been painted by them and do you like to stay behind your countrymen?

No most honourated Sir, you will not do that! I am sure about that! But it will be you an honour to make possible by your powerful support the edition of a book, that else by no one of my countrymen would be desired, by no body would be bought and that no one on earth would have costed a moment of joy.

Have I gained the pleading?

Ah! it is true! I have forgotten something! You know literal nothing about my person!

But what can I say you that is able to awake faith and confidence? When I tell you pretty things from myself, then do you think: the man lies of course!, and I do not obtain my preface. When I confess on the other hand honestly my bad deeds en qualities, then do you think: I have immediately thought that there was something wrong with this man and who knows what he yet keeps back. And I do not obtain my preface not at all.

Nevertheless I do not like to say no anything and in order to show you that my will is good, I communicate you, that my length is 1.61 meter, my complexion is bleach, eyes blue, hairs flaxen, and I bear a beard. Nose common, ears common, mouth common, one fore-tooth fails. Bears black dress of dubious stuff, black hat, marked C.W., white nether garments, marked J.A.B., C.B. and P.B., save the collar which is dirty and the pocked handkerchief which is marked K.S.D. Boots black, weared off and in a great time not polished. Has in his pockets a pipe, a notebook without leafs, an ivory haft of an Indian sword and presumptively his neck-cloth.

It is not much like you see, but I do not know more that is guaranteed sure. It is the description that the police gave of me eight years ago, when I had gone away on a New Years evening to gratulate an old friend but had stand away about twenty four hours, because a dried ditch, the place where I had seen him the last time, was freezed now and I not had could understand in what manner such an important mutuation can happen in the two or three month that had passed since.

And might you find that all this is not sufficient to trust me in the affair from which is the question, then, most honoured Sir offer I docily my good name and beg you to agree me that what I ask you for disdain; I am with joy well pleased therewith.

Receive in each case the declaration of my most respectful sentiments and admiration

Your dediated reader
Pieter Bausch.
(nom de plume "Peet Boetser."

P.S. When perhaps you have to make a present of some weared off or superfluous humours, I recommend myself politely for sending.

P.S. My wife who had read this letter, says that you will problably send me a physician and not a preface and that you will believe that all this is foolishness. And your preface would help us so good through the winter, she says. I have answered her of course that this physician, when [if] he came soon, still could draw me a bad tooth, for though there is something in her words that is just, the prosperity and peace of our home forbid me to avow this. Nevertheless I will not wholly neglect her observation and declare also that all that I have written here is deep earnest, especially that what belongs the preface. Farther that it wood be very kind from you were so officious and that this preface, when [if] you came to day or to morrow in the neighbourhood of our house threatens you with the grateful cries of a whole family. We do not have children, so that you will be obliged to renounce of their voice, at our regret, but the parents have very good lungs on the other hand.

That is it almost what my wife said, but translated by me in pathetic stile and therwith does she have her will too.

9 Dec. '08

Amsterdam
Vrolikstraat 333 III
Holland

Dictated Christmas Day, 1908

Ten days ago Robert Collier wrote me that he had bought a baby elephant for my Christmas, and would send it as soon as he could secure a car for it and get the temporary loan of a trainer from Barnum and Bailey's winter-quarters menagerie at Bridgeport. The cunning rascal knew the letter would never get to my hands, but would stop in Miss Lyon's on the way and be suppressed. The letter would not have disturbed me, for I know Robert, and would have suspected a joke behind it; but it filled Miss Lyon with consternation—she taking it in earnest, just as he had expected she would. She and Ashcroft discussed the impending disaster together, and agreed that it must be kept from me at all costs. That is to say, they resolved to do the suffering and endure the insomnia and save me. They had no doubts about the elephant. They knew quite well that if Robert was inspired to do a kindness for a friend, he would not consider expense, but would buy elephants or any other costly rarity that might seem to him to meet the requirements.

Miss Lyon called up New York on the telephone and got into conversation with Robert. She timidly suggested that we had no way of taking care of an elephant here, it being used to a warm climate and—

"Oh, that's all right, put him in the garage," interrupted Robert cheerfully.

"But there's nothing but a stove there, and so—"

"The very thing! There couldn't be anything better."

Defeated. Miss Lyon hunted up another excuse.

"But the pony lives in the garage, Mr. Collier, and she's a timid little thing, and if an elephant should come, she—"

"Oh, that's all right, Miss Lyon, give yourself no trouble. This elephant loves ponies above everything, and will fondle the pony and—"

"Mr. Collier, she would jump out through the roof! Oh we never never can shut them up together. Between his caresses and her frenzies they would wreck the whole place."

"Oh, *I* have it! The loggia! the loggia! Spacious—enclosed with glass—steam-heated—cheerful surroundings—bright sunshine—adorable scenery—oh, the very place! Put him in the loggia!"

"But Mr. Collier, I think it would never do—I am afraid it wouldn't—indeed I am sure. We play cards there—"

"Just the thing! He has a passion for cards. Oh, games of any kind! They're just in his line. He'll take a hand, don't you doubt it."

Miss Lyon despairingly invented excuse after excuse, with failing hope, but Robert turned them all to the elephant's advantage; and so at last her invention-mill broke down and she hung up the receiver, beaten at all points.

That was ten days ago. Miss Lyon has worried about the impending elephant by day and by night ever since, and Ashcroft has done the best he could to find reasons that could make an elephant's society endurable here. Among other emollients he kept prominently in the foreground the fact that this was only a baby elephant, not an adult.

Meantime telegrams came from Robert now and then reporting progress—progress that was slow and disappointing, but full of hope, full of encouragement—all this concerned the car for the elephant; heavy Christmas traffic in the way, etc.; but at last came cordial word that the car had been secured. Miss Lyon had been hoping, a little, and then a little more and a little more—but this news mashed those frail hopes into the mud.

Day before yesterday came a telegram saying ten bales of hay—one ton—had been shipped to us by fast freight, and along with the hay twenty bushels of carrots and fruit. All for the elephant. Freight prepaid.

Early yesterday morning the railway office, three miles away, reported the arrival of this provender, and an hour later it arrived here and was stored in the garage. Miss Lyon—however, her despair had already reached bottom.

At nine this morning, Mr. Lounsbury telephoned that there was a man at the station with a letter from Robert Collier; man said he was an elephant trainer from Barnum and Bailey's, and had been sent here to train an elephant for Mr. Clemens. Bring him over? Yes, bring him. So Lounsbury brought him. Lounsbury is always awake, and always has his pump with him. On the way over, he did a little pumping:

"Where is the elephant?"

"He will arrive at noon."

"Where is he going to be housed?"

"In the loggia."

"What kind of an elephant is it?"

"A baby elephant."

"How big?"

"About as big as a cow."

"How long have you been with Barnum and Bailey?"

"Six years."

"Good. Then you know a couple of old friends of mine there—Billy Brisbane and Hank Roberts."

"Yes, indeed. Good boys, too."

"There aren't any better. How are they?"

"Billy was ailing a little, last week—rheumatism, I think—but Hank's as sound as a nut."

Mental remark by Lounsbury: "They've been dead as much as two years; this fellow's a fraud; there's a nigger in this woodpile somewhere."

Miss Lyon received the trainer (Robert Collier's butler in disguise), as cheerfully as she could, and she and Ashcroft took down his instructions concerning the right and safe way to get on the good side of an elephant, and which end of him to avoid when he was angry: then the trainer drove away with Lounsbury to get the animal, and Ashcroft was sent to my room to say that the decorating of the loggia (with greenery and so on) had been delayed, and would I remain abed for an hour or two longer? They had sent the pony to a neighbor's house, and wanted to get the elephant stowed out of sight in the garage before I should have my Christmas spoiled by finding out the disaster that had befallen us.

In about half an hour the elephant arrived, but Miss Lyon got herself out of the way; she could not bear to look at him. Yet there was no occasion to be afraid of him: he is only two feet long, is built of cloth, and goes on wheels.

Robert has come out ahead. No, it is the pony: for she has the ton of hay and the other delicacies.

Dictated at Stormfield, January 5, 1909

I saw only three references to that curious Presidential performance of two or three weeks ago—the one where the Chief Magistrate treated a young girl harshly. One of these was in the New York *Times*. The substance of it, as I remember it, was to this effect. An article or an editorial in the *Sun* charged Mr. Roosevelt—who was out riding in the country, with friends—with striking, with his "crop," the horse of a young girl who violated etiquette by riding past him. It was further charged that Mr. Roosevelt sternly rebuked the girl, besides, for her lack of manners. Continuing, the *Times* added some elephantine attempts at sarcasm, to the effect that the girl and her father were arrested and sent to a military dungeon to be tried by court martial, etc. I could make nothing out of the thing. I could not make out whether anything *at all* had happened or not. There seemed to have been a Rooseveltian incident, but the size and style of it were hopelessly obscured by the *Times*'s unhappy attack of clumsy and idiotic satirics.

But we have a visitor, to-day, who furnishes what he claims to be the facts. He got them from a friend of the girl's father. To wit. The President, with three friends, was out in the country taking a horseback ride. Presently a girl of fifteen appeared in the rear—on horseback. She closed the interval, and was intending to ride by, when she recognized the President by his shoulders, or perhaps his ears, and slackened her pace and fell back a few paces. After a little, the Head of the Greatest Nation on Earth whirled about and charged rearward and exclaimed to the child—

"Don't you know who I am? You have followed me long enough. Where are your manners?"

The frightened girl explained.

"I was in a hurry, and was going to ride by, but when I saw it was the President, I—"

"Never mind about that! Yonder's a side-road—take it. Go!"

The girl burst into sobbings and said—

"It is the road to my father's house, sir. I was going to take it as soon as—"

"Go—will you!"

Which she did. The father wrote a note to the President complaining, but got no reply.

Have we ever had a President before of whom such a story could be told and find believers? Certainly not. It would be recognized as a foolish and extravagant invention, a manifest lie; for we have never had a President before who was destitute of self-respect and of respect for his high office; we have had no President before who was not a gentleman; we have had no President before who was intended for a butcher, a dive-keeper or a bully, and missed his mission by compulsion of circumstances over which he had no control. Will the story be believed now? Yes, and justifiably. No one who knows Mr. Roosevelt will doubt that in its essence the tale is true. This is the same ruffian whose subordinate ruffian brutally treated a lady in the waiting-room of the White House three years ago, and was rewarded for it by being appointed postmaster of Washington.

Dictated at Stormfield, January 11, 1909

From away back towards the very beginning of the Shakspeare-Bacon controversy I have been on the Bacon side, and have wanted to see our majestic Shakspeare unhorsed. My reasons for this attitude may have been good, they may have been bad, but such as they were, they strongly influenced me. It always seemed unaccountable to me that a man could be so prominent in Elizabeth's little London as historians and biographers claim that Shakspeare was, and yet leave behind him hardly an incident for people to remember him by; leave behind him nothing much but trivialities; leave behind him little or nothing but the happenings of an utterly commonplace life, happenings that could happen to the butcher and the grocer, the candlestickmaker and the undertaker, and there an end—deep, solemn, sepulchral silence. It always seemed to me that not even a distinguished horse could die and leave such biographical poverty behind him. His biographers did their best, I have to concede it, they took his attendance at the grammar-school; they took his holding of horses at sixpenny tips; they took his play-acting on the other side of the river; they took his picturesque deer-stealing; they took his diligent and profitable Stratford wool-staplings, they took his too-previous relations with his subsequent wife; they took his will—that monumental will!—with its solemnly comic second-best bed incident; they took his couple of reverently preserved and solely existent signatures in the which he revealed the fact that he didn't know how to spell his own name; they took this poor half-handful of inconsequential odds and ends, and spun it out, and economised it, and inflated it to bursting, and made a biography with a capital B out of it. It seemed incomprehensibly odd to me, that a man situated as Shakspeare apparently was, could live to be fifty-two years old and never a thing happen to him.

When Ignatius Donnelly's book came out, eighteen or twenty years ago, I not only published it, but read it. It was an ingenious piece of work and it interested me. The world made all sorts of fun of it, but it seemed to me that there were things in it which the thoughtful could hardly afford to laugh at. They have passed out of my mind now, or have grown vague with time and wear, but I still remember one of those smart details of Donnelly's. According to my recollection he remarked that it is quite natural for writers, when painting pictures with their pens, to use scenery that they are familiar with in place of using scenery that they only know about by hearsay. In this connection he called attention to the striking fact that Shakspeare does not use Stratford surroundings and Stratford names when he wants to localize an event, but uses scenes familiar to Lord Bacon instead; hardly even mentioning Stratford, but mentioning St. Albans three-and-twenty times!

Ignatius Donnelly believed he had found Bacon's name acrostified—or acrosticised—I don't know which is right—cryptically concealed all through the Shaksperean plays. I think his acrostics were not altogether convincing; I believe a person had to work his imagination rather hard sometimes if he wanted to believe in the acrostics. Donnelly's book fell pretty flat, and from that day to this the notion that Bacon wrote Shakspeare has been dying a slow death. Nowadays one hardly ever sees even a passing reference to it, and when such references have occurred they have uniformly been accompanied by a gentle sneer.

Well, two or three weeks from now a bombshell will fall upon us which may possibly woundily astonish the human race! For there is secretly and privately a book in press in Boston, by an English clergyman, which may unhorse Shakspeare permanently and put Bacon in the saddle. Once more the acrostic will be in the ascendant, and this time it may be that some people will think twice before they laugh at it. That wonder of wonders, Helen Keller, has been here on a three days' visit with her devoted teachers and protectors Mr. and Mrs. John Macy, and Macy has told me about the clergyman's book and bound me to secrecy. I am divulging the secret to my autobiography for distant future revealment, but shall keep the matter to myself in conversation. The clergyman has found Bacon's name concealed in acrostics in more than a hundred places in the plays and sonnets. I have examined a couple of the examples and I feel that just these two examples all by themselves are almost sufficient to discrown Shakspeare and enthrone Bacon. One of the examples is the Epilogue to "The Tempest." In this acrostic Bacon's name is concealed in its Latin form—Francisco Bacono. You take the last word of the Epilogue (free) and move your finger to the left to the beginning of that last line, then to the right along the next line above, then to the left again to the beginning of the third line and so on and so on, going left then right then left until you find a word which begins with R. You will find it in the fifth line from the bottom; your finger will then be moving to the left; it will encounter an A at the beginning of the sixth line and will thence move to the right; it will move to the left through the seventh line and to the right again along the eighth line and will encounter an N in that line. Nine lines above, it will find C and I; two lines above that it will find S. In this acrostic no letters are used that occur within a word or at the right-hand end of it; continue the process and you find the C and the O properly placed; only letters that *begin* words and letters that stand *by themselves* are used.

"Bacono" begins with the word "be" at the end of the next to the last line, and proceeds right and left as before, picking up initial letters as it goes along until it reaches the first line of the Epilogue, and that line furnishes the close of the name "Bacono."

Through the last page of "King Lear" is scattered the acrostic "Verulam," spelt backwards. It begins with the last word of the last line, which is a stage-direction (*"Exeunt with a dead march"*). That line furnishes two of the letters, M and A, the line immediately above furnishes the L; you travel upward nine lines before you come to a word beginning with U; four lines higher up you find a word beginning with R; twenty-one lines above that you find a word beginning with E, and you do not find it any earlier; you find the V in the line immediately above that and the acrostic stands completed.

One may examine these two examples until he is tired, hoping that these two names got distributed in this orderly and systematic way without a hitch anywhere, by *accident,* and he will have only his interesting labor for his pains. If he had only one example he might, by clever and possibly specious reasoning, convince himself that the thing was an accident; but when he finds two examples strictly following the law of the system he will know, for sure, that not both of them are accidents; and he will probably end by conceding that nineteen-twentieths of the probabilities are that both are results of design and neither of them a miracle. For he will know that nothing short of a miracle could produce a couple of such elaborate and extraordinary accidents as these.

Mr. Macy says that there are between 100 and 150 examples in the plays and sonnets that are the match of these two. This being so, the likelihood that Shakspeare riddled his works with Bacon's name and Bacon's titles and forgot to acrosticise his own anywhere is exceedingly remote—much remoter than any distance measurable on this planet, indeed remoter than that new planet of Professor Pickering's which is so far outside Neptune's orbit that it makes Neptune seem sort of close to us and sociably situated.

These acrostics have been dug out of the earliest and least doctored editions of Shakspeare. Sometimes in the much-edited editions of our day changes in the text break up the acrostic. The general reader will not have access to the folio of 1623 and its brethren, therefore photographic facsimiles will be made from those early editions and placed before the reader of the clergyman's book, so that he can trace out the acrostics for himself. I am to have proof sheets as fast as they issue from the galleys, and am to behave myself and keep still. I shall live in a heaven of excited anticipation for a while now. I have allowed myself for so many many years the offensive privilege of laughing at people who believed in Shakspeare that I shall perish with shame if the clergyman's book fails to unseat that grossly commercial wool-stapler. However, we shall see. I shan't order my monument yet.

The house at 21 Fifth Avenue, where Clemens and his daughters lived from 1904 to 1908. Culver Pictures.

Clemens being interviewed aboard the SS *Minneapolis* upon his arrival in England, 18 June 1907. Mark Twain House and Museum, Hartford.

Ralph Ashcroft, Mr. and Mrs. John Henniker Heaton, and Clemens on their way to the royal garden party at Windsor Castle, 22 June 1907. Mark Twain House and Museum, Hartford.

The royal garden party at Windsor Castle; Queen Alexandra is in the foreground, King Edward in the center facing Clemens. From a drawing by W. Hatherell of the London *Graphic,* reprinted in *Harper's Weekly,* 27 July 1907.

The procession from All Souls College at Oxford to the Sheldonian Theatre, where the honorary doctorates were awarded, 26 June 1907. Clemens is sixth in line, behind Sidney Colvin, with Sidney Lee at his side and Rudyard Kipling behind him.

Clemens with Sir William Ramsay near the Sheldonian Theatre, smoking despite the risk of being "fined a guinea, and perhaps hanged later," 26 June 1907.

Clemens watching the Oxford Pageant, Christ Church Meadow, 27 or 28 June 1907. Photograph by Gillman and Co. of St. Aldates, Oxford. Special Collections Research Center, University of Chicago.

Clemens with Frances Nunnally at the studio of Henry Walter Barnett, London, 1907.

House of Commons, 2 July 1907. *Left to right:* John Samuel Phene, Edmund Gosse, Montague Horatio Mostyn Turtle Piggott, Arthur Fraser Walter, John Henniker Heaton, Clemens, Hugh McCalmont, Sydney Charles Buxton, unidentified, and Thomas Power O'Connor. Photograph by Sir Benjamin Stone. National Portrait Gallery, London.

House of Commons, 9 July 1907. *Seated:* former prime minister Arthur Balfour, Japanese Ambassador Komura Jutaro, and Clemens, guests of honor at a luncheon given by Sir Benjamin Stone, who also photographed the gathering.

James N. Gillis. Photograph from the Sonora (Calif.) *Banner and Sonora News,* unknown date.

Stephen Gillis at Jackass Hill, March 1907. Photograph by Albert Bigelow Paine.

Joseph T. Goodman at the former site of the Gillis cabin, Jackass Hill, March 1907. Photograph by Albert Bigelow Paine.

Irene Gerken, Clemens, Henry H. Rogers, Elizabeth Wallace, and William E. Benjamin, Hamilton, Bermuda, 1908. Photograph by Isabel Lyon.

Clemens and Rogers at the Princess Hotel, Hamilton, Bermuda, 1908. Photograph by Isabel Lyon.

Reginald and Maude, the donkey, with Clemens and Margaret Blackmer, Hamilton, Bermuda, 1908. Photograph by Elizabeth Wallace.

Dorothy Quick dressed as an Indian princess during her visit to Tuxedo Park, New York, 1907. Photograph by Isabel Lyon.

Mary (Paddy) Madden and Clemens on the RMS *Bermudian,* March 1907. Photograph by Isabel Lyon.

Clemens and Helen Allen swimming near her home in Bermuda, 1908. Photograph by Isabel Lyon.

NOTICE.

To the next Burglar.

There is nothing but plated ware in this house, now and henceforth. You will find it in that brass thing in the dining-room over in the corner by the basket of kittens. If you want the basket, put the kittens in the brass thing. Do not make a noise — it disturbs the family. You will find rubbers in the front hall, by that thing which has the umbrellas in it, chiffonier, I think they call it, or pergola, or something like that. Please close the door when you go away!

Very truly yours

S L Clemens

The notice "illuminated" by Dorothy Sturgis from Clemens's "rude original," as he recorded in the Stormfield guestbook, 18 September 1908.

Henry S. Williams, one of the Stormfield burglars and author of *In the Clutch of Circumstance*. Photograph from the Brooklyn *Eagle*, 8 March 1925.

Clemens speaks to the builders of Stormfield, 27 June 1908. Photograph by Isabel Lyon.

Clemens playing cards with Dorothy Harvey, Louise Paine, and Joy Paine, "first week at Stormfield," late June 1908. Photograph (and dating note) by Albert Bigelow Paine.

Clara and Samuel Clemens, Stormfield, 1908.
Photograph by Isabel Lyon.

Clemens and Laura Hawkins Frazer, Stormfield,
October 1908. Library of Congress.

Franklin and Harriet Whitmore with Clemens,
Stormfield, 1908. Photograph by Isabel Lyon.

Helen Keller, Anne (Sullivan) Macy, and John
Macy with Clemens, Stormfield, January 1909.
Photograph by Isabel Lyon.

Clemens with Isabel Lyon and Ralph Ashcroft, Stormfield, 1908.

The "Lobster Pot" or "Summerfield," the house deeded to Isabel Lyon and later returned to Clemens, before and after renovations. Photographs by Isabel Lyon.

Stormfield as it appeared on 5 January 1909. Photograph taken for Paul Thompson, who published it in *Burr McIntosh Monthly,* March 1909.

Archibald Henderson, Ralph Ashcroft, Isabel Lyon, and Clemens in the library at Stormfield, December 1908. Photograph by Alvin Langdon Coburn. Mark Twain House and Museum, Hartford.

Portrait of Clemens painted by Francis D. Millet in 1877. Hannibal (Mo.) Free Public Library.

Francis D. Millet in 1875. Photograph by Antonio Perini, Venice. Courtesy of Special Collections Research Center, Syracuse University Libraries.

Portrait of Samuel Moffett clipped by Clemens from the 15 August 1908 issue of *Collier's Weekly*.

Nellie and Pieter Bausch's carte-de-visite sent to Clemens on 27 February 1909, inscribed on the back "to Mark Twain, the splendid man and famous humorist." Photograph by M. H. Laddé, Amsterdam.

The wedding of Ossip Gabrilowitsch and Clara Clemens, 6 October 1909, at Stormfield. *Left to right:* Samuel Clemens, Jervis Langdon, Jr., Jean Clemens, Ossip Gabrilowitsch, Clara Clemens Gabrilowitsch, and the Rev. Joseph Twichell. Photograph by Frank J. Sprague.

Jean Clemens, ca. 1908. Mark Twain House and Museum, Hartford.

Ossip and Clara, Stormfield, 1910. Photograph by Albert Bigelow Paine.

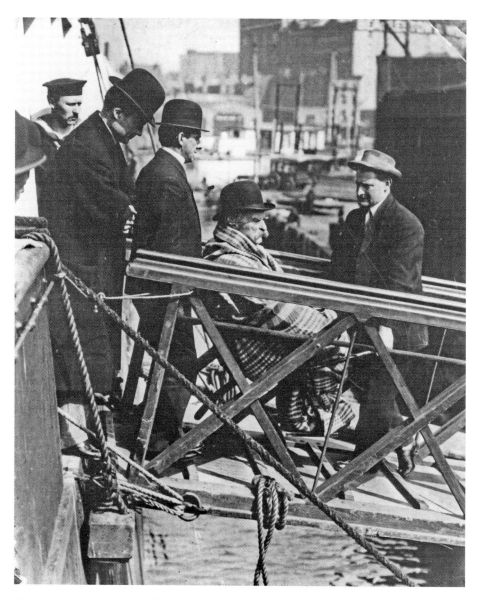

Clemens disembarking from the SS *Oceana* in New York harbor upon his return from Bermuda. Paine wrote on the verso of his copy: "Last photograph made of M.T. Brought home from Bermuda by A.B.P. April 14, 1910. He died one week later, April 21 *6 PM*." Photograph by National News Association.

Dictated March 10, 1909

Miss Lyon came into the billiard room an hour ago, where I was busying myself in the freedom of a dressing-gown, in perfecting myself in a new wonder-compelling shot which I discovered by accident last night—perfecting myself in it with the idea of playing it in a casual and indifferent way before Ashcroft when he comes to-night; also with the idea that when, after he has seen the shot executed, and shall proclaim that notwithstanding this successful execution of it, the shot is impossible and can never be made again; also, with the further intention on my part of assuring him that I have never seen the shot attempted until now, but that I believe I can achieve it again. So I was practising as I say, and when Miss Lyon came in I had made myself so capable in it that I could make it four times out of five, and was already entirely sure of astonishing Ashcroft this evening. We drifted into an incident of a few weeks ago, where I called at the private school in New York to see one of my little angel-fishes, Irene, and was refused permission to see her. The austere old virgin to whom the school belongs informing me it was against the rules for her young girls to receive visitors during school hours. My vanity was badly hurt, my dignity had been trampled under foot; I had been treated just like an ordinary human being, instead of as clay of the salt of the earth, and I could not endure it. I got a letter right away, as soon as I was back in Stormfield, from Irene, saying that her special teacher, Miss Brown, was ashamed of the fact that I had been treated just as the rules required ordinary visitors to be treated, but if she had known it was I she would have dismissed her class immediately, and I could have had Irene into my taxicab and carted her off to her home.

This incident naturally brought up another. In '93, when the charming Carey, the bright Carey, the lovely Carey, the incomparable Carey, was still with us in the land of the living, and was still occupying his long-time high post on the staff of the *Century Magazine*, he came along the hall one day, that leads to the editorial rooms, and there in the dingy twilight he found a venerable and profoundly-revered and illustrious citizen of the United States waiting for admission. Carey's banks overflowed, and he poured out a flood of apologies, and escorted that citizen at once to the editorial sanctum. Then he went to his own place, and sent for the boy. The boy conceded that the great citizen had been waiting there a good while; also, the boy defended himself quite competently by saying he had only obeyed the rule of the house. Carey stormed at him, and said:

"The rule of the house! A child ought to know, and if a child doesn't know, then somebody ought to inform the child that there was never yet in the world a rule that can be or ought to be enforced upon all occasions. There must always come a time, in the life of any rule, when the occasion rises away above the rule, and automatically abolishes it. At these rare times the person in charge must remember that a part of his duty is to now exercise his discretion, and let the rule go."

Meantime Carey had ranged three large lithograph portraits alongside each other— Washington, Lincoln and Shakspeare—and he said to the boy:

"Now, impress these faces on your memory; burn them into your memory, so that they will stay there forever. Now then, if either of these gentlemen should ever call, and want to see the editor of this magazine, suspend the rule instantly, and take him to the sanctum."

Further along in the conversation, I remarked that while I was shaving this morning, I made another Lotos Club–Carnegie speech; that this one did not resemble the Lotos Club–Carnegie speech I made in the bath-tub four days ago; that when I get up to speak at that Carnegie dinner on the 17th of this month, I shall be sure to make a third speech; that the third speech will bear little resemblance to its two predecessors, and will rank with them as a brass farthing ranks with a government bond in the matter of value. I enlarged upon the inspiration that is furnished by inanimate things: by friendly and sympathetic and uncritical bath-tubs and old familiar chairs and rugs, and chests of drawers, and the other voiceless objects that make one's private quarters the homiest of homes, and the most inspiring audience any speaker ever faces. Yes, and it's true. One doesn't have to watch the chairs and things to see how his talk is being received; one doesn't have to observe sharply and take account of that subtle devil, the atmosphere of an audience; that atmosphere that invades the speaker's soul and tells him without utterance or gesture that he is doing handsomely, or that he is making a failure.

This naturally reminded me of an incident of forty-three years ago, which remains vividly in my memory now, and has never suffered even the slightest shade of change from the night it happened until now. I was a brand-new lecturer, and timid. I was to lecture in San Jose, fifty miles below San Francisco, and I arrived late. I hurried to my place on the platform, weak and quaking with trepidation. An audience had been sitting there an hour and a quarter, waiting for me. There was a scowl upon their faces that stretched from the stage to the doors, and darkened the place like a thundercloud. For the first time in my brief oratorical career, I was received in silence; there was not a hand-clap, there was not a movement, there was not a gesture. I was sick, sick clear to the heart. I began—timidly of course—and of course that made matters worse, for timidity gains no friends in most company, especially among human beings who are ready to eat a person. Uttering jokes timidly is not a good way; there are no laughs, there are only sneers, and you can read the sneers as plainly as if they were written on those faces in large print.

My despairing eye went wandering around over that hostile house, and suddenly it fell upon, as it were, the sun flashing through a rift in a stormcloud. Dear me! the surprise of it, the welcome of it, the uplift, the inspiration! It was the dear sweet friendly face of a girl of about eighteen, and it was all alight with happy expectancy—altogether the most beautiful face I have ever seen, I suppose; a judgment which perhaps is a little tinged with prejudice. All my trepidation, all my distress, all my despair, all my discomfort, vanished away in an instant. I sailed breezily and comfortably away on my theme as upon a summer sea. It was not a large place; the people were all packed together on the floor, in number about three hundred: that darling sat in the very centre of the place. I looked her straight in the eye, I made every remark straight to her and nobody else; it was easy and friendly and unconventional as if we were holding a private talk in a private place; I broke her all up with my first remark, because under her inspiration the remark was made in a natural way; she let fly the care-free laugh of her blessed youth, and from that to the end we had a triumph together. I could hear continuously, constantly, a great outbreak of laughter, and sometimes the applause, and I vaguely knew that it came from the audience; but I was not interested in it; I had but the one audience, that girl; to me the rest of the three hundred were outsiders and not concerned in this matter so far as I was concerned. I have never in my life had a more delightful evening, and yet my audience was as slender as I have described. It consisted of but one person, and that person a stranger. Well, it shows what a person can do when he is all by himself, just as when he is talking to sympathetic and uncritical furniture in the privacy of his bed-chamber; his imagination has a freedom then and a wider spread of wing than it can ever have before an audience of human beings. But next to furniture, for a splendid inspiration, give me that girl again!

March 25, 1909

About two months ago I was illuminating this Autobiography with some notions of mine concerning the Bacon-Shakspeare controversy, and I then took occasion to air the opinion that the Stratford Shakspeare was a person of no public consequence or celebrity during his lifetime, but was utterly obscure and unimportant. And not only in great London, but also in the little village where he was born, where he lived a quarter of a century, and where he died and was buried. I argued that if he had been a person of any note at all, aged villagers would have had much to tell about him many and many a year after his death, instead of being unable to furnish inquirers a single fact connected with him. I believed, and I still believe, that if he had been famous, his notoriety would have lasted as long as mine has lasted in my own village out in Missouri. It is a good argument, a prodigiously strong one, and a most formidable one for even the most gifted, and ingenious, and plausible Stratfordolater to get around or explain away. To-day a Hannibal *Courier-Post* of recent date has reached me, with an article in it which reinforces my contention that a really celebrated person cannot be forgotten in his village in the short space of sixty years. I will make an extract from it:

> Hannibal, as a city, may have many sins to answer for but ingratitude is not one of them or reverence for the great men she has produced, and as the years go by her greatest son Mark Twain, or S. L. Clemens as a few of the unlettered call him, grows in the estimation and regard of the residents of the town he made famous and the town that made him famous. His name is associated with every old building that is torn down to make way for the modern structures demanded by a rapidly growing city and with every hill or cave over or through which he might by any possibility have roamed, while the many points of interest which he wove into his stories, such as Holiday Hill, Jackson's Island, or Mark Twain cave, are now

monuments to his genius. Hannibal is glad of any opportunity to do him honor as he has honored her.

So it has happened that the "old timers" who went to school with Mark or were with him on some of his usual escapades have been honored with large audiences whenever they were in a reminiscent mood and condescended to tell of their intimacy with the ordinary boy who came to be a very extraordinary humorist and whose every boyish act is now seen to have been indicative of what was to come. Like Aunt Beckey and Mrs. Clemens they can now see that Mark was hardly appreciated when he lived here and that the things he did as a boy and was whipped for doing were not all bad after all. So they have been in no hesitancy about drawing out the bad things he did as well as the good in their efforts to get a "Mark Twain story," all incidents being viewed in the light of his present fame, until the volume of "Twainiana" is already considerable and growing in proportion as the "old timers" drop away and the stories are retold second and third hand by their descendants. With Mark some seventy-three years young and living in a villa instead of a house he is a fair target, and let him incorporate, copyright, or patent himself as he will there are some of his "works" that will go swooping up Hannibal chimneys as long as gray beards gather about the fires and begin with "I've heard father tell" or possibly "Once when I."

The Mrs. Clemens referred to is my mother—*was* my mother.

And here is another extract from a Hannibal paper. Of date twenty days ago:

Miss Becca Blankenship, Sister of "Huckleberry Finn" Died Yesterday Aged 72 Years.

Miss Becca Blankenship died at the home of William Dickason, 408 Rock street, at 2:30 o'clock yesterday afternoon, aged 72 years. The deceased was a sister of "Huckleberry Finn," one of the famous characters in Mark Twain's "Tom Sawyer." She had been a member of the Dickason family—the housekeeper—for nearly forty-five years and was a highly respected lady. For the past eight years she had been an invalid, but was as well cared for by Mr. Dickason and his family as if she had been a near relative. She was a member of the Park Methodist church and a Christian woman.

I remember her well. I have a picture of her in my mind which has remained there, clear and sharp and vivid, sixty-three years. She was about nine years old, and I was about eleven. I remember where she stood and how she looked; and I can still see her bare feet, her bare head, her brown face, and her short tow-linen frock. She was crying. What it was about, I have long ago forgotten. But it was the tears that preserved the picture for me, no doubt. She was a good child, I can say that for her. She knew me nearly seventy years ago. Did she forget me, in the course of time? I think not. If she had lived in Stratford in Shakspeare's day, would she have forgotten him? Yes. For he was never famous during his lifetime, he was utterly obscure in Stratford, and there wouldn't be any occasion to remember him after he had been dead a week.

"Injun Joe," "Jimmy Finn" and "General Gaines" were prominent and very intemperate ne'er-do-weels in Hannibal two generations ago. Plenty of gray-heads there remember them to this day, and can tell you about them. Isn't it curious that two "town-drunkards" and one half-breed loafer should leave behind them, in a remote Missourian village, a fame a hundred times greater and several hundred times more particularized in the matter of definite facts than Shakspeare left behind him in the village where he had lived the half of his lifetime?

Dictated April 16, 1909

For the second time I have heard Clara sing in public. It was in New York. I was vastly pleased with her singing, and also with her perfect carriage on the stage. A fine and graceful and dignified and sweetly-winning stage carriage is an unusual thing in a beginner. I went to the concert with Mr. and Mrs. H. H. Rogers, and when I found that Mrs. Rogers had had the thoughtfulness to provide herself with a great bouquet of choice roses to hurl at the singer in case the singer's performance might warrant it, I was ashamed that I, the singer's own father, had been less thoughtful. I will refer to this detail again, presently. Here is a notice, culled from the New York *Evening Post:*

Miss Clemens and Miss Littlehales.

There was an audience of unusual distinction at Mendelssohn Hall last night when Miss Clara Clemens and Miss Lillian Littlehales gave a joint recital. Literature was represented as well as music; Mark Twain was there to witness his daughter's triumph, and W. D. Howells applauded as if he belonged to a paid claque. After the second group of songs, bouquets were passed to Miss Clemens, the last one being carried by her venerable father; and as she was a little slow in coming out again, he deposited it on the stage for her to pick up.

Miss Clemens was heard in the same hall in a group of songs some weeks ago, but she was then affected by a cold, which prevented her from doing herself justice. Last night her voice was in fine condition, and she gave much pleasure to the audience by her singing, while those who cared not for her songs could listen with their eyes and wonder if they had ever seen a concert singer with such an attractive stage presence. In the concert hall, as in the opera house, it is an advantage to have the charms of visible and audible beauty combined.

The programme included nearly two dozen songs; it suffered from the disadvantage of a lack of variety in the moods, and some of the numbers were not master-songs, which was a pity; for by her singing of Schubert's "An die Musik," "Nacht und Träume," and Schumann's "Frühlingsnacht" and "Intermezzo," Miss Clemens showed that she can interpret mastersongs with intelligence and feeling. She was nervous when she began her opening number, Handel's "Ah, mio cor," and this affected her voice; but thenceforward, from number to number, the quality of her tones improved, as is so often the case with opera singers, who are best in the last act. She had to repeat "Flow gently, sweet Afton," and made other climaxes especially in the group of songs rendered in English. Other songs were sung in French, German, and Italian, with full appreciation of their poetic content. Miss Clemens's voice has the true contralto quality, so rare in these days; yet there is great beauty also in her highest tones. If Mme. Schumann-Heink, who sings soprano as well as mezzo and contralto, had charge of her voice, great things might be accomplished with it.

And here is another notice. This is from the New York *Herald:*

> It isn't every evening that you can go to a song recital and see Mark Twain leave his seat and carry to the stage a bunch of flowers tied with a pink streamer ribbon. But that was the interesting sight the audience in Mendelssohn Hall saw and enjoyed last evening. Of course, it follows, too, that it isn't every singer for whom Mark Twain would leave his seat and carry flowers. Last night the singer was none other than his daughter, Miss Clara Clemens, who was giving a song recital, assisted by Miss Lillian Littlehales, 'cellist.
>
> After the second group of songs, when the audience applauded, Miss Clemens came out and received some roses and a bunch of violets. Then she retired to the artists' room, but the applause continued, and then her father had his chance. When the silvery haired humorist got to the footlights his daughter had not reached there, so he gently laid the immense bouquet on the platform and walked away. When Miss Clemens came out and saw the roses she smiled down at her father, who had returned to his seat, and there was the tiniest suspicion of a mischievous wink. Then daughter and father wirelessed signals of gratification at each other.
>
> Miss Clemens has been heard here before. Last night she captivated her audience by her winsome and serious manner, and she sang a lengthy and interestingly varied programme of songs and displayed her deep contralto voice to advantage. Miss Littlehales gave a finished performance of a Galliard sonata and earned hearty applause.

Providence does often protect the witless, and steer them comfortably out of their difficulties. During one of the outbursts of applause following one of Clara's triumphs, a man passed up the middle aisle, carrying a lot of bouquets to give to her. Mr. Rogers snatched Mrs. Rogers's bouquet, and gave it to me, and said:

"When that man comes back, ask him to deliver this one."

But the man did not come back; he sheered off to port, and went down the other way. Without thinking what I was about, I did a very happy thing: without thinking that I was about to filch a credit properly belonging to Mrs. Rogers, I got up and walked down the aisle, and laid the bouquet on the stage. Then the audience broke out with vehement approval, and I recognized that it meant, "Here is a father to be proud of; a father who loves and admires his daughter, and has the courage to testify it before all the world, instead of employing a hireling to do it for him; a father, too, who is considerate and thoughtful, and brings his flowers with him, instead of forgetting all about it, as other fathers would." That cordial praise went straight to my heart, and did me as much good as if I had deserved it. Providence does take care of us, and I am grateful.

I have another compliment to-day, and again I am pleased with myself, and happy. It is from Clara; she closes her letter with it:

"Father, you were as cunning and well-mannered and orderly and winning at my concert as you could possibly be, and you made it an historic event."

It is fulsome flattery, but I can stand a good deal in that line.

Note to Chapter . . .

As concerns the certainty that a writer who ventures to use the professional technicalities and freemasonries of a trade which he has not served in his own person will never fail to make mistakes which will "give him away" to the master of that trade—oh, well, literature is crowded with instances.

Chapter X of Alice Kegan Rice's new book ("Mr. Orr") opens with a scene on a Mississippi steamboat which will sound ever so sane and natural and correct to the average passenger familiar with those boats, but it will sorely befog the trained steamboatman. There's a generous supply of steamboaty details, and they ought to enable him to locate the scene of the episode, but they won't. He may examine them till he is tired, he will remain a defeated man: he will not be able to determine *which end* of the boat the thing happened on.

Thirty-seven or thirty-eight years ago, when John Hay and I were young and he was on the *Tribune* staff, he gathered his Pike County Ballads together for publication in book form, and he asked me for advice concerning the ballad of the "Prairie Belle." Was there anything steamboatfully incorrect in it?

"Yes, but nothing worth the trouble of correcting, since the error is so small and so technical that the great public will never detect it. You make the engineer of the burning boat the hero. It is he who bravely resolves to hold the steamer's 'nozzle to the bank till the last galoot's ashore.' He couldn't do it by himself; he couldn't see where the nozzle was, from his place on the main deck amidships; he would have to have intelligent orders from the pilot-house, by bells or speaking tube. In that case there would be *two* heroes, and the pilot would be the chief one, since his post would be some thirty or forty times as perilous as the engineer's."

So Hay made no change, and the poem remains now as he originally wrote it.

In the ballad of the "Heathen Chinee," there's a euchre-game wherein Bret Harte's Chinaman, the sly rascal, has fourteen cold decks up his sleeve. Did the great public deride this extravagant departure from the likelihoods? No, the great public didn't; it suffered no damage, for it doesn't know the game.

Three years ago I emptied into this Autobiography a correspondence which I had been having with a bugler who had bugled in Butterfield's brigade all through the war. I had published a short story called "A Horse's Tale," and in it had introduced several of the regular army's bugle calls, and had added thereto a call which wasn't in the regulation-list. My secretary filched it for me out of the opening bars of an opera. That veteran bugler was distressed; he said there was never a bugle in the world that could handle that combination of notes, and he wanted me to snatch it out of the book, for my reputation's sake, before my ignorant error should be discovered, and I be laughed at. I explained to him why I believed it not worth while to squelch that call.

Last month, in New York, another bugler woke up. He came to me with a most earnest appeal to remove that call—on the same old grounds: there never was a bugle that could deliver that combination of notes, and I would be found out, etc., etc. I couldn't remember just what I had said to the former complainant, but I could come near enough to it to make my point; so I asked—

"When did you come across the story?"

"Yesterday. And I was going to write you, but I saw by the papers that you were here, so I thought it would be better to come in person."

"How many people are there in the United States?"

"Eighty or ninety millions, as I understand it."

"How many men in the army?"

"Seventy thousand."

"How many buglers? Seventy thousand?"

"Lord, no! Only about—"

"Never mind about exactnesses. Call it seven hundred."

"It's too many. There's only about—"

"Never mind, we'll call it seven hundred. In three years I have heard from two of them. It is one bugler per year and a half. It will take me 469 years to hear from the others—I mean those that do not die in the meantime. I'm writing a sea-story now. In it the great scene, the central scene, the most thrilling episode, is where the young hero's foot slips and he falls from the garboard strake to the futtock shrouds and fractures his skull by collision with the maintogallant stunsl boom on the way. How does it strike you? Isn't it good?"

"*Good?* Well, I should *say* so! By gracious it sounds just splendid!"

"Does it thrill? That's the main thing—does it *thrill?*"

"Oh, don't you worry about *that!* it thrills you from your scalp to your heels."

"Now that is mighty satisfactory, for all I've given you is only the naked *plunge,* nothing more—no embroideries. You wait till I've dressed it out with the dramatic accessories—*then* see! There's a race on, you know; everybody on deck—crowds of passengers and sailors and officers—and everybody excited; captain on the capstan, thundering orders to the men; the hero's happy mother and little sister standing in the binnacle, his proud sweetheart standing erect, statuesque and beautiful in the light of the cat-heads, her eyes and all eyes riveted upon her daring hero; and at that supreme moment he falls! falls, strikes, and the next moment there he lies gasping in death at the feet of her who loves him, adores him, worships him more than life itself! What do you think of it?"

"By George, it's great! *I* think it's just splendid!"

"To be frank, so do I. Do you understand it? I mean, *all* of it?"

"Well, no, not the ship-talk, but that's no matter, I get the *thrill*—I get the *whole* of it, and my, but it's just grand!"

"All right, then, that's all I'm after, and I shan't alter a word. There are eighty-five millions of people in America that don't know you can't fall from the garboard strake, because it's under the bottom of the ship."

Dictated October 21, 1909

Little by little the evidence comes out as to Miss Lyon's drinking habits. Stromeyer's man was here yesterday, and he spoke of an incident in this line, which occurred in the days when this house was being finally equipped inside for occupancy. He was here to put up window-shades and curtains. He heard Miss Lyon scream, and he ran into the room where she was. She seemed to be overmastered by hysterics, and cried out, "Hold my hands! hold my hands!" He held her hands. A dozen workmen came running to see what the screaming was about, and there they found the dramatic situation which I have just described. Among the inflow was Lounsbury. He was calm; he knew Miss Lyon's breed of hysterics; he had had experience of them before; and he knew what to do. He drew a flask of whisky and said, "Give her this, it will quiet her." It got a welcome reception.

Miss Lyon was drunk, and Lounsbury knew it. On another occasion when she was hysterically drunk, she demanded whisky, and they gave her a third of a glass, which emptied the bottle. She demanded more, and was told there was no more to be had immediately, because Claude had the key of the wine-closet, and he was not about. She flew into a rage, and dashed the glass against the wall, and broke it. I think Lounsbury was present on that occasion, too, but I will ask him, and make sure.

When Katy, Claude, and Miss Lyon were completing the clearing out of the house in Fifth Avenue, in September of last year, Miss Lyon ran out of liquor, and demanded a fresh supply. There wasn't any. She said she could not do this kind of work without the help of restoratives, and ordered Claude to fetch a bottle of Scotch whisky from the Brevoort—which he did. By the testimony of Claude and Katy, she finished that bottle before bedtime.

Stromeyer's young man said yesterday, that during the housebuilding—so the workmen said—Miss Lyon was not only pretty customarily and manifestly under the influence of liquor, but that she was quite generous with it with the men; in hurrying them up, she would encourage them with whisky, remarking that she herself found that she could work better with the help of a little stimulant of that kind.

A few days after she was discharged from here last spring, she visited the house one day, and before going asked Claude for a glass. He brought it, and also brought the whisky bottle, supposing she would want that also; but she said no, she had found brandy a better restorative when she was fagged than whisky. She produced a flask, and poured out a quantity measuring something more than a claret-glass, and drank it off neat, without water.

Katy says Miss Lyon always kept a bottle of cocktails in her room, in a cupboard, both in New York, and here at Stormfield, and that a bottle lasted her only about a day, and she was drinking a good deal of whisky, besides. Ashcroft was doing the same. Claude and Katy say he was a liberal drinker.

In the sixty-two days of July and August of last year, this house ordered—and also consumed—forty-eight quarts of Scotch whisky. Yesterday I examined the guest-book, and found there the names of a couple of generous drinkers of Scotch whisky. Apparently one of them was here two days and two nights, and the other one night. It is possible that between them they drank three quarts. In that two months two other men were here, who drink Scotch whisky, but as they drink it only at dinner, with water, in the English fashion, their consumption of that kind of whisky was necessarily slender, and they were only here one or two days anyway. In those days I drank Scotch whisky once in every twenty-four hours; and always after I was in bed, and ready for sleep. I took the same quantity always, a liqueur-glassful. While in those days I probably consumed a quart of Scotch whisky in a fortnight, nowadays a quart lasts me a month. If we allow that three or four guests drank four bottles in those two months, and I four, that makes eight. Miss Lyon always kept the key of the wine-closet herself, after we moved into this house, and perhaps she, with the help of Ashcroft, would be able to explain what went with the other forty quarts of Scotch whisky consumed under this roof in the sixty-two days of July and August, 1908.

We had many a guest in those old times. Nowadays a number of them speak quite freely of Miss Lyon's drunks, as observed by them; also they speak rather frankly of my dulness in not perceiving that she was a drunkard; and when they don't speak of my dulness in this connection, they doubt that I am telling the strict truth when I say that I did not know that she was a heavy drinker. And so, no matter which attitude they take, I come out without a compliment. I don't deny that I knew Miss Lyon to be a drinker, and that I knew it all of two years ago, but I did not know she was a heavy drinker. She came to my room with great frequency, both in the night and in the day, to borrow some of my whisky, saying she was out, and not feeling well, and my bottle was nearer than the wine-closet. Now, inasmuch as she is a convicted thief, and misused my check-book to steal money from me, it is quite likely, that upon a pinch she would steal whisky also. Katy says Miss Lyon used to hold up my bottle, and say somebody had been filching from it, and that without doubt it was Teresa. Teresa was born and reared in a land of light wines; circumstantial evidence points, not to her, but to Miss Lyon, as the whisky thief.

Closing Words of My Autobiography

Stormfield, Christmas Eve, 11 a.m., 1909.

Jean is dead!

And so this Autobiography closes here. I had a reason for projecting it, three years ago: that reason perishes with her.

The reason that moved me was a desire to save my copyrights from extinction, so that Jean and Clara would always have a good livelihood from my books after my death. I meant that whenever a book of mine should approach its forty-two-year limit, it should at once be newly issued, with about 20,000 words of Autobiography added to its contents. This would be copyrightable for a term of twenty-eight years and would practically keep the whole book alive during that term. I meant to write 500,000 words of Autobiography, and I did it.

That tedious long labor was wasted. Last March Congress added fourteen years to the forty-two-year term, and so my oldest book has now about fifteen years to live. I have no use for that addition, (I am seventy-four years old), poor Jean has no use for it now, Clara is happily and prosperously married and has no use for it.

Man proposes, Circumstances dispose.

———

Has any one ever tried to put upon paper all the little happenings connected with a dear one—happenings of the twenty-four hours preceding the sudden and unexpected death of that dear one? Would a book contain them? would two books contain them? I think not. They pour into the mind in a flood. They are little things that have been always happening every day, and were always so unimportant and easily forgetable before—but now! Now, how different! how precious they are, how dear, how unforgetable, how pathetic, how sacred, how clothed with dignity!

Last night Jean, all flushed with splendid health; and I the same, from the wholesome effects of my Bermuda holiday, strolled hand in hand from the dinner table and sat down in the library and chatted, and planned, and discussed, cheerily and happily (and how unsuspectingly!) until nine,—which is late for us—then went up stairs, Jean's friendly German dog following. At my door Jean said, "I can't kiss you good night, father: I have a cold, and you could catch it." I bent and kissed her hand. She was moved—I saw it in her eyes—and she impulsively kissed my hand in return. Then with the usual gay "Sleep well, dear!" from both, we parted.

At half past seven this morning I woke, and heard voices outside my door. I said to myself, "Jean is starting on her usual horseback-flight to the station for the mail." Then Katy entered, stood quaking and gasping at my bedside a moment, then found her tongue:

"Miss Jean is dead!"

Possibly I know now what the soldier feels when a bullet crashes through his heart.

In her bath-room there she lay, the fair young creature, stretched upon the floor and covered with a sheet. And looking so placid, so natural, and as if asleep. We knew what had happened. She was an epileptic: she had been seized with a convulsion and could not get out of the tub. There was no help near, and she was drowned. The doctor had to come several miles. His efforts, like our previous ones, failed to bring her back to life.

It is noon, now. How lovable she looks, how sweet and how tranquil! It is a noble face, and full of dignity; and that was a good heart that lies there so still.

In England, thirteen years ago, my wife and I were stabbed to the heart with a cablegram which said "Susy was mercifully released to-day." I had to send a like shock to Clara, in Berlin, this morning. With the peremptory addition, "You must not come home." Clara and her husband sailed from here on the 11th of this month. How will Clara bear it? Jean, from her babyhood, was a worshipper of Clara.

––––––––

Four days ago I came back from a month's holiday in Bermuda in perfected health; but by some accident the reporters failed to perceive this. Day before yesterday, letters and telegrams began to arrive from friends and strangers which indicated that I was supposed to be dangerously ill. Yesterday Jean begged me to explain my case through the Associated Press. I said it was not important enough; but she was distressed and said I must think of Clara. Clara would see the report in the German papers, and as she had been nursing her husband day and night for four months and was worn out and feeble, the shock might be disastrous. There was reason in that; so I sent a humorous paragraph by telephone to the Associated Press denying the "charge" that I was "dying," and saying "I would not do such a thing at my time of life."

Jean was a little troubled, and did not like to see me treat the matter so lightly; but I said it was best to treat it so, for there was nothing serious about it. This morning I sent the sorrowful facts of this day's irremediable disaster to the Associated Press. Will both appear in this evening's papers?—the one so blithe, the other so tragic.

––––––––

I lost Susy thirteen years ago; I lost her mother—her incomparable mother!—five and a half years ago; Clara has gone away to live in Europe; and now I have lost Jean. How poor I am, who was once so rich! Seven months ago Mr. Rogers died—the best friend I ever had, and the nearest perfect, as man and gentleman, I have yet met among my race; within the past four weeks Gilder has passed away, and Laffan—old, old friends of mine. Jean lies yonder, I sit here; we are strangers under our own roof; we kissed hands good-bye at this door last night—and it was forever, we never suspecting it. She lies there, and I sit here—writing, busying myself, to keep my heart from breaking. How dazzlingly the sunshine is flooding the hills around! It is like a mockery.

Seventy-four years old, twenty-four days ago. Seventy-four years old yesterday. Who can estimate my age to-day?

––––––––

I have looked upon her again. I wonder I can bear it. She looks just as her mother looked when she lay dead in that Florentine villa so long ago. The sweet placidity of death! it is more beautiful than sleep.

I saw her mother buried. I said I would never endure that horror again; that I would never again look into the grave of any one dear to me. I have kept to that. They will take Jean from this house to-morrow, and bear her to Elmira, New York, where lie those of us that have been released, but I shall not follow.

Jean was on the dock when the ship came in, only four days ago. She was at the door, beaming a welcome, when I reached this house the next evening. We played cards, and she tried to teach me a new game called "Mark Twain." We sat chatting cheerily in the library last night, and she wouldn't let me look into the loggia, where she was making Christmas preparations. She said she would finish them in the morning, and then her little French friend would arrive from New York—the surprise would follow; the surprise she had been working over for days. While she was out for a moment I disloyally stole a look. The loggia floor was clothed with rugs and furnished with chairs and sofas; and the uncompleted surprise was there: in the form of a Christmas tree that was drenched with silver films in a most wonderful way; and on a table was a prodigal profusion of bright things which she was going to hang upon it to-day. What desecrating hand will ever banish that eloquent unfinished surprise from that place? Not mine, surely. All these little matters have happened in the last four days. "Little." Yes—*then*. But not now. Nothing she said or thought or did, is little, now. And all the lavish humor!—what is become of it? It is pathos, now. Pathos, and the thought of it brings tears.

All these little things happened such a few hours ago—and now she lies yonder. Lies yonder, and cares for nothing any more. Strange—marvelous—incredible! I have had this experience before; but it would still be incredible if I had had it a thousand times.

————

"Miss Jean is dead!"

That is what Katy said. When I heard the door open behind the bed's head without a preliminary knock, I supposed it was Jean coming to kiss me good morning, she being the only person who was used to entering without formalities.

And so—

I have been to Jean's parlor. Such a turmoil of Christmas presents for servants and friends! They are everywhere; tables, chairs, sofas, the floor—everything is occupied, and over-occupied. It is many and many a year since I have seen the like. In that ancient day Mrs. Clemens and I used to slip softly into the nursery at midnight on Christmas Eve and look the array of presents over. The children were little, then. And now here is Jean's parlor looking just as that nursery used to look. The presents are not labeled—the hands are forevermore idle that would have labeled them to-day. Jean's mother always worked herself down with her Christmas preparations. Jean did the same yesterday and the preceding days, and the fatigue has cost her her life. The fatigue caused the convulsion that attacked her this morning. She had had no attack for months.

————

Jean was so full of life and energy that she was constantly in danger of overtaxing her strength. Every morning she was in the saddle by half past seven, and off to the station for the mail. She examined the letters and I distributed them: some to her, some to Mr. Paine, the others to the stenographer and myself. She dispatched her share and then mounted her horse again and went around superintending her farm and her poultry the rest of the day. Sometimes she played billiards with me after dinner, but she was usually too tired to play, and went early to bed.

Yesterday afternoon I told her about some plans I had been devising while absent in Bermuda, to lighten her burdens. We would get a housekeeper; also we would put her share of the secretary-work into Mr. Paine's hands.

No—she wasn't willing. She had been making plans herself. The matter ended in a compromise. I submitted. I always did. She wouldn't audit the bills and let Paine fill out the checks—she would continue to attend to that herself. Also, she would continue to be housekeeper, and let Katy assist. Also, she would continue to answer the letters of personal friends for me. Such was the compromise. Both of us called it by that name, though I was not able to see where any formidable change had been made.

However, Jean was pleased, and that was sufficient for me. She was proud of being my secretary, and I was never able to persuade her to give up any part of her share in that unlovely work. I paid her the compliment of saying she was the only honest and honorable secretary I had ever had, except Paine. It is true that Jean had furnished me no statements, but I said I hadn't ever wanted them from her, for she was honest, and the lack of them had never caused me any uneasiness.

Oh, that unfortunate conversation! Unwittingly I was adding to her fatigues, and she was already so tired. Before night she suspended her Christmas labors, and drew up a detailed statement for November, and placed it in my hands. I said, "Oh, Jean, why did you do it? didn't you know I was only chaffing?"

But she was full of the matter, and eager to show me that her administration had been care-taking and economical. The figures confirmed her words. In the talk last night I said I found everything going so smoothly that if she were willing I would go back to Bermuda in February and get blessedly out of the clash and turmoil again for another month. She was urgent that I should do it, and said that if I would put off the trip until March she would take Katy and go with me. We struck hands upon that, and said it was settled. I had a mind to write to Bermuda by to-morrow's ship and secure a furnished house and servants. I meant to write the letter this morning. But it will never be written, now.

For she lies yonder, and before her is another journey than that.

————————

Night is closing down; the rim of the sun barely shows above the skyline of the hills.

I have been looking at that face again that was growing dearer and dearer to me every day. I was getting acquainted with Jean in these last nine months. She had been long an exile from home when she came to us three-quarters of a year ago. She had been shut up in sanitariums, many miles from us. How eloquently glad and grateful she was to cross her father's threshold again!

Would I bring her back to life if I could do it? I would not. If a word would do it, I would beg for strength to withhold the word. And I would have the strength; I am sure of it. In her loss I am almost bankrupt, and my life is a bitterness, but I am content: for she has been enriched with the most precious of all gifts—that gift which makes all other gifts mean and poor—death. I have never wanted any released friend of mine restored to life since I reached manhood. I felt in this way when Susy passed away; and later my wife; and later Mr. Rogers. When Clara met me at the station in New York and told me Mr. Rogers had died suddenly that morning, my thought was, Oh, favorite of fortune—fortunate all his long and lovely life—fortunate to his latest moment! The reporters said there were tears of sorrow in my eyes. True—but they were for *me,* not for him. He had suffered no loss. All the fortunes he had ever made before were poverty compared with this one.

———

Why did I build this house, two years ago? To shelter this vast emptiness? How foolish I was. But I shall stay in it. The spirits of the dead hallow a house, for me. It was not so with other members of my family. Susy died in the house we built in Hartford. Mrs. Clemens would never enter it again. But it made the house dearer to me. I have entered it once since, when it was tenantless and silent and forlorn, but to me it was a holy place and beautiful. It seemed to me that the spirits of the dead were all about me, and would speak to me and welcome me if they could: Livy, and Susy, and George, and Henry Robinson, and Charles Dudley Warner. How good and kind they were, and how lovable their lives! In fancy I could see them all again, I could call the children back and hear them romp again with George—that peerless black ex-slave and children's idol who came one day—a flitting stranger—to wash windows, and stayed eighteen years. Until he died. Clara and Jean would never enter again the New York hotels which their mother had frequented in earlier days. They could not bear it. But I shall stay in this house. It is dearer to me to-night than ever it was before. Jean's spirit will make it beautiful for me always. Her lonely and tragic death—but I will not think of that, now.

———

Jean's mother always devoted two or three weeks to Christmas shopping, and was always physically exhausted when Christmas Eve came. Jean was her very own child—she wore herself out present-hunting in New York these latter days. Paine has just found in her desk a long list of names—fifty, he thinks—people to whom she sent presents last night. Apparently she forgot no one. And Katy found there a roll of bank notes, for the servants. Also two books of signed checks which I gave her when I went to Bermuda. She had used half of them.

Her dog has been wandering about the grounds to-day, comradeless and forlorn. I have seen him from the windows. She got him from Germany. He has tall ears and looks exactly like a wolf. He was educated in Germany, and knows no language but the German. Jean gave him no orders save in that tongue. And so, when the burglar alarm made a fierce clamor at midnight a fortnight ago, the butler, who is French and knows no German, tried to interest the dog in the supposed burglar. He remembered two or three of Jean's German commands (without knowing their meaning), and he shouted them to the eager dog. "Leg' Dich!" (lie down!) The dog obeyed—to the butler's distress.

"Sei ruhig!" (be still!) The dog stretched himself on the floor, and even stopped batting the floor with his tail. Then Jean came running, in her night clothes, and shouted "Los!" (go! fly! rush!) and the dog sped away like the wind, tearing the silences to tatters with his bark. Jean wrote me, to Bermuda, about the incident. It was the last letter I was ever to receive from her bright head and her competent hand. The dog will not be neglected.

Paine has come in to say the reporters want photographs of Jean. He has found some proofs in her desk—excellent ones, and evidently not a fortnight old. This is curiously fortunate, for she has not been photographed before for more than a year.

———

There was never a kinder heart than Jean's. From her childhood up she always spent the most of her allowance on charities of one kind and another. After she became secretary and had her income doubled she spent her money upon these things with a free hand. Mine too, I am glad and grateful to say.

She was a loyal friend to all animals, and she loved them all, birds, beasts and everything—even snakes—an inheritance from me. She knew all the birds; she was high up in that lore. She became a member of various humane societies when she was still a little girl—both here and abroad—and she remained an active member to the last. She founded two or three societies for the protection of animals, here and in Europe.

She was an embarrassing secretary, for she fished my correspondence out of the waste-basket and answered the letters. She thought all letters deserved the courtesy of an answer. Her mother brought her up in that kindly error.

She could write a good letter, and was swift with her pen. She had but an indifferent ear for music, but her tongue took to languages with an easy facility. She never allowed her Italian, French and German to get rusty through neglect.

Her unearned and atrocious malady—epilepsy—damaged her disposition when its influence was upon her, and made her say and do ungentle things; but when the influence passed away her inborn sweetness returned, and then she was wholly lovable. Her disease, and its accompanying awful convulsions, wore out her gentle mother's strength with grief and watching and anxiety, and caused her death, poor Livy! Jean's—like her mother's—was a fine character; there is no finer.

The telegrams of sympathy are flowing in, from far and wide, now, just as they did in Italy five years and a half ago, when this child's mother laid down her blameless life. They cannot heal the hurt, but they take away some of the pain. When Jean and I kissed hands and parted at my door last, how little did we imagine that in twenty-two hours the telegraph would be bringing me words like these!

> "From the bottom of our hearts we send our sympathy, dearest of men and dearest of friends."

For many and many a day to come, wherever I go in this house, remembrancers of Jean will mutely speak to me of her. Who can count the number of them?

She was an exile so long, so long! There are no words to express how grateful I am that she did not meet her fate in the house of a stranger, but in the loving shelter of her own home.

———

"Miss Jean is dead!"
It is true. Jean is dead.
A month ago I was writing bubbling and hilarious articles for magazines yet to appear, and now I am writing—this.

———

Christmas Day. Noon. Last night I went to Jean's room at intervals, and turned back the sheet and looked at the peaceful face, and kissed the cold brow, and remembered that heart-breaking night in Florence so long ago, in that cavernous and silent vast villa, when I crept down stairs so many times, and turned back a sheet and looked at a face just like this one—Jean's mother's face—and kissed a brow that was just like this one. And last night I saw again what I had seen then—that strange and lovely miracle—the sweet soft contours of early maidenhood restored by the gracious hand of death! When Jean's mother lay dead, all trace of care, and trouble, and suffering, and the corroding years had vanished out of the face, and I was looking again upon it as I had known it and worshiped it in its young bloom and beauty a whole generation before.

———

About three in the morning, while wandering about the house in the deep silences, as one does in times like these, when there is a dumb sense that something has been lost that will never be found again, yet must be sought, if only for the employment the useless seeking gives, I came upon Jean's dog in the hall down stairs, and noted that he did not spring to greet me, according to his hospitable habit, but came slow and sorrowfully; also I remembered that he had not visited Jean's apartment since the tragedy. Poor fellow, did he know? I think so. Always when Jean was abroad in the open he was with her; always when she was in the house he was with her, in the night as well as in the day. Her parlor was his bedroom. Whenever I happened upon him on the ground floor he always followed me about, and when I went up stairs he went too—in a tumultuous gallop. But now it was different: after petting him a little I went to the library—he remained behind; when I went up stairs he did not follow me, save with his wistful eyes. He has wonderful eyes—big, and kind, and eloquent. He can talk with them. He is a beautiful creature, and is of the breed of the New York police-dogs. I do not like dogs, because they bark when there is no occasion for it; but I have liked this one from the beginning, because he belonged to Jean, and because he never barks except when there is occasion—which is not oftener than twice a week.

In my wanderings I visited Jean's parlor. On a shelf I found a pile of my books, and I knew what it meant. She was waiting for me to come home from Bermuda and autograph them, then she would send them away. If I only knew whom she intended them for! But I shall never know. I will keep them. Her hand has touched them—it is an accolade—they are noble, now.

And in a closet she had hidden a surprise for me—a thing I have often wished I owned: a noble big globe. I couldn't see it for the tears. She will never know the pride I take in it, and the pleasure. To-day the mails are full of loving remembrances for her; full of those old, old kind words she loved so well, "Merry Christmas to Jean!" If she could only have lived one day longer!

At last she ran out of money, and would not use mine. So she sent to one of those New York homes for poor girls all the clothes she could spare—and more, most likely.

————

Christmas Night. This afternoon they took her away from her room. As soon as I might, I went down to the library, and there she lay, in her coffin, dressed in exactly the same clothes she wore when she stood at the other end of the same room on the 6th of October last, as Clara's chief bridesmaid. Her face was radiant with happy excitement then; it was the same face now, with the dignity of death and the peace of God upon it.

They told me the first mourner to come was the dog. He came uninvited, and stood up on his hind legs and rested his forepaws upon the trestle, and took a long last look at the face that was so dear to him, then went his way as silently as he had come. *He knows.*

At mid-afternoon it began to snow. The pity of it—that Jean could not see it! She so loved the snow.

The snow continued to fall. At six o'clock the hearse drew up to the door to bear away its pathetic burden, Paine playing Schubert's "Impromptu," which was Jean's favorite. Then he played the "Intermezzo"; that was for Susy; then he played the "Largo": that was for their mother. He did this at my request. Elsewhere in this Autobiography I have told how the "Intermezzo" and the "Largo" came to be associated, in my heart, with Susy and Livy in their last hours in this life.

From my windows I saw the hearse and the carriages wind along the road and gradually grow vague and spectral in the falling snow, and presently disappear. Jean was gone out of my life, and would not come back any more. The cousin she had played with when they were babies together—he and her beloved old Katy—were conducting her to her distant childhood home, where she will lie by her mother's side once more, in the company of Susy and Langdon.

————

December 26. The dog came to see me at eight o'clock this morning. He was very affectionate, poor orphan! My room will be his quarters hereafter.

The storm raged all night. It has raged all the morning. The snow drives across the landscape in vast clouds, superb, sublime—and Jean not here to see.

————

2.30 p.m. It is the time appointed. The funeral has begun. Four hundred miles away, but I can see it all, just as if I were there. The scene is the library, in the Langdon homestead. Jean's coffin stands where her mother and I stood, forty years ago, and were married; and where Susy's coffin stood thirteen years ago; where her mother's stood, five years and a half ago; and where mine will stand, after a little time.

Five o'clock. It is all over.

When Clara went away two weeks ago to live in Europe, it was hard, but I could bear it, for I had Jean left. I said *we* would be a family. We said we would be close comrades and happy—just we two. That fair dream was in my mind when Jean met me at the steamer last Monday; it was in my mind when she received me at this door last Tuesday evening. We were together; *we were a family!* the dream had come true—oh, preciously true, contentedly true, satisfyingly true! and remained true two whole days.

And now? Now, Jean is in the grave!

In the grave—if I can believe it. God rest her sweet spirit!

Mark Twain

End of the Autobiography.

THE ASHCROFT-LYON MANUSCRIPT

Editorial Preface

Mark Twain wrote this long manuscript, which he left untitled, over a period of more than four months, from May to September 1909. Presumably among the last additions to the text was a separately paginated preface, "To the Unborn Reader," which he signed "Mark Twain" and dated simply "1909, autumn." Scholars have dubbed the text "The Ashcroft-Lyon Manuscript," a title of convenience adopted here. It records in detail the events that led Clemens to dismiss, for malfeasance, Ralph W. Ashcroft (his business manager since 1907) and Isabel V. Lyon (his secretary and housekeeper, and then companion, since 1902). (Biographical information about Ashcroft and Lyon prior to 1909 may be found in the notes at 331.40, 332.35–36, 333.6–10, and 333.16, and in *AutoMT2*, 473 n. 27.22.)

Ashcroft and Lyon had married in March of 1909, a "queer event" (p. 340) that Clemens believed was merely a strategy to ensure their mutual loyalty and complicate any exposure of their duplicity. Before the first stirrings of trouble in 1908, Clemens had regarded both of them as practically members of the family, and by his own account had "absolute confidence in their honesty, their truthfulness, & their devotion" to him (p. 335). But after investigating allegations made by his daughter Clara, he concluded that Ashcroft was a liar and swindler who had—among other lesser misdeeds—tricked him into signing a power of attorney that "transferred all my belongings, down to my last shirt, to the Ashcrofts, to do as they pleased with" (p. 388). It was Lyon, however, who was the primary target of his anger. He came to believe that she had been stealing money from his household account, and had deceived him into paying for renovations to the "Lobster Pot," the property near Stormfield that he had given her. Worse than these "thefts" was Lyon's having conspired to keep his daughter Jean, who suffered from epilepsy, "exiled in dreary & depressing health-institutions a whole year & more after she was well enough to live at home without damage to her well-being" (p. 341). Lyon became in his eyes "a liar, a forger, a thief, a hypocrite, a drunkard, a sneak, a humbug, a traitor, a conspirator, a filthy-minded & salacious slut pining for seduction & always getting disappointed, poor child" (6 Mar 1910 to CC, ViU; for a discussion of how Lyon's gender might have contributed to Clemens's bitterness see Stoneley 1992, 149–58).

Sixty years elapsed between Mark Twain's death and the first time modern scholars saw or read this manuscript. Paine doubtless read it, but because Clara wanted Isabel Lyon completely expunged from his account of her father's life, he made little if any use of it.[1] And the 433 leaves of manuscript were never part of the Mark Twain Papers, which the author placed under Paine's and Clara's supervision as his literary executors when he died in 1910.[2] The manuscript was instead placed in the care of his attorney,

---

1. Paine's only comment on the whole affair was that "there had befallen him that year one of those misfortunes which his confiding nature peculiarly invited—a betrayal of trust by those in whom it had been boundlessly placed" (*MTB*, 3:1528).

2. Article 7 of Mark Twain's last will and testament, signed on 17 August 1909: "As I have expressed to my daughter, Clara Langdon Clemens, and to my associate Albert Bigelow Paine, my ideas and desires

Charles T. Lark, and then by Lark in the hands of Clemens's executors, specifically Edward Eugene Loomis (1864–1937), the husband of Clemens's niece Julia Olivia Langdon (1871–1948). Loomis evidently passed on the document to his business partner, Harold R. German. German died in March 1964 without leaving any instructions about what was to be done with it, and his daughter, Janet German Harbison Penfield, found it in a shoe box among other papers about to be destroyed. She recognized its importance, rescued it, and reasoned that Mark Twain must have given it to Edward Loomis, and that Loomis gave it to German, making her (Penfield) and her brother the rightful owners. In January 1970, through John S. Van E. Kohn of Seven Gables Bookshop, Penfield sold the manuscript to the Henry W. and Albert A. Berg Collection of the New York Public Library for $27,500. But her ownership of the manuscript, and therefore her right to sell it, were challenged successfully in 1972 by one of the daughters of Edward and Julia Loomis, Olivia Loomis Lada-Mocarski (1905–93), who maintained that her parents had never given the document to German, even though it was manifestly in his possession when he died, sixteen years after the death of her mother. The sale to the Berg Collection was rescinded, and the manuscript returned to Lada-Mocarski and her sister, Mrs. Bayard Schieffelin, who gave it to the Mark Twain Papers in March 1973.

Hamlin Hill was the first to study the manuscript while it was (briefly) at the Berg Collection. He made extensive use of it in *Mark Twain: God's Fool* (1973). Hill found that "the Clemens family comes off more poorly than the Ashcrofts do in the 'Ashcroft-Lyon Manuscript'; all three Clemenses were illogical and lacking in compassion; and Clara's and Jean's harassment of the defenseless and high-strung secretary and her mother was needlessly vicious. The manuscript is a geyser of bias, vindictiveness, and innuendo. It proceeds in no systematic order, and it ends with the quite irrelevant and almost irrational comment about Peary and Cook both discovering the North Pole" (Hill 1973, 231). Thirty years later Karen Lystra's *Dangerous Intimacy: The Untold Story of Mark Twain's Final Years* (2004) took a more generous view of the author while also distributing blame more evenly. Drawing on numerous documents not available to Hill, especially Jean's diaries, to better judge the facts from different points of view, she also summarized the evidence from Clemens's financial records to support the charge of dishonesty (Lystra 2004, xii–xiv). Laura Skandera Trombley, in *Mark Twain's Other Woman* (2010), defends Lyon and described the manuscript as a "fiction about his family's squabbles," expressed in language that "could have been directly lifted from the melodramatic and sensational press." She claimed that Clara, whose friendship with Lyon had turned to enmity, pressured Clemens to dismiss Lyon out of a "need for retri-

---

regarding the administration of my literary productions, and as they are especially familiar with my wishes in that respect, I request that my executors and trustees above named confer and advise with my said daughter Clara Langdon Clemens, and the said Albert Bigelow Paine, as to all matters relating in any way to the control, management and disposition of my literary productions, published and unpublished, and all my literary articles and memoranda of every kind and description, and generally as to all matters which pertain to copyrights and such other literary property as I may leave at the time of my decease."

bution," and that both father and daughter feared what she would reveal about Clara's relationship with the married Charles Wark (Trombley 2010, 205, 211, 216–17; see AD, 6 Oct 1908, note at 267.36–37). In the same year, Michael Shelden's *Mark Twain, Man in White: The Grand Adventure of His Final Years* (2010) made a well-informed examination of the life from 1906 onward, and offered a corrective to the partisans of Miss Lyon.

Written as a letter (never to be sent) to William Dean Howells, the manuscript is the only known example of a "splendid scheme" which Clemens had recently "invented" as a better way than dictation to compose autobiography. He described the plan to Howells on 17 April 1909:

> When I wrote you at 3 this morning I did not know I was laying an egg that would hatch out in the course of a few hours & produce a cunning & handy scheme, but I know it now. I am glad. For I like to see my mind perform according to the law which I have laid down in "What Is Man": the law that the mind works automatically, & plans & perfects many a project without its owner suspecting what it is about; the mind being merely a machine, & not in even the slightest degree under the control of its owner or subject to his influence.
>
> My mind's present scheme is a good one; I could not like it better if I had invented it myself. It is this: to write letters to friends & *not send them.*
>
> I will now try it on you as a beginning, & see how it works. Dictating Autobiography has certain irremovable drawbacks.
>
> 1. A stenographer is a lecture-audience; you are always conscious of him; he is a restraint, because there is only one of him, & one alien auditor can seldom be an inspiration; you *pay out* to him from your own treasury, whereas if there were five hundred of him you would pay out from *his:* he would furnish the valuable part of your discourse—that is, the soul & spirit of it—& you would only have to furnish the words.
>
> 2. You are not talking to yourself; you are not thinking aloud—processes which insure a free & unembarrassed delivery—for that petrified audience-person is always there, to block that game.
>
> 3. If it's a she person, there are *so* many thousands & thousands of things you are suffering to say, every day, but mustn't, because they are indecent.
>
> 4. If it's a religious person, your jaw is locked again, several times a day: profane times & theological times. I had a person of that breed for a year or two. The profanity cruelly shocked her at first; soon she became reconciled to it; presently she got to liking it, next she couldn't get along without it; but from the beginning to the end there was never a time when she could stand my theology. She said she wouldn't give a Gatun Dam for it.
>
> 5. Often you are burning to pour out a sluice of intimately personal, & particularly private things—& there you are again! You can't make your mouth say them. It won't say them to any but a very close personal friend, like Howells, or Twichell, or Henry Rogers.
>
> But that scheme—that newborn scheme—that splendid scheme—that all-comforting, all-satisfying, all-competent scheme—blows all these obstructing and irritating difficulties to the winds! I will fire the profanities at Rogers, the indecencies at Howells, the theologies at Twichell. Oh, to think—I am a free man at last!
> (NN-BGC and MH-H, in *MTHL,* 2:844–45)

On 10 September 1909—three days after the last date that Clemens recorded in the manuscript—he, his daughters, and Paine signed a document releasing the Ashcrofts from all the debts for which Clemens had threatened to sue them (MiD). The Ashcrofts, for their part, dropped their threatened lawsuit for defamation of character. On that day Clemens noted in a memorandum, "Everything cleaned up & arranged with the Ashcrofts." Ashcroft had presented a bill for services, which included the pay he was due for his work as manager of the Mark Twain Company: "His bill was for $8,000; he gets $1,000 & 6 months' commission, beginning March 13 & ending Sept. 13 (say $750); & gives up 18 months' commission . . . say $3,000. Resigned the management, by request, to keep from being thrown out. He required, as a condition of his resignation, a note of regret from me, & withdrawal of all my charges against Miss Lyon. Both refused. . . . On my side I get back the Lobster Pot." On September 18 he added, "we are entirely rid of those thieves at last" (memorandum in CU-MARK). The final details were worked out on 26 September (19 and 27 Sept 1909 to Twichell, CtY-BR). Just a month before his death, Clemens summed up the sad affair in a letter to John Hays Hammond: "First & last, in one way & another, that putrescent pair cost me $50,000—& yet I have come out ahead. For they are tied together for life, & I was the unwitting reason of it" (22 Mar 1910 to Hammond, secretarial copy in CU-MARK).

Clara, however, had not heard the last of the Ashcrofts. In July 1910, only three months after Clemens's death, the Ashcrofts tried to sell the manuscript of "Is Shakespeare Dead?" According to attorney Lark:

> About a year after Mr. Clemens, through us, had had an accounting and had settled with the Ashcrofts, we learned that Ashcroft, then residing in Racine, Wisconsin, was offering this Shakespearian manuscript for sale in New York City, although we did not know that he had the same or claimed any right thereto. At the request of Mr. and Mrs. Ossip Gabrilowitsch, and as the representative of the Hon. John B. Stanchfield, attorney for the Clemens Estate, I went west, saw Ashcroft and secured the manuscript for a nominal consideration, on July 15, 1910. (TS "Note," signed, attached to the manuscript of "Is Shakespeare Dead?," DFo)

Just a few weeks later, Clara described the same incident in a letter to her friend Harriet E. Whitmore (Lyon's quondam employer and friend):

> I must just tell you that only ten days or two weeks ago we had what I *hope* is our last battle with the Ashcrofts. They had stolen some of father's manuscripts & were offering them to dealers and publishers here in N.Y. which we discovered because the dealers came to us to know if they were genuine. At the same time either Miss Lyon or Mr. Ashcroft sent me a blackmailing letter (which I will tell you about when I see you) apparently thinking that this letter would frighten me into letting them have anything they wanted and thus at least avoid some more of their scandalous talk in the newspapers. But Father left me *one* weapon to use in case they troubled me any more & I used it.—He wrote out a full description of their entire story of dishonesty which I was to publish if there was no other way to keep

them quiet.—So we sent the lawyer out to Chicago (where they are now), who threatened them with the publication of this M.S. if they did not give back to me all the stuff of Father's that they had in their possession & desist from annoying me in any way. It was successful. A paper was signed before a notary & I *believe* that we may for a time lead a peaceful private life. (CC to Harriet E. Whitmore, 5 Aug 1910, CtHMTH)

So far as is known, this incident was the last time that Clara was threatened by the Ashcrofts. The other stolen manuscripts that she mentions have not been identified.

In 1913 the Ashcrofts moved to Montreal, where Ashcroft worked as advertising director for the Dominion Rubber Company. From 1916 to 1920 he held the same position with the United States Rubber Company, and as of 1920 they were living in Dobbs Ferry, New York, with Isabel's mother. The couple separated in 1923 and divorced in 1927, and Ashcroft returned to Canada, where he later became the general manager of the Trans-Canada Broadcasting Company. He remarried, but Lyon remained single, living in a small apartment in New York's Greenwich Village and working for twenty-five years for the Home Title Insurance Company in Brooklyn ("Business Leader Friend and Aide of Mark Twain," Toronto *Globe and Mail,* 9 Jan 1947, 7; *Westchester Census* 1920, 1276:23B; Trombley 2010, 249; Lystra 2004, 265–66; Shelden 2010, 416–17).

Mark Twain's manuscript, including the holographic, typed, and printed items he inserted into it, is transcribed in plain text, which aims to reproduce the original documents as fully and reliably as possible (see the Note on the Text). The symbols and conventions used in the transcription are defined in the list below. Textual aspects of the manuscript not susceptible to transcription are reported in the Textual Commentary at *MTPO.* Also recorded there are Clemens's jottings in the margins of his manuscript—gnomic reminders that are not part of the narrative—and two pages of more extensive working notes. Several invoices annotated by Clemens, which could not be intelligibly transcribed, have been reproduced in facsimile. See the Appendix "Ashcroft-Lyon Chronology" for a summary of the events relevant to Clemens's narrative.

Editorial and Authorial Signs

a̶ cance- deletions, make the $100,000	Cancellation is signified by a slash for a single character or by a horizontal strikethrough for two or more characters; canceled words within a passage or phrase that was then entirely canceled are indicated by a double rule.
marking it ˄up˄	Insertion is signified by one caret beneath a single character or by two carets enclosing two or more characters.
◊	A hollow diamond stands for a character that the editors have not been able to read.

Stormfield	Words underscored once are transcribed in italic type, words with a wavy underscore are transcribed in boldface type—typographical conventions assumed by Clemens and other writers of the period.
Believe	
RALPH W. ASHCROFT	Extra-small small capitals with no initial capitals signify printed text, such as letterhead.
shaded words ‸can be‸ revised ~~From~~ letter in fact— unstrung	Gray background identifies text originated and inscribed or typed by someone other than Clemens; when Clemens made insertions, deletions, or underscores in such a text his changes appear without the gray background.
[*note by CC:*] [*written in the margin: P. S.*] Mrs. Ashcroft[']s an[d] A[s]hcroft	Square brackets enclose editorial notes and text characterized or described; superscript or subscript brackets enclose words or characters unintentionally omitted by the writer and interpolated by the editors.
⟦Some silence.⟧	The author's square brackets are transcribed thus to distinguish them from editorial brackets.
	Ruled borders are an editorial convention to represent the edges of a newspaper clipping; boxed text is shown without a gray background.
sort, ‸OVER she bought . . . OVER ‸	Text following 'OVER' (in small capital letters) was inscribed on the back of the manuscript leaf; a second 'over' (in small capital letters or in lowercase letters and placed on a separate line) signals that Clemens resumed writing on the front of the leaf; these additions are by definition insertions and are so marked with carets.
ⱡ	Canceled caret
¶	Paragraph sign
⁓	Paraph

[THE ASHCROFT-LYON MANUSCRIPT]

To the Unborn Reader.

———

In your day, a hundred years hence, this Manuscript will have a distinct value; & not a small value but a large one. If it can be preserved an ten centuries it will still have a still larger value—a value augmented tenfold, in fact. For it will furnish an intimate inside view of our domestic life of to-day not to be found in naked & comprehensive detail outside of its pages. Its episodes have occurred in all lands & in all ages, but they have never been linked together in progressive order & sequence & set down as plain narrative of fact before; heretofore certain of them have been used in romances, but not otherwise. That employment of them has weakened them, not strengthened them, because, so used, they fail of the priceless quality of authenticity.

There are three conspicuous characters in this true tale of mine, this queer & shabby & pitiful tale—to-wit, I a pair of degraded & sufficiently clumsy sharpers, & I the born ass, their easy victim. The These three characters have figured as clever inventions in many romances, but in this Manuscript we are not inventions, we are flesh & blood realities, & the silly & sordid things we have done & said are facts, not fancies.

I have set this history down in the form of a Letter—a letter to an old & sympathetic friend, a friend of thirty-five years' standing, the novelist William Dean Howells. This was to give me freedom, utter freedom, limitless freedom, liberty to talk right out of my heart, without reserve. I could not talk like that to the general public, I could not strip myself naked before company.

Howells is all refinement, by nature & training. Now & then, when I have been obliged to be robust & indelicate in my speech, Howells was an embarrassment to me; I found I could not say things to him which I could not say to a lady. In these cases I have gotten over the difficulty by imagining I was talking to Colonel George Harvey. He is as robust as I am myself.

This original Manuscript will be locked up & put away, & no copy of it made. Your eye, after mine, will be the first to see it.

If the Paston Letters had been a free-spoken private communication to a Howells of four & a quarter centuries ago, imagine the light it would throw upon domestic life in England in that old day! a life which is hidden in deep night, a life which is a sealed book to the world forever; & imagine the value of it!

Mark Twain

Stormfield, 1909, autumn.

———

Insert Ashcroft's Letter received yesterday, May 1/09.

————

RALPH W. ASHCROFT
24 STONE STREET
NEW YORK

April 29, 1909.

Dear Mr. Clemens:

I saw Mr. Rogers at his office this morning ₐat his requestₐ. His auditor will be here in a day or two, and will go over your accounts and affairs for the last two years; so that, in a very few days, your mind will be set at ease on that score, and your present worries lessened by the knowledge that your affairs have been honestly and conscientiously looked after by Miss Lyon and me.

Mr. Rogers seems to be of the same opinion that many of your other friends are, viz: that the ghastly treatment accorded to Miss Lyon during the past few weeks by a member of your family is a mightily poor return for the way in which she has, since Mrs. Clemens' death, looked after you, your daughters and your affairs. While it is, of course, impossible for her calumniator to make any reparation; I and other of your friends trust that you will, in this matter, uphold your reputation for fairness and justice, and make what reparation you yourself can. As you have already stated, the charges emanated from a brain diseased with envy, malice and jealousy, and it is only when one forgets this fact that one views them seriously. However, irresponsibly conceived or not, they have been and are serious in their effect upon your comfort and well-being, and upon that of others, and must therefore be viewed from that standpoint.

There is no reason on earth why the rest of your days should be spent in an atmosphere of artificiality, restraint and self-sacrifice; and, while I don't suppose that the happiness that was your lot during the last six months of 1908 will recur in all its fulness and entirety, still I trust that you will, regardless of your philosophical theories, exercise your prerogatives of fatherhood and manhood in a way that will be productive of the greatest benefit to yourself. This I say regardless of what effect the expression of the sentiment may have on my relationships with you.

I am,

Yours, most sincerely,
R. W. Ashcroft

Stormfield, May 2/09,

Dear Howells: Those resentful & rather disrespectful references are to Clara Clemens. They are earned; for it was she that found the Ashcrofts out. You are acquainted with them, you like drama & melodrama in real life: we've been having it—strenuously—right under our roof for three years & never suspected it till now. Other people have suspected it almost from the beginning,—Harvey, Dunneka, Major Leigh and David Munro for a year past, & Albert Bigelow Paine for two years—but Clara & I remained peacefully asleep. Lounsbury, that shrewd Yankee neighbor of ours, classified Miss Lyon & Ashcroft as "crooked" before he had known them a month. Our house-servants had arrived at a similar verdict more than a year ago, while we were still living in New York. Broughton & John Hays Hammond set Ashcroft down for a rascal & an Ananias as early as two years ago. H. H. Rogers read "fraud" all over Ashcroft the first time he saw him. So did Edward Loomis.

And yet—how dull I have always been, in reading character!—I had the most absolute & uncompromising faith in the honesty, fidelity & truthfulness of that pair of rotten eggs all the while. Yes, & so had Clara. Clara & Miss Lyon were like lovers. They called each other by pet names. Clara called Miss Lyon "Nana;" Clara's pet name was "Santa Clara." Uttered in their presence now, these names would act ₐupon themₐ as emetics.

Dear me, what a revolutionary work a couple of months can do! It is about that long ago that Clara's suspicions were aroused. By Dʳ Quintard. He thought Miss Lyon & Ashcroft ought to be asked to furnish an account of their stewardship. Ashcroft told me he heard Quintard tell Miss Lyon he believed she was dishonest. Ashcroft was d̶o̶ indignant, & so was I.

But Clara was not in a good-natured mood, & she wanted to carry out Quintard's suggestion. Her mood resulted from two or three little things which had been happening. Well, little things can do large work sometimes; a lucifer match can start a small fire that will burn down a metropolis. One day Clara rang up a servant & gave an order; Miss Lyon heard of it & countermanded the order, & added that all orders must pass thro' *her*. Another day Miss Lyon told me Katy had been angering the servants by refusing to eat at their table—"wouldn't eat with Italians." It was strange conduct for Katy, who had served us 27 years & had not been accused of putting on airs before. Miss Lyon told me she got it from Teresa & Giuseppe. (Both denied it promptly.) I gave Katy a scolding. She seemed most thoroughly & comprehensively amazed; & said she had never said nor even thought of saying the thing which had been charged upon her. Clara was in a fury, & stood by Katy, & said that Katy's denial of the charge was sufficient, & made the charge a falsehood. Then Miss Lyon assured me, in her oily way, that *it was not she* that brought the charge to me! I wish to be damned if I didn't **believe** her!

Howells, this is a very remarkable little tale that I am unfolding in this answer to Ashcroft's letter above quoted: & ~~one~~ my principal reason for addressing my answer to *you* is, that your trained & alert literary instincts & appreciations are the best & most inspiring I know of to display it before;ₐ an audience that will beguile me into dwelling leisurely & lovingly upon it, & enjoying the taste of it in my mouth. It is a darling tale, & I can't consent to spoil it by writing it to A[s]hcroft. It would degrade my dignity beyond ~~healing~~ re-elevation to lower it to the level of that cad. I suppose you see he *is* a cad? He is 34 years old & a cipher in the world; I am nearly 74 & a figure in the world, yet he blandly puts himself on an equality with me, & insults me as freely & as frankly as if I were his fellow-bastard & born in the same sewer. And do you know—he stepped in, yesterday afternoon as ˄on the heels of his letter, as˄ smily & congenial as if nothing had happened. Paine was there (billiard room), & I was glad. It saved me from calling Ashcroft a son of a bitch—language which I never allow myself to use in society. I mean to keep my temper, for I have a purpose. If I keep it & leave him unanswered, he will snow me under with similar letters, & I will add them to my tale, & you shall have them all. You would never guess how rich they will be. But I know about this; for he fell upon John Hays Hammond two or three years ago, with his pen, & rained filth & fury and unimaginable silliness upon him during two or three weeks—daily? No—almost hourly. A man like Hammond— ˄lately an˄ aspirant to the Vice Presidency of the United States—couldn't afford to reply to a louse like Ashcroft, of course, & so he remained silent. Ashcroft thought he was afraid! Man, let me tell you, Ashcroft would consider himself quite competent to carry on a literary war with me. Now that is true; I am speaking seriously. He *is* clever—& in many ways, too—but not with his pen. He does not suspect this. Do you know—he even composes poetry; & gets it printed, & gives it to the poor. I have read it, & not all of it is bad; some of it is tolerably good.

II

I began at the end of my tale; I think I must go back & give you a word of introduction. In London, in ~about 1900,~ ˄in 1899,˄ I took $25,000 of the stock of the Plasmon Syndicate, ˄& paid the money down;˄ (total capital, $150,000.) I became a director. By May, 1900, we had the enterprise on its feet & doing a ~prosperous~ ˄promising˄ business. Then some Americans wanted the rights for America. Of them was John Hays Hammond, ~mi~ South African millionaire & famous engineer. I knew his South African history, & had a great respect for him & confidence in him—a man of sterling character. I had had objections, but I withdrew them when I found that Hammond was of the party. The trade was made, & the American ˄company˄ was presently started in New York. Henry A. Butters of California was one of the promoters & directors. He swindled me out of $12,500 & helped Wright, a subordinate, to swindle me out of $7,000 more.

Two of the directors—Butters & another—proceeded to gouge the company out of its cash capital. By about 1905 they had sucked it dry, & the company went bankrupt. At that time Ashcroft was secretary or treasurer, or both, & I became acquainted with him & liked him & believed in him. Mind, it is not yet proven that he is ˄persistently & constantly˄ dishonest, he is merely under suspicion, that is all.

About two years ago (say 1907), he became my self-appointed business-man & protector,˄—without salary. There was hardly anything for him to do except errands & small matters, but he was prompt and clever˄ at these things—none could do them better than he˄ did.

Presently he started a Spiral Pin company & I put in ten or twelve thousand dollars & hoped he would make a success of his enterprise. I don't know how it˄ ˄the company˄

stands: it never makes an official report, & ˅also˅ refrains from declaring dividends. But it doesn't matter; I have had similar experiences before. ~~I only went into it because he was charging me no salary.~~ I was of use to him now & then, in the way of ~~introducing~~ making him acquainted with prominent & useful people.

Is that enough introduction for the hero of this sordid little romance?

A word, then, about the heroine. Isabel V. Lyon. She came to us ˅in 1902˅ when we were living at Riverdale on the Hudson. She was to be Mrs. Clemens's secretary, at $50 a month & board & lodge in the house, or $70 & board & lodge outside. She had been ˅child's˅ governess in the family of a Mr. Dana, & afterwards in the family of our old Hartford friends the Whitmores. She was slender, petite, comely, 38 years old by the almanac, & ~~18~~ ˅17˅ in ways ˅& carriage˅ & dress. I liked her, but did not see much of her in those days. She boarded out. She was without order, without system, without industry, but she got along well enough, for there wasn't much for her to do. However, in one thing she was industrious, & commendably so: this was in making pincushions to sell at the Ladies' Exchange in Hartford. They had a ready sale—at a dollar apiece, I think she told me. She said she was ~~helping to~~ support˅ing˅ her mother, & I believe it was true. After she was authorized to sign checks for me, three years ago or along there somewhere, she ceased from making pincushions. I mention this as an incident, & not as ˅necessarily˅ connecting the two facts. During the past two or three years she has bought out the Bermuda shawl & scarf & silk & bead & bricabrac shops, & unloaded some New York shops of their overplus of rugs, & brass pots, & copper pots, & general jimcrackery of a luxurious & tasteful sort, OVER she bought a single bicycle & a double one to ride around the "oval" on, she helped Ashcroft & Freeman make me a fifty-dollar present the other day (carom-rails for the billiard table), ˅she's bought~~ no end~~ expensive books, ˅—she has done all these luxurious things, OVER˅ & has done it on $50 a month & supported her mother besides, & I have never known anybody who was more dutiful or could make $50 work harder. It was not good financial judgment, for there was a mortgage on her ˅little˅ Farmington ~~house,~~ ˅cottage,˅ & perhaps she could have lifted it if she had tried. I think so, because when I gave her a house & "five or ten" acres of land, she lifted ten more out of me, & put it in the deed. I ˅read, reflected,˅ signed, & said nothing. According to my habit. All my life I have ˅read, reflected,˅ signed & said nothing,. ~~And all my life I have never even read, with deliberation & understanding, a document before signing it~~ if I had confidence in the honor & honesty of the person presenting ~~it~~ ˅a document˅ to me for signature. In this ~~case~~ present case the considerable augmentation of the acres struck me unpleasantly, & I was ashamed of Miss Lyon for confiscating them without previously telling me ˅—just as a grace—that˅ she was going to do it, ~~—just as a grace.~~ I should not have offered an objection. I had also another feeling: I was ashamed of *myself* for not having thought of making the allotment 20 acres in the first place. I felt just the shame a person feels who is caught in a stinginess.

But damnation, I had never been used to 20-acre ownerships! ~~of land~~ The "grounds" of our Buffalo house, in the dim days of the Long Ago, consisted of only half an acre; father Langdon's ~~sum~~ spacious grounds in Elmira covered only three acres; our grounds in Hartford covered but a scant three acres; the grounds of the house we bought at Tarrytown—five acres—seemed large to me; the habitable & usable part of the grounds of our Riverdale house covered but four acres. And so, by old habit of mind I was land-stingy, & thought I was pretty liberal in giving away "five or ten" acres all in one great pile; indeed I was privately proud of myself. But "she"—well, she knew me. She knew she could pump ten or fifteen extra acres into the deed & I would sign & say nothing.

Why didn't she make it 40 acres? She knows me, but also I know *her;* & I know she has reviled herself many a time for not having struck for 40.

She early found out one incurable defect of my character—that I would promise almost *anything* to a friend, if I could be caught suddenly & not allowed a chance to ~~reflect.~~ ,sleep on the matter., From that time forth she practised upon that defect—with exasperating results to me. I used to implore her to refrain from springing important matters upon me without giving me a chance ~~to think~~ ,stu, ,to carefully study, them over before saying yes; & I used to say, often & often, "Always give me 24 hours; & when you come with other people's projects, protect me! be *my* friend, not theirs! make them give me 24 hours, for ~~God's~~ ,goodness', sake!"

Which she always did—if *she* wanted the project damned; but not otherwise. She damned Albert Bigelow Paine's project, in the matter of a literary executorship. There *was* a delay, for reflection; but she did the reflecting for me. She persuaded me that Paine had dark & evil designs, in that matter.

And not in that one alone, but in many others. She made me believe Paine was always spying around; always clandestinely reading letters he hadn't any business to read; always dishonorably slipping away with important letters & papers, & leaving behind him no list of them & no receipt; & she ~~go so cr◊~~ so saturated me with the superstition that Paine would cram so many of my old letters into his Biography of me that her & Clara's ~~Life~~ & ,volumes of, "Letters of Mark Twain" would be in a manner impoverished thereby, & commercially damaged.

And so I actually wrote Colonel Harvey to limit Paine to "extracts" ~~& to~~ ,& such-like, snippings from my letters. This would be funny, if it weren't so— ,so—, but I can't use the only ,worthy, word, it being unprintable. Day before yesterday I wrote Harvey to ~~can~~ annul that order of mine. He has done it promptly. I have his letter to-day (May 5.)

I have just said, a while ago, "I know her." It is true. I have known her *nearly a month.* She has been with me 7 years.

I have known *one side* of her for 7 years. There was another side to her, but nobody would venture to expose it to me, for everybody ,knew, I wouldn't listen ~~for a moment to~~ ,to, any attack upon her character or conduct, no matter who or what the source might be. It reminds me of three warnings brought to me by friends a good while ago, & which I rejected angrily & said I wanted no dealings with spies: one of them was a warning—accompanied by facts & figures—that Bliss of Hartford was swindling me. It took me nine years to discover that the charge was true; by that time my rejection of it had cost me $60,000. Another of them was a warning against Paige; my rejection of it cost me $170,000. The third was a warning against Webster's book-keeper & against

Webster's incompetence. I would not listen; later I had to pay the cost, which was $36,000 for believing in the bookkeeper, & something more than three times as much for believing in Webster's competency.

III

To resume (May 27.) Clara persisted in wanting the stewardship of Miss Lyon & Ashcroft looked into. I opposed it, & called it nonsense. I said they would be far from opposing it, for it could not hurt them—they would come out of it clear & clean. I wrote Clara that her mind had been poisoned by prejudiced people; that I knew this couple better than I knew anybody else in the world (including Clara herself by implication); & that I had absolute confidence in their honesty, their truthfulness, & their devotion to me; that Miss Lyon was invaluable when guests were in the house, because of her attractions as a talker & entertainer; that she had many talents & had acquired a graceful & effective literary style—& so on, & so on, & so on. I poured out my admiration, my gratitude & my ~~affection~~ ₐesteemₐ without stint. (And all the while—unsuspected by me, & by me alone—this pair of ~~sneak thieves~~ ₐverminₐ were pillaging me & conspiring together to rid the house of Clara & of the suspicious servants, & make the pillaging a permanent industry!) I am ashamed of that letter now, & would like to forget it; still, it will interest you, so I will put it in here, & let you see it blush.*

~~(Letter to Clara)~~

Honestly, I did think she had acquired a literary style, but that was a mistake. I was deceived by certain letters which she wrote to Betsy. They were bright & good. Were they inspirations? I suppose so. When she first came to us, seven years ago, her English was a curiosity. It was a child's English; I mean, an ignorant child's; clumsy, & incoherent & sprawling. When I would get through erasing & interlining, her page looked like a printer-apprentice's galley-proof. And the letter wasn't English *then*. There was no art that could turn her verbal slovenlinesses into English.

But I must be just, & say there was no pretentiousness about her performances. They could never remind a body of Ashcroft's. Ashcroft's are all wind, & sham, & ~~conscious~~ self-complacency, & labored & conscious effort at what he regards as fine writing. And my, when he is hitching together a ₐsophomoricₐ gravel-train of nine-jointed ₐcommonplaceₐ words, with the private conviction that every car in it is a Pullman, how gifted he does feel, & how eloquent & awful & impressive! I would rather be the author of his prose-poem at the top of this letter than have the ~~gonnorhea,~~ ₐpiles,ₐ I give you my word—I would, honest.

But to hark back to Clara's proposed investigation of the pair. Ashcroft got wind of it, & called her up on the telephone & said he was quite willing, but did *she* want to

---

ₐ* I have removed it to Chapter ~~XIV.~~ M.T.ₐ

risk the venture? It seemed an astonishing remark, & she asked for an explanation. His explanation was, that if the investigation were instituted it would reveal to her father how much money she had been costing him for some months past!

Two or three insults in a single remark! By implication, her father was a fool (plenty true enough), & knew nothing about his daughter's affairs, nor how they were affecting his own; by implication, she was concealing her expenditures from me; by implication, I would make trouble if I knew how much she was costing me; by implication the pair of conspirators were generously *protecting* her from exposure & calamity by shirking a duty to me in order to hide her derelictions & save her from sorrow.

By God, Howells, it shows that even the cleverest people can lose their heads & degenerate into idiots when they get scared.

In reply to Ashcroft's foolish "explanation," Clara naturally resented the idea that she had anything to conceal from me. Ashcroft mentioned her expenses for ~~the~~ a recent month—about $865̸0. Clara denied the figures & challenged Ashcroft to furnish them. He promised. As he has been asked for those figures once or twice since but has not yet forwarded them, it is possible that his statement was not true. Still it is not at all unlikely that he was speaking the truth; for Clara is like all the artist breed, & like myself—foggy in matters pecuniary. She could easily have doubled her monthly expenses upon occasion & not been aware of it.

I must do Miss Lyon this justice: she was faithful & diligent in persuading me (when Clara was on the other side of the water) to send her only two or three hundred dollars whenever she asked for five hundred, upon the argument that the ~~larger sum~~ more money she had on hand the more careless & squanderous she would be with it. Miss Lyon persuaded me to scrimp Jean, too. In fact she scrimped everybody but herself. Herself & Stormfield. ˄*OVER˄

But I needn't use both words. She & Stormfield were one—& she was the one. That was her idea. She believed her dominion ~~as~~ was permanently established. She fully expected to make it absolute & perpetual. And she would have succeeded, but for Clara's fortunate outbreak. She said to every servant,

"I want you to understand that I am sole mistress in this house, & that you are responsible to me, & to me only.˄," when Miss Clemens is not here."

That was the form for a time. But the lust of power & the sense of sovereignty grew apace, & before very long she left the Miss Clemens off. She had a passion for power, & she wanted *all* of it—no division. She couldn't bear anybody near her throne—even on the bottom step of it. Not even Clara. Once when Clara was visiting me & wanted her 5 o'clock tea sent to her own parlor, she rang for Teresa & order₍ed₎ it. Miss Lyon's door

˄(Footnote)
*Since I dismissed her, we have discovered that in paying the servants for February she paid two of them by the day instead of by the month, thus robbing them of a few shillings. With no advantage to herself except that she ~~hated~~ ˄disliked˄ those two. This is reducing meanness to mathematics, ain't it? Jean made the discovery & squared-up.

OVER ˄

always stood open, so that she could watch me & the rest of her subjects; she saw Teresa passing by, & called her in & asked her errand. ~~Tereesa~~ Teresa told her, & got this retort:

"Don't you ever answer Miss Clemens's bell again without first reporting to me. Then *I*'ll tell you whether to answer it or not."

She commanded one of the maids to never answer *my* ring at all! Miss Lyon informed me that when I wanted anything I could ring for Horace the butler. Not Elizabeth—Elizabeth's hands were more than full, she said, whereas she found difficulty in supplying Horace with work. Perhaps I could have believed that that was her reason, if she hadn't revealed a better one a week or so earlier—to wit, having the maids serve me, could make talk; *was* making talk, all over the countryside,—was, indeed, making a *scandal;* that she (Miss Lyon) was doing everything she could to protect my character, & to save Stormfield from obloquy, & she begged me to help her. She was thinking about me only, she said; she was only trying to save *my* name from scandal.

The damned impudence of it! Why, Howells, every week-end was spent by her & Ashcroft in her bedroom, part of every day & at night, too s◊—sometimes till past midnight, & with the door shut! All the servants knew this, & so did everybody else. I mentioned this circumstance, & said I thought she & Ashcroft could be depended upon to furnish scandal enough for *one* countryside without help from me; & in honor of their efforts I offered to change the house's name to Scandal Hall.

One night last October or September—it was after the burglary, anyway—there was an incident. At about 2 in the morning, the servants were awakened by a noise—burglars, of course!—& they flew to Ashcroft's room to rout him out with his gun—& found his bed empty & the bedding undisturbed; nobody had been in it! Miss Lyon's room was across the hall. She stormed out of it, & berated the servants soundly—her usual fashion—& ordered them to always knock at her door first, before meddling with Ashcroft's.

The servants couldn't stand Miss Lyon & her ~~insulting~~ ₐslave-driverₐ violences of speech, & they presently gave notice & left in a body. Do you know, she was vain of those verbal violences of hers; she thought they were something fine, something heroic, something majestic. She used to come to me after an exhibition of the kind, & give me the details of the explosions she had let off,—~~laughed~~ & the high & autocratic manner of it, & brag about it! I told her more than once that it was not a thing to boast of, but to be ashamed of; but it had no effect. She had always been a servant during her woman-hood, consequently she despised servants & did not know how to treat them. She had never had any money; now she had my check-book, & was using it with a free & lavish & unwatched hand. Put a pauper in a motor-car, etc., etc., etc. She was on her way. It was Clara that punched her tyre.

ₐ**IV**ₐ

However, she was not herself in those days. ~~W~~ In fairness we must allow for that. She had hysterics;~~—~~not ₐjustₐ occasionally, but frequently; not merely frequently, but very frequently. Hysterics—that was Ashcroft's name for it. But the truth is, she was drunk.

Drunk daily. On cocktails, on whisky, & on bromides. I did not know it, I never even suspected the whisky part of it—which was the main part. Everybody on the place knew it but me. The guests knew it, & discussed it among themselves. One witness saw her take three cocktails, one after the other—without visible effect. ~~Another~~ ˄Two other entirely trustworthy witnesses˄ said that that was homeopathy for her; & added that they had seen her take *more than half a tumbler* of whisky *straight*—not a drop of water in it—and march away as upright as a derrick.

Howells, she's a daisy! One day I rang for Elizabeth. I was in Miss Lyon's room at the time, & Ashcroft was present. I went to my room & then returned. Miss Lyon was greatly excited, & asked, in a slave-driver-to-slave tone, what I had wanted with Elizabeth. ¶ "To find for me a batch of mislaid manuscript."

Then she burst out—oh, like Vesuvius!

"What business has Elizabeth in there? She *hasn't* any business in there! What does *she* know about manuscript? Ashcroft, go & find the manuscript, & send Elizabeth to the kitchen!"

Ashcroft meekly departed on his errand, & I as meekly for the billiard room.

Unquestionably she was drunk at the time, but I was not ˄then˄ aware that she was a drinker. After a little, Ashcroft came down & ˄to the billiard room &˄ said—

"She is very sorry, & apologizes, & ~~he~~ asks you to forgive her. You must overlook it; she didn't mean any harm, but she is not herself. She's got one of those frightful three-day headaches, she is hysterical, she is all worn out in your service, & you must be gentle & considerate with her. She is all gone to pieces, she is a mere wreck, & ˄her life is in danger,˄ the doctor says she is right on the verge of nervous prostration."

I mastered my anger with an effort, & only said—

"The trouble with *her* is, that she's a God damned fool!"

She is a born spy. She always kept her door open all day & until she went to bed at night, & nobody could pass along the hall unobserved by her. Whenever a bell rang she would summon the servant whose bell it was, & inquire who had rung it & what was wanted.

And dear, dear, what a luxurious mendicant she was! She would get herself up in sensuous oriental silken flimseys of dainty dyes, & stretch herself out on her bepillowed lounge in ˄her bedroom, in˄ studied enticing attitudes, with an arm under her head & a cigarette between her lips, & imagine herself the Star of the Harem waiting for the eunuchs to fetch the Sultan; & there she would lie by the hour enjoying the imaginary probabilities. If she wanted any little thing, she would ring up a servant ˄from down stairs˄ to hand it to her. She was the only member of the family that never did anything for herself.

She was much the laziest white person I have ever seen, except myself. She had half a dozen duties which she greatly liked; those she did well, & gladly, & with alacrity, but she shirked all the others, never performing a single one of them that she could get around. She would promise—& promise—& promise; & never perform. When reproached, she humbly furnished an excuse: usually a pathetic one, intended to move ~~your compassion~~

your pity; customarily an artful one; & always a lie, I do now suppose. But in those days I often believed them genuine. She had two excuses that she worked particularly hard: one was, she had "been *so* driven," etc., etc.; the other was, she had been utterly prostrated by one of her three-day "sick-headaches." The fact is, she had been drunk, but in those days I never suspected that. I finally got so tired of those ‸two‸ monotonous old sl stand-byes that I fell to shutting them off when she opened her mouth to throw them up. Still I did pity those imaginary headaches, most sincerely, for she certainly did look sick.

Oh, but she was a glib promiser! She was always going to do things, right away. Always ‸"‸going to." I find that she had a name which I never chanced to hear in those days: "Miss Always-Going-to."

She always made the stenographer do her secretary-work—even to filling out checks; & by & by she got to letting a good part of it accumulate day by day for a week, then make Ashcroft slave a whole day over it at the week-end, while she did the Star of the Harem act on the sofa & puffed her cigarette & longed for the Sultan. Or even the eunuch.

After dismissing her, I found ‸among her secretarial leavings‸ an unpaid bill of Altman's three months old! She quite well knew it had been the law of our house for thirty-five years to pay all bills as soon as they were presented. I now sent ~~inquiries~~ to Putnam, Wanamaker, Altman, & others, & got them to go back over their books & tell me the result. Howells, that shirk had had the *custom* of leaving our bills unpaid for months ‸& months‸ on a stretch! I used to consider the Countess Massiglia the lowest-down woman on the planet. Well, when I get through examining Miss Lyon I shall realize that I have been doing the Countess a wrong.

Three years ago, when we were summering in the New Hampshire hills she got Albert Bigelow Paine to fill out checks for her one day. He tells me it took him all of an hour of swift writing to fight the accumulation of bills to a stand-still, so high was the pile. All but about a dozen of those bills had been lying unpaid for periods covering from six weeks to ~~five~~ ‸four‸ months!

She had then been signing checks for me about a year, & it is possible that she had begun these neglects when she first began to sign; at any rate we know she began before her authority was seven months old. Her authority was limited: she could not draw above ~~₫~~ $1000 on a single check. That authorization ‸(now revoked)‸ still exists. The Lincoln National Bank has it. No ‸similar‸ authorization, *not criminally procured,* has been granted by me to *anybody* within the past 7 years. More of this matter by & by.

V

Six years ago Miss Lyon accompanied us to Italy, & we lived outside the walls of Florence about eight months. ~~Mi~~ She did not live in the villa with us, but in a cottage in the grounds, therefore we did not see much of her. I had seen but little of her the previous year. I liked her. I did not perceive that she was made up of shams & artificialities ‸&

affectations, & hadn't a sincere fibre in her anywhere. When we returned to America five years ago & took a house in New York, she lived with us & was necessarily pervasive, for she was to all intents & purposes a member of the family. She sat at table & in the drawing-room when there was company & when there wasn't; our intimates became her intimates; they visited her & she visited them; of her own motion & by her own desire she became housekeeper. ~~Clara & Jean & I~~ It was in those days that she began to evolute, began to develop.

Not swiftly. No, quite slowly, and by stages: one affectation, one sham, one artificiality at a time. Even I was able to notice some of them, dull as I am. But to me they were not offensive except now & then when she overdid them. On those occasions there was fine company present, as a rule, & she was showing off. ~~She~~ Perhaps her pet sham was this: she would start to tell what purported to be a humorous thing, a killingly humorous thing, & a thing quite too funny for this world; & she would break into throes of artificial laughter as she went along, & bow, & bend, & writhe, & twist in her chair, in sham convulsions of mirth, & finally finish her tale with broken ejaculations & "oh, dears," & with heavings & pantings and gaspings! By God, Howells, it was the most degraded exhibition that ever was.

The disposition to show off grew upon her; she long ago ceased from saving it for company & began to practice it upon us. Even upon me all by myself. During the past two years, ~~she~~ showing-off has been a habit with her, not to say a passion. ~~In~~ I think it reached the limit in this past year. Circumstances are responsible for this. It is just about ~~y~~ a year since I moved into this new house; we have had shoals of guests; Miss Lyon was in full command, Clara being absent almost all the time, & Jean *all* the time (by grace of Miss Lyon's own plottings & ˌviciousˌ ingenuities); the guests made much of her; she could blow up the servants whenever she wanted to; she felt her sovereignty, she adored it, she prized it above her soul's salvation, she ~~rh~~ intended to make it ~~perma-~~ absolute over me, & permanent, & drive the children away for good & all. But ~~she~~ to *rob* us, strip us naked, take the roof from over our heads, was not a part of her plan—until after she married Ashcroft. Or at least until within two or three months of that queer event.

Yes, her head got turned, you see. She had acquired "position;" she could freely enter front doors, now, whose back ones she & Ashcroft couldn't enter a few years earlier; she had never had anything, now there seemed to be no valuable thing that she *hadn't;* she had always lived down cellar, so to speak, now she was living on the roof, along with the lightning-rod; she had always been an obscurity, now she was in correspondence with people all over the globe; between the Human Race & the Great Humorist she stood, erect, impressive, & all alone, ˌlike Liberty Enlightening New Jersey,ˌ & no unit of that Race could get a chance to lay a prayer at his feet without her permission. You see, she had always been just a chicken-coop, now she was an aeroplane.

Yes, she was turned inside out, like a sausage, & all her contents exposed; all her shams, all her affectations. She had used to gush periodically, like the Great Geyser, but now she was practically an Unintermittent. By my halidome it was worth a king's ransom to hear her gush out this ~~enthu~~ rapturous remark about Ashcroft recently, right after the insane marriage—to hear her gush it out, I say, & see her roll her happy eyes around, & languorously close them, & smile the contented smile of the cat that is digesting the canary: "Isn't he *dear?---*and so *honest!*"

Honest! *Such* a compliment—from such a source! Howells, it is like one ^old^ prostitute praising another's chastity.

VI

Miss Lyon, as I am now aware, was guilty of many meannesses, ~~many basenesses,~~ & many small frauds, & of a vast deal of wanton & malicious lying, & she was also guilty of one great crime, one ~~infamous~~ ^cruel^ & unforgivable crime. Do I mean the crime of spreading a report here a year ago (while she was pretending to be Clara's most loving & devoted friend), that Clara was insane? No, that was bad enough, but the crime I refer to was worse. It was the crime of keeping Jean exiled in ~~damnable~~ ^dreary & depressing^ health-institutions a whole year & more after she was well enough to live at home without damage to her well-being.

How was she able to accomplish this outrage? By various devices. Mainly by keeping me persuaded that ^the cure of^ Jean's ~~cure~~ ^pathetic malady—epilepsy—^ would be disastrously interrupted if she came home, where there would be company & distractions & excitements, & where she would lack the strict control & the exacting regime so necessary to her improvement. No, the sanitarium was the right place, the best place, the only healthful & wholesome place for that poor ~~child—~~ ^guiltless prisoner—^ that was the unvarying tune.

She even persuaded me not to read Jean's letters, but to let *her* read them & tell me such of their contents as I needed to know. This upon the plea that they contained complaints which were unreasonable & were figments of Jean's imagination; also that they contained requests which it would be impossible to grant, & projects which it would not be possible to entertain. I am aware, now, that in ~~almost~~ ^nearly^ all these instances Miss Lyon was ~~lying.~~ ^feeding me with falsehoods.^ It cuts me to the heart, now, to know that Jean made many ~~a pathetic~~ ^an imploring & beseeching^ appeal to me, her father, & could not get my ear; that I, who should have been her best friend, forsook her in her trouble to listen to this ~~snake in the grass~~ ^designing hypocrite^ whom I was coddling in the place which should have been occupied by my forsaken child. It is pitiful to know, now, that in those shameful days Jean, ^in her distress, even^ tried to get my ear through outside & roundabout ways; & ^tried, &^ could not succeed. ^The relatives OVER appealed to were afraid to come to me with Jean's prayers & petitions, lest Miss Lyon find it out & they be visited with her enmity. Even my niece, Julie Langdon Loomis, & Jean's aunt, Susan Langdon Crane, were afraid to speak to me in Jean's behalf. It shows how impregnable Miss Lyon's fortress was believed to be, & how unchallengeable her sovereignty over me & my belongings. One of Jean's appeals (which never reached me,) was for a summer lap-robe. Miss Lyon refused it—on the score of economy—& Jean had to use her winter lap-robe all summer.

~~OVER~~

,At that same time Miss Lyon was treating herself to any & every small luxury she wanted, & footing the bills with pilferings from me.

over,

Miss Lyon kept Jean scrimped in the matter of money; & Clara, alas; but I could not perceive that she scrimped herself. She always had money in her own pocket, & was a free spender—money cribbed from my bank account, ,in some cases,, by misuse of my signature, as now appears; & procured, in other instances, by graft levied upon tradesmen. She always said she had no resources but her wage ($50 a month,) & that out of her wage she supported her mother. In her latest letter to me—at the time I dismissed her—she even uses the word "entirely."

(Insert the pencil-letter)

Last year the Stanchfields, while on a visit here spoke very highly of a German specialist whom they had employed, & with Dr. Peterson's assent we sent Jean to him. Miss Lyon kept her sufficiently short of money. Jean was doubtful of the Berlin doctor, & sent home one of his prescriptions. Dr. Peterson said, "This will not do; order her home at once." Which we did, by cable. Jean responded with a cable saying she was well ,enough,, & asking leave to remain in Berlin at her own expense & support herself by teaching English. This grace was denied her. I would have denied it myself if I had known about it, but I would not have added "on account of financial stringency," for there wasn't any. Jean was never once at the opera, while in Berlin, although the doctors were willing that she should enjoy that refreshment frequently; Miss Lyon kept her too short of money. There was never any occasion to do her that unkindness.

~~As I have said, Miss Lyon kept~~

Jean couldn't go to the opera, but Miss Lyon & Ashcroft could indulge in expensive single (& even ~~dob~~ double) bicycles by means of my check. Bicycles in these hills! There isn't a stretch of three hundred yards in this region that is bicyclable without traveling a mile to find it. They paraded around the oval in front of the house a couple of evenings, ~~then took~~ on those things, then took them down & stabled them in Miss Lyon's house & we never saw them again until the explosion came, last March, & I dismissed Miss Lyon; soon after which they smuggled them into my garret when no one was watching, & left them there: a confession that they bought them with money not ~~there~~ their own & were afraid of the possible consequences.

As I have said, Miss Lyon kept Jean's home barred against ,her, during more than a year after her health had become normal & satisfactory. Meantime she had privately kept Dr. Peterson, the specialist, persuaded that *I* couldn't bear to have Jean in the ~~home~~ house, because she would make me nervous! ~~The heartless miscreant!~~ ,Howells, could you forgive that? & would you?, Early last summer Miss Lyon secured for Jean a comfortable & very pretty cottage on the seashore about ~~fou~~ three miles below Gloucester,

Massachusetts, & Jean took a couple of good friends to that place to keep house & be company for her. No ailing, grieving & complaining invalids present this time! Which reminds me that Jean & these friends had had a house to themselves in Greenwich, Connecticut the year before; so she was probably well enough to have come home *then,* if there had been no ~~Miss~~ Lyon in ~~the way.~~ ˄the path.˄

Miss Lyon was always objecting to my visiting Jean; she said the sight of me would remind Jean of home, & fill her heart with longings which she ought to be spared. Miss Lyon was not thinking of my going to Gloucester, or she would have prevented it. She & Ashcroft were keeping tender & solicitous watch over me all the time, like a pair of anxious & adoring nurses, & I couldn't even go to Bermuda, & not even to New York (an hour & a half distant), without one or both of them along to see that I didn't catch cold or get run over by a baby wagon. ˄And I liked that nursing & petting, & was vain of being a person who could call out such homage, such devotion. The pair were laughing at me all the time, but I never suspected.˄

But I did go to Gloucester—by a sort of accident. Paine & I had a call to Portsmouth, New Hampshire, to attend ~~the~~ Thomas Bailey Aldrich's memorial services, & we took that opportunity to run down & pay Jean a call. We were charmed & surprised to see how well she was, ˄, how sound & vigorous in mind & body.˄ When we got home to Stormfield I broke the ~~joyful~~ ˄good˄ news to Miss Lyon in an outburst of enthusiasm, & said D^r. Peterson must cancel her exile & let her come home at once. Miss Lyon did her best to look glad, & said she would write the doctor, but there was frost upon her raptures, even I was able to notice it.

The minute my back was turned she sent a telegram to D^r. Peterson telling him to absolutely refuse his consent to Jean's removal to Stormfield! Lounsbury carried the telegram, & read it.

That evening Ashcroft & Miss Lyon walked the hall in agitated conversation, & ~~Miss~~ ˄Paine˄ heard Miss Lyon say, with emphasis:

"This is the *last time!* He shall never leave this place again without one of us *with* him!" ˄OVER˄

Doesn't it sound like print? Isn't it exactly the way it would happen in a book? Howells, the whole great long Lyon-Ashcroft episode is just as booky as it can be; so booky that sometimes its facts & realities seem mere cheap commonplace shopworn artificialities ˄to me,˄ & as if they hadn't ever happened, but had straggled into my half-asleep consciousness out of some paltry & fussy & pretentious ~~rom~~ old-time novel of that hallowed ancient day when. . . . when. . . . well, you see, yourself, how dam *stagey* the whole thing is!

To resume. Neither Paine

over˄

~~Neither Paine~~ nor Lounsbury tried to tell me these things. They believed I wouldn't listen. Well, they were right. I would not have allowed any one to say a word in criticism of those worshiped pets of mine. To every man & woman in this region they were a pair of transparent rascals, but to me they were worthy of the Kingdom of heaven—may they soon land there! Everybody was laughing at me, but I didn't know it.

The conspirators "won out" with the doctor, & I failed to get Jean home.

VII

================

June 19. Let me go away back, now, to where Clara was urging an examination of these carbuncles that had fastened themselves upon me, & I was ¢ telling her to go on with her project if she thought she must—they would be perfectly sure to come out of the ordeal unscathed. I said they would be *glad* to be inspected. I proudly repeated this to Ashcroft. To my astonishment he didn't look glad, he looked sick. I said,

"Do you mean to tell me you have *objections?*"

He floundered, & hesitated, & stammered, & finally managed to get out an answer: the examination by expert accountants would humiliate *me,* because they would tell all about my private affairs to reporters—& *then* what! I was ashamed of him, & could hardly refrain from saying so, fond as I was of him. In the end he agreed to the examination. It s scope was to cover a couple of years, & would be a quite simple & easy thing, he said, & would take almost no time. (A mistake; it took a it is taking a very long time.)

Clara went to see Mr. Rogers, & he did according to his incomparable nature, the unselfishest I have known: he heard her story, then said he would send for Ashcroft & talk with him, & have him bring the check books & vouchers to the Standard Oil offices, where they would be examined by his own expert without prejudice to either party of the parties to the interests involved. Which was done. Very well, the examination was begun. He did not live to see the result. He died suddenly in the early morning of the 19th of April. May. In losing him I lost my best friend.

February was a cold month, as far as sentiment goes, between "Santa Clara," "Nana" & "The Bishop of Benares"—pet names, all. And all withered by that frost. Withered, rotted, squshed. Squshed & discarded. For all time. But I was still on affectionate terms with Nana & Benares, & was still their champion & sturdy believer in their purity.

Until that time when Ashcroft consented to be inspected. Consented reluctantly. Reluctantly! when I was expecting joyous alacrity! The frost touched me, then; but it was only a touch, it did not invade my bones right away. This was about the first of March.

In one particular the atmospheric change was quite noticeable, as regarded Miss Lyon: she was troubled, anxious, excitable. Ashcroft said it was overwork ; overwork in my service: in entertaining company, keeping house, doing secretary-work, village library-work, etc. That was partly an overstatement, I judge. She liked entertaining, & she liked shopping. In these pleasures she was quite capable of working herself down, & was always ready & anxious to do it; but the rest of Ashcroft's diagnosis was a work of his extravagant, not to say scrofulous, imagination. There was a better explanation of her distressed & excited condition than the one he had furnished: she was afraid of the contemplated inspe investigation of her stewardship.

She had reason to be afraid of it; & without doubt Ashcroft knew it. But I was serenely in the dark, I did not suspect her. Suspicions of Ashcroft himself had been bred in me by that reluctance of his, but they were very slight; indeed of little or no consequence.

In truth, that pair were in a state of consternation in those days, but Ashcroft did not show it. He was pleasant, he was charming, he was his usual self. Exteriorly. But he was not a happy man inside. Against custom, he ~~remained~~ ˄took to staying ~~here~~˄ here something more than half his time. In her room, mostly, & ostensibly hard at work preparing the investigation-statement. I now think they were discussing the outlook, & inventing precautions. I also think they eventually decided to gag each other, & do it so effectually that neither of them could for personal safety's sake sacrifice the other.

~~Then came a day when things happened! Ashcroft brought me four nicely-typed & disrespectfully-worded contracts to examine & sign—right away, as usual! *See Appendix.* I read~~

The frost went on gathering. Soon it was becoming apparent to me that the parting of the ways was approaching˄,˄ & that I was likely to lose one or both of these ~~helpers~~ ˄crutches˄ of mine. I was willing to lose Miss Lyon, if I must, but I was not willing to lose Ashcroft. I had supposed I could not do without either of them, & they were quite evidently of that opinion too; but Miss Lyon had grown so aggressive, & high-handed, & masterly, & fractious, & hysterical & insolent of late that if I didn't presently turn her out of the house she would turn me out. So I was beginning to cast an eye around for somebody to take her place.

VIII

————

The domestic barometer was getting down toward 29; the atmosphere was full of uncertainty, uneasiness, expectancy; apparently something was going to happen. Miss Lyon kept to her couch, right along, during several days, with Ashcroft for company. She was having one of her spells, & looked it. The doctor came daily. One day, after he had gone, Miss Lyon told me he had said she was on the very verge of a nervous breakdown, & must pack up & go away at once, & take two weeks of absolute rest—absolute rest, uncompromising rest, in solitude. It is possible that he said it, it ˄is˄ possible that he didn't. But ~~But~~ I have not asked him, therefore I have no evidence one way or the other. However, I believed he had said it, so I told her she ought not to hesitate, nor tarry, nor stop to consider my convenience, nor her own, nor anybody else's, but go at once. She yielded, with artful & touching reluctance, & ordered her trunk to be packed.

There was nothing the matter with her. There was a game on hand, & she was playing her part in it. Ashcroft took her to Hartford & lodged her at Heublind's, the most expensive hotel in the place. She stayed there three days, in a solitude consisting of two or three friends. She was then rested-up & all right; so she went to New York for five ~~days~~ ˄days˄, to drowse in the healing thunder of the traffic & the screaming of the whistles,˄ then came home as sound as a nut. [[And sober.]]

Ashcroft had been buying a near-by farm for me. The day after Miss Lyon went away he completed the purchase & brought the deed. He had paid for the property. That surprised me. How had he managed it, the check-signer being absent? It meant (as I thought), that

Miss Lyon had signed blank checks & left them behind her, ˄when she went cavorting around rest-curing.˄ It seemed to me that that was not a good business method, & I˄ thought I would take an early opportunity to tell her to refrain from it in future.

The truth was, Ashcroft could sign checks for me, too, but *I didn't know it!* I will explain this, by & by. ˄¶. Come—*isn't* it ˄just˄ like an old-time machine-made novel? ˄

¶ In the billiard room, that afternoon, the unexpected happened again: Ashcroft, ˄shamefaced, embarrassed, hesitating, told me he & Miss Lyon had concluded to *get married!* It was as amazing as if he had said they had concluded to hang themselves.

I said it was an insane id He asked my judgment upon the matter, & I gave it. I said it was an insane idea, & unbelievable.

He hastened to say they would not carry it out if it would cause me inconvenience; that they would put it aside if I wished it.

Necessarily I said it was not my affair, & I could not be put in that position: they must go their own way, & take the responsibilities themselves.·

He said they would postpone it if I wished, & as long as I pleased.

But I said I was not willing to be a party to the freak in any way.

Then he said they would be willing to get married secretly and—

But of course I said they ought not to think of such a thing; it could get us all into hot water presently.

He was of the opinion that the marriage would not inconvenience me, & would change nothing: the bride would live in the ˄my˄ house & conduct things at the old stand in the old way, & he would continue to live with his sisters in Brooklyn, & come up here for his week-ends.

That seemed to me to be the wildest proposition of all, & I said so. I said I wouldn't have any married people in the house, nor any babies.

He answered, with confidence & conviction, that there would not be any; that this was not that kind of a marriage; that there was nothing animal about it; that he had none of that feeling for Miss Lyon.

He said it in the coolest way, the calmest way, ˄just as if he was perfectly sane & then it wasn't a matter of any consequence anyway. I said,

"Why, how you talk! won't you love her?"

He said, composedly, "not in that way."

"Then what in the world are you marrying her for? what is your reason?"

Howells, he was marrying her out of pity, charity, benevolence! That was the sense of his reply, though not the words. He said she had worn herself out in my service & was a physical wreck & her life was in danger;/ nothing could save her but watchful care & tender nursing. He was going to marry her˄ & save her.

I could not know what was back of these hypocrisies, I only knew there was a mystery back of them somewhere, & that this marriage had a *real* purpose in view, if one could but guess what it was.

I said a marriage without love was foolish & perishable, & that this one would go to ruin inside of two years.

You see, *I* couldn't know that this was a marriage for revenue only; I never suspected it. I took it for a marriage of fools, I didn't know it was a marriage of sharpers. The fact is, it was both, but I didn't perceive it.

He offered a palliation: he said it was not wholly without love; no, for *she loved him.* Yes, she loved him, & he had a ~~very~~ great respect for her character & qualities, & also compassion for her unprotected condition.

Isn't it refreshing! Howells, have you ever come across this kind of a frog?

We wandered back to the baby question; or at least he did, & said there wouldn't be any—he knew it; knew it perfectly. I offered to bet him ten dollars to one, & he took me up. (In ~~partheis~~ parenthesis, I will remark that when Miss Lyon got back *she* wanted a chance in this speculation; she wanted to put up a dollar against ten that there would be no babies, & I took her up. I do not know how my chances stand, but I suppose they are about the same as theirs: he is 34, she is 11 years older; she is fire & he is frost; it is a case of iceberg & volcano, you see; there may be an ~~freshet~~ irruption, there may be a ~~freeze—let us wait & see.~~ litter of kitty icebergs—let us wait & see.

Ashcroft resumed the suggestion that nothing would be changed by the marriage; all our affairs would go on as before.

I said they couldn't, for I would not have any married people in the house.

Later events showed that he did not believe me; that he believed I couldn't conduct my house without his wife; that he could billet her on me for good & all; that he & she owned me body & soul & I couldn't help myself; that all in good time they would be indisputably supreme here, & I another stripped & forlorn King Lear. All this to be brought about by a deep & dark & spectacular scheme which I was to accidentally stumble upon the track of by & by, three months ~~later, &~~ which later; a scheme so darkly & shudderingly & mysteriously showy & romantic that they must surely have lifted it out of an old-time novel, no modern mind could have invented it. You'll see, when I get to it.

~~VIII~~ IX

I have stated the young Ashcroft's reasons for selecting the ~~mature~~ overdue Miss Lyon for a wife: reasons of a sort to tell to the marines; reasons that would not bear close examination, by the old sailors. He had other & better ones, but kept them to himself. Miss Lyon had reasons for selecting ~~As~~ the young Ashcroft for a husband. She told one of them to Mrs. Lounsbury. It had wisdom in it. She said there could be an explosion at Stormfield one of these days & a sudden house-clearing—& what would become of *her?* What she was going to need was a refuge & a support—somebody to lean upon, somebody to stand by her & take care of her. She did not say anything about being in love with Ashcroft. In fact she wasn't. She greatly liked him, but so did the rest of us. She was not warmer than we were. The most of our friends liked him greatly, & greatly liked

& admired her, too. A few of them had vague suspicions of the pair, (as it now appears,) but only two or three had definite ~~&~~ ˄ones & harsh ones—Mr. Rogers & Mr. Broughton, for instance. We had an average of twenty guests per month, & they stayed with us from one or two days up to ten. Clara & Jean were absent, & Miss Lyon was hostess. Capable? Yes. She made them happy, she made them cheerful, she made them gay, she delighted them. In the ~~art~~ ˄matter˄ of making people glad ˄that˄ they had come, & in shopping for bricabrac of a quality she couldn't afford, she was at home & competent. My paths have never been pleasanter than they were during her reign.

The couple decided to get married *soon*. At first they were inclined to be very quiet, & tell the news to friends only. That certainly looked right enough, for none but the friends could be interested in the matter. However, Miss Lyon's native love of showing off got the best of her, & she "announced" the engagement in a Hartford paper, thus fondly giving it the aspect of a "society" event. Which was not right, not righteous, not godly, for the ignorant would be sure to get that ˄very˄ idea of it, & be taken in.

Next, the wedding-day was appointed—March 18. Then those two shams turned their vain little souls entirely loose, & fairly reveled in imitation aristocratic pomps & glories. They got out announcement-cards—engraved ones—Italian script, & all that—cards announcing that on the 18th of March they would be married in the Church of the Assumption by Rev. ˄Percy˄ Stickney Grant, D D., & these they ~~sent~~ ˄mailed˄ to everybody they had ever heard of. I judge so, because there was a mountain of them on the floor by Ashcroft's chair that reminded me of the Matterhorn, & of Mont Blanc, & of the Great Pyramid, & of Aconcagua, & impressed me more than all of those humps put together; because I ~~thought~~ ˄judged˄ I knew who was paying that postage & standing sponsor for that stationery.

Gay times! oh, gay! The radiant bride, the beaming eye, & all that!

Then there was another mountain. Engraved cards again. Making this final announcement:

> Mr. & Mrs. R. W. Lyon-Ashcroft
> At Home
> Saturdays in June.
> "Summerfield," Redding, Conn.

Aren't those sweet little apings of swelldom just too-too!—the hyphenated name, the At Home, ~~the "Summerfield,"~~ & all that? What do you suppose they sent out those thirteen barrels of At Homes for?—to impress the village postmaster? For, outside of my friends & acquaintances, Miss Lyon hadn't any friends that were likely to make a railway journey just to see what she might look like in her wickyup & prefposterously married. She couldn't bed them, she couldn't shelter them, if there should be a freshet of three in one cloudburst; & there wasn't an inn nor a hotel within eight miles of that wickyup. Very well, Ashcroft hadn't any friends that would know what "At Home" meant, therefore madame would look for no freshet from that quarter.

But no matter. Let us anticipate. The fates had decided that when the seventy-five necessary days should elapse & the first June Saturday arrive, there wouldn't be anybody at home at "Summerfield;" nor any one there on the three succeeding Saturdays. Yesterday (June 26) was the last one; & the hyphenated Lyon-Ashcrofts—where are they? Many meridians of longitude curve about the globe's rotundity betwixt them & the wickyup. They are traveling for Miss Lyon's "health."

To go back to the early March days. Things moved swiftly after Miss Lyon's "announcement" of her engagement in the society-column of the¢ newspaper. I repeated my remark that I could not have any married people in the house. Relations were now strained—strained all around. On the 13th, Ashcroft brought me four contracts & a Memorandum to sign. One of them formally constituted him my universal business agent; another constituted him Manager of the Mark Twain Corporation, ˄for two years,˄ with authority to collect all moneys earned by me, & charge a commission for that service. Whenever I should have any instructions to give him, they must in all instances be conveyed "in writing." He was not to report to me oftener than once every three months. The language was that of master to slave, I being the slave. By grace of this document he would have no duty to perform but collect his commission on my income; & that would be easy, since the Harper checks would go to him by mail (instead of to me, as before); he would not have to go after them. I was content. The other document was the one I prized. By its terms he was obliged to take care of all my business affairs, & save me that annoyance & trouble. I noticed that he could annul the contract by a week's notice, but I did not mind that, as I meant to make him satisfied with the position & be willing to continue in it. However, I did *not* notice, or rather did not perceive the importance of the fact, that it said nothing about compensation, & was therefore valueless & unbinding. I supposed the other ˄paper˄ covered & compensated these duties. A mistake. It didn't. I signed both. [[Inside of three ˄of five˄ weeks Ashcroft dropped the unlucrative one for good & all, & without a word.]]

I signed the other two contracts, too, & quite willingly—for they made the getting rid of Miss Lyon easy & unembarrassing. One of them constituted Miss Lyon my "social secretary"—a quite new office, I believe, & not thitherto known to this sordid & unromantic planet. By its terms Miss Lyon condescended to act as my "social" secretary—which meant that she would invite my guests for me, & preside at table & in the drawing-room & entertain them, but would most distinctly ˄& decidedly˄ not do any social penmanship for any one *else* on the premises—meaning Clara. Ashcroft explained that all other secretarying, of whatever kind, would have to be done by the stenographer. That did not trouble me, & exploded no bomb of surprise under me, for the stenographer had already been doing it three years. Also, Miss Lyon was most distinctly & decidedly not to be called upon to take any part in the work of housekeeping. Miss Lyon's wage must be $100 a month, as Social Secretary & Ornament, & she must be housed & fed at Stormfield!

This did n̸ seem to me to be immensely impudent, after all I had said about not allowing married persons to live in the house. However, I could dissolve the contract ˄at any time˄ by a month's notice, & so I made no comment, but gratefully signed it. I had recently been getting a little acquainted with Miss Lyon at last, & was growing anxious to be rid of her. She has a marvelous art in concealing her character; good judges, people of old experience,—like D.ʳ Quintard, for instance—tell me they have never seen anything to approach it. Quintard was up here yesterday, & he said that for three years she deceived him completely. All through that period he regarded her word as gold, her spirit as beautiful, her ideals lofty, & so on, & so on: in a word, she had seemed to him without spot or blemish, altogether admirable, altogether lovely & lovable. Yet she is rotten to the very heart. If she has a heart. Which is doubtful.

The other contract promised that Miss Lyon would get to work "promptly" at the "Letters of Mark Twain," & prepare them for the press. For this service she would accept of no compensation. This was positive. I could annul the contract with a week's notice, & so could she.

~~Ashcroft astonished me~~

Of course this paper would annul the agreement made with her three years ago, which gave her a ₐpermanentₐ one-tenth interest in the book's royalties.

Ashcroft explained why she was so calmly throwing that one-tenth interest overboard. He said, with quite marked contempt,

"It is petty, & she doesn't care for it."

I could have said,

"Why, you ass, it will be three or four volumes, & for fifty-six years will pay her a larger annual income than she has ever had in her life or ever will have."

But I didn't say it, I kept it to myself, & made no comment. On the terms of that old contract I could get a *competent* person—which she certainly wasn't, & was aware of that fact herself; though during my long-time admiration of her I had believed her equal to that work or almost any other. I gratefully signed.

The humor of that document! She was going to take hold of the Letters "promptly!" I had been beseeching her for three years to take hold of them. In ~~December~~ ₐAugust lastₐ I had begged her to throw a volume of them together helter-skelter & without interspersed comments, so that Colonel Harvey could use it upon his directors to persuade them to renew my guaranty of $25,000 a year for a second term of five years, but to no purpose: seven months afterward she hadn't begun.

I knew Miss Lyon ~~was~~ ₐ& Ashcroft wereₐ well enough acquainted with my royalty-~~income~~ -affairs to know that that one-tenth interest in the Letters was valuable & would cost but three months' literary work, & so I was naturally surprised when it was contemptuously flung aside. I would not have been so surprised if I had known that they already had something so much larger up their sleeve that by comparison that tenth-interest was indeed "petty"—petty & contemptible.

X

I signed the four contracts in Ashcroft's presence. Nobody else was present. Nobody else was ever present when I was signing papers presented by Ashcroft. And there were

never any duplicates. There were originals only, & he always carried them away. If I afterward wanted to see what it was I had been signing, he would bring me an unsigned copy—at least what purported to be a copy. I can see, now, that some of his ways—in fact all of his ways—were suspicious; but during three or four years that idea did not occur to me.

On that memorable 13ᵗʰ of March Ashcroft did certainly come loaded—loaded for a complete & comprehensive clean-up; a clean-up which would wash the slate & leave nothing indefinite between us, nothing to argue over, or dispute about, or re-arrange. The four contracts having been signed, he produced a Memorandum, type-written on a little piece of paper. I read it & signed it.

And finally he produced what he said was four notes, for $250 each—*his* notes, he said; remarking that he wished to assume Miss Lyon's debt of a thousand dollars to me; & that, furthermore, she would presently return to me ~~and~~ the $500 which I had given her at Christmas, as she did not wish to accept it. Ɖ He didn't say where she was going to get the $500, & he didn't say where he was going to get the $1000 to pay the notes with. Both of them were living upon me & had no other source of support, & both of them knew that I knew it.

But they also knew I didn't know they had a by & by fortune up their sleeve.

I didn't look at the notes. I cared nothing for them. I never meant to collect them. I told Ashcroft to put them away & keep them for me. Which he probably did; I did not see them again.

Have I told about the Christmas present to Miss Lyon? Anyway, the way of it was this. While Stormfield was being built, Miss Lyon was mending-up "Summerfield"—called the "Lobster Pot" at that time—the old farm-house which I had given her a couple of years before. A year ago, when I arrived here for the first time, she remarked that she had no money to make repairs with, & was going to raise a thousand dollars by putting a mortgage on a cottage she owned in the village of Farmington. Perhaps she had forgotten that there was already a mortgage on that cottage that was making the shingles crack with its weight. But no matter, I understood her hint: she wanted to borrow of me. I told her to do so.

Very well, the repairing went on. Close upon Christmas she came to me & joyfully said the restitutions & patchings were finished, & had cost $1500. I gave her a receipt for $500 of it as a Christmas present.

~~The day after~~

On Christmas Day Ashcroft reported to me that she was much pleased. I said I was going to give her the other thousand, by & by, $500 at a time, in the form of receipts. After an interval of twenty-four hours he came to me in the library, with a receipt for a thousand dollars in his hand, & said—

"As long as you are going to give it to her eventually anyway, would you mind si—"

ⁿ I exclaimed with some feeling,ⁿ

"What ~~the hell~~ have *you* got to do with it?ⁿ!ⁿ ~~Won't you be good enough to mind your own business, for a change?"~~

Four contracts & a Memorandum, on the memorable 13th of March, General Clean-Up Day. Here is the Memorandum. It is couched in Ashcroft's deliciousest & impudentest style—a style uncopyable, inimitable, unapproachable, for self-complacent impertinence. The Jeames style; for Ashcroft, has served long as a lackey, in England, & I doubt if there was ever a better one.

∧(Insert it Here.)∧

_∧Memorandum

RALPH W. ASHCROFT
24 STONE STREET
NEW YORK

April 7, 1909.

This is to certify that, until a few weeks ago, Mrs. Ralph Ashcroft (formerly Miss Lyon), acted as my secretary, housekeeper, hostess in the absence of Miss Clemens, financial representative, attorney-in-fact, and in divers other capacities—having full supervision of the building of my present home "Stormfield"—and that I compensated her for such services, as follows: By a fee of $50. per month, and board, residence and medical attendance; by allowing her to purchase, for my account, such items of clothing as were necessary or desirable for the proper maintenance of her position as hostess of my house; by deeding her about 20 acres of my land at Redding, Conn., and the cottage thereon built; by allowing ∧her∧ to renovate and rehabilitate said cottage with money advanced by me, of which money I presented her, Christmas Day last, $500.

[The lower right corner of the leaf, which presumably contained SLC's signature, is torn away]

I read the Memorandum through while Ashcroft stood waiting; then I signed it & he carried it away ∧to New York∧ with the other documents. That night I fell to wondering what the idea of that Memorandum could be. It ~~itemised~~ ∧invoiced∧ Miss Lyon's services in ∧solemn & impressive∧ detail.⫽ Why? Did I need the information? Certainly not.⫽ Who, then, needed it? Ashcroft? No—he was familiar with the facts. Why did he want them in writing, & signed?

Blest if I could guess! By & by it occurred to me that there must be a nigger in that woodpile somewhere—there must be a̲n̲ ~~secret~~ ∧important∧ *reason* secreted in that chaff, if I could only find it. Very well, I found it. At least I believed so. It could not be the doctor-bills;⫼ Miss Lyon had known for years that I paid all the household doctor bills myself. So it must be the clothes! She was always buying them, & she generally had the village dressmaker in the house.⫽ a̲At two dollars a day. I knew she had told that woman she should want her ∧practically∧ the whole winter. I knew it because Miss Lyon had told me so herself—in one of her bragging moods—& told me how surprised & glad the woman was. Miss Lyon was just thoughtless enough to give herself away like that. It did not occur to her that I might ˄possibly (though not probably)˄ put two & two together & arrive at this result: that her frequently-exhibited pride in the fact that she spent little or nothing on herself, but her $50 ~~a month~~ ˄salary˄ on her mother's support, didn't tally very well with this new source of pride. If it cost $50 a month$ to merely manufacture the gowns & things, how much did the *materials* cost?

It seemed plain that the clothing-item must be the sensitive place in the Memorandum. Did she want me to concede, in writing, that I had authorized her to buy those clothes? There was trouble in the air, ˄,˄ as she & the rest of us knew.˄ If it came to separation & a quarrel,, might she not need such a paper as a protection if she should chance to be accused of misusing my check-book?

Next morning I ~~asked~~ ˄requested˄ her to telephone Ashcroft & ask him to bring back the Memorandum & let me read it again. He brought it; & said, without waiting for me to examine it—

"The clothing, she—well, she spent only ˄about˄ three hundred dollars, &—well, she was authorized to buy clothing."

"Who authorized her?"

"Miss Clemens said that as she had to meet so much company she ought to be properly dressed; so she authorized her to buy such as was needed."

"Ashcroft, Miss Lyon knew Miss Clemens's authorization was without value. You knew it, too."

So that was really the tender spot in the Memorandum. It wasn't any matter, it possessed no consequence—except in one way: while this was a very small depredation & possibly had ~~not~~ cost me but little per year, it offered strong presumptive evidence that the depredator or depredatoress who would depredate in clothes, would not stop there, but would go further——*had* gone further.

I put the Memorandum away & locked it up, Ashcroft making no comment. ~~I copy it here:~~

~~Insert Memorandum.~~
here

˄Months later I was to find out that the clothes were cunningly put in to conceal the real nigger in the woodpile. That real nigger was in the *closing sentence.*˄

Contract Day! Cleaning-Up Day! The Busy Day! Wonderful Thirteenth of March, the Unforgetable! How much was crowded into it, when you come to think! Not into the whole Day—no, into one hour.

As a result, I was Miss Lyon's slave & also Mr. Ashcroft's slave; & had confessed it in writing, & had bound myself to pay wages for the place & get absolutely nothing in return—nothing, at any rate, that couldn't be had in the market for half the money.

But I was happy. I still had my Ashcroft, my precious, & we should now get back into the old delightful comradeship again right away—I not knowing about that Thing they had up their Sleeve. As for Miss Lyon, I would not be too abrupt: I would wait thirty days before dismissing her.

XI

Five days slipped by. Then came the wedding. I was there. It was a binding together of a pair of conspirators, for protective purposes. Each knew of the other's crimes, & neither was willing to trust the other, ungagged. No, not quite that, perhaps. Ashcroft was probably not concerned about crimes already committed by him, because he had ‸almost certainly‸ covered them cunningly up—even from Miss Lyon, probably; what he was afraid of was, ‸I think,‸ that if she were not gagged she might some time or other expose ~~the fut~~ *contemplated* crimes—crimes planned by the two for future execution. Otherwise, why was he tying himself to her? He didn't want her. He had never proposed to her. He told me so, himself. He told me she had proposed the marriage, & had also urged it. ‸[[It was OVER that day in the billiard room, & the "urgency" had seemed to me to translate itself into *compulsion*. This was a justifiable guess, in view of a thousand familiar circumstances, but not as good a guess as I could make now. Now that I know what they had up their sleeve.]]

over ‸

The church was cold & clammy, which was quite proper. Miss Lyon's mother was there, some Ashcrofts were there, the ‸two‸ Freemans were there, I was there. Also Mrs. Martin W. Littleton‚ ‸,‸ and God. ‸If‸ God ‸He‸ was there‚ ~~I didn't see him.~~ Reverend Percy Grant intimated that He was‚; ~~But that was probably merely an ordinary wedding-convention, with nothing in it.~~ ‸even *said*‸ He was. Nine in all.‸

Miss Lyon acted the happy young bride to admiration. She almost made it look real. The reality itself could hardly have been more sweetly and gushingly ‸& artfully artlessly‸ girlish. And when she knelt on a prie-dieu & bowed her head reverently, with her bridal veil flowing about it, & Percy Grant stood ‸grandly up‸ in his consecrated livery, with hands & chin uplifted, & prayed over her—well, it was stunningly impressive & rotten, & I was glad I was there to see.

There was no bridal trip. Mr. & Mrs. R. W. Lyon-Ashcroft came back ~~"home."~~ ‸&‸ took up night-quarters at their house & day-quarters at mine.‸

In these days we had guests in the house all the time, & the new bride was in great form as salaried Social Secretary & Ornament. She was the liveliest of the lively, the gayest of the gay. Clara was now in command, as housekeeper. The Ashcrofts & I were soon very friendly & sociable again, & I hoped & believed these conditions would continue. Clara hoped the opposite.

On the 30th of March Clara reported to me that Horace ‸Hazen‸ wanted an advance of wages & another afternoon & evening off. I said "satisfy him if you can." He wasn't much of a butler, but he was improving. He was a country lad, nineteen years old, very slim, & apparently nineteen feet high, but this was an optical delusion, he was only 6 feet

2. He was a good fellow, & of good character, & was the son of a farmer-neighbor whose forbears had occupied the farm since the earliest times. His wage was high enough—$35 a month—but he was learning, & would soon be worth more.

Clara & I left for New York the next morning. In the course of the three-mile drive to the station I asked about Horace, & she said he & she had agreed upon $45 per month & the extra off-time he had asked for.

I spent that night at the house of H. H. Rogers, & arranged for next day's journey. To Norfolk, Virginia, to speak at a banquet in his honor, & witness the glories which were to be poured out upon him by the people—for he had built a great railway 446 miles long, ~~down~~ all by himself, down there, & secured for that region a vast & permanent prosperity. ~~for~~ Ashcroft was to go with me & take care of me, & baby me, & protect me from drafts, & so-on & so-on, just in the old-time way, the old charming way, the old happy way, & just as if nothing had ever happened to interrupt our heaven-born relations.

We went by boat, ₍sailing at 3 p.m.,₎ along with the other guests. We were together, & ever so content & comfortable until midnight, when he tucked me in, placed my books, tobacco, pipes, cigars, matches, & hot-whisky outfit conveniently, ~~undressed me,~~ then went his way. We had sat together at dinner; we sat together at breakfast in the morning; we drove together to the hotel in Norfolk; we ₍were₎ inseparable in all our goings & comings that day. It was all exceedingly pleasant & sociable.

Then came an incident. Toward dinner time he came into my room with an open letter in his hand, & astonished me by saying,

"Miss Clemens has discharged Horace!"

"No such thing; she's done nothing of the kind."

"Yes, but she *has!*" & his little rat-eyes twinkled with malicious joy.

"How do you know she has?"

"Horace *says* so. This letter is from Horace, & he says just that; uses that expression."

"Does his saying so make it so?"

"Yes, it does, because Horace is absolutely truthful—absolutely. He doesn't know *how* to lie."

"He has lied this time, all the same, unless something has been happening since I left to cause his discharge."

"Well, he wasn't going to stay, anyway."

"He wasn't? How do you know?"

"He told me so, himself. He said he would not serve under Miss Clemens for any wages in the world."

"*He* said that to you?"

"Yes."

"Did you recognise that he had insulted you? Did you try to knock him down?" ⟦Ashcroft's silence meant No.⟧ "Were you skunk enough to take that?" ⟦Some more silence.⟧

~~"When did he~~

"When did he tell you these things?"

"The night before you left."

"Why, you were in New York! You went down that morning."

That seemed to embarrass him for a moment or two, then he said,

"I had to go back to attend to some things."

"Then Horace must have told you those things in my house. Did he?"

"Yes."

"You knew my daughter & I were going away in the morning. Why didn't you report that conversation to me, so that we could secure a butler in New York?"

He was getting pretty uncomfortable; words did not flow easily with him. He finally made out to say he hadn't believed Horace was in real earnest, but was only irritated about something & would cool off & change his mind. Then he added:

"But it didn't happen. He has been discharged; & as it was without notice, he is entitled to a month's wages, & wants it."

"Wants it, merely on *his* testimony, uncorroborated, that he has been peremptorily discharged? Well, he won't get it right away, *that* I know."

Those rat-eyes glinted again joyfully, & Ashcroft said—

"He's already got it!"

"What do you mean?"

"That was his check that you signed this morning, & I sent it off in the noon mail."

"Well, upon my word! You do seem to be in a most extravagant hurry. You are my salaried business conscience, my business adviser, my business nurse, my business sentinel on the watch-tower to see that nobody slips up on me with an undocumented & unverified claim, & *this* is your first official act! Why, Ashcroft, child as I am, I know more about business than that, myself. Get that check back! And don't lose any time about it."

He pretty meekly confessed that perhaps he had been a little premature, & said he would go at once & telegraph Horace.

I would give a ~~thousand dollars,~~ good deal now, if I had kept still & allowed that check to be collected. But I didn't know Ashcroft then, & so I lost my chance, ~~to jail him.~~

I took Horace's letter, read it, & put it in my pocket. There was no envelop. There had never been one, but I didn't know that. I insert it here. For certain good & sufficient reasons, it is an interesting document.

Redding, Conn.
Mar 31ˢᵗ 09

Mr S. L. Clemens.

Dear Sir;— Having been discharged from your services on this 31ˢᵗ day of March 1909. by Miss Clara Clemens but, having agreed to stay until April 5ᵗʰ 1909, according to my contract I am entitled to a months salary for which I would consider a favor if you would send me on or before that time.

No words can express ý my gratitude for your kindness shown me since being in your employment, and believe me my dear sir I feel greatly indebeted to you.

Again thanking you and hoping to hear and see you often,

I beg to remain,
Your humble servent,
H. W. Hazen.

[*note by CC:*]

I did not discharge Horace. On the contrary before I left Redding the new arrangement was that Horace was to ₐhaveₐ his wages raised to $45 a month and be allowed one extra night a week.—

Horace has discharged himself.

Clara Clemens

April 7ᵗʰ 1909

We reached New York from Norfolk late on Tuesday the 6ᵗʰ of ~~May~~ April. I stayed at Mr. Rogers's house, & went to Clara's apartment in Stuyvesant Square the next morning. I had telegraphed Clara on the 4ᵗʰ that Horace had pronounced himself discharged. She had sent at once for Claude. He had a place, but could give notice & come to us on the 15ᵗʰ—"& very gladly," he said, "on condition that he was not to serve under Miss Lyon." ⟦She was still "Miss Lyon" to everybody—including her husband.⟧ Clara had telephoned the news to Katy, at Stormfield,/ who telep₍h₎oned back, "I told Miss Lyon right away, & she was so scared she was as white as a ghost, for *she* knows what Claude thinks about that two-o'clock-in-the-morning incident, & that was why she made up her mind to drive him off the place & keep him from talking."

I showed Horace's letter to Clara, & she said it was totally false; that she hadn't discharged him, & hadn't thought of such a thing. I asked her to put the gist of it in writing—which she did, on the back of the letter. I was perplexed to a stand-still. I was not able to construct a plausible guess at how Horace had come to write the letter. Neither could Clara, but she chanced the idea that "those Ashcroft's are in it somewhere."

At mid-afternoon Ashcroft saw me to the station—for the last time—& bought my tickets & helped me aboard the train, according to old custom. Then he telephoned the lioness at "Summerfield," & she called up Stormfield & said to Terese excitedly—

"Get Horace out of the house! Get him out at once! Mr. Clemens is coming, & is in a perfect rage."

In a rage! Another of her lies. I hadn't anything to rage about. For I hadn't found out, yet.

Miss Lyon was at Stormfield when I arrived, & she exclaimed with the most gushing & best-acted delight her art could furnish,

"Oh, I am *so* glad Claude is coming back! The best servant that ever was; the most honest, the most competent; I did so *hate* to lose him, & he said he would walk over burning ploughshares any time, to serve me. He's just a *dear!*"

XII

I was able to tell Miss Lyon some news of a sort that pleased me very much. News of the kind brough₍t₎ back from Gloucester by Paine & me nine months before. I said––

"Clara ~~has~~ had a call from Jean this morning, & I happened in just in time. Jean is in fine condition! She had come over to see Dʳ· Peterson, & she was on her way there now. Presently she drove thitherward in a deluge of rain. Clara & I were sure, *very* sure she is well enough to come home, & she called the doctor up & made an appointment with him for four o'clock to-morrow afternoon. This time he will consent, sure!"

Miss Lyon flushed, her eyes spewed fire, & she was hysterical in a moment. She broke out intemperately—

"Indeed he will not! Jean come home? It isn't to be thought of for a moment; she is far worse than she looks; she has convulsions two & three times a month."

I was surprised.

"How do you know?"

"From Anna. She keeps me posted all the time."

"How?"

"By letter."

The slave was lying, but I didn't know it. I supposed she was telling the truth, & I judged Clara's visit to Peterson would meet with no success. I was not to know, until June 25 (five days ago,) from Anna's own lips, that Jean had had only three convulsions since her return from Germany. And they were a month apart. Anna has been in Jean's service four years.

There is no reasonable doubt that Miss Lyon telephoned Ashcroft to forestal Clara's visit to Peterson & fill his mind with lies. I base this upon the fact that Clara found him resolutely unwilling to ~~lis~~ allow Jean to come home. She was astonished at his attitude & asked why he was so unwilling. It was because *I* would be disturbed by Jean's presence here!

I have already told how he believed Clara was not speaking the truth when she told him that that notion was utterly groundless; & how she got Dr Quintard to go & reason with him; & how Quintard could not convince him; & how, when I went to Peterson, in my turn, he wouldn't believe *me,* at first. That was about the 20th ˌ14^thˌ of April. He had been up here the day before, in my absence, & had been listening to Miss Lyon's falsities all day.

¶ All I could get out of Peterson was permission to allow Jean to come home for one week. If the experiment was not a failure it could be tried a little longer & its results noted.

So Jean arrived here on the 26th of April; so glad to be in her own home once more, that she hadn't any words for her gratitude. She is here yet, & is as healthy as the very rocks. Not a single symptom of her cruel malady has ever shown itself. She is up at six in the morning & is busy & active thence till bedtime at nine in the evening. She rakes & mows on her farm; superintends her men; directs the repairs upon her house & barn; buys chickens & ducks from the farmers around & feeds & cares for them herself; walks home at eleven, examines & annotates the mail, then answers the letters & draws the checks for all bills; & in ~~an~~ two hours has cleared off all my secretary-work for the day—a most pleasant & satisfactory change from the shirking ways of that lazy & incompetent former secretary of mine, who couldn't write English, whereas Jean can. Jean spends the afternoon riding horseback & driving until her five o'clock tea. Imagine it—I could have had her at home two years ago, ˌ(as I have at last discovered,)ˌ but for the schemings of that pitiless pair & my own inexcusable stupidity!

Well, they themselves have avenged me. For they are married. Two months & a half. ~~Th~~ By this time they loathe each other. They didn't want to marry, they were scared into it. They smelt bad weather coming. Each is a millstone around the other's neck, & each wishes the other was in ~~hell.~~ ˌNew Jersey.ˌ They have over-avenged me; I couldn't wish ~~a dog~~ ˌmy dearest enemyˌ such luck as theirs.

As I have said, I reached Stormfield on the 7th of April. Things were buzzing, so to speak. Ashcroft came up a day or two later. Meantime I had ~~seen~~ not happened to see anything of Horace, & was too busy to look into his case. When Ashcroft arrived he paid Horace to date, & I signed the check. He paid him at the old rate—a confession, apparently, that Horace had *not* been "discharged," & that Ashcroft knew it.

Yes, things were buzzing. Clara wanted Miss Lyon discharged & sent out of the house at once. I said her first month on the March 15 contract would be compted on the 15th of the current month & I would then give her a month's notice & let her retire to her own house.

Clara wanted Miss Lyon's trunks, in the attic, searched for stolen goods. This astonished me! Did she think Miss Lyon *that* kind of a thief? Yes, she thought she was; & believed she had more than merely plausible reasons for it.

On the 12th ~~or 13~~ I went down to attend Clara's concert on the 13th. I went to the concert with the Rogerses. No Ashcrofts along. A month earlier, it had been planned that the Ashcrofts & I would go there together; but things were changed, now; that pair wanted none of Clara's music, & Clara was not yearning for any Ashcrofts.

On the 14ᵗʰ I was still in New York I suppose, ‸(a part of the day),‸ because I had a talk with Ashcroft which I think must have occurred about that time. He told me Clara's feeling against Miss Lyon had reached such a pass that Miss Lyon believed Clara was going to have her trunks searched; also that she was going to have her arrested—& so Miss Lyon was in a state of pitiable humiliation & distress.

Then Ashcroft cried.

I said—

"Arrest her? Nonsense. On what ground?"

"Because she has a suspicion that—"

"Well, *that* is nonsense, too. Clara would apply to a lawyer, & the lawyer would not allow her to proceed upon a mere suspicion."

Miss Lyon's fright was a self-accusation, but I didn't know it, & was not suspecting it. Clara's suspicions were well grounded, but I thought they were merely grounded upon resentment & dislike.

On the 15ᵗʰ I was at home again, & sent & received this ‸a letter from Clara, about a housekeeper to take Miss Lyon's place. Miss Lyon had stipulated in her contract of a month earlier that she was to be Social Secretary only, & have nothing to do with the housekeeping. The Miss Hindhaugh mentioned was a lady who was highly educated but h & had been rich but had lost her money three years before, & from that date had been serving as housekeeper & secretary in the family of a Columbia-University professor at $50 30 a month. That is, for nine months of the year. The family went away each summer, but left her behind, without salary. She was very willing to come to us at Clara's offer—$50 a month—but she didn't come, because when the professor heard about it he raised her wage to $50—vacation included. She liked the family very much, & they liked her as much.

This is Clara's letter:

(Insert it here)

Dearest Marcus

Even if Miss Hindhaugh can not come on the 1ˢᵗ of May we can get along perfectly without anyone for awhile as Jean will be ~~in Redding~~ ˄at Stormfield˄ and I shall be there a great deal & with such servants as Claude and Teresa the house almost runs itself.—Of course I don't believe Horace because he could never for a minute have fancied that I DISCHARGED him whatever else he might have missunderstood.

I think it was a little scheme to make you ~~the~~ pay the higher wages for otherwise he would have addressed me on the subject instead of you. But fortunately it ~~was~~ ˄has been˄ a benefit to us instead of an annoyance. Somebody else may have put the idea into his head. Who knows?

Last night I sang at a small musicale without nervousness & consequently with success.

Tomorrow we go to Boston & I shall stop with Katie at Marie Nichols' home
1100 Beacon Street.

I am glad that you are well again.

With a great deal of love.
Clara

You will give Miss Lyon her notice *right away* I hope.—

But I must go back two or three days, now, for I find I have left out a letter to me from Miss Lyon which bears date April 12. It is about the Memorandum & the clothes. The Memorandum has no date, but I have supposed it was offered along with those other documents, for signature, March 13. That is still (July 5) my impression, but I am probably wrong. However, it isn't important.

But the letter is.

I recognise in it a better, ~~& clearer, & sorrier, &~~ portrait of her character ˄(as I am now acquainted with it)˄ than any camera has ever made of her face. ~~To-wit:~~ ˄⟦"Benares"—her pet name for Ashcroft:⟧˄

(Insert the letter in pencil, of Apl. 12

April 12/09

Dear M^r. Clemens

Please read this, for M^r. Ashcroft tells me that there has been some misunder-standing about the few garments I've bought~~+~~, but which I never would have bought if Miss Clemens in all sweetness & generosity did not tell me to buy, after a morning about 2 years ago when I had been angry because Miss Hobby was draw-ing five dollars a day & was shirking her work. She came from your room & said that she had said to you that it was wrong for Miss Hobby to be paid just double the amount of salary that I drew, & that I must at least buy my clothes since I would not accept an advance of salary. She said I had to travel about with you etc. etc. Then I *did* buy a little suit at Altman's & told her, but she was very very dear, & said "Oh don't mention those little things." She was the dearest creature, & said that you felt it was only right that I should have my garments—as I had my Mother to support entirely from my salary. I have bought very little, but can so eas-ily itemize all of it. I have some silk here that I bought to wear only in your house, & fortunately it has never been cut into, so it is yours, as I have said to Benares—& the other articles I shall be so very glad to pay for.

One thing more. I have been careful not to buy things where Miss Clemens would buy so that there could be no conflicting of accounts[.] I shall be so glad to have you show this letter to Miss Clemens, & she will know by what I own & wear, how little I have purchased. I have—but never mind.

I. V. Lyon.

"The few garments I've bought." "Few" must be a slip of the pen. Katy maintains that ~~she~~ ₍Miss Lyon₎ had more clothes, ~~& costlier ones,~~ than Clara. I am aware, myself, that her closets overflowed with gowns, & jackets, & silken shawls, & the daintyiest & delicatest auxiliary things that go to the setting off & heightening the effects of such raiment. I am also aware that in 1905–6–7–8 she had a dressmaker in attendance ~~with~~ several times to Clara's once. When she had been in Stormfield a while, Paine asked her about the village dressmaker, Miss Banks, & said his wife had some work for her & would like to know something about her abilities & prices. Miss Lyon blew cold upon the matter, & said she should keep Miss Banks employed all the winter herself. Necessarily on those "few garments" she had bought. She repeated that ~~grandiloquent~~ ₍boastful₎ remark to Paine on another occasion. She made it good, too, in a large measure. Last winter I got ~~tha~~ very tired of that dressmaker's presence, for she did her sewing in a room across the hall from mine, ₍& persisted in keeping her door open;₎ & as I always kept mine open, too, neither of us had any privacy. It is my custom to keep to my room, in night dress, until mid-afternoon, & intersperse my work with trampings up & down, to aid reflection & composition. This kept me under the eye of that stranger, & was an annoyance which damaged my labors by banishing from them the needed reposefulness of spirit. Several times I asked her to keep her door closed. She would comply for a day or two, then ‸conveniently‸ forget, & resume her former habit. By command of Miss Lyon, I now suppose, who was a spy upon us all, in those days.

Yes, she certainly did indulge in a few garments, on $50 a month which went "entirely" to the support of her mother. ~~Oh, certainly!~~ ‸"ENTIRELY." It is a strong word.‸ During the years I have mentioned, she brought dainty & expensive things home so often, with the remark, sweetly & laughingly & girlishly ~~expressed,~~ ‸burbled out,‸ "They *would* make me take it—they insisted—they wouldn't listen to a no—& they put it down to nearly nothing, & said if I didn't buy I'd have to take it as a *gift*—& so—well, I couldn't resist any longer, *could* I?"—with a birdlike upward cant of the innocent face:┼made that kind of remark so often, I say, that it became the joke of the house, & even the servants got to mimicking ~~her~~ ‸those‸ airs & speeches. She would fetch home a lovely silken fabric—always lovely, for she had perfect taste in materials, qualities, colors, harmonies—& spread it over a cha‸ir‸,~~t~~, & arrange its sweep & its folds effectively; & ‸then‸ stand off & ~~worshiping~~ worshiping it critically a minute, ‸OVER‸ cocking her head first one side then t'other;

over ‸

then step forward & give it another artistic touch-up with her practised hand, then step back & worship again. And all the time her face would beam with rapture & she would winningly & jocosely chatter about how "they" just *made* her take it, & ~~it~~ how they put the price down to next to nothing, & said it was the *very* thing for her, ‸*the very thing*,‸ & if she wouldn't buy ‸it‸ they'd make her take it anyway. Once when she was opening her mouth to begin a performance of this kind, Mary Lawton, who didn't like her, interrupted & said—

"Never mind, I know the tune, ~~I know the~~ I'll sing it for you. It's worth forty-seven dollars & they made you take it at four & a half. Because they love you so."

Katy tells about a shopping-incident of Clara's—to this effect. Clara was ‸longingly‸ examining a delicate piece of underwear, which was ravishingly belaced, & embossed, & ~~or~~ embroidered, or inlaid, or enameled, or whatever you call it, & when she put it aside Katy asked her why she didn't buy it, & she said she couldn't afford it. Katy said—

"Why, Miss Clara, Miss Lyon's got lots of those things."

This was ~~early in~~ ‸in the first week of‸ March last, & Clara's allowance had just been raised to four hundred dollars a month. Katy reminded her of this, & said—

"Miss Lyon affords it, & so I don't see why you can't."

"Because she can sign checks for my father. I can't."

By that time Clara was detesting & despising Miss Lyon most cordially & diligently, & Miss Lyon was hating Clara with her whole heart. If I didn't tell you this, you might be misled by some of the expressions in Miss Lyon's letter. Such as "Miss Clemens, in all sweetness & generosity;" and "she was very very dear;" & "she was the dearest creature‸,‸" ~~& she~~

Yes, Miss Lyon had bought a few garments—as many as that, anyway, during the years which I have mentioned. Ashcroft said she had bought none recently, except some silks & such things—not more than three hundred dollars' worth; anyway— ‸then‸ correcting himself;┼ "not at the outside more than ~~four~~ ‸three‸ hundred & fifty dollars' worth."

She remarks in her letter that those silks are mine. Did she think I would send for them? Indeed she didn't. Had she any intention of sending them to me? Indeed she hadn't. She knew me long ago; by this time I was beginning to know her.

In her letter she is illogical—however she was always that. She refuses an advance of salary, & imagines that ˄that˄ justifies her in buying ~~cost~~ clothes at my expense without asking leave. She ought to have been able to say she *had* to take money not her own because she couldn't *get* a raise of salary. Better still, she ought to have *asked* for a raise instead of refusing it. Or, she could have asked for the clothes. But somehow she couldn't think of any way to acquire the clothes but a ~~disreputable~~ ˄discreditable˄ one. She was not an easy creature to understand. Once when I gave her a check to get a gown with, she took it; six ~~or se~~ months later, when I offered her a similar check for a similar purpose she declined it & said she had all the clothes she needed.

And isn't she a hardy talker! She says Clara "will know by what I own & wear, how little I have purchased." Why, bless you she had a whole milliner's outfit in her trunks & closets!

And observe that shot at poor Miss Hobby the stenographer. What business had she with Miss Hobby's affairs? Miss Hobby took dictation from me an hour & a half every forenoon, & typewrote the result every afternoon, putting in a matter of three hours on that detail of her work. She was not my secretary, she was my stenographer, & did the work she was hired to do, & did it well, & earned her money. Miss Lyon was my secretary, but she gradually unloaded three-fourths of her work onto Miss Hobby & shirked half of the other fourth. Yet she works herself into a virtuous rage at the thought of anybody's intruding upon her special privilege of doing all the shirking herself. Miss Hobby earned her $5 a day. Miss Lyon received about half as much, but she didn't earn it.

Miss Lyon had to "travel about" with me? It is an overstatement. I never required it of her. Whenever I projected a journey she promptly said "I shall go along; I shall not let you go unlooked-after." I was glad to have her company, but her going along was her own affair, not mine. ~~Th~~ Howells, she was a most competent & eloquent flatterer—I knew that; also she was a rank & rotten hypocrite. *That* I didn't know, but sometimes I did in a kind of a sort of a ˄limited˄ measure suspect it.

Do you remember that holy look she used to put on sometimes when there was an audience? Examine this picture, which I have cut out of the New York *American,* & see if you can get on the track of it.

Insert it here.

MISS LYON.

XIII

———

Sunday. July 11, 1909. The Twichells (Rev. J. H. & Harmony) spent yesterday & the previous day here. That made an interruption. But this letter can stand interruptions; there is no hurry about finishing it. It is my only employment; also my only diversion, except billiards—daily from 5 to 7 p.m. with Paine; for I have at last acquired a "smoker's heart," by 60 years' diligent effort in that direction, & am forbidden to make journeys, or take walks, or run up stairs, or accumulate fatigue in any other way. I have to hold still, & keep quiet. Very well, I have a talent for it.

As I have said, I reached home from Virginia April 7th.

On the 15th I gave Miss Lyon a month's notice—sent it to her room by a maid. In the forenoon.

Claude (butler) arrived at noon.

In the afternoon Miss Lyon sent me her reply by a maid. She had been married about a month, but was still called by her unwedded name, & she was still using it herself, & so it came natural to her to sign the present note in that way.

(Insert the Note)

REDDING
CONNECTICUT

April 15/09

Dear M^r. Clemens

Thank you so much for doing in so kind a way, the thing that I have been expecting.

The original letters ee that I have had charge of, are all in the house, & I shall be glad to inform Miss Clemens about the collecting which has not gone beyond the letters M^r. Howells sent.

And I now accept my dismissal from your service, to take place at any time you shall cho[o]se within the month, with thanks inexpressable, for the wonder & beauty you have brought into my life. (over)

I am

with great respect & homage.
Your secretary
Isabel V. Lyon.

The "collecting!" She had been for two years under written contract to collect my Letters, preparatory to arranging them for publication. At the end of which liberal period her "collecting" "has not gone beyond the letters Mr. Howells sent." Always when it came to shirking work she was a daisy.

A ∅ singular character, & most difficult to understand—now that at last I am acquainted with it. I learned yesterday that only 8 days before she wrote that note she not only telephoned Teresa to get Horace out of the house at once inasmuch as I was homeward bound "in a rage," but warned her to get *all* the servants out of the house before my arrival, as I was going to discharge all ˄the whole˄ of them immediately. They believed her, & packed their things. They expected a storm to break, but as I was not aware that one was required, I did not furnish it. ˄So they stayed.˄

At the very time that she was trying to ~~get~~ ˄make trouble & vexation for Clara & me by getting˄ my servants to leave me in a body, she was accepting wages under a contract in which she particularly & especially declined to have anything to do with the housekeeping. And with this ~~shabby~~ ˄rather base˄ conduct of hers still fresh in her memory, she ~~is~~ ˄was˄ able to say—without a blush, so far as I can see—those words with which she closes her note: *"with thanks inexpressable, for the wonder & beauty you have brought into my life."*

She had been serving under the 13th of March contract about a month when I discharged her on the 15th of April, therefore she was entitled to two months' pay. I paid it, signing the check myself, for I had revoked her check-signing power a while before. ~~I think~~

It was Ashcroft who brought the checks to be signed. Another gent would have credited the $200 on his notes, but Ashcroft is not that kind of a gent. What I always admired about Ashcroft, was his diligence & single-mindedness in looking out for Number One. An act which would look shabby to another gent would not look so to Ashcroft, let the act be what it might, if its object was to confer an advantage upon Number One.

Up to this time Ashcroft had rendered a weekly Statement every Saturday in accordance with the requirements of one of those 13th of March contracts (the φ ingenious one that cunningly neglected to mention any "consideration" & was therefore worthless); & he slipped in on that errand on Saturday the 17th; did the work, then slipped away again. I saw him from my windows disappearing down the road in the distance, & have never seen him since, I think.

Miss Lyon lingered along about ~~nine~~ ˄a few˄ days. She came mornings about 10, & went home to her cottage about 5. She had nothing ˄official˄ to do, for I was attending to the secretary-work myself, with Mr. Grumman the stenographer. Still, she lingered, fussing at her trunks in the attic & busying herself in various ways with her ˄own˄ affairs.

I wished she would go, but I couldn't tell her so.

The next thing that happened was, that Horace appeared. I asked him to explain the mystery of the Norfolk letter.

"How did you come to say Miss Clara had discharged you when it wasn't true?"

He was very penitent, & said he was ashamed of himself & sorry he had done it.

"Well, then, what possessed you to do it, Horace?"

Then it came out that Ashcroft *made him do it!*

"Ashcroft? How could Ashcroft make you do it, & he away down in Virginia?"

"No, Mr. Clemens, he was *here*˄, ~~th~~ On the ~~31st~~ 30th of March I had my talk with Miss Clemens, & she raised my wages to $45 & an extra evening, & ~~in the morning I told her I was satisfied, & glad to stay.~~ ˄I was satisfied. Mr. Ashcroft was not˄ here then; he had gone to New York on the noon train. Next morning—31st—you & Miss Clemens went to New York by the 10. 31, & Mr. Ashcroft came up by the noon train & got to the house about 2. He told me I was going to be discharged,˄, & I'd better quit before I was discharged. He said Miss Clemens was going to discharge all the servants. He told me to write a letter to you, & he made me say 'discharged.' That was his word. I said it wasn't right, because I hadn't been discharged, but he said *use that word,* & he made me use it, & said it would be worth a month's wages to me."

"Why, this is splendid; it's like a romance! Go on."

"Mr. Clemens, I don't think I would have sent that letter that way, I would have changed it."

"Why didn't you?"

"I couldn't, because as soon as it was finished he took it."

"Took it away with him?"

"Yes, sir. I didn't see it any more. He left for New York next morning, April 1, by the 7 o'clock train."

Isn't it interesting? And isn't it just like that cheap villain in a seventh-rate play?

On the 2ᵈ I took Ashcroft with me to lunch with two ladies at the Hotel Gotham, & he was very sweet & nice, & the ladies liked him ever so much, & he had that letter in his pocket all the time, & was under contract, since March 13ᵗʰ, to look after my business matters & take good care of them. We joined Mr. Rogers & the others on the boat at mid-afternoon, & Ashcroft, with that letter in his pocket, dined with those people, swapped anecdotes & other sociabilities with them, & in these & in all ways allowed them to treat him just as if he were a gentlemen. And three of them were fellow-countrymen of his—Englishmen: Mr. Broughton & Mr. Coe, sons-in-law of Mr. Rogers, & Mr. Lancaster of Liverpool, the city Ashcroft was born in.

Clear till bedtime Ashcroft, was with that letter in his pocket, was as tenderly & watchfully & affectionately attentive to my slightest needs or desires as ever; & next day in Norfolk it was the same; & I think it was late afternoon of that day that he came into my room looking greatly surprised, with Horace's open letter in his hand, & said—

"It's from Horace—Miss Clara has discharged him!"

Isn't it romantic! Isn't it stagy & charming!

Horace looked in again on the 26ᵗʰ of April, the day that restored Jean to me, & we had another talk. He is a nice boy, a simple farmer lad, & without guile. His mother says he cried the most of the day following the spiriting-away of his letter, for he wanted to keep his place. I asked Horace to go home & write the history of the letter for me; & not to deal in generalities, but in particulars. He did so.

Insert his letter

Mr S. L. Clemens:--

Dear Sir:--

Referring to our conversation of the 26th ulto. in which you asked me to give you a written statement concerning the conversation between Mr R. W. Ashcroft, and myself, in which I was advised ˄(by Ashcroft)˄ to write my letter to you, stating my discharge.

On Mar 14th. I asked Mʳ Ashcroft for an advance in salary and more time off. He told me I would have to talk with Miss Lyon—During Mr Ashcroft and my conversation, "he say's." (Horace no one expected to see you here as long as this). (I say's) Why how is that? (He says! I suppose you know there is going to be a change here.) I told him, I was not aware of it. (He say's. Miss Clare Clemens wants to run her own house.) He say's I tell you this so that you may know what to expect.) I asked him if he thought it would make any difference in my position. ¶ (He said, Miss Clara, has *hated* you from the very first of you begining work here˄, and was determined to FIRE you out, but Miss Lyon wouldn't stand for it. He, (Mr Ashcroft) then said Miss Clara even went to her father and demanded of him that I should not remain in their house, and you said you were satisfied with me. So I was not let know anything about it. ¶ Mr Ashcroft then said (But of coarse she will not have you now.) I then made this remark˄. "Had I known˄ that Miss Clara had such a dislike for me, I never would have remained under her roof."

¶ Up to that time Mr Clemens I knew nothing of the troubles of your house, and˄ from that time on Mr Ashcroft, gave me the impression that I would be discharged by Miss Clara, as was her intention to do with all the help. So he said he advised every-one of the help to leave before they got kicked out. ¶ Soon after my talk with Mr Ashcroft regarding salary & time off I spoke to Miss Lyon about it. (She said) "I have nothing to say about it, you'l have to see what Miss Clara says about it.

On Miss Clara return home to Redding I spoke to her about my salary and time. I didn't explain to her as I should have done, that Miss Lyon had promised to advance my salary until I should receive (Sixty dollars) $60.⁰⁰ per month, but know˄ing˄ or) at'least as I had been told her feelings towards me, I thought it of little use to even ask for the position, although I did ask her for more time off and Fifty Dollars ($50.⁰⁰) per month.

She, Miss Clara, said Mr Clemens would give me Forty five ($45.⁰⁰) per Mo. but would rather let me go than to pay $50.⁰⁰ per mo.

The following day Mr Ashcroft, say's to me "I hear you got discharged." I told him I didn't know as it was exactually a discharge, simpley Miss Clara and I didnot come to any exact agreement, on either salary or time off. (He say's) "Didn't I tell you it was her intentions to discharge all the help." And I knew of no reason why Mr Ashcroft shouldn't know the plans of your house as he was supposed to be your Acting Secretary.

He, (Mr Ashcroft,) then said (Under my advise you write ˄a letter˄ to Mr Clemens and tell him, you have been discharged by Miss Clemens and I will give it to him, and have him sign a check and will send it to you, of which he did for a full month salary, and which I received, and returned it to him (Mr Ashcroft,) upon his return to ~~home~~ ˄Redding˄ from Norfolk Via. with Mr Clemens, and I told him I only wanted what was due me.

Now concerning the remarks Mr Ashcroft claims I made about Miss Clara, I never had any occasion to pass even the simplest remark: for Miss Clara had alway's used me like a perfect Lady should in all her dealing's with me. I was never called to serve her in her rooms or in any part of the house but what her appearance was alway's presentable. I never heard her express a vulgar expression of any kind, she never even gave me a look nor word that would give me the impression she was not satisfied with me and I am sure I had no occasion to pass any remarks and I *never* did and if Mr Ashcroft claims I did, he tells an untruth. I am sure I have manly principal enough about me to know when I am dealing with a lady. And I am sure the respect I received from both your-self, and Miss Clara has always been both respectifull & honorable.

Trusting that after considering the position I was in you will see I was greatly influenced, and hoping that both yourself & Miss Clemens, will not judge me to harshly, I beg to remain

A true & worthy friend
Horace

XIV

Miss Lyon had long been Supreme High Chief, but Horace's second paragraph indicates that Ashcroft had been promoted, & was now sharing the throne with her—an arrangement which I was ignorant of, & about which I had not been consulted. And so, the butler ignores ciphers like Clara & me when he wants his wages raised, goes to Ashcroft about it. In turn, Ashcroft tells him he will "have to talk with Miss Lyon." Why, hang him, Miss Lyon had formally & distinctly & haughtily retired from her housekeeping-sovereignty just the day before—had he forgotten it already?

You notice, this matter of Horace's was being discussed by these three servants of ours sixteen days before Clara & I ever heard of it. The Lyon-Ashcroft impudence has not its ~~mate~~ fellow anywhere; it is a new kind.

In Horace's third paragraph Ashcroft gives wings to his imagination, & lies freely, briskly, glibly, but not with good art, as it seems to me. He has talent, but he is ignorant & does not know how to use it. I could have done it better. "Miss Lyon wouldn't stand for it!" Isn't it good? The dear little heroine! why, Howells, you can just *see* her,˄— plucky little ~~hou~~ clothes-pin˄—standing erect & gallant, between that coal-oil derrick & harm!

Observe, *she* wouldn't stand for it!—which naturally settles it. Apparently we couldn't dismiss a servant $\phi_{\wedge}$if ~~she that for~~ that uncompleted little three-weeks' foetus declined to "stand for it."

Horace mentions, in his fourth paragraph, that Ashcroft advised "every one of the help to leave before they got kicked out." It is even so. He rang them all in, & delivered that remark to them in person.

It sometimes seems to me, that in secretly & slyly & surreptitiously conspiring with our servants, under the hospitable shelter of our own roof, & trying to get them to leave us, & thus put us to great inconvenience & discomfort, Ashcroft was not quite loyal to the contract he had signed earlier in the month, & which bound him to look out for my interests, & take care of them to the best of his ability. Howells, his conduct almost smacks of treachery.

Horace closes his letter with the suggestion that he was "greatly influenced." Yes, that is what happened.

It was a bright pair, a sharp pair, an unusually clever pair. But not always. Sometimes they made a mistake. Sometimes they anticipated conditions which apparently were on the point of arriving, apparently were sure to arrive, but *hadn't* arrived. In the present case *absolute sovereignty* over me was apparently on the verge of arriving, but it hadn't quite arrived. They ought to have waited until they were firmly seated in the sovereignty before they undertook to drive the servants away & replace them with minions of their own selection.

XIV

I have left out certain things that happened in March. One was a letter which I wrote to Clara on the 11th; I will insert it by & by. Another was a matter concerning the Safe Deposit box in the Produce Exchange. There were two keys to the box—both in the hands of my pets. Under Clara's persuasions I revoked their authority to use the keys, & took them into my own possession.

Next, Clara wanted the contents of the box examined, to see if the securities, contracts, etc., were still there. So I sent a key to Mr. Dunneka, of the Harper & Brothers' business-staff, together with a written authorization to use it, & asked him to overhaul the box's contents & send me a list of the same. *I* hadn't a list. My secretary never kept a list of *anything*. She was always going-to, but never did. She never knew which stocks paid dividends, nor when the dividends were due. She was always going-to inform herself (during 7 years,) but she never did. In some regards she was the most remarkable secretary that ever secretaried in this world.

However, it turned out that Ashcroft had a list of the box's contents. He is a shrewd, & sharp, & careful, & watchful, & observant creature, & can be depended upon to have a list of the contents of any box, or cabinet, or closet, or bank vault, or stable, or rat hole or bawdy house or cesspool he can get access to, by fair means or foul. He went with Dunneka, & took his list along.

Dunneka reported to me, March 12, by letter, enclosing a list of the box's contents, & saying the contents agreed with Ashcroft's list.

Now lo & behold, the list failed to mention the organization-papers of the "Mark Twain" Company!" It mentioned the *stock,* & the fact that all the 50 shares were present, & all in ~~my name~~ my control: that is, 45 in my name, & three in Ashcroft's (transfer signed), & 2 in Miss Lyon's (transfer signed). But there was no mention of those organization papers.

I was troubled. One—or two—or three months earlier—I couldn't remember when—Ashcroft had come to me with some documents to sign. And he was in a hurry. He was always in a hurry when documents were to be signed. I was going to read these documents—there were three of them—but he said it wasn't worth the trouble; that they were merely organization-papers of the Mark Twain Company, purely perfunctory, & worded according ~~to the unvarying~~ to the stereotyped form furnished by the statute-book.

So I signed them.

I don't know why I supposed they would be kept in the Safe Deposit, but I had that notion. When they failed to appear in Dunneka's list, I was uneasy.

Uneasy, I didn't quite know why. ~~But I had a vague notion that~~ Except that I had noticed the phrase *"real estate"* in one of those organization-papers when I was signing it. It didn't startle me at the time, but it did now. What business had the Mark Twain Company with real estate? Its business was supposably confined to ˄my˄ literary copyrights.

Very well, I was uneasy. Then another thing happened; Dunneka sent me a private oral message to this effect: Do you think it safe to sign the transfers on the back of your ~~stocks~~ securities & *trust an outsider with the key?"*

Of course that was an insane thing$ to do,, & I asked Ashcroft if I had done it. He said yes. I asked him why he had allowed me to do it? He said he had felt, at the time, that it was not wise, but that as I wanted to do it he could not very well object.

Pretty soon I went down to New York, & Ashcroft & I went to the vault, & he sat opposite me at a table while I took out the ~~papers~~ ˄securities,˄ one by one, & scratched my name from the transfer-blank. I was hoping, but not quite expecting, to find the organization-papers, but they were not there. I searched, & searched, & searched, examining each & every fold of each & every paper, over & over again—to no purpose. Ashcroft sat there smiling his gentle Memphistophelian smile, & never saying a word. I believed he knew what I was after. When my search was ended, I believed he had stolen the document, from under my nose, & had it upon his person. It was not a long-lived belief. We went to 44 Wall & I took John Larkin privately aside & asked him if the Mark Twain corporation had any authority over my real estate? He said no—over nothing but the copyrights.

So I was relieved & content. Also, sorry I had suspected Ashcroft.

Now we will jump back into April, & cavort around in that month again for a while. On Shakspeare's birthday Clara went to Mr. Rogers's house, 3 East 78ᵗʰ street &

talked our matters over with him. In the course of the day he wrote me from the Standard Oil offices, as follows:

(Insert letter dated April 23)

In my own talk with Mr. Rogers he had told me his plan of procedure. He said he would see that the examination was conducted with perfect fairness to all concerned; that he would put the matter in the hands of a man who had been in his employ twenty-five years, & had been busy at this kind of work all that time; that if there was a single instance of crookedness in the Ashcroft accounts, that man would find it—it couldn't be hidden from him.

You notice what he says:

"I think I have read between the lines. In the last two or three years I had my suspicion of things."

You note also what he says about Clara's statement of the case:

"Her story was very convincing."

And yet, only six days later, according to that Croton reservoir of oratorical veracity, Ashcroft, "Mr. Rogers seems to be of the same opinion that many of your other friends are, viz., that the ghastly treatment accorded to Miss Lyon during the past few weeks by a member of your family is a mightily poor return for the way in which she has, since Mrs. Clemens's death, looked after you, your daughters & your affairs."

For instance, the way in which she has looked after my invalid daughter Jean—by keeping her exiled among strangers many months after her health was restored & she should have been in the comfort & shelter of her own home.

"As you have already stated, the charges emanated from a brain diseased with envy, malice & jealousy," etc.

No, I didn't say it. That language is much too fine for me. I wouldn't ever be able to soar to those ~~gaudy~~ ₍glittering₎ heights. What I said to Clara was set down in just plain ordinary human English, without any Ashcroftian rainbows & firecrackers: I said she had allowed her mind to be poisoned by prejudiced friends. That was it. I read it to Ashcroft before I mailed it. I read it to him to show him that I was doing the best I could to defend Miss Lyon & modify Clara's feeling against her. Why, Howells, I *never* could have said "emanated"—it is too fine, too exquisite, too voluminous, too ~~aris~~ literary, too aristocratic. I would have used a humbler form; I would have said it squirted from her brain, or something like that. And I wouldn't have said "diseased" brain—it is much too lofty, much too ornate₍,₎ I would have said rotten.

And of course I ~~d~~₍w₎ouldn't have said "envy" & "jealousy," because they wouldn't mean anything in that connection₍,₎ you can see it yourself. What was there about Miss Lyon for Clara to envy? Why should she envy my housekeeper? She might as well envy the cook. And what was there about Miss Lyon for Clara to be jealous of? Howells, I wish I may be damned before my time if I can guess. Clara is young, Clara is beautiful, Clara is highly gifted, Clara is accomplished, Clara's intimates are the choicest people in the land: why should she be jealous of this talentless, positionless, inconsequential poor old domestic?

Oh, well, I suppose Ashcroft's ~~muse~~ fired off his remark about envy & jealousy not because it had any sense in it, but because it had a stately sound—which it *has* Howells, there is no denying it. It fairly thrills you when you come upon it all of a sudden. Ashcroft really has a remarkable ear for sound, though none for sense. And he is refined, in his phrasing, beyond any other writer of our time, I think. ~~Always far beyond me.~~ Always he ~~says organs of transmission where I say guts.~~ says "Ah, me," where others say "Oh, hell."

I think it is time to insert his grand letter again. The oftener I read it the more I enjoy it & the more precious it becomes to me. Howells, it hasn't its match anywhere. It stands in a class by itself: it is *the* Literary ~~Emetic~~ ₍Vomit₎ of the Ages. What could he have been feeding on? What do *you* think?

(Insert letter of Apl 29 again)

April 29, 1909.

Dear Mr. Clemens:

I saw Mr. Rogers at his office this morning, at his request. His auditor will be here in a day or two, and will go over your accounts and affairs for the last two years; so that, in a very few days, your mind will be set at ease on that score, and your present worries lessened by the knowledge that your affairs have been honestly and conscientiously looked after by Miss Lyon and me.

Mr. Rogers seems to be of the same opinion that many of your other friends are, viz. that the ghastly treatment accorded to Miss Lyon during the past few weeks by a member of your family is a mightily poor return for the way in which she has, since Mrs. Clemens' death, looked after you, your daughters and your affairs. While it is, of course, impossible for her calumniator to make any reparation, I and other of your friends trust that you will, in this matter, uphold your reputation for fairness and justice, and make what reparation you yourself can. As you have already stated, the charges emanated from a brain diseased with envy, malice and jealousy, and it is only when one forgets this fact that one views them seriously. However, irresponsibly conceived or not, they have been and are serious in their effect upon your comfort and well-being, and upon that of others, and must therefore be viewed from that standpoint.

There is no reason on earth why the rest of your days should be spent in an atmosphere of artificiality, restraint and self-sacrifice; and, while I don't suppose that the happiness that was your lot during the last six months of 1908 will recur in all its fulness and entirety, still I trust that you will, regardless of your philosophical theories, exercise your prerogatives of fatherhood and manhood in a way that will be productive of the greatest benefit to yourself. This I say regardless of what effect the expression of the sentiment may have on my relationships with you.

I am,
Yours, most sincerely,

R. W. Ashcroft

XV

Ashcroft was bitter against Clara, as it is sufficiently indicated by his letter. After I dismissed his wife on the 15th of April she still lingered, day after day, still haunted the place, still infested it with her unwelcome presence, still tried to let on that our relations were as pleasant as ever, whereas the insolences & impertinences of her contract of March 13th were rankling in me & the sight of her exasperated me.

She would come up from her house at ten every morning & occupy her room till late in the afternoon. Now & then she would sail into my room, artificially radiant & girlish with something killingly funny to tell me, & would stand by my bed & detail it with all sorts of captivating airs & graces & bogus laughter—& get no response. Seeing she wasn't going to be asked to sit down, she would presently supply the defect & cover her embarrassment by slumping into a chair as if overcome by her humorous emotions. I found it useless to wait for her to take a hint from my unsympathetic attitude & vacate the place: I always had to *tell* her I was busy & wanted to be alone.

Once in a burst of affectionate regard she started to tell me what a sacrifice she had made for my sake in getting married: that she had not wanted to marry, but saw it was the only way that she & Ashcroft could save me from depression in my lonely estate, & take of me the watchful & devoted care I needed—& she was going on and on; but I interrupted her, not over-gently, & said I had had enough of that offensive nonsense already from Ashcroft, & didn't want any more of it. I said the pair had done a silly thing, with a purpose in view—"God knows what, *I* can't guess!"—& it couldn't be palmed off on me as having been done for *my* sake.

I think she kept coming until a couple of days before Jean's arrival on the 26th. She spent a good deal of time in the attic among the accumulated trunks, & said she was removing her things to her house; also that she was arranging her secretarial matters so that her successor would not find them in disorder, but systematised. A very proper duty & a necessary thing to do. This being the case, it goes without saying that she shirked it; shirked it utterly, leaving her secretarial affairs in an almost miraculous condition of confusion.

She left my manuscripts in the same confusion—dumped helter-skelter into drawers. They had been in her loose custody so long that portions of several of them had been misplaced & lost.

Clara wanted to examine her trunks. She demanded her keys, & got them. I was discomforted by this; in fact a good deal distressed, & I persuaded Clara—much against her will—to spare her that humiliation.

It was a mistake. The trunks should have been searched. Miss Lyon had an almost insane fondness for pretty things, dainty things, jewels, trinkets, bricabrack, & so on; and—....however the search was not made, & I am glad of it, at this late day. Provided she got away with no mementos, heirlooms, things sacred from association.

It turned out, later, that she did filch one such thing—a string of large carnelian beads; beads worn, long & long ago, by Mrs. Clemens.

Paine was familiar with the incident. By my request he has he put it upon paper—as follows: for possible use by my lawyer—as follows:

(Paine's letter to Lark)

Incident of the Carnelian Necklace.

———

From letter to Mr. W Lark, dated June 7, 1909.

———

When Miss Clemens was examining the contents of certain trunks in the attic here with Miss Lyon, in preparation for the departure of the latter, she happened to remember having seen, in an old cabinet up there, some large carnelian beads—a most unusual necklace—unique in fact—unstrung. This necklace had been the property of Mrs. Clemens, and was highly valued. Miss Lyon had also seen the necklace. Miss Clemens now went to the cabinet, and found the beads were gone. She turned to Miss Lyon, and said,

"Where are those carnelian beads that were in this cabinet some time ago?"

Miss Lyon, looking somewhat startled, replied,

"Mr. Wark (a friend of the family) took them, when we were packing, in New York." (That is to say, twelve months earlier.)

Miss Clemens replied,

"It was not in New York, but here, that I saw them a few weeks ago."

To this Miss Lyon made no reply whatever, and was unable to return Miss Clemens's look. Miss Dorothea Gilder, and Katie Leary, Miss Clemens's maid, were present. Miss Clemens did not mention the necklace again for perhaps twenty minutes, and then said;

"Miss Lyon, I wish you'd find that necklace for me."

Miss Lyon said,

"I?"

"Yes," Miss Clemens said, "You!"

Again Miss Lyon could not answer, and the subject was dropped. Miss Lyon then removed her effects from the Clemens household, and made no further mention of the necklace to any member of it, but gave it out to acquaintances that she had "even been accused of stealing a carnelian necklace."

Some two weeks ago, a housemaid named Teresa and her husband Giuseppe—the latter Mr. Clemens's cook—were leaving Redding for New York. Before leaving returning to the city, Teresa visited Miss Lyon, presumably to bid her good-bye. Next day she saw Katie Leary in New York City, and said to her,

"Miss Lyon says 'tell Miss Clemens she will find the carnelian necklace in a trunk in the attic.[,]'"

Teresa added,

"I asked Miss Lyon if she meant the green necklace, and she said, 'No, the beads I mean are like this one,' and she took a large carnelian bead from her work-basket, and held it up for me to see."

Miss Clemens and Katie Leary came to Redding a day or two later, and upon examining the only unlocked trunk in the attic, they found, in a pasteboard box, the carnelian necklace. But it had not been there long; Katie Leary herse lf had put the pasteboard box in the trunk; it had contained nothing but a few artificial flowers; and the necklace, instead of being unstrung, ⟨(as formerly,)⟩ was strung on a piece of new green wrapping-twine.

Thinking the matter out, the following conclusions seem inevitable: that Miss Lyon had the necklace in her possession at the time of the examination by Miss Clemens; that she had taken the unstrung beads and had them in her work-basket; that she had strung them, and had overlooked one bead; that as time passed, she was possessed with a terror that she was to be arrested for theft; that she was afraid to destroy the beads and decided to return them; that she got some one connected with the household ⟨[[Teresa?]]⟩ to place them where they were subsequently found; that in her disordered state of mind, due to fear and the use of drugs and liquor, she forgot that the beads had not been strung when she carried them away; that even after the beads were restored, she was filled with a fear that they might lie there in that old trunk for years, and that she was still in no less danger of prosecution because of their disappearance, and that she confided the matter to Teresa, because Teresa was on friendly terms with the members of the Clemens household. It does not seem likely, however, that Teresa was the one who restored the beads, or could have known positively of their theft, for she would hardly have been likely to have invented the incident of the extra bead and work-basket. That has a sound of actuality, and would seem to indicate that the beads were restored by another hand; perhaps by Teresa's husband, who was a favorite with Miss Lyon, or by Miss Lyon's own husband, who had the run of the household for two weeks after Miss Lyon herself had gone.

⟨It⟩ is a wee little event, yet it is a tragedy, for it stabs a character to death. The Social Secretary & Ornament was a thief! This fact was established, beyond cavil or question. I had to concede it myself, strongly & persistently as I had believed in & championed her honesty before, in my disputes with Clara. Since ~~she~~ ⟨Miss Lyon⟩ would steal ⟨hallowed⟩ keepsakes,⟨ sacred memorials,⟩ might there be anything she *wouldn't* steal?

Ashcroft's wee little shabby performance regarding Horace was a tragedy, too, for it exposed *his* character for good & all, & killed it. Two character-suicides in one family inside of two months!⟨

XVI

On the great Cleaning-Up Day, March 13th, Miss Lyon, as per signed & sealed contract, had retired from ~~all coarse~~ all vulgar & useful activities, & had become high-throned Social Secretary & Society Ornament, with nothing to do but charm the guests & collect her augmented salary. She would need the check-book no longer; so, next day I told her to cancel her power of attorney with the banks & leave the signing of checks to me in future.

A month later (April 15), as I have already remarked, I dismissed her.

Five days later (April 20), Ashcroft brought me a penciled paper, in the loggia, & said he had directed Mr. Lounsbury to smooth the roadway around the "oval," & this was his ₐ(Lounsbury's)ₐ estimate of the cost—$54. Ashcroft ₐsaid heₐ had told him to go ahead. He asked me if that was right. I said yes. Afterward I wondered what business *he* ₐAshcroftₐ had to be meddling with the road. It looked like an impertinence. Then I examined the road, & found that it needed no repairing & that there was no occasion to waste money on it. But I found a place beyond the oval that needed repairing, & needed it very much. I went over it with Lounsbury, who said the cost would be $250. I told him to let the oval entirely alone, & proceed with this work—which he did. When Ashcroft next arrived from New York he ~~inquired~~ asked Lounsbury who had authorized him to mend that road? Lounsbury told him. Ashcroft said, "Go on with it, *if you want to take the risk.*"

Lounsbury couldn't understand this, ₐextraordinary remark.ₐ He reported it to me, & I couldn't understand it. It had a meaning, but at that time it was too deep for me.

April 29ᵗʰ Ashcroft wrote his already-several-times-quoted letter.

May arrived.

Along in the first days of May, I learned something that troubled me a little. Mr. Rogers had said he would put the ~~inspection~~ ₐinvestigationₐ of Miss Lyon's accounts in the hands of a man in the Standard Oil who had done nothing but that kind of work for twenty-five years; & that if there was anything crooked in the accounts he would be certain to find it, the Ashcrofts would not be able to conceal it from him.

The thing that was troubling me now, was, that Mr. Rogers had put the investigation into the hands of a woman! It was his second secretary, Miss Watson. I knew her. I believed the Ashcrofts would wring her heart with the cruel injuries I had heaped upon them, & make her their devoted friend & champion, instead of judge. They would "explain" everything to her satisfaction. In the meantime I should have no chance to explain their explanations.

However, I was not very much disturbed, for Miss Watson's report would have to be laid before Mr. Rogers, finally; then if there were any crookednesses, I believed he would be absolutely certain to find them.

~~Just at this time~~ ₐAbout the 9ᵗʰ or 10ᵗʰₐ Paine & I started to New York on business, & Lounsbury drove us to the railway station. On the way, reference was made to the cost of the rehabilitation of Miss Lyon's house—$1500. Lounsbury said—

"Fifteen hundred? Why, it cost thirty-five hundred!"

I said no, it couldn't be so, because Miss Lyon had given me the exact figures a day or two before Christmas—fa shade less than $1500—& had told me that the work was all finished & that that was the sum spent upon it.

But Lounsbury held his ground. He got out his deadly memorandum book, in which he sets down everything, & from it he furnished the figures, the names, & the dates. The dates showed that Miss Lyon had spent about $2,000 of my money on her house *before* I had offered to assist her with a loan. This was plain, simple, stark-naked *theft*.

I did not find Mr. Rogers at the Standard Oil, but I gave the figures to Miss Harrison,

Mr. Rogers's first secretary,, & said I should intrude only this once upon the ~~Examination,~~ ‸Investigation,‸ but I would like to have these figures placed before Miss Watson. They probably made Miss Watson pretty sick—later it had that look. And they probably made Miss Watson detest me—with a little Ashcroftian help in that direction; later it had that look.

~~About May 25~~

They gave the Ashcrofts a most difficult nut to crack. We now have the evidence of ~~his~~ Ashcroft's attempts to crack it—attempts which sorrowfully failed. By & by I will exhibit those attempts, for they are interesting. So also is the letter to Mr. Rogers which accompanies them. If he saw the letter & Mr. Ashcroft's abortive figures, he passed from this life knowing Miss Lyon for what she was—a pretty hardy & very deliberate thief.

If Mr. Rogers had lived he would have settled the case privately. It could still ‸— even then—‸ be settled privately if wisely handled. I put it into the hands of John B. Stanchfield.

I speak of it as a "case." It was become that, by this time. Originally it wasn't a "case," it was an inquiry; an inquiry instituted to satisfy Clara; an inquiry from which the Ashcrofts would emerge with characters pure ‸and‸ clean, white as snow, as I believed & proclaimed; an inquiry which would cover Clara with confusion & the Ashcrofts with glory.

But that stage had had its day, & was gone by. Things had happened—things like the Norfolk episode, which revealed Ashcroft as a very very small liar, sneak & swindler, & made me desire to get rid of him; also to get rid of the Ashcroft neighborship. So I had a "case." Mr. Ashcroft must be invited to ~~resign~~ cancel the Mark Twain Company contract of March 13, & his wife must be invited to deed her house & ground back to me.

About the 25ᵗʰ of May, Paine & I went down to New York. Stanchfield wanted the examination of checks & vouchers transferred to a *man,*—a public & responsible accountant, ‸,‸ incorruptible by injured-servant tears & maudlin sentimentality.‸ So Paine & I went to the Standard Oil, & I delivered my message to ~~her~~ ‸Miss Watson‸ in one of the private offices. She was very frosty; whereby I knew Miss Lyon had been crying down the back of her neck & saying damaging things about me; & that Miss Watson was further incensed against me because those deadly figures had damaged the Ashcrofts in her estimation, & she had failed to find any way to *un*damage them.

She was just a little inconsistent. In the beginning she remarked, gloomily, that the examination had cost her ten days of exhausting & frightful labor; whereas toward the end of her talk she remarked that the labor had been very light, because the ~~accounts &~~ vouchers & checks tallied so well that it was but little trouble to check them ~~off.~~ ‸up.‸

"Check them ~~off.~~ ‸up.‸" That was her expression. She used it again, a month later, when she sent her bill:

Evidently she thought I might dispute the bill—otherwise there was no occasion to
make that opening remark. I sent the check, & observed that I was aware that Mr. Rogers
had made the remark. Which was true. But he didn't make it in *that* form; he didn't say
"this office," he spoke of a *person*—a he, not a she—& he was jesting at the time. At his
dwelling-house, speaking seriously, he had said, "Our man will not charge you as much
as a public accountant."

When Stanchfield's expert took hold of the matter *he* didn't find it so very simple
& easy, he found it considerably tangled & obscure in places, & not bearing any strong
resemblance to a "checking-up" picnic.

He worked over it a couple of weeks, translated it into good clear figures, ʃ put his
fateful finger on the sore places, & charged me only $250; & when he was done. . . . but
I haven't come to that, yet.

XVII

———

Leaving the Standard Oil, Paine & I went chatting along up town in the Subway,
& got out at Astor Place. The talk was to this effect: since Miss Lyon had made so free
with my check-book in rehabilitating her house, perhaps we might find other instances
of this license besides those exposed by Mr. Lounsbury if we should inaugurate a hunt.
Paine believed we could discover cases of "graft," at any rate. He mentioned one which
had the look of a certainty: he was with Miss Lyon one day at Boiajin's (the Armenian
rug-dealer) when she bought a ninety-dollar rug, & borrowed half of the money from
Paine & said she would send the other half to the dealer by check. I will anticipate by

remarking that the investigation-discloses revealed the fact, a few weeks later, that she had kept her word: she had paid the $45 with my check.

Then there was the Strohmeyer case. Miss Lyon had employed Strohmeyer to refit & re-upholster a couple of car-loads of furniture for us, & she said he was so grateful for her custom that he had rebuilt & perfected a large old mahogany table for her whi for nothing, & had told her he would have charged any one else $65 for this work. We went to Strohmeyer & asked him if he had repaired the table, & he—innocent man!—suspecting nothing, told us all about it. He said it was a very fine old table, but just a ruin when it came to him. It was as good as new when he was done with it. He produced his work-shop's itemised bill—half a page of details—whereby it appeared that he had paid his workmen $33 for the work, & that he had charged Miss Lyon only $10. At the bottom of the bill the $10 was acknowledged. About this time he began to grow suspicious & a little nervous, & said no, he wouldn't have charged a stranger $65, but probably only $45. This didn't mend the matter much, since it was a confession that he had given Miss Lyon $33 worth of work for $10—a very plain case of graft. Paine remarked privately that it had been perfectly natural & characteristic in Miss Lyon to lie about the matter & boast of getting the work for nothing when she had really paid ten dollars for it. He said she *couldn't* tell the truth in any circumstances whatsoever—she had never learned how.

Strohmeyer caught the sinister drift of our inquiries, & he was a good deal embarrassed, & said perhaps he had charged Miss Lyon the full rate—yes, undoubtedly! The ledger would show. The ledger was brought. Unhappily it confirmed the $10. But also unhappily, it didn't stop there. There were several entries, & I asked leave to examine them. It couldn't gracefully be excused. There was a bedstead & a mattrass—for whom? Miss Lyon's mother. It went to Summerfield. (Pure waste of stolen money; our attic¢ was well stocked with bedsteads & mattrasses in perfect condition—there was no occasion for Miss Lyon to buy such things.) And there was a seventy-dollar chair. My, but that was sumptuous! Whose palace was it for? Miss Lyon's. The several items in the ledger-account, bunched together, aggregated $115. At that time Miss Lyon had not been invited to borrow money of me. Evidently she was a capable provider for herself, when unwatched.

Next, Paine & I thought we would look into Miss Lyon's habit of delaying the payment of bills—if she really had that lazy & vicious habit. By letter we ‚had already‚ asked two or three of the big department-stores to go back over their books a year or two years, & tell me the a◊ dates when bills were mailed, & the dates when they were paid. ‚Two or three had responded in the early days of the month (May.)‚

I had already ‚previously‚ come across one such bill. It arrived when Miss Lyon had been gone about a week. It was 3 months old, & had a wail in it. To-wit:

201

First rendered February 1.

L F 566   *Statement.*   MAY 1 1909

New York, _____ 190_

Mr. S. L. Clemens

Redding

Ct.

To B. Altman & Co.
Fifth Avenue
34th and 35th Streets.

TERMS { SETTLEMENTS REQUIRED THE
FIRST PART OF EACH MONTH.

To Mdse   13 95

PAID
may 3

Unpaid bill 3 months old.

Kindly favor us with a remittance & greatly oblige
Yours respectfully
B. Altman & Co.

I paid it by check, May 3.

The new record rendered by Altman at my request showed payments delayed 3 months, & even 5 months:

It was enough to make a person want to wring that indolent creature's neck. I did want to do it, but I refrained, on account of the talk it would make.

The contracts with architect & builder—for the building of Stormfield—were signed before President Roosevelt's infamous panic broke out & paralysed all industries in the land & made money very difficult to get, even for common necessities; but for once in my life I had been deep & wily & cautious: I had placed in bank in a sacred deposit by itself, the sum required to pay those contracts in full, as they matured. Nevertheless, without shadow of excuse Miss Lyon kept the contractors out of their money until in some cases their men said they must quit, & hunt for work where they could get their pay, for their families were running sho[r]t of food to eat.

How do I explain Miss Lyon's conduct? I could not have explained it in those days, but I can explain it now: in the first place she was too indolent to draw the checks, & in the second, the muscle in her chest that does duty for a heart, is nothing but a potatoe. She has no feeling. She cares for no one but herself; even her ostentatious affection for her mother goes to pieces under even a slight pressure.

Wanamaker's report is a spectacle!

Bill Rendered	Feb. 1/06	50.34	Paid	Feb. 13
" "	Mar. 1/06	17.13	"	Mar. 26 *-25 day*
" "	Apr. 1/06	5.85 } *— 50 days*		May 23 *22 "*
" "	May 1/06	26.02 }	"	
" "	June 1/06	31.27	"	June 14 *-13 "*
" "	July 1/06	50.23 } *— 2 months + 10 days*		
" "	Aug. 1/06	8.05 } *— 40 days*		
" "	Sept 1/06	6.00 }	"	Sept 11
" "	Oct. 1/06	24.12	"	Oct. 16 *-15 day*
" "	Nov. 1/06	44.55 } *— 3 months + 1 week*		
" "	Dec. 1/06	36.76 } *— 2" " ".. 6 ".*		
" "	Jan. 1/07	36.83 }	"	Feb. 8 *-37 day*
" "	Feb. 1/07	15.20 } *— 4 months*		
" "	Mar. 1/07	116.37 } *— 3 "*		
" "	Apr. 1/07	8.88 } *— 2 "" *		May 31
" "	May 1/07	20.53 } *1 month*		
" "	June 1/07	62.34 } *3 weeks*		June 20
" "	July 1/07	77.50	"	July 19 *-18 day*
" "	Aug. 1/07	52.40	"	Aug. 22 *21 "*
" "	Oct. 1/07	15.00	"	Oct. 17 *16 "*
" "	Nov. 1/07	19.93	"	Nov. 11 *10 "*
" "	Dec. 1/07	128.97	"	Dec. 16 *15 "*
" "	Jan. 1/08	10.00	"	Jan. 9 *- 8 "*
" "	Feb. 1/08	126.14	"	Feb. 8 *— 7 "*
" "	Mar. 1/08	66.94 *1 month*	"	Apr. 4
" "	Apr. 1/08	1.40	"	Apr. 27 *-26 "*
" "	May 1/08	9.44	"	May 20 *19 "*
" "	June 1/08	119.55	"	June 5
" "	July 1/08	97.35	"	July 23 *22 "*
" "	Oct. 1/08	107.50	"	Oct. 5
" "	Nov. 1/08	115.66	"	Nov. 4
" "	Dec. 1/08	.25.22	"	Dec. 8
" "	Jan. 1/09	51.85	"	Jan. 20 *-19 "*
" "	Feb. 1/09	32.73	"	Feb. 16 *15 "*

Samuel L. Clemens,
Redding, Ct.

The first thing I ever noticed about Miss Lyon was her incredible laziness. Laziness was my own specialty, & I did not like this competition. Dear me, I was to find out ‸ in the course of time,‸ that in the matter of laziness I was a runaway train on a down grade & she a-standing still. At my very laziest I could hear myself whiz, when *she* was around.

I will add Putnam's report, now, & close with it; ‸a supplementary from Altman;‸ with the remark that as a delayer, & a conscienceless one, a pitiful one, a shameless one, Miss Lyon stands elected:

209   Mr. S. L. Clemens.   *Altman*   *(Concealed) Delays*

Date.	Tuxedo Park,	Redding Conn.,	21-5th Ave.	When paid.	
Sept. 1907	24.07		3.33	Oct. 17, 1907	*6 days*
Oct. 1907	9.95		76.76	Nov. 25, 1907	*7 weeks*
Nov. 1907			137.69	Jan. 9, 1908	*2¼ months*
Dec. 1907			165.09	Jan. 9, 1908	*40 days*
Jan. 1908			123.36	Feb. 21, 1908	*7 weeks*
Feb. 1908			212.60	Apr. 17, 1908	*2½ months*
Mar. 1908			35.70	Apr. 17, 1908	*6 weeks*
Apr. 1908			99.66	May 6, 1908	*4 weeks*
May 1908			117.42	July 24, 1908	*3 months*
June 1908		462.22	42.26	July 24, 1908	*7 weeks*
July 1908		17.88	.73	Sept. 8, 1908	*9 weeks*
Aug. 1908		19.80	.50	Sept. 8, 1908	*5 weeks*
Sept. 1908		20.29	16.00	Oct. 5, 1908	
Oct. 1908		3 1.51	.43	Oct. 5, 1908	

XVIII

Toward the end of May our tempest in a teapot was puffing away at a great rate, & making a lively stir amongst the farms & hamlets scattered in the woodsy hills & vales of our neighborhood. Every day brought its fresh little event & added a new text for gossip. Whatever either side did or said was known next day all around, & discussed.

As soon as I had begun, in the front end of the month to ask merchants for two-year-old statements, Ashcroft heard of it. In one case I was only looking for delayed payments, but he supposed I was on a still-hunt for graft. He probably knew Miss Lyon had covered her tracks fairly well in most cases, but he must have known she had been unwary in the Strohmeyer case, for he took measures to forestal me there. He wrote & asked Strohmeyer about Miss Lyon's dealings with him, & inquired if they had been entirely straight & correct. Strohmeyer's answer was an almost rapturous *Yes*. Before he knew that Paine & I were spies, he showed us that correspondence. A sorrowful man was he, later, I reckon, when Ashcroft found he had revealed everything to us & rendȷered the rapturous Yes worthless, as evidence, to be laid before the investigation-experts.

In those latter May days it was rumored that the Ashcrofts were getting uneasy, nervous, worried. Lounsbury said they were trying to mortgage Summerfield for $1500. What did they want with the money? They wanted it, according to Ashcroft, to square up with me. A month earlier, that amount would have sufficed for it, but not now. I had lent Miss Lyon $1500, but we were now aware that she had taken a couple of thousand more, before anything had been saidȷ about borrowing or lending.

Well, then, what *did* they want with the money? To *run away* with? Yes, that impression went around, & was believed & discussed.

Next, it transpired that they had acquired the $1500.

About the 28th, Ashcroft made one [of] his blunders. With all his smartness he was sure to do a foolish thing now & then—just as in the case of Horace & the imaginary "discharge." The present blunder was a peculiarly stupid one. Young Harry Lounsbury was driving him from the station, & the two were exchanging gossip, when Harry spoke of a rumor that I was proposing to do so & so.

"He!" said Ashcroft, scornfully, "I can sell his house, over his head, for a thousand dollars, whenever I want to!"

Harry told this at home. His father told Paine; & ~~ca~~ Paine, greatly worried, came at once to me with it. I said there was nothing in it, it was only brag. But Paine was not satisfied. He said it meant that Ashcroft could do as he said. Had he a power of attorney? I said no—& nothing resembling one. I said Miss Lyon had a power of attorney to sign checks—nothing more, & that I had revoked it orally on the 14th of March.

~~Now~~

He advised me to revoke it in writing; which I did—& sent it by Lounsbury, who waited, & brought back Miss Lyon's written acknowledgment.

I was now satisfied, but Paine & Clara were not. They were still worrying over that boastful remark of Ashcroft's. On Sunday the 30th they drove over to Nickerson's place, & he remember´ed acknowledging my signature to a general power of attorney back in November or December. He thought it conferred power upon both Miss Lyon & Ashcroft. They came back & reported. I said Nickerson's memory was astray & there was nothing to fret about, for I had not given a general power to anybody.

That was Decoration Day. Paine said I might be wrong & Nickerson right; so we must take no chances; we must go to New York & rummage the banks. We went down the next morning, Monday, & while I loafed in the Hotel Grosvenor, Paine went to the banks. Sure enough, in the Liberty National he found a power of attorney! A stately one, a liberal one, an all-comprehensive one! By it I transferred all my belongings, down to my last shirt, to the Ashcrofts, to do as they pleased with.

So this was what they had had up their sleeve all the time! This was why Ashcroft could say to Lounsbury about the road-mending, "Go ahead *if you want to take the risk!*" This was why Miss Lyon was able to say to the servants, "I am the only person in authority in this house, my word is law, & the only law, & I want you to understand it!" This was why Ashcroft could summon the servants on the 31st of March & say to them, "You better resign at once & save your faces, for you are all going to be discharged."

Ashcroft had had this fraudulent document placed on record in New York, just as if it had been a deed. To this he had ~~had~~ added another unusual precaution: he had had Nickerson's authority as a notary certified in the Fairfield county clerk's office, & the certification recorded. Nickerson's seal wasn't enough for him!

This swindling paper had been in force ever since November 14, 1908—about six & a half months—& I had never suspected it.

I will insert here ˄a copy of˄ that formidable power of attorney, & the ~~original~~ revocation:

KNOW ALL MEN BY THESE PRESENTS, that, WHEREAS, I, SAMUEL L. CLEMENS, of the Town of Redding, County of Fairfield, State of Connecticut, in and by my letter of attorney bearing date the 14th day of November, 1908, made, constituted and appointed Isabel V. Lyon and Ralph W. Ashcroft my true and lawful attorneys, as by the aforesaid letter of attorney will more fully and at length appear; and

WHEREAS, the said Ralph W. Ashcroft subsequently married the said Isabel V. Lyon, and the former now writes his name Ralph W. Lyon-Ashcroft, and the latter now subscribes herself as Isabel V. Lyon-Ashcroft, and it having become necessary and desirable for me to revoke the said power of attorney above mentioned;
NOW KNOW YE, that I, the said Samuel L. Clemens have revoked, countermanded, annulled and made void, and by these presents do revoke, countermand, annul and make void the said letter of attorney above mentioned, and all the power and authority thereby given, or intended to be given, to the said Isabel V. Lyon and Ralph W. Ashcroft, a copy of which said letter of attorney is hereto annexed and made a part hereof marked "Exhibit A", and the original of which said letter of attorney was filed in the office of the Register of the County of New York, State of New York, on or about the 23rd day of November, 1908.

IN WITNESS WHEREOF, I have hereunto set my hand and seal the first day of June, in the year One thousand nine hundred and nine.

Signed, sealed and delivered
in the presence of:

ˬCharles T. Larkˬ   ˬSamuel L. Clemensˬ (L. S.)
ˬAlbert Bigelow. Paineˬ
ˬCLARA CLEMENS !!ˬ

STATE OF NEW YORK,   ⎫
                          ⎬ ss.
COUNTY OF NEW YORK,   ⎭
    On this first day of June, 1909, before me personally came and appeared Samuel L. Clemens, to me personally known to be the individual described in and who executed the foregoing instrument, and he acknowledged to me that he executed the same.

                                                            ˬCharles T. Larkˬ

        [*stamped:* NOTARY PUBLIC, NEW YORK COUNTY,
                NO. 12. CERTIFICATE FILED IN KINGS COUNTY.]

[*embossed seal:* CHARLES T. LARK,
NEW YORK COUNTY. NOTARY -*- PUBLIC]

EXHIBIT A.

Know All Men By These Presents, That I, Samuel L. Clemens, of the Town of Redding, County of Fairfield, State of Connecticut, have made, constituted and appointed, and by these presents do make, constitute and appoint, Isabel V. Lyon, and Ralph W. Ashcroft my true and lawful attorneys for me and in my name, place and stead, to exercise a general supervision over all my affairs and to take charge of and manage all my property both real and personal and all matters of business relating thereto; to lease, sell and convey any and all real property wheresoever situate which may now or which may hereafter at any time belong to me; to demand, receive and collect rentals of such real property, to make repairs to any buildings thereon, to keep any and all buildings insured; to remand, receive and collect all dividends, interests and moneys due and payable to or to become due and payable to me; to satisfy and discharge mortgages; to sell, assign and transfer any and all stocks, bonds and mortgages belonging or which may at any time belong to me; to change any or all of my investments and to make any investment of any or all of the moneys belonging to me; to draw checks or drafts upon any banks, banker or Trust Company or any financial institution with which or whom I have or may at any time hereafter have moneys on deposit or to my credit; to endorse either for deposit, collection or transfer any and all notes, checks, drafts or bills of exchange now or hereafter payable to me or to my order; to prosecute, defend, compromise and settle suits and legal proceedings and to retain and employ attorneys and counsel for such purpose or otherwise, to protect my interests; to release and discharge as my attorneys may deem proper any and all claims and demands in my favor of any kind or nature, and to make, sign, seal, acknowledge and deliver any and all receipts, acquittances, discharges, satisfaction pieces, transfers, assignments, agreements, deeds or other instruments under seal or otherwise, which in the judgment of my said attorneys may be necessary, appropriate or proper, giving and granting unto my said attorneys, and unto either of them individually, full power and authority to do and perform any act or thing requisite and necessary to be done in and about the premises as fully to all intents and purposes as I might or could do if personally present, with full power of substitution and revocation, hereby ratifying and confirming all that my said attorneys or attorney, or their or her or his substitutes or substitute shall lawfully do or cause to be done by virtue hereof.

In Witness Whereof I have hereunto set my hand and seal this 14th day of November, 1908.

Samuel L. Clemens (L.S.)

Signed, sealed and delivered in the presence of

Horace W. Hazen
Harry Ives.

STATE OF CONNECTICUT   }

COUNTY OF FAIRFIELD   Redding

On this 14th day of November, 1908, before me personally came Samuel L. Clemens, to me personally known to be the individual described in and who executed the foregoing instrument, and he acknowledged to me that he executed the same.

John W. Nickerson,
Notary Public within and
for the State of Connecticut.

(Seal)
(Residing at Redding)

XIX

It makes a body gasp to read it! It takes possession of everything belonging to me except my soul.

This was the card they had had up their sleeve all this time, & I not suspecting it. I had been their property, their chattel, more than half a year, & didn't know it.

These people had not asked me for a power of attorney, & I had not conferred one upon them. The subject had never been mentioned.

How did they get it, then? I do not know. The original is still in the possession of my lawyers, & I have not seen it yet; so I do not know whether I signed it or whether the signature is forged. Mr. Stanchfield & Mr. Lark think I wrote the signature myself. If I did, then how did I come to do it?

I can only guess. Ashcroft probably (while my back was turned) substituted this paper which I had not seen, for one which I had read & approved, & in this way got me to sign the latter.

There were two occasions when he could have managed this. When I gave Miss Lyon the "Lobster Pot" (Summerfield), we were still living in New York & I had never visited this region up here. Paine (at Redding), sent the deed to New York & I signed it. Miss Lyon had it recorded at Redding. A little later she told Clara & Paine that she didn't want to accept the gift as a permanency, but only for her lifetime & her mother's; therefore she was going to make the change, & would do it either in a will or incorporate it in a new deed. The idea was her own; I did not suggest it or desire it.

A year or two later, when "Stormfield" was finished & furnished, I came up, & ~~entered the~~ saw the place for the first time, & entered into occupation—June 18 of last year, 1908. By & by,—in the autumn, I think—Ashcroft brought a new deed to my bedroom to be signed. I read it over. I found nothing in it that I recognized as being new. I supposed it would mention the life-ownership, but it didn't. I said—

"I don't see anything in this about returning the property to me eventually."

He offered no explanation, but simply said, quite unemotionally,

"There *isn't*."

I wondered at that a little, but made no comment, further than to say *I* had never suggested the change, it was Miss Lyon's own idea. Also I wondered why *two* deeds should be wanted—& so I asked. Ashcroft said Miss Lyon had neglected to record the first one, & now she couldn't find it. That was a good enough reason, so I asked no more questions. We were standing seven or eight feet from the centre-table. He took the deed, & turned away & carried it to the table, & arranged it there conveniently for signing; then at his call I went there and wrote my signature.

Ashcroft was lying. The first deed *had* been recorded, long ago, when it first came up from New York. We found this out when we the dis Ashcroft's unguarded remark to young Harry Lounsbury at the end of last May (that he could sell me out whenever he wanted to & I couldn't help myself) sent Paine & Clara flying to Redding on a hunt suspicious-document hunt.

Yes, the first deed was on record, & the second one wasn't.

Then what did Ashcroft want with the second one, since it could have no possible value, to Miss Lyon or any one else?

It could have this value: Ashcroft could take it from my hand, walk away with his back to me, sh slip it into his breast-pocket, slip out the General Power of Attorney, sp arrange the latter on the table, conveniently folded for signature, with nothing in sight but the blanks for the signatures—& thus get my signature to a most undesirable & dangerous document which I had never seen no[r] heard of before.

What became of that second deed? Only the Ashcrofts can tell. It had served its purpose; it went into the fire no doubt.

There was another time when a like substitution could have been made. And quite simply & easily. That was when Ashcroft brought me a type-written document which he said was the charter of the Mark Twain Company.

I didn't need to read it. It would be like any other charter granted under a general law. He showed me where to sign, & I signed. This could have been the General Power of Attorney in disguise. I signed. This time I signed at the bottom of a whole big type-written page. I remembered afterward that in that page I glimpsed the phrase "real estate," & wondered what a copyright-corporation could have to do with landed property.

By & by, when the teapot-tempest rose in this house I remembered that circumstance, & that was why I got scared & took Ashcroft with me to the Safe Deposit, the time that I went there to remove my signature from stock-transfers. I believed I had signed a document which transferred my copyrights, real estate & everything else, to Ashcroft, disguised as the Mark Twain Company, & so I was badly frightened.

Very well, I *had* transferred everything to Ashcroft—& not only in one way, but in two. One was by transfer-signature on the Mark Twain stock. I rectified that. Ashcroft sat there privately smiling to himself I reckon, he knowing (I suppose) that I was hunting anxiously & despairingly for a charter which wasn't there & which I had never signed; &

he being also aware that my destruction of those signatures couldn't do me any good, since he could restore them whenever he pleased, by authority of a colossal ˄General˄ Power of Attorney which he had acquired of me by fraud, & of whose existence I had no suspicion.

XX

Why did that couple want *both* of their names in the General Power of Attorney? What could be the occasion for that? It was almost beyond question that Miss Lyon would remain a member of my household (indeed to all intents & purposes a member of my *family,* honored, esteemed & beloved) all the rest of her life; she would be on the premises all the time; I ˄also˄ would be present all the time: how could *three* persons be needed?—for *what?* To sell ~~securities? there~~ securities, once or twice in the year? there was nothing else to ~~sll~~ sell. To buy securities, once or twice in the year? there was nothing else to buy. To employ legal counsel for me? I already had a lawyer—had had him five years & was satisfied with him.

What possible occasion had I to give *any* one a General Power of Attorney? Even if I wanted to do so unnecessary a thing, so silly a thing, so insane a thing, why give the power to *two* persons? Why give an entire two persons absolute power over me & be their slave? Wouldn't one master be enough?

I think the solution of this mystery is the one that seemed to explain that astonishing marriage: viz., both were criminals, also fellow-criminals, each was afraid of the other, they must stand or fall *together;* separate, they would betray each other, when, in an emergency, it came to a matter of turning State's evidence.

We know many things now (August) which we didn't know then. We know that Miss Lyon had been stealing money from me for two years, & that Ashcroft had been living on it & was guiltily accessory to it. Without a doubt it was Ashcroft who turned Miss Lyon into a thief. The check-stubs show that up to 1907 she was honest. He & she became friendly & sociable in the latter half of 1906 & excessively friendly & sociable in the beginning of 1907, & then the stealing began, as per the check-stubs. I don't mean that they fell in love with each other—in a clean way. That would be impossible—at least on his part, though not on hers. I suppose she never had any principle, but I think she had been protected from dishonesty by fear until he beguiled her & showed her how to cover up her tracks—a lesson which she sometimes disastrously forgot, as the check-stubs reveal.

As to that question, Why did they want ~~both names in~~ the General Power of Attorney, when I was going to be here all the time in person & could have no use for such a thing? We have discussed the matter all around, & have concluded that Ashcroft had conceived the idea of robbing me on a comprehensive & exhaustive scale, & he did not feel safe to carry out his plan without first closing Miss Lyon's mouth. He must make her a confederate. The surest way to accomplish this would be to put her into the General Power along with himself.

She was persuadable; & if she wasn't she was at least scarable: he knew that, quite well. He could expose her stealings whenever he might choose to do it; & he could prove them up to the hilt, too.

We think they were not proposing to be in a hurry about using the Power. I was 73. They could go on living upon me comfortably until I should some day get sick unto death, then ˄they could˄ sell my securities & transfer to themselves & my Mark Twain stock & decamp. Or remain, & furnish death-bed approvals of their acts, done ˄worded˄ in the first person, & with my name signature forged to them. (A week ago, August, 4, Ashcroft revealed a sample of his work of exactly this sort.)

XXI

If I had died while my transfer-signature was still attached to the stocks, bonds, & Mark Twain Company stock in the Safe Deposit vault! The Ashcrofts had a key & could have removed them & conveyed the ownership to themselves. It would have been difficult for a court to find an objection to it. The Mark Twain stock was paying worth a million dollars, & the other stuff about two hundred thousand. The children would have been paupers. However, I didn't die.

It does not appear that Ashfield sold anything (so far as we as yet know), except a piece of property which was not in the Deposit. The Knickerbocker Trust Company failed in the fall of 1907, & caught me. I had $51,000 on deposit there. After a few months the company got on its feet again, & began to repay the depositors in instalments. Toward the end of 1908 it had paid us 70 per cent in cash, & 30 per cent in bank stock drawing 4 per cent. I wanted that stock. It was worth 80 & would soon reach par. We found that eleven days after the date of the General Power of Attorney Ashcroft had sold it, through a shady broker, at 75 & that the broker had sold it on the same day for 80. There was no occasion to sell it, for we had a large balance in bank. There was $800 brokerage on the transaction, & Ashcroft probably got half of this graft, but no more.

We now arrive at June 4. Stanchfield's official expert was getting toward the end of his examination of Miss Lyon's check-stubs & vouchers, & was asking her some rather embarrassing questions. There were things which she could not explain satisfactorily— things which proved her a thief; proved it beyond question. The Ashcrofts were getting very nervous.

When they got married—as before remarked—they had sent out some bushels of copper-plate cards announcing that the aristocratically-hyphenated Mr. & Mrs. R. W. Lyon Ashcrofts would be "At Home" at Summerfield "Saturdays in June." When Friday the 4th arrived the countryside flocked along the country roads & to the little railway station to see the fine city-birds that would come. But they didn't see them. What they saw was the highly-hyphenated Ashcrofts slipping out & gliding away on the New York train! They never reappeared during that month.

They were scared. They were in flight, to save Miss Lyon from arrest. They believed ~~they were~~ ^she was^ in danger of spending her At Homes in the Danbury jail. They privately took passage in an obscure steamer for Holland, for a date half-way between the first & second At Homes (Tuesday, June 8.) Their intention was suspected.

On the 12th, Stanchfield's subordinate, Mr. Lark, sent the following news to Mr. Paine:

CHARLES A. COLLIN.   LAW OFFICES OF
JOHN L. WELLS.   COLLIN, WELLS & HUGHES,
THOMAS L. HUGHES.   5 NASSAU STREET,

CHARLES T. LARK.
WILLIAM M. PARKE.

NEW YORK.

June 12, 1909.

Mr. A. B. Payne,
"Stormfield",
Redding, Conn.

My Dear Mr. Payne:–

In reply to your note of the 11th inst. I beg to state that Mr. Weiss has not as yet been able to complete any further statement for your consideration, but I will advise you concerning the statement at the earliest possible moment and come up to Redding if my engagements permit.

With reference to our friend Mr. Ashcroft, I was informed over the telephone by someone at his office that he sailed for Europe on Tuesday the 8th inst., the very day you and Mr. Clemens were here in the office, although Mr. Ashcroft had told me on Monday that he had not engaged passage and had no idea whatever as to when he would sail, in fact, he told me at that time that his wife's condition was such that he might have to put her in a sanitarium and then not go at all for the present.

Awaiting your further wishes, believe me,

Yours very truly,
Charles T. Lark

So the soiled birds had flown.

They had reason to be frightened, for, as a precautionary measure, Mr. Lark ~~had~~ ^was intending to^ ~~asked~~ the district attorney of Fairfield count~~yry~~ to place Miss Lyon's case before the grand juror for said county & let him summon her, the grand juror to proceed whenever he should get further instructions. ~~These preliminaries had been accomplished.~~ Nothing further was to be done in this direction until all effort to settle the matter out of court should fail. It was my duty as a citizen to jail Miss Lyon, but she was a woman & the thing was so revolting that my citizenship was ~~not~~ ˄hardly˄ equal to it. If it had only been Ashcroft! That would have been another matter, & my citizenship would have stood the strain most elegantly.

~~It is time to peruse Ashcroft's majestic oratory again:~~

It is time to insert the midnight letter I wrote to Clara in those March days when I still believed in the honesty of the Ashcrofts, heart & soul, & still wanted to keep my precious Ashcroft & not lose him˄¦

That first date is March 11, two days before the grand Cleaning-Up Day, the Diarrhea of Contracts, March 13ᵗʰ of sacred memory; the postscript is dated the day after that spectacular flux:

> ˄Strictly *PRIVATE*. If these contents must be revealed to Mr. Jackson, I am willing, but no detail of them must go to any other person.˄
> ~~P.P.S.~~

REDDING

CONNECTICUT

March 11/09

½ past 2 in the morning:

Clara dear, I am losing sleep again over this matter.

When I wrote you, I believed I had placed ~~th~~ it in a sound & effective way of settlement—a clear & understandable way. I believed that an itemised report to me, covering a year or two, of income & outgo, would furnish the information required. I am of that opinion yet.

The materials are all here: Publishers' statements; Bank deposits, checkbooks, &c. And so I had asked Ashcroft ~~&~~ to get up that report. The report for the past 12 months will be gotten up now; the previous 12 to follow.

———

I supposed everything was peaceful & serene again. But your letter abolished that dream. It indicated that you & Mr. Jackson are not satisfied. You had asked for something which Ashcroft had met with a couple of objections. That surprised me. *I* had already asked him for all the essentials & had encountered no objections.

(To-night he explained.) In formulating an answer to your letter I had already set down as one of its ~~nφ~~ items an objection on my own part: I would not allow the check-books to go out of the house.

Yes, Ashcroft objected. ~~He had~~ It had been proposed to put my affairs into the hands of professional accountants. That is premature, & must be postponed till there is occasion for it. ˄That is to say,˄

When Ashcroft hands me the two reports I have asked for. They can be examined by competent friends of mine ˄& yours,˄ & compared with the check-books & bank deposits. If they fail to tally; if there are discrepancies that look suspicious, let the accountants take hold of the matter.

To put them on the work now, argues suspicion of Miss Lyon's honesty, & Ashcroft's—*charges* it, substantially. I have no such charge to offer, there being no evidence before me to found it on,, & there being no suspicions in my own mind to base it on.

We will wait for Ashcroft's reports. Unless you can furnish evidence. Not theory, not guess, but evidence.

If you can do this, we will proceed. If you cannot, we will wait for the reports, & see what competent friends have to say after examining them.

And so you have no further use for a lawyer until the reports arrive. Say that to him when you get this letter.

In my belief, you will not need a lawyer's services again.

Continuation.

Among the notes I made (for letter) this was one: "While we are hunting eagerly for *dis*service, are we forgetting to hunt for service?"

It is a thought which does not make me feel very comfortable.

Miss Lyon came to your mother as secretary, at $50 a month. She has never asked for more. Yet she has been housekeeper 4 or 5 years, with its many vexations & annoyances. She could not have been replaced at any price, for she was qualified to meet our friends socially & be acceptable to them. This service has been beyond computation in money, for its like was not findable.

And she has been a housebuilder. In this service—a heavy one, an exacting one, & making her liable to fault-finding—she labored hard for a year. I would not have done it at any price, neither would you. Would you have undertaken that job? I think not. Could we have found anybody, so competent as she, to take it? Or half so willing, or half so devoted? There isn't a decorator in New York who can compare with her for taste & talent. These services of hers have been very valuable; but she has charged nothing for them. ~I never knew n, or asked what we paid our idiot in New York, but Mrs. Littleton has paid hers $4,000 for her grotesque services in planning her parlor-floor suite. She must have studied mainly from the nude; the place looks naked.~

[SLC tore away the bottom half of one MS page and the top half of the next, removing as many as 120 words]

Anybody can get his mind poisoned, & I have not wholly escaped, as regards Miss Lyon. But it is healthy again. I have no suspicions of her. She was not trained to business & doubtless has been loose & unmethodical, but that is all. She has not been dishonest, even to a penny's worth. All her impulses are good & fine. She makes friends of everybody, & she loses no friends. The Whitmores & the Danas she served under their roofs for years, & they have nothing but affection & praise for her. She has several talents, & they are much above common; & in the last three or four years she has developed literary capacities which are distinctly remarkable. She has served me with a tireless devotion, & I owe her gratitude for it—& I not only owe it but feel it. I have the highest regard for her character.

She has wrought like a slave for that little library & has set it firmly on its feet—almost alone, & without charge.

And all by herself she has beaten the game that was to have robbed a poor old neighbor of ours of his homestead.

[written sideways in the margin of the MS page that begins with the next paragraph:

P.S. I am empowering Mr. Dunneka to examine the Safety Deposit box & report to me its contents, together with the nature & scope & ownership of the Mark Twain Co. I will keep this letter until I can add his report to it. Till Saturday or Sunday.]

And what shall I say of Ashcroft? He has served me in no end of ways, & with astonishing competency—brilliancy, I may say. During 7 4 years he has fought my ˄Plasmon˄ fight against desperate odds˄—a night-&-day month-in-and-month-out struggle, through lawsuit after lawsuit & machination after machination, never complaining, never losing hope, & has won out at last, scoring victory all along the line. In not a single suit did the old company of thieves win their case. It has not cost me a hundred dollars. The result is a rescued property which is now solely in the hands of himself, myself & the London company. He has always reported to me every move he made, & its result. He has persistently kept after Sir Thomas Lipton (who greatly admires him) for two years, with steady progress toward success, & to-day it looks as if he is going to land him. In any case he has pulled that great property out of what seemed to me & to others a disastrous & hopeless hole, & it is safe & secure now.

He (first, I think—certainly independently of Larkin) invented the Mark Twain Co—a stroke of genius, & this family owns all of the stock. It may supersede copyright-law some day.

He has now completed the purchase (this is not to be mentioned for a while yet, till the deed is recorded) of the adjoining farm of ~~175~~ ˄125˄ acress, farm buildings & stock, for ~~$72,000~~ $7,200 & saved us $600 thereby.

He has put my London Plasmon interest in good shape, & that concern has begun to prosper again.

However, his services have been absolutely endless—& they are daily, & constant. ~~I think I told you how near he came to making $100,000 ˄house-building costs—& more—˄ for me at the storm-centre of the panic. I was sending an order to buy a copper-stock at 25—it was selling at 27. He advised me not to risk losing a small fortune by trying to get the last cent out of the chance—he said give the order to *buy at market*. If I had done it I'd have gotten it at 27—but I didn't. It took me 24 hours to get wise, then it was too late—the Trust Co failed, & swallowed ˄nearly˄ all my cost, & by & by I had to sell good securities below cost, to get money for my necessities & obligations. It was my fault alone that he didn't make the $100,000 ˄small fortune˄ for me. The purchase at 27, of 2,000 shares would have increased my holding to 3,750 shares & leveled the whole cost down to 38. When I owned 500 shares (cost 53) he wanted me to sell at 65; I took Mr. Rogers's advice & *bought* instead. I would by ˄buy˄ that stock to-day at 47 (the last quotation I have noticed) if I had the money to spend. For it will be back at 65 & maybe 70 before the year is out. I once bought it at 43 & sold it at 69.~~

I know Ashcroft & Miss Lyon better & more intimately than I have ever known any one except your mother, & I am quite without suspicion of either their honesty or their honorableness.

Miss Lyon is a sick & broken-down woman, & I want her to be left in peace until the Ashcroft reports exhibit evidence to go upon in exposing my private affairs to the professional accountants, & her to unnecessary & unjustifiable humili₍a₎tion. Dismiss your lawyer until then—unless, as I have before suggested, you have in your hands something definitely & demonstrably incriminating.

I wouldn't let Jean ˄(four years ago),˄ charge Brush's ~~se~~ Italian servant with theft **upon suspicion** & demand his arrest. Jean was resentful at the time, but felt better about it when Mrs. Brush (3 months later) found the silver where she had put it herself & long ago & forgotten it. Meantime the man—dismissed, with ~~rep~~ public reproaches)—was gone. Also his character.

Good-bye, dear heart, it is half past 6, & I am tired. With lots of love

Father.

P. S.

Sunday, Mch 14.

Nothing is as it was. Everything is changed. Sentiment has been wholly eliminated. All things in this house are now upon a strictly business basis. All duties are strictly defined, under several written contracts, signed before a notary.

[SLC tore away the bottom third of one MS page, removing as many as 40 words]

All services rendered me are paid for, henceforth.

But there is no vestige of ugly feeling, no *hostility* on either side. The comradeship remains, but it is paid for; also the friendship. Stormfield was a home; it is a tavern, now, & I am the landlord.

Dunneka's Report. He examined the box & made a list of its contents. After which, he asked for Ashcroft's list & compared the two. They tallied exactly.

He examined the Mark Twain Co, & found that I am the Co in my own person, with full control.

Zoe Freeman becomes Vice Pres & director, in place of Miss Lyon.

I sign all checks, in future.

Ashcroft assumes the remaining $1000 of money borrowed of me by Miss Lyon to renovate her house, & ~~I have~~ ˄gives˄ his notes (4) for $250 each.

Jesus, what a week!

Most lovingly
Father

Indeed, yes, I believed in those people thoroughly.

I didn't even glance at the notes offered me by Ashcroft. It fretted me, shamed me, to be put in the attitude of dickering with a devoted & affectionate old servant like Miss Lyon on that paltry sum—a sum which I had no intention of ˄ever˄ collecting or accepting. I told Ashcroft to keep the notes himself; that if I took them I should lose them. He put them in his pocket, & nothing more was said. That is, nothing more was said until his imagination supplied some more in a newspaper about five months afterwards.

The birds had flown. This was not discovered until a while after the event. They had slipped away very privately. Ashcroft's office man was not able to furnish particulars; he said he didn't know what ship they had sailed by, he was only able to say their objective point was England, where Ashcroft needed to see Sir Thomas Lipton on business connected with the ~~P~~ Milk ~~F~~ Products Company (Ashcroft's new name for the wrecked & robbed & ruined old Plasmon Company.)

A search of the passenger registers of the big English lines failed to produce any Ashcrofts. Apparently they had sailed under fictitious names. But they hadn't. They had been smarter than that: They had gone by way of Holland ~~in~~ per a Dutch line not heard of before. They were fleeing from arrest; that is, fleeing from a spectre—Mr. Stanchfield would not ḍ have arrested Miss Lyon, because she was a woman. Not much of a woman, still a woman.

I was not troubled about Sir Thomas Lipton, for I had not endorsed Ashcroft to him, but had only formally introduced the two to each other one day in an English railway train; but the case was different with Lord Northcliffe. He had visited me at Stormfield in the winter when the Ashcrofts were practically members of my family, & I had strongly praised Ashcroft to him, & had as uncompromisingly endorsed him. So I sent I was now afraid Ashcroft would try to use Northcliffe & all his 58 newspapers; so I sent him word by a private hand that I was not endorsing Ashcroft now.

Mr. Stanchfield now suggested that we attach Miss Lyon's "Summerfield" in part payment of the money she had stolen from me to repair it with. Not the borrowed money, but money stolen by her before anything was said about borrowing. So we attached the said "Lobster pot."

The sheriff wasted no time, but conveyed the fact to the newspapers right away. It went straight to the London journals by cable, & made a large personage of ⅄ the little Ashcrofts immediately. The interviewers & correspondents flocked in. Ashcroft knew them all, through me. He had gone over with me in the summer of 1907 when I was summoned by Oxford University to receive a degree, & during all the six weeks of our stay he received the newspaper men & photographers daily, in my place, & was never so proud & happy in his life before. And they treated him well; treated him as a gentleman, which was kind of them, for they knew, by certain signs, that he was not a gentleman according to British standards. Certain words of his gave him away. For instance he always said "anythin," like a costermonger, whereas the British gentleman adds the *g.*

When the As₍h₎crofts fled, Mr. Weiss, the expert had not finished his examination of Miss Lyon's book-keeping. He had found that she had filched money for house-repairs, & that she had tried to cover up some of the filchings by altering the check-stubs with all-too-recent ink.

We had further claims against her, but not all of these had been examined when she fled. They were for money stolen by her & entered in the stub as "house money." House money was cash. It was used only for trifling expenses which could not be paid by check. We never needed more than $300 or $400 cash in a year. This was provable by the check-books of many years; provable also by the check-books of 1906—a sorrowful witness against Miss Lyon, for she was in charge of those check-books then, & got along quite well with $25 to $30 a month house-money. But there was a jump, as soon as Ashcroft needed a support, in 1907, & taught her to steal.

In a year & ten months she drew nearly ten thousand dollars, house-money! Also she drew various other cash-amounts and charged them to "C. C.,"—that is, Clara Clemens—& stole 90 per cent of *that.* In one cash she drew $500 & charged it to Clara when Clara was away down South at the time, & living upon checks drawn upon *her own* bank account.

Memoranda from Mr. Weiss's statement.

Amount spent on the "Lobster Pot", discovered to date,   3431.37

Amount of "cash" cheques, Feb 26, 1907, to Jan. 9, 19079, (97 weeks) (11 months) 1.y. & 10 m.   97790.00
An average of 100.00 a week.
On several cheque stubs the words "Lobster Pot" and the initials "I.V.L." appear to have been added lately—the ink being less darkened by age.

On his statement made to Mr. Rogers, Ashcroft had acknowledged 2717.33 spent on the "Lobster Pot", though immediately under this acknowledgement he gives Miss Lyon's figures of about 1500.00, as being the amount shown by his audit to date—a direct contradiction of the statement just above.

And now the cable began to twang. Thus:

'Twain Charges False,' Declares Mrs. Ashcroft

———

Humorist's Former Secretary, Whose Gift House Was Attached, Coming Back for Vindication.

———

Special Cable to New York American.
London, July 1.—Mr. and Mrs. Ralph Ashcroft, the latter formerly private secretary for Mark Twain, arrived in London to-day and received from America clippings from the New York American enumerating Miss Clemens's charges and telling of the sheriff's attachment upon the farmhouse, which is the bone of contention between Mrs. Ashcroft and the humorist.

Mrs. Ashcroft told The American correspondent the charges were false, but that in view of their widespread publicity she intends, contrary to her original intention, to sail on the Mauretania on Saturday to vindicate her position. Mr. Ashcroft will remain in England[.]

Both Mr. and Mrs. Ashcroft told The American correspondent they could not understand Miss Clemens's attitude in the matter.

"If she is as familiar with her father's affairs as she claims to be," they said, "she must know that every step taken in the restoration of the farmhouse in Connecticut was with her father's knowledge and approval. Furthermore, for every cent expended Mrs. Ashcroft incurred liability to pay, and Mark Twain possesses notes amounting to nearly $1,000 signed by Mr. Ashcroft when the first rough estimate was made of the cost of rehabilitation, while the humorist made a written agreement with Mr. Ashcroft to accept his notes for the balance of the indebtedness outstanding upon the completion of repairs.

> "There has been no request made by Mark Twain for repayment of any money spent, while Miss Lyons several times refused suggestions on his part to consider the cost of renovation as a present from him."
>
> Mrs. Ashcroft in conclusion told The American correspondent: "I sail on Saturday to vindicate my position and prove that every one of the charges brought against me is false."

We wondered how "Miss Clemens" came to ˄be˄ talking about this matter to newspaper people. It is against the rule of the house to discuss our matters in print; & so this was an astonishing breach, & wholly unexpected.

Alas & alas! ˄it was not Miss Clemens,˄ it was Jean!

She had long been an exile in the sanitariums; she had forgotten the rule of the house, & she was caught off her guard. She happened, most unfortunately, to be the only person around when the telephone bell rang; instead of declining to talk, she talked.

It was a great pity. It gave the Ashcrofts their chance. It lifted them out of obscurity & insignificance, & made them objects of interest & importance for a moment in a far country. What a dear & welcome opportunity it afforded the little lioness to whet up with half a pint or so ˄of puissant old Scotch,˄ & air her sweet-sixteen dramatics & listen to herself gabble! To be called on, by metropolitan newspapers, to spread her little "Lobster pot" affairs before the thronged millions of the world's capital! Well, a-well, I can *see* her at it, just as plain!—I know ˄her˄ every trick & gesture & intonation, I know all those machine-made enchantments of hers, & that bewitching die-away light that she turns on, at the climaxes, from her handsome black eyes. I know that that little thing swelled, & swelled, & swelled until she felt as big & tall & imperial as our Goddess of Liberty Enlightening the World with her extinguish˄ed˄ torch down yonder in New York harbor. Wasn't it the proudest day of her life? Oh, sure.

I don't know why Jean's "charges" should have stirred up so much virtue in Miss Lyon. She was a thief; & she knew she was a thief; she believed that the proof was in the hands of the expert when she ran away—(for her "health's" sake, as Ashcroft put it.) Now why did she get into such a ˄virtuous˄ frenzy, & want to rush back & "vindicate her position"?—& she *so* sick, according to Ashcroft.

How could she be so illogical? What *was* her "position"? She hadn't any. She couldn't vindicate what she hadn't, could she? But there it is, you see: going to illogically fly right back, at deadly peril to her "health" & go to vindicating like Sam Hill! Vindicating *what? She* didn't know. It was a noble large word & she had to heave it out, she couldn't help it. Well, it was just like her, she was always that way—born so. Always ready to do a spectacular thing when she had an audience, & explain it to herself later when the whisky got out of her head.

She was always a kind & willing liar, but she had no gift. She would do the best she could, but her best had no considerable value, because, with all its art it was so artless, so transparent, so undeceptive. Now in the present case she wrought poorly, when she had the opportunity of her life; the opportunity to make a European reputation, a planetarian reputation; a reputation which could set her away up high, and bracket her ~~her~~ with the most revered & illustrious liars of history; but she wasted it.

Look at her effort! The eyes of the world upon her, everlasting renown waiting upon her impending words: And when they come, oh, how disappointing! Begin with her fourth paragraph, & read to the end.

Although each & every statement is a separate & distinct lie, *that* is no merit—anybody can tell lies: there is no merit in a *mere* lie, it must ~~po exhibit art~~ possess *art,* it must exhibit a ~~persuasiveness,~~ splendid & plausible & convincing *probability;* that is to say, it must be powerfully calculated to *deceive.*

If she had been a real artist she would have reflected—like this: Mr. Clemens is known, I am not; he has a reputation to watch over & take care of, I have not; if I charge him with misconduct, furnishing no evidence but my *word,* will that convince a nation that knows him favorably & knows me not at all? won't these people say "it is not a bit like Clemens to do these things wantonly; without a doubt he has a reason for it, & a *good* one?"

Without any doubt she did me great injury in England. Without any doubt, old & dear & valued friends & admirers of mine over there were saddened, & said—

"This person was under Clemens's personal tuition for seven years, ~~yet~~ —& look at the result: she exhibits no more art than if she had been under a bishop. She is a mere blundering, unscientific, ignorant amateur, & Clemens is to blame."

But what could *I* do? she couldn't learn, it wasn't in her.

Another thing: she hasn't any presence of mind; she breaks out with a heroic irruption just because it sounds grand & fine, & there she is—committed! Many's the time she has cursed herself for saying she was coming back to go vindicating around; for she hadn't the least notion of coming back & risking the jail; but she was committed, & she had to come.

And when she came, she ⸮ told that lie again—said she had come back vindicating. She didn't stir in the matter: we had to place the subject before her ourselves. And we even had to *crowd* her! Yes, she was that unwilling to face us.

Very well, she came. In three ships. Three are mentioned, at any rate, as undertaking the exodus; or the leviticus, or whatever the proper name for it is. She came, poor mistaught, inartistic little abuser of facts, & resumed relations with the newspaper lads on the pier. We saved two or three of her interviews; & now that they are a month old I find them freshly interesting—partly because of things which have happened since; things which do not allow me to be sorry for her, much as she stands in need of compassion. Without greatly deserving it. This is from the Evening Telegram of (apparently) July 13:

Cut Short Honeymoon Hearing Mark Twain Attached Gift

———

**Mrs. R. L. Ashcroft, Author's Former Secretary,
Hurries Back to Probe Stories.**

———

LEFT HUSBAND IN EUROPE;
HE WILL RETURN LATER

———

**Cannot Understand Reported Action
in Placing Lien of $4,000 on House He Gave Her.**

———

Mrs. Ralph L. Ashcroft, whose maiden name was Lyon, and who, prior to her marriage two months ago, was private secretary to Mr. Samuel L. Clemens (Mark Twain), arrived from England on the Cunard liner Carmania to-day.

Mrs. Ashcroft interrupted her wedding trip to come over here and investigate the stories published a week ago to the effect that Mr. Clemens had placed an attachment for $4,000 on a house which he had given her in Redding, Conn., when she was his secretary.

"I cannot understand the situation at all," said the humorist's former secretary. "Mr. Clemens is one of the most lovable of men and no one has known him better than I. I am confident that this reported action on his part was not made voluntarily."

Mrs. Ashcroft refused to state outright whom she believed responsible for the placing of the attachment on her house. While discussing her relationship with Miss Jean Clemens, daughter of Mark Twain, she said:—

"I think Miss Clemens has been ill advised in this matter, but she is a most lovable woman."

Questioned as to whether she was financially indebted to Mr. Clemens, Mrs. Ashcroft replied that at the time he gave her the house he had also advanced her $4,000 to rehabilitate it.

"But that money was to be paid back at my leisure," she added.

Mr. Ashcroft did not accompany his wife over. He will remain in England for a week or so and will then come to New York. Mrs. Lyon, mother of Mrs. Ashcro[f]t was at the pier to meet her daughter. They started for the house in Redding, Conn., immediately.

MRS. RALPH ASHCROFT.

Don't you notice? *At last* she emits one bright little ray of artistic invention—she turns her scramble out of the country, where the jail's jaws were gaping, to a *honeymoon* trip! But is that really her work? It seems a pity to take it away from her, & yet it may be that reporter's performance.

Jean gets Clara's share of notice, & it serves her right. It was she that emptied Miss Lyon into the London papers & gave her the chance of her life.

When it comes to grinding out ₍historical₎ elevations, depressions, inflations, extinctions, & other discrepancies, I will back Miss Lyon to beat anybody in the profession, except her husband. Let me see: I lent her $1500 about Xmas of last year, (rehabilitation-money), she concealing the fact that she had already filched about $2,000 from me & spent it on her house. Now she enlargeds these sums to $4,000 & says id I *"advanced"* it to her.

I think our adventure with the burglars, the 18th of last September, has disordered her financial dictionary a little. I "advanced" the burglars some silverware, but *I* didn't know it. I was asleep up stairs at the time.

The $4,000 "was to be paid back at my leisure." I think she is the foolishest creature I know, except myself. And Ashcroft. She had only $50 a month salary; wouldn't allow me to increase it, according to her own story; was supporting her mother "entirely" out of that $50, according to her written statement. It would have required about seventy-five years of her leisure to pay it back. She was foolish in not telling me she had spent $3,500, & would like to make it a charge against her share of the royalties on "Mark Twain's Letters"—the book she & Clara were to prepare. That security would have been ample.

But why should she care about a little matter like $4,000? At that very time she & Ashcroft had had the forged Power of Attorney up their sleeve five weeks, & were ready & waiting to rob the Clemens family of its last farthing the moment I should fall gravely ill. Why should she care for a fifteen or twenty thousand dollar share in a book, when she knew she had a secret & unsuspected death-grip upon my entire remains?

She quite well knew the value of her share in that book. I was astonished when she threw it away on the 13th of March. But I seems to understand it now. Ashcroft despised it, & called it "petty"—which greatly surprised me. But it doesn't now.

How sure they were of their undislodgeable grip upon me in those days! And how insolent was their manner & attitude, & how calmly & masterfully dictatorial was their phrasing in the impertinent contracts they brought me to sign! They were my Piers Gavestons, my pets, my idols, & they were feeling absolutely sure they could turn me against Clara, drive her off the place, & reign over Stormfield & me in autocratic & sovereignty. I am aware now, just lately, by the testimony of a trustworthy witness, that in one of their indiscreet outbursts they said Jean wouldn't be allowed to ever cross my threshold again. I know Miss Lyon has a cruel nature & is unforgiving & unrelenting—but Ashcroft? Yes, I think he is just about her match in these particulars.

Miss Lyon looks sad in that picture. I think I pity her, but I hope to be damned if I *want* to.

The next of my preserved clippings seems to be from the *American:*

SHE WILL MAKE TWAIN EXPLAIN
HIS $4,000 SUIT

———

Humorist's Former Secretary Feels Sure Miss Clemens
Investigated Action.

———

TROUBLE OVER FARM.

———

Mrs. Ashcroft Says Mr. Clemens and She
Were Like Father and Daughter.

———

Mrs. Ralph W. Ashcroft, who used to be Mark Twain's private secretary and whose farm in Connecticut, given to her by the humorist, was recently attached by him, arrived in New York to-day on the Carmania, after a honeymoon abruptly broken into. She blames the whole trouble on the "artistic temperament" of Miss Clara Clemens, the writer's daughter.

Mrs. Ashcroft is a pretty, Quakerish-looking little woman, the kind you expect to wear a folded kerchief over her shoulders and dove-colored frocks. She was Miss Isabel Lyon and was married to Mr. Ashcroft, who was also an adviser of Mark Twain, on March 18. They sailed for Europe on June 9 and a few days after the house and sixteen acres belonging to Mrs. Ashcroft and adjoining Mark Twain's place near Redding, Conn., were attached by a deputy sheriff in a suit to recover $4,000.

It was claimed that Mrs. Ashcroft had used more of the humorist's money than he had given her permission to use in making repairs on the farm house. Miss Clemens put the matter into the hands of the late Henry H. Rogers, who employed an expert to go over Mark Twain's books, and later John B. Stanchfield directed the investigation.

"I have come back to vindicate myself," Mrs. Ashcroft said to-day, and in discussing the matter her eyes filled with tears and she had difficulty in restraining her emotions. "I heard nothing of the suit until a friend sent me a newspaper clipping to London, and I took the first boat I could get. I had to leave Mr. Ashcroft over there for t little while and I won't be able to go back because we can't afford it.

"It is a terrible shock to me," she continued. "I loved Mr. Clemens like a father and he treated me like a daughter. No one was closer to him for years, I believe, and I don't think the bringing of this suit was his doing. It was his daughter who did it, I am sure, and I think that back of her action therr are eenmies of mine who persuaded her.

"It is all on account of her artistic temperament—it is always leading her to do things she is sorry for afterward. Mr. Clemens told me to take what money I needed for the repairs and there has never been a request to me for r[e]payment. On the contrary, I have often refused his offer to consider the costs of the renovation a present from him. I am going right up to Redding to-day and will see Mr. Clemens. I am sure that he will treat me fairly and justly and that I can disprove every one of these charges."

Mrs. Ashcroft and Her Mother
Here to Answer Mark Twain Suit.

(Especially Photographed by an Evening World Staff Artist.)

MRS. ASHCROFT AND HER MOTHER
MRS. LYONS.

I enjoy the vigorous head-lines. "She will *make* Twain explain." Oh, *that* she will!
I can just see that little bantam stepping ~~threatingly~~ ˄fiercely˄ around with her feathers ruffled up, & making the blood of those reporters run cold in their veins with
apprehen/sion—~~just~~ ˄perfectly˄ sickening apprehension. I doubt if even the most excited
& bloody-minded butterfly could inspire a more ghastly terror.

But when we come to think of it there *is* something fine, something gallant, something heroic in her brave defiance, something that compels our admiration. Compels it because we know that in her circumstances *we* couldn't do it. We should meanly want to hide. The haunting consciousness of being a detected thief, an exposed fraud, a social ruin, an outcast, would weaken us, & take the noise out of us.

Her closing paragraph is rich enough in lies, but they are clumsy, loose, inartistic. She never never *never* will learn. Evidently she makes no preparation, but always trusts to inspiration, & lies upon the spur of the moment. As a result, she spews up any lie that occurs to her, & nine times in ten it isn't the best one for the emergency, & is sure to lack grace & finish besides.

Still, there is one agreeable feature about these lies—novelty. They are fresh, they are not shopworn. Also they have ₫ ˄an easy & ˄breezy inconsistency which tastes good. She has "often refused his offer to consider the costs of the renovation a present from him." The dear thing! she had only one chance, (the $500-one) & she didn't refuse that one. She was never offered the rest of the borrowed $1500.

And that other one: "Mr. Clemens told me to take what money I needed for the repairs."

Naughty I[s]abel! she had already stolen two thousand dollars before there was ever any conversation about the repairs. We had only the one conversation upon the subject. She named the sum she would need ("about $1500") & I said borrow it of me. Just before Xmas 1908 she said her house was done & the cost had fallen a few pennies within the $1500. But she forgot to say anything about the two thousand (nearly) which she had stolen.

Isabel is a little unfair, in one particular: she puts upon Clara's shoulders the crime of bringing the suit; whereas she knows I am the person to blame. I̶ ̶a̶m̶ ̶I̶ ̶a̶m̶ ̶t̶o̶ ̶b̶l̶a̶m̶e̶ I didn't bring it until I knew she was a thief & had run away to avoid the jail. It was my duty as a citizen to put her in jail, but for *my* sake I haven't done it. Not for hers, only for mine.

There's ˄"never been any request to her for repayment." Says it with such a fine air! an air which indicates, & practically asserts, that all I needed was to *ask* for the money & get it. That is just wild! Why she hadn't a penny in the world—an unstolen one, I mean—& her opportunity to pay me back with my own check was gone, gone for good & all. She a̶d̶ says, her own self, that she can't return to her blatherskite over the water because "we can't afford it."

"I am sure. . . . I can disprove every one of these charges."

She certainly is *not* a good liar. The more I see of her efforts, the more I am discouraged about her.

She thinks there are "enemies" of hers who persuaded Clara. That is a distinct & definite slap at *Paine.* I am sorry for Paine; sorry for any one upon whom the blight of our angel's disapproval has fallen. I don̸ not know what to compare such a calamity to, so I will leave it alone & not strain myself.

Another one with some attractive display-heads:

MARK TWAIN MUST EXPLAIN

———

Mrs. Ashcroft Back From Europe to Learn Why He Has Attached House He Gave to Her.

———

PUTS BLAME ON HIS DAUGHTER

———

Writer's Family Jealous of Her, the Former Secretary Declares, in Telling of Relations.

———

Mrs. Ralph W. Ashcroft, the former secretary of Samuel L. Clemmens (Mark Twain), who learned shortly after she had arrived in London two weeks ago that the humorist had obtained an attachment of $4,000 against the house in Redding, Conn., he had given to her, arrived to-day on the steamship Oceanic of the Cunard line, "to learn," she said, "the true inwardness of the attachment and to see if the matter, which must have been the result of a misunderstanding, cannot be straightened out."

Mrs. Ashcroft declared that Mr. Clemens was influenced by a daughter to take this legal step against her, and added that in her belief the humorist was led to take out the attachment because of the jealousy of members of his household had of her. Mrs. Ashcroft, who left her husband in London on business, was met at the dock by her mother, Mrs. Lyon, who volunteered the information that her daughter would rest one day in New York begore going in to see Mr. Clemens at his country home, "Stormfield."

As Miss I. N. Lyon, Mrs. Ashcroft was the secretary of the humorist for several years, looking after his correspondence, and being more closely associated with him in his business affairs than any other person.

"I am at a loss to understand why this attachment should be brought against the property Mr. Clemens gave me," she declared, in speaking freely of her associations with the humorist and the circumstances under which he gave the house to her.

"Let me begin at the beginning. Two weeks ago I received a letter while in London, informing me of this step Mr. Clemens had taken. The house against which he has sworn out an attachment of $4,000, he gave to me. I decided to come directly back, I leaving my husband in London.

"I am sure I can straighten this matter out," continued Mrs. Ashcroft. "I am heartbroken over it. For several years I was closely associated with Mr. Clemens as his secretary. I loved him as a daughter would love a father. For seven years I relieved him of every care I could. He gave me the house at Redding and later lent me money with which to furnish the house. It was understood between us that I should return him the money as soon as I could possibly do so.

"When I left Mr. Clemens he was as nice to me as when I had been his secretary. It cannot be possible that Mr. Clemens put that attachment on my house. He is not that kind of a man. It is my firm belief that the whole trouble has been caused by his younger daughter, Miss Jean Clemens. She is of a highly artistic temperament that is apt to lead her at times in a wrong direction. I do not believe that even she would make this trouble for me of her own volition. I believe she was badly advised by people who were jealous of me because of my former close associations with Mr. Clemens.

"I am of the impression that Miss Jean Clemens did not fully understand the conditions that existed, and took a step on that account she would not have taken if she properly understood the mistake she was making. I intend to do everything possible to clear myself of the charges that have been made against me. You may rest assured that there is not the least doubt in my mind but that I will displove to the satisfaction of every one every charge that has been made.'"

Mrs. Ashcroft, who is a small woman hardly more than 5 feet tall, added that she would go to Redding to-morrow to see Clemens personally.

I "must" explain. Certainly. She is coming right up here to Stormfield to take me by the scruff of the neck & squeeze the explanation out of me. I never saw such a violent pterodactyl.

As literary discharges, ₐall ofₐ these unpremeditated interviews are interesting to me, because they contain so much variety. They all play substantially the same tune, but it isn't monotonous, because the prodigal variations save it.

She is "at a loss to understand." However, that isn't a new lie, she has told that before.

~~And~~

But that about lending her money with which to "furnish" her house hasn't been used before. It is fresh from the factory. She filched money to furnish with, but I didn't lend her any for that purpose.

"It was understood between us that I should return him the money as soon as I could *possibly* do so." That is new, too; she hasn't said that before. "Possibly" is a good strong word. It indicates that I was anxious about that money, & wasn't willing to be deprived of it long. Also, the lie in this fresh form furnishes the suggestion that I was uneasy about that money, & that she flew back to soothe me & reassure me—sweet girl! Flew back to hearten me, flew back to revive my fainting courage, flew back to save me from despair—darling bird! Damnation, she's improving—this is almost art!

"I intend to do everything possible to clear myself." That is an improvement. Heretofore she has been too blustery; she gave the world the impression that she was an escaped hurricane & was going to come blasting & blighting & lashing & thrashing & crashing up here, destroying everything that opposed her course & leaving the leveled hills & forests smoking in her wake— & restore her purity absolutely. ₐAbsolutely & sudden.ₐ But now she is only going to try. Trying is better. It is a distinct improvement. This is much better than violence. We can chain up the dog again, now.

Once more it is Jean who is to blame, not Clara. It is Jean's "highly artistic temperament" that has made the trouble. It is another improvement, for it is in the line of delicacy. A year ago she told all these farmers around here that Jean was exiled to sanitariums—for life—because she was "crazy." It is much kinder to change it to a highly artistic temperament. It isn't true, for Jean is not artistic, but eminently business-like & practical, but I like the new lie better than the old one. It isn't permanent, though; she only made the change for the occasion; she will resume the other one when occasion shall require it; she made the present change to get another swipe at Paine. Paine is the bad adviser. He is the jealous one.

However, Jean didn't take any "steps." The lawyers did it. It was the lawyers that siezed "Summerfield," otherwise the "Lobster pot," to partly make good the thefts Miss Lyon had perpetrated. Miss Lyon was aware of that.

Very well, Miss Lyon did come up here, but she didn't "prove, to the satisfaction of every one every charge that had been made." Moreover, she didn't try. There wasn't any way to do it, & there wasn't any place to begin.

Naturally those interviews woke up the reporters & they flocked to us by every train—day-trains & night-trains both. But we gave them nothing. I did not care to make important people of the Ashcrofts, & they couldn't do it themselves, without my help. They were unknown & insignificant adventurers, & the only reason a newspaper would make room for their grievances was because there might be a chance that I would reply.

I didn't reply, of course. But every time a reporter applied, I sent him away empty, & then eased my anger against the Ashcrofts by putting on paper what I would have *liked* to say. It is the best way to quiet your indignant soul. It is efficient. I have practised it for forty years.

~~Sample.~~

Sample. Written, & laid aside:

"It is a case for lawyers & expert accountants to examine, & ₍for₎ Courts to ₍decide₎, not newspapers. The verdict will be in my favor; no other is possible.

"There ~~was~~ ₍is₎ nothing romantic about ~~it,~~ ₍the case,₎ nothing sentimental, no pathos, no tears, nothing for the gallery; it deal~~t~~₍s₎ merely with ~~graft. a gross~~ ₍an unsavory₎ business matter; the attempts made to pump sentiment into it ~~were~~ ₍are₎ out of place."

Another Sample:

"~~This~~ ₍Mrs. A's₎ matter is too serious for trial by newspaper; it can only be competently adjudicated by the grand jury & a cou₍r₎t. And so, where is the profit in talking about it? I have nothing to say.

"If it suits Mrs. A's ideas of propriety to wash her private linen in public, let her do it, it is her privilege; I never wash mine at all." ~~And so, where is the profit in talking about it?~~

[*SLC wrote the two previous paragraphs on a penciled note from Jean,
folded and addressed to 'Monsieur' on the outside of the folder:*]

> Grenouille dear,
>   I am deserting my post early but I shall get the necessary mail ready right after lunch. There is nothing pressing now & my hay needs attention.
>   I am afraid you did not sleep as much as you needed to. I saw your light when I retired & again at 3.30 A.M. & I was very sorry to do so.
>   Much love, dear Heart   J.L.C.

Another Sample:

"I have refrained from talking about the Ashcroft matter in the newspapers. I have nothing to say, except that I have been generous to Mrs. Ashcroft, because she is a woman. She belongs in jail, if the evidences in my hands are as damning as lawyers & expert-accountants think they are. In sparing her I have been false to my duty as a citizen, & have had no thanks for it."

Another Sample. I was very strongly moved to send the following one to the Chief Manager of the Associated Press for publication all over the world, but I held my grip on myself, & didn't do it:

_∧(To be given to the Associated Press *only*. Send it to
Melville Stone.)_∧

"The case between Mrs. Ashcroft & me has been in the hands of the lawyers for several months, & it is ~~her~~ ∧Mrs. Ashcroft[¹]'s∧ own fault that it was not settled ~~privately~~ by them without publicity in June. Apparently she wants to try it in the newspapers. To this end she has unloaded upon them many statements—mainly falsehoods. I have not responded in print, but perhaps I ought to abandon that policy & say a word or two publicly.

"The case is simple, there is nothing complex or difficult about it. For several years she signed checks for me. I never watched her, I had full confidence in her. Last spring, however, circumstances moved me to inquire into her stewardship. The examination of her accounts for the preceding two years was begun by an expert accountant. Evidences of crookedness appeared. She ~~proposed to go abroad, but was requested to remain & face the result of the expert's work. The promise was given—by her husband—on the 8ᵗʰ of June, accompanied by the remark that the pair had not taken passage-tickets. Nevertheless they~~ ~~fled to~~ ~~vanished to~~ ~~fled to~~ ∧departed for∧ England immediately. This fact was not discovered until some days later.

"According to the newspapers she has come back, now, to rehabilitate her character. She had the opportunity to try ∧to do∧ it before she went away; she has the opportunity once more. All that is asked of her is, that she explain why she told me the work on her house was finished & had cost $1482.47 (money borrowed of me), ~~& forgot to tell me~~ & refrained from telling me that the money-part of this statement was deliberately untrue. She had spent a couple of thousands more, & this fact she concealed. She went on concealing it; & when it was at last discovered, the ~~dis~~ unearthing was accomplished without any help ~~or thanks~~ ~~or conversation~~ from her or encouragement from her.

"It is also desirable that she explain why she drew from my bank account $9,970 in two years ~~lacking a month—~~ an unprecedented amount of "house money," as she called it in the check-stubs. ~~She had~~ We had no use for any more than about one-tenth of that cash—for stamps, railway tickets, express charges, car fares & one or two other trifles. The other expenses were paid by check.

"There are other details that need explaining, such as "doctored" check-stubs—emergency check-stubs, so to speak—check-stubs doctored to meet the exigencies of an expert-inquest.

"Mrs. Ashcroft has more than once endeavored to relieve me of the responsibility of inviting her to ~~allow~~ submit to an investigation of her stewardship by transferring it to my daughter. This is kind, but it is not quite fair. I am the responsible person, not my daughter.

[SLC tore away the bottom half of the page, removing as many as 75 words]

"I consider that I have been very patient with this noisy lady, up to now; & very charitable, in that I have not instituted criminal proceedings against her for acts committed on ~~the 16th of October, 1907. & Jan. 3, 1908, May 22, 1908 & July 2, 1908, as it was my duty as a citizen to do.~~ Nov. 18, 1907, Aug. 31, 1908, & July 2, 1908, I have spared her because of her sex; I would not have spared a man."

S L. Clemens

~~S L. Clemens~~

"P. S. There are other details that need explaining. She has her opportunity.

"At present I have nothing to say about her husband, except this. On the 31st of March & the 3d of April he was guilty of two or three sly & underhand treacheries, perfidies, & shameless & pathetically small dishonesties—the smallest & shabbiest that have been practised upon me in my lifetime. The average thimble-rigger would be ashamed of them. While he was doing these things against me he was in my employ & serving me for pay. Also he was my trusted & familiar friend. He earned a month in jail, that time, & he ought to have had it."

SLC

Miss Lyon & her mother came straight up to "Summerfield"—in order to make good her boast to the reporters? Perhaps so. We couldn't know that that was all she had in mind. Possibly she might really be intending to arrange a settlement with us. So Mr. Lark came up from New York to conduct our end of it.

But Miss Lyon had gotten over her ferocious eagerness to "make" Mark Twain answer to her for the outrage he had been committing in siezing her property under the false pretence that she had been feloniously appropriating money belonging to him; yes, & she had gotten over her desire to "beard him in his den"—that was one of the phrases—& find out the nature of the "misunderstanding" & how it had originated. She didn't come to us, she didn't send any ambassadors. All day long she didn't. Next day she didn't. Up to luncheon she hadn't. At 2 p.m. she still hadn't. ^Nor at night.^

Evidently she had been "bluffing" all the while, to fool reporters & other innocents; evidently she didn't want a settlement. And why should she? She had no case, she hadn't a leg to stand on; she had stolen money, we had the proofs, & the settlement *we* wanted was a deed of her property, to extinguish a part of her debt.

Next morning the ~~cond~~ ^situation^ remained unchanged. Mr. Lark said we must take the initiative ourselves. He proposed to go to "Summerfield" & open the negotiations. But he wanted a witness, he did not wish to go alone. The wary man! He was quite right; for his mission was to a woman who couldn't put five sentences together that didn't contain a lie; a woman who could get fifteen lies into five sentences when she had her hand ~~it~~ in; a liar who hadn't her match under petticoats; nor in breeches either, if you except her husband.

Yes, Lark must have a witness. Paine? Oh, *hell* no! Me? Oh, *hell* no! It wouldn't be a conference, it would be a riot, right at the start. And who would get the worst of it? Paine & me. That cat would scratch our eyes out.

Then where were we to get that witness? Would Jean go? I hoped she would say yes; ~~& she~~ for she would maintain her dignity, whatever might happen; she would carry with her the best head & the sanest & fairest, except Mr. Lark's; & she would remember what was done & what was said, & be able to state it in a court ~~without~~ in ^a^ plain & simple & straightforward words free from embellishments ~~or~~ ^&^ exaggerations. There couldn't be a better witness. She despised Miss Lyon, but she did not hate her, there not being enough of Miss Lyon for a self-respecting person to hate. Miss Lyon hated Jean, & that was natural, for she had been merciless to Jean, cruel to her, brutal to her, when Jean was suffering from an awful malady & was exiled from home and ~~friends (chiefly~~ friends by Miss Lyon's machinations & falsehoods & treacheries. And Miss Lyon had boasted, when she was at the height of her power under my roof, that Jean should never cross my threshold again during life. Yes, she hated Jean. She had hated her long ago; do you imagine the feeling had diminished any, now that she was down & out & in disgrace, & Jean was invested with the sovereignty she had been criminally planning for *herself*? Not likely.

I told Jean to take sharp note of everything, for she might have to go into court some day as a witness concerning this matter; also I should want her to write it out before it got dim in her memory, & read *that* in court when called upon to testify.

She & Lark went down to the Lobster pot ~~on foot.~~ ^together.^

Here is her narrative. She wrote it ~~next~~ out in the rough next day, & made clean copy for me a week later. I will paste it in, in this place:

On Saturday, July seventeenth, I accompanied Mr. Lark when he went down to "Summerfield" between 10. 30 and 11 o'clock A.M. He wished to see Mrs. Ashcroft, but we were met at the door by Mrs. Lyon, her mother, and told that Mrs. A. was ill and consequently unable to see us. When Mr. Lark asked whether there was any likelihood of his seeing Mrs. Ashcroft in the afternoon, her mother answered that there might be and that she would let him know by telephone.

We had hardly reached "Stormfield" when the message was sent, that Mrs. Ashcroft would see Mr. Lark between two and half past. At the same time, the request was made that he go alone, ʃ which he was unwilling to grant, as he wished me to be there as witness of everything that was said and done.

Immediately after lunch, we again drove down to "Summerfield". This time we were admitted ʃ. Mrs. Lyon being dressed, now, in a black satin or satiene waist and black stuff skirt.

Mrs. Lyon said she would call her daughter, but I had not as yet seated myself on the sofa, beside Mr. Lark, when she entered at the other end of the room, which runs lengthwise across the width of the house.

Mrs. Ashcroft was very simply dressed in a white waist, skirt and belt. She wore no ornaments of any kind; merely her wedding- and a seal-ring. Mrs. Ashcroft didn't speak to me. She bowed as she came in, looking at Mr. Lark, while I merely pronounced her name, as I seated myself.

Mrs. Lyon sat down in a large arm-chair nearly opposite Mr. Lark, only a few feet away, while Mrs. Ashcroft ~~sat~~ seated herself in a very small chair a little at my left, so that I was between her and Mr. Lark.

For several moments nothing was said. Then Mr. Lark began by saying that as we had ˄read˄ in the papers that Mrs. Ashcroft had returned from Europe, in order to settle the difficulty with Mr. Clemens and was going to Redding for that purpose, it had been considered best for him ˄(Mr. L.)˄ to go down and see her, since she had not appeared at "Stormfield". Mrs. Lyon broke in, there, and begged Mr. Lark to treat her daughter like a lady, whereupon Mrs. Ashcroft pretty shortly asked her mother to keep still and not interfere, while Mr. Lark answered that he had no intention of treating her otherwise than as a lady. Then he suggested, that, as some of the things he had to say would be trying for her to hear, perhaps Mrs. Lyon would prefer to withdraw. No attention was paid to the suggestion, so he continued with the matter in hand.

For some time Mrs. A. pretended ignorance of what the attachment was made for. Then, when she saw that it was useless to deny her knowledge of the cause, she tried to make out that she had been allowed to see no check-books and been unable to ~~make~~ ˄prepare˄ ˄make˄ any statement whatsoever. Mr. Lark told her that she and Mr. Ashcroft, together, had made an ~~itemized~~ statement of the cost of putting her house in order and that that statement was absolutely incorrect. Mrs. A. then said that if she could have the bills she would prove that the amount stated as above her estimate, was incorrect. Mr. Lark asked ~~if she had had~~ by whom most of the work had been done, after telling her that in one instance, when the work on "Stormfield" had amounted to $61.00 and that at "Summerfield" to over

$450.—she had paid the whole with one check and written on ˄the˄ stub "for "Stormfield."" Mrs. A. said that the only people who had worked for both places, were Adams, the carpenter, Lounsbury, (Jack of all Trades,) and Hull, the plumber and that their work had all been s amounted to very little. To that Mr. Lark answered that it was Hull's bill of over $400.⁰⁰ which she had put down as work done at "Stormfield." That silenced her for a moment and she changed her tack, trying to look Mr. Lark out of countenance with a long, pathetic, absolutely unwinking gaze. She failed, of course, and wearily said ˄she˄ was "very sorry," if she had done wrong.

In the course of the conversation, Mrs. Ashcroft said, in answer to the accusation that she had drawn checks to pay for the repairs on her house with Father's money, as far back as the summer spent in Tuxedo (1907), that Father had told her to do so. Mr. Lark said Father had no recollection of giving her permission to borrow of him until the spring ˄summer˄ of 1908, when she had said she would have to mortgage her place, in order to pay for the repairs.

Mr. Lark finally stated that if she Mrs. Ashcroft would deed back the property, he *believed* Father would drop his suit. That is to say, if she deeded the property and paid the mortgage, which, after what she had once said, she had no right to do. Then he went on to explain that when Father had given her the property, she had suggested that it be only a life possession for herself & her mother, reverting to Clara & me upon their death, which Father had not considered necessary but had not declined. That clause was not in the deed, however, but ˄that˄ Mrs. Ashcroft had said she would never sell the place, whereas in mortgaging it, she had already practically sold it. She answered that there was no paper showing that she mustn't sell the place, to which Mr. Lark acceded but said she had broken ʃher word in the matter.

Then he drew attention to the amazing checks drawn for "house money" which had amounted to $4000 ˄($7,000?)˄ which we had not succeeded in explaining, as no such amount had been used before. The servants were almost invariably paid by check and so were all bills of any consequence. Mr. Lark went on to say that if she deeded the property & paid the $1500 mortgage, Father would still be the loser of about $3000 but that, to put it bluntly, what he most wanted, was to get her out of the neighborhood. At intervals, Mrs. Ashcroft said she *couldn't* give up her home, that she would raise the money to pay everything back with, although ˄that˄ she had borrowed from Father with the understanding that she was to pay when she was able to, that she was very sorry, must think a while, first, was unable to do so, must talk it over with her mother, must see her lawyer before deciding.

Mr. Lark asked Mrs. Ashcroft if she was supporting her mother in part of 1907 & '08 to which she answered that she was, in the winter, that during the summer of 1907 her mother had lived with her sister, (Mrs. Ashcroft's) in Hartford. When Mr. Lark drew attention to the fact that Mrs. Lyon's board would use up the greater part of Miss Lyon's salary of fifty dollars per month, they both answered that the board had never exceeded eight and a half dollars per week. After which he remarked that that left Miss Lyon fifteen dollars to dress on, to which she responded that Father had given her permission to buy such clothing as she needed, because she had several times declined a higher salary. I told Mr. Lark that that permission had not been given in New York but here, last winter.

In reference to the large amount of house money drawn, Mrs. Ashcroft made a feeble effort to make out that she had used a large amount of it in paying for the furnishings of "Stormfield," which had to be paid for in cash, at Macy's. She volunteered that she could explain the excess, if only she were allowed to see the books and also, that she never had a bank account that amounted to anything. Mr. Lark caught her at once on the furnishing statement & showed her the item in the accountant's record of her checks, where she had paid for the furnishing. A little later, he caught her again. When speaking of the mortgage, she said she could pay it all, as she hadn't touched it since she had deposited it. When asked how it happened that she had just said she hadn't an account, she explained that she had placed the mortgage-money in the Liberty Bank, whereas her other small account was at the Lincoln.

Mr. Lark explained that Father was making this offer of settling the matter out of court, because Mrs. Ashcroft was a woman, that if the trouble had been with a man he wouldn't have thought of it and that he, personally, the believed him far more generous than *he* would be in similar conditions. He also said that as the matter remained unsettled, Father was growing more and more angry about it, realizing, as he did, the ingratitude of her conduct, after being treated practically as a member of the family for nearly seven years, and that he was also feeling that he was not doing his duty as a citizen. He went on to say that if Mrs. Ashcroft felt unwilling to accept the proposition now made, that the complaint had been made out by the Grand Juror of the district and would be handed in. When she didn't understand what that meant, he explained that the complaint would be given to the prosecuting attorney of this county. Mrs. Lyon showed that she knew what that meant, but either Mrs. Ashcroft didn't fully grasp the idea, or she controlled herself admirably.

Once Mrs. Ashcroft seemed on the point of breaking down, whereupon her mother went & soothed her for a few moments.

Mrs. Lyon asked just what would be included in the deed, whether any of the furniture, or not, to which Mr. Lark responded that it meant merely the house, barn and land, which were the same, except for the water improvements, ƒ for which Father had paid, as when he gave them.

Mrs. Ashcroft repeated that she was very sorry, at least four times and twice that she would raise the money to pay everything back with., once before, and once after, she had told Mr. Lark to do as he chose, that she and her mother "had each other" and were satisfied with that.

When Mrs. Ashcroft wanted to see her lawyer before deciding & then go in to New York to see Mr. Stanchfield, Mr. Lark suggested that that might not be desired, because in doing so, she would be out of the jurisdiction of the state.

Finally, at 3. 35 P.M. Mrs. Ashcroft gave in and Mr. Lark said he would return with the deed, for signature, Monday morning, July nineteenth. As we were leaving, they both very nearly had histerics and as it was, were weeping in each other's arms.

Once, w after saying she was sorry, Mrs. Ashcroft called on her mother to back up her statement that she had never drawn up any checks falsely, saying: "You know I wouldn't do such a thing, don't you, Mother"?, to which Mrs. Lyon of course answered: "No, dear, of course you wouldn't." To which Mr. Lark said: "Mrs. Lyon, you are were not the a witness on those occasions, the checks are the witnesses of that fact."

After we reached "Stormfield," it was found that the deed could be obtained from Mr. Nickerson at once, thus saving Mr. Lark ⱡ the trip on Monday.

So once more I went down to "Summerfield," this time on foot, accompanied by Mr. G. M. Acklom. We were met at their entrance, at 5. 45 ₍6. 15₎ P.M.. Mr. Acklom remained with the horse, while Mr. Nickerson, Mr. Lark & I went in. We found M̶r̶ the ladies quieted down somewhat, but ready to break down.

While Mr. Nickerson read the deed aloud to Mrs. Ashcroft, in the small back parlor, Mr. Lark & I remained in the large room, while Mrs. Lyon did the same, sitting with her back to us, looking out of the window opening down the hill. When the reading was over, Mrs. Ashcroft showed no unwillingness to sign it, or to draw the mortgage-check, although she was very nervous, indeed. She wasn't sure of the date & for a moment, seemed uncertain of how to draw the check. Mrs. Lyon once more asked about the furniture, saying she had brought a lot of it from Farmington. She was again told the furniture would not be taken and then, when they asked how soon they ₍must₎ move out, tearfully remarking that they had nowhere to go to, as the Farmington house was let, Mr. Lark first said they could remain until Sept. 15th, which was the date Mrs. Lyon asked for, but after we stepped outside, I reminded him that Sept. 15, gave them within two days of two months and that Sept. 1st seemed sufficient to me, so he stepped back and told them that after all, six weeks ought really to suffice them in finding a place to move to.

When Mr. Nickerson handed Mrs. Ashcroft the dollar bill, necessary, to make such a proceeding legal, she tore it in half, half screaming and exclaiming that she would not take it. So Mr. Nickerson carefully picked the two pieces up and put them in his wallet.

Just before leaving, Mr. Lark told Mrs. Ashcroft that he thought Father ₍would₎ now release the lien on t̶h̶e̶i̶r̶ her Farmington house.

Soon after we reached "Stormfield," Mrs. Lyon again telephoned, asking whether they must still live in daily dread of further trouble. In answering her, Mr. Lark said he was pretty sure that Father would bring no other suit, but that that was of course for him to decide.

Jean L. Clemens.

July 24, 1909.

Mr. Lark & Jean call her "Mrs. Ashcroft." It is an unfamiliar sound. Ever since the marriage the countryside have continued to call her Miss Lyon; likewise my family & my servants; likewise Ashcroft himself. Apparently nobody was impressed with the idea that the marriage was a real one—not even the husband himself. Meantime, what has become of that aristocratic high-flying hyphenated name? It seems to have died an early death. In those newspaper interviews Miss Lyon has discarded it herself.

In them she is plain undecorated "Mrs. Ashcroft." It is good wisdom; it is best to go before a democratic public unhyphenated when a person has returned from a foreign flight to patch-up & poultice a damaged character.

When Miss Lyon chose the hyphenated name she said it was because she was not willing to sink her own well known name ˄(Lyon)˄ out of sight of a name the world had never heard of (Ashcroft.) She certainly was known to all the newspapers of the country as my secretary. She was proud of her celebrity & often said so. She mistook it for fame, which was an error. It was perishable, it was evanescent; it dropped out of use only three months ago, yet it is already forgotten. She is become "Mrs. Ashcroft," the cipher, the unknown, the unpetted, the uninvited. It is a pity, too for she dearly loved notoriety.

She was sick when Jean & Lark made their forenoon visit. I used to believe in her sicknesses, but I have my doubts about them now. She could always get over them expeditiously—more expeditiously then anybody *I* ever encountered before—& then she was straightway just as sound & spry & good as new. It was because she had been drinking, & had slept off her "jag˄," but I didn't know that, in those bygone days. Nobody told me. And I wouldn't have listened, anyway, & would have shut the slanderer up. They all knew that, & they did not choose to instruct me & get no thanks for it. But there are plenty of witnesses now: Katy, our ancient maid; also Katy the laundress; the contractors & a dozen or so of their men; the architect's assistant; the Lounsburys; Paine; Clara. Finally Claude, the French butler—whom Miss Lyon always said didn't know what dishonesty was, with either his tongue or his pen. He says she emptied two quarts of Scotch whisky in her room, per week, ˄(& sometimes three),˄ besides what she drank in the evening down stairs. Also that she drank two & sometimes three bottles of cocktails in her room per week, besides the cocktails she drank before dinner down stairs. Katy endorses these statements, & says Miss Lyon was so addicted to robbing the guestrooms, both here & in New York, that she (Katy) had to watch those rooms, & visit them when guests arrived—as a precaution. A necessary precaution, for she generally found that Miss Lyon had been there & created a drouth.

Miss Lyon often came to my room away in the night, both here & in New York to get whisky—she being sick again. Once, & possibly oftener—but once anyway, I flew out at her & said, "Why in the nation don't you keep whisky in your room, when you are so often ill & need it in the night?" These whisky-raids of hers ˄would˄ certainly have attracted the attention of an intelligent person, but they never attracted mine. John Stanchfield (as I have remarked some score or so of pages back) told me he saw her drink three cocktails one after the other & walk off erect & steady; Mrs. Stanchfield has since told me that that was right after Miss Lyon had refreshed her works with a glass of straight whisky.

It was Miss Lyon that introduced the cocktail to us. This was five years ago, after we came back from Italy. We never had any real use for that deadly drink, nor any desire for it; & since Miss Lyon went away, four months ago, we have never seen a cocktail—nor asked for one. She left a supply behind her, but we have it yet. When she didn't know she was going to be dismissed, she laid in wine, whisky & cocktails enough to start a saloon with—oh, an astonishing invoice! & the first thing she did when she retired to the Lobster pot was to order twelve quarts of Scotch whisky, with cocktails, brandy, etc., in proportion. At that time Lounsbury carted five barrels of liquor bottles away from our cellar. He had carted away ten barrels of empties earlier.

I think I have spoken of the fact that in July & August of last year (with only three drinkers among the guests, & they not present more than three days in the two months) we consumed 48 quarts of Scotch whisky! Since Miss Lyon departed, one ~~bott~~ quart a week has sufficed for the household & the guests. The bottle that stands upon my night table shows no perceptible decline—which is natural enough, for I have taken but three drinks from it in five weeks. A bottle used to last me a week or ten days; I expect the present one to last me several months. Miss Lyon's departure has been a valuable moral investment for us.

Yes, when Lark & Jean paid their forenoon visit, she was sick.

I like Jean's account very much; it is simply-worded & direct, & it not only furnishes facts, but pictures, also. At least for me; for I know that sofa & that house, & I know the actors & their characteristics; & so when they do a thing, I *see* them do it. I can see that shrewd, & wise, & alert—but courteous & self-possessed—young fellow, Lark; I can see that slender & little & shapely Miss Lyon, outwardly merely vicious & angry, but with hellfire boiling & raging inside; I can see Jean, grave, attentive, compassionate; & I can see—& pity—that gentle, shrinking, timid, meek little mother, that worthy, esteemed, respected, blemishless little fat commonplace thing who is miserable, wretched, ashamed, hurt to the heart by her daughter's disgrace, & in fact is doing about ten times as much suffering over the situation as is the said daughter that brought it about.

The idea of that humble little thing, that soft little thing, clouding up, cold, & queenly & sombre, & rebuking that young stranger—*that* I am not able to see! that picture is lost to me. I have seen a worm turn, & so I know what it is like—but Mrs. Lyon? No, it is beyond me.

Treat her daughter "as "like a lady." There is something pathetic about that appeal, it was so irrelevant & so conspicuously premature, seeing that poor little Lark hadn't done a thing, & the daughter wasn't a lady anyhow. No, I can't see that picture, but I can see, vividly, the next picture—Miss Lyon, with snapping eyes, turning insolently upon her poor little champion & shutting her up! Yes, I can see that—I know exactly how Miss Lyon looked. And I can see her mother wilt. I can see it quite plainly; for I saw Miss Lyon wilt her mother once, in New York. It was by accident. They didn't know I saw it, but I did.

It didn't hurt me, grieve me, shame me as it ought to have done. I suppose, because I had an aversion for Mrs. Lyon—merely because she was so meek & harmless. Character-less, you know. It was not a strong aversion, but just an aversion; about the aversion an emperor would feel for a doughnut; mere indolent disfavor, without passion, without fire, without malignity; in fact, just the way *any* large-minded person would feel about a doughnut. Well, Mrs. Lyon is a doughnut; just a humble, unassuming Christian doughnut, it is all you can say for her.

Her case is pitiful, poor little woman. The Ashcrofts have been in hell for several months, & she has been in it with them, most undeservedly.

Another picture I can see: Miss Lyon, defeated, silenced, staring across the interven-ing Jean at Mr. Lark, with her wicked eyes, trying to look him out of countenance. I know that exhibition; she treated me to it more than once. I recognize the "long, pathetic, absolutely unwinking gaze." Pathetic. Yes, she was doing the pathetic by art; the kind of art that fools no one.

Miss Lyon's remark that there was "no paper" (no writing) showing that the place was to revert to my daughters upon her death & her mother's is a startling instance of the influence of environment upon a person's morals. Until she fell under Ashcroft's influence I am quite sure she would have felt outraged & indignant if any one had suggested that her spoken promise wasn't a sufficient security, without being backed up by writings.

I am glad to know that Mr. Lark was frank & truthful about my main reason for bringing the suit—"to get her out of the neighborhood." He was representing me, & that is what I would have said, myself.

She must have been hard pushed to account for "house-money" outgo when she said she had to pay Stormfield furnishing-bills at Macy's in cash! Macy's people would have taken her check.

The "complaint" referred to as having been made out by the grand juror had been hanging over Miss Lyon's head several days; it was the first step toward sending her to jail. It was my duty as a citizen to send her to jail, but I was doing what any other weak man would do—shirking it.

Tearing up the dollar bill & squealing—*that* is Miss Lyon! Miss Lyon under the "influence." I believe that that creature is just as sensitive to insult, & as sharply pained by it, as even an actual lady could be. And yet she is a brute; just a plain, simple, heartless brute, & rotten to the spine.

Paine went down to New York yesterday (which was the 24th of August) to remove my stuff to the Lincoln Deposit, which is in 42d street & handier. In the train, on his way back, he saw Mr. & Mrs. Peck, who have that big place over yonder on ¢top of the ridge, the other side of our valley. Peck said he had seen Miss Lyon drink astonishingly, here at Stormfield; & Mrs. Peck said she had seen her in a Pullman car when she was stupid with liquor, & smelling of it, too. I must be miraculously dull, & miraculously unsuspicious, never to have noticed these things—*at the time.* ₐEvidentlyₐ When she was drunk to everybody else, I took it for hysterics—which was Ashcroft's name for it. If I had known how heavy our liquor bills were, I should have been obliged to suspect Ashcroft or Miss Lyon, one or the other, but I never looked at bills of any kind. Consequently I knew nothing of these liquor-freshets until the expert's investigation of Miss Lyon's checks revealed them.

To return to the subject of digging the Ashcroft's out of the Lobsterpot ("Summerfield.["]") Mr. Lark was suspicious of the Ashcrofts. ~~Mrs~~ Miss Lyon, by deeding back the property, had clearly & unequivocally confessed her thefts. Upon reflection she might regret that confession & try to nullify it by endeavoring to get the deed set aside. So he proposed to go down & clinch the matter by giving her a lease of the place until the 1st of September, which would further validate the transfer.

Clara was to go with him, as a witness. Not a pleasant error, since (according to the interviews) this whole trouble had arisen out of Clara's "jealousy" of Miss Lyon. Jealousy based upon what? However, Miss Lyon had to find an explanation of some kind, & one explanation would answer as well as another, as long as for her reputation's sake Miss Lyon couldn't afford to furnish the real one. The interviews indicated that Miss Lyon's mind had been in a condition of pretty wild disorder, for more than once she named Jean as the jealous one! Whereas Jean had never even been on the place, & ~~w/~~ the insurrection was under full headway two months & a half before ~~Jean~~ she had a chance to hear of it.

I asked Clara to make a narrative of her visit to the Lobster pot while the details were fresh in her memory, to be used on the witness stand if this matter ever got into Court. She did it.

ₐCLARA'S NARRATIVE.ₐ

On Thursday the 20th of July Mr. Lark came out to Redding with the intention of presenting a lease to Mrs. Ashcroft which would permit her and her mother to remain in the house 'till the first of September; they had asked for this permission in the interview on the preceding Saturday at which my sister was present.

Mr. Lark was obliged to wait while Mr. Nickerson prepared the lease which required nearly two hours and then desiring a witness Mr. Lark asked me to accompany him to Mrs. Ashcroft's house. Mr. Lounsbury also went with us but on arriving there we were first asked by Wells, their man, to wait a moment and were then met by Mrs. Lyon instead of Mrs. Ashcroft.

Mrs. Lyon came onto the porch by the kitchen door with the announcement that Miss Lyon was ill in bed. Never having known Mrs. Lyon except as a calm reserved woman it was a surprise to see her attack Mr. Lark in great excitement and anger. Her face was flushed and she gesticulated nervously as she addressed him in a loud tone of voice:

"You took an unfair advantage of us last Saturday and did not keep your word for you promised us to go away and bring back the deed in two or three days but instead of that you came back with it the same day and therefore it is not *legal*. My daughter does not even *know* what she ₐsignedₐ and we are both of us *crazy;* you intimidated her into giving ₫ her signature by threatening to arrest her if she didn't—and you *never* would have *dared* to do such a thing if there had been a *man* in the house"—by this time she was fairly screaming and although Mr. Lark attempted to interrupt her and deny her statement that he had threatened her daughter with arrest on the previous Saturday she would not listen to him but continued to talk in a stream of ₵ words expressing resentment and rage.

Mrs. Lyon had not once looked at me, nevertheless at this point I turned to her and said—

"Mrs. Lyon I don't see why it should ever have been necessary for us to *ask* your daughter to return this property, why wasn't she eager to do it of her own accord?"

It was evident now by her reply that up to this moment she had merely been reciting a part which had been taught her either by her daughter or her daughter's attorney for when she answered my question it was with a burst of genuine feeling that could no longer be suppressed by legal advice. "Do you think *I* want to stay here another day, do you think I want this horrible land or house or anything remotely connected with the Clemens family? No—no—no. We're packing to get out as fast as we can"—

"Very good then Mrs. Lyon—I interrupted—that is all that your daughter signed last Saturday, she merely returned what you do not want yourselves & what we have no use for as property but what we do want because of the circumstances which make your daughter's presence so unpleasant." To this Mrs. Lyon made no direct reply but half sobbing exclaimed "if you had any pity any *pity*"

"I have great pity for you Mrs. Lyon I answered but none whatever for your daughter—"

She wailed on "I have never had one happy day in this house not *one*" and here Mr. Lark ventured an unfortunate remark which threw Mrs. Lyon into hysterics. He said:

"I know how unhappy you must have been for your daughter treated you so horribly."—

"My daughter treated me horribly? She screamed rushing up to Mr. Lark, how *dare* you say such a thing? She has always been good to me, how dare you, how *dare* you?"

Mr. Lark and I tried to appease her and persuaded her to sit down on a bench at the back of the porch; the others then having withdrawn a little, Mrs. Lyon still weeping began to talk with me somewhat more quietly. "How could you accuse her of such things after her seven years' of devotion to your family, she *lived* for you all and worked so hard in your interest—"

"That was what we believed I said and we appreciated it and for that reason my father gave her this place & lent her money for the repairs—"

"She worked so very hard, Mrs. Lyon continued—looking after the Servants and the household"

"And Mrs. Lyon that is why we offered to get a housekeeper which she refused—or to raise her salary which she refused. We tried to make her feel that she was one of us and when she did not wish to accept a higher salary for her increased services I told her to at least buy herself dresses now and then which she was willing to do.

But I can't talk about all this with you Mrs. Lyon, there are so many things that are impossible to say to you about your own daughter."

"But what is it all anyway asked Mrs. Lyon, *we* have'nt any money we have'nt a bit—"

"*You* have'nt any—no" I replied

"Nor has Isabel"—she said

"No I suppose not"—I replied (over

"Well then who do you think has it, Mr. Ashcroft?" she asked.

"It does not matter who has it Mrs. Lyon for it is not the money we want, it's merely this house and land and that you have relinquished."

She was still sobbing and moaning all the time she talked.

"Why did your father give power of attorney to my daughter and then deny it afterwards?"

"He denied, I replied, having seen the extraordinary paper by which Miss Lyon could possess herself of everything and ruin us if she chose."

"But she did'nt use it" Mrs. Lyon said

"No, Mrs. Lyon she had'nt yet and I do not believe that your daughter did all these things by herself. Of course she was influenced but it was a terrible thing for her to *be* influenced when she held that powerful and trusted position."

"Yes—yes—Mrs. Lyon muttered as if dazed by it all, and then repeated the remark she had made earlier about her faithful devotion to us.

"I used to think so, I answered until I heard from various sides in N.Y. that she was telling lies about me and betraying my confidences—she changed very much in the past two years."

"Yes she has changed, Mrs. Lyon admitted, but she has been very ill for some time; and then why did you not answer the letter she sent your father asking whether it would be all right for her to go to England instead of waiting 'till she got over there and then shaming her by attaching her property and letting it all come out" in the newspapers?"

"My father never received any such letter, I answered and besides Mr. Stanchfield telephoned to Mr. Ashcroft in N.Y. and told him not to go to England as he needed him & Mrs. Ashcroft here. The whole thing got into the ~~Bridgeport~~ papers through the Bridgeport ~~papers~~ notary and not through us for certainly we did not care for this newspaper talk"—then feeling somewhat irritated that I should be filling the position of the accused I called upon to account for my actions I broke out rather vehemently and said

"Mrs. Lyon your daughter is guilty—*guilty*"

"Guilty of what?" she asked At these words she rose with a gesture that made me draw back but rushing past me she appealed to Mr. Lounsbury & Wells who were standing a few steps away from the porch out on the grass, repeating over & over again at the top of her lungs

"Do you hear what Miss Clemens says? She says my daughter has been guilty of stealing of stealing—of **stealing**"

Her screams were heard up at my father's house some distance away. (Half a mile, or nearly that.)

I regretted my remark and once more we all had to make an effort to quiet her begging her to think no more of any of it but she was half crazy with unhappiness and reiterated many times that she had never been in such a position before and could not live through the disgrace of it. Finally she turned to me & said: "Why didn't you come and settle it all with us instead of going to law about it and ruining our name for life?"

I might have gone to *you* I replied but what good would it have done to go to your daughter? Didn't she live for weeks in the same house with me after she knew that there was something the matter without offering to make any explanation of any kind? We lunched and dined together daily after she knew that she was suspected but she remained silent. There never would have been all this trouble anyway if she had simply left our vicinity instead of insisting upon staying here."

"But she has done nothing wrong, Mrs. Lyon continued, she *couldn't*. Yet think what we have got to face. All her friends ask her why she does not refute these accusations but of what use is it for *her* to refute them, your father is the only one who can do that, / oh! I have always believed in my God in Heaven. I had faith in my Redeemer., but what trouble I have had and still have."◊ She had such a tragic expression in her face that one or two tears dropped from my ~~voice~~ eyes onto her onto her dress and when she saw them she drew me down with one arm about my neck and poured forth a fresh appeal for her daughter's name. "Please say in the paper that she never did anything that wasn't perfectly honorable and straight"—

I glanced at Mr. Lark and then said "Would you like us to say that she has made restitution and that her accounts had gotten mixed because of overwork?"

At first Mrs. Lyon said yes but then concluded it was better to say nothing more. She seemed suddenly to be almost prostrated and kept exclaiming "I feel so sick, so sick"—so we helped her into the house and got her onto the sofa.

When I leaned over her to say goodbye she said in a low tone "you nearly killed her when you suspected her of taking things that time in the garret when Dorothea Gilder was there—" I replied that I had only asked her about some beads which had been in an old cabinet for years & were now missing.

"Well did'nt you find them?" she asked "yes, I answered, but not in the same place."

Then Mrs. Lyon in the midst of sobs drew me down still nearer and whispered in my ear "if she ever did anything wrong it was because she was ill."

Mr. Lark then suggested our going & we left her in the care of Wells.

———

It is pitiful. That poor old mother had done no harm, & yet she is doing the main part of the suffering. The Ashcrofts have the relief of cursing me (Miss Lyon knows that art) & planning vengeances with me ~~for the~~ ^as^ victim, but Mrs. Lyon hasn't ^any^ relief to resort to. Malignities & vengeances are not for her; she is more gently made.

It was like Miss Lyon's heartlessness to stay up stairs & leave her mother to fight her battle for her. It is true that she was up stairs, & doubtless "sick"—in the usual way—but she was not in bed. Lounsbury saw her at a window, looking down upon the fracas.

Clara's report, as far as it goes, agrees with Mr. Lark's, but his goes further. Mrs. Lyon said her daughter would not ac₍c₎ept the lease; that her daughter had signed the deed without knowing what it was, & it was therefore without value in law, & that she would take measures with her lawyer to annul that paper.

Pretty wild talk, in view of the fact that the notary *read the deed aloud,* from be₍ginn₎ing to end, to Miss Lyon before she signed it. I tell you a body needs to be well fortified with witnesses when he deals with the Ashcroft firm of professional liars.

So Mr. Lark's lease-scheme didn't work, but he was not troubled. He said Miss Lyon's lawyer would not be at all likely to allow her to try to annul the deed. He believed the tribe would vacate the Lobster pot the 1ˢᵗ of September, & drop the idea of resistance.

Very well, we have arrived this far: that Miss Lyon, in re₍s₎toring the property & handing back the mortgage-money ($1500) has quite ~~definitely~~ ₍concretely₎ acknowledged herself a thief, wh₍i₎le denying it in the abstract with her mouth.

I wonder if she agrees with her mother that if a person signs a paper without knowing what ~~the paper~~ ₍it₎ contains, the paper is invalid & of no force? If so, I wonder what she thinks of the formidable Power of Attorney which purports to have been signed by me?—a paper which I never saw nor heard of until six & a half months after the date on which I (ostensibly) signed it.

In one of those interviews poor Mrs. Lyon makes one remark of a rather striking sort; where, in her despair & sense of forlornness, & referring to her daughter, she finds refuge & solace in this blessed fact: "We have each other." It would have been inexcusable cruelty if Lounsbury had added, aloud instead of to himself, "and our dear Ashcroft."

For without a doubt they have had enough & more than enough of the dear Ashcroft long before this. Indeed they began to realize the hole they had sprung into straightway after ~~their~~ marriage their panic fright had driven them into. They came from New York in the train with my niece & her husband, Julia & Edward Loomis, & they stayed apart not only in the train but after they reached this house. They addressed no remarks to each other at dinner; they kept well apart during the evening, & all of the next two days. They could not have been a colder pair if they had been on the ice a week. The room next to mine had been prepared for them, because it had a double bed in it; but they provoked further remark by taking separate rooms. They continued this as long as they ~~remained~~ ₍slept₎ in the house, which was ten or twelve nights.

~~Ten or twelve days~~ ₍Shortly₎ after Miss Lyon re-deeded the property, her husband arrived in New York from England. He called on Mr. Lark, ₍some days later,₎ & wanted a settlement arranged, & was evidently anxious about it & eager to get it accomplished & done with. He said he would do anything in reason & was willing to put trifles aside & deal with essentials only.

That was on the 3ᵈ of August—& Miss Lyon was on her way down, that same afternoon,₍,₎ ~~to meet him.~~ Mr. Lark telephoned us the pleasant news, & said everything would be amicably & satisfactorily settled next day & the long wrangle ended.

But he didn't know Miss Lyon was on her way down! On her way down, & ravenous to take a hand! But he knew it the first thing next morning, when the New York Times came out with another Ashcroftian interview. The Times was just the place for it, for it keeps the standing sign at its head, "All the news that's fit to print." And whenever it can get hold of any that isn't fit to print, it prints that, too. For example:

ASHCROFT ACCUSES MISS CLARA CLEMENS

**Says Mark Twain's Daughter Made Charges
Because She Was Jealous of Her Success.**

QUOTES HUMORIST'S LETTER

**In It He Praised His Secretary and Rebuked Daughter for
Complaints—No Diversion of Funds.**

Ralph W. Ashcroft, manager of the Mark Twain Company at 24 Stone Street, whose wife, for years before her marriage was private secretary to Mr. Clemens, was sued by the humorist to recover $4,000, gave out a statement yesterday in which he warmly defends his wife against insinuations that she misused Mr. Clemens's money.

Mr. Ashcroft, in his statement, accuses Miss Clara Clemens, daughter of the humorist, of having been envious of Miss Lyon's achi[e]vements as secretary to her father. Miss Clemens, he says, wanted to have Miss Lyon removed from her place.

Mr. Ashcroft declares that it was without the knowledge of the humorist's New York lawyers that the cottage at Redding, Conn., adjoining the Clemens estate, which he gave to Miss Lyon, was attached in his recent suit. He gives excerpts from the author's letters to indicate the high opinion he once had of Miss Lyon. This is the statement:

"Since my return from Europe, a week ago, I have thoroughly investigated the occurrences connected with quarrels forced on Mrs. Ashcroft by Mary Twain's daughters, and have heard what both sides have to say in the matter.

"To understand the matter in its true light, it is necessary to hark back to the Summer of 1904, when Mrs. Clemens died in Italy. Mrs. Ashcroft (then Miss Lyon) was Mark Twain's secretary. When his wife died, Mark Twain was like a ship without a rudder, and, as Henry H. Rogers said to me a few days before he died: 'At that crisis in his life, Clemens needed just such a person as Miss Lyon to look after him and his affairs, and Miss Lyon came to the front and has stayed at the front all these years and no one has any right to criticise her.'"

Daughters Jealous of Miss Lyon.

"For two years or more after their mother's death, both girls were in sanitaria most of the time, and the younger daughter has been under the care of nerve specialists ever since. Under these circumstances, Miss Lyon naturally became

---

Mr. Clemens's hostess and person of affairs, and how well she fulfilled the position is known to all who met her in those capacities. Both daughters, however, became jealous of her, were afraid that Mark Twain would marry her, and of[t]en indeavored to destroy his confidence in her. She probably would have been supplanted two or three years ago, but the elder daughter had musical and other ambitions, and thought more of them than of taking care of her old father and filling her mother's place.

"One's vocal ambitions, however, sometimes exceed one's capacities in that direction, and the bitter realization of this has, in this instance, caused the baiting of a woman who has earned and kept the admiration and respect of all of Mark Twain's friends. Mark Twain well has said of her: 'I know her better than I have known any one on this planet, except Mrs. Clemens.' When one of his daughters made an attack on her about two years ago, he wrote this:

> I have to have somebody in whom I have confidence to attend to every detail of my daily affairs for me except my literary work. I attend to not one of them myself; I give the instructions and see that they are obeyed. I give Miss Lyon instructions—she does nothing of her own initiative. When you blame her, you are merely blaming me—she is not open to criticism in the matter. When I find that you are not happy in that place, I instruct her to ask Drs. Peterson and Hunt to provide change for you, and she obeys the instructions. In her own case I provide no change, for she does all my matters well, and, although they are often delicate and difficult, she makes no enemies, either for herself or me. I am not acquainted with another human being of whom this could be said.

> It would not be possible for any other person to see reporters and strangers every day, refuse their requests, and yet send them away good and permanent friends to me and herself—but I should make enemies of many of them if I tried to talk with them. The servants in the house are her friends, they all have confidence in her, and not many people can win and keep a servant's friendship and esteem—one of your mother's highest talents. All Tuxedo likes Miss Lyon—the hackmen, the aristocrats and all. She has failed to secure your confidence and esteem, and I am sorry. I wish it were otherwise, but it is no argument since she has not failed in any other person's case. One failure to fifteen hundred successes means that the fault is not with her.

The Expense Accounts Explained.

"The only person, so far as I know, who has charged Mrs. Ashcroft with dishonesty is Clara Clemens. Mark Twain has not, and his lawyers have not. As is the custom in all large households, so it was in the Clemens household— money was drawn from the bank in cash to pay the thousand-and-one debts and expenses that it is not convenient to pay by check. When Mark Twain placed all of his financial responsibilities on Miss Lyon's shoulders (in addition to her other manifold duties) he did not tell her to employ a bookkeeper to keep a set of books, and she simply followed the custom that had been in vogue under Mr. Clemens's régime, to wit: no books of account were kept (other than the check book) and no itemized or other record was kept of cash expenditures. Miss Lyon was never asked to keep any such record, and did not do so.

"Clara Clemens now insinuates that Miss Lyon embezzled a large part of the money she drew from the bank in cash. Fortunately Miss Lyon is in a position to prove that the bulk of the money was paid to Clara Clemens herself for the expenses of concert tours and the delightful experience of paying for the hire of concert halls destined to be mainly filled with 'snow' or 'paper,' for the maintenance of her accompanist, Charles E. Wark, and to defray other cash expenditures that an embryonic Tetrezzini is naturally called upon to make. Returning home one day from an unsuccessful and disheartening tour Clara Clemens simply couldn't stomach the sight of Miss Lyon's successful administration of her father's affairs. So it became a case of 'get rid of her by hook or crook;' and she endeavored to enlist my sympathies and services along these lines, with the result that—well, I married Miss Lyon.

"Mr. Clemens's New York lawyers now state that Mrs. Ashcroft's cottage was attached without their knowledge or advice. They also now state that they did not know that Mr. Clemens and I had made an agreement regarding the money he advanced for the rehabilitation of the cottage, which agreement makes his suit against Mrs. Ashcroft for this indebtedness absolutely groundless and farcical, in that no one can sue for a debt which has been partially paid and the balance of which is not due.

"The agreement is as follows:

Redding, Conn., March 13, 1909.
Received from R. W. Ashcroft his notes for the sum of $982.47, being estimated balance due on money advanced to Isabel V. Lyon for the renovation of "The Lobster Pot," this receipt being given on the understanding that said Ashcroft will pay in like manner any further amounts that his examination of my disbursements for the fiscal year ending Feb. 23, 1909, shows were advanced for like purposes.
S. C. CLEMENS. (Seal.)

I agree to the above and to make said examination as promptly as my other duties will permit.
R. W. ASHCROFT. (Seal.)

An Amicable Settlement.

"The matter has been settled amicably as far as Mark Twain, Mrs. Ashcroft, and I are concerned, and the adjustment will be consummated as soon as the proper papers can be drawn up, although it may be necessary for Mrs. Ashcroft to commence suit against Mark Twain to set aside the deed transferring the cottage to him, simply to protect her legal rights for the time being; as, while we believe that Mark Twain and his lawyer, John B. Stanchfield, will abide by their promises, still there is always the contingency of the death of either or both to be provided against. If Mr. Rogers had not died so suddenly and unexpectedly the affair would have been settled long ago without any publicity. It is an unfortunate occurrence all around. I am still manager of the Mark Twain Company, and shall so remain for the present. My contract has nearly two years to run."

Efforts to talk with Mr. Clemens at his home at Redding last night were futile. A TIMES reporter called up the humorist's home on the telephone, was informed that he had retired, and that, under no circumstances, would any word of Mr. Ashcroft's statement be conveyed to him. It was stated that Miss Clemens was at home, but that she, too, had retired, and that no communication would be taken to her until morning. It was also found impossible to reach John B. Stanchfield, Mr. Clemens's lawyer.

That shell surprised Mr. Stanchfield & Mr. Lark when it fell in their camp. They were familiar with converted criminals, but this was new: they had never seen one get unconverted again so suddenly. Still, it did not surprise them so much as it would have done a matter of three weeks earlier: the time Ashcroft tacitly promised that he ˄& his century plant˄ would stay & face the investigation, then clandestinely ran away to Europe the same night.

I enjoy this interview, because it is such a matchless portrayal of Ashcroft's charafcter. And so innocent, too; so unconscious. He is not aware that he [is] exposing himself. He thinks the reader will be admiring him.

At *last* we know why Clara Clemens was jealous of little Miss Lyon! she was jealous of Miss Lyon's "achievements" as my secretary. It is definite, but it has a defect: it lacks adequacy. And it has another defect: it puts forward a weak reason, when there was a strong one in stock. I think Clara could, or might, or maybe ought, to be jealous of Miss Lyon's achievements as a *house-decorator, & deviser of charming & eloquent & effe[c]tive harmonies in color,* for that woman's achievements in that line are *real* achievements—soft, delicate, dainty, unobtrusive, caressing, inviting, enchanting—damnation, Howells, they *are* achievements, it's the right name for them!

And yet this dull & blind ass leaves them unnoticed, unmentioned, unpraised, to bray about her "achievements" as my secretary! Whereas, there weren't any. *He* knew, long ago, what I *didn't* know, to-wit, that she deliberately & persistently left every duty of her secretaryship undone that she could shirk. He also knew, & confesses, that she adopted my loose & systemless fashion of keeping my accounts, & made no effort to institute better methods—as any ~~other~~ secretary not idiotic & not lazy would have done. He knew, what I didn't know, that when I wrote the private letter to my daughter which he has come by dishonestly & has dishonorably used in print, it contained not a single compliment that was deserved, save one—her soothing & ingenious & suc[c]essful ways with reporters & interviewers. He knew, what I didn't know, that the Tuxedo people disliked her, & were not thankful to me for pushing her into their social life. He knew, what I didn't know, that from the beginning of her life with us to the end of it, she made enemies, not friends. He knew, what I didn't know, that he *and* Miss Lyon worked hard during three years—through lies told to Drs. Hunt & Peterson—to keep Jean exiled from her father's house, & still kept her exiled during the third year when she was well enough, all that year, to come home. (She has now—August 30—been under my roof more than four months & is the healthiest person on the place.) He knew, what I didn't know, that he & she told friends of ours that Jean would be a trouble at home & that they should keep her away the rest of her life—for *my* sake! He knew, what I didn't know, that we have never had a servant that didn't detest Miss Lyon. And he knew, what I didn't know, that during the last two years Miss Lyon spent in my house she was stealing money from me by the handful & supporting him with it.

It is an error to say I have not charged dishonesty upon Miss Lyon. Ashcroft knows I have charged it everywhere except in print. He knows I can't say anything in print; for, he is aware a Major General cannot waive rank & dispute in public with a sutler's clerk.

Ashcroft says, "Mark Twain well has said of her: 'I know her better than I have known any one on this planet, except Mrs. Clemens.'"

He does not explain that this is from a private letter of mine, & that he came by it by theft. Stolen in this way: that Miss Lyon copied it before mailing it. No—*that* is not the crime—keeping a copy of it was of no consequence; but letting him have it to for publication was a crime; a crime of such baseness, too, that it puts the final stamp of treachery upon her character, & is ample evidence that she is capable of any dishonorable act that has a place in the list of human shabbinesses.

Ashcroft is curiously illogical. He is apparently defending & reinstating Miss Lyon's character; & as an argument in her favor he uses my *former* high opinion of her. My *later* opinion of her is the only one that has value now, & can be worth quoting as evidence now—& *that* one accuses her of being a thief; & she, by reconveying her house to me, has distinctly & definitely *confessed* that at the charge, is true.

When it comes to lying, Ashcroft seems to have *no* reserves, no modesties. "Mr. Ashcroft declares that it was without the knowledge of the humorist's New York lawyers that the cottage was attached."

He was saying this right after his talk with Mr. Lark; & so, when he said it he knew it was Mr. Lark himself who had had the cottage attached.

Ashcroft is even shabby enough put to drag the dead out of the grave to give false evidence. "Mr. Rogers said to me, etc., etc." It is a plain simple lie; Mr. Rogers said nothing of the kind. Read it, Howells! You knew the grave, ungushing, unexcitable Chief of the Standard Oil—try to imagine him losing his cool & placid self-control & breaking out with a volcanic & adoring eulogy like that, about *anybody!* It would have been as impossible to him to do that, as it was impossible to him to say one thing to Clara;—on about Miss Lyon—on a Monday, say for instance—& then say the opposite to Ashcroft on the Tuesday. He had known & liked Clara for sixteen years, & he talked to her without reserve. He said he had never liked Miss Lyon, & had always been suspicious of her; & that if she & Ashcroft came out of the investigation clean & honest it would surprise him.

Mr. Rogers saw Ashcroft *after* his talk with Clara; & according to Ashcroft, he faced clear around the other way!

Howells, you knew Mrs. Clemens, from the fall of 1871 until her death in 1904, & I wonder if you are able to believe I could ever find a person who would seem to me to be her match, & thus be moved to marry again? Would it occur to you that if I found such a person it might, would or could be Miss Lyon? In all my (nearly) seventy-four years I have seen only the one person whom I would marry, & I have lost her. Miss Lyon compares with her as a buzzard compares with a dove. (I say this with apologies to the buzzard.)

Thus we arrive at yet one more reason why Clara & Jean were "jealous" of that little old superannuated virgin—they were "afraid I would marry her!" We have now reached the absolute limit of burlesque; burlesque ~~cam~~ can go no further than that. What a fine & large & splendid & radiant & rotten imagination that Liverpool bastard has! Miss Lyon is good company, agreeable company, delightful company, drunk or sober, but there is nothing about her that invites to intimate personal contact; her caressing touch—& she was always finding excuses to apply it—arch girly-girly pats on the back of my hand & playful little spats on my cheek with her fan—& these affectionate attentions always made me shrivel uncomfortably—much as happens when a frog jumps down my bosom. Howells, I could not go to bed with Miss Lyon, I would rather have a waxwork.

Was I unaware that before the middle of 1906 she had made up her mind to marry me? No—I was aware of it. I am uncommonly lacking in insight, uncommonly unobservant, but I was able to see that. So were the servants, & Jean & Clara, & some of the friends— Mrs. H. H. Rogers, for instance, & Mr. Broughton & Mr. Benjamin (sons-in-law) who noticed it in Bermuda & spoke of it. But I didn't bite. Then, when Ashcroft escorted me to England in the summer of 1907, a paragraph appeared in an English paper reporting a rumor that I was engaged to my secretary Miss Lyon. Ashcroft brought it to me eagerly. I had introduced him to a few dozen London reporters, & I suspected that the report was his work & had been done by Miss Lyon's request. I think so yet. By that time Miss Lyon was stealing money from me every day, so to speak, & she was in deep enough to be getting ~~afraid~~ ˄scared—˄—& Ashcroft too, perhaps, for without doubt he was living on her thefts, & she would naturally be afraid of *him,* as knowing him much better than I did, & being therefore aware that if her contributions failed he would betray her at any moment that he could get an advantage out of it. The report was cabled to America & circulated in the newspapers, & I began to be waylaid by reporters & correspondents who wanted the facts. So I departed from my custom & furnished them. To-wit that the report was untrue.

Before that—no, before it or after it, I don't remember which, Miss Lyon threw out a feeler: she came, looking ever so arch, & girly-girly & engaging, & gave me one of those little love-pats, & said—

"What do you reckon they say?"

"Well, what do they say?"

"That we are going to get married!" ⟦Burst of girly-girly stage-laughter to indicate how killingly funny & wildly absurd an idea it was.⟧

"Who say it?"

"Everybody. It's all over the town!"

"Oh, well, it isn't any matter. It wasn't started for fun, it was started for a purpose. We don't know what the purpose was, we only know that the person that started it is going to get left, as the slang phrase goes."

I have stopped the press to call Clara in & ask her if she & Jean were ever afraid sh I would marry Miss Lyon.

"No, we were not; but we were afraid she would marry *you*."

"Really & truly afraid, Clara?"

"Yes, really & truly."

"When?"

"When you came back to New York from Tuxedo—& *in* Tuxedo, too. We knew—& so did the friends—that she was aiming to marry you, & she seemed to have gotten such a hold upon you that she could make you do whatever she pleased. She was supreme. She had everything her own way in the house. She had stopped making requests, she only gave orders. You never denied her anything. Very well, as we knew she was intending to marry you, we were afraid you would submit—in fact, we *expected* you to submit. Mary Lawton, the psychist, said ý she had hypnotised you, & it certainly looked like it."

Clara went on & cited some other instances:

"Twice you allowed me to arrange with Mr. Jackson the lawyer for the Ashcrofts to be investigated by him; both times the Ashcrofts got around you & hypnotised you into breaking up the arrangement & stopping the inquest. Mr. Jackson had one interview with Ashcroft, & he said Ashcroft was so frightened he couldn't talk coherently. He couldn't furnish a single rational reason against the investigation, but was full of distress because it would reveal to you how expensive I had been!—as if I must go to *him* for protection from my father!

"The very same thing happened in the case of Mr. Rogers. Twice I was to see Mr. Rogers at his house about our difficulties, & both times you told the Ashcrofts & they talked you out of it & broke it up. Hypnotised you, we all thought, & think yet. We never could depend on you to stick to a purpose, they always talked you out of it. You were putty in their hands, father, & they could mould you to any shape they pleased. That had not been your way, before; you had a will of your own before the Ashcrofts came. When I made my third engagement with Mr. Rogers, I kept it secret from you. If you had known about it you would have told the Ashcrofts & they would have squelched it."

She added:

"Once you wrote a letter to Jean—& it was probably a *real* letter—a letter from father to daughter—a letter with some feeling in it, some sympathy, not a page or two of empty & unexcitable commonplaces such as Miss Lyon was accustomed to dictate to you as replies to that poor friendless exile[1]'s appeals—"

"By God I can't stand it, Clara! it makes me feel like a dog—like the cur I was; if I could land Miss Lyon in hell this minute, I hope to be damned if I wouldn't do it—& it's where I belong, anyway. Go on."

["]It was probably a *real* letter. I think so for this reason. It had been your custom to write merely a few empty lines to Jean & hand the result to Miss Lyon to edit; to edit out of it such suggestions of feeling & affection as might have intruded into it, under impulse. You then rewrote the vacuum & returned it to Miss Lyon for the post. But this time you forsook that custom. You wrote a *thick* letter. Also, you sealed it. Also, you didn't give it to Miss Lyon to mail with the other letters. You waited for a chance to get it out of the house clandestinely. You saw—from your bedroom window—Mr. Lounsbury approaching the house, & you ran down & overhauled him in the hall & gave him the letter & asked him to mail it. Miss Lyon was in the telephone closet & overheard it all. You went back up stairs. Lounsbury passed on, to the kitchen. He was there a quarter of an hour, & when he came out Miss Lyon was standing at the foot of the stairs, looking as if she had been sent down on an errand./ She said—

"'I've been waiting for you, Mr. Lounsbury. Mr. Clemens says he has given you a letter, & he wants it again, to add something to it which he forgot.'"

"She took the letter, & Lounsbury went away, saying 'there's a nigger in that woodpile somewhere'—for him b Lounsbury saw through Miss Lyon the first day she was ever in this region—the night she slept at his house & said she was dying with sick headache & must have whisky, & he gave her a quart & she drank it all up in two hours & was as drunk as a porter, & rolled over off the sleeping couch onto the floor, & he & his wife heard the noise & went in there & inspected her; & from that night until now, the Lounsburys have had their own opinion of Miss Lyon, & it is not a complimentary one. Very well; Lounsbury didn't see the letter any more. Of course Jean doesn't know whether she ever got it or not, it is so long ago; but she is of the opinion that she never got a *real* letter & a *fat* one until this insurrection broke out & you discovered that Miss Lyon had been Jean's enemy for three years & had by her lies to Dr. Peterson had kept her out of this house a whole year after she was sound in her body & clear in her head, & hadn't any further use for sanitariums & their privations & social horrors & distresses. Do you think that that letter ever reached Jean, father?"

"No, I *don't* think it. I think that that misgotten gutter-rat destroyed it."

Well, that's all. I don't want Clara to come in here any more. I like the truth sometimes, but I don't care enough for it to hanker after it. And besides, I have lived with liars so long that I have lost the tune, & a fact jars upon me like a discord.

My, but that Ashcroft is fertile in surprises! This one interview contains one—a masterpiece in its way. Necessarily it is prefaced with a lie or two. Because Ashcroft had to open his mouth. When he opens his mouth there can be but one result. He says my lawyers didn't know he & I had "made an agreement regarding the money advanced" by me for the rehabilitation of Miss Lyon's cottage. Then he prints the "agreement."

There you have it, all written out, & dated, & signed by me!

Why, Howells, I hope I may land in perdition before I finish this sentence if I ever heard of that piece of writing until I saw it in that interview in the Times, on the afternoon of the 4th of August. Never heard of it, never heard it mentioned, never saw it, never signed it.

Isn't it admirable "cheek," as the vulgar say?

At first I thought he had built it & forged my name to it on the 3d of August for use in the interview, but I now think that it didn't happen in that way. I think he had the little document with him when he brought the four notes on the famous Cleaning-Up Day—the 13th of March.

I didn't take the notes, & didn't look at them, but told him to keep them himself & preserve them with the rest of my business papers. He probably was not expecting that, & it nonplussed him for the moment & he didn't quite know what to do next.

It may be that he did not attach my signature at that time, but later; most probably on the 3d of August, when he wanted to print the little paper in his interview. I wonder if he *forged* the signature? Perhaps he took a safer way: removed, with acids, my writing from a letter-page (above my genuine signature), & then filled the vacancy with his rascally "agreement." Mr. Lark is going to ask him for a sight of it. He certainly won't get it.

The paragraph that follows the alleged "agreement" is interesting. There *was* an "amicable settlement" between Mr. Lark & Ashcroft on the 3d of August; the papers were to be drawn & signed on the 4th, & everybody was to drop the matter then & there, & shut up for the future. One of our main desires was to get Ashcroft to hand in his resignation as manager of the Mark Twain Company; to dismiss him by formal vote of the board of directors would start the newspaper-chatter again. He agreed to do it, & he & Lark parted well content with their interview's results.

But as I have remarked before, Miss Lyon was at that ~~moment~~ moment *on her way down to New York.* Yes, & full of suppressed shame, & wrath & the spirit of vengeance! Full of a determination, no doubt, to smash any agreement that had been arrived at if a certain couple of requirements happened to be absent from it. Well, they were not in it. Ashcroft had offered them, & had tried to get them inserted, but had failed. I reckon she was the author of them, & she *may* have been insane enough to imagine they would be conceded, for she *is* pretty damned insane, Howells, by reason of these many weeks of exasperation, & whisky, & bad dreams & troubled sleep; & in these seven years she has come to know me so well that she would *have* to be insaner than normal before her imagination could get so out of control, & so wild & so reckless as to beguile her into the notion that I would concede those two things. Why, dear me, I *couldn't* concede them; I couldn't dream of such a thing.

They are gems! Examine them.

1. Ashcroft will resign the post of manager & director of the Mark Twain Company; *provided* I write a note regretting the loss of his services in those capacities; and also

2. *Provided* I will write a note clearing ~~Mrs_iss_ R. W. L~~ Mrs. Ashcroft of dishonesty & regretting that by an unfortunate mistake she has been wrongly charged with it.

Sho, I can tell literary lies as fast as anybody, & of standard size, too; but when it comes to lying a couple of thieves and blatherskites into the confidence of an unoffending public, I'm not equal to it. I am under the deadly reputation of being a man whose word, in serious matters, is worth par; & if you had such a reputation, Howells, you would know what a slave it makes of a ^person, & how useless it is to repine—it can't be helped, you've got to stand by that reputation, there is no getting around it. May you never be in my situation, Howells, dear old friend of my long-vanished youth! However, there is no use in my going into hysterics about it, you are not in any danger I reckon.

My lawyers—backed by Paine,—who knew what my ƒ answer would be—declined to entertain that pair of provisos, & that paralysed the◊ agreement-proceedings.

I did write a note of regret, just to see if I could do it & not seem to be artificial & insincere, but Lark did not think it would be satisfactory to Ashcroft, so it was suppressed, & I only insert here to show I had good intentions:

> ^Whereas,^ As I understand it, Mr. Ashcroft, who has been requested to hand in his resignation as manager & director of the Mark Twain Company, will comply on condition that I write a note expressing regret for the loss of his services in those capacities.
>
> Therefore,
>
> Recognizing, by a certain incident of date March 31–April 3, that he is a liar, ~~a blackguard,~~ a traitor, ~~a coward,~~ a sneak, & a would-be thief, it is matter of deep regret to me that the Mark Twain Company must lose his services as manager & director; for, the above defects aside, he possesses high capacities for those positions, he being notably shrewd, inventive, enterprising, & tirelessly diligent, watchful, & persistent in the administration of all business affairs that interest him & furnish play for his talents.
>
> S L Clemens, President

What a delightful thing a coincidence is! There isn't anybody to whom that mysterious conjunction which we call a coincidence is a matter barren of interest. Well, one has just been hatched out in my own nest, here in these closing days of August.

We were discussing the Ashcrofts in the evening. We are usually discussing the Ashcrofts. The question came up—how did they come to get such an ascendancy over me? It was strange, exceedingly strange, for all the chief requirements ψ necessary to the creation and maintenance of an infatuation were lacking, & only a lot of minor ones present. I greatly liked to have Miss Lyon around, yet I had never much liked her; she was artificial, insincere, vain, gushy, & full of foolish affectations—& I had an aversion for these things; she was an old, old virgin, & juiceless, whereas my passion was for the other kind. To nearly everybody but me she was a transparent fraud, but to me she was not. I believed utterly in her honesty & in her loyalty to me & to my interests. She was master, & I was slave. She could make me do anything she pleased. In time—& no long time—she would have become permanently supreme here, & Clara & ~~Jean~~ would not have been able to stay in the house, nor Jean to enter it. By ~~as~~ means of the forged Grand

Power of Attorney, she & Ashcroft would by & by have stripped the children bare, when I died—a purpose which they unquestionably had in view.

And look at Ashcroft! A sneaky little creature, with beady, furtive, treacherous little eyes, & *all* the ways of a lackey—obsequious, watchful, attentive, and looking as if he wanted to lick somebody's boots. I was never able to get to my room in time to take my clothes off unassisted—he was always at my heels, he always stripped me, he put my night-shirt upon me, he laid out my clothes for next day, & there was no menial service which he omitted. I despised him, yet I liked him, & liked his company. I was always ready to say yes to anything he proposed; & do it without reflection, too. The thing I would promptly refuse to nearly any other friend of mine, I would as promptly grant to him.

No one was able to influence me against these people. Efforts in that direction were essayed but once, & not repeated.

When D⁻ Quintard called Clara to a serious consultation & said that that pair were robbing me & *must* be investigated, *I* was perfectly willing to mention the matter to Ashcroft, & was sure he & the Lyon would be glad to be investigated. And I think the first real jolt I got was when I discovered by Ashcroft's manner that the prospect of being investigated did not fill him to the chin with joy—as I had thought it was going to do.

So, as I say, were were discussing these Ashcrofts, & trying to account for the master-ship they had acquired over me. Clara finally said—

"It's *hypnotism!* it accounts for it all."

I had never thought of that. The suggestion looked reasonable—particularly since no *other* plausible way had been discovered of accounting for the enslaved condition I had been in for the past two or three years.

The "coincidence" heretofore referred to, was this: the first piece of print my eye fell upon when I went up to bed, was an article in the September number of *The World's Work* on hypnotic suggestion, & the paragraph my eye first fell upon was this one—which did certainly seem to fit my case to admiration!

> Old people, though in all appearance still independent and responsible, are often entirely under the suggestive influence of some masterful or interested per-son. I have seen cases of rich old men, apparently normal, who acted entirely against their original character, against their true inclinations, against their own interests, under the influence of some nurse or attendant who had succeeded in mastering the master's mind. In such cases the intriguer knew how to apply his suggestions so as to rule at last the whole household, cheating the legitimate heirs out of their rights or bringing about a marriage contract.

It describes my case ~~with~~ minutely, exactly, vividly, & with most humiliating truthful-ness. It is odd that I should have come upon it just when I did—which was just the right time—just when that talk was fresh & hot in my mind. If I had read it a day earlier it would probably have roused no interest in me & made no impression upon me.

Some more gossip. Paine met Z. at the Players the other day, & they talked. I cannot recall any of Z's name but the initial, but no matter, I used to know him slightly in Hartford eighteen or twenty years ago, where he had a good character, & was of some prominence. He told Paine Miss Lyon & his wife are good friends from away back— many many years, but that Mrs. Z. is aware that she came near getting into difficulties, once, when she was manager of the Exchange, for the Hartford ladies,—the institution for which she used to make pin cushions when she came with us in 1902. (And didn't make any more pin cushions after she got to signing checks for me.) She got short in her accounts, & Mrs. Z., & the Whitmores & other friends got the lacking money together & saved her, when there was imminent danger of a scandal.

Miss Lyon started a bank account when she had been with us a little while, & I have a transcript of it, procured from the bank. On a wage of $50 a month she deposited $700 in the first 7 months. It proves nothing against her honesty, but nothing in favor of it. ~~Two years~~ Three years later she was pilfering, in a small way, according to the testimony of Miss Hobby, my stenographer, & she finally made me discharge Miss Hobby—because Miss Hobby knew too much, Miss Hobby says.

I have not been able to believe—quite—that Miss Lyon was never a thief until she fell under the influence of Ashcroft; & the Woman's Exchange incident half persuades me that she began as much as ten years earlier than that. However, I guess it was Ashcroft that made a *large* thief out of her.

And how tactless she was! When she got married, she sent a twelve-dollar cablegram to Paine, in Egypt, to announce the fact! It was a week's wages.

And when she went to Hartford, last spring to rest & get back her strength, she took up her quarters at Heublein's hotel, where ₍she₎ couldn't live for anything s₍h₎ort of ten dollars a day! And she bragged to Paine that she would have work for Miss Banks the dressmaker the whole winter! If I had been H. H. Rogers, instead of myself, these extravagancies would have looked suspicious, & there would have been an immediate overhauling of her accounts. But *moi?*—I was hypnotised, & it never occurred to me.

MEMORANDUM.

September 7, 1909. ~~Five~~ ₍Six₎ days ago Dr. Cook sent a telegram from the Arctic regions announcing his *discovery of the North Pole* on the 21st of April 1908, & his name has been thundering around the whole globe ever since. During the past five days he has been the guest of the King of Norway, while the newspapers of all Christendom have been shouting his glories, not in columns, but by whole pages of costly telegraphic clatter.

And now, last night comes a telegram from Commander Peary, from up among the icebergs, saying *he* has discovered the North Pole! Discovered it a year later than Cook, according to the dates.

Half the world believed Cook, the other half didn't. But the entire world believes Peary. I believe both are speaking the truth.

Well, it is a pity that *two* men did it. While it was the achievement of one man it placed him alongside of Columbus, away up in the very sky—apparently to remain there forever—discoverers whose feat could never be repeated, there being no more worlds to discover, & no more poles *worth* discovering. But now that the honor is divided—well, the bulk of the value is gone.

Apparently Dr Cook sat down among the icebergs to waste a year—in writing about the discovery? If he really was so foolish as all that, he deserves to take second place—along with Adams, who didn't push his discovery of Neptune, but let Leverrier get in ahead of him & take first place for good & all.

#

EXPLANATORY NOTES

These notes are intended to clarify and supplement Autobiographical Dictations in this volume by identifying people, places, and incidents, and by explaining topical references and literary allusions. In addition, they attempt to point out which of Clemens's statements are contradicted by historical evidence, providing a way to understand more fully how his memories of long-past events and experiences were affected by his imagination and the passage of time. Although some of the notes contain cross-references to texts or notes elsewhere in this volume and in Volumes 1 and 2, the Index is an indispensable tool for finding information about a previously identified person or event.

All references in the notes are keyed to this volume by page and line: for example, 1.1 means page 1, line 1 of the text. All of Clemens's text is included in the line count except for the date titles of the dictations. Most of the source works are cited by an author's name and a date, a short title, or an abbreviation. Works by members of the Clemens family may be found under the writer's initials: SLC, CC (Clara), and JC (Jean). All abbreviations, authors, and short titles used in citations are fully defined in References. Most citations include a page number ("*L1*, 74" or "Rugoff 1981, 53–62"), but citations to works available in numerous editions may instead supply a chapter number or its equivalent, such as a book or act number. All quotations from holograph documents are transcribed verbatim from the originals (or photocopies thereof), even when a published form—a more readily available source—is also cited for the reader's convenience. The location of every unique document or manuscript is identified by the standard Library of Congress abbreviation, or the last name of the owner, all of which are defined in References.

Autobiographical Dictation, 1 March 1907

3 *title*   March 1, 1907] This Autobiographical Dictation is actually a series of three dictations strung together under a single date; it was probably completed on 4 or 5 March.

3.5–12   Isabella Beecher Hooker is dead . . . They are all dead] Clemens first touched on the Hooker family in the Autobiographical Dictation of 29 January 1907, four days after the death of Isabella Beecher Hooker (*AutoMT2*, 400–409, 626 n. 403.30–32). The "Beecher brotherhood and sisterhood" were all children of the Reverend Lyman

Beecher (1775–1863). With his first wife, the former Roxana Foote (1775–1816), he had eight children who survived infancy: three daughters and five sons, all of whom became ministers. Catharine (1800–1878) devoted her career to promoting the education of women, founding the Hartford Female Seminary (in 1823) and several other schools; she never married. Mary (1805–1900) helped Catharine found the seminary and taught there briefly, but retired to private life in 1827 when she married Thomas Perkins, a prominent Hartford attorney. Harriet is best known for her 1852 novel *Uncle Tom's Cabin;* she and her husband, Calvin Stowe, were Nook Farm neighbors of the Clemenses' (*AutoMT1,* 574 n. 310.37–38). Clemens does not mention (and was probably unacquainted with) the three oldest sons, William, Edward, and George. The two youngest, Henry Ward Beecher (1813–87) and Charles Beecher (1815–1900), together attended the newly founded Lane Theological Seminary in Cincinnati, whose first president was their father. Henry was, as Clemens says, "internationally famous," and served his entire career as the pastor of Plymouth Church in Brooklyn, even managing to survive the scandal of a public trial for adultery with one of his parishioners in 1872–75 (see *AutoMT1,* 575 n. 314.38–315.1). Charles attempted a music career before he was ordained and began his ministry, first at a church in Fort Wayne (Indiana), then in Newark (New Jersey), and finally Georgetown (Massachusetts). In all three positions his unorthodox religious views disturbed some of his parishioners; in 1873 a Congregational council convicted him of heresy (reversed by a later council). Thomas Kinnicut Beecher (1824–1900) and James Chaplin Beecher (1828–86) were the second and third children Lyman had with his second wife, the former Harriet Porter (1790–1835). (Her first child was Isabella: see the note at 4.3–5.) For forty-six years Thomas was the beloved—although unconventional—pastor of the First Congregational (later Park) church in Elmira, New York, one of whose founders was Jervis Langdon, Olivia's father. In 1870 Thomas officiated at the Clemenses' wedding. James went to sea after graduating from Dartmouth. He attended Andover Theological Seminary but left to minister to seamen in China, where he remained for five years. During the Civil War he raised a black regiment in North Carolina, which he led and served as chaplain. He was later a pastor of churches in Owego and Poughkeepsie, New York, and then worked with the poor in Brooklyn. Suffering from severe mood swings, he spent several years in institutions before committing suicide at age thirty-eight (Rugoff 1981, xvi–xvii, 53–62, 142–43, 194, 205–13, 406–15, 444–65).

4.3–5   Isabella Beecher Hooker threw herself into the woman's rights movement . . . all the rest of her life] Isabella Beecher (1822–1907) was the eldest child of Lyman Beecher's second marriage. She began to question the legal status of women soon after she married lawyer John Hooker in 1841, but it was not until 1868 that she became active in the women's rights movement. In that year she helped to establish the New England Woman Suffrage Association and wrote "Two Letters on Woman Suffrage," published anonymously in the November and December issues of *Putnam's Magazine* (Hooker 1868a, 1868b). In 1869 she became one of the founders of the Connecticut Woman Suffrage Association in Hartford, serving as its president until 1905. That same year she met Susan B. Anthony and Elizabeth Cady Stanton and joined the national struggle for female suffrage and equal rights (see the note at 4.6–7). In 1870 she began promoting a bill granting property rights to married women, which the Connecticut legislature finally passed in 1877. Her tireless campaigning and generous financial support soon made her a leader of the movement, and she continued her work for over thirty years. In 1892 she received the honor of being chosen to join Stanton, Anthony, and Lucy Stone in testifying before the Senate Committee on Woman Suffrage (Hooker 1905; Barbara A. White 2003, 119, 127–35, 147–48, 250, 303, 326). Clemens had not always admired Isabella Hooker. In November 1872 he asked Olivia not to associate with her because of her connection with the notorious feminist and free-love advocate Victoria Woodhull, and because she believed her brother Henry guilty as charged in the adultery scandal. For the same reasons her own family and members of the Nook Farm community ostracized her until late 1875 (MEC and SLC to JLC and PAM, 26 Nov 1872, *L5,* 229–32; Barbara A. White 2003, 112–13, 172–74, 213–15, 246–49). Before his own marriage in 1870 Clemens may not always have looked with full approval on women's suffrage: in 1867 he published four articles poking fun at its proponents, but slyly included powerful rebuttals from imagined women readers (SLC 1867c–f). At any rate, in 1874, in a letter to the editor of the London *Evening Standard,* he expressed unequivocal support for female suffrage: "I wish we might have a woman's party now, & see how that would work. I feel persuaded that in extending the suffrage to women this country could lose absolutely nothing & might gain a great deal" (12 Mar 1874, *L6,* 69, 72–73 n. 10).

4.6–7 Susan B. Anthony, Elizabeth Cady Stanton, and Mrs. Livermore . . . in 1848] Susan Brownell Anthony (1820–1906) and Elizabeth Cady Stanton (1815–1902) founded the National Woman Suffrage Association in 1869, which Stanton served as president until 1890. In addition to planning campaigns, making speeches, and appearing before government committees, they coedited (with Matilda Joslyn Gage) the first three volumes of *History of Woman Suffrage* (1881–86). Mary Ashton Rice Livermore (1820–1905) began her political work alongside her husband, Daniel, fighting for the abolition of slavery. During the Civil War she was an organizer with the U.S. Sanitary Commission. Afterwards she became a popular lecturer, speaking in support of temperance and women's rights. She also wrote two books, *My Story of the War* (1887) and *The Story of My Life* (1897). Although Clemens could have met her in the early 1870s, when they both lectured for James Redpath's Boston Lyceum Bureau, no evidence has been found that he did so.

4.16–17 Clara is singing in New England . . . North Attleboro, Massachusetts] Clara Clemens, an accomplished contralto (or mezzo-soprano, as she was often described), had made her professional debut in Norfolk, Connecticut, the previous September (*AutoMT2,* 240, 567 n. 240.6–8). On 19 February she began touring with Boston violinist Marie Nichols, accompanied on the piano by Charles Edmund Wark (for more on Nichols and Wark, see AD, 19 Feb 1908, note at 210.8–9, and AD, 6 Oct 1908, note at 267.36–37). Only a few of their engagements have been identified: one, on 21 February in Portsmouth, New Hampshire, and six in as many Massachusetts towns: 25 February in Springfield, 28 February in Greenville, 1 March in Pittsfield, 4 March in North Adams, 6 March in Fitchburg, and 7 March in Shelburne Falls ("City Briefs," Portsmouth *Herald*, 21 Feb 1907, 8; "Miss Clemens at Washington Hall," Greenville *Gazette and Courier*, 23 Feb 1907, 6; Springfield *Republican*: "Concert by Miss Clemens," 26 Feb 1907, 4; "Berkshire County. Pittsfield," 2 Mar 1907, 14; "Shelburne Falls," 7 Mar 1907, 11; Shelden 2010, 29, 438–39 n. 19). It has not been confirmed that Clara sang in North Attleboro (the dictation typescript originally read "North Adams" before Clemens revised it: see the note at 4.28–36). No letter from the "stage management" has been found. On 26 February the Springfield *Republican* reported on the "agreeable concert" of the previous evening:

> The singer is dark and somber, even to a suggestion of the tragic muse; the violinist a blonde with brio. They set each other off. What development Miss Clemens has made in her art could not be fairly judged last evening, because she was evidently troubled by a cold, which interfered not a little with the freedom and openness of her upper tones. The quality of her voice, which is an uncommonly expressive and sympathetic instrument, could best be felt in the andante of "Death and the Maiden," which was sung with a fine sustained legato.

The reviewer concluded that "both artists received generous applause, and the audience would gladly have had an encore number or two" ("Concert by Miss Clemens," 4). Despite generally positive reviews, the audiences were small. Clemens's secretary, Isabel Lyon, noted in her journal on 28 March (referring to Clara as "C.C." and quoting Clemens, who used the family's pet name, "Ben"):

> Oh the King is so great. C.C. has come back from her tour & it has cost at least $2500[00]—a financial loss, but when I talked with him this morning about the chances of proceeding for another 4 weeks, he said "Pay the bills & tell Ben to go ahead." He was shaving & with his face covered with lather he said in substance that she was learning her trade & the only way she can learn it is to know how to sail her ship in adverse winds—he said that if she had come home with twenty thousand dollars in her purse it would not be of the value to her that this experience has been; the big enthusiastic audiences are not the ones that are of greatest help—but the smaller, cold audiences that you win over are the ones that help you most. (Lyon 1907)

Clara evidently did extend her tour: on 17 April she and her colleagues performed in Seneca Falls, New York ("Clemens Recital This Evening," Syracuse *Post Standard*, 17 Apr 1907, 9).

4.27–28   Professor William M. Sloane ... now of Columbia University] William Milligan Sloane (1850–1928) graduated from Columbia College and received a doctoral degree from the University of Leipzig, then served for a time as private secretary to George Bancroft, U.S. minister to Germany. He taught Latin and history at Princeton University until 1896, when he became a professor of history at Columbia University.

Among his many publications were *The French War and the Revolution* (1893) and *Life of Napoleon Bonaparte,* serialized in the *Century Magazine* (1894–96) and then issued as a book. Clemens and Olivia had known him since at least 1886.

4.28–36 North Attleboro . . . this product was forwarded to every State in the Union] As originally dictated, this text referred to the town of North Adams. Clemens altered the name to "North Attleboro" on the typescript, presumably because he remembered belatedly that the latter was the correct name of the town known for its "cheap gimcrack jewelry." According to tradition, the earliest jewelry maker in Attleboro (which became North Attleboro in 1887) was an unnamed Frenchman, who began practicing his craft in 1780. The flourishing industry that Clemens describes here was built up over the course of the next century. By the 1890s dozens of firms were making inexpensive plated jewelry. Their products, marketed primarily through offices in New York and Philadelphia, were sold throughout the United States—sometimes by itinerant salesmen—and were also exported (Daggett 1894, 367–98).

5.13 Feather-Duster Man] In an 1886 notebook entry Clemens wrote, "'I'm a *feather-duster* man,' Prof. Sloan"; in 1894 he jotted a reminder to "Write up the 'Feather-Duster Man,'" making similar notes in 1895 and 1897 (*N&J3*, 223; Notebook 33, TS p. 58; Notebook 36, TS p. 11; and Notebook 41, TS pp. 16, 34, CU-MARK; for more about feather-duster salesmen see Krausz 1896, 130).

Autobiographical Dictation, 6 March 1907

10.19 The watch was a Jürgensen] Jürgen Jürgensen (1748–1811), watchmaker to the Danish court, established a watchmaking business in 1780. His grandsons, Urban (1806–67) and Jules (1808–77), continued the family tradition, building a factory in Switzerland in 1838 that produced watches of the highest quality.

Autobiographical Dictation, 26 March 1907

13.14–15 I have eighty thousand dollars in a 10 per cent stock] Clemens owned 1,500 shares of preferred stock in the Utah Consolidated Mining Company, which was supposed to pay a 10 percent annual dividend: see the Autobiographical Dictation of 27 March 1907, where he discusses this stock in more detail.

13.20–22 John Howells has been architecting a house . . . bought a year and a half ago] The house being designed by John Howells, son of Clemens's good friend William Dean Howells, was to be built in Redding, Connecticut, on a site suggested by Albert Bigelow Paine (for John Howells see *AutoMT2*, 509 n. 102.40). In 1905 Paine had purchased land in the area and renovated an old house on the property; by 1906 he was living there with his wife, Dora, and three daughters, Joy, Louise, and Frances. His enthusiastic descriptions of the landscape prompted Clemens, who had been thinking of leaving New York, to buy a neighboring property in March 1906. After buying additional parcels of land in May and September of that year, he owned about two hundred acres, comprising an entire hilltop overlooking the Saugatuck River valley (*MTB,* 3:1293–94; "Estate of Samuel L. Clemens" 1910, 1–3). By August 1906 he had engaged John Howells to draw up plans for a house. On 3 August he told the elder Howells that he wanted "John & Clara to take hold of that house now, & build it—out of the Review money. I shall bank it by itself for that purpose, as I have just been telling Clara." The "Review money" was Clemens's anticipated earnings from "Chapters from My Autobiography," the series of excerpts that he and George Harvey had just agreed to publish in the *North American Review* (see *AutoMT1,* 51–54, 557 n. 267.35). At thirty cents a word, he expected to earn at least thirty thousand dollars, the expected cost of construction. Ultimately, the house cost at least forty thousand dollars, and probably more; in October 1908 he claimed it was "double what I had expected" (12 Oct 1908 to Butler, transcript in CU-MARK; see also AD, 27 Mar 1907). At first he thought to call it Autobiography House, as he told Howells: "How's that for a name for it? Seems good. It is Miss Lyon's suggestion" (3 Aug 1906 to W. D. Howells, MH-H, in *MTHL,* 2:817). By the time the house was finished he had renamed it Innocence at Home, and then, finally, Stormfield (3 Aug 1906 to CC, photocopy in CU-MARK; John Howells to Lyon and SLC, 19 Sept 1906, and John Howells to SLC, 7 May 1907, CU-MARK; for more on the house and its naming, see AD, 17 April 1908, note at 221.17–19; AD, 3 July 1908; and AD, 6 Oct 1908).

13.31   another trip to Bermuda a week or two ago] On 16 March Clemens left for a "flying" trip to Bermuda accompanied by Isabel Lyon and Mary (Paddy) Madden, a pretty nineteen-year-old whose company he had enjoyed on his return trip from Bermuda on 7–9 January (see *AutoMT2,* 611 n. 359.27–28). On 11 March Lyon noted in her journal:

> The King is restless— The gout seems better—& I painted the foot again tonight—
> (I hear him sneeze.) He cannot dictate & he is much in need of a change. We have
> been talking up a trip to Bermuda. We should have but one night there for the
> Bermudian sails every Saturday from here—but the King won't care— He will
> have 5 days away from home, & so I telephoned first to M^r. Howells to ask if he
> were not planning to go to Bermuda, but he isn't—& then after foraging about in
> his thoughts he suggested Paddy Madden, & I telephoned the invitation to her &
> delighted her soul. (Lyon 1907)

Also on board the outgoing voyage, on the RMS *Bermudian,* was Charles William Eliot (1834–1926), president of Harvard University. According to Lyon,

> That pretty creature Paddy proves a delightful bait for the very nicest men on
> board— She sat beside President Elliot & seemed to delight him with her empty
> little remarks— She loves ice cream, but not candy, & she never drinks coffee all
> of which . . . she says with a conviction that makes you interested in what she is
> saying. She wears white when the fellows come to see her. She says a 5 page prayer

to the virgin 5 times a day when she isn't too sleepy & so & so on, & she is so pretty. (Lyon 1907, entry for 17 Mar)

The travelers spent one day sightseeing before returning to the ship, which departed the next day and arrived back in New York on 21 March.

13.36–37   Clara has been barnstorming . . . she has learned her trade] See the Autobiographical Dictation of 1 March 1907, note at 4.16–17.

14.14   Thomas Bailey Aldrich has passed from this life, seventy years old] Clemens met Aldrich—a poet, novelist, journalist, and editor of the *Atlantic Monthly* from 1881 to 1890—in November 1871, and remained his lifelong friend, until his death on 19 March 1907. In his 1904 sketch "Robert Louis Stevenson and Thomas Bailey Aldrich," Clemens wrote that Aldrich "never had his peer for prompt and pithy and witty and humorous sayings" (*AutoMT1*, 229, 539 n. 229.8). Clemens discusses Aldrich and the memorial museum that his wife, Lilian, established in his honor in the Autobiographical Dictations of 3 and 6 July 1908.

14.32–33   that object was to distribute it through my existing books . . . new copyright life of twenty-eight years] In January 1904 Clemens first expressed his plan to publish his autobiography as "*notes* (copyrightable) to my existing books" to add twenty-eight years to their copyrights and thereby create income for his daughters. The notes would "add 50% of matter to each book, & be some shades more readable than the book itself" (16 Jan 1904 to Howells, MH-H, in *MTHL*, 2:779). For a discussion of this "copyright extension gambit" and why it never came to pass, see *AutoMT1*, 23–24; see also *AutoMT2*, 285–86, 585 n. 285.40–286.3, and "Closing Words of My Autobiography."

14.38–39   Mrs. Kinnicutt, dined with us two or three nights ago . . . Mrs. Draper] The dinner party took place on 22 March. Eleonora Kissel Kinnicutt (1837–1910), wife of noted physician Francis P. Kinnicutt (1846–1913), was a trustee of Barnard College and, since 1896, manager of the Manhattan State Hospital for the Insane on Wards Island (New York *Times*: "Mrs. F. P. Kinnicutt Dead," 27 Oct 1910, 11; "Dr. Kinnicutt Dies at Doctors' Meeting," 3 May 1913, 11; *Manhattan Census* 1910, 1037:1A). Mary Palmer Draper (1839–1914) was the widow of Henry Draper (1837–82), a professor of astronomy at Harvard and a pioneer in astronomical photography. She worked with her husband in the Harvard College Observatory, becoming an accomplished astronomer herself. She remained active in the field; in 1905 and 1906 she had invited Clemens to meet the members of the Astronomical and Astrophysical Society at her home on Madison Avenue. Upon her death she made bequests totaling more than $1 million to the New York Public Library and Harvard University, among other institutions ("Mrs. Draper Wills $400,000 to Library," New York *Times*, 20 Dec 1914, 1; New York Public Library 2013). The other guests at the dinner included Count Tcherep-Spiridovitch (see AD, 28 Mar 1907, note at 18.1–2); Dorothea Gilder (1882–1920), a friend of Clara's and daughter of Richard Watson Gilder; Melville Stone (see AD, 19 Aug 1907, note at

104.23); and Governor Edwin Warfield of Maryland (1848–1920) and his wife, Emma (Lyon 1907, entry for 22 March).

14.40–41   Mrs. Kinnicutt said—but I will refer to this later] Lyon recorded a remark that was probably the one Clemens promised to return to "later"—but never did:

> Last night M^rs. Kinnicutt said a thing that interested me. She said that when Karl Schurtz was writing his autobiography he was unable to write the early part of it—his German life—in English; he was obliged to write it in German & have it translated. M^rs. Kinnicutt said he would labor with it & write in stilted English[,] impossible English—& finally would give it up & go back to the German. (Lyon 1907, entry for 23 Mar)

For Carl Schurz see the Autobiographical Dictation of 19 August 1907, note at 104.22. Eleonora Kinnicutt collaborated with Schurz in translating his *Reminiscences,* published in three volumes in 1907–8.

Autobiographical Dictation, 27 March 1907

15.13–14   he told me to buy that copper stock which I have been talking about] Henry Huttleston Rogers, a vice-president of Standard Oil and a highly successful expert on the stock market, had advised Clemens to buy stock in the Utah Consolidated Mining Company, whose president was Rogers's son-in-law, Urban H. Broughton. As of April 1906, Rogers himself owned 5,025 shares (for Rogers see *AutoMT1*, 192–94, 522 n. 192.15–17; for Broughton see AD, 18 May 1907, note at 51.37–38). The company, a consolidation of several smaller companies, had been established in 1903; in addition to copper ore it mined gold and silver. The rate of production peaked in 1906, and then fell in 1907, when its net earnings declined by more than half. When Clemens died in 1910 his 1,750 shares (worth about $81,000) were by far his largest investment after the $200,000 that he owned in "capital stock of the Mark Twain Company" ("Utah Consolidated. President Broughton Says a Good Dividend Can Be Maintained in Spite of Copper Prices," *Wall Street Journal,* 20 Apr 1906, 5; Stevens 1908, 1374–77; 14 Feb 1910 to Paine, WU-MU; "Estate of Samuel L. Clemens" 1910; for the Mark Twain Company see AD, 25 Mar 1909, note at 304.16).

16.31–33   wireless telephone . . . records the messages which it receives] Clemens refers to the Telegraphone, invented in 1898 by Valdemar Poulsen (1869–1942) of Denmark. It was not itself a telephone, but rather a device that could be attached to a telephone to record messages; it could also be used for dictation (see also the note at 16.38–39). Clemens's confusion is understandable. In late 1906 and early 1907 the newspapers printed numerous articles about the invention and development of wireless transmission of the voice. The technology, however, was still impractical for widespread use because of its limited range. In 1903 Poulsen had patented an arc-transmitter that could increase the range, and he licensed the rights to several companies that made premature claims of commercial success to attract investors. Within about ten years the arc-transmitter was made obsolete by vacuum-tube technology ("American Telegraphone Company Introduces Wonderful Invention," San Francisco *Chronicle*, 3 Mar 1907, 32; "May Telephone Across Ocean," Los Angeles *Times*, 4 Feb 1907, 14; Thomas H. White 2012).

16.38–39   I found that I could get a hundred shares of the stock at ten dollars] The Sterling Debenture Corporation of New York sent a promotional letter to Clemens on 19 January 1907, offering stock in the American Telegraphone Company (CU-MARK):

> The first issue of the company's stock is now being sold for the purpose of equipping a factory in Wheeling, W. Va., to enable the company to manufacture all its machines in this country instead of importing them from Denmark, the home of the invention.
> These shares are $10 each, and you may subscribe for one or ten or fifty up to one hundred, but no one person will be allowed to take more than one hundred shares. . . .
> As soon as the Telegraphones can be manufactured in quantities to supply the orders that are already on file, the value of these shares will advance as rapidly as did that of the Bell Telephone shares under like conditions.

17.15–17   my own experience of twenty-nine years ago with Bell Telephone stock . . . early chapters of this Autobiography] Wireless companies typically marketed their stock by citing the example of the highly profitable Bell Telephone Company. The United Wireless Telegraph Company, for example, claimed that "inasmuch as the Wireless is destined to supplant the telegraph, telephone and cable, its shares should prove even more profitable than those of the Bell Telephone, wherein an original investment of $100 represents a value to-day of $200,000" ("United Wireless Telegraph Company," New York *Tribune*, 17 Mar 1907, 7). For Clemens's account of his failure to invest in the telephone in 1878 see the Autobiographical Dictation of 24 May 1906 (*AutoMT2*, 56–57, 491–92 nn. 56.37–57.8, 57.15–18).

17.25–26   I sent a thousand dollars this morning and captured a hundred shares of this gamble] Clemens actually paid a $20 deposit and received a temporary stock certificate dated 28 March 1907, for a hundred "shares of capital stock of the American Telegraphone Company, fully paid and non-assessable (at $10 per share)"; a permanent certificate was to be "promptly forwarded upon receipt of the amount, $980" (CU-MARK). The Sterling Debenture Company succeeded in selling 100,000 shares of this stock at $10 a share, but kept $800,000 in commissions and paid only $200,000 to the Telegraphone Company. Between 1906 and its forced closure in December 1912, this brokerage firm sold large quantities of stock in legitimate companies at inflated prices, and further cheated buyers by aggressively marketing worthless securities. In April 1914 its officials were convicted of mail fraud and received sentences ranging from three to six years in prison (Dater 1913; "Sterling Debenture Co. Sentences," *Wall Street Journal*,

8 Apr 1914, 8). Fraud was in fact so widespread throughout the wireless industry that in early 1907 journalist Frank Fayant published a series of articles exposing the "financial jugglery" of companies engaging in what he called the "wireless telegraph bubble," describing its "chief figure," Abraham White of the United Wireless Telegraph Company, as "a modern Colonel Sellers" (Fayant 1907a, 1907b).

Autobiographical Dictation, 28 March 1907

18.1–2   Yesterday I went to the plutocratic St. Regis Hotel . . . dined with us a week ago] The luncheon was hosted by Count Tcherep-Spiridovitch (1858–1926), who sent Clemens a printed invitation (in the original Mark Twain Papers). The count dined at Clemens's house on 22 March. The two men had probably first met ten days earlier, when on 12 March they shared a box at a benefit performance by Ethel Barrymore in *Carrots* at the Hudson Theatre (Lyon 1907, entries for 12 and 22 Mar; see also AD, 26 Mar 1907, note at 14.38–39). Tcherep-Spiridovitch, a major general in the Russian Army (although no longer in active service), owned several sugar factories as well as a commercial fleet on the Volga River, and was a major shareholder in many oil and mining companies. He was touring America in his capacity as president of the Pan-Slavic League, which advocated the unification of all Slavic peoples. In September 1907, after his return to Russia, he wrote to Clemens, "Am sending You my heartiest remembrances from old Moscow, which by its warm hospitality, reminds me of ever dear America." He sent his "compliments" to Miss Lyon—despite her failure to send a promised photograph of Clemens (2 Sept 1907, CU-MARK). By 1920, when he emigrated to the United States, Tcherep-Spiridovitch was an ardent anti-Bolshevik and antisemite. In 1926 he published *The Secret World Government,* a political screed that denounced the Jews as "heirs of Satan" and warned that "the White Race is facing a most terrific World Revolution staged by the Judeo-Mongol Hidden Hand which may put an end to civilization based on Christianity" (Cherep-Spiridovitch 1926, 24, 41; Russia Culture 2012; "Russian Cup for Roosevelt," New York *Times,* 18 Jan 1907, 8; "Count Cherep-Spiridovich, Russian Anti-Semite Agitator, Found Dead in Room," *Jewish Daily Bulletin,* 25 Oct 1926, 2).

18.17–21   Mr. John Bigelow . . . he being past ninety] Bigelow (1817–1911), aged eighty-nine at the time of the luncheon, had a distinguished career as a diplomat and author. He was admitted to the New York bar in 1838, and from 1848 to 1861 was coeditor and part owner of the New York *Evening Post.* Appointed consul general at Paris in 1861, he later served as minister to France (1865–67). He had a large role in establishing the New York Public Library, and served as president of its board of trustees from 1895 until his death. His published works included numerous histories and biographies, as well as ten volumes of the complete writings of Benjamin Franklin.

18.41   I was publicly known to be on the side of the revolutionists] Clemens had publicly advocated assassination of the Romanoff house in "The Czar's Soliloquy," published in the *North American Review* in March 1905 (SLC 1905a). In April 1906 he sent a letter to be read by Maxim Gorky at a meeting in New York, in which he said his sympathies were "with the Russian revolution, of course" and that he hoped the tsar and the grand dukes would soon be as scarce in Russia "as I trust they are in heaven" ("Arms to Free Russia, Tchaykoffsky's Appeal," New York *Times,* 30 Mar 1906, 9, in *AutoMT1,* 463–64). In a subsequent interview he identified himself as "a revolutionist in my sympathies, by birth, by breeding and by principle. I am always on the side of the revolutionists, because there never was a revolution unless there were some oppressive and intolerable conditions against which to revolute" ("Gorky Sent from Hotel," New York *Tribune,* 15 Apr 1906, 2, reprinted in Scharnhorst 2006, 542–43). That same month a newspaper cartoon depicted him upsetting the tsar's throne ("A Yankee in Czar Nicholas's Court," New York *World,* 13 Apr 1906, 8; Schmidt 2014).

19.4–5   it could make you and me seem to be in sympathy with the Czar's side of the question] Clemens's mere presence at the luncheon sparked the kind of criticism Bigelow feared. The New York *Worker,* a Socialist Party newspaper, printed the following article on 27 April 1907 (4):

> What has come over Mark Twain, the fearless, outspoken, stimulating Mark Twain, the Mark Twain whom we had come to look upon as free from the cant that characterizes so many "popular" writers? What does he mean by attending a banquet given by General Spiridovitch and there sit, silent and apparently unashamed, as that supporter of the Russian autocracy emits fulsome eulogy of the Tsar and all his detestable court, the same Tsar whom Mark Twain so bitterly satirized a few years ago? Are we to reckon Mark as among the lost from now on? Last year he snubbed Maxim Gorky, when the newspapers opened their mud batteries on that splendid genius. Now he sits at the feet of the Tsar himself and pays homage to a coarse and blatant toady of the infamous regime at St. Petersburg. The cause of progress has not suffered from this so much as Mark Twain himself has lost by it.

Gorky caused a scandal when he visited the United States in April 1906 accompanied by a woman who was not his wife. Clemens had initially agreed to speak at a dinner to raise funds for the Russian revolution, but he and Howells (and others) withdrew their support when Gorky's offense was revealed (see Budd 1959).

19.24–26   I got up and made the speech . . . Government has been carrying on daily for two years] A single report of Clemens's speech has been found, in the New York *Times,* stating only that he "paid some compliments" to the count ("Count Spiridovitch Gives a Luncheon," 28 Mar 1907, 9). For the slaughter of Jews in Russia see the Autobiographical Dictation of 22 June 1906 (*AutoMT2,* 132–33, 524 nn. 132.35–133.3, 133.11–12).

19.28–32   the Count got up and made a political speech . . . adulations of the Russian Emperor] The New York *Times* reported four paragraphs of the count's speech—presumably an excerpt:

"I thank you for your sympathetic interest, which I attribute to my having come from Russia, that old and sincerest friend of the United States.

"While I, as a soldier, would willingly die for the Czar, the liberal-minded and brave Emperor prefers that every one of his people should live for the progress of not only Russia, but the whole human race. He has already immortalized himself in history first by declaring against wars in the world outside and bringing about the creation of The Hague conference, and in the second place by granting to his people a Constitution regardless of dangers and obstacles.

"The Constitution has been definitely introduced, but necessarily half a thousand politically trained men to work in the Parliament cannot be produced in a day. We must wait a generation. Andrew Carnegie, one of your best men, has already materialized the idea of the Czar by building a Temple of Peace in The Hague.

"The Russian people remember that the American Nation is formed from the cream of the best European peoples, and Russia is infinitely more proud of every expression of American sympathy than of all other expressions." ("Count Spiridovitch Gives a Luncheon," 28 Mar 1907, 9)

For the International Peace Conference at The Hague and Carnegie's Palace of Peace, see the Autobiographical Dictation of 8 April 1907, note at 22.6–16, and *AutoMT2*, 172, 541 n. 172.26–34.

19.34–35   a practised talker like Choate] Jurist, diplomat, and wit Joseph H. Choate (see *AutoMT1*, 572 n. 303.2–10).

20.6–15   Some months ago I commented . . . large interest for Susy] See the Autobiographical Dictation of 21 December 1906 (*AutoMT2*, 326–34, 600–601 nn. 327.3–6, 329.4–5, 329.21–27).

Autobiographical Dictation, 8 April 1907

21.3   the last survivor of the battle of Navarino is dead] In the Battle of Navarino, fought off the coast of southern Greece in 1827 during its War of Independence, the allied navies of Britain, France, and Russia defeated the Egyptian-Turkish fleet. The war ended in 1832 with the creation of the independent Kingdom of Greece. The March 1907 death of the battle's "last survivor," ninety-nine-year-old John Stainer, was widely reported in newspapers ("Last Survivor of Navarino," Bendigo [Australia] *Advertiser*, 19 Apr 1907, 3).

21.15   it was in the Lepanto fight that Cervantes was wounded] The Spanish novelist and poet Miguel de Cervantes Saavedra (1547–1616) received a wound in the Battle of Lepanto (1571), which permanently maimed his left hand. The battle, a major victory for the Hapsburg forces over the Ottomans, was—like the Battle of Navarino—fought off the coast of Greece. Cervantes also fought in a battle at Navarino (1572).

21.26–35   a party of us representing the *Quaker City* Excursion . . . a hotel in Venice] In 1867 Clemens traveled to Europe and the Holy Land on the *Quaker City* with about seventy-five passengers, only a handful being members of Henry Ward Beecher's

Plymouth Church in Brooklyn, where the idea for the excursion had originated. Clemens revised his newspaper correspondence with the San Francisco *Alta California* and the New York *Tribune* and used it for more than half the text of *The Innocents Abroad* (1869). On 5 July he and two companions (Daniel Slote and Dr. Abraham Reeves Jackson) took the train from Marseilles to Paris, where they stayed for a week. At the time, Nicholas I (1841–1921), prince (and later king) of Montenegro, was in Paris visiting the International Exposition. Neither the newspaper correspondence nor the book mentions the encounter with Nicholas I, but it almost certainly occurred, since ten years later Clemens referred to it in an 1878 notebook. In the fall of 1878 Clemens stayed in Venice with his family (and Olivia's friend Clara Spaulding). They arrived on the evening of 25 September after an exhausting day's travel from Bellagio, on Lake Como. They stayed at the Grand Hôtel d'Italie, whose south side was on the Grand Canal. The preemption of their rooms at some other hotel by the Prince of Montenegro has not been confirmed, but in late September Clemens wrote in his notebook, "Ran across the Prince of Montenegro again to-day. At tomb of Napoleon in 67" (*N&J2*, 197).

22.6–16 William T. Stead . . . American contingent of this roving commission] Stead, an English political reformer, journalist, and spiritualist, had admired Clemens's work since at least 1890, and had met him personally on a transatlantic voyage in 1894. As a longtime friend of Andrew Carnegie's, he had come to America to attend the ceremony on 11 April at the Carnegie Institute in Pittsburgh in honor of Founder's Day and the opening of the greatly enlarged library ("W. T. Stead Here to Talk of Peace," New York *Times*, 4 Apr 1907, 7; see *AutoMT2*, 541 n. 172.26–34, 604 n. 336.32–337.2). Stead was also scheduled to address the National Arbitration and Peace Congress in New York on 14–17 April, whose purpose was to decide on the position of the United States at the upcoming Second International Peace Conference at The Hague. Stead wanted to select twelve American "Pilgrims of Peace," who would travel to London, Paris, and Rome to gather additional representatives from European nations, so that "100 would finally round up at The Hague to present their petition to the conference." Stead's primary objective was to establish an arbitration process so that "in case of a conflict being imminent between two countries neither of them can open hostilities until a period of 15 or 20 days has elapsed. During this period two friendly Powers will always have the right to intervene and to endeavour to settle the quarrel amicably" ("Mr. W. T. Stead and the Peace Conference," London *Times*, 9 Jan 1907, 5; "Stead Unfolds His Idea," Chicago *Tribune*, 8 Apr 1907, 3; James Brown Scott 1907). The Second International Peace Conference, which took place from 15 June to 18 October 1907, had first been proposed by President Roosevelt but was officially convened by Nicholas II of Russia. The delegates, representing forty-four countries, approved thirteen articles pertaining to the rules of warfare, including one to establish an International Prize Court, as well as a declaration in support of the principle of obligatory arbitration (on which the United States abstained from voting). Ultimately, however, the article creating the world court was not ratified (New York *Times:* "Peace

Compromise Spurned by Choate," 12 Oct 1907, 4; "Shelves Knox Peace Plan," 3 Sept 1910, 4; Hull 1908).

22.34   Stead is not popular in England, where he belongs] Stead, an indefatigable crusader against vice, social injustice, and war, was considered a visionary by his supporters, but his critics objected to his extreme tactics (such as pretending to buy a child prostitute, for which he was imprisoned), and derided his belief in the spirit world. After he perished on the *Titanic* in 1912, his acts of heroism were reported by several survivors.

22.40–23.1   the following letter . . . I will leave out the introductory remarks] The essay transcribed here by Clemens's stenographer, Josephine Hobby, was sent with the following cover letter (CU-MARK):

Ottawa, Canada, April 3rd. 1907

Samuel L. Clemens,
New Haven,
Conn.

Dear Sir,
    At the outset I must apologise for intruding upon you. You will forgive me perhaps when I say that I am asking for nothing except the privilege of telling you how keenly I have enjoyed your writings, more especially your great satires.
    Today, men laud your humor, in ages to come they shall stand uncovered in the memory of the Titanic force and directness of your philosophy.
    That men do not think deeply is evidenced by the fact that "Gulliver's Travels" is still classed as a book for children.
    You are more fortunate because conditions permit the use of less disguised methods and in that there is a great element of hope.
    I am sanguine enough to believe that our race will survive the crises and eventually win to intellectual freedom.
    My belief is based on the existence of such men as Swift and yourself. That Swift is dead is a small matter, you have yourself attained honorable age yet so far as human needs are concerned you are both immortal and that is an element of continued hope.
    I do not believe in personal immortality, it is an egoistic dream but when will Shakespeare die? Not while Man lives.
    The real history of Mankind is the history of its thinkers and their thought.
    The true kings of men have rarely found thrones and the true saviors have found the stake oftener than the altar and oblivion oftener than either. You are fortunate in that you have found none of these but bid fair to be well remembered.
    I believe that good work is its own reward, you should be a happy man. In my small way I am happy also.

With kind wishes,
I remain,
Yours very truly,
Mark G. McElhinney

Lyon noted Clemens's response on the bottom of the letter, "Thank him for his letter & say that by & by when his philosophy is printed he will send him a confidential copy."

23.23 "The altar-cloth of one age becomes the door-mat of the next."] Mark Twain used this maxim, a "Punjabi proverb" from "Pudd'nhead Wilson's New Calendar," as an epigraph for chapter 23 in *More Tramps Abroad,* the English edition of *Following the Equator* (SLC 1897b). It does not appear in the American edition, which also has different chapter breaks.

23.35 Jah] An element of "Yahweh," one of the names of the God of Israel in the Hebrew Bible, traditionally represented by the tetragrammaton YHWH.

24.6 Chinese Gordon] Major General Charles George Gordon (1833–85), an officer in the British Army Corps of Engineers, earned the nickname "Chinese Gordon" for commanding a force of Chinese soldiers who in 1863–64 suppressed the Taiping Rebellion, a major uprising against the Qing imperial government. While serving as governor general of Sudan, he was killed by Muslim fundamentalists in revolt against Anglo-Egyptian rule, who stormed his palace at Khartoum after a thirty-one-day siege. Gordon was a popular hero in Britain because of his incorruptibility, his bravery, and his dedication to helping the poor.

24.13 Mark G. McElhinney] McElhinney (b. 1868) was originally from Nova Scotia. He became a dental surgeon who, according to a 1916 advertisement, treated "certain of the cognoscenti" (*Ottawa Naturalist* 30 [Apr 1916]: ii). He was also a writer, poet, and, in 1910, the inventor of a machine he called the "Telelectron," which used electricity as a form of anesthesia (McElhinney 1922, 1927; "Invents Sleep Producer," Manitoba *Free Press,* 10 Jan 1911, 1).

Autobiographical Dictation, 9 April 1907

24.14 The "Wapping Alice" story] None of the present text was actually dictated. The first four paragraphs, in which Clemens introduces the "Wapping Alice" story, are based on a manuscript written in April 1907. He wrote the story itself in 1897 or 1898, either in Weggis, Switzerland, or in Vienna. He revised it slightly in 1907 for inclusion in the autobiography. In the Autobiographical Dictation of 10 April he "tells the facts" of the "dramatic episode," which took place in July 1877 (for the full history of composition see AD, 10 Apr 1907, note at 39.9–10).

24.15 banquet in honor of Ambassador Tower, last night] The dinner was hosted at the Manhattan Club by Herman Ridder, publisher and editor of the *New-Yorker Staats-Zeitung,* to honor Charlemagne Tower, the American ambassador to Germany since 1902 (see *AutoMT1,* 500 n. 124.17, and *AutoMT2,* 639–40 n. 432.15–18). The evening's speeches stressed the importance of friendly relations between the United States and Germany, which were negotiating a new trade agreement to prevent high import tariffs on American goods ("Tariff Peace Near with the Kaiser," New York *Times*, 9 Apr 1907, 2).

24.15–22 I encountered a guest . . . a very dramatic episode which enacted itself in our house] When he attended the Tower dinner, Clemens had probably already decided to insert "Wapping Alice" into his autobiography: Lyon noted in her journal on 8 April that he had "read 'Wapping Alice'—that darling condemned sketch—to me. It has got to go into print as Auto—or as something for it is perfectly delightful" (Lyon 1907). Clemens's remarks about the "banquet-guest" are presumably his pretext for including the story, since no evidence has been found linking it with anyone at the dinner.

24.26–27 they are all dead these many years, except . . . one other] Clemens presumably meant the Reverend Joseph H. Twichell, his lifelong friend, whose name he suppressed in this version of the story. Clemens identifies him in the Autobiographical Dictation of 10 April 1907 (see also *AutoMT1*, 479 n. 73.13).

24.31–34 Wapping Alice . . . Alice, the colored cook] "Wapping Alice" was Clemens's fictional name for Lizzie Wills, Susy Clemens's English nurse, who was apparently hired in the fall of 1874. The live-in cook's name was Mary (OLC to Crane, Sept–Dec 1874, transcript in CU-MARK; 17 May 1877 and 17 July 1877 [1st] to OLC, CU-MARK).

25.39–40 George . . . Patrick] George Griffin, the Clemenses' butler, and Patrick McAleer, their coachman (*AutoMT1*, 579 n. 322.31–42, 583 n. 335.28–32).

26.10–11 he meant *my* family, not his] At this point in his manuscript Clemens wrote, "Consider this further light: my grand-father owned George's grand-father, my father owned George's father, and George owned *me*—at any rate that is what the family said." He deleted the sentence when revising Hobby's typescript in 1907.

28.21 Mr. C—] Clemens wrote merely "Mr. ——" in his manuscript. Later, on the typescript, he inserted the name "Charles Hopkins Clark" before deciding on the anonymous "Mr. C—." Clark was a friend and an editor on the Hartford *Courant* (*AutoMT1*, 576 n. 317.33).

30.4–5 A young Swede he was, by the name of Bjurnsen Bjuggersen Bjorgensen] Lizzie's friend was Willie Taylor, an unemployed mechanic, whom Clemens described to Olivia as a "tall, muscular, handsome fellow of 35" (17 and 18 July 1877, CU-MARK).

31.41–42 Major Kinney, and Mr. Bunce, and Mr. Robinson, and Mr. Hubbard, and Gen'l] John C. Kinney, Stephen A. Hubbard, and General Joseph Roswell Hawley were all associated with the Hartford *Courant*: Kinney as assistant editor, Hubbard as business manager and part owner, and Hawley as editor and part owner (*N&J2*, 383 n. 79; *AutoMT1*, 576 n. 317.23–24, 577 n. 319.22–23). Edward M. Bunce, a bank cashier, was a close family friend; George M. Robinson was an Elmira furniture manufacturer and Clemens's summer billiards partner (*AutoMT1*, 576 n. 316.13–14; *AutoMT2*, 620 n. 378.14–15).

34.17–20   we telephoned for Reverend Thomas X. . . . Reverend Joe Twichell was off on his vacation] As Clemens explains in the Autobiographical Dictation of 10 April, the fat, perspiring Thomas X. was a fiction; it was Twichell who was summoned. Clemens's first telephone was not installed until December 1877 or January 1878; it connected him only to the office of the Hartford *Courant* (*AutoMT2*, 491 n. 56.37–57.8).

34.33   chief of police] Walter P. Chamberlain (1815?–90), Hartford's chief of police in 1860–71 and 1875–81 (Beckwith 1891, entry for May 1890 in "Chronicle of Events"; Thomas S. Weaver 1901, 16, 54–55).

Autobiographical Dictation, 10 April 1907

39.9–10   I diverged from fact . . . because I wanted to publish the thing in a magazine] Clemens evidently considered writing up the story of Lizzie Wills as early as May 1891, when he wrote in his notebook, "How we made an honest woman of the English servant girl" (Notebook 30, TS p. 43, CU-MARK). When he finally drafted his account in 1897–98, he used the participants' real names, including his own and Patrick McAleer's. In the fall of 1898, however, when he decided to offer the story to James J. Tuohy of the New York *World,* he prepared the manuscript for publication by substituting (albeit inconsistently) the fictional names of "Jackson" and "Dennis" for the original "Clemens" and "Patrick," and disguising the city names of Rochester, Northampton, and Springfield. He had the manuscript typed with the fictional names, explaining to Tuohy that he had made "fiction of this tale," because

> the public won't give shucks for fact when it can get fiction—& besides I've always been a little sore over this cussed adventure, & I couldn't bring myself to substitute my own name for "Jackson's" if I should try. However, some day in my Autobiography I intend to get over that delicacy. The thing happened in my house fifteen years ago—I have changed one large but not essential detail—& the participants are mainly dead by this time, perhaps. But my pastor the Rev. Joe Twichell isn't, & he took out the licence, sweated 3 hours in the bathroom, married the couple, & gave me his tearful blessing for my good deed. (10 Nov 1898 to Tuohy, photocopy in CU-MARK)

Tuohy rejected the story, despite the "detail" that had been changed for the sake of propriety—the gender of the protagonist. In April 1899 Clemens offered the typed version to John B. Walker of *Cosmopolitan,* who also declined to print it. By August of that year he had decided that the tale was not "publishable" as drafted and, as he told Rogers, he had no interest in rewriting it (5 Apr 1899 to Walker, photocopy in CU-MARK; 22 Aug 1899 to Rogers, Salm, in *HHR,* 407). In January 1906, when Clemens told the story in an after-dinner speech at The Players club, he called Lizzie "English Mary" and altered several other details, but he did acknowledge his own role in the forced marriage (for a text of the speech see *AutoMT1,* 662–63). By April 1907, when he decided to insert the manuscript into his autobiography (setting aside the typed version), he was ready to make the same admission in writing: he added a note to his typist, "Wherever 'Jackson' appears, change it to CLEMENS, & 'Dennis' to PATRICK. SLC" (see the Textual Commentary at *MTPO*). Clemens made one more attempt to publish the story, in August 1907, when he sent it to Frederick Duneka for the Christmas issue of *Harper's Monthly* (the version has not been identified). Duneka rejected it in favor of extracts from "Captain Stormfield's Visit to Heaven." "Wapping Alice" remained unpublished until 1981 (Duneka to SLC, 2 Aug 1907, CU-MARK; SLC 1907–8, 1981).

40.28–29 Garvie and Hills, the contractors who built your house] The Clemenses' house at 351 Farmington Avenue in Hartford, designed by Edward Tuckerman Potter, was built in 1873–74 by John B. Garvie, a general contractor, and John R. Hills, a stonemason.

40.30 Mr. George Warner] George H. and Lillie Warner were the Clemenses' neighbors (*AutoMT1,* 580 n. 327.14; for Bunce, Robinson, and Hawley see AD, 9 Apr 1907, note at 31.41–42).

41.1 I have now told all the facts and removed all the fictions] Clemens wrote a factual account of the events in three letters to Olivia in July 1877, when it took place. On 17 July he told her that "there has been no burglar in the house, but only one or both of Lizzie's two loafers." His main concern at that point was to confirm that neither she nor her "loafers" had stolen anything. When confronted with the fact that Taylor had left the house early one morning, Lizzie claimed that she "was sent for to the nursery one evening (it was later than he ought to have remained) & while she was gone the alarm was put on. She knew no other way to do than to leave him in her room all night & go herself and sleep with Mary." When Mary denied that Lizzie had slept with her, Clemens told Lizzie, "'Your friend slept with *you* the night he left this house so early in the morning.' She confessed." He thereupon "laid a plan" to force Taylor to marry her. He went himself to the courthouse to get the marriage license, then called on the chief of police. Upon his return home he discovered that Lizzie was not in the house, so he sent a note to summon her. She was present when Taylor arrived, and remained, "crying straight along," while Clemens questioned him. Twichell officiated at the wedding ceremony, and "Lizzie cried through the service & the prayer, & then her husband put his arm about her neck & kissed her & shed a tear & said 'Don't cry'" (17 July 1877 to OLC [1st and 2nd], and 17 and 18 July to OLC, CU-MARK).

41.3–4 The tremendous Thaw trial . . . an extract from it] Clemens returns to a subject he discussed in the Autobiographical Dictation of 28 February 1907: the trial of wealthy playboy Harry K. Thaw for the June 1906 murder of architect Stanford White. Thaw sought revenge for White's seduction of his wife, Evelyn Nesbit—an artist's model and chorus girl—when she was a sixteen-year-old virgin (see *AutoMT2,* 647 n. 454.3–7). Delphin M. Delmas (1844–1928) studied law at Yale University and was admitted to the bar in California in 1866. He practiced law in San Jose, and then in San Francisco, serving also as district attorney of Santa Clara County and as a regent of the University of California. Considered a great courtroom orator, he was said to resemble Napoleon because of his short stature and the "little brow wisp of hair" that he used to disguise his baldness. Thaw's other two attorneys summoned Delmas from California to deliver the closing argument and "win the fight for Thaw's life" ("Delmas Opens Plea for Thaw," New York *Times*, 9 Apr 1907, 1).

42.5–8   Stanford White … heard the shriek of horror and anguish of the victim] Delmas thought that Thaw's only hope of acquittal lay in pleading insanity, and he tried to withdraw from the case when Thaw insisted that his defense be based on the "unwritten law" that justified his act of revenge. Delmas used his closing argument to excoriate White and paint a lurid picture of the seduction scene to persuade the jury that "Providence had sent Thaw to avenge the wrong" ("Thaw His Own Lawyer," Washington *Post*, 16 Apr 1907, 15; "Delmas to Jury," Los Angeles *Times*, 9 Apr 1907, I1). He was partially successful: a mistrial was declared on 12 April after the jury failed to agree on a verdict. When Thaw was retried in 1908 he was found not guilty by reason of insanity and committed to an insane asylum.

42.16–18   Chief Magistrate of this nation recently said … punished by death] In his address to Congress on 4 December 1906, President Roosevelt condemned the lynch law and recommended the death penalty for crimes against women:

> Every colored man should realize that the worst enemy of his race is the negro criminal, and above all the negro criminal who commits the dreadful crime of rape; and it should be felt as in the highest degree an offense against the whole country, and against the colored race in particular, for a colored man to fail to help the officers of the law in hunting down with all possible earnestness and zeal every such infamous offender.

In addition, he said the "members of the white race" should realize that "no man can take part in the torture of a human being without having his own moral nature permanently lowered" ("Summary of the Features of Message," Chicago *Tribune*, 5 Dec 1906, 13).

Autobiographical Dictation, 11 April 1907

43.4–5   Many months ago I extracted … the Children's Record] Clemens inserted excerpts from "A Record of the Small Foolishnesses of Susy & 'Bay' Clemens (Infants)," a manuscript he wrote between 1876 and 1884, in the Autobiographical Dictation of 5 September 1906. In the extracts that follow, Clemens adapts rather than "quotes" his manuscript (for the complete text see *FamSk*, 51–93; *AutoMT2*, 222–25).

43.23   Aunt Sue] Susan Langdon Crane, Olivia Clemens's foster sister. She and her husband, Theodore, owned Quarry Farm, near Elmira, where the Clemens family spent their summers from 1871 to 1889 (*AutoMT1*, 480 n. 74.1, 579 n. 324.32).

43.24   "I love Jesus because He first loved me."] This is the last line of a refrain in several different hymns. The most popular, written by Anglican clergyman Frederick Whitfield (1829–1904), was first published in 1855 with the title "The Name of Jesus," and was commonly sung to an American folk melody (Julian 1908, 1276).

44.7–8   Mary Lewis, the colored wife of John T. Lewis, (the colored lessee of Quarry Farm,)] Mary Stover (1841?–94) was born in Virginia. Lewis married her in 1865, a year after he had settled in Elmira, and she worked as a servant at Quarry Farm. They had one child, Susanna, born in 1871 or 1872 (see *AutoMT2*, 541–42 n. 172.40–173.1; *Chemung Census* 1880, 817:235C; Gretchen Sharlow, personal communication, 10 Aug 1990, CU-MARK; Thomasson 1985).

44.11–15   Maggie O'Day . . . Lizzie Botheker] Maggie O'Day has not been further identified. Clemens omitted here a further comment on Lizzie Botheker that he had recorded in the "Children's Record": he "had to pay her worthless husband $60 to let her come, beside her wages of $5 per week (*FamSk*, 54).

44.16   Patrick's wife, Mary McAleer] Patrick, the Clemenses' coachman, was married to the former Mary Reagan (b. 1846?). Their first child, James, was about the same age as Clara (*AutoMT1*, 579 n. 322.31–42; *Hartford Census* 1880, 97:117C).

44.17–18   Maria McManus . . . To me, but not to Mrs. Clemens, Maria was a delight] Maria McLaughlin ("McManus" was Clemens's invention) was indeed not a "delight" to Olivia. In a letter of 23 April 1875 she told Elinor Howells about her "wet nurse that is tractable and good when I am in the house but who gets drunk when I go away" (MH-H). In "A Family Sketch," a series of reminiscences begun in 1896 and then added to and revised through 1906, Clemens wrote another colorful description of the inimitable Maria, calling her "the Egyptian" (*FamSk*, 31–32).

44.35–36   Gillette place] The home built in 1857 by Francis Gillette, a cofounder of the Nook Farm community and the father of William Gillette and Lilly Gillette Warner (*AutoMT1*, 580 n. 327.14, 584 n. 336.18).

45.12–14   A couple of years after Clara was done . . . gave me as a reference] In January 1876, less than a year after leaving the Clemenses, Maria was "waiting her confinement" at the New York Infant Asylum, a charitable institution for unwanted children and unwed or indigent mothers. When she was caught with some "fine-cut tobacco . . . and a bottle of liquor," she spoke of her former employment to the superintendent, who wrote to Clemens:

> The managers of this institution are ready to dismiss her, but I begged them to wait a little and have just had a talk with her when she told me of having been in your service. She says you were very good to the poor, that you helped her to coal, paid her rent, &c when her husband was out of work.
>
> Have I any need to apologize for asking from you a good word for the girl if she deserves it? (Ranstead to SLC, 13 Jan 1876, CU-MARK)

Clemens's reply is not known to survive.

45.15–16   eleven thousand Virgins of Cologne] According to Christian martyrology, Saint Ursula, a Romano-British maiden, and eleven thousand virgin companions were slaughtered in the third century while defending their purity and faith against the Huns. Their relics were discovered buried near Cologne, where a church was erected in their honor. The legend has evolved into many different versions through a series of implausible interpretations and rationales.

45.25–26   Frank D. Millet, the young artist . . . remained with us a fortnight] Francis Davis Millet (1846–1912) grew up on a farm in East Bridgewater, Massachusetts. After serving as a drummer boy in the Union army, he graduated in 1869 from Harvard College with a degree in literature. He then turned his interest to painting, which he studied in Italy and Belgium, and enjoyed a successful career as a journalist, writer, painter, and muralist. He was deeply mourned when he died on the *Titanic*. Millet visited Hartford in early 1877, completing Clemens's portrait on 17 January. On that day Clemens wrote a friend, "the artist has made a most Excellent portrait of me, & besides has given us a week of social enjoyment, for his company is a high pleasure. We have to lose him tomorrow" (17 Jan 1877 to Boyesen, CtHMTH). For a photograph of the portrait see Schmidt 2005.

46.6   He had . . . been appointed war correspondent by the London *Daily News*] During the early months of the Russo-Turkish War of 1877–78, Millet corresponded for the New York *Herald,* but in the fall of 1877 he moved to the London *Daily News* (see the note at 46.9–10). Clemens was actually in Elmira when he received Millet's letter announcing his first assignment:

> I had been in London a day or two to see the pictures there and had steadily refused offers to go to the war as correspondent because I could not bear to leave my work. After my return to Paris I received a letter from the manager of the European correspondence of the N.Y. Herald requesting me to meet him. . . . I immediately started down to see him and on the way as I was stopped at a crowded crossing I blundered right into his carriage and he was on his way up to find me having that moment learned my address. He said "Will you go to Romania with me"? I said "yes"! (Millet to SLC, 9 June 1877, CU-MARK)

46.9–10   MacGahan and Archibald Forbes, those daring knights of the pen] Januarius Aloysius MacGahan (1844–78) was born in Ohio, the son of an Irish immigrant. His career in journalism began in 1870, when he was hired by the New York *Herald* to report on the Franco-Prussian War (1870–71). He earned a reputation for bravery and endurance when he accompanied the Russian Army on their 1873 expedition into Central Asia, eluding the Cossack horsemen sent to arrest him. He later corresponded from Cuba, and then from Spain during the Carlist insurrections in 1874–75. His 1876 dispatches on the Turkish atrocities in Bulgaria swayed the British to support the Russians in their 1877–78 war to end Turkish rule there. He corresponded for the London *Daily News* during that war, which resulted in the liberation of Bulgaria and made him a popular hero. He died in Constantinople of typhoid fever while nursing a friend (Bullard 1914, 115–54). Archibald Forbes (1838–1900), a Scotsman, was arguably the most famous and intrepid war correspondent of his day. After a brief stint with the London *Morning Advertiser,* he was hired by the London *Daily News,* for which he covered the Franco-Prussian War and other conflicts throughout the 1870s, including the Russo-Turkish War, the Afghan War (1878), and the Anglo-Zulu War (1879). Although his colorful exploits brought him fame, his critics were skeptical, "suggesting that he exaggerated, over-dramatized and occasionally falsified reports and sometimes took credit for other correspondents' stories" (Brake and Demoor 2009, 224; Bullard 1914, 69–114). In 1877 Millet, Forbes, and MacGahan worked cooperatively in Bucharest. When Forbes fell ill in September, Millet was offered his place on the London *Daily News* for triple the salary he had received from the *Herald,* and he became a "special artist" for the London *Graphic.* He wrote of his new position to Clemens from Bulgaria on 18 October, adding a comment about the conduct of the war: "The poor, patient soldiers, the devoted, brave officers of the line, the gallant colonels and brigadiers have to go up and be slaughtered because a stupid, idiotic major general is taking his tea in the middle of the day and has given the order without the very slightest idea of the state of affairs" (CU-MARK; Bullard 1914, 98–99).

46.10   He was in the centre of the hottest fire at Plevna] For five months, beginning in July 1877, the Turks—armed with Winchester rifles—defended the Bulgarian town of Plevna (now known as Pleven) against the superior forces of the Russian and Romanian armies before capitulating in December. In his dispatches Millet described the battle scenes and the horrible carnage he observed afterwards in the ruined city.

46.11–12   the Emperor was his friend, and decorated him on the field, for valor] On 18 October 1877 Millet wrote to Clemens about receiving this honor from Tsar Alexander II (1818–81): "I have been presented to the Emperor for decoration with the cross 'pour valour militaire' in company with several officers.... If they would give me a commission to paint *his majesty* instead of a tin cross, I'd thank 'm heartily" (CU-MARK). Millet was awarded the Cross of St. Stanislaus and the Cross of St. Anne by the Russian government, and he received several additional decorations for bravery under fire, including one for his care of the wounded (Maynard 1912, 654). Clemens wrote to Mary Mason Fairbanks on 6 March 1879, "I have seen these decorations, but Millet himself does not speak of them, for he is an exceedingly modest fellow" (*Letters 1876–1880*).

46.18–19   When the war was over he returned to Paris ... We were at the wedding] After the war Millet traveled to Sicily, Spain, and London before returning to Paris. On 1 June 1878 he wrote to Clemens (CU-MARK):

> I was so disgusted in London with the swagger and bluster of some of the war correspondents there that I hid my head. As I was the only one who made the whole campaign I think I know more about it than the rest and never have told half the story in my letters. But when I heard the rest of the men yarning at 20 knots an hour about battles and adventures where I was myself it made me hate the trade.

After his return to Paris, Millet was married, on 11 March 1879, to Elizabeth (Lily) Greeley Merrill, the sister of a college friend. Clemens wrote to Fairbanks on 6 March, "We're expecting Frank D. Millet, a very dear young artist friend of ours here, every moment, to dinner, with the lovely girl he is to marry next Tuesday—with I & 3 friends as witnesses,—& Livy & Clara S. & I & 6 or 8 more will eat the wedding breakfast in his studio" (*Letters 1876–1880;* Baxter 1912, 636, 638). Clemens may have considered Elizabeth "lovely" in 1879, but in 1894 he described her to Olivia in less flattering terms:

> Mrs. Millet was as prodigious an improvement upon herself as—well there isn't *any* comparison that will describe it. She was pretty, she was unstunningly dressed, hardly the top of the crevice between her breasts was exposed, she was dignified & reposeful, her feverish eagerness to jabber & jabber & jabber was gone, she said many rational things & got badly caught out only once.

When Clemens praised Thomas Bailey Aldrich as "the one man in this earth who was *always* witty, *always* brilliant,"

> It was Mrs. Millet's opportunity to expose herself, & she said with large calm superiority:
> "I think you cannot have met him *very* often. My experience differs from yours. I have met him at dinners often & over again when he was dull, monosyllabic—yes, & even *silent* during long intervals."
> I saw poor Millet wince! And yet nevertheless I was not mollified, but said (gently & without emphasis, but *said* it)—
> "Yes, there *are* dinner companies that can do even that miracle." (8 or 9 Feb 1894 to OLC, CU-MARK)

46.23–25 the World's Exposition in Chicago . . . artists of repute under him] Millet's experience with expositions in Paris and Vienna brought him to the attention of the organizers of the 1893 World's Exposition in Chicago, held in celebration of the four-hundredth anniversary of Columbus's landing in America. He was placed in charge of decorating the principal buildings in Jackson Park, for which he chose only American artists. The buildings, covered in white plaster of paris, became known as the "White City." In addition, he painted the highly praised murals in the exposition's Liberal Arts building and the grand hall of the New York State building ("Artist Millet and Assistants," Chicago *Tribune,* 22 Oct 1892, 18; Baxter 1912, 638).

46.40–47.1 I went in there to get the ends of my hair clipped off . . . disaster that had befallen] Samuel Johnson Woolf (1880–1948), a graphic artist who sketched Clemens in February 1906 for a painting, recalled being shown Millet's portrait and hearing the following story:

> "It's all mine, except the hair," he remarked. I looked in bewilderment. "It was this way," he explained, "when I started sitting for that one, my hair was fairly long, but as the sittings continued, it grew until it was uncomfortable. So one day,

without saying anything to Millet about it, I went to the barber to have it trimmed. Unfortunately, I grew sleepy in the comfortable chair, and when I woke up I saw that I had lost all likeness to my portrait. I didn't know what to do, for I was afraid of Millet in those days, so on the day for the next sitting I hired a wig and went to the studio. When I got there Millet at once noticed how fine my hair looked and painted it, and it wasn't until the session was ended that I took it off." (Woolf 1910, 43)

47.34–35 Miss Hesse ceased from her office of private secretary . . . leave of us to-day] Fanny C. Hesse (1821?–1907) served as Clemens's secretary in 1876–77. From 1882 to 1893 she was in charge of Hatfield House at Smith College in Northampton, Massachusetts (*Vermont Vital Records* 1760–1954, record for Fanny C. Hesse; Smith College Alumnae Association 1911, 12).

48.5 Rosa] Rosina Hay (see *AutoMT2*, 568 n. 242.34).

48.14 George] George Griffin.

Autobiographical Dictation, 20 April 1907

48.34–35 that phrase which . . . is the blackest one that exists in any language] The newspaper article that Clemens read has not been identified. The subject of this "dictation," however (which is in fact based on a manuscript), leaves no doubt that he refers to the phrase "age of consent" (see the note at 49.36–38).

49.36–38 the age of consent . . . before the age of sixteen] Clemens appears to be misinformed: in the state of New York, the age of consent had been raised from sixteen to eighteen in 1895.

Autobiographical Dictation, 18 May 1907

51.8 In March, after a second trip to Bermuda] See the Autobiographical Dictation of 26 March 1907, note at 13.31.

51.21–22 I had put together enough Autobiography . . . twenty-eight years' renewal of copyright life] See the Autobiographical Dictation of 26 March 1907, note at 14.32–33.

51.34–35 I helped to open the Actors' Fund Fair on the 6th of this present month] The fair was held at the Metropolitan Opera House to raise funds for aged or infirm actors. The main hall, transformed into a Shakespearean village with shops and dwellings, provided one of the numerous entertainments, which also included games of chance, palmists and fortune tellers, and vaudeville performers. Clemens's "famous white suit and white hair made him a conspicuous figure from the minute he entered the hall" ("Actors' Fund Fair Opens with Vim," New York *Times*, 7 May 1907, 5).

51.36–37 I went down to Jamestown in Mr. Rogers's yacht . . . the opening of the World's Fair there] The Jamestown Exposition was held from 26 April through November 1907 to commemorate the three-hundredth anniversary of the first permanent English settlement in America. It took place at Sewell's Point, Virginia, a peninsula north of Norfolk and south of Jamestown Island, where the original colony had been founded. On 24 April Clemens and several other guests departed New York on the *Kanawha*, Rogers's fast yacht, to attend the elaborate opening ceremonies. On the day before the opening, they made an early tour of the fair, which included numerous exhibit buildings, animal acts, and amusement rides. The following day, 26 April, they viewed from the deck of the *Kanawha* a "dazzling naval pageant" performed by warships of the United States and thirteen other nations, which welcomed President Roosevelt with a fusillade of gun salutes. Clemens mentions the fair again in the Autobiographical Dictation of 26 September 1907 (Lyon 1907, entry for 24 April; "Roosevelt Day at Jamestown," Washington *Post*, 27 April 1907, 1; for the *Kanawha* see *AutoMT2*, 506 n. 82.9–10; for a complete description of the trip see Shelden 2010, 57–65).

51.37–38 Two or three days of fog followed . . . all the guests except Mr. Broughton and I got tired and went back home by rail] Clemens was "marooned" on the yacht by heavy fog because it was unsafe to return to New York by sea, and he preferred not to take the train ("Mark Twain in Gloom," Washington *Post*, 1 May 1907, 5). Rogers had already left, accompanied by most of the other guests: Henry H. Rogers, Jr. (see AD, 26 Sept 1907, note at 142.30); William Evarts Benjamin, one of his sons-in-law (see *AutoMT2*, 622 n. 387.8–10); and Charles Lancaster, a capitalist from Liverpool (see "The Ashcroft-Lyon Manuscript," note at 368.18–20). Clemens's remaining companion was Urban H. Broughton (1857–1929). Born in Worcester, England, he was trained as a civil engineer and emigrated to the United States in 1887. In 1895, while working on a drainage project in Fairhaven, Massachusetts, he met and married Cara Leland Rogers (1867–1939), Rogers's widowed daughter. He became an officer in several mining, financial, and railway companies—most of which were connected with Rogers—and president of the Utah Consolidated Mining Company (*HHR*, 736; "Urban H. Broughton Dies in London at 71," New York *Times*, 31 Jan 1929, 23).

52.1–3 we got to sea and came through to New York . . . carried us along with it] On 4 May the New York *Times* ran a front-page article—"Twain and Yacht Disappear at Sea"—reporting that the *Kanawha*, on which Clemens had sailed from Old Point Comfort three days earlier, was missing at sea. According to the Washington *Post*, Rogers had "sent out a frenzied call to the wireless station at Cape Henry to look out for his yacht" ("Joke on Mark Twain," 5 May 1907, 14). The following day the *Times* reported that Clemens was safe ("Mark Twain Investigating," 2):

> "You can assure my Virginia friends," said he, "that I will make an exhaustive investigation of this report that I have been lost at sea. If there is any foundation for the report, I will at once apprise the anxious public. I sincerely hope that there

is no foundation for the report, and I also hope that judgment will be suspended until I ascertain the true state of affairs."

To his friend, Milt. Goodkind of 121 West Forty-second Street, Mr. Clemens sent the following telegram as soon as he had read a report from Norfolk telling of the fear there that he was lost on the bosom of the briny deep:

> Latitude 43 degrees 5 hours and 41 seconds west by southeast of Central Park West. Kanawha heading toward nowhere; terrific cyclone raging; all the houses down in our vicinity; trees and telegraph poles interfering with our progress; vessel leaking badly; passed a school of whales and several elephants at dawn. Fire Department badly crippled; extension ladder out of commission; water very low; two of our crew lost overboard last evening. Please send airship and some bock beer at once; crew starving.
>
> Deny report that I am dodging Mrs. Eddy or Actors' Fund Fair. Ship sinking; send financial relief at once.
>
> MARK TWAIN.

The Washington *Post* announced that Clemens had in fact arrived home safely on 1 May, the same day he had left Virginia, and reported his suspicion that the rumor had originated with Rogers, who was "having fun" with him:

> The Standard Oil wizard showed a remarkable willingness to let the newspapers into the workings of his mind—and the narrative of the missing humorist was born.
>
> Mark Twain, who has been safe at home since last Wednesday, seemed to be more amused than annoyed at the report that he had been lost at sea. . . . The only way he was lost at sea, he added, was for something to do. ("Joke on Mark Twain," 5 May 1907, 14)

52.4–5   I have been invited by Oxford University . . . shall sail on that quest on the 8th] See the Autobiographical Dictations of 23 May, and 25, 26, and 30 July 1907.

52.14–16   a complimentary poem . . . by a judge on the bench] The poem was sent by John A. Kirlicks (CU-MARK):

JOHN A. KIRLICKS,   B. F. FREDERICK
JUDGE   CLERK

OFFICE OF
CORPORATION COURT
CITY OF HOUSTON

HOUSTON TEXAS, May 9th 1907.

Sam[l] L. Clemens, Esq.
(Mark Twain)
New York City,
N. York.

Dear Sir:

I take the liberty of enclosing you a few verses that are justified by your life.

I have tried to avoid fulsomeness, and attempted only to say what is true.

I have been asked for permission to publish some, but have doubted the propriety of doing so without first submitting the lines to you.

If the piece does not displease you, and you can afford to hear the truth about yourself, even when uttered by a stranger, I would prefer it to be given to the public in some New York City publication.

I am with profound respect,

Your Obedient Servant,
John A. Kirlicks

Kindly excuse the worn appearance of the manuscript; I have worn it in my coat pocket so long, to permit it to cool off, and thereby enable me to detect and eliminate any error of fact, sentiment or meter.

Kirlicks (1852–1923) was born in Prussia and emigrated to Texas as a young boy. He was a member of the Texas bar, and served as a Democrat in the state legislature in 1887–89. For a time he was the deputy sheriff of Galveston, and for much of his career he occupied the bench of the Houston Corporation Court, a municipal court that tried misdemeanor offenses (*Galveston Census* 1900, 1637:7A; Legislative Reference Library of Texas 2012, entry for John Kirlicks). Clemens replied to Kirlicks on 15 May (MS facsimile, Houston *Post,* 24 Apr 1910, 8):

It is a beautiful poem & has touched me deeply. If I might venture to suggest, I should say that the proper place for it is either the "Century" or "Harper's Monthly"—preferably the "Century," because I am not connected with it, except by old ties of friendship, whereas I am connected with "Harper's" commercially.

Very gratefully yours
S L. Clemens

Kirlicks submitted his poem to the *Century Magazine,* which rejected it, and then to *Harper's Monthly,* whose editor replied, "We are sorry that we are obliged to return your poem, 'To Mark Twain,' as it is not available for our use" (18 June 1907, CU-MARK). Kirlicks told Clemens of his disappointment on 8 July 1907, regretting the magazine's judgment that "you have no right to hear what the people say about you while you live" (CU-MARK). He did ultimately publish the poem in the Houston *Daily Post* shortly after Clemens's death (24 Apr 1910, 8), and included it in a collection of verse he published in 1913, *Sense and Nonsense in Rhyme,* along with a facsimile of Clemens's 15 May letter (63, 65).

Autobiographical Dictation, 23 May 1907

53.14–15   A cablegram arrived from England . . . honorary degree on the 26th of next month] The telegram was sent from London on 3 May by Whitelaw Reid, the American ambassador to Great Britain (ViU):

OXFORD UNIVERSITY WOULD CONFER DEGREE OF DOCTOR OF LET-
TERS ON YOU ON JUNE 26TH BUT PERSONAL PRESENCE NECESSARY
CABLE ME WHETHER YOU CAN COME

WHITELAW REID

Lyon noted Clemens's reply on the telegram: "I will come with greatest pleasure" (for Reid see *AutoMT1*, 534 n. 222.9–11). Clemens attributed the honor in part to the influence of C. F. Moberly Bell (see AD, 23 Aug 1907, note at 109.27).

53.26–27   ten years later, in Keokuk, that I found a fifty-dollar bill in the street] Clemens describes this incident, which probably occurred in the fall of 1856, in the Autobiographical Dictations of 29 March and 2 October 1906 (*AutoMT1*, 460–61; *AutoMT2*, 237–38).

53.28–31   in San Francisco . . . I found a ten-cent piece in the crossing at the junction of Commercial and Montgomery streets] In chapter 59 of *Roughing It* Clemens tells of the "silver ten-cent piece" that he "would not spend" when in financial straits in San Francisco (*RI 1993*, 405–6). The *Morning Call* building—where he worked from June to October 1864–was at 612 Commercial Street, at the corner of Montgomery (*AutoMT2*, 514 n. 117.21–22).

54.1–7   two from Yale and one from Missouri University . . . Missouri University made me a Doctor of Laws] Yale University conferred a Master of Arts degree on Clemens in June 1888, and a Master of Letters in October 1901. On the first occasion he was unable to attend, but on the second he went to New Haven and participated in the ceremony, which took place during the university's bicentennial celebration (see AD, 14 July 1908, and the note at 257.10–12). In June 1902 he traveled to Columbia to receive a Doctor of Laws degree from the University of Missouri, and took the opportunity to visit Hannibal and St. Louis for the last time (see *AutoMT1*, 353, 589 n. 353.28–29).

Autobiographical Dictation, 24 May 1907

55.5–6   Tuxedo Park is not more than a quarter of a century old] Tuxedo Park, an exclusive gated community in the Ramapo Mountains about forty miles northwest of New York, was built in 1885–86 by tobacco heir Pierre Lorillard IV (1833–1901). It was originally conceived as a sporting resort, with a large lake and six thousand acres of land stocked with fish and game, but later also included a golf course and tennis courts. The Tuxedo Club, to which all residents belonged, offered social activities in a club house on the lake designed by architect Bruce Price (1845–1903). Local property owners H. H. Rogers, Jr., and his wife, Mary, may have suggested to Clemens that he would enjoy the congenial community. The house he rented from 1 May to 1 November 1907 had been built in 1904 by W. H. Neilson Voss on the shore of Wee-Wah Lake (5 Mar 1907 to JC, photocopy in CU-MARK; 3 June 1907 to H. H. Rogers, Jr., and Mary Rogers, NNC;

"The New Tuxedo Park," New York *Times*, 16 Dec 1885, 2; Emily Post 1911; "Mark Twain in Orange Co.," Kingston *Freeman*, 16 May 1907, 8).

55.42   Captain Bush] Gilmore G. Bush, chief of the Tuxedo Park police ("Dinsmore Silver Found," Kingston *Freeman*, 2 Aug 1907, 9).

56.29–30   Gentile or the Shunammite, or the good Samaritan] Clemens conflates the parable of the Shunammite woman in 2 Kings 4:8–37 with the compassionate Samaritan in Luke 10:30–37.

Autobiographical Dictation, 26 May 1907

57.22–24   Through Mr. Paine I learn that Jim Gillis is dead . . . Mr. Paine went with Mr. Goodman to see him] In the spring of 1907 Albert Bigelow Paine gathered material for his biography by traveling to Hannibal and then the West Coast to talk with "those old friends of Mark Twain's who were so rapidly passing away" (*MTB*, 3:1376). In California he met Joseph T. Goodman, former owner of the Virginia City *Territorial Enterprise* and Clemens's lifelong friend (see *AutoMT1*, 535 n. 225.3–5, 544 n. 252.32–253.1). Clemens knew James, Stephen, and William Gillis from his years in Nevada and San Francisco, in the early 1860s (no George is listed in the family genealogy: see *AutoMT1*, 295, 569 n. 295.5–15). James died on 13 April 1907 at age seventy-six. Although he was well read and trained in herbal medicine, he spent his life as a miner, living from 1862 until his death at Jackass Hill, in Tuolumne County, California, prospecting for "pockets" of gold. It was there, in the winter of 1864–65, that Clemens stayed with him, his brother Billy, and Dick Stoker (see the note at 58.25; "James N. Gillis—His Life and Death," Sierra *Times*, 14 Apr 1907, unknown page; 26 Jan 1870 to Gillis, *L4*, 36–37 n. 1; *AutoMT1*, 552–53 n. 261.21–24; *AutoMT2*, 514 n. 113.21–23, 621 n. 384.16–19).

57.24–25   Steve Gillis's end is also near at hand . . . in the sylvan Jackass Gulch country] Steve had been a typesetter and colleague of Clemens's on the *Territorial Enterprise*. He worked on newspapers until 1894, when he joined his brothers at Jackass Hill. Paine described the visit to Tuolumne County in his biography:

> Joe Goodman, still full of vigor (in 1912), journeyed with me to the green and dreamy solitudes of Jackass Hill to see Steve and Jim Gillis, and that was an unforgetable Sunday when Steve Gillis, an invalid, but with the fire still in his eyes and speech, sat up on his couch in his little cabin in that Arcadian stillness and told old tales and adventures. When I left he said:
>   "Tell Sam I'm going to die pretty soon, but that I love him; that I've loved him all my life, and I'll love him till I die. This is the last word I'll ever send to him." Jim Gillis, down in Sonora, was already lying at the point of death, and so for him the visit was too late, though he was able to receive a message from his ancient mining partner, and to send back a parting word. (*MTB*, 3:1377)

Steve Gillis survived eleven more years, dying in 1918 at age seventy-nine.

57.27–28   Steve and George and Billy have large crops of grandchildren] Steve married Catherine Robinson (1843–75) in Virginia City in 1867. Two of their four children survived to adulthood: Marguerita (1868–1962) and James Alston (1870–1944). In 1867 Billy joined his brother Steve in Virginia City, where he worked as an *Enterprise* reporter. He and his wife, Elizabeth, had at least one child, Charles Alston (1876–1944), and—by 1907—two grandchildren. Billy and Elizabeth both died in 1929, when he was eighty-nine and she was about seventy-two ("Friend of Mark Twain Dies," New York *Times*, 21 Aug 1929, 27; Gillis 1930, xiii, 11, 117; "Ancestral File" 2012; *California Death Index 1940–97*, record for Charles A. Gillis; *Tuolumne Census* 1880, 85:176A; 1930, 224:1B).

58.14–20   small book which I wrote . . . military genius, a shoemaker by trade] Clemens refers to his character Absalom Jones, military genius and bricklayer (not shoemaker), in chapter 4 of "Captain Stormfield's Visit to Heaven" (Baetzhold and McCullough 1995, 177; for the history of this "small book," see *AutoMT2*, 193–94, 550–51 nn. 193.39–194.2, 194.17–18).

58.25   Dick Stoker] Jacob Richard Stoker (1820–98) was born in Kentucky. He enlisted in the army in 1847 and fought in the Mexican War. In 1849 he joined the California Gold Rush and settled at Jackass Hill, where he remained for the rest of his life, eking out a living as a pocket miner. In chapter 61 of *Roughing It*, Clemens described him as "gray as a rat, earnest, thoughtful, slenderly educated, slouchily dressed and clay-soiled, but his heart was finer metal than any gold his shovel ever brought to light—than any, indeed, that ever was mined or minted" (*RI 1993*, 416, 704–5 n. 416.4).

58.26–27   Jackass Gulch . . . of which I have already spoken] See the Autobiographical Dictation of 23 January 1907 (*AutoMT2*, 384–87).

58.34–38   "The Tragedy of the Burning Shame." . . . how gorgeous in its unprintable form] In chapter 23 of *Adventures of Huckleberry Finn*, Clemens modified the title of the tale as well as its details: in the "Thrilling Tragedy of the King's Cameleopard or the Royal Nonesuch" the king entertains an all-male audience ("ladies and children not admitted") by capering around the stage naked and painted with stripes, a performance that Huck finds "awful funny." Jim Gillis's "unprintable" version evidently included a further detail—a lighted candle inserted into the performer's posterior. Gillis's title may have derived from the expression "burning shame," defined in Francis Grose's 1785 *Classical Dictionary of the Vulgar Tongue* as "a lighted candle stuck into the private parts of a woman" (*HF 2003*, 194–96, 438–39 n. 195.1–4). Although Gillis told the story, Stoker willingly enacted the skit, as Clemens recalled in a letter to Gillis of 26 January 1870: "And wouldn't I love to take old Stoker by the hand, & wouldn't I love to see him in his great specialty, his wonderful rendition of 'Rinaldo' in the 'Burning Shame!' Where *is* Dick, & what is he doing? Give him my fervent love & warm old remembrances" (*L4*, 35–36).

58.39–40 "The Tramp Abroad," . . . woodpeckers tried to fill up a house with acorns] From chapters 2 and 3 of *A Tramp Abroad* (1880), where Jim Baker's yarn is about blue jays, not woodpeckers.

59.2–3 in one of my books—the story of Jim Baker's cat . . . Tom Quartz. Jim Baker was Dick Stoker] In chapter 61 of *Roughing It,* the character Dick Baker tells the story of a cat who is asleep in a mining shaft when the miners "put in a blast" to dislodge the rock, and as a result becomes permanently "prejudiced agin quartz mining" (*RI 1993,* 416–19).

Autobiographical Dictation, 29 May 1907

61.32 He had a letter from you once, and it was the prize of his heart] Only two letters to Gillis are known to survive, dated 26 January 1870 and 2 July 1871. (There are photocopies of both in the Mark Twain Papers, but the current location of the manuscripts is not known.) The earlier letter is probably the one that Gillis enjoyed showing to his "rare old cronies": Steve Gillis made it available to Paine for his volume of *Mark Twain's Letters,* and the manuscript was evidently so worn that it had to be repaired (*L4,* 35–39, 428–29, 601–2, 674–75). In it, Clemens told Gillis of his upcoming marriage to "Miss Olivia L. Langdon" and reminisced about his winter with the Gillises, recalling the day he heard the "Jumping Frog" tale that made him famous (SLC 1865):

> You remember the one gleam of jollity that shot across our dismal sojourn in the rain & mud of Angel's Camp—I mean that day we sat around the tavern stove & heard that chap tell about the frog & how they filled him with shot. And you remember how we quoted from the yarn & laughed over it, out there on the hillside while you & dear old Stoker panned & washed. I jotted the story down in my notebook that day, & would have been glad to get ten or fifteen dollars for it—I was just that blind. But then we were *so* hard up. I published that story, & it became widely known in America, India, China, England,—& the reputation it made for me has paid me thousands & thousands of dollars since.

The letter concluded with a teasing allusion to the incident of the sour plums: "P. S. California plums *are* good, Jim—particularly when they are stewed" (*L4,* 35–36; see *AutoMT2,* 46–49).

61.39 Crittenden Hampton] Hampton (1862–1948) was born in Tuolumne County, California, and was a teacher in nearby Inyo County before relocating to Sonora, the Tuolumne County seat, where he was an attorney and notary. He was also a Mason and a member of the American Bar Association (*California Death Index* 1940–97, and *California Great Registers* 1866–98, records for Crittenden Hampton). Clemens dictated the following reply (CSoM):

Tuxedo Park.
May 27, 1907.

Dear Mr. Hampton:—

I dictated a long and admiring and affectionate chapter about Jim Gillis, yesterday, and some day or other, in the by and by, it will appear in my Autobiography. It will then be seen that I, and perhaps not another person in the world, knew Jim Gillis for what he was, namely: a man with a fine, and I may say even wonderful imagination, and that he was also a born humorist of the first order. Of course Jim must have known that he was a humorist, but I am quite sure that he never once suspected that his place was in the top rank of the guild.

I thank you very much for your letter.

Sincerely yours,
S L. Clemens

62.1–2   Rev. Dr. Long, who is a naturalist equipped with a pleasant and entertaining pen] William Joseph Long (1866?–1952) earned degrees from Harvard College (1892), Andover Theological Seminary (1895), and the University of Heidelberg (1897). From 1899 to 1903 he was pastor of the First Congregational Church in Stamford, Connecticut. He was also an avid outdoorsman who made frequent visits to the northern woods to observe wildlife, often accompanied by his wife and children. Although he wrote many literary and historical works, as well as children's fiction, he was best known for his nature and animal studies, which portrayed the natural world as a source of moral wisdom, free from the corrupting influence of human civilization. The first of these, *Ways of Wood Folk,* was issued in 1899, and by 1907 he had published many more (Lutts 1990, 55–60, 161–62, 182, 185, 205–6). Clemens owned at least three of his books: *Beasts of the Field* (1901), *Fowls of the Air* (1902 copy, first published in 1901), and *School of the Woods* (1902) (Gribben 1980, 1:419).

62.2–3   a heavy-weight like John Burroughs] Burroughs (1837–1921) grew up on a farm in upstate New York and for a time worked as a schoolteacher. In 1863 he took a job with the U.S. Treasury Department and moved to Washington, D.C., where he became a lifelong friend of Walt Whitman's. A veteran nature writer, he published his first collection of essays in 1871, *Wake Robin,* which was praised for its vivid descriptions of birds. Burroughs ultimately wrote more than two dozen nature studies that combined accurate description with eloquent commentary and expressed his conviction that animals acted solely on instinct, not on acquired knowledge. Clemens owned at least three of his books: *Birds and Bees* (1887), *Songs of Nature* (1901), and *Bird and Bough* (1906); he mentions Burroughs again in the Autobiographical Dictation of 19 August 1907 (Gribben 1980, 1:116–17). The "scrap" began in March 1903, when Burroughs published an article in the *Atlantic Monthly* attacking Long's claim that animals teach their young (see the note at 64.28–30). Roosevelt, who had long admired Burroughs, shared his view that Long was a deliberate fraud whose nature writings were idealized interpretations. He invited Burroughs on a trip to Yellowstone National Park, and the two men became fast friends. The *Atlantic Monthly* article set off a prolonged controversy, carried on by Burroughs, Long, and other naturalists in the *Century Magazine,* the *North American Review,* the *Atlantic*

Monthly, Harper's Monthly, and *Everybody's Magazine.* Roosevelt refrained from public comment on the subject until 1905, when he dedicated his book *Outdoor Pastimes of an American Hunter* to Burroughs (see the note at 64.31–33; Lutts 1990, 4–9, 37, 40–43, 50–55, 60–73, 222 nn. 28–29, 31–32, 34–35; for more on Roosevelt's hunting see the ADs of 18 and 21 Oct 1907).

62.15–20   got himself interviewed for the *Outlook* ... wild bird mend its broken leg] The interview was published in *Everybody's Magazine,* not in the *Outlook,* a weekly journal (see the note at 64.9–16). Roosevelt first took aim at Jack London for claiming in *White Fang* that a bulldog could fend off a wolf, and that a lynx could kill one: "This is about as sensible as to describe a tom cat tearing in pieces a thirty-pound fighting bull terrier." Then he focused his attack on Long, objecting in particular to his description of a wolf killing a caribou fawn with a bite to the heart. The interview did not include a mention of Long's controversial essay "Animal Surgery," in which he described a bird who made itself a cast for a broken leg (see the notes at 65.1–4, 65.6–7, and 65.17–18). Clemens likens the "noise" Roosevelt made to the historic Battle of Tsushima, fought on 27–28 May 1905, in which Japanese battleships destroyed two-thirds of the Russian fleet (see *AutoMT2,* 525 n. 134.38–135.1).

62.23–25   Did he not fling the faithful Bowen out of office, and ... deodorize the mephitic Loomis] In early 1905 Herbert Wolcott Bowen (1856–1927), a career diplomat who was appointed minister to Venezuela in 1901, accused Assistant Secretary of State Francis B. Loomis (1861–1948), the former minister, of having engaged in improper financial transactions in connection with asphalt interests in Venezuela. Roosevelt, who believed in Loomis's innocence, launched an official inquiry. At its conclusion, in June 1905, Loomis was exonerated, and Roosevelt dismissed Bowen from office for "circulating unfounded charges" ("The Progress of the World" and "Record of Current Events," *American Monthly Review of Reviews* 32 [July 1905]: 18, 19).

62.25   Didn't he promulgate the illegal Order 78] Roosevelt's Executive Order 78 added advanced age to the list of disabilities that qualified Civil War veterans for a pension. It went into effect on 13 April 1904, and was projected to cost as much as $15 million. Many considered the act unconstitutional, and criticized Roosevelt for exceeding his power in order to win votes from veterans (see *AutoMT2,* 615–16 nn. 371.42–372.15, 372.29).

62.25–26   Hasn't he tunneled so many subways under the Constitution] Roosevelt expanded the power of his office by issuing more than a thousand executive orders, far more than any of his predecessors. He explained in his autobiography:

> I declined to adopt the view that what was imperatively necessary for the Nation could not be done by the President unless he could find some specific authorization to do it. My belief was that it was not only his right but his duty to do anything that the needs of the Nation demanded unless such action was forbidden by the Constitution or by the laws. Under this interpretation of executive power I did

and caused to be done many things not previously done by the President and the heads of the departments. I did not usurp power, but I did greatly broaden the use of executive power. (Roosevelt 1922, 357)

62.27–28   Didn't he send a bouquet and a broken heart to lay upon the corpse of Mr. Quay] Matthew Stanley Quay (1833–1904), a Republican politician from Pennsylvania, was an exceptional tactician and organizer. In 1885 he was elected state treasurer and became a member of the Republican National Committee, becoming the political "boss" of his state. In 1887–99 and 1901–4 he served in the U.S. Senate. He was indicted for misuse of state funds in 1898, but was acquitted the following year. When he died in May 1904, Roosevelt sent his widow a "wreath of American beauty roses and white peonies, with maiden hair fern interwoven," and added a message of "profound sympathy, official and personal," praising Quay as a "stanch and loyal friend" ("A Curious Collocation," New York *Times*, 1 June 1904, 8; "Last Rites for Senator Quay," Chicago *Tribune*, 1 June 1904, 7).

62.31   foot-ball and base ball, and molly-coddles] In 1905 the alarmingly high number of injuries (and even fatalities) among college football players prompted Roosevelt to summon the coaches of several universities to discuss reforming the game. Harvard—for whose team Theodore Roosevelt, Jr., played—was among the schools that appointed a committee to investigate and make recommendations. In February 1907, shortly before its report was delivered, Roosevelt commented on the issue in a speech to the students:

> As I emphatically disbelieve in seeing Harvard or any other college turn out mollycoddles instead of vigorous men, I may add that I do not in the least object to a sport because it is rough. Rowing, baseball, lacrosse, track and field games, hockey, football are all of them good. Moreover, it is to my mind simple nonsense, a mere confession of weakness, to desire to abolish a game because tendencies show themselves, or practices grow up which prove that the game ought to be reformed. ("No Mollycoddles, Says Roosevelt," New York *Times*, 24 Feb 1907, 1)

The report suggested new rules that would discourage unsportsmanlike behavior and allow plays like the forward pass which favored "speed and skill" over "brute force." Harvard President Charles William Eliot approved the adoption of these reforms, which he agreed would make football less dangerous, but maintained that it was still an "undesirable game for gentlemen to play or multitudes of people to witness" ("Roosevelt in New Crusade," Chicago *Tribune*, 10 Oct 1905, 1; "The New Game of Football," New York *Times*, 30 Sept 1906, SM5; Washington *Post*: "If Not Football, What," 1 Jan 1906, 8; "Football Too Fierce," 7 Mar 1907, 9; John J. Miller 2012).

64.9–16   The title of this article is 'Roosevelt on the Nature Fakirs.' . . . unfounded charge at the end] The article, in *Everybody's Magazine* for June 1907, was by Edward B. Clark of the Chicago *Evening Post*, who spent an evening at the White House conversing with the president (Lutts 1990, 101–2). Roosevelt wrote to Burroughs in March 1907, "I finally proved unable to contain myself, and gave an interview or statement, to a very fine fellow, in which I sailed into Long and Jack London and one or two other of the more preposterous writers of 'unnatural history'" (quoted in Lutts 1990, 101). The "Editor's Note" introducing the interview explained that Roosevelt was especially concerned about the use of Long's books in the classroom:

> It is about time to call a halt upon misrepresentative nature studies. Utterly pre-posterous details of wild life are placed before school children in the guise of truth. Wholly false beliefs have been almost standardized. Only by an authoritative pro-test can the fraud be exposed. At this juncture it is fitting that the President should come forward. From every point of view he is the person in the United States best equipped for the task, and we are fortunate in being able to fire the first gun, so to speak, with a charge of Mr. Roosevelt's vigorous, clear-cut, earnest English. (Clark 1907, 770)

The article begins with a quotation from the chief of the U.S. Biological Survey: "Theodore Roosevelt is the world's authority on the big game mammals of North America. His writings are fuller and his observations are more complete and accurate than those of any other man who has given the subject study." At the conclusion of the interview, Roosevelt said that it was "startling to think of any school authorities accepting" Long's story about a "caribou school": "If the child mind is fed with stories that are false to nature, the children will go to the haunts of the animal only to meet with disappointment. The result will be disbelief, and the death of interest. The men who misinterpret nature and replace fact with fiction, undo the work of those who in the love of nature interpret it aright" (Clark 1907, 770, 774).

64.28–30   a violent attack was made upon me ... every honest argument it con-tained was frankly answered] In his March 1903 article, "Real and Sham Natural His-tory," Burroughs called Long's *School of the Woods* "ridiculous," objecting especially to his claim that an animal's survival did not depend upon instinct but upon parental training. Long was understandably offended by the personal nature of Burroughs's criticism: "Mr. Long's book reads like that of a man who has really never been to the woods, but who sits in his study and cooks up these yarns from things he has read in Forest and Stream, or in other sporting journals. Of real observation there is hardly a vestige in his book; of deliberate trifling with natural history there is no end" (Burroughs 1903, 303, 306). Long "answered" Burroughs's attack in the May 1903 issue of the *North American Review,* where he argued that nature study was not science, but a world of "suggestion and freedom and inspiration": "In a word, the difference between Nature and Science is the ... difference between the woman who cherishes her old-fashioned flower-garden and the professor who lectures on Botany in a college class-room." He claimed that for "over twenty years, I have gone every season deep into the woods; have lived alone with the animals for months at a time. ... I have gone fifty miles out of my course to interview some famous old Indian or hunter, and ask for his verification or denial of my own observations." He also defended the stories Burroughs had found unbelievable, giving specific examples of young animals who learned from their parents (Long 1903b, 688–89, 691–92).

64.31–33 Roosevelt . . . goes far out of his way for the sake of repeating his friend's attack] Roosevelt's *Outdoor Pastimes of an American Hunter,* published in October 1905, included a dedication to Burroughs:

> I wish to express my hearty appreciation of your warfare against the sham nature-writers—those whom you have called "the yellow journalists of the woods." . . . It is unpardonable for any observer of nature to write fiction and then publish it as truth, and he who exposes and wars against such action is entitled to respect and support. You in your own person have illustrated what can be done by the lover of nature who has trained himself to keen observation, who describes accurately what is thus observed, and who, finally, possesses the additional gift of writing with charm and interest. ("To John Burroughs," in Roosevelt 1905)

64.34–38 a short time ago I wrote a series of articles . . . a sort of brutal thoughtlessness] Long's articles were published in *Brier-Patch Philosophy by "Peter Rabbit"* (1906). The chapter entitled "Heroes Who Hunt Rabbits" is a scathing rebuke of those who slaughtered animals for entertainment and promoted such sport as a way to develop courage. Roosevelt was not named, but was clearly recognizable as one of the men described by Long, who were "killing mother bears with young, or collecting numerous heads of game unfit to eat, or killing more deer and ducks than they can use," and then urging "all honest men to spare and protect the diminishing wild animals" (Long 1906, 170–71).

65.1–4 the most improbable thing I ever wrote—a story of a woodcock . . . eight witnesses] Long's article "Animal Surgery" appeared in the *Outlook* in September 1903 and was reprinted as "A Woodcock Genius" in *A Little Brother to the Bear, and Other Animal Stories* (Long 1903a, 101–6, 1903c). Early in 1904, it elicited several indignant letters to *Science* magazine. In the issue of 14 May, Long defended himself in an article entitled "Science, Nature and Criticism," which included the evidence and testimony he mentions here (Long 1904; see also Lutts 1990, 76–82).

65.6–7 Mr. Roosevelt . . . certain statements concerning the Canada lynx] Roosevelt pointed out "all kinds of absurdities" in the story "Upweekis the Shadow," from *Beasts of the Field* (Long 1901). In particular, he was incredulous of Long's claim that a "number of lynxes gathered around the nearly eaten carcass of a caribou, while a menagerie of smaller beasts, including a pine marten, circulates freely among them," and rejected as implausible his account of a lynx that stalked him "hour after hour through the wilderness" (Clark 1907, 773).

65.9–12 Dr. Long, opening one of Mr. Roosevelt's books . . . literally inexplicable] The quotations are from "Wolves and Wolf-Hounds," chapter 8 of *Hunting the Grisly and Other Sketches,* first published in 1893 and widely reprinted (Roosevelt 1893a).

65.17–18   mathematical impossibility is that a huge wolf should kill . . . by biting into the deer's chest] "The Way of the Wolf," a chapter in Long's *Northern Trails,* included a brief mention of a caribou fawn that was killed by "one quick snap of the old wolf's teeth just behind the fore legs," which "pierced the heart more surely than a hunter's bullet" (Long 1905, 85–86). Long was so incensed by Roosevelt's accusation that when he reprinted the story in 1907, in *Wayeeses the White Wolf,* he devoted a large part of his preface to a defense of his story, explaining that since it

> would surely be read by many children, I had to make the death scene as free as possible from bloody and repulsive details.
>   As I knew from my own observation and from the testimony of my Indians that wolves sometimes kill in this way, cleanly and quickly, I accordingly used it as the least repulsive method consistent with strict truth. (Long 1907, x–xi)

66.1–2   read Roosevelt's 'Wilderness Hunter,' and then read 'Wild Ways,' which he condemns] *The Wilderness Hunter* (1893b) and Long's *Wilderness Ways* (1900).

66.9   LONG ASKS APOLOGY FROM THE PRESIDENT] Clemens's source for this article, containing Long's letter to the president of 28 May 1907, has not been identified. Long sent copies of his letter to newspapers throughout the country; it appeared in full or part in at least five New York newspapers (the *Times, Sun, Tribune, World,* and *Evening Telegram*), but none of these versions matches the one that Hobby transcribed into the autobiography (Lutts 1990, 110–11).

66.30   Dr. Long submits an affidavit] Long's letter, much of which is omitted from this partial account, included a "signed and witnessed statement of an educated Sioux Indian," Stephen Jones Hepidan, who was "fitting himself to be a teacher and missionary among his own people," and spoke "solely in the interest of truth and justice." Hepidan certified that he and "three or four others" of his tribe had seen two horses killed by wolf bites to the chest ("Long Offers Proof," New York *Times,* 29 May 1907, 6).

66.43   Private Secretary Loeb] William Loeb, Jr. (1866–1937), secretary to President Roosevelt from 1901 to 1909.

67.4   The President will pay no further attention to Dr. Long] Long persisted in his campaign to defend his honor: on 2 June 1907 he was interviewed in a Sunday feature article in the New York *Times,* "'I Propose to Smoke Roosevelt Out'—Dr. Long: Clergyman Whom the President Has Aroused Proves to Be a Real Fighter When His Honor Is Questioned" (SM2). Once again he claimed that Roosevelt was no better than "a man of the stone age who sallied forth with his club to brain some beast and drag it home to display before his wives." Burroughs retaliated a week later in an interview of his own, published in the *Times* under the headline "John Burroughs Supports the President: Veteran Naturalist Analyses Dr. Long's Animal Stories and Declares Them Impossible—Instances of Errors, Inaccuracies, Gullibility, and Absurdity" (9 June 1907, SM2). Roosevelt did not keep his resolve to "pay no further attention" to the matter.

In the September issue of *Everybody's Magazine* he published "'Nature Fakers,'" which characterized Long as "the most reckless and least responsible" of those writers who were guilty of "deliberate invention, deliberate perversion of fact" (Roosevelt 1907, 428). In October Long was still fighting back, but his career as a nature writer was coming to a close, and by the end of 1908 his books were no longer ubiquitous in the classroom ("Roosevelt, Only Nature Faker—Long," New York *Times*, 8 Oct 1907, 10; "Long Calls Killing She Bear Butchery," Boston *Herald*, 23 Oct 1907, 2; see Lutts 1990, 127–37).

Autobiographical Dictation, 30 May 1907

67.13–17　I think it is not wise . . . citizen whose trade he knows nothing valuable about] See the Autobiographical Dictation of 29 May 1907 for details of the controversy Clemens continues to discuss here.

67.22　Pliny] The *Naturalis Historia* of Pliny the Elder (23–79 A.D.) records many legendary peoples and animals, and attributes improbable qualities to real ones.

67.22　Sir John Mandeville] The pseudonymous medieval *Travels of Sir John Mandeville,* originally composed in French, gives improbable descriptions of foreign lands and peoples. Clemens read and annotated the translation in Thomas Wright's *Early Travels in Palestine;* reading of "people that have ears so long that they hang down to their knees," he wrote, "Vision of a modern Congress" (Wright 1848, 229; Gribben 1980, 2:789).

67.30　the ravens fed Elijah] 1 Kings 17.

68.14–15　I lectured for one of the great charities . . . young members of the imperial family] Clemens lectured in Vienna on 1 February 1898 for the benefit of a charity hospital. In a letter of 5 and 6 February he told Rogers, "We had a staving good time. Many of the seats were $4 each. Packed house, & lots of 'standees.' Six members of the Imperial family present and four princes of lesser degree, & I taught the whole of them how to steal watermelons"—referring to his "watermelon story," which had been in his lecture repertoire since 1894 (Salm, in *HHR,* 318; *MTB,* 2:981).

68.16　a grand duchess whose married title was the Countess di Bardi] Princess Adelgunde, Countess of Bardi (1858–1946), was the daughter of King Miguel I of Portugal and Adelaide of Löwenstein-Wertheim-Rosenberg. On 3 February 1898 Clemens wrote to Twichell:

> The other night I lectured for a Vienna charity; & at the end of it Livy & I were introduced to a princess who is aunt to the heir apparent of the imperial throne—a beautiful lady, with a beautiful spirit, & very cordial in her praises of my books & thanks to me for writing them; & glad to meet me face to face & shake me by the hand—just the kind of princess that adorns a fairy tale & makes it the prettiest tale there is. (*MTL,* 2:657–60)

The countess (princess), born into the House of Braganza, became a member of the House of Bourbon-Parma through her marriage in 1876 to Prince Henry, the Count of Bardi. The "heir apparent" was the stepson of Archduchess Maria Theresa, her sister (see the note at 68.26–27).

68.18–19 Madame Laszowska, wife of a lieutenant general] Jane Emily Gerard (1849–1905) was born in Scotland; in 1869 she married Miecislas de Laszowska, an Austrian army officer. A resident of Vienna since 1885, she wrote novels, travel books, and articles about—as well as reviews of—German literature. Through her publisher, William Blackwood, she obtained a letter of introduction to Clemens, who wrote Blackwood himself on 7 November 1897 to thank him (StEdNL; McKeithan 1959). On 19 November Madame Laszowska wrote to Blackwood:

> Mark Twain himself is older looking than I had expected and strikes one at first as an excessively serious almost solemn person— I don't think I have seen him smile and only a curious sort of twinkle in his wonderfully expressive eyes betrays the real man at times— . . . He was here yesterday to afternoon tea and talked almost incessantly for an hour and a half on every possible subject— Mrs Clemens is also very intelligent and charming in manner but looks delicate— They are all still in deep mourning and have evidently not yet recovered ₍from₎ the loss of an eldest daughter. (StEdNL, in McKeithan 1959, 64–65)

68.26–27 the palace of another grand duchess of the imperial family] The Countess of Bardi was staying with her sister, Archduchess Maria Theresa (1855–1944), the recent widow of Archduke Karl Ludwig (1833–96), the younger brother of Emperor Franz Joseph I of Austria. After the death of Franz Joseph's son Rudolph, in 1889, Karl Ludwig had briefly been the heir presumptive, but he renounced the throne in favor of his eldest son (by his second wife), Franz Ferdinand.

69.21 "what larks!"] Joe Gargery's catchphrase in *Great Expectations*.

70.32–33 grand duchesses appeared at the head of the stairs . . . and took up their line of march toward us] Clemens told Twichell the same anecdote, with slightly different details, in his letter of 3 February 1898. In that version he and Olivia were waiting in a drawing room when "the door spread wide & our princess & 4 more" entered (*MTL*, 2:659). Accompanying "our princess" (the Countess of Bardi) and her sister, Archduchess Maria Theresa, was a third sister, Princess Maria Josepha (see the note at 71.10–13). The other two women have not been identified.

71.10–13 a little lady . . . who had given his life to the study of diseases of the eye] The "revered grand duke" was Carl Theodor, duke in Bavaria (1839–1909), the brother of Empress Elisabeth, wife of Franz Joseph I (see *AutoMT1*, 568 n. 293.15–30). He studied medicine in Munich, Vienna, and Zurich, specializing in diseases of the eye. In the hospitals and clinics that he established, he treated patients without charge, and over the course of his career he performed more than five thousand cataract surgeries. His clinic in Munich, Augenklinik Herzog Carl Theodor, is still open today. In 1874 he married

Princess Maria Josepha (1857–1943), who served as his assistant. The "little duke" was presumably their son, nine-year-old Franz Joseph (1888–1912). The "little lady" and the other children have not been identified: Clemens told Twichell that there were "2 young girl Archduchesses present, & . . . 3 little princes" (3 Feb 1898 to Twichell, *MTL*, 2:659).

Autobiographical Dictation, 24 July 1907

72.1   Mr. Ashcroft] For Ralph W. Ashcroft, see "The Ashcroft-Lyon Manuscript," especially the editorial preface and the note at 331.40. Clemens, who had met Ashcroft through his investment in the Plasmon Company of America, asked him to be his traveling secretary on a trip to Egypt in October 1906. That trip was canceled; but Ashcroft, as an Englishman, was a natural choice to serve as secretary on the trip to England which followed in June–July 1907. In October, Clemens invited Ashcroft to come stay with him at Tuxedo Park, and he began to establish himself as part of the household (Lystra 2004, 117–19).

72.18–23   very sweet child of seventeen . . . Her name was Carlotta] Carlotta Welles (1889–1979), the daughter of Americans resident in Europe, was eighteen years old when Clemens met her aboard the SS *Minneapolis*. She was traveling, chaperoned by three teachers from her boarding school in Pennsylvania, to her parents' house in France. Writing to Dixon Wecter in 1947, she recalled that, after Clemens invited her to sit with him at dinner, she "was forthwith installed with him and really spent every waking moment with him," although Clemens's attentions were not always welcome: "I used to get restless and chafed at times at being expected to sit quietly with him when my inclination was to race around." She added:

> I felt, in Mr. Clemens' attitude toward me, something tender and very sad. He talked quite a bit about "Susy." . . . There was a heart-broken quality about him but, as you know well, there were also effervescent spirits and at any moment, his eyes were ready to twinkle with mischief and out would come the most unexpected & picturesque remarks! (Carlotta Welles Briggs to Wecter, 4 Nov 1947, CU-MARK)

After Clemens's return to America, a few letters passed between him and Carlotta, but they did not meet again in person (Schmidt 2009).

72.24–36   On the last night out there was the usual concert . . . In my talk I departed from the humorous] This concert, featuring music and recitations by passengers, was given in the saloon of the *Minneapolis* on the evening of 15 June 1907. Clemens's talk for this concert was entitled in the concert program "A Page from My Autobiography"; Carlotta Welles recalled that "the night of the concert, his talk was based on pages from Susy's diary, and he almost broke down" (Carlotta Welles Briggs to Wecter, 4 Nov 1947, CU-MARK). Proceeds from the auction of "unimaginably poor caricatures" benefited the Liverpool Seamen's Orphanage, founded in 1868 to care for the children of sailors lost at sea. The master of ceremonies and auctioneer was the theologian Francis L. Patton (1843–1932), from 1888 to 1902 president of the College of New Jersey, which became Princeton University in 1896 (Leitch 1978, 354–57).

73.3   At the end of nine days we reached the dock at Tilbury] The *Minneapolis* reached Tilbury Docks, the principal port of London, at about 4 a.m. on 18 June. A special train took Clemens and Ashcroft to St. Pancras rail station in London, where Clemens spoke to journalists; he was then escorted to Brown's Hotel by his friend of many years, the British librarian J. Y. W. MacAlister. Newspaper articles reporting Clemens's arrival are reprinted in *Mark Twain's Four Weeks in England, 1907* by the late Edward Connery Lathem, to which these notes are greatly indebted (Lathem 2006, 15–22).

Autobiographical Dictation, 25 July 1907

73.16–17   Bernard Shaw . . . Mr. Henderson] The most recent plays of George Bernard Shaw (1856–1950), at the time of this meeting with Clemens in St. Pancras Station, were *Man and Superman, Major Barbara,* and *Caesar and Cleopatra.* For Clemens's luncheon with Shaw on 3 July, see the Autobiographical Dictation of 23 August 1907. Archibald Henderson (1877–1963) was an instructor in mathematics at the University of North Carolina, Chapel Hill, when he "discovered" the works of Shaw in 1903, and undertook to write a biography of him. Henderson would later correspond with Clemens, visit him at Stormfield, and write one of the earliest books about him. See also the Autobiographical Dictation of 4 September 1907 (Holroyd 1988–92, 2:211–13; Lathem 2006, 18–19; Henderson 1912).

73.34–35   I will leave room in this place . . . to insert them or not] Clemens never inserted anything in the blank space he called for at this point in the typescript.

74.15–21   In the hotel I stumbled upon . . . Francesca] Frances Nunnally (1891–1981), the daughter of James H. Nunnally, the wealthy owner of an Atlanta candy factory, was sixteen when Clemens met her at Brown's Hotel. She and her mother were taking a European summer vacation; in September they accepted Clemens's invitation to visit him in Tuxedo Park. Frances was among the first manifestations of Clemens's "fad" of "collecting young girls"; starting in the next year, he would begin to call this his Aquarium Club, with himself as "Admiral" and the girls as "angelfish." The first angelfish, by Clemens's reckoning, was fourteen-year-old Dorothy Butes, who visited him in New York with her mother in the spring of 1907 (see the ADs of 17 and 18 Apr 1908). Frances's graduation from St. Timothy's School for Girls, near Baltimore, on 9 June 1909 was the occasion for Clemens's last public speech (AD, 12 Feb 1908; Cooley 1991, 33–35, 191–95; "Atlanta Industries," *Wall Street Journal,* 28 Aug 1906, 7; Carson 1998; Schmidt 2009).

74.24–38   a dinner at Dorchester House . . . Mr. Sidney Lee] Whitelaw Reid, U.S. ambassador to the Court of St. James from 1905 until his death in 1912, rented the luxurious Dorchester House in Park Lane and used it as the embassy during his term as ambassador. Guests at this 21 June 1907 dinner included: Edwin Abbey (1852–1911), expatriate American painter; Sir Joseph Norman Lockyer (1836–1920), astronomer; Hallam, Baron Tennyson (1852–1928), eldest son of the poet; Sir Edward Poynter (1836–1919) and Sir Ernest Albert Waterlow (1850–1919), artists; Sir George Goldie (1846–1925), founder of the Royal Niger Company; Algernon Borthwick, Baron Glenesk (1830–1908), newspaper owner; Robert Newton Crane (d. 1927), American diplomat; Sir George Reid (1841–1913), Scottish painter and illustrator; Sir Hubert von Herkomer (1849–1914), Bavarian-born painter and Oxford professor of fine art; Alfred Austin (1835–1913), the poet laureate; Edward, Lord Macnaghten (1830–1913), judge; Edward Cooper Willis (1831–1912), lawyer; Sir Arthur Conan Doyle (1859– 1930), author, creator of Sherlock Holmes; Anthony Hope Hawkins (1863–1933), writer of romances; Sir Lawrence Alma-Tadema (1836–1912), painter; and Sidney Lee (1859–1926), Shakespearean scholar ("Finest American Embassy," Pittsburgh *Press,* 22 June 1906, 9; "Robert N. Crane Dies; Was King's Counselor," New York *Times,* 7 May 1927, 17; London *Times:* "Court Circular," 22 June 1907, 12; "Mr. E. Cooper Willis, K.C.," 27 July 1912, 9; for Whitelaw Reid see *AutoMT1,* 534 n. 222.9–11, and the ADs of 27 and 28 Aug 1907).

74.38–39   Mr. H.W. Lucy, of *Punch*] See the Autobiographical Dictation of 31 August 1907, note at 124.8.

74.40–41   luncheon tendered by the London Society of the Pilgrims] The Pilgrims Society of Great Britain was founded in 1902 with the declared purpose of promoting "good-will, good-fellowship, abiding friendship, and everlasting peace between the United States and Great Britain." A "brother" society in New York was established in 1903. The Pilgrims supported the imperial ambitions of both nations, stressing "the proud traditions of the Anglo-Saxon race" and "the great mission of the Anglo-Saxon race towards peace and civilization" (Baker 2002, 11–14; Chicago *Tribune:* "Pilgrims Honor British Leader," 9 Aug 1902, 2; "Pilgrims Outwit Sea," 30 Jan 1904, 1).

75.11   Augustine Birrell] Birrell (1850–1933) was an essayist and a Liberal member of parliament. In January 1907 he had been appointed Chief Secretary for Ireland.

75.15   the letters "O.S."] Verses printed in *Punch* under these initials were by Owen Seaman (1861–1936), who became the magazine's editor in 1906.

76.17–23   Mr. HARRY BRITTAIN … George Wilson, Pilgrims, New York] Henry Ernest Brittain (1873–1974), journalist and Conservative politician, was the moving force behind the creation of the Pilgrims Society. Knighted in 1918, he promoted solidarity between the British Empire and the United States. George T. Wilson, an American insurance executive, helped found the London society and was the moving force behind the New York society ("George T. Wilson," *English Speaking World* 3 [Feb 1920]: 27).

76.46–47   they rule us from their urns] Lord Byron, *Manfred,* act 3, scene 4: "The dead, but sceptred sovereigns, who still rule / Our spirits from their urns."

77.16   a quartern loaf . . . Otway] The English poet Thomas Otway (1652–85) was traditionally represented as having died by choking on the first mouthful of "a quartern loaf" (a four-pound loaf of bread; Byron 1900, 92).

77.20   Maecenas] Proverbial for a generous patron of literature; from Gaius Maecenas, the patron of Virgil and Horace.

77.20   Chatterton . . . who perished in his prime] Birrell (or the newspaper report of his speech) misquotes Wordsworth, "Resolution and Independence": "I thought of Chatterton, the marvellous Boy, / The sleepless Soul that perished in his pride" (Wordsworth 1815, 2:29). For the poet Thomas Chatterton, see *AutoMT2,* 570 n. 247.2–3.

77.24–26   great burden of debt . . . Sir Walter Scott] Two publishing houses in which Scott was financially interested failed in 1826 with enormous debts: James Ballantyne and Company, and Archibald Constable and Company. Scott undertook to pay those debts by creating a new, revised and annotated edition of his collected novels, which was still underway when he died in 1832. His responsible behavior in this crisis enhanced his status as "the supreme model of career closure—and, indeed of noble dying" in English and American literature (Millgate 1992, 1).

77.48   "Tom Brown's Schooldays"] Novel of schoolboy life by Thomas Hughes (1857).

78.11–13   a few words of preface . . . "the moralist of the Main."] Mark Twain's first collection, *The Celebrated Jumping Frog of Calaveras County, and Other Sketches,* was published in New York in May 1867 by Charles Henry Webb (John Paul), who wrote the prefatory "Advertisement" that Birrell quotes here. In Britain an unauthorized edition was published by George Routledge and Sons (*ET&S1,* 546; SLC 1867a, 1867b).

78.48–79.2   Professor Norton . . . by marriage with Darwin] The date of this visit to Harvard professor Charles Eliot Norton has not been identified. Clemens recorded Norton's account of the soporific effect on Darwin of his books in an 1882 notebook entry. Norton's sister-in-law was married to Darwin's eldest son, William (*N&J2,* 486 n. 185; Norton 1913, 304).

79.23–32   "Darwin's Life and Letters" . . . that quality is atrophied] Clemens's paraphrase bears a resemblance to a letter written by Darwin to his friend, botanist Sir Joseph Hooker (1817–1911), on 17 June 1868 and published in *Life and Letters of Charles Darwin* (Darwin 1887, 2:273–74); but it resembles still more closely a passage from his *Autobiography,* published in the same collection, in which Darwin describes his "curious and lamentable loss of the higher aesthetic tastes. . . . My mind seems to have become a kind of machine for grinding general laws out of large collections of facts, but why this should have caused the atrophy of that part of the brain alone, on which the higher tastes depend, I cannot conceive" (Darwin 1887, 1:81).

79.41–42   "Mark Twain Arrives Ascot Cup Stolen."] The Gold Cup Race for thoroughbred horses is run in June as an event in the annual Royal Ascot Festival. In 1907, the trophy was reported stolen on the afternoon of 18 June, the day Mark Twain arrived in England, and the theft was widely reported in newspapers the next day. The Cup was never seen again; a replacement was commissioned from the original manufacturers, Crown jewelers Garrard and Company (Lathem 2006, 159; HorseRacing.co.uk 2013; Culme 2010).

80.7   luncheon party . . . Archdeacon Wilberforce] Basil Wilberforce (1841–1916) would become an archdeacon in 1900, but at the time of the luncheon party mentioned here (3 July 1899) he was Canon of Westminster. He came of a distinguished line of political and evangelical figures: his father was Samuel Wilberforce (1805–73), bishop and famed opponent of Darwinism, and his grandfather was William Wilberforce, the abolitionist (1759–1833). A liberal and progressive-minded cleric, he shared Clemens's interests in animal rights and spiritualism. Clemens wrote in the evening to Wilberforce, informing him that they had inadvertently switched hats (*MTB*, 2:1085–86); he also retailed the anecdote in letters of the same day to Howells and Twichell (3 July 1899 to Howells, NN-B, in *MTHL*, 2:703–5; 3 July 1899 to Twichell, CtY-BR; SLC 2010a, 272–75, 310–11; 17 Apr 1900 to Wilberforce, photocopy in CU-MARK).

80.8–9   the Westminster Battery] Wilberforce was Canon of Westminster; the pun on "canon/cannon" was always irresistible to Clemens.

Autobiographical Dictation, 26 July 1907

81.34   "England's Ovation . . . Sydney Brooks] Brooks (1872–1937) was the London correspondent for *Harper's Weekly*. The article quoted in the text appeared in July, while Clemens was still abroad (Brooks 1907).

81.35–36   a chapter of this Autobiography . . . when Clara made her début] See *AutoMT2*, 243–45.

82.29   Lord Curzon] George, Lord Curzon of Kedleston (1859–1925) was Viceroy of India from 1899 to 1905. He had been installed as Chancellor of Oxford University in May 1907; as such his duties included the conferring of honorary degrees, which was (and is) done at the Encaenia, the annual ceremony in commemoration of the university's founders and benefactors ("Lord Curzon at Oxford," London *Times*, 13 May 1907, 4; Lathem 2006, 3).

82.31–35   Prince Arthur of Connaught . . . General Booth, of the Salvation Army] Clemens mentions: Prince Arthur of Connaught (1883–1938), a grandson of Queen Victoria often deputized by King Edward VII to represent the Crown on ceremonial occasions; Sidney Colvin (1845–1927), scholar of art and literature; Sidney Lee (see AD, 19 Aug 1907); and William Booth (1829–1912), founder and general superintendent of the Salvation Army.

83.2   Sir William Ramsay] British chemist (1852–1916), who discovered helium.

83.22 Mr. Whitelaw Reid] The American ambassador, with whom Clemens had a sometimes acrimonious relationship; see the Autobiographical Dictations of 27 and 28 August 1907.

83.35 the Prime Minister] Sir Henry Campbell-Bannerman; see *AutoMT2*, 227 and notes on 559.

83.36 Sir Evelyn Wood] Field Marshal Sir Evelyn Wood (1838–1919), British Army officer.

84.24–26 I doubt whether Mark Twain … condemned by all the proprieties to silence] For advice about his conduct at the Oxford ceremony, Clemens consulted Ian MacAlister (1878–1957), the Oxford-educated son of his friend J. Y. W. MacAlister. In 1938, Ian MacAlister recalled:

> He was stopping at Brown's Hotel. … He had sent for me for this reason. He was going to take this Honorary Degree and he wanted to know about the ceremony— what he was to do and say and all about it. He had an idea that on these occasions there was a great crowd of undergraduates who ragged the people who got the Degrees, and he wanted to get ready. He had got it into his head that he had to exchange witticisms with them, and stand up for himself. I had to explain to him that I was sorry there was nothing of that kind. He must not say a word. He must look quite solemn and dignified and quite ignore the gallery. I think he was really a bit disappointed. I think he had been looking forward to a kind of duel of wit with these fellows in the gallery. But he promised to be good. (MacAlister 1938, 144)

84.28–30 *Vir jucundissime … concutis*] "You, Sir, a gentleman most amiable, most charming, most witty, who shakes the sides of the whole world with your inborn merriment" (translation by Norman A. Doenges, in Lathem 2006, 169).

84.39 Mrs. Riggs (Kate Douglas Wiggin)] See *AutoMT2*, 579 n. 270.20–22.

84.45 "Mark Twain's Pageant" it was called by one of the papers] The London *Daily Chronicle* of 28 June 1907 (Lathem 2006, 60). For the Oxford Pageant see the Autobiographical Dictation of 30 July 1907.

Autobiographical Dictation, 30 July 1907

85.5 a dinner … at one of the colleges] This 26 June 1907 dinner was at Christ Church. Clemens arrived after the dinner and responded to a toast. Whitelaw Reid, also present, wrote later that the speech was "rather longer than was expected, rambling, and, as the English said, thin in straining for humor to which he did not attain," but that it was redeemed by gracious closing compliments to Prince Arthur of Connaught and Rudyard Kipling (Lathem 2006, 173).

86.8–12 a phrase which I had used ten years before … a Presbyterian in hell] Clemens alludes to his article "Diplomatic Pay and Clothes," written in Vienna in January

1899, where he describes a black-clad American official at a Continental court "scuffling around in that sea of vivid color, like a mislaid Presbyterian in perdition" (SLC 1899, 26; Lathem 2006, 173).

86.28   The Oxford Pageant] Oxford's historical pageant of 1907, an early instance of a rage for historical pageantry that would sweep Britain and America in the years to follow, was organized by British actor-producer Frank Lascelles (1875–1934). Using huge forces both professional and amateur—"3,500 men, women and children," according to Clemens—it presented fifteen extravagantly costumed scenes drawn from Oxford history and legend. The pageant was staged in Christ Church Meadow, on the banks of the River Cherwell; the price of admission was one shilling. The performance, which lasted between three and four hours, was given six times, from 27 June through 3 July 1907. Clemens attended the first performance, on 27 June. Although he does not mention it in the *Autobiography,* he saw the pageant again the following day (Porter to SLC, 20 June 1907, CU-MARK; 30 June 1907 to CC, photocopy in CU-MARK; 30 June 1907 to JC, MoHM; 8? July 1907 to Hervey, CU-MARK; Lathem 2006, 177; Ryan 2007, 63–64, 69–70, 76).

87.27   the Grand Chain] A ledge of rock in the Mississippi River about thirty miles above the mouth of the Ohio River; a menace to navigation (Baldwin 1941, 70).

87.38   Fair Rosamond] The legendary mistress of King Henry II, kept by him in a labyrinth at Woodstock, and buried at Godstow, just outside Oxford.

87.41   Roger Bacon] See the note at 90.12–13.

87.41–42   Queen Elizabeth . . . never swore once] In his privately circulated dialogue *Date 1601,* Clemens represents Queen Elizabeth I and her court as coarse and indecent speakers (SLC 1996).

88.2   King Harold Harefoot] See the note at 89.40–43.

88.17–18   Royalty was detained, and did not come] Princess Louise, King Edward VII's sister, had been expected (Lathem 2006, 177).

88.34   "supe"] Short for "supernumerary," an extra in a theatrical production.

89.4   THE LEGEND OF ST. FRIDESWIDE] Here and later, Clemens inserts passages from a book printed as a program or souvenir for pageant spectators (*Oxford Historical Pageant* 1907).

89.40–43   the year 1036 . . . Harold Harefoot] King Harold I, made king at Oxford around 1036.

90.12–13   Friar Bacon . . . his legendary Brazen Head] The Oxford pageant followed legend in representing the historical Roger Bacon (ca. 1214–92) as the inventor of an oracular head made of brass.

90.24–25   the Masque of the Mediaeval Curriculum . . . the creation of a young American] The masque was written by Francis Hartman Markoe, Jr., of New York, a recent Yale graduate who was taking a year of study at Oxford ("The 'Masque of Medieval Learning,'" *Independent,* 1 Aug 1907, 298).

90.26   Wolsey] Cardinal Thomas Wolsey (1470?–1530), Henry VIII's chief minister, was educated at Oxford and founded Cardinal College, later renamed Christ Church, on whose grounds the 1907 pageant was performed.

90.38   the Book of the Pageant] See the note at 89.4.

94.12–13   University Press . . . Dr. Hart] Oxford University Press traces its origins to the sixteenth century; in the early twentieth century it was the largest press in the world, issuing millions of volumes each year. Horace Henry Hart (1840–1916) was controller of the press and printer to the university (Oxford University Press 2013; Donald 1903, 70–71; Lathem 2006, 178).

94.38–95.3   I knew, through Mr. John Murray . . . *perpetual* copyright to the Bible] Clemens was indignant that Oxford University Press (and two other publishers) held perpetual copyright in the English Bible, while modern authors enjoyed no such entitlement to their own works. He spoke on this subject in 1900 before a House of Lords committee on copyright; see the Autobiographical Dictations of 24 November and 26 December 1906 (*AutoMT2,* 288–92, 334–42). John Murray (1851–1928) was the fourth of that name to head the eponymous London publishing firm; it is not known when Clemens spoke with him.

95.8   Robert Porter] Robert P. Porter was a British-born, American-naturalized journalist. Clemens stayed at his house in Oxford throughout his time there ("R. P. Porter Dead; Founded N.Y. Press," New York *Times,* 1 Mar 1917, 13; "Mark Twain Sobered," Washington *Post,* 30 June 1907, 10; see AD, 5 Oct 1907, note at 154.29–35).

95.13–14   Louis Stevenson and I dubbed the Suppressed Fame] For suppressed or "submerged" fame, see "Robert Louis Stevenson and Thomas Bailey Aldrich" (*AutoMT1,* 229).

95.22–23   to talk to the Rhodes scholars at their club] The Rhodes scholarships were established in 1903 according to the terms of the will of British imperialist Cecil Rhodes (1853–1902). They provided, initially, for three years of study at Oxford University for fifty-seven recent college graduates from the United States, the British Empire, and Germany; more scholarships, and other countries, were added in the following years (Rhodes Trust 2013).

96.19–20   ten millions with which Mr. Rockefeller has endowed that Institution] John D. Rockefeller's initial (1903) gift to the medical institute that bears his name was $1.2 million; he later added a vast endowment, but not until after the date of this dictation. In saying "ten millions" Clemens may be thinking of Rockefeller's 1905 gift to the General Education Board, a national charity (New York *Times:* "Rockefeller Plans for Vast Institute," 22 Feb 1903, 1; "Rockefeller Gift of $10,000,000," 1 July 1905, 1).

96.20–21 endowed with ten millions by Mr. Carnegie in Washington . . . devoted to medical research] See the Autobiographical Dictation of 12 December 1907, note at 193.32.

96.23–25 Within the past two or three months Mr. Rockefeller's Institution has removed . . . cerebro-spinal meningitis] See the Autobiographical Dictation of 21 May 1908, note at 231.14–23.

96.32–33 I always detested Mr. Rhodes] Clemens wrote at length about Cecil Rhodes in *Following the Equator* (SLC 1897a, 141–50, 283, 652–66, 690–91, 708–10; see also Budd 1962, 171–72).

96.39–40 while I was in Oxford a thing happened . . . wise and far-seeing document it was] At this point in the typescript, five leaves are missing. They were last seen by Arthur G. Pettit, who quotes from them in his 1970 University of California dissertation, "Merely Fluid Prejudice: Mark Twain, Southerner, and the Negro," later reworked and published as *Mark Twain and the South* (Pettit 1974). Absent the approximately 1,100 missing words, one cannot know precisely what Clemens said. The best that can now be done is to reproduce the passage from Pettit where he quotes and paraphrases from the now missing typescript:

> Occasionally, the manner in which Clemens chose to prepare the way with cheerfulness was rather ambiguous and unsuccessful. While in London in 1907 to pick up his Oxford degree, Clemens became embroiled in "a small storm, which could easily grow into a large one" among the American Rhodes Scholar students, who were up in arms over the election of a Negro student. Assured by officials that the white students "would willingly listen to me, and give respectful attention to any advice I might offer," Clemens agreed to "do my best to convince them that their position was not wise, and not just."
>
> At first he considered stressing the "wise" rather than the "just" part of the position—to appeal to the white students on rather businesslike terms, to the effect that they should fulfill the contractual agreement they had made to accept any student elected to membership. When he found that the Negro youth had scored high on every criteria of measurement except popularity, however, Clemens backed off. Though he readily conceded that the Negro's unpopularity was due to his color, he decided that to grant the Negro a scholarship would be "to defeat one of Mr. Rhodes's dearest purposes"; that is, popularity. Rather than puffing "the Negro lad" as he had been urged to do, Clemens upheld Cecil Rhodes and the white students, and, when he talked to them in London, "refrained from any reference to the matter in dispute, and confined my talk to other and cheerfuler things." (Pettit 1970, 527–28)

The black scholar was Alain Leroy Locke (1885–1954), a recent Harvard graduate in philosophy. As soon as he was elected a Rhodes scholar in March 1907, a group of Rhodes scholars hailing from the American South sent a delegation to the Rhodes Trust protesting his participation; Clemens's attempted intervention, and capitulation, were in June. In the fall of 1907, with "influential Americans" still threatening the trust with the declaration that "the admission of a negro on equal terms with white students will create a prejudice against the educational work of the trust," Locke was not invited to the American Rhodes scholars' Thanksgiving dinner. Trust officials declined to interfere in what they termed an "American question." Locke took no degree at Oxford, but went on to study at Berlin and Paris, and got his doctorate at Harvard. He edited the seminal literary anthology *The New Negro* (1925), and became an influential cultural critic ("Color Line at English College," San Jose *Evening News,* 7 Oct 1907, 8; "Negro Student Objected to by the Americans," Denver *Post,* 7 Oct 1907, 6; "Southern Asses Abroad!" Cleveland *Gazette,* 19 Dec 1908, 2; Stewart 1993).

Autobiographical Dictation, 10 August 1907

97 *title* Dictated August 10, 1907] This "dictation" is in fact based on a manuscript.

97.15–16 Two or three years ago . . . I went over and asked the librarian about it] This must refer to the restrictions placed on *Huckleberry Finn* by the Brooklyn Public Library in 1905 (see *AutoMT2,* 27–33 and notes on 473–76). No record of an actual visit to the library has been found.

98.9–25 Once I was a hero . . . I braced up and read my verse and hers too] Clemens lectured in Hudson, Massachusetts (not "Hudson, New York"), on 21 December 1869. The incident he describes must have happened at the home of his sponsor there, the Reverend H. G. Gay. From an 1879 notebook entry it appears that the offending biblical verse was 2 Kings 18:27: "Hath my master sent me to thy master, and to thee, to speak these words? hath he not sent me to the men which sit on the wall, that they may eat their own dung, and drink their own piss with you?" (*N&J2,* 302–3; 21 Dec 1869 to OLL, *L3,* 434–35 n. 3).

Autobiographical Dictation, 16 August 1907

98.27–99.2 I met Marie Corelli . . . therefore I accepted by return mail] Marie Corelli (1855–1924), born Mary Mackay, became Britain's most popular novelist, and commanded much public attention with her pronouncements on issues of the day. Clemens first met her at Bad Homburg in the summer of 1892. Since 1899 she had lived in Stratford-on-Avon, where she was a public advocate for the preservation and restoration of the town's Shakespearean monuments. On 20 June 1907 she wrote an effusive letter to Clemens, praising him extravagantly and lamenting that she was "apparently 'left out' and forgotten by your numerous hosts who ask other writers to meet you" (CU-MARK). Clemens replied to her "love-letter" on 21 or 22 June (Vyver 1930):

> You very dear Marie Corelli,
>   It is lovely of you to feel & say those affectionate things, & they have made a choking in my throat which is more eloquent response than any that can be built out of words. If I were not so hard-driven, daily & nightly & hourly, by

this dear, hospitable, & heart-bewitching England, I would go & hunt you up & revive the Homburg days. As it is, I suppose I shall never see you again, & that is a sorrowful thought for me. But I send you my loving good-bye, & may you be happy always!

S. L. Clemens.

Corelli replied by mail: "But you *will* see me, won't you?—you must not go back across the sea without coming to Shakespeare's *own* town!" (Corelli to SLC, 23 June 1907, CU-MARK). Clemens accepted this invitation, as he says, "by return mail" (Ashcroft for SLC to Corelli, 24 June 1907, MS draft, CU-MARK).

99.8–9   a speech at the Lord Mayor's to follow] See the note at 101.10.

99.41   Shakspeare's church, but I canceled that] Stratford's Holy Trinity Church, where Shakespeare was baptized and is buried, is informally spoken of as "his" church. According to a Stratford newspaper, Clemens declined the invitation to visit Holy Trinity in these words: "I am sure that if Shakespeare knew how very kind my friends are to me, and how very near I am to being killed with kindness, even he would excuse me" (Lathem 2006, 182, quoting "Mark Twain at Stratford-on-Avon," *Stratford-upon-Avon Herald and South Warwickshire Advertiser,* 5 July 1907, 2).

100.10–11   she had been purchasing the house which the founder of Harvard . . . lived in] John Harvard (1607–38) was not from Stratford, although his maternal family were. Marie Corelli campaigned for the restoration of the house of Harvard's ancestors in Stratford High Street. It was purchased by a wealthy American and presented in 1909 to Harvard College for use as a club for American visitors (Dilla 1928, 103–4).

100.30–32   fifty pupils of a military school . . . asked me to make a little speech] Clemens's remarks to the boys of the Army School, Stratford, apparently touched on his own military career: "he had once himself been a soldier for two weeks during the American Civil War, and that his experiences were such that he did not much care to remember them" (Lathem 2006, 183, quoting "Mark Twain at Stratford-on-Avon," *Stratford-upon-Avon Herald and South Warwickshire Advertiser,* 5 July 1907, 2).

101.10   I spoke at the Lord Mayor's banquet that night, and it was a botch] On 29 June 1907 London's Lord Mayor, Sir William Treloar, gave a dinner in Mark Twain's honor at Mansion House, the guests being about two hundred and fifty of his fellow members of the Savage Club. It is not clear why Clemens considered his performance "a botch"; according to the report in the *Telegraph,* which printed his speech, it was acclaimed with "loud cheers" (Lathem 2006, 76–78, quoting "Mark Twain Stories," London *Telegraph,* 1 July 1907, 13; Fatout 1976, 564–66).

Autobiographical Dictation, 17 August 1907

101.12–13   Sir Gilbert and Lady Parker] Gilbert George Parker (1860–1932), Canadian-born British novelist and statesman, and his wife, the American heiress Amy Vantine.

102.4–12   Winston Churchill . . . Sir William Vernon Harcourt] The dinner at Sir Gilbert Parker's house where Clemens met Winston Spencer Churchill (1874–1965) was probably on 26 March 1900. Churchill was then a war correspondent, recently returned from the South African conflict. When Churchill came to New York as a public lecturer later that year, Clemens introduced his lecture at the Waldorf-Astoria on 12 December (Notebook 43, TS p. 6, CU-MARK; Gribben 1980, 2:526; Fatout 1976, 367–69). For Sir William Vernon Harcourt, see the Autobiographical Dictation of 7 September 1906 (*AutoMT2*, 228, 560 n. 228.21–22).

Autobiographical Dictation, 19 August 1907

102.25   Dined with Sidney Lee at the Garrick Club] British man of letters Sidney Lee (1859–1926) was born in London and educated at Oxford. A prominent scholar of Elizabethan literature, he was also coeditor (with Leslie Stephen) of the *Dictionary of National Biography,* and published biographies of Shakespeare (1898) and Queen Victoria (1902). This dinner with Lee at the Garrick Club occurred on 1 July 1907; Clemens describes his first acquaintance with Lee in the latter part of this dictation (Ashcroft 1907, 3).

102.25–26   Mrs. Macmillan's . . . Lady Jersey] Margaret Child-Villiers (1849–1945), countess of Jersey, was active in imperialist and antisuffragette causes. She was a founder of the Victoria League, a "predominantly female" association for disseminating imperialist propaganda (Riedi 2002, 572). Clemens had known her and her husband, the seventh earl of Jersey, since at least 1900. Associated with Lady Jersey in some of these causes was Helen Macmillan, wife of publisher Maurice Macmillan, and mother of future prime minister Harold Macmillan (Riedi 2002, 576; Notebook 43, TS pp. 16–17, CU-MARK).

102.27–29   I encountered J. M. Barrie . . . in London twice, seven years ago, and once in New York] These meetings with Scottish playwright and novelist J. M. Barrie (1860–1937), the author of *Peter Pan,* have not been traced.

102.35–36   at Bateman's . . . whitewashing of the fence by Tom Sawyer] Clemens refers to Hezekiah Bateman, the American manager of the Lyceum Theatre in London (for whom see AD, 1 Oct 1907, note at 144.33–35), and three of his associates in the London theater: Henry Irving, the actor (1838–1905); John Lawrence Toole (1830–1906), actor; and William Gorman Wills (1828–91), playwright. The occasion on which Clemens narrated the white-washing episode to Irving and Wills must have been in 1872 (*L5:* 15 Sept 1872 to OLC, 159–60 n. 2; 6 July 1873 to Fairbanks, 402–9 n. 6).

103.3–6   long-forgotten occasion . . . Tom Hughes and Leveson-Gower] This dinner in honor of Joaquin Miller (1839–1913), the American author, was given at the Garrick Club on 7 July 1873 by Anthony Trollope (1815–82). The guests included Tom Hughes (1822–96), British children's writer and social reformer, author of *Tom Brown's School Days* (1857); and Granville George Leveson-Gower (1815–91), second earl Granville, Liberal politician, at this time foreign secretary. The "obliterated" guest was Edward Levy-Lawson (1833–1916), editor of the London *Telegraph* (6 July 1873 to Fairbanks, *L5,* 402–9 n. 11).

103.27–28   doubtless the obliterated guest is dead; Joaquin Miller is white-headed, and mute and quiet in his dear mountains] Levy-Lawson, who had been elevated to the peerage in 1903, was still alive. Joaquin Miller was living on his estate in the hills above Oakland, California, and was still writing and publishing.

103.31–32   he was of the blood of . . . "Charley," tenth Lord Fairfax] For Charles Snowden Fairfax, see "My Autobiography [Random Extracts from It]" (*AutoMT1,* 203, 526 n. 203.10–18). The Fairfax scion Clemens met at the Macmillans' house has not been identified.

104.3–5   I had not seen Sidney Lee since 1902 . . . at 92d street and Fifth Avenue] Andrew Carnegie's dinner in honor of Sidney Lee took place on 28 March 1903. Lee was in the midst of a lecture tour of America which stretched from February into May; in his capacity as a trustee of Shakespeare's Birthplace, he may have wished to discuss Carnegie's offer to Stratford of a public library ("Court Circular," London *Times,* 19 May 1903, 10; "Carnegie's Gift Is Defended," Washington *Post,* 28 June 1903, 3).

104.21   John Burroughs] See the Autobiographical Dictation of 29 May 1907.

104.22   Carl Schurz] Schurz (1829–1906) was a German-born American Civil War general, Republican senator from Missouri, and secretary of the interior under Rutherford B. Hayes. Clemens had introduced him at a Hartford political rally in 1884, and eulogized him in the brief essay "Carl Schurz, Pilot" (SLC 1906b; Fatout 1976, 186–87).

104.23   Melville Stone] Stone (1848–1929) was the general manager of the Associated Press from 1892 to 1921 ("A.P. Resolution Pays Tribute to Melville Stone," New York *Herald Tribune,* 23 Apr 1929, 17).

104.23–24   Horace White] White (1834–1916) had been chief editor of the Chicago *Tribune* and the New York *Evening Post.* Regarded as "a survivor of the distinguished group of New York journalists which included Charles A. Dana and Whitelaw Reid," he was also an authority on finance ("Horace White, Publicist, Dies," New York *Tribune,* 17 Sept 1916, 13).

106.7   Mr. Hornblower] William Butler Hornblower (1851–1914), prominent New York lawyer.

Autobiographical Dictation, 22 August 1907

106.21   Lunched with Henniker Heaton] John Henniker Heaton (1848–1914) had lived in Australia for many years, and on becoming a British member of parliament labored to improve communications among territories of the Empire. By 1898 he had succeeded in creating an Empire-wide penny postage (except for Australia, New Zealand,

and the Cape Colony) and his goal was now a universal penny postage. This luncheon at the House of Commons took place on 2 July 1907. Clemens clarified his interest in British postal matters for the New York *Sun*'s correspondent:

> I am taking up this matter on this side because it is a curious commentary on our Government that once England introduces a new system it is very easy to get the United States to follow suit. The mere fact that England has done this or that acts with wonderful effect on Congress, and if we glance back along the line of governmental reforms and ideas we find that America only adopted them after England had tried them and found them desirable. ("Mark Twain for Penny Post," New York *Sun,* 2 July 1907, 2)

106.26   T. P. O'Connor] Thomas Power O'Connor (1848–1929) was an Irish radical journalist and politician, known as "T. P." (given its Irish pronunciation of "Tay Pay," as Clemens explains in the dictation of 2 October 1907). He was a member of parliament representing first Galway, then (from 1885) a largely Irish district of Liverpool. A prolific chronicler of the British political and literary scenes, he founded several newspapers. At the time of Clemens's visit he was the editor of two weekly magazines, *T. P.'s Weekly* and *P.T.O.*

106.27   the Earl of Crawford and Balcarres] James Ludovic Lindsay, twenty-sixth earl of Crawford and ninth earl of Balcarres (1847–1913). His presence at this meeting in the interest of postal reform was owing to his status as an eminent stamp collector and postal historian ("Earl of Crawford Sells His Stamps," New York *Times,* 9 Nov 1915, 19).

107.15–17   My project was a postal check … completed in the summer and fall of 1898] Clemens's "Proposition for a Postal Check," written in Vienna in 1898–99, advocated a scheme whereby the U.S. government would print and sell checks—prepaid, and in fixed denominations (like stamps), which would be cashable at a post office (like postal orders).

107.27–28   It named a member of Congress … a bill for a postal check] A bill mandating the issue of $50 million worth of "post check notes" was introduced in Congress on 16 March 1900. Congress took no action on the bill, which was reintroduced, with no action taken again, in 1902 ("A Postal Check System," Washington *Post,* 17 Mar 1900, 4; "Post-Check Currency," Los Angeles *Times,* 23 Mar 1902, B4; U.S. Congress 1902, 26).

107.39–108.2   I read in the *American Review of Reviews* … Dr. Shaw] An article by R. R. Bowker in the March 1905 *American Review of Reviews* endorsed a postal check system. It said nothing about any "Northern Congressman." The editor of the *Review* was Albert Shaw (Bowker 1905, 331).

108.10–21   House Bill 7053 … the "invention" of a Mr. W. C. Post] Clemens had before him a copy of H.R. 7053 (session of 1905–6). He mistakes the name of the originator of the bill, cereal magnate C. W. Post (1854–1914). He is also mistaken in the question of priority: Post was publicly advocating a postal check in 1898, when Clemens's article was not yet written (U.S. Congress 1906; C. W. Post 1898; "C. W. Post of Battle Creek Kills Himself," Grand Rapids [Mich.] *Press,* 9 May 1914, 1, 15).

108.22–24   he stands ready to confer it upon the Government as a free gift . . . In '98 I wrote John Hay, from Vienna] Clemens misdates his 11 March 1899 letter to John Hay, who was at this time the U.S. secretary of state. And even though he implies here that he expected no royalties on sales of his postal checks, his letter to Hay shows otherwise:

> I merely want a royalty for a while—no lump sum. I only want the government to issue & sell a thing which is as simple as a post-card, & pay me a royalty of *one per cent* on the sales *for twelve years.* The government would derive other revenues from this scheme, but in those I could not share. . . . Suppose the sales were only $5,000,000 a year, & brought an additional revenue of $5,000,000; I shouldn't receive a royalty on both sums, but only on the first-mentioned. *That* wouldn't make me any richer than I ought to be—you know it yourself.
>
> Can't you get the government to instruct you to say to me that it will grant me that royalty if upon examining the idea it concludes to use it? (11 Mar 1899 to Hay [1st], DLC)

Later the same day Clemens wrote to Hay again, asking him not to "mention my scheme for a postal-cheque to any one. It could get into print ahead of me, for much talking is done in Vienna" (11 Mar 1899 to Hay [2nd], ViU). No reply from Hay has been found.

108.31–32   I will inter that old postal-check article of mine in an Appendix] See the Appendix "Proposition for a Postal Check."

Autobiographical Dictation, 23 August 1907

109.4   Luncheon with George Bernard Shaw] The luncheon was at Shaw's flat in Adelphi Terrace; also present were Mrs. Shaw, Archibald Henderson, and Max Beerbohm (misidentified in the press as his half-brother, Herbert Beerbohm Tree) (Lathem 2006, 192–94).

109.13–16   William Morris . . . encomium upon "Huck Finn"—things which Mr. Shaw had already said to me in a letter] Shaw related William Morris's opinion in a letter written just after this luncheon:

> Once, when I was in Morris's house, a superior anti-Dickens sort of man (sort of man that thinks Dickens no gentleman) was annoyed by Morris disparaging Thackeray. With studied gentleness he asked whether Morris could name a greater master of English. Morris promptly said "Mark Twain." This delighted me extremely, as it was my own opinion; and I then found that Morris was an incurable Huckfinomaniac. This was the more remarkable, as Morris would have regarded the Yankee at the Court of King Arthur as blasphemy, and would have blown your head off for implying that the contemporaries of Joan of Arc could touch your own contemporaries in villainy. (Shaw to SLC, 3 July 1907, CU-MARK)

109.27   There was a choice company at Moberly Bell's] C. F. Moberly Bell (1847–1911), manager of the London *Times* since 1890, had been instrumental in arranging Clemens's Oxford degree—or so Clemens believed. Clemens wrote him on 3 May 1907, "Your hand is in it! & you have my best thanks. Although I wouldn't cross an ocean again for the price of the ship that carried me, I am glad to do it for an Oxford degree" (CU-MARK, in *MTL*, 2:806).

109.30–36   in London seven years ago . . . had lately been making Cecil Rhodes's life uncomfortable] Princess Catherine Radziwill (1858–1941), descended from impoverished Polish nobility, first tried to attach herself to Cecil Rhodes in 1899, when she followed him from London to the Cape Colony. She seems to have started rumors that she was his mistress and that he had proposed marriage. The princess was in London from April to June 1900; the Clemenses probably met her at Moberly Bell's on 4 May. She returned to South Africa shortly thereafter, continuing her pursuit of Rhodes. When he died suddenly in 1902, she was on trial for forging his signature; she was convicted and served sixteen months in prison (Roberts 1969, 179–225, 361, and passim; Notebook 43, TS p. 9, CU-MARK).

Autobiographical Dictation, 26 August 1907

110.16   Sir James Knowles's] As secretary of the Metaphysical Society and the founding editor of the influential monthly *The Nineteenth Century*, journalist-architect Sir James Knowles (1831–1908) was in contact with most of the intellectual and political leaders of his time. His house was next door to Queen Anne's Mansions (see the note at 110.19–20).

110.16–17   banquet in celebration of Independence Day] See the Autobiographical Dictation of 29 August 1907.

110.19–20   the Queen Anne Mansions] Queen Anne's Mansions, a luxury apartment complex overlooking St. James's Park, Westminster, was built from 1873 to 1890 by the entrepreneur Henry Hankey. With its tallest part reaching 160 feet, it was for a long time London's tallest residential structure and, some said, its ugliest. Adjacent to the burgeoning development was Queen Anne's Lodge, the house leased by Sir James Knowles, who in 1888 brought suit against the Mansions and sought to organize public opposition to their latest extension. Queen Anne's Mansions, which took the form of a central court surrounded by residential blocks, was also a hotel; the Clemenses stayed there from 30 September until 14 October 1899, when they moved to an apartment at 30 Wellington Court (Dennis 2008, 233–38; Metcalf 1980, 299–308).

110.25   guide-boards] Signposts giving directions, of the kind found at a crossroads.

110.33   circular check] An early form of bank money order, issued by certain American banks in the last years of the nineteenth century (Branch 1903, 68–69).

111.20   an English gentleman who had sent in his card after dinner] Unidentified.

111.21–29   Relations between England and the Transvaal . . . war would break out in eleven days] See *AutoMT2,* 526 n. 137.40–138.21.

111.32   luncheon . . . in honor of a Prussian princess] Sir James Knowles's luncheon of 4 July was in honor of Princess Marie Louise of Schleswig-Holstein (1872–1956). A granddaughter of Queen Victoria, she lived in England after separating from her husband in 1900. She was musical, well-read, and a patron of the arts (Knowles to SLC, 27 June 1907, CU-MARK).

Autobiographical Dictation, 27 August 1907

112.3–11   Whitelaw Reid's afternoon reception . . . most palatial private residence in London] Reid's Fourth of July reception was at his residence, Dorchester House; see the Autobiographical Dictation of 25 July 1907.

112.13   the King's great garden party at Windsor] This had occurred on 22 June 1907. On Ashcroft's typed record of the Oxford trip's events, Clemens marked the entry for 22 June and wrote in the margin, *"Put it last"* (Ashcroft 1907, 2). He discusses King Edward VII's garden party in the Autobiographical Dictation of 1 October 1907.

112.16–18   Reid's salary is $17,500 . . . His town house rent is a hundred thousand dollars a year] Clemens correctly states the salary of Reid (and all U.S. ambassadors, at that time). The rent he paid on Dorchester House was $40,000; he also leased a country estate in Bedfordshire from the earl of Cowper. The total outlay of his household was conjectured to be perhaps $300,000. Whatever the exact figures, it was much remarked in the press that magnificence on this scale was attainable by private millionaires, not public servants ("Pays Twice His Salary in Rent; Ambassador Reid Gratifies Fancy," Chicago *Tribune,* 26 June 1905, 6; "Finer than the King's," San Francisco *Chronicle,* 22 July 1906, 5; "Mr. Reid's Salary Not Enough for Flowers," New York *Times,* 28 July 1907, SM2).

112.20–21   salaried members of the New York *Tribune* staff . . . married unnumbered millions of dollars] As managing editor of Horace Greeley's New York *Tribune,* Reid recruited John Hay to the editorial staff (1870) and encouraged Clemens's occasional contributions. Upon Greeley's death in 1872, Reid borrowed heavily from Jay Gould to buy the *Tribune,* and parlayed his control of America's foremost newspaper into a political career. Hay and Reid were both married to the daughters of wealthy railroad magnates: Reid to a daughter of Darius O. Mills in 1881, and Hay to a daughter of Amasa Stone in 1874 (5 Dec 1872 to Reid, *L5,* 242–43 n. 1).

113.12–13   Leonard Wood] Clemens denounced Wood's ruthless military actions in the Philippines, and his controversial appointment by Roosevelt to the rank of major general, in the Autobiographical Dictations of 12 and 14 March 1906 (see *AutoMT1,* 403–9 and notes on 615–19).

113.13–14   Theodore Roosevelt . . . implored by the whole nation to accept a third term] For more on Roosevelt's terms of office, see the Autobiographical Dictation of 14 July 1908, note at 255.18.

Autobiographical Dictation, 28 August 1907

113.20–28   MR. ROOSEVELT'S EXACT PORTRAIT . . . meddling America] The speech given by Representative Samuel W. McCall (1851–1923) on 22 August 1907 at Marshfield, Massachusetts, was widely reported. This extract comes from the New York *World,* which continued to reprint it on its editorial page during the ensuing week (New York *World:* "M'Call Fears an American Autocrat," 23 Aug 1907, 5; "Is This Mr. Roosevelt's Exact Portrait?," 27 Aug 1907, 6).

113.30–33   Reid and Edward H. House had a falling out . . . I ranged myself on House's side] For Edward H. House see *AutoMT1,* 598 n. 375.23. Clemens misrepresents this contretemps: House, in actuality, was a casualty of Clemens's own "falling out" with Reid. In May 1873 Reid, as editor of the New York *Tribune,* refused to assign House the duty of reviewing *The Gilded Age.* House had read the novel in manuscript during a recent visit to the Clemenses in Hartford, and he approached Reid, who "abused him & charged him with bringing a dishonorable proposal" from Clemens (SLC 1890, 8). Reid stated his own views on the subject to Kate Field:

> I hear he [Mark Twain] says that he has a quarrel with *The Tribune.* If so, it is simply that *The Tribune* declined to allow him to dictate the person who should review his forthcoming novel. His modest suggestion was that Ned House should do it, he having previously interested House in the success of the book by taking him into partnership in dramatizing it. There is a nice correspondence on a part of the subject which would make pleasant reading. (Reid to Field, 17 May 1873, DLC, in *L5,* 369 n. 2)

Eight years later, Clemens and Howells organized a similar scheme to promote *The Prince and the Pauper,* Howells offering to review the work in the *Tribune.* The time was ripe, for Reid was overseas, and John Hay was deputizing as editor; from Vienna, however, Reid warned Hay: "As to Twain. It isn't good journalism to let a warm personal friend & in some matters literary partner, write a critical review of him in a paper wh. has good reason to think little of his delicacy & highly of his greed" (Reid to Hay, 25 Sept 1881, RPB-JH, in *L5,* 368 n. 2). Hay disobeyed his superior, and Howells's review was printed (unsigned). Early in 1882, inflamed by reports that the *Tribune* was engaged in a campaign against him, Clemens made notes for a "revenge" biography of Reid; he abandoned the project when no evidence of such a campaign could be found (*N&J2,* 355–56, 417–25, 431–32, 439–45).

114.1   dinner at Dorchester House the other day] See the Autobiographical Dictation of 25 July 1907.

114.18–25 I had been helping the London newspaper men fetch the Shah of Persia over from Ostend . . . he lightly borrowed it of me] Nasr-ed-Din, the shah of Persia, made a diplomatic tour through Europe in June 1873. Clemens (accompanied by Olivia, Susy, and Clara Spaulding) was in London making notes for a projected book about England. For the New York *Herald* he dispatched five articles on the Shah's visit, which, upon publication, he found had been printed with "added paragraphs & interlineations, & not pleasant ones, either." The New York *Herald*'s London correspondent was journalist-physician George W. Hosmer (1830–1914; 4 Aug 1873 to Yates, *L5,* 430–31 n. 3). For his work in the *Herald,* Clemens seems to have received £69 (then worth about $350); House met up with Clemens in London and borrowed £61 from him (about $300). Months later, in a November 1874 letter to Clemens, House wondered whether his recent letters had been miscarrying, among them his "new note for the money borrowed in England," and offered repayment through his uncle's firm on Wall Street (*L5:* 17 or 18 June 1873 to Young, 383–84 n. 1; 1 July 1873 to Conway, 394; 2 Aug 1873 to Bliss [2nd], 425 n. 1; 4 Aug 1873 to Yates, 430–31 nn. 1, 3; SLC 1873a–e; House to SLC, 13 Nov 1874, CU-MARK).

114.26–27 his New York banker had failed, at cost to him of twenty-five thousand dollars] No particulars of this alleged bank failure have been found, nor is it known if House's debt was ever repaid.

114.32–34 About 1882, or along there somewhere, House came back from Japan . . . disabled by rheumatism] House, who relocated frequently in his efforts to influence Western policymakers, "came back" from Japan more than once. Clemens confuses one such return, spanning the period 1880–82, with another, in 1886, when House's chronic gout had become incapacitating (since about 1883 he had been confined to a bed or wheelchair). He arrived in New York in May 1886, with his adopted daughter, Koto, and a servant, Eijiro Ninomiya (see the notes at 114.34–35 and 115.13). Clemens visited him several times, and wrote him frequently. House, who had stayed with the Clemenses in Hartford in 1881–82, was there again from May 1886 through October 1888, staying sometimes with the George Warner household and sometimes with the Clemenses. House became a favorite with Susy and Clara, with whom he kept up a lively and whimsical correspondence when he was in New York (Huffman 2003, 176, 185, 201–3, 204–5, 214; "House v. Clemens" 1890, 26).

114.34–35 He brought with him a bright and good-natured and wonderfully muscular Japanese lad] Eijiro Ninomiya had served House since about 1885. In January 1891, however, a quarrel arose; he left House's service and joined a New York book-binding business (Ninomiya to SLC, 1 June 1891, CU-MARK).

114.41–115.1 literary work on "Arrah-na-Pogue," . . . Boucicault laughed at it and said it was a straight lie] The true extent of House's involvement with the successful play *Arrah-na-Pogue; or, The Wicklow Wedding* is unknown. It premiered in Dublin in 1864 as the work of Irish actor-playwright Dion Boucicault (1820–90), but House was named as coauthor in the 1865 American production (and in the subsequent litigation). In 1890, in "Concerning the Scoundrel Edward H. House," Clemens wrote that "a theatre manager assures me that Mr. House merely wrote a few lines in 'Arrah no Pogue' to protect Mr. Boucicault's rights here against pirates" (SLC 1890, 19–20; "Amusements," New York *Times*, 10 July 1865, 4; Tice L. Miller 1981, 82, 171 n. 33; Huffman 2003, 38–39; McFeely 2012, 55–56; *N&J3*, 545–46 n. 188).

115.3–6   "The Prince and the Pauper," . . . I proposed that House dramatize the book. He was indifferent, and declined] Clemens wrote to House, then living in New York, on 17 December 1886:

> You had spoken of the Prince & Pauper for the stage. That *would* be nice; but I can't dramatize it. The reason I say this is because I *did* dramatize it, & made a bad botch of it. But *you* could do it. And if you will, for ½ or ⅔ of the proceeds, I wish you would. Shan't I send you the book? The work might afford you good amusement when the pains mercifully retire at times. (ViU)

House did not "decline" this offer; he wrote immediately that he was "well pleased to undertake a dramatization" and could start "in a day or two." (House's side of this correspondence is missing, except for such passages as he introduced, from his copies, in the 1889–90 proceedings in the case of *House v. Clemens et al.*) He requested a copy of the book, "the commonest copy you have, as I shall use it roughly" (House to SLC, 24 Dec 1886, transcript in CU-MARK). Clemens sent the book. In June 1887, while staying with Clemens in Hartford, House read to him the completed first act (Clemens later called this a "skeleton of the first act": "House v. Clemens" 1890, 77). House would later testify that he had reported the play's completion in September 1887, and that he had been shocked to discover, early in 1889, that Clemens had asked another writer to dramatize the book. He wrote to Clemens, who replied: "I gather the idea from your letter that you would have undertaken the dramatization of that book. Well, that would have been joyful news to me about the middle of December [1888], when I gladly took the first offer that came and made a contract" (26 Feb 1889 to House, New York *Times*, 27 Jan 1890, 5). Clemens's contract was with Abby Sage Richardson (for whom see the note at 115.6–11). A week later, Clemens wrote again to House, urgently requesting evidence of any contract he might "heedlessly, ignorantly, forgetfully" have made with him (2 Mar 1889 to House, facsimile in CU-MARK). House replied, and on 19 March Clemens stated his position:

> The case is quite plain, quite simple: I have lately made a contract for the dramatization of the Prince & Pauper. I must live up to it unless there is an earlier contract in existence. If you have one, send me a copy of it, so that I can take measures to undo my illegal action, & I will at once proceed in the matter.
> I made the re[c]ent contract with simply this ancient impression in my memory: That two years or more ago you signified a willingness to dramatize that book; that some months later, the willingness to dramatize it had modified itself to a willingness to *sketch out a plan* for me to fill up myself—at which point I lost all

interest in the matter—no, *began* to lose interest in it, & by & by did lose interest in it—for the reason, as I suppose, that you gradually abandoned the matter & ceased to speak of it. I still remember somewhat of the sketch you made for a part of the first act. But I do not remember that it was anything more than that, or that you were then thinking of writing the act yourself. I carried away the impression that you had no such idea in your mind.

From that day to this, if the play has ever been referred to by you, I have no recollection of it. (19 Mar 1889 to House, ViU)

115.6–11   I hunted up another dramatist—Mrs. Abby Sage Richardson . . . Elsie Leslie] Abby Sage Richardson (1837–1900) was inevitably best known for the events of 1869, when her ex-husband, Daniel McFarland, mortally wounded her lover, journalist Albert D. Richardson, in the offices of the New York *Tribune*. She was married to Richardson on his deathbed. Her subsequent career would be bound up with that of Daniel Frohman (1851–1940). Frohman, as an eighteen-year-old *Tribune* employee, had witnessed Albert D. Richardson's murder; he became a friend to Mrs. Richardson, quit journalism, and by the 1880s he was the manager of New York's Lyceum Theatre. The widowed Mrs. Richardson developed a modest reputation as an essayist and lecturer. On 4 December 1888 she wrote to Clemens proposing that she adapt *The Prince and the Pauper* (CU-MARK). Clemens promptly gave his permission, in a letter not now extant, suggesting "that she try to get House to help her" (this paraphrase is from "Concerning the Scoundrel Edward H. House," SLC 1890, 48). Mrs. Richardson replied that what she needed was not "literary" assistance but "some one who knows 'behind the scenes' thoroughly, and I can get that sort of suggestion from the manager of a theatre who would be interested in the play if I did it"—hinting that Frohman would produce it; she also suggested child actor Elsie Leslie for the dual role of Tom Canty and the Prince (Richardson to SLC, 9 Dec 1888, CU-MARK). They made a contract on 3 January 1889, Clemens offering her half the profits, and a commitment from Daniel Frohman to produce the play was soon obtained. The play opened in Philadelphia on 24 December 1889 and in New York on 20 January 1890. Between those dates, House brought suit for an injunction against the performances. Clemens himself had not yet read the script written by Richardson (with Frohman's assistance), and did not see a performance until the New York premiere, at which he made a dutiful curtain-speech. A few days later he wrote a letter (never sent) to Frohman, calling the play a "mess of idiotic rubbish & vapid twaddle" and itemizing its "infinite repulsivenesses"; the dramatist had "merely transferred *names* from the book, & often left the *characters* that belonged to them behind" (2 Feb 1890 to Frohman, photocopy in CU-MARK). Critics broadly agreed, though Elsie Leslie's performance drew praise, and the production would run seven weeks in New York before doing two years as a touring production ("Abby Sage Richardson Dies in Rome, Italy," New York *Times*, 6 Dec 1900, 9; Stern 1947, 286–87; Richardson to SLC, 4 Dec 1888, CU-MARK; *N&J3*, 453 n. 155, 466 n. 202, 487 n. 21, 542–43 n. 183, 543–44 n. 184; Fatout 1976, 256–57; Huffman 2003, 218; for Elsie Leslie, see *AutoMT2*, 557–58).

115.13 a young Japanese girl, Koto] Aoki Koto (1859?–1939) was a student of House's at a state-sponsored school for girls in Japan; married in 1874, she was soon divorced. To "save her from subsequent humiliation"—reportedly she intended to commit suicide—House legally adopted her (Huffman 2003, 87–89).

115.14–15 they were our guests during two or three months] Edward and Koto House stayed with the Clemenses from mid-May through June 1887. House testified in 1890 that during this six-week visit he was working on the play and sharing his progress with Clemens (see the note at 115.3–6); this Clemens denied. In this dictation he wrongly places the Houses' visit *after* Clemens's commissioning of Mrs. Richardson in December 1888 (*N&J3*, 292 n. 223; "House v. Clemens" 1890, 28; Huffman 2003, 204–5, 214).

115.15–20 House notified me, through his lawyer, Robert G. Ingersoll, to take it off . . . discharged him, and hired Howe and Hummel in his place] House retained Robert G. Ingersoll early in 1889, many months before Mrs. Richardson's dramatization was staged. House soon dismissed Ingersoll, but he did not hire Howe and Hummel; in fact, they represented Clemens's codefendants, Frohman and Richardson. By the time court proceedings began, House was represented by Morgan and Ives. Clemens's counsel was his regular lawyer, Daniel Whitford (Ingersoll to House, 29 Mar 1889, ViU; Ingersoll to SLC, 29 Mar 1889, ViU; New York *Times:* "Mark Twain Hauled Up," 27 Jan 1890, 5; "Two Ways Left Open," 10 Mar 1890, 5; for Ingersoll, see *AutoMT1,* 474 n. 69.15–17; for Whitford, see *AutoMT2,* 493 n. 2.18).

115.20 Hummel is in the penitentiary, now] Abraham Hummel (1849–1926), since 1902 the head of the eminent New York law firm of Howe and Hummel, was convicted of suborning perjury in May 1907. He was disbarred and served ten months in prison ("Hummel Given a Year," Washington *Post,* 11 May 1907, 1; "Hummel Leaves the Island To-day," New York *Times,* 19 Mar 1908, 5).

115.22–29 The case came before Judge Daly in chambers . . . Judge Daly's decision went against me] House's application for an injunction requiring that performances of the Richardson-Frohman play cease, and that Clemens "join" House in the staging of his own dramatization, was decided on 8 March 1890 by Judge Joseph F. Daly of New York's Court of Common Pleas. House's deposition quoted extensively from his correspondence with Clemens in order to establish the existence of an oral contract. For his part, Clemens deposed that he had "never agreed to accept" House's dramatization, nor given him "the exclusive right" to the property, and that after the May–June 1887 visit he had heard nothing about House's dramatization. Judge Daly granted a temporary injunction, holding that the correspondence of the parties in December 1886 established a contract, and that there was no bar to its being honored ("House v. Clemens" 1890; Daly 1892, 8–9, 14; *N&J3,* 542–43 n. 183).

115.30–32 the veracity of a sick man . . . was more to be depended upon than the oath of a man who was well] Clemens is recalling a passage in Judge Daly's decision, bearing upon House's and Clemens's contradictory accounts of their conversations after June 1887:

In the multitude of professional work pressing upon so busy and popular an author as Mr. Clemens, much may have escaped his recollection that would not be forgotten by an invalid like the plaintiff, confined to his bed or his chair, and conceded to be a man of methodical habits in recording the details of his correspondence or conversations. (Daly 1892, 9)

The judge went on, however, to say that letters or conversations after the initial agreement, or the absence of same, "in no way affected the rights of the parties based upon the original proposition and its acceptance."

115.34–37   A temporary injunction was upon the box-office ... decided one way or the other] Judge Daly's 8 March 1890 injunction prohibited performance of the play unless House's consent was obtained. Clemens was not averse to the play's closure, but Frohman was. On 11 March House agreed with Frohman that performances might continue as long as Clemens's royalties were held in an escrow account until legal proceedings were concluded. Clemens was not a party to this agreement, so its validity was questionable (Huffman 2003, 218; N&J3, 548 n. 196).

115.37–116.9   Then House and his little family removed to Hartford ... he had already skipped, and was safe] House's dramatization of *The Prince and the Pauper* opened on 6 October at the Amphion Academy in Brooklyn. It starred Tommy Russell, a child actor who had alternated with Elsie Leslie in a dramatization of *Little Lord Fauntleroy*. Frohman successfully applied for an injunction against the production, and House's play closed on 18 October. Nothing has been found to confirm Clemens's claim that House lived in Hartford at this time. He certainly did not flee the United States at the time Clemens alleges: House and Koto lived in New York until mid-1892, when they returned to Japan. He was, as his biographer says, "mired in legal sloughs," but nothing is known of any fraud against the French bank Crédit Lyonnais. Charles E. Gross was a Hartford lawyer (N&J3, 451–52 n. 150, 582 n. 32; Huffman 2003, 223; Spalding 1891, 119).

116.12–17   I instructed Mr. Bainbridge Colby to go and get my share ... I do not now know what became of them] Bainbridge Colby (1869–1950), later an eminent statesman but at this time a young Wall Street lawyer, handled legal matters for Rogers and Clemens before being appointed assignee in the bankruptcy of Webster and Company in April 1894. The case of *House v. Clemens et al.* never came to trial. After House's departure for Japan, the matter was left unattended until Whitford moved for a dismissal, which was granted in January 1894, and the temporary injunction was removed. In February of that year Clemens ordered that suit be brought against Frohman to collect his share of the royalties, which he estimated at "only five or six thousand dollars" (7 Feb 1894 to OLC, CU-MARK). In 1896, he was bitter against Frohman: "Colby will never collect the money that is owing to me by that Lyceum Theatre Jew" (20 Oct 1896 to Rogers, Salm, in *HHR,* 240–42). Later, after the restoration of his fortunes, he was readier to forgive, recalling that years later Frohman and he "met in the Lotus Club, & chaffed each other about it, each claiming that the other owed money—but they went to playing billiards &

dropped the subject" (Lyon for SLC to Chapin, on or after 19 Aug 1906, CU-MARK; *N&J3,* 582 n. 32; *HHR,* 42 n. 3).

Autobiographical Dictation, 29 August 1907

116.29–117.1   My first experience of a banquet in a foreign country . . . mine in the place of honor—the last] Clemens misremembers some of the details of his experience at the Inauguration Banquet of Sheriffs at Guildhall on 28 September 1872. About two hundred and fifty guests were present. He was not "there by appointment, to respond to a regular toast": he attended as the guest of Sir John Bennett, who asked him during the meal to respond to the toast "Success to Literature." The London *Observer*'s report shows that he took his very lack of preparation as his text. He wrote his wife that night: "Imagine my situation, before that great audience, without a single word of preparation—for I had expected nothing of this kind—I did not know I was a lion. I got up & said whatever came first, & made a good deal of a success—for I was the only man they consented to hear *clear through*—& they applauded handsomely. . . . I think it was a sort of lame speech I made, but it was splendidly received" (28 Sept 1872 to OLC, *L5,* 183–88).

117.6   Sir John Bennett] Sir John Bennett (1814–97), a watchmaker by trade and a London politician by vocation, was noted for flamboyant display. He was a sheriff of London and Middlesex in 1871–72, during which term he was knighted. Clemens had recently been befriended by Bennett, and was at this Lord Mayor's Dinner by his invitation (*L5:* 25 Sept 1872 to OLC, 180 n. 3; 28 Sept 1872 to OLC, 185–86 n. 1).

117.24–27   banquet to General Grant . . . I was No. 16] At the banquet to General Grant given in Chicago on 13 November 1879, Clemens gave a celebrated speech in response to the toast to "The Babies," the last of fifteen toasts and the only speech of the evening that caused Grant himself to laugh ("Banquet of the Army of the Tennessee," New York *Times,* 15 Nov 1879, 1; see "The Chicago G.A.R. Festival," *AutoMT1,* 67–70).

117.34–35   Sir Mortimer Durand . . . speech of considerable length] Durand (1850–1924) was ambassador to the United States from December 1903 to November 1906, when he was recalled by his government; he never held an official post again (Washington *Post:* "Durand Is Presented," 3 Dec 1903, 9; "Bryce Is Ambassador," 22 Dec 1906, 3).

118.1–3   Sir Mortimer Durand still remains unconvinced . . . I did not take the Ascot Cup] See the Autobiographical Dictation of 25 July 1907. Sir Mortimer had said, in proposing the toast to the president:

> The race feeling [shared by England and America] is not gone. I am certain that the remains of it will long endure—just as certain as I am that, in spite of his protestations, Mark Twain has got that Cup. It is not the first cup your people have lifted here, and I daresay it won't be the last. How he will get it through the Custom House I don't know. (Lathem 2006, 199, quoting the American Society

in London's *Report of the Speeches at the Independence Day Banquet, July 4th, 1907*)

118.8   England has been trying to take a Cup of ours for forty years] The America's Cup, the trophy of the international yacht race of the same name, was held by the New York Yacht Club—as it had been since 1851, and as it would be until 1983. Britain had challenged the American defenders frequently since 1870 (Lathem 2006, 196).

118.9–12   Sir Mortimer Durand . . . had to sit all night in his regimentals] In his toast, Sir Mortimer told how, at his last American Society in London dinner, he had "listened with so much interest and pleasure that I lost my last train into the country, and had to spend the night in full warpaint in the waiting room at Victoria" (Lathem 2006, 199).

118.15–29   Two or three years ago in New York . . . I lost my train, and it was I who broke the Sabbath] Clemens refers to a speech he made at a banquet given by the British Schools and Universities Club of New York, at Delmonico's on 9 November 1901. Clemens followed two speakers, who seem to be conflated in his portrait of a "very famous and very great British clergyman": the British-born Rev. D. Parker Morgan (1843–1915), and Francis L. Patton, the Presbyterian minister and president of Princeton University (see AD, 24 July 1907, note at 72.24–36). From Clemens's speech it is clear that Patton changed places with Clemens in the speaking order:

> If I never do another creditable thing, I have at least got the Rev. Dr. Patton's train for him, and I have lost my own. To-morrow his Sabbath will suffer no damage, but I have to break mine. But if you will consider the self-sacrifice that I make, think of it. He can afford it better than I. He has a record to fall back on, and, sadly, so have I. [Laughter.] I also enjoy a kindness. I am glad to have him catch his train. The sooner he goes the more liberally I can afford to speak. ("Britons Here Toast Their King, Edward," New York *Times,* 10 Nov 1901, 9)

118.38–45   when night shuts down, that pandemonium will begin . . . we cripple and kill more people than you would imagine] The dangers of the Fourth of July as a result of firecrackers, gunfire, and gunpowder became a widespread concern at the turn of the twentieth century. Deadly tetanus could follow from even minor burns or lacerations. In 1899, the Chicago *Tribune* launched its continuing "Campaign for a Sane Fourth," a series of articles tabulating the injuries and deaths caused by Fourth of July celebrations across the nation. In 1906 the American Medical Association reported 5,308 injuries—including the loss of eyes, limbs, and fingers—and 158 deaths. There was mockery and resistance, but by 1911 Chicago and many other cities limited or banned fireworks (Chicago *Tribune:* "Fourth of July Slaughter," 10 July 1905, 6; "Call the Roll of July 4th Deaths," 1 Sept 1905, 6; "Medical View of the Fatal Fourth," 17 Aug 1906, 5; Nickerson 2012).

119.23–24   Sir Mortimer Durand . . . did it with some reluctance] In his toast to the president Sir Mortimer said, "Since England came to the conclusion, a hundred and thirty years ago, somewhat reluctantly if I remember right, that she had no further use for her American Colonies, our ways have diverged" (Lathem 2006, 199).

120.9–11   that memorable proclamation . . . set the black slave free] The Emancipation Proclamation, issued by Abraham Lincoln on 1 January 1863, freed the slaves in territories which were in rebellion against the Union. Slavery throughout the United States was abolished by the Thirteenth Amendment to the Constitution in 1865.

120.15   England led the way, for she had set her slaves free] The Slavery Abolition Act of 1833 outlawed slavery in the British Empire (with the exception of some territories).

120.18–20   when a slave . . . sets his foot upon English soil, his fetters by that act fall away] In the case of *Shanley v. Harvey* (1762), the Lord Chancellor, Robert Henley, first earl of Northington, ruled that "as soon as a man sets foot on English ground he is free" (Hurd 1858–62, 1:186). This referred literally to England, and not to its colonies.

120.30   President Murray Butler] Nicholas Murray Butler (1862–1947) was president of Columbia University from 1902 to 1945. He was in England in 1907 to receive an honorary degree from Cambridge (Lathem 2006, 200).

Autobiographical Dictation, 30 August 1907

121.5   *Friday, July 5.* Dined with the Earl and Countess of Portsmouth] Newton Wallop, sixth earl of Portsmouth (1856–1917), was a Liberal politician, and a member of the cabinet of premier Henry Campbell-Bannerman. Clemens had dined with him and his countess, Beatrice, on 24 March 1900 (Notebook 43, TS p. 6, CU-MARK).

121.7–8   *Saturday, July 6.* Breakfasted at Lord Avebury's . . . Sir Archibald Geikie] This breakfast was given by Lord Avebury (Sir John Lubbock, 1834–1913), a banker, politician, scientific writer, and philanthropist. Clemens read and admired Lubbock's *Ants, Bees, and Wasps* on publication in 1882. He returned to it when traveling the Indian Ocean in 1896, and mined it for information in *What Is Man?* (Gribben 1980, 1:427–28; SLC 1906a). Lubbock had written to Clemens in advance that he would "ask a few literary & scientific friends to meet him" (20 June 1907, CU-MARK), among whom Clemens mentions physicist William Thomson (Lord Kelvin, 1824–1907) and the geologists Sir Charles Lyell (see *AutoMT2,* 555 n. 212.28) and Sir Archibald Geikie (1835–1924).

121.9–11   Quarters at the hotel occupied by invasion of photographers . . . will sit no more] Clemens adapts Ashcroft's original memorandum of the day's occurrences, which reads: "Sat 22 times for photos, 16 at Histed's." The photographer Ernest Walter Histed (1862–1947) specialized in celebrity portraits. His studios were at 42 Baker Street (Ashcroft 1907, 4; Histed to SLC, 11 July 1907, CU-MARK). It is true that on this trip Clemens was pestered with requests to sit for his portrait (for a sampling, see Lathem 2006, 205).

121.12–13   Savage Club dinner ... Brennan mono-rail car exhibited in action] At the dinner given in his honor by the Savage Club on 6 July, Clemens wore for the first time in England the white suit he had introduced to American audiences in 1906 (see *AutoMT2*, 249–50). After his speech, he was presented with a gilt plaster replica of the Ascot Cup, in allusion to his alleged theft of the original, which had become a running joke in the newspapers. The fake trophy was provided by Garrard and Company, the makers of the authentic cup. Irish inventor Louis Brennan (1852–1932) gave a demonstration of his monorail car, which ran "around the dining room tables on wire cables. The wonderful six foot model ran curving between the bottles and candlesticks, going backwards and forwards fast and slow to Mark Twain's great delight" ("British Acclaim Twain in White," Chicago *Tribune,* 7 July 1907, 8; for Clemens's speech on this occasion see Fatout 1976, 572–76).

121.14–16   Sir Norman Lockyer ... Admiral Sir Cyprian Bridge, whom I had known in Australia in '95] Clemens mentions: Sir Joseph Norman Lockyer (1836–1920), astronomer; Linley Sambourne (1844–1910), illustrator and *Punch* cartoonist; and Admiral Sir Cyprian Bridge (1839–1924), commander of the Australian naval station when Clemens traveled there in 1895.

121.17   Drove two hours and a half returning calls, with little Francesca] On the afternoon of July 7, with Frances Nunnally in tow, Clemens called on J. Y. W. MacAlister and family (see *AutoMT2*, 640–41 n. 434 *title*); Edwin A. Abbey, American artist (see AD, 25 July 1907, note at 74.24–38); John Rolls, Baron Llangattock (1837–1912) and family; the earl and countess of Portsmouth (see the note at 121.5); Annie Colt McCook, the widow of Major General Alexander McCook (Clemens had known them both at Old Point Comfort, and Mrs. McCook was now resident in London); and Lord and Lady Avebury (see the note at 121.7–8; 7 July 1907 to Nunnally, CSmH; McCook to SLC, 26 June 1907 and 4 July 1907, CU-MARK; for Nunnally see AD, 25 July 1907, and note at 74.15–21).

121.19   *Monday, July 8.* Lunched with Plasmon Directors at Bath Club] For the British Plasmon Company, see the note at 122.10–16.

121.20   Dined privately at Moberly Bell's] For C. F. Moberly Bell, see the Autobiographical Dictation of 23 August 1907, note at 109.27.

121.21–23   *Tuesday, July 9.* Lunched at the House of Commons with Sir Benjamin Stone ... Japanese ambassador] Sir Benjamin Stone (1838–1914), a Conservative member of parliament, gave this luncheon at the "Harcourt" dining room of the House of Commons. Clemens's fellow guests of honor were Conservative Party leader and ex-prime minister Arthur Balfour (1848–1930) and the Japanese ambassador to Britain, Komura Jutaro (1855–1911). In his remarks, Balfour pled for "the necessity of guarding the purity of the English language." Clemens thanked him "for his recognition of his services in keeping the English language pure and undefiled, and assured him he would not allow it to deteriorate in his hands" ("Twain Takes Up Task for Briton," Chicago

Tribune, 10 July 1907, 3). Stone, an amateur photographer, took pictures of the luncheon gathering outside the Houses of Parliament (see the photographs following page 300).

121.24   *Punch* dinner in the evening] See the note at 122.18–19.

121.33–35   little maid of sixteen . . . during two hours paying calls] Frances Nunnally.

122.10–16   Seven years ago I assisted in founding the Plasmon Company . . . amounting to thirty-two thousand dollars] In 1900 Clemens made a £5,000 investment (roughly equivalent to $25,000) in the newly formed British Plasmon Company. How he arrived at his 1907 valuation of the investment at "eighty thousand dollars" is not known (8–9 Apr 1900 to Rogers, Salm, in *HHR,* 438–42).

122.18–19   For fifty years the *Punch* staff has assembled once a week in *Punch*'s own quarters] The offices of London humor magazine *Punch* at 10 Bouverie Street included a dining room, where the contributors' traditional Wednesday dinners took place. The dinner to Clemens on Tuesday, 9 July, however, was "an off day, not the Wednesday dinner" (Lucy 1909, 1:364; Young 2007, 41–42).

122.26–123.12   MARK TWAIN LEAVES ENGLAND . . . Punch's Tribute to Mark Twain] The newspaper article is a clipping from the Syracuse (N.Y.) *Herald* of 14 July 1907, which also reprints a cartoon from *Punch* (issue of 26 June 1907, 453). On the clipping Clemens inscribed a simplified version of *Punch*'s original caption, which was: "TO A MASTER OF HIS ART. MR. PUNCH (*to* MARK TWAIN). 'SIR, I HONOUR MYSELF BY DRINKING YOUR HEALTH. LONG LIFE TO YOU—AND HAPPINESS—AND PERPETUAL YOUTH!'" The original drawing, by Bernard Partridge, was presented to Clemens at the dinner; see the Autobiographical Dictation of 31 August 1907.

Autobiographical Dictation, 31 August 1907

124.6–7   Mr. Agnew, the editor-in-chief] Clemens refers to Philip L. Agnew (1863–1938), a proprietor of *Punch* and also its managing director. The editor was Owen Seaman ("Mr. P. L. Agnew," London *Times,* 9 Mar 1938, 16).

124.8   Linley Sambourne, Sir Francis Burnand, and Mr. Lucy] For Linley Sambourne see the Autobiographical Dictation of 30 August 1907, note at 121.14–16. Sir Francis Burnand (1836–1917) was the editor of *Punch* from 1880 to 1906. Henry William Lucy (1843–1924) covered Parliamentary proceedings for *Punch* under the pseudonym of "Toby, M.P." For the recollections of *Punch* contributors who were present at this meeting, see Lathem 2006, 212–14.

124.10   Leech, Tenniel, Douglas Jerrold] Illustrators John Leech (1817–64) and Sir John Tenniel (1820–1914); playwright and humorist Douglas Jerrold (1803–57).

124.23–24   The little sprite was Joy Agnew, eight years of age] Enid Jocelyn Agnew (1898–1921) was called Joy by her parents, Philip L. Agnew and his wife, Georgette (Whitaker 1907, 12; Farthingstone Village 2014; "Mr. P. L. Agnew," London *Times,* 9 Mar 1938, 16).

125.29–30   "Fair as a star when only one / Is shining in the sky."] From Wordsworth's "She dwelt among the untrodden ways" (Wordsworth 1815, 1:130).

126.10–11   Owen Seaman, and Partridge] For *Punch* editor Owen Seaman, see the Autobiographical Dictation of 25 July 1907, note at 75.15. John Bernard Partridge (1861–1945) was the magazine's cartoonist from 1891.

Autobiographical Dictation, 4 September 1907

126.22–24   Professor Henderson . . . a copy of "What is Man?"] Archibald Henderson was the official biographer of George Bernard Shaw (see AD, 25 July 1907, note at 73.16–17). Clemens composed his philosophical dialogue *What Is Man?* between 1898 and late 1905, and had a limited edition printed for private distribution in 1906 (*AutoMT2,* 602–3 n. 332.35–36; SLC 1906a).

126.38–127.2   I laid one chapter of my gospel before the Monday Evening Club . . . denying that there is any such thing as personal merit] Clemens addressed the Monday Evening Club on 19 February 1883, reading an essay entitled "What Is Happiness?" To judge from a notebook entry a little before this, the essay is the germ from which *What Is Man?* would spring: "Is *any*body or any *action* ever unselfish? (Good theme for Club Essay)" (*N&J2,* 498 n. 214). Clemens's essay, as given before the club, formed no part of the eventual book *What Is Man?* (see the note at 127.31–33; *WIM,* 4, 11–20, 124–214; for the Monday Evening Club, see *AutoMT1,* 558 n. 269.1–6).

127.23–24   as pointed out by Lord Bacon some centuries ago] Francis Bacon (1561–1626) held that philosophical progress is impeded by "idols"—inherited prejudices and inherent frailties. In his *Novum Organum* (1620) he called for "entirely abolishing common theories and notions, and applying the mind afresh, when thus cleared and levelled, to particular researches" (Francis Bacon 1841, 3:362).

127.31–33   in Vienna in 1898, I wrote out and completed one chapter . . . Frank N. Doubleday, who was passing through Vienna, and he wanted to take it and publish it] The compositional history of *What Is Man?* is complicated; for an account of it, see *WIM,* 603–9. Frank Nelson Doubleday (1862–1934) was a publisher; in 1897 he had just set up a publishing firm with S. S. McClure; in 1900 it became Doubleday, Page and Company. What Clemens read to Doubleday was presumably the manuscript "What Is the Real Character of 'Conscience?,'" written in Vienna and Kaltenleutgeben in April and July 1898. After revisions, reshuffling, and a change of title, this would form about one-half the matter of *What Is Man?* (*WIM,* 11–15, 603–9). In his memoirs, Doubleday disclaims any personal interest in Clemens's philosophy: "I thought that the whole thing was a crazy piece of business and urged him to forget it, but he thought it the best thing he had ever written.... It was, I always thought, a poor thing, and I think so yet" (Doubleday 1972, 87–88).

127.36–38   destroying the concluding chapter, whose subject was "The Moral Sense."... that one was disrespectful—in fact riotous] "The Moral Sense," probably written in July 1898, was removed from the first typescript of *What Is Man?* and does not appear in the printed edition; but other manuscript and typed versions survive in the Mark Twain Papers. It argues that mankind would be better off in the condition of the animals, lacking the moral sense and not subject to moral standards. It is not especially "riotous," however, and Clemens may be thinking of another omitted chapter, entitled "God," which he seems to have considered briefly as a replacement for the omitted "Moral Sense" (*WIM*, 472–75, 476–92).

127.41   two hundred and fifty copies printed for me] Copyright was registered to J. W. Bothwell (not "Boswell"), the general manager of the De Vinne Press. Two hundred and fifty copies were ready in August 1906.

128.23–25   Is it not Goethe who says... to prevent him from doing other great things] From Goethe's *Conversations with Eckermann:* "If you do anything for the sake of the world, it will take good care that you shall not do it a second time" (Goethe 1930, 38).

129.6   *mot d'ordre*] "Watchword."

129.7   *Ich kann nicht anders*] "I cannot do otherwise": words attributed to Martin Luther, addressing the Diet of Worms in 1521.

129.30   *Fais ce que tu veux*] In *Gargantua* (1534) by Rabelais, the motto of the Abbey of Thélème is "Fais ce que tu voudras" ("Do what thou wilt").

130.1   I have not read Nietzsche or Ibsen] Clemens was not absolutely innocent of acquaintance with these authors. In 1890 Olivia remarked in a letter that she was reading Ibsen's *A Doll's House* (in German, apparently), and intended to read *Ghosts* next. Clemens mentioned Ibsen as a leading man of the times in the manuscript fragment "Ancients in Modern Dress" (1896–97), without implying familiarity with his work; later, in 1906, he owned a volume of Ibsen's collected works containing *Hedda Gabler* and *The Master Builder* in the translations of Edmund Gosse and William Archer. Clemens had also looked over Nietzsche's *Thus Spake Zarathustra,* in Isabel Lyon's copy, on 8 August 1906—reportedly exclaiming afterward "Oh damn Nietzsche! He couldn't write a lucid sentence to save his soul" (Gribben 1980, 1:343, 2:508; OLC to King, 25 Feb 1890, photocopy in CU-MARK; Brahm and Robinson 2005).

Autobiographical Dictation, 6 September 1907

130.21–24   Lady Stanley... when I first knew her, a proud and happy young bride] Clemens called on Dorothy, Lady Stanley (1855–1926), the widow of Henry M. Stanley, on the afternoon of 20 June 1907. Born Dorothy Tennant, she was an artist and illustrator. She married Stanley in 1890, having earlier had liaisons with Andrew Carnegie and other prominent men. The newlywed Stanleys visited the Clemenses in Hartford in December 1890, in the course of Stanley's lecture tour of 1890–91 (*N&J3*, 587 n. 49).

130.27–28 Mrs. Myers, her widowed sister, was the wife . . . British Psychical Society] Lady Stanley's sister, Eveleen Tennant (1856–1937), was the widow of the wealthy essayist and psychical researcher Frederic William Henry Myers (1843–1901), a founder, in 1882, of the Society for Psychical Research, devoted to the scientific examination of psychic phenomena. The society invited Clemens to join them in 1884; his letter of acceptance, published in the society's *Journal,* expressed "a very strong interest" and belief in "thought-transference, as you call it, or mental telegraphy as I have been in the habit of calling it" (Barrett 1884, 166). Clemens was a frequent reader of the society's publications and, in his own writings, gave it public encouragement and credit: "They have penetrated toward the heart of the matter . . . and have found out that mind can act upon mind in a quite detailed and elaborate way over vast stretches of land and water. . . . They have done our age a service" (SLC 1891, 95). The society's records indicate that Clemens remained a member until 1902. He had no great opinion of Myers as an investigator, writing of him just after his death: "I am afraid he was a very easily-convinced man. We visited two mediums whom he & Andrew Lang considered wonderful, but they were quite transparent frauds" (26 Mar 1901 to McQuiston, CtHMTH; Barrett to SLC, 26 Sept 1884, CU-MARK; *N&J3*, 260–61 n. 111; Horn 1996, 10–12).

131.12–15 Stanley had left behind him an uncompleted autobiography . . . Lady Stanley is preparing it for publication] For the life of Henry Morton Stanley, and Clemens's acquaintance with him, see *AutoMT2*, 583 n. 280.28–33. Stanley's manuscript autobiography, written in the 1890s, sets forth—"freely," though not "frankly"—the events of his life up through August 1862, when he had recently been discharged from the Union army. In 1909, Lady Stanley published the autobiography, "completed" by her using Stanley's journalism, notebooks, and other material. In February 1910, Howells recommended "the autobiography of Stanley" to Clemens as "about the livest book I ever read" (Stanley 1909, ix, 215, 219; McLynn 1989, 43; McLynn 1991, 384, 389; Howells to SLC, 11 Feb 1910, CU-MARK, in *MTHL,* 2:852–53).

131.22 I will mix my dates again] Clemens "mixes" his dates in order to juxtapose the credulous Lady Stanley, whom he saw on 20 June, with the similarly credulous Archdeacon Basil Wilberforce, whom he saw on 23 June. For Wilberforce, see the Autobiographical Dictation of 25 July 1907, note at 80.7.

131.27 the Immaculate Conception] See *AutoMT2,* 523 n. 130.33.

132.5–8 *Sunday, June 23.* In the afternoon Mr. Clemens visited Archdeacon Wilberforce . . . seventy-five or a hundred others were there] This "note of Ashcroft's" is a creative expansion by Clemens; Ashcroft's real note is more terse: "Had tea at Wilberforce's and saw The Holy Grail" (Ashcroft 1907, 2).

132.10–24   the long lost Holy Grail had at last been found . . . All this had happened a week or ten days before this present conversation of June 23d] The saucer-like vessel displayed at Wilberforce's home had been brought there the day before by Wellesley Tudor Pole (1884–1968), a Bristol grain merchant and clairvoyant. For the last five years, Tudor Pole had been making pilgrimages to Glastonbury, believing that he, in association with "a triad of maidens" (his sister and two friends), had a pivotal role in "preparing the Way for the Coming of the Holy Graal." In September 1906 he told the maidens to search "a certain Holy Well" near Glastonbury Abbey, where they found the vessel. Pole showed it to an acquaintance, Dr. J. A. Goodchild, who volunteered the surprising information that he himself had secreted the item in the well. Goodchild said he had purchased it in an antiques shop in Italy in 1885; later, spirit voices revealed to him that it was the Grail, and told him to place it in the well, where a pure woman would, at the appointed time, discover it. Early in 1907 Tudor Pole began to submit the vessel to the scrutiny of antiquarians, clerics, and spiritualists, with varying results. Wilberforce was enthusiastic, and so, at first, was Sir William Crookes (1832–1919), a scientist and spiritualist. At Wilberforce's house on 20 July 1907, before an invited audience of some forty interested persons, Wilberforce exhibited the vessel; Tudor Pole told his story, and Crookes was given a week to investigate the artifact. Meanwhile, the "find" became a short-lived newspaper item (see AD, 12 Sept 1907, note at 134.5–6). Crookes, in his report, declined to state whether the vessel was of ancient or modern manufacture; in January 1908 a panel of experts concluded that it was "fairly modern" (Benham 1993, 59–82; *Annals of Psychical Science* 1907; Lathem 2006, 156–58).

Autobiographical Dictation, 12 September 1907

133.2–3   this was the very vessel . . . delivered to Nicodemus] The expected reference here would be to Joseph of Arimathea, who is supposed to have brought the Grail to England. Nicodemus, in the Gospel of John, is a Pharisee who cooperates with Joseph of Arimathea in the burial of Jesus (John 19:39).

134.5–6   Two or three weeks after the 23d a brief account was published in a London paper] The London *Express* broke the Holy Grail story on 26 July 1907. For a sampling of press coverage, see Lathem 2006, 156–58.

Autobiographical Dictation, 13 September 1907

134.16–31   President Roosevelt . . . the names of the men who furnished the money, and the amounts which each contributed] This scandal concerns the 1904 presidential election. In late October of that year, the Democratic candidate, Judge Alton B. Parker, made a speech in which he said that "the trusts are furnishing the money with which they [the Republicans] hope to control the election" ("Genesis of the Famous Election Fund

Raised by Harriman at Roosevelt's Request," New York *World,* 9 Sept 1907, 3). Congress had recently passed legislation forbidding corporations to contribute to political campaigns. Incumbent president Theodore Roosevelt denied any impropriety. In April 1907, railroad magnate E. H. Harriman renewed the charge in a letter leaked to the New York *World.* Harriman said that Roosevelt, fearing he might not carry his home state of New York, had called upon Harriman to raise $250,000 in election funds, and had promised in return to appoint Republican Senator Chauncey Depew as ambassador to France, and to relax his attack on corporate interests. Once elected, Roosevelt did neither of these things. Such was Harriman's account; Roosevelt hit back in public, calling Harriman's story a lie, and publishing their 1904 correspondence. The *World* renewed the attack on 9 September, publishing the names of the corporate contributors to the election fund, with the amounts they gave ("Harriman Lies, Says President," Washington *Post,* 3 Apr 1904, 1; "Heads of Corporations Came Up with the Cash to Elect Roosevelt," New York *World,* 9 Sept 1907, 3; Lewis 1919, 231–34).

134.32   three of them are Standard Oil monopolists] Among the three Standard Oil chiefs reported as having contributed to Roosevelt's 1904 election fund was Clemens's close friend and benefactor Henry Huttleston Rogers (the other two were John D. Archbold and William Rockefeller). If true, the donation by Rogers of $30,000 is surprising, since, on the testimony of fellow tycoon Thomas W. Lawson, he had despised Roosevelt for years (Lawson 1904). This matter of campaign donations was still being fought out years after Roosevelt's presidency and Rogers's death in 1909 (New York *Times:* "Standard Oil Gave $100,000," 9 Sept 1907, 1; "Roosevelt Says Big Gifts Didn't Purchase Favor," 5 Oct 1912, 1).

135.2–7   In a printed statement, Judge Parker now says . . . willing to sell them] Parker's statement appeared in the New York *World* on 11 September 1907, and was widely reprinted.

135.11–16   For years the rich corporations have furnished vast sums . . . Mr. Roosevelt saw that it would be popular to attack the great corporations] The Republican party had traditionally been friendly to big business and enjoyed its support; but Roosevelt's first term gave unmistakable signs that he aimed to restrict the power of corporations along the lines mandated by the Sherman Antitrust Act of 1890. In 1902 he shocked Wall Street by filing an antitrust suit against the Northern Securities Company. The next year, he clashed with Standard Oil by sponsoring antitrust legislation; and upon reelection in 1904, he ordered an investigation of the petroleum industry, intending to break up Standard Oil. In this context, Clemens's claim that Roosevelt had been bought by the corporations, but failed to "stay bought," hardly seems tenable (Murphy 2011, 156–60; "President Threatens an Extra Session," New York *Times,* 8 Feb 1903, 1; "Investigation of Standard Oil Ordered," San Francisco *Chronicle,* 19 Nov 1904, 1).

135.21–22   This judge has fined the Standard Oil Company twenty-nine million . . . dollars, upon a quibble] On 13 April 1907, in the Chicago federal court of Judge Kenesaw

Mountain Landis, a jury found Standard Oil of Indiana guilty of multiple violations of the Elkins Act. Standard Oil had accepted illegal discounted rates, or "rebate," on transportation of its oil by the Chicago and Alton Railway Company. Because the indictment treated each delivery of oil as a separate criminal act, the indictment contained 1,903 counts, each of them bearing a substantial fine. In August 1907, Judge Landis imposed fines totaling $29.24 million. In his notebook, Clemens recorded the quip of an unidentified person—Rogers, perhaps: "Fining the Standard Oil Co $29,240,000 reminded him of the June bride's remark: 'I expected it but didn't suppose it would be so big'" (Notebook 48, TS p. 19, CU-MARK; New York *Times:* "Standard Oil Found Guilty," 14 Apr 1907, 1; "Judge's Decision Imposing the Fine," 4 Aug 1907, 2).

135.23–24   It is quite unlikely that a higher court will affirm the decision] On appeal, Judge Landis's August 1907 decision was reversed, and a new trial was ordered. Judge Anderson, of the district of Indiana, disallowed the counting of each shipment as an individual act, reducing the number of counts and the size of any possible fines. At the close of proceedings in March 1909, Judge Anderson instructed the jury to acquit. The government abandoned the case. Standard Oil was broken up under antitrust law in 1911 ("Government Abandons $29,240,000 Case against the Standard Oil Co.," *Wall Street Journal,* 11 Mar 1909, 2).

135.26   He has sent Secretary Taft around the world] From September to December 1907 William Howard Taft, then Roosevelt's secretary of war, made a 123-day tour around the world, sailing from Seattle and visiting heads of state in Japan, the Philippines, and Russia before returning via the Atlantic ("Taft Home Again, Mum on Politics," New York *Times,* 21 Dec 1907, 1).

135.28–29   He is sending the United States navy to San Francisco . . . all for advertisement] See the Autobiographical Dictation of 18 October 1907, note at 173.10.

135.41–136.3   In six months he has reduced the value of every species of property . . . it is not worth more than ninety billions now] Clemens blames Roosevelt's antitrust policy for the slump of 1907 (which would soon be eclipsed by the panic of the same year; see AD, 1 Nov 1907). The total wealth of the United States was reported in early 1907 as slightly more than $107 billion, not the $114 billion that Clemens asserts. An article in the New York *Times* of 15 August 1907 estimated that stock values had declined $3 billion over the last three weeks. Clemens could have applied this conjectural rate of loss to the last six months to arrive at his figure of $24 billion lost, giving a new value of "ninety billions" (New York *Times:* "U.S. Wealth in 1904 Was $107,104,192,410," 24 Mar 1907, 10; "Roosevelt Blamed for Wall St. Slump," 15 Aug 1907, 1, 2).

136.10–18   he is going to review the Mississippi . . . to ameliorate the condition of that useless river—apparently that, really to feed the Republican vote] In May 1907 Roosevelt announced that he planned to make an October journey down the Mississippi by steamboat. The excursion was sponsored by the Lakes-to-the-Gulf Deep Waterways Association, a group of businessmen who lobbied for the improvement of the Mississippi and its tributaries. If artificially deepened to accommodate freight ships, the river system, which was public property, could offer competition to the railroads, which were owned and controlled by wealthy men. The project had Roosevelt's approval, but Clemens's contrary view of "the Mississippi Improvement conspirators" was not purely reactive: improvements of this kind had been discussed for decades, and Clemens derided them in chapter 28 of *Life on the Mississippi* (1883). His claim that the river-improvements lobby fed "the Republican vote" has not been substantiated; at this period, both Democrats and Republicans favored the improvements ("Jaunt for President," Washington *Post,* 19 May 1907, 12; "World's Greatest Waterway Indorsed by President," New York *Times,* 6 Oct 1907, SM1; Democratic National Committee 1908, 15).

136.25–33   Three or four weeks ago the Mayor of Cairo invited me . . . which said I had "declined" to pilot the President's boat] Clemens, staying in Tuxedo Park in July 1907, declined an invitation from the mayor of Cairo, Illinois, where the presidential tour was going to be launched, on 29 July. A few days later he received and declined an invitation from the city of Memphis, where the tour would end with a convention of the Lakes-to-the-Gulf Association (29 July 1907 to Parsons, InU-Li; Lakes-to-the-Gulf Association to SLC, 31 Aug 1907, CU-MARK; 26 and 27 Sept 1907 to Edmonds, Baton Rouge *State Times–New Advocate,* 20 Feb 1911, 2).

136.35–36   some poetry has resulted . . . it advertises me] The poem that follows is by Clemens's second cousin William James Lampton, the grandson of one of Jane Clemens's paternal uncles. He became a journalist in the 1870s, and was best known as a contributor of satirical verses to the New York papers (*AutoMT1,* 642 n. 450.13–19; "Colonel W. J. Lampton, Newspaper Poet, Dead," *Editor and Publisher* 49 [2 June 1917]: 29).

Autobiographical Dictation, 26 September 1907

137.40   Commodore Cornelius Vanderbilt] Cornelius Vanderbilt III (1873–1942) was the great-grandson of the first Cornelius Vanderbilt (1796–1877), who gained a fortune from shipping, railroads, and finance. Cornelius III earned several degrees at Yale, including one in mechanical engineering, and patented more than thirty devices for railroads. An avid yachtsman, he was commodore of the New York Yacht Club from 1906 to 1908 ("Gen. C. Vanderbilt Dies on His Yacht," New York *Times,* 2 Mar 1942, 21, 24).

137.40–41   challenge of Sir Thomas Lipton . . . for the America's Cup was rejected] Sir Thomas Lipton (1848–1931), the tea merchant, challenged the New York Yacht Club for the America's Cup five times between 1899 and 1930, always in vessels named *Shamrock.*

138.4   Lewis Cass Ledyard . . . J. Pierpont Morgan] Lewis Cass Ledyard (1851–1932), a preeminent New York lawyer, was personal counsel to ultra-rich financier J. Pierpont Morgan. Both were prominent members of the New York Yacht Club ("L. Cass Ledyard, Noted Lawyer, Dies," New York *Times,* 28 Jan 1932, 21).

138.11   the *Columbia,* the *Reliance*] The *Columbia,* built in 1899 for J. Pierpont Morgan, successfully defended the America's Cup against Lipton's challenges in 1899 and 1901. The *Reliance,* owned by a consortium of eight members of the New York Yacht Club, defeated Lipton's *Shamrock III* in 1903. Both vessels were extreme examples of design for speed alone, and were unsuited to any use except racing ("Big Sloops Are Ready," New York *Tribune,* 20 Aug 1903, 1).

138.22   with none so poor to do it honor] Compare *Julius Caesar,* act 3, scene 2: "And none so poor to do him reverence."

138.23   a World's Fair has been struggling along at Jamestown, Virginia] For the Jamestown Ter-Centennial, see the Autobiographical Dictation of 18 May 1907, note at 51.36–37. Unlike the admired and remunerative World's Fairs in Chicago (1893), Buffalo (1901), and St. Louis (1904), the Jamestown fair was not a success. Its site (at Norfolk, Virginia) had poor accommodations and bad transportation, the planning committee was plagued with controversy, and low revenues landed the fair in debt and bankruptcy (de Ruiter 2013).

138.25   the first effort of white people to establish a colony in America] Jamestown might be called the first enduring colony of Europeans in North America, but it was not the "first effort" in that line, having been preceded by various Spanish and French settlements, and by Sir Walter Raleigh's failed colony at Roanoke, Virginia.

138.26–28   I went down with Mr. H. H. Rogers . . . opening of the Fair] See the Autobiographical Dictation of 18 May 1907, note at 51.36–37.

138.32–34   Cornelius Vanderbilt is President of the Robert Fulton Monument Fund Association . . . Major General Fred Grant] For the Robert Fulton Memorial Association and Frederick D. Grant, see *AutoMT1,* 426–28 and notes on 630–31. For its president, Cornelius Vanderbilt, see the note at 137.40.

138.37   the dishonorable Funston] Clemens criticized Frederick Funston for his treacherous capture of Emilio Aguinaldo, the leader in the fight for Filipino independence, in the Autobiographical Dictation of 14 March 1906 (see *AutoMT1,* 408, 618 n. 408.30–42).

140.35–141.1   Very well, our orator had failed . . . go down in the yacht and introduce him] Clemens and the Fulton Day planners learned in July 1907 that Grover Cleveland would be unavailable to speak at the 23 September festivities. "But we can get Choate," wrote Clemens, "he said he would come to the rescue if Mr. Cleveland failed us. So I am comfortable" (27 July 1907 to CC, CtHMTH). Clemens offered Joseph H. Choate the oratorship and passage to the exposition on board Rogers's yacht (Rogers was not going himself, having suffered a serious stroke on 22 July). The invitation was a blunder: Rogers and Choate were on bad terms, and Choate was unwelcome on the *Kanawha.* Now Choate proved to be unavailable, and Clemens tried to beg off, pleading exhaustion, but the organizers of Fulton Day were insistent on his presence. Clemens now had Isabel

Lyon write to Mrs. Rogers to ask if Columbia University president Nicholas Murray Butler would be an "acceptable" guest on the *Kanawha*. Rogers himself replied:

> I note that you are getting into trouble in that Jamestown matter. I think you make a mistake in trying to advertise a man like Butler. People of Virginia don't want to see him. They want Mark Twain. If you cannot see that, I can. . . . If you do not want to speak, just get into the background, and take along with you such good fellows as W. J. Howells, Peter Dunne and Geo. Harvey. . . .
>
> If your modesty prevents you from making a suggestion in the matter, just send this letter along to Mr. Tucker, chairman of the Committee. I don't think since you have been in Europe you know as much as you used to. I am sure that this is right because I am always so. You had better consider yourself under orders at once. However, if you and your stupidity have a different idea, why let us have that, but you will never make any success unless you do what people want you to do. (Rogers to SLC, 30 Aug 1907, CU-MARK, in *HHR,* 636–37)

Clemens replied:

> *No,* sir! no literary ragtag & bobtail for *me*—on a gala excursion. Why, Uncle Henry, down there there's going to be fireworks, & balls & banquets & receptions & all kinds of light & frolicsome goings-on, & the elderly people you have mentioned would be quite out of harmony with it. And besides, I don't like the society of old people, anyway; I am not suited to it, I am not used to it, & I'll be d & I'm—
>
> —Never mind, this is Sunday, & no proper time to discuss such a d— such an ——
> Oh, let it *go!* I never heard of such a godda—
>
> ———
>
> *Noon.* I have read a chapter, & oh, the healing of the perturbed spirit that is in the Good Book. (1 Sept 1907 to Rogers, IEN)

When Butler declined, the oratorship fell to Martin W. Littleton (29 July 1907 to Rogers, CtHMTH, in *HHR,* 630–32 n. 2; 3 Aug 1907 to Choate, facsimile in CU-MARK; Emilie Rogers to SLC, 15 Aug 1907, CU-MARK, in *HHR,* 632–33; SLC *per* Lyon to Emilie Rogers, 27 Aug 1907, Salm, in *HHR,* 634–35).

141.5   Mr. Littleton, of New York] Martin W. Littleton (see AD, 1 Nov 1907, note at 179.28).

141.34–35   a pair of little black cheese-box models of Ericsson's *Monitor*] The *Monitor,* designed for the Union navy by inventor John Ericsson (1803–89), was a pioneering ironclad warship with an armored revolving turret. Ridiculed at first as resembling "a cheese-box on a raft," on 9 March 1862 the *Monitor* proved its worth at the Battle of Hampton Roads (just off the site of the 1907 Jamestown Exposition), and gave its name to an entire class of vessels. Present on Fulton Day was the *Canonicus,* the last remaining vessel of the monitor type, which had been expensively refurbished for the fair but which seems to have attracted little interest. Clemens omits, but newspapers reported, the four-mile long parade of "a score or more vessels . . . representing every type of steam craft, from the time of Robert Fulton to the present" ("Mark Twain's Wit Delights Them All," Richmond [Va.] *Times-Dispatch,* 24 Sept 1907, 1, 2; "Battle Ships of Five Nations," [Boise] *Idaho Statesman,* 28 Apr 1907, 7; "Monitor Fails to Attract," Washington *Post,* 15 Nov 1907, 11).

142.2–3   Admiral Harrington . . . followed by Captain Collins of the *Brooklyn*] Rear admiral P. F. Harrington came out of retirement to officiate on Fulton Day. Captain John B. Collins was commander of the armored cruiser *Brooklyn,* which was on loan to the exposition (Syracuse University Library 2013; U.S. Bureau of Navigation 1908).

142.29–30   Robert Fulton Cutting consented to introduce the others] Cutting was a wealthy New York philanthropist (see AD, 8 Dec 1908, note at 283.37).

142.30   Harry and my adoptive niece, his wife] Henry Huddleston Rogers, Jr. (1879–1935), was his father's youngest child and only son. He was an energetic teenager when Clemens first knew him; he called him "the Prince of Activity" and "the Electric Spark." In 1900 Rogers married Mary Benjamin (1879–1956), who was from a cultured New York family. Starting in earnest in 1906, Clemens developed a particularly close friendship with Mary; she was then twenty-five and the mother of two young children (Lewis Leary 1961, 12, 37–38; *HHR,* 743, 744).

142.34   Fulton's boat, the *Clermont*] Fulton's pioneering steam vessel was registered as the *North River Steam Boat* but came to be known, erroneously, as the *Clermont.* Its successful run from New York to Albany in 1807 demonstrated that steam power could be used for river transportation.

142.36   the great banqueting hall of the Chamberlin] The luxurious 554-room Hotel Chamberlin opened in 1896 at Old Point Comfort, across the harbor from the site of the Jamestown Exposition (Quarstein and Clevenger 2009, 54–58).

142.38–39   brilliant speech by Mrs. McLean] Mrs. McLean (1859–1916), born Emily Ritchie in Frederick, Maryland, was a charter member of the Daughters of the American Revolution and a noted public speaker ("Mrs. Donald McLean Dead," New York *Times,* 20 May 1916, 11).

Autobiographical Dictation, 1 October 1907

144.4–5   Mr. and Mrs. Henniker Heaton] For John Henniker Heaton, see the Autobiographical Dictation of 22 August 1907, note at 106.21.

144.5   the King's garden party at Windsor] On the afternoon of 22 June 1907 King Edward VII hosted a gigantic garden party on the grounds of Windsor Castle. There were an estimated eight thousand guests, drawn from the ranks of aristocracy, government, the military, and artists (Lathem 2006, 25–30).

144.6   Sir Thomas Lipton] See the Autobiographical Dictation of 26 September 1907, note at 137.40–41.

144.30–31   Ellen Terry . . . her new husband] For Ellen Terry, and Clemens's (presumed) 1872 meeting with her and Henry Irving, see *AutoMT2,* 467 nn. 19.4–7, 19.17–18. She had married her third husband, American actor James Carew (1876–1938), in March 1907. Carew was thirty-one. The marriage broke up in 1910.

144.33–35   the first meeting was at a large dinner-party at Mr. Bateman's house—the father of the "Bateman Children." . . . in St. Louis, in 1858] Hezekiah L. Bateman (1812–75) was born in Maryland and began his theatrical career as an actor. He devoted many years to furthering the career of his daughters, the child-actress duo of Kate (1842–1917) and Ellen (1844–1936), who won fame in America and England with their precocious acting of scenes from classic drama and comedy afterpieces. Clemens later remembered Kate Bateman as "a gentle-looking little school girl of 12 or 13 when I used to see her in her front yard playing, every day" (28 Nov 1869 to OLL, *L3,* 412–14). The Batemans were based in St. Louis from November 1855 until 1859; Clemens did not reside there during this time, but could have seen Kate Bateman on a visit to the city, where his mother and Pamela were living. In 1871, Hezekiah Bateman assumed the management of the Lyceum Theatre in London. The dinner party Clemens remembers at Bateman's house in London is undocumented (28 Nov 1869 to OLL, *L3,* 412–14, n. 5; "Mark Twain's 1872 English Journals," *L5,* 629 n. 92).

145.10–12   "The Bells" or "The Lyons Mail" . . . He astonished Irving by asking him to take his place] Clemens is mistaken in asserting that Irving took over from Bateman as the tragic lead. It was Irving who was keen to play in *The Bells* (a melodrama, adapted by Leopold Lewis from the French)—so much so that, even though he was substantially an unknown, he made it a condition of his contract with Bateman's theater company. Bateman was reluctant to stage the play, and never had any intention of playing the lead. Irving's triumph in *The Bells,* an overnight success in 1871, inaugurated his climb to the head of his profession. *The Lyons Mail,* a melodrama adapted by Charles Reade from a French original, was first performed in 1854. Irving revived it at the Lyceum Theatre in 1877, playing two lead roles; the play was strongly identified with him and remained in his repertoire to the end of his life (Richards 2005, 159, 401–3).

145.17   Duke of Connaught and his heir; the King of Siam and his heir] Clemens mentions: Arthur, Duke of Connaught (1850–1942), third son of Victoria and Albert; his son, Prince Arthur, who a few days later would receive an honorary degree from Oxford at the same ceremony as Clemens (see AD, 26 July 1907, note at 82.31–35); Chulalongkorn, the westernizing King of Siam (1853–1910); and his son, Prince Vajiravudh (1881–1925).

145.23–35   newspaper said I patted his Majesty on the shoulder . . . newspaper which said I talked with her Majesty with my hat on] All the details of which Clemens complains appeared in dozens of newspapers worldwide; see, for example, "Mark Twain at Windsor," London *Observer,* 23 June 1907, 7, and "Garden Party Splendour," London *Express,* 24 June 1907, 1 (both excerpted in Lathem 2006, 26–29). For Clemens's earlier meeting with the future Edward VII at Homburg, see *AutoMT2*, 179–82, 546 n. 181.31–36.

Autobiographical Dictation, 2 October 1907

146.6–7 Liverpool . . . Lord Mayor's banquet in the evening] Clemens initially declined the invitation of the Lord Mayor of Liverpool (John Japp); but he subsequently decided to extend his stay in England by one week, and informed the Lord Mayor he would be able to visit on 10 July (4? May 1907 to Japp; Ashcroft for SLC to Japp, 19 June 1907 and 21 June 1907; all in CU-MARK).

146.14–17 T. P. O'Connor . . . we made the trip together—in quite unusual comfort] Clemens left London for Liverpool on 10 July, accompanied by Ashcroft and T. P. O'Connor (for the latter, see AD, 22 Aug 1907, note at 106.26). To a request from Liverpool's Lord Mayor, John Japp, W. N. Turnbull of the London and North Western Railway replied that Clemens would be provided with a "saloon with one bed made up, to be attached to the 12-10 p.m. train from Euston to Liverpool on July 10th., and this vehicle will be retained for the return journey the next day, and I shall be glad if you will advise me the train by which Mr. Clemens will leave for London. An Attendant will be sent with the Saloon." According to the London *Globe*, "Mr. Clemens at once retired on entering the car, and Mr. T. P. O'Connor, who made the journey with him, stated that he had had a bad night, and needed rest." (The *Punch* dinner was the night before.) The London *Evening Standard* noted that the car "was formerly the Prince of Wales's saloon." The train arrived at Liverpool's Lime Street Station at about four o'clock (Turnbull to Japp, 29 June 1907, enclosed with Japp to SLC, 1 July 1907, CU-MARK; "Mark Twain Goes North," London *Globe*, 10 July 1907, unknown page, in Scrapbook 31:128, CU-MARK; Lathem 2006, 106, quoting "Mark Twain," London *Evening Standard*, 10 July 1907, 9).

146.27–28 The banquet was just over when he conducted me into the banqueting hall, so the speech-making began at once] The timing was specified by Clemens, who instructed Ashcroft to write to the Lord Mayor from London on 22 June (CU-MARK):

> My dear Lord Mayor:
> Mr. Clemens directs me to say that, in his own country, when attending banquets—even those given in his honor—he is usually granted the privilege of arriving towards the end of the dinner, in order that he may not be fatigued when he is called upon to speak. He would very much like that this privilege be extended to him by you at the proposed banquet in Liverpool next month.
> While Mr. Clemens is remarkably well and vigorous for a man of his years, he easily tires; and I know that, if you will grant him the privilege he asks for, he will be in better form for addressing those present. He will go to bed as soon as he arrives in Liverpool in the afternoon, and remain there until it is time for him to join you at the Town Hall.

146.30 I copy from the newspaper] The newspaper passages quoted in this dictation are from an article entitled "Mark Twain in Liverpool," in the Liverpool *Post* of 11 July 1907. Ashcroft pasted the entire article into Scrapbook 32 (32:130–32, CU-MARK) and Clemens revised it in ink, correcting and adapting it for use in the *Autobiography*.

147.21–23 as I ventured to say . . . some time ago, Mark Twain has come to his own] O'Connor refers to his article published on 29 June in his magazine *P.T.O.* (T. P. O'Connor 1907, in Scrapbook 32:65–66, CU-MARK).

147.35–37 In a speech which I heard . . . he uttered something approaching to an apology for the humour of his works] O'Connor attended the luncheon given for Mark Twain by the London Society of Pilgrims on 25 June, where he asked the audience to "forgive" his "chaffing and chaffing and chaffing here": see the Autobiographical Dictation of 25 July 1907, 80.41–42.

148.14 the poem of James Russell Lowell] O'Connor alludes to a line from Lowell's "Ode Recited at the Harvard Commemoration" (1865): "New birth of our new soil, the first American."

148.29–38 Sir Walter Scott became a member of a great publishing firm . . . he died in his work] O'Connor picks up this comparison from the speech made by Augustine Birrell at the Pilgrims' luncheon on 25 June. See the Autobiographical Dictation of 25 July 1907 and the note at 77.24–26.

149.41–42 an anecdote in Dana's "Two Years Before the Mast."] For the process by which Clemens, over many years, adapted and transformed this anecdote from chapter 35 of the best-known work of Richard Henry Dana, Jr. (1815–82), see Gribben 1980, 1:171–73.

150.21–22 thirty-five years before . . . I had once lectured there] Clemens first performed in Liverpool on 20 October 1873, giving his Sandwich Islands lecture just before sailing for home with Olivia and Susy. Returning to Britain unaccompanied in November, he again appeared in Liverpool on the homeward leg of his journey, giving his "Roughing It" and his Sandwich Islands lectures on 9 and 10 January 1874, respectively (22 Oct 1873 to Unidentified, *L5,* 458 n. 1; 12 Jan 1874 to Finlay, *L6,* 19–20 n. 1).

150.24 some final dissipations on the 12th] Clemens's activities on 12 July 1907 included a visit to the National Gallery, as the guest of its recently appointed director, Sir Charles Holroyd (1861–1917), and lunch with Lord and Lady Portsmouth (for whom see AD, 30 Aug 1907, note at 121.5; Ashcroft 1907, 5).

Autobiographical Dictation, 3 October 1907

150.31–32 Lieutenant General Nelson A. Miles] Nelson Appleton Miles (1839–1925) had a brilliant military career, despite his lack of formal education. He fought in the Civil War and was wounded four times. After the war, in July 1866, he become a colonel in the regular army, and in March 1867 was awarded the brevet of brigadier general for distinguished gallantry at the Battle of Chancellorsville. From 1869 until the early 1890s he campaigned against Indian tribes in the West, and afterward he fought in the Spanish-American War. In 1880 he became a brigadier general in the regular army, and in 1901 was advanced to the rarely used rank of lieutenant general. From 1895 until his retirement in 1903 he was Commanding General of the U.S. Army. During these years his outspoken criticism of military and administrative policies brought him into conflict with the War Department and with President Roosevelt, who privately called him a "dangerous foe and slanderer of the army which he was supposed to command" (Ranson 1965–66, 191–200).

150.32   was given a great dinner party in New York] No New York dinner honoring Miles has been identified. Clemens is probably remembering an occasion of 12 March 1907, when he shared a box with Miles at an afternoon performance at the Hudson Theatre and afterwards attended a dinner party hosted by banker and railroad director Colgate Hoyt and his wife. Lyon reported in her journal: "Mr. Clemens dined at the Hoyts where Gen. Miles was a guest, he had a very good time, the lady who sat on his right 'was very intelligent, she talked about adultery as if she knew all about it'" (Lyon 1907, entry for 12 Mar; see also AD, 28 Mar 1907, note at 18.1–2).

150.38–151.5   Washington in 1867 . . . brigadier-generalship in the regular army] Clemens spent the winter of 1867–68 in Washington, where he worked briefly as a secretary for Senator William M. Stewart of Nevada and corresponded for several newspapers (*AutoMT1*, 472–73 n. 67.6–13). At that time Miles was a colonel; he did not attain the rank of brigadier general in the regular army until 1880, nor had he yet campaigned in the Indian Wars (see the note at 150.31–32)

151.13–14   *Quaker City* Excursion . . . Bliss of Hartford to write "The Innocents Abroad."] Clemens describes his early dealings with Elisha Bliss of the American Publishing Company and the publication of *The Innocents Abroad* (1869) in the Autobiographical Dictation of 21 May 1906 (*AutoMT2*, 48–49 and notes on 486–87).

151.16–19   William Swinton, brother of the historian . . . first Newspaper Syndicate on the planet] Clemens discusses his association with Swinton, a former Civil War correspondent for the New York *Times,* in the Autobiographical Dictation of 15 January 1906. Swinton's older brother, John, was a journalist and social reformer. None of the letters published through the syndicate has been positively identified, although at least two works reprinted in the Cincinnati *Evening Chronicle* on 9 and 13 March 1868 ("An Important Question Settled" and "General Spinner as a Religious Enthusiast") could easily be products of this syndicate, since their place of first publication is not known (SLC 1868a, 1868b; *AutoMT1*, 281–82, 562–63 n. 281.39–41).

154.25   Now then, that is the tale] Clemens soon retold this story in a speech at a dinner given in his honor by the Pleiades Club in New York on 22 December 1907 ("How Mark Twain 'Worked' Gen. Miles," New York *Times,* 23 Dec 1907, 5).

Autobiographical Dictation, 5 October 1907

154.29–35 Robert Porter arrived from England ... by cable, without expense]
Robert P. Porter (1852–1917) was born in England, but emigrated to the United States in
the mid-1860s and became a journalist, working for a succession of newspapers including
the Chicago *Inter-Ocean,* the Rockford (Ill.) *Gazette,* the Philadelphia *Press,* and the New
York *Tribune.* He married in 1874, but in 1884 he divorced his first wife and married Alice
Russell Hobbins (1853–1926), also born in England but raised in Madison, Wisconsin;
they had four children. A newspaper correspondent in her own right, Alice was on the
staffs of the New York *Daily Graphic* and the Chicago *Inter-Ocean,* successively. Robert
founded the New York *Press* in 1887, with Alice on the staff. In the 1890s the couple lived
in Washington, D.C., where Robert served as director of the Eleventh United States
Census, traveling also on special assignments for the government. In 1904 he joined the
London *Times,* becoming its principal Washington correspondent in 1906. The "special
mission" which brought him to America in 1907 has not been identified. On 12 September, aboard the *Lusitania,* he received Clemens's invitation to Tuxedo Park; he was
met by Ashcroft at the dock in New York, and arrived in Tuxedo Park on 14 September.
Lyon described him in her journal as "a sturdy chunky Englishman, & very agreeable &
hearty. He enjoyed his food & the house & Tuxedo & seemingly everything" ("Robert
P. Porter," Chicago *Tribune,* 12 June 1884, 3; Jackson and Jackson 1951, 13; Willard and
Livermore 1893, 2:582–83; Lyon 1907, entries for 12 and 14 Sept; Porter to SLC, 13 Sept
1907, CU-MARK; for the *Lusitania* see the note at 155.33–41).

155.25–28 Mr. Bryan's name ... permanent candidate for the Presidency] See the
Autobiographical Dictation of 14 July 1908, note at 258.18–19.

155.33–41 When the *Lusitania* was half way across the Atlantic ... correct figure
by only *six minutes*] At the time of her maiden voyage, the Cunard RMS *Lusitania* was
the largest steamship in the world, measuring 790 feet and accommodating twenty-two
hundred passengers with a crew of over eight hundred. The transatlantic crossing from
Queenstown (Ireland) to Sandy Hook, from 7 to 13 September 1907, established a speed
record of slightly over five days, about six hours less than the previous record. As a special
correspondent for the London *Times,* Porter described the crowds assembled to cheer the
ship's departure and arrival, and explained that fog and a desire not to strain the steam-
powered propellers prevented an even faster crossing. After arrival on 13 September he
reported: "I find that I am a few minutes wrong in my calculations of the probable length
of the Lusitania's passage sent to *The Times* by wireless telegraphy during the week. I
apologize. The time was 5 days 54 min., not 5 days 1 hour. The average speed was 23.01
knots, not 23, as I estimated" ("The Lusitania's Voyage," London *Times,* 14 Sept 1907,
5; "Lusitania's Maiden Trip," *Wall Street Journal,* 14 Sept 1907, 7; "Lusitania Here at 9
A.M. To-day," New York *Times,* 13 Sept 1907, 1).

156.1–2 Francesca and her mother ... spent a couple of days with us] Frances Nunnally and her mother, Cora, visited Tuxedo Park on 28–30 September. Lyon recorded in

her journal that Clemens was "so gay & sweet & pretty in his ways with 'Francesca' who is a dear grave girl of 16, with the most wonderful little slender hands." The weather was poor, and the party spent much of the time playing hearts (Lyon 1907, entries for 28 and 30 Sept; for Nunnally see AD, 25 July 1907, and note at 74.15–21).

156.2–3   Ten days earlier Dorothy . . . society during seven days and nights] Clemens had met ten-year-old Dorothy Gertrude Quick (1896–1962) of Plainfield, New Jersey, on board the SS *Minnetonka,* while coming home from England in July 1907. She was traveling with her mother, Emma Gertrude Quick, and her grandparents (her father was no longer living with his family). Her 3–12 September visit to Tuxedo Park was the second since their return; she had first stayed there on 5–9 August. On 15 August Clemens wrote to her mother, "Every day & every hour of her brief stay, Dorothy was a delight & a blessing, & every night it cost me a pang to let her go to bed. Hers is a most beautiful & lovable character, & she will never lack for adoring friends while she lives" (Quick 1961, 11; 1 Aug 1907 and 15 Aug 1907 to Quick, CU-MARK; Lyon 1907, entries for 3 and 12 Sept; Schmidt 2009). Clemens's warm friendship with Dorothy continued until his death. She bequeathed her letters from Clemens to the Mark Twain Papers; their extensive correspondence is published in *Mark Twain's Aquarium* (Cooley 1991).

156.8–9   Dorothy is possessed with the idea of becoming a writer . . . privilege to me to egg her on] In a letter written after Dorothy's first visit, Clemens advised her:

> It is a good idea, to choose a name in advance, & then fit the literature onto it when the literature comes. I will keep on the lookout for a fortunate name, dear. Write another little story, now, & send it to me. It will take you several years to learn to do a story even *tolerably* well, & it will cost lots of good hard work, & patient thought, & sharp attention, & close observations, & ever so much tearing-up & re-writing—but no matter, it's worth the trouble; & no trade is ever well learned on any other terms. (17, 18, 19, 21, and 22 Aug 1907, CU-MARK, in Cooley 1991, 52–54)

For Dorothy's pen name Clemens suggested "Nebraska Chesterfield," "Oregon Trail," and "Oregon de Baragay" (Lyon 1907, entry for 23 Aug). Quick ultimately did become a writer, producing several volumes of poems, mystery novels, and a memoir of her friendship with Mark Twain (Quick 1961). In addition to recounting her meeting with Clemens, her visits to Tuxedo Park (and later, to Stormfield), and his encouragement, she described him working on the autobiography:

> Mr. Clemens would walk up and down the room while he was dictating, and the dictation sounded more as though he were talking conversationally than creating a story. He would pace back and forth, his hands behind his back, speaking continuously in his slow, drawling way. Often he would say things that the stenographer would think were just funny little by-comments on the story, but which he actually meant to be in the completed manuscript. Thinking they were Mr. Clemens' personal observations or for her own benefit, she would leave them out of the script.
> Later, when he had finished dictating and turned to correcting the typed manu-

script of the work of the day before, he would discover this and break out into fiery explosions of rage because she had left out something he had particularly wanted in the manuscript. His anger would last several minutes, and then he would calm down very suddenly and dismiss it entirely from his mind, for the time being at any rate. (Quick 1961, 62)

Autobiographical Dictation, 7 October 1907

158.6–7   Mrs. M. was here yesterday afternoon] Clemens's visitors were Marion Peak Mason (1872?–1929) and her husband, George Grant Mason (1868–1955). The Masons had become suddenly wealthy in May 1907, when George inherited $12 million from an uncle. They moved to New York from South Dakota, where he had worked as a division superintendent for a railroad. Mrs. Mason was a Christian Scientist, and Clemens engaged her in a spirited conversation, in which (according to Lyon) he "pointed out how God isn't good in a single instance, & those 2 Masons sat amazed & enchanted & horrified. He said things the like of which they had never even imagined a person could say" (Lyon 1907, entry for 6 Oct; *Tuxedo Census* 1910, 1060:24A; "Mrs. George G. Mason Dies at Tuxedo Park," New York *Times,* 4 Aug 1929, N33; "Smith Heir Quits Work," Chicago *Tribune,* 17 May 1907, 9).

158.7–9   a story which she said was on its rounds in Tuxedo Park . . . a lady for whom I have a strong but concealed aversion] Repeating this anecdote to H. H. Rogers on 8 October, Clemens added: "It is all wrong, I give you my word. It didn't happen in Tuxedo at all; it was New York. And more than a year ago, at that. And it wasn't a lady, it was a man. A man whom I detest" (Salm, in *HHR,* 641–42).

158.28–30   Sioux Falls, S.D. . . . Dear Sir:] This anecdote was written on a postcard sent by a music dealer in Sioux Falls to the Ziegler Publishing Company in New York, which forwarded it to Clemens. He wrote on it, "Received from the Zeigler people & dictated into my Autobiog. Oct. 7" (CU-MARK). On 11 January 1908 Clemens used a version of this anecdote in a speech he gave at the Lotos Club on "collecting compliments" (Fatout 1976, 603–11).

159.4–15   extracts from Omar Khayyam on the first page of this morning's Courant . . . 1879] This Autobiographical Dictation is the unique source for the letter from Joseph H. Twichell, which was written in 1875 (not 1879). The article Twichell refers to, which appeared on the front page of the Hartford *Courant* of 22 December 1875 ("Omar Khayyam. The Astronomer-Poet of Persia"), comprised biographical information about the poet followed by forty-two quatrains quoted "at random" from the book. No mention was made of the translator, Edward Fitzgerald; none of the editions published before his death, in 1883, included his name. Clemens eventually owned several editions of the poem, by more than one translator (see Gribben 1980, 2:516–19; Potter 1929, 141).

Autobiographical Dictation, 10 October 1907

160.3 This morning's paper contains the following instances] The "instances" are all from the New York *World* of 10 October.

Autobiographical Dictation, 11 October 1907

162 *title* Dictated October 11, 1907] This Autobiographical Dictation was evidently created over the course of four days, with each day's work introduced by a summary. Presumably Clemens gathered the texts under one date because they treat the same topic, the art of platform reading.

163.3–4 impending marriage of Gladys . . . Vanderbilt, with Count Széchényi] Gladys Vanderbilt (1886–1965), a granddaughter of the first Cornelius Vanderbilt (see AD, 26 Sept 1907, note at 137.40), inherited $12.5 million when she turned twenty-one in August 1907. She met Count László Széchényi von Sárvár-Felsövidék (1879–1938) in Salzburg, and was formally betrothed at his family's home in Hungary; the pair were married in January 1908. The count—described in the New York *Times* as "a good sportsman and a charming type of the Hungarian cavalier"—came from a rich and powerful family of ancient Magyar lineage (New York *Times:* "Szechenyi Very Wealthy," 4 Oct 1907, 11; "Romantic Wooing of Miss Gladys Vanderbilt," 6 Oct 1907, SM5; "Count Szechenyi's Family Delighted with His Betrothal to Miss Vanderbilt," 27 Oct 1907, SM7; "Countess Laszlo Szechenyi, 78, Former Gladys Vanderbilt, Dies," 30 Jan 1965, 27).

163.8 I knew the head of it in Vienna nine or ten years ago] Clemens refers to László's older brother, Count Dionys Széchényi (1866–1936), who became the head of the family in March 1898 when his father died. He was the only one of his brothers to pursue a diplomatic career. A highly cultured and educated man, he earned a Doctor of Laws degree and served, among other assignments, as the Austro-Hungarian secretary of legation in Dresden and Munich. Clemens wrote in the notebook he used in Vienna in 1897–99, "Count (Sagehenyi) & his mother" and "Count Szecsen (Foreign Office)" (Notebook 42, TS pp. 5, 10, CU-MARK; "Count Szechenyi's Family Delighted with His Betrothal to Miss Vanderbilt," New York *Times,* 27 Oct 1907, SM7).

163.27–28 John Hay . . . Austrian court as our chargé d'affaires] Hay served as the chargé d'affaires in Vienna in 1867–68 (*AutoMT1,* 534 n. 222.9).

163.30–31 In Vienna Mrs. Clemens and I visited . . . a lady whom I had known when she was a young girl] Unidentified.

163.38–39 a young Scotch officer . . . saved the young Emperor's life] Maximilian Karl Lamoral Count O'Donnell (1812–95) was born in Vienna to a noble Irish family. He pursued a career in the Austrian army, becoming aide-de-camp to Emperor Franz Joseph I. In February 1853 he foiled an assassination attempt on the emperor by wounding his attacker, a Hungarian nationalist, with his saber. As a reward, the emperor made O'Donnell (already the son of a count) a count of the Austrian Empire, awarded him the cross of St. Leopold, and augmented his family arms to reflect these honors. In 1860 he married Franziska Wagner, a commoner, a union that Viennese society frowned upon (Burke 1866, 408–9).

163.40   *Hof-fähig*] Literally, "court admissible": admission to the court of Franz Joseph I required sixteen great-great-grandparents of noble blood, with the exception of military officers, whose rank qualified them (Johnston 1972, 39).

164.24–25   I had made my good-night bow to an audience in a South African town two years before] Clemens's last three scheduled performances on his world lecture tour were on 9, 10, and 11 July 1896 at the one-thousand-seat Opera House in Cape Town, South Africa. They were so well received that his agent booked a fourth and final appearance, on 12 July, at the Town Hall in nearby Claremont (Cooper 2000, 309–10).

164.31–32   I read for a charity the first time, in Vienna . . . the second time that I learned the art] Both of Clemens's readings for Vienna charities were at the request of Countess Misa Wydenbruck-Esterházy, a patroness of the arts who introduced the Clemenses to Viennese society and became their good friend. On the first occasion, 1 February 1898, the stories he told (from memory) included "Stolen Watermelon | Grandfather's Old Ram | Golden Arm. | Poem (Ornithorhyncus)"—all standard pieces from his 1895–96 world tour (Notebook 42, TS p. 55, CU-MARK). His second reading took place on 8 March 1899, when he shared the platform with the actress Auguste Wilbrandt-Baudius (1843–1937) (Dolmetsch 1992, 118, 132–38). In his notebook he wrote, "*March 8, '99, Vienna.* Read, this afternoon, with the poet Wilbrandt's wife, for one of the Countess Wydenbruck-Esterhazy's charities. [Lucerne Girl & Interviewer—had to leave out the Mexican Plug for lack of time.]" (Notebook 40, TS p. 56, CU-MARK). Later that year he told Howells of the "trick" he had learned in Vienna, presumably at this March event, where he read from a copy of the Tauchnitz edition of *Huckleberry Finn,* which he had marked and annotated (see "Mark Twain's Revisions for Public Reading, 1895–1896," *HF 2003,* 617–54):

> I meant to *read* from a Tauchnitz, because I knew I hadn't well memorised the pieces; & I came on with the book & read a few sentences, then remembered that the sketch needed a few words of explanatory introduction; & so, lowering the book & now & then unconsciously using it to gesture with, I talked the introduction, & it happened to carry me into the sketch *itself,* & then I went on, pretending that I was merely talking extraneous matter & would come to the sketch *presently.* It was a beautiful success. I knew the substance of the sketch & the *telling* phrases of it; & so, the throwing of the rest of it into informal talk as I went along limbered it up & gave it the snap & go & freshness of an impromptu. . . . Try it. You'll never lose your audience—not even for a moment. (26 Sept 1899 to Howells, NN-BGC, in *MTHL,* 2:705–6)

165.4   Charles Dickens . . . brought the idea with him from England in 1867] Dickens had great success with his public readings, and became strongly identified with the art of platform performance. He first read from his works in public in December 1853, reading his Christmas stories to a Birmingham adult school; five years later, financial necessity (and histrionic inclination) led him to tour commercially, giving selections from his novels. His performances were immensely popular and remunerative, and until the end of his life he returned to the platform regularly when he was not writing. His first American reading tour (he had toured there as a lecturer in 1842) began in Boston on 2 December 1867 and ended in New York on 20 April 1868. The tour's manager was George Dolby, who later arranged Clemens's 1873–74 lecture tour in Britain. Despite poor health, Dickens endured a grueling schedule and earned £19,000—the equivalent of over $2 million in today's dollars (Collins 2011; see 15 Sept 1872 to OLC, *L5*, 160 n. 1).

165.12   The family went to the Dickens reading, and I accompanied them] The "sweet and timid and lovely young girl" was of course Clemens's future wife, Olivia Langdon (on the date of this meeting, see *AutoMT1*, 355, 577 n. 320.32–34; and, for Clemens's newspaper report of the Dickens reading, *AutoMT1*, 508–9 n. 148.25–27).

165.22   the storm scene in which Steerforth lost his life] *David Copperfield*, chapter 55.

165.27–28   curious and artless industry called Authors' Readings] Clemens describes this "new and devilish invention" in the Autobiographical Dictation of 26 February 1906 (*AutoMT1*, 383–85).

165.33–166.6   I entered it in 1868 . . . I remained in the lecture field three seasons] Clemens relates some of his lecturing experiences in "Lecture-Times" and "Ralph Keeler" (*AutoMT1*, 146–54). His first tour, in the winter of 1868–69, was managed by G. L. Torbert. The second and third tours, in 1869–70 and 1870–71, were managed by the Boston Lyceum Bureau, run by James Redpath and George L. Fall. Temperance lecturer John B. Gough, liberal pastor Henry Ward Beecher, women's rights advocate Anna Dickinson, and social reformer Wendell Phillips were among Redpath's most popular lecturers in 1869–73. Clemens's fees typically ranged from $75 to $150, but occasionally reached $200; he paid his own expenses and gave Redpath a 10 percent commission (see *AutoMT1*, 508 n. 148.8, 511 n. 151.12–14; "Lecture Schedule, 1868–1870," *L3*, 481–86; *L4*: 8 Jan 1870 to Redpath, 11 n. 5; "Lecture Schedule, 1871–1872," 557–60; 23 Feb 1874 to Redpath, *L6*, 43 n. 1).

166.10–11   when I returned to the platform for a season, in 1884] See the note at 166.21–23.

166.15–17   Cable . . . had been born with a natural talent for it] George Washington Cable's career on the platform had barely begun—he had given only a few lectures and even fewer readings—when Clemens arranged and promoted his first public appearance in the North, on 4 April 1883 in Hartford. The reviewer for the Hartford *Courant* reported that Cable spoke "in a simple, unaffected manner, as if he were talking with friends in a drawing-room, in a fine and small voice, but sweet and penetrating." Nevertheless, neither he nor Clemens was satisfied with the performance. Cable feared that he had failed to project his voice sufficiently in the large hall; Clemens was ostensibly critical of the material, not the delivery. But on the following day Cable was enthusiastically received by the girls of the Saturday Morning Club. Clemens wrote to Cable's sister that "George W. partially defeated himself night before last by not making a good selection of reading matter; but he swept that all away by a splendid triumph yesterday morning" (6 Apr 1883 to Cox, CtHMTH; 9 Mar 1883 to Cable [1st], LNT; Rubin 1969, 120–31; "Mr. Cable's Readings," Hartford *Courant,* 5 Apr 1883, 2).

166.17–20   he prepared himself for his public work by taking lessons ... not half as pleasing and entertaining] Soon after his Hartford appearance, Cable began voice training with Franklin Haven Sargent (1856–1923), a noted elocution and drama coach who had taught at Harvard and founded what later became the American Academy of Dramatic Arts in New York. The immediate result, according to friends who heard him on 23 April at the Madison Square Theatre, was not an improvement, but a loss of richness in tone and variety of expression. Despite his belief that Sargent had not helped Cable, Clemens wrote to Pond in September 1884 that he wanted "Cable's elocutionist to give me a few lessons in strengthening up my voice for the platform campaign" in the coming winter (Turner 1956, 142, 172; 1 Sept 1884 to Pond, photocopy in CU-MARK).

166.21–23   I hired Major Pond ... we started out on our venture] After visiting Cable in New Orleans in the spring of 1882, Clemens proposed a joint tour with Cable, William Dean Howells, Charles Dudley Warner, Thomas Bailey Aldrich, and Joel Chandler Harris ("Uncle Remus")—an idea he had abandoned by late June, when none of the proposed readers was interested except Cable. By July 1884, however, he had revived the idea, inviting only Cable to join him. Lecture impresario James B. Pond acted on Clemens's behalf and negotiated a financial agreement with Cable, who agreed to be paid $450 (not $600) a week plus expenses. Pond would receive 10 percent of the net proceeds, with Clemens paying Pond's train fares but not hotel bills. The tour lasted from early November to the end of February 1885, taking in more than sixty cities in the East, Midwest, and Canada, with over a hundred performances. Clemens earned an estimated $17,000 after expenses (*AutoMT1,* 600 n. 381.14; Pond 1900, 490–96; Rubin 1969, 120–21; Cardwell 1953, 8–11).

166.24   I had selected my readings well enough] Clemens prepared two programs for use in cities where he appeared twice. The first consisted of readings from the forthcoming *Huckleberry Finn.* The second one varied, comprising four selections from a repertoire of about ten possible choices, none of them from *Huck* (see "Mark Twain's Revisions for Public Reading, 1884–1885," *HF 2003,* 578–616). Cable, in addition to reading from his novels and stories, sang Creole songs. The months spent together on tour did not improve their friendship. In fact, Clemens developed an intense aversion to many of Cable's habits—his tendency to usurp Clemens's time on the platform, his miserliness, and his strict observance of the Sabbath by refusing to travel—and he no longer admired Cable's reading skill; he now complained of his "self-complacency, sham feeling & labored artificiality" (5 May 1885 to Howells, NN-BGC, in *MTHL,* 2:527–29; 22 Dec 1884 to Pond, NN-BGC; 27 Feb 1885 to Howells, NN-BGC, in *MTHL,* 2:520–21; Cardwell 1953, 107–9).

166.35–36   One of the readings . . . "His Grandfather's Old Ram."] See *Roughing It,* chapter 53 (*RI 1993,* 361–68).

171.2–3   Pratt and Whitney's ingenious machine . . . five-millionth part of an inch] From 1882, the Hartford manufacturing firm of Pratt and Whitney invented and refined a succession of precision measuring machines. They also built for Clemens a prototype of the Paige typesetter (Pratt and Whitney 1930; "The Machine Episode," *AutoMT1,* 101–6 and notes on 494–98).

171.5–6   when I went reading around the world for the benefit of Mr. Webster's creditors] Clemens's 1895–96 world tour was undertaken to pay off the debts incurred by the failure of his publishing firm, Charles L. Webster and Company, whose titular head was his nephew (see *AutoMT2,* 57–59, 74–80, and notes on 492–504).

171.10–21   story of "The Golden Arm" . . . I had the pause rightly measured that time] See "My Autobiography [Random Extracts from It]," *AutoMT1,* 532–33 n. 217.25–27. Clemens quotes Susy's account of this Vassar reading in the Autobiographical Dictation of 7 March 1906 (*AutoMT1,* 394–95).

Autobiographical Dictation, 18 October 1907

172.13–15   Burns . . . for a' that] The lines are loosely quoted from the last verse of "Song: 'For a' That and a' That'" by Robert Burns (1795).

172.16   (Lord) LOREBURN, Lord High Chancellor of England] Robert Reid, Baron Loreburn (1846–1923), a Liberal politician, served as Lord Chancellor from 1905 to 1912.

172.26   (Ven. William Macdonald) SINCLAIR] William Macdonald Sinclair (1850–1917) was the archdeacon of London from 1889 to 1911.

172.30–32   Yesterday, for the first time . . . wireless messages sent entirely across the Atlantic] Guglielmo Marconi (1874–1937) of Italy received a British patent for a system of wireless telegraphy in 1896, and the following year founded the Wireless Telegraph and Signal Company of Britain. Although his device first transmitted a message from Newfoundland to Cornwall in December 1901, it was nearly six years before a regular transatlantic service was launched ("Dream of Marconi Realized at Last," Los Angeles *Times,* 18 Oct 1907, I4; "Marconi Opens Regular Service over Atlantic," New York *World,* 18 Oct 1907, 1).

172.32–173.3   on that same day the President . . . scour the State of Louisiana in search of the great hunter] The newspapers printed frequent front-page reports of President Roosevelt's October bear-hunting trip; the specific article that Clemens read has not been identified (see, for example, "Bear Escapes Roosevelt," New York *Times,* 17 Oct 1907, 1; "Bear Ran Other Way," Washington *Post,* 17 Oct 1907, 1). He treats this subject at greater length in the Autobiographical Dictation of 21 October 1907.

173.7–8   Rev. Dr. Long, the "nature fakir," came along and explained that it was a cow track] For the ongoing quarrel between William Joseph Long and Roosevelt see the Autobiographical Dictation of 29 May 1907 and notes. Clemens's joke anticipates an actual interview that appeared four days later in the New York *World,* in which Long derided Roosevelt for "chasing a timid animal with a pack of dogs and then shooting him from a safe distance when he can't do a thing to save or defend himself" ("Calls Roosevelt Bearkilling Pure Brute Cowardice," New York *World,* 22 Oct 1907, 1).

173.10   his scheme of provoking a war with Japan with his battleships] In 1906–7, tensions arising from Japanese territorial claims in Asia and the treatment of Japanese immigrants in California fueled an existing controversy over the proposed deployment of United States warships to the Pacific. When in August 1907 it was announced that Roosevelt was planning to send a fleet of sixteen battleships to the Pacific, purportedly on a practice cruise, several newspapers—notably the New York *World* and New York *Sun*—denounced the maneuver as bound to provoke a war; Roosevelt replied that his intentions were peaceful, and that the show of naval power was intended to avert trouble with Japan. The fleet departed in December, but there was no official announcement until March 1908 that it would undertake a world cruise (a plan that the newspapers had reported as early as September 1907). The Japanese, choosing to regard the action as a friendly demonstration and not a provocation, formally invited the fleet, and received it hospitably in October 1908. Roosevelt considered the cruise of the "Great White Fleet"—as it came to be known—one of his greatest contributions to world peace (Bailey 1932, 389–403, 408, 413–14, 421–22; John M. Thompson 2011, 227; for Roosevelt's role in ending the Russo-Japanese War see *AutoMT1,* 462–63, 647–48 n. 462.33–36).

173.12   He was in a skirmish once at San Juan Hill] Roosevelt was second in command of the First Volunteer Cavalry, known as the Rough Riders, who captured San Juan Hill in Cuba on 1 July 1898 during the Spanish-American War.

173.14   Brander Matthews's] See *AutoMT1,* 548 n. 255.24.

173.23–24   I met Mr. Marconi in London . . . with Sir Hiram Maxim] Nothing is known of this meeting, beyond Clemens's notebook entry, "Met Marconi & Sir Hiram Maxim, 1900" (Notebook 48, TS p. 12, CU-MARK). In that year, American-born inventor Hiram Stevens Maxim (1840–1916) became a British subject; he was knighted the following year. Best known for the machine gun that bears his name, he also experimented with flying machines and incandescent lamps. Several of Maxim's letters to Clemens survive, in which he expounds at length his opposition to the work of Christian missionaries in China. He praises Clemens's writings on the subject as "of very great value to the civilization of the world," there being "no man living whose words carry greater weight than your own as no one's writings are so eagerly sought after by all classes" (17 Apr 1901, CU-MARK). Clemens's letters to Maxim have not been found.

173.27   Professor Morse, and Graham Bell] It is not known when Clemens met Samuel Finley Breese Morse (1791–1872), acknowledged here as the inventor of the telegraph—although elsewhere Clemens noted that "Professor Henry, the American, Wheatstone in England, Morse on the sea, and a German in Munich, all invented it at the same time" (SLC 1891, 98). Neither is it known when Clemens met Alexander Graham Bell.

173.27   Edison] Clemens met Thomas Alva Edison (1847–1931) on one documented occasion, in June 1888: see the Autobiographical Dictation of 14 February 1908, note at 205.24 (1st).

173.32–34   in the summer of 1858 when the first electric message was sent . . . by cable] The first transatlantic cable was laid in August 1858, after several failed attempts, but it stopped working after only three weeks. It was not until 1866 that a functioning cable was successfully put in place.

173.36–37   That was the year of the great comet] Donati's comet was first sighted by Giovanni Battista Donati (1826–73) of Italy on 2 June 1858. The brilliance of its tail captured public interest while it was visible to the naked eye, from September 1858 to March 1859. The comet will not return until 3808.

174.6–11   It was not my fortune to be present . . . worked the key himself and exchanged messages] On 10 June 1871 a bronze statue of Morse was unveiled in New York's Central Park, and he was honored that evening at a reception in the Academy of Music. The climax of the event occurred when an operator sent a message over all the wires in America: "Greeting and thanks to the telegraph fraternity throughout the land. Glory to God in the highest, on earth peace, good-will to men." Morse then sat at the keyboard himself and transmitted "S. F. B. Morse," which was greeted with a "wild storm of enthusiasm" (Prime 1875, 718–20). Clemens was in Elmira on that day, plotting another lecture tour (10 June 1871 to Redpath and Fall, *L4,* 398–402).

Autobiographical Dictation, 21 October 1907

175.1–9   ROOSEVELT TELLS OF HUNTING TRIP . . . After the Kill] These headlines appeared on the front page of the New York *Times* of 21 October.

175.15–176.16   The bear slain by the President . . . seem to have] This article (including the brief excerpts from it quoted earlier) was published in the New York *World* on 21 October. The McKenzies owned a plantation near the hunting camp, where two Secret Service men stayed. Alex Ennolds was an African American hunting guide ("Bear's Turn Today," Washington *Post,* 7 Oct 1907, 1; "In the Canebrakes," Omaha *Morning World-Herald,* 22 Oct 1907, 4).

Autobiographical Dictation, 25 October 1907

176 *title*   Dictated New York, October 25, 1907] This "dictation" is actually based on a manuscript.

176.23   Mr. O.] Unidentified.

176.23–26   Baron Tauchnitz . . . following in the footsteps of the honest father] Baron Christian Karl Bernhard von Tauchnitz had run the publishing house established by his father, the first Baron Tauchnitz, since the latter's death in 1895 (see *AutoMT2,* 599 n. 323.1–11).

176.34   steals an author's book in the 42d year of its age] At this date United States law stipulated a copyright term of twenty-eight years, renewable for another fourteen (*AutoMT2,* 585 n. 285.40–286.3).

Autobiographical Dictation, 1 November 1907

177.10   I find it in the morning papers] The article that follows was published in the New York *Times* on 1 November.

177.12–13   John W. Alling] Alling (b. 1842?), the son of a woolen manufacturer, had practiced law in New Haven since at least 1864 (*New Haven Census* 1870, 109:22A; Rockey 1892, 2:28).

177.14   F. A. Agar of this city] Unidentified.

177.15   Henry Clews] Clews (1834–1923) was head of a prominent Wall Street brokerage firm ("Henry Clews Dies in His 89th Year," New York *Times,* 1 Feb 1923, 1).

177.26–27   The financial panic calls for an opinion as to how far 'my policies' are responsible for it] The panic of 1907 began in October when the Knickerbocker Trust Company, one of the largest banks in the country, suspended operations. The series of events leading up to the closure began with the involvement of its president, Charles T. Barney (see AD, 27 Apr 1908, note at 223.5–7), with F. Augustus Heinze (1869–1914), head of the Mercantile National Bank, in a failed attempt to corner the market in United Copper Company stock. On 16 October worried depositors began to withdraw their funds from the Mercantile and other banks associated with Heinze; crisis was averted when the New York Clearing House agreed to clear Mercantile checks, provided Heinze retired from banking. But on 21 October Barney was forced to resign from the Knickerbocker when his involvement with the copper maneuver was revealed, and the next day the National Bank of Commerce announced that it would not honor the Knickerbocker's checks. The result was a run on the Knickerbocker; after paying out about $8 million the bank had no cash to meet further demand. This in turn precipitated two weeks of bank runs and panic selling; many banks collapsed, and a sharp depression followed. Financial conservatives blamed Roosevelt's antitrust and rate-regulation legislation, which threatened business profits and undermined public confidence in railroad securities; see, for example, *The Roosevelt Panic of 1907* (Edwards 1907). Roosevelt, however, blamed irresponsible speculation and stock manipulation by "certain malefactors of great wealth" (Moen 2001; Campbell 2008b; Pringle 1956, 304–8). Clemens blames Roosevelt for the 1907 economic slump in the Autobiographical Dictation of 13 September 1907 (see the note at 135.41–136.3).

177.32–36   President Roosevelt is alone responsible for raising this railroad rate question . . . Democrat Senator Tillman] One of Roosevelt's most controversial policies during his second term, which began in 1905, was his push for greater government oversight of the railroads, to curb alleged abuses such as favoritism in setting shipping rates. (One of the companies that Roosevelt accused of profiting greatly from special rates was Standard Oil, of which Clemens's friend Henry Rogers was a vice-president: see AD, 13 Sept 1907, notes at 135.21–22 and 135.23–24.) Roosevelt enlisted Representative William P. Hepburn of Iowa to introduce a bill that would give the Interstate Commerce Commission the power to oversee railroad operations; he also resorted to a temporary alliance with his constant detractor, Democratic Senator Benjamin Tillman of South Carolina, who successfully ushered the bill through the Senate. The Hepburn Act, enacted on 29 June 1906, was the most significant domestic legislation of Roosevelt's presidency. It enlarged the Commission's jurisdiction over the railroad industry, granting it the power to determine reasonable shipping rates; its rulings, however, were subject to judicial review (Pringle 1956, 292–99; Murphy 2011, 160–65).

178.39–40   the millionaire "bandits" whom the President is so fond of abusing . . . stayed the desolation] J. Pierpont Morgan, John D. Rockefeller, and several other wealthy bankers made available a pool of $25 million to brokerage houses under pressure during the October 1907 panic. In addition, the secretary of the treasury, George B. Cortelyou, agreed to make available $25 million in treasury funds to help national banks ease the cash shortage. Roosevelt was not personally involved; on 24 October he wrote to Cortelyou, commending him and the financiers who collaborated with him; the president's letter was widely reprinted ("Deluge of Money Drowns Out Fear," Chicago *Tribune*, 25 Oct 1907, 1; "Roosevelt Indorses Cortelyou's Work," New York *Times*, 27 Oct 1907, 1; Pringle 1956, 306–11; Campbell 2008b).

178.42–179.1   The great financiers saved every important bank and trust company in New York but one—the Knickerbocker Trust Company] Although at first Morgan and his associates claimed they would help the Knickerbocker, late in the evening of 22 October they decided that the company's capital and surplus were insufficient to justify a rescue. Morgan "did not care to assume the responsibilities of previous poor management"; privately, he reportedly said, "I can't go on being everybody's goat" (Pringle 1956, 308; New York *Times*: "Knickerbocker Will Be Aided," 22 Oct 1907, 1; "Knickerbocker Will Not Open," 23 Oct 1907, 1). The Morgan associates' decision deterred other institutions from offering substantial aid as well (Moen 2001).

179.3–7 No one will lose by the temporary suspension . . . I had fifty-one thousand dollars there] Lyon recorded in her journal on 22 October:

> Oh its too dreadful. Every penny the King has—fifty one thousand dollars—is in the Knickerbocker Trust Co—& it has suspended payment— It has gone crashing into a terrible state. I was in town and reading of the panic in the Times & Ashcroft & I went to the bank at 34th St and Fifth Ave to find crowds of people there, with bank books in their quivering hands. And then I came back to Tuxedo to find the King in bed—& so cheerful & beautiful & brave—& trying not to show his anxiety. He had telephoned in to me to withdraw the money, but by the time I could do anything it was too late. (Lyon 1907)

The next day she noted Clemens's plan to sell bonds to finance the house he was building in Redding and to rely on royalty payments for living expenses:

> This morning the financial outlook was a bad one. Yesterday's paper said aid would be given to the Knickerbocker, but it wasn't forthcoming. This morning when I went to the King's room his face looked grey, but he was brave & cheerful & talked over what we must do: Sell the Steel bonds a few at a time to build the Redding house with—for the Autobiography money is in the Knickerbocker—& live on what comes from the Harpers. (Lyon 1907, entry for 23 Oct)

On the morning of this dictation, the Knickerbocker's directors announced that the suspension was only temporary, because its assets were sufficient to pay all depositors. It was not able to resume business, however, until March 1908, because of the difficulty of formulating a workable plan that was acceptable to all parties—the directors, the depositors, the stockholders, and the court (New York *Times:* "Knickerbocker Can Pay All," 1 Nov 1907, 2; "Knickerbocker Will Open on March 26," 8 Mar 1908, 12). Clemens himself registered his approval of the plan in a letter of 17 January 1908 to the "Other Depositors" (CtHMTH):

> The time is very short. It expires to-morrow. Mr. Grover Cleveland, a depositor, has approved the Satterlee plan for resumption, & it seems to me that that ought to satisfy every depositor that that plan is safe & wise. If we accept it & support it we shall lose no part of our money; if we do not accept it the Knickerbocker will be delivered over to a permanent receivership. I have already tried a permanent receivership once, & did not like the results. It costs more to keep a permanent receiver than it does to keep a harem. Anybody who has had experience in these matters will endorse this statement. In the long run—in the very long run—we got some of our money, but not enough of it to keep a harem with. All the depositors said so, & were disappointed, & there was much regret. If we accept the Satterlee plan, & do it immediately, it will be well for us; if we refuse, we invite & insure a shrinkage which the patients will not find enjoyable. I have not been invited to say those things, still it has seemed worth while to say them.
>
> Very respectfully
Mark Twain

Clemens's letter was circulated by the planners and found its way into the newspapers. Most of Clemens's money was restored in cash (70 percent), the rest in stock (30 percent) (see "The Ashcroft-Lyon Manuscript," p. 394; "Mark Twain Hit by Failure," Portland *Oregonian,* 11 Jan 1908, 3; "Mark Twain on Receivers," San Luis Obispo [Calif.] *Telegram,* 12 Feb 1908, 5).

179.8–9   I think I have spoken of that Young Christian . . . earlier chapter of this Autobiography] See the Autobiographical Dictation of 15 March 1906 (*AutoMT1,* 409–12).

179.25   The directors of the Lincoln Trust Company were hard pressed by their depositors] By 24 October the Lincoln Trust Company had paid out "nearly $7,000,000 since the quiet run began on the institution right after the failure of the Knickerbocker." The company's president said that it had "been a little rough," but by calling in its loans, it had raised the money to meet all demands ("Has Paid Out $7,000,000," Washington *Post,* 25 Oct 1907, 2). See the note at 179.27 for an explanation of the truncated text.

179.27   [*one page and all but two lines of the following page (about 420 words) are missing*] When Bernard DeVoto prepared this dictation for publication in *Mark Twain in Eruption,* he discarded one page and all but two lines of a second page of the original typescript. The missing pages contained a section of text he decided to omit, which is now lost. The summary paragraph at the head of the dictation indicates that the lost section concluded the discussion of the Lincoln Trust Company, and contained a letter to the Knickerbocker Trust Company. No text of that letter has been found; there exists, however, a draft of a letter written by Clemens to the Knickerbocker directors a little later (ca. 22–26 November), which may convey a similar sentiment. It reads in part (NN-BCG):

> You discriminated against me by accepting two deposits from me after some had been warned to take their money out. Instead of putting your hands in your pockets, & paying your debts, like the Lincoln Trust & other respectable concerns, you have been shillyshallying for a month trying to escape your obligations & find some more economical & less reputable way to resume. Why do you wish to resume? Do you suppose any one will risk money with you again? Next time you will bring up in jail, where you probably ought to have been many & many a year ago. At large, you are a common danger, whereas in jail you would be useful—useful, as an example. Also happy, for you would be at home; at home, & among sympathetics; sympathetics, & all harmonious, all wearing the same handsome stripes. Oh, you must not think of resuming, it would make the people to laugh, as the French say. And they would say the most sarcastic things about you, just as they are doing now. They would remember that the government & the capitalists hastened to rescue the Lincoln & the other reputable trusts, but hadn't a kind word for you, nor a dollar. I am your friend, & I assure you it will be a mistake for you to resume.
>
> Affectionately,
M. T.

179.28   Mr. L. was here last night] Martin W. Littleton (1872–1934) was one of nineteen children born to a poor family in Roane County, Tennessee. Almost entirely self-educated, he became a lawyer, a Brooklyn district attorney, and a Democratic party politician. In 1908 he defended Harry K. Thaw in his second trial for murder (see *AutoMT2,* 647 n. 454.28–29). Littleton was Clemens's friend and neighbor in New York—though never "Mr. Clemens's lawyer," as the summary paragraph asserts—and visited to play billiards occasionally, even after Clemens moved to Stormfield on 18 June 1908. Clemens recorded a witticism of Littleton's which concerns the autobiography: "When I break into hellfireworks of speech, Miss Lyon sets down the words in a book. Mr. Littleton says it takes three historians to record me: a biographer, an autobiographer, and a naughty biographer—Paine, myself, & Miss Lyon" (21 Dec 1907 to JC, typescript in CU-MARK). Littleton later represented New York's First District in Congress ("M. W. Littleton Sr., Lawyer, Dies at 62," New York *Times,* 20 Dec 1934, 1; Crowell 1922; *MTB,* 3:1406).

179.31–33   where my father and mother lived eighty years ago, along with Colonel Mulberry Sellers . . . "The Gilded Age."] Clemens's parents lived in and near Jamestown, in Fentress County, Tennessee, from 1827 to 1835. In the first chapter of *The Gilded Age* (coauthored with Charles Dudley Warner) Clemens describes life in Obedstown, a fictional version of Jamestown. That book's character Colonel Sellers had the first name "Eschol" in early printings; when a real Eschol Sellers threatened a lawsuit, Clemens and Warner changed the name to "Beriah Sellers." In the *Gilded Age* play, and in *The American Claimant* (1892), he became "Mulberry Sellers" (see *AutoMT1,* 206–8 and notes on 528–29).

Autobiographical Dictation, 2 December 1907

181 *title*   Dictated December 2, 1907] Under this date Clemens groups four dictations about Andrew Carnegie, clearly the work of several days.

181.17–20   Mr. Bryce, the British Ambassador . . . have also revered him] James Bryce (1838–1922), ambassador to the United States from 1907 to 1913, had been a leading Liberal member of parliament from 1880 to 1907. He first met Clemens sometime before 1899, for in June of that year he invited Clemens to lunch to "renew" their acquaintance (Bryce to SLC, 14 June 1899, CU-MARK; Notebook 40, TS p. 58, CU-MARK).

182.16–17   Gilder, of *The Century* . . . General Carl Schurz] Richard Watson Gilder, editor of the *Century Magazine* since 1881, had been a friend of Clemens's for over twenty years (*AutoMT1,* 486 n. 77 *footnote*). Clemens visited Carl Schurz shortly before his death, in May 1906 (see AD, 19 Aug 1907, note at 104.22).

182.31   King Edward's visit to him at Skibo Castle in Scotland] Carnegie bought Skibo Castle, overlooking Dornoch Firth in the Scottish Highlands, in 1897, and renovated it extensively. King Edward VII's visit was in September 1902 ("King Edward Visits Carnegie at Skibo," New York *Times,* 7 Sept 1902, 4).

182.41   loaded to the guards] Steamboat language for heavily loaded—loaded even on the extensions, called guards, of the main deck past the hull (*ET&S1*, 443).

183.31   President Roosevelt's motive when he issued that lawless Order 78] See the Autobiographical Dictation of 29 May 1907, note at 62.25.

184.35–36   I want to tell you about my meeting with the Emperor] See the notes at 185.32–186.4 and 186.6–19.

185.14   wee bit of a lawyer there, by the name of Clarke] Unidentified.

185.32–186.4   We went aboard the *Hohenzollern,* Tower and I . . . Bring him to me] Carnegie wrote in his autobiography that he was invited to meet Wilhelm II, emperor of Germany and king of Prussia, after the monarch read Carnegie's 1902 rectorial address to the students of the University of St. Andrews, which appealed to the emperor to "use his influence toward the eventual creation of the United States of Europe, under the form of a political and industrial union" ("Andrew Carnegie on Industrial Supremacy," New York *Times,* 23 Oct 1902, 9). The meeting was delayed, however, until June 1907, when Carnegie and his wife traveled to Kiel, where Charlemagne Tower, the U.S. minister to Germany, took him aboard the emperor's yacht, the *Hohenzollern* (Carnegie 1920, 366–69).

186.6–19   I know you for a confirmed and incurable independent . . . your mighty place in the world] Carnegie gave a similar account of this conversation in his autobiography: when Wilhelm said, "I have read your books. You do not like kings," Carnegie replied that he did not, "but I do like a man behind a king when I find him." Writing on the eve of World War I, he praised the emperor as "fine company . . . an earnest man, anxious for the peace and progress of the world," and stated that "the peace of the world has little to fear from Germany," despite the agitations of the "military caste," on whom he would later blame the outbreak of war (Carnegie 1920, 369–72; Nasaw 2006, 785).

187.15   his recent visit—by request—to the President] Carnegie met with Roosevelt several times in October–December 1907, lobbying for peace initiatives and consulting on the financial crisis (Nasaw 2006, 692–95).

187.16–19   his departure from his last year's requirement of a new battleship per year . . . sixty-nine million dollars] For several years Roosevelt's administration deemed the building of one U.S. battleship a year sufficient. But after the representatives at the 1907 International Peace Conference at The Hague failed to reach an agreement to limit the number or size of warships, he decided on an increase in production. In the fall of 1907 the secretary of the navy, Victor H. Metcalf, urged Congress to authorize the construction of four battleships, in addition to twenty-six other vessels of various types, at a projected total cost of $96 million. His proposal was reported in newspapers on the day of this dictation ("Our Navy Second as to Efficiency," New York *Times,* 2 Dec 1907, 8). Congress authorized only two of the requested battleships, but in January 1909, after a second appeal, it approved two more. During Roosevelt's presidency, a total of fourteen battleships were launched, more than doubling the size of the navy ("Roosevelt Urges

Need of Battleships," New York *Times,* 15 Apr 1908, 5; Hodge 2011, 264–71; Washington *Post:* "Congress and the Navy," 16 Feb 1908, E4; "For 2 Battleships," 23 Jan 1909, 1; see also *AutoMT2,* 525 n. 134.38–135.1, and AD, 8 Apr 1907, note at 22.6–16).

187.20–22   Mr. Roosevelt's . . . the recipient of the Nobel Prize] Roosevelt won the Nobel Peace Prize in December 1906 for his role in negotiating the Treaty of Portsmouth, which ended the Russo-Japanese War. Clemens called the treaty, signed in September 1905, "the most conspicuous disaster in political history," claiming that the restoration of peace enabled the Russian tsar to "resume his medieval barbarisms" against his own people (Trani and Davis 2011, 374–75; see *AutoMT1,* 462–63 and notes on 647–48).

188.4–8   to introduce the name of God into the Constitution . . . the legend, "In God We Trust."] In 1861, a small Protestant sect called the Covenanters renewed earlier efforts to introduce an affirmation of the Christian God into the Constitution. Other Christian denominations joined the cause, and early in 1864 the National Reform Association was founded, with the goal of securing "such an amendment to the Constitution of the United States as will declare the nation's allegiance to Jesus Christ and its acceptance of the moral laws of the Christian religion." The association also sought to incorporate religion into other aspects of government, such as family law, education, and observance of the Sabbath. It found little support in Washington (Allison 2013). In 1863 Secretary of the Treasury Salmon P. Chase, having received more than one letter requesting (in the words of one such letter) "the recognition of the Almighty God in some form on our coins," mandated the addition of the motto "In God We Trust" to U.S. coinage. The change was ratified by Congress in the Coinage Act of 1864. The motto was added to the two-cent coin that year, and two years later it appeared on several others, including the ten-dollar gold eagle and twenty-dollar double eagle (U.S. Department of the Treasury 2013).

188.11–16   ordered that remark to be removed . . . this was a profanation of the Holy Name] In late 1905 Roosevelt commissioned Augustus Saint-Gaudens to redesign the U.S. coinage. The first of the new coins, the ten-dollar gold eagle, was released in early November 1907, a few months after the sculptor's death. The obverse shows the head of Liberty in profile wearing an Indian headdress, and the reverse an eagle perched on a branch. According to Saint-Gaudens's son, his father omitted the motto "In God We Trust" because he considered it an "inartistic intrusion," and Roosevelt concurred. Its absence caused an immediate outcry. Roosevelt claimed responsibility for the decision, but did not defend it on aesthetic grounds, arguing instead that it was "eminently unwise to cheapen such a motto by use on coins, just as it would be to cheapen it by use on postage stamps or in advertisements." Public pressure eventually led to the passage of the McKinley bill in May 1908, which reinstated the motto on all subsequent mintings of coins on which it had formerly appeared (Levine 2011, 145–47; Saint-Gaudens 1913, 2:329–32; "New Eagles Lack Motto," New York *Times,* 7 Nov 1907, 8).

188.28–32   removal of the motto fetched out a clamor . . . that this is a Christian country] Numerous religious bodies protested against the removal of "In God We Trust" from the new coinage. Clemens may refer to a resolution introduced at an 11 November 1907 meeting of the Presbyterian Ministers' Association, where the Reverend William J. Peck was reported as saying the nation "was lapsing into barbarism" ("To Condemn Omission of 'In God We Trust,'" Boston *Herald,* 12 Nov 1907, 1). A week later the association, which included Presbyterian, Reformed, and Reformed Episcopal ministers, adopted the resolution that "the motto 'In God We Trust' is in harmony with historical and religious sentiment of our land," and should be retained "in the interest of religion and morality." The debate over the coins coincided with a controversy over the legality of Christmas activities in the New York public schools, prompting debate as to whether the United States is "a Christian country" ("Want 'In God We Trust,'" Baltimore *Sun,* 19 Nov 1907, 1; "Want the Motto Back," Washington *Post,* 19 Nov 1907, 5; "Board of Education Put on Defensive," New York *Times,* 26 Nov 1907, 5).

Autobiographical Dictation, 10 December 1907

189.8–12   Three seasons ago I was still keeping up the banqueteering habit . . . three times in every week for six months] Clemens should have said "two seasons ago." In April 1906 he announced his intention to lecture only "when I am not paid to appear and when no one has to pay to get in," and evidently also declined a number of banquet invitations during the 1906–7 season, as he explained to George Harvey on 5 October 1907: "I attended no banquets last year. That was a restful & blessed year! I will duplicate it this season" (photocopy in CU-MARK; *AutoMT2,* 14, 15).

189.31–33   Mr. Fritz . . . took hold of it with Mr. Holley] John Fritz (1822–1913), the chief engineer of the Bethlehem Iron Company, revolutionized steel production through the application of the Bessemer process. Alexander L. Holley (1832–82) bought the American rights to the Bessemer process in 1863 and became the country's foremost steel-plant engineer.

189.35–38   The dinner was in honor of Mr. Carnegie . . . twelve hundred thousand dollars] The banquet was "officially the christening of the new home of the Engineers' Club," according to the New York *Times,* and three or four hundred members attended ("Mark Twain Jeers at Simple Spelling," 10 Dec 1907, 2). It honored Carnegie for donating $1.5 million to finance the construction of two adjoining buildings, which connected internally, on 39th and 40th Streets near Fifth Avenue. On 40th Street, the twelve-story Renaissance Revival building designed for the Engineers' Club featured public and social areas, plus sixty-six private rooms (NYC Circa 2011). The 39th Street building, of thirteen stories, housed the Associated Societies of Engineers and comprised a large auditorium as well as lecture halls, administrative offices, and libraries. Clemens conflates the two buildings and organizations.

192.3–14   at last the chairman called me up . . . Look at his pestiferous Simplified Spelling] The speech that Clemens quotes below is thematically the same as the one reported in the New York *Times,* but it differs in its details (see "Mark Twain Jeers at Simple Spelling," 10 Dec 1907, 2). Clemens treats the subject of Carnegie's Simplified Spelling movement in the Autobiographical Dictations of 7 November and 19 November 1906 (see *AutoMT2,* 266–69, 273–77).

Autobiographical Dictation, 12 December 1907

193.32   Carnegie Institute] The Carnegie Institution in Washington, founded in 1902 with a gift of $10 million, supported research in all the sciences ("Carnegie Institution," Washington *Post,* 5 Jan 1902, 5).

194.6   following telegram from the newspaper] The article appeared in the New York *World* on 11 December 1907.

194.11   R. S. Woodward] Robert Simpson Woodward (1849–1924), a mathematical physicist, was president of the Carnegie Institution from 1905 to 1920 ("Dr. R. S. Woodward, Carnegie Scientist, Dies at Age of 75," Washington *Post,* 30 June 1924, 10).

194.29–32   seventeen years ago, in Germany, I was one of the guests ... Prince of Wales and is now King and Emperor] The dinner took place at Bad Homburg on 25 August 1892, four days after Clemens was introduced to the prince (see *AutoMT2,* 181, 546 n. 181.31–36). He described the occasion in his notebook: "Dined at the Kursaal with Sir Charles Hall, to meet the Prince of Wales. 7 present. Sat at the Prince's left. [Chauncey] Depew at his right.... Much talk, many yarns, everything sociable, pleasant, no formality. Two hours delightfully spent" (Notebook 32, TS p. 22, TxU-Hu). Sir Charles Hall (1843–1900) was a judge and Conservative politician who was close to the royal family.

Autobiographical Dictation, 13 January 1908

195 *title*   Dictated January 13, 1908] This dictation was undoubtedly the work of two days; the second section (beginning with the summary at 198.11–13) was created on or after 16 January.

195.5–10   Elinor Glyn ... a romance which she is purposing to write] Glyn (1864–1943) was the author of best-selling society novels and romances, some of them considered risqué. Clemens had met her on 27 October 1907 at a small dinner party hosted by Daniel Frohman and his wife. She had arrived in New York on 4 October, on a tour to promote her novel *Three Weeks* (see the note at 195.11–12), which took her through the eastern states and as far as California. She was also on a "literary quest" to study Americans, particularly the men, and then possibly "set forth my conclusions in a new book when I get home" (New York *Times:* "Mrs. Glyn Praises American Men," 5 Oct 1907, 6; "What Elinor Glyn Thinks of New York City," 12 Oct 1907, 1; Frohman to SLC, 21 Oct 1907, CU-MARK). Upon her return to England Glyn recorded her observations in

Elizabeth Visits America (1909), a gushy epistolary novel. She later became a Hollywood scriptwriter, and is credited with coining the use of "It" to denote sexual magnetism (Anthony Glyn 1968, 157–58, 223, 279, 301–2, 305–7).

195.11–12   The source of this notoriety is a novel of hers called "Three Weeks."] *Three Weeks* (1907) dealt, scandalously for the period, with adultery, and was supposedly inspired by Glyn's recent romance, possibly unconsummated, with the much younger Lord Alastair Robert Innes-Ker (1880–1936) (Hardwick 1994, 113–18, 148; "Roxburghe, Duke of," in Cracroft 2012). She was not embarrassed by the "storm-wind" her book had aroused, nor by condemnatory reviews. Of the nay-sayers she had recently remarked:

> I know that critics have condemned the book severely, . . . but what of that? It does not disturb me in the least. With 50,000 copies sold last month and the book still selling, I think I can stand a little criticism, don't you? You know why I don't mind the words of critics? I will tell you. A critic is a man who has failed. He is a pessimist; he has failed in what he attempted to do, and he would make others fail. . . . In England a young woman came to see me just before I sailed, and you ought to have seen that interview. Not a word of it was correct. . . . I guess the young woman must have been a critic: she was such an idiot. ("Critics Idiots—Mrs. Glyn," New York *Times,* 17 Nov 1907, 1)

195.33   stars] That is, asterisks.

196.4   she has a daughter fourteen years old] Glyn had two daughters: Margot, born in 1893, and Juliet, born in 1898 (Hardwick 1994, 67, 78–79).

197.24–27   when I publicly attacked the American missionaries in China . . . I had to obey and take the consequences] In "To the Person Sitting in Darkness" (first published in February 1901 in the *North American Review* and then issued as a pamphlet by the Anti-Imperialist League of New York), Clemens condemned the American missionaries in China as a front for imperialism. He also criticized the imperialist actions in China and elsewhere of England, Germany, Russia, and the United States (SLC 1901a, 1901b). The article elicited much praise, but also much condemnation, which Clemens answered in "To My Missionary Critics," in the *North American Review* for April 1901 (SLC 1901c). For a discussion of the entire episode, see Foner 1958, 269–82.

198.4   her husband, in England] Elinor had married Clayton Glyn (1857–1915), an indebted and spendthrift landowner, in 1892. Glyn was indifferent to his wife and daughters, and the couple's incompatibility led to an unhappy marriage (Hardwick 1994, 60–64, 71–79).

198.28–29   The lady had not been sent by Mrs. Glyn . . . had studied Mrs. Glyn's report of our conversation] Glyn's friend has not been identified. If she came without Glyn's knowledge, it is unlikely that she left a copy of the "report"; the five-page typescript that survives in the Mark Twain Papers is accompanied by a note from Glyn herself, dated three days after Clemens made this dictation (CU-MARK):

Plaza Hotel
Jan *16ᵗʰ*

Dear Mʳ· Clemens

    I am sending you my report of the interview we had, & I think you will be amused to find what an accurate "reporter" I am! Even if you feel you would rather I did not publish it, I shall always keep it in memory of a delightful afternoon with a delightful American gentleman.

    Greetings & kind regards from

Yˢ sincerely
Elinor Glyn

    P.S. I wonder if you knew how charming you were that afternoon?! & if you remember what wise things you said?

Most of Glyn's report of their conversation accords well with what Clemens recalls here. In addition, she quotes him as saying that "his 'law' was to protect his daughters," and that the woman in her novel was moved by "this immense unfettered force of the first great law of all things, to give herself to her mate," because she had no children and therefore felt no "mother instinct" to protect them. Glyn also claimed that Clemens had called her book "a fine piece of writing." Clemens characterized her report in his reply to her:

21 Fifth Avenue,
Jan. 24, 1908.

Dear Mrs. Glyn:—

    It reads pretty poorly. I get the sense of it, but it is a poor literary job; however, it would have to be that because nobody can be reported even approximately except by a stenographer. Approximations, synopsized speeches, translated poems, artificial flowers, and chromos all have a sort of value, but it is small. If you had put upon paper what I really said, it would have wrecked your type-machine. I said some fetid and over-vigorous things, but that was because it was a confidential conversation. I said nothing for print. My own report of the same conversation reads like Satan roasting a Sunday School. It, and certain other readable chapters of my autobiography, will not be published until all the Clemens family are dead—dead and correspondingly indifferent. They were written to entertain me, not the rest of the world. I am not here to do good—at least not to do it intentionally. You must pardon me for dictating this letter; I am still sick a-bed and not feeling as well as I might.

Sincerely yours,
S. L. Clemens

Glyn printed the typescript of her interview with Clemens, as well as his 24 January letter, in *Mark Twain on "Three Weeks,"* a privately circulated pamphlet (Elinor Glyn 1908, 8, 10, 13–14 [the unique source of Clemens's letter]). When a staff member of the New York *American* showed Clemens a copy, he complained that Glyn had "put into my mouth humiliatingly weak language" ("Twain Says He Told Her 'Book a Mistake,'" New York *American,* 27 Sept 1908, 2:1; see Schmidt 2013a, which reprints the pamphlet, and Shelden 2010, 188–93, 278–79). In her 1936 autobiography, *Romantic Adventure,* Glyn gave a one-paragraph account of her encounter with Clemens, reporting that she had "a thrilling afternoon with him in his own sitting-room," and calling him "the wittiest creature imaginable," "exquisitely whimsical," and a "dear old man" (Elinor Glyn 1936, 144).

199.9   King Leopold of Belgium] See *AutoMT1,* 557 n. 268.24–25.

199.9   the Children's Theatre] The Children's Theatre, on the lower east side of Manhattan, was founded in 1903 under the auspices of the Educational Alliance, which had begun in 1889 as a social service agency for Eastern European Jewish immigrants. The casts of the Theatre—and to a great extent its audiences—were made up of neighborhood youngsters, and its programs included dramatized fairy tales and Bible stories, condensed versions of Shakespeare's plays, and, on more than one occasion, *The Prince and the Pauper.* In 1907 Clemens became an enthusiastic supporter of the Theatre, speaking often at its productions, and in April 1908 he became "honorary President" of its board of directors. In "The Great Alliance," written around the time of this dictation, he praised the good work of the Alliance, and especially of the Theatre, which he described later in 1908 as his "pet & pride" and "the only teacher of morals & conduct & high ideals that never bores the pupil" (Oct 1908 to Hookway, draft in CU-MARK; SLC 1908; Educational Alliance 2013; New York *Times:* "Mark Twain Tells of Being an Actor," 15 Apr 1907, 9; "An Educational Theatre," 15 Sept 1907, 8; "Children Flock to Biblical Tableaus," 25 Nov 1907).

199.15–16   The Fulton Memorial Fund . . . one lecture] See *AutoMT1,* 426–28, 630–31 nn. 426.13–15, 426.20–21. No evidence has been found that Clemens's attendance at the opening of the Jamestown Exposition in April 1907 was at the behest of the Robert Fulton Memorial Association (see AD, 18 May 1907), but while he was there, the association's vice-president approached him with a request to speak on Robert Fulton Day in Jamestown the following September (see AD, 26 Sept 1907).

199.17–19   The movement propagated by Miss Holt for . . . adult blind persons] Winifred T. Holt was a founder of the New York State Association for Promoting the Interests of the Blind (see *AutoMT1,* 464 and notes on 649–50), of which Clemens was an honorary vice-president. On 14 January 1908 Holt wrote to Clemens asking to use his name in promoting a fund-raising event, noting that it "would help so much towards the success of the occasion" (CU-MARK).

199.20   The American movement in the interest of those Russian revolutionists] See *AutoMT1,* 462–64 and notes on 647–49.

200.29   "Yes."] The dictation ends here, the last line in a full, normally typed page, but in the midst of a manifestly incomplete thought. It seems likely that Clemens originally continued his thought on at least one further page, now lost. Since the page now ending with "Yes" is numbered 2439 and the first page of the next dictation is 2440, he must have removed an original page 2440 before beginning the next dictation one month later.

Autobiographical Dictation, 12 February 1908

201.22   I have been to Bermuda again; this is the fifth time] Clemens's previous visits were: 11–15 November 1867, on the return trip from the Holy Land aboard the *Quaker City;* 20–24 May 1877, the trip with Joseph H. Twichell that he described in "Some Rambling Notes of an Idle Excursion" (SLC 1877–78); 4–7 January 1907, with Twichell and Lyon, mentioned in the Autobiographical Dictation of 6 January 1907 (*AutoMT2,* 359–61 and notes on 611–12); and 18–19 March 1907, with Lyon and Paddy Madden, a young friend from the January trip (see AD, 26 Mar 1907, and the note at 13.31). For details of all of Clemens's trips to Bermuda, see Hoffmann 2006.

201.27–30   We made the passage in forty-five hours . . . stayed eight days longer] Clemens, accompanied by Ashcroft, boarded the RMS *Bermudian* on Saturday, 25 January, and arrived two days later in Hamilton. He registered at the Princess Hotel, where he had stayed in January 1907. He departed on the RMS *Bermudian* on Monday, 3 February, and docked in New York three days later (Hoffmann 2006, 89, 100, 157).

201.31–32   I allowed the physicians to send Mrs. Clemens . . . to Italy] In the fall of 1903, following her physicians' prescription of a mild climate, Clemens took Olivia and the rest of his family to Florence. He described their unhappy stay, which culminated in Olivia's death in June 1904, in his "Villa di Quarto" dictation (see *AutoMT1,* 230–49 and notes on 539–42).

202.13   I collect pets: young girls] Clemens describes his collection of "angelfish" at length in the Autobiographical Dictation of 17 April 1908 (see also AD, 25 July 1907, note at 74.15–21, and AD, 13 Feb 1908, note 203.7).

Autobiographical Dictation, 13 February 1908

203.7   it's Blackmer] Margaret Gray Blackmer (1896–1987) was the daughter of Henry M. Blackmer and his first wife, Helen. Blackmer (1869–1962) was a wealthy lawyer, financier, banker, and oilman, who in 1924 was implicated in the Teapot Dome naval oil reserves scandal and fled the United States to avoid prosecution for tax evasion. Margaret and her mother had been in Bermuda since 9 December 1907 (Schmidt 2009; "Henry Blackmer, Oil Man, 92, Dies," New York *Times,* 27 May 1962, 9; Hoffmann 2006, 89).

204.20   Miss W.] Elizabeth Wallace (1865–1960), an 1886 graduate of Wellesley College, was an instructor in French literature and a college dean at the University of Chicago. She had arrived at the Princess Hotel on 30 December 1907 on holiday and soon after befriended Margaret Blackmer, and then Clemens. In 1913 she published *Mark Twain and the Happy Island,* a memoir of her friendship with him, which continued after his Bermuda sojourn. She also devoted a chapter to him in her 1952 autobiography, *The Unending Journey* (University of Chicago Library 2006; Wallace 1952, 154–69; Hoffmann 2006, 89–91).

205.23　the electric telegraph] See the Autobiographical Dictation of 18 October 1907 and the note at 173.32–34.

205.24　the phonograph] In 1877 Thomas Edison invented the first phonograph, which used metal cylinders to record sound and play it back; ten years later he began using wax cylinders. In 1888 Clemens considered using a phonograph to dictate *A Connecticut Yankee,* and in June of that year he visited Edison in his New Jersey laboratory. Edison later recalled that he "told a number of funny stories, some of which I recorded on the phonograph records. Unfortunately, these records were lost in the big fire which we had at this plant in 1914" (Edison to Cyril Clemens, 10 Jan 1927, photocopy in CU-MARK). In 1891 Clemens experimented with dictating *The American Claimant,* but was dissatisfied with the result and presumably discarded the four dozen cylinders he had filled (Library of Congress 2013; *N&J3,* 386–87 nn. 289, 292; *MTHL,* 2:637–42). In 1908–9 representatives of the Edison Manufacturing Company asked Clemens to make a recording for commercial distribution. Lyon noted his response on one of the letters: "This is a business matter. Very fond of Mr. Edison but do not want business mixed up with friendship" (note on Martin to Dyer, 10 Aug 1908, CU-MARK). In 1909, however, Clemens did allow the company to produce a moving picture version of *The Prince and the Pauper* (Plimpton to Ashcroft, 1 June 1909, CU-MARK). The film is not known to survive; it was probably lost in the 1914 fire. A moving picture of Clemens at Stormfield, made as part of the project, is now at the Mark Twain Home Foundation, in Hannibal, Missouri.

205.24　the wireless, and with the telephone] For Marconi's development of wireless telegraphy see the Autobiographical Dictation of 18 October 1907, note at 172.30–32. Clemens discusses the attempts to market a "wireless telephone" in the Autobiographical Dictation of 27 March 1907. The most practical application of wireless technology was the radio, which Marconi patented in 1904. For the telephone see the note on that dictation at 17.15–17.

205.24–27　the Hoe press . . . compare that wee marvel with to-day's press] Clemens recalls his 1854 visit to a Washington newspaper office, where he saw for the first time a rotary press, the invention of Richard M. Hoe (see 17 and 18 Feb 1854 to the Muscatine *Journal, L1,* 40–44). In 1908, state-of-the-art newspaper presses, such as the Hoe Double Octuple Rotary Machine, could produce two hundred thousand copies per hour, cut and folded, of a two-sided eight-page paper.

205.28–30　the autochrome . . . the Lumière process] A complex color photography process invented, and patented in 1904 and 1906, by the brothers Auguste and Louis Lumière, who with their father, Antoine, had a famous photographic firm in Lyons, France (Jones 1912, 46–47, 344–45).

205.36–37　I was born in the same year that the lucifer-match was born] Phosphorus friction matches, sometimes called "lucifer" matches, were patented in the United States in 1836, the year after Clemens's birth (*HF 2003,* 393).

206.2–4 he wanted a picture of me for use as one of the illustrations ... Margaret must be put into the picture with me] No article by the "amateur" has been found, and no copy of the color photograph is known to be extant. Lyon, however, took several photographs of Clemens with Margaret in the donkey cart (see the photographs following page 300).

206.23–24 Francesca and Dorothy ... two other Dorothies besides—an American one and an English one] For Frances Nunnally see the Autobiographical Dictation of 25 July 1907 and the note at 74.15–21; for Dorothy Quick see the Autobiographical Dictation of 5 October 1907 and the note at 156.2–3. The American was Dorothy Harvey (1894–1937), the only child of George Harvey and his wife, Alma (Schmidt 2009). The English girl was Margaret Dorothy Butes: see the Autobiographical Dictation of 17 April 1908 and the note at 219.24–28.

207.4 Mark Twain, speech ... Dorothy Quick] In her 1961 memoir of her friendship with Clemens, Quick confirmed his account of this incident, and included a text of the concert program that billed him as "Mark Twain (By courtesy of Miss Dorothy Quick)." She recalled that he explained his delegation of authority to her by saying: "You're my business manager for this trip, anyway, and I'm strongly considering giving you the job for life." At the concert, "He talked about the improvement of the conditions of the adult blind and repeated the story he had told in *A Tramp Abroad* of having been caught with a companion in Berlin in the dark for an hour or more, enlarging on his horror at not being able to see for even so short a time" (Quick 1961, 26–30). The episode in the dark is in chapter 13 of *A Tramp Abroad,* where it occurs in Heilbronn, not Berlin.

207.5 last September when Dorothy spent a week with us in Tuxedo] See the Autobiographical Dictation of 5 October 1907 and the note at 156.2–3.

208.15 Dorothy came last Saturday and stayed over Sunday] Lyon arranged this visit, Quick's first to 21 Fifth Avenue, by telephone on Friday, 7 February 1908. On 8 February she noted in her journal: "Dorothy arrived today & the King was so impatient, pacing up & down the big rooms & going to the front door when ever the bell rang & standing there in his white clothes in an icy blast of wind." After Dorothy's departure two days later Lyon wrote, "All day the King has been playing with Dorothy, & when she left this afternoon, he went up stairs quite lonely, but tired too & so he slept" (Lyon 1908, entries for 7, 8, and 10 Feb). Quick made only a brief mention of this visit in her memoir (Quick 1961, 109).

208.21 a game of "500"] A popular card game combining features of euchre and bridge.

209.3–4 Dorothy Quick, continued ... letter recently received from her] This portion of the dictation was added no earlier than 19 February. Quick dated her letter "Feb 18th 1908," which Clemens canceled before Hobby transcribed it.

209.12 Miss Clara's musical] See the Autobiographical Dictation of 19 February 1908 and the note at 210.8–9.

Autobiographical Dictation, 19 February 1908

210.6   I wrote Jean] Jean was living in Greenwich, Connecticut, under care for her epilepsy (see "The Ashcroft-Lyon Manuscript," note at 342.36–343.4).

210.8–9   Clara's musicale of last night . . . 140 of the 160 guests invited came] Clara's performance, with her accompanist, Charles Wark, and Boston violinist Marie Nichols, was at the Clemenses' 21 Fifth Avenue residence on the evening of 13 February. The New York *Times* reported the event the next day, listing about sixty of the guests, including Mr. and Mrs. Henry H. Rogers, Mr. and Mrs. Henry H. Rogers, Jr., Mr. and Mrs. Richard Watson Gilder, Mr. and Mrs. John Howells, Mr. and Mrs. Frank N. Doubleday (see the note at 211.20–21), and Mr. and Mrs. Andrew Carnegie ("Miss Clemens's Musicale," 14 Feb 1908, 7). In her journal Lyon called the concert "a great success" and noted: "There were some very lovely people here—140 I should say. And after everything was over I understood the hitches that occurred—the waiters got drunk" (Lyon 1908, entry for 13 Feb). Marie Nichols (1879–1954) had also performed at Clara's 22 September 1906 professional debut in Norfolk, Connecticut, and on her New England tour in the spring of 1907 (see *AutoMT2*, 240, 567 n. 240.6–8, and AD, 1 Mar 1907, note at 4.16–17). Nichols had a successful concert career of her own, touring the United States and Europe, appearing with the Boston Symphony and the Berlin Philharmonic, among other orchestras. After retiring from the concert stage, she taught violin and was director of music at Sarah Lawrence College (New York *Times:* "Miss Nichols of Boston Pleases Musical Berlin," 1 Nov 1903, 4; "Violinist, 75, Is Dead," 23 Nov 1954, 33; for Wark see AD, 6 Oct 1908, note at 267.36–37).

210.24–25   a big supper and ball at Sherry's . . . till 4.05 a.m.] Lyon noted: "It was 4:30 this morning when the King came in from a Valentine party at Sherry's. . . . I heard the mobile [automobile] come down the avenue like a tragic giant June-bug, & so I went to look over the ballusters & see the King come running up the stairs, like a happy exhilarated boy" (Lyon 1908, entry for 14 Feb). Sherry's, named for proprietor Louis Sherry, was an elegant restaurant at Fifth Avenue and 44th Street, patronized by New York high society.

210.31   Robert Collier . . . and that sweet and beautiful girl, his wife] Robert J. Collier (1876–1918) was associated with his father, Peter F. Collier, in the management of their publishing house, P. F. Collier and Son, and had been the editor of *Collier's Weekly* from 1898 to 1902. In 1909, upon his father's death, he became head of the publishing house, and served again as the editor of *Collier's* in 1912–13. In 1902 he had married Sara Steward Van Alen (1881–1963), a member of the Astor family ("R. J. Collier Dies at Dinner Table," New York *Times,* 9 Nov 1918, 13; Mott 1957, 453–57, 462–65).

210.33–34   John Hay's poet-daughter, Mrs. Payne Whitney] Helen Hay Whitney (1876–1944) married banker and financier Payne Whitney (1876–1927) in 1902. Between 1898 and 1910 she published several volumes of poetry under her maiden name. She later became prominent in horse racing, owning one of the largest stables in the world and producing two Kentucky Derby winners. She was also known for her extensive philanthropy.

210.35   her mother's . . . limitless millions] Helen Hay Whitney's mother, Clara Louise Stone Hay (1849–1914), was the daughter of Cleveland millionaire Amasa Stone (25 Feb 1874 to Fairbanks, *L6, 49* n. 3).

210.36–38   Mrs. Harry Payne Whitney . . . slaves daily and enthusiastically and faithfully at her statuary work] Sculptor Gertrude Vanderbilt Whitney (1875–1942), great-granddaughter of the original Cornelius Vanderbilt, had married financier Harry Payne Whitney (1872–1930), brother of Payne Whitney, in 1896. She distinguished herself not only with her own sculpture, but also with her generous patronage of other artists through monetary awards and by establishing, in 1908, a gallery in her New York studio building where they could show their work. She went on to found the Whitney Museum of American Art, which opened in 1931.

210.40–211.2   Prince Troubetskoi . . . His wife is Amélie Rives, the poet] Portrait painter Prince Pierre Troubetzkoy (1864–1936), a member of an aristocratic Russian family, was the second husband of American novelist, poet, and playwright Amélie Rives (1863–1945).

211.2–6   Ethel Barrymore, actress . . . carried off every valuable thing she had in the world] Barrymore (1879–1959), a leading stage actress and later a supporting actress in films, was the daughter of actors Maurice Barrymore (1849–1905) and Georgiana Drew Barrymore (1856–93). She had recently ended a two-month run at New York's Hudson Theatre in a play entitled *Her Sister* ("Theatrical Notes," New York *Times,* 16 Feb 1908, 11; Kotsilibas-Davis 1977, 12). Barrymore had been robbed on 9 February:

> The actress left her apartment to visit Mr. and Mrs. Sidney Drew, her uncle and aunt, on Sunday evening about 9:30 o'clock, and did not return until late at night. When she returned the window in her sleeping room was wide open.
>   The apartment had been completely ransacked and the bureau drawers were all open. The most serious money loss was an envelope containing $500 in cash and some smaller sums. The loss which Miss Barrymore felt more keenly, however, was a locket and necklace that belonged to her mother and some other pieces of jewelry she valued highly as keepsakes. ("Ethel Barrymore Robbed," New York *Times,* 11 Feb 1908, 1)

Barrymore's mother was never a widow, having predeceased her husband. Her uncle Sidney and his wife, Gladys, enjoyed moderately successful careers in the theater and were still performing; no evidence has been found that she helped support them or anyone else in the Drew family (Kotsilibas-Davis 1977, 319–20, 356–57, 425).

211.8–13   Nazimova, the illustrious Russian actress . . . then she took lessons and acquired her native tongue] Alla Nazimova (1879–1945) was born in Russia and educated in Switzerland before returning to Odessa to study the violin. She later studied acting in Moscow under Stanislavski and was already an established actress when she emigrated to New York in 1905. By 1906 she had learned English, and in that year made her first great success in the title role in Ibsen's *Hedda Gabler.* She enjoyed a long career as a leading stage actress (particularly as an interpreter of Ibsen), became a popular star of silent films, and was still performing character roles in movies up until her death ("Alla Nazimova, 66, Dies in Hollywood," New York *Times,* 14 July 1945, 11).

211.17–20   a Ben Jonson masque . . . acting which I had not seen approached before by amateurs] On 19 February 1908 the New York *Times* reported: "The eighth annual entertainment of the Junior League, formed of the season's débutantes, yesterday afternoon at the Plaza was a brilliant success. Previous débutantes have never given a more beautiful and finished performance. Ben Jonson's famous masque, 'The Hue and Cry After Cupid,' formed the setting for all that followed" ("Debutantes Give Charity Pantomime," 7). The paper noted Clemens's attendance with his daughter Clara.

211.20–21   I dined out in the evening at the Doubledays' . . . to the Guinnesses', in Washington Square] Frank Doubleday (see AD, 4 Sept 1907, note at 127.31–33) was married to the former Neltje De Graff (1865–1918), a naturalist and prolific nature writer under the pen name Neltje Blanchan. Benjamin S. Guinness (1868–1947), a retired British naval officer, had made a fortune as a Wall Street banker and business executive. His wife, the former Bridget Henrietta Frances Williams-Bulkeley (d. 1931), was the daughter of a baronet and a noted society hostess (New York *Times:* "Mrs. B. S. Guinness, Noted Hostess, Dies," 6 Jan 1931, 25; "Benjamin S. Guinness," 17 Dec 1947, 29). Lyon noted the occasion in her journal:

> That queenly creature Neltje Blanchan Doubleday, talked to me again about Kipling, & said that he never puts a poem down on paper until he has gone over & over it in his head, & eliminated every superfluous word. When they were visiting him last summer in Sussex & motored about with him, his head was full of delightful verses that went in time to the rhythm of the mobile wheels, & he would recite them as they sped along.
> The King put me down at the house & he went on to M^{rs}. Guinness's where he stayed until past midnight. (Lyon 1908, entry for 18 Feb)

211.22–23   The illustrious Caruso] The famed tenor was appearing at the Metropolitan Opera House, most recently in Puccini's *Manon Lescaut* on the evening of 17 February ("Cavalieri Falls on Stage," New York *Times,* 18 Feb 1908, 7).

211.26   a distant cousin of mine, Mrs. William Waldorf Astor] Nancy Langhorne Astor (1879–1964) was a member of the prominent Langhorne family of Virginia. Clemens's middle name was in honor of a friend of his father's who evidently belonged to that same family. That did not, of course, make Clemens even a "distant cousin" to Nancy Astor. A famous beauty, she had become part of the British branch of the wealthy Astor family in 1906, when she married Waldorf Astor (1879–1952), son of William Waldorf Astor (1848–1919). In 1919 she would become the first woman to serve in the British Parliament. In February 1908 she was in New York to raise funds for the " 'poor whites' of the Blue Ridge section of Virginia," whom she described as "utterly poor, often hungry, and without the slightest means of educating themselves," and forced to "live on a par with animals" ("Mrs. Waldorf Astor Pleads a Good Cause," New York *Times,* 14 Feb 1908, 7; Lampton 1990, 96).

211.34–35   Cliveden . . . that wonderful place] The Astors' mansion, with its hundreds of acres of gardens and woodlands, overlooked the Thames midway between Oxford and London. It was the site of lavish parties attended by politicians, writers, artists, and intellectuals of all kinds.

211.36   Peter Dunne ("Mr. Dooley")] Humorist Finley Peter Dunne (see *AutoMT2,* 619 n. 377.3).

211.38–40   leaving for Bermuda . . . absolutely necessary for H. H. Rogers] Rogers had suffered a stroke in July 1907 and, according to Lyon, was still "a sick sick man" when he joined her and Clemens on 22 February for the voyage to Bermuda (Lyon 1908, entry for 22 Feb). For more on the seven-week excursion, see the Autobiographical Dictation of 16 April 1908.

Autobiographical Dictation, 16 April 1908

212.3–4   Miss Lyon and the Rogerses and I arrived back from Bermuda . . . absence of seven weeks] Clemens's party, which included Lyon, Rogers, Rogers's valet, and one of his sons-in-law, William E. Benjamin, arrived in Bermuda on 24 February. Rogers's wife, Emilie, joined them in mid-March. The entire group boarded the RMS *Bermudian* on 11 April for the return trip. For details see Hoffmann 2006, 102–26.

212.5–6   I talked twice in that fairyland . . . benefit of the Aquarium] Clemens appeared on behalf of the Cottage Hospital on 5 March in the ballroom of the Princess Hotel. As the master of ceremonies he introduced several other entertainers, then told his story of the three-dollar dog (recounted in full in the AD of 3 Oct 1907). According to Lyon, "He broke down into a hearty boyish laugh" when he reached the "point where the general asked if he would sell that dog." The reviewer for the Bermuda *Royal Gazette* noted that it was impossible to describe Clemens's "infinite variety of tone, the queer whimsical voice and the charm of the handsome white head and brilliant eyes" (Lyon 1908, entry for 5 Mar; "Entertainment at Princess Hotel in Aid of the Cottage Hospital," Bermuda *Royal Gazette,* 7 Mar 1908, unknown page; see also Hoffmann 2006, 110–15). In his appeal for donations Clemens suggested that "the ladies may contribute their jewels and the gentlemen their letters of credit, or express checks, properly indorsed" ("Samuel Langhorne Clemens [1835–1910]," *Bermuda Historical Quarterly* 34 [Autumn 1977]: 54–59). The benefit for the Bermuda Biological Station and Aquarium, constructed on nearby Agar's Island out of a former powder magazine used by the Royal Army, took place on 9 April at the Colonial Opera House. Clemens told three of his stock anecdotes: his theft of a green watermelon, which he returned for a ripe one; his shocking discovery of a corpse in his father's office; and his disastrous attempt to ride a Mexican plug (from *Roughing It,* chapter 24) ("Lecture at the Colonial Opera House," Bermuda *Royal Gazette,* 11 Apr 1908, unknown page; see also Hoffmann 2006, 123–25).

212.10   Chief Justice] Henry Cowper Gollan (1868–1949), chief justice of Bermuda from 1904 to 1911.

212.14–16   their Excellencies Governor Wodehouse and . . . Earl Grey, Governor-General of Canada] Josceline Heneage Wodehouse (1852–1930) was governor of Bermuda in 1907–8; he had married Mary Joyce Wilmot-Sitwell in 1901. Albert Henry George, fourth earl Grey (1851–1917), was the governor-general of Canada from 1904 to 1911. Although some of his pro-imperialist policies made him unpopular, especially in Quebec, he had a reputation for integrity and conscientiousness. He successfully promoted Canadian-American cooperation, and was responsible for the creation of numerous cultural and sporting events. He and his wife, the former Alice Holford, had been married since 1877 and had five children.

213.2   the time that the slave woman plucked me out of Bear Creek] Clemens describes this incident—and his other near drownings—in the Autobiographical Dictation of 9 March 1906 (*AutoMT1,* 401–2).

213.9–10   One of my angel-fishes was along—a diffident Boston schoolgirl of sixteen years] Dorothy Sturgis: see the Autobiographical Dictation of 17 April 1908, notes at 220.40 and 221.9–13.

213.19   mother in Israel] A virtuous and faithful woman; the term derives from the biblical prophetess Deborah, a wise judge and courageous leader (Judges 5:7).

Autobiographical Dictation, 17 April 1908

213.27   One day at Riverdale-on-the-Hudson] The Clemens family lived principally in Riverdale from 1 October 1901 until their departure for Italy in the fall of 1903 (*AutoMT2,* 506 n. 82.4–9, 507–8 n. 99.16–19, 651).

213.27–214.9   Mrs. Clemens and I were mourning . . . departed this life August 18, 1896] This "dictation" is actually a transcription of two manuscripts. One of them, on which Clemens wrote "Dictated April 17/08," contains the two prose sections of the text. The inserted poem is in a second manuscript, which he finished at York Harbor, the resort in Maine where the family spent the summer of 1902. Dated "August 18, 1902," it was written to commemorate the sixth anniversary of the death of Susy Clemens at age twenty-four, from meningitis (SLC 1902). The "lost little ones" were Clara, born in 1874, and Jean, born in 1880 (see the Appendix "Family Biographies"). The poem is a revised version of "Broken Idols," written in Kaltenleutgeben, Austria, on 18 August 1898 (SLC 1898). Many lines of the 1902 poem are identical to the 1898 version, but other sections are new, or rearranged. In both poems the old woman and her lost child clearly represent Olivia and Susy (for a full discussion of "Broken Idols" see Bush 2007, 246–50).

216.36–217.7 But turned sixteen . . . In roses pearled with dew—so sweet, so glad] At age seventeen Susy wrote and staged *A Love-Chase,* a play "formed upon Greek lines." Clemens described the occasion in his "Memorial to Susy" (see *AutoMT1,* 327, 580 n. 327.11–13, and the photograph following page 204).

218.20–28 "And I not by! . . . For mother-help, and got for answer—Silence!"] Susy died in the family home in Hartford while her parents and sister were abroad: see the Autobiographical Dictation of 2 February 1906 (*AutoMT1,* 323–25).

219.24–28 Dorothy Butes . . . we correspond] Margaret Dorothy Butes (1893–1975), Clemens's first angelfish, was born in London to Alfred and Janet Butes. Her father, a skilled stenographer, was for many years the confidential secretary of New York publisher Joseph Pulitzer. Dorothy met Clemens in the fall of 1906 through George Barr Baker, an associate editor of *Everybody's Magazine,* who chatted with Dorothy at a dinner and wrote Clemens of her desire to "know where Mark Twain lives" (Baker to SLC, 21 Oct 1906, CU-MARK). Three days later, on 24 October, Dorothy herself wrote Clemens, enthusiastically praising his works, and on 30 October her mother took her to meet him (CU-MARK; Lyon 1906, entry for 30 Oct; Lyon 1907, entry for 28 Aug). In early 1907 Dorothy submitted at least one story to *St. Nicholas* magazine: the March issue included her on a list of those whose work "entitled them to encouragement" (34:474). In mid-1907 Alfred Butes resigned his position with Pulitzer (forfeiting his role as a trustee of Pulitzer's estate and a fifty-thousand-dollar legacy) and accepted a secretarial job with the English publisher Lord Northcliffe (see AD, 24 Nov 1908, note at 278.21–38). Dorothy returned to England with her family in July; Clemens was "heartsick" to see her go (Lyon 1907, entry for 25 July; see Schmidt 2009, an important source for the biographical information in many of the notes for this dictation). Ten of Dorothy's letters survive in the Mark Twain Papers, but only three of Clemens's to her have been found. Much of the correspondence between Clemens and his angelfish has been published in *Mark Twain's Aquarium* (Cooley 1991, 285–93).

219.29–33 Frances Nunnally . . . Europe-bound] See the Autobiographical Dictation of 25 July 1907 and the note at 74.15–21. Frances and Clemens planned to meet in New York before her departure for Europe, but the date had not yet been fixed. They saw each other on 12 June, the day before she embarked (Nunnally to SLC, 30 Apr 1908, CU-MARK; 29 May 1908 to Welles, CU-MARK).

219.34–36 Dorothy Quick . . . How many chapters have I already talked about her] See the Autobiographical Dictations of 5 October 1907 and 14 February 1908.

220.13–21 Margaret Blackmer . . . I am to say a few words] Clemens describes his first meeting with Margaret, in Bermuda, in his Autobiographical Dictation of 13 February 1908 (see also the note at 203.7). She was a pupil at the Misses Tewksbury's School for Girls in Briarcliff Manor, in Westchester County. Her letter of "five days ago" does not survive; on 15 April Clemens replied to it:

> So I will look for you about the 23ᵈ. I am the honorary President of the Children's Theatre, & on the 23ᵈ the children will give a performance in aid of one of the great charities. Ah, they are great, those gifted children. Of course I shall be there (for I have to speak a few words,) & it would be lovely if you could go there with Miss Lyon & me. Can you? Will you? (CtY-BR, in Cooley 1991, 136)

Lyon noted in her journal that on 23 April she and Clemens attended an evening performance at the Children's Theatre with publisher Robert J. Collier and his wife (like Clemens, Collier was on the newly formed board of directors); she made no mention of Margaret (Lyon 1908, entry for 23 April; for the Children's Theatre see AD, 13 Jan 1908, note at 199.9 [2nd]). According to the New York *Times,* Clemens gave a "short address" on the occasion, while the entire staff of the Children's Theatre "ranged itself behind the curtains, with an eye at every possible peep hole, and an ear at every crack" to hear him ("Child Actors Warm to Their Mark Twain," 24 Apr 1908, 9).

220.22–23 Irene Gerken . . . of twelve summers] Clemens "found" Irene (1896–1969) in Bermuda on 25 February 1908 (Lyon 1908, entry for 25 Feb). Her parents, Frederick and Charlotte Gerken, were both immigrants from Germany. Frederick was a wealthy businessman and real estate developer; one of his enterprises was a casino in Deal, New Jersey, where the family spent their summers. His interests included yachting and horse racing. In 1915 Irene married Joseph L. Egan, an attorney who later became the president of the Western Union Telegraph Company.

220.31 Hellen Martin, of Montreal, Canada] Hellen Elizabeth Martin (b. 1897) was the daughter of Robert Dennison Martin, born in Ontario, and the former Helen Moncrieff Morton, an immigrant from Scotland; they had lived in Montreal since 1899. Martin was a highly successful grain merchant. He died in 1905 at age fifty, leaving his widow with five young children, of whom Hellen was the second oldest. In about 1947 she married Rudolf James Waeckerlin, the Swiss consul to Jamaica (Atherton 1914, 3:94–97; Lowrey 2013).

220.33 Jean Spurr, aged thirteen the 14th of last March] Clemens met Jean Woodward Spurr (1896–1979) in Bermuda no later than 20 March, when Lyon noted in her journal, "Jean wears a blond wig & has no eyebrows or lashes, but the King doesn't care about a detail like that. He sees into her fair young soul & is very glad" (Lyon 1908). She was the daughter of Harriet and Edwin Robert Spurr of New Jersey. Spurr was a contractor of cut stone; his company, founded by his father, supplied stone for many important buildings in New York. Jean graduated from Vassar College in 1917, and in 1919 married Walter Wood Gamble of Jersey City, an engineer in the oil industry (*Connecticut Death Index* 1949–2001, record for Jean Woodward Spurr; *Vassarion* 29 [1917]: 86).

220.35   Loraine Allen, nine and a half years old] Loraine Allen (1898–1984) was the only child of the former Grace Fanshawe and George Marshall Allen of New York. In 1904 her father incorporated the Bermuda Electric Light, Power and Traction Company, which began to supply electric current in May 1908. In 1917 Loraine married Allan MacDougall, a coffee merchant; they divorced in 1941. She later married Godfrey Stephen Beresford.

220.38   Helen Allen, aged thirteen, native of Bermuda] Helen Schuyler Allen (1895–1956) was the daughter of William Henry Allen, the American vice-consul to Bermuda, and his wife, Marion. Clemens noticed Helen when she came to the Princess Hotel to watch the dancing, and two days later she invited him to her home, Bay House. There he learned that he had met Helen's grandfather, Charles Maxwell Allen, who had been the U.S. consul to Bermuda when the *Quaker City* stopped there on its return to New York in 1867. And he discovered an even more remarkable coincidence: as a child, Olivia Clemens had been acquainted with Helen's grandmother, Susan Elizabeth Allen, whom he visited in Flatts Village to reminisce about the Langdon family. The Allens became warm and hospitable friends; in 1910, during his last trip to Bermuda, Clemens made his home at Bay House. In 1913 Helen's mother recorded her memories of his stay in a magazine article, "Some New Anecdotes of Mark Twain" (Allen 1913; Hoffmann 2006, 120). In 1915, at age nineteen, Helen married Percy Walker Nelles, who had a successful career in the Royal Canadian Navy, retiring in 1945 as an admiral.

220.40   Dorothy Sturgis, aged sixteen, of Boston] Dorothy Sturgis (1891–1978) was visiting Bermuda with her parents and older brother while her mother recovered from an operation. Clemens became acquainted with her at the Princess Hotel; he had already met her father, prominent architect Richard Clipston Sturgis (1860–1951), at the Tavern Club in Boston. Dorothy, who attended the prestigious Winsor School for girls (housed in a Boston building designed by her father), was interested in art. She later studied at the Boston Museum of Fine Arts, worked as a draftsman at the Portsmouth (N.H.) Naval Shipyard, and had a successful career as a bookplate designer and book illustrator (Harding 1967, 3–4; "Social Life," Boston *Herald,* 12 Apr 1908, 2; American Antiquarian Society 2013).

221.1–5   On the voyage . . . made a perilous and thundersome event of it] In a letter to Clemens of 14 April 1908, Dorothy commented on the dramatic accounts of their misadventure: "I suppose you saw what they said in the newspapers about our being caught by that wave. The account in the Boston Herald was really very funny, and of course mostly incorrect!" (CU-MARK, in Cooley 1991, 135). The *Herald* story was entitled "Mark Twain Near Death from Huge Wave":

> The humorist was one of a very few that ventured on the deck during the 60-mile gale and his companion was Miss Dorothy Sturgis, daughter of a well known New York architect. Mr. Clemens had Dorothy by the arm, and they were making great sport of their hazardous progress down the promenade deck, slipping from side to side as the wind buffeted them and the spray dashed in their faces.
> Suddenly a giant comber hurled itself slantwise at the ship and burst in a delug-

ing cloud of water over the rail. A swirl of the water descended upon Mark Twain and the young girl and snatched her from his protecting arm. She was swept from him and down into the scuppers. Then Mr. Clemens' feet went out from under him as another wave pounded over the side, but he managed by an agile movement to catch the rail and save himself.

As soon as he could gain his feet he worked his way down the scuppers to where Miss Sturgis lay gasping and in a perfect swoon. He caught the young girl in his arms and carried her safely to a gangway and down into the shelter of the cabin. (14 Apr 1908, 16)

The story was picked up by newspapers across the country: see, for example, "Mark Twain a Hero," in the Waterloo (Iowa) *Courier* (15 Apr 1908, 4), and "Twain Nearly Goes Overboard" in the Los Angeles *Times* (14 Apr 1908, 11).

221.9–13   All the ten schoolgirls in the above list are my angel-fishes ... their Club the Aquarium] Clemens visited the Bermuda aquarium on 1 March (see AD, 16 Apr 1908, note at 212.5–6). According to Paine, it was the angelfish he saw there—which "suggested youth and feminine beauty"—that inspired him to establish his club for young girls (*MTB*, 3:1440). Lyon noted in her journal on 1 April: "He has his aquarium of little girls—& they are all angel fish—while he wears a flying fish scarf pin, though he says he is a shad. Off he goes with a flash when he sees a new pair of slim little legs appear; & if the little girl wears butterfly bows of ribbon on the back of her head then his delirium is complete" (Lyon 1908, entries for 1 Mar and 1 Apr). The roster of "The Aquarium" in Clemens's June 1908 notebook (Notebook 48, TS p. 3, CU-MARK) includes two members whom he does not mention in his autobiography: Marjorie Breckenridge (1893–1980), daughter of Maude Breckenridge and stepdaughter of her second husband, attorney John M. Dater, Redding neighbors of Clemens's; and Louise Paine (1894–1968), the oldest daughter of Albert Bigelow Paine and his wife, Dora. The roster includes Dorothy Harvey, whom he refers to only as his "American" Dorothy in the Autobiographical Dictation of 14 February 1908. He also makes no mention in the autobiography of Gertrude Natkin (1890–1969), whom he did not consider an official angelfish, possibly because she was more mature than the others. (He addressed her as "Marjorie," after Marjory Fleming, the precocious Scottish girl whose writing he admired: see *AutoMT1*, 581 n. 328.12.) Clemens met Gertrude in New York in December 1905, and corresponded with her frequently until April 1906, when she turned sixteen. His letters then became brief and intermittent (most of their correspondence is in CU-MARK). On her birthday he wrote her: "*Sixteen!* Ah, what has become of my little girl? I am almost afraid to send a blot [kiss], but I venture it. Bless your heart it comes within an ace of being improper! Now back you go to 14!—then there's no impropriety" (8 Apr 1906, CU-MARK, in Cooley 1991, 1–3, 24–25).

221.17–19   A year or two ago I bought a lovely piece of landscape ... We'll spend the coming summer in it] See the Autobiographical Dictation of 26 March 1907, note at 13.20–22. Paine described the house as "simple and severe in its architecture—an Italian villa, such as he had known in Florence, adapted now to American climate and needs." Clemens left all the oversight of design and construction details to Clara Clemens and Isabel Lyon, preferring not to see the house, he said, "until the cat is purring on the hearth" (*MTB*, 3:1446, 1450): "I was not willing to discuss the plans nor look at the drawings. I merely said I wanted three things—a room of my own that would be quiet, a billiard-room big enough to play in without jabbing the cues into the wall, and a living-room forty by twenty feet" (Dugmore 1909, 608). The builders, William W. Sunderland and his son, Philip, of Danbury, Connecticut, broke ground on 23 May 1907. As work progressed, Lyon enthusiastically took on the job of decorating and furnishing the new home; by early June she was working "night & day" to prepare it for occupancy (14 June 1908 to Quick, CU-MARK). On 18 June Clemens, accompanied by Paine, traveled by train to Redding, where he entered the house for the first time. He wrote to Clara, who was in London on a concert tour:

> I have been in residence two days, now, & I realize that this is the most satisfactory house I was ever in & also about the most beautiful. The Hartford house was a lovely home, but the architect damaged many of its comfort-possibilities & wasted a deal of its space. The New York house is a roomy & pleasant home, but it is sunless not beautiful. This house is roomy & delightful & beautiful, & no space has been wasted. The sun falls upon it in such floods that you can hear it. Miss Lyon has achieved wonders, I think. (20 June 1908, photocopy in CU-MARK)

Clemens at first intended to live in Redding only during the summer, spending the rest of the year at 21 Fifth Avenue. On 18 July, however, he wrote to Clara, "I do so delight in this home that the thought of ever going back to that crude & tasteless New York barn, even to stay over night, revolts me. I do not wish to live anywhere but here" (CSmH); and by mid-August he had decided to "stay here winter & summer both" (13 Aug 1908 to Allen, BmuHA). For a detailed description of the house, with photographs and architectural plans, see Mac Donnell 2006.

221.23–24 There's a letter from the little Montreal Hellen. I will begin an answer . . . finish it later] Although Clemens wrote "Dictated April 17, 1908" on the manuscript that is the source of this "dictation," he may well have finished it some days later. Neither of the two letters that Hellen wrote by mid-April could have arrived by 17 April, but either one might have been delivered on 18 April. Her first letter, dated 7 April, was sent to Bermuda; the postmark indicates that it was not forwarded to New York until 16 April (CU-MARK):

Westmount
1 Murray Ave
April 7th 1908

Dear Mr Clemens
We arrived at home on Sunday morning April 5th, We stayed five day's in New York and had a fine time there. We found our cat had run away on saturday eve-

ning, We did not get him back until Monday morning. Our dog was delighted at our coming back. How are you feeling. I was very sick on the boat and so was Mother, it was very rough coming back. The snow is going away very slowly. It is a lovely day and quite warm we seem to have brought good weather with us. I have not started my lessons yet. My little dickie Bird sing's beautifully. We were down town yesterday. I wish you a Bright and Happy Easter. I am feeling quite well now. Lots of Love from xxxxxxxxxxxx

Your Little friend
Hellen Martin

P. S. Please write soon.

Hellen's second letter, undated but postmarked in Montreal on 17 April (at 6 p.m.), was sent directly to New York (CU-MARK):

Dear Mr Clemens

I wrote you a letter but was just to late for the mail for Bermuda. I hope you had a pleasant voyage coming back. My Brother Charlie who is at Boarding School, is coming Back for the Easter Holidays. How are you feeling now? I am feeling fine, Lots of Love from

Your Loving Little friend
Hellen Martin

P. S. Wishing you a very Happy Easter. H. M.

No reply from Clemens other than the fragment in this dictation has been found. He did finish and send it, however: Hellen acknowledged his letter on 24 April, saying "I also miss you very much indeed" (CU-MARK).

221.27–28   rain, you know, which falls upon the just and the unjust alike] A paraphrase of Matthew 5:45.

221.31–32   Reverend Twichell is coming down from Hartford . . . a word of welcome] Twichell had written (CU-MARK):

Hartford.
Apr. 15. 1908

Dear Mark:

You were doubtless grieved to learn—if you did learn—on your arrival home that you had missed the honor and privilege of my "keep" over last Sunday.

But dry your tears. It is wonderful how Providence does favor some people. I am called to New York again:—this time to attend a meeting in Carnegie Hall next Monday evening (Apr. 20) and I will lodge with you then if you say so.

But there's no *compulsion* about it, you understand.

Yours aff
Joe

On Sunday, 12 April 1908, Twichell, a former Union army battlefield chaplain, had been in New York to participate in a service of the Military Order of the Loyal Legion of the

United States, commemorating the end of the Civil War. The meeting that he planned to attend on 20 April was "held under the auspices of the Laymen's Missionary Movement"; the featured speaker was Secretary of War Taft. Afterward, Twichell did "lodge" with Clemens at 21 Fifth Avenue. Presumably Clemens sent him a "word of welcome," but perhaps not exactly the one he drafted here: the source of our text is a manuscript that remained in his possession; the letter he mailed to Twichell has not been found ("Agents of Trade Hurt Us in Orient," New York *Times,* 21 Apr 1908, 3; *AutoMT1,* 287, 312, 430–31, 632–33 nn. 430.29–30, 430.40–431.7; Twichell 1874–1916, entries for 11–13 and 20–21 Apr 1908).

221.33–37 "new movement" up your way . . . Christian Science, with some of the ear-marks painted over] In 1906 Elwood Worcester (1862–1940), rector of the Emmanuel Episcopal Church in Boston, established a clinic to treat people with "nervous disorders," guided by the principles of psychology developed by Sigmund Freud and William James (among others), which emphasize the connection between physical and emotional health. Worcester rejected most of the theology of Christian Science, especially its repudiation of traditional medicine, but accepted its central idea of the healing power of Christ. He and his associate rector, Samuel McComb (1864–1938), treated only ailments which, in their judgment, originated in the mind or soul, such as melancholia, neurasthenia, anxiety, and alcohol addiction. Their techniques included psychotherapy, hypnosis, and the power of suggestion, which they described in a book published in May 1908 entitled *Religion and Medicine: The Moral Control of Nervous Disorders* (Worcester, McComb, and Coriat 1908). McComb became the primary spokesman for the Emmanuel movement. His lecture in Hartford on 31 January 1908 excited much interest among ministers and doctors ("Dr. McCombe Tells of His Clinics," Hartford *Courant,* 1 Feb 1908, 6).

221.39–222.3 The Jews steal a God . . . Christian Science arrives and steals the Christian outfit] For similar comments see the Autobiographical Dictations of 20 June and 22 June 1906 (*AutoMT2,* 130–32, 136, 525–26 n. 136.10–12).

222.10–12 Christian Science, disguised . . . the Theological Factory] William D. Mackenzie, president of the Hartford Theological Seminary, was concerned that physicians and ministers in Hartford without adequate training might immediately begin to offer treatments like those being implemented at Emmanuel Church. To avert such a "hazardous" undertaking he arranged two courses of lectures at the seminary on nervous diseases. The first, by a doctor, was to cover their "physical basis." The second, by Samuel McComb, would address "their psychology, their relation to the spiritual life, the therapeutic value of prayer and mental suggestion in dealing with them" ("The Healing of Sick Minds in Sick Bodies" and "Letters from the People: A Notable Announcement," Hartford *Courant,* 11 Mar 1908, 8). According to the New Haven *Register,* Mackenzie's "announcement can hardly do less than rivet the attention of students of the times everywhere. It is probably the most important indication so far given of the new turn toward the healing of the body which the church is taking" ("The Simpson-McComb Lectures," Hartford *Courant* [reprinting the New Haven *Register*], 14 Mar 1908, 8).

222.12–14   largely built out of stolen money . . . his pals of the American Publishing Company] Clemens believed that Newton Case, a director of the American Publishing Company, had been complicit when Elisha Bliss, as the company's secretary, falsely claimed that the royalties on Clemens's books, which ranged from 5 to 10 percent, represented at least half the profits. After Bliss's death in 1880, the account statement furnished by the board convinced Clemens that Bliss had been swindling him ever since he signed the contract for *Roughing It* in 1870. Clemens tried to buy his book contracts, but Case refused, prompting him to publish with another company. His next book, *The Prince and the Pauper*, was issued in 1881 by James R. Osgood. Case was also a trustee and generous benefactor of the Hartford Theological Seminary. By 1890 he had donated at least one hundred and fifty thousand dollars—money that Clemens claimed was "stolen"—to build a library (*AutoMT1*, 370–72, 498 n. 112.20, notes on 596–97; *AutoMT2*, 52–53, 488 n. 53.19–20; "Obituary. Newton Case," Hartford *Courant*, 16 Sept 1890, 1).

Autobiographical Dictation, 27 April 1908

222.21–22   District-Attorney Jerome . . . The newspaper report says] William Travers Jerome (1859–1934), a graduate of Columbia Law School, was the district attorney of New York City from 1901 to 1909. He was known for his vigorous crusade against crime and vice, and was a persistent foe of the corrupt Tammany Hall political machine. Clemens supported his reelection in 1905, donating twenty-five dollars to the campaign. In 1909, at a dinner honoring Jerome, Clemens made a brief speech expressing regret that as a Connecticut resident he was no longer eligible to cast a vote for him. He concluded, "I am not a Congress, and I cannot distribute pensions, and I don't know any other legitimate way to buy a vote" (New York *Times:* "Jerome Reviews His Official Years," 8 May 1909, 1–2; "Jerome Dies at 74; Long Tammany Foe," 14 Feb 1934, 19; 14 Oct 1905 to Jerome, CU-MARK). Jerome delivered his speech at the annual dinner of the St. George's Society, a charity founded in 1770 to assist needy British people living in New York. The dinner was held on 23 April 1908 at the Waldorf-Astoria Hotel; the text that Clemens inserts here is from the New York *World* of the following day ("Jerome Rails at 'Government by Newspapers,'" 2).

222.23–24   British Ambassador, Mr. Bryce] James Bryce (see AD, 2 Dec 1907, note at 181.17–20).

222.27–28   Pat. McCarren, Charley Murphy, Fingy Conners and Packy McCabe] Patrick Henry McCarren (1849–1909) served as a Democratic state senator from 1890 until his death, except for a single term. In 1903 he became the political "boss" of Brooklyn, but remained independent of Tammany Hall. According to his obituary, he was "accused of the basest and lowest forms of political fraud and criminality," but "remained the most strongly intrenched political leader in New York State." Charles Francis Murphy (1858–1924) was the Democratic leader of Tammany Hall from 1902 until his death.

William James ("Fingy") Conners (1857–1929), a Buffalo newspaper publisher and Great Lakes shipping magnate, became chairman of the State Democratic Committee in 1906. Patrick ("Packy") McCabe (1860–1931) was the leader of the Democratic party in Albany County for twenty years. He was elected county clerk in 1899, and in 1904 became a member of the State Democratic Committee (New York *Times:* "M'Carren Is Dead; Lingered All Day," 23 Oct 1909, 1; "Chief Is Stricken Suddenly," 26 Apr 1924, 1; "William J. Conners Dies in Buffalo," 6 Oct 1929, N6; "P. E. M'Cabe Dies; Once Albany Boss," 3 Nov 1931, 24).

223.5–7   the head of a great financial institution killed himself . . . private life] On 14 November 1907 Charles T. Barney (1851–1907), ousted three weeks previously as president of the Knickerbocker Trust Company (see AD, 1 Nov 1907, note at 177.26–27), shot himself and died several hours later. His financial problems were merely temporary, and he was not suspected of any wrongdoing; according to his friends, it was his "mental anguish" over being asked to resign that drove him to suicide ("C. T. Barney Dies, a Suicide," New York *Times,* 15 Nov 1907, I13). Several newspapers speculated that his reasons were more personal, reporting that his wife was divorcing him on account of his illicit relationship with a "prominent society woman" ("Barney's Home Life Notoriously Unhappy," Los Angeles *Times,* 15 Nov 1907, I1). The New York *Daily People* (and probably other newspapers) went even further: according to a lurid story printed only three days after Barney's death, letters found in his desk had revealed that he was having an affair with a second woman—the former mistress of a "French prince"—whom he supported in luxury. She ended the relationship when she learned that he was in "financial straits": "Coming on the top of the financial crash, after he realized that he had sacrificed his family and everything else, this proved the hardest blow" ("Barney's Secrets. The Skeleton Peeps Out of the Family Closet," 17 Nov 1907, 1). Moments before he died, Barney signed a new will, reinstating his estranged wife as sole legatee; its primary purpose, however, was (according to his lawyers) "to facilitate as much as he could the payment of his creditors"—presumably the "atonement" Jerome alluded to in his speech ("Died a Brave Man," Washington *Post,* 16 Nov 1907, 1).

223.7   He had two lovely daughters growing up] Barney and his wife, Lilly, had two married daughters, Helen and Katherine ("C. T. Barney Dies, a Suicide," New York *Times,* 15 Nov 1907, 1).

223.11–12   A large advertiser in Philadelphia . . . committed suicide here. Not a paper in Philadelphia chronicled it] On 18 April 1907 Benedict Gimbel (1869–1907), part owner, with his brothers, of a large department store in Philadelphia, was arrested in New York for molesting a sixteen-year-old boy. The boy's mother had called the police when she learned that Gimbel was spending time with her son and giving him money. Gimbel offered the arresting officer $2,100 for his release and was further charged with attempted bribery. After posting bail, Gimbel went to a hotel in Hoboken, New Jersey, where he slit his throat and wrists; he died several days later. A correspondent for the Chicago *Tribune* reported, "Evidence of the tremendous influence the Gimbels have in Philadelphia and also the peculiar methods of the Philadelphia newspapers is found in the fact that up to today not a prominent Philadelphia daily paper has published anything about Gimbel's arrest or his attempt at suicide." In addition, the Philadelphia chief of police forbade the sale there of New York papers containing news of the "disgrace" ("Gimbel's Wealth Hides Disgrace," Chicago *Tribune,* 21 Apr 1907, 6; "Gimbel Welcomed Death," Washington *Post,* 23 Apr 1907, 3). The news was only briefly suppressed. On 21 April the Philadelphia *Inquirer* reported the incident, but tried to soften the facts as much as possible by claiming that the boy's mother had "sent the police to find her son" because she was "frightened over the recent kidnapping stories," and that Gimbel's family attributed his behavior to a mental breakdown caused by overwork ("Benedict Gimbel Reported Better," 2).

223.16–17   a prominent man in this city was shot dead in a department store . . . where it was done] Unidentified.

223.22–27   One of our great papers investigated ice . . . netted the young man $5,000] In the summer of 1906 New York experienced a shortage of ice. The American Ice Company was accused of causing the shortage by using monopoly practices to control the Maine ice fields, thereby reducing supply and raising prices. After a lengthy investigation, the grand jury declined in March 1908 to make an indictment (New York *Times:* "Ice Up to 40 Cents and a Famine in Sight," 2 Mar 1906, 16; "State Sues Ice Trust; Wants It Dissolved," 21 Dec 1906, 3; "No Ice Trust Indictment," 17 Mar 1908, 1). The "young man" who "went up to Maine" has not been identified.

223.34   I was called a thief] Jerome was repeatedly criticized in the press for his alleged failure to prosecute the executives of large, powerful corporations. In particular, he was accused of laxness in pursuing several insurance companies involved in the scandals of 1905, in return for fifty thousand dollars donated to his second-term reelection campaign (see *AutoMT1,* 549 n. 257.6–9, and *AutoMT2,* 493 n. 59.5–8). More than one attempt was made to remove Jerome from office for malfeasance, but after a lengthy investigation he was completely exonerated. Before that outcome, however, he attempted to defend his reputation by suing several newspapers for libel. One insignificant lawsuit, against the editor of the Yonkers (N.Y.) *Herald,* was successful, but Jerome was awarded only $250 in damages. Of greater significance were the lawsuits he initiated in March 1906 against two New York newspapers owned by a longtime political enemy, William Randolph Hearst, which evidently were unsuccessful. At the time of his speech, Jerome was still under fire in regard to several cases involving corporate misconduct (New York *Times:* "Jerome Raps Hearst and Some Editors," 19 July 1907, 1; "Libel on Jerome Costs $250," 16 Oct 1907, 2; "Jerome's Removal Asked on Charges," 28 Feb 1908, 5; "Jerome Exonerated in Hand's Report," 25 Aug 1908, 1; Chicago *Tribune:* "Jerome Sues for Libel," 13 Mar 1906, 7; "Jerome Defends Course," 30 Mar 1906, 3; "Jerome Is Accused," Washington *Post,* 8 June 1906, 1; Richard O'Connor 1963, 254–64).

223.35–38   the Public Service bill was up in Albany . . . the Eighty Cent Gas bill]
The Public Utilities Law was passed by the New York state legislature and signed into
law in June 1907. It created a commission to oversee and control the corporations that
provided gas, electricity, and mass transportation within the city of New York and its
suburbs, for the purpose of improving services and lowering rates ("How Utilities Bill
May Aid the Public," New York *Times*, 9 June 1907, 3). A "new law providing that gas
shall be 80 cents instead of $1 a thousand feet in this city" had gone into effect a year
earlier, on 1 May 1906 ("Eighty-Cent Gas To-day," New York *Times*, 1 May 1906, 1).

224.15–34   SORROWS OF CUPID IN GOULD FAMILY . . . separation of the
couple] This newspaper article, describing the marital travails of the children of financier
and railroad magnate Jay Gould, appeared in the New York *World* on 18 April 1908 (for
Gould see *AutoMT1*, 364, 594 n. 364.19). Howard Gould (1871–1959), a financier and
yachtsman, was educated at Columbia University. To counter the charges of cruelty
brought against him by his wife, Katherine Clemmons (1874–1930), he alleged that
she had lied about her premarital relationship with "Buffalo Bill" (William F. Cody,
1846–1917), who had financed her unsuccessful stage career, and that she had carried
on an adulterous affair with Dustin Farnum (1874–1929), a well-known actor. In 1909
Mrs. Gould was exonerated and granted a separation with alimony of thirty-six thousand dollars a year ("Gould's Answer Attack on Wife," Chicago *Tribune*, 7 Apr 1908,
1; New York *Times:* "Howard Gould Dies Here at 88," 15 Sept 1959, 39; "Mrs. Howard
Gould Dies in Virginia," 25 Dec 1930, 21). Anna Gould (1875–1961) married Hélie de
Talleyrand-Périgord, Duke of Sagan, in July 1908 after he converted to Protestantism, the
Pope having denied their appeal for an annulment of her first marriage ("To Plead with
Pope," Los Angeles *Times*, 1 May 1908, I16; "Mme. Gould's Wedding To-day," New York
Times, 7 July 1908, 1; "Anna Gould Buried after Rites in Paris," Chicago *Tribune*, 3 Dec
1961, K38). Frank Jay Gould (1877–1956) graduated from the College of Engineering of
New York University in 1899; while still a young man he proved himself an able financier.
His marital difficulties began in 1906, but Mrs. Gould had only recently applied for a
legal separation ("Frank Goulds Parted," Washington *Post*, 18 Apr 1908, 3; "Frank Jay
Gould Dead on Riviera," New York *Times*, 1 Apr 1956, 88).

Autobiographical Dictation, 28 April 1908

225.2–3   Lord Dundreary has been revived . . . played by Sothern's son] Edward
Askew Sothern (1826–81), an English comedian, first portrayed the witless peer Lord
Dundreary in Tom Taylor's *Our American Cousin* in October 1858, when the play opened
at Laura Keene's Theatre in New York (see the note at 225.25). His son, Edward Hugh
Sothern (1859–1933), a leading romantic and Shakespearean actor, revived the character
fifty years later, in January 1908, at New York's Lyric Theatre, where the play had a successful fifteen-month run. Clemens attended a performance on 25 April, accompanied

by Isabel Lyon (New York *Times:* "History of 'Our American Cousin,'" 26 Jan 1908, SM10; "Amusements," 14 April 1909, 9; Lyon 1908, entry for 25 Apr).

225.6–8   I can distinctly remember . . . it was in Hartford] Clemens evidently saw the elder Sothern perform as Lord Dundreary in Hartford in March 1874. Sothern had first enacted the role there in January 1872, when Clemens was absent on a lecture tour ("Sothern's Father Played Here in '72," Hartford *Courant,* 1 Apr 1922, 6; "Lecture Schedule, 1871–1872," *L4,* 559–60; 26 Apr 1875 to Jennings, *L6,* 468–69 n. 6).

225.18–20   Dundreary made in London the first long-run record . . . when a hundred nights was a long run] After a successful six-month run in New York in 1858–59, Sothern took the play to London. At first it was a failure, but after the manager of the Haymarket Theatre "papered" the house for six weeks, according to the New York *Times,* "Lord Dundreary became the cynosure of all eyes, and 'The American Cousin' was played to crowded and enthusiastic audiences for 477 consecutive nights" ("History of 'Our American Cousin,'" New York *Times,* 26 Jan 1908, SM10).

225.24   Daniel Frohman and his wife have been dining with us] Clemens had known Frohman since at least 1886, when Frohman planned to produce the play *Colonel Sellers as a Scientist,* a project conceived by Clemens and Howells but never produced. In 1889–90 he mounted Richardson's short-lived stage adaptation of *The Prince and the Pauper* (*N&J3,* 237 n. 39; see AD, 28 Aug 1907, notes at 115.6–11 and 115.34–37). Under Frohman's management, from the mid-1880s until 1898, the younger Sothern became a star, and in 1900 noted actress Margaret Illington (1879–1934) made her debut on Frohman's stage. Despite the nearly thirty years' difference in their ages, she and Frohman married in 1903 ("E. H. Sothern Dies of Pneumonia at 73," New York *Times,* 30 Oct 1933, 1; Schmidt 2009). Clemens was very fond of Illington, and dined with the Frohmans several times in 1908, most recently on 26 April (Lyon 1908, entries for 5 Jan, 19 and 26 Apr, and 10 May). On 12 May Clemens wrote to Dorothy Quick, "Margaret Illington has been trying to get into our Aquarium, & I wouldn't let her; but Sunday night she came here to dinner with her husband (Daniel Frohman), & she was dressed for 12 years, & had pink ribbons at the back of her neck & looked about 14 years old; so I admitted her as an angel-fish, & pinned the badge on her bosom" (CU-MARK, in Cooley 1991, 154). The Frohmans were divorced in 1909, and Illington was remarried a few days later to Edward J. Bowes, a wealthy real estate developer. On 26 January 1910 Clemens wrote to her, "I am so glad to know you are happy! for I love you so. Some are born for one thing, some for another; but you were specially born to love & be loved, & be happy—& so, things are with you now as they ought to be" (photocopy in CU-MARK, in Cooley 1991, 270–71).

225.25   Laura Keene accepted the play and staged it here in New York] Keene (1826–73) was born in England and emigrated to the United States in 1852. Within a few years she had established herself as a successful theater manager as well as an accomplished actress. According to the New York *Times,*

Tom Taylor wrote the comedy for the English stage, and his idea was to exploit the uncouth sort of American who was coming into humorous literature on both sides of the Atlantic. . . . The author sent the play over to Laura Keene, then in the height of her glory in New York, perhaps because the London comedians could not see any sympathetic interest in the part of Asa Trenchard, or did not believe that the London public would be interested in the American yokel so differentiated from the English Tony Lumpkin type which held so large a place on the English stage. ("History of 'Our American Cousin,'" New York *Times,* 26 Jan 1908, SM10)

Although Keene "did not see great possibilities" in the script, she decided to stage it to fill a schedule gap. She asked Joe Jefferson (1829–1905), a member of her stock company, to play the "yokel" Asa Trenchard—the character that was soon eclipsed by Sothern's creative impersonation of Lord Dundreary.

Autobiographical Dictation, 29 April 1908

226 *title*   Dictated April 29, 1908] This "dictation" is in fact based on a manuscript.

226.7–8   He is about thirty-five years old] Henry van Dyke was born in 1852.

226.11–13   It is a grand Catholic day . . . there is to be great doings] The Catholics of the city were participating in festivities held to commemorate the founding of the Diocese of New York, which began on 26 April with a thanksgiving mass at St. Patrick's Cathedral and ended on 2 May with a parade down Fifth Avenue. The climax of the week was a pontifical mass celebrated at the cathedral on 28 April by Michael Cardinal Logue of Ireland; at its conclusion Archbishop John M. Farley of New York read a congratulatory message from Pope Pius X (New York *Times:* "Primate of Ireland Here for Centennial," 26 Apr 1908, 16; "Papal Greeting to New York Catholics," 29 Apr 1908, 3; "Big Parade to End Church Centennial," 2 May 1908, 5).

227.39   I clipped it out of the *Atlantic* last night] The passage inserted below was originally published in "Some Remarks on Gulls," an article by van Dyke in *Scribner's Magazine* for August 1907 (van Dyke 1907, 142). Clemens found it quoted in "Shall We Hunt and Fish? The Confessions of a Sentimentalist," an essay by Episcopal minister Henry Bradford Washburn which appeared in the May 1908 issue of the *Atlantic Monthly.* Washburn used van Dyke's words as a "point of departure" to describe and explain his "positive aversion to the processes and the results of sportsmanship entailing death": "It is bolder still to say that the sentimentalist is the only consistent Christian, that he is the one man who has reached that point where he dislikes all things that entail suffering or the curtailing of natural freedom, the man who cannot add to the total of necessary pain the agony incident to sport" (Washburn 1908, 672, 674, 678).

228.36–37   my privately printed, unsigned, unacknowledged and unpublished gospel, "What is Man?"] See the Autobiographical Dictation of 25 June 1906 (*AutoMT2,* 140–43, 527 n. 142.14, 602–3 n. 332.35–36).

Autobiographical Dictation, 21 May 1908

229.6–7 a note from a son of a former schoolmate of mine ... "Buck" Brown] Clemens's recollection of "W. B. Brown" in this dictation closely resembles his description of "Bill Brown" in a letter to William Bowen of 6 February 1870. But his mention of the nickname "Buck" suggests that he was not remembering William Lee Brown (1831?–1903), but his older brother, James Burnett (or Burkett) Brown (1827–1915), who was known as "Doc Buck Brown." James, a druggist, served as mayor of Hannibal in 1882–83, and Clemens had seen him in 1902 during his last visit to Hannibal. His son's "note" has not been found (*Inds*, 20–23, 308; Edgar White 1924, 52; Wecter 1952, 305 n. 16; Find a Grave Memorial 2013b; *Marion Census* 1870, 791:524B; Holcombe 1884, 910; *MTB*, 3:1168).

229.9–10 my father died ... I was never in school after that event] According to the 1850 Hannibal census, compiled in October, Clemens had been in school "within the year," which suggests that he received at least some schooling after his father's death (*Inds*, 314).

229.24–25 Will Bowen and John Briggs] See *AutoMT1*, 614 n. 402.16–33, 627–28 n. 420.17–18.

229.35 Aldine Club] According to *Publishers' Weekly,* the Aldine Club was incorporated in 1889 "to encourage literature and art" and also to give New York publishers "a congenial place in which to lunch and talk shop." Although in 1898 it consolidated with the Uptown Association and was then to be officially known as the Aldine Association, it continued "to be identified in the popular mind with the original name" ("The Aldine Association," 25 Mar 1899, 552). On 4 December 1900, the Aldine had given an elaborate dinner to Clemens, called "the most notable event of the kind that has ever taken place at that club" ("Mark Twain at the Aldine Club," New York *Times,* 15 Dec 1900, BR8; see also the note at 231.8–13).

230.10–12 The corporations were the creation of the atrocious tariffs imposed upon everything by the Republican party] The issue of protective tariffs was a major point of political debate in the late nineteenth and early twentieth centuries, especially during the 1908 presidential election (see AD, 16 July and 12 Sept 1908, note at 260.4–9). Clemens voices the position of the Democrats, who claimed that duties on foreign goods were more of a hardship for small businesses than for powerful monopolies, which could better afford the high cost of materials and, by limiting production, raise consumer prices. Henry O. Havemeyer, head of the sugar-refining industry, called the tariff the "mother of all trusts"—a phrase that became the motto of the antiprotectionists. The Republicans, on the other hand, "endorsed the principle of protection as being highly advantageous to both labor and industry" by making domestic products cheaper than foreign ones (Hornig 1958, 241–43; Hardesty 1899, 185). In their view, trusts were the inevitable result of a market economy (see the note at 230.16–17).

230.16–17 they have persisted in attacking the symptoms and in letting the disease carefully alone] Roosevelt expressed the Republican position in his first Annual Message, delivered on 3 December 1901: "The creation of these great corporate fortunes has not been due to the tariff nor to any other governmental action, but to natural causes in the business world." Moreover, in a speech on 4 April 1903 he asserted that lowering the tariff would not

> have any substantial effect in solving the so-called trust problem. Certain great trusts or great corporations are wholly unaffected by the tariff. Almost all the others that are of any importance have as a matter of fact numbers of smaller American competitors; and of course a change in the tariff which would work injury to the large corporation would work not merely injury but destruction to its smaller competitors; and equally of course such a change would mean disaster to all the wage-workers connected with either the large or the small corporations. (Roosevelt 1908, 1:164, 211)

230.18–21 the vast election contributions of the money . . . has merely indulged in wordy bluster] Clemens's statement here is at odds with his earlier complaint that Roosevelt did not honor his "contract" with the Republican party to protect the monopolies in return for campaign donations (see AD, 13 Sept 1907, and the note at 135.11–16). Roosevelt accomplished less with his antitrust crusades than he is sometimes credited with. Not only was he occupied with other matters, he was hampered by the existing law and by clever corporate defense attorneys. But he did bring the public's attention to the importance of curbing monopolies, which set the stage for further reforms under his successor, President Taft, who initiated nearly double the number of successful proceedings against them (Pringle 1956, 300).

230.22–23 the chief sinner selected for attack was the Standard Oil Company] See the Autobiographical Dictation of 13 September 1907 and the note at 135.21–22.

230.28–29 The Company has been in existence about forty-five years . . . never had a strike] The company was founded in 1870 by John D. Rockefeller, Sr., and several partners, and by the early 1880s dominated the oil industry. Its workers first went on strike in 1915.

231.8–13 Doubleday came here a few days ago . . . see what he might look like in there] Frank N. Doubleday wrote to Clemens on 15 May 1908 (CU-MARK):

> Dear Mr. Clemens:
>   As I telephoned Miss Lyon, I saw Mr. Rogers, and he agreed to come to our luncheon at one o'clock on Wednesday, May 20th, at the Aldine Club, 111 Fifth Avenue if he was in town. Mr. Rogers, I think, will come *if he is in town,* but I am almost afraid that he will run away so that he will not have to come, and I hope you will corral him for the good of the cause. I will be there to meet you, or will come to your house and meet you and Mr. Rogers together if you would prefer to have me.
>   I have invited young Mr. John Rockefeller and Mr. Walter Jennings, and hope

that they will also be present. There are to be no reporters, and it will be entirely informal and friendly.

Very sincerely yours,
F N Doubleday.

Walter Jennings (1858–1933), son of Oliver Burr Jennings, one of the original stockholders in the Standard Oil Company, became a director of the Standard Oil Company of New Jersey in 1903 and served as its secretary in 1908–11 ("Walter Jennings Dies in the South," New York *Times,* 10 Jan 1933, 21).

231.14–23   Mr. Rockefeller's Institute for Medical Research ... death-rate from 75 per cent of the persons attacked to 25] In 1901, after his three-year-old grandson died of scarlet fever, Rockefeller established the first institute in this country whose sole purpose was to study and cure diseases. By May 1908 he had given a total of $4.5 million to build a laboratory building and hospital on the East River at 66th Street, together with a large endowment to ensure its future. The first important medical discovery at the Rockefeller Institute was made by Simon Flexner (1863–1946), the director, who in 1907 developed a treatment for meningococcal meningitis. He proved that an antiserum that had previously been ineffective when injected subcutaneously could, when injected directly into the spinal column, dramatically reduce the number of fatalities ("From a Child's Death Came a Medical Institute," New York *Times,* 25 Feb 2001, RE7; "Rockefeller Gives Hospital," Chicago *Tribune,* 31 May 1908, 6; Rockefeller University 2013; Fitzpatrick 1941).

231.27–28   the one hundred and thirty-eight million dollars he has publicly contributed] Although estimates of Rockefeller's charitable gifts vary, Clemens's figure of $138 million for public donations is high. According to the Chicago *Tribune* of 1 January 1908, Rockefeller's contributions totaled about $70 million, of which $45 million was given in 1907 ("Banner Year of Philanthropy," 6).

231.35   sister-in-law] Almira Geraldine Goodsell Rockefeller (1844–1920), the wife of William Rockefeller (1841–1922), John D.'s younger brother ("Mrs. W. Rockefeller Dies Suddenly at 75," New York *Times,* 18 Jan 1920, 22).

233.20   This was nearly three months ago. The child is well and flourishing now] The blood transfusion was administered in March 1908 to the infant daughter of Dr. Adrian V. S. Lambert (1872–1952), a prominent New York surgeon. She was suffering from melena neonatorum, a rare disease that causes bleeding in the digestive tract. The attending physician was Dr. Alexis Carrel (1873–1944), a Frenchman who worked at the Rockefeller Institute from 1906 to 1939. In 1912 he was awarded the Nobel Prize in medicine for successfully transplanting organs in animals, and for discovering the technique that Clemens describes here, in which the blood vessels of the patient and the donor are sutured together. The procedure was sometimes fatal, because the concept of incompatible blood types was still unknown ("Alexis Carrel, 'Robot' Heart Inventor, Dies," Chicago *Tribune,* 6 Nov 1944, 23; Lambert 1908, 885).

Autobiographical Dictation, 22 May 1908

233.33–234.8 The Harpers have now been my publishers four years and a half . . . "Tom Sawyer," 41,000] Harpers became Clemens's exclusive publishers in October 1903 (see *AutoMT2*, 528 n. 143.34–144.5, 539 n. 160.32–36). The sales and royalty figures listed here, as well as those in the next two paragraphs, are from a Harpers statement entitled "Volumes of Mark Twain Sold from Nov 1—1903 to Oct 31—1907" (CU-MARK). In the Autobiographical Dictation of 3 June 1908, Clemens inserts a newspaper clipping of a speech he gave to the American Booksellers' Association on 20 May, in which he recited the same statistics.

234.17–18 This accuracy has been conceded by Andrew Lang . . . from his verdict there is no appeal] Andrew Lang, a prominent British author and critic, was an expert on Joan of Arc, having published two books about her, in 1895 and 1906. He had reviewed Clemens's *Personal Recollections of Joan of Arc* in the *St. James Gazette* on 18 May 1896. While acknowledging that the story had "errors in detail," he enjoyed its portrait of Joan as "pure, perfect, adorable, unexampled in her life," praising the author's "modern rendering" because "his heart is in it": "The colour is modern, the taste in humour and dialogue is Mississippian; the historic sense of time and manners is absent. But the book is honest, spirited, and stirring" (Budd 1999, 384–86; for Lang see *AutoMT2*, 606 n. 348.1–3). In April 1908 Lang wrote a letter to Clemens (now lost) in which he harshly criticized a newly published biography of Joan by Anatole France, *Vie de Jeanne d'Arc*. According to Paine's summary of the letter, Lang called France an "egregious ass" and accused him of following "every step of her physical career at the expense of her spiritual life, which he was inclined to cheapen." Clemens replied on 25 April that he would wait for an English translation, but agreed to write an article ridiculing France's book if Lang would—as he had offered—provide him with "a complete set of what the authorities say, and of what this amazing novelist says that they say" (25 Apr 1908 to Lang, *MTL*, 2:810–11; Lang to SLC, 4 May 1908, CU-MARK). No evidence has been found that Clemens actually attempted such an article, but Lang attacked France in a biography of his own, *The Maid of France*, published later in 1908 (see Searle 1976, 66).

234.23 when it appeared serially in *Harper's Monthly*, I concealed the authorship] *Joan of Arc* was serialized in 1895–96 and published as a book in 1896. For Clemens's concealment of his authorship see *AutoMT2*, 353, 608–9 n. 353.10–19.

234.41–235.6 Jack Van Nostrand was among the excursionists . . . a hope which was disappointed] Clemens initially formed a poor impression of John A. Van Nostrand (1847?–79) of Greenville, New Jersey, and New York City but later grew to like the "good-hearted and always well-meaning" youngster (*N&J1*, 330; link note following 8 June 1867 to McComb, *L2*, 64). Clemens describes his ill-fated business dealings with Daniel Slote, a blank-book manufacturer, in his Autobiographical Dictation of 24 May 1906 (*AutoMT2*, 55, 489 nn. 54.15–16 and 54.26, 490 n. 55.14–16). According to

William R. Denny, a fellow *Quaker City* passenger, Slote had a "pretty face" and was a "though'er man of the world, and that harms no one if he can help it, clever to a fault." Julius Moulton (1843?–1916), the son of a railroad engineer, wrote travel letters during the voyage to the St. Louis *Missouri Republican.* Clemens described him in 1907 as "quiet & rather diffident"; Denny noted that he was "tall, slender and kind" (Denny 1867, entry for 11 Sept; link note following 8 June 1867 to McComb, *L2,* 64–65). Joshua William Davis (1840?–1900), a New York banker and stockbroker, established his own firm in 1874. Denny recorded that he was "more of a worldling than strict Christian . . . he is a good fellow[,] tries to please and agree with you without comprising his opinions" (*Richmond Census* 1880, 923:359C; New York *Times:* "Copartnership Notices," 1 Dec 1874, 10; "Death of Joshua W. Davis," 24 Feb 1900, 7). William F. Church (b. 1819?), an insurance adjuster from Cincinnati, was appointed state insurance commissioner in 1872. According to Denny he had an "open good countenance and a lip that shows determination of purpose." Church lectured on the excursion in March 1870; according to the Cincinnati *Gazette,* his story—"in a very different vein from the narrative of the humorist"—was "pleasantly and clearly told" ("A Cincinnatian's Reminiscences of the Holy Land," 23 Mar 1870, 2; *Hamilton Census* 1860, 974:284). In September 1867 these five men in Clemens's "clique," together with two others (Denny and Dr. George Birch), made a three-week side trip on horseback from Beirut to Damascus, then through Palestine to Jerusalem, and finally to Jaffa, where they rejoined the ship (*N&J1,* 373, 416–43).

235.15–16   a young journalist who visited us a year ago] Unidentified.

Autobiographical Dictation, 3 June 1908

236.4   I clip the following from the newspapers] The source of the clipping transcribed here has not been identified.

236.29–30   my publishers had to account to me for 50,000 volumes . . . whether they sold them or not] The contract of 22 October 1903 stipulated a minimum royalty of $25,000 a year for five years, not a specific number of copies (*HHR,* 694; *AutoMT2,* 539 n. 160.32–36).

Autobiographical Dictation, 26 June 1908

237 *title*   Innocence at Home] Clemens's first name for his Redding house; in October he decided to call it Stormfield: see the Autobiographical Dictation of 6 October 1908.

237.12   We entered into occupation of this new house eight days ago] See the Autobiographical Dictation of 17 April 1908, note at 221.17–19.

237.13–18   In an earlier chapter I have told . . . I published that true story in a magazine] The sketch, published in *Harper's Monthly* in December 1902, was inserted into the Autobiographical Dictation of 4 June 1906. Clemens also touches on the subject of "unveracity" in the dictation of 6 June 1906, and describes Clara's struggle to keep things from Olivia in the dictation of 7 June 1906 (*AutoMT2*, 80–108, 506 n. 83.16–17).

237.22   DOUBLE BLOW FOR FATHER] The article that begins here was published in the New York *Times* on 26 June.

238.12   ARRESTS IN BALLOON CASE] This article, like the one inserted earlier in the dictation, appeared in the New York *Times* on 26 June.

238.34   Senator Hoar of Massachusetts] George Frisbie Hoar (1826–1904), a graduate of Harvard University and Law School, served Massachusetts in Congress for thirty-five years, in 1869–77 as a representative and in 1877–1904 as a senator. He championed the civil rights of black men and worked for the New England Woman's Suffrage Association; and as an anti-imperialist he supported self-determination for Puerto Ricans and Filipinos. Moreover, he staunchly opposed the spoils system and promoted merit-based government appointments.

238.35   Grover Cleveland, twice President of the United States, who died yesterday] Cleveland, Democratic president in 1885–89 and 1893–97, died on 24 June at age seventy-one. Clemens was one of the "mugwumps" who voted for him in 1884, when he defeated Republican James G. Blaine. Clemens talks about the election, and about his cordial encounters with Cleveland and his wife, in the Autobiographical Dictations of 24 January, 5 March, and 6 March 1906 (*AutoMT1*, 315–19, 385–92, 602 n. 385.35–36).

238.41–239.1   It is said that Mr. Cleveland has left but little for his family to live on ... but she will not get it] On 28 June the New York *Times* announced that Congress was expected to authorize a $5,000 annual pension for Frances Cleveland, the late president's popular wife. (Similar pensions had been granted to the widows of presidents who had not seen military service; widows of former soldiers received military pensions.) Although more than one newspaper reported that Cleveland "died a comparatively poor man," he left his wife a sizable inheritance, and she refused the pension that Congress offered her ("Pension for Mrs. Cleveland," New York *Times*, 28 June 1908, 1; "Few Presidents Rich," Washington *Post*, 11 July 1908, 11, reprinting the Brooklyn *Eagle*; Watson 2012, 369).

Autobiographical Dictation, 3 July 1908

239.8   Hell-fire Day, that English holiday] See Clemens's speech about the Fourth of July in the Autobiographical Dictation of 29 August 1907.

239.24–30   Thirty-five years ago, in Edinburgh ... the other half something more than a hundred] The oak mantelpiece—purchased in Edinburgh in the summer of 1873—had been in Ayton Castle, built in 1851. To the armorial carvings of its original owner the Clemenses added the date of its installation in the Hartford house (1874); they also added a brass plate engraved with a quotation from Emerson: "The ornament of a house is the friends who frequent it" (Courtney 2011, 60; Emerson 1870, 115).

239.35–36   When we sold the Hartford house, several years ago] The house was sold in May 1903 to Richard M. Bissell, a Hartford Fire Insurance Company executive, for $28,800. This was at a considerable loss, given that in 1906 Clemens (although probably with some exaggeration) put the cost of "house and grounds and furniture" at between $150,000 and $167,000 (*AutoMT2,* 79, 159, 504 n. 79.2–3; Courtney 2011, 123; for the construction of the house see AD, 10 Apr 1907, note at 40.28–29).

240.27–30   citizens of the Sandwich Islands . . . the fireplace is waiting for that ornament] The koa-wood mantelpiece and accompanying breadfruit plaque, gifts from the people of Hawaii, were carved by Frank N. Otremba (1855–1910), a German-born woodcarver and cabinetmaker who had settled in Honolulu in about 1882. The mantelpiece was installed on 30 November 1908, Clemens's seventy-third birthday. Clemens sent his thanks that day in letters to Otremba (WU-MU) and to H. P. Wood, secretary of the Hawaiian Promotion Committee. In the latter he coined his famous description of Hawaii as "the loveliest fleet of islands that lies anchored in any ocean" (*MTH,* 241–43, facsimile of letter facing 243; Rose 1988, 131–32).

240.31–33   personally conducted me to . . . the Thomas Bailey Aldrich Memorial Museum] Aldrich had died in March 1907 (see AD, 26 Mar 1907, note at 14.14). The dedication of the Aldrich Memorial Museum took place on 30 June 1908 at the Portsmouth Music Hall; Clemens was a featured speaker ("Dedication of the Thomas Bailey Aldrich Memorial," program in CU-MARK). For details of his remarks, see the Autobiographical Dictation of 9 July 1908.

240.39–40   Aldrich was born in his grandfather's house . . . seventy-three years ago] Aldrich was born in Portsmouth in 1836, but not in his grandfather's Court Street house. A few years later he moved with his parents to New York City, and then to New Orleans, before he returned to Portsmouth in 1849 to live with his grandfather until 1852. He fictionalized Portsmouth, the house, and his grandfather in 1869 in his semiautobiographical novel *The Story of a Bad Boy* (Walk Portsmouth 2011; Aldrich Home 2013).

240.40–241.7   His widow has lately bought that house . . . to act as advertisement and directors] Lilian Woodman Aldrich (1845?–1927), who had married Aldrich in 1865, organized the Thomas Bailey Aldrich Memorial Association at a meeting held in Portsmouth on 8 July 1907. Wallace Hackett, the mayor of Portsmouth, was president of the association and presided over the 1908 dedication ceremony (see AD, 8 July 1908, and the note at 249.40). Among the "elected" directors were several of Clemens's friends and acquaintances, including William Dean Howells and Finley Peter Dunne. Clemens had also been made a director, but on 25 July 1907 he asked Lyon to notify Charles A. Hazlett, the association's secretary, that he refused the position,

> for the reason that he does not approve of public memorials that have to be paid
> for by subscription. This does not in any way indicate that M^r. Clemens's warm

friendship & love for M^r. Aldrich has in any way abated; but that for many years he has declined to be sponsor for such memorials, & has repeated[ly] expressed himself as being most unwilling to have any such distinction paid to himself either living or dead. (CU-MARK)

After Aldrich's time in Portsmouth, the Court Street house had been used as an orphanage and then as the town's first hospital. In 1911 Lilian Aldrich recalled that "a fund of ten thousand dollars" was

> raised by popular subscription, in sums from one dollar to one thousand dollars. The house . . . was bought and work at once begun to restore the house and garden to their former condition. . . . Not only are the material things restored, but that which is much more difficult, the atmosphere of the past, which is so tangible there that the stranger feels impelled to hasten his visit ere the family return and find him. (Aldrich 1911, 206)

Today the Aldrich House Museum is one of the historic homes of Portsmouth's Strawberry Banke Museum (New York *Times:* "Memorial to T. B. Aldrich," 1 July 1908, 16; "Mrs. Thomas B. Aldrich," 23 May 1927, 21; *New York Passenger Lists* 1820–1957, 400:888:38; Hazlett to SLC, 9 July 1907, CU-MARK; Walk Portsmouth 2011; Aldrich Home 2013).

241.36   Edmund Clarence Stedman] The poet, critic, and editor whom Clemens blamed for contributing to the failure of Charles L. Webster and Company (see *AutoMT2,* 78, 503 n. 78.19–28). He was another of the elected directors of the memorial association.

242.3–4   I conceived an aversion for her the first time I ever saw her . . . thirty-nine years ago] Clemens and Lilian Aldrich had met unhappily in Boston in January 1872 (not in 1869), when Aldrich brought him home unannounced to a dinner that Lilian stuffily and pointedly refused to serve, having misinterpreted Clemens's appearance and drawling speech as signs of intoxication. She gave a vivid account of the episode, and of her own chagrin upon learning that it was Mark Twain whom she had slighted, in her 1920 memoir, *Crowding Memories* (Aldrich 1920, 128–32, reprinted in 15 and 16 Mar 1874 to Aldrich, *L6,* 80–81 n. 11).

242.7–8   we never saw a great deal of him because we couldn't have him by himself] On occasion at least, Clemens was able to suppress his dislike of Lilian Aldrich. In her memoir, she recalled a convivial 7–10 March 1874 visit she and her husband had made to the Clemenses in Hartford, with Clemens at his prankish best, particularly one morning before breakfast and then at the table, when "loud was the laughter, and rapid the talk" (Aldrich 1920, 146–48, 157–60, reprinted almost entirely in 24 Mar 1874 to Aldrich, *L6,* 93–94 n. 13). The Aldriches and Clemenses met more than once in Paris in May 1879, after which Clemens wrote, "We (all the tribe) felt an awful vacancy here when the Aldriches left" (25 May 1879 to Aldrich, DLC; OLC to OLL, 13 and 16 May 1879,

CtHMTH). And Lilian Aldrich recalled "the wit, the chaff, the merry dinners ... the gaiety and laughter" of the Paris occasions (Aldrich 1920, 229).

242.10–12   three years ago ... visit the Aldriches at "Ponkapog,"] On 21 October 1905 Clemens went to Boston "to fill various social engagements (with my jaw) & I will finish up *that* end of the country—if the weapon holds out; she used to be pretty effective when Samson had her. I shall be there a week; possibly a couple" (20 Oct 1905 to Rogers, Salm, in *HHR,* 602–3). While in Boston, he spoke at the College Club on 24 October, at the Authors Club on 25 October, and at the Round Table on 26 October. He spent the next few days with the Aldriches at Redman Farm, the remodeled farmhouse they had acquired in the fall of 1874 in Ponkapog, a village twelve miles south of Boston. On 4 November he spoke again in Boston at the Twentieth Century Club, and returned to New York on 6 November (Lyon 1905b, entries for 21 Oct, 24–26 Oct, and 6 Nov; Schmidt 2008; 24 Mar 1874 to Aldrich, *L6,* 92–93 n. 12; see also the Autobiographical Dictation of 6 July 1908, note at 243.7–8).

242.12–13   wheedled out of poor old Mr. Pierce years ago by that artful lady, a number of years before the old gentleman died] Henry L. Pierce (1825–96) was a chocolate manufacturer, Massachusetts legislator (1860–62, 1866), two-time mayor of Boston (1873, 1878), Republican congressman from Massachusetts (1873–77), philanthropist, and Ponkapog neighbor of the Aldriches'. Lilian Aldrich, recalling her husband's twenty-five-year friendship with Pierce, reported that "it was exceptional (if they were in the same city) if a day passed in which they did not meet; and after Mr. Pierce's death the miserable feeling of loneliness changed for a long time Mr. Aldrich's world" (Aldrich 1920, 278–80). Neither she, nor Ferris Greenslet, Aldrich's biographer, mentions any of the gifts Clemens catalogs here. When Pierce died, however, he left the Aldrich family a substantial bequest: $200,000 to Thomas and Lilian and $100,000 to each of their twin sons, the house at Ponkapog with all its furnishings, and 155 acres of adjoining land with all the buildings on it ("The Gifts to Mr. Aldrich," New York *Times,* 26 Dec 1896, A1). Pierce accompanied the Aldriches on a 10 May 1879 visit to the Clemenses in Paris (OLC to OLL, 13 and 16 May 1879, CtHMTH).

242.15–16   a great dwelling-house at 59 Mount Vernon Street, Boston ... a small cottage at the seaside] In 1883, after previously owning houses on Pinckney Street and Charles Street, Aldrich

> bought the beautiful, ample house at 59 Mount Vernon Street, which as time went
> on was to become a treasure-house of choice books, literary relics, autographs, and
> objects of art. There through the winters Aldrich, in his hours of ease in his study
> under the roof, read innumerable French and Spanish novels, or descended with
> cheerful reluctance to the drawing-room to play the perfect host to the visitors who
> thronged his hospitable portals.

In 1893 the Aldriches built "'The Crags' at Tenant's Harbor on the Maine coast, a summer place that the poet came to be immensely fond of" (Greenslet 1908, 85–86, 94, 151 161).

242.20   the Aldrich appetite for travel] The Aldriches traveled abroad frequently and extensively—for example, in March–October 1875, in the summers of 1890–92 and 1900, and in the winters of 1894–95 and 1898–99, when they made round-the-world tours (Greenslet 1908, 117, 119, 161).

242.23–25   Mrs. Aldrich entertained Mrs. Clemens and me . . . in the presence of Aldrich and of poor old Mr. Pierce] Nothing is at present known of this occasion.

242.34–35   Worth, the celebrated Parisian ladies' tailor] Charles Frederick Worth (see *AutoMT2*, 483 n. 43.27–29).

Autobiographical Dictation, 6 July 1908

243.3   Joel Chandler Harris is dead] Harris, Clemens's correspondent since 1881 and personal friend since 1882, had died on 3 July (see *AutoMT1*, 532–33 n. 217.25–27, and *AutoMT2*, 260, 264–65).

243.7–8   I had gone to Boston to spend a week with a friend] Clemens's Boston hosts in October–November 1905 were stockbroker Sumner B. Pearmain and his wife, Alice. They had been his Dublin, New Hampshire, neighbors in the summer and fall of 1905 and again in the summer of 1906 (*AutoMT2*, 548 n. 190.37–191.8; Lyon 1905a, entries for 21 Oct and 2 Nov).

243.18–23   They had an automobile . . . Bar Harbor in July] According to his biographer, "The summer of 1905 was spent by Aldrich cruising along the coast in his son's yacht, the Bethulia, and touring in his automobile,—an engine that always had for his imagination something of the mysterious potency of Aladdin's carpet" (Greenslet 1908, 232). The *Bethulia* belonged to the Aldriches' son Talbot. Nothing is known of Clemens's visit to Bar Harbor, Maine, in July 1905.

244.17–22   Young Aldrich was a bachelor . . . the girl escaped] Talbot Aldrich (1868–1957) became engaged in early 1906 to Eleanor Lovell Little (1884–1978), and they were married in June 1906. She was a recent graduate of Bryn Mawr College; her father, David M. Little, was a naval architect who had been the mayor of Salem, Massachusetts, in 1900 but never governor. Clemens was evidently mistaken about her father's office (Greenslet 1908, 232; *Salem Census* 1900, 647:2A; "A Noon Wedding at Salem," Boston *Evening Transcript*, 30 June 1906, 3).

Autobiographical Dictation, 7 July 1908

244.35   Murat Halstead is dead] Halstead (b. 1829) had died on 2 July 1908. During a fifty-year career in journalism he was a staff member, editor, owner, and war correspondent of the Cincinnati *Commercial*, editor of the Cincinnati *Commercial Gazette*, and editor of the Brooklyn *Standard-Union*. Later he wrote several historical works ("Murat Halstead, Editor, Is Dead," New York *Times,* 3 July 1908, 7; Mott 1950, 459–60).

245.32–38   I sailed for Germany in the steamer *Holsatia* . . . he had to remain with us] The *Holsatia,* carrying Clemens and his family on the first leg of their 1878–79 European travels, actually departed from Hoboken, New Jersey, on 11 April 1878, but was forced to anchor overnight off Staten Island and make a fresh start the next morning because of difficulty in disembarking a large group that had come to bid farewell to Bayard Taylor (see the note at 245.42). As a result of the delay, Halstead, who had "intended only to make a short trip to the Narrows, to see his family well on their way to France," made "the suddenly conceived plan of turning his excursion into a voyage. He was led to this by the fact that he must go to Paris in two months, and could attend to his business there about as well now" (New York *Tribune:* "Bayard Taylor's Farewell," 12 Apr 1878, 5; "Farewells to Bayard Taylor," 13 Apr 1878, 2).

245.42   Bayard Taylor] Taylor (1825–78) was a prolific poet, travel writer, and translator, and from 1870 to 1877 professor of German literature at Cornell University. Of great repute in his day, but of little after, in 1878 he was appointed U.S. minister to Germany and was aboard the *Holsatia* en route to take his post. He had been in ill health before his appointment, however, and died in Berlin in December of that year.

246.18–19   Halstead was editor and proprietor of the Cincinnati *Enquirer*] Halstead never was connected with the *Enquirer,* the rival of his *Commercial Gazette*.

246.39   the best of all English translations of Goethe's "Faust."] Taylor's two-volume translation, published in 1871, was highly regarded in its day, but is now considered mediocre.

246.40–42   two very fine songs . . . an Arab lover to his sweetheart] Taylor's "Song of the Camp," collected in 1863 in *The Poet's Journal,* describes British soldiers during the eleven-month siege of Sebastopol (1854–55) in the Crimean War. They sing the old Scottish song "Annie Laurie," which is based on a poem generally credited to William Douglas, with music and additional lyrics by Alicia Scott. The poem about the Arab lover is "Bedouin Song," collected in Taylor's *Poems of the Orient* (1854).

247.12–13   a negro manservant . . . looking as fine as a rainbow] Taylor described his servant in an 1878 letter from Berlin:

> You should see Harris, in his navy-blue dress, with gilt buttons, white cravat, stove-pipe hat with broad gold band, etc. No one else, except Prince Carl, the Emperor's brother, has a darkey; and when we drive out with Harris on the box as footman, we make a sensation. We find him singularly ignorant of many little details of service (the result of serving in a gentlemen's club), but very anxious to learn, and perfectly honest. Marie and I have entire faith in him, and believe that we have done well in taking him along. But I must tell you one funny circumstance, illustrating the man's naïveté. Two days after I called at the Palace . . . Harris came to me and said: "I went to the Palace the next day after your Excellency. A gentleman

in military clothes invited me in, and I wrote my name down in a book, as a well-wisher to the King"!!—I don't know what he will do next; but a "dark-complected" person may take many liberties in Berlin. (10 June 1878 to Richard and Elizabeth Stoddard, in Bayard Taylor 1997, 489–91)

Autobiographical Dictation, 8 July 1908

248.36   an old gull's alms] The legacy of Henry L. Pierce (see AD, 3 July 1908, note at 242.12–13).

249.22–26   the governor of Massachusetts . . . will have to be a staff officer] Curtis Guild, Jr. (1860–1915), editor and owner of the Boston *Commercial Bulletin*, was the Republican governor of Massachusetts from 1906 to 1909. Talbot Aldrich served on his staff as an aide-de-camp, with the rank of major, having been commissioned on 27 December 1907 (*U.S., Adjutant General Military Records* 1631–1976, report years 1907, 1908). His twin brother, Charles (1868–1904), had died of tuberculosis contracted in 1901.

249.32   the tin-pot boy] "The ancient fashion of carrying drinking water through the cars in a battered tin tea kettle still prevails in some parts of New England. At least I am told so" ("Irrigation Excursions," *Railroad Gazette*, 26 Apr 1895, 261).

249.39–40   to wait until the house should be full] There were "about a thousand admirers" in attendance, including "several hundred . . . men and women writers" ("Tributes to Aldrich," Boston *Evening Transcript*, 1 July 1908, 13).

249.40   the mayor] Wallace Hackett (1856–1939), a lawyer and mayor of Portsmouth in 1907–8 (Foss 1998, 51).

Autobiographical Dictation, 9 July 1908

251.14–19   Colonel Higginson . . . when he charged with his regiment and led it to bloody victories] During the Civil War, Unitarian minister and author Thomas Wentworth Higginson (1823–1911) was colonel of the First South Carolina Volunteers, the first black regiment in the Union army. The regiment saw significant combat, although not in any major battles.

251.19   Howells's speech was brief] Howells "read an original poem, written for the occasion" ("Literary Hosts Do Honor to Aldrich," Boston *Herald*, 1 July 1908, 2). The text of his speech has not been recovered.

251.24–25   twelve minutes of . . . desecrating nonsense] Clemens read an excerpt about Aldrich from his own "Robert Louis Stevenson and Thomas Bailey Aldrich," which had appeared in the *North American Review* in September 1906 (*AutoMT1*, 228–30). Whatever else he said, Lilian Aldrich did not consider it "desecrating nonsense." She wrote him on 2 July 1908, "I am most grateful for your tribute of friendship you brought on Tuesday to little 'Tom Bailey,' and to your older and dearer friend, 'Tom Aldrich.'" She recalled a late visit Aldrich had paid to Clemens, "and on his return the old friendship and love seemed to burn with fresh fire; I am glad to remember the affectionate things he said of you then" (CU-MARK). Tom Bailey is the main character of *The Story of a Bad Boy,* recognized as an influence on *The Adventures of Tom Sawyer* ("Literary Hosts Do Honor to Aldrich," Boston *Herald,* 1 July 1908, 2; "Following Journal Lead Literary Men Honor Thomas Bailey Aldrich," Boston *Journal,* 1 July 1908, 6; *TS,* 5).

Autobiographical Dictation, 10 July 1908

251.34–35   I wrote John Howells some . . . praises of his work as architect of this house] Clemens had promised the elder Howells at the 30 June Aldrich Memorial dedication ceremony in Portsmouth that he would write to John praising the new house in Redding. John himself wrote Lyon on 2 July (CU-MARK) to express how much he would "prize" such a letter, and Clemens complied the following day (DLC):

July 3/08.

Dear John:
  You have set up a charming Italian villa here & made it look native & at home among these Yankee woods & hills. It is a fine feat. It is a shapely & stately & handsome house, & grows more & more impressive & satisfying and beautiful the more I enlarge my acquaintance with it. I am speaking of its outside. Inside it is sane,—a compliment which cannot be applied to any other Italian villa, I suppose. The distribution of the rooms is rational, no space is wasted, all space is profitably utilized. It has four times as much useful & usable room in it as was findable in that last Florentine villa of ours, although that one was 200 feet long, 60 feet wide, 3 stories high, & had a cellar under the whole silly mass. You couldn't even get to one bedroom without passing through somebody else's; & it had only 3 *good* bedrooms in it.
  All of our visitors are as delighted with the house as I am. Go on, John. Introduce the American-Italian villa, & spread it over the land. It is the ideal house, the ideal home.

Affectionately
SL. Clemens

For Clemens's recollections of the unsatisfactory Villa di Quarto, which he and his family rented in Florence in 1903–4, see *AutoMT1,* 230–44.

252.3–4   it and its father came down to Hartford . . . thirty years ago] Clemens recalls the 11–12 March 1876 visit to Hartford by the Howellses, father and son (see *MTHL,* 1:126–27).

252.5   the colored butler, George] George Griffin (see *AutoMT1,* 583 n. 335.28–32).

253.40   a slice of ripe, fresh watermelon] At least as early as 1869, some physicians had recommended watermelon as a cure for dysentery. Beginning in 1893, if not earlier, Clemens promoted its use, in both his literary works and his personal correspondence. Dr. K. Patrick Ober has compiled an exhaustive account of Clemens's advocacy, but was unable to add a scientific endorsement: "From a twenty-first century perspective, it is appealing to think that watermelon may have been beneficial to dysentery victims through replenishing fluid and sugar (or by other undefined mechanisms), despite the absence of any evidence of antimicrobial action" (Ober 2011, 879).

Autobiographical Dictation, 14 July 1908

254.26–28   Norman Hapgood wrote that paragraph . . . intimately acquainted with as I am with him] The paragraph (inserted later in this dictation) was not the "principal," but only one of twelve short editorials in the 11 July 1908 issue of *Collier's Weekly*, edited by Hapgood since 1903. He and Clemens saw each other with some regularity during this period, usually at dinner or lunch (see *AutoMT1*, 598 n. 375.2).

255.18   he dexterously secured Mr. Taft's nomination] Roosevelt had succeeded to the presidency on 14 September 1901 after the assassination of William McKinley. He was elected to his own term in 1904, and as early as election night, 8 November of that year, announced that he would not seek reelection. In 1907 he chose Taft, his secretary of war, as his successor, and orchestrated his nomination as the Republican candidate in 1908. Taft took office in March 1909, but soon alienated Roosevelt by abandoning some of his progressive policies in favor of an increasingly conservative agenda. This led Roosevelt to challenge him for the 1912 Republican presidential nomination and then, after failing, to oppose him in the general election as the candidate of the Progressive Party (popularly known as the Bull Moose Party). This split in the Republican party insured the election of Democrat Woodrow Wilson.

255.23–25   he jumped that horse-doctor, Leonard Wood . . . by help of the famous "interval,"] Roosevelt's first appointment of Wood to the rank of major general in August 1903 was met with opposition in the Senate; on 7 December 1903, during the brief interval between two sessions of Congress, Roosevelt renewed his nomination, which was finally confirmed in March 1904 (see *AutoMT1*, 409, 619 n. 409.1–17).

255.39–40   springing enthusiastically to the aid of HENEY, SPRECKELS . . . in San Francisco] Rudolph Spreckels (1872–1958), sugar magnate and organizer of the First National Bank of San Francisco, was a prime mover and financier of the 1906–8 investigations and convictions for corruption of San Francisco Mayor Eugene Schmitz, Republican political boss Abraham Ruef, and several city officials. The lead attorney in the spectacular trials was Francis J. Heney (1859–1937), a noted federal prosecutor and San Francisco assistant district attorney. In the process Spreckels, Heney, and their supporters came under attack from several wealthy and influential San Franciscans. On 8

June 1908 Roosevelt sent a long letter of support to Spreckels, urging him and Heney not to feel "downhearted when you see men guilty of atrocious crimes, who for some cause or other succeed in escaping punishment, and especially when you see men of wealth, of high business, and, in a sense, of high social standing, banded together against you." He exhorted them to "not be discouraged; don't flinch" and to "keep up the fight" (New York *Times*: "Keep Up Graft War, Roosevelt Urges," 21 June 1908, 8; "Service Tomorrow for Francis Heney," 2 Nov 1937, 25; "Rudolph Spreckels Dies at 85," 5 Oct 1958, 86).

256.1   in his praise of CLEVELAND] Grover Cleveland, the former two-time Democratic president (1885–89, 1893–97), died on 24 June 1908. On 27 June, Roosevelt attended the funeral in Princeton, New Jersey, at which, exclusively for the members of Cleveland's two cabinets, he delivered "an exquisite eulogy on the life and death of Cleveland. It was the only eulogy at the funeral, and even this was delivered behind closed doors, to men who once were much in the public eye" ("Eulogy by President," Washington *Post*, 28 June 1908, 3).

256.3–4   a good Police Commissioner . . . a good President] See *AutoMT2*, 464 n. 13.1–2.

256.25–26   vigorous fighter for civil service reform . . . spoils system] Roosevelt had been a leader in reforming the spoils system, by which government offices were routinely awarded according to party affiliation, so that there could be wholesale turnover after elections. He served as the U.S. Civil Service Commission's most vigorous member from 1889 to 1895.

256.28–29   to represent his interests at the Republican Convention in Chicago] Largely by means of political patronage, Roosevelt dominated the convention that met in the Chicago Coliseum on 16–19 June 1908 and nominated Taft, his chosen successor.

257.1–2   He invited a negro to lunch with him at the White House . . . Booker T. Washington] On 16 October 1901 Roosevelt hosted Washington, the famous black leader, at a family dinner, not lunch, in the White House, to discuss the Republican party's position in the South. This was the first time that a black person had dined in the White House. Clemens does not exaggerate the "storm" of reaction, particularly from Southern whites, who demanded Roosevelt's impeachment. Some in Roosevelt's camp tried to limit the political fallout by claiming the event was only an impromptu business lunch in the presidential office. Roosevelt himself, dismayed by the abuse, reportedly threatened to invite Washington to dinner again. He did not do so, but did continue to consult with him. For a detailed account of the dinner and its repercussions, see Davis 2012, 187–247.

257.3–4   whose shoe-latchets Mr. Roosevelt is not worthy to untie] Echoing Mark 1:7: "the latchet of whose shoes I am not worthy to stoop down and unloose"; also Luke 3:16 and John 1:27.

257.10–12   a freshet of honorary degrees at Yale . . . gowned and hooded for baptism] The occasion was the elaborate closing ceremony of Yale University's bicentennial celebration, on 23 October 1901. Booker T. Washington attended as one of the invited academics, and Roosevelt was there to receive an honorary doctor of laws degree. Clemens was honored with a doctor of letters degree; among those who received the same distinction were his friends Thomas Bailey Aldrich, William Dean Howells, and Richard Watson Gilder. In conferring Clemens's degree, Yale President Arthur T. Hadley remarked, "It would be supererogation to enlarge upon his attainments" ("Yale Commemorates Her Bi-Centennial," New York *Times,* 24 Oct 1901, 1–2; Davis 2012, 219–23).

257.28 Alexander VI] Pope Alexander VI (see *AutoMT2,* 525 n. 134.28).

257.28–258.3 the Brownsville incident . . . testimony that could go to the favor of those men] The "incident" began with a racial melee in Brownsville, Texas, on 13 August 1906, which resulted in the death of one white civilian and the wounding of another. White Brownsville residents blamed the black soldiers of the Twenty-fifth Infantry, who had recently been stationed at nearby Fort Brown. In what is regarded as the worst mistake of his presidency, Roosevelt ordered the discharge of all 167 black soldiers, costing them their careers, pay, pensions, and honors, without a military trial, and despite the fact that white officers testified that they were in their barracks at the time of the fracas. Nevertheless, a 1907–8 Senate investigation supported Roosevelt's action. Further inquiry in 1909 and 1910 resulted in the reenlistment of a small number of the dismissed soldiers. But it wasn't until 1972 that the army, after a new investigation, declared the soldiers innocent and made restitution to the two who were still alive.

258.3–5 the testimony of Captain McDonald . . . Government and its agents acted in a shabby and dishonest and dishonorable way] William Jesse McDonald (1852–1918) was a famed Texas Ranger captain from 1891 until 1907, who also served in 1905 as one of Theodore Roosevelt's bodyguards (Texas Ranger Hall of Fame and Museum 2013). Convinced of the guilt of the soldiers accused in the Brownsville incident, he tried to arrest them for civil prosecution. The military authorities refused to hand them over, however, and, contrary to what Clemens says here, did in fact listen to "testimony that could go to the favor of those men," ultimately finding the evidence against them insufficient for indictment. Clemens's characterization of McDonald was no doubt influenced by Paine, who gave a complimentary account of his actions in a book published in 1909, *Captain Bill McDonald, Texas Ranger.* But Paine also makes it clear that McDonald was intemperate and vainglorious, and asserted that his damning report to Roosevelt precipitated the president's Draconian action (Paine 1909, 315–56). A 1970 study that prompted the investigation leading to the soldiers' exoneration throws a harsh light on McDonald's inflammatory and prejudicial behavior (John D. Weaver 1970, 80–87).

258.14–15 I find this editorial in . . . a New York *Herald* of something more than a month ago] The four paragraphs that follow were extracted from a longer article in the New York *World,* not the *Herald,* of 19 June 1908.

258.18–19   provided the Democratic National Convention nominates William J. Bryan] Attorney, editor, and populist leader William Jennings Bryan (1860–1925), a twice-defeated presidential candidate (1896, 1900), was nominated at the Democratic convention in Denver in July 1908. He lost to Taft by a wide margin in the November election.

258.26   Andrew Johnson, in his periods of sobriety] Johnson had been drunk at his inauguration as Lincoln's vice-president on 4 March 1865. A few weeks later he succeeded to the presidency upon Lincoln's assassination and, after barely surviving an impeachment attempt in 1868, finished out Lincoln's second term. In March of 1869, as Johnson was leaving office, Clemens lampooned him and his dubious record in "The White House Funeral," written for the New York *Tribune* but not published (SLC 1869b; for its text, see the enclosure with 8–10 Mar 1869 to Young, *L3,* 458–66).

Autobiographical Dictation, 16 July and 12 September 1908

258 *title*   Dictated July 16 and September 12, 1908] This "dictation" is actually based on a manuscript; the first part is dated 16 July, and the second is dated 12 September. The manuscript is continuously paged, however, so it is clear that the sections were intended as a single essay, despite the fact that on 16 August Clemens paused to write a eulogy for his nephew, Samuel E. Moffett.

258.38–39   Thirty-five years ago in a letter to my wife ostensibly, but really to Mr. Howells] Clemens inserts this letter later in his manuscript.

259.1–2   when the Monarchy should replace the Republic] For Clemens's earlier remarks on this allegedly inevitable process, see the Autobiographical Dictations of 13 December 1906 and 15 January 1907 (*AutoMT2,* 312–15, 370–74), and, in this volume, 26 September 1907.

259.4–5   a letter which preceded it . . . treated the coming Monarchy seriously] The earlier letter is not known to survive.

259.33   Mr. Cleveland's couple of brief interruptions] See the Autobiographical Dictation of 14 July 1908, note at 256.1. In the fifty years prior to 1908, there actually had been two Democratic presidents in addition to Cleveland: James Buchanan (1857–61) and Andrew Johnson (1865–69).

259.41–260.1   by the voice of a Secretary of State it has . . . Supreme Court with judges friendly to its ambitions] Clemens discusses Elihu Root, Roosevelt's secretary of state, and his belief in centralized governmental power in the Autobiographical Dictation of 13 December 1906 (see *AutoMT2,* 312–14 and notes on 595). In May 1908 Root was named as a possible nominee for chief justice; at the time, six of the nine Supreme Court justices were Republican appointees, and Taft, during his administration, made six appointments, more than any previous president ("Root May Head Supreme Court," Chicago *Tribune,* 18 May 1908, 1).

260.4–9   it has created a number of giant corporations . . . puts off that assault till "after election."] See the Autobiographical Dictation of 21 May 1908, note at 230.10–12. Taft proposed revisions in the law that would lower some tariff rates while increasing others, to be implemented immediately after his inauguration by a special session of Congress. Bryan, his Democratic opponent, claimed that the Republicans were "too deeply obligated to protected corporate interests to pay off such promises." Taft asserted that the monopolies could be controlled by strict enforcement of antitrust laws, which would eliminate unfair practices. His stance drew much adverse criticism, some of it from Republican supporters of the Democratic plan to impose tariffs to produce revenue rather than corporate profits (Hornig 1958, 240–43, 262).

260.14–16   formerly our Monarchy went through the form of electing its Shadow . . . *appointed* the succession-Shadow] The "Shadow," Roosevelt, chose his "succession-Shadow," Taft.

260.25–26   so long as a Titus succeeds a Vespasian, and we shall best not trouble about a Domitian] The Roman emperor Vespasian (r. A.D. 69–79) succeeded in passing the throne to his son Titus; all earlier emperors had either been selected by adoption or proclaimed by the Praetorian Guard. Vespasian and Titus (r. A.D. 79–81) were considered by later historians to have presided over a period of "transient felicity" (Gibbon 1880, 1:311). The crimes of Domitian—Titus's brother, successor, and (probably) assassin—are chronicled in Suetonius's *The Twelve Caesars,* one of Clemens's favorite books (Suetonius 1876, 479–505).

260.32–33   thirty-five years ago, I wrote the letter to Mr. Howells, while ostensibly writing it to my wife] On 8 July 1908 Howells sent "a huge mass of your letters" for Clemens to review before making them available to Paine (NN-BGC, in *MTHL,* 2:830–31; see "The Ashcroft-Lyon Manuscript," note at 334.21–22). The letter, written on 20 November 1874, was evidently transcribed by Hobby from the holograph that Howells had preserved and returned to Clemens for use in Paine's biography. Clemens then made a few minor revisions on her typescript before having it retranscribed by his second typist for the autobiography. The original letter is now in the Berg Collection.

260.38–39   Rt. Hon. the Marquis of Ponkapog (Thomas Bailey Aldrich—on whom be peace!)] Aldrich had died in March 1907; he did much of his writing at his country retreat in the village of Ponkapog, near Boston (see AD, 26 Mar 1907, and the note at 14.14; AD, 3 July 1908, note at 242.10–12).

261.18–19   I walked hither, then, with my precious old friend] See the note at 263.34–35.

261.31   his Duchess] The former Elinor Gertrude Mead (1837–1910) of Brattleboro, Vermont, who married William Dean Howells in 1862. She had been a close friend of the Clemenses' since the mid 1870s (Howells 1988, 3–4).

262.4   Osgood] Boston publisher James R. Osgood (*AutoMT1,* 498 n. 112.20).

262.22   Lady Harmony] Wife of Joseph H. Twichell (*AutoMT1,* 632 n. 430.9).

262.26   the author of "Gloverson and His Silent Partners"] Ralph Keeler: see the last paragraph of this dictation.

263.9   the Irishman had been with us only about thirty years] Clemens alludes to the more than one and a half million Irish who emigrated to the United States between 1847 and 1854, during and after the Great Potato Famine of 1845–50.

263.15–16   the German came next] Between 1845 and 1855 more than a million Germans emigrated to the United States to escape economic hardship and the political unrest that led to the revolution of 1848.

263.29   Marconi] See the Autobiographical Dictation of 18 October 1907, note at 172.30–32.

263.34–35   walk from Hartford to Boston with Twichell . . . a hundred miles and more] On the morning of 12 November 1874, Clemens and Twichell set out from Hartford, intending to walk all the way to Boston. They good-naturedly gave up the attempt the following morning, after a total of about thirty-five miles, and then completed the journey by train. They remained in Boston until the night of 16 November, when they returned to Hartford, also by train (for details see the letters written to OLC from 12 to 14 Nov 1874, *L6,* 277–85).

263.40–264.1   Twichell . . . had been chaplain of a marching regiment all through the war] See *AutoMT1,* 287–88, 430–31, 566 nn. 287.34, 288.12–26.

264.8   Young's Hotel] A small, elite Boston hotel, known for years for its comfortable beds and fine restaurant (10 and 11 Nov 1869 to OLL, *L3,* 395 n. 4).

264.11–12   Day before yesterday . . . the brothers Wright broke the world's record] On 3 September 1908 Orville Wright began demonstrating his airplane for the U.S. Army at Fort Meyer, Virginia. Over the course of two weeks he repeatedly set new records for flight duration, remaining aloft for nearly an hour and six minutes on 10 September. (His brother, Wilbur, was giving similar demonstrations in France at the time.) His trials were interrupted on 17 September, when he was seriously injured in a crash that killed his passenger (New York *Times:* "Wright Flies Over an Hour," 10 Sept 1908, 1; "Wright Ship Up Over 70 Minutes," 12 Sept 1908, 1; "Fatal Fall of Wright Airship," 18 Sept 1908, 1; see also *AutoMT2,* 612 n. 360.40).

264.24–30   poor Ralph Keeler . . . only one copy was sold] See "Ralph Keeler" (*AutoMT1,* 150–54, 510 n. 150.17–23, 513 n. 154.35–41).

Autobiographical Dictation, 16 August 1908

264.33–265.1   Samuel E. Moffett, was drowned . . . they struck the life out of him] The source of this eulogy to Moffett is a manuscript, not a dictation. He perished while swimming in the ocean near Sea Bright, New Jersey. Although rescued from the surf, he could not be revived; the physicians who were present "decided that death had been due to apoplexy superinduced by fright and overexertion and not to drowning" ("Editor Moffett Dies, Struggling in Surf," New York *Times,* 2 Aug 1908, 1).

265.7–14   a working journalist, an editorial writer, for nearly thirty . . . got the berth and kept it sixteen years] In the Autobiographical Dictation of 27 March 1906, Clemens recalled that Moffett was "obliged to hunt for something to do by way of making a living" in 1886, at age twenty-six. It is clear, however, that his career in journalism began soon after leaving the University of California in 1882. According to obituaries in the New York *Times* and *Collier's,* Moffett was chief editorial writer for the San Francisco *Evening Post* by 1885. Over the next twenty years he worked for several other newspapers and journals in California and New York. In January 1905 he began to edit a department in *Collier's* called "What the World Is Doing" (see *AutoMT1,* 450–51 and notes on 642–43).

265.24–33   I was laboriously constructing an ancient-history game . . . without effort] The history game that Clemens ultimately developed was patented in 1885. Moffett evidently worked on an early version while on a visit to Buffalo, when he was ten years old (*AutoMT1,* 643 n. 450.31).

265.34–39   back in '80 or '81, when the grand irruption of Krakatoa . . . He came to the office and swiftly wrote it all up] The volcanic eruption on Krakatoa, an island in the Sunda Strait between Java and Sumatra, occurred in August 1883. It destroyed the island, creating new land masses and causing an immense tsunami. A report in the San Francisco *Chronicle* estimated that as many as one hundred thousand people perished ("Further Details of the Java Calamity," San Francisco *Chronicle,* 3 Sept 1883, 3; "The Yawning Earth. Thousands of People Swallowed up—Awful Scene in Java," Washington *Post,* 31 Aug 1883, 1).

266.30–33   He leaves behind him wife, daughter and son . . . This boy will be distinguished] Moffett married Mary Elvish Mantz (1863–1940), an accomplished painter living in San Jose, California, in 1887. They had two children, Anita Moffett (1891–1952) and Francis Clemens Moffett (1895–1927). Anita graduated *magna cum laude* from the University of California. She became an indexer for the annually bound volumes of *Publishers' Weekly.* She died intestate; her Clemens letters and scrapbooks were purchased by the University of California in 1954 and are now in the Moffett Collection of the Mark Twain Papers (see "Description of Provenance," *L6,* 736–37). Francis, who earned an M.A. from Columbia University, went into the advertising business and wrote short stories. He died suddenly of heart disease at age thirty-one ("Samuel E. Moffett," *Collier's* 41 [15 Aug 1908]: 23; "News Notes," *Antiquarian Bookman,* 17 Oct 1953, 1079; New York *Times:* "Clemens Moffett," 6 Mar 1927, 26; "Mrs. Samuel E. Moffett," 3 Oct 1940, 25).

Autobiographical Dictation, 6 October 1908

267 *title*   Dictated at Stormfield, October 6, 1908] Between 14 July and 6 October, Clemens nearly stopped working on his autobiography, producing only two manuscripts—the one he began on 16 July and completed on 12 September, and the one he wrote on 16 August. On 28 July he commented on this period of low productivity in a letter to Jean: "I am doing very very very very little work. I am sorry, but I can't help it—without an effort, & I have ceased from having a liking for efforts. I seem to greatly prefer cards, & billiards, & reading, & smoking, & lying around in the shade" (photocopy in CU-MARK). Two weeks later he wrote to Howells, "I have discharged my stenographer, & have entered upon a holiday whose other end is in the cemetery" (12 Aug 1908, NN-BGC). The Autobiographical Dictation of 14 July was the last one taken down by Josephine Hobby, who was dismissed on 4 August. The present dictation was recorded by a new employee, Mary Louise Howden (b. 1880?), whom Clemens found to be "competent & ladylike, & educated & agreeable" (12 Oct 1908 to JC, photocopy in CU-MARK; *Scotland Census* 1901, CSSCT 1901:327; "Approximate Pay Roll March 1ˢᵗ '07 to Feb'y 28ᵗʰ '09," Schedule 8 of "Accountants' Statements and Schedules" 1909). Howden had replied to an advertisement in the New York *Herald* for a "beginner at stenography who is willing to work in the country." She learned later that Clemens preferred someone inexperienced because "he dictated so slowly," pausing so long between his sentences that "watchful waiting was more desired than rapid fire speed" (Saunders 1925). In her letter of application she wrote:

> I have worked for a year in the office of the Y.W.C.A. in Paris and have just mastered the Remington machine as used in this country. I graduated from Pitmans school in London as a stenographer, one year ago but have worked only 6 months out of that year owing to my leaving Europe and coming to America. I am a Scotch girl, an Episcopalian, refined and well educated. (Howden to SLC, 23 Sept 1908, CU-MARK)

In 1925 Howden published a long and interesting article about her experience at Stormfield, describing Clemens's habit of dictating either in his bedroom or in the billiard room, his deadpan style of dictating humorous remarks, and his preference for adding his own punctuation to the typescripts, not allowing his stenographer "to add so much as a comma" (Howden 1925). She worked for Clemens until February 1909, when she was replaced by William E. Grumman (see "The Ashcroft-Lyon Manuscript," note at 367.25).

267.8–11   I got all of the necessary money for it . . . "Captain Stormfield's Visit to Heaven."] Although George Harvey of Harpers had rejected "Captain Stormfield's Visit" in September 1906—facetiously calling the story "too damn godly for a secular paper like the Magazine"—he accepted it a year later for publication in *Harper's Monthly,* where it appeared in two installments in December 1907 and January 1908 (Harvey to

SLC, before 7 Sept 1906, NNC; SLC 1907–8; see *AutoMT2*, 550–51 nn. 193.39–194.2, 194.17–18). In 1909 Clemens recalled, "I got out that rusty little batch of paper and counted the words and saw that there was enough of them to build the loggia; so I sent the 'Visit' to *Harper's Monthly* and collected the money" ("Stormfield, Mark Twain's New Country Home," *Country Life in America* 15 [Apr 1909]: 607–11, 650–52). In February 1907 Sunderland, the builder, gave an estimate of $4,100 for the loggia; the addition of a sleeping porch for Clara on the upper level brought the total cost to $4,550. This figure is consistent with the amount that Clemens earned for the story: thirty cents a word for approximately fifteen thousand words (letters in CU-MARK: Sunderland to Howells and Stokes, 20 Feb 1908, enclosed with Howells and Stokes to SLC, 21 Feb 1908; Howells and Stokes to SLC, 23 Mar 1908).

267.23   The burglars made a good deal of noise] The burglary took place early in the morning of 18 September. For the burglars, Henry Williams and Charles Hoffman, see the Autobiographical Dictation of 12 November 1908, notes at 276.10 and 278.18–20.

267.24–25   the butler] Claude Beuchotte (see the note at 268.34–35).

267.34   Mr. Lounsbury, our nearest neighbor] Harry A. Lounsbury (1873–1938), listed in the Redding census as a "farmer," was a "Jack of all trades" who supervised the construction of Stormfield and served as the overseer of the house and grounds, including its livery stable. Clemens relied on his "talents in many fields" (*Redding Census* 1910, 127:7A; *MTB*, 3:1463; Find a Grave Memorial 2013a; Howells and Stokes to SLC, 19 July 1907, CU-MARK).

267.36–37   Mr. Wark] Charles Edmund ("Will") Wark (1877–1954), a pianist born in Ontario, Canada, was Clara's accompanist during her concert tours in New England in early 1907 and in Europe in 1908 (see *AutoMT2*, 567 n. 240.6–8; AD, 1 Mar 1907, note at 4.16–17). Wark, although a married man (he was estranged from his wife), developed a romantic relationship with Clara, which by the fall of 1908 had become a subject of gossip. On 7 September 1908, shortly after their return from Europe, the New York *World* reported that the couple were expected to announce their engagement. Lyon forcefully denied the rumor when approached by reporters, and scandal was averted. Nevertheless, Clara soon ended her association with Wark, both personal and professional, and by mid-December had resumed her interrupted relationship with Ossip Gabrilowitsch (Shelden 2010, 91–92, 261–65, 301, 456 nn. 47, 49; Stormfield guestbook, entry for 18 Dec 1908, CU-MARK; also Trombley 2010, 160–67).

268.34–35   four days ago the butler gave up trying to sleep, and took his departure; the cook and the maids handed in their resignations the next day] According to Katy Leary (the family's longtime housekeeper), Claude Joseph Beuchotte (b. 1877), the French butler, first worked for the Clemenses during their residence in Riverdale (1901–3). He was again employed at 21 Fifth Avenue on 1 May 1907, but was among the group of servants who left Stormfield on 1 October 1908. (In "The Ashcroft-Lyon Manuscript," Clemens says the servants left because of Lyon, and not because of the burglary.) Claude returned in April 1909 and remained until Clemens's death ("Approximate Pay Roll March 1ˢᵗ '07 to Feb'y 28ᵗʰ '09," Schedule 8 of "Accountants' Statements and Schedules" 1909; for the other servants see "The Ashcroft-Lyon Manuscript," note at 337.26–27). Henry Rogers, Jr., later hired Beuchotte to manage the Tabitha Inn, the hotel that his father had built in Fairhaven, Massachusetts (Schmidt 2013b).

269.13–14   NOTICE. To the next Burglar] Seventeen-year-old Dorothy Sturgis, an angelfish who arrived for a visit on 18 September, inscribed this humorous instruction in ornamental letters on a large card (see the reproduction following page 300). Clemens described it in his Stormfield guestbook: "The illuminated 'Notice to the Next Burglar,' which hangs in the billiard room, is Dorothy's work ~~copied~~ ₐengrossedₐ from my rude original" (CU-MARK; Lyon 1908, entry for 18 Sept; for Dorothy see AD, 17 Apr 1908, note at 220.40). Clemens also posted the text on his front door, and it became an enduring newspaper item ("Burglars Invade Mark Twain Villa," New York *Times,* 19 Sept 1908, 9).

Autobiographical Dictation, 31 October 1908

269 *title*   Dictated October 31, 1908] The source of this "dictation" is actually a manuscript.

269.26–33   Widow Provided For, Butters Fortune Goes to Student Son . . . South African tramway line] Railroad magnate and businessman Henry A. Butters (b. 1850), of Piedmont, California, died of pneumonia on 26 October. His first business success had been in mining, in Colorado and then in South Africa, where he then made a fortune by building an electric railway. At the time of his death he was president of the Northern Electric Railroad in California. In 1891 he married Lucie Beebee Sanctella (1849–1909) and they had one son, Henry, Jr. (b. 1892). Mrs. Butters had been twice widowed. By her second marriage she had two daughters, whom Butters adopted: Marie Sanctella Butters (b. 1883) and Marguerite Sanctella Butters (b. 1885). In 1907, Butters quarreled with his wife when he found himself short of working capital for his business interests and she refused to return to him a "large amount of property" he had previously transferred to her. It was also "common gossip" (according to the Oakland *Tribune*) that their estrangement resulted from Butters's relationship with his "handsome secretary-stenographer" ("Mrs. Butters' Children to Contest Her Will: Henry A. Butters Gave His Stenographer $100,000 in Gifts," 9 July 1909, 1). In February 1908 Butters abandoned his wife. He left virtually his entire estate in trust for his sixteen-year-old son, Henry, Jr., bequeathing nothing to his wife and only five dollars to each of his adopted daughters, with the explanation that he had already "amply provided" for their "support and comfort" (Oakland *Tribune:* "Full Text of Will of Late Henry A. Butters," 3 Nov 1908, 9; "Mrs. Henry A. Butters' Heirs Declare Her Will Is Fraud," 12 Aug 1909, 1–2; *Lassen Census* 1900, 88:9A; San Francisco *Chronicle:* "Oakland Capitalist Succumbs to Pneumonia," 27 Oct 1908, 4; "Made Her Will to Win Her Husband," 13 Aug 1909, 1–2; *AutoMT1* mistakenly gives Butters's year of birth as 1830).

269.34 So Butters has escaped] For Clemens's dealings with the Plasmon Company of America see "The Ashcroft-Lyon Manuscript," pp. 332, 398–99, and the notes at 332.7–8, 332.28–29, and 398.9–10.

269.34–35 William C. Prime's. Prime was a gushing pietist] Clemens had targeted Prime, a journalist and travel writer, forty years earlier in chapters 46 and 48 of *The Innocents Abroad* (see *AutoMT1*, 481 n. 74.31).

270.7 Edmund M. Stanton] Edwin M. Stanton (1814–69), secretary of war from 1861 to 1865.

270.8–9 his brother-in-law . . . Hammond Trumbull] See *AutoMT1*, 559–60 n. 272.31–32. Prime married J. Hammond Trumbull's sister Mary (1827–72) in 1851. Clemens knew Trumbull well enough to have heard this story from him.

270.27 his lawyer, William W. Baldwin] William Woodward Baldwin (1862–1954) was the New York attorney for the Plasmon Company of America. He had served as third assistant secretary of state in 1896–97 under Grover Cleveland ("Office for W. W. Baldwin," New York *Herald,* 18 Feb 1896, 6; "Obituaries," Chicago *Tribune,* 18 Oct 1954, C6).

270.31 John Hays Hammond] Hammond (1855–1936) was a mining engineer who helped to develop gold mining in South Africa. Clemens met him there in May 1896, while on his world lecture tour; Hammond was then in prison for participating in the Jameson Raid, an abortive attempt to overthrow the Boer government of the Transvaal. Clemens judged Hammond to be "square—when not being used as a convenience" by Butters and his associates (16 Jan 1906 to MacAlister, ViU).

270.40–42 Three years ago, in a short story entitled "A Horse's Tale" . . . a libel suit] In chapter 6 of "A Horse's Tale," written in 1905 and first published in *Harper's Monthly* in 1906, one of the horses says, "I recognized your master. He is a bad sort. Trap-robber, horse-thief, squaw-man, renegado—Hank Butters—I know him very well." "Hank Butters" was Clemens's alteration in magazine proofs (SLC 1905b, 48; SLC 1906c, 336). No libel suit brought by Butters has been traced, but Clemens did at least intend to elicit such an action. Writing from Florence in January 1904, he told his lawyer: "As soon as I get back we will pull Butters into Court, & I guess we can jail him. We will try, anyhow. And I will add that libel, & see if he has grit enough to prosecute me" (29 Jan 1904 to Stanchfield, CU-MARK). In the unfinished "Three Thousand Years Among the Microbes" (1905), Clemens appropriated Butters's name for the character of a "bucket-shop dysentery-germ"; see also the Autobiographical Dictations of 28 January 1907 (based on a 1905 manuscript; *AutoMT2*, 393, 399) and 8 February 1906; the latter was published, with slight modifications, in NAR 4 (Oct 1907; *AutoMT1*, 54, 342; *WWD*, 545).

271.7–13 A Brooklyn evening paper of yesterday . . . she is young and handsome and good] The newspaper has not been identified. No evidence has been found that Lucie—who was nearly sixty years old—was Butters's second wife. Mrs. Butters had two married daughters (and three sons) from her first marriage; they had no legal relationship with Butters and were not mentioned in his will.

Autobiographical Dictation, 2 November 1908

271.14–22 an unpublished philosophy of mine . . . in Vienna in '97 or '98] See the Autobiographical Dictation of 4 September 1907, notes at 127.31–33 and 127.41. In that dictation Clemens correctly recalls the number of copies printed (two hundred and fifty). Here he again mangles the name of the general manager of the De Vinne Press, J. W. Bothwell.

271.32–33 Doubleday sent a copy to Kipling's father, a very intelligent man] Doubleday had become acquainted with Kipling's father, J. Lockwood Kipling, on a transatlantic voyage in 1899. The elder Kipling (1837–1911) was an artist, teacher, and author who worked in India for nearly thirty years. According to Edward Bok, who was also aboard, he was an "encyclopaedia of knowledge" and a "rare conversationalist." Today he is best known as the illustrator of his son's works (Bok 1922, 309–12; see also *AutoMT2,* 644 n. 446.16). His opinion of *What Is Man?* has not been discovered.

271.36 With Andrew Carnegie the result was the same] Carnegie's reaction to *What Is Man?* (evidently presented to him without authorship information) was forwarded to Clemens by Doubleday: "Thanks for the volume. It will startle the ordinary man, but I don't see that it goes much deeper than we were before. . . . What comes of us we fortunately know not, nor why we feel or do as we do; but this remains: 'All is well since all grows better.' Our only duty is to obey the Judge within" (Doubleday to SLC, 17 or 18 Dec 1906, CU-MARK).

271.36–37 The same with Bernard Shaw's biographer] Clemens inserted Archibald Henderson's letter about *What Is Man?* in the Autobiographical Dictation of 4 September 1907 (see also AD, 25 July 1907, note at 73.16–17).

272.8–16 a Canadian friend of his . . . The following letters reached me this morning from Mr. Norris] Little is known about Ashcroft's friend, Charles G. Norris of Toronto. He carried on a brief correspondence with Clemens, writing him at least four letters between September and December 1908, one of which is inserted in this dictation. In another letter, sent on 9 October 1908, he enclosed an essay in which he mentions that his father was a Congregational clergyman. Norris's essay expounds his personal philosophy, which embodies the tenets of Freemasonry and holds that "Truth is the only authority" (CU-MARK). Clemens wrote at least two letters to Norris, only one of which survives. On 17 September 1908 he replied to a letter from Norris that is now lost:

> What I have desired, & what I still desire is, to have What is Man examined by *unpreoccupied* (& CAPABLE) minds. *Examined*—not glanced at. To accomplish this, the authorship must be concealed—for the present. To publish the book with my name to it would defeat this. I want a backing of several hundred capable men before I come out of hiding—men who have read *unprejudiced,* & have approved. Then they are *committed,* & will stand to their guns; & will persuade others.
>
> I marvel that you have found several persons who were able to put their training aside sufficiently to enable them to understand the book. I have placed it (clandestinely) before 5 or 6 competent persons—with deliciously sad results! I have

read it—with comments & explanations—to six persons; three understood, three didn't. Since I finished this house & moved into it on the 18ᵗʰ of June, we have had about three dozen guests—all educated, all intelligent—but I have not brought the matter before one of them. They would not have understood.

I got my first lesson 23 years ago, when I threw out a feeler among 12 men of very superior intellect. Not one of them could understand & accept the proposition that *personal* merit is an impossible thing.

Yes, typewrite as many copies as you please, adding "copyright by J. W. Bothwell." I hope your printed copy will get worn out by & by; then Ashcroft will send you another. (NN-BGC)

272.20–23   David Grayson . . . "Adventures in Contentment" and "The Open Road,"] David Grayson was the pseudonym of Ray Stannard Baker (1870–1946), a journalist and author who was also coeditor and part owner of the *American Magazine.* "Adventures in Contentment," his series of essays on country life, appeared there from November 1906 to November 1907, followed by a sequel, "The Open Road," in January and March 1908.

272.34–39   Elbert Hubbard . . . his candid plea of guilty] Hubbard (1856–1915) was a printer, journalist, and moralist. Inspired by William Morris, in 1895 he established the Roycroft Press; the community of Roycroft artisans, based near Buffalo, New York, exemplified the American Arts and Crafts movement. Hubbard expressed his social and political views—a mixture of radicalism and conservatism—in the pages of *The Philistine,* cofounded (and finally entirely written) by himself. An 1899 editorial of his, reprinted as "A Message to Garcia," brought him national fame. His lecture "What Is Man" (titled, like Clemens's book, from Psalms 8:4) was advertised in *The Philistine* in 1908. Norris's remark about "guilt" refers to Hubbard's adulterous relationship with Alice Moore, who bore him a daughter in 1894. His 1907 tribute to Alice, *White Hyacinths,* praises her character in extravagant terms and admits, but does not apologize for, their relationship ("Elbert Hubbard Lectures," *Philistine* 27 [Sept 1908]: unnumbered advertisement; "'Greatest of Women,' Elbert Hubbard's Remarkable Tribute to His Wife," Washington *Post,* 10 July 1907, 2).

272.40–42   Edward Carpenter, the English philosopher . . . "Leaves of Grass,"] Carpenter (1844–1929) was an English social theorist, author, and early champion of gay rights. After reading Walt Whitman's *Leaves of Grass* in 1868 he became a socialist, and later made an extensive study of Eastern religions; his personal philosophy combines these interests. His best-known writing is his Whitmanesque poetry collection *Towards Democracy* (1883). He lived a quiet life with his partner at his country home near Sheffield, which became a mecca for his admirers. His numerous writings on socialism, pacifism, and homosexuality influenced writers such as E. M. Forster and D. H. Lawrence (Dawson 2013).

272.42–43   Count Leo Tolstoy . . . might wish to reveal yourself] In her journal entry of 2 November, Lyon described the circumstances of this dictation:

This morning a letter from M^r. Norris telling of his sending What is Man to David Grayson & Tolstoy has inspired the King to dictation. He came into my room in his red silk gown, & seated by the window said that his head was bursting with fancies that he had no physical ability to give birth to. Oh why couldn't he live until the time when a man's thoughts could be taken down by the wonderful the simple machine that is to be invented—perhaps is invented, & all you have to do is to turn the crank of it, & the grey cloud of thought will come back to you visualized, verbalized as it existed in the brain before the machine delivered it. There he sat, with eyes flashing, & deploring the fact that the Great Giant within him would be strangled at birth, & its force expended in disrupted temper.

The King regrets so that Tolstoy is a Christian—"a Hell of a Christian." (Lyon 1908)

No indication has been found that Tolstoy received or read a copy of *What Is Man?*

273.10–13 Dr. Isaac K. Funk . . . "Standard Dictionary."] Funk (1839–1912) was a Lutheran minister and lexicographer who cofounded the Funk and Wagnalls Company in 1877. Best known as the editor of *A Standard Dictionary of the English Language,* he also wrote on psychic and spiritual phenomena. *The Next Step in Evolution* (1902) considered the "probability, significance, and character of a second coming of Christ" ("New Books," Washington *Post,* 2 Feb 1903, 7; "Dr. Isaac K. Funk, Publisher, Is Dead," New York *Times,* 5 Apr 1912, 13).

Autobiographical Dictation, 5 November 1908

273.35 an accomplished lady . . . in one of the great female colleges] Unidentified.

274.12 that thief Mr. Clemens had before him in court not long ago] This cannot refer to the trial of the Stormfield burglars, which would not take place until 10 November. Clemens had, however, attended the arraignment in the chambers of a Redding judge on 18 September, wearing his white suit and accompanied by Clara and Charles Wark ("Mark Twain Enjoys Being the Goat," Boston *Journal,* 19 Sept 1908, 6; Springfield *Republican:* "Burglars Rob Mark Twain," 19 Sept 1908, 16; "Mark Twain on Witness Stand," 11 Nov 1908, 14).

275.17–18 For several days I have been trembling for Prince von Bulow] Bernhard, Prince von Bülow (1849–1929), was Wilhelm II's foreign minister when Clemens knew him in Vienna in 1897–98. From 1900 to 1909 he was chancellor of Germany and prime minister of Prussia; he became a prince in 1905. His "blunder" was failing to prevent publication of an interview with the emperor that appeared in the London *Telegraph* on 28 October 1908. In it, Wilhelm intemperately announced that he was friendly to the British, although the majority of Germans were not; that he had proposed the plan that helped the British to win the Second Boer War; and that British apprehensiveness about the growing German navy was "mad" and "unworthy." Von Bülow had received the manuscript of the interview for vetting, but failed to read it. The "Daily Telegraph Affair" offended not only the British and the Germans but also the French and the Russians, and swiftly led to von Bülow's resignation ("Britons Ingrates, Kaiser Declares," Chicago *Tribune,* 28 Oct 1908, 1; "German Chancellor Offers Resignation," New York *Times,* 1 Nov 1908, C3).

275.18–19 for two days I have been trembling for Mr. Taft] Taft had been elected president on 3 November. On that day Lyon noted in her journal, "The King said that if he had a preference it would be Taft, but that he regretted seeing the Republican Party continue in power" (Lyon 1908).

275.30–39 Senator Foraker... he is a crushed man to-day] In the fall of 1908 newspaper mogul William Randolph Hearst (1863–1951) campaigned on behalf of the Independence Party's presidential candidate (Thomas L. Hisgen, 1858–1925), accusing both the Democratic and Republican parties of corruption. On 17 September he focused his attack on Senator Joseph B. Foraker of Ohio (1846–1917), revealing the contents of letters written to Foraker by a Standard Oil executive, John D. Archbold. The letters, which had been stolen from the company's offices, revealed that, during his first senatorial term, Foraker had received large cash payments from Standard Oil in return for opposing legislation unfavorable to the company. In December 1908 Foraker, facing inevitable defeat, withdrew his bid for reelection to the Senate (Page 1908; New York *Times:* "Roosevelt Hits at Foraker Now," 22 Sept 1908, 1; "Burton for Senator; Taft, Foraker Out," 1 Jan 1909, 8; "Foraker Speaks in Own Defense," San Francisco *Chronicle,* 26 Sept 1908, 2).

Autobiographical Dictation, 12 November 1908

276.10 Charles Hoffman and Henry Williams] For Clemens's account of the burglary see the Autobiographical Dictation of 6 October 1908; he inserts a letter from Williams in the Autobiographical Dictation of 8 December 1908. Little is known about Hoffman; according to the New York *Times,* he was "aged 30, of South Norwalk." Henry Spengler Williams was born in Sprendlingen, Germany, in 1882. According to his autobiography, he was orphaned at fourteen. Arriving in the United States as a stowaway in 1898, he worked odd jobs until he was arrested for vagrancy and sent to prison "on a trumped-up charge." Upon his release, embittered toward society, he became a burglar. After another conviction in 1902 he spent five more years in prison. In 1908 he decided to marry; but making a home for his future wife "called for money, and lots of it," so when he read about Clemens's move to Stormfield he decided that it would be an easy target (Williams 1922, 13, 35–41, 46–50, 59–60, 81, 110–11, 168–69; "Clemens Burglar Is Out of Prison, Going Straight," Hartford *Courant,* 24 Oct 1916, 1, 2).

276.21 Stiles Judson] Judson (1862–1914) served several terms in the Connecticut state legislature and was appointed state's attorney for Fairfield County in 1908 (Pullman 1916).

277.16–17   my memory transported me to Warwick in England, across . . . thirty-five years] Clemens attended the assizes (periodical criminal court) at Warwick in July 1873, perhaps as a side trip of his 8–10 July excursion to Stratford-on-Avon with Olivia and Moncure Conway. In his notebook he wrote that at Warwick he saw "a woman convicted of passing 2-shilling pieces. Second offense. . . . She was sentenced to prison for 5 years which was very kind" (*N&J1*, 566).

278.18–20   condemned to four years in the penitentiary . . . prison for nine years] Hoffman was sentenced to "not less than three nor more than five years in State prison." Williams received five to six years for the burglary, and another four for assault, and was sent to the Connecticut state prison at Wethersfield. He was granted an early release for good behavior in October 1916. While in prison he organized a chapter of the Humanitarians, a charity dedicated to helping prisoners and ex-convicts, and after his release he continued his work to improve prison conditions. In 1917 Clara Clemens Gabrilowitsch helped him to get training as an automobile mechanic; he later married his former sweetheart and settled in Brooklyn. In 1922 he published an anonymous memoir, *In the Clutch of Circumstance*. Billing himself as "the Mark Twain Burglar," he was active as a lecturer on prison reform as late as 1931 (Williams 1922, 255–58, 268–72; New York *Times:* "Burglars Invade Mark Twain Villa," 19 Sept 1908, 9; "Twain Burglars Sentenced," 12 Nov 1908, 4; Hartford *Courant:* "Clemens Burglar Is Out of Prison, Going Straight," 24 Oct 1916, 1, 2; "Continues Story of State Prison," 25 Oct 1916, 2; "'Mark Twain Burglar' in Forum Talk," 11 Jan 1930, 4; untitled advertisement, Brooklyn *Eagle*, 28 Nov 1931, 10).

Autobiographical Dictation, 24 November 1908

278.21–38   Lord Northcliffe came up with Colonel Harvey . . . London *Times*] Harvey brought Lord Northcliffe (Alfred Charles William Harmsworth, 1865–1922) to Stormfield on 20–21 November 1908 (Stormfield guestbook, CU-MARK). Harvey had probably introduced the two men in January 1901 (Notebook 44, TS p. 3, CU-MARK). Harmsworth was born in Ireland, but his family soon moved to London. He established himself as a journalist in the early 1880s. In 1888 he married Mary Elizabeth Milner against his mother's wishes, and in the same year founded his own publishing business; by the early 1890s, in partnership with his brother Harold, he was issuing numerous popular magazines with combined sales of over a million copies a year. He bought the failing *Evening News* in 1894, and made it profitable by tailoring it to middle-class tastes. Two years later he launched the *Daily Mail,* and over the next few years added several more newspapers to his media empire. In March 1908 he purchased the London *Times* for £320,000. He was made a baronet in 1904, and in December 1905 was granted a peerage, taking the title Baron Northcliffe of the Isle of Thanet.

279.11–12   I believe I can work it through Congress this winter] On 11 December 1908 Clemens wrote to Champ Clark, a Democratic congressman from Missouri and an ally in his campaign to reform copyright law, to tell him of Harmsworth's visit (MoHM). According to Paine, the scheme that Clemens outlines in this dictation was made at Clark's suggestion, but was never introduced in Congress (*MTB*, 3:1640).

279.16   Copyright] The text that follows, Clemens's explanation of his copyright "scheme," is based on a manuscript.

279.20–22   Nineteen or twenty years ago . . . in the interest of Copyright] Clemens may be referring to either of two occasions. In January 1886 he and James Russell Lowell both spoke before the Senate Committee on Patents, which was considering two international copyright bills. Three years later, in January 1889, he again went to Washington to lobby for one of the bills. The debate in Congress continued until 1891, when a law was adopted that made foreign publications eligible for copyright, provided their country of origin recognized the copyrights of U.S. authors. For Lowell and Putnam (secretary of the American Publishers' Copyright League), and a discussion of the Senate hearings, see *AutoMT2*, 584 n. 283.25–284.16, 597–98 nn. 317.29–36, 318.21–22, 318.39–40.

279.22   Senator Platt of Connecticut] Orville H. Platt (1827–1905) was a Republican senator from 1879 until his death. He served on the Senate Committee on Patents for nearly his entire career, and was its chairman in 1881–87 and again in 1895–99. An ardent proponent of international copyright, he was largely responsible for passage of the 1891 act (Coolidge 1910, 70, 90–110).

279.26–27   still the policy of Congress to-day] The first copyright law in the United States, passed in 1790, provided a term of fourteen years, renewable for another fourteen; in 1831, the term was extended to twenty-eight years plus another fourteen. That law remained unchanged until March 1909, when a bill was passed allowing a term of twenty-eight years, renewable for another twenty-eight (*AutoMT2*, 585 n. 286.12–13).

Autobiographical Dictation, 8 December 1908

281.3   the worst and toughest of our two burglars—Williams] For information on the 18 September 1908 burglary and the two perpetrators, Henry Williams and Charles Hoffman, see the Autobiographical Dictations of 6 October and 12 November 1908.

282.3–4   "genuine gentleness, honest symphaty, brave humanity and sweet kindliness"] This phrase (without the misspelled "sympathy") is from "Biographical Criticism," an essay by Brander Matthews that was included in the first volume, *The Innocents Abroad*, of numerous collected editions of Mark Twain's works, issued by the American Publishing Company and Harper and Brothers beginning in 1899 (Matthews 1899; for information on the various editions see Schmidt 2010).

282.11   necessity knows no law . . . to borrow one of your own expressions] Clemens took credit for this ancient proverb in chapter 51 of *The Innocents Abroad* (SLC 1869a, 542).

282.13–16   "Old age and experience . . . in the wrong."] A close paraphrase of lines from "A Satire Against Mankind" (1679) by John Wilmot, second earl of Rochester.

282.21   "Father forgive them, they know not what they did."] A close paraphrase of Jesus's words, as reported in Luke 23:34.

282.21–22   Being my first offence against the law] Williams had already served a five-year prison term (see AD, 12 Nov 1908, note at 276.10).

282.23–25   "Oh what a fatal time . . . thinking being!"] From Victor Hugo's *Les Misérables* (1862), as translated in *Masterpieces of Ancient and Modern Literature* (Peck et al. 1899, 12:6331).

282.34–35   "warum ich traure in des Lebens Blüthezeit."] From Friedrich Schiller's poem "Der Jüngling am Bache" ("The Youth at the Brook"), variously translated, but meaning "why I mourn in the flowering of life."

283.37   Robert Fulton Cutting] Cutting (1852–1934), the great-nephew of steamboat inventor Robert Fulton, was a New York financier and businessman, philanthropist, and officer of several educational and social welfare agencies, which earned him the epithet "first citizen of New York." Cutting and Clemens were among the organizers, in January 1906, of the Robert Fulton Memorial Association, which intended to build a Fulton monument in New York City. Clemens was the association's first vice-president and a member of its executive committee (see *AutoMT1*, 426–28, 630 n. 426.13–15; New York *Times:* "For a Monument to Fulton," 18 Jan 1906, 8; "R. Fulton Cutting, Civic Leader, Dies," 22 Sept 1934, 15).

284.6   he would hunt down his fellow convict and kill him] Williams held his accomplice, Charles Hoffman, responsible for rousing the Stormfield household during the burglary when he "stumbled and fell heavily over" a brass bowl that Williams had placed "noiselessly" on the floor. And Williams was no doubt infuriated because Hoffman's momentary escape from the pursuing "posse" left him to take the brunt (by his telling) of a brutal capture that left him bloodied and unconscious (Williams 1922, 172, 175–77).

Autobiographical Dictation, 10 December 1908

284.14   the expense of building a house for our little library] A few months after moving to Redding in June 1908, Clemens, along with some of his neighbors, founded the Mark Twain Library Association. The Mark Twain Library opened, in a former chapel, on 28 October 1908. Clemens then raised money for a new building with stratagems such as the one he describes in this dictation. After the sudden death of Jean Clemens on 24 December 1909 (see "Closing Words of My Autobiography"), her house and property on the Stormfield grounds were sold and, a few days before his own death in April 1910, Clemens gave the $6,000 in proceeds to construct what became the Jean L. Clemens Memorial Building, which was formally dedicated in February 1911. The core of the library's collection consisted of about three thousand of Clemens's own books, several hundred donated by Clemens himself and the rest donated by Clara after his death (Mark Twain Library 2014a–b; Gribben 1980, 1:xxvii–xxviii; "Twain Books for Library," New York *Times,* 10 July 1910, 1; see also "The Ashcroft-Lyon Manuscript," note at 345.37).

285.13   Robert Collier] See the Autobiographical Dictation of 19 February 1908, note at 210.31.

285.23   Theodore Adams] In a speech delivered at the opening of the library, Clemens had suggested that Theodore Adams provide the land for a new building. Adams, whose great-grandfather had settled in Redding around 1760, had recently returned to the area after working for thirty-five years with a carriage manufacturer in Springfield, Massachusetts (Todd 1906, 222–23). Although Clemens's remark took him by surprise, Adams promptly offered to donate a "most desirable site" (*MTB,* 3:1471–73; Fatout 1976, 630–31). On 19 December 1908 Lyon noted in her journal, "It made me ill in my soul to see the men pacing off double the quantity of land needed, & to see M^r. Adams's expression of distress when he saw them devouring the land with mighty strides" (Lyon 1908).

285.23   Mr. Sunderland] Philip N. Sunderland worked for his father's contracting firm, which built Stormfield.

286.6   TORONTO] Clemens revised the original of this letter before it was transcribed into the autobiography, canceling the letterhead ("Virtue and Company, Publishers and Importers of Fine Editions of Special and Standard Works," a Toronto firm) and the writer's signature, "J B Sutherland."

286.12–13   last March, when you were speaking in aid of the Sailors' Hospital] Clemens spoke at a benefit for the Cottage Hospital (not the Sailors' Hospital) in Bermuda on 5 March 1908 (see AD, 16 Apr 1908, and the note at 212.5–6).

286.14   the Toronto Saturday Night] *Toronto Saturday Night* was a weekly magazine devoted to public affairs and the arts. Established in 1887, it appeared in a variety of formats until 2005. The issue of 5 December 1908, which evidently printed Clemens's "To My Guests" circular, was not available for examination.

286.21   I have read your autobiography] That is, the twenty-five "Chapters from My Autobiography" published in the *North American Review* between September 1906 and December 1907, or reprints of them.

286.36   "Baker's blue-jay yarn"] In chapters 2 and 3 of *A Tramp Abroad.*

287.10   I have explained to him] Clemens's reply to Mönch is not known to survive.

Autobiographical Dictation, 16 December 1908

287.16   Howard P. Taylor] Taylor (1838–1916), a native of Louisville, Kentucky, went to California while still a boy. There he worked as a printer's devil for the San Francisco

Argonaut, later becoming an editorial writer. In the early 1860s, when Clemens first knew him, he was a typesetter on the Virginia City *Territorial Enterprise* and then, briefly, part owner and publisher of the Virginia City *Evening Bulletin.* After relocating to New York City, Taylor wrote a number of popular plays. Clemens had last been in touch with him not "forty-five or fifty" years ago, but in 1889–90, when he agreed to let Taylor dramatize *A Connecticut Yankee.* By 15 July 1890 Taylor had finished his play, which he believed had "barrels of money" in it, but lacked the means to produce it. He struggled to find a theater manager willing to take it on, but met with objections that it was a "one-man piece" and too expensive to stage (Taylor to SLC, 15 July 1890, 16 Dec 1890, CU-MARK). In January 1891 Taylor informed Clemens of a proposal from a wealthy but faded Jewish comic actor, M. B. Curtis (1852–1921), who had enjoyed great success in the early 1880s with a comic melodrama entitled *Sam'l of Posen; or, The Commercial Drummer.* Curtis was willing to stage the *Yankee* play if he was allowed to "make a modern American Jew" of Hank Morgan and call the piece "Sam'l of Posen at King Arthur's Court" (Taylor to SLC, 24 Jan 1891, CU-MARK). Although Clemens assented, the project was dropped. Finally, in April 1891, Taylor signed a production contract for his own dramatization with a New York management firm, but the play was never produced (Taylor to SLC, 29 Apr 1891, CU-MARK; Doten 1973, 3:2251; Angel 1881, 323; Kelly 1863, 286; "Howard P. Taylor Dead," New York *Times,* 8 July 1916, 9; 29 Jan 1891, 9 Mar 1891, 30 Apr 1891 to Taylor, MS secretarial copies, CU-MARK; Erdman 1995, 28, 32, 41–43).

287.28   you didn't seem "bigger than a paragraph,"] An allusion to *A Connecticut Yankee,* chapter 2 (*CY,* 61).

287.39–40   Joe Goodman ... somewhere in Southern California] Goodman had sold the Virginia City *Territorial Enterprise* in 1874, then lived in San Francisco until 1880, when he became a raisin farmer in Fresno, California. In 1891 he moved to Alameda, California (*AutoMT1,* notes on 544–45).

287.40   Jim Townsend] James W. E. Townsend had been a staff member on the Virginia City *Territorial Enterprise,* the San Francisco *Golden Era,* and other California newspapers. Known as "lying Jim" for his facility with the tall tale, he reportedly was the prototype for Truthful James in Bret Harte's "The Heathen Chinee," and has also been credited with originating Clemens's "Jumping Frog" tale, a short version of which appeared in the Sonora *Herald* in 1853, during Townsend's tenure on that paper (*N&J1,* 69 n. 3).

287.41–288.1   Jim Gillis ... Dan de Quille] De Quille (William H. Wright) was Clemens's predecessor and then his colleague on the Virginia City *Territorial Enterprise;* Gillis was his Jackass Hill, California, mining friend (*AutoMT1,* 543 n. 251.32–38; see AD, 26 May 1907, and the note at 57.22–24, and AD, 29 May 1907).

288.1   Denis and Jack McCarthy] Denis McCarthy was co-owner of the *Territorial Enterprise* and Clemens's lecture agent briefly in 1866. His brother Jack was a pressman on the *Enterprise* (*AutoMT1,* 537 n. 227.7–9 and notes on 544–45; Doten 1973, 3:2251).

288.1–2   Pit Taylor, Jack McGinn, Mike McCarthy, George Thurston] Pitney Taylor was an associate editor of the Virginia City *Union;* Mike McCarthy (not known to be related to Denis and Jack) and George Thurston were *Enterprise* typesetters (Doten 1973, 2:835–36, 3:2251). Jack McGinn has not been identified.

288.40   Poultney A. Bigelow] Bigelow (1855–1954) was a lawyer, Spanish-American War correspondent, and the author of several books on international politics and travel. He and the Clemenses saw each other socially in London in 1896–97, but the occasion described here has not been independently documented.

289.24–25   summer of 1857 . . . not seen Keokuk since the January of that year] Clemens lived in Keokuk, Iowa, most of the time from June 1855 until October 1856 (not until January 1857, as he says here), while working in his brother Orion's Ben Franklin Book and Job Office. He subsequently visited in July 1860, while he was piloting on the Mississippi; in January 1885, while he was on his reading tour with George Washington Cable; and in July 1886, when he took his family to visit his mother (link notes following 5 Mar 1855 to the Muscatine *Tri-Weekly Journal* and 5 Aug 1856 to Henry Clemens, and 11 Aug 1860 to Stotts, *L1,* 58–59, 69, 101 n. 1; *AutoMT2,* 356–58, 591 n. 302.41–42; *N&J3,* 242 n. 60).

290.1–3   grand account of the banquet . . . which appeared in *Harper's Weekly*] In his Autobiographical Dictation of 12 January 1906, Clemens discussed the banquet that George Harvey held in honor of his seventieth birthday at Delmonico's restaurant in New York. He also considered inserting there the "grand account," which filled a sizable portion of the 23 December 1905 issue of *Harper's Weekly,* but did not do so. A facsimile of the magazine is available at *MTPO* (*AutoMT1,* 267–68, 558 n. 268.28, 657–61).

Autobiographical Dictation, 22 December 1908

290 *title*   Dictated December 22, 1908] The first three paragraphs of this "dictation"—that is, Clemens's introduction to the letter from Bausch—are actually based on a manuscript.

290.26   what Irwin has done, with his delightful Japanese schoolboy] Wallace Irwin (1875–1959) was a prolific journalist, author, humorist, and staff writer for *Collier's* magazine. In the voice of a Japanese "schoolboy," Hashimura Togo (actually a thirty-five-year-old domestic servant), Irwin wrote letters in fractured English on American society and politics. These were serialized in *Collier's* between November 1907 and February 1909 (although not in every issue). The series was tremendously popular in its day, and remained so for decades, but is now regarded as stereotypical and racist ("Wallace Irwin, Humorist, Dead," New York *Times,* 15 Feb 1959, 87; Irwin 1909, 3; Uzawa 2006). Clemens had written to the magazine the previous July:

July 6/08.

Hon. Collier Weekly which furnish Japanese Schoolboy to public not often enough, when is his book coming out? I shall be obliged if you will send me the earliest copy, or at least the next earliest. That Boy is the dearest & sweetest & frankest & wisest & funniest & delightfulest & lovablest creation that has been added to our literature for a long time. I think he is a permanency, & I hope so, too.

Truly yours

S. L. Clemens

Collier's published a facsimile of Clemens's letter on 8 August 1908 (41:22), and Irwin wrote to thank Clemens (undated letter, CU-MARK):

Dear Mr. Clemens:—

May I drop a line to say how deeply grateful I feel for your appreciation of my Japanese kid, which has just reached me through Collier's. A word of praise from you is more than I ever hoped to merit; and suddenly, out of a clear sky, to receive your praise in such hearty quantities—well, little Togo is still scratching his Japanese pompadour and wondering if it's all true.

No, the Japanese schoolboy is not out in book form yet, but we have been approached by some publishers and hope to have it inside covers in time. When it *does* come out in book form, may I be permitted to send you the first copy off the press?

Hoping that I may teach Hashimura to live up to the good things you have said about him, I am

Very sincerely yours

Wallace Irwin

When the book was published in February 1909, Irwin sent an early copy to Clemens, who responded by letter on 8 March: "The aged & mouldy, but good & wise Mark Twain, benefactor of the human race,—say-so of Hon. public—has received the book of Japanese Schoolboy, other benefactor of Hon. human race, & sends very heartiest thanks, & cannot keep from reading it all the time, & chuckling & enjoying" (CU-BANC).

291.14–15 Esperanto or Volapück] Artificial international languages, both created in the late nineteenth century. Esperanto was invented by Ludwig L. Zamenhof of Russia, and was based largely upon words common to the principal European languages. At various times Esperanto has been used by governmental and international agencies, including the U.S. Army, but no country has adopted it officially. Volapük, which Esperanto supplanted, was invented by Johann Martin Schleyer, a German Catholic priest; it was based chiefly on English, but used some root words from German, French, and Latin.

293.16 your travels through our country—you rambles it at all sides] Clemens and his family visited the Netherlands in mid-July 1879, during the European sojourn that provided material for *A Tramp Abroad* (*N&J2*, 48). He made only brief mention of that part of the trip, at the end of the last chapter: "From Paris I branched out and walked through Holland and Belgium, procuring an occasional lift by rail or canal when tired, and I had a tolerably good time of it 'by and large'" (SLC 1880, 580). That there were extensive "rambles" is clear, however, from Olivia Clemens's letter of 20 July 1879 to her mother, in which she reported on "fascinating" outings in and around Rotterdam, Amsterdam, Haarlem, and The Hague (CtHMTH).

294.15–21   my length is 1.61 meter . . . neck-cloth] On 27 February 1909 Bausch completed this self-portrait by sending Clemens a photograph of himself and his wife, Nellie (see the photograph following page 300).

295.9   Holland] Clemens was so amused by Bausch's letter that he published this entire Autobiographical Dictation in *Harper's Weekly* on 20 February 1909 (SLC 1909d). Four additional letters from Bausch survive in the Mark Twain Papers, written between 27 February and 22 June 1909, but none of Clemens's replies has been found. It is clear, however, that Clemens answered him twice, sending both the requested preface (now lost) and fifty dollars, as compensation for his contribution to the *Harper's* article. Bausch thanked Clemens in a semicoherent twenty-six-page letter of 17 March, in which he remarked:

> And then the compliment which you makes me! Until now it was indeed only my cat who it is sitting warm and calm on my knees when I write, who found pleasure in my work! And then the preface! And then the fifty dollar! . . . One of the first results has been that my mother in law has now nothing to criticise more at my work. . . . And that was not yet all. For when one of my brothers in law, who is a dealer in chease, and who feels himself therefore always me superior, heard from your letter, he came immediately to my home to do tell him all. . . . I comprehended very well, of course, that this was the beginning of the glory and a fore-token of that what will be mentioned at my regard in the newspapers, when I will be a famous man and will be interviewed about all sorts of things, wherewith I have nothing to do and will be obliged to say my meaning about all sorts of questions from which I do not know only anything, just as is done by all famous men at their turn.
>   And all this I thank your preface! (CU-MARK)

On 27 April Bausch expressed his gratitude yet again (in a letter only ten pages long), in which he described his financial difficulties and noted that "the 50 dollar which your letter contained, have saved our life." At this point Clemens grew weary of the correspondence; on the envelope of this letter he wrote: "No answer. NEVER try to do a stranger a kindness" (CU-MARK). His failure to respond led Bausch to write a fourth letter on 22 June, this time evidently addressed to *Harper's Weekly,* to inquire "wether mr. Clemens is indisposed or is hindered to answer for some other reason" (enclosed with Duneka to SLC, 2 July 1909, CU-MARK).

Autobiographical Dictation, Christmas Day, 1908

295 *title*   Dictated Christmas Day, 1908] This "dictation" is actually based on a manuscript.

295.10–11   Robert Collier . . . bought a baby elephant for my Christmas] No letter from Collier with this news is known to survive. He may not actually have sent such a letter, intending, as Clemens claims, for Lyon to intercept it. On the contrary, Collier communicated directly with her, but not until 19 December, when she noted in her journal: "Tonight just after I got into bed at 9:30, M^r. Robert Collier telephoned to say that he is going to send a baby elephant—a real elephant up for the King's Christmas" (Lyon 1908). It is likely that Clemens's account of this episode, including the chronology, is not strictly factual.

295.12   Barnum and Bailey's winter-quarters menagerie at Bridgeport] Phineas T. Barnum combined his "Greatest Show on Earth," founded in 1871, with James A. Bailey's circus in 1881. Barnum died in 1891, and after Bailey's death in 1906, the circus was sold to the Ringling Brothers, who continued to produce it separately from their own circus for many years. In 1875 the Clemenses had visited the Barnums at their summer home in Bridgeport, Connecticut, which was also the site of the circus's winter quarters (3 Feb 1875 and 7 June 1875 to Barnum, and link note following 11 Oct 1875 to Blaine, *L6*, 368–71, 491–92, 555–56).

295.15–16   it filled Miss Lyon with consternation] In her journal on 24 December Lyon noted:

> At 3^{30} just as I was away up on top of a step ladder on top of a table tying a Xmas ball to the gas-nub, the elephant trainer arrived—& said that the little creature was on its way, that it was about as big as a cow, that the Garrage must be warmed—heated—that it must have half a bale of hay a day, & bread & carrots; that it cant come into the house, that there is a ton of hay out at the station—& my distress was genuine, for I know the wave of feeling that will rush over the King at having a wild creature in captivity. (Lyon 1908)

297.14–15   Miss Lyon . . . could not bear to look at him] In her journal on 25 December Lyon admitted that even after she helped unpack the toy elephant she was not clear about the joke and "flew to the telephone to talk to M^r. Lounsbury about it" (Lyon 1908).

Autobiographical Dictation, 5 January 1909

297 *title*   Dictated at Stormfield, January 5, 1908] This "dictation" is actually based on a manuscript.

297.19–30   Presidential performance of two or three weeks ago . . . *Times*'s unhappy attack] The account of the riding incident, involving "Miss May Rhodes, daughter of a wealthy resident of Los Angeles," appeared in the New York *Sun* on 19 December 1908 ("Girls Angry at Roosevelt," 3). The following day, the *Times* printed an article accusing the *Sun* of "grossly imperfect reporting" that betrayed an obvious inclination to belittle the importance of the incident, to make out as good a case as possible for Mr. ROOSEVELT, in The Sun's accustomed way. Why suppress the fact that the President, drawing a hammerless, self-cocking revolver of the machine gun type from his right hip pocket, shot the horse and sent the girl rider, although she was severely injured by the fall of her mount, to Fort Monroe?

Only the poor thing's parents and those of her companions, who were placed in irons and sent to Washington to await the inquiry of a secret tribunal, have known until now how hard the mailed hand of authority can bear upon the offenders in such a case as this. A weak, piffling attempt to make light of an incident which must have its influence on all the future history of the country, to treat of it in print in so trivial a manner as to make the ordinary reader regard it as a "fake," or at best as an exaggeration of a gossiping school girl's all but baseless yarn, deserves the severest condemnation. ("Careless Reporting," 10)

297.31 we have a visitor, to-day, who furnishes what he claims to be the facts] Two visitors came to Stormfield on 5 January 1909, but it is not known which one furnished "the facts." On 21 December 1908 Paul Thompson, an agent for authors and photographers, had written to Clemens: "Several English and European publications whom I represent have asked me to secure photographs of you and your family in your new home.... If you can see your way clear to permit my sending a photographer to Redding to take them I will appreciate it very much" (CU-MARK). Thompson (1878–1940), a Yale graduate, and his photographer ("Mr. Taylor," according to the Stormfield guestbook) visited Stormfield on 5 January: "There the humorist was snapped playing billiards, writing at his desk and in other familiar positions. The immediate sale of this set of pictures brought in $1,000, which became the initial capital for the establishment of Mr. Thompson as an independent news photographer" ("Paul Thompson, 62, Early Cameraman," New York Times, 28 Nov 1940, 23; Stormfield guestbook, entry for 5 January 1909, CU-MARK). Four of the photographs taken at Stormfield appeared in the March 1909 issue of The Burr McIntosh Monthly (Paul Thompson 1909; see the photograph following page 300).

298.9 The father wrote a note to the President ... but got no reply] No letter of complaint from the girl's father, Alonzo Willard Rhodes, a prominent Los Angeles banker and financier, has been found; but her mother wrote to Roosevelt "to deny that her daughter's horse had been struck by the President while riding past her in a road near Washington" ("Thanked by Roosevelt: President Writes to Mother of Girl," New York Times, 9 Feb 1909, 1; "A. W. Rhodes, Financier, Dies," Los Angeles Times, 5 Nov 1937, A23). Roosevelt replied in early February:

My Dear Mrs. Rhodes, I thank you for your letter of the 20th ultimo, and am glad to hear from you that your daughter denied the story that I struck her horse. Of course, I never struck her horse or any other lady's horse. The whole story was so absurd as not to be worth denial. Numerous stories of this kind are started from time to time by foolish or malicious people. Occasionally I am obliged to deny them, but as a rule I find it best simply to ignore them, because denying them calls attention to them and gives a chance to mischief-makers to mislead well-meaning people by further repetitions of the stories.

Sincerely yours,
THEODORE ROOSEVELT.

298.18–19   subordinate ruffian brutally treated a lady . . . postmaster of Washington] Benjamin F. Barnes, an assistant presidential secretary, forcibly ejected Mrs. Minor Morris from the White House in January 1906. Clemens discusses the incident at length in the Autobiographical Dictations of 10, 15, and 18 January 1906, and again on 3 and 4 April 1906 (*AutoMT1*, 256–59, 279–81, 292–93, 551 n. 258.34; *AutoMT2*, 6–12).

Autobiographical Dictation, 11 January 1909

298.20–21   From away back towards the very beginning of the Shakspeare-Bacon controversy I have been on the Bacon side] The theory that Sir Francis Bacon (Lord Verulam, 1561–1626) wrote the plays usually ascribed to William Shakespeare was first put forward by Delia Bacon (1811–59), of Hartford. In a magazine article published in 1856 and a book published the next year, she asserted that the plays' author had to be of better birth and education than Shakespeare, the "stupid, ignorant, illiterate, third-rate play-actor" of Stratford. If Clemens's account in *Is Shakespeare Dead?* (1909) is to be trusted, "Delia Bacon's book" made him a Baconian in 1856 or 1857; evidence is against this. He recorded some doubts about Shakespeare's authorship in an 1873 notebook, but as a rule his adherence to the Baconian party is not apparent before 1887 (see the note at 299.4–5; Delia Bacon 1856, 19; Delia Bacon 1857; SLC 1909a, 4–17; *N&J1*, 562–63; Berret 1993; Gribben 1980, 2:633–36).

298.32–37   his holding of horses . . . his couple of reverently preserved and solely existent signatures] These incidents (of varying degrees of verifiability) in the life of Shakespeare are discussed in standard biographies, such as Sidney Lee's *Life*, and in studies of Shakespearean biography such as S. Schoenbaum's *Shakespeare's Lives* (Sidney Lee 1908; Schoenbaum 1991).

299.4–5   When Ignatius Donnelly's book came out . . . I not only published it, but read it] Ignatius Donnelly (1831–1901) was a Minnesota politician, lawyer, and author. In *The Great Cryptogram* (1888) he claimed Bacon wrote the plays, scattering clues to his authorship, written in a cipher, throughout the text of the 1623 First Folio edition. Donnelly's theory was much discussed in newspapers before publication. Clemens's memory that he published Donnelly's book is erroneous. On 9 July 1887 he wrote from Elmira to Fred Hall (deputizing for Charles Webster): "Couldn't we get Ignatius Donelly's Shakspeare-cipher book?—or has Thorndike Rice captured it?" He crossed out that sentence, however, and wrote: "No—we don't want it" (NPV, in *MTBus,* 384). Hall replied that "Donnelly offered us his Shakespeare book, but Mr. Webster thought it best to decline it, especially as the author wanted all the profits" (10 Aug 1887, CU-MARK). Clemens then forgot his earlier letter, and blamed Webster for a decision that merely duplicated his own. He wrote to Orion on 7 September that Webster "had the hardihood to turn Donelly's Shakspeare book away without asking me anything about it . . . Of course he didn't know he was throwing away $50,000; he was merely ignorant; had probably never heard of Bacon & didn't know there was a controversy. This won't happen again" (CU-MARK; *N&J3,* 324 n. 73). On the same day, Susy Clemens wrote to Edward H. House (ViU):

> There is a great discussion in our family at the present time, upon . . . the author-ship of Shakespeares plays.
> The notices of Mr. Donnelrys book are not very favorable to poor old William. It would be a revolution if Shakespeare should be dethroned and Bacon, placed upon his long occupied pedestal.
> Mamma revolts at the mere idea, but papa favors Bacon, & so do I.

The Great Cryptogram received wide (but mostly contemptuous) press coverage, and was a financial failure (Friedman and Friedman 1957, 27–50; Fish 1892, 115).

299.25–30   a book in press in Boston . . . Macy has told me about the clergyman's book] Helen Keller, with her guardians Anne (Sullivan) Macy and John Macy, arrived at Stormfield on 8 January 1909. Isabel Lyon noted in her diary that John Macy had brought the galleys of a new book on the Bacon-Shakespeare controversy: "The King was instantly alert." The book, William Stone Booth's *Some Acrostic Signatures of Francis Bacon,* was yet another attempt to show Bacon's authorship through ciphered messages in the First Folio text. "He has convinced the King of this truth," wrote Lyon, "and the King has seized upon it with a destroying zeal . . . you'd think both men had Shakespeare by the throat righteously strangling him for some hideous crime." At Macy's urging, Clemens began to write *Is Shakespeare Dead?* on 11 January and finished it on 9 March; Harper and Brothers published it in April (Lyon 1909; Booth 1909; SLC 1909a). The British-born writer William Stone Booth (1864–1926) was not a "clergyman," as Clemens repeatedly calls him.

299.36–37   One of the examples is the Epilogue to "The Tempest." . . . Francisco Bacono] This example is specifically discussed by William Friedman and Elizebeth Friedman, who show that, using Booth's methods, it is just as easy to extract the "signature" of Ben Jonson or several other Tudor luminaries (Friedman and Friedman 1957, 120–21).

300.29   that new planet of Professor Pickering's] In the first days of 1909 it was reported that Harvard astronomer William H. Pickering (1858–1938) had concluded, from analysis of the "perturbations" of Neptune's orbit, that a ninth planet existed. (Pickering's conjectural planet is not identical with Pluto, which would be discovered in 1930.) On 4 January, Clemens wrote his short sketch "The New Planet," which was published in *Harper's Weekly* at the end of the month (New York *Times:* "Report a New

Planet," 2 Jan 1909, 1; "Finding the Orbit of the New Planet," 4 Jan 1909, 3; "To Verify New Planet," 10 Jan 1909, 4; SLC 1909a, 1909b; Hoyt 1976).

Autobiographical Dictation, 10 March 1909

301.12–18   to see one of my little angel-fishes, Irene . . . her special teacher, Miss Brown] Irene Gerken (see AD, 17 Apr 1908, note at 220.22–23). Neither her school nor her teacher has been identified.

301.22–25   charming Carey . . . *Century Magazine*] William Carey (1858–1901) served on the editorial staff of the *Century Magazine* for twenty years. According to Arthur John, in *The Best Years of the Century,* he acted as "liaison between editors and production men . . . shuttling proofs from author to printer and back," and the *Century's* editor Richard Watson Gilder relied upon him "in all matters of taste and judgment" (John 1981, 116). Known for his exceptional kindness, he was also a brilliant conversationalist and immensely popular with authors. William Webster Ellsworth, secretary of the Century Company, reported that "Mark Twain called him the wittiest man he ever knew" ("William Carey Dead," Boston *Herald,* 19 Oct 1901, 2; Ellsworth 1919, 31–35; "William Carey," *Century Magazine* 63 [Jan 1902]: 477–78; *N&J3,* 495 n. 43).

302.7–9   when I get up to speak at that Carnegie dinner . . . make a third speech] On 17 March 1909 Andrew Carnegie was the guest of honor at a Lotos Club dinner in recognition of his generosity during the financial panic of 1907. He had enabled the club to continue with the construction of a new home at 110 West 57th Street; the dinner was the first held at the new venue. Clemens made a brief speech in which he chaffed Carnegie for his assumed diffidence toward the lavish compliments he received and for his frequent mentions of Scotland in his speech ("Carnegie Honored by Club He Financed," New York *Times,* 18 Mar 1909, 9; for a text of the speech see Fatout 1976, 637–39).

302.19–22   forty-three years ago . . . I was to lecture in San Jose] Clemens delivered his Sandwich Islands lecture in San Jose, California, on 21 November 1866. He had made his platform debut with this talk on 2 October in San Francisco, and toured with it afterwards in Nevada and California, making his final appearance in San Francisco again on 10 December (see *L1:* link note following 25 Aug 1866 to Bowen, 361–62; 29 Oct 1866 to Howland, 362 n. 1; 2 Nov 1866 to JLC and family, 366–67 n. 4). He received mixed reviews in the San Jose newspapers. The *Evening Patriot,* for example, said there was "much beauty of imagery and expression—parts sublimely beautiful—which elicited applause—some useful information which gratified—a great deal of humorous wit at which the audience laughed immoderately," but diluted this praise by saying there was also "too much buffoonery which we confess to Mr. Twain, privately, was not in our line, and was almost as hard to digest as the old missionary was to the cannibal" (22 Nov 1866, 3).

Autobiographical Dictation, 25 March 1909

303.15–16   two months ago I was illuminating this Autobiography . . . concerning the Bacon-Shakespeare controversy] See the Autobiographical Dictation of 11 January 1909. The present text is based on a manuscript.

303.27   Hannibal *Courier-Post* of recent date has reached me, with an article] Clemens gave a clipping of the article—whose date of publication has not been determined—to his typist to transcribe. He had undoubtedly received it in a letter from Laura Frazer (née Hawkins), a former Hannibal playmate and sweetheart and the prototype of Becky Thatcher in *The Adventures of Tom Sawyer*. Laura had visited Stormfield in October 1908, and had subsequently corresponded with Clemens about childhood friends. In a letter of 16 March she wrote, "Enclosed you will find several clippings which I think will interest you" (CU-MARK; see *Inds,* 323).

303.38   Holiday Hill, Jackson's Island, or Mark Twain cave] Holliday Hill and McDowell's cave—fictionalized as Cardiff Hill and McDougal's cave—figure in chapters 29–33 of *Tom Sawyer.* Jackson's Island—based on the real Glasscock's Island—is the scene of the boys' adventures in chapters 13–16 (see *AutoMT1,* 515 n. 158.22–25, 624 n. 418.29–30; *HF* 2003, 393–94 n. 41.35).

304.16   copyright, or patent himself] At Ashcroft's suggestion, Clemens had recently taken two steps to prevent unauthorized use of his name, in an effort to ensure his daughters' financial future. In November 1907 Ashcroft registered patents, in his own name, on Mark Twain's pseudonym, photograph, and autograph for use on whiskey bottles and cigars. He explained the registration to an interviewer for the Brooklyn *Eagle,* who noted, "Down in the United States patent office the celebrated author and humorist is registered under four serial numbers just like a toilet soap or some new fangled breakfast food," and quoted Ashcroft:

> We acted chiefly out of precaution. It was a protective measure to keep the use and value of a noted name in the family of the man who made it famous. . . .
>   While Mr. Clemens is not going into this from a purely commercial motive, he will be compelled to sell whisky and tobacco under his name in order to protect his patent rights and serial numbers. . . . It may be that the trade will be restricted and made as private as possible. ("'Mark Twain' Whisky under Patent Rights," Brooklyn *Eagle,* 5 Jan 1908, 1)

Ashcroft further clarified that only "one bottle of whiskey and a few cigars would be turned out" to satisfy the law ("A Mark Twain 'Smile,'" New York *Tribune,* 6 Jan 1908, 7). On 22 December 1908 Clemens adopted a second strategy to protect his rights: he created a corporation called the Mark Twain Company, and transferred to it the rights to his name and to his literary properties ("Certificate of Incorporation" 1908). According to the *Wall Street Journal,*

Mark Twain is making himself a Christmas present of a majority of the stock of the Mark Twain Co., incorporated Wednesday at Albany, with a capital of $5,000. The directors consist of the humorist and his two daughters, Miss I. V. Lyon, his private secretary, and R. W. Ashcroft, his business agent, and the stock is owned entirely by them. The duration of the corporation is to be perpetual, and its purpose is to acquire from Samuel L. Clemens all his rights, titles and interest in and to the name "Mark Twain."

Mr. Clemens is president of the company, Miss Lyon vice-president, and Mr. Ashcroft secretary and treasurer. By incorporating himself, Mark Twain ensures to his family all future benefits that may accrue from the use of the name which he has made famous. ("Mark Twain Co. Incorporated," 24 Dec 1908, 2)

Many companies have used the name "Mark Twain" on cigars and whiskey, but no clear evidence has been found that they did so with Clemens's authorization. After his death, the Mark Twain Company retained the rights to his name and likeness, and held his assets in a trust for his daughter Clara. When she died the income from the trust passed to her husband, Jacques Samossoud, and upon his death to Dr. William Seiler. When Seiler died in 1978, the property in her estate was used to create the Mark Twain Foundation, as stipulated in Clara's will. The foundation succeeded the former company, and now owns the rights (Rasmussen 2007, 2:776–77). The Mark Twain Company, and later the foundation, also retained the rights to Clemens's published and unpublished works. In fact, Clemens's principal reason for incorporating was actually to "keep the earnings of Mr. Clemens's books continually in the family, even after the copyright on the books themselves expires." This strategy was not foolproof, because it might not prevent his works being pirated under the name of "Samuel L. Clemens." Clemens had argued that his pseudonym was a trademark in at least three lawsuits against literary pirates, in 1873, 1883, and 1901, but only the first was successful (New York *Times*: "Mark Twain, Plaintiff," 27 Mar 1901, 6; "Mark Twain Turns Into a Corporation," 24 Dec 1908, 2; *N&J2*, 271 n. 112; "A Nom de Plume Is Not a Trade-Mark," Chicago *Tribune*, 9 Jan 1883, 7; *AutoMT2*, 534 n. 152.28). According to a lawyer interviewed by the New York *Times* in 1908, even if Clemens added material to a work to secure a new copyright, "The Misses Clemens could assert that the reprint of the original unamended works under a different name to that under which they were originally published was not the publication of the genuine book, and that it was interfering with the publication of the genuine book. An injunction, at least, could be issued on these grounds" ("Mark Twain Turns Into a Corporation. The Pen Name Is Incorporated to Save Daughters from Literary Pirates," New York *Times*, 24 Dec 1908, 2; see also AD, 26 Mar 1907, and the note at 14.32–33, and "Closing Words of My Autobiography"). Because the Mark Twain Foundation maintains that the author's name is a valid trademark in at least some states, his works published before 1923 (and therefore in the public domain) have sometimes been issued under the name "Samuel L. Clemens." Copyright on works published between 1923 and 2002 is owned by the Foundation (for further details see Mark Twain Project 2014; Rasmussen 2007, 2:775; Judith Yaross Lee 2014).

304.21   another extract from a Hannibal paper ... twenty days ago] The extract was typed from a newspaper clipping, probably also sent by Laura Frazer (see the note at 303.27). The newspaper, presumably an issue of 5 March, has not been identified.

304.22   Miss Becca Blankenship, Sister of "Huckleberry Finn"] Elizabeth (Becca) Blankenship was the sister of Tom Blankenship, the model for Huckleberry Finn (see *AutoMT1,* 609 n. 397.20–26).

304.43   "Injun Joe," "Jimmy Finn" and "General Gaines"] See *AutoMT1,* 531–32 nn. 213.33–36, 213.36–37.

Autobiographical Dictation, 16 April 1909

305.7   For the second time I have heard Clara sing in public] Clemens attended Clara's recital at Mendelssohn Hall in New York on the evening of 13 April 1909. He had previously seen her perform in Norfolk, Connecticut, on 22 September 1906 ("Miss Clemens in New York," Hartford *Courant,* 15 Apr 1909, 6; see *AutoMT2,* 240, 243–44, 567 n. 240.6–8).

305.10   Mr. and Mrs. H. H. Rogers] Rogers married Emilie Augusta Randel Hart (1847?–1912), his second wife, on 3 June 1896 (*HHR,* 217 n. 1; "Mrs. H. H. Rogers Dies on a Train," 31 Aug 1912, 7).

305.14   Here is a notice, culled from the New York *Evening Post*] The clipping is from the issue of 14 April, the day after Clara's recital.

305.15   Miss Littlehales] Lillian Littlehales (1874?–1949) was born in Canada. After studying with Pablo Casals, she enjoyed a successful career as a cellist, playing for many years with the Olive Mead String Quartet. In the late 1920s she taught at Vassar College, and in 1929 published a biography of her famous mentor ("Lillian Littlehales, Long a 'Cellist, 75," New York *Times,* 9 Aug 1949, 25).

305.38   "Flow gently, sweet Afton,"] A setting of Robert Burns's poem by Jonathan Edwards Spilman (1812–96).

306.2   Mme. Schumann-Heink] Ernestine Schumann-Heink (1861–1936), born in Lieben, Bohemia (now part of Prague), was the most celebrated contralto of her time, with a career spanning more than five decades.

306.5   This is from the New York *Herald*] This article was clipped from the issue of 14 April.

306.24   a Galliard sonata] One of the six sonatas for cello (or bassoon) and keyboard written by German composer Johann Ernst Galliard (1687–1747). The name of the accompanist was not mentioned in the newspaper accounts.

Note to Chapter . . .

307.8–9   Chapter X of Alice Kegan Rice's new book ("Mr. Orr") opens with a scene on a Mississippi steamboat] Clemens refers to *Mr. Opp*, by Alice Hegan Rice (1870–1942), mistaking both her middle name and the book's title. Rice was best known for her popular novel *Mrs. Wiggs of the Cabbage Patch* (1901). She had met Clemens in July 1904, when he rented a cottage from Richard Watson Gilder next door to the Gilders' own cottage in Tyringham, Massachusetts (13 June 1904 to Langdon, CtHMTH; Gilder to Woodberry, 4 Aug 1904, in Gilder 1916, 361–62). Rice and her husband, Cale Young Rice, called on Clemens on 26 July while visiting the Gilders. Lyon noted in her journal: "I ought not to say I was disappointed in M^rs. Rice, but I was. She seemed very unliterary and inconsequent. M^r. Clemens says that 'M^rs. Wiggs' is not literature so there is less need than might be for a literary flavor to M^rs. Rice" (Lyon 1903–6, entry for 26 July). According to Rice in her autobiography, Gilder warned her that Clemens was a "blasphemous and unhappy old man"; Clemens devoted much of their conversation to unflattering anecdotes about Bret Harte (Rice 1940, 76–80). Clemens probably read *Mr. Opp* soon after it was published in April 1909, and wrote "Note to Chapter . . ." in May or June. The scene of the novel is the Ohio River, not the Mississippi, but the name of the river is not revealed until chapter 11. The present essay is not a dictation, but is based on an unfinished manuscript. Not only is the title incomplete, but the text ends in the middle of a sentence; the editors have altered a semicolon after "ship" to a period. Nevertheless, the mention of "this Autobiography" (at 307.32) signifies Clemens's intention to include it.

307.15–27   John Hay and I were young . . . the poem remains now as he originally wrote it] Hay's poem "Jim Bludso, of the Prairie Bell" appeared in the New York *Tribune* on 5 January 1871 and was collected later that year in *Pike County Ballads and Other Pieces*. Neither Hay's letter asking for advice nor Clemens's reply has been found. Hay answered Clemens's letter on 9 January: "I owe you many thanks for your kind letter. I think the pilot is a much more appropriate and picturesque personage and should certainly have used him except for the fact that I knew Jim Bludso and he was an engineer and did just what I said" (quoted in *L4*, 299–300 n. 1; for Hay see *AutoMT1*, 534 n. 222.9). In a 1905 letter to the editor of *Harper's Weekly*, Clemens explained that Hay's technical error was a "very slight one, but it could not have been corrected without dividing the heroism between two persons, and that would have spoiled the poem; so Hay left it as it was" (SLC 1905c).

307.28–29   the "Heathen Chinee," . . . has fourteen cold decks up his sleeve] Harte's poem "Plain Language from Truthful James," better known as "The Heathen Chinee," appeared in the *Overland Monthly* in September 1870 and brought him immediate fame (*AutoMT2*, 520 n. 120.6–17). It describes a euchre game in which two miners try to cheat the Chinese character Ah Sin, who instead wins with cards concealed up his sleeves. The poem was intended as a satire of racial prejudice, but was often misinterpreted as anti-Chinese, and was even used to support the Chinese Exclusion Act of 1882 (Penry 2010).

307.32–34 Three years ago . . . I had published a short story called "A Horse's Tale,"]
In October 1906 Clemens received a letter from bugler Oliver W. Norton, commenting
on "A Horse's Tale," which had appeared recently in *Harper's Monthly* (SLC 1906c; see
AutoMT2, 547 n. 189.43–190.4):

> It is evident that you appreciate the sentiment of the bugle and you may possibly
> accept my criticism of your music for the bugle call by which the little girl sum-
> moned her horse, when I say that except the first strain it could not possibly be
> played on a bugle or trumpet. These instruments are without keys, and, whatever
> the size or pitch, they are alike in having only five notes. (Norton to SLC, 3 Oct
> 1906, CU-MARK)

Norton had fought in the Civil War under Brigadier-General Daniel Butterfield (1831–
1901), and in July 1862 was the first bugler to play "Taps," which Butterfield had adapted
from a traditional bugle call. Clemens revised Norton's typed letter as if he intended to
insert it into a dictation, but never did so (Villanueva 2014).

307.36 My secretary filched it for me out of the opening bars of an opera] Soldier
Boy's bugle call is "lifted" from the introduction to the Pizzicato of the ballet *Sylvia,* by Léo
Delibes, as Clemens acknowledged in "A Horse's Tale" (SLC 1906c, 539; SLC 1907, viii, 81).

308.21 I'm writing a sea-story now] Unidentified.

Autobiographical Dictation, 21 October 1909

309.3–4 Stromeyer's man] C. F. Stromeyer, located on East 9th Street in New
York, was a provider of furniture, upholstery, and "decorative painting." Lyon relied on
his services when decorating Stormfield (Stromeyer to SLC, 1 Dec 1908, CU-MARK).

309.17 Claude] Claude Beuchotte, the butler (see AD, 6 Oct 1908, note at 268.34–35).

309.20 Katy] Katy Leary.

309.23–24 the Brevoort] The Brevoort Hotel, very near Clemens's rented house
at 21 Fifth Avenue.

309.31 A few days after she was discharged from here last spring] Lyon was dismissed on 15 April (see "The Ashcroft-Lyon Manuscript," p. 375).

310.31–32 Teresa was born and reared in a land of light wines] Household servant
Teresa Cherubini (see "The Ashcroft-Lyon Manuscript," note at 331.27).

Closing Words of My Autobiography

310 *title* Closing Words of My Autobiography] The source of the present text is a
manuscript that Clemens wrote over three days—24, 25, and 26 December 1909.

310.38–311.8   desire to save my copyrights from extinction . . . oldest book has now about fifteen years to live] Mark Twain's oldest book, *The Innocents Abroad,* was published in 1869. Under the previous law, its copyright could not be renewed beyond 1911; the law passed in March 1909 extended it until 1925 (for more of Clemens's comments about copyright see *AutoMT2,* 337–42, and AD, 24 Nov 1908).

311.10   Clara is happily and prosperously married] Clara had married Ossip Gabrilowitsch at Stormfield on 6 October 1909. Born in St. Petersburg, Russia, Gabrilowitsch (1878–1936) was a musical prodigy who studied piano under Theodor Leschetizky in Vienna. It was there that he met Clara, his teacher's new pupil, in 1898. Over the next decade he established himself as a successful concert pianist, touring in Europe and America, while he and Clara maintained a turbulent relationship. They were briefly engaged twice, Clara breaking it off in each case. Gabrilowitsch renewed his courtship in the fall of 1908, when Clara ended her romantic attachment to Charles Wark. In the summer of 1909, Clara cared for Gabrilowitsch at Stormfield while he recovered from a dangerous illness; she accepted his third proposal late in September (see AD, 6 Oct 1908, note at 267.36–37; Shelden 2010, 93–95, 301–4, 378–80; CC 1938, 1–51).

311.20–21   from the wholesome effects of my Bermuda holiday] Clemens traveled to Bermuda on 20 November, accompanied by Paine, and returned on 20 December.

311.41–312.1   In England, thirteen years ago . . . "Susy was mercifully released today."] Clemens received notice in London of Susy Clemens's death in Hartford on 18 August 1896, while Olivia and Clara were en route to New York (see *AutoMT1,* 323–25).

312.3   Clara and her husband sailed from here on the 11th of this month] Clara and Ossip had planned to sail for Germany, where Ossip had concert engagements, ten days after their wedding; but their honeymoon in Atlantic City was interrupted when he suffered an appendicitis, and was operated on at a New York sanatorium. His European engagements had to be canceled. Clara and he were not able to sail for Germany (where they stayed with his parents) until December (CC 1938, 51–52; "Operation on Gabrilowitsch," New York *Tribune,* 19 Oct 1909, 7).

312.8–19   I was supposed to be dangerously ill . . . the one so blithe, the other so tragic] Reporters who greeted Clemens upon his return from Bermuda reported that he "did not look well" and was suffering from a "severe pain in his chest." He told them, "I have five or six unfinished tasks, including my autobiography, and do not know when I will finish them. I have done almost nothing in the last three years. I may take up my autobiography again in a few weeks. I have published 100,000 words and expect to have 500,000 published, mostly after I am dead" ("Mark Twain Back in Poor Health," San Francisco *Chronicle,* 21 Dec 1909, 1; "Mark Twain Comes Home Ill," Chicago *Tribune,* 21 Dec 1909, 5). On 23 December he issued the following "blithe" statement: "I hear the newspapers say I am dying. The charge is not true. I would not do such a thing at my time of life. I am behaving as good as I can. Merry Christmas to everybody!" Jean's death was announced on Christmas Day (New York

Times: "Twain's Merry Christmas," 24 Dec 1909, 6; "Miss Jean Clemens Found Dead in Bath," 25 Dec 1909, 1).

312.23–25   Seven months ago Mr. Rogers died . . . Gilder has passed away, and Laffan] Henry H. Rogers died on 19 May at age sixty-nine; Clemens learned the shocking news when he arrived at Grand Central Station, on his way to Rogers's home. Richard Watson Gilder, editor of the *Century Magazine,* died at age sixty-five on 18 November. William Mackay Laffan, editor of the New York *Sun,* died the following day at age sixty-one (New York *Times:* "H. H. Rogers Dead, Leaving $50,000,000. Apoplexy Carries Off the Financier Famous in Standard Oil, Railways, Gas, and Copper" and "Mark Twain Grief-Stricken," 20 May 1909, 1; "R. W. Gilder Dies of Heart Disease," 19 Nov 1909, 1; "W. M. Laffan Dead of Appendicitis," 20 Nov 1909, 11).

313.6   her little French friend] Marguerite (Bébé) Schmitt (see "The Ashcroft-Lyon Manuscript," note at 342.15–21).

313.39   the stenographer] William E. Grumman (see "The Ashcroft-Lyon Manuscript," note at 367.25).

315.16   George] Griffin (*AutoMT1,* 583 n. 335.28–32).

315.17   Henry Robinson] Attorney Henry C. Robinson (1832–1900), a Hartford friend (*AutoMT1,* 560 n. 272.36–37).

315.33–34   Her dog . . . She got him from Germany] See "The Ashcroft-Lyon Manuscript," note at 342.15–21.

318.23   Schubert's "Impromptu," which was Jean's favorite] Probably op. 142, no. 2 (D.935, no. 2), also one of Clemens's favorite pieces (*MTB,* 3:1309).

318.25–27   I have told how the "Intermezzo" and the "Largo" came to be associated, in my heart, with Susy and Livy] The autobiography contains no mention of the "Intermezzo," from Mascagni's *Cavalleria Rusticana,* or of Handel's "Largo," from the opera *Xerxes.* But Lyon recorded in her journal their special significance for Clemens:

> I have been playing to Mr. Clemens, playing his favorites—and after I had played many things that he loves, I took up the Largo— He sat in the big green tufted chair quite near me, with his back toward me, and when I had finished it he said— "If you're not tired play the Susie one." That is the Intermezzo. I played it & he said "I can fit the words to both those pieces, as the coffins of Susie & her mother are borne through the dining room & the hall & the drawing room of the Hartford house, Susie calls to me in the Intermezzo & her mother in the Largo—& they are lamenting that they shall see that place no more—" (Lyon 1906, entry for 2 Mar)

318.30–31   The cousin she had played with when they were babies together] Jervis Langdon, Jr. (1875–1952), the son of Olivia's brother, Charles J. Langdon (*MTB,* 3:1548).

319.18   *End of the Autobiography*] In *Mark Twain: A Biography,* Paine printed a passage he said Clemens had "omitted" from "Closing Words of My Autobiography."

No manuscript of this text has been found in the Mark Twain Papers. It is reprinted here from Paine's transcription (*MTB,* 3:1552):

> *December* 27. Did I know Jean's value? No, I only thought I did. I knew a ten-thousandth fraction of it, that was all. It is always so, with us, it has always been so. We are like the poor ignorant private soldier—dead, now, four hundred years—who picked up the great Sancy diamond on the field of the lost battle and sold it for a franc. Later he knew what he had done.
>
> Shall I ever be cheerful again, happy again? Yes. And soon. For I know my temperament. And I know that the temperament is *master of the man,* and that he is its fettered and helpless slave and must in all things do as it commands. A man's temperament is born in him, and no circumstances can ever change it.
>
> My temperament has never allowed my spirits to remain depressed long at a time.
>
> That was a feature of Jean's temperament, too. She inherited it from me. I think she got the rest of it from her mother.

[The Ashcroft-Lyon Manuscript]

329.29–31   Paston Letters . . . domestic life in England in that old day] The letters and papers of the Paston family of Norfolk, England, written primarily between 1422 and 1509 and first published in 1787, are an important source of information about the English gentry of the time. Clemens had been familiar with them since at least 1896 (Stoker 1995; Notebook 39, TS pp. 12, 15–16, CU-MARK; Gribben 1980, 2:535).

330.34   R. W. Ashcroft] Clemens wrote on the envelope of Ashcroft's typed and signed letter: "Letter from a sniveling hypocrite—who is also a skunk, & a professional liar. It is precious, it has no mate in polecat literature——don't let it get lost. SLC."

331.1   Harvey, Dunneka, Major Leigh and David Munro] For George Harvey, Frederick Duneka, and David Munro see *AutoMT1,* 557 n. 267.35, 564 n. 284.7, and *AutoMT2,* 527 n. 143.22. Frederick T. Leigh (1864–1914) had reached the rank of major in the National Guard when Harvey brought him to Harper and Brothers in 1899; he was treasurer of the company starting in 1900 ("Lieut. Col. F. T. Leigh Dead," New York *Times,* 11 Nov 1914, 13; "Obituary Notes," *Publishers' Weekly,* 14 Nov 1914, 1565; "Frederick T. Leigh," *North American Review* 200 [Dec 1914]: unnumbered page).

331.3   Lounsbury] Harry A. Lounsbury (AD, 6 Oct 1908, note at 267.34).

331.5   Broughton] Urban H. Broughton, Rogers's son-in-law (AD, 18 May 1907, note at 51.37–38)

331.6   John Hays Hammond] See the note at 332.7–8.

331.6   Ananias] Ananias and his wife, Sapphira, lied about the money they received for their land; their subsequent deaths were deemed punishments from God (Acts 5:1–11).

331.8   Edward Loomis] Railroad executive Edward Eugene Loomis, who married Julia Olivia Langdon, daughter of Olivia Clemens's brother Charles, in 1902 (*AutoMT1*, 610 n. 398.12–15).

331.15   Dr Quintard] Dr. Edward Quintard (1867–1936) was a physician and professor of medicine at the New York Post-Graduate School and Hospital (later part of Columbia University), as well as a published writer of prose and poetry. A close family friend, he treated Clemens and his daughters in New York and at Stormfield, and would be present at Clemens's deathbed (*MTB*, 3:1511, 1563, 1577–78; New York *Times:* "Mark Twain Is Dead at 74," 22 Apr 1910, 1; "Dr. Quintard Dies; Medical Educator," 13 Feb 1936, 20; 20 May 1905 to CC, MoHM; Lyon 1903–6, entry for 24 Dec 1904; Lyon 1906, entry for 2 Feb).

331.27   Teresa & Giuseppe] Teresa and Giuseppe Cherubini. Teresa worked as a housemaid for the Clemenses at the Villa di Quarto in Florence, and after Olivia's death in 1904 she returned with the family to the United States. She became ill early in 1906 and left their employ temporarily. For a while she served as caretaker at 21 Fifth Avenue after Clemens moved to Stormfield in June 1908; she joined the staff at Stormfield that fall with her husband, Giuseppe, who was hired to replace Mary Walsh as the cook (see the note at 337.26–27). The couple fell out with the family in 1909 after being implicated in what Clemens termed the "Incident of the Carnelian Necklace" (pp. 377–78), and they were suspected as accomplices in some of Lyon's alleged deceptions. They left the household on 19 May 1909 and may have returned to Italy (Notebook 47, TS p. 16, CU-MARK; JC 1900–1907, entry for 18 Oct 1906; Lyon 1906, entry for 6 Feb; Lyon 1908, entries for 8 Oct and 3 Nov; 18 Feb 1906 to CC, CU-MARK; 2 and 3 Oct 1906 to CC, photocopy in CU-MARK; 6–9 Oct 1908 to Blackmer, CtY-BR; JC to Twichell, 14 June 1909, CtHSD; JC to Brush, 8 July 1909, DSI-AAA; "Approximate Pay Roll March 1st '07 to Feb'y 28th '09," Schedule 8 of "Accountants' Statements and Schedules" 1909).

331.40   He is 34 years old & a cipher in the world] On 14 February 1910 Clemens wrote to Paine:

> In the 5 years that I have intimately known Ashcroft I have never heard him utter a single word about his past history except that his birthplace was Liverpool, that he retains his English subjectship, & that his father was a dissenting minister. He is absolutely corked-up & sealed, concerning himself. I have encountered nothing resembling this before.
>
> I am sure he has been either a bedroom steward or a valet—perhaps both. He knows the latter trade to perfection.
>
> Daily during 2 years he heard us talk of Redding & the house-building, yet never once mentioned that he had lived there in his boyhood in a prominent family! The Driggs's arrived here at the house a year ago in a motor car & "Ralph'd" him & gushed over him & took him home for a day! The first time we ever heard of them. (WU-MU)

Ashcroft (1875–1947) was one of nine children born to Robert Ashcroft, a Congregational minister of Rock Ferry, England, near Liverpool. After his mother died in 1889, he emigrated to the United States with his father and older sister Dora, and they settled in Brooklyn. Five more siblings arrived early in 1890. (Nothing has been found to confirm his association with Frederick Driggs, who owned a summer home near Redding.) The 1900 Brooklyn census describes Ashcroft as a traveling salesman; by December 1901 he was manager of the export firm of Davis, Allen and Company in New York. In June 1902 he was hired as assistant manager of the Plasmon Company of America, then became secretary and treasurer in December (*AutoMT1,* 586 n. 342.31; "Business Leader Friend and Aide of Mark Twain," Toronto *Globe and Mail,* 9 Jan 1947, 7; *Brooklyn Census* 1900, 6A; *New York Passenger Lists* 1820–1957, 540:1485:41–43, 543:81:2–6; Ashcroft 1904, 3, 8; Ashcroft to SLC, 19 Sept 1904, CU-MARK; Todd 1906, 181–82).

332.7–8   he fell upon John Hays Hammond ... & rained filth & fury and unimaginable silliness upon him] Ashcroft represented Clemens in his successful fight against his enemies among the Plasmon stockholders, including Hammond (see the notes at 332.30 and 332.31). Ashcroft exulted in Hammond's defeat, pestering him with a series of vitriolic letters and even ridiculing him in a puerile parody of Byron's *Childe Harold's Pilgrimage* (Ashcroft 1905a). He also filed a lawsuit for libel against Hammond—for calling him "incompetent, or worse" in a 1904 telegram—which he ultimately lost (for Hammond see AD, 31 Oct 1908, note at 270.31; Hill 1973, 101–3; Ashcroft to SLC, 19 July 1905 and 3 Aug 1905, CU-MARK; 20 July 1905 to Ashcroft, photocopy in CU-MARK; Ashcroft to SLC, 23 Aug 1905, CU-MARK, enclosing typed copies of Ashcroft's letters to Hammond of 5, 19, 22, and 23 Aug 1905; "John Hays Hammond Sued," New York *Times,* 16 Oct 1907, 7; "Privileged Communications," *Moody's Magazine* 9 [Apr 1910]: 304).

332.9–10   an aspirant to the Vice Presidency of the United States] In 1908 Hammond was considered as a candidate for vice-president under William Howard Taft, whom he had known at Yale.

332.14–15   he even composes poetry; & gets it printed] On 25 August 1905 Ashcroft sent Clemens a typescript of his *Childe Harold* parody, explaining: "I have turned into a poet / And thought I would let you know it" (CU-MARK). He also had it printed as a pamphlet (Ashcroft 1905a).

332.20–21   In London ... I became a director] See the Autobiographical Dictation of 30 August 1907, note at 122.10–16.

332.28–29   Henry A. Butters ... swindled me out of $12,500 & helped Wright, a subordinate, to swindle me out of $7,000 more] For Butters see the Autobiographical Dictation of 31 October 1908, note at 269.26–33. Howard E. Wright (1867–1942) was the general manager of the Plasmon Company of America. In the early 1860s Clemens had known his father, Samuel H. Wright (d. 1904), in Virginia City, where the elder Wright was a longtime district judge. At first Clemens discussed his doubts about the Plasmon management with Wright, but later came to view him as complicit in the misuse of funds. Clemens believed that his original 1902 purchase of 250 shares from Butters for $25,000 made him an "original subscriber," entitling him to an equal number of bonus shares. He never received these bonus shares, however, because of the way the sale was recorded. He believed Butters had deliberately defrauded him, whereas Butters claimed the error was inadvertent. In January 1904 Clemens refused an offer from Butters to "restore" to him "the 250 shares which he stole from me" provided that he "buy some more (at a price above its value)" (29 Jan 1904 to Stanchfield, CU-MARK). Clemens's loss of "$7,000 more" (or $7,500, according to other sources) was a loan to Wright, which was never repaid (14 Jan 1902 to Wright, photocopy; Wright to SLC, 4 Feb 1903; 5 Feb 1903 to Wright, *per* Lyon; 12 Dec 1907 to Plasmon Co.; Ashcroft to SLC, 19 Sept 1904; all in CU-MARK; Kramer 1997, 1, 9; "Death Calls Noted Jurist," San Francisco *Call,* 27 Aug 1904, 6; "Estate of Samuel L. Clemens" 1910, 4; Ashcroft 1904, 9–13; Ashcroft 1905b; "Mark Twain Concern Gives Up the Ghost," New York *Times,* 21 Dec 1907, 6; "Mark Twain Makes Merry over Losses," San Francisco *Chronicle,* 1 Dec 1907, 23).

332.30   Two of the directors—Butters & another—proceeded to gouge the company] The second director that Clemens blames for the failure of the American Plasmon company was Harold Wheeler (1857–1936), a San Francisco attorney (*California Death Index* 1905–39, record for Harold Wheeler; *San Francisco Census* 1900, 106:14A).

332.31   By about 1905 they had sucked it dry, & the company went bankrupt] Clemens implies that the Plasmon company went bankrupt in 1905, when in fact it survived two more years. In September 1904, as a result of bitter disagreements among the directors over the company's management, Ashcroft had arranged the election of a new board. The former directors refused to relinquish control, and their allies among the stockholders filed a lawsuit to have the election declared invalid. On 10 February 1905 Hammond, Butters, and others who supported the old board filed a petition for bankruptcy. The lawsuit, which went to the Supreme Court of New York on 29 September 1905, was ultimately unsuccessful, and the bankruptcy petition was withdrawn on 16 January 1906. On that day Clemens wrote to J. Y. W. MacAlister (a director of International Plasmon), "There was a conspiracy to throw the American Co. into bankruptcy, capture its patents & other belongings, & freeze the English Co & me utterly out" (ViU; "Petitions in Bankruptcy," New York *Times,* 11 Feb 1905, 11; Ashcroft to the shareholders of the Plasmon Company of America, 29 Apr 1905, CU-MARK; Ashcroft to SLC, 15 June 1906, CU-MARK). The Plasmon company did not succeed in marketing its product, however, and became insolvent. In December 1907 its creditors filed an involuntary bankruptcy petition, which was approved by the court in January 1908. At that time its liabilities totaled $26,843, with assets of only $1,395, consisting of $945 in cash and accounts, $100 worth of patents, $200 of manufacturing machinery, and "30,000 pounds of spoiled casein" worth $150. Clemens told the newspapers that his total loss was $32,500, which represents his original $25,000 investment plus the bad loan to Wright ("Mark Twain Makes Merry over Losses," San Francisco *Chronicle,* 1 Dec 1907, 23; "Twain Is an Easy 'Mark,'" Chicago *Tribune,* 21 Dec 1907, 2; Ashcroft

1905b; New York *Times:* "Business Troubles," 23 Apr 1908, 13; "Bankruptcy Notices," 24 Apr 1908, 13; "Business Troubles," 7 May 1908, 10). Despite the bankruptcy, Clemens continued to believe in the viability of Plasmon, and in late 1908 he established a new company (see the note at 398.9–10).

332.35–36   About two years ago (say 1907), he became my self-appointed business-man & protector] Ashcroft acted as Clemens's secretary on the trip to England in June 1907 (see the ADs of 24 through 30 July 1907). After their return, he became a frequent visitor at Tuxedo Park, occasionally taking care of Clemens's correspondence. In late January 1908 he accompanied Clemens to Bermuda, and after Clemens's move to Stormfield in June he spent nearly every weekend there. As their friendship grew, he gradually took over the management of Clemens's business affairs. He earned a salary from the Plasmon Company of America, and received income from his investments, but was not paid by Clemens for his services (AD, 24 July 1907, note at 72.1; Ashcroft to SLC, 19 July 1905, CU-MARK).

332.39   Presently he started a Spiral Pin company] In 1904 Ashcroft suggested that Clemens invest in the International Spiral Pin Company and its subsidiary the Koy-lo Company, producers of safety pins and metal and celluloid hairpins. Ashcroft's uncle, W. D. Garside of Melbourne, Australia, was a stockholder in the companies and Ashcroft was secretary and treasurer of Koy-lo. At Clemens's death, his 133 shares of International Spiral Pin and 345 shares of Koy-lo were "believed to be worthless" ("Estate of Samuel L. Clemens" 1910, 4; *HHR,* 623; Hill 1973, 102; Ashcroft to SLC, 19 Sept 1904; International Spiral Pin Company to SLC, 10 May 1906 and 30 July 1906; Ashcroft to SLC, 18 Apr 1907; all in CU-MARK).

333.6–10   She came to us in 1902 ... the family of our old Hartford friends the Whitmores] Lyon was employed as governess for the six children of Harriet and Franklin Whitmore from about 1884 to 1890. The Whitmores were friends and neighbors of the Clemenses', and Franklin served as Clemens's Hartford business agent. From 1890 to at least 1894 Lyon worked for the family of Charles Edmund Dana (1843–1914) of Phila-delphia, an art critic and professor at the University of Pennsylvania, but she remained friends with Harriet Whitmore, who recommended her to Olivia Clemens in June of 1902. She began employment with the Clemenses in October of that year (*AutoMT1,* 496 n. 105.17; *AutoMT2,* 473 n. 27.22; Trombley 2010, 8, 12–13, 17–20; OLC to Har-riet Whitmore, 30 June 1902, CtHMTH; CC to Harriet Whitmore, 10 Dec 1902, CtHMTH; *MTB,* 2:678–79).

333.16   She said she was supporting her mother] Lyon's mother, Georgiana Van Kleek Lyon (1838–1926), was widowed in 1883. With Isabel and her younger children, Charles and Louise, she moved from Tarrytown, New York, to Farmington, Connecticut, where they rented Oldgate, a landmark house. Charles died in 1893, a probable suicide (as Lyon later confided to Jean Clemens). Louise married Jesse Moore (at one time a reporter for the Hartford *Courant*) and they built a house in Farmington. Isabel bought an adjacent lot from her sister and built a cottage on it, which she shared with her mother, whom she also helped support (*AutoMT2*, 473 n. 27.22; Trombley 2010, 12, 17–18; Rafferty 1996, 43–44; *Hartford Census* 1910, 131:1B; "Died," New York *Times*, 20 Jan 1926, 25).

333.17–18   she was authorized to sign checks for me ... along there somewhere] Clemens granted Lyon power of attorney on 7 May 1907 ("Power of Attorney" 1907). See also the note at 388.12–16.

333.23   Freeman] Zoheth (Zoe) Sparrow Freeman (1875–1932) was a banker and one of the trustees of Clemens's estate. The Freeman family often visited Clemens at Stormfield, and Mrs. Freeman (Grace Hill "Sheba" Freeman) was apparently a friend of Lyon's. In 1909, after Clemens dismissed Lyon, Zoe Freeman replaced her as a director and vice-president of the Mark Twain Company (16 Nov 1908 to Zoheth Freeman, photocopy in CU-MARK; *MTB*, 3:1528; "Deaths: Freeman," New York *Times*, 24 July 1932, 22).

333.29   I gave her a house & "five or ten" acres of land] On 8 June 1907 Clemens deeded to Lyon twenty acres of land and a farmhouse (Lystra 2004, 106; JC to Twichell, 14 June 1909, CtHSD; Hill 1973, 172).

334.1–2   grounds of the house we bought at Tarrytown—five acres—seemed large to me] After Susy Clemens died in 1896, the Clemenses decided not to return to their beloved Hartford house, which they had not lived in since leaving for Europe in 1891. In April 1902, while they were renting a house in Riverdale, Olivia bought a property in Tarrytown, about sixteen miles further up the Hudson River, for $45,000. The estate—a house built in 1882 and nineteen acres of land (not five, as Clemens recalls)—was the largest they had ever owned. But Olivia's plans to renovate the house and then her illness prevented the family from occupying it before their departure for Italy in October 1903. Clemens finally sold the property in December 1904 for $47,000, six months after Olivia's death (*MTB*, 3:1141–42, 1152; 14 Apr 1902 to Rogers, MFi, in *HHR*, 484–85; OLC to Katharine B. Clemens, 4 May 1902, CtHMTH; 11 May 1903 to Rogers, Salm, in *HHR*, 526–27; Clute to SLC, 16 Dec 1904, CU-MARK; Benjamin to SLC, 21 Dec 1904, CU-MARK; Hill 1973, 43–44; Courtney 2011, 123).

334.18   Paine's project, in the matter of a literary executorship] In her diary entry for 25 December 1906, Lyon noted that Clemens was having papers drawn up "to make AB literary executor—but that isn't the place for AB—& CC would not wish him to occupy it—so he will be surprised to learn of an annulment of that situation." Less than a month later, on 14 January 1907, she noted that Clemens had amended his will to give Clara Clemens "full authority over all literary remains" (Lyon 1906, Lyon 1907). Clemens's final will, dated 17 August 1909, stipulated that his executors and trustees "confer and advise with my said daughter Clara Langdon Clemens, and the said Albert Bigelow Paine, as to all matters relating in any way to the control, management and disposition of my literary productions, published and unpublished" (SLC 1909e, 7).

334.21–22   Paine was always spying around ... reading letters he hadn't any business to read] After months of discussing the project with Clemens, Paine contracted with

Harper and Brothers in August of 1906 to write his biography. By the end of 1906 he had received permission to collect Clemens's letters and other papers, and over the next few years he organized the material that Clemens had in his possession and gathered other correspondence from his friends and colleagues. Lyon and Paine initially worked together, and she even expressed her admiration for his work: "Mr. Paine IS a 'find'— He is doing the very thing that I have longed to have some worshipping creature do with M[r]. Clemens's papers & letters & clippings & autobiographical matter. He is bringing the mass into order—reducing the great chaos that I have always longed to be able to touch but have never found time for" (Lyon 1906, entry for 19 Jan). By January 1908, however, Lyon had begun to mistrust Paine's methods and suspected that he was copying letters without Clemens's permission—in particular, those to Howells. Supported by Ashcroft, she expressed her misgivings to Clemens (contract between Paine and Harper and Brothers dated 27 Aug 1906, photocopy in CU-MARK; unsigned SLC memorandum, drafted by Paine, dated "Washington D.C. Dec. 10, 1906," NPV; Lyon 1908, entries for 22, 23, 24, 26 Jan, 7 Feb, 26 July, and 8 Aug; 30 July 1908 to Harvey, Lyon transcript, photocopy in CU-MARK; SLC 1909e). On 22 January 1908 Clemens wrote to Howells, clearly in reaction to Lyon's concerns:

> I find that Sam Moffett has been lending old letters of mine to Mr. Paine without first submitting them to me for approval or the reverse, & so I've stopped it. I don't like to have those privacies exposed in such a way to even my biographer. If Paine should apply to you for letters, please don't comply. I must warn Twichell, too. A man should be dead before his private foolishnesses are risked in print. (MH-H, in *MTHL,* 2:828)

Howells replied that he had already given Paine some dozen letters, but agreed to let Clemens review the "vast bulk" of them, which he had not yet sent (Howells to Clemens, 4 Feb 1908, CU-MARK, and 8 July 1908, NN-BGC, in *MTHL,* 2:829–31). On 28 January 1908 Paine wrote to Lyon, objecting to her accusations (author's transcript in CU-MARK):

> It is *absolutely necessary* that I should know all there is to know, whatever it may be, in order that I may build a personality so impregnable that those who, in years to come, may endeavor to discredit and belittle will find themselves so forestalled at every point that the man we know and love and honor will remain known as *we* know him, loved and honored through all time.
>
> If I can have the King's fullest confidence and co-operation I feel that I shall have the strength and the understanding and the perseverance and the expression to do this thing. But if, on the other hand, I am to be shut off on one avenue of research, and another; if I am to be handicapped by concealments, and opposition, and suspicion of ulterior motives; if I am to be denied access to the letters written to such men as Howells and Twichell; in a word, if I am to become not *the* biographer but simply *a* biographer—one of a dozen groping, half-equipped men, then I would better bend my energies in the direction of easier performance and surer and prompter return, not only in substance, but in credit, for us all.

334.24–27   so saturated me with the superstition . . . impoverished thereby, & commercially damaged] In June 1905, six months before Paine began his work on the biography, Clemens devised a plan for publication of his letters. He described it to Clara on 18 June (photocopy in CU-MARK):

> I'm appointing you & Jean to arrange & publish my "Letters" some day—I don't want it done by any outsider. Miss Lyon can do the *work*, & do it well. There's plenty Letters here & there & yonder to select from; Twichell has 250, Howells used to have a bushel, Mr. Rogers has some, & so on. Miss Lyon can do the actual work, & take a tenth of the royalty resulting.

In early 1906 Paine made progress in organizing the material for his book, but Lyon was stalled, despite the help she received from Ashcroft in collecting the letters. The two projects eventually converged, and she began to fear that Paine's work would supersede any volume of hers (2 Aug 1908 to Fairbanks, CtHMTH; 6 June 1905 to Duneka; 30 July 1908 to Goodman, Lyon transcript, photocopy; Ashcroft to Henderson, 13 Feb 1909, photocopy; all in CU-MARK; Lyon 1905b, entry for 6 June; Lyon 1906, entries for 12 Jan, 19 Jan, and 4 Feb; Lyon 1907, entries for 27 Mar, 11 July, and 12 July; Lyon memorandum dated 5 Sept 1905, NPV; contract dated 13 Mar 1909, giving Lyon the right to publish Clemens's letters, CU-MARK).

334.28–31   And so I actually wrote Colonel Harvey to limit Paine to "extracts" . . . I have his letter to-day] On 10 August 1908 Clemens described his agreement with Harvey in a letter to Clara in Europe. That letter is now lost, but on the same day he quoted it in a letter to Harvey (MH-H):

> By the original understanding with Paine I was to edit the Biography, with power to approve & disapprove with finality. But I have turned that editing over to Col. Harvey, & he has accepted the job. . . . He is to limit *letters* of mine, & *excerpts* from letters of mine (when paragraphed *apart* from Paine's text) to an *aggregate* of 10,000 words for the *whole* Biography. . . . But Paine may sprinkle single & double sentences & brief remarks here & there & yonder *IN* his text with considerable freedom. [This would help your & Miss Lyon's volumes of "Letters," not hurt them.]

Neither Clemens's 3 May 1909 letter annulling this agreement, nor Harvey's reply, has been found.

334.38–41   one of them was a warning . . . my rejection of it had cost me $60,000] In March 1872 Clemens dismissed an accusation made by his brother Orion, then an employee of the American Publishing Company, that Elisha Bliss had overstated the production costs of *Roughing It,* thereby circumventing his agreement to share profits equally with Mark Twain. It was not until 1879 that he came to believe that the royalty terms (10 percent, supposedly the equivalent of half the profits) were a swindle. He devotes much of the Autobiographical Dictations of 21 February and 23 May 1906 to excoriating Bliss. In the dictation of 17 July 1906 he says Bliss robbed him of only half the amount he claims here (7 Mar 1872 to OC and 20 Mar 1872 to Bliss, *L5*, 55–56, 68–69; *AutoMT1*, 370–72 and notes on 596–97; *AutoMT2*, 50–52, 143, 527–28 n. 143.30–31).

334.41–42 Another of them was a warning against Paige; my rejection of it cost me $170,000] Clemens describes his ill-fated investment in the typesetter invented by James W. Paige in "The Machine Episode," written primarily in 1890 (*AutoMT1*, 101–6, 494–95 n. 102.10).

334.42–335.3 The third was a warning against Webster's book-keeper . . . for believing in Webster's competency] Clemens gives his account of how Charles L. Webster caused the failure of the Webster publishing company in the Autobiographical Dictation of 2 June 1906. There he claims the firm owed him and Olivia $125,000 in "borrowed money" and about $96,000 to other creditors. He also describes bookkeeper Frank M. Scott's embezzlement, correctly recalling the amount—$26,000 (*AutoMT2*, 74–80, 498–99 nn. 75.10–20 and 76.2–7, 504 n. 79.7–9; see also *AutoMT1*, 486 n. 79.21–22, 644 n. 455.1–2).

335.21–22 I was deceived by certain letters which she wrote to Betsy] Clemens refers to Elizabeth Wallace (see AD, 13 Feb 1908, note at 204.20). Lyon felt a great affection for her, describing her as "wonderful" and "a living throbbing woman" who deserved "to be living a stronger throbbinger life" (Lyon 1908, entry for 24 Mar). Their correspondence is not known to survive. In 1912 Paine asked Wallace not to discuss Lyon in her book, *Mark Twain and the Happy Island,* because Clara did not want Lyon mentioned in accounts of her father's life (Paine to Wallace, 9 and [22] Mar 1912, CU-MARK; Wallace 1913).

335 *footnote* *I have removed it to Chapter XIV.] The letter is inserted in chapter 21 (pp. 396–99).

337.6 Horace the butler. Not Elizabeth] For Horace Hazen see the note at 354.37–355.2. Elizabeth Dick, "a nice girl of 17 or so" and a relation of groundskeeper Harry Iles, was hired in October 1908 "to help Teresa in the upstairs work" (Lyon 1908, entry for 11 Oct).

337.20 after the burglary] The burglary that occurred on 18 September 1908 (see the ADs of 6 Oct and 12 Nov 1908).

337.26–27 The servants couldn't stand Miss Lyon . . . they presently gave notice & left in a body] At first the family thought that the staff left because they were frightened by the burglary, not because they objected to Lyon (see AD, 6 Oct 1908). The servants who gave notice and left on 1 October were Claude Beuchotte, the butler (see AD, 6 Oct 1908, note at 268.34–35); Mary Walsh, the cook; Katie Murray, the laundress (all of whom later returned); and Katherine Gregory, the waitress. George O'Conner, Jean's coachman, also left, because Jean had departed for Berlin ("Approximate Pay Roll March 1ˢᵗ '07 to Feb'y 28ᵗʰ '09," Schedule 8 of "Accountants' Statements and Schedules" 1909; 6–9 Oct 1908 to Blackmer, CtY-BR; 12 Oct 1908 to Emilie Rogers, MFai; JC to Lyon, 27 and 28 Oct 1908, CU-MARK; 30 Nov 1908 to JC, NN-BGC; *Redding Census* 1910, 127:18A).

339.18   Putnam, Wanamaker, Altman] Stores that Clemens regularly patronized. Besides being publishers, G. P. Putnam's Sons of New York were booksellers, stationers, and printers. John Wanamaker's department store was one of the first and largest in the country, with flagship stores in Philadelphia and New York City. B. Altman and Company was another large New York department store.

339.20–21   Countess Massiglia the lowest-down woman on the planet] In "Villa di Quarto" Clemens describes his family's stay outside Florence in 1903–4 and his exasperating conflicts with the owner of the property, the American-born Countess Massiglia (Frances Paxton) (*AutoMT1*, 230–44, 540–41 n. 231.13).

340.36   like Liberty Enlightening New Jersey] Bedloe's Island, home since 1886 of the Statue of Liberty Enlightening the World, lies within the boundaries of New Jersey, but belongs to New York State.

340.40–41   She had used to gush periodically, like the Great Geyser, but now she was practically an Unintermittent] Geology distinguishes between geysers, which erupt sporadically, and "unintermittent" springs. The Great Geyser is in Iceland.

341.13–15   the crime of keeping Jean exiled in dreary & depressing health-institutions . . . well-being] Jean began treatment under Dr. Frederick Peterson (1859–1938), a well-known epilepsy specialist, in February 1906. After suffering a series of seizures, she agreed to go to his private sanatorium in Katonah, New York, on 25 October, where she stayed until 9 January 1908 (Lyon 1906, entry for 5 Feb; New York *Times:* "Dr. Peterson Dead," 11 July 1938, 17; "Medical Pioneer," 24 July 1938, 57; Lystra 2004, 80–85, 123–24).

342.14   (Insert the pencil-letter)] Clemens originally intended to place Lyon's letter of 12 April 1909 at this point in this manuscript, but changed his mind and inserted it later (p. 362).

342.15   the Stanchfields] Clara Spaulding, a dear childhood friend of Olivia's, married attorney John B. Stanchfield in September 1886 ("John B. Stanchfield, Lawyer, Dies at 66," New York *Times,* 26 June 1921, 23; see the note at 380.14–15).

342.15–21   a German specialist . . . This grace was denied her] The Berlin specialist, Dr. Hofrath von Renvers, had treated the Stanchfields' daughter, Alice. After leaving Katonah in January 1908, Jean lived with friends for several months (see the note at 342.36–343.4). Although by July 1908 Clemens had decided to bring her home, Lyon insisted (and Peterson evidently concurred) that she consult Dr. von Renvers. She left for Germany on 26 September, accompanied by her maid, Anna Sterritt (see the note at 358.27), and Marguerite (Bébé) Schmitt, a former French governess of Peterson's. Although she enjoyed Berlin, her stay was cut short when Peterson objected to a drug she was given, and on 17 December Clemens ordered her to return. Upon her arrival, in January 1909, she was moved to a farm in Babylon, on Long Island, with paid caretakers, a situation that proved especially disagreeable and dreary. Clara learned of her plight, and by March had arranged a place for her in a private care facility, "Wahnfried," in

Montclair, New Jersey. In late April, however, with Lyon in disgrace, Clemens and Clara finally convinced Peterson to allow Jean to come home (*AutoMT1,* 600 n. 380.28–29; 17 Dec 1908 to JC, CU-MARK; Lystra 2004, 142–43, 149–51).

342.36–343.4 Miss Lyon kept Jean's home . . . in Greenwich, Connecticut the year before] After leaving Katonah Jean moved to Greenwich with a fellow patient, Mildred Cowles, her sister, Edith Cowles, and Marguerite Schmitt. In May 1908 the entire household moved to Gloucester, Massachusetts, to be closer to Peterson (Lystra 2004, 123–26).

343.15–16 But I did go to Gloucester . . . Thomas Bailey Aldrich's memorial services] Clemens's longtime friend died on 19 March 1907 (see AD, 26 Mar 1907). Over a year later his widow, Lilian Aldrich, invited Clemens to speak at the dedication of the Aldrich Memorial Museum, held on 30 June 1908. Clemens traveled with Paine to Boston en route to Portsmouth on 29 June (see AD, 3 July 1908, and the notes at 240.31–33 and 240.40–241.7). They visited Jean in Gloucester after the ceremony, returning to Redding on 2 July (Lystra 2004, 139–40). Jean had invited her father to stay with her in Gloucester, but Peterson refused to allow it. Clemens wrote her on 19 June (photocopy in CU-MARK):

> Certainly it *is* a pity that I can't stay all night in your house, but your health is *the* important thing, & I must *help* D.ʳ Peterson in his good work, & not mar it & hinder it by going counter to his judgment & commands.
> I am very grateful to him for the wonderful work he has done for you, & I feel that you & I ought to testify our thankfulness by honoring his lightest desire.

Jean had hoped to move to Redding with her father, and during his visit she asked if she could occupy an old farmhouse near Stormfield. He wrote her upon his return, "Dear Jean I am disappointed, distressed, & low-spirited, for that dream of yours & mine has come to nothing. That house turns out to be a poor trifling thing, like the rest of the ancient farmhouses in this region, it has no room in it" (2 July 1908, photocopy in CU-MARK). The following spring, in March 1909, Clemens did purchase such a property for Jean (see the note at 345.37).

344.20–21 He died suddenly in the early morning of the 19th of May] See "Closing Words of My Autobiography," note at 312.23–25.

344.23 "The Bishop of Benares"] Both Lyon and Clemens used this nickname for Ashcroft, derived from a popular drama, *The Servant in the House,* by Charles Rann Kennedy. Clemens called the play "noble" after seeing it performed on 6 June 1908, and he dined with the author the next evening. In the play, the Bishop of Benares in India arrives at the home of his brother, an English vicar. Disguised as a butler, he "takes on the personality of the reincarnated Christ" in order to redeem his brother and "enroll him in the cause of a universal brotherhood" ("News of the Theaters," Chicago *Tribune,* 18 Aug 1908, 8; Gribben 1980, 1:368).

344.31–32 village library-work] See the Autobiographical Dictation of 10 December 1908, note at 284.14.

345.32   lodged her at Heublind's] The popular Heublein Hotel in Hartford was owned by the Heublein brothers, Gilbert and Louis, who were also in the alcohol distribution business. Lyon was suffering what at the time Clemens termed "a sort of nervous break-down, attributable to too much work & care" (9 Feb 1909 to Nunnally, CSmH; G. F. Heublein and Bro. to SLC, invoice dated 1 Jan 1881, CU-MARK).

345.37   Ashcroft had been buying a near-by farm for me] In the early spring of 1909, Ashcroft negotiated with one of Clemens's neighbors, Stephen E. Carmina, to buy his property. Clemens wrote to Clara, "He has now completed the purchase (this is not to be mentioned for a while yet, till the deed is recorded) of the adjoining farm of 125 acres, farm buildings & stock, for $7,200 & saved us $600 thereby" (11 and 14 Mar 1909, CU-MARK). Even though Jean was living in Montclair, New Jersey, when the farm was bought, Clemens clearly expected her to return to Stormfield and take charge of it, as Jean explained to her friend Nancy Brush:

> After I got up here [Stormfield] & even before, Father began to call it my farm & I had the tiresome prospect of waiting all these best months before being able to do a thing. But last night the owner-lessee came up & found that some one had either drunk or sold a barrel of cider he had anticipated drinking, which made him so mad that he decided that he wanted to be rid of the place at *once* & was willing to relinquish his lease at considerably easier terms than he had been a few weeks ago. (13 June 1909, DSI-AAA)

In March 1910, after Jean's death, Paine sold the house and forty acres of the land on Clemens's behalf for $6,000. Clemens asked if he could uproot the wisteria growing on the house and move it to Stormfield, to remind him of Jean, and donated the proceeds from the sale to fund a new building for the Redding library (see AD, 10 Dec 1908, note at 284.14; "Samuel L. Clemens, Esq., to R. A. Mansfield Hobbs, Attorney and Counsellor at Law," invoice dated 8 Apr 1909, CU-MARK; 17 and 18 Feb 1910 to Paine, *per* Helen Allen, CU-MARK; 6 Apr 1910 to Lark, *MTL*, 2:843; 12 Mar 1910 to CC and Gabrilowitsch, photocopy in CU-MARK; *MTB*, 3:1565–66).

347.34   Mrs. Lounsbury] Edith L. Boughton Lounsbury (1872–1927), wife of Harry A. Lounsbury, was a friend of Lyon's and worked with her to establish the Redding library (*Connecticut Death Index* 1650–1934, record for Harry Lounsbury; Lyon 1908, entry for 20 Aug; AD, 6 Oct 1908, note at 267.34).

348.12   she "announced" the engagement in a Hartford paper] The announcement appeared in the "Personal Mention" section of the Hartford *Courant:*

> Mrs. G. V. Lyon of Farmington announces the engagement of her daughter, Isabel Lyon, to Ralph Ashcroft of New York. The marriage will take place very soon. Miss Lyon has been private secretary to Samuel L. Clemens (Mark Twain) for seven years and expects to make no change in her professional duties. Mr. Ashcroft is an Englishman and a warm personal friend of Mr. Clemens. (11 Mar 1909, 7)

348.19   Rev. Percy Stickney Grant] Rev. Dr. Percy Stickney Grant (1860–1927) was a progressive Episcopalian minister and rector of the Church of the Ascension in New York from 1893 to 1924. Lyon attended his services when she lived in the city with the Clemenses (Lyon 1905a, entry for 23 Apr).

349.10–12   On the 13th, Ashcroft brought me four contracts & a Memorandum . . . Manager of the Mark Twain Corporation] Only three of the contracts have been found; they are described in the next three notes. The contract that made Ashcroft manager of the Mark Twain Company is not known to survive. The reference to a "Memorandum" is unclear: see the note at 352.1.

349.19–21   The other document was the one I prized . . . he could annul the contract by a week's notice] According to this contract, Ashcroft agreed to supervise Clemens's "financial receipts and expenditures" and submit a weekly report thereof, and to "audit his bank accounts periodically, and, in a general way, to watch over and care for his financial affairs." Either man could terminate the agreement by giving one week's notice in writing (contract between Clemens and Ashcroft dated 13 Mar 1909, CU-MARK).

349.28–36   One of them constituted Miss Lyon my "social secretary" . . . the stenographer had already been doing it three years] By this agreement Lyon agreed to "perform the duties of social and literary secretary" for a salary of $100 a month plus "board and residence in his house 'Stormfield.'" It also stipulated that she would "not be required to supervise, direct or attend to" the affairs of any other member of his household. On it Clemens noted, "Canceled Apl. 15 by written notice, to take effect May 15/09. [¶] Two months' salary paid by check. SLC" (first contract between Clemens and Lyon dated 13 Mar 1909, CU-MARK). Clemens had employed three stenographers over the previous three years: see *AutoMT1*, 25–27, 543 n. 250.19–21 (Hobby); AD, 6 Oct 1908, note at 267 *title* (Howden); and the note at 367.25 (Grumman).

350.8–14   The other contract promised that Miss Lyon would get to work "promptly" . . . one-tenth interest in the book's royalties] According to the contract, Lyon "expressly agrees that she is to receive no compensation whatever for the compilation of said manuscript." Clemens noted on it, "Canceled Apl 15 by written notice at the same time that the other paper of this date was canceled. SLC" (second contract between Clemens and Lyon dated 13 Mar 1909, CU-MARK). Clemens's original agreement with Lyon to allow her to edit his letters has not been found, but in June 1905 he had already decided that she would do the work and receive one-tenth of the royalties (see the note at 334.24–27).

350.28–29   Colonel Harvey could use it upon his directors . . . my guaranty of $25,000 a year for a second term of five years] Clemens refers to a proposed extension of the agreement reached in 1903 with Harper and Brothers (*AutoMT2*, 539 n. 160.32–36).

350.39–40   Nobody else was ever present when I was signing papers] The three original documents that survive were witnessed. Ashcroft's contract was witnessed by Teresa Cherubini and Horace Hazen; Lyon's contracts were witnessed by Ashcroft and

Hazen. The documents were also notarized by the Redding area judge John N. Nickerson, possibly without Clemens having to appear in person.

351.11–12   And finally he produced what he said was four notes, for $250 each . . . Miss Lyon's debt of a thousand dollars to me] As Clemens explains below, he loaned money to Lyon to renovate the cottage he had given her. In his letter of 30 July 1909 to Stanchfield, Ashcroft provided a typed transcription of the receipt that he claimed Clemens had signed on 13 March 1909 (see the Appendix "Ralph W. Ashcroft to John B. Stanchfield, 30 July 1909"). The entire "agreement" was published in the New York *Times* on 4 August 1909, a clipping of which Clemens inserted later in this manuscript (p. 430).

352.1   Memorandum, on the memorable 13ᵗʰ of March] Despite his repeated mentions of a memorandum of 13 March, Clemens inserts a memorandum dated 7 April that alludes to Lyon as Mrs. Ashcroft—clearly not a document that he could have signed on 13 March, five days before she was married. It is possible that Ashcroft redrafted the memorandum to reflect her new married status, preserving the contents of the original.

352.4   Jeames] A name for a ludicrous footman or flunky, derived from the title character in William Makepeace Thackeray's story "The Diary of Jeames de la Pluche," first published in *Punch* magazine in 1845–46.

353.23–27   So that . . . gone further] Pinned to the manuscript page, covering this paragraph, is a clipping from an unidentified newspaper, which reads:

CONDUCTOR'S STEALINGS.

His Book Showed That They Ran from $2.80 to $11.05 a Day.

Judge Dike in the County Court, Brooklyn, yesterday sentenced Frederick Lehefeld, who had been convicted of pilfering from the Brooklyn Rapid Transit Company while working as a conductor, to not less than two and a half years or more than five years in Sing Sing.

The defendant, it was shown, kept a memorandum book carrying an account of his stealings or profits from the company, which varied from $2.80 to $11.05 a day.

"It is no wonder," remarked Judge Dike in imposing sentence, "that the Brooklyn Rapid Transit Company declared a dividend while you were in court."

It is not known why Clemens preserved the article or where, if anywhere, he intended to use it in the text.

353.28–31   I copy it here: | Insert Memorandum. | here] Clemens decided to insert the memorandum several pages earlier; see the note at 352.1.

354.20–22   the two Freemans . . . Reverend Percy Grant] The Reverend Grant (see the note at 348.19) officiated at the wedding at the Church of the Ascension in New York City. Maud Wilson Littleton (b. 1874) was the wife of Martin W. Littleton (see AD, 1 Nov 1907, note at 179.28). For the Freemans see the note at 333.23. According to at least one newspaper account, Clara was also present ("Ashcroft-Lyon. Marriage of Mark Twain's Business Agent and His Secretary," Hartford *Courant*, 19 Mar 1909, 6).

354.37–355.2   Horace Hazen ... whose forbears had occupied the farm since the earliest times] Horace W. Hazen (1890–1930) was hired in October 1908 to replace Claude Beuchotte. He was the son of George E. Hazen (1868–1950), a neighboring farmer who sometimes sold produce and meat to the household. Lyon noted in her journal, "He has never been in service of any kind, but he feels that it is an honor to be given the privilege just to try to be the King's butler" (Lyon 1908, entry for 9 Oct; *Redding Census* 1900, 134:10A–B; "Employees, S. L. Clemens," undated memorandum in CU-MARK; *Connecticut Death Index* 1650–1934 and 1934–2001, records for George E. and Horace W. Hazen).

355.7–10   To Norfolk, Virginia, to speak at a banquet in his honor ... great railway 446 miles long] Rogers built the Virginian Railway, his last great project, in partnership with engineer William Nelson Page. When the panic of 1907 made it difficult to sell bonds, Rogers financed the project largely from his personal fortune. It was one of the most successful railways of its era, serving primarily to carry coal from southern West Virginia to the port at Hampton Roads. Rogers, Clemens, and several companions (see the note at 368.18–20) sailed from New York on the Old Dominion liner, SS *Jefferson*, on 1 April to attend the banquet celebrating the opening of the railroad, which took place on 3 April. Clemens was one of several speakers; when the chairman compared Rogers to Caesar, he quipped, "Yes, Caesar built a lot of roads in England, and you can find them. But Rogers has only built one road, and he hasn't finished that yet. I like to hear my old friend complimented, but I don't like to hear it overdone" (Fatout 1976, 640; "Mark Twain a Banquet Orator," San Francisco *Chronicle,* 4 Apr 1909, 37; *HHR*, 647–48; New York *Times:* "H. H. Rogers Off to Virginia," 2 Apr 1909, 1; "Rogers Road Open from Coast to Mines," 3 Apr 1909, 6).

357.22   Clara's apartment in Stuyvesant Square] Clara moved into a rented two-bedroom flat at 17 Livingston Place in Stuyvesant Square on 2 October 1908. Charles Wark, her accompanist and presumed lover, had an apartment in the same building (2 Oct 1908 to JC, photocopy in CU-MARK; 1 Dec 1908 to Quintard, MoHH; AD, 6 Oct 1908, note at 267.36–37; Trombley 2010, 169–70).

357.24   Claude] Beuchotte.

357.29   that two-o'clock-in-the-morning incident] That is, when Ashcroft's bed was found empty one night "last October or September—it was after the burglary" (see p. 337).

358.11–12   walk over burning ploughshares] According to legend, Queen Emma of Normandy (d. 1052), mother of Edward the Confessor, proved herself innocent of adultery by walking unharmed over nine red-hot ploughshares.

358.27   Anna] Jean's Irish maid, Anna Sterritt (b. 1859) (*New York Passenger Lists 1820–1957*, 1190:4:28).

359.40   Clara's concert on the 13th] See the Autobiographical Dictation of 16 April 1909.

361.14   Marie Nichols' home] See the Autobiographical Dictation of 19 February 1908, note at 210.8–9.

361.21–24   The Memorandum has no date . . . but I am probably wrong] Clemens seems to refer to the memorandum he inserted earlier, which, however, is clearly dated 7 April (see the note at 352.1). Moreover, Lyon's 12 April letter, inserted below, refers to the clothing expenditures, which suggests that it was written in response to the 7 April memorandum.

362.6–7   Miss Hobby was drawing five dollars a day] At first Hobby was paid one dollar per hour of dictation and five cents per one hundred typed words (*AutoMT1*, 26). By March 1907, however, she was receiving a salary of $100 a month. Lyon received $50 a month ("Approximate Pay Roll March 1st '07 to Feb'y 28th '09," Schedule 8 of "Accountants' Statements and Schedules" 1909).

362.29   his wife] Dora Locey Paine (b. 1868), who married Albert Bigelow Paine in 1893 (U.S. National Archives and Records Administration 1795–1925, passport application for Dora Locey Paine, issued 18 June 1923).

363.21   Mary Lawton] An actress and Clemens family friend (*AutoMT2*, 18–19, 466 n. 18.34–36).

365.7–366.1   I have at last acquired a "smoker's heart,"] Clemens's attacks of angina pectoris had prompted Dr. Quintard to advise him in the summer of 1909 to smoke less and avoid activities such as his lifelong habit of "lightly skipping up and down stairs" (*MTB*, 3:1498, 1503–5, 1527–28).

367.25   Mr. Grumman the stenographer] William Edgar Grumman (1854–1925) was the last stenographer Clemens used for his autobiographical dictations; he replaced Howden in February 1909 and remained until at least October. Only four pieces in the autobiography were typed by Grumman, one of them transcribed from Clemens's manuscript (see the ADs of 10 Mar, 25 Mar, 16 Apr, and 21 Oct 1909). In the later months, he worked primarily on Clemens's correspondence. A local resident and historian, he had written about Redding's part in the Revolutionary War. He also served as librarian at the Mark Twain Library in Redding for many years. Clemens wrote to Jean, "We've got a new stenographer—a *he* one this time—to whom I can dictate cuss-words if I want to" (8 Feb 1909 to JC, MiD; *MTB*, 3:1472–73; *AutoMT1*, 27 n. 68, 669; 16 Sept 1909 to Thayer, DSI-AAA; "Funeral Today for William E. Grumman," Bridgeport *Telegram*, 27 Mar 1925, 6; Grumman 1904).

368.12   On the 2^{d} I took Ashcroft with me to lunch with two ladies at the Hotel Gotham] The ladies attending this luncheon (on 1, not 2, April) at the elegant Hotel Gotham, at Fifth Avenue and Fifty-fifth Street, have not been identified (Hotel Gotham restaurant bill, 1 Apr 1909, CU-MARK).

368.18–20 And three of them were fellow-countrymen of his . . . Mr. Coe, sons-in-law of Mr. Rogers, & Mr. Lancaster of Liverpool] Broughton was from Worcester, England. William R. Coe (1869–1955), the husband of Rogers's youngest daughter, Mai (Mary), was born in Stourbridge, also in Worcestershire; his wealth came primarily from investments in coal and real estate (*HHR*, 737). Charles Lancaster was co-partner in the Liverpool and London engineering firm of Hughes and Lancaster (Lancaster to SLC, 14 June 1907, CU-MARK).

372.1 Dunneka reported to me, March 12, by letter] The report from Frederick A. Duneka has not been found.

372.17–19 Except that I had noticed the phrase *"real estate"* . . . when I was signing it] Clemens is probably recalling a paragraph in the certificate of incorporation for the Mark Twain Company, signed and dated on 22 December 1908, which, among other things, gives the company the right to "buy, sell, deal in, lease, hold or improve real estate." The language of the document is standard; it also stipulates, for example, that the company may "construct dams, reservoirs, water towers and water ways" ("Certificate of Incorporation" 1908; for the Mark Twain Company see AD, 25 Mar 1909, note at 304.16).

372.36 John Larkin] The attorney who handled Clemens's tax, real estate, and copyright affairs (*AutoMT2*, 531 n. 149.11–17).

372.41 On Shakspeare's birthday] Though his actual date of birth is unknown, Shakespeare's birthday is traditionally observed on 23 April.

374.17–18 I said she had allowed her mind to be poisoned by prejudiced friends] Clemens refers to his letter to Clara of 11 and 14 March 1909, written after she first accused Ashcroft and Lyon of stealing. The letter is inserted later in the narrative (see pp. 396–99).

376.36–377.3 my lawyer—as follows . . . letter to Mr. Lark, dated June 7, 1909] John B. Stanchfield, the lawyer investigating Ashcroft and Lyon (see the note at 380.14–15), was assisted by attorney Charles T. Lark, who also helped Clemens with various personal legal matters, such as revising his will and preparing the document to establish the Redding Library building (see the note at 345.37; *MTB*, 3:1528, 1566; 6 Apr 1910 to Lark, *MTL*, 2:843).

377.14 Mr. Wark] Pianist Charles E. Wark.

377.30 Teresa and her husband Giuseppe] Cherubini.

379.23 his second secretary, Miss Watson] Not further identified.

379.42 Miss Harrison] Katharine I. Harrison (1866–1935) had been Rogers's secretary for about twenty years. She was indispensable to Rogers, and, with a reputed $10,000 salary at the turn of the century, was one of the highest paid women working on Wall Street ("Henry H. Rogers," in *AutoMT1*, 193–94; *HHR*, 738–39; U.S. National Archives and Records Administration 1795–1925, passport application for Katharine I. Harrison, issued 3 July 1896).

380.14–15   I put it into the hands of John B. Stanchfield] Attorney John Barry Stanchfield (1855–1921) had previously helped Clemens build a case against the Plasmon directors (see the note at 332.7–8). Aside from his law practice, Stanchfield was active in politics, serving as Chemung County district attorney (1880–85), mayor of Elmira (1886–88), state assemblyman (1895–96), and Democratic candidate for governor of New York (1900).

381.33–34   Boiajin's (the Armenian rug-dealer)] Boyajian Twin Brothers, the Fifth Avenue oriental rug company operated until 27 August 1909 by N. M. and K. M. Boya-jian ("The Twin Brothers in Bankruptcy," *American Carpet and Upholstery Journal,* 10 Sept 1909, 49).

382.3   Strohmeyer] C. F. Stromeyer (see AD, 21 Oct 1909, note at 309.3–4).

384.1–2   The new record rendered by Altman . . . & even 5 months] Clemens's note at the top of the bill reproduced here reads: "Delays in paying bills. Due to LAZINESS. The house-building bills were so delayed (without any excuse at all), that Lounsbury's men had difficulty in getting along." Next to the paid date "April 24th, 1908," he wrote "nearly 5 months"; below that, for the months of February and March, he wrote "3 ½ months" and "in effect five " " (ditto marks under "months").

384.40   President Roosevelt's infamous panic broke out] Clemens describes the 1907 financial crisis in the Autobiographical Dictation of 1 November 1907 (see also AD, 13 Sept 1907, and the note at 135.41–136.3).

388.4   Young Harry Lounsbury] The son of Harry A. and Edith Lounsbury, born in 1896 (AD, 6 Oct 1908, note at 267.34; *Redding Census* 1910, 127:7A).

388.12–16   Miss Lyon had a power of attorney to sign checks . . . Miss Lyon's writ-ten acknowledgment] Lyon's power of attorney was broader than Clemens thought: it granted her the right to "manage all my property both real and personal and all matters of business relating thereto; to lease, sell and convey any and all real property wheresoever situated which may now or which may hereafter at any time belong to me" ("Power of Attorney" 1907). He revoked it on 29 May 1909 in a letter, witnessed by Paine, in which he reminded her that it had already been "orally revoked some months ago" (author's copy, CU-MARK). Her "written acknowledgment" has not been found.

388.23   Decoration Day] The former name for Memorial Day, traditionally observed on 30 May. The latter term came into common usage after World War II; in 1971 the observance was moved to the last Monday in May.

390.2–5   I, Samuel L. Clemens . . . do make, constitute and appoint, Isabel V. Lyon, and Ralph W. Ashcroft my true and lawful attorneys] This transcription of the 14 November 1908 power-of-attorney agreement, which comprises "Exhibit A" of the revocation document, is the only text known to be extant. But there can be no doubt that Clemens signed at least two originals, which were sold by Charles Hamilton Auto-graphs in 1966 (Catalog 15, item 281, transcription in CU-MARK) to the Detroit

Public Library (but cannot now be located). Clemens's signatures on the documents were verified with a notary's gold-paper seal, and one of them was certified by County Clerk William T. Haviland.

390.39   Harry Ives] Harry Iles (b. 1877), the groundskeeper who was hired to work at Stormfield in June 1908 (JC to Lyon, 5 Aug 1908, CU-MARK).

392.16   Yes, the first deed was on record, & the second one wasn't] The only deed currently known to exist is dated 8 June 1907 (see the note at 333.29).

393.13–14   I already had a lawyer—had had him five years & was satisfied with him] Either John B. Stanchfield or John Larkin, both of whom had handled business for Clemens since 1904.

394.19–20   The Knickerbocker Trust Company failed in the fall of 1907, & caught me] See the Autobiographical Dictation of 1 November 1907 and notes at 177.26–27 and 179.3–7.

395.2–4   They privately took passage . . . for a date half-way between the first & second At Homes (Tuesday, June 8.)] The couple sailed for Rotterdam, evidently on the luxurious Holland America SS *Nieuw Amsterdam*. According to Ashcroft, he had business to transact with a "Holland Company" ("Shipping and Mails," New York *Times*, 8 June 1909, 13; Holland America Line 2014; Lark to Paine, 17 June 1909, CU-MARK).

395.19   Mr. Weiss] The firm of W. F. Weiss, certified public accountants, at 128 Broadway, New York, handled the investigation into the management of Clemens's 1907–9 accounts (Weiss to SLC, 27 Sept 1909, CU-MARK).

396.11   Mr. Jackson] The lawyer Clara hired to assist her with the case against the Ashcrofts, not further identified.

397.25–27   I never knew nor asked what we paid our idiot in New York, but Mrs. Littleton . . . planning her parlor-floor suite] The New York house at 21 Fifth Avenue was being redecorated in the winter of 1904 and early 1905. Lyon wrote to Harriet Whitmore on 8 January 1905, "The house is not yet entirely settled. Some of the wall papering must be done over, because the decorator employed is a woman of execrable taste,—and a great deal of the paper is an 'offense' to Mr. Clemens" (CtHMTH). According to Lyon's notes on household accounts for the winter of 1904–5, $598.02 was spent on household furnishings, and Mrs. Mason C. Davidge was paid $390.66 for "house furnishing." Davidge had made a career for herself by furnishing fine hotels in New York and decorating the houses of friends and acquaintances ("Rooms in Woman's Hotel," New York *Tribune,* 7 Feb 1902, 7; Kirkham 2000, 314).

397.43–44   a poor old neighbor of ours] Unidentified.

398.9–10   The result is a rescued property which is now solely in the hands of himself, myself & the London company] After the bankruptcy of the American Plasmon Company, Clemens gained the rights to the U.S. and Canadian patents for the product as well as the machinery for making it. In November 1908 he incorporated a new Plasmon Milk Products Company, with a capital of $100,000; in addition to himself, the directors were Ashcroft and R. A. Mansfield Hobbs (Ashcroft's attorney, who established the Mark Twain Company the following month). Clemens invested $35,000 in the new enterprise, which was not successful. Two years later, when an inventory was made of his estate, the stock shares in the "rescued" company were listed as "practically worthless" ("Estate of Samuel L. Clemens" 1910, 3; "Mark Twain in Milk Products Co.," New York *Times,* 26 Nov 1908, 6; Ashcroft to Lark, 2 Nov 1909, CU-MARK; Lark to Loomis, 9 Nov 1909, CU-MARK).

398.11–13 He has persistently kept after Sir Thomas Lipton . . . it looks as if he is going to land him] Lipton had met Ashcroft in June 1907, when he accompanied Clemens to England (see AD, 1 Oct 1907, and AD, 26 Sept 1907, note at 137.40–41). When he was in London, in 1900, Clemens had thought of approaching Lipton to invest in the International Plasmon Company. In December 1908, soon after incorporating his new Plasmon Milk Products Company, he asked Ashcroft to go to England to persuade Lipton to "act as our selling agent in this country" (Ashcroft to Lark, 2 Nov 1909, CU-MARK). The following spring Ashcroft appeared to be making progress with Lipton, and in the summer he returned to England, this time with Lyon as his wife. Lipton continued to stall, however, and ultimately declined (8 Mar 1900 to MacAlister, ViU; *AutoMT1,* 622 n. 413.33–35; Hill 1973, 212, 251–52; Lyon 1908, entry for 28 Dec; Loomis to Paine, 6 Nov 1909, CU-MARK).

398.25–38 I think I told you how . . . I once bought it at 43 & sold it at 69] Clemens also discusses his investments in copper stock in the Autobiographical Dictation of 27 March 1907.

398.47–48 I wouldn't let Jean (four years ago), charge Brush's Italian servant with theft **upon suspicion** & demand his arrest] Painter George de Forest Brush and his family were residents of the Dublin, New Hampshire, artists' colony. In 1905, when the Clemenses were summering there, Jean became friends with two of the Brush children, Nancy (b. 1890) and Gerome (b. 1888) (*Oxford Census* 1900, 596:3B; *AutoMT2,* 553 n. 200.6; Lystra 2004, 47). No other mention of this incident has been found.

399.33 until his imagination supplied some more in a newspaper about five months afterwards] That is, in the interview published in the New York *Times* on 4 August 1909 (see the clipping transcribed on pp. 428–31).

400.3–5 I had not endorsed Ashcroft to him . . . Lord Northcliffe] Alfred Charles William Harmsworth, Lord Northcliffe, evidently met Ashcroft and Lyon when he accompanied Colonel Harvey to stay at Stormfield on the night of 20 November 1908. According to Lyon, when Ashcroft went to England the following month, Clemens supplied him with "appreciative letters" to both Lipton and Northcliffe (see AD, 24 Nov 1908, and the note at 278.21–38; Lyon 1908, entries for 20 Nov and 28 Dec).

400.37   In a year & ten months she drew nearly ten thousand dollars, house-money]
Weiss's accounting included all the checks Lyon had written from March 1907 through
December 1908—a total of $5,225 expended in "house-money." Added to $650 (dis-
counting a check for $1,000 "not passed through Bank") in checks cashed for reasons
"not specified," and to $3,662 in "checks to be accounted for," the total expended was
$9,537, that is, Clemens's "nearly ten thousand dollars" ("Recapitulation" of Schedule 5
of "Accountants' Statements and Schedules" 1909). Lyon claimed to have used much of
the house money to pay the household servants in cash. In fact, in the statement that
Ashcroft submitted to Stanchfield on her behalf, he listed cash wages of $2,625. At the
bottom of the document Paine noted, "Where did A. get these figures? Did he have
mem.? Or are they just inspiration? A.B.P." (Ashcroft 1909). Weiss noted that out of a
total two-year payroll of about $7,560, Lyon "did actually pay to the servants in cash,
$2097.80, a difference of over $500" ("Statement of Disbursements" 1909, 7; "Approximate Pay Roll March 1st '07 to Feb'y 28th '09," Schedule 8 of "Accountants' Statements
and Schedules" 1909).

400.37–38   Also she drew various other cash-amounts and charged them to "C. C.,"]
Weiss's accounting lists about $22,903 in checks "paid to or stated or assumed to have
been paid" to Clara over two years. He also noted that "Miss Lyon, in that period"
claimed to have "given to Miss Clemens out of the house-money she drew, $1950"
("Statement of Disbursements" 1909, 7; "Recapitulation" of Schedule 4 of "Accountants'
Statements and Schedules" 1909).

403.39–40   Evening Telegram of (apparently) July 13] Clemens clipped this article
from the issue of 14 July 1909.

406.21–22   They were my Piers Gavestons] Piers Gaveston, first earl of Cornwall (d.
1312), was the favorite of King Edward II; accused of misleading the young king, he was
exiled and ultimately executed by his enemies at court.

406.30   The next of my preserved clippings seems to be from the *American*] The
clipping is actually from the New York *Evening World* of 14 July 1909.

410.1   MARK TWAIN MUST EXPLAIN] The source of this clipping has not
been identified.

414.30–31   he was in my employ & serving me for pay] It seems unlikely that
Clemens misremembered the fact that he did not pay Ashcroft; his earlier deletion of
the words "without salary" at 332.36 suggests that he preferred not to admit it.

417.2–5   the only people who had worked for both places . . . Hull's bill of over
$400.00] Lark's remarks were based on the statement prepared by Weiss, who reviewed
the construction invoices and identified several unauthorized payments that Lyon made
for work on her cottage. Among these payments were three to Eugene Adams totaling
$1,031, two to Lounsbury totaling $365, and one to F. A. Hull and Son that combined
$466 for work on the cottage with $62 for work on Stormfield ("Statement of Disbursements" 1909, 1–6; "Money of Mr. Samuel L. Clemens" 1909).

417.38–39   during the summer of 1907 her mother had lived with her sister, (Mrs. Ashcroft's) in Hartford] That is, in nearby Farmington. See the note at 333.16.

419.4   Mr. G. M. Acklom] George Morebye Acklom (1870–1954), an Englishman, was an editor and poet. The Clemenses had become friendly with his parents, Robert E. Acklom (1846–1926) and his wife, Annabella (b. 1848), when traveling in Agra, Jaipur, and Ajmeer, India, in 1896, and they remained in touch. In 1897 Robert was named inspector general of police and jails for the Central Province. George arrived at Stormfield for a visit on 16 July 1909 (7 Mar 1896 to Robert and Annabella Acklom and 7 Mar 1896 to Robert Acklom, ViU; Annabella Acklom to SLC, 5 Aug 1897, CU-MARK; Stormfield guestbook, entry for 16 July 1909, CU-MARK; 18 July 1909 to CC, CU-MARK).

422.25   Mr. & Mrs. Peck] Lester and Laura Peck had a farm at Redding Ridge, near Stormfield, as well as a house on West End Avenue in New York (Peck to SLC, 25 Dec 1909, CU-MARK; William Harrison Taylor 1912, 224).

426.29–30   some beads which had been in an old cabinet for years & were now missing] See Paine's account of this incident on pp. 377–78.

428.2–3   New York Times came out with another Ashcroftian interview] Clemens cut this article from the front page of the 4 August 1909 issue.

428.40–41   both girls were in sanitaria most of the time] In 1904 and 1905 Clara spent time in rest-cures in New York City and Norfolk, Connecticut, recovering from the death of her mother (28 Feb 1905 to Luchini, photocopy in CU-MARK; 26 Mar 1905 to Higginson, Paine typescript in CU-MARK; 16 July 1905 to MacAlister, ViU). For Jean's sequestrations, see the notes at 341.13–15, 342.15–21, and 342.36–343.4.

429.12–13   When one of his daughters made an attack on her about two years ago, he wrote this] No evidence of Jean's "attack" has been found. Clemens's reply to her, probably written in June 1907, survives only in Ashcroft's two transcriptions: the one printed in the *Times,* and the one quoted in his letter of 30 July 1909 to John B. Stanchfield, reproduced in an Appendix to this volume.

429.20   Drs. Peterson and Hunt] Edward Livingston Hunt—not Frederick Hunt, as previously thought (Hill 1973, Lystra 2004)—was a physician who worked with Peterson at the sanatorium at Katonah and personally handled Jean's treatment (Hunt to Lyon, 22 Feb 1907, CU-MARK; JC to Nancy Brush, 2 Oct 1907, DSI).

430.11   Tetrezzini] That is, Luisa Tetrazzini (1871–1940), the Italian operatic soprano.

430.24   The agreement is as follows] A handwritten copy of this agreement, made by Ashcroft and signed by him and Clemens, survives in the Detroit Public Library (MiD).

433.34–36   The report was cabled to America … who wanted the facts] It is not known which English paper printed the original report in early July 1907, but the story was cabled to the New York *Herald,* which printed Clemens's vehement denial on 5 July ("Mark Twain Will Not Wed," 9; see also *AutoMT2,* 565 n. 236.1–6).

436.3–9   Never heard of it . . . four notes on the famous Cleaning-Up Day—the 13th of March] This agreement was also mentioned, but not quoted, in the article Clemens inserted from the New York *American* of 2 July (see the text on pp. 401–2 and the note at 351.11–12).

437.9   that paralysed the agreement-proceedings] No draft of this aborted agreement has been found.

437.18–19   a certain incident of date March 31–April 3 . . . a sneak, & a would-be thief] In an undated letter written sometime in September, Clemens wrote the board of the Mark Twain Company to suggest that Ashcroft "be asked to resign his position as Manager of the Company" because he was "not a fit person to serve that office":

> In Norfolk, Virginia, in the early days of April last, he procured a sum of money from me on false pretenses, by methods distinctly criminal in their character. He assisted his process by lies of his own, & by beguiling another man, through threats & persuasions, to lie for him. I have the evidence, & am ready to furnish it to you in *detail.* (5–9 Sept 1909 to the Board of Directors of the Mark Twain Company, MS facsimile, *Twainian* 53 [Sept 1997]: 1–4)

No further details of the incident have been found. Ashcroft had already offered to resign his position in a letter of 30 July: see the Appendix "Ralph W. Ashcroft to John B. Stanchfield, 30 July 1909." He later did so as part of the Ashcrofts' final settlement with Clemens.

438.25–26   an article in the September number of *The World's Work*] Clemens refers to "Curing by Suggestion" by Dr. Frederick van Eeden, in the September 1909 issue (van Eeden 1909).

438.40   Paine met Z. at the Players] "Z." has not been identified. The Players was a club founded in New York in 1888 for actors and their friends in the arts; Clemens was a member for many years (see *AutoMT1,* 431–32, 546–47 n. 255.18–19).

439.13–15   according to the testimony of Miss Hobby, my stenographer . . . knew too much] Lyon noted in her journal that she personally dismissed Hobby on 4 August 1908, giving no reason (Lyon 1908, entry for 4 Aug).

439.21   Paine, in Egypt] In February 1909 Paine had gone on a voyage to retrace Clemens's 1867 *Quaker City* travels, described in *The Innocents Abroad.* He returned in late April and gave an account of the trip in *The Ship-Dwellers,* published the following year (Paine 1910; *MTB,* 3:1480, 1484).

439.29–440.9   *MEMORANDUM* . . . for good & all] It is not clear why Clemens ended his manuscript with this "memorandum." He alludes to an announcement in the newspapers on the morning of 7 September 1909 that Robert E. Peary (1856–1920) had reached the North Pole, six days after the same claim had been made by Frederick A. Cook (1865–1940). A bitter dispute erupted over who should receive credit for the feat. Cook asserted that he had arrived at the pole in April 1908, a year before Peary, but had been unable to return until the following spring. After an examination of all the evidence, the National Geographic Society awarded the honor to Peary. Cook's claim was rejected, and he was denounced as a fraud. A modern researcher has concluded that probably neither explorer was successful ("London Applauds Peary's Exploit," New York *Times,* 7 Sept 1909, 1; Warren E. Leary 1997; see Bryce 1997, 447–56 and passim). English astronomer John Couch Adams (1819–92) and French mathematician Urbain Jean Joseph Le Verrier (1811–77) both calculated the position of Neptune, but Le Verrier was the first to announce his prediction, which was confirmed in 1846. Both men are now credited with the discovery.

APPENDIXES

SAMUEL L. CLEMENS: A BRIEF CHRONOLOGY

1835　Born 30 November in Florida, Mo., the sixth child of John Marshall and Jane Lampton Clemens. Of his six siblings, only Orion, Pamela, and Henry lived into adulthood. (For details, see the next appendix, "Family Biographies.")

1839–40　Moves to Hannibal, Mo., on the west bank of the Mississippi River; enters typical western common school in Hannibal (1840).

1842–47　Spends summers at his uncle John Quarles's farm, near Florida, Mo.

1847　On 24 March his father dies. Leaves school to work as an errand boy and apprentice typesetter for Henry La Cossitt's Hannibal *Gazette*.

1848　Apprenticed to Joseph P. Ament, the new editor and owner of the Hannibal *Missouri Courier*. Works for and lives with Ament until the end of 1850.

1851　In January joins Orion's newspaper, the Hannibal *Western Union*, where he soon prints "A Gallant Fireman," his earliest known published work.

1853–57　After almost three years as Orion's apprentice, leaves Hannibal in June 1853. Works as a journeyman typesetter in St. Louis, New York, Philadelphia, Muscatine (Iowa), Keokuk (Iowa), and Cincinnati.

1857　On 16 February departs Cincinnati on the *Paul Jones,* piloted by Horace E. Bixby, who agrees to train him as a Mississippi River pilot.

1858　Henry Clemens dies of injuries from the explosion of the *Pennsylvania*.

1859　On 9 April officially licensed to pilot steamboats "to and from St. Louis and New Orleans." By 1861 has served as "a good average" pilot on at least a dozen boats.

1861　Becomes a Freemason (resigns from his lodge in 1869). Works as a commercial pilot until the outbreak of the Civil War. Joins the Hannibal Home Guard, a small band of volunteers with Confederate sympathies. Resigns after two weeks and accompanies Orion to Nevada Territory, where Orion will serve until 1864 as the territorial secretary. Works briefly for Orion, then prospects for silver.

1862   Prospects in the Humboldt and Esmeralda mining districts. Sends contributions signed "Josh" (now lost) to the Virginia City *Territorial Enterprise,* and in October becomes its local reporter.

1863–64 On 3 February 1863 first signs himself "Mark Twain." While writing for the *Enterprise* he becomes Nevada correspondent for the San Francisco *Morning Call.* To escape prosecution for dueling, moves to San Francisco about 1 June 1864 and for four months works as local reporter for the *Call.* Writes for the *Californian* and the *Golden Era.* In early December visits Jackass Hill in Tuolumne County, Calif.

1865   Visits Angels Camp in Calaveras County, Calif. Returns to San Francisco and begins writing a daily letter for the *Enterprise.* Continues to write for the *Californian.* "Jim Smiley and His Jumping Frog" published in the New York *Saturday Press* on 18 November.

1866   Travels to the Sandwich Islands (Hawaii) as correspondent for the Sacramento *Union,* to which he writes twenty-five letters. In October gives his first lecture in San Francisco.

1867   His first book, *The Celebrated Jumping Frog of Calaveras County, and Other Sketches,* published in May. Gives first lecture in New York City. Sails on *Quaker City* to Europe and the Holy Land. Meets Olivia (Livy) Langdon in New York on 27 December. In Washington, D.C., serves briefly as private secretary to Senator William M. Stewart of Nevada.

1868   Lectures widely in eastern and midwestern states. Courts and proposes to Livy, winning her consent in November.

1869   *The Innocents Abroad* published. With Jervis Langdon's help, buys one-third interest in the Buffalo *Express.*

1870   Marries Olivia on 2 February; they settle in Buffalo in a house purchased for them by Jervis Langdon. Son, Langdon, born prematurely on 7 November.

1871   Sells *Express* and the house and moves to Hartford, Conn. For the next two decades the family will live in Hartford and spend summers at Quarry Farm, in Elmira.

1872   Daughter Olivia Susan (Susy) Clemens born 19 March; son Langdon dies 2 June. *Roughing It* published in London (securing British copyright) and Hartford. Visits London to lecture in the fall.

1873   Takes family to England and Scotland for five months. Escorts them home (Livy is pregnant) and returns to England alone in November. *The Gilded Age,* written with Charles Dudley Warner, published in London and Hartford.

1874   Returns home in January; daughter Clara Langdon Clemens born 8 June. The family moves into the house they have built in Hartford.

1875–76 *Mark Twain's Sketches, New and Old* (1875) and *The Adventures of Tom Sawyer* (1876) published.

1878–79 Travels with family in Europe.

1880 *A Tramp Abroad* published. Daughter Jane (Jean) Clemens born 26 July.

1881 Begins to invest in Paige typesetting machine. *The Prince and the Pauper* published.

1882 Revisits the Mississippi to gather material for *Life on the Mississippi,* published 1883.

1884–85 Founds publishing house, Charles L. Webster and Co., named for his nephew by marriage, its chief officer. Reading tour with George Washington Cable (November–February). *Adventures of Huckleberry Finn* published in London (1884) and New York (1885). Publishes Ulysses S. Grant's *Memoirs* (1885).

1889 *A Connecticut Yankee in King Arthur's Court* published.

1891–94 Travels and lives in France, Switzerland, Germany, and Italy, with frequent business trips to the United States. Henry H. Rogers, vice-president of Standard Oil, undertakes to salvage Clemens's fortunes. In 1894 Webster and Co. declares bankruptcy, and on Rogers's advice Clemens abandons the Paige machine. *The Tragedy of Pudd'nhead Wilson* published serially and as a book in 1894.

1895 In August starts an around-the-world lecture tour to raise money, accompanied by Olivia and Clara; lectures en route to the Pacific Coast and then in Australia and New Zealand.

1896 Lectures in India, Ceylon, and South Africa. *Personal Recollections of Joan of Arc* published. On 18 August Susy dies from meningitis in Hartford. Jean is diagnosed with epilepsy. Resides in London.

1897 *Following the Equator* published in London and Hartford. Lives in Weggis (Switzerland) and Vienna.

1898 Pays his creditors in full. Lives in Vienna and nearby Kaltenleutgeben.

1899–1901 Resides in London, with stays at European spas. The family returns to the United States in October 1900, living at 14 West 10th Street, New York, then in Riverdale in the Bronx. Publishes "To the Person Sitting in Darkness" (February 1901).

1902 Makes last visit to Hannibal and St. Louis. Olivia's health deteriorates severely. Isabel V. Lyon, hired as her secretary, is soon secretary to Clemens.

1903 Moves family to rented Villa di Quarto in Florence. Harper and Brothers acquires exclusive rights to all Mark Twain's work.

1904   Begins dictating autobiography to Lyon; Jean types up her copy. Olivia dies
        of heart failure in Florence on 5 June. Family returns to the United States.
        Clemens leases a house at 21 Fifth Avenue, New York.

1905   Spends summer in Dublin, New Hampshire, with Jean. Writes "The
        War-Prayer."

1906   Begins Autobiographical Dictations in January. Excerpts will appear
        in the *North American Review,* 1906–7. Rents Upton House, Dublin.
        Commissions John Mead Howells to design a house to be built at Redding,
        Conn. *What Is Man?* printed anonymously for private distribution.

1907   *Christian Science* published. Hires Ralph W. Ashcroft as business assistant.
        Travels to England to receive honorary degree from Oxford University.

1908   Moves into the Redding house ("Innocence at Home," then "Stormfield").

1909   Dismisses Lyon and Ashcroft. Jean rejoins Clemens at Stormfield. Clara
        marries Ossip Gabrilowitsch, pianist and conductor, on 6 October. Jean
        dies of heart failure on 24 December.

1910   Suffers severe angina while in Bermuda; with Paine leaves for New York on
        12 April. Dies at Stormfield on 21 April.

For a much more detailed chronology, see *Mark Twain: Collected Tales, Sketches,
Speeches, & Essays, 1852–1890* (Budd 1992a, 949–97).

FAMILY BIOGRAPHIES

Biographies are provided here only for Clemens's immediate family—his parents, siblings, wife, and children. Information about other relatives, including Olivia Clemens's
family, may be located through the Index.

John Marshall Clemens (1798–1847), Clemens's father, was born in Virginia. As a
youth he moved with his mother and siblings to Kentucky, where he studied law and in
1822 was licensed to practice. He married Jane Lampton the following year. In 1827 the
Clemenses relocated to Jamestown, Tennessee, where he opened a store and eventually
became a clerk of the county court. In 1835 he moved his family to Missouri, settling
first in the village of Florida, where Samuel Clemens was born. Two years later he was
appointed judge of Monroe County Court, earning the honorific "Judge," which young
Clemens unwittingly exaggerated into a position of great power. In 1839 he moved the
family to Hannibal, where he kept a store on Main Street and was elected justice of the
peace, probably in 1844. At the time of his death, he was a candidate for the position of
clerk of the circuit court, but died some months before the election. He was regarded
as one of the foremost citizens of the county, scrupulously honest, but within his family
circle he was taciturn and irritable. A contemporary reference to John Clemens's "shat-
tered nerves," together with his extensive use of medicines, may point to some chronic

condition. His sudden death from pneumonia in 1847 left the family in genteel poverty. When his father died Clemens was only eleven; he later wrote that "my own knowledge of him amounted to little more than an introduction" (*Inds,* 309–11; 4 Sept 1883 to Holcombe, MnHi).

Jane Lampton Clemens (1803–90), Clemens's mother, was born in Adair County, Kentucky. Her marriage to the dour and humorless John Marshall Clemens was not a love match: late in life she confided to her family that she had married to spite another suitor. She bore seven children, of whom only four (Orion, Pamela, Samuel, and Henry [1838–58]) survived at the time of her husband's death in 1847. The widowed Jane left Hannibal, Missouri, and between 1853 and 1870 lived in Muscatine, and possibly Keokuk, Iowa, and in St. Louis, Missouri, initially as part of Orion Clemens's household and then with her daughter, Pamela Moffett. After Clemens married and settled in Buffalo, New York, in 1870, Jane set up house in nearby Fredonia with the widowed Pamela. In 1882 she moved to Keokuk, Iowa, where she lived with Orion for the rest of her life. She was buried in Hannibal's Mount Olivet Cemetery, alongside her husband and her son Henry. Her Hannibal pastor called her "a woman of the sunniest temperament, lively, affable, a general favorite" (Wecter 1952, 86). She was the model for Aunt Polly in *Tom Sawyer* (1876), *Huckleberry Finn* (1885), and other works. After her death in 1890 Clemens wrote a moving tribute to her, "Jane Lampton Clemens" (*Inds,* 82–92, 311).

Orion (pronounced O'-ree-ən) Clemens (1825–97), Clemens's older brother, was born in Gainesboro, Tennessee. After the Clemens family's move to Hannibal, Missouri, he was apprenticed to a printer. In 1850 he started the Hannibal *Western Union,* and the following year became the owner of the Hannibal *Journal* as well, employing Clemens and Henry, their younger brother, as typesetters. In 1853, shortly after Clemens left home to travel, Orion moved with his mother and Henry to Muscatine, Iowa. There he married Mary (Mollie) Stotts (1834–1904), who bore him a daughter, Jennie, in 1855. He campaigned for Lincoln in the presidential election of 1860, and through the influence of a friend was rewarded with an appointment as secretary of the newly formed Nevada Territory (1861). Mollie and Jennie joined him there in 1862; Jennie died in 1864 of spotted fever. That year Nevada became a state, and Orion could not obtain a post comparable to his territorial position. Over the next two decades he struggled to earn a living as a proofreader, inventor, chicken farmer, lawyer, lecturer, and author. From the mid-1870s until his death in 1897, Orion was supported by an amused and exasperated Clemens, who said that "he was always honest and honorable" but "he was always dreaming; he was a dreamer from birth" (*Inds,* 311–13; see *AutoMT1,* 451–55 and notes on 643–44).

Pamela (pronounced Pə-mee'-la) A. (Clemens) Moffett (1827–1904), also known as "Pamelia" or "Mela," was Clemens's older sister. Born in Jamestown, Tennessee, after the Clemens family's move to Hannibal she attended Elizabeth Horr's school and in November 1840 was commended by her teacher for her "amiable deportment and faithful application to her various studies." Pamela played piano and guitar, and in the

1840s helped support the family by giving music lessons. In September 1851, she married William Anderson Moffett (1816–65), a commission merchant, and moved to St. Louis. Their children were Annie (1852–1950) and Samuel (1860–1908). From 1870 Pamela lived in Fredonia, New York. Clemens called Pamela "a lifelong invalid"; she was probably the model for Tom's cousin Mary in *Tom Sawyer, Huckleberry Finn,* and other works (*Inds,* 313).

Olivia Louise Langdon Clemens (1845–1904), familiarly known as "Livy," was born and raised in Elmira, New York, the daughter of wealthy coal merchant Jervis Langdon (1809–70) and Olivia Lewis Langdon (1810–90). The Langdons were strongly religious, reformist, and abolitionist. Livy's education, in the 1850s and 1860s, was a combination of home tutoring and classes at Thurston's Female Seminary and Elmira Female College. Always delicate, her health deteriorated into invalidism for a time between 1860 and 1864. "She was never strong again while her life lasted," Clemens said in 1906. Clemens was first introduced to the shy and serious Livy in December 1867; he soon began an earnest and protracted courtship, conducted largely through letters. They married in February 1870 and settled in Buffalo, New York, in a house purchased for them by Livy's father; their first child, Langdon Clemens, was born there in November. In 1871 they moved, as renters, to the Nook Farm neighborhood of Hartford, Connecticut, and quickly became an integral part of the social life of that literary and intellectual enclave. They purchased land and built the distinctive house which was their home from 1874 to 1891. Young Langdon died in 1872, but three daughters were born: Olivia Susan (Susy) in 1872, Clara in 1874, and Jane (Jean) in 1880. Clara later recalled her mother's "unselfish, tender nature—combined with a complete understanding, both intellectual and human, of her husband"; she took "care of everything pertaining to house and home, which included hospitality to many guests," and made "time for lessons in French and German as well as hours for reading aloud to my sisters and me" (CC 1931, 24–25). To her adoring husband, whom she addressed fondly as "Youth," Livy was "my faithful, judicious, and painstaking editor" (*AutoMT1,* 354–59). In June 1891, with their expenses mounting and Clemens's investments draining his earnings as well as Livy's personal income, they permanently closed the Hartford house and left for a period of retrenchment in Europe; thenceforth Livy's life was spent in temporary quarters, hotel suites, and rented houses. When Clemens was forced to declare bankruptcy in April 1894, the family's financial future was salvaged by the expedient of giving Livy "preferred creditor" status and assigning all Clemens's copyrights to her. In 1895–96 she and Clara accompanied Clemens on his round-the-world lecture tour. The death of her daughter Susy in 1896 was a blow from which she never recovered. She died of heart failure in Italy in June 1904.

Olivia Susan Clemens (1872–96), known as "Susy," was Clemens's eldest daughter. Her early education was conducted largely at home by her mother and, for several years starting in 1880, by a governess. Her talents for writing, dramatics, and music were soon apparent. At thirteen, she secretly began to write a biography of Clemens, much of which he later incorporated into his autobiography; it is a charming portrait of idyllic family life. Susy accompanied her parents to England in 1873 and for a longer stay abroad in 1878–79. In the fall of 1890 she left home to attend Bryn Mawr College in Pennsylvania, but completed only one semester. In June 1891, the Clemenses closed the Hartford house, and the family, including Susy, left for a period of retrenchment in Europe that would last until mid-1895. Susy attended schools in Geneva and Berlin and took language and voice lessons, but increasingly she suffered from physical and nervous complaints for which her parents sought treatments including "mind cure" and hydrotherapy. After the European sojourn Susy chose not to go with her father, mother, and sister Clara on Clemens's lecture trip around the world (1895–96); she and her sister Jean stayed at the Elmira, New York, home of their aunt Susan Crane. In August 1896, while visiting her childhood home in Hartford, Susy came down with a fever, which proved to be spinal meningitis. She died while her mother and sister were making the transatlantic journey to be with her. "The cloud is permanent, now," Clemens wrote in his notebook (Notebook 40, TS p. 8, CU-MARK; see *AutoMT1*, 323–28).

Clara Langdon Clemens (1874–1962), called "Bay," was Clemens's second daughter. Born in Hartford, Connecticut, she was mostly educated at home by her mother and governesses. During the family's sojourn in Europe between 1891 and 1895, Clara enjoyed more independence than her sisters, returning alone to Berlin to study music. She was the only one of Clemens's daughters to go with him and Livy on their 1895–96 trip around the world. The death of her sister Susy, and the first epileptic seizure of her other sister, Jean, both came in 1896: "It was a long time before anyone laughed in our household," Clara recalled (CC 1931, 179). The family settled in Vienna in 1897. Clara aspired to be a pianist, studying under Theodor Leschetizky, through whom she met the young Russian pianist Ossip Gabrilowitsch (1878–1936). By 1898 Clara's vocation had changed from pianist to singer, a career in which she found more indulgence than acclaim. After her mother's death in 1904 Clara suffered a breakdown and was intermittently away from her family at rest cures in 1905 and 1906. She was financially dependent on her father but spent less and less time in his household, traveling and giving occasional recitals. Increasingly suspicious of the control exerted by Isabel V. Lyon and Ralph Ashcroft over her father and his finances, Clara convinced Clemens to dismiss the pair in 1909. She married Gabrilowitsch in 1909; their daughter, Nina Gabrilowitsch (1910–66), was Clemens's last direct descendant. Between 1904 and 1910 Clara lost her mother, her sister Jean, and her father; at the age of thirty-five, she was sole heir to the estate of Mark Twain, which was held in trust for her, not to be disposed in its entirety until her own death. For the rest of her life she used her influence to control the public representation of her father. Gabrilowitsch died in 1936; in 1944 Clara married Russian conductor Jacques Samossoud (1894–1966). Her memoir of Clemens, *My Father, Mark Twain,* was published in 1931. She spent the last decades of her life in Southern California. Clara's bequest of Clemens's personal papers to the University of California, Berkeley, in 1962, formed the basis of the Mark Twain Papers now housed in The Bancroft Library.

Jean (Jane Lampton) Clemens (1880–1909), Clemens's youngest daughter, was named after his mother but was always called Jean. Like her sisters, she was educated largely at home. In 1896, however, she was attending school in Elmira, New York, when she suffered a severe epileptic seizure. Sedatives were prescribed, and for the next several years her anxious parents tried to forestall the progress of her illness, even spending the summer of 1899 in Sweden so that she could be treated by the well-known osteopath Jonas Kellgren. Her condition, which worsened after her mother's death in 1904, and the household's frequent relocations, gave Jean little chance to develop an independent existence. In late 1899 she began teaching herself how to type so that she could transcribe her father's manuscripts. She also loved riding and other outdoor activities, and espoused animal and human-rights causes. In October 1906 Jean was sent to a sanatorium in Katonah, New York, and remained in "exile" until April 1909, when she rejoined her father at Stormfield, in Redding, Connecticut. Over the next months she enjoyed a close, happy relationship with him and took over Isabel Lyon's duties as secretary. Jean died at Stormfield on 24 December 1909, apparently of a heart attack suffered during a seizure. Over the next few days Clemens wrote a heart-breaking reminiscence of her entitled "Closing Words of My Autobiography."

CLEMENS'S 1873 AUTOBIOGRAPHICAL NOTES, AND BIOGRAPHICAL SKETCH BY CHARLES DUDLEY WARNER

On 27 and 28 January 1873 Clemens replied to a request from Michael Laird Simons for a biographical sketch, to be published in a revised edition of the *Cyclopaedia of American Literature* (first issued in 1856), which Simons was preparing. Clemens prepared eleven pages of autobiographical notes and suggested several excerpts from his own works for the anthology. He then "furnished the data to Chas. Dudley Warner," who had agreed to write the essay. Warner's unsigned biographical sketch, based on Clemens's notes, was published in the revised edition of the *Cyclopaedia,* together with one passage from *Roughing It* and two from *The Innocents Abroad.* The *Cyclopaedia* appeared serially in 1873–74, and was then published in two volumes in 1875 (27 and 28 Jan 1873 to Simons, *L5,* 283–87). Clemens's autobiographical notes, now at the Pierpont Morgan Library in New York (NNPM), are transcribed according to a system of manuscript notation called "plain text," which represents the original document as faithfully as possible, including the author's revisions. (For an explanation of the characters and conventions used in the transcription see "Editorial and Authorial Signs," p. 327.) Supplementary details of inscription too complex to show here are reported in the Textual Commentary at *MTPO.* Clemens's 1873 autobiographical notes are followed by Warner's sketch, as published in 1875.

Most of the information in Clemens's notes has been annotated in the three volumes of the *Autobiography,* and can be located through the indexes. The "chap" Clemens mentions in the last paragraph, who was translating *The Innocents Abroad* into German, was

Moritz Busch (for whom see Griffin 2010, 131 n. 8); his two-volume edition appeared in 1875: *Die Arglosen auf Reisen* and *Die Neue Pilgerfahrt* (Leipzig: Grunow).

———

[Autobiographical Notes, 1873]

Samuel Langhorne Clemens.

⸺

Born Nov. 30, 1835, in village of Florida, Monroe County, ~~Mo.~~ Missouri.

Attended the ordinary western common school in Hannibal, Mo., from the age of 5 till near the age of 13. That's all the ~~education—if~~ schooling—if playing hookey & getting licked for it may be called by that name.

Education continued in the offices of the Hannibal "Courier" & the "Journal," as an apprenticed printer. Afterward worked at that business in St Louis, Cincinnati, Philadelphia & New York while yet a boy—& belonged to the Typographical Unions in those cities, by a courtesy which forebore to enforce the rule requiring 21 years age for eligibility.

About 1855, aged 20, started to New Orleans, with about ten or twelve dollars, after paying steamboat passage, intending in good earnest to take shipping there for the port of Para, & explore the river Amazon & open up a commerce in the marvelous herb called coca, which is the concentrated bread & meat of the tribes (when on long, tedious journeys) that inhabit the country lying about the headwaters of the Amazon. Broken-hearted to find that a vessel would not be likely to leave N. O. for Para during the next generation. Got some little comfort out of the fact that I had ~~not~~ at least not arrived too late, if I *had* arrived too soon, for no ship had ever ₍yet₎ left N. O. for Para in preceding generations.

Had ~~learn~~ made friends with the pilots & learned to steer, on the way down; so they had ~~com~~ good-will enough to engage to make a St Louis & N. O. pilot of me for $500, payable upon graduation. They kept their word, & for 18 months I went up & down, steering & studying the 1275 miles of river day & night, supporting myself meantime by helping the freight ~~clerks & standing the sho~~ clerks on board & the freight watchmen on shore. Then I got my U.S. license to pilot, & a steady berth at $250 a month—which was a princely salary for a youth in those days of low wages for mechanics.

~~Foll~~ While ₍I was₎ still an apprentice pilot, the most ancient pilot in the whole west, (Capt. Isaiah Sellers) used to write paragraphs now & then for the N O Picayune, which he signed "Mark Twain;" it is a leadsman's term & signifies a depth of two fathoms of water. In his articles he always spoke of this present high water being higher than he had ever seen it before, or lower than he had ever seen it before, since 18— always naming a date so long before any other man on the river was born, that he was an aggravating eyesore to a hundred river men who wanted to be considered veterans. And he was always referring to islands nobody had ever heard of before; & then he would add in an exasperatingly naive way that they had washed away during such and such a remote generation. My first literary venture was a communication ˄of a column & a half˄ to the N. O. True Delta, ~~about 18~~ over a fictitious signature in which I ante-dated *him* about sixty years, recalled high water & low¢ water which "laid over" his most marvelous recollections, introduced islands which had joined the main land & become States & Territories before he was born—& thus won the gratitude of all the other veterans & Capt. Sellers's undying animosity. He never wrote again.

Early in 1861, my brother was appointed Secretary to the then Territory of Nevada, & I went out there with him as ~~pr~~ his private Secretary. Got the silver fever & fought the mines with a spade & shovel for a year or more; was really worth a million dollars for just ten days, as related in "Roughing It," & lost it through my own indolent heedlessness. Then I ~~worke~~ shoveled quartz in a silver mill at ten dollars a week, for one entire week, & then resigned, with the consent & even the gratitude of the entire mill company.

Meantime had written an occasional letter to the Virginia City "Enterprise" over a fictitious signature; & in the winter of 1862–3 their city editor went to the States on a visit & I was offered his berth for 3 months at $25 a week. Gladly took it, & held it nearly 3 years. Part of the time reported Legislative proceedings for my paper (from Carson the capital˄) Wrote a letter every Saturday to sum up results, & therefore needed a signature. In the nick of time Capt. Sellers's death came over the wires & I "jumped" his nom de plume before the old man was cold.

Went to San Francisco when the silver collapse came, & reported five months on the "Morning Call,"˄◊ Got too lazy to live, & too restless & enterprising. Went up to Calaveras County & worked in the surface gold diggings 3 months without result. Came back to San F & made a living writing newspaper correspondence & literary sketches several months.

Then went down early in ~~1867~~ 1866, to the Sandwich Islands for the Sacramento Union. Wrote from there 5 or 6 months. Came back with a high Pacific Coast fame & lectured on my own hook in the city & all around California & Nevada.

Went east with more worldly gear than I was accustomed to.

Published "The Jumping Frog & Other Sketches" in the spring of '67. It had a fair sale here & a good sale in England, where Routledge republished it.

In August 1869, published "The Innocents Abroad," 650 pp. 8vo, illustrated. It sold 125,000 copies in 3 years & has good steady sale yet.

Entered the lecture field here 1869–70.

In March 1872, published "Roughing It," illustrated, 600 pp. 8vo. It ~~has~~ sold 91,000 copies in 9 months—have n't got the yearly return yet.

In England the Routledges & Hotten have gathered together & published all my sketches; a great many that have not appeared in book form here. There are four volumes of these sketches. "Roughing It" & the "Innocents Abroad" are republished in England, 2 vols. each, & have a good sale.

Residence, Hartford, Conn.

Baron Tauchnitz proposes to issue my books complete, on the Continent in English.

And there's a chap going to issue them in Germany in the German Language he says. Is now translating the Innocents.

———

[Biographical Sketch by Charles Dudley Warner]

SAMUEL LANGHORNE CLEMENS,

WHO is widely known by his signature of "Mark Twain," an American humorist of decided and peculiar originality, and the possessor of a descriptive style of great vigor and clearness, was born in the village of Florida, Monroe County, Missouri, November 30, 1835. His only schooling was in the ordinary district school at Hannibal, from the age of five to thirteen, when he was apprenticed to the printing business in a newspaper office of that town. He worked at his trade in St. Louis, Cincinnati, Philadelphia, and New York, after the manner of travelling journeymen, and was a member of the Typographical Union, though under age. At the age of twenty he started for New Orleans, with a capital of about twelve dollars, after paying his steamboat fare, and the intention of shipping thence for the port of Para, exploring the Amazon, and opening up a trade in coca, which he had understood was the concentrated bread and meat of the tribes about the head waters of the river. This commercial venture was frustrated by finding that no vessel was likely to leave New Orleans for Para during the next generation; but he had the comfort of knowing that he had not arrived too late, if he had arrived too soon, for no vessel had ever left New Orleans for Para in the preceding generations.

Having made the acquaintance of some pilots and learned to steer on the way down, he determined to become a Mississippi river pilot. The members of the craft agreed to teach him for $500 on graduation; and for eighteen months he went up and down, studying the river night and day, and supporting himself by helping the freight clerks and standing tricks with the shore watchmen. Obtaining his license as a pilot, he had steady work at a salary of $250 a month, a princely sum in those days of low wages to mechanics. While he was still an apprentice, there was on the river a noted pilot, Capt. Isaiah Sellers, who wrote paragraphs occasionally for the New Orleans papers signed "Mark Twain"—the leadsman's term signifying a depth of two fathoms of water. Sellers was an aggravation to all the other pilots, by reason of his assumption of ancient knowledge of the river. If it was high water, he would say it was higher than he had ever seen it before since 18—, naming a date before any other man on the river was born; and he was always referring to islands which nobody had ever heard of before, and naively adding that they had washed away in such and such a remote generation. He was a nuisance to all the other pilots who wanted to be considered veterans. The first literary venture of young Clemens was a communication a column and a half in length to the New Orleans

True Delta, under a fictitious signature, in which he ante-dated Capt. Sellers about sixty years, recalling high and low water which belittled his most marvellous recollections, and introducing islands which had joined the mainland and become territories and States before he was born. The communication squelched Capt. Sellers; he never wrote again, and Clemens became the pet of the river men.

Early in 1861 Mr. Clemens went to Nevada as private secretary to his brother, who was appointed Secretary of the Territory. His adventures there are graphically related in his volume called *"Roughing It."* He had the silver fever, and fought the mines with pick and spade for a year or more, and was actually, as he relates in his book, the owner of a claim worth a million dollars for several days, but lost it by his heedlessness in not taking some necessary steps to secure it. Plunged at once from riches to poverty, he hired out to shovel quartz in a silver mill, at ten dollars a week, but resigned at the end of a week, with the consent and even gratitude of the entire mill company. Meantime he had written an occasional letter to the Virginia City *Enterprise,* and in 1862–3 he became its city editor, at $25 a week, and continued in that post for three years. In reporting the legislative proceedings, and writing a weekly letter summing up results, which was no doubt rather personal in its comments, he needed a signature, and at the nick of time hearing of the death of Capt. Sellers, he appropriated the *nom de plume* of "Mark Twain," which he has since been identified with.

When the silver collapse came, he went to San Francisco and reported for five months on the *Morning Call;* became lazy or enterprising, and travelled to Calaveras county and worked at surface gold digging for three months without result. Returning to San Francisco, he lived by reporting and sketch writing till early in 1866, when he visited the Sandwich Islands and remained there six months, writing diligently to the Sacramento *Union.* Coming back he found he had a high Pacific coast reputation, and he lectured with great success in California and Nevada. He went East with a pocket-book much fuller than it was accustomed to be. In the spring of 1867 *The Jumping Frog and Other Sketches* was published in New York. It had a fair sale in this country, and a better in England, where it was reprinted.

In 1868 Mr. Clemens made a pilgrimage, with a party of excursionists in the Quaker City, to the Mediterranean and the Holy Land. He corresponded during his absence with the San Francisco *Alta* and the New York *Tribune;* and upon his return he published, in 1869, a very humorous and picturesque account of his travels, called *The Innocents Abroad,* an illustrated octavo volume of 650 pages, which sold 125,000 copies in three years. In 1869–70 he lectured everywhere to large audiences in the Northern States. In March, 1872, he published *Roughing It,* in the main a true account of his Pacific coast experiences, with exact pictures of a wild frontier society—an illustrated octavo volume of 600 pages, which sold 91,000 copies in nine months. The fall of 1872 Mr. Clemens spent in England. He was married in 1870 to Olivia L., daughter of Jervis Langdon, Esq., of Elmira, New York. His residence is Hartford, Connecticut.

All the books of Mr. Clemens have been reprinted in England, most of them by two publishers, who have gathered together, besides, four volumes of sketches, many of which have not been in book form here. The author was most cordially received in England, where his writings are in great favor. Tauchnitz proposes to issue his books complete in English on the Continent; and a translation of *The Innocents,* to be followed by others, is now being made into German.

Mr. Clemens and Mr. Charles D. Warner wrote in 1873 a joint novel, *The Gilded Age,*—a social and political satire of the times.

CLEMENS'S 1899 AUTOBIOGRAPHICAL NOTES, AND BIOGRAPHICAL SKETCH BY SAMUEL E. MOFFETT

On 31 March 1899 Clemens wrote from Vienna to Frank Bliss, who was preparing the Autograph Edition of the Writings of Mark Twain (the first of many uniform editions) for the American Publishing Company:

> Mrs. Clemens wants some *more* new copyright matter added—viz., a brief biographical sketch of me. So I stopped writing this letter to jot down a skeleton for it. She wants this skeleton to be handed to my nephew Samuel E. Moffett, editor of the New York Journal, & she wants him to put it in his own language, & add to it or elaborate it, according to his judgment. (31 Mar and 2 Apr 1899 to Bliss, CtHMTH and NN-BGC)

He enclosed the fourteen-page "skeleton" with his letter, noting at the top, "[[Mrs. Clemens wishes you to ask Sam Moffett, my nephew (editor New York Journal) to write the biographical sketch from these notes, & then she would like to see it before it is printed.]]"

As requested, Moffett expanded Clemens's notes into a biographical sketch, which he sent to Clemens for review. Clemens evidently returned his draft with suggestions for revision. (This earlier text survives as a typescript in the Mark Twain Papers, and is transcribed at *MTPO.*) Moffett submitted a rewritten sketch on 26 June 1899, which Clemens approved in a letter dated 14 July (but postmarked a day earlier):

> Sanna
> Rosendala
> Sweden, July 14/99.

Dear Sam:
> *This* biographical sketch suits me entirely—in simplicity, directness, dignity, lucidity—in all ways. All previous ones have made me ashamed of myself.
> Bliss can leave it all out, if he needs the room, but if he uses it he must not shorten it or alter it, & *he must not put any other in its place.* (CU-MARK)

Before being published in 1900 in the Autograph Edition (in volume 22, *How to Tell a Story and Other Essays*), the sketch appeared in the October 1899 issue of *McClure's*

Magazine (Moffett 1899). Moffett's mother, Pamela, wrote him several days after it appeared, objecting to certain inaccuracies:

> My dear Son:
>
> I noticed two or three errors in your biographical sketch that troubled me a good deal, but I said nothing about it, because I thought it was too late to correct them. But your aunt Molly [Clemens] insists that there is still time to change them for the book, and that it would be very unfortunate to allow them to go into permanent form.
>
> There are plenty of people who know that your grandma did not belong to the bluegrass region of Kentucky. She was born and brought up in Columbia Adair Co. in the southern part of the state, quite outside of the bluegrass region. She never lived in Lexington, and I doubt if she ever even saw the place.
>
> Another mistake was in saying that my father had just been elected county judge at the time of his death. *He had been county judge*—appointed to fill out an unexpired term. At the time of his death he was a candidate for the county clerkship, and as good as elected though the election hadn't come off.
>
> The other two errors are of comparatively slight importance—alluding to *North* instead of *Nye* as governor of Nevada, and leaving off part of Jean's name. She had herself babtised Jean Lampton, in Elmira, while her parents were away.
>
> Now to my mind there are two or three reasons why these mistakes should not be allowed to stand: first *Truth* is of preeminent importance. second: there are plenty of people who know that your grandma could not claim to be a daughter of the bluegrass region, and in their minds such fundamental errors would impair the credibility of the whole: and of course they would influence others. But what troubles me most in this connection next to the importance of *truth* itself is, that as your uncle Sam gave his unqualified approval to your sketch, it might look as if he were anxious to give the family a prestige they did not deserve. This would certainly show a weakness unworthy of the strength and dignity of his character. (PAM to Moffett, 15 Oct 1899, CU-MARK)

There was in fact time to revise the sketch "for the book"—as Bliss wrote to Moffett on 26 October: "We had not yet put your article in type, so that the corrections from the McClure are all in good time" (CU-MARK). Moffett took the opportunity to make revisions in the text. He corrected the information about John Marshall Clemens's judgeship, dropped "bluegrass" from Jane Clemens's history, and changed "Lexington" to "Columbia" and "Governor North" to "the governor" (John W. North was an associate justice of the supreme court of Nevada Territory, not the governor). The 1900 book version also has information not found in the *McClure's* text, material which had been in Moffett's manuscript but was deleted on the magazine proofsheets (now in CU-MARK), evidently to save space: two additional paragraphs about piloting from chapter 13 of *Life on the Mississippi* (657.20–40); a passage about Clemens's presence at a session of the Austrian Reichsrat in 1897 (662.14–18), when the Viennese police "dragged and tugged and hauled" the "representatives of a nation . . . down the steps and out at the door" (SLC 1898a, 540); and observations on Clemens's universality and dramatizations of his works (662.20–24).

Most of the information in Clemens's notes has already been explained in the three volumes of the *Autobiography,* and can be located through the indexes. Clemens makes one statement, however, that is not found elsewhere in his autobiography—that he was almost "captured by Colonel Ulysses S. Grant" at the start of the Civil War (652.18–19). He did serve a brief stint in the Missouri State Guard, under the command of General Thomas A. Harris (1826–95), in June 1861 (see *AutoMT1,* 527 n. 205.29–36). But his claim cannot be accurate, because Colonel Ulysses S. Grant did not arrive in Missouri in pursuit of the confederates until mid-July. Clemens made the same claim in his famous semifictional account, "The Private History of a Campaign That Failed," which appeared in the *Century Magazine* in December 1885 (SLC 1885b; Fulton 2010, 28–33).

Clemens's autobiographical notes, now in the Berg Collection in the New York Public Library (NN-BGC), are transcribed according to a system of manuscript notation called "plain text," which represents the original document as faithfully as possible, including the author's revisions. (For an explanation of the characters and conventions used in the transcription see "Editorial and Authorial Signs," p. 327.) Moffett's biographical sketch is based on the 1899 magazine text, but incorporates the changes in the 1900 Autograph Edition that the editors believe to be revisions made by the author.

[Autobiographical Notes, 1899]

Samuel L. Clemens.

Samuel Langhorne Clemens.

Born in Florida, Mo., Nov. 30, 1835. Son of John Marshall Clemens, of Virginia, & Jane Lambton of Kentucky. An ancestor (Jeoffrey Clement), was ambassador to Spain under Charles I., married a Spanish wife & introduced a strain of Spanish blood into the Clemens stock which shows up ~~in~~ now & then in a descendant yet. (Clara is an instance.) This Clement sat as one of Charles's judges on the trial that rendered the death-verdict.

The Lambtons still ~~occupy~~ ₍possess₎ in England the lands occupied by their ancestors of the same name before the invasion of the Conqueror.

The childhood of S. L. Clemens was spent in the village of Florida, his boyhood in the town of Hannibal, on the Mississippi. Before he was 13 he had been rescued in a substantially drown condition nine times—3 times from the Mississippi & 6 times from Bear creek. His mother's comment was, "People who are born to be hanged are safe in the water."

S. L. C.'s parents began their young married life in Lexington, Ky., with a small property in land & six inherited slaves. They presently removed to Jamestown, Tennessee; & later to Florida, Mo., & finally to Hannibal, where Mr. C. served as a magistrate some years & was then elected County Judge, but died (1847) before he was invested with the office.

S. L. C was educated in the common school at Hannibal, & in his brother's newspaper office, where he served in all capacities, including staff-work. His literature attracted the town's attention, "but not its admiration"—(his brother's testimony.)

He ran away in 1853 & visited the World's Fair in New York. After a year's absence he in the Atlantic States he was obliged by financial dis stress to reveal his whereabouts to the family. He returned to the West & lived in St Louis, Muscatine & Keokuk until 1857; he spent the next 4 years on the river, between St Louis & New Orleans, in the pilot house. On his last tri

In the su

He was in New Orleans when Louisiana went out of the Union, Jan. 26, 1861, & started North the next day. Every day on the trip a blockade was closed by the boat, & the batteries at Jefferson Barracks (below St Louis) fired two shots through her chimneys the last night of her voyage.

At the beg

In June he joined the Confederates in Ralls county, Mo., ₐas a 2ᵈ lieutenantₐ under General Tom Harris, & came near having the distinction of being captured by Colonel Ulysses S. Grant. He resigned, after 2 weeks' service in the field, explaining that he was "incapacitated by fatigue" through persistent retreating; became private secretary to his brother, who had been appointed Secretary of the Nev new Territory of Nevada, & crossed the Plains with him in the overland coach—an 18 day-&-night trip.

After a year spent in the silver mines of the Humboldt and Esmeralda regions he became local editor of the *Territorial Enterprise* at Virginia, Nevada, & also legislative correspondent for that paper from Carson City, the capital. He wrote a weekly letter to the paper; it appeared Sundays, & on Mondays the legislative proceedings were obstructed by the complaints of members, as a result. They rose to questions of privilege & answered the criticisms of the correspondent with bitterness, customarily describing him with elaborate & uncomplimentary phrases, for lack of a briefer way. To save their time he presently began to sign the letters, using the Mississippi leadsman's call, "Mark Twain" (2 fathoms = 12 feet) for their this purpose.

Dueling was in that day a custom there—a temporary one. The weapons were always Colt's navy revolvers; distance, 15 paces; fire, & advance; six shots allowed. M. T. & Mr. Laird, editor of the Virginia *Union* got into a newspaper quarrel, & a duel was appointed for dawn in a mountain gorge outside the town. Neither man was capable with a pistol; but this did not appear on the field, for an accident caused Mr. Laird to withdraw & apologise. The accident was this. The seconds of both parties were practicing the their men in neighboring gorges with a concealing ridge between. Mr. Laird was making fairly good practice, but M. T. was hitting nothing. A small bird flew by & lit on a sage-bush 30 yards away, & M. T.'s second, who was an expert, fired & knocked its head off. Just then the adverse party came over the ridge to compare notes, & when they saw the dead bird & learned the distance, they were troubled interested. When they further learned

~erroneously~ (from Gillis, M. T.'s second) that Twain had done the shooting, & that it was not a remarkable feat for him, they were troubled. They drew aside & consulted, then returned & made a formal apology & the duel was "off."

There was a new & stringent law which provided two years' imprisonment for any one who should send a challenge, carry a challenge, or receive one. The noise of the proposed duel had reached the capital, 18 miles distant. Governor North was very angry, & gave orders for the arrest of all concerned in the preliminaries of the duel; he said he would make an example that would be remembered. But a friend of the duelists got wind of the matter & outrode the officers of the law, arriving in time to hurry the parties over the frontier into California & save them from well-earned punishment.

M. T. took service of the San Francisco *Morning Call* as city editor, & held the place a couple of years; then spent three months in the "pocket" mines of Calaveras county at Jackass Gulch, but found no pockets.

He returned to San Francisco & wrote letters to the Virginia *Enterprise for the Sacramento Union; Enterprise* for a while, & was then sent to the Sandwich Islands by the Sacramento *Union* to write about the sugar interest. While in Honolulu the survivors of the clipper "Hornet" (burned on the line), arrived, mere skin-&-bone relics, after a passage of 43 days in an open boat on 10 days' provisions, & M. T. worked all day & all night & produced a full & complete account of the matter & flung it aboard a schooner which had already cast off. It was the only full account that went to California, & the *Union* paid M.T. $100 a column for it, which was ten-fold the current rates. for it.

On his return to California after a half-year's absence he ~profitably~ delivered several lectures & cleared $1500, then went east & ~(1867)~ & joined the "Quaker City" Excursion to Europe & the Holy Land; was gone five or six months, & upon his return wrote & published "The Innocents Abroad," ~(1869)~ which was an account of the voyage. The sale reached 100,000 copies in the first year, & doubled it later.

In 1869 he entered the lecture field & traversed the eastern and western States. ~Remained in the field 4 years.~

In ~the beginning of February,~ 1870 he was married to Miss Olivia L. Langdon, & took up his residence in Buffalo, N.Y., where he bought a third interest in the *Express,* a daily newspaper, & joined its staff. In the following November a son (Langdon) was born to him. (Died 1872.)

In ~October~ 1871 he removed to Hartford, Conn., & presently built a house, which the family still retain.

In 1872 Susan Olivia Clemens was born. "Roughing It" written. Also "The Gilded Age" (in collaboration with Charles Dudley Warner.)

In 1873 the family spent some months in England & Scotland; M.T. lectured a few weeks in London.

In the succeeding years various books were written. In 1874 Clara ~Langdon~ Clemens was born. In 1878 the family went to Europe & spent 14 18 months. "A Tramp Abroad" resulted. Jean Clemens born, 1880.

In 1885 M.T. financed the publishing house of Charles L. Webster & Co., in New

York. Its first issue was the Memoirs of General Grant, which achieved a sale of more than 600,000 volumes. The first check received by the Grant heirs was for $200,000; it was followed a few months later by a check for $150,000. These are the largest checks ever paid for an author's work on either side of the Atlantic.

In 1886–89 M. T. spent $170,000 ₌a large sum of money₌ on a type-setting machine, the invention of one James W. Paige, a fraud ₌which was a failure₌. The money was all lost.

The publishing house was incapably conducted, & wasted all the money that came into its hands. M. T. contributed $65,000 in efforts to save its life, but to no purpose. It finally failed, ₌(1894)₌ with liabilities of $96,000 & assets worth less than a third of that amount. The debts The privilege of paying the debts fell to M. T.'s share.

In 1895₌–6₌ M. T., with his wife & second daughter, made a lecturing tour around the world, wrote "Following the Equator," & paid off the debts.

The years 1897–98

Near the close of this absence of 13 months the eldest daughter, who had remained at home, died, aged 24 years.

The years 1897–98–99 were spent by the family in England, Switzerland & Austria. M. T. was present in the Austrian Reichsrath on the memorable occasion when the House was invaded by 60 policemen & 16 refractory Members dragged roughly out of it.

A number of his books have been translated & published in France, Germany, Russia, ₌Italy₌ Sweden, Norway & Hungary. Dramatisations of " the Gilded Age," Tom Sawyer, Prince & Pauper and Puddnhead Wilson made good successes on the stage.

#

MARK TWAIN.

A BIOGRAPHICAL SKETCH.

By Samuel E. Moffett.

In 1835 the creation of the Western empire of America had just begun. In the whole region west of the Mississippi, which now contains 21,000,000 people—nearly twice the entire population of the United States at that time—there were less than half a million white inhabitants. There were only two States beyond the great river, Louisiana and Missouri. There were only two considerable groups of population, one about New Orleans, the other about St. Louis. If we omit New Orleans, which is east of the river, there was only one place in all that vast domain with any pretension to be called a city. That was St. Louis, and that metropolis, the wonder and pride of all the Western country, had no more than 10,000 inhabitants.

It was in this frontier region, on the extreme fringe of settlement "that just divides the desert from the sown," that Samuel Langhorne Clemens was born, November 30, 1835, in the hamlet of Florida, Missouri. His parents had come there to be in the thick of the Western "boom," and by a fate for which no lack of foresight on their part was to blame, they found themselves in a place which succeeded in accumulating 125 inhabitants in the next sixty years. When we read of the westward sweep of population and wealth in the United States, it seems as if those who were in the van of that movement must have been inevitably carried on to fortune. But that was a tide full of eddies and back currents, and Mark Twain's parents possessed a faculty for finding them that appears nothing less than miraculous. The whole Western empire was before them where to choose. They could have bought the entire site of Chicago for a pair of boots. They could have taken up a farm within the present city limits of St. Louis. What they actually did was to live for a time in Columbia, Kentucky, with a small property in land and six inherited slaves; then to move to Jamestown, on the Cumberland plateau of Tennessee, a place that was then no farther removed from the currents of the world's life than Uganda, but which no resident of that or any other part of Central Africa would now regard as a serious competitor; and next to migrate to Missouri, passing St. Louis, and settling first in Florida and afterward in Hannibal. But when the whole map was blank, the promise of fortune glowed as rosily in these regions as anywhere else. Florida had great expectations when Jackson was President. When John Marshall Clemens took up 80,000 acres of land in Tennessee, he thought he had established his children as territorial magnates. That phantom vision of wealth furnished later one of the motives of "The Gilded Age." It conferred no other benefit.

If Samuel Clemens missed a fortune, he inherited good blood. On both sides, his family had been settled in the South since early colonial times. His father, John Marshall Clemens, of Virginia, was a descendant of Gregory Clement, who became one of the judges that condemned Charles I. to death, was excepted from the amnesty after the Restoration in consequence, and lost his head. A cousin of John M. Clemens, Jeremiah Clemens, represented Alabama in the United States Senate from 1849 to 1853.

Through his mother, Jane Lampton (Lambton), the boy was descended from the Lambtons, of Durham, whose modern English representatives still possess the lands held by their ancestors of the same name since the twelfth century. Some of her forbears on the maternal side, the Montgomerys, went with Daniel Boone to Kentucky, and were in the thick of the romantic and tragic events that accompanied the settlement of the "Dark and Bloody Ground;" and she herself was born there, twenty-nine years after the first log-cabin was built within the limits of the present commonwealth. She was one of the earliest, prettiest, and brightest of the many belles that have given Kentucky such an enviable reputation as a nursery of fair women, and her vivacity and wit left no doubt in the minds of her friends concerning the source of her son's genius.

John Marshall Clemens, who had been trained for the bar in Virginia, served for some years as a magistrate at Hannibal, holding for a time the position of county judge. With his death, in March, 1847, Mark Twain's formal education came to an end, and his education in real life began. He had always been a delicate boy, and his father in consequence had been lenient in the matter of enforcing attendance at school, although he had been profoundly anxious that his children should be well educated. His wish was fulfilled, although not in the way he had expected. It is a fortunate thing for literature that Mark Twain was never ground into smooth uniformity under the scholastic emery wheel. He has made the world his university, and in men and books and strange places and all the phases of an infinitely varied life has built an education broad and deep on the foundations of an undisturbed individuality.

His high school was a village printing-office, where his elder brother, Orion, was conducting a newspaper. The thirteen-year-old boy served in all capacities, and in the occasional absences of his chief he reveled in personal journalism, with original illustrations hacked on wooden blocks with a jackknife, to an extent that riveted the town's attention, "but not its admiration," as his brother plaintively confessed. The editor spoke with feeling, for he had to take the consequences of these exploits on his return.

From his earliest childhood young Clemens had been of an adventurous disposition. Before he was thirteen he had been extracted three times from the Mississippi and six times from Bear Creek in a substantially drowned condition, but his mother, with the high confidence in his future that never deserted her, merely remarked: "People who are born to be hanged are safe in the water." By 1853, the Hannibal tether had become too short for him. He disappeared from home, and wandered from one Eastern printing-office to another. He saw the World's Fair at New York and other marvels, and supported himself by setting type. At the end of this *Wanderjahr,* financial stress drove him back to his family. He lived at St. Louis, Muscatine, and Keokuk until 1857, when he induced the great Horace Bixby to teach him the mystery of steamboat piloting. The charm of all this warm, indolent existence in the sleepy river towns has colored his whole subsequent life. In "Tom Sawyer," "Huckleberry Finn," "Life on the Mississippi," and "Pudd'nhead Wilson" every phase of that vanished estate is lovingly dwelt upon.

Native character will always make itself felt, but one may wonder whether Mark Twain's humor would have developed in quite so sympathetic and buoyant a vein if he had been brought up in Ecclefechan instead of in Hannibal, and whether Carlyle might not have been a little more human if he had spent his boyhood in Hannibal instead of in Ecclefechan.

A Mississippi pilot in the later fifties was a personage of imposing grandeur. He was a miracle of attainments; he was the absolute master of his boat while it was under way; and just before his fall, he commanded a salary precisely equal to that earned at that time by the Vice-President of the United States or a justice of the Supreme Court. The best proof of the superlative majesty and desirability of his position is the fact that Samuel Clemens deliberately subjected himself to the incredible labor necessary to attain it—a labor compared with which the efforts needed to acquire the degree of Doctor of Philosophy at a university are as light as a summer course of modern novels. To appreciate the full meaning of a pilot's marvelous education one must read the whole of "Life on the Mississippi," but this extract may give a partial idea of a single feature of that training—the cultivation of the memory:

"First of all, there is one faculty which a pilot must incessantly cultivate until he has brought it to absolute perfection. Nothing short of perfection will do. That faculty is memory. He cannot stop with merely thinking a thing is so and so; he must *know* it; for this is eminently one of the exact sciences. With what scorn a pilot was looked upon, in the old times, if he ever ventured to deal in that feeble phrase 'I think,' instead of the vigorous one 'I know!' One cannot easily realize what a tremendous thing it is to know every trivial detail of 1,200 miles of river and know it with absolute exactness. If you will take the longest street in New York and travel up and down it, conning its features patiently until you know every house and window and door and lamp-post and big and little sign by heart, and know them so accurately that you can instantly name the one you are abreast of when you are set down at random in that street in the middle of an inky black night, you will then have a tolerable notion of the amount and the exactness of a pilot's knowledge who carries the Mississippi River in his head. And then if you will go on until you know every street crossing, the character, size, and position of the crossing stones, and the varying depth of mud in each of those numberless places, you will have some idea of what the pilot must know in order to keep a Mississippi steamer out of trouble. Next, if you will take half of the signs on that long street and *change their places* once a month, and still manage to know their new positions accurately on dark nights, and keep up with these repeated changes without making any mistakes, you will understand what is required of a pilot's peerless memory by the fickle Mississippi.

"I think a pilot's memory is about the most wonderful thing in the world. To know the Old and New Testaments by heart, and be able to recite them glibly, forward or backward, or begin at random anywhere in the book and recite both ways, and never trip or make a mistake, is no extravagant mass of knowledge, and no marvelous facility, compared to a pilot's massed knowledge of the Mississippi, and his marvelous facility in handling it . . .

"And how easily and comfortably the pilot's memory does its work; how placidly effortless is its way; how *unconsciously* it lays up its vast stores, hour by hour, day by day, and never loses or mislays a single valuable package of them all! Take an instance. Let a leadsman say: 'Half twain! half twain! half twain! half twain! half twain!' until it becomes as monotonous as the ticking of a clock; let conversation be going on all the time, and the pilot be doing his share of the talking, and no longer consciously listening to the leadsman; and in the midst of this endless string of half twains let a single 'quarter twain!' be interjected, without emphasis, and then the half twain cry go on again, just as before: two or three weeks later that pilot can describe with precision the boat's position in the river when that quarter twain was uttered, and give you such a lot of head marks, stern marks, and side marks to guide you that you ought to be able to take the boat there and put her in that same spot again yourself! The cry of 'Quarter twain' did not really take his mind from his talk, but his trained faculties instantly photographed the bearings, noted the change of depth, and laid up the important details for future reference without requiring any assistance from him in the matter."

Young Clemens went through all that appalling training, stored away in his head the bewildering mass of knowledge a pilot's duties required, received the license that was the diploma of the river university, entered into regular employment, and regarded himself as established for life, when the outbreak of the Civil War wiped out his occupation at a stroke and made his weary apprenticeship a useless labor. The commercial navigation of the lower Mississippi was stopped by a line of fire, and black, squat gunboats, their sloping sides plated with railroad iron, took the place of the gorgeous white side-wheelers whose pilots had been the envied aristocrats of the river towns. Clemens was in New Orleans when Louisiana seceded, and started North the next day. The boat ran a blockade every day of her trip, and on the last night of the voyage the batteries at the Jefferson Barracks, just below St. Louis, fired two shots through her chimneys.

Brought up in a slave-holding atmosphere, Mark Twain naturally sympathized at first with the South. In June he joined the Confederates in Ralls County, Missouri, as a second lieutenant under General Tom Harris. His military career lasted for two weeks. Narrowly missing the distinction of being captured by Colonel Ulysses S. Grant, he resigned, explaining that he had become "incapacitated by fatigue" through persistent retreating. In his subsequent writings he has always treated his brief experience of warfare as a burlesque episode, although the official reports and correspondence of the Confederate commanders speak very respectfully of the work of the raw countrymen of the Harris Brigade. The elder Clemens brother, Orion, was *persona grata* to the Administration of President Lincoln, and received in consequence an appointment as the first Secretary of the new Territory of Nevada. He offered his speedily reconstructed junior the position of private secretary to himself, "with nothing to do and no salary." The two crossed the plains in the overland coach in eighteen days—almost precisely the time it will take to go from New York to Vladivostok when the Trans-Siberian Railway is finished.

A year of variegated fortune-hunting among the silver mines of the Humboldt and Esmeralda regions followed. Occasional letters written during this time to the leading newspaper of the Territory, the "Virginia City Territorial Enterprise," attracted the attention of the proprietor, Mr. J. T. Goodman, a man of keen and unerring literary instinct, and he offered the writer the position of local editor on his staff. With the duties of this place were combined those of legislative correspondent at Carson City, the capital. The work of young Clemens created a sensation among the lawmakers. He wrote a weekly letter, spined with barbed personalities. It appeared every Sunday, and on Mondays the legislative business was obstructed with the complaints of members who rose to questions of privilege and expressed their opinion of the correspondent with acerbity. This encouraged him to give his letters more individuality by signing them. For this purpose he adopted the old Mississippi leadsman's call for two fathoms (twelve feet)—"Mark Twain."

At that particular period dueling was a passing fashion on the Comstock. The refinements of Parisian civilization had not penetrated there, and a Washoe duel seldom left more than one survivor. The weapons were always Colt's navy revolvers—distance, fifteen paces; fire and advance; six shots allowed. Mark Twain became involved in a quarrel with Mr. Laird, the editor of the "Virginia Union," and the situation seemed to call for a duel. Neither combatant was an expert with the pistol, but Mark Twain was fortunate enough to have a second who was. The men were practising in adjacent gorges, Mr. Laird doing fairly well, and his opponent hitting everything but the mark. A small bird lit on a sage bush thirty yards away, and Mark Twain's second fired and knocked off its head. At that moment the enemy came over the ridge, saw the dead bird, observed the distance, and learned from Gillis, the humorist's second, that the feat had been performed by Mark Twain, for whom such an exploit was nothing remarkable. They withdrew for consultation, and then offered a formal apology, after which peace was restored, leaving Mark Twain with the honors of war.

However, this incident was the means of effecting another change in his life. There was a new law which prescribed two years' imprisonment for any one who should send, carry, or accept a challenge. The fame of the proposed duel had reached the capital, eighteen miles away, and the governor wrathfully gave orders for the arrest of all concerned, announcing his intention of making an example that would be remembered. A friend of the duelists heard of their danger, outrode the officers of the law, and hurried the parties over the border into California.

Mark Twain found a berth as city editor of the "San Francisco Morning Call," but he was not adapted to routine newspaper work, and in a couple of years he made another bid for fortune in the mines. He tried the "pocket mines" of California this time, at Jackass Gulch, in Calaveras County, but was fortunate enough to find no pockets. Thus he escaped the hypnotic fascination that has kept some intermittently successful pocket miners willing prisoners in Sierra cabins for life, and in three months he was back in San Francisco, penniless, but in the line of literary promotion. He wrote letters for the "Virginia Enterprise" for a time, but, tiring of that, welcomed an assignment to visit Hawaii for the "Sacramento Union" and write about the sugar interests. It was in Honolulu that he accomplished one of his greatest feats of "straight newspaper work." The clipper "Hornet" had been burned on "the line," and when the skeleton survivors arrived after a passage of forty-three days in an open boat on ten days' provisions, Mark Twain gathered their stories, worked all day and all night, and threw a complete account of the horror aboard a schooner that had already cast off. It was the only full account that reached California, and it was not only a clean "scoop" of unusual magnitude, but an admirable piece of literary art. The "Union" testified its appreciation by paying the correspondent ten times the current rates for it.

After six months in the islands, Mark Twain returned to California, and made his first venture upon the lecture platform. He was warmly received, and delivered several lectures with profit. In 1867 he went East by way of the Isthmus, and joined the "Quaker City" excursion to Europe and the Holy Land as correspondent of the "Alta California," of San Francisco. During this tour of five or six months the party visited the principal ports of the Mediterranean and the Black Sea. From this trip grew "The Innocents Abroad," the creator of Mark Twain's reputation as a literary force of the first order. "The Celebrated Jumping Frog of Calaveras County" had preceded it, but "The Innocents" gave the author his first introduction to international literature. A hundred thousand copies were sold the first year, and as many more later.

Four years of lecturing followed—distasteful, but profitable. Mark Twain always shrank from the public exhibition of himself on the platform, but he was a popular favorite there from the first. He was one of a little group, including Henry Ward Beecher and two or three others, for whom every lyceum committee in the country was bidding, and whose capture at any price insured the success of a lecture course.

The "Quaker City" excursion had a more important result than the production of "The Innocents Abroad." Through her brother, who was one of the party, Mr. Clemens became acquainted with Miss Olivia L. Langdon, the daughter of Jervis Langdon, of Elmira, New York, and this acquaintance led, in February, 1870, to one of the most ideal marriages in literary history.

Four children came of this union. The eldest, Langdon, a son, was born in November, 1870, and died in 1872. The second, Susan Olivia, a daughter, was born in the latter year, and lived only twenty-four years, but long enough to develop extraordinary mental gifts and every grace of character. Two other daughters, Clara Langdon and Jean, were born in 1874 and 1880 respectively, and still live (1899).

Mark Twain's first home as a man of family was in Buffalo, in a house given to the bride by her father as a wedding present. He bought a third interest in a daily newspaper, the "Buffalo Express," and joined its staff. But his time for jogging in harness was past. It was his last attempt at regular newspaper work, and a year of it was enough. He had become assured of a market for anything he might produce, and he could choose his own place and time for writing.

There was a tempting literary colony at Hartford; the place was steeped in an atmosphere of antique peace and beauty, and the Clemens family were captivated by its charm. They moved there in October, 1871, and soon built a house which was one of the earliest fruits of the artistic revolt against the mid-century Philistinism of domestic architecture in America. For years it was an object of wonder to the simple-minded tourist. The facts that its rooms were arranged for the convenience of those who were to occupy them, and that its windows, gables, and porches were distributed with an eye to the beauty, comfort, and picturesqueness of that particular house, instead of following the traditional lines laid down by the carpenters and contractors who designed most of the dwellings of the period, distracted the critics, and gave rise to grave discussions in the newspapers throughout the country of "Mark Twain's practical joke."

The years that followed brought a steady literary development. "Roughing It," which was written in 1872, and scored a success hardly second to that of "The Innocents," was, like that, simply a humorous narrative of personal experiences, variegated by brilliant splashes of description; but with "The Gilded Age," which was produced in the same year in collaboration with Mr. Charles Dudley Warner, the humorist began to evolve into the philosopher. "Tom Sawyer," appearing in 1876, was a veritable manual of boy nature, and its sequel, "Huckleberry Finn," which was published nine years later, was not only an advanced treatise in the same science, but a most moving study of the workings of the untutored human soul in boy and man. "The Prince and the Pauper," 1882; "A Connecticut Yankee at King Arthur's Court," 1890, and "Pudd'nhead Wilson," first published serially in 1893–94, were all alive with a comprehensive and passionate sympathy, to which their humor was quite subordinate, although Mark Twain never wrote, and probably never will write, a book that could be read without laughter. His humor is as irrepressible as Lincoln's, and like that it bubbles out on the most solemn occasions; but still, again like Lincoln's, it has a way of seeming, in spite of the surface incongruity, to belong there. But it was in the "Personal Recollections of Joan of Arc," whose anonymous serial publication in 1894–95 betrayed some critics of reputation into the absurdity of attributing it to other authors, notwithstanding the characteristic evidences of its paternity that obtruded themselves on every page, that Mark Twain became most distinctly a prophet of humanity. Here at last was a book with nothing ephemeral about it—one that will reach the elemental human heart as well among the flying-machines of the next century as it does among the automobiles of to-day, or as it would have done among the stage-coaches of a hundred years ago.

And side by side with this spiritual growth had come a growth in knowledge and in culture. The Mark Twain of "The Innocents," keen-eyed, quick of understanding, and full of fresh, eager interest in all Europe had to show, but frankly avowing that he "did not know what in the mischief the Renaissance was," had developed into an accomplished scholar and a man of the world for whom the globe had few surprises left. The Mark Twain of 1895 might conceivably have written "The Innocents Abroad," although it would have required an effort to put himself in the necessary frame of mind; but the Mark Twain of 1869 could no more have written "Joan of Arc" than he could have deciphered the Maya hieroglyphics.

In 1873, the family spent some months in England and Scotland, and Mr. Clemens lectured for a few weeks in London. Another European journey followed in 1878.

"A Tramp Abroad" was the result of this tour, which lasted eighteen months. "The Prince and the Pauper," "Life on the Mississippi," and "Huckleberry Finn" appeared in quick succession in 1882, 1883, and 1885. Considerably more amusing than anything the humorist ever wrote was the fact that the trustees of some village libraries in New England solemnly voted that "Huckleberry Finn," whose power of moral uplift has hardly been surpassed by any book of our time, was too demoralizing to be allowed on their shelves.

All this time fortune had been steadily favorable, and Mark Twain had been spoken of by the press sometimes with admiration as an example of the financial success possible in literature, and sometimes with uncharitable envy as a haughty millionaire, forgetful of his humble friends. But now began the series of unfortunate investments that swept away the accumulations of half a lifetime of hard work, and left him loaded with debts incurred by other men. In 1885 he financed the publishing house of Charles L. Webster & Company, in New York. The firm began business with the prestige of a brilliant coup. It secured the publication of the Memoirs of General Grant, which achieved a sale of more than 600,000 volumes. The first check received by the Grant heirs was for $200,000, and this was followed a few months later by one for $150,000. These are the largest checks ever paid for an author's work on either side of the Atlantic. Meanwhile Mr. Clemens was spending great sums on a type-setting machine of such seductive ingenuity as to captivate the imagination of everybody who saw it. It worked to perfection, but it was too complicated and expensive for commercial use, and, after sinking a fortune in it between 1886 and 1889, Mark Twain had to write off the whole investment as a dead loss.

On top of this the publishing house, which had been supposed to be doing a profitable business, turned out to have been incapably conducted, and all the money that came into its hands was lost. Mark Twain contributed $65,000 in efforts to save its life, but to no purpose; and when it finally failed, he found that it had not only absorbed everything he had put in, but had incurred liabilities of $96,000, of which less than one-third was covered by assets. He could easily have avoided any legal liability for the debts; but as the credit of the company had been based largely upon his name, he felt bound in honor to pay them. In 1895–96 he took his wife and second daughter on a lecturing tour around the world; wrote "Following the Equator," and cleared off the obligations of the house in full.

The years 1897, 1898, and 1899 were spent in England, Switzerland, and Austria. Vienna took the family to its heart, and Mark Twain achieved such a popularity among all classes there as is rarely won by a foreigner anywhere. He saw the manufacture of a good deal of history in that time. It was his fortune, for instance, to be present in the Austrian Reichsrath on the memorable occasion when it was invaded by sixty policemen, and sixteen refractory members were dragged roughly out of the hall. That momentous event in the progress of parliamentary government profoundly impressed him.

Mark Twain, although so characteristically American in every fiber, does not appeal to Americans alone, nor even to the English-speaking race. His work has stood the test of translation into French, German, Russian, Italian, Swedish, Norwegian, and Magyar. That is pretty good evidence that it possesses the universal quality that marks the master. Another evidence of its fidelity to human nature is the readiness with which it lends itself to dramatization. "The Gilded Age," "Tom Sawyer," "The Prince and the Pauper," and "Pudd'nhead Wilson" have all been successful on the stage.

In the thirty-eight years of his literary activity Mark Twain has seen generation after generation of "American humorists" rise, expand into sudden popularity, and disappear, leaving hardly a memory behind. If he has not written himself out like them, if his place in literature has become every year more assured, it is because his "humor" has been something radically different from theirs. It has been irresistibly laughter-provoking, but its sole end has never been to make people laugh. Its more important purpose has been to make them think and feel. And with the progress of the years Mark Twain's own thoughts have become finer, his own feelings deeper and more responsive. Sympathy with the suffering, hatred of injustice and oppression, and enthusiasm for all that tends to make the world a more tolerable place for mankind to live in, have grown with his accumulating knowledge of life as it is. That is why Mark Twain has become a classic, not only at home, but in all lands whose people read and think about the common joys and sorrows of humanity.

PROPOSITION FOR A POSTAL CHECK

Mark Twain wrote "Proposition for a Postal Check" in Vienna in 1898–99. He discusses the development of his idea at length in the Autobiographical Dictation of 22 August

1907, which concludes with the remark, "I will inter that old postal-check article of mine in an Appendix, where the curious may find it if they want it." Although the article has little importance among Mark Twain's writings, the vigorous process of revision that he lavished upon it shows how much he expected of his brainchild (see the Textual Commentary at *MTPO*).

———

Proposition for a Postal Check.*

Statesman. You were proposing to distribute cheap books and a multitude of other articles by mail. To order them from headquarters——

Wisdom Seeker.—Will be unhandy and inconvenient? Yes, it will. I have been thinking out a way to remedy that. It is necessary to find a smooth and easy way out of a couple of difficulties which at present badly cripple purchase and sale in things of trifling cost—and in things of larger cost, too.

S. What are they?

W.S. Well, the first one is this. Take books, for instance. The bookseller cannot keep samples of *all* books in stock—he hasn't room. When he is out of a book he offers to order it for you, but if you are the average man you say never mind, let it alone. That is a damage. Because of it, a book which should sell ten thousand copies sells only three thousand. Again, you read a review of a book, and want a copy; but if you have to go all the way to the bookstore to get it or order it—well, if you are the average man, that cools your desire and you drop the matter out of your mind, or you forget it. *Another* damage: twenty thousand copies fail of purchase in *that* way. And so, a book which would sell thirty thousand copies if things were handier, sells only three thousand.

S. What is the other difficulty?

W.S. This: that there is at present no good way to beguile a man into ordering the book *himself.* Therein lies the prodigious damage—the incalculable damage! If he could order it without stirring from his chair, and without any trouble or bother, the usual three-thousand-copy book would sell—well, a ton or two. But there is no way. If he proposes to send postage-stamps to the publisher, he finds he is just out of stamps; if he needs to send several dollars, his check will not be good with a publisher who doesn't know him; if he enclose bank notes—but that is too risky; very well, there's no help for it—he must go to the postoffice and get a postal money-order, with all which that means of bother and red tape and waste of time.

S. Isn't the postal order a convenience?

W.S. Yes. So is the stage-coach.

S. But *is* there so much bother and waste about it?

W.S. Yes, in Austria, and it must be so in all countries. Here is a man who sends me a money-order for two dollars from Kaltenleutgeben, ten miles from Vienna. The

---

* Written in Austria five years ago, i.e. in 1898–9. M.T.

pen-work in it consists of 319 letters—the equivalent of sixty-four words! When I have a sentence of twenty words already planned out in my head, I can swiftly put it on paper in one minute. Then how long would it take me to fill the blanks in this money-order with those sixty-four words?

S. Three minutes.

W.S. It is a mistake. The words consist of unfamiliar *names,* and with figures about which I must be very careful, lest I make a costly mistake. It would take me *six* minutes.

S. Is that a serious matter?

W.S. It looks so to me. But that isn't all. The sixty-four words have to be also entered in the postmaster's record-book. Six minutes more. At the other end of the line a number of the words have to be written again. The mere penmanship expended on this two dollars' worth of money-order has cost about twenty minutes—and time is money.

S. It really has a rather serious aspect.

W.S. We haven't reached the end, yet. The man who *sent* the order lost fifteen minutes in his trip to the postoffice and back. Add that: thirty-five minutes altogether. All for two dollars.

S. It grows formidable.

W.S. Yes. An output of a hundred thousand money-orders per day with a total loss of a half hour's time on each would be sure to rob the country's industries of fifty thousand hours per day of more or less valuable time. For it is time taken from the ten hours of daylight. In a year the country's industries would lose in wasted labor-time about 5,500 years. At $600 a year for wages, and $600 more for the product of the labor, the country's cash loss is more than $6,000,000 for the year.

S. Of course that is disastrous, but does any country buy a hundred thousand money-orders per day—working-day?

W.S. It is only one and a quarter orders per working-day for each thousand of the population of the United States.

S. Will your scheme save that wasted time?

W.S. Substantially. Nine-tenths of it, let us say.

S. Then you are not proposing to restrict it to books?

W.S. By no means! Books are not even 1 per cent of the commerce the scheme would cover.

S. Very good. What is the scheme?

W.S. I will try to develop it. When you enclose half a dozen postage-stamps or a bank note to a reputable firm, what risk are you running?

S. Merely the risk that some thief may steal the enclosure on the road.

W.S. But it *is* a risk?

S. Yes. Of course it is.

W.S. When you enclose a check drawn to the order of a reputable firm are you running any risk?

S. No.

W.S. Is the firm running a risk?

S. Yes; if you are a bankrupt stranger and the firm choose to chance you and endorse and collect.

W.S. Which the firm wouldn't do?

S. I think not.

W.S. Now, then, couldn't the *Government* issue blank checks for you or anybody to fill up?

S. The Government! How do you mean?

W.S. Well, the postage-stamp is really the Government's check drawn to "bearer"— and so is the greenback. When you ship these things through the mail the Government runs no risk, but *you* do. Now then, why shouldn't the Government sell you checks with *no* risk attaching, to either itself or you? Checks to be sent in an envelope, along with your order, like any other checks.

S. Checks to "bearer?"

W.S. No. Checks to "order."

S. How does that differ from a postal money-order?

W.S. In convenience, handiness, and economy of time. I will explain. This check should be a simple thing, and as small as a post-card, or smaller; and it should say "Pay to order of (*blank for name.*)" These checks should be of five several values* (5 cents, 25 cents, $1 and $3 and $5), and the figure-value should be printed large on the check and also a few times in small letters or figures, after the custom used in the case of the greenback. At the postoffice you would buy a basketful of these checks, of the several denominations, and carry them home and lock them up in your desk, and when you wished to buy a book, or a patent medicine, or a fountain pen, or an umbrella, or a Waterbury, or a theatre ticket, or wanted to subscribe to a magazine, or a charity, or a church-fund, or anything, you could fill-in the check-blank and attend to it in two minutes; you could ship any amount you pleased, and do it without stirring out of your chair.

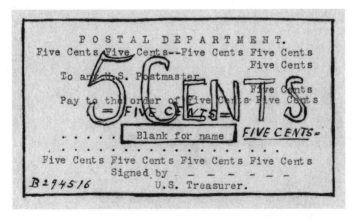

Picture of the check.

---

* In order that you may be able to make up any sum you please which does not require the division of a half-dime.

S. It looks very good.

W.S. Dear sir, I believe it *is* good. The Government is the all-sufficient endorser; the check is not collectable by an unknown person; no one runs any risk; the thing is speedy and convenient, and the slow and cumbersome postal money-order (the American one, at least,) is done away with. Think of the lost time we spoke of; but the poor and the Government *must* lose it on the money-order, since the poor have no safe way to send money but that. It is a pathetic and unchristian fact—but a fact. If we get this scheme going there won't be a man, woman or child in America too poor to keep a bank account and carry checks in his or her pocket to draw upon it with. And it will be a very good bank, too—the United States Treasury.

S. Would the checks be single, like bank notes?

W.S. Some of them. The high-figure ones with a stub on the end for you to tear off and keep.

S. What material would you use for your Universal-Check-and-Everybody's-Time-Saver?

W.S. Greenback-paper, I think, so as to beat the counterfeiter. In Great Britain, English bank-note paper.

S. Size and shape?

W.S. The shape of the greenback, but as much as a third smaller, and by that much handier to carry in purse or vest pocket.

S. Why do you want it handy for the pocket?

W.S. Because as long as the blank in it was unfilled it could pass from hand to hand as money.

S. Come, you are restoring the old postal currency!

W.S. Yes, but with a large difference. With the blank filled you can send it through the mails without fear of thieves.

S. Suppose a village postmaster should suddenly be called upon to cash postal checks to the amount of a thousand dollars—how is he going to find that money?

W.S. You know how he would find it to-day to pay that amount in money-orders, don't you?

S. Yes. The Government would prepare him. Let us suppose the orders originated in New York, and the receiving village was in the middle of Arkansas; the Government would send the thousand dollars and it would arrive at the village in time to cash the orders.

W.S. But suppose each order was for a dollar. Ten clerks would fill a part of the blanks in the thousand orders; enter the thousand sums and the two thousand names and addresses of payer and payé in their books; then the thousand sums and the two thousand names would be written out on a blanket and the same mailed to the Arkansas village along with a thousand dollars in one-dollar bills. It would take each of the ten clerks nine hours to do the red-taping for his hundred money-orders. It is ten days' working-time for one man; it costs $40 in wages. All that labor and expense to ship a thousand dollars to Arkansas. Add five hundred hours wasted by the thousand senders—$250 or more. Isn't it too costly in time and wages?

S. It looks so.

W.S. But suppose the thousand dollars went from a thousand different villages? Could the Government come to the Arkansas postmaster's rescue in that case?

S. I don't know, but I suppose not. But how are you proposing to protect *your* village-postmaster when a thousand-dollar cold-wave strikes him?

W.S. The thousand checks would arrive drawn to the order of this, that and the other villager. The village banker would know the men, and would cash the checks at a trifling discount.

S. Suppose there was no bank?

W.S. The village storekeepers would perform the banker's function.

S. Then what would *they* do with the checks?

W.S. Endorse them and pay their debts to the big merchants in the big city with them.

S. And what would the big merchants do with them?

W.S. Endorse them and send a clerk to the general postoffice to collect the money. The Government keeps a large money-reserve in great general postoffices.

S. It seems sound and simple. Would you expect a large sale of these checks?

W.S. Yes. I should expect fifty million people to buy an average of five dollars' worth a year.

S. Isn't that a rather large order?

W.S. Ah, well, you see, they are so seductively handy! You must not overlook that feature. I am trading on human nature, now. A man is always an easy victim to handiness. There are a thousand things which he will not put himself to the least trouble about, but if you make them perfectly handy and convenient, he is your prey. Consider what the postage-stamp and the telephone have done. When I was a boy I knew none but merchants and professionally-busy people who wrote more than about one letter in a month or two. Postage was 10, 15, and 25 cents, and one had to walk half a mile to post a letter. The cheap and handy stamp and post-card and the handy letter-box have changed all that; in our day the kitchen girl writes more letters in six months than the United States Senator used to write in a year. When we used to have to go all the way down town to order things which we didn't absolutely need, we did without them. But now by telephone we order every unnecessary thing that comes into our heads. The telephone has doubled the world's local business—yes, and made domestic life infamously expensive. The postal check will greatly increase commerce in books and all sorts of little merchandise, and make every man and woman in the land spend from $5 to $100 more per year than he or she spends now.

S. This is all an advantage to the Government?

W.S. And the express companies? And general commerce? And manufacturers? Yes. Because you must multiply the output of a cheap article ten-fold above its present output, for one thing. The letter that carries an order and a check must bear a postage-stamp, and the mails will carry back a considerable share of the articles ordered—a couple of profitable advantages for the Government.

S. Are there other advantages for the Government?

W.S. Blank checks will get into circulation, as money. A percentage of them will get worn out or lost. They have been paid for, and the Government has the money.

S. Will that hurt silver? Will it drive it out?

W.S. The great majority of users of the checks will not buy them oftener than once a month, and then not so much as a dollar's worth, perhaps. Those people buy with silver, not greenbacks.

S. You feel sure that this scheme will increase the output of cheap articles?

W.S. Yes, ten-fold, I am quite sure of it. I know what other people are, because I know what I am myself. The non-existence of the handy postal check saves me a good deal of money every year; for it is the *instant* ability to order books and things without leaving my chair that beguiles me; if I must go down town to leave an order at a merchant's or a bookstall, or even down stairs to struggle with the telephone, it gives me time to reflect—*and that is fatal to commerce*. I have never bought a postal order; I would rather go hungry for a thing a century than take all that trouble about it; but I would keep a basketful of those postal checks in my desk all the time and ruin myself every year.

S. What becomes of the retailer in the towns and villages and cities?

W.S. He will order and sell double as many cheap articles as he dares to order now.

S. Why?

W.S. Because the great postal check sales will advertise the things finely and he will get the benefit of that advertising. And there is one kind of customer that can never be taken from him.

S. What customer is that?

W.S. The men and women that won't buy an article until they have had a chance to examine it.

S. True. If you could persuade the Government to try your scheme right away, when would your ten-fold boom begin?

W.S. It would begin before very long; I think it would not be a long wait.

S. And the extent of it?

W.S. When it was under full headway I think it quite likely that a cheap and useful novelty that sells three thousand examples by the present methods would sell a hundred thousand then.

S. Would the Government think this postal check scheme a wise and promising one?

W.S. Well, the Government could not absolutely *know* without trying it. But why not try? The cost of a trial on a small scale would be very light.

S. What custom should it first bid for?

W.S. At *first* for that which I have heretofore indicated: that which is too small for the money-order traffic.

S. For instance—as to details?

W.S. One doesn't take the trouble to buy a money-order for 10 cents, nor for 25, nor 50, nor for a dollar. If a person wants to send for an article which costs one of those sums, he must send stamps or a dollar bill. Thousands of people do that, every day, but many other thousands do *not* do it,—merely because of the risk of loss by theft. The checks would remove the temptation to steal, stop the stealing, and dispose of the fears of the sender. Three good things. These would justify the Government in trying the check-experiment on a small scale.

S. The removal of the temptation to steal is not without value.

W.S. Yes. The Government does not like to have its servants tempted, but at present there is no way to help it.* A merchant's mail consists largely of envelopes containing small bank-bills. You have noticed that.

S. Yes.

W.S. In the postal-currency times they came by the basketful. This kind of small trade fell off heavily when the postal currency was abolished. But that currency was always unsafe and improper matter for the mails. By and by you will see everywhere this addition to mercantile advertisements: *"Send by mail no form of money but postal checks and certified bank-checks."*

Mark Twain.

Vienna, Feb. 9, 1899.

---

* "Any person who sends money or jewelry in an unregistered letter not only runs a risk of losing his property but exposes to temptation every one through whose hands his letter passes, and may be the means of *ultimately bringing some clerk or letter-carrier to ruin."*—(*From U.S. Official Postal Guide.*)

ASHCROFT-LYON CHRONOLOGY

Late 1880s	Clemens meets Lyon at a card party at the home of their mutual friends, Franklin and Harriet Whitmore.
June 1902	Clemens buys stock in the Plasmon Company of America, of which Ashcroft is assistant manager.
October 1902	Lyon begins working as secretary for the Clemens family while they are living at Riverdale-on-the-Hudson.
October 1903	The Clemenses, accompanied by Lyon, leave for Italy, where they rent the Villa di Quarto near Florence.
5 June 1904	Olivia Clemens dies in Italy, after which Lyon takes on a more substantial role as Clemens's household manager.
Summer 1904–Fall 1905	Clara is placed under the care of doctors, after suffering a nervous collapse brought on by grief over her mother's death. She is not often with the family in New York City or in Dublin, New Hampshire.
18 June 1905	Clemens writes Clara that she and Jean should compile his letters for publication. Lyon is to help them and share in the royalties.

January 1906	Albert Bigelow Paine receives permission from Clemens to write his biography; he begins to spend time with the family and has access to Clemens's personal papers.
February 1906	Jean begins treatment by Dr. Frederick Peterson, an authority on epilepsy.
27 August 1906	Paine contracts with Harper and Brothers to write the biography.
25 October 1906	At the urging of Lyon and Dr. Peterson, Jean moves to a sanatorium at Katonah, New York. She is a resident there for fifteen months.
Late December 1906	Clemens considers making Paine his literary executor.
14 January 1907	Clemens amends his will to name Clara as his literary executor.
19 February–28 March 1907	Clara is on a concert tour throughout New England.
7 May 1907	Lyon is given power of attorney over Clemens's affairs, including the authority to sign checks.
8 June 1907	Clemens deeds to Lyon a cottage and twenty acres of land on his property in Redding, Connecticut, where a new house is under construction.
8 June–22 July 1907	Clemens visits England, accompanied by Ashcroft, to receive an honorary degree from Oxford University.
December 1907	The creditors of the Plasmon Company of America file a petition for involuntary bankruptcy, which the court approves a month later.
January 1908	Lyon begins to mistrust Paine's handling of Clemens's letters and informs Clemens of her misgivings.
9 January 1908	Jean leaves the Katonah sanatorium and moves to a cottage in Greenwich, Connecticut, with sisters Edith and Mildred Cowles and Marguerite (Bébé) Schmitt.
May 1908	Jean and her companions move to a cottage in Gloucester, Massachusetts, where they are nearer to Dr. Peterson.
16 May–9 September 1908	Clara is on a European concert tour.
18 June 1908	Clemens moves into his new home in Redding, Connecticut, ultimately called Stormfield.
18 September 1908	Burglars break into Stormfield early in the morning and are chased off, then captured.

26 September 1908	Jean departs for Berlin with two companions and lives there under the care of Dr. Hofrath von Renvers.
1 October 1908	Clemens's butler, Claude Beuchotte, and a number of other servants leave Stormfield, allegedly in reaction to Lyon's harsh treatment.
2 October 1908	Clara moves into an apartment in Stuyvesant Square in New York City.
28 October 1908	The Mark Twain Library in Redding opens in temporary quarters. Lyon greatly assists Clemens in its establishment.
November 1908	Ashcroft becomes a director of the new Plasmon Milk Products Company.
14 November 1908	Clemens signs a document giving both Ashcroft and Lyon broad powers of attorney. He later does not remember signing it.
17 December 1908	Clemens instructs Jean to return from Berlin.
22 December 1908	The Mark Twain Company is officially incorporated, with Lyon and Ashcroft on its board of directors. Ashcroft also serves as manager and secretary.
Christmas 1908	Clemens makes a gift to Lyon of $500 to be used in renovating the cottage he gave her.
January 1909	Jean returns from Berlin and moves to a farm on Long Island with paid caretakers.
February 1909	Paine goes abroad to retrace Clemens's 1867 *Innocents Abroad* travels.
23 February 1909	Lyon, suffering from nervous prostration, leaves for several days' recuperation at the Heublein Hotel in Hartford.
24 February 1909	Ashcroft informs Clemens of his engagement to Lyon.
Early March 1909	Jean moves to a private care facility, Wahnfried, in Montclair, New Jersey.
Early March 1909	Clemens agrees to an audit of the household finances as proposed by Clara, who has begun to suspect that Ashcroft and Lyon are dishonest. H. H. Rogers will oversee the investigation, and Ashcroft is asked to voluntarily assist by handing over the relevant records. At this time, Clemens is not convinced that Ashcroft and Lyon are guilty of any wrongdoing.
13 March 1909	The "great Cleaning-Up Day." A number of documents are brought for Clemens to sign, detailing Lyon's and Ashcroft's duties and responsibilities as well as some financial arrangements.

14 March 1909	Clemens orally revokes Lyon's 7 May 1907 power of attorney to sign checks.
18 March 1909	Ashcroft and Lyon marry.
31 March–6 April 1909	Clemens and Clara go to New York City. From there, Clemens, Ashcroft, and Rogers go to Norfolk, Virginia, for the opening of Rogers's Virginian Railway.
2 April 1909	Ashcroft informs Clemens that Clara has discharged butler Horace Hazen.
7 April 1909	Clemens sees Clara in New York on his way home from Norfolk and questions her about Hazen. She insists that she did not dismiss him; later Hazen claims that Ashcroft forced him to say that she had.
13 April 1909	Clemens attends Clara's concert at Mendelssohn Hall in New York City. Lyon and Ashcroft do not attend, as formerly planned, and instead they summon Dr. Peterson to confer about Jean's condition.
15 April 1909	Clara secures permission from Dr. Peterson for Jean to come to Stormfield for a week. Clemens gives Lyon a month's notice to leave Stormfield. Claude Beuchotte returns as Clemens's butler.
22–25 April 1909	Lyon packs to leave before Jean's arrival. Clara notices that her mother's carnelian beads are missing and accuses Lyon of stealing them.
Late April 1909	Paine returns from his trip abroad; Jean arrives to live at Stormfield.
29 April 1909	Ashcroft writes to assure Clemens that he and Lyon have been handling his affairs "honestly and conscientiously."
2 May 1909	Clemens begins writing "The Ashcroft-Lyon Manuscript," prefacing it with Ashcroft's letter.
Early May 1909	Miss Watson, one of Rogers's secretaries, is put in charge of investigating the Ashcrofts' handling of Clemens's money.
9 or 10 May 1909	Clemens learns from Harry Lounsbury that work on Lyon's house cost close to $3,500, not $1,500, as Lyon reported. According to Lounsbury, she spent close to $2,000 of Clemens's money before he offered her a loan at Christmas, 1908.
19 May 1909	H. H. Rogers dies in New York City. Clemens puts the Ashcroft-Lyon investigation into the hands of attorney John B. Stanchfield.

29 May 1909	Clemens revokes in writing Lyon's 7 May 1907 power of attorney to sign checks.
1 June 1909	In Clemens's bank in New York City, Paine discovers the power of attorney that Clemens signed for Ashcroft and Lyon on 14 November 1908. Clemens revokes it that day.
8 June 1909	Ashcroft and Lyon leave the country for an extended stay in England. Ashcroft conducts business there for Clemens and the Plasmon Milk Products Company.
14 July 1909	Lyon returns to the United States after discovering that Clemens wants the Redding cottage returned to him and has put a lien on her property in Farmington, Connecticut.
17 and 20 July 1909	Clara, Jean, and attorney Charles Lark visit Lyon's cottage to negotiate its transfer back to Clemens and arrange her departure.
27 July 1909	Ashcroft returns from England.
30 July 1909	Ashcroft writes Stanchfield protesting his and Clemens's treatment of Lyon. He lists various conditions to be met by Clemens before they can consider all business between them finished. The letter is transcribed in the Appendix "Ralph W. Ashcroft to John B. Stanchfield, 30 July 1909."
4 August 1909	The New York *Times* prints Ashcroft's invective against Clara: "Ashcroft Accuses Miss Clara Clemens."
17 August 1909	Clemens's final will gives Clara and Paine joint authority over his published and unpublished literary works.
7 September 1909	Last date recorded in "The Ashcroft-Lyon Manuscript."
10 September 1909	Clemens, through his lawyers, reaches a settlement with the Ashcrofts to avoid any lawsuits (except for a few minor details); Ashcroft agrees to resign his position with the Mark Twain Company.
13 September 1909	An article in the New York *Times,* "Mark Twain Suits All Off," presents Ashcroft's false claims that Clemens and Clara have retracted all their charges and that he has been asked to remain an officer of the Mark Twain Company. Clemens makes no public comment.
26 September 1909	Final details of the settlement are worked out; Clemens severs all connection with the Ashcrofts.
6 October 1909	Clara marries Ossip Gabrilowitsch. In December they depart for Europe, where they plan to live.
24 December 1909	Jean dies at Stormfield.

21 April 1910	Clemens dies at Stormfield.
13 June 1927	Ashcroft and Lyon divorce, having separated on 24 May 1923. Ashcroft remarries on 1 October 1927.
8 January 1947	Ashcroft dies in Toronto.
4 December 1958	Lyon dies in New York City.
19 November 1962	Clara dies in San Diego, California.

RALPH W. ASHCROFT TO JOHN B. STANCHFIELD, 30 JULY 1909

Ashcroft vigorously defended Isabel Lyon (his wife, as of 18 March 1909) when she came under suspicion of malfeasance in handling Clemens's household accounts (see "The Ashcroft-Lyon Manuscript"). Among the documents that he provided to Clemens's attorneys was his own record of the cash disbursements, totaling $7,049, which he claimed Lyon had made on Clemens's behalf between February 1907 and February 1909. He also listed a number of services for which he wanted compensation, since Clemens did not pay him a salary. Among these were $500 for "checking over Miss Lyons' account" and $880 for "accompanying Mr. Clemens to England" (Ashcroft 1909; Lark to Paine, 10 Aug 1909, CU-MARK). Clemens responded to this request with characteristic ire, compiling his own list of losses in lawyers' fees, poor investments recommended by Ashcroft, and miscellaneous "pilferings," totaling some $30,000. Through his lawyers, he reached a financial settlement with the Ashcrofts on 10 September 1909, but refused Ashcroft's request for a signed statement that Lyon was innocent of any wrongdoing. When the remaining details were resolved on 26 September, the ugly conflict finally came to an end (see the editorial preface to "The Ashcroft-Lyon Manuscript," p. 323).

The letter that Ashcroft wrote to attorney John B. Stanchfield on 30 July is his fullest defense of Lyon against Clemens's accusations. It is transcribed below from Ashcroft's own typed copy, now at the Mark Twain House and Museum (CtHMTH). On another copy of the letter, now in the Mark Twain Papers, attorney Charles T. Lark annotated the claim that "Mr. Lark expressly states that Mr. Clemens or your office do not charge Miss Lyon with any moral turpitude, embezzlement or defalcation" with the comment, "I made no such statement. C.T.L."

July 30, 1909.

John B. Stanchfield, Esq.,
    5 Nassau Street, New York.

Dear Mr. Stanchfield:

As doubtless you have been informed, yesterday, together with my attorney, Mr. R. A. Mansfield Hobbs, I had a talk with your Mr. Lark, and at his request write you this letter.

My surprise in London at hearing that Mrs. Ashcroft's real estate in Connecticut had been attached in a suit against her by Mr. Clemens, turned to amazement when I discovered on my return on the 27th inst. on the S.S. Caronia that she had been inveigled into transferring her cottage and land at Redding to Mr. Clemens.

As you are aware, Mrs. Ashcroft returned from Europe two weeks before me, immediately on receipt of information regarding the attachment, solely for the purpose of protecting her name and reputation. Three days after her arrival, without being permitted the benefit of counsel, when alone with her mother in the cottage, and, as she says, by threats and intimidations, and what she is led to believe, misrepresentations, she was induced to sign a paper, the purport of which she knew not, and give a check for $1,500., the amount of the mortgage she had raised on the property. All of which transpired at a time when, as her doctor says, she was a physical and nervous wreck.

Mrs. Ashcroft was with Mr. Clemens for about seven years, first, when Mrs. Clemens was alive, as his secretary, and, on her decease, and owing to the disability of the two daughters, was necessarily forced to take complete charge of Mr. Clemens' household. As Mr. H. H. Rogers said a few days before he died: "When Mrs. Clemens died, Clemens needed such a person as Miss Lyon at that crisis of his life, to look after him and his affairs, and she came to the front and has stayed at the front all these years, and no one has any right to criticize her." You personally are familiar with the position she latterly occupied with the family. It was that, practically, of a daughter. She was Mr. Clemens' hostess and person of affairs. Her position is more adequately described by him in this letter to his daughter:

"Jean dear, if your mother were here she would know how to think for you and plan for you and take care of you better than I do; but we have lost her, and a man has no competency in these matters. I have to have somebody in whom I have confidence to attend to every detail of my daily affairs for me except my literary work. I attend to not one of them myself; I give the instructions and see that they are obeyed. I give Miss Lyon instructions—she does nothing of her own initiative. When you blame her you are merely blaming me—she is not open to criticism in the matter.

When I find that you are not happy in that place I instruct her to ask Drs. Peterson and Hunt to provide a change for you, and she obeys the instructions. In her own case I provide no change, for she does all my matters well, and although they are often delicate and difficult she makes no enemies, either for herself or me. I am not acquainted with another human being of whom this could be said. It would not be possible for any other person to see reporters and strangers every day, refuse their requests, and yet send them away good and permanent friends to me and to herself—but I should make enemies of many of them if I tried to talk with them. The servants in the house are her friends, they all have confidence in her: and not many people can win and keep a servant's friendship and esteem—one of your mother's highest talents. All Tuxedo likes Miss Lyon—the hackmen, the aristocrats and all. She has failed to secure your confidence and esteem and I am sorry. I wish it were otherwise, but it is no argument since she has not failed in any other person's case. One failure to fifteen hundred successes means that the fault is not with her.

I am anxious that Dr. Peterson shall place you to your satisfaction, and I have not a doubt that he will find such a place if it exists. God Almighty alone is responsible for your temperament, your malady and all your troubles and sorrows. I cannot blame you for them and I do not.

Lovingly and compassionately,
Your Father."

The present differences, as you are aware, originated through women's jealousy, Mr. Clemens at first siding with Miss Lyon. Latterly her opponents solely having his ear, his leaning seems to be in their direction. At the incipiency of the matter, Miss Lyon courted a rigid investigation, and I, at the request of Mr. Clemens, spent nearly two months of my time making up the account to be submitted to Mr. H. H. Rogers, who, as you know, had one of his accountants go over the same, who reported that the account was correct. Unfortunately, Mr. Rogers died before this could be reported to Mr. Clemens, who then turned the account over to you; and the account and figures you have are mine, thus submitted, without, however, being completely classified, as, on the decease of his father, Mr. H. H. Rogers, Jr., refused to allow the accountant to have anything further to do with the matter.

Mr. Lark expressly states that Mr. Clemens or your office do not charge Miss Lyon with any moral turpitude, embezzlement or defalcation. Should any such charge be made by any responsible person, please consider the after part of this letter withdrawn, and we will immediately prove to the satisfaction of a court or jury that not $1. was ever misappropriated or misapplied by Miss Lyon, and will justify her reputation by holding those responsible for the defamation, in addition to enforcing whatever rights she may have in the matter.

This letter is not alone to you in the capacity of Mr. Clemens' attorney, but as an old friend of all concerned. You have known Miss Lyon for several years, and I think that you will agree that any imputation of dishonesty against her is cruel, unjust and malicious. She is hurt to the quick; and this matter and its attendant notoriety have made her a nervous wreck. She loved Mr. Clemens as a daughter;

anticipated his every wish and desire; labored day and night for seven years for him, and indulged in a sort of hero-worship; and the return that Mr. Clemens made her for these services and sacrifices has broken her down in health and spirit.

No accounts were ever kept of the household expenditures, nor was Miss Lyon ever requested or instructed to do so. The items Mr. Lark seems to question are cash items. According to Mr. Rogers' audit, during this time $6789. was drawn in cash, an average of $282. per month—a mere bagatelle when you consider the receipts and disbursements passing through her hands, which were: receipts, $342,751.; disbursements, $279,536. Out of this $6789., part of the servants' wages was paid—the pay-roll for servants amounting to about $5,000.; also, out of this $6789., the sum of approximately $3,000. was paid in cash to Miss Clara Clemens for her accompanist, Mr. Wark, her manager, Mr. Charlton, part of the expense of her concert trips, a trip to Nova Scotia, and many other items. Every cent of the balance was used for the expenses of the house, traveling expenses, and other payments in Mr. Clemens' or his daughters' interests.

As a practical man, you are aware that it is extremely difficult, if not impossible, to go back two years, and take a stub entry showing an amount of say $100. drawn in cash, and technically account for each cent of it. The only records ever kept were the brief stub entries, which was the manner in vogue when Miss Lyon assumed her duties. It can only be said that not $1. was spent dishonestly, and it was all disbursed for the best interests of Mr. Clemens. Never during her administration was she asked to make an accounting or to keep any record of cash expenditures. She was practically a member of the family and treated as such.

There was no occasion for Mr. Clemens to attach her property, especially in her absence temporarily in Europe, and the resultant notoriety is only chargeable to him. The bone of contention seems to have been the cottage, and its acquisition by Mr. Clemens could have been accomplished amicably and equitably to the satisfaction of all, on her return, instead of by the discreditable means employed. I am advised that Mrs. Ashcroft would have little difficulty in setting the deed aside; there was *no consideration for the transfer;* it was procured by threats, intimidation and duress; she did not know what she was signing, only that it was represented to her that if she signed such a paper, it would mean a complete ending of the matter.

I think until my talk with Mr. Lark yesterday, by his surprise, you were unaware of the following agreement:

"Redding,
Connecticut"

$982.47

Received from R. W. Ashcroft his notes for the sum of $982.47, being estimated balance due on money advanced to Isabel V. Lyon for the renovation of "The Lobster Pot"; this receipt being given on the understanding that said Ashcroft will pay in like manner any further amounts that his examination of my disbursements for the fiscal year ending February 28/09 shows were advanced for like purposes.

S. L. Clemens (Seal)

I agree to the above and to make said examination as promptly as my other duties will permit.

R. W. Ashcroft. (Seal)

March 13/09.

Mr. Clemens gave this cottage and 20 acres of land to Miss Lyon as some appreciation of her unique and extraordinary services to him. When she wanted to mortgage it for the purpose of raising money to rehabilitate it, Mr. Clemens told her to use what money of his, was, in her judgment, necessary for that purpose. This she did to the amount of about $2,700., with the full knowledge of Mr. Clemens, who voluntarily made her a present of $500. of this amount as per the following:

"Stormfield
Redding
Connecticut

December 24, 1908.
Received from Miss I. V. Lyon Five Hundred Dollars and interest to date, in part payment of money borrowed to rehabilitate the house called The Lobster Pot.
(signed) S. L. Clemens."

Consequently Mr. Clemens has, by the tactics alluded to, become possessed of the *record* title to the cottage: has my personal notes for $982.47; is under agreement with me to take my notes for the balance of the money he loaned; has taken back his present of $500. to Miss Lyon; has $1,500. in money, the proceeds of the mortgage (which we do not know whether the deed recited or not, and which mortgage, so far as we are aware, has not been, as yet, satisfied with the proceeds of the same, to wit: the said $1,500.): has not repaid Mrs. Ashcroft the sum of approximately $100. to $150. recently expended on the cottage (details of which I can furnish later.)

I have endeavored to give you by this long letter, both sides of the controversy. Any further details that you wish that I can supply, please ask me for them. Your representative, Mr. Lark, at our conference yesterday at Mr. R. A. Mansfield Hobbs' office, wanted to know my attitude, which briefly is:

Neither Mrs. Ashcroft nor I have any desire to be belligerent or litigious, but we are both extremely hurt by Mr. Clemens' actions, attitude and ingratitude (I personally having performed many services for him for several years under sometimes difficult and trying circumstances, without any compensation whatsoever, but purely out of my fondness and respect for him), and fully intend to protect our rights and Mrs. Ashcroft's reputation before our friends and the public, regardless of whom it will now affect. If this can be accomplished without further litigation and notoriety, we shall be pleased, but the following conditions must be complied with, not that I state them arbitrarily, but only in justice and protection to ourselves:

First: An exchange of general releases for all acts or actions to date, between Mr. Clemens and Mrs. Ashcroft, and Mr. Clemens and me.

Second: A signed letter from Mr. Clemens to Mrs. Ashcroft, in about the following form:

"My dear Mrs. Ashcroft:
    With reference to our recent misunderstandings, and the unfortunate airing of the same in the press due to my attachment of your property, I beg to state that I have had your administration of my financial and other affairs investigated and find the same to have been properly and satisfactorily conducted by you, and I regret that any criticism by any one of you in this respect should have occurred.
                                                    Yours, sincerely,
                                                    S. L. Clemens."

Third: Satisfaction of the mortgage on the property at Redding, with the $1,500. received from Mrs. Ashcroft for that purpose.

Fourth: Withdrawal of the attachment on Mrs. Ashcroft's property at Farmington, Conn.

Fifth: Return of my notes, and release from my obligation to provide further notes.

Sixth: Return of the present of $500. to Mrs. Ashcroft, and reimbursement of the recent expenditures on the cottage, amounting to about $100. to $150., details to be furnished by me.

Seventh: I should be equitably reimbursed for my two months' work and expenses, on the accounting and auditing, which I made at Mr. Clemens' request.

—:—:—:—

On my part, if the above settlement is made, I will retire from my connection with the Mark Twain Company, and will consent to the cancellation of my contract with the Company, on payment of my percentage to date of cancellation, and payment of the Company's debts contracted during my administration of its affairs; a certified copy of some suitable resolution of regret at my resignation and satisfaction with my services, to be passed by the directors, to be given to me; no interference with my work and the proposed contract with Sir Thomas Lipton in regard to the Plasmon Milk Products Co. to be permitted, Mr. E. E. Loomis now representing Mr. Clemens' interests in the Company. Of course, it would be understood that with the exchange of releases, no action would be brought by us to set aside the deed of the property at Redding, Conn.

With kind regards, and again assuring you as I did before my departure for England that I am only too willing to give you any and all information in my power, believe me,

Yours, sincerely,

PREVIOUS PUBLICATION

Below is a list of each piece in this volume, identifying its earliest publication, if any. Separate publications of the various writings that Clemens incorporated into the *Autobiography,* such as speeches, letters, and literary works, are not tracked, unless the published text was based on the autobiographical dictation. The designation "partial" may mean publication of anything from an excerpt to a nearly complete piece. Short quotations from the typescripts in critical or biographical works are not accounted for. Charles Neider, the editor of *The Autobiography of Mark Twain (AMT),* reordered and recombined excerpts to such an extent that all publication in his volume is considered "partial." At the end of this appendix is a list of the "Chapters from My Autobiography" published in NAR installments between 7 September 1906 and December 1907. All works cited by an abbreviation or short title are fully cited in References.

Autobiographical Dictations, March 1907–December 1909

1 Mar 1907: previously unpublished.
6 Mar 1907: previously unpublished.
26 Mar 1907: previously unpublished.
27 Mar 1907: previously unpublished.
28 Mar 1907: NAR 18, 118–19, partial.
8 Apr 1907: previously unpublished.
9 Apr 1907: SLC 1981.
10 Apr 1907: SLC 1981, partial.
11 Apr 1907: Salsbury 1965, 33–34, 38, 58, 60, 62, partial.
20 Apr 1907: previously unpublished.
18 May 1907: previously unpublished.
23 May 1907: *AMT,* 348–49; Lathem 2006, 4–5.
24 May 1907: previously unpublished.
26 May 1907: *MTE,* 358–66; *AMT,* 138–43.
29 May 1907: *MTE,* 19–22.
30 May 1907: *MTE,* 22–24, partial.
24 July 1907: Lathem 2006, 11–12.
25 July 1907: Lathem 2006, 22–23, 38–45.

26 July 1907: NAR 23, 169–71, partial; Lathem 2006, 45–46, 54–57.

30 July 1907: NAR 23, 171–73, partial; *MTE,* 320–23, partial; Lathem 2006, 57–59, 62–70.

10 Aug 1907: SLC 2010b, partial; *L3,* 435, partial.

16 Aug 1907: *MTE,* 323–28; *AMT,* 350–53.

17 Aug 1907: *MTE,* 328–31; Lathem 2006, 79–80.

19 Aug 1907: *MTE,* 331–38, partial; Lathem 2006, 82–84, partial.

22 Aug 1907: Lathem 2006, 85–87.

23 Aug 1907: Lathem 2006, 88–89.

26 Aug 1907: Lathem 2006, 91–93.

27 Aug 1907: Lathem 2006, 93–94.

28 Aug 1907: Lathem 2006, 94–97.

29 Aug 1907: Lathem 2006, 97–101.

30 Aug 1907: Lathem 2006, 108–9, partial.

31 Aug 1907: Lathem 2006, 109–12.

4 Sept 1907: *MTE,* 239–43, partial.

6 Sept 1907: *MTE,* 338–42.

12 Sept 1907: *MTE,* 342–46.

13 Sept 1907: *MTE,* 14–19 [dated 7 Sept 1907], partial.

26 Sept 1907: previously unpublished.

1 Oct 1907: Lathem 2006, 30–32.

2 Oct 1907: Lathem 2006, 112–17.

3 Oct 1907: NAR 25, 489–94; *MTE,* 351–58; *AMT,* 154–58.

5 Oct 1907: Cooley 1991, 73–75, partial.

7 Oct 1907: previously unpublished.

10 Oct 1907: previously unpublished.

11 Oct 1907: *MTE,* 213–28, partial; *AMT,* 174–83.

18 Oct 1907: *MTE,* 7–10, partial; SLC 2010a, 231–32, partial.

21 Oct 1907: *MTE,* 10–14; SLC 2010a, 232–35.

25 Oct 1907: previously unpublished.

1 Nov 1907: *MTE,* 4–7, partial.

2 Dec 1907: *MTE,* 36–51.

10 Dec 1907: *MTE,* 51–60.

12 Dec 1907: previously unpublished.

13 Jan 1908: *MTE,* 312–19, partial; *AMT,* 353–57.

12 Feb 1908: previously unpublished.

13 Feb 1908: Cooley 1991, 102–6.

14 Feb 1908: Cooley 1991, 106–7 [dated Apr 1908], 127–31, partial.

19 Feb 1908: previously unpublished.

16 Apr 1908: previously unpublished.

17 Apr 1908: Arthur L. Scott 1966, 116–22, partial; Cooley 1991, 137–41, partial.

27 Apr 1908: previously unpublished.

28 Apr 1908: previously unpublished.

29 Apr 1908: SLC 2009, 87–94.

21 May 1908: *MTE,* 96–105, partial.

22 May 1908: previously unpublished.

3 June 1908: previously unpublished.

26 June 1908: *MTE,* 347, partial.

3 July 1908: *MTE,* 292–95, partial; *AMT,* 357–60.

6 July 1908: *AMT,* 360–62.

7 July 1908: *MTE,* 303–9; *AMT,* 290–94.

8 July 1908: *MTE,* 295–301; *AMT,* 362–66.

9 July 1908: *MTE,* 301–3; *AMT,* 366–67.

10 July 1908: *AMT,* 368–70.

14 July 1908: *MTE,* 24–33, partial.

16 July and 12 Sept 1908: *MTE,* 1–4, 34, partial; *MTB,* 3:1633–36, partial.

16 Aug 1908: SLC 1923a, 351–54.

6 Oct 1908: SLC 2004, 56–57, partial.

31 Oct 1908: *MTE,* 349–51, partial.

2 Nov 1908: previously unpublished.

5 Nov 1908: previously unpublished.

12 Nov 1908: previously unpublished.

24 Nov 1908: *MTB,* 3:1640–42, partial.

8 Dec 1908: previously unpublished.

10 Dec 1908: previously unpublished.

16 Dec 1908: previously unpublished.

22 Dec 1908: SLC 1909d.

Christmas Day, 1908: SLC 2010, 235–38.

5 Jan 1909: previously unpublished.

11 Jan 1909: Shapiro 2014, 353–57.

10 Mar 1909: Cooley 1991, 254–55, partial.

25 Mar 1909: SLC 1909a, 144–50.

16 Apr 1909: previously unpublished.

"Note to Chapter . . . ": previously unpublished.

21 Oct 1909: previously unpublished.

"Closing Words of My Autobiography": SLC 1911, partial; *AMT,* 371–80.

"Chapters from My Autobiography" in the *North American Review,* 1906–1907

The texts listed below in italic type were published in full or nearly so—that is, with no more than a paragraph or occasional sentence omitted.

Installment	*Published*	*Contents*
NAR 1	7 Sept 1906	AD 26 Mar 1906 (Introduction); My Autobiography [Random Extracts from It] (first part)
NAR 2	21 Sept 1906	AD, *21 May 1906;* Scraps from My Autobiography. From Chapter IX (first part); *[Robert Louis Stevenson and Thomas Bailey Aldrich];* AD, 3 Apr 1906
NAR 3	5 Oct 1906	ADs, 1 Feb 1906, 2 Feb 1906, 5 Feb 1906
NAR 4	19 Oct 1906	ADs, 7 Feb 1906, *8 Feb 1906*
NAR 5	2 Nov 1906	ADs, *9 Feb 1906, 12 Feb 1906*
NAR 6	16 Nov 1906	ADs, 26 Feb 1906, *7 Mar 1906,* 22 Mar 1906
NAR 7	7 Dec 1906	ADs, 5 Mar 1906, 6 Mar 1906, 23 Mar 1906
NAR 8	21 Dec 1906	AD, 19 Jan 1906
NAR 9	4 Jan 1907	ADs, *13 Dec 1906, 1 Dec 1906, 2 Dec 1906*
NAR 10	18 Jan 1907	ADs, 28 Mar 1906, 29 Mar 1906
NAR 11	1 Feb 1907	ADs, 29 Mar 1906 (misdated 28 Mar in the NAR), 2 Apr 1906
NAR 12	15 Feb 1907	[John Hay]; ADs, 5 Apr 1906, 6 Apr 1906
NAR 13	1 Mar 1907	My Autobiography [Random Extracts from It] (second part)
NAR 14	15 Mar 1907	ADs, *6 Dec 1906,* 17 Dec 1906, 11 Feb 1907 (misdated 10 Feb in the NAR), *12 Feb 1907,* 17 Jan 1906
NAR 15	5 Apr 1907	ADs, *8 Oct 1906, 22 Jan 1907*
NAR 16	19 Apr 1907	ADs, 12 Jan 1906, 13 Jan 1906, 15 Jan 1906
NAR 17	3 May 1907	AD, 15 Oct 1906; Scraps from My Autobiography. From Chapter IX (second part)
NAR 18	17 May 1907	ADs, 21 Dec 1906, 28 Mar 1907
NAR 19	7 June 1907	ADs, 21 Dec 1906 (with note dated 22 Dec), 19 Nov 1906, 30 Nov 1906, *5 Sept 1906*

NAR 20	5 July 1907	*Notes on "Innocents Abroad";* AD, 23 Jan 1907
NAR 21	2 Aug 1907	ADs, 8 Nov 1906, 8 Mar 1906, *6 Jan 1907*
NAR 22	Sept 1907	ADs, *10 Oct 1906,* 19 Jan 1906 (dated 12 Mar 1906 in the NAR, with note dated 13 May 1907), *20 Dec 1906*
NAR 23	Oct 1907	ADs, 9 Mar 1906, *16 Mar 1906,* 26 July 1907, 30 July 1907
NAR 24	Nov 1907	ADs, *9 Oct 1906, 16 Oct 1906,* 11 Oct 1906, *12 Oct 1906,* 23 Jan 1907
NAR 25	Dec 1907	ADs, 11 Jan 1906, *3 Oct 1907*

NOTE ON THE TEXT

The present volume consists of Mark Twain's last autobiographical dictations, and the manuscripts that he labeled as dictations or included in his *Autobiography*. They are arranged chronologically, completing the series begun in Volume 1 (which ended with the dictation of 30 March 1906) and continued in Volume 2 (which ended with the dictation of 28 February 1907). This volume begins with the dictation of 1 March 1907 and ends with "Closing Words of My Autobiography," a moving tribute to Jean Clemens written shortly after her death on 24 December 1909. The history of Mark Twain's work on his autobiography, from the preliminary manuscripts and dictations he produced between 1870 and 1905 through the dictation series that began in early 1906, is given in the Introduction to Volume 1, and the editorial rationale for choosing between variants and for correcting errors is likewise given in that volume, in the Note on the Text (pp. 1–58, 669–79). Both are also available in the electronic edition published at Mark Twain Project Online (*MTPO*). The editorial practices described there have been applied without change to the texts in this third and final volume.

With few exceptions, these typescripts and manuscripts have been in the Mark Twain Papers since their creation. There is little reason to doubt that their author intended all of them to be published eventually, as signaled by his including them in the archive of literary manuscripts that he entrusted to Albert Bigelow Paine. It is that intention to publish on which the editors have relied in constructing the authorially intended text from the relevant documents.

The case is rather different for the so-called "Ashcroft-Lyon Manuscript," which is published here for the first time. Written in the form of a letter to William Dean Howells between May and September 1909 (but never sent), it is by Clemens's own account his latest experiment in autobiography. He could easily have made it part of the *Autobiography*—but he did not.

Apart from its use as a "weapon" (see p. 326), Clemens had in mind another purpose, which required at least that the manuscript be preserved, though not necessarily published. In his address to the "Unborn Reader" he says, "In your day, a hundred years hence, this Manuscript will have a distinct value" as authentic documentation of "an intimate inside view of our domestic life of to-day not to be found in naked & comprehensive detail outside of its pages." Then he grows even more explicit: "This original Manuscript will be locked up & put away, & no copy of it made. Your eye, after mine, will be the first to see it." He did *not* have the manuscript typed, even though he had secretarial help readily available, and instead of putting it into Paine's and Clara's hands along with his other literary manuscripts, he entrusted it to his attorney, Charles T. Lark. It is hard to think of this document as anything but distinctly private.

Publishing it now, just a little more than one hundred years after Clemens stopped adding to it, the editors' goal is to create a typographical transcription that is a readable and reliable substitute for the original manuscript, just as it was when the author ordered it "locked up & put away." We therefore accord it the same treatment we give to other private documents, such as letters and notebooks—a treatment that is not designed to satisfy authorial expectations for publication, but rather the modern reader's legitimate expectations for accuracy and completeness. Since 1988, the editors have had at their disposal a system, called "plain text," designed to transcribe manuscripts "as fully and precisely as is compatible with a highly inclusive *critical text*—not a literal, or all-inclusive one, but a typographical transcription that is optimally legible and, at the same time, maximally faithful to the text that Clemens himself transmitted" ("Guide to Editorial Practice," *L6,* 698). Although this system was originally designed for publishing manuscript letters, it serves just as well for transcribing the intensely private Ashcroft-Lyon manuscript. Transcription into plain text is not "diplomatic" or "literal" or "all-inclusive" because it does not undertake, among other things, to reproduce the original lineation or pagination of the manuscript, except where lineation has meaning (in addresses and signatures for letters, for example). It does, however, undertake to change or omit as little as possible. It therefore includes errors and abbreviations in the original holographic or typewritten document, shows its cancellations and insertions, and represents as many quirks of the holograph as possible, so long as the editorial rendering does not itself become more difficult to read than the original. It is a critical text, above all, because the editors are charged with deciding which classes of detail to include (and when to make exceptions), and their choices are often constrained by whether those details can be intelligibly transcribed. The editorial symbols and conventions used in the text are defined at pp. 327–28. All textual details of the original deemed not susceptible to intelligible transcription are reported in the Textual Commentary at *MTPO*. For a detailed account of the transcription policy see "Guide to Editorial Practice" in *Mark Twain's Letters, Volume 6.*

WORD DIVISION IN THIS VOLUME

The following compound words that could be rendered either solid or with a hyphen are hyphenated at the end of a line in this volume. For purposes of quotation each is listed here with its correct form.

3.23–24	second-hand
5.16–17	feather-duster
10.35–36	watch-works
27.21–22	bookshelves
27.38–39	horse-races
31.28–29	best-hearted
74.32–33	water-colors
78.31–32	dreamland
101.27–28	good-fellowship
140.8–9	grandchildren
141.16–17	daytime
225.3–4	graveyard
232.26–27	hand-shake
250.13–14	boyhood
253.5–6	second-hand
290.26–27	schoolboy
291.22–23	openhearted
293.32–33	clergyman
305.31–32	mastersongs
342.10–11	tradesmen
368.15–16	mid-afternoon
416.38–39	check-books

REFERENCES

This list defines the abbreviations used in this volume and provides full bibliographic information for works cited by an author's name and a date, a short title, or an abbreviation. Works by members of the Clemens family may be found under the writer's initials: SLC, CC, and JC.

"Accountants' Statements and Schedules." 1909. "S. L. Clemens. Holder No. 1. Accountants' Statements and Schedules." Includes Schedules 1–12, financial spreadsheets for 1 March 1907 to 10 May 1909, CU-MARK.

AD. Autobiographical Dictation.

Aldrich, Lilian W.
 1911. "The House Where the Bad Boy Lived." *Outlook* 98 (27 May): 205–12.
 1920. *Crowding Memories.* Boston: Houghton Mifflin Company, Riverside Press.

Aldrich Home. 2013. "Aldrich Home: Mrs. Aldrich Tour." http://seacoastnh.com/postcards/aldrich/index.html. Accessed 6 August 2013.

Allen, Marion Schuyler. 1913. "Some New Anecdotes of Mark Twain." *Strand Magazine* 46 (August): 166–72.

Allison, Jim. 2013. "The NRA (National Reform Association) and the Christian Amendment." http://candst.tripod.com/nra.htm. Accessed 2 May 2013.

American Antiquarian Society. 2013. "Dorothy Sturgis Harding Papers, 1921–1976." http://www.americanantiquarian.org/Findingaids/dorothy_sturgis_harding.pdf. Accessed 17 June 2013.

AMT. 1959. *The Autobiography of Mark Twain.* Edited by Charles Neider. New York: Harper and Brothers.

"Ancestral File." 2012. Privately compiled genealogy of the Gillis family. https://family search.org. Accessed 12 December 2012.

Angel, Myron, ed. 1881. *History of Nevada.* Oakland, Calif.: Thompson and West. Index in Poulton 1966.

Annals of Psychical Science. 1907. "The Strange History of the Discovery of the 'Holy Grail.'" *Annals of Psychical Science* 6 (July–December): 228–31.

Ashcroft, Ralph W.
 1904. "Plasmon's Career in America. As recounted by R. W. Ashcroft." TS of twenty leaves, dated 22 September, CU-MARK.
 1905a. *The XXth Century Childe Harold. By Ralph W. Ashcroft, Manager of the Childe Harold Smelting and Refining Company.* New York: Published by the Society

for the Prevention of freeze-outs of minority stockholders; for the exposure of California shysters, and for the instruction as to the rudiments of New York State corporation law (which A B C they seem to have forgotten), of Messrs. Bugler, Burn Pulverizer & Clay-Moulder, Attorneys-at-law.

1905b. "Statement of R. W. Ashcroft in regard to S. L. Clemens' purchase of shares in the Plasmon Company of America." TS of nine leaves numbered [1]–6 and [1]–3, dated 24 February, CU-MARK.

1907. "What Happened. June 8 to July 22, 1907." TS of five leaves, CU-MARK.

1909. "Statement submitted in behalf of Mrs. Ashcroft, at the request of Mr. Stanchfield, in which are classified (E. & O. E.) the cash disbursements made by Mrs. Ashcroft for Mr. Clemens during the two years ending February 28, 1909." TS of six leaves, written ca. 10 August, CU-MARK.

Atherton, William Henry. 1914. "Robert Dennison Martin." In *Montreal, 1535–1914*. 3 vols. Montreal: S. J. Clarke Publishing Company.

AutoMT1. 2010. *Autobiography of Mark Twain, Volume 1*. Edited by Harriet Elinor Smith, Benjamin Griffin, Victor Fischer, Michael B. Frank, Sharon K. Goetz, and Leslie Diane Myrick. The Mark Twain Papers. Berkeley and Los Angeles: University of California Press. Also online at *MTPO*.

AutoMT2. 2013. *Autobiography of Mark Twain, Volume 2*. Edited by Benjamin Griffin, Harriet Elinor Smith, Victor Fischer, Michael B. Frank, Sharon K. Goetz, and Leslie Diane Myrick. The Mark Twain Papers. Berkeley and Los Angeles: University of California Press. Also online at *MTPO*.

Bacon, Delia.

1856. "William Shakespeare and His Plays; an Inquiry Concerning Them." *Putnam's Monthly* 7 (January): 1–19.

1857. *The Philosophy of the Plays of Shakspere Unfolded*. With a preface by Nathaniel Hawthorne. Boston: Ticknor and Fields.

Bacon, Francis. 1841. *The Works of Francis Bacon, Lord Chancellor of England*. A New Edition; with a Life of the Author, by Basil Montagu, Esq. 3 vols. Philadelphia: Carey and Hart.

Baetzhold, Howard G., and Joseph B. McCullough, eds. 1995. *The Bible According to Mark Twain: Writings on Heaven, Eden, and the Flood*. Athens: University of Georgia Press.

Bailey, Thomas A. 1932. "The World Cruise of the American Battleship Fleet, 1907–1909." *Pacific Historical Review* 1 (December): 389–423.

Baker, Anne Pimlott. 2002. *The Pilgrims of Great Britain: A Centennial History*. London: Profile Books.

BAL. 1955–91. *Bibliography of American Literature*. Compiled by Jacob Blanck. 9 vols. New Haven: Yale University Press.

Baldwin, Leland D. 1941. *The Keelboat Age on Western Waters*. Pittsburgh: University of Pittsburgh Press.

Barrett, William Fletcher. 1884. "Mark Twain on Thought-Transference." *Journal of the Society for Psychical Research* 1 (October): 166–67.

Baxter, Sylvester. 1912. "Francis Davis Millet: An Appreciation of the Man." *Art and Progress* 3 (July): 635–42.

Beckwith, George. 1891. *Old and Original Beckwith's Almanac, Volume 44.* Edited by Mrs. M. L. Beckwith Ewell. Birmington, Conn.: Bacon and Co.

Benham, Patrick. 1993. *The Avalonians.* Glastonbury: Gothic Image.

Berret, Anthony J. 1993. *Mark Twain and Shakespeare: A Cultural Legacy.* Lanham, Md.: University Press of America.

BmuHA. Bermuda Archives, Hamilton, Bermuda.

Bok, Edward W. 1922. *The Americanization of Edward Bok.* New York: Charles Scribner's Sons.

Booth, William Stone. 1909. *Some Acrostic Signatures of Francis Bacon, Baron Verulam of Verulam, Viscount St. Alban: Together with Some Others, All of Which Are Now for the First Time Deciphered and Published.* Boston: Houghton Mifflin Company.

Bowker, R. R. 1905. "The Post Office: Its Facts and Its Possibilities." *American Monthly Review of Reviews* 31 (March): 325–32.

Brahm, Gabriel Noah, and Forrest G. Robinson. 2005. "The Jester and the Sage: Twain and Nietzsche." *Nineteenth-Century Literature* 60 (September): 137–62.

Brake, Laurel, and Marysa Demoor. 2009. *Dictionary of Nineteenth-Century Journalism in Great Britain and Ireland.* Ghent: Academia Press.

Branch, James R., ed. 1903. *Proceedings of the Twenty-ninth Annual Convention of the American Bankers' Association.* New York: n.p.

Brooklyn Census. 1900. *Population Schedules of the Twelfth Census of the United States, 1900. Roll 1059. New York: Kings County, Borough of Brooklyn, Ward 22.* Photocopy in CU-MARK.

Brooks, Sydney. 1907. "England's Ovation to Mark Twain." *Harper's Weekly* 51 (27 July): 1086–89.

Bryce, Robert M. 1997. *Cook and Peary: The Polar Controversy, Resolved.* Mechanicsburg, Pa.: Stackpole Books.

Bryn Mawr College. 1907. *Program: Bryn Mawr College, Academic Year—1907–08.* Philadelphia: John C. Winston Company.

Budd, Louis J.

    1959. "Twain, Howells, and the Boston Nihilists." *New England Quarterly* 32 (September): 351–71.

    1962. *Mark Twain: Social Philosopher.* Bloomington: Indiana University Press.

    1992a. *Mark Twain: Collected Tales, Sketches, Speeches, & Essays, 1852–1890.* The Library of America. New York: Literary Classics of the United States.

    1992b. *Mark Twain: Collected Tales, Sketches, Speeches, & Essays, 1891–1910.* The Library of America. New York: Literary Classics of the United States.

    1999. *Mark Twain: The Contemporary Reviews.* Cambridge: Cambridge University Press.

Bullard, F. Lauriston. 1914. *Famous War Correspondents.* Boston: Little, Brown and Co.

Burke, Bernard. 1866. *A Genealogical History of the Dormant, Abeyant, Forfeited, and Extinct Peerages of the British Empire.* New ed. London: Harrison.

Burroughs, John. 1903. "Real and Sham Natural History." *Atlantic Monthly* 91 (March): 298–309.

Bush, Harold K. 2007. *Mark Twain and the Spiritual Crisis of His Age.* Tuscaloosa: University of Alabama Press.

Byron, George Gordon, Lord. 1900. *The Works of Lord Byron with His Letters and Journals, and His Life by Thomas Moore.* Edited by Richard Henry Stoddard. Volume 13. Boston: Francis A. Niccolls and Co.

California Death Index.

1905–39. *California Death Index, 1905–1939* [online database]. http://ancestry.com. Accessed 8 May 2014.

1940–97. *California Death Index, 1940–1997* [online database]. http://ancestry.com. Accessed 13 December 2012.

California Great Registers. 1866–98. *California Great Registers, 1866–1898* [online database]. http://ancestry.com. Accessed 13 December 2012.

Campbell, Ballard C.

2008a. *American Disasters: 201 Calamities That Shook the Nation.* Edited by Ballard C. Campbell. New York: Checkmark Books.

2008b. "1907: Financial Panic and Depression." In Campbell 2008a, 202–6.

Cardwell, Guy E. 1953. *Twins of Genius.* [East Lansing]: Michigan State College Press.

Carnegie, Andrew. 1920. *Autobiography of Andrew Carnegie.* Boston: Houghton Mifflin Company, Riverside Press.

Carson, John C. 1998. "Mark Twain's Georgia Angel-Fish Revisited." *Mark Twain Journal* 36 (Spring): 16–18.

CC (Clara Langdon Clemens, later Gabrilowitsch and Samossoud).

1931. *My Father, Mark Twain.* New York: Harper and Brothers.

1938. *My Husband, Gabrilowitsch.* New York: Harper and Brothers.

"Certificate of Incorporation." 1908. "Certificate of Incorporation of Mark Twain Company." Document signed and dated on 22 December and recorded on 23 December, State of New York, Book 252:645, photocopy in CU-MARK.

Cherep-Spiridovitch, Arthur. 1926. *The Secret World Government or "The Hidden Hand": The Unrevealed in History.* New York: Anti-Bolshevist Publishing Association.

Clark, Edward B. 1907. "Roosevelt and the Nature Fakirs." *Everybody's Magazine* 16 (June): 770–74.

Collins, Philip. 2011. "Public Readings." In *The Oxford Reader's Companion to Dickens.* Edited by Paul Schlicke. Online version. Oxford: Oxford University Press. http://www.oxfordreference.com/view/10.1093/acref/9780198662532.001.0001/acref-9780198662532. Accessed 14 February 2013.

Connecticut Death Index.

    1650–1934. *Connecticut, Deaths and Burials Index, 1650–1934* [online database]. http://ancestry.com. Accessed 20 June 2014.

    1949–2001. *Connecticut Death Index, 1949–2001* [online database]. http://ancestry.com. Accessed 28 June 2013.

Cooley, John, ed. 1991. *Mark Twain's Aquarium: The Samuel Clemens–Angelfish Correspondence, 1905–1910.* Athens: University of Georgia Press.

Coolidge, Louis A. 1910. *An Old-Fashioned Senator: Orville H. Platt of Connecticut.* New York: G. P. Putnam's Sons.

Cooper, Robert. 2000. *Around the World with Mark Twain.* New York: Arcade Publishing.

Courtney, Steve. 2011. *"The Loveliest Home That Ever Was": The Story of the Mark Twain House in Hartford.* Mineola, N.Y.: Dover Publications.

Cracroft-Brennan, Patrick, ed. 2012. *Cracroft's Peerage: The Complete Guide to the British Peerage and Baronetage.* http://www.cracroftspeerage.co.uk. Accessed 26 February 2013.

Crowell, Merle. 1922. "The Amazing Story of Martin W. Littleton." *American Magazine* 94 (December): 16–17, 78–86.

CSmH. Henry E. Huntington Library, Art Collections and Botanical Gardens, San Marino, Calif.

CSoM. Tuolomne County Museum, Sonora, Calif.

CtHMTH. Mark Twain House and Museum, Hartford, Conn.

CtHSD. Stowe-Day Memorial Library and Historical Foundation, Hartford, Conn.

CtY-BR. Yale University, Beinecke Rare Book and Manuscript Library, New Haven, Conn.

CU-BANC. University of California, The Bancroft Library, Berkeley.

Culme, John. 2010. "Mark Twain and the Ascot Gold Cup of 1907." http://www.myfamilysilver.com/blog/index.php/2010/05/mark-twain-and-the-ascot-gold-cup-of-1907. Accessed 13 December 2012.

CU-MARK. University of California, Mark Twain Papers, The Bancroft Library, Berkeley.

CY. 1979. *A Connecticut Yankee in King Arthur's Court.* Edited by Bernard L. Stein, with an introduction by Henry Nash Smith. The Works of Mark Twain. Berkeley and Los Angeles: University of California Press.

Daggett, John. 1894. *A Sketch of the History of Attleborough, from Its Settlement to the Division.* Boston: Press of Samuel Usher.

Daly, Charles P. 1892. *Reports of Cases Argued and Determined in the Court of Common Pleas for the City and County of New York.* New York: Banks and Brothers.

Darwin, Charles. 1887. *The Life and Letters of Charles Darwin, Including an Autobiographical Chapter.* Edited by Francis Darwin. 2 vols. New York: D. Appleton and Co.

Dater, John Grant. 1913. "Financial Department." *Munsey's Magazine* 48 (February): 824–27.

Davis, Deborah. 2012. *Guest of Honor: Booker T. Washington, Theodore Roosevelt, and the White House Dinner That Shocked a Nation.* New York: Atria Books.

Dawson, Simon. 2013. "Biographical Note. The Edward Carpenter Archive." http://www.edwardcarpenter.net/ecbiog.htm. Accessed 20 November 2013.

Democratic National Committee. 1908. *The Campaign Text Book of the Democratic Party of the United States, 1908.* Chicago: Democratic National Committee.

Dennis, Richard. 2008. "'Babylonian Flats' in Victorian and Edwardian London." *London Journal* 33 (November): 233–47.

Denny, William R. 1867. MS journal of the *Quaker City* excursion kept by "William R Denny | Winchester | Frederick County | Virginia | U. States, of America." First volume, 8 June–10 September, pages 1–141 plus newspaper clippings; second volume, 11 September–20 November, pages 142–276 plus newspaper clippings, CU-MARK.

de Ruiter, Brian. 2013. "Jamestown Ter-Centennial Exposition of 1907." *Encyclopedia Virginia.* http://www.encyclopediavirginia.org/ Jamestown_Ter-Centennial_Exposition_of_1907. Accessed 25 July 2013.

DFo. Folger Shakespeare Library, Washington, D.C.

Dilla, Geraldine. 1928. "Shakespeare and Harvard." *North American Review* 226 (July): 103–7.

DLC. United States Library of Congress, Washington, D.C.

Dolmetsch, Carl. 1992. *"Our Famous Guest": Mark Twain in Vienna.* Athens: University of Georgia Press.

Donald, Robert. 1903. "The Most Famous Press in the World." *World's Work and Play* 2 (June–November): 70–76.

Donnelly, Ignatius. 1888. *The Great Cryptogram: Francis Bacon's Cipher in the So-Called Shakespeare Plays.* Chicago: R. S. Peale and Co.

Doten, Alfred. 1973. *The Journals of Alfred Doten, 1849–1903.* Edited by Walter Van Tilburg Clark. 3 vols. Reno: University of Nevada Press.

Doubleday, F. N. 1972. *The Memoirs of a Publisher.* Garden City, N.Y.: Doubleday and Co.

DSI. Smithsonian Institution, Washington, D.C.

DSI-AAA. Smithsonian Institution, Archives of American Art, Washington, D.C.

Dugmore, A. Radclyffe. 1909. "Stormfield, Mark Twain's New Country Home." *Country Life in America* 15 (April): 607–11, 650, 652.

Duyckinck, Evert A., and George L. Duyckinck, eds. 1875. *Cyclopaedia of American Literature: Embracing Personal and Critical Notices of Authors, and Selections from Their Writings, from the Earliest Period to the Present Day; with Portraits, Autographs, and Other Illustrations.* Edited to date by M. Laird Simons. 2 vols. Philadelphia: William Rutter and Co. Citations are to the 1965 reprint edition, Detroit: Gale Research Company.

Educational Alliance. 2013. "Our History." http://www.edalliance.org. Accessed 6 February 2013.

Edwards, Adolph. 1907. *The Roosevelt Panic of 1907.* 2d ed. New York: Anitrock Publishing Company.

Ellsworth, William Webster. 1919. *A Golden Age of Authors: A Publisher's Recollection.* Boston: Houghton Mifflin Company.

Emerson, Ralph Waldo. 1870. *Society and Solitude.* Boston: Fields, Osgood and Co.

Erdman, Harley. 1995. "M. B. Curtis and the Making of the American Stage Jew." *Journal of American Ethnic History* 15 (Fall): 28–45.

"Estate of Samuel L. Clemens." 1910. "To the Court of Probate of and for the District of Redding. Estate of Samuel L. Clemens, Late of Redding in Said District—Deceased." Inventory of "all the property belonging to Samuel L. Clemens at the time of his death," prepared by Albert B. Paine and Harry A. Lounsbury, 15–18 October. Photocopy in CU-MARK.

ET&S1. 1979. *Early Tales & Sketches, Volume 1 (1851–1864).* Edited by Edgar Marquess Branch and Robert H. Hirst, with the assistance of Harriet Elinor Smith. The Works of Mark Twain. Berkeley and Los Angeles: University of California Press.

ET&S2. 1981. *Early Tales & Sketches, Volume 2 (1864–1865).* Edited by Edgar Marquess Branch and Robert H. Hirst, with the assistance of Harriet Elinor Smith. The Works of Mark Twain. Berkeley and Los Angeles: University of California Press.

FamSk. 2014. *A Family Sketch, and Other Private Writings by Mark Twain; Livy Clemens; Susy Clemens.* Edited by Benjamin Griffin. Oakland: University of California Press.

Farthingstone Village. 2014. "The History of the Joy Mead Gardens." http://www .farthingstone.org.uk/joymead/Joymead_history.html. Accessed 20 May 2014.

Fatout, Paul. 1976. *Mark Twain Speaking.* Iowa City: University of Iowa Press.

Fayant, Frank.
  1907a. "Fools and Their Money—IV." *Success Magazine* 10 (January): 9–11, 49–52.
  1907b. "The Wireless Telegraph Bubble." *Success Magazine* 10 (June): 387–89, 450–51.

Find a Grave Memorial.
  2013a. "Harry A. Lounsbury." http://www.findagrave.com. Accessed 12 September 2013.
  2013b. "James Burnett Brown." http://www.findagrave.com. Accessed 22 July 2013.

Fish, Everett W., ed. 1892. *Donnelliana: An Appendix to "Caesar's Column."* Chicago: F. J. Schulte and Co.

Fitzpatrick, Rita. 1941. "How Meningitis Toll Was Cut Told by Expert." Chicago *Tribune,* 17 May, 11.

Foner, Philip S. 1958. *Mark Twain: Social Critic.* New York: International Publishers.

Foss, Gerald D. 1998. *Portsmouth.* Dover, N.H.: Arcadia Publishing.

Friedman, William P., and Elizebeth S. Friedman. 1957. *The Shakespearean Ciphers Examined.* Cambridge: Cambridge University Press.

Fulton, Joe B. 2010. *The Reconstruction of Mark Twain: How a Confederate Bushwhacker Became the Lincoln of Our Literature.* Baton Rouge: Louisiana State University Press.

Galveston Census. 1900. *Population Schedules of the Twelfth Census of the United States, 1900. Roll T623. Texas: Galveston County.* Photocopy in CU-MARK.

Gibbon, Edward. 1880. *The History of the Decline and Fall of the Roman Empire.* With notes by Dean Milman, M. Guizot, and Dr. William Smith. 6 vols. New York: Harper and Brothers. SLC copy in CU-MARK.

Gilder, Rosamond. 1916. *Letters of Richard Watson Gilder.* Boston: Houghton Mifflin Company.

Gillis, William R. 1930. *Gold Rush Days with Mark Twain.* New York: Albert and Charles Boni.

Glyn, Anthony. 1968. *Elinor Glyn.* Rev. ed. London: Hutchinson and Co.

Glyn, Elinor.

    1908. *Mark Twain on "Three Weeks."* Printed for Mrs. Glyn (for private distribution only). London: Elinor Glyn.

    1936. *Romantic Adventure, Being the Autobiography of Elinor Glyn.* London: Ivor Nicholson and Watson.

Goethe, Johann Wolfgang von. 1930. *Conversations of Goethe with Eckermann.* Translated by John Oxenford. London: J. M. Dent.

Greenslet, Ferris. 1908. *The Life of Thomas Bailey Aldrich.* Boston: Houghton Mifflin Company.

Gribben, Alan. 1980. *Mark Twain's Library: A Reconstruction.* 2 vols. Boston: G. K. Hall and Co.

Griffin, Benjamin. 2010. "'American Laughter': Nietzsche Reads *Tom Sawyer.*" *New England Quarterly* 83 (March): 129–41.

Grumman, William E. 1904. *The Revolutionary Soldiers of Redding, Connecticut, and the Record of Their Services.* Hartford: Hartford Press.

Hamilton Census. 1860. *Population Schedules of the Eighth Census of the United States, 1860. Roll M653. Ohio: Hamilton County.* Photocopy in CU-MARK.

Hardesty, Jesse. 1899. *The Mother of Trusts: Railroads and Their Relation to "The Man with the Plow."* Kansas City, Mo.: Hudson-Kimberly Publishing Company.

Harding, Dorothy Sturgis. 1967. "Mark Twain Lands an Angel-fish." *Columbia Library Columns* 16 (February): 3–12.

Hardwick, Joan. 1994. *Addicted to Romance: The Life and Adventures of Elinor Glyn.* London: Andre Deutsch.

Hartford Census.

    1880. *Population Schedules of the Tenth Census of the United States, 1880. Roll T9. Connecticut: Hartford County.* Photocopy in CU-MARK.

    1910. *Population Schedules of the Thirteenth Census of the United States, 1910. Roll T624. Connecticut: Hartford County.* Photocopy in CU-MARK.

Henderson, Archibald. 1912. *Mark Twain.* New York: Frederick A. Stokes Company.

HF 2003. 2003. *Adventures of Huckleberry Finn.* Edited by Victor Fischer and Lin Salamo, with the late Walter Blair. The Works of Mark Twain. Berkeley and Los Angeles: University of California Press. Also online at *MTPO.*

HHR. 1969. *Mark Twain's Correspondence with Henry Huttleston Rogers.* Edited by Lewis

Leary. The Mark Twain Papers. Berkeley and Los Angeles: University of California Press.

Hill, Hamlin. 1973. *Mark Twain: God's Fool.* New York: Harper and Row.

Hodge, Carl Cavanagh. 2011. "The Global Strategist: The Navy as the Nation's Big Stick." In Ricard 2011, 257–73.

Hoffmann, Donald. 2006. *Mark Twain in Paradise: His Voyages to Bermuda.* Columbia: University of Missouri Press.

Holcombe, Return I. 1884. *History of Marion County, Missouri.* St. Louis: E. F. Perkins. [Citations are to the 1979 reprint edition, Hannibal: Marion County Historical Society.]

Holland America Line. 2014. "Holland America Blog: The Nieuw Amsterdam (I) of 1906." http://www.hollandamericablog.com/holland-line-ships-past-and-present/the-nieuw-amsterdam-i-of-1906/. Accessed 22 July 2014.

Holroyd, Michael. 1988–92. *Bernard Shaw.* 4 vols. New York: Random House.

Hooker, Isabella Beecher.

    1868a. "Two Letters on Woman Suffrage. I." *Putnam's Magazine* 12 (November): 603–6.

    1868b. "Two Letters on Woman Suffrage. II." *Putnam's Magazine* 12 (December): 701–11.

    1905. "The Last of the Beechers: Memories on My Eighty-third Birthday." *Connecticut Magazine* 9 (April–June): 286–98.

Horn, Jason Gary. 1996. *Mark Twain and William James: Crafting a Free Self.* Columbia: University of Missouri Press.

Hornig, Edgar A. 1958. "Campaign Issues in the Presidential Election of 1908." *Indiana Magazine of History* 54 (September): 237–64.

HorseRacing.co.uk. 2013. "Ascot Gold Cup." http://www.horseracing.co.uk/horse-racing/flat-racing/ascot-gold-cup.html. Accessed 1 February 2013.

"House v. Clemens." 1890. "New York Court of Common Pleas. Edward H. House, Plaintiff, against Samuel L. Clemens et al, Defendant. Certified copy of injunction order, undertaking, summons, complaint, affidavits, and orders." TS of eighty-nine leaves, CU-MARK.

Howden, Mary Louise. 1925. "Mark Twain as His Secretary at Stormfield Remembers Him." New York *Herald,* 13 December, section 7:1–4. Reprinted in Scharnhorst 2010, 318–25.

Howells, Elinor Mead. 1988. *If Not Literature: Letters of Elinor Mead Howells.* Edited by Ginette de B. Merrill and George Arms. Columbus: Ohio State University Press.

Hoyt, William Graves. 1976. "W. H. Pickering's Planetary Predictions and the Discovery of Pluto." *Isis* 67 (December): 551–64.

Huffman, James L. 2003. *A Yankee in Meiji Japan: The Crusading Journalist Edward H. House.* Lanham, Md.: Rowman and Littlefield Publishers.

Hull, William I. 1908. "Obligatory Arbitration and the Hague Conferences." *American Journal of International Law* 2 (October): 731–42.

Hurd, John Codman. 1858–62. *The Law of Freedom and Bondage in the United States.* 2 vols. Boston: Little, Brown and Co.

IEN. Northwestern University, Evanston, Ill.

Inds. 1989. *Huck Finn and Tom Sawyer among the Indians, and Other Unfinished Stories.* Foreword and notes by Dahlia Armon and Walter Blair. The Mark Twain Library. Berkeley and Los Angeles: University of California Press. Also online at *MTPO.*

InU-Li. Indiana University Lilly Rare Books, Bloomington.

Irwin, Wallace. 1909. *Letters of a Japanese Schoolboy.* Illustrated by Rollin Kirby. New York: Doubleday, Page and Co.

Jackson, Alice F., and Bettina Jackson. 1951. *Three Hundred Years American: The Epic of a Family.* N.p.: State Historical Society of Wisconsin.

JC (Jean Lampton Clemens). 1900–1907. *Diaries of Jean L. Clemens, 1900–1907.* 7 vols. MS, CSmH.

JLC. Jane Lampton Clemens.

John, Arthur. 1981. *The Best Years of the Century: Richard Watson Gilder, "Scribner's Monthly," and "Century Magazine," 1870–1909.* Urbana: University of Illinois Press.

Johnston, William M. 1972. *The Austrian Mind: An Intellectual and Social History, 1848–1938.* Berkeley: University of California Press.

Jones, Bernard E., ed. 1912. *Cassell's Cyclopaedia of Photography.* London: Cassell and Co.

Julian, John, ed. 1908. *A Dictionary of Hymnology Setting Forth the Origin and History of Christian Hymns of All Ages and Nations.* 2d rev. ed. London: John Murray.

Kelly, J. Wells, comp. 1863. *Second Directory of Nevada Territory.* San Francisco: Valentine and Co.

Kirkham, Pat, ed. 2000. *Women Designers in the USA, 1900–2000.* New Haven: Yale University Press.

Kirlicks, John A. 1913. *Sense and Nonsense in Rhyme.* Houston: Rein and Sons.

Kotsilibas-Davis, James. 1977. *Great Times, Good Times: The Odyssey of Maurice Barrymore.* Garden City, N.Y.: Doubleday and Co.

Kramer, Julia Wood. 1997. "My Grandfather and Mark Twain." TS of twelve leaves, CU-MARK.

Krausz, Sigmund. 1896. *Street Types of American Cities.* Chicago: Werner Company.

L1. 1988. *Mark Twain's Letters, Volume 1: 1853–1866.* Edited by Edgar Marquess Branch, Michael B. Frank, and Kenneth M. Sanderson. The Mark Twain Papers. Berkeley and Los Angeles: University of California Press. Also online at *MTPO.*

L2. 1990. *Mark Twain's Letters, Volume 2: 1867–1868.* Edited by Harriet Elinor Smith, Richard Bucci, and Lin Salamo. The Mark Twain Papers. Berkeley and Los Angeles: University of California Press. Also online at *MTPO.*

L3. 1992. *Mark Twain's Letters, Volume 3: 1869.* Edited by Victor Fischer, Michael B. Frank, and Dahlia Armon. The Mark Twain Papers. Berkeley and Los Angeles: University of California Press. Also online at *MTPO.*

L4. 1995. *Mark Twain's Letters, Volume 4: 1870–1871.* Edited by Victor Fischer, Michael

B. Frank, and Lin Salamo. The Mark Twain Papers. Berkeley and Los Angeles: University of California Press. Also online at *MTPO.*

L5. 1997. *Mark Twain's Letters, Volume 5: 1872–1873.* Edited by Lin Salamo and Harriet Elinor Smith. The Mark Twain Papers. Berkeley and Los Angeles: University of California Press. Also online at *MTPO.*

L6. 2002. *Mark Twain's Letters, Volume 6: 1874–1875.* Edited by Michael B. Frank and Harriet Elinor Smith. The Mark Twain Papers. Berkeley and Los Angeles: University of California Press. Also online at *MTPO.*

Letters 1876–1880. 2007. *Mark Twain's Letters, 1876–1880.* Edited by Victor Fischer, Michael B. Frank, and Harriet Elinor Smith, with Sharon K. Goetz, Benjamin Griffin, and Leslie Myrick. *Mark Twain Project Online.* Berkeley and Los Angeles: University of California Press. [To locate a letter text from its citation, select the Letters link at http://www.marktwainproject.org, then use the "Date Written" links in the left-hand column.]

Letters NP1. 2010. *Mark Twain's Letters Newly Published 1.* Edited by Victor Fischer, Michael B. Frank, Sharon K. Goetz, and Harriet Elinor Smith. *Mark Twain Project Online.* Berkeley and Los Angeles: University of California Press. [To locate a letter text from its citation, select the Letters link at http://www.marktwainproject.org, then use the "Date Written" links in the left-hand column.]

Lambert, Samuel W. 1908. "Melaena Neonatorum with Report of a Case Cured by Transfusion." *Medical Record* 73 (30 May): 885–87.

Lampton, Lucius Marion. 1990. *The Genealogy of Mark Twain.* Jackson, Miss.: Diamond L Publishing.

Lassen Census. 1900. *Population Schedules of the Twelfth Census of the United States, 1900. Roll T623. California: Lassen County.* Photocopy in CU-MARK.

Lathem, Edward Connery. 2006. *Mark Twain's Four Weeks in England, 1907.* Hartford: The Mark Twain House and Museum.

Lawson, Thomas W. 1904. "Standard Oil's Fight on Theodore Roosevelt." Chicago *Tribune,* 22 October, 8.

Lawton, Mary. 1925. *A Lifetime with Mark Twain: The Memories of Katy Leary, for Thirty Years His Faithful and Devoted Servant.* New York: Harcourt, Brace and Co.

Leary, Lewis, ed. 1961. *Mark Twain's Letters to Mary.* New York: Columbia University Press.

Leary, Warren E. 1997. "Who Reached the North Pole First? A Researcher Lays Claim to Solving the Mystery." New York *Times,* 17 February, 10.

Lee, Judith Yaross. 2014. "Brand Management: Samuel Clemens, Trademarks, and the Mark Twain Enterprise." *American Literary Realism* 47 (Fall): 27–54.

Lee, Sidney. 1908. *A Life of William Shakespeare.* 6th ed. London: Smith, Elder and Co.

Legislative Reference Library of Texas. 2012. *Texas Legislators: Past and Present* [online database]. http://www.lrl.state.tx.us/legeLeaders/members/membersearch.cfm. Accessed 7 December 2012.

Leitch, Alexander. 1978. *A Princeton Companion*. Princeton, N.J.: Princeton University Press.

Levine, Stephen L. 2011. "'A Serious Art and Literature of Our Own': Exploring Theodore Roosevelt's Art World." In Ricard 2011, 135–53.

Lewis, William Draper. 1919. *The Life of Theodore Roosevelt*. Philadelphia: John C. Winston Company.

Library of Congress. 2013. "American Memory: Edison Sound Recordings." http://memory.loc.gov/ammem/edhtml/edsndhm.html. Accessed 5 March 2013.

LNT. Tulane University, New Orleans, La.

Long, William J.

    1900. *Wilderness Ways*. Boston: Ginn and Co.

    1901. *Beasts of the Field*. Boston: Ginn and Co.

    1903a. *A Little Brother to the Bear, and Other Animal Stories*. Boston: Ginn and Co.

    1903b. "The Modern School of Nature-Study and Its Critics." *North American Review* 176 (May): 688–98.

    1903c. "Animal Surgery." *Outlook* 75 (12 September): 122–27.

    1904. "Science, Nature and Criticism." *Science* 19 (13 May): 760–67.

    1905. *Northern Trails: Some Studies of Animal Life in the Far North*. Boston: Ginn and Co.

    1906. *Brier-Patch Philosophy by "Peter Rabbit."* Boston: Ginn and Co.

    1907. *Wayeeses the White Wolf.* Boston: Ginn and Co.

Lowrey, Linda. 2013. "Hellen Elizabeth Martin" in "The Morton Family: From Lanark and Perthshire, Scotland, to Canada." http://ancestry.com. Accessed 16 January 2013.

Lucy, Henry W. 1909. *Sixty Years in the Wilderness: More Passages by the Way*. London: Smith, Elder and Co.

Lutts, Ralph H. 1990. *The Nature Fakers: Wildlife, Science and Sentiment*. Golden, Colo.: Fulcrum Publishing.

Lyon, Isabel V.

    1903–6. MS journal of seventy-four pages, with entries dated 7 November 1903 to 14 January 1906, CU-MARK.

    1905a. Diary in *The Standard Daily Reminder: 1905*. MS notebook of 368 pages, CU-MARK. [Lyon kept two diaries for 1905, this one and Lyon 1905b; some entries appear in both, but each also includes entries not found in the other.]

    1905b. Diary in *The Standard Daily Reminder: 1905*. MS notebook of 368 pages, photocopy in CU-MARK. [In 1971 the original diary was owned by Mr. and Mrs. Robert V. Antenne and Mr. and Mrs. James F. Dorrance, of Rice Lake, Wisconsin; its current location is unknown. Lyon kept two diaries for 1905, this one and Lyon 1905a; some entries appear in both, but each also includes entries not found in the other.]

    1906. Diary in *The Standard Daily Reminder: 1906*. MS notebook of 368 pages, CU-MARK.

    1907. Diary in *Date Book for 1907.* MS notebook of 368 pages, CU-MARK.

1907–8. Stenographic Notebook #4, with entries dated 5 October 1907 to 17 February 1908, CU-MARK.

1908. Diary in *The Standard Daily Reminder.* MS notebook of 368 pages, CU-MARK.

1909. Diary entries transcribed in Lyon to Howe, 6 February 1936, NN-BGC.

Lystra, Karen. 2004. *Dangerous Intimacy: The Untold Story of Mark Twain's Final Years.* Berkeley and Los Angeles: University of California Press.

MacAlister, Ian. 1938. "Mark Twain: Some Personal Reminiscences." *Landmark* 20 (March): 141–47.

Mac Donnell, Kevin. 2006. "Stormfield: A Virtual Tour." *Mark Twain Journal* 44 (Spring/Fall): 1–68.

Manhattan Census. 1910. *Population Schedules of the Thirteenth Census of the United States, 1910. Roll T624. New York: Manhattan.* Photocopy in CU-MARK.

Marion Census. 1870. *Population Schedules of the Ninth Census of the United States, 1870. Roll M593. Missouri: Marion County.* Photocopy in CU-MARK.

Mark Twain Library.

2014a. "History of the Mark Twain Library." http://www.marktwainlibrary. org/1aboutus-folder/history-of-the-mark-twain-library.htm. Accessed 11 February 2014.

2014b. "Samuel Clemens and the Mark Twain Library." http://www.marktwain library.org/9samuelclemens-folder/samuel-clemens-and-the-mark-twain-library .htm. Accessed 11 February 2014.

Mark Twain Project. 2014. "Copyright and Permissions." http://www.marktwainproject .org/copyright.shtml. Accessed 27 February 2014.

Matthews, Brander. 1899. "Biographical Criticism." In *The Innocents Abroad,* Volume 1 of the Autograph Edition of the Writings of Mark Twain, v–xxxiii. Hartford: American Publishing Company. [The essay also appeared in later collected editions.]

Maynard, George W. 1912. "Francis Davis Millett—A Reminiscence." *Art and Progress* 3 (July): 653–54.

McElhinney, Mark G.

1922. "Under the Whispering Pines." *Dental Digest* 28 (June): 355–61.

1927. *Morning in the Marsh: Poems for Lovers of the Great Outdoors.* Ottawa: Graphic Publications.

McFeely, Deirdre. 2012. *Dion Boucicault: Irish Identity on Stage.* Cambridge: Cambridge University Press.

McKeithan, Daniel Morley. 1959. "Madame Laszowska Meets Mark Twain." *Texas Studies in Literature and Language* 1 (Spring): 62–65.

McLynn, Frank.

1989. *Stanley: The Making of an African Explorer.* London: Constable.

1991. *Stanley: Sorcerer's Apprentice.* London: Constable.

MEC. Mary E. (Mollie) Clemens.

Metcalf, Priscilla. 1980. *James Knowles: Victorian Editor and Architect.* Oxford: Clarendon Press.

MFai. Millicent Library, Fairhaven, Mass.

MH-H. Harvard University, Houghton Library, Cambridge, Mass.

MiD. Detroit Public Library, Detroit, Mich.

Miller, John J. 2012. "How Teddy Roosevelt Saved Football." New York *Post* online, posted 12 May 2011, updated 22 January 2012. http://nypost.com/2011/04/17/how-teddy-roosevelt-saved-football/. Accessed 21 February 2014.

Miller, Tice L. 1981. *Bohemians and Critics: American Theatre Criticism in the Nineteenth Century.* Metuchen, N.J.: Scarecrow Press.

Millgate, Michael. 1992. *Testamentary Acts: Browning, Tennyson, James, Hardy.* Oxford: Clarendon Press.

MnHi. Minnesota Historical Society, St. Paul.

Moen, Jon. 2001. "The Panic of 1907." In *EH.Net Encyclopedia of Economic and Business History.* Edited by Robert Whaples. http://eh.net/encyclopedia/the-panic-of-1907/. Accessed 14 March 2013.

Moffett, Samuel E.

  1899. "Mark Twain. A Biographical Sketch." *McClure's Magazine* 13 (October): 523–29.

  1900. "Mark Twain: A Biographical Sketch by Samuel E. Moffett." In *How to Tell a Story and Other Essays,* Volume 22 of the Autograph Edition of the Writings of Mark Twain, 314–33. Hartford: American Publishing Company. [The essay also appeared in later collected editions.]

MoHH. Mark Twain Home Foundation, Hannibal, Mo.

MoHM. Mark Twain Museum, Hannibal, Mo.

"Money of Mr. Samuel L. Clemens." 1909. "Money of Mr. Samuel L. Clemens used by Miss Lyon. For the reconstruction and rehabilitation of her cottage. March 1, 1907 to February 28, 1908." TS of 1 leaf, CU-MARK.

Mooney, Michael Macdonald. 1976. *Evelyn Nesbit and Stanford White: Love and Death in the Gilded Age.* New York: William Morrow and Co.

Mott, Frank Luther.

  1950. *American Journalism: A History of Newspapers in the United States through 260 Years, 1690 to 1950.* Rev. ed. New York: Macmillan Company.

  1957. *A History of American Magazines, 1885–1905.* 2d printing [1st printing, 1938]. Cambridge: Belknap Press of Harvard University Press.

MS. Manuscript.

MTA. 1924. *Mark Twain's Autobiography.* Edited by Albert Bigelow Paine. 2 vols. New York: Harper and Brothers.

MTB. 1912. *Mark Twain: A Biography.* By Albert Bigelow Paine. 3 vols. New York: Harper and Brothers. [Volume numbers in citations are to this edition; page numbers are the same in all editions.]

MTE. 1940. *Mark Twain in Eruption.* Edited by Bernard DeVoto. New York: Harper and Brothers.

MTH. 1947. *Mark Twain and Hawaii.* By Walter Francis Frear. Chicago: Lakeside Press.

MTHL. 1960. *Mark Twain–Howells Letters*. Edited by Henry Nash Smith and William M. Gibson, with the assistance of Frederick Anderson. 2 vols. Cambridge: Belknap Press of Harvard University Press.

MTL. 1917. *Mark Twain's Letters*. Edited by Albert Bigelow Paine. 2 vols. New York: Harper and Brothers.

MTLP. 1967. *Mark Twain's Letters to His Publishers, 1867–1894*. Edited by Hamlin Hill. The Mark Twain Papers. Berkeley and Los Angeles: University of California Press.

MTPO. Mark Twain Project Online. Edited by the Mark Twain Project. Berkeley and Los Angeles: University of California Press. [Launched 1 November 2007.] http://www.marktwainproject.org.

Murphy, Gary. 2011. "Theodore Roosevelt, Presidential Power and the Regulation of the Market." In Ricard 2011, 154–72.

N&J1. 1975. *Mark Twain's Notebooks & Journals, Volume 1 (1855–1873)*. Edited by Frederick Anderson, Michael B. Frank, and Kenneth M. Sanderson. The Mark Twain Papers. Berkeley and Los Angeles: University of California Press.

N&J2. 1975. *Mark Twain's Notebooks & Journals, Volume 2 (1877–1883)*. Edited by Frederick Anderson, Lin Salamo, and Bernard Stein. The Mark Twain Papers. Berkeley and Los Angeles: University of California Press.

N&J3. 1979. *Mark Twain's Notebooks & Journals, Volume 3 (1883–1891)*. Edited by Robert Pack Browning, Michael B. Frank, and Lin Salamo. The Mark Twain Papers. Berkeley and Los Angeles: University of California Press.

NAR 1. 1906. "Chapters from My Autobiography.—I. By Mark Twain." *North American Review* 183 (7 September): 321–30. Galley proofs of the "Introduction" only (NAR 1pf) at ViU.

NAR 2. 1906. "Chapters from My Autobiography.—II. By Mark Twain." *North American Review* 183 (21 September): 449–60. Galley proofs (NAR 2pf) at ViU.

NAR 3. 1906. "Chapters from My Autobiography.—III. By Mark Twain." *North American Review* 183 (5 October): 577–89. Galley proofs (NAR 3pf) at ViU.

NAR 4. 1906. "Chapters from My Autobiography.—IV. By Mark Twain." *North American Review* 183 (19 October): 705–16. Galley proofs (NAR 4pf) at ViU.

NAR 5. 1906. "Chapters from My Autobiography.—V. By Mark Twain." *North American Review* 183 (2 November): 833–44. Galley proofs (NAR 5pf) at ViU.

NAR 6. 1906. "Chapters from My Autobiography.—VI." *North American Review* 183 (16 November): 961–70. Galley proofs (NAR 6pf) at ViU.

NAR 7. 1906. "Chapters from My Autobiography.—VII. By Mark Twain." *North American Review* 183 (7 December): 1089–95. Galley proofs (NAR 7pf) at ViU.

NAR 8. 1906. "Chapters from My Autobiography.—VIII. By Mark Twain." *North American Review* 183 (21 December): 1217–24. Galley proofs (NAR 8pf) at ViU.

NAR 9. 1907. "Chapters from My Autobiography.—IX. By Mark Twain." *North American Review* 184 (4 January): 1–14. Galley proofs (NAR 9pf) at ViU.

NAR 10. 1907. "Chapters from My Autobiography.—X. By Mark Twain." *North American Review* 184 (18 January): 113–19. Galley proofs (NAR 10pf) at ViU.

NAR 11. 1907. "Chapters from My Autobiography.—XI. By Mark Twain." *North American Review* 184 (1 February): 225–32. Galley proofs (NAR 11pf) at ViU.

NAR 12. 1907. "Chapters from My Autobiography.—XII. By Mark Twain." *North American Review* 184 (15 February): 337–46. Galley proofs (NAR 12pf) at ViU.

NAR 13. 1907. "Chapters from My Autobiography.—XIII. By Mark Twain." *North American Review* 184 (1 March): 449–63. Galley proofs (NAR 13pf) at ViU.

NAR 14. 1907. "Chapters from My Autobiography.—XIV. By Mark Twain." *North American Review* 184 (15 March): 561–71.

NAR 15. 1907. "Chapters from My Autobiography.—XV. By Mark Twain." *North American Review* 184 (5 April): 673–82. Galley proofs (NAR 15pf) at ViU.

NAR 16. 1907. "Chapters from My Autobiography.—XVI. By Mark Twain." *North American Review* 184 (19 April): 785–93.

NAR 17. 1907. "Chapters from My Autobiography.—XVII. By Mark Twain." *North American Review* 185 (3 May): 1–12. Galley proofs (NAR 17pf) at ViU.

NAR 18. 1907. "Chapters from My Autobiography.—XVIII. By Mark Twain." *North American Review* 185 (17 May): 113–22.

NAR 19. 1907. "Chapters from My Autobiography.—XIX. By Mark Twain." *North American Review* 185 (7 June): 241–51. Galley proofs (NAR 19pf) at ViU.

NAR 20. 1907. "Chapters from My Autobiography.—XX. By Mark Twain." *North American Review* 185 (5 July): 465–74.

NAR 21. 1907. "Chapters from My Autobiography—XXI. By Mark Twain." *North American Review* 185 (2 August): 689–98. Galley proofs (NAR 21pf) at ViU.

NAR 22. 1907. "Chapters from My Autobiography.—XXII. By Mark Twain." *North American Review* 186 (September): 8–21.

NAR 23. 1907. "Chapters from My Autobiography.—XXIII. By Mark Twain." *North American Review* 186 (October): 161–73.

NAR 24. 1907. "Chapters from My Autobiography.—XXIV. By Mark Twain." *North American Review* 186 (November): 327–36. Galley proofs (NAR 24pf) at ViU.

NAR 25. 1907. "Chapters from My Autobiography.—XXV. By Mark Twain." *North American Review* 186 (December): 481–94. Galley proofs (NAR 25pf) at ViU.

Nasaw, David. 2006. *Andrew Carnegie*. New York: Penguin Press.

NElmHi. Chemung County Historical Society, Elmira, N.Y.

New Haven Census. 1870. *Population Schedules of the Ninth Census of the United States, 1870. Roll M593. Connecticut: New Haven.* Photocopy in CU-MARK.

New York Passenger Lists. 1820–1957. *Passenger Lists of Vessels Arriving at New York, New York, 1820–1957* [online database]. http://ancestry.com. Accessed 6 August 2013.

New York Public Library. 2013. "Henry and Mary Anna Palmer Draper Papers, Manuscripts and Archives Division." http://archives.nypl.org/mss/838. Accessed 18 December 2013.

Nickerson, Matthew. 2012. "How the Fourth Became a Day of Celebration Rather than a Day of Carnage." Chicago *Tribune,* 1 July, 25.

NjWoE. Rutgers, The State University of New Jersey, Thomas A. Edison Papers Project.

NN-BGC. New York Public Library, Albert A. and Henry W. Berg Collection, New York, N.Y.

NNC. Columbia University, New York, N.Y.

NNPM. Pierpont Morgan Library, New York, N.Y.

"Nook Farm Genealogy." 1974. TS by anonymous compiler, CtHSD.

Norton, Charles Eliot. 1913. *Letters of Charles Eliot Norton. With Biographical Comment by His Daughter Sara Norton and M. A. DeWolfe Howe.* 2 vols. Boston: Houghton Mifflin Company.

NPV. Vassar College, Poughkeepsie, N.Y.

NYC Circa. 2011. "Bryant Park Place." http://nyccirca.blogspot.com/2011/07/virtually -every-building-in-new-york.html. Accessed 16 May 2013.

Ober, Karl Patrick. 2011. "Mark Twain's 'Watermelon Cure.'" *Journal of Alternative and Complementary Medicine* 17 (October): 877–80.

OC. Orion Clemens.

O'Connor, Richard. 1963. *Courtroom Warrior: The Combative Career of William Travers Jerome.* Boston: Little, Brown and Co.

O'Connor, T. P. 1907. "Mark Twain." *P.T.O.* 2 (29 June): 801–2.

OLC. Olivia (Livy) Langdon Clemens.

OLL. Olivia (Livy) Louise Langdon.

Oxford Census. 1900. *Population Schedules of the Twelfth Census of the United States, 1900. Roll T623. Maine: Oxford County, Lovell Township.* Photocopy in CU-MARK.

Oxford Historical Pageant. 1907. *The Oxford Historical Pageant. In Aid of the Radcliffe Infirmary, Oxford Eye Hospital, &c.* 2d ed. Oxford: n.p.

Oxford University Press. 2013. "A Short History of Oxford University Press." http:// global.oup.com/about/oup_history/?cc=us. Accessed 7 January 2013.

Page, Walter Hines. 1908. "The Archbold-Foraker Letters." *The World's Work* 17 (November): 10851–55.

Paine, Albert Bigelow.

1909. *Captain Bill McDonald, Texas Ranger: A Story of Frontier Reform.* New York: J. J. Little and Ives Company.

1910. *The Ship-Dwellers: A Story of a Happy Cruise.* New York: Harper and Brothers.

PAM. Pamela Ann Moffett.

Peck, Harry Thurston, et al., eds. 1899. *Masterpieces of Ancient and Modern Literature.* 20 vols. N.p.

Penry, Tara. 2010. "The Chinese in Bret Harte's *Overland:* A Context for Truthful James." *American Literary Realism* 43 (Fall): 74–82.

Pettit, Arthur G.

1970. "Merely Fluid Prejudice: Mark Twain, Southerner, and the Negro." Ph.D. diss., University of California, Berkeley.

1974. *Mark Twain and the South.* Lexington: University Press of Kentucky.

Pond, James B. 1900. *Eccentricities of Genius: Memories of Famous Men and Women of the Platform and Stage.* New York: G. W. Dillingham Company.

Post, C. W. 1898. "Postal Currency." *North American Review* 167 (December): 628–30.

Post, Emily. 1911. "Tuxedo Park: An American Rural Community." *Century Magazine* 82 (October): 795–805.

Potter, Ambrose George. 1929. *A Bibliography of the Rubáiyát of Omar Khayyám, Together with Kindred Matter in Prose and Verse Pertaining Thereto.* London: Ingpen and Grant.

Poulton, Helen J. 1966. *Index to History of Nevada.* Reno: University of Nevada Press.

"Power of Attorney." 1907. "Power of Attorney. S. L. Clemens to S. V. Lyon." Record copy dated 7 May 1907, CU-MARK. Published in Trombley 2010, 136.

Pratt and Whitney. 2014. "History." http://prattandwhitney.com/Content/History.asp. Accessed 6 May 2014.

Prime, Samuel Irenaeus. 1875. *The Life of Samuel F. B. Morse, LL.D., Inventor of the Electro-Magnetic Recording Telegraph.* New York: D. Appleton and Co.

Pringle, Henry F. 1956. *Theodore Roosevelt: A Biography.* New York: Harcourt, Brace and World.

Pullman, John S. 1916. "Obituary Sketch of Stiles Judson." In *Cases Argued and Determined in the Supreme Court of Errors of the State of Connecticut, December, 1914–December, 1915,* 722–23. Edited by James P. Andrews. New York: Banks Law Publishing Company.

Quarstein, John V., and Julia Steere Clevenger. 2009. *Old Point Comfort Resort: Hospitality, Health and History on Virginia's Chesapeake Bay.* Charleston, S.C.: History Press.

Quick, Dorothy. 1961. *Enchantment: A Little Girl's Friendship with Mark Twain.* Norman: University of Oklahoma Press.

Rafferty, Jennifer L. 1996. "'The Lyon of St. Mark': A Reconsideration of Isabel Lyon's Relationship to Mark Twain." *Mark Twain Journal* 34 (Fall): 43–55.

Ranson, Edward. 1965–66. "Nelson A. Miles as Commanding General, 1895–1903." *Military Affairs* 29 (Winter): 179–200.

Rasmussen, R. Kent. 2007. *Critical Companion to Mark Twain: A Literary Reference to His Life and Work.* 2 vols. New York: Facts on File.

Redding Census.

 1900. *Population Schedules of the Twelfth Census of the United States, 1900. Roll T623. Connecticut: Fairfield County, Redding Township.* Photocopy in CU-MARK.

 1910. *Population Schedules of the Thirteenth Census of the United States, 1910. Roll T624. Connecticut: Fairfield County, Redding Township.* Photocopy in CU-MARK.

Rhodes Trust. 2013. "History of the Rhodes Trust." http://www.rhodeshouse.ox.ac.uk/rhodes-trust/history. Accessed 7 February 2013.

RI 1993. 1993. *Roughing It.* Edited by Harriet Elinor Smith, Edgar Marquess Branch, Lin Salamo, and Robert Pack Browning. The Works of Mark Twain. Berkeley and Los Angeles: University of California Press. [This edition supersedes the one published in 1972.]

Ricard, Serge, ed. 2011. *A Companion to Theodore Roosevelt.* Chichester, West Sussex: Wiley-Blackwell.

Rice, Alice Hegan.

    1909. *Mr. Opp.* New York: The Century Company.

    1940. *The Inky Way.* New York: D. Appleton-Century Company.

Richards, Jeffrey. 2005. *Sir Henry Irving: A Victorian Actor and His World.* London: Hambledon and London.

Richmond Census. 1880. *Population Schedules of the Tenth Census of the United States, 1880. Roll T9. New York: Richmond County.* Photocopy in CU-MARK.

Riedi, Eliza. 2002. "Women, Gender, and the Promotion of Empire: The Victoria League, 1901–1914." *The Historical Journal* 45 (2002): 569–99.

Roberts, Brian. 1969. *Cecil Rhodes and the Princess.* London: Hamish Hamilton.

Rockefeller University. 2013. "The First Effective Therapy for Meningococcal Meningitis." http://centennial.rucares.org/index.php?page=Meningitis. Accessed 25 January 2013.

Rockey, J. L., ed. 1892. *History of New Haven County, Connecticut.* 2 vols. New York: W. W. Preston and Co.

Roosevelt, Theodore.

    1893a. *Hunting the Grisly and Other Sketches.* New York: G. P. Putnam's Sons.

    1893b. *The Wilderness Hunter.* New York: G. P. Putnam's Sons.

    1905. *Outdoor Pastimes of an American Hunter.* New York: Charles Scribner's Sons.

    1907. "'Nature Fakers.'" *Everybody's Magazine* 17 (September): 427–30.

    1908. *The Roosevelt Policy: Speeches, Letters and State Papers, Relating to Corporate Wealth and Closely Allied Topics, of Theodore Roosevelt.* With an introduction by Andrew Carnegie. 2 vols. New York: Current Literature Publishing Company.

    1922. *Theodore Roosevelt: An Autobiography.* New York: Charles Scribner's Sons.

Rose, Roger G. 1988. "Woodcarver F. N. Otremba and the Kamehameha Statue." *Hawaiian Journal of History* 22 (1988): 131–46.

RPB-JH. Brown University, John Hay Library of Rare Books and Special Collections, Providence, R.I.

Rubin, Louis D., Jr. 1969. *George W. Cable: The Life and Times of a Southern Heretic.* New York: Pegasus.

Rugoff, Milton. 1981. *The Beechers: An American Family in the Nineteenth Century.* New York: Harper and Row.

Russia Culture. 2012. "Maj Arthur I. Cherep-Spiridovich." http://www.findagrave.com/cgi-bin/fg.cgi?page=gr&GRid=99180758. Accessed 4 December 2012.

Ryan, Deborah Sugg. 2007. "'Pageantitis': Frank Lascelles' 1907 Oxford Historical Pageant, Visual Spectacle and Popular Memory." *Visual Culture in Britain* 8 (2007): 63–82.

Saint-Gaudens, Homer, ed. 1913. *The Reminiscences of Augustus Saint-Gaudens.* 2 vols. New York: The Century Company.

Salem Census. 1900. *Population Schedules of the Twelfth Census of the United States, 1900. Roll T623. Massachusetts: Essex County, Salem Township.* Photocopy in CU-MARK.

Salm. Collection of Peter A. Salm.

Salsbury, Edith Colgate, ed. 1965. *Susy and Mark Twain: Family Dialogues.* New York: Harper and Row.

San Francisco Census. 1900. *Population Schedules of the Twelfth Census of the United States, 1900. Roll T623. California: San Francisco.* Photocopy in CU-MARK.

Saunders, Hortense. 1925. "Says Mark Twain's Private Secretary: 'I Was Afraid to Laugh at His Jokes.'" Elmira *Star Gazette,* 27 December, clipping in Scrapbook 145:55, NElmHi.

Scharnhorst, Gary, ed.

    2006. *Mark Twain: The Complete Interviews.* Tuscaloosa: University of Alabama Press.

    2010. *Twain in His Own Time.* Iowa City: University of Iowa Press.

Schmidt, Barbara.

    2005. "A Strange Case of the Disputed Millets." http://www.twainquotes.com/disputedmillets.html. Accessed 5 December 2005.

    2008. "Chronology of Known Mark Twain Speeches, Public Readings, and Lectures." http://www.twainquotes.com/SpeechIndex.html. Accessed 24 October 2008.

    2009. "Mark Twain's Angel-Fish Roster and Other Young Women of Interest." http://www.twainquotes.com/angelfish/angelfish.html. Accessed 20 May 2009.

    2010. "A History of and Guide to Uniform Editions of Mark Twain's Works." http://www.twainquotes.com/UniformEds/toc.html. Accessed 19 November 2010.

    2013a. "Mark Twain and Elinor Glyn." http://www.twainquotes.com/interviews/ElinorGlynInterview.html. Accessed 31 January 2013.

    2013b. "Mark Twain's Last Butler: Claude Joseph Beuchotte." http://www.twainquotes.com/beuchotte.html. Accessed 10 September 2013.

    2014. "Mark Twain on Czars, Siberia and the Russian Revolution." http://www.twainquotes.com/Revolution/revolution.html. Accessed 1 April 2014.

Schoenbaum, S. 1991. *Shakespeare's Lives.* New ed. Oxford: Clarendon Press.

Scotland Census. 1901. *Scotland Census. Lanarkshire: Govan* [online database]. http://ancestry.com. Accessed 20 March 2014.

Scott, Arthur L. 1966. *On the Poetry of Mark Twain, with Selections from His Verse.* Urbana: University of Illinois Press.

Scott, James Brown. 1907. "Editorial Comment: The National Arbitration and Peace Conference at New York." *American Journal of International Law* 1 (July): 727–29.

Searle, William. 1976. *The Saint and the Skeptics: Joan of Arc in the Work of Mark Twain, Anatole France, and Bernard Shaw.* Detroit: Wayne State University Press.

Shapiro, James, ed. 2014. *Shakespeare in America: An Anthology from the Revolution to Now.* The Library of America. New York: Literary Classics of the United States.

Shelden, Michael. 2010. *Mark Twain, Man in White: The Grand Adventure of His Final Years.* New York: Random House.

SLC (Samuel Langhorne Clemens).

    1865. "Jim Smiley and His Jumping Frog." New York *Saturday Press* 4 (18 November): 248–49. Reprinted in *ET&S2,* 282–88.

1867a. *The Celebrated Jumping Frog of Calaveras County, and Other Sketches.* Edited by John Paul. New York: C. H. Webb.

1867b. *The Celebrated Jumping Frog of Calaveras County, and Other Sketches.* Edited by John Paul. London: George Routledge and Sons.

1867c. "Female Suffrage. Views of Mark Twain." St. Louis *Missouri Democrat,* 12 March, 4, clipping in Scrapbook 1:64, CU-MARK. Reprinted in Budd 1992a, 214–16.

1867d. "Female Suffrage. A Volley from the Down-Trodden." St. Louis *Missouri Democrat,* 13 March, 4, clipping in Scrapbook 1:64, CU-MARK. Reprinted in Budd 1992a, 216–19.

1867e. "Female Suffrage. The Iniquitous Crusade Against Man's Regal Birthright Must Be Crushed." St. Louis *Missouri Democrat,* 15 March, 4, clipping in Scrapbook 1:65–66, CU-MARK. Reprinted in Budd 1992a, 219–23.

1867f. "Female Suffrage." New York *Sunday Mercury,* 7 April, 3. Reprinted in Budd 1992a, 224–27.

1868a. "An Important Question Settled." Letter dated 4 March. Cincinnati *Evening Chronicle,* 9 March, unknown page.

1868b. "General Spinner as a Religious Enthusiast." Cincinnati *Evening Chronicle,* 13 March, 3.

1869a. *The Innocents Abroad; or, The New Pilgrims' Progress.* Hartford: American Publishing Company.

1869b. "The White House Funeral." Written on 7 March for the New York *Tribune,* but not published. One sheet of *Tribune* galley proof, CU-MARK. Published in *L3,* 458–66.

1873a. "The Man of Mark Ready to Bring Over the O'Shah." Letter dated 18 June. New York *Herald,* 1 July, 3. Reprinted in SLC 1923a, 31–46.

1873b. "Mark Twain Executes His Contract and Delivers the Persian in London." Letter dated 19 June. New York *Herald,* 4 July, 5. Reprinted in SLC 1923a, 46–57.

1873c. "Mark Twain Takes Another Contract." Letter dated 21 June. New York *Herald,* 9 July, 3. Reprinted in SLC 1923a, 57–69.

1873d. "Mark Twain Hooks the Persian out of the English Channel." Letter dated 26 June. New York *Herald,* 11 July, 3. Reprinted in SLC 1923a, 69–78.

1873e. "Mark Twain Gives the Royal Persian a 'Send-Off.'" Letter dated 30 June. New York *Herald,* 19 July, 5. Reprinted in SLC 1923a, 78–86.

1876. *The Adventures of Tom Sawyer.* Hartford: American Publishing Company.

1877–78. "Some Rambling Notes of an Idle Excursion." *Atlantic Monthly* 40 (October–December 1877): 443–47, 586–92, 718–24; *Atlantic Monthly* 41 (January 1878): 12–19.

1880. *A Tramp Abroad.* Hartford: American Publishing Company.

1885a. *Adventures of Huckleberry Finn.* New York: Charles L. Webster and Co.

1885b. "The Private History of a Campaign That Failed." *Century Magazine* 31 (December): 193–204. Reprinted in Budd 1992a, 863–82.

1889. *A Connecticut Yankee in King Arthur's Court.* New York: Charles L. Webster and Co.

1890. "Concerning the Scoundrel Edward H. House." MS of fifty-two leaves, CU-MARK.

1891. "Mental Telegraphy." *Harper's New Monthly Magazine* 84 (December): 95–104.

1892. *The American Claimant.* New York: Charles L. Webster and Co.

1896–1906. "Memorial to Susy." MS of 104 leaves, various drafts and parts, CU-MARK.

1897a. *Following the Equator: A Journey around the World.* Hartford: American Publishing Company.

1897b. *More Tramps Abroad.* London: Chatto and Windus.

1898a. "Stirring Times in Austria." *Harper's New Monthly Magazine* 96 (March): 530–40.

1898b. "Broken Idols." MS of eleven leaves, written on 18 August, CU-MARK.

1899. "Diplomatic Pay and Clothes." *Forum* 27 (March): 24–32. Reprinted in Budd 1992b, 344–53.

1901a. *To the Person Sitting in Darkness.* New York: Anti-Imperialist League of New York.

1901b. "To the Person Sitting in Darkness." *North American Review* 172 (February): 161–76. Reprinted in Zwick 1992, 22–39.

1901c. "To My Missionary Critics." *North American Review* 172 (April): 520–34.

1902. "In Dim and Fitful Visions They Flit Across the Distances." MS of eleven leaves, written on 18 August, CU-MARK.

1905a. "The Czar's Soliloquy." *North American Review* 180 (March): 321–26.

1905b. "A Horse's Tale." Manuscript of 174 leaves, written in September, NN-BGC.

1905c. "John Hay and the Ballads." Letter to the editor dated 3 October. *Harper's Weekly* 49 (21 October): 1530.

1906a. *What Is Man?* New York: De Vinne Press.

1906b. "Carl Schurz, Pilot." *Harper's Weekly* 50 (26 May): 727.

1906c. "A Horse's Tale." *Harper's Monthly Magazine* 113 (August–September): 327–42, 539–49.

1907. *A Horse's Tale.* Illustrated by Lucius Hitchcock. New York: Harper and Brothers.

1907–8. "Extract from Captain Stormfield's Visit to Heaven." *Harper's Monthly Magazine* 116 (December 1907): 41–49; (January 1908): 266–76.

1908. "The Great Alliance." MS of twenty-nine leaves, written on 16 January, CU-MARK.

1909a. *Is Shakespeare Dead? From My Autobiography.* New York: Harper and Brothers.

1909b. "The New Planet." MS of four leaves, written on 4 January, CU-MARK.

1909c. "The New Planet." *Harper's Weekly* 53 (30 January): 13.

1909d. "A Capable Humorist." *Harper's Weekly* 53 (20 February): 13.

1909e. "Last Will and Testament of Samuel L. Clemens. Dated August 17th, 1909." Typescript of eight leaves, witnessed by Albert Bigelow Paine, Harry A. Lounsbury, and Charles T. Lark. Original on file at Probate Court, District of Redding, Redding, Connecticut, photocopy in CU-MARK.

1911. "The Death of Jean." *Harper's Monthly Magazine* 122 (January): 210–15.

1923a. *Europe and Elsewhere.* With an introduction by Albert Bigelow Paine and an appreciation by Brander Matthews. New York: Harper and Brothers.

1923b. *Mark Twain's Speeches.* With an introduction by Albert Bigelow Paine and an appreciation by William Dean Howells. New York and London: Harper and Brothers.

1962. *Mark Twain: Letters from the Earth.* Edited by Bernard DeVoto, with a preface by Henry Nash Smith. New York: Harper and Row.

1981. *Wapping Alice: Printed for the First Time, Together with Three Factual Letters to Olivia Clemens; Another Story, the McWilliamses and the Burglar Alarm; and Revelatory Portions of the Autobiographical Dictation of April 10, 1907.* With an introduction and afterword by Hamlin Hill. Berkeley: Friends of The Bancroft Library.

1996. *1601, and Is Shakespeare Dead?* Foreword by Shelley Fisher Fishkin. Introduction by Erica Jong. Afterword by Leslie A. Fiedler. The Oxford Mark Twain. New York: Oxford University Press.

2004. *Mark Twain's Helpful Hints for Good Living: A Handbook for the Damned Human Race.* Edited by Lin Salamo, Victor Fischer, and Michael B. Frank. Berkeley and Los Angeles: University of California Press.

2009. *Who Is Mark Twain?* Edited, with a note on the text, by Robert H. Hirst. New York: HarperStudio.

2010a. *Mark Twain's Book of Animals.* Edited by Shelley Fisher Fishkin. Berkeley and Los Angeles: University of California Press.

2010b. "Excerpt from 'The Autobiography of Mark Twain.'" *Newsweek,* 9 August, 41.

Smith College Alumnae Association. 1911. *Catalog of Officers, Graduates and Nongraduates of Smith College, Northampton, Mass., 1875–1910.* N.p.: Alumnae Association of Smith College.

Spalding, J. A., comp. 1891. *Illustrated Popular Biography of Connecticut.* Hartford: J. A. Spalding.

Stanley, Henry Morton. 1909. *The Autobiography of Sir Henry Morton Stanley.* Edited by Dorothy Stanley. Boston: Houghton Mifflin Company.

"Statement of Disbursements." 1909. "Statement of Disbursements, etc., as made by Miss Lyon, as shown by Expert Accountant's Report." TS of seven leaves, CU-MARK.

StEdNL. National Library of Scotland, Edinburgh [formerly UkENL].

Stern, Madeleine B. 1947. "Trial by Gotham 1870: The Career of Abby Sage Richardson." *New York History* 28 (July): 271–87.

Stevens, Horace J., comp. 1908. *The Copper Handbook: A Manual of the Copper Industry of the World, Vol. VIII.* Houghton, Mich.: Horace J. Stevens.

Stewart, Jeffrey C. 1993. "A Black Aesthete at Oxford." *Massachusetts Review* 34 (Autumn): 411–28.

Stoker, David. 1995. "'Innumerable Letters of Good Consequence in History': The Discovery and First Publication of the Paston Letters." *Library* 17 (June): 107–55.

Stoneley, Peter. 1992. *Mark Twain and the Feminine Aesthetic.* Cambridge: Cambridge University Press.

Suetonius Tranquillus, C. 1876. *The Lives of the Twelve Caesars. By C. Suetonius Tranquillus; to Which Are Added, His Lives of the Grammarians, Rhetoricians, and Poets.* Translated by Alexander Thomson. Revised and corrected by T. Forester. Bohn's Classical Library. London: George Bell and Sons. SLC copy in CU-MARK.

Syracuse University Library. 2013. "Biographical History," Purnell Frederick Harrington Collection. http://library.syr.edu/digital/guides/h/harrington_pf.htm#d2e88. Accessed 9 September 2013.

Taylor, Bayard. 1997. *Selected Letters of Bayard Taylor.* Edited by Paul C. Wermuth. Lewisburg, Pa.: Bucknell University Press.

Taylor, William Harrison. 1912. *Legislative History and Souvenir of Connecticut, Vol. VIII, 1911–1912.* Hartford: William Harrison Taylor.

Texas Ranger Hall of Fame and Museum. 2013. "William Jesse McDonald." http://www.texasranger.org/halloffame/McDonald_Jesse.htm. Accessed 16 October 2013.

Thomasson, Kermon. 1985. "Mark Twain and His Dunker Friend." *Messenger* 134 (October): 16–21.

Thompson, John M. 2011. "Theodore Roosevelt and the Press." In Ricard 2011, 216–36.

Thompson, Paul. 1909. "A Day with Mark Twain." *Burr McIntosh Monthly* 18 (March): unnumbered pages.

Todd, Charles Burr. 1906. *The History of Redding, Connecticut.* New York: Grafton Press.

Trani, Eugene P., and Donald E. Davis. 2011. "The End of an Era: Theodore Roosevelt and the Treaty of Portsmouth." In Ricard 2011, 368–90.

Trombley, Laura Skandera. 2010. *Mark Twain's Other Woman: The Hidden Story of His Final Years.* New York: Alfred A. Knopf.

TS. Typescript.

TS. 1980. *The Adventures of Tom Sawyer; Tom Sawyer Abroad; and Tom Sawyer, Detective.* Edited by John C. Gerber, Paul Baender, and Terry Firkins. The Works of Mark Twain. Berkeley and Los Angeles: University of California Press.

Tuolumne Census.
> 1880. *Population Schedules of the Tenth Census of the United States, 1880. Roll T9. California: Tuolumne County.* Photocopy in CU-MARK.
> 1930. *Population Schedules of the Fifteenth Census of the United States, 1930. Roll T626. California: Tuolumne County.* Photocopy in CU-MARK.

Turner, Arlin. 1956. *George Washington Cable: A Biography.* Durham, N.C.: Duke University Press.

Tuxedo Census. 1910. *Population Schedules of the Thirteenth Census of the United States, 1910. Roll T624. New York: Orange County, Tuxedo Township.* Photocopy in CU-MARK.

Twichell, Joseph H. 1874–1916. "Personal Journal." MS of twelve volumes, Joseph H. Twichell Collection, CtY-BR.

TxU-Hu. Harry Ransom Humanities Research Center, University of Texas, Austin.

University of Chicago Library. 2006. "Guide to the Elizabeth Wallace Papers, 1913–1955." Chicago: University of Chicago Library.

U.S., Adjutant General Military Records. 1631–1976. *U.S., Adjutant General Military Records, 1631–1976* [online database]. http://ancestry.com. Accessed 9 September 2013.

U.S. Bureau of Navigation. 1908. *Annual Report of the Chief of the Bureau of Navigation to the Secretary of the Navy.* Washington: Government Printing Office.

U.S. Congress.

1902. *Proceedings and Conclusions of the Committee Appointed . . . to Consider the Advisability of Adopting the "Post-Check."* Washington: Government Printing Office.

1906. *Post-Check Bill (H.R. 7053) and Postal Notes: Hearings before the Committee on the Post-Office and Post-Roads of the House of Representatives, Fifty-ninth Congress.* Washington: Government Printing Office.

U.S. Department of the Treasury. 2013. "History of 'In God We Trust.'" http://treasury.gov/about/education/Pages/in-god-we-trust.aspx. Accessed 2 May 2013.

U.S. National Archives and Records Administration. 1795–1925. *U.S. Passport Applications, 1795–1925* [online database]. http://ancestry.com. Accessed 26 March 2014.

Uzawa, Yoshiko. 2006. "'Will White Man and Yellow Man Ever Mix?': Wallace Irwin, Hashimura Togo, and the Japanese Immigrant in America." *Japanese Journal of American Studies* 17 (2006): 201–19.

van Dyke, Henry. 1907. "Some Remarks on Gulls." *Scribner's Magazine* 42 (August): 129–42.

van Eeden, Frederick. 1909. "Curing by Suggestion." *The World's Work* 18 (September): 11993–99.

Vermont Vital Records. 1760–1954. *Vermont Vital Records, 1760–1954* [online database]. https://familysearch.org. Accessed 4 December 2012.

Villanueva, Jari. 2014. "An Excerpt from Twenty-Four Notes That Tap Deep Emotions: The Story of America's Most Famous Bugle Call." http://tapsbugler.com/an-excerpt-from-twenty-four-notes-that-tap-deep-emotions-the-story-of-americas-most-famous-bugle-call. Accessed 11 February 2014.

ViU. University of Virginia, Charlottesville.

VtMiM. Middlebury College, Middlebury, Vt.

Vyver, Bertha. 1930. *Memoirs of Marie Corelli.* London: Alston Rivers.

Walk Portsmouth. 2011. "Aldrich House." http://walkportsmouth.blogspot.com/2011/08/aldrich-house.html. Accessed 6 August 2013.

Wallace, Elizabeth.

1913. *Mark Twain and the Happy Island.* Chicago: A. C. McClurg and Co.
1952. *The Unending Journey.* Minneapolis: University of Minnesota Press.

Ward, Edwin A. 1923. *Recollections of a Savage.* London: Herbert Jenkins.

Warner, Charles Dudley. 1875. "Samuel Langhorne Clemens." In Duyckinck and Duyckinck, 2:951–55.

Washburn, Henry Bradford. 1908. "Shall We Hunt and Fish? The Confessions of a Sentimentalist." *Atlantic Monthly* 101 (May): 672–79.

Watson, Robert P. 2012. *Affairs of State: The Untold History of Presidential Love, Sex, and Scandal, 1789–1900.* Lanham, Md.: Rowman and Littlefield Publishers.

Weaver, John D. 1970. *The Brownsville Raid.* New York: W. W. Norton and Co.

Weaver, Thomas S. 1901. *Historical Sketch of the Police Service of Hartford from 1636 to 1901.* Hartford: Hartford Police Mutual Aid Association.

Wecter, Dixon. 1952. *Sam Clemens of Hannibal.* Boston: Houghton Mifflin Company, Riverside Press.

Westchester Census. 1920. *Population Schedules of the Fourteenth Census of the United States, 1920. Roll T625. New York: Westchester County, Village of Dobbs Ferry.* Photocopy in CU-MARK.

Whitaker, Robert Sanderson. 1907. *Whitaker of Hesley Hall, Grayshott Hall, Pylewell Park, and Palermo.* London: Mitchell Hughes and Clarke.

White, Barbara A. 2003. *The Beecher Sisters.* New Haven: Yale University Press.

White, Edgar. 1924. "The Old Home Town." *Mentor* 12 (May): 51–53.

White, Thomas H. 2012. "United States Early Radio History: Arc-Transmitter Development (1904–1928)." http://earlyradiohistory.us/sec009.htm. Accessed 10 September 2012.

Willard, Frances E., and Mary A. Livermore, eds. 1893. *A Woman of the Century: Fourteen Hundred-Seventy Biographical Sketches Accompanied by Portraits of Leading American Women in All Walks of Life.* Buffalo: Charles Wells Moulton.

Williams, Henry. 1922. *In the Clutch of Circumstance: My Own Story, by a Burglar.* New York: D. Appleton and Co.

WIM. 1973. *What Is Man? And Other Philosophical Writings.* Edited by Paul Baender. The Works of Mark Twain. Berkeley: University of California Press.

Woolf, Samuel Johnson. 1910. "Painting the Portrait of Mark Twain." *Collier's: The National Weekly,* 14 May, 42–44.

Worcester, Elwood, Samuel McComb, and Isador H. Coriat. 1908. *Religion and Medicine: The Moral Control of Nervous Disorders.* New York: Moffat, Yard and Co.

Wordsworth, William. 1815. *Poems: Including Lyrical Ballads, and the Miscellaneous Pieces of the Author.* 2 vols. London: n.p.

Wright, Thomas, ed. 1848. *Early Travels in Palestine.* Bohn's Antiquarian Library. London: Henry G. Bohn. SLC copy in CU-MARK.

WU-MU. Madison Memorial Union Library, University of Wisconsin, Madison.

Young, Alan R. 2007. *"Punch" and Shakespeare in the Victorian Era.* Oxford: Peter Lang.

Zwick, Jim. 1992. *Mark Twain's Weapons of Satire: Anti-Imperialist Writings on the Philippine-American War.* Syracuse: Syracuse University Press.

INDEX

Boldfaced page numbers indicate principal identifications or short biographies. All literary works are by Clemens unless otherwise noted: his major writings are listed only by title; the minor ones are listed both by title and under "Clemens, Samuel Langhorne: WORKS." Other literary works are found only under their authors' names. Place names are indexed only when they refer to locations SLC lived in, visited, or commented upon. Foreign cities are listed only by country. Newspapers are listed by city, other periodicals by title. Bullets (•) designate people and places represented in the photographs following page 300.

Banks (deputy sheriff), 267–68
Banks, Miss (dressmaker), 362–63, 439
Bardi, Countess of (Princess Adelgunde),
    68, 70, **478–79**
Barnard College, 447
Barnes, Benjamin F., 298, 603
Barney, Charles T., 223, 532, **560**
Barney, Helen, 223, 560
Barney, Katherine, 223, 560
Barney, Lilly, 560
Barnum, Phineas T., 187, 601
Barnum and Bailey circus, 295–96, 601
Barrie, J. M., 102, **491**
Barrymore, Ethel, 211, 450, **548**
Barrymore, Georgiana Drew, 211, 548
Barrymore, Maurice, 548
Bateman, Ellen, 144–45, **518**
Bateman, Hezekiah, 102, 144–45, 491, **518**
Bateman, Kate, 144–45, **518**
Bath Club (London), 121
•Bausch, Nellie, 294–95, 600
•Bausch, Pieter, 290–95, 598, 600
Beecher, Catharine, 442
Beecher, Charles, 3, 442
Beecher, Edward, 442
Beecher, Harriet Porter, 442
Beecher, Henry Ward, 3, 166, 442–43, 452,
    527, 660
Beecher, George, 442
Beecher, Isabella (Mrs. John Hooker), 3–4,
    115, 441, **442–43**
Beecher, James Chaplin, 3, 442
Beecher, Lyman, 441–42
Beecher, Roxana Foote, 442
Beecher, Thomas K., 3–4, 442
Beecher, William, 442
Beerbohm, Max, 494
Belgium, 114, 599
Bell, Alexander Graham, 173, 531
Bell, C. F. Moberly, 109–10, 121, 468, **495**
The Bells, 145, 518
Bell Telephone Company, 17, 449
Ben Franklin Book and Job Office, 598
•Benjamin, William Evarts, 433, 465, 550
Bennett, John, 117, 503
Beresford, Godfrey Stephen, 554
•Bermuda: 13–14, 51, 201–6, 209–13,
    220–21, 311–12, 314, 316–17, 343,

433, 446–47, 544, 553–56, 611, 617,
    640; SLC's readings for charity, 212,
    286, 550–51, 596
Bermuda Biological Station and Aquarium,
    212, 550–51, 555
Bermuda *Royal Gazette,* 550
•*Bermudian* (ship), 13, 446–47, 544, 550
Beuchotte, Claude Joseph, 268, 309–10,
    315, 357–58, 361, 366, 420, **586**–87,
    621, 627, 671–72
Bible, 177, 516; copyright, 94–95, 487;
    corrupting influence on children, 97–98;
    violation of the law of Nature, 196
CHARACTERS: Adam, 88; Ananias, 331,
    613; David, 193; Deborah, 551; Goliath,
    193; Jonah, 67; Joseph of Arimathea, 511;
    Nicodemus, 133, 511; Sapphira, 613
REFERENCES: dung and piss (2 Kings), 98,
    489; "Father forgive them" (Luke), 282,
    595; Immaculate Conception (Virgin
    Birth), 131; just and unjust (Matthew),
    221, 557; mother in Israel (Judges), 213,
    551; ravens feeding Elijah (1 Kings), 67,
    478; Samaritan (Luke), 56, 469; shoe
    latchets (Mark, Luke, John), 257, 579;
    Shunammite woman (2 Kings), 56, 469;
    "sinner that repenteth" (Luke), 282;
    "Strait is the way and narrow is the gate"
    (Matthew), 188; "what is man" (Psalms),
    590
Bigelow, John, 18–19, **450–51**
Bigelow, Poultney A., 288–89, **598**
Birch, George, 569
Birrell, Augustine, 75–81, **482–83**, 520
Bissell, Richard M., 571
Bixby, Horace, 136, 637, 656
Blackmer, Helen, 202, 544
Blackmer, Henry M., 220, **544**
•Blackmer, Margaret Gray, 202–5, 220, **544,**
    552–53
Blackwood, William, 479
Blaine, James G., 570
Blanchan, Neltje (Mrs. Frank Nelson
    Doubleday), 547, **549**
Blankenship, Elizabeth (Becca), 304, 608
Blankenship, Tom, 304, 608
Bliss, Elisha P., Jr., 151, 334, 521, 559,
    620–21

Bliss, Francis E., 649–50
Boer War (second, 1899–1902), 111, 180–81, 591
Bok, Edward, 589
Bonaparte, Napoleon, 21, 23, 58, 185, 453, 459
Boone, Daniel, 655
Booth, William, 82–83, **484**
Booth, William Stone, 299, 604
Borthwick, Algernon (Baron Glenesk), 74, **482**
Boston and Maine Railway, 241, 248, 251
Boston *Commercial Bulletin,* 576
Boston *Herald,* 554–55
Boston Lyceum Bureau, 165, 443, 527
Boston Museum of Fine Arts, 554
Botheker, Lizzie, 44, 460
Bothwell, J. W. (called "Boswell" and "Bosworth"), 127–28, 271, 509, 589–90
Boucicault, Dion, 114–15, **498–99**
Bowen, Herbert Wolcott, 62, **473**
Bowen, William, 229, 565
Bowes, Edward J., 563
Bowker, R. R., 493
Boyajian Twin Brothers (rug dealers), 381, 630
Breckenridge, Marjorie, 555
Breckenridge, Maude, 555
Brennan, Louis, 121, 506
Brevoort Hotel (New York), 309, 610
Bridge, Cyprian, 121, **506**
Bridget (maid?), 28
Briggs, John, 229, 565
British Parliament, 106–7, 121, 146, 279, 487, 493, 506, 549
British Plasmon Company (Plasmon Syndicate). *See* Plasmon
British Schools and Universities Club (New York), 118, 504
Brittain, Henry Ernest, 75–76, 106, **482**
Brittain, Mrs. Henry Ernest, 106
"Broken Idols," 551–52
Brooklyn (warship), 142, 517
Brooklyn *Eagle,* 606
Brooklyn Public Library, 97, 489
Brooklyn *Standard-Union,* 575
Brooks, Sydney, 81, 83–84, **484**
Broughton, Cara Leland Rogers, 465

Broughton, Urban H., 51, 331, 348, 368, 433, 448, **465,** 629
Brown, James Burnett, 565
Brown, Miss (teacher), 301, 605
Brown, W. B., 229, 565
Brown, William Lee, 565
Brown's Hotel (London), 73, 98, 121, 481, 485
Brownsville incident, 257–58, 580
Brush, George de Forest, 398, 632
Brush, Gerome, 632
Brush, Mrs. George de Forest, 399
Brush, Nancy, 624, 632
Bryan, William Jennings, 155, 258, 260, **581–82**
Bryce, James, 181, 222, **536**
Bryn Mawr College, 122, 574, 643
Buffalo (N.Y.), 333, 638, 641–42, 653, 660
Buffalo *Express,* 638, 653, 660
Bull Moose Party (Progressive Party), 578
Bunce, Edward M., 31, 40, 456
Burnand, Francis, 124, **507**
Burns, Robert, 172, 305, 529, 608
Burroughs, John, 62–64, 68, 104–5, **472–77**
Busch, Moritz, 644–45, 647
Bush, Gilmore G., 55–57, 469
Butes, Alfred, 552
Butes, Janet, 219, 552
Butes, Margaret Dorothy, 206, 219, 481, **552**
Butler, Nicholas M., 120, **505,** 516
Butt, Fred, 161
Butterfield, Daniel, 307, **610**
Butters, Henry A., 122, 269–71, 332, **587–88,** 615–16
Butters, Henry, Jr., 269, 271, 587
Butters, Lucie Sanctella, 269, 271, 587
Butters, Marguerite Sanctella, 269, 271, 587
Butters, Marie Sanctella, 269, 271, 587
•Buxton, Sydney Charles, 106
Byron, George Gordon, 76, 482, 615

Cable, George Washington, 166, 527–29, 598, 639
Caesar, Julius, 23, 58, 185, 627
Cairo (Ill.), 136, 514
Californian (periodical), 638

Cambridge University, 505
Campbell-Bannerman, Henry, 83, 144, 485, 505
Canonicus (warship), 516
"A Capable Humorist" (Pieter Bausch), 290–95, 600
"Captain Stormfield's Visit to Heaven," 58, 267, 458, 470, 585–86
Carew, James, 144, 518
Carey, William, 301–2, **605**
"Carl Schurz, Pilot," 492
Carl Theodor (duke), 71, **479–80**
Carlyle, Thomas, 656
Carmania (ship), 404, 407
Carmina, Stephen E., 624
Carnegie, Andrew, 172, 453, 510, 547; characterized by SLC, 104–5, 181–94; Engineers' Club banquet, 189–93, 539–40; Lotos Club tribute, 302, 605; philanthropy, 96, 182–83, 189, 194, 452, 492, 539–40, 605; reaction to *What Is Man?*, 271, 589; simplified spelling movement, 192–93, 539–40; visit of Edward VII to Skibo Castle, 182, 187, 536; visit with Wilhelm II, 184–86, 191, 537
Carnegie, Louise Whitfield, 104, 537, 547
Carnegie Institute (Pittsburgh), 453
Carnegie Institution (Washington), 193–94, 540
Carpenter, Edward, 272, **590**
Carrel, Alexis, **567**
Caruso, Enrico, 211, 549
Casals, Pablo, 608
Case, Newton, 222, 559
The Celebrated Jumping Frog of Calaveras County, and Other Sketches, 78, 483, 638, 646, 648, 659
Century Magazine, 104, 182, 301–2, 445, 467, 472, 536, 605, 612, 651
Cervantes Saavedra, Miguel de, 21, **452**
Ceylon, 639
Chamberlain, Walter P., 34, **457–58**
"Chapters from My Autobiography" *(North American Review),* 16, 286, 446, 576, 596, 611, 640, 683–84
Charles I (king of England), 87, 119, 651, 655
Charles Hamilton Autographs, 630

Charles L. Webster and Company. *See* Webster, Charles L., and Company
Chase, Salmon P., 538
Chatterton, Thomas, 77–78, 483
Cherep-Spiridovitch, Arthur (count), 18–19, 447, **450–52**
Cherubini, Giuseppe, 331, 377–78, 614
Cherubini, Teresa, 310, 331, 336–37, 358, 361, 366, 377–78, 610, 614, 625
Chicago and Alton Railway Company, 513
Chicago *Inter–Ocean,* 522
Chicago *Tribune,* 492, 504, 561, 567
"Children's Record," 43–45, 47–48, 459–60
Children's Theatre (New York), 199, 220, 543, 553
Child-Villiers, Margaret (countess of Jersey), 102–3, **491**
Child-Villiers, Victor (earl of Jersey), 103, 491
China, 197, 199, 264, 541
Chinese Exclusion Act (1882), 609
Choate, Joseph H., 19, 452, 515
Christian Science, 640
Christian Science (Church of Christ, Scientist), 147, 160, 199, 221–22, 524, 558
Christian Union (periodical), 20
Chulalongkorn (king of Siam), 145–46, **518**
Church, William F., 235, **569**
Churchill, Randolph, 102
Churchill, Winston, 102, **491**
Church of the Ascension (New York; called "Assumption"), 348, 625–26
Cincinnati, 637, 645, 647
Cincinnati *Commercial* and *Commercial Gazette,* 574
Cincinnati *Enquirer,* 246, 575
Cincinnati *Evening Chronicle,* 521
Cincinnati *Gazette,* 569
Civil War (1861–65), 131, 136, 151, 180, 188, 251, 254, 307, 443, 473, 490, 492, 510, 516, 520–21, 557–58, 576, 610; SLC's service, 637, 651–52, 658
Clark, Champ, 593–94
Clark, Charles Hopkins (called "Mr. C—"), 28, 456
Clark, Edward B., 64, 474

Clemens, Samuel Langhorne (SLC):

CHARITABLE ACTIVITIES (continued)
State Association for Promoting the
Interests of the Blind, 199, 515, 543;
Robert Fulton Memorial Association,
138–42, 199, 515, 543; Russian revolutionists, 199; Vienna charities, 68, 164,
172, 478, 526

FOREIGN TRAVELS: around-the-world tour,
81, 148, 164, 171, 526, 529, 588, 634,
639, 642–43, 654, 662; Europe, 114,
242, 575, 599, 618, 643, 653, 661. See
also Austria; Bermuda; England; France;
Germany; Italy; Quaker City excursion;
Scotland; Switzerland

LECTURES, SPEECHES, AND READINGS:
Adventures of Huckleberry Finn, 526,
528; after Clara's debut, 81–82; Aldine
Club, 232; Aldrich museum dedication, 251, 571, 576–77, 623; American
Booksellers' Association, 236–37, 568;
American Rhodes Scholars Club, 95,
488–89; Army School (Stratford-on-
Avon), 100, 490; around-the-world tour,
81, 148, 164, 171, 526, 529, 588, 634,
639, 642–43, 654, 662; Authors Club,
573; "The Babies" (Grant banquet), 117,
503; "The Begum of Bengal," 149–50,
520; British lecture tours (1872–74),
527, 638, 653, 661; British Schools and
Universities Club, 118, 504; Carnegie
banquets, 190, 192–93, 302, 539–40,
605; Cape Town and Claremont (South
Africa) lectures, 164, 526, 639; "Collecting Compliments," 524; College Club,
573; "The Day We Celebrate" (Fourth
of July banquet), 117–20; decision to
stop speaking at banquets and for pay,
164, 189, 539; "discovery of a corpse,"
550–51; early lectures, 98, 165–66,
302–3, 443, 527, 531, 563, 605, 638,
646, 648, 653, 659–61; "The Golden
Arm," 171, 526, 529; "Grandfather's
Old Ram," 166–71, 526; Guildhall
banquet, 116–17, 503; House of Commons luncheon, 506; House of Lords
copyright committee, 487; Hudson
(Mass.) lecture, 98, 489; introduction

of Churchill, 491; Jerome dinner, 559;
Liverpool, 150, 520; Liverpool Lord
Mayor's banquet, 149–50; London Lord
Mayor's banquet, 99, 101, 490; Lotos
Club, 302, 524, 605; "Lucerne Girl &
Interviewer," 526; "The Mexican Plug,"
526, 551; Oxford University banquet,
85–86, 485; "A Page from My Autobi-
ography," 72, 480; Pilgrims Society luncheon, 75, 78–82, 147, 520; The Players
club, 457; Pleiades Club, 521; "Poem
(Ornithorhyncus)," 526; The Prince and
the Pauper play premiere, 500; "Robert
Louis Stevenson and Thomas Bailey
Aldrich" excerpt, 576; Rogers's Virginian
Railway banquet, 355, 627; "Roughing It" lecture, 520; Round Table, 573;
Sandwich Islands lecture, 302–3, 520,
605, 653, 659; Savage Club dinner, 506;
SLC-Cable reading tour, 166, 527–29,
598, 639; "Stolen Watermelon," 478,
526, 550; St. Timothy's School for Girls
(last public speech), 481; Tcherep-Spiri-
dovitch luncheon, 18–19, 451; "three-
dollar dog," 152–54, 521, 550; Tuxedo
(N.Y.) reading, 164; Twentieth Century
Club, 573; Vassar reading, 171; Young
Men's Christian Association (Majestic Theatre), 179. See also Clemens,
Samuel Langhorne (SLC): CHARITABLE
ACTIVITIES

LETTERS: See Letters from SLC; Letters to
SLC

OCCUPATIONS: authorial history, 51, 245,
637–40, 645–49, 652–54, 656–62;
freight clerk and watchman, 645, 647;
inventor, 265, 584; journalist, 114, 148,
245, 287–88, 453, 468, 498, 521, 581,
597, 638, 646–48, 652–53, 655–56,
658–60; magazine contributor, 16, 20,
234, 237, 245, 270, 286, 307–8, 446,
450–51, 457–58, 471, 485–86, 492,
541, 568–70, 576, 585–86, 588, 596–
97, 600, 604, 610–11, 638–40, 651, 653,
659, 683–84; miner and quartz-mill
laborer, 148, 245, 637–38, 646, 648,
652–53, 659; newspaper syndicator,
151, 521; Orion's secretary in Nevada,

Clemens, Samuel Langhorne (SLC)
(continued)

READING: Aldrich's writings, 241, 571,
577; Arabian Nights, 93, 252; Aristotle,
67–68; *Atlantic Monthly,* 226–28, 564;
Delia Bacon's writings on Shakespeare,
603; Francis Bacon's *Novum Organum,*
127, 508; Burroughs's *Birds and Bees,
Songs of Nature,* and *Bird and Bough,*
472; Coleridge's "Rime of the Ancient
Mariner," 182; *Collier's Weekly,* 254, 266;
Dana's *Two Years Before the Mast,* 149–
50; Darwin's *Life and Letters* and *Autobiography,* 79, 483; Dickens's *Great Expectations* and *David Copperfield,* 69, 165, 479,
527; Emerson's essays, 159, 571; Marjory
Fleming's writings, 555; Glyn's *Three
Weeks,* 195–97, 541; Goethe's *Faust,* 246,
575; Harte's "Heathen Chinee," 307, 609;
Hay's "Jim Bludso, of the Prairie Belle"
and *Pike County Ballads,* 307, 609; Ibsen's
Hedda Gabler and *The Master Builder,*
509; Irwin's Japanese schoolboy letters,
290, 598–99; Khayyám's *Rubáiyát,* 158–
59, 524; Long's *Beasts of the Field, Fowls
of the Air,* and *School of the Woods,* 472;
Lubbock's *Ants, Bees, and Wasps,* 505;
Mandeville's *Travels,* 67, 478; Nietzsche's
Thus Spake Zarathustra, 509; Paston letters, 329, 613; Pliny the Elder's *Naturalis
Historia,* 67, 478; Rice's *Mr. Opp,* 307,
609; Shakespeare's plays, 99, 138, 208,
299–300, 347, 515, 604; *Journal of the
Society for Psychical Research,* 510; Taylor's
poetry and translation of *Faust,* 246, 575;
Thackeray's "The Diary of Jeames de la
Pluche," 352, 626; van Dyke's writings,
226–28, 564; van Eeden's "Curing by
Suggestion," 438, 635; Washburn's "Shall
We Hunt and Fish?," 226, 564; Wordsworth's "She dwelt among the untrodden
ways," 125, 508; *The World's Work* (periodical), 438, 635; Wright's *Early Travels
in Palestine,* 478. *See also* Bible

RESIDENCES: *See* Dublin; Elmira; Hart-
ford; Italy; New York City; Riverdale;
Stormfield; Tarrytown; Tuxedo Park;
Tyringham; York Harbor

WORKS: *The American Claimant,* 536,
545; "Ancients in Modern Dress," 509;
"Broken Idols," 551–52; "A Capable
Humorist" (Pieter Bausch), 290–95,
600; "Captain Stormfield's Visit to
Heaven," 58, 267, 458, 470, 585–86;
"Carl Schurz, Pilot," 492; *Christian Sci-
ence,* 640; *Colonel Sellers as a Scientist*
(play), 563; *Colonel Sellers* (Gilded Age
play), 536, 654, 662; "Concerning the
Scoundrel Edward H. House," 499–500;
"Copyright," 279–80, 594; "The Czar's
Soliloquy," 450–51; *Date 1601,* 486;
"Diplomatic Pay and Clothes," 86, 485–
86; English book (projected), 498; "A
Family Sketch," 460; "Forty-three Days
in an Open Boat," 653, 659; "A Gallant
Fireman," 637; "General Spinner as a
Religious Enthusiast," 521; "God," 509;
"The Great Alliance," 543; "A Horse's
Tale," 270, 307–8, 588, 610; *How to
Tell a Story and Other Essays,* 649–50;
"An Important Question Settled," 521;
"In Dim and Fitful Visions They Flit
Across the Distances," 214–19, 551–52;
Is Shakespeare Dead?, 326–27, 603–4;
"Jim Smiley and His Jumping Frog," 78,
471, 597, 638; "King Leopold's Solilo-
quy," 147; "Lecture Times," 527; "The
Machine Episode," 621; *Mark Twain's
Sketches, New and Old,* 639; "Memo-
rial to Susy," 552; "The Moral Sense,"
127, 509; *More Tramps Abroad,* 455;
"My Autobiography [Random Extracts
from It]," 103, 492; "The New Planet,"
604; notes for Moffett's biographical
sketch, 649–54; notes for Warner's
biographical sketch, 644–47; •"Notice.
To the next Burglar," 269, 587; *Personal
Recollections of Joan of Arc,* 78, 234, 236,
494, 568, 639, 661; "The Private History of a Campaign That Failed," 651;
"Proposition for a Postal Check," 107–8,
493–94, 662–69; "Pudd'nhead Wilson's New Calendar," 23, 455; "Ralph
Keeler," 527; "A Record of the Small
Foolishnesses of Susy & 'Bay' Clemens
(Infants)," 43–45, 47–48, 459–60;

"Robert Louis Stevenson and Thomas Bailey Aldrich," 447, 487, 576, 683; Shah of Persia letters, 114, 498; "Three Thousand Years Among the Microbes," 588; "To My Guests," 285, 596; "To My Missionary Critics," 197, 541; "To the Person Sitting in Darkness," 197, 541, 639; *The Tragedy of Pudd'nhead Wilson,* 639, 654, 656, 660, 662; "Villa di Quarto," 544, 622; "Wapping Alice," 24–41, 455–58; "Was It Heaven? Or Hell?," 237, 569–70; "What Is Happiness?," 126–27, 508; "What is the Real Character of 'Conscience?,'" 508; " 'What Ought He to Have Done?': Mark Twain's Opinion" (*Christian Union* article), 20; "The White House Funeral," 581. See also *Adventures of Huckleberry Finn; The Adventures of Tom Sawyer; The Celebrated Jumping Frog of Calaveras County, and Other Sketches; A Connecticut Yankee in King Arthur's Court; Following the Equator; The Gilded Age; The Innocents Abroad; Life on the Mississippi; The Prince and the Pauper; Roughing It; What Is Man?*

Clemens family servants: Claude Beuchotte (butler), 268, 309–10, 315, 357–58, 361, 366, 420, 586–87, 621, 627, 671–72; Lizzie Botheker (Clara's wet nurse), 44, 460; Bridget (maid?), 28; Giuseppe Cherubini (cook), 331, 377–78, 614; Teresa Cherubini (housekeeper and caretaker), 310, 331, 336–37, 358, 361, 366, 377–78, 610, 614, 625; Elizabeth Dick (housekeeper), 337–38, 621; Katherine Gregory (waitress), 621; George Griffin (butler), 25–35, 38–40, 48, 252, 315, 456; Rosina Hay (nurse), 48; Horace Hazen (butler), 337, 354–59, 361, 366–71, 378, 388, 390, 625, 627, 672; Harry Iles (groundskeeper), 390, 621, 631; Katy Leary (housekeeper), 309–11, 313–15, 318, 331, 357, 362–63, 377, 420, 586; Mary (Alice; cook), 24–25, 456, 458; Patrick McAleer (coachman), 25–26, 28, 33, 44, 456–58; Maria McLaughlin (Maria McManus; Clara's

wet nurse), 43–45, 460; Katie Murray (laundress), 420, 621; George O'Conner (coachman), 621; Mary Walsh (cook), 621; Lizzie Wills (Wapping Alice; Susy's nurse), 24–41, 455–58

Clements, Gregory (called "Jeoffrey Clement"), 651, 655

Cleopatra, 45

Clermont (steamboat), 142, 517

Cleveland, Frances Folsom, 140, 238–39, 570

Cleveland, Grover, 139–40, 143, 238, 256, 259, 515, 534, 570, 579, 581

Clews, Henry, 177, **532**

Cliveden, 211, 550

"Closing Words of My Autobiography," 310–19, 610–13, 644

Cody, William F. ("Buffalo Bill"), 224, 562

Coe, Mai (Mary) Rogers, 629

Coe, William R., 368, **629**

Coinage Act of 1864, 538

Colby, Bainbridge, 116, **502**

Cole, Arabella Mae, 161

Coleridge, Samuel Taylor, 182

"Collecting Compliments," 524

College Club (Boston), 573

Collier, Peter F., 547

Collier, Robert J., 210, 285, 295–97, **547,** 553, 601

Collier, Sara Steward Van Alen, 210, **547,** 553

Collier's Weekly, 254, 265–66, 285, 547, 578, 584, 598–99

Collins, John B., 142, 517

Colonel Sellers as a Scientist (play), 563

Colonel Sellers (Gilded Age play), 536, 654, 662

Colonial Opera House (Bermuda), 212, 550

Columbia (yacht), 138, 515

Columbia University, 4, 120, 360, 444, 505, 516, 559, 562, 584, 614

Columbus, Christopher, 46, 134, 440

•Colvin, Sidney, 82, **484**

"Concerning the Scoundrel Edward H. House," 499–500

Connecticut State Prison (Wethersfield), 281, 593

Dunne, Finley Peter (Martin Dooley), 211, 516, 550, 571
Durand, Mortimer, 117–20, **503**–5

Ebbitt House (Washington, D.C.), 152
Eddy, Mary Baker, 466
Edison, Thomas Alva, 173, 189, 531, 545
Edison Manufacturing Company, 545
Educational Alliance (New York), 543
Edward II (king of England), 633
•Edward VII (king of England), 112, 117, 134, 144–46, 182, 187, 484, 486, 496, 504, 517, 536; meetings with SLC, 145, 194, 519, 540
Edward the Confessor (king of England), 627
Egan, Joseph L., 553
Eijiro Ninomiya, 114, 498
Eliot, Charles William, 446
Elisabeth Amalie Eugenie (empress of Austria), 479
Elizabeth I (queen of England), 87–88, 486
Elkins Act, 513
Ellsworth, William Webster, 605
Elmira (N.Y.), 3, 40, 312, 333, 442, 461, 531, 603, 642–44; Quarry Farm, 44, 48, 459–60, 638
Elmira Female College, 642
Emancipation Proclamation, 120, 505
Emerson, Ralph Waldo, 159, 571
Emma (queen of Normandy), 627
Emmanuel movement (Emmanuel Episcopal Church, Boston), 221, 558
Engineers' Club and Associated Societies of Engineers (New York), 189–93, 539–40
England, 111, 119–20, 541; Ascot Cup joke, 79, 84, 118, 121, 483–84, 503, 506; SLC's Oxford degree trip, 52–54, 71–96, 98–112, 116–24, 128, 130–34, 140, 144–50, 154, 206–7, 219, 400, 480–96, 503–7, 509–11, 523, 546, 640, 670; SLC's pre-1907 lecture tours and visits, 527, 598, 632, 638–39, 648, 653–54, 632, 661–62; SLC's works published, 638–39; Stratford-on-Avon, 98–99, 489, 492, 593; Tilbury, 73, 95, 146, 150, 481; Warwick, 277–78, 593; Windsor Castle garden party, 112, 134, 144–46, 496, 517

Ennolds, Alex, 175–76, 531
Ericsson, John, 141, **516**
Everybody's Magazine, 473–74, 478, 552

Fairbanks, Mary Mason, 462–63
Fairfax, Charles Snowden, 103, 492
Fall, George L., 527
"A Family Sketch," 460
Farley, John M. (archbishop), 564
Farnum, Dustin, 224, **562**
Field, Kate, 497
First Congregational Church (Park Church; Elmira, N.Y.), 3, 442
First South Carolina Volunteers, 251, 576
Fitzgerald, Edward, 524
Fleming, Marjory, 555
Flexner, Simon, 567
Florence. *See* Italy
Florida (Mo.), 637, 640, 645, 647, 651, 655
Following the Equator, 455, 488, 639, 654, 662
Football, 62, 474
Foraker, Joseph B., 275, 592
Forbes, Archibald, 46, **462**
Forster, E. M., 590
"Forty-three Days in an Open Boat," 653, 659
France, 639; Paris, 21, 46, 240, 453, 572–73, 599
France, Anatole, 568
Franz Ferdinand (emperor of Austria), 479
Franz Joseph (duke of Austria), 480
Franz Joseph I (emperor of Austria), 71, 163, 479, 525–26
•Frazer, Laura Hawkins, 606–8
Frederick, B. F., 466
Fredonia (N.Y.), 641
Freeman, Grace Hill (Sheba), 354, **618**
Freeman, Zoheth (Zoe) Sparrow, 333, 354, 399, 618
Freemasons, 589, 637
Freud, Sigmund, 558
Frideswide, Saint, 89, 486
Fritz, John, 189–91, **539**
Frohman, Daniel, 115, 225, **500**–502, 540, 563
Frohman, Margaret Illington, 225, 540, **563**

Griffin, George, 25–35, 38–40, 48, 252, 315, 456

Grose, Francis, 470

Gross, Charles, 116, 502

Grumman, William E. (stenographer-typist), 313, 349, 367, 585, 606, 612, 625, **628**

Guild, Curtis, Jr., 249–50, **576**

Guildhall (London), 116–17, 503

Guinness, Benjamin S., 211, **549**

Guinness, Bridget Wiliams-Bulkeley, 211, **549**

Hackett, Wallace, 249–50, 571, **576**

Hadley, Arthur T., 580

The Hague, 600

Hall, Charles, 540

Halstead, Murat, 244–46, **574–75**

Hammond, John Hays, 270, 326, 331–32, **588,** 615–16

Hampton, Crittenden, 61, **471–72**

Handel, George Frederick, 93, 305, 318, 612

Hankey, Henry, 495

Hannibal (Mo.), 303–5, 468–69, 545, 565, 606, 637, 639–41, 645, 647, 651–52, 655–56

Hannibal *Courier-Post,* 303–4, 606

Hannibal *Gazette,* 637

Hannibal Home Guard (Marion Rangers), 637

Hannibal *Journal,* 641, 645

Hannibal *Missouri Courier,* 637, 645

Hannibal *Western Union,* 637, 641

Hapgood, Norman, 254–56, 258, 578

Harcourt, William Vernon, 102

Harmsworth, Alfred Charles William (Lord Northcliffe), 278–79, 400, 552, **593–94,** 632

Harmsworth, Harold, 593

Harmsworth, Mary Milner, 279, 593

Harold I (king of England), 88–89, 486

Harper and Brothers, 285, 371, 594, 613; SLC's contract, sales and royalties, 233–34, 236–37, 349–50, 534, 568–69, 625, 639

Harper's Monthly, 234, 237, 267, 285, 458, 467, 474, 568–69, 585–86, 588, 610

Harper's Weekly, 81, 107–8, 285, 290, 484, 492, 598, 600, 604, 609

Harriman, E. H., 134–35, 512

Harrington, P. F., 142, 517

Harris (Bayard Taylor's servant), 247, 575–76

Harris, Joel Chandler (Uncle Remus), 104, 243, 528, 574

Harris, Thomas A., 651–52, 658

Harrison, Katharine I., 379–81, **629**

Hart, Horace Henry, 94, **487**

Harte, Bret, 307, 597, 609

Hartford (Conn.): Clemenses' arrival and departure, 618, 638, 642–43, 653; Clemenses' house, 25, 239, 315, 333–34, 458, 556, 570–71, 642, 660; Clemenses' neighbors, 3, 25, 315, 442, 458, 460, 617, 642, 660

Hartford *Courant,* 159, 456–57, 524, 527–28, 617

Hartford Female Seminary, 442

Hartford Fire Insurance Company, 571

Hartford Theological Seminary, 222, 558–59

Harvard, John, 100, **490**

Harvard College and University, 78, 100, 446–47, 461, 472, 474, 483, 488–90, 528, 570, 604

Harvey, Alma, 546

•Harvey, Dorothy, 206, 546, 555

Harvey, George, 285, 331, 350, 446, 516, 539, 546, 585, 625; characterized by SLC, 207–8, 329; Clemens's seventieth birthday banquet, 289, 598; Paine's biography, 334, 620; visit to Stormfield, 278, 632

Havemeyer, Henry O., 565

Haviland, William T., 631

Hawaii. *See* Sandwich Islands

Hawkins, Anthony Hope, 74, **482**

Hawkins, Laura Frazer, 606–8

Hawley, Joseph Roswell, 31, 40, 456

Hay, Clara Stone, 496

Hay, John, 108, 112, 163, 210, 307, 494, 496–97, 525; writings, 307, 609

Hay, Rosina (Mrs. Horace K. Terwilliger; nurse), 48

Hayes, Rutherford B., 492

Hubbard, Stephen A., 31, 456
Hudson (Mass.), 98, 489
Hudson Theatre (New York), 450, 521, 548
Hughes, Thomas, 77, 103, 483, **491**
Hugo, Victor, 282, 595
Hull, F. A., 417, 633
Humanitarians (charity), 593
Hummel, Abraham, 115, **501**
Ingersoll, Robert G., 115, 501
Hunt, Edward Livingston, 429, 432, 634, 676
Hunt, Frederick, 634

Ibsen, Henrick, 129–30, 509, 549
Iles, Harry (called "Ives"), 390, 621, **631**
Illington, Margaret (Mrs. Daniel Frohman, later Mrs. Edward J. Bowes), 225, 540, **563**
"An Important Question Settled," 521
Inauguration Banquet of Sheriffs (London), 503
Independence Party, 592
India, 634, 639
Indian Wars, 521
"In Dim and Fitful Visions They Flit Across the Distances," 214–19, 551–52
Ingersoll, Robert G., 115, 501
Innes-Ker, Alastair Robert (lord), 541
The Innocents Abroad, 151, 521, 588, 661, 671; composition, 453, 660; copyright, 280, 311, 611; German translation, 644–65, 649; popularity and sales, 234–36, 646, 648, 653, 659–60; price, 280; publication, 638, 644, 646, 648, 653; quoted, 282, 595; uniform editions, 594. See also *Quaker City* excursion
International Peace Conference (The Hague, 1907), 22, 452–53, 537
International Plasmon Company. *See* Plasmon
International Spiral Pin Company, 332–33, 617
Irving, Henry, 102, 144–45, **491**, 518
Irwin, Wallace, 290, **598**–99
Is Shakespeare Dead?, 326–27, 603–4
Italy, 201, 316, 420, 428, 551, 618, 639; Florence, 201–2, 312, 317, 339, 544, 555, 577, 588, 614, 622, 639–40, 669; Venice, 21, 453

•Jackass Hill (or Gulch, Calif.), 57–58, 61, 245, 469–70, 597, 638, 646, 648, 653, 659
Jackson, Abraham Reeves, 453
Jackson, Mr. (Clara's lawyer), 396, 398, 434, 631
James, William, 558
Jamestown (Tenn.), 536, 640, 651, 655
Jamestown (Va.) Exposition (Ter-Centennial), 51, 138–39, 140–42, 465, 515–17, 543; Robert Fulton Day fiasco, 139–43, 515–17, 543
Japp, John (Lord Mayor of Liverpool), 146–47, 149, 519
Jefferson, Joseph, 564
Jefferson (ship), 627
Jennings, Oliver Burr, 567
Jennings, Walter, 566–67
Jerome, William Travers, 222–24, **559**–61
Jerrold, Douglas, 124, **507**
Jews, 19, 221, 450–51
"Jim Smiley and His Jumping Frog," 78, 471, 597, 638
John, Arthur, 605
John (king of England), 119
Johnson, Andrew, 258, 581
Jonson, Ben, 211, 549, 604
Judson, Stiles, 276, **592**
Jürgensen watch company, 445

Kanawha (Rogers's steam yacht), 51, 138–39, 141, 465–66, 515–16
Karl Ludwig (archduke of Austria), 479
Keeler, Ralph, 262, 264, 583
Keene, Laura, 225, **563**–64
•Keller, Helen, 299, 604
Kellgren, Jonas, 644
Kennedy, Claude Rann, 623
Keokuk (Iowa), 53, 289, 468, 598, 637, 641, 652, 656
Khayyam, Omar, 158–59, 524
"King Leopold's Soliloquy," 147
King of England's Cup, 140
Kinney, John C., 31, 456
Kinnicutt, Eleanora Kissel, 14, **447**–48
Kinnicutt, Francis P., 447
Kipling, Caroline Starr, 88
Kipling, J. Lockwood, 271, **589**

•Kipling, Rudyard, 82–83, 88, 94, 190, 271, 485, 549, 589
Kirlicks, John A., 52–53, 466-**67**
Knickerbocker Trust Company, 179, 223, 394, 398, 532–35, 560
Knowles, James, 110–11, 132, **495**–96
Kohn, John S. Van E., 324
•Komura Jutaro, 121, 506
Koy-lo Company, 617
Krakatoa, 265, 584

La Cossitt, Henry, 637
Lada-Mocarski, Olivia, 324
Laffan, William Mackay, 312, 612
Laird, James L., 652–53, 658–59
Lambert, Adrian V. S., 567
Lampton, William James, 136–37, 514
Lancaster, Charles, 368, 465, 629
Landis, Kenesaw Mountain, 135, 512–13
Lang, Andrew, 234, 510, 568
Langdon, Charles Jervis (Olivia's brother), 165, 612–13, 660
Langdon, Jervis (Olivia's father), 3, 333, 442, 638, 642, 648, 660
•Langdon, Jervis, Jr., 318, 612
Langdon, Julia Olivia (Mrs. Edward Eugene Loomis), 324, 341, 427, 614
Langdon, Olivia Lewis (Olivia's mother), 642
Lark, Charles T., 324, 326–27, 376–78, 389, 391, 395, 431–32, 629; characterized by SLC, 421; negotiates Ashcroft-Lyon settlement, 414–27, 436–37, 633, 673–78
Larking, John, 372, 391, 398, 629, 631
Lascelles, Frank, 486
Laszowska, Jane Emily Gerard, 68, 479
Laszowska, Miecislas de, 68, 479
Lawrence, D. H., 590
Lawson, Thomas W., 512
Lawton, Mary, 363, 434, 628
Leary, Katy, 309–11, 313–15, 318, 331, 357, 361–63, 377, 420, 586
"Lecture Times," 527
Ledyard, Lewis Cass, 138, **514**
Lee, Sidney, 74, 82, 102–6, 481–82, 484, **491**-92, 603
Leech, John, 124, 507

Lehefeld, Frederick, 626
Leigh, Frederick T., 331, **613**
Leopold II (king of Belgium), 147, 199, 543
Lepanto (battle), 21–22, 452
Leschetizky, Theodor, 611, 643
Leslie, Elsie, 115, 500, 502
Letters from SLC: SLC's insistence on reviewing for biography, 618–19
TO FAMILY MEMBERS: Clara, 312, 335, 374, 396–99, 432, 556, 621, 624, 629; Jean, 210, 429, 431, 434–35, 536, 585, 623, 628, 675–76; Olivia, 458, 463, 502–3; Orion, 604
TO OTHER PEOPLE: "an accomplished lady," 274–75; Joy Agnew, 125–26; Pieter Bausch, 600; Moberly Bell, 495; Margaret Blackmer, 553; William Blackwood, 479; Francis E. Bliss, 649; William Bowen, 565; Margaret Dorothy Butes, 552; Nicholas M. Butler, 446; Frederic Chapin, 502–3; Nikolai Chaykovsky, 451; Champ Clark, 593–94; Grover Cleveland, 140; *Collier's Weekly,* 598–99; Marie Corelli, 98–99, 489–90; Frances Cox, 528; Frederick Duneka, 371; Edison Manufacturing Company, 545; Mary Mason Fairbanks, 462–63; Daniel Frohman, 500; James Gillis, 470–71; Elinor Glyn, 542; Milton Goodkind, 466; Frederick J. Hall, 603; John Hays Hammond, 326; Crittenden Hampton, 472; William Harmsworth (Lord Northcliffe), 400, 632; *Harper's Weekly,* 609; George Harvey, 334, 539; John Hay, 108, 307, 494, 609; Edward H. House, 499–502; John Mead Howells, 251, 577; William Dean Howells, 258–64, 325, 366, 446–47, 484, 526, 529, 585, 619–20; Margaret Illington, 563; Wallace Irwin, 599; John Japp, 519; John A. Kirlicks, 467; Knickerbocker Trust Company depositors, 534–35; Knickerbocker Trust Company directors, 535; Andrew Lang, 568; Thomas Lipton, 632; London *Evening Standard,* 443; Isabel Lyon, 388, 630; J. Y. W. MacAlister, 616; Hellen Elizabeth Martin, 221, 557; Hiram Maxim, 531;

Mark G. McElhinney, 455; Samuel E. Moffett, 649; Kurt Mönch, 287, 596; Gertrude Natkin, 555; Charles G. Norris, 589–90; Oliver W. Norton, 307, 610; Frank N. Otremba, 571; Albert Bigelow Paine, 614; James B. Pond, 528; Dorothy Quick, 523, 556, 563; Emma Quick, 523; Whitelaw Reid, 53, 468; Abby Sage Richardson, 500; Emilie Rogers, 515–16; Henry H. Rogers, 457, 478, 502, 516, 524; Michael Laird Simons, 644; Society for Psychical Research, 510; John B. Stanchfield, 588; Melville Stone, 413–14; James J. Tuohy, 457; Joseph H. Twichell, 221–22, 478–80, 484, 558; Basil Wilberforce, 484; H. P. Wood, 571

Letters to SLC: invitation to introduce Clara, 4; invitation to introduce Cleveland, 139; invitations to Roosevelt tour, 136, 514; stock offer, 16, 449

FROM FAMILY MEMBERS: Clara, 306–7, 357, 360–61; Jean, 413

FROM OTHER PEOPLE: Joy Agnew, 124–25; Lilian Aldrich, 576–77; Ralph W. Ashcroft, 330, 374–75, 379, 613, 615; Pieter Bausch, 290–95, 598, 600; Margaret Blackmer, 553; Margaret Dorothy Butes, 552; James Bryce, 536; Frances Folsom Cleveland, 140; Robert Collier, 295, 601; Marie Corelli, 98, 489–90; Frank N. Doubleday, 566–67, 589; Frederick Duneka, 372, 629; Laura Hawkins Frazer, 606; Irene Gerken, 301; Elinor Glyn, 542; Frederick J. Hall, 603–4; Crittenden Hampton, 61, 471; George Harvey, 334, 585–86, 620; John Hay, 307, 609; Horace Hazen, 355–57, 367–71; Archibald Henderson, 126, 128–29, 589; Winifred T. Holt, 543; Edward H. House, 498–99, 501–2; William Dean Howells, 252, 510, 619; Wallace Irwin, 599; John A. Kirlicks, 52–53, 466–67; Andrew Lang, 568; John Lubbock, 505; Isabel Lyon, 342, 361–64, 366, 388, 425, 622, 630; Hellen Elizabeth Martin, 221, 556–57; Hiram Maxim, 530–31; Mark G. McElhinney, 23–24, 454–55; Francis D.

Millet, 462; Kurt Mönch, 286–87; Gertrude Natkin, 555; Charles G. Norris, 272–73, 589, 591; Oliver W. Norton, 307, 610; James B. Pond, 528; Dorothy Quick, 209, 220; C. C. Ranstead, 460; Whitelaw Reid, 53, 467–68; Abby Sage Richardson, 500; Henry H. Rogers, 373–74, 516; George Bernard Shaw, 109, 494; Michael Laird Simons, 644; Sioux Falls music dealer, 158, 524; Sterling Debenture Corporation, 449; J. B. Sutherland, 286, 596; Howard P. Taylor, 287–88; Arthur Tcherep-Spiridovitch, 450; Paul Thompson, 602; Joseph H. Twichell, 158–59, 524, 557; A. Watson, 381; Basil Wilberforce, 80; Henry Spengler Williams, 281–84; Ziegler Publishing Company, 524

Le Verrier, Jean Joseph, 440, 636

Leveson-Gower, Granville (earl Granville), 103, **491**

Levy-Lawson, Edward ("obliterated guest"), 103, **491–92**

Lewis, John T., 44, 460

Lewis, Leopold, 518

Lewis, Mary Stover, 44, **460**

Lewis, Susanna, 460

Liberty National Bank, 388, 418

Life on the Mississippi, 283, 514, 639, 650, 656–57, 661

Lincoln, Abraham, 58, 120, 148, 270, 505, 581, 641, 658, 661

Lincoln National Bank, 339, 418, 422

Lincoln Trust Company, 179, 535

Lindsay, James Ludovic (earl of Crawford and Balcarres), 106, **493**

Lipton, Thomas, 75, 137–38, 143–44, 398–400, **514**–15, 632, 679

Little, David M., 574

Littlehales, Lillian, 305–6, **608**

Littleton, Martin W., 141, 179–80, 516, **535–36**

Littleton, Maud Wilson, 354, 397, 626

Livermore, Daniel, 443

Livermore, Mary Ashton Rice, 4, **443**

Liverpool, 146–47, 150, 519–20

Liverpool *Post,* 520

Liverpool Seamen's Orphanage, 72, 480–81

349, 395, 398, 402, 420–21, 425–26,
439, 624, 675–77; house-money dispute, 400–401, 414, 417–18, 422, 633;
journals, 444, 446–48, 456, 521–24,
534, 536, 546–47, 549–50, 552–53,
555, 590–92, 596, 601, 604, 609, 612,
618–19, 621, 627, 632, 635; laziness and
shirking, 338–39, 364, 366–67, 371,
376, 382–87, 431, 630; legal action in
SLC dispute, 326, 407, 409, 417–19,
422–26, 428, 430, 673, 677; letters written for SLC, 455, 468, 502–3, 515–16,
545, 571–72; "Letters of Mark Twain"
plan, 334, 350, 366, 406, 620, 625, 669;
"Lobster Pot" ("Summerfield") gift from
SLC, 323, 333–34, 391–92, 404, 618,
671; "Lobster Pot" money for renovation (gift and loan from SLC), 323,
351–52, 367, 387, 399–402, 404–7,
409–11, 413, 417, 424, 430, 435, 618,
626, 671–72, 677–79; "Lobster Pot"
repossession/attachment by SLC, 326,
401, 404, 410, 414–26, 675, 679; management of Stormfield staff, 336–40,
357–59, 366–71, 377–78, 388, 424,
429, 586, 621, 625, 633, 676–77; Mark
Twain Company, 372, 399, 607, 618,
671; Mark Twain Library, 344, 397,
624, 671; marriage and divorce, 323,
327, 340, 346–48, 354, 359, 366, 376,
393–94, 404, 407, 419, 427, 430, 439,
624, 626–27, 671–72, 674; marriage
designs on SLC, 429, 433–34, 634–35;
misappropriations and thefts, 323, 333,
342, 348, 359, 376–82, 387, 393–94,
400–402, 405–18, 422, 425–27, 430,
432–33, 439, 633, 672, 676; newspaper
interviews, 401–2, 404–5, 407–8, 410–
15, 423, 425, 427–31; photographs,
365, 405–6, 408; Power of Attorney
plot, 323, 347, 350–51, 388–94, 406,
425, 427, 437–38, 630–31, 670–73;
premarital relationship with Ashcroft,
337–38, 357, 627; relationship with
Clara, 326–27, 330–31, 335–37, 341–
42, 344, 349, 353–54, 359–60, 362–63,
374, 376, 400, 406–7, 414, 423, 425,
428–29, 633, 672; resents and dismisses

Hobby, 362, 364, 439, 635; Rogers's
opinion, 373–74, 428, 432–33, 675;
salary, 333, 342, 349, 351–52, 362–64,
378, 397, 406, 417, 424, 439, 625, 628;
SLC's praises and defense, 323, 331,
333–36, 344, 348, 378, 396–99, 429,
431–34, 437–38, 556, 675–76; smoking, 338–39; social status, 337, 340;
sovereignty over SLC, 340–41, 343,
347, 353, 371, 393, 406, 434, 437–39,
643; Stormfield burglary, 267–68, 276,
406; Stormfield design, construction,
and decoration, 309, 352, 384–85, 397,
417–18, 422, 431, 556, 577, 610, 630;
support of mother, 333, 342, 362–63,
385, 406, 417, 618
Lyon, Louise, 417, 617, 634
The Lyons Mail, 145, 518

MacAlister, Ian, 485
MacAlister, J. Y. W., 481, 485, 616
MacDougall, Allan, 554
MacGahan, Januarius Aloysius, 46, **461–62**
"The Machine Episode," 621
Mackenzie, William D., 558
Macmillan, Harold, 491
Macmillan, Helen, 102–3, 491–92
Macmillan, Maurice, 103, 491–92
Macnaghten, Edward (lord), 74, **482**
•Macy, Anne Sullivan, 299, 604
•Macy, John, 299–300, 604
•Madden, Mary (Paddy), 446–47
Maecenas, Gaius, 77, 483
Magna Carta, 119
Mandeville, John, 67, 478
Manhattan Club, 455
Mansion House (London), 490
Marconi, Guglielmo, 172–74, 263, **529–30,**
545
Maria Josepha (princess of Austria), 479–**80**
Maria Theresa (archduchess of Austria), 479
Marie Louise (princess of Schleswig-Hol-
stein), 111, **496**
Majestic Theatre (New York), 179
Markoe, Francis Hartman, Jr., 486–87
Mark Twain: A Biography, 323, 334, 469,
582, 612–13, 618–20, 670. *See also*
Paine, Albert Bigelow

Mark Twain Company, 304, 326, 349, 372, 392, 398–99, 428, 431, 436–37, 448, 606–7, 618, 625, 635, 671, 673, 679

Mark Twain Foundation, 607

Mark Twain in Eruption (DeVoto), 535

Mark Twain Library (Redding, Conn.), 284–86, 344, 595–96, 624, 628–29, 671

Mark Twain's Sketches, New and Old, 639

Martin, Helen Moncrieff Morton, 553

Martin, Hellen Elizabeth, 220–21, **553,** 556–57

Martin, Robert Dennison, 553

Mary (Alice; Clemenses' cook), 24–25, 456, 458

Mary (queen of Scots), 88

Mascagni, Pietro, 318, 612

Mason, George Grant, **524**

Mason, Marion Peak, 158, **524**

Massiglia, Countess (Frances Paxton), 339, 622

Matthews, Brander, 173, 594

•Maude (donkey), 203–4

Maxim, Hiram Stevens, 173, **530–31**

McAleer, James, 460

McAleer, Mary, 44, 460

McAleer, Patrick, 25–26, 28, 33, 44, 456–58

McCabe, Patrick, 222, 560

McCall, Samuel W., 113, **497**

McCarren, Patrick Henry, 222, **559**

McCarthy, Denis, 288, 597

McCarthy, Jack, 288, 597

McCarthy, Mike, 288, 598

McClure, S. S., 107, 508

McClure's Magazine, 649–50

McComb, Samuel, 558

McCook, Alexander, 506

McCook, Annie Cole, 506

McDonald, William Jesse, 258, **580**

McElhinney, Mark G., 23–24, 454–**55**

McFarland, Daniel, 500

McGinn, Jack, 288, 598

McKinley, William, 578

McKinley bill (1908), 538

McLaughlin, Maria (Maria McManus; Clara's wet nurse), 43–45, 460

McLean, Emily Ritchie, 142, **517**

"Memorial to Susy," 552

Memphis (Tenn.), 136, 514

Mendelssohn Hall (New York), 305–6, 608, 672

Mental telegraphy, 20, 263, 510

Mercantile National Bank, 532

Metaphysical Society, 495

Metcalf, Victor H., 537

Metropolitan Opera House (New York), 464, 549

"The Mexican Plug," 526, 551

Miguel I (king of Portugal), 478

Miles, Nelson Appleton, 150–54, **520–21**

Miller, Joaquin, 103, **491–92**

Millet, Elizabeth Merrill, 463

•Millet, Francis D., 45–48, **461–64**

Mills, Darius O., 496

•*Minneapolis* (ship), 71–73, 480–81

Minnetonka (ship), 206–7, 523, 546

Mississippi River, 87, 136, 245, 486, 513–14, 637, 639

Missouri State Guard, 651

Moffett, Anita, 266, 584

Moffett, Annie, 642

Moffett, Francis Clemens, 266, 584

Moffett, Mary Mantz, 266, **584**

Moffett, Pamela A. Clemens (SLC's sister), 518, 637, 650; biographical information, **641–42**

•Moffett, Samuel E. (SLC's nephew), 264–66, 581, 583–84, 619, 642; biographical sketch of SLC, 649–51, 654–62

Moffett, William A., 642

Monday Evening Club, 126–27, 508

Monitor (warship), 141, 516

Moore, Alice, 590

Moore, Jesse, 617

Moore, Louise Lyon, 617

"The Moral Sense," 127, 509

More Tramps Abroad, 455

Morgan, D. Parker, 504

Morgan, J. Pierpont, 96, 138, 202, 514–15, 533

Morgan and Ives, 501

Morris, Mrs. Minor, 298, 603

Morris, William, 109, 494, 590

Morse, Samuel Finley Breese, 173–74, **531**

Moulton, Julius, 235, **569**

Mount Olivet Cemetery (Hannibal, Mo.), 641

Munro, David, 331, 613

Murphy, Charles Francis, 222, **559**

Murray, John, 94, **487**

Murray, Katie, 420, 621

Muscatine (Iowa), 637, 641, 652, 656

"My Autobiography [Random Extracts from It]," 103, 492, 683

My Father, Mark Twain (Clara Clemens), 643

Myers, Eveleen Tennant, 130, 132–33, **510**

Myers, Frederic William Henry, 130, 510

"The Name of Jesus" (hymn), 43, 460

Nasr-ed-Din (shah of Persia), 114, 498

National Arbitration and Peace Conference, 453

National Bank of Commerce, 532

National Gallery (London), 520

National Geographic Society, 636

National Reform Association, 538

National Woman Suffrage Association, 443

Natkin, Gertrude, 555

Navarino (battle), 21–22, 452

Nazimova, Alla, 211, **548–49**

Nelles, Percy Walker, 554

Nero (Roman emperor), 63

Nesbit, Evelyn, 41–42, 458–59

Netherlands (Holland), 290, 295, 395, 399, 599–600; The Hague, 22, 452–53, 537, 600

Nevada, 163, 245, 469, 605, 637–38, 641, 646, 648, 650, 652–53, 658

New England Woman's Suffrage Association, 442

New Haven *Register,* 558

New Orleans, 528, 637, 645, 647, 652, 658

New Orleans *Picayune,* 645

New Orleans *True Delta,* 646, 648

"The New Planet," 604

New York *American,* 364, 401–2, 406, 542, 633, 635

New York City: Clara's residence, 357, 627, 671; SLC attends World's Fair (1853), 652, 656; SLC employed as a typesetter, 637, 645, 647; •SLC's residences, 340,

397, 546–47, 556, 558, 586, 614, 631, 639

New York Clearing House, 532

New York *Daily Graphic,* 522

New York *Daily People,* 560

New-Yorker Staats-Zeitung, 455

New York *Evening Post,* 305–6, 450, 492, 608

New York *Evening Telegram,* 403–4, 633

New York *Herald,* 114, 258, 306, 461, 498, 580, 608, 635

New York Infant Asylum, 45, 460

New York *Journal,* 649

New York Post-Graduate School and Hospital, 614

New York *Press,* 522

New York Public Library, 324, 447, 450, 651

New York *Saturday Press,* 638

New York State Association for Promoting the Interests of the Blind, 199, 543

New York *Sun,* 297, 530, 601–2, 612

New York Supreme Court, 616

New York *Times,* 177–78, 237–38, 297, 428–31, 436, 451–52, 465–66, 521, 531–32, 553, 570, 601–2, 626, 634, 673; characterized by SLC, 428

New York *Tribune,* 112, 264, 307, 453, 496–97, 522, 581, 609, 648

New York *Worker,* 451

New York *World,* 66–67, 97, 113, 134, 160–62, 172, 175–76, 194, 222–23, 269, 407–8, 457, 497, 500, 511–12, 525, 530–31, 540, 559, 580

New York Yacht Club, 137–39, 143, 504, 514–15

New Zealand, 639

Nicholas I (prince of Montenegro), 21, **453**

Nicholas II (tsar), 19, 199, 451–53, 538

Nichols, Marie, 210, 361, 443–44, **547**

Nickerson, John N., 388, 391, 419, 423, 626

Nietzsche, Friedrich, 129–30, 509

The Nineteenth Century (periodical), 495

Nook Farm (Hartford), 442–43, 460, 642

Norfolk (Va.), 81–82, 355–58, 366–68, 370, 380, 443, 547, 608, 627, 635, 672

Norris, Charles G., 272–73, 589–91

North, John W., 650

Reid, Whitelaw *(continued)*
467–68, 481–82, 485, 496; character-
ized by SLC, 112–13, 116; correspon-
dence with SLC, 53, 467–68; falling out
with SLC, 113–14, 497; marriage, 112,
496; New York *Tribune* career, 112, 492,
496–97; Oxford degree, 83–84
Reliance (yacht), 138, 515
Republican Party, 134–35, 161–62, 188,
230, 256, 259–60, 474, 512, 565–66,
578–79, 592
Revolutionary War, 119, 504–5, 628
Rhodes, Alonzo Willard, 297–98, 601–2
Rhodes, Mrs. Alonzo Willard, 602
Rhodes, Cecil, 96, 109, 487–88, 495
Rhodes, May, 297–98, 601–2
Rice, Alice Hegan, 307, 609
Rice, Cale Young, 609
Rice, Thorndike, 603
Richard I (king of England), 90
Richardson, Abby Sage, 115–16, 499,
500–501
Richardson, Albert D., 500
Richelieu (cardinal), 148
Ridder, Herman, 455
Riggs, Kate Douglas Wiggin, 84, 485
Ringling Brothers, 601
Riverdale (N.Y.), 213, 333–34, 551, 586,
618, 639, 669
Rives, Amélie (Mrs. Pierre Troubetzkoy),
211, **548**
Robert Fulton Memorial Association, 138–
41, 199, 543, 595
"Robert Louis Stevenson and Thomas Bai-
ley Aldrich," 447, 487, 576, 683
Robinson, George M., 31, 40, 456
Robinson, Henry C., 315, 612
Rockefeller, Almira Geraldine Goodsell,
231, 567
Rockefeller, John D., Jr., 230, 232, 566–67
Rockefeller, John D., Sr., 96, 230–33, 487–
88, 533, 566–67
Rockefeller, William, 134, 512, 567
Rockefeller Institute, 231–33, 487, 567
Rockford (Ill.) *Gazette,* 522
Rogers, Emilie Augusta Randel Hart, 212,
305–6, 359, 433, 516, 547, 550, 608
•Rogers, Henry H., 148, 325, 502, 547, 587,

629; Aldine Club dinner with SLC,
230–32, 566; Ashcroft-Lyon investigation, 330–31, 344, 372–75, 379–81,
401, 407, 431–34, 439, 672, 676–77;
Bermuda trip with SLC, 211–12, 550;
characterized by SLC, 312, 344, 432;
Clara's concert, 305–6, 359; correspondence with SLC, 373–74, 457, 478, 502,
516, 524, 620; death, 312, 315, 344, 431,
612, 672, 675–76; financial advice for
SLC, 15–17, 398, 448, 639; health, 211,
515, 550; Jamestown (Va.) excursions,
51, 138–39, 465–66; opinion of Ashcroft, 331, 348; opinion of Lyon, 428,
432–33, 675; sense of humor, 466, 513,
516; Virginian Railway, 355, 368, 627,
672. *See also* Standard Oil Company
Rogers, Henry H., Jr. (Harry), 139, 141–42,
465, 468, **517,** 547, 587, 676
Rogers, Mary Benjamin, 141–42, 468, **517,**
547
Rolls, John (Baron Llangattock), 506
Roosevelt, Theodore, 113, 117, 138, 146,
155, 228, 453, 465, 503, 521, 581; abuse
of executive power, 62, 143, 176–77,
258–60, 473–74, 581–82; antitrust
crusades, 135, 230–31, 512, 532–33,
566, 578; bear hunting, 161–62, 172–
76, 529–31; Booker T. Washington
controversy, 257, 579; Brownsville incident, 257–58, 580; campaign donation
scandal, 134–35, 511–12; civil service
reform, 256, 579; economic policies
criticized, 135–36, 177–78, 384, 512–
13, 532–33; eulogy for Cleveland, 256,
579; football reform, 62, 474; horseback
riding incident, 297–98, 601–3; "In
God We Trust" controversy, 188, 538;
lynch law condemnation, 459; meeting
with Carnegie, 184, 187–88; militarism,
135, 187, 258, 530, 537–38; Nobel
Peace Prize, 187, 538; pensions for
veterans, 62–63, 183, 473; personality,
173, 187, 254–56; popularity, 22, 173,
254; presidential career, 578; promotion
of Wood, 113, 255, 496, 578; quarrel
with Long, 62–68, 173, 472–78, 530;
SLC's refusal to accompany, 136–37,

South Africa, 111, 164, 180, 526, 639
Spanish-American War, 173, 521, 530, 598
Spaulding, Clara L. (Mrs. John B. Stanch-
field), 342, 420, 453, 463, 622
Spreckels, Rudolph, 255, **578–79**
Spurr, Edwin Robert, 553
Spurr, Harriet, 553
Spurr, Jean Woodward, 220, **553**
Stainer, John, 21, 452
Stanchfield, Alice, 622
Stanchfield, Clara L. Spaulding, 342, 420,
453, 463, 622
Stanchfield, John B., 326, 342, 380–81, 391,
394–95, 399, 418, 420, 425, 430–31,
437, 588, 622, 629–**30**, 631, 633, 672–
73; letter from Ashcroft, 626, 673–80
Standard Oil Company, 134–35, 148, 230–
31, 275, 379–81, 432, 466, 512–13, 533,
566–67, 592, 639; defended by SLC,
230–31
Stanislavski, Konstantin, 548
Stanley, Dorothy Tennant, 130–31, **509–10**
Stanley, Henry M., 130–31, 509–10
Stanton, Edwin M., 270, 588
Stanton, Elizabeth Cady, 4, **443**
Statue of Liberty, 340, 402, 622
Stead, William T., 22, 453–54
Stedman, Edmund Clarence, 14, 241, 572
Steinway Hall (New York), 165
Stephen, Leslie, 491
Sterling Debenture Company, 16–17, 449
Sterritt, Anna, 358, 622, 627, 671
Stevenson, Robert Louis, 95
Stewart, William M., 521, 638
St. George's Society, 559
St. James Gazette (periodical), 568
St. Louis (Mo.), 144, 468, 518, 637, 639,
641–42, 645, 647, 652, 656
St. Louis *Missouri Republican,* 569
St. Nicholas (periodical), 552
St. Nicholas Hotel (New York), 165
Stoker, Dick, 58–59, 469–**70**, 471
Stone, Amasa, 496, 548
Stone, Benjamin, 121, **506**–7
Stone, Lucy, 443
Stone, Melville, 104–5, 210, 413–14, 447,
492
•Stormfield (Clemenses' house in Redding,

Conn.): burglary, 267–69, 276–78,
281, 283, 337, 406, 586–87, 591–92,
670; cost and financing (land, design,
and construction), 13, 221, 267, 384–
85, 417–18, 445–46, 534, 555–56,
585–86, 630, 640, 670; descriptions
and praises, 239–40, 267, 556, 577;
guests, 278, 284–86, 297, 299–300,
310, 340, 342, 348, 354, 365, 400, 421,
481, 577, 587, 593, 602, 604, 606,
632, 634; Hawaiian mantelpiece, 240,
571; naming, 239, 267, 337, 446, 640;
SLC's arrival, 391, 536, 556, 617, 670;
staff, 268, 309–11, 313–15, 318, 331,
336–38, 354–59, 361–63, 366–71,
377–78, 388, 390, 417, 420, 586–87,
610, 614, 621, 625, 627, 631, 633, 671–
72, 676–77. *See also* Lyon, Isabel Van
Kleek: Stormfield design, construction,
and decoration
Stowe, Calvin, 442
Stowe, Harriet Beecher, 3, 442
St. Patrick's Cathedral (New York), 226,
564
Strawberry Banke Museum (Portsmouth,
N.H.), 572
St. Regis Hotel (New York), 18, 20
Stromeyer, C. F., 309, 382, 387, 610
St. Timothy's School for Girls, 481
Sturgis, Dorothy, 213, 220–21, **554**–55,
587
Sturgis, Richard Clipston, 554
Sunderland, Philip and William W. (build-
ers), 240, 285, 384–85, 556, 586, 596
Swift, Jonathan, 454
Swinton, John, 151, 521
Swinton, William, 151–52, 521
Switzerland, 455, 639, 654, 662
Syracuse (N.Y.) *Herald,* 507
Széchényi, Dionys, 163, **525**
Széchényi, László, 163, **525**

Tabitha Inn (Fairhaven, Mass.), 587
Taft, William Howard, 135, 254–58, 260,
275–76, 513, 558, 566, 578–79, 581–
82, 592, 615
Taiping Rebellion, 455
Talleyrand-Périgord, Anna Gould, 224, 562

University of California, 584
University of Chicago, 544
University of Missouri, 54, 468
University of North Carolina, 481
University of St. Andrews, 537
Ursula, Saint, 461
U.S. Army and Navy, 151, 173, 520–21, 583, 599; battleship fleet, 135, 173, 187, 530, 537–38; Brownsville incident, 257–58, 580; bugle corps, 307–8, 610; Rough Riders (First Volunteer Cavalry), 173, 530
U.S. Civil Service Commission, 579
U.S. Congress, 239, 259, 279, 443, 478, 512, 537, 559, 570, 578, 582; Coinage Act of 1864, 538; copyright acts, 311, 532, 594, 611; Elkins Act, 513; Hepburn Act, 533; House Bill 7053 (postal reform), 107–8, 493–94; McKinley bill, 538; Roosevelt's message, 42, 459; Sherman Antitrust Act, 512
U.S. Constitution, 119, 188, 505, 536, 538. See also Roosevelt, Theodore: abuse of executive power
U.S. Department of War, 108, 257, 521
U.S. economy, 135–36, 177–79, 184, 384, 512–13, 532–34, 537, 605, 627
U.S. Sanitary Commission, 443
U.S. Supreme Court, 259, 581–82
U.S. Treasury Department, 136, 183. 472, 533, 538
Utah Consolidated Mining Company, 13, 15–16, 445, 448, 465

Vajiravudh (prince of Siam), 145, 518
Vanderbilt, Cornelius, 137, **514,** 525, 548
Vanderbilt, Cornelius III, 137–43, 163, **514**–15
Vanderbilt, Gladys, 163, **525**
van Dyke, Henry, 226–28, 564
van Eeden, Frederick, 438, 635
Van Nostrand, John A. (Jack), 234–35, **568**
Vassar College, 171, 529, 553, 608
Vespasian (Roman emperor), 260, 582
Victoria (queen of England), 113, 484, 491, 496, 518
Victoria League, 491
Vienna. See Austria

Villa di Quarto, 577, 614, 639, 669. See also Italy
"Villa di Quarto," 544, 622
Virgil, 483
Virginia City (Nev.), 245, 289, 615
Virginia City Evening Bulletin, 597
Virginia City Territorial Enterprise, 245, 287–88, 469–70, 597–98, 638, 646, 648, 652–53, 658–59
Virginia City Union, 598, 652, 658
Virginian Railway, 355, 627, 672
Virgins of Cologne, 45, 461
von Bülow, Bernhard (prince), 275, **591**–92
von Renvers, Hofrath, 342, 622, 671
Voss, W. H. Neilson, 468

Waeckerlin, Rudolf James, 553
Waldorf-Astoria Hotel (New York), 491, 559
Walker, John B., 457
•Wallace, Elizabeth (Betsy), 204, 206, 335, **544,** 621
Wallop, Beatrice (countess of Portsmouth), 121, 505–6, 520
Wallop, Newton (earl of Portsmouth), 121, **505**–6, 520
Walsh, Mary, 614, 621
Wanamaker's (department store), 339, 385, 622
"Wapping Alice," 24–41, 455–58
Warfield, Edwin, 448
Warfield, Emma, 448
Wark, Charles Edmund (Will), 267–68, 325, 377, 430, 443–44, 547, **586,** 591, 611, 627, 677
Warner, Charles Dudley, 115, 315, 528, 536, 638, 649, 653, 660; biographical sketch of SLC, 644, 647–49
Warner, George H., 40, 115–16, 458, 498
Warner, Elisabeth Gillette (Lilly), 458, 460, 498
Washburn, Henry Bradford, 227, 564
Washington (D.C.), 150–51, 279, 521, 545, 594, 638
Washington, Booker T., 257, 579–80
Washington, George, 241
Washington Post, 465–66

The Mark Twain Project is housed within the Mark Twain Papers of The Bancroft Library at the University of California, Berkeley. The Papers were given to the University by Mark Twain's only surviving daughter, Clara Clemens Samossoud, and form the core of the world's largest archive of primary materials by and about Mark Twain. Since 1967 the Mark Twain Project has been producing volumes in the first comprehensive critical edition of everything Mark Twain wrote, as well as readers' editions of his most important texts. More than thirty-five volumes have been published, all by the University of California Press.

The Mark Twain Papers and *The Works of Mark Twain* are the ongoing comprehensive editions for scholars. Full list of volumes in the Papers at http://www.ucpress.edu/books/series/mtp.php Full list of volumes in the Works at http://www.ucpress.edu/books/series/mtw.php

The Mark Twain Library is the readers' edition that reprints texts and notes from the Papers and Works volumes for the benefit of students and the general reader. Full list of Library volumes at http://www.ucpress.edu/books/series/mtl.php

Mark Twain Project Online is the electronic edition for the Mark Twain Project. *Autobiography of Mark Twain, Volumes 1, 2,* and *3,* are now published there. All volumes in the Papers and Works as well as the Library will eventually be made available at http://www.marktwainproject.org

Jumping Frogs: Undiscovered, Rediscovered, and Celebrated Writings of Mark Twain brings to readers neglected treasures by Mark Twain—stories, tall tales, novels, travelogues, plays, imaginative journalism, speeches, sketches, satires, burlesques, and much more. Full list of Jumping Frogs volumes at http://www.ucpress.edu/books/series/jf.php

Editorial work for all volumes in the Mark Twain Project's Papers, Works, and Library series has been supported by grants from the National Endowment for the Humanities, an independent federal agency, and by donations to The Bancroft Library, matched equally by the Endowment.

TEXT: 10.75 / 14 GARAMOND PREMIER PRO
DISPLAY: AKZIDENZ GROTESK
COMPOSITOR: BOOKMATTERS, BERKELEY CA
PRINTER AND BINDER: MAPLE PRESS